THE FOUR LORDS
OF THE DIAMOND

THE FOUR LORDS
OF THE DIAMOND

LILITH: A Snake in the Grass
CERBERUS: A Wolf in the Fold
CHARON: A Dragon at the Gate
MEDUSA: A Tiger by the Tail

Jack L. Chalker

Nelson Doubleday, Inc.
Garden City, New York

Published by arrangement with
Del Rey/Ballantine Books
A Division of Random House, Inc.
201 East 50th Street
New York, New York 10022

Printed in the United States of America

CONTENTS

THE WARDEN DIAMOND

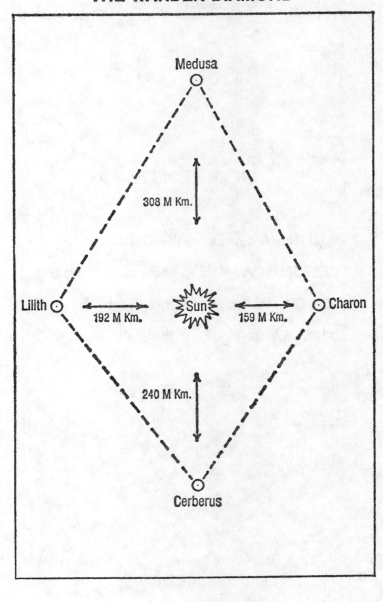

THE FOUR LORDS
OF THE DIAMOND

LILITH:
A Snake in the Grass

For Lou Tabakow,
a great unsung friend
of science fiction for
almost fifty years,
and a man whose kindness
and friendship
I will always treasure

CONTENTS

Background to Trouble

I

The little man in the synthetic tweed jacket didn't look like a bomb. In fact, he looked much the same as most of the other clerks, junior computer operators, and political men on the make in Military Systems Command. Two beady little brownish eyes set a bit too far apart by a hawk nose, a twitchy little mouth above a lantern jaw—the kind of nebbish nobody ever looked at twice. That's why he was so dangerous.

He wore all the proper entry cards, and when handprints and retinal patterns were taken at doors that could trap or even destroy if the slightest thing was wrong he was passed without so much as an electronic pause. He carried a small briefcase, unusual only in that it was merely clasped and not chained to him or attached in some other way. Still, that caused no notice or alarm—it was probably tuned to his body, anyway.

Occasionally along brightly lit halls he'd meet another of his apparent ilk, and they'd pass, perhaps nodding as if they knew each other but more often simply ignoring one another as they would in a crowd or on any street corner. There was nothing exceptional about them, nothing to mark them as something apart from the common herd, because, except for their jobs and job location, there *wasn't* any real difference. Except for this one little man. He was definitely exceptional, being a bomb.

Finally he reached a small room in which a single computer access element was placed in front of a comfortable-looking chair. There were no warning symbols, no huge guards or robot sentinels about, even though this particular room was the gateway to the military secrets of an interstellar empire of vast proportions. There was no need. No single individual could activate that access element; doing so required the combined and nearly simultaneous consent of three different human beings and two robot backups, each of whom received a different coded order from a different source. Any attempt to use it without the actions of all the others would result not only in a dead computer and blank terminal but also in a warning flashed to security.

The little man sat down in the chair, adjusted it for proper operating position, then leaned over and casually opened his briefcase. Removing a small crystalline device, he idly flicked it on with a thumb motion and then it set against the activation plate of the terminal.

The screen flickered, came to life. Printed on it were all the access codes as if it had received them and the question of whether the user preferred voice or CRT communication. There was no question of a print-out. Not with *this* computer.

"CRT only, please," the little man idly said, in a thin, dry, nasal voice that bore no trace of accent. The machine waited. "Defensive files C-476-2377AX and J-392-7533DC, please, at speed."

The computer seemed to blink at that last; at speed would be at roughly four hundred lines a second, the limit of the CRT to form the images in the first place. Nonetheless, the computer went to work. Both plans were delivered up and snapped past the little man in less than a second.

He was pleased. So much so that he decided then and there to press his luck a little and ask for more. "Run the master defense emergency plans, please, at speed, in order," he told the machine casually.

The machine obeyed. Because of the volume of material it took almost four minutes.

The little man glanced at his watch. It was so tempting to continue, but every second he was here increased his chances of somebody just looking in or some random check. That wouldn't do, not at all.

He placed his device back in his briefcase, snapped it closed, stood up, and walked out. At that point he made one minor mistake, one he would not be expected to know. You had to tell the damned thing to clear and reset the codes. If you didn't, this computer didn't react like all others and simply stay on—intolerable, with access to such secrets—or shut itself down. When it "saw" that the operator had left the room without resetting it, the machine advised control personnel of that fact, then locked in emergency shutdown until reset.

As the little man reached the first checkpoint door on his way out, things were already starting to crack around him.

The young woman glared for a moment at the red alert light that had flashed on her console. She ran a quick check to make sure there was no internal malfunction, then punched up the trouble—the Eyes Only Storage Computer.

Although she was one of those with part of the code that would activate the computer, she could not ask it any questions on its information storage from where she was—but she could get *security* information. She knew she had given no access so far today, so she punched two buttons and instructed, "Run tape last operation."

The little man's face showed clearly. Not only his face, but his retinal pattern, thermal pattern, everything about him that could be read by remote sensors and recorded. She brought in the rest of the computer net. "Identify!" she commanded.

"Threht, Augur Pen-Gyl, OG-6, Logistics," came the computer's reply. Before her hand could hit the alarm it had already been hit by two of her associates.

No alarms sounded, no flashing lights and whistling bells that would panic or tip off a spy. Instead, as Threht reached the third and last security door, peered into the oculator, and pressed his palm on the identiplate, it simply refused to open.

He realized at once that security, both human and robotic, was already closing in on him from all sides, and decided in a flash that the least security would be on the other side of the door. He raised his left hand, paused for a moment, frozen, as if marshaling all he had, then struck the door near its locking mechanism. The area buckled, and he leaned forward and without seeming effort pushed until the door slid back enough for him to squeeze through.

Once he was inside, the door slammed shut behind him, and he could hear the secondary seals slide into place. It formed an effective trap, between the inner and outer door. The chamber itself was airtight; so if someone got this far, the air inside the chamber could be rapidly withdrawn. No chances, not with somebody this good.

The vacuum hardly bothered him. He kicked at the outer door once, twice; on the third try, it gave. He leaned forward with all his might, opening a crack and holding the door open against the massive inrush of air until the pressure equalized. At that point he threw it open and strode through into the main entrance hall.

His guess had been correct; security forces were only now reaching the hall area, and stunned personnel throughout the hall prevented a quick shot. Four sleek black security robots sped toward him. Apparently unafraid, he let them advance. Then, just before they reached him, he suddenly ran right at the two in the lead, pushing one into the other and spilling both to the floor. The scene was incredible: a tiny, ordinary-looking fellow tumbled four tons of animated metal without so much as recoiling.

He moved quickly now, directly for the clear windows at the front of the hall. He moved with such tremendous speed, speed beyond human and most robots, that when he reached the windows he leaped straight into them. The panes were tremendously thick, able to resist even conventional bombs hurled against them, but they cracked and shattered like ordinary glass as he sailed through; he then dropped the twelve meters to the ground, landing on his feet with perfect balance, and started to run across the broad courtyard.

By then he had lost the element of surprise. Realizing from the point at which he'd battered in the first door that they were dealing with some

8 THE FOUR LORDS OF THE DIAMOND

clever sort of robot, the security forces had assumed the worst and were ready for him with killer robots, human troops, even a small laser cannon.

He stopped in the center of the grassy knoll and looked around, sizing up the situation but appearing cool and efficient. Then, suddenly, turning to look at the massive amounts of firepower trained on him, he grinned; the grin became a laugh, a laugh that rose in pitch until it became eerie, inhuman, maniacal, echoing back from the building's walls.

The order was given to open fire, but as the beams tore into the spot on which he stood he just wasn't there any more. He was going up, rising into the air silently and effortlessly at a tremendous rate of speed.

Automatic weapons tried to follow him but couldn't match his rate of climb. One officer stared up into the empty sky, laser pistol drawn. "The thing that pisses me off most is that he didn't even tear his pants."

Control shifted instantly to Orbital Command, but they weren't prepared for the suddenness of the little man's departure, nor could they be certain of how high he would rise or to where. Thirty-seven commercial and sixty-four military ships were in orbit at that point, plus over eight thousand satellites of one sort or another—not to mention the five space stations. Sophisticated radar would spot him if he changed course or attitude and decided to land elsewhere on the planet, but while he remained in space they would have to wait until he did something to draw their attention. There were simply too many things in orbit, and he was too small to track unless first spotted so they could lock onto him.

So they waited patiently, ready to shoot the hell out of any ship that made a break for it or simply decided to change position. And they closely monitored each ship; should someone try to board from space they'd know it.

The robot played the waiting game for almost three full days. By then its primary mission was a total failure—the plans it had stolen were now known, so quite obviously obsolete at that point—but what it had stolen was of some value, since they revealed strengths and current positions, and when analyzed by a specialist in military affairs would show a prospective enemy how the thinking of the Military Command and its bosses ran. Still, it couldn't wait forever—the force positions could not be so easily or quickly changed, and any contingency plan for their dispersion must be a variation of the original. For the present, their range of options was narrowed, but the options would increase geometrically with each elapsed hour. The robot had to make its move, and it did.

A small planetary satellite officially on the records as an obsolete weather-control monitor station came within three thousand meters of a small corvette. The ship, a government courier boat, would ordinarily be unmanned while keeping station, but no ships were left unguarded at this point.

The robot, still looking like the perfect clerk, emerged from the satellite through a hatch that should not have been there. But, then, the satellite was only superficially what it appeared to be, having long ago been copied and replaced with something infinitely more useful.

With seeming effortlessness, the robot sped to the corvette and stuck to the outer hull. It reached to its belt and pulled off a small weapon whose dangling line it attached to a small terminal that was otherwise invisible under its left arm. The robot had spent the past three days drawing enormous energy reserves to itself with the devices in the satellite; now, at capacity, it discharged through the weapon. A strong beam emerged from the thing, quickly cutting a hole the size of an orange in the corvette's hull. It had chosen its spot well: there were only two guards, one human and one robot, on the ship, and both were in the compartment directly under the point at which the beam went through the elaborate triple hull and into the opening. No one would ever know if it was decompression or the beam that killed the unlucky human guard; the robot, obviously, was shorted out by the sudden dispersion of energy within the compartment.

The enemy robot then tripped the airlock in the forward compartment and entered effortlessly, finding no apparent alarms and no opposition. The instant acceleration from a standing start would have killed any living thing on board.

2

The young man sat in absorbed silence, listening to the taped narrative. He was in much the same mold as most of his fellow humans at this point in human history, the perfection of the physical body. From the viewpoint of earlier times he was almost a superman; genetic engineering had made that possible. But every man and woman these days was at this peak of perfection, so among his fellow humans he was merely average-looking, somewhere around thirty with jet-black hair and reddish-brown eyes, at the legal norm height of 180 centimeters, and the legal norm weight of 82 kilograms. But he was neither average nor normal in more than one specific area, and that was why he was here.

He looked over at Commander Krega as the narrative stopped at the fleeing ship. "You had all the available ships under close watch and trace, of course?" It wasn't a question, merely a statement of fact.

Krega, an older version of the norm himself in whom the experience of an additional forty years' service showed on his face and particularly in his eyes, nodded. "Of course. But merely to have destroyed the thing at that point, when he'd already come so far and done so much, would have been a waste. We simply placed a series of tracers on everything that could conceivably move in orbit and waited for him . . . it . . . whatever. It was just a robot, after all, albeit a striking one. We had to know whose. At least who it worked for. You know something about subspace ballistics, I take it?"

"Enough," the younger man admitted.

"Well, once we had his angle and speed—and *what* speed from a standing start!—we knew where he'd have to come out. Fortunately, tightbeams can outrun any physical object, so we had someone in the area when he emerged a few subjective minutes later. Close enough, anyway, to get his next set of readings. That much wasn't difficult. He made seven blind switches, just to try to throw us off the track, but we never lost him. We were able to move in within a few minutes of the point in time at which he began transmitting the data—a safeguard just in case we were as efficient as we actually are. We closed in immediately then, though, and fried him and the ship to atoms. No other way around it. We'd seen firsthand just some of the things that baby could do."

The younger man shook his head. "Pity, though. It would have been interesting to disassemble the thing. It's certainly not any design I know of."

The commander nodded. "Or any of us, either. The fact is, the thing was just about at the limits of our own technology, if not a bit beyond. It fooled x-ray scanners, retinal scanners, body heat and function sensors— you name it. It even fooled the friends of the poor civil servant it was pretending to be, implying memory and possibly personality transfer. At any rate, even though its clever little orbital base blew up after it departed, there was enough left to piece together some of its insides—and I'll tell you, it's not ours. Not anything close. Oh, you can deduce some of the functions and the like, but even where the function is obvious, it isn't done the way *we'd* do it, nor are the materials similar to ours. We have to face the ugly fact that the robot and its base were built, designed, and directed by an alien power of which we are totally ignorant."

The young man showed mild interest. "But surely you know something about it now?"

The commander shook his head sadly. "No, we don't. We know more than we did, certainly, but not nearly enough. These bastards are wickedly clever. But I'll get to that in a minute. Let's first look at what we do know, or can deduce, about our enemy." He turned in his desk chair and punched a button. A blank wall blinked and became a visor screen showing an enormous collection of stars, thousands of which blazed a reddish color.

"The Confederacy," the commander stated needlessly. "Seven thousand six hundred and forty-six worlds, by last count, over a third of a galaxy. Quite an accomplishment for a race from a single planet out there on that one little arm. Planets terraformed, planets where the people were adapted to the place, even planets with sixty other intelligent native life forms on them, all now nicely acculturated to our way of doing things. We own it, we run it our way, and we've always had our own way. Not a single one of those other races was ever in any position to challenge us. They had to accept us and our way, or they died in much the manner our own native world was pacified so many centuries ago. We're the boss."

The young man didn't respond. He felt no need to. Born and raised in this culture, he simply took what Krega was saying for granted, as did everyone else.

"Well, we've now met our technological equals, perhaps even slight technological superiors," the commander continued. "Analysis made the obvious deductions. First, we're always expanding. Obviously there is another dominant race and culture doing the same from some other point in the galaxy. They discovered us before we discovered them—bad luck for us. They scouted, probed, and analyzed us, and came up with several facts. Second, our ultimate collision is unavoidable. We're starting to compete for the same space. Third, they are probably smaller than we, numerically weaker, as it were, but with a slight technological edge. They assume war, but they are not certain they could win it. If they *had been* sure they'd have attacked by now. That means they need information—lots of it. How our military organization is set up. How our defenses are established and would be used. And most important, how we think. A total understanding of us while we remained in ignorance of their ways would give them and their war machines a tremendous edge, assuming equal firepower. Fourth, they've been at this for some time, which means our collision is still way off, perhaps years. Finding us was probably accidental, some scout of theirs who got overextended, lost, or just overly ambitious. They've been around long enough, though, to make robots that pass for humans, to put spy stations in orbit around Military Systems Command, of all things, and to work out a deal with some of our own to help sell us out."

The young man suddenly looked interested. "Ah," he breathed.

"Exactly," the commander grumbled. "The last deduction is that they themselves are physically so alien to us that there is simply no way in hell they could move among us undetected, no physical disguise even possible. That leaves human-mimicking robots—who knows how many? I'm getting so I suspect my own staff—and human traitors. That last becomes the province of this office, naturally."

In earlier times the Operational Security Office might have been referred to as a secret police, which it most certainly was. Unlike the earlier models, though, it had little to do with the day-to-day life of the citizenry in the specific sense. Its mandate was broader, more generalized.

Mankind had perfected a formula long ago, one that worked. It was neither free in a libertarian sense nor in a personal sense, but it was efficient and it worked—not just for one world but for every world, across an interstellar empire so vast that only total cultural control could keep it together. The same system everywhere. The same ideas and ideals, the same values, the same ways of thinking about things—everywhere. Flexible, adaptable to different biomes and even, with some wrenching adjustments made mercilessly, adaptable to alien cultures and life forms. The formula was all-pervasive, an equalizing force in the extreme, yet it provided some play for different conditions and a measure of social mobility based on talent and ability.

There were of course populations that could not or would not adapt. In some instances, they could be "reeducated" by means of the most sophisticated techniques, but in others they could not. These were not merely alien worlds where the formula simply couldn't be tried because of their very alienness—those were ruthlessly exterminated as a last resort. Every system also bred individuals who could circumvent it and had the will and knack of doing so. Such people could be extremely dangerous and had to be hunted down and either captured for reeducation or killed outright.

"In the early days, however, the powers that be were much softer on those who couldn't otherwise be dealt with," Commander Krega told him. "They had not yet reached the absolute perfection of our present system. The result was permanent exile in the Warden Diamond, as you know. We still send a few there—the ones with particular talents and abilities we need or those who show potential for some great discovery. It's paid off, too, that policy, although we ship barely a hundred a year out there now."

The young man felt a nervous twinge in his stomach. "So that's where your alien race went for help. That's where your robot fled—the Warden Diamond."

"You got it," Krega agreed.

In a galaxy whose system was based on perfect order, uniformity, harmony, and a firm belief in natural laws, the Warden Diamond was an insane asylum. It seemed to exist as a natural counterpoint to everyplace else, the opposite of everything the rest of the Confederacy was or even believed in.

Halden Warden, a scout for the Confederacy, had discovered the system nearly two hundred years earlier, when the Diamond was far outside the administrative area of the Confederacy. Warden was something of a legend among scouts, a man who disliked most everything about civilization, not the least other people. Such extreme antisocial tendencies would have been dealt with in the normal course of events, but there was an entire discipline of psychology devoted to discovering and developing antisocial traits that could benefit society. The fact was, only people with personalities like Warden's could stand the solitude, the years without companionship, the physical and mental hardships of deep-space scouting. No sane person in Confederation society, up to Confederation standards, would ever take a job like that.

Warden was worse than most. He spent as little time as possible in "civilization," often just long enough to refuel and reprovision. He flew farther, longer, and more often than any other scout before or since, and his discoveries were astonishing in their number alone.

Unfortunately for his bosses back in the Confederacy, Warden felt that discovery was his only purpose. He left just about everything else, including preliminary surveys and reports, to those who would use his beamed coordinates to follow him. Not that he didn't make the surveys—he just communicated as little with the Confederacy as possible, often in infuriating ways.

Thus, when the signal "4AW" came in, there was enormous excitement and anticipation—four human-habitable planets in one system! Such a phenomenon was simply unheard of, beyond all statistical probabilities, particularly considering that only one in four thousand solar systems contained anything remotely of use. They waited anxiously for the laconic scout to tell them what he would name the new worlds and to give his preliminary survey descriptions of them, waited anxiously not only in anticipation of a great discovery, but also with trepidation at just what Crazy Warden would say and whether or not his message could be deciphered.

And then came the details, confirming their worst fears. He followed form, though, closest in to farthest out from the sun.

"Charon," came the first report. "Looks like Hell."

"Lilith," he continued. "Anything that pretty's got to have a snake in it."

"Cerberus," he named the third. "Looks like a real dog."

And finally, "Medusa: Anybody who lives here would have to have rocks in his head."

The coordinates followed, along with a code confirming that Warden had done remote, not direct, exploration—that is, he hadn't landed, something that was always his option—and a final code, "ZZ," which filled the Confederacy with apprehension. It meant that there was something very odd about the place, so approach with extreme caution.

Cursing Crazy Warden for giving them nothing at all to go on, they mounted the standard maximum-caution expedition—a full-scale scientific expedition, with two hundred of the best, most experienced Exploiter Team members aboard, backed up by four heavy cruisers armed to the teeth.

The big trouble with Warden's descriptions was that they were almost always right—only you never figured out quite what he meant until you got there. Appearing out of hyperspace, the follow-up party gazed upon a strange sight—a hot, F-type star, with a huge solar system containing ringed gas giants, huge asteroids, and numerous solid planets. But in the midst of it, close to the sun, were four worlds with abundant oxygen, nitrogen, and water, four jewels that screamed "life." Although the four planets were in far different orbits—from a little more than 158 million kilometers from their sun to 308 million kilometers out—when the party first encountered them, they were in a rare configuration. For a brief period, the four were at almost exact right angles to one another. Although that configuration was a fluke and rarely observed since, the system's four worlds became known as the Warden Diamond. And diamonds they were despite the orbital coincidence at their discovery—sparkling gems with potential untold riches.

Still, even some of the most materialistic among the observers took the diamond configuration as some sort of omen, just as Warden himself might have. And so, like Warden, they didn't land immediately. They poked and they probed and they analyzed, but found nothing at all suspicious. There was no evidence of supernatural meddlings here, despite the incredible impossibility of four worlds so closely matched to permit life. So they laughed at themselves for their foolishness, their superstition, their sudden infusion with primitive fears they all believed themselves well beyond, and they relaxed a little. Some suspected that the Warden Diamond was the result of some ancient civilization terraforming to suit—but if it was, there was no sign of that now.

They moved cautiously in on the planets. Charon was hot and steamy, closest of the four to the sun. It rained much of the time there, and the small, nasty dinosaurlike saurians that lived there seemed formidable, perhaps even dangerous—but not unmanageable. There might be more dangerous stuff in the seas that covered much of the world, but only a permanent expedition could find that out. In the meantime, this jungle world, with an axial tilt of under 6 degrees, had a temperature range of from roughly 28 to 60 degrees centigrade. Thanks to the land distribution it was habitable and usable—but not inviting.

Charon did indeed look like Hell.

Next out was Lilith, almost a textbook perfect world. Slightly smaller than Charon, it was roughly 70 percent water but far more temperate and far gentler in its landscape. Mountains were low, and there were broad plains and swamps. A nice variety of landforms without serious extremes or violence, and an axial tilt of 84 degrees—almost a world on its side, which meant little seasonal variation. It was very hot all over, with days of 40 degrees centigrade or more, with 20 to 25 considered absolutely frigid.

Its junglelike forests were the most verdant green, and though the foliage was alien, it wasn't all *that* alien, bearing large amounts of fruits and other products that proved edible by humans. The dominant animal life was apparently exclusively insects, from giant behemoths down to tiny creatures smaller than the head of a pin. It was the kind of world Confederacy terraformers aimed for and rarely achieved artificially; now, here it was, apparently natural, the beautiful Edenlike paradise of Lilith. And not a snake in sight—yet.

Cerberus was harsher. Its 25-degree axial tilt gave it extreme seasonal variations that ranged from its frozen polar caps to a hot 40-degree centigrade at the equator. The oddest thing about Cerberus was its land surface, which appeared almost covered with enormous varicolored forests. It took the actual landing to discover that Cerberus in fact had no land area at all, but was almost covered by enormous plants growing up from the ocean bottom, some many kilometers, so tremendously dense in many places that they formed an almost solid surface. On the tops of these great waterlogged forests whole new varieties of plants grew, forming a unique botanical ecosystem. The visible wildlife seemed to be birdlike in appearance, although there were some insects as well, but animal life was sparse on Cerberus, it seemed—unless it lay beneath the omnipresent waters of the surface. Still, so dense and enormous were the plants of this water world that men could live there, perhaps even build cities in the trees—an alien but not impossible world. With no apparent natural resources beyond wood and no way to bring in a truly modern lifestyle, settlement there would be precarious. Inhabitable, yes, but from the standpoint of modern man it *was* something of a dog.

Last and least pleasant of all was Medusa, a planet with frozen seas, blinding snow, and jagged, towering peaks. Its 19-degree axial tilt gave it seasons, all right, but it was a bad to worse situation, with summer in the tropics averaging 20 degrees centigrade or less and going to the impossibly cold polar regions. Although in heavy glaciation, it was the only one of the four Warden worlds with signs of volcanic activity. There were some forests, but mostly tundra and grasslands, although it had what appeared to be mammalian life in the form of herds of odd grazing animals and some very fierce and nasty carnivores. It was a harsh, brutal world that could be tamed and lived on; still, the Exploiter Team had to agree with Warden—to *want* to go and live there, you'd have to have rocks in your head.

Four worlds, from a steaming hell to frozen tundra. Four worlds with temperature extremes that could be borne and air and water that could be used. It was incredible, fantastic—and true. And so the Exploiter Team went in, set up its main base just off a tropical lagoon out of the most romantic travel poster—on Lilith, of course. Smaller expeditions went from there to the other three worlds for preliminary testing, poking, and probing.

Warden had been right about three of them, but his suspicion of Lilith seemed to be just the natural suspicion of somebody who sees something too good to be true. Or perhaps it was some sixth sense, developed from so many years in isolation and poking and probing into so many alien systems. Perhaps it was . . .

Once down, the Exploiter Teams were in effective quarantine from the military and from all commerce with the Confederacy. The initial exploration would take at least a year, during which they would be both scientists and guinea pigs, poking and probing one another as much as they poked and probed each planet. They had shuttlecraft capable of traveling between the planets if necessary and ground and air transportation to carry on their own work, but nothing interstellar. The risk was too great. Man had been burned too many times before to take such chances.

It took Lilith's snake about six months to size up the newcomers.

By the time all their machinery ceased to function it was already too late. They watched first as all the power drained out of the machinery and equipment as if being drunk by an eager child. Within forty-eight hours the machinery, the equipment—in fact, all artifacts—started to break up into so much junk. Four died as a result, and the rest watched in helpless horror as their corpses, too, rapidly began to decompose.

Within a week there was simply no sign that anything alien had ever landed. Cleared places seemed to grow over almost overnight; metal, plastics, organic and inorganic compounds—everything rotted, dissolved, and eventually was nothing more than a fine powder quickly absorbed by the rich soil. There was nothing left—nothing but sixty-two stunned, stark-naked scientists both bewildered and scared, without even the most rudimentary instruments to help explain what the hell had happened to them.

Just a week earlier direct contact between the parties on the four planets had been resumed. A small group from each of the other three worlds had come to Lilith to share their findings and decide what to do next. They had come, talked, analyzed, filed preliminary reports with the guardian cruiser still in space nearby, then returned to their own planets, unknowingly taking with them the snake.

The science section on the cruiser immediately jumped on the problem. And with remote robot-controlled labs they finally found the one thing everybody but Warden's sixth sense had missed. The snake was an alien organism, microscopic beyond belief and acting in colonies within the cells. It was not intelligent in the sense that it possessed anything humans would recognize as thought processes, but it did seem to have an amazing set of rules it enforced on an entire planet and an incredible capacity for adjusting to new conditions and bringing them to heel. Though its life span was a sparse three to five minutes, somehow this microorganism operated at a time rate hundreds, perhaps thousands, of times faster than anything around it. On Lilith, it still had taken the organism six months to adapt to these new things that had been introduced to its world, and it had finally evolved enough to adapt the aliens to its comfortable, symbiotic system.

But the other planets were different—different atmospheric balances, different gravity, different radiation intensities, all sorts of great differences. It could not adapt such alien environments to its system, so it adapted to them instead. In some cases—Medusa, for one—it adapted the host organism, the people, and quickly, the animals and plants. On Charon and Cerberus it struck a balance in the hosts that was to its liking; this produced by-products of physical change not relevant to it but rather resulting from where, in those bodies, it was most comfortable.

The Warden Diamond was, sadly, quarantined while scientists looked for a cure. Removing some of the unlucky victims in isolation chambers did not work: something linked the organisms to the Diamond, and they died when removed from the system, killing their hosts in the process, since the organisms resided in the hosts' cells and took over, really, rearranging things to suit themselves. Without their managers, the cells rapidly went berserk, causing an ugly and painful, although mercifully swift, death.

Oddly, those on one of the planets could still move in-system to the others, the organism having mutated so much inside them that it no longer even recognized Lilith as its home and, having struck a comfortable balance, having no further reason to change.

Humans *could* live and work and build on the Warden Diamond, but once there they could never leave.

That did not stop the scientists, of course, and they came and set up their colonies, although doing so was difficult on Lilith, where nothing not native to the planet seemed to be allowed. They came prepared and they came to study and uncover the secrets of the Warden Diamond. After two centuries their descendants were still at it, joined occasionally by others—but very little progress had been made. The planets, the organism, even the changes defied them. That only spurred them on all the more.

But it wasn't the scientists who were to settle the Diamond, but the antisocials. Early on, when the magnitude of the problem was realized, came the idea of setting up the four worlds as the perfect prison.

The misfits were sent there in droves—all those whose connections could avoid the psych boys, who had genius or some sort of talent that would be destroyed by reeducation, political prisoners from countless worlds—all sent there rather than killed or mentally altered in the hope that some future successful rival would remember they didn't kill or psych the deposed but exiled them. Male, female, it didn't matter. The best antisocials, the political-criminal elite. And there they lived and bore their children and died, and their children lived and bore *their* children, and so on.

So these worlds were run, dominated in fact, by a criminal elite imprisoned forever and with little love for or feeling of kinship with the masses of the Confederacy. Nonetheless, they had commerce. The organism could be killed, sterilized out, in a complex process, on unmanned ships. So other criminal geniuses, those not yet caught or in charge of governments, could establish caches of money, jewelry, precious art, and stolen goods of all types on the Warden worlds with no fear that the Confederacy could touch them.

At the same time the strongest, the smartest, the most ruthless of the exiles clawed their ways to the top of these four strange worlds, until they controlled them and their own trade. Lilith, where nothing physical could be stored, was the perfect place for storing such information as special bank account numbers, official secrets even the Confederacy had to be kept ignorant of, things of that sort—the kind of information one never put into a computer because all computers are vulnerable to a genius technician. No matter how foolproof the machine, the foolproof system was devised by someone and could therefore be broken by someone else.

So these great criminal kings—the Four Lords of the Diamond, alien now from their ancestral race, geniuses all yet bitterly exiled nonetheless—had the secrets, the stolen goods, the blackmail of the Confederacy, and their influence extended throughout the Confederacy even though they were forever barred from seeing it.

* * *

"Then the Four Lords are selling us out," the young man sighed. "Why not simply destroy all four worlds? Good riddance anyway, I'd say."

"So would I," Commander Krega agreed. "Only we can't. We let them go on too long—they're politically invulnerable. Too much wealth, too much power, too many secrets are there. There is simply no way to get them any more—they have the goods on just about anybody who would be high up enough to make those decisions."

The young man cleared his throat. "I see," he responded a little disgustedly. "So why not place agents on those worlds? Find out what's what?"

"Oh, that was tried from the first," Krega told him. "It didn't work, either. Consider—we're asking someone to exile himself permanently and allow himself to be turned, equally permanently, into something not quite human. Only a fanatic would agree to that—and fanatics make notoriously poor spies. The Four Lords are also not exactly easy marks, you know. They keep track of who's coming in, and their own contacts here tell them just about everything they want to know about any newcomers. We might sneak one agent, one really good agent, in on them—but a lot? Never. They'd quickly catch on and just kill the lot, innocent and guilty alike. They also are supremely confident of human psychology—the agent is going to have to be *damned* good to get away with such an assignment. Anybody with that much on the ball is also going to realize that he is trapped there and that he'll have to live there, on the Four Lords' worlds, until he dies. Loyalty comes hard, but even the most loyal and committed agent is going to have the brains to see which side his future bread will be buttered on. So he switches sides. One of the current Lords is in fact a Confederacy agent."

"Huh?"

Krega nodded. "Or was, I should say. Probably the best infiltrator in the business, knew all the ins and outs, and found the Diamond not threatening but fascinating. The Confederacy bored him, he said. We dropped him on Lilith just to worm his way into the hierarchy—and he sure did. In spades. Only we received almost no information from him while feeding him a great deal—and now he's one of the enemy. See what I mean?"

"You have a tough problem," the young man sympathized. "You don't have any reliable people on the Warden worlds, and anybody capable of doing what has to be done winds up on the other side. And now they're selling us out to an alien force."

"Exactly." Krega nodded. "You see where this puts us. Now, of course, we *do* have some people down there. None are a hundred percent reliable, and all of them would slit your throat in an instant if doing so was in their best interests. But we find occasional inducements—small payoffs of one sort or another, even a little blackmail on ones with close relatives back in the Confederacy—that gives us a little edge. A little, but not much, since the Four Lords are pretty ruthless when it comes to what they perceive as treason. Our only advantage is that the worlds are still fairly new to us and so therefore relatively sparsely settled. There is no totalitarian control on any of them, and there are different systems and hierarchies on each."

The young man nodded. "I have the uneasy feeling that you are leading up to something—but I must remind you of what you told me about past agents, and also that, even kicking and screaming, I'd be but one man on one world."

Commander Krega grinned. "No, it's not quite like that at all. You're a damned good detective and you know it. You've tracked down and upset rocks in places nobody else looked at twice; outmaneuvered and outguessed sophisticated computers and some of the best criminal minds ever known, even though you are still quite young. You are the youngest person with the rank of Inspector in the history of the Confederacy. We have two different problems here. One, we must identify this alien force and trace it back to its origin. We must find out who they are and where they are and what their intentions are. Even now it may be too late, but we must act as if it were not. Two, we must neutralize their information conduit, the Four Lords. How would you do it?"

The young man smiled thoughtfully. "Pay the Four Lords more than the aliens do," he suggested hopefully. "Put 'em to work for us."

"Impossible. We already thought of that," the commander responded glumly. "It's not profit—they have more than they need. And it's not power—that, too, they have in abundance. But we have cut them off forever from the rest of the universe, trapped them there. Before, they could do nothing—but now, with an alien force as their ally, they can. I'm afraid such people are motivated by revenge, and *that* we cannot give them. We can't even commute their sentence, short of a scientific breakthrough—and nobody has more people working on that angle than they do. No, making a deal is out. We have no cards."

"Then you need somebody good down there on each world, looking for clues to the aliens. There has to be some sort of direct contact: they have to get their information out and their little play-toys, like that fancy robot, programmed and in. An agent might turn traitor, but if he was a volunteer he wouldn't be motivated by revenge and would sure as hell feel closer to humanity than to some aliens of unknown appearance and design."

"Agreed. And it would have to be the very best for all four. Someone who could survive, even prosper under their conditions while having the ability to collect enough data and get it out. But how do we buy the time we also need?"

The young man grinned. "Easy. At least easy to say—maybe nearly impossible to do. You kill all four Lords. Others would take their places, of course, but in the interim you'd buy months, maybe years."

"That was our thinking," Krega agreed. "And so we ran it through the computers. Master detective, loyal, willing to volunteer, and with an As-

sassin's License. Four needed, plus a coordinator, since they all would
have to be put to work simultaneously and would obviously have no likely
reason or means to contact one another. Plus for insurance, of course,
spares that could be sent in if something happened to one or more of the
originals. We fed in all these attributes and requirements and out you
popped."

The young man chuckled dryly. "I'll bet. Me and who else?"

"Nobody else. Just you."

For the first time the man looked puzzled. He frowned. "Just me?"

"Oh, lots of secondaries, but they were slightly less reliable for one
reason or another, or slightly weaker in one or another way, or, frankly,
were engaged on other vital business or located halfway around the Confederacy."

"Then you've got two problems," the young man told Krega. "First, you
have to figure out how the hell I'd volunteer willingly for an assignment
like this, and, second, how you're going to make . . ." His voice trailed off
and he suddenly sat up straight. "I think I see . . ."

"I thought you would." Krega sounded satisfied and confident. "It's
probably the most guarded secret in the Confederacy, but the Merton Process works now. Almost a hundred percent."

The other nodded absently, thinking about it. When he'd received his
promotion to Inspector over a year ago, they'd taken him into an elaborate
and somewhat mystifying laboratory and put him into some sort of hypnotic state. He was never quite sure what they had done, but he'd had a
headache for three days and that had aroused his curiosity. The Merton
Process. The key to immortality, some said. It had taken a hell of a lot of
spare-time detective work to come even that close to it, and all he'd been
able to determine in the end was that the Confederacy was working on a
process wherein the entire memory, the entire personality, of an individual
could be taken, stored in some way, and then imprinted on another brain,
perhaps a clone brain. He had also learned that every time it had been
tried, the new body either had become hopelessly insane or had died. He
said as much.

"That used to be the case," Krega agreed, "but no more. The clone
brains just couldn't take it. Raised in tanks, they had developed different
brain patterns for the autonomic functions, and those were always
disrupted in the transfer. Still, we had been able to remove all the conscious part of the brain from someone and then put it back just the way
it was in the original body while also keeping the original information on
file. That led, of course, to trying it with other bodies—remove the cerebral
part, as it were, just like erasing a recording, then put someone else's personality and memories in there. It's a ticklish business—only works once in
a while, when loads of factors I don't understand very well, and maybe
Merton doesn't either, match. The new body has to be at least two years
younger than the original, for example. On the other hand, some impor-

tant factors like sex or planetary origin seem to be irrelevant. Still, we get a perfect transfer about one in twenty times."

He stirred uneasily. "What happens to the other nineteen?"

Krega shrugged. "They die, or are nuts and have to be destroyed. We use only minor antisocials anyway, those who would have to be psyched and programmed or simply eliminated. We took your print fourteen months ago—you must know that. Now we can make four of you. Different bodies, of course, but you inside in every single detail. More than four, if necessary. We can drop you on all four planets simultaneously, complete with criminal record and past history. We can drop you on all four and still keep *you* here, as you are, to correlate the data from the others."

The young man said nothing for almost a minute, then: "Well, I'll be damned."

"Four times damned, yet also not damned at all," the commander came back. "So you see, there's no risk. We already *have* your imprint."

He considered the facts. "Still, there'd have to be a more recent one," he noted. "It wouldn't do to have four of me wake up en route to the Warden Diamond in different bodies with no knowledge of the last fourteen months, not to mention this conversation."

Krega nodded. "You're right, of course. But I have mine updated annually, anyway. Except for the headache, if the process worked the first time it'll work ever after."

"That's reassuring," the man replied uncomfortably, considering that they had done it to him without his knowledge before—and the commander's words implied that sometimes it *didn't* work. Dismissing that idea from his mind, he asked, "But how do I get the data to correlate? Even supposing that these four versions of me are able to ferret out everything you want to know—how do *I* know it?"

Krega reached into a desk drawer and pulled out a small box. He opened it gingerly and pushed it over to the young man. "With this," he said flatly.

The man looked at the object. "This" turned out to be a tiny little bead of unknown substance so small it could hardly be seen with the naked eye even in its black velveteen setting.

"A tracer implant?" The young man was skeptical. "What good does that do us?" The device was familiar to all cops; it could be implanted anywhere on a body with no chance of detection and with no operation necessary. Once in place, someone could follow its signal to just about anywhere—a common police tool.

"Not a tracer," the commander told him. "Based on it, I'll admit, but more a by-product of the Merton researches. It is implanted directly into a specific point in the brain—I'm sorry I don't have enough technical biology to explain further. You'll get one, too. It only works when two bodies have exactly the same brain pattern; otherwise you get gibberish. Using the tracer part, a special receiver can locate the wearer anywhere on a planet, then lock onto him, receive, and enormously amplify what it receives, which then is fed to a Merton recorder. From that another imprint can be made, a 'soft' one, that will give its matched mate a record of just what happened after the new body awoke until we took the readout. It's soft—they tell me the sensation is kind of like seeing a movie all at once. But it's a record of everything your counterpart said and did. We'll put you on a guard picket ship, very comfortable, and take almost continuous soft imprints using monitor satellites. You'll have your information, all right. And the thing's actually a quasi-organic substance, so even on Lilith, which hates everything alien, it will continue to function as part of the body. We know. We have a couple of people with tracers down there now—they don't know it, of course. Just a test. Works fine."

The young man nodded. "You seem to have thought of everything." He paused a moment. "And what if I refuse after all this? Or to put it another way, what if I say to go ahead and my, ah, alter egos decide once down there not to cooperate?"

Krega grinned evilly. "Consider what I'm offering. We have the capacity to make you immortal—if you succeed. If you succeed, no reward would be high enough. You are an atheist. You know that when you go, you go forever—unless you succeed. Then you, and because of the soft imprints, your alter egos as well will continue to exist. Continue to live on. I think that is quite an inducement."

The young man looked thoughtful. "I wonder if *they* will see it that way?" he mused, only half aloud.

Four Lords of the Diamond. Four enormously powerful, clever people to kill. Four keys to an enigma that could spell the end of humanity. Five problems, five puzzles.

Krega didn't really have to offer a reward. The assignment was irresistible.

3

The base ship was seven kilometers long. It floated there off the Warden system, about a quarter of a light-year from the sun. Designed as a floating base, almost a mini-world, the ship was completely self-contained, and were it not for the feeling of isolation all around, a pretty comfortable duty.

From its lower decks sped the picket ships: one-man or often totally automated vessels that encircled the Warden system and kept the base ship in constant touch with every section of space around and inside the solar system itself. All commerce had to come here first, then be transferred to automated craft for an in-system run. No one but the military was allowed beyond the perimeter the picket ships established, and even military personnel never landed. The penalty for any violation was simple—capture if possible, elimination if not possible. Between the automatic guardians and the manned patrols a violator might get by one or two, but he would have to run a gauntlet of several hundred to get anywhere meaningful—and do so against the best defensive computers known.

For this reason, the pinpointing of the Warden Diamond as the center of some alien conspiracy was met with a great deal of skepticism by the organized military forces, most of which believed that the alien robot had simply practiced misdirection in desperation after being discovered.

The analytical computers and strategic specialists thought otherwise. At least, they couldn't afford *not* to think otherwise, which explained the arrival of a very special man at the base ship. They all knew he was special, and rumors abounded as to who he was, whom he worked for, and what he was doing there; but no one, not even the commanding admiral, really knew for sure.

With the man came a complete module that interlocked to the building-block nature of the base ship in the security control section. From here the mysterious man would do whatever he was doing, away from all others, surrounded by security guards who had no idea who he was or what he was doing—and who could not enter the module any more than the admiral could. It was keyed to the man's own brain waves, voice print, retinal pattern, gene structure, and just about everything else any paranoid security division had ever figured out. Anyone else attempting entry would be instantly stopped and neatly packaged for security. Any nonliving thing that tried would be instantly vaporized.

Although the man had been there for months, not a soul even knew his name. Not that he was totally withdrawn—on the contrary, he joined in the sports games in Recreation, ate his meals in the Security Mess, even wined and dined some female soldiers and civilians aboard, many of whom were simply intrigued by this man of mystery. He was likable, easygoing, relaxed. But in all those months he had not revealed the slightest thing about himself, not even to those with whom he'd been most intimate—although, security officers noted, he'd had a positive knack of finding out the most private things about the people with whom he'd come in contact. They admired him for his total self-control and absolute professionalism, and even the highest-ranking of them were scared stiff of him.

He spent several hours most days in his little cubicle, and always slept there. They all wondered and guessed at what was inside until they were almost crazy with curiosity, but they never guessed the truth.

He heard the buzzer sounding as he entered the command module and for the first time felt genuine excitement and anticipation. Long ago he'd accomplished all he could with the physical data, but for too long now it had been a boring exercise. The computer filed what it could from the memory traces but gave him a picture that was too emotional and incomplete when examined in his own mind to make much sense. Hoping this time would be different, he headed for the master command chair and sat comfortably in it. The computer, sensing its duty, lowered the small probes, which he placed around his head, then administered the measured injections and began the master readout.

For a while he floated in a semihypnotic fog, but slowly images started forming in his brain as they had before. Only now they seemed more definite, clearer, more like his own thoughts. The drugs and small neural probes did their job. His own mind and personality receded, replaced by a similar, yet oddly different pattern.

"The agent is commanded to report," the computer ordered, sending the command deep into his own mind, a mind no longer his own.

What would happen, or so the techs had advised him, would amount to a sort of total recall from the mind of his counterpart down below, information his own mind would sort, classify, and edit into a coherent narrative.

Recorders clicked on.

Slowly the man in the chair cleared his throat several times. It still took more than three hours to get him to do anything beyond mumbling some odd words or sounds, but the computers were nothing if not patient, knowing that the man's mind was receiving a massive amount of data and was struggling to sort and classify it.

Finally the man began to speak.

CHAPTER ONE

Rebirth

After Krega's talk and a little preparation to put my own affairs in order—this would be a long one—I checked into the Confederacy Security Clinic. I'd been here many times before, of course, but never knowingly for this purpose. Mostly, this was where they programmed you with whatever information you'd need for a mission and where, too, you were reintegrated. Naturally, the kind of work I did was often extralegal, a term I prefer to illegal, which implies criminal intent—and much of it was simply too hot ever to be revealed. To avoid such risks, all agents had their own experience of a mission wiped from their minds when it involved sensitive matters.

It may seem like a strange life, going about not knowing where you have been or what you've done, but it has its compensations. Because any potential enemy, military or political, knows you've been wiped, you can live a fairly normal, relaxed life outside of a mission structure. No purpose is served in coming after you—you have no knowledge of what you've done, or why, or for or to whom. In exchange for those blanks, an agent of the Confederacy lives a life of luxury and ease, with an almost unlimited supply of money, and with all the comforts supplied. I bummed around, swam, gambled, ate in the best restaurants, played a little semipro ball or cube—I'm pretty good, and it keeps me in shape. I enjoyed every minute of it, and except for my regular requalification training sessions—four- to six-week stints that resemble military basic training, only nastier and more sadistic—I felt no guilt at my playboy life. The training sessions are to make sure that your body and mind don't turn soft from all that good living. Permanently implanted sensors constantly monitor and decide when you need a good refresher.

I often wondered just how sophisticated those sensors were. The thought that a whole security staff might see all my debauchery and indiscretions used to worry me, but after a while I learned to ignore it.

The life offered in trade is just too nice. Besides, what could I do about it? People on most civilized worlds these days had such sensors, although hardly to the degree and sophistication of mine. How else could a population so vast and spread out possibly be kept orderly, progressive, and otherwise peaceful?

But when a mission came up you naturally couldn't forgo all the past experience you'd had. A wipe without storage simply wouldn't have been very practical, since a good agent gets better by not repeating his mistakes.

So the first thing you did was go to the Security Clinic, where they stored everything you ever experienced, and get the rest of you put back so you would be whole for whatever they'd dreamed up this time.

It always amazed me when I got up from that chair with my past fully restored. Even the clear memories of the things I'd done always amazed me, that I, of all people, had done this or that. The only difference this time, I knew, was that the process would be taken one step further. Not only would the complete "me" get up from that table, but the same memory pattern would be impressed on other minds, other bodies—as many as needed until a "take" was achieved.

I wondered what they'd be like, those four other versions of myself. Physically different, probably—the kind of offender they got here wasn't usually from one of the civilized worlds, where people had basically been standardized in the name of equality. No, these people would come from the frontier, from the traders, and miners and freebooters who existed at the edge of expansion, and who were necessary in an expanding culture, since a high degree of individuality, self-reliance, originality, and creativity was required in the dangerous situations in which they lived. A stupid government would have eliminated all such, but a stupid government degenerates or loses its vitality and potential for growth by standardization.

That, of course, was the original reason for the Warden Diamond Reserve. Some of these hard-frontier types are so individualistic that they become a threat to the stability of the civilized worlds. The trouble is, anybody able to loosen the bonds that hold our society together is most likely the smartest, nastiest, meanest, cleverest, most original sort of mind humanity can produce—and therefore not somebody who should be idly wiped clean. The Diamond could effectively trap people of this sort forever, allowing them continued creative opportunities which, when properly monitored, might still produce something of value for the Confederacy—if only an idea, a thought, a way of looking at something that nobody else could come up with.

And the felons down there were naturally anxious to please as well, since the alternative was death. Eventually, such creative minds made themselves indispensable to the Confederacy and ensured their continued survival.

The damned probe hurt like hell. Usually there was just some tingling followed by a sensation much like sleep, and you woke up a few minutes later in the chair once again yourself. This time the tingling became a painful physical force that seemed to enter my skull and bounce around, then seize control of my head. It was as if a huge, giant hand had grabbed my brain and squeezed, then released, then squeezed again in excruciating pulses. Instead of drifting off to sleep, I passed out.

I woke up and groaned slightly. The throbbing was gone, but the memory was still all too current and all too vivid. It was several minutes, I think, before I found enough strength to sit up.

The old memories flooded back, and again I amazed myself by recalling many of my past exploits. I wondered if my surrogate selves would get similar treatment, considering that they couldn't be wiped after this mission as I could. That realization caused me to make a mental note that those surrogates would almost certainly have to be killed if they did have my entire memory pattern. Otherwise, a lot of secrets would be loose on the Warden Diamond and many in the hands of people who'd know just what sort of use to make of them.

No sooner had I thought of that than I had the odd feeling of *wrongness*. I looked around the small room in which I'd awakened and realized immediately the source of that feeling.

This wasn't the Security Clinic, wasn't anyplace I'd ever seen before. It was a tiny cubicle, about twelve cubic meters total, including the slightly higher than normal ceiling. In it was a small cot on which I'd awakened, a small basin and next to it a standard food port, and in the wall, a pulldown toilet. That was it. Nothing else—or was there?

I looked around and spotted the most obvious easily. Yes, I couldn't make a move without being visually and probably aurally monitored. The door was almost invisible and there was certainly no way to open it from inside. I grasped immediately where I was.

It was a prison cell.

Far worse than that, I could feel a faint vibration that had no single source. The sensation wasn't irritating; in fact it was so faint as to be hardly noticeable, but I knew what it was. I was aboard a ship, moving somewhere through space.

I stood up, reeling a little bit from a slight bout of dizziness that soon passed, and looked down at my body. It was tremendously muscular, the body of a miner or some other sort of heavy laborer. There were a few scars on it that obviously had been treated by someone other than a meditech, and I recognized two of them as knife wounds.

My entire body was almost covered in thick, coarse, black hair—more hair on my chest, arms, and legs than I'd ever seen on anything but an animal. I couldn't help noticing, though, that I was better endowed sexually than I had believed humanly possible. I just stood there, stunned, for I don't know how long.

I'm not me! my mind screamed at me. *I'm one of them—one of the surrogates!*

I sat back down on the cot, telling myself that it just wasn't possible. I knew who I was, remembered every bit, every detail, of my life and work.

My shock gave way after a while to anger—anger and frustration. I was a copy, an imitation of somebody else entirely, somebody still alive and kicking and perhaps monitoring my every move, my every thought. I hated that other then, hated him with a pathological force that was beyond reason. He would sit there comfortable and safe, watching me work, watching me do it all—and when it was over, he'd go home for debriefing, return to that easy life, while I . . .

They were going to dump me on a world of the Warden Diamond, trap me like some kind of master criminal, imprisoned there for the rest of my life—of this body's life, anyway. And then? When my job was done? I'd said it myself upon awakening, passed my own sentence. The things I knew! I would be monitored at all times, of course. Monitored and killed if I blew any of those secrets. Killed anyway at the completion of the mission just for insurance.

My training came into automatic play at that point, overriding the shock and anger. I regained control and considered everything I knew.

Monitor? Sure—more than ever. I recalled Krega saying that there was some sort of organic linkup. Are you enjoying this, you son of a bitch? Are you getting pleasure from vicariously experiencing my reaction?

My training clicked on again, dampening me down. It didn't matter, I told myself. First of all, I knew just what he must be thinking—and that was an advantage. *He,* of all people, would know that I would be a damned tough son of a bitch to kill.

It was a shock to discover that you were not who you thought you were but some artificial creation. It was a shock, too, to realize that the old life, the life you remembered even if you personally didn't experience it, was gone forever. No more civilized worlds, no more casinos and beautiful women and all the money you could spend. And yet as I sat there, I adjusted. That was what they picked men like me for from the start: we had the ability to adjust and adapt to almost anything.

Although this was not my body, I was still me. Memory and thought and personality made up an individual, not his body. This was no more than a biological disguise, I told myself, of a particularly sophisticated sort. As to who was really me—it seemed to me that this personality, these memories, were no more that other fellow's than my own. Until I got up from that chair back in the Security Clinic I had really been somebody else anyway. A lot of me, my memories and training, had been missing. That old between-missions me was the artificial me, the created me, I thought. He, that nonentity playboy that currently did not exist, was the artificial personality. The real me was bottled up and stored in their psychosurgical computers and only allowed to come out when they needed it—and for good reason. Unleashed, I was as much a danger to the power structure as to whomever they set me against.

And I was good. The best, Krega had called me. That's why I was here now, in this body, in this cell, on this ship. And I wouldn't be wiped and I wouldn't be killed if I could help it. That other me, sitting there in the console—somehow I no longer hated him very much, no longer felt anything at all for him. When this was all over he'd be wiped once more— perhaps killed himself if my brother agents on the Diamond and I found out too much. At best he'd return to being that stagnant milquetoast.

Me, on the other hand . . . Me, I would still be here, still live on, the *real* me. I would become more complete than he would.

I was under no illusions, though. Kill me they would, if they could, if I didn't do their bidding. They'd do it automatically, from robot satellite, and without a qualm. *I* would. But my vulnerability would last only until I mastered my new situation and my new and permanent home. I felt that with a deep sense of certainty, for I knew their methods and how they thought. I'd have to do their dirty work for them, and they knew it—but only until I could find a way around it. They could be beaten, even on their own turf. That was why they had people like me in the first place: to uncover those who expertly covered over their whole lives and activities, who managed to vanish totally from their best monitors—to uncover them and get them.

But there'd be no new expert agent sent to get me if *I* beat them. They'd just be putting somebody else in the same position.

I realized then, as they had undoubtedly figured, that I had no choice but to carry out the mission. Only as long as I was doing what they wanted would I be safe from them while still in that vulnerable stage. After that—well, we'd see.

The thrill of the challenge took over, as it always did. The puzzle to be solved, the objectives to be accomplished. I like to win, which is even easier when you feel nothing about the cause, just the challenge of the problem and the opponent and the physical and intellectual effort neces- sary to meet that challenge. Find out about the alien menace. It no longer concerned me either way—I was trapped on a Warden world from now on anyway. If the aliens won the coming confrontation, the Wardens would survive as allies. If they lost, well, it wouldn't make a damned bit of difference, only continue the current situation. That meant the alien problem was purely an intellectual challenge, which made it perfect.

The other objective created a similar situation. Seek out the Lord of that particular Diamond world and kill him if I could. In a sense accomplishing that would be more difficult, for I'd be operating on totally unfamiliar ground and would therefore require time and perhaps some allies. Another challenge. And if I got him, it could only increase my own power and position in the long term. If he got me instead, of course, that would solve everybody's problem—but the thought of losing is abhorrent to me. That set the contest in the best terms, from my point of view. Track down assassination was the ultimate game, since either you won or you died and did not have to live with the thought that you lost.

It suddenly occurred to me that the only real difference between me and a Lord of the Diamond was that I was working *for* the law and he—or she—against it. But no, that wasn't right, either. On his world *he* was the law and I would be working against that. Fine. Dead heat on moral grounds.

The only thing wrong at this point, I reflected, was that they were starting me at a tremendous disadvantage. The normal procedure was to program all pertinent information into my brain before setting me off on a mission—but they hadn't done that this time. Probably, I thought, because they had me once on the table for four separate missions, and the transfer process, to a new body, was hard enough without trying to add anything afterward. Still, this method put me in a deep pit. I thought sourly that somebody should have thought of that.

Somebody did, but it was a while before I discovered how. About an hour after I had awakened a little bell clanged near the food port and I went over to it. Almost instantly a hot tray appeared, along with a thin plastic fork and knife I recognized as the dissolving type. They'd melt into a sticky puddle in an hour or less, then dry up into a powder shortly after that. Standard for prisoners.

The food was lousy, but I hadn't expected better. The vitamin-enriched fruit drink with it, though, was pretty good; I made the most of it, keeping the thin, clear container (not the dissolving type) in case I wanted water later. Everything else I put back in the port, and it vaporized neatly. All nice and sealed.

About the only thing they couldn't control was bodily functions, and a half-hour or so after eating my first meal as a new man, you might say, nature called. On the far wall was a panel marked "toilet" and a small pull ring. Simple, standard stuff. I pulled the ring, the thing came down—and damned if there wasn't a small, paper-thin probe in the recess behind it. And so I sat on the john, leaned back against the panel, and got brief and relief at the same time.

The thing worked by skin contact—don't ask me how. I'm not one of the tech brains. It was not as good as a programming, but it enabled them to talk to me, even send me pictures that only I could see and hear.

"By now I hope you're over the shock of discovering who and what you are," Krega's voice came to me, seemingly forming in my brain. I was shocked when I realized that not even my jailers could hear or see a thing.

"We have to brief you this way simply because the transfer process is delicate enough as it is. Oh, don't worry about it—it's permanent. But we prefer to allow as much time as possible for your brain patterns to fit in and adapt without subjecting the brain to further shock, and we haven't the time to allow you to 'set in' completely, as it were. This method will have to do, and I profoundly regret it, for I feel you have the most difficult task of all four."

I felt the excitement rise in me. The challenge, the challenge . . .

"Your objective world is Lilith, first of the Diamond colonies," the commander's voice continued. "Lilith is, scientifically speaking, a madhouse. There is simply no rational, scientific explanation for what you will find there. The only thing that keeps all of us from going over the brink is that the place does have rules and is consistent within its own framework of logic. I will leave most of that to your orientation once you make planetfall. You will be met and briefed as a convict—along with the other inmates being sent there with you—by representatives of the Lord of Lilith, and that will be more effective than anything I can give you secondhand.

"Though the imprint ability of this device is limited," he continued, "we can send you one basic thing that, oddly, you will not find on Lilith itself. It is a map of the entire place, as detailed as we could make it."

I felt a sharp back pain followed by a wave of dizziness and nausea; this quickly cleared and I found that in fact I had a detailed physical-political map of the entirety of Lilith in my head. It would come in very handy.

There followed a stream of facts about the place not likely to be too detailed in any indoctrination lecture. The planet was roughly 52,000 kilometers around at the equator or from pole to pole, allowing for topographic differences. Like all four of the Warden Diamond worlds, it was basically a ball—highly unusual as planets go, even though everybody including me thinks of all major planets as round.

The gravity was roughly .95 norm, so I'd feel lighter and be able to jump further. That would take a slight adjustment of timing, and I made a note to work on that first and foremost. It was also a hair higher than the norm for oxygen, which would make me feel a tad more energetic but also would make fires burn a little easier, quicker, and brighter. Not much, though. The higher concentration of water than normal combined with its 85-degree axial tilt and slightly under 192,000,000 kilometer distance from its sun—made this world mostly hot and very humid with minimal seasons. Latitude and elevation would be responsible for the main temperature variations on Lilith, not what month it was. Elevation loss was a near-standard 3 degrees centigrade per 1,800 meters.

And even latitude wasn't all that much of a factor. Equatorial temperatures were scorchers—35 to 50 degrees centigrade, 25 to 34 or so in the midlatitudes, and never less than 20 degrees even at the poles. No ice caps on Lilith. No ice, either, which in itself might explain why there was only one enormous continent on Lilith, along with a bunch of islands.

A day was 32.2 standard hours, so it would take some adjusting to the new time rate. A lot, I thought. That was over 8 hours more than I was used to. But I'd coped with almost as bad; I could cope with this one, too. A year was 344 Lilith days. So it was a large world, as worlds go, but with low gravity, which meant no metals to speak of. Pretty good prison, I thought.

"The Lord of Lilith is Marek Kreegan," Krega continued. "Most certainly the most dangerous of the Four Lords, for he alone is not a criminal or convict but instead was, like you, an agent of the Confederacy, one of the best. Were he able to leave the Warden system, he would probably be considered the most dangerous man alive."

I felt a thrill go through me for more than one reason. First, the absolute challenge of tracking down and hitting one like myself, one trained as I was and considered the most dangerous man alive—it was fantastic. But more than that, this information offered me two rays of hope that I'm fairly sure Krega hadn't considered. If this man was a top agent sent down on a mission, he'd have been in the same position as I would be upon its completion—and he hadn't been killed. There could be only one reason for that: they had no way of killing him. He'd figured the way out and taken it. Perfect. If Kreegan could do it, so could I.

And he'd worked himself up to being the Lord of Lilith.

The logic still held. If he and I were judged at least equal, then that meant that I potentially have the same powers as he has—greater powers than anyone else on the planet or somebody else would be Lord. And what he could do, I could do.

"Still, to find Kreegan, let alone kill him, could prove to be an almost impossible task," Krega continued. "First of all, he rarely makes an appearance, and when he does, he is always concealed. Everyone who discovers what he looks like is killed. He has no fixed base, but roams the world, always in disguise. This keeps his underlings on their toes and relatively honest, at least toward him. They never know who he might be, but fear him tremendously, as he can kill them and they can do nothing to him. At last count there were a little over 13,244,000 people on Lilith—that's a rough estimate, of course. A very small population, you'll agree—but Kreegan can be any one of them."

Well, actually he couldn't, I noted to myself. For one thing, Kreegan was a standard from the civilized worlds. That meant he was within fairly definite physical limits, thus eliminating a lot of people. Of course, since I knew he was male that eliminated close to half the population right there. He was also seventy-seven, but he'd been on Lilith for twenty-one years, which would change him a great deal from any picture of him as a younger man. Still, he'd be an older man, and on Lilith older men would stand out anyway—it would be a rough world. So we call him middle-aged, standard height and build, and male. When you were starting with 13,000,000, that narrowed the field down more than, I suspect, Krega himself realized.

A challenge, yes, but not as impossible as it sounded. Even more important, as the Lord and administrator there would be certain places he'd have to hit, and certain functions he'd have to attend. Still more narrowing down, and I wasn't even on the planet yet.

The rest of the briefing was pretty routine. After it was over I simply got off the john and pushed it back in the wall. I heard a flushing sound and, the next time I used it, discovered that my waste wasn't the only thing that had disappeared. Because it had been a direct neural transmission, less than a minute was needed to get all the information they could pack into it, too.

Extremely efficient, the security boys, I told myself. Even my ever-vigilant jailers on the other end of those lenses and mikes would have no idea that I was anybody other than who I was supposed to be.

As to who that was, I'd gotten my first mental picture of myself from the briefing. Brutish, my old self might have said, but in many ways I was not all that bad-looking and definitely oversexed—something I really didn't mind at all.

I was Cal Tremon, a lone-wolf pirate, murderer, and all-around bad boy. Over two meters tall, 119 kilos of pure muscle and gristle. My face was square and tough-looking, with a shock of coal-black hair fading into a beard that framed it like some beast's mane, with a big, bushy mustache that connected to the sideburns. A broad mouth, thick-lipped, atop which sat a slightly flattened but very large nose. The eyes were large and a deep brown, but what made the effect so menacing was the bushy black eyebrows that actually connected at the bridge of the nose.

I looked and felt like some primordial caveman, one of our remotest ancestors. Yet the body was in good condition, tremendously powerful and formidable—far more powerful than my own had been. The muscles bulged. It would take some getting used to, this huge, brutish body, but once fine-tuned it would, I was certain, be an enormous asset.

On the other hand, the one thing Cal Tremon had never been and never would be is a cat burglar. He was about as petite as a volcano.

He. I, my mind corrected. Now and forever after I was Cal Tremon.

I lay back down on the cot and put myself in a light trance, going over all the briefing information, filing, sorting, thinking. The data on Tremon's own life and colorful, if bloody, career was of particular import. Although he didn't seem like the kind of guy who would have any friends, there was a world full of crooks down there. Somebody must have known him.

CHAPTER TWO

Transportation and Exposure

Except for regular meals I had no way to keep track of time, but it was a fairly long trip. They weren't wasting any money transporting prisoners by the fastest available routes, that was for sure.

Finally, though, we docked with the base ship a third of a light-year out from the Warden system. I knew it not so much by any sensation inside my cloister but by the lack of it—the vibration that had been my constant companion stopped. Still, the routine wasn't varied; I supposed they were waiting for a large enough contingent from around the galaxy to make the landing worthwhile. I could only sit and go over my data for the millionth time, occasionally reflecting on the fact that I probably wasn't very far from my old body (that's how I'd come to think of it). I wondered if perhaps he didn't even come down and take a peek at me from time to time, at least out of idle curiosity—me and the three others who probably were also here.

I also had time to reflect on what I knew of the Warden situation itself, the reason for its perfection as a prison. I had not of course swallowed that whole—there was no such thing as the perfect prison, although this one had to come close. Shortly after I was landed on Lilith and started wading in and breathing its air I would be infected with an oddball submicroscopic organism that would set up housekeeping in every cell of my body. There it would live, feeding off me, even earning its keep by keeping disease organisms, infections, and the like in check. The one thing that stuff had was a will to live, and it only lived if you did.

But it needed something, some trace element or some such that was only present in the Warden system. Nobody knew what and nobody had been able to do the real work to find out, but whatever it needed other than you was found only in the Warden system. Whatever it was wasn't in the air, because shuttles ran between the worlds of the Diamond and in them you breathed the purified, mechanically produced stuff with no ill effect. It wasn't in the food, either. They'd checked that. It was possible for one of the Warden people to live comfortably on synthetics in a totally isolated lab such as a planetary space station. But get too far away, even with Warden food and Warden air, and it died; and since it had modified your cells to make itself at home, and those cells depended on the organism to keep working properly, you died, too—painfully and slowly, in horrible agony. That distance was roughly a quarter of a light-year from the sun, which explained the location of the base ship.

All four worlds were more than climatologically different, too. The organism was consistent in what it did to you on each planet, but—possibly because of distance from the sun, since that seemed to be the determining factor in its life—it did different things to you depending on which world you were first exposed to it, and whatever it did stuck in just that fashion even if you went to a different world of the Diamond.

The organism seemed somehow to be vaguely telepathic in some way, although nobody explained how. It certainly wasn't an intelligent organism; at least it always behaved predictably. Still, most of the changes seemed to involve the colony in one person affecting the colony in another —or others. You provided the conscious control, if you could, and that determined who bossed whom. A pretty simple system, even if nobody had yet been able to explain it.

As for Lilith, all I would remember was that it was some sort of Garden of Eden. I cursed again not having been fed the proper programming to make me fully prepared. Learning the ropes there would take time, possibly a lot of it.

About a day and a half—five meals—after I'd arrived at the base ship, a lurching and a lot of banging around forced me to the cot and made me slightly seasick. Still, I wasn't disappointed. No doubt they were making up the consignments and readying for the in-system drop of these cells. I faced the idea with mixed emotions. On the one hand, I wanted desperately to be out of this little box, which provided nothing but endless, terrible boredom. On the other, when I next emerged from the box it would be into a much larger and probably prettier box—Lilith itself, no less a cell for being an entire planet. And what it would make up for in diversion, challenge, excitement, or whatever, it would also be, unlike this box, very, very final.

Shortly after the banging about started, it stopped again, and after a short, expectant pause, I again felt a vibration indicating movement— much more pronounced than before. Either I was on a much smaller vessel or located nearer the drives. Whatever, it took another four interminable days, twelve meals, to reach our destination. Long, certainly—but also fast for a sublight carrier, probably a modified and totally automated freighter. The vibration stopped and I knew we were in orbit. Again I had that dual feeling of being both trapped and exhilarated.

There was a crackling sound, whereupon a speaker I'd never even known was there suddenly came to life. "Attention, all prisoners!" it commanded, its voice a metallic parody of a man's baritone. "We have achieved orbit around the planet Lilith in the Warden system," it continued, telling me nothing I didn't know but probably informing the others, however many there were, for the first time. I could understand what they must be going through, considering my own feelings. A hundred times mine, probably, since at least I was going in with my eyes open even if no more voluntarily than they. I wondered for a fleeting instant about Lord Kreegan. *He* had gone in voluntarily, the only one I ever knew about. I couldn't help but wonder why. Perhaps there were things about the War-den Diamond that were outside the knowledge of the Confederacy.

"In a moment," the voice continued, "the doors to your cells will slide open and you will be able to leave. We strongly recommend you do so, since thirty seconds after the doors open they will close again and a vac-uum pump will begin sterilization operations within the cells. This would be fatal to anyone who remains."

Nice touch, I thought. Not only did their method ensure against break-outs en route, you moved or you died on their schedule. I couldn't help wonder whether anybody chose death.

"Immediately after you enter the main corridor," the voice continued, "you will stand in place until the cell doors close once again. Do not at-tempt to move from in front of your cell door until it closes or automatic guard equipment will vaporize you. There will be no talking in the corri-dor. Anyone breaking silence or failing to obey orders precisely will be dealt with instantly. You will receive further instructions once the doors close. Ready to depart—*now!*"

The door slid open and I wasted no time in stepping out. A small white box, complete with marks for feet, indicated where you were to stand. I did as instructed, galling as all this was. Being totally naked and isolated on a ship controlled only by a computer humbled you more than was right, gave you a sense of total futility.

I could still look around and saw that I'd been right. We were standing in what was basically a long, sealed hall, along the sides of which were at-tached the little cells. I looked up and down and counted maybe a dozen, certainly no more than fifteen. The cream of the crop, I thought sourly. A dozen men and women—about half and half—naked and bedraggled, beaten prisoners about to be dropped and left. I wondered why these had been selected for transport rather than wiped, considering the trans-portation expense alone. What had the computers and psych boys found in these dejected specimens that dictated that they should live? *They* didn't know, that was for sure. I wondered who did.

The doors snapped shut. I waited expectantly, listening perhaps for the scream of somebody who didn't move fast enough as the air was pumped out, but there was no hint of melodrama. If anybody had taken that way out, the fact was not evident.

"At my command," the voice barked from speakers along the ceiling, "you will turn right and walk slowly, in single file, as far forward as you can. There you will find a special shuttle that will take you to the surface. You will take seats from the front first, leaving no empty seats between you. Immediately strap yourselves in."

"Sons of bitches," I heard a woman ahead of me mutter. At once a brief but very visible spurt of light from a side wall hit with an audible hiss just in front of her foot. She started in surprise, then muttered, "All right, all right." She was silent once more.

The voice had paused, but now took up its instructions with no reference to the incident. "Right turn—*now!*" it commanded, and we did as instructed. "Walk slowly forward to the shuttle as instructed."

We walked in silence, definitely in no hurry. The metal floor of the corridor was damned cold, though—in fact, the place wasn't any too comfortable as a whole—and this made the shuttle at least preferable to this damned refrigerator.

The shuttle itself was surprisingly comfortable and modern, although the seats weren't made for naked bodies. I found a seat about four rows back and attached the safety straps, then waited for the rest to enter. My first impression had been close, I noted. The shuttle itself could seat twenty-four, but there were only fourteen of us, eight males and six females.

The hatch closed automatically, and I heard the hiss of pressurization. Then, without further fanfare, there was a violent lurch and we were free of the transport and on our way down.

The shuttle was much too modern and comfortable for mere prisoner transport, I told myself. This, then, had to be one of the interplanetary ships regularly used for transportation between the worlds of the Warden Diamond.

The overhead speakers crackled, and a much nicer female voice that actually sounded human came on. It was a great improvement.

"Welcome to Lilith," the voice said, sounding for all the world as if it meant it. "As has no doubt been explained to you, Lilith is your final destination and new home. Although you will be unable to leave the Warden system after debarking, you will no longer be prisoners but citizens of the Warden Diamond. Confederacy rule ended when you entered this shuttle, which is owned in common by the Warden Worlds, one of a fleet of four shuttlecraft and sixteen freighters. The System Council is a corporate entity fully recognized as internally sovereign by the Confederacy and even with a seat in the Confederation Congress. Each of the four worlds is also under separate administration, and the governments of each planet are unique and independent. No matter who you were or what you might have been or done in the past, you are now citizens of Lilith and nothing more. You are no longer prisoners. Anything done prior to now is past history that will not be remembered, filed, or referred to ever again. Only what you do from this point on, as citizens of Lilith, Warden System, will matter."

It—or she, I really wasn't sure—paused for that piece of information to sink in. The contrast between the attitude and tone taken now and the one we'd all just been subjected to was enormous.

"Because of the unique properties of Lilith," the voice continued, "the shuttle cannot remain long or it might become disabled. Furthermore, it has a schedule to keep, and others need to use it. We therefore would appreciate your debarking as soon as the hatch opens. Someone will be there to meet you, answer your questions and assign you to your new homes. Please cooperate with this individual, as Lilith is a primitive world and extremely dangerous to newcomers. We will arrive in approximately five minutes."

Although the lid was off, nobody really said anything for the rest of the ride—partly because we were still conditioned by our recent imprisonment; the rest was nerves, me included. This was it, I told myself. Here we go.

A sudden sensation of falling as if we'd hit an air pocket in some flying craft was followed by the reimposition of weight and a hard thump. They had come in as fast as was safely possible, and I wondered for a moment what their hurry was. Then the hatch hissed and opened; to my surprise, a sudden rush of tremendously warm, moist air hit us.

We lost no time doing as instructed—no use in alienating our new lords and masters before we even got the lay of the land—and debarked quickly. I was surprised to find a moving walkway extending from the shuttlecraft itself down to the bare ground. No spaceport, nothing. In a matter of moments we were standing, naked and disoriented and already beaded with sweat from the heat, on a grassy plain or meadow.

We had arrived on Lilith—and even as that first warm rush of native air had hit us our bodies were being systematically invaded.

CHAPTER THREE

Orientation and Placement

I was aware of others around now—not the mechanics and service personnel one would expect but just other people—passengers for the outbound, I realized. A half-dozen or so wearing loose-fitting skirts or even shiny robes but not looking very different from the run-of-the-mill frontier individual I knew well. Not very different from us, really. After the last of us emerged, they moved quickly to replace us on the craft, a sleek, saucerlike vessel. The ramp retracted and the hatch closed almost immediately.

"They sure don't waste any time, do they?" a man near me remarked, and I had to agree.

Reflecting for a moment on the passengers I *did* realize one odd thing about them that separated them from any passengers on any interplanetary craft I'd ever known. None of them, not one, carried any sort of luggage—and there certainly had not been time to load any before we got off. In fact, none of them had anything at all except the flimsy-looking clothes they had worn.

We were well clear of the craft and watched it come to life, then rise very quickly. The ship was gone in an instant, yet all of us followed it with our eyes, continuing to stare at the exact spot where it had vanished into the deep blue sky. It was as if that shuttle represented our last link with the old culture, our last line to the places we'd been and the people we'd known—and the people we had been, too.

I was among the first to look down and spotted a very attractive woman approaching us. Wearing only one of those flimsy but colorful skirts and what looked like a pair of flat sandals, she was extremely tall—almost 180 centimeters, surely—with long black hair, her skin tanned very dark, almost black.

"Hello!" she called out in a deep, throaty, yet pleasant voice. "I am your orientation guide and teacher. Will you all please follow me and we'll get you settled in?"

A few of the others continued to look skyward as if spellbound or hypnotized for a few moments, but eventually all of us turned and followed her. We were all survivors and life went on.

The Garden of Eden description of Lilith I'd heard was mostly an impression of a warm, resort-type world. At least that had been how I'd pictured it. But nearly naked women and grass huts were a bit more primitive than I'd imagined—or been used to.

Yet grass huts they were, with yellow reed walls and thatched roofs. I could see the others having thoughts similar to my own. We'd been prepared for almost anything, but we'd grown up in a slick, automated world. Even those in the lowest classes were used to glancing at their watch for time, date, and whatever; to lights turning on when you entered rooms; to having food ready to be ordered when you were hungry with a command and a touch of a wall plate. A primitive place was one where the weather wasn't always controlled and buildings might be made of stone or wood, things like that—and a place with grass and trees. But this—not only did I now look like some prehistoric man, but I was living the part.

We all sat down in front of one of the huts and the woman introduced herself to us. "I am Patra," she told us, trilling the r sound slightly. "Like you, I was a convicted felon sentenced here about five years ago. I won't reveal what my offenses were, nor my old name—such things are not asked on the Warden worlds, although the information is sometimes freely given. It remains your choice to tell as much or as little about your past as you wish, and to whomever you wish. It is also your choice to use your old name or to choose any new one you like, as I did."

There were murmurs and nods at that, and I liked the idea myself. Barring a chance meeting with someone who had known the old Cal Tremon, I'd be spared the embarrassing questions and consequent chances of being tripped up somewhere.

"You will stay here a few days," Patra continued. "For one thing, you are now on a new and very hostile world. I realize that many of you have been on new and hostile worlds before, but never one quite like this one. In the past, you've had maps, charts, reference computers, all sorts of mechanical aids—not to mention effective weapons. There is none of that here, so you will have to get your information from me. Furthermore, as you are no doubt aware, the Warden organism invades our bodies and lives within us, and during the first few days, that process can have some unpleasant side effects. I don't want to alarm you—mostly some dizziness, disorientation, stomach upset, things like that. You won't be really sick, just a little uncomfortable from time to time. The discomfort passes quickly, and you'll never even think about it again. And it has some advantages."

"Yeah, keeps us planeted on this rock," somebody muttered.

Patra just smiled. "Not exactly, although it keeps us in this solar system. It's a fact of life, so accept that fact. Don't even think about escape, beating *this* system. Not only can't it be done—and some of the best minds in the galaxy have tried—but the death it brings is the worst, most horrible sort imaginable."

She paused to let that sink in, knowing it probably wouldn't, then continued. "The advantage of the organism is that you'll never have to worry about even the slightest ailment again. No toothaches, no colds, no infection, nothing. Even pretty large wounds, if not fatal or of an extremely critical nature, will heal quickly, and tissue regeneration is possible. There has never been a need for any doctor on Lilith, nor will there be. In other words, the Warden organism pays for what it takes."

She went on for a while, detailing some of the basics of the planet that I had already gotten from the briefing; then it was time for food. That took the most getting used to. The cuisine of Lilith seemed to consist of cooked insects of all sorts and lots of weeds, sometimes mixed with a grain of some sort that was a very unappetizing purple in color.

There were a few of my group who just couldn't manage the food for a while, but of course everybody would come around eventually. For a few it might be really tough going, or prove to be a very effective form of dieting.

Getting used to insect stews and chewy purple bread was going to be tough, I told myself, but I would have to learn to eat it and like it or else. Over the next few days I did manage to adjust to eating the food and to crapping in the bushes, using leaves instead of automatic wipers, and all the rest. As I said earlier, we were chosen for our ability to adapt to just about anything—and this was the "just about" the training manuals had implied.

Patra was also right about the side effects of the organism's invasion. I experienced strong dizziness, some odd aches and pains, and a feeling of itching all over inside—damned unpleasant, but I could live with it. We all had the runs, too, but I suspect that was mostly due to the food, not to the organism.

So far, though, Patra's orientation lectures had mostly covered things I already knew about, and though they went into greater detail than any I'd had before and were therefore welcome, she hadn't covered the facts I needed so far. On the fourth very long day—it was hell sleeping in that climate as it was, without the days and nights being so much longer—she finally got around to material of more interest.

"I know a lot of you have been wondering and asking why there are no machines, no spaceport, no modern buildings or conveniences here," she began. "So far I've put you off, simply because this was important enough for me to want you all to be through most of the ill effects of arrival. The reason is easy to explain but damned difficult to accept, but it's the explanation for everything you've seen around here." She seemed to look at each of us in turn, a half-smile on her face.

"Lilith," she said, "is alive. No, that doesn't make sense—but none of the Wardens do. I am going to tell you what *is* in terms that can only be approximations of what is going on.

"I want you to imagine that every single thing you see—not just the grass and trees, but *everything*: rocks, the very dirt under your feet—is alive, all cells of a single organism, each of which has its own Warden organism inside it in the same symbiotic relationship as it is establishing in your bodies. That organism likes the world *exactly* the way it is. It maintains it. Chop a tree down and another grows from its stump in record time. Meanwhile the original starts decaying with equal speed—in a full day it's started to decompose; within three it's completely gone, absorbed into the ground. Same for people. When you die you'll be completely gone to dust in under three days. That's why our food is what it is. It's what can be caught, killed, and prepared within a day. You probably have noticed that people arrive with our rations every morning."

There were a few nods, but I frowned. "Wait a minute. If that's true, then how do these grass huts stay up? They're dead matter."

She smiled again. "A good question. The truth is, they *aren't* dead. They're single living *hunti* plants, related to those yellow stalks you see growing here and there in the woods."

"You mean they obligingly grow into houses for us?" a woman asked skeptically.

"Well, not exactly," came the reply. "They grow into houses because they were ordered to do so."

Eyebrows shot up at this. "Ordered by whom?" somebody else asked.

"Life is a contest of wills everywhere," Patra responded. "On Lilith, it is more so. That is at the heart of the culture we've built here. You see, though the Warden organism isn't intelligent, at least as we understand such things, it is a truly alien organism that more or less becomes an integral part of whatever it lives in—and it lives in everything. You are no longer human beings. You are something else now—alien creatures, really. If you master your own body and if your mind is strong enough and has enough natural ability and sheer willpower, you can sense the Warden organism in all things around you. Sense it, and in a way talk to it. Somehow, nobody knows how, all Warden organisms are linked together. You might think of them as single, independent cells of a great creature. Unlike our cells, they don't adjoin, but like our cells, they are linked together somehow in a manner we don't yet understand. They communicate. You can make them communicate. You might, if strong enough and powerful enough, instruct Warden organisms not a part of you to do just about anything."

A sense of stunned unbelief swept over the group, but I was a little better prepared. Even so, I found the idea hard to visualize.

"The power of the individual over the organism," Patra explained, "varies wildly. Some people never get much of anything—the majority, I'm afraid, remain as you are now—and thus are at the mercy of more powerful minds that have more control and thus can control Warden organisms necessary to you—for food, for shelter, even within your own bodies. There are also those wild talents with the ability to exercise power, sometimes considerable power, but not under any sort of control. Like the majority, they are essentially powerless—but they get a little more respect, particularly if their wild talents are dangerous or deadly. The degree of control you have is fixed. We have no idea why some have it and others don't. But I *can* tell you that for some reason non-natives in general tend to possess a higher level of power than those born here. Perhaps this is because the Warden organism remains alien, something we are always aware doesn't belong in us. If you have the power, it'll show up on its own. Once it does, though, training and practice are required to bring you up to your full potential—and that's when you'll find out where you fit in this world."

It was something to think about, and worry about—a wild-card factor beyond my control, and I felt more than a little nervous. Whether or not I'd go far around here depended on how well I got along with the little buggers in my cells.

"Lilith is divided into political regions," she explained. "These areas, or districts, are based on population. As of this moment, each District contains roughly twenty-eight thousand people and there are a total of four hundred and seventy of them, each headed by an official called a Duke. They are enormously powerful, having the ability to stabilize dead matter. As a result, they live in fine mansions and often have art, dinnerware—all the finer things you can think of. And weapons, too.

"The Duke of a District is the most powerful Knight in his District. Therefore the officials below him are called Knights, and each Knight rules an area called a Keep. Knights also have some control over dead matter, but nothing like on the scale of a Duke—there's really no difference in power between Dukes and Knights with regard to the rest of the population. A Duke is only the most powerful of Knights. The Keeps, by the way, vary in size from very small to huge, depending on the number of people living in them. The more powerful the Knight, the more people he or she controls and the larger the Keep. The Duke, also being a Knight, has the largest Keep, of course."

I nodded to myself. Knights and Dukes had their way around here. The place was beginning to sound like a monarchy, but one determined by some indefinable natural ability, not heredity. Well, at least it kept dynasties down.

"Keeps," Patra went on, "are administered by Masters. Think of them as department heads. Each runs a particular area of Keep administration. Masters can control living things, but their ability to stabilize dead matter is very, very limited. A Master could make these *bunti* grow into a house, though, to his or her particular design.

"Below Masters are Supervisors, who are just what the term says. They manage the actual work. Their ability to stabilize dead matter is limited to usually a few articles of basic clothing, but they still have power over living things—mostly destructive. However, they can regenerate parts of themselves, even whole limbs, and can cause regeneration in others—as can, of course, Masters, Knights, and Dukes. I must warn you, they can also do the opposite—cause a limb to wither, inflict pain by sheer will."

"Which are you?" a man asked.

"None of the above," she laughed. "I am a Journeywoman. Basically my power is similar to a Master's, but I don't belong to a Keep. Dukes need people to travel between Keeps, to carry messages, to work out commerce, to—well, give orientation talks to newcomers. We're salespeople, ambassadors, couriers, you name it—answerable only to our Dukes. It's mostly a matter of temperament whether you're Journey or Master class. There are pluses and minuses for both jobs, and the fact that I'm a Journeywoman now doesn't mean I might not take a Master's position sometime."

"You've covered all the high spots," I noted. "You've accounted for maybe several thousand people, but you said there were more than thirteen million on the planet. What about the rest?"

"Pawns," she answered. "They do the work. In fact they do just about anything they're told to do. Consider—pawns need those more powerful to feed them, to provide shelter, to protect them against the savage beasts of the planet. They are in no position to do anything else."

"Slaves," the man next to me muttered. "Just like the civilized worlds, only reduced to the lowest common denominator."

I didn't agree with the man's comparison at all, but I could understand him completely now and why he was there.

"You've left somebody out," a woman—I think the one who was defiant back on the prison ship—spoke out. "The guy who runs the place. What kind of power does it take to be the Lord?"

Patra appeared to be slightly embarrassed by the way in which the question was put, but she answered it anyway. "There's only one Lord," she pointed out. "Right now it's the Lord Marek Kreegan. He got there because he challenged the previous Lord and killed him, thereby proving his power. Lords, of course, have all the powers of Dukes plus one extra ability that almost no one has—the ability to stabilize alien matter. They can possess a device that is not of this world. All alien matter except that stabilized by the Lord or his almost-as-powerful administrative aide, Grand Duke Kobé, decomposes. As well as undergoing extreme decontamination procedures, our two shuttles were stabilized by Lord Kreegan. If that weren't so, even the shuttles would decompose here."

Well, there it was: the unbelievable reality of the pecking order on Lilith and what individuals could—and could not—do, and the reason those folks didn't have any luggage. This also explained the clothing, and lack of it, seen around. Since your ability to "stabilize dead matter" was what counted, the more clothes you could comfortably wear, the higher your rank. I wondered idly if Dukes wore so much clothing they looked like moving clothes racks; if so, there would be disadvantages to higher rank, which would seem to *require* that outer badge of office. No wonder Lord Kreegan wanted to remain anonymous. The ceremonial robes of office alone would probably suffocate him.

On Lilith, clothes made the man or woman—and the man or woman made the clothes. That meant that because we remained naked, we all started out as low rank on the social scale. Well, at least on Lilith one wouldn't freeze to death. However, a certain sense of social modesty had been ingrained in me—not that I really minded here, surrounded by a lot of new prisoners in the same state. But in a strange land and civilization I knew I was going to feel more than a little self-conscious, particularly around the midsection.

Later that afternoon small blood samples were taken from each of us. I had no idea how they could analyze it, but apparently the results were satisfactory to everyone. Later that evening, Patra called us together for the last time as a formal group.

"Tomorrow," she told us, "the shuttle will return for you and take you to widely scattered Keeps. From then on you will be on the rolls of a specific Keep—I have no idea which—and will be assigned work. Your first few weeks will be an education, I think, in the powers of this world and the way it operates. Whether you remain pawns or whether you rise will depend on you. You *will* rise to your proper level—you won't be able to avoid it, really—but the timing will vary from weeks to months to years. Just remember that almost three million on Lilith came here as you did; the rest are native born to the generations past and present that came here. You have the same potential as they."

There were murmurings from the group. This seemed to be the worst kind of culture to enter: a totally combative one that relied on powers the strength of which was totally beyond the individual's control.

I slept very little that evening. I suppose few of us got much rest, considering the new day. As for me, I was feeling several emotions I had not experienced in a very long time and facing a situation I felt uncomfortable about. I felt doubt within me, and a sagging confidence in myself and my abilities. And there was still so much I didn't know about this world— things I *had* to learn, even as I learned where this odd system would place me. The only thoughts that consoled me were that Marek Kreegan had come here from the same background as me and that he had risen to rule it. Most importantly, he was a man like me, a person, a human being. He had enormous power, it was said, but he was mortal, and he could die.

Besides, I already knew an awful lot about him. I knew his age, sex, and general appearance, and I knew that he had a passion for anonymity and disliked the soft life. That meant he had to masquerade as a Journeyman, in order to be able to travel about and observe both great and small. Naturally others would also have figured this out, so he obviously had extra tricks up his sleeve to preserve his disguise. But, I realized, though Journeymen might have only the power of a Master, they would have a more exalted position, particularly the middle-aged men. Not even the greatest Duke could avoid being paranoid about such people. Journeyman would be the rank I'd find best suited to my own purposes, I decided—but that was a factor beyond my control.

That idea brought the depression back once again, and I consoled myself with the thought that, here only a few days and having seen almost none of this strange world, I had already narrowed my suspects down to a mere handful, perhaps less than a thousand.

Yeah, sure. The assignment was becoming simple.

CHAPTER FOUR

Zeis Keep

The shuttle that had brought us to the orientation point—I was never sure where that was on Lilith—had been silver; although the one that took us to our new homes was a dull rusty-red color, it looked like the first on the inside. I wondered whether it was the same one. Maybe it got a new paint job every time it reached orbit, to replace what was lost. Undoubtedly the schedule for the shuttle, which had to operate from an orbital base, had to be carefully worked out in advance. Somebody had to do it without benefit of transceivers—that meant a representative of all the Dukes and the Lord of Lilith, since the schedule would have to be coordinated well in advance, yet be available as need arose.

I still hadn't much of a clue as to what this special "power" might be like, either in execution or from the standpoint of just seeing it work. Nothing had dissolved around me, nobody had shot thunderbolts from their fingertips, nothing like that. If I never saw the power in operation, I didn't know how I could find out whether I had it myself. If I didn't, and in sufficient quantity, I'd lose before I had really started. I had to have some faith in Security there. Their computers had carefully selected me for this job, and that would have been one of the prime considerations— factors favorable to great power. But those same computers and the best scientists in the galaxy had absolutely no nice, normal, and natural physical explanation for the Warden phenomena, either.

I kept coming back to Kreegan. He'd known what he was getting into, and he'd voluntarily and confidently consigned himself to Lilith. Obviously the man had a strong reason to expect gaining great power or he wouldn't have done it.

Before it was my turn we landed four times, picking up and discharging not only those from my party but regular passengers as well. It was not wasted on me that we newcomers were the only passengers without clothing. Then we landed once again—the shuttle made orbit between stops to cleanse itself, which meant a slow journey—and the speaker called my seat number. The hatch hissed and opened, the ramp extended, and I walked out once more onto the surface of Lilith.

The scene was incredible. It was a beautiful valley surrounded by tall mountains, some of which had slight traces of snow on them. The valley itself was out of some children's fairy tale: broad fields in which long, leafy plants grew up to three meters in the air, all in nice, neat rows; a few small lakes that looked shallow enough to be paddies of some sort; and a meadow where really hideous-looking livestock grazed. This was my first look at the kinds of things that went into those stews, and my stomach automatically recoiled. Giant insects that resembled monstrous roaches except for their enormous, glittering, multifaceted eyes on stalks and their thick, curly brown fur. I'd seen an awful lot of alien life in my travels, including some creatures even more repulsive than those, but I'd never eaten them.

To one side stood groves of fruit trees. The fruit was unfamiliar but large and of different varieties. Another area seemed to be devoted to bushes covered with berries. They all at least looked comfortably edible.

But what made the pastoral scene so unreal was the castle in the middle, set against the mountains and built on a possibly man-made ledge right into the mountainside at an elevation of perhaps a hundred meters. The stone building came complete with towers, parapets, and battlements; it was the kind of place found *only* in fantasy.

Below the castle, in the valley itself, was what looked like a complex of straw huts much like those we'd used for orientation but a lot denser. That, then, was where the common folk lived, or at least the area around which their lives centered. I did note that there were other clusters of huts in various parts of the valley.

I heard a rumbling and turned to see a very plain sledlike wagon made of some thick plant material. It was being pulled by a large green thing with a shiny, almost round shell and who knew how many legs underneath. The tiny head, which seemed to be a horn-like snout atop which sat two dim little red dots and a couple of thin antennae, was all that was visible.

The man sitting on a crudely fashioned seat behind the creature was a large, dark, nasty-looking fellow, but that didn't really bother me—after all, I was now a large, dark, nasty-looking fellow myself. It did, however, seem interesting that he had no reins, no steering or other controls in his hands or attached to his body at all. He was just sitting there looking bored, letting the green beast pull him.

I realized in an instant that I was seeing the first demonstration of this mysterious power. He *was* controlling that thing, but not with any mechanical apparatus.

The wagon came up to me and stopped, whereupon the man rose to his feet and just stood there, staring down at me. He was an imposing figure—solid muscle, a weightlifter's physique—yet he wasn't really a big man. His squat build and muscles just made him seem so. He wore what appeared to be a yellow jockstrap, around which, oddly, was a wide belt of some pliable dark-brown material, from which a nasty-looking coiled whip hung at his side.

"Well?" he growled. "You just gonna stand there gawking or are you gonna get aboard?"

Welcome to your new home, I thought sourly as I climbed up and sat next to him on the bench. It was, like a lot on this world, made from some kind of thick, hard plant material, possibly bark. Without another word the huge green creature started off again, almost knocking me off the seat.

The other man chuckled. "Yeah, it's a rough ride," he commented, "but you get used to it. Not that you have to worry much—pawns don't do much ridin'." He paused a moment, giving me a good look. "Nice muscles, good build. We can use you, all right. You got any skills from your old life that maybe would make you a little more useful? Carpentry? Masonry? Animal care?"

I almost laughed at the question. The concept of anybody from the civilized worlds even knowing the meaning of those terms was ridiculous. I checked my reaction because I remembered that this was not my old body, but that of a frontiersman from a rough life, an impression I wanted to maintain as long as possible.

So I just shook my head and replied, "No, sorry, nothing I can think of. Electrical and power systems, weapons, things like that."

He snorted. "Electrical! Haw! Around here that don't mean shit. You're just a common laborer now. The only electricity we got on Lilith is lightning from the thunderstorms, and the only power is what some people got. Nope. Best forget the old comforts—you're a pawn of Zeis Keep now. I'm Kronlon, work supervisor for this section. You'll be workin' fer me. You call me 'sir' and you obey orders from me, nobody else."

"I'm not used to taking orders," I muttered, low and deep but deliberately loud enough for him to hear. I expected this to provoke him and gain his measure, but he laughed instead. The wagon stopped in the middle of a field about halfway to a group of huts to the left of the castle.

"Get down," he ordered, his tone more casual than menacing, gesturing with a beefy hand. "Go ahead. Get down."

I shrugged and did as instructed. Ordinarily I'd have expected a menacing tone or perhaps a swing, but if this was any kind of fight preparation he was definitely the cool one.

He jumped down after me, then walked right up to me. I towered over him, but that seemed to increase his pleasure. "Okay, go ahead. Take a swing at me. Go on—swing!" He thrust out his jaw. So it *was* a showdown after all.

I shrugged again, then hauled off and punched as hard as I could. Only I couldn't. My arm was suddenly stopped in midswing, fist tightly clenched. I couldn't move it, not forward, back, up, or down. I felt my muscles, tensed for the punch, start to hurt from the unreleased tension, but I could do nothing to release that energy. The fist was only a few centimeters from his out-thrust jaw.

He hauled off and hit me in my midsection with a blow that seemed designed to shatter ribs. I went down hard, with a groan and yelp of surprise and pain. Lying there on my back, gasping for breath, I realized that my right arm was still stiffly clenched.

He walked over and grinned. "See? Kind of hard to believe, isn't it?" He was clearly enjoying himself.

I felt my arm suddenly unfreeze, and lying there on the road, I completed the swing, almost rolling over in the process.

Kronlon laughed derisively, then turned and started to walk back to the wagon.

Marshaling my strength, I leaped up and rushed his back, attempting to tackle him. He might have heard me, but there was no way he could have seen me, and the combination of my new body and the low gravity gave me both force and speed. Suddenly, just a few meters from him, my legs seemed to turn to rubber. I stumbled, cried out, and crashed to the ground once again.

He stopped and turned to look down on me, grinning like mad. "See? You can't even sneak up on me. Listen—I got your number, see? I got your pattern inside my skull." He tapped it for emphasis. "You don't make a move against me I don't know it ahead of time and tell your body to screw up. Okay, get up. You ain't hurt."

I got slowly to my feet, starting to feel a few slight bruises. My mind raced, first in frustration and fury that this man had me completely at his mercy, and second, because now that I'd seen this power in operation I still knew nothing about how it worked. And this guy was the lowest rung on the power structure!

He unhooked his whip from his belt and for a moment I was afraid he was going to use it on me—but to my surprise, he tossed it to me.

"Here, catch. Uncoil it. You know how to use one of these? All right, use it, then. Whip the living shit out of me!"

I was mad enough to do it, and though the whip was crude and fashioned out of some sort of shiny braided material, it was well balanced and long. I snapped it a few times, getting the feel of it, then took him at his word.

He just stood there and laughed. Try as I might, I could not make any part of that whip touch him. I could, after a little bit, pick up a stone or cut grass with it, but no matter how dead on my aim, the whip always seemed to miss him just slightly. I couldn't believe it and kept at it for several minutes while he just stood there, laughing and taunting but not flinching.

"Okay, fun's over," he said at last, seeming bored with it all. "Now you see your problem. Drop a twenty-kilo boulder on my head from a fall of less than a meter and it'll still miss me. *But not the other way around!*" He reached out and the whip seemed almost to leap from my hand to his, then coil back into its storage position. To my relief, he replaced it on his belt loop.

The grin grew wider. "I know what you're thinkin'. I can see it on your face. You're glad I didn't use the whip on you. Want to know why? It's just a badge of office—all supervisors carry 'em. I got it from Boss Tiel himself, matched to me, and I don't like it to get mussed up or broke." The grin vanished, and so did the casual tone. Menace now dripped from his lips.

"Now, you got two choices and that's all," Kronlon growled. "You obey orders. You listen, you live, for my orders, and then you obey 'em. You don't ask no questions, you don't wonder why or figure anything out. You just do it. Do that and you live. The other choice is you kill yourself. *I* won't kill you. I don't hav'ta. I can do much worse."

Suddenly my whole body was consumed with the most horrible, agonizing pain I had ever known. I cried out and fell, senseless to anything but the pain, rolling about the grassy earth in sheer agony. I could not bear it; the pain was so intense, so all-encompassing. Almost immediately I longed for death, for anything to give me release.

And just as suddenly the pain was gone. The relief was tempered by echoes of the agony in my nervous system and the burning memory in my brain. I just lay there face up on the grass, panting.

"Get up!" Kronlon ordered.

I hesitated, still in shock and unable to get my bearings fully. Instantly the pain was back, if only for a fleeting second that seemed like an eternity. I turned, I crawled, I scrambled to my feet, still trembling and gasping.

Kronlon watched, a look of amused satisfaction on his face. He had done this many times before. I hated him worse than I ever hated anyone in my life.

But he still wasn't through.

"What's your name?" he asked.

"Tre—Tremon," I gasped. "Cal Tremon."

The agony was back, knocking me down again; then it was released.

"Get up!" the supervisor commanded. I tried to get back to my feet once more, making it on the second try. He waited patiently until I succeeded.

"Now, you'll address me as 'sir' always," he warned. "You will put 'sir' at the beginning of every statement to me, and you will put 'sir' at the end of it. You will stand straight when I am around and face me always, and when you are given an order you will bow slightly and then do it. You will speak to anyone not of your class only when spoken to, and only in reply to their questions or commands. Understand that?"

I was still gasping for breath. "Yes . . . sir," I responded. The pain returned.

"Not what I ordered, Tremon! What kind of a dumb shit are you? Now get up, you bastard, and we'll try it again."

For a moment I was confused, hesitant, until I realized he was deadly serious. The pain and agony he could inflict without moving a muscle was horrible, intense. By now I feared that more than anything, the memory so vivid that I would do almost anything to avoid it. It was horrible to know that I had been so easily humbled and beaten, so quickly broken—but broken I was. I wasn't even thinking straight any more. I just wanted to avoid that pain.

We spent what felt like hours out in that field, with quick applications of the pain followed by increasing demands, over and over again, a terrible torturer's delight. It was a process not unfamiliar to me, but one in which I'd never participated on the receiving end. Keep at the victim: administer pain, then demands, then pain again. Never be pleased, never be satisfied. Agents were trained to black out after a certain threshold was reached, but I found even that suddenly beyond my power. Agents could also will themselves to death, of course, but that was the one point at which he was not going to win, not yet.

If I were being interrogated about a mission, or jeopardizing a mission, other people, anything, I would not have hesitated to take the death-wish route—but such was not the case. Nor was any torture mechanism being used—just one short, squat, brutish man standing there in a field, doing nothing at all.

As Kronlon had warned, there were only two routes for any thinking human being to take in this situation—death, or absolute, unquestioning obedience. My ego shattered in the waning sun, and my will seemed to recede into nothingness. Before sunset I was, on command, licking his stinking, dirty feet.

As we rode into the small village, me sitting dully at his side, a small corner of the old me, all that seemed to remain on the conscious level, kept saying over and over, "And a Master is ten times as powerful as a Supervisor and a Knight is ten times a Master and a Duke is ten times a Knight and a Lord is like a god. . . ."

I don't even remember entering the little village of straw and mud huts. It was nearly sunrise when I awoke.

CHAPTER FIVE

Village Routine

The pawns lived a miserably primitive life, I soon discovered, sleeping crammed into those huts with only more of the strawlike *bunti* plant that formed the hut covering the floor so deeply that it actually gave slightly under the weight of human bodies.

For several days I remained in nearly complete withdrawal, going through the motions like an automaton, thinking little and feeling nothing The other pawns seemed to understand what a newcomer went through, even though most of them were native-born and had been raised on this horrible system and probably hadn't gone through quite what I had. There was no attempt to rush me, or to establish normal contact with me. They seemed content to wait until I snapped out of it, if I ever did, and initiated the contact myself.

We were routed out at dawn, and everybody crowded into a huge communal eating area in the center of the "village," as it were, where food-service pawns put out enormous, mostly tasteless rolls and a fair supply of good-tasting pulpy yellow fruit. Then the supervisor arrived; actually, he lived right there, in a hut just like the rest of us, only privately. But his food, the same as ours, was served to him by the food-service pawns in his hut—and someone would clean the place while work was being done.

Incredibly, despite the enormous power Kronlon possessed, on Lilith he was only a slight notch, just a hair really, above us, the lowest of the low. Just one look at his modest *bunti* hut and that castle up on the mountain told of the gulf separating him from his own bosses.

The work consisted mostly of loading and hauling. How soft mankind has become, even on the frontier. On Lilith, life was frozen in the stone age all labor was manual; all tools were crudely fashioned and usually temporary.

Two rivers flowed from the mountains down to those small lakes, causing the twin problems of flood control and irrigation. It rained heavily at some point almost every day, yet the duration was short, the runoff quick. The mountains clearly absorbed the brunt of the storms on their other faces and allowed only the worst to get over to Zeis Keep. Therefore irrigation canals had to be dug by hand; the mud and muck was carried out by hand to carts, then hauled by men pulling those carts to fill areas near the lakes, where the silt would be formed into crude earthen dikes. Hundreds of kilometers of drainage and irrigation canals were constantly silting up; so when you finished the whole route, it was time to start again.

Men and women worked equally in the fields and in those jobs. Of course the strongest and hardiest took on the heaviest labor, and job assignment was clearly based on physique, age, and the like. Children—some as young as five or six I guessed—worked along with their elders, doing what they could under the watchful eyes of the oldest and most infirm. The social system was crude and primitive but well thought out. It worked, on the most basic, tribal level. Once, when mankind evolved on its mother world into what we now know as human beings, all people must have lived something like this.

Days were long, punctuated regularly by very short breaks and by four food breaks during the sixteen-hour work cycle. When darkness finally fell across the valley and the distant castle blazed with light was there rest. But the nights, too, were long. Zeis Keep was only 5 degrees south of the equator, which made the periods roughly equal all year.

Social time for the pawns was at night, and it was as basic and primitive as everything else. They had some dances and songs, for anybody who was in any condition to join in, and they talked and gossiped in an elementary way. They also made love then, seemingly without regard for any family unit or other permanent attachments. Marriage and such seemed alien concepts to these people, though if both partners felt like it, they married.

They were a lively, yet somewhat tragic group, largely ignorant of anything beyond their own miserable existence, which they accepted as normal and natural because they knew nothing else. So thoroughly ingrained was the system that I cannot recall a single instance in which a supervisor had to exercise his or her terrible powers.

As for me, I was in a curious state of mental catalepsy. I functioned, did my job as ordered, ate and slept, but basically didn't think. Looking back on the period now, I can see the reasons and understand, although I can't really forgive myself. It was not the defeat at Kronlon's hands or the crushing blow to my ego and pride that was inexcusable. What bothers me, really, is that I retreated into being a mental vegetable at the end of the contest.

I don't know how long I remained that way—days, weeks; it was hard to be sure, since there are no watches or calendars on Lilith. Still, slowly my mind struggled for some kind of control, some sort of reassertion of identity—first in dreams, then in fleeting memories. The real danger in this situation was that I could have gone mad, could have retreated into some sort of fantasy world or unreal existence. I realize now that the inner struggle was caused by compulsions placed on me by the Security Clinic programmers. They were not ones to take chances, and they could always program another body—but once a body was programmed and sent to the Warden System, they had to make sure it would remain true to them.

Find the aliens . . . kill the Lord. . . .

These commands echoed in my dreams and became the supports to which other parts of my shattered ego could cling.

Find the aliens . . . kill the Lord. . . .

Slowly, very slowly, night after night another fragment would return and coalesce around those deeply hidden commands, commands I might never have known were there had this not occurred.

Find the aliens . . . kill the Lord. . . .

And rationality finally returned to me. In the evening hours and just before falling asleep, I was able to try to sort out just what the hell had happened to me, to regain some of my confidence. I needed hope, and the only hope I could have was in reasoning a way out of my predicament.

The logic chain I forged may have been faulty, but it worked, and that alone was important. First and foremost was the realization that everyone who came here had undergone substantially the same treatment I had. It *had* cowed them all, driven them into some sort of grudging submission from which they'd had to learn to cope. Was that insanity, or perhaps a fatalistic acceptance?

Patra, that Knight up there in his fairyland castle, even Lord Marek Kreegan. There were no inherited positions or titles on Lilith, except perhaps for those skilled in things useful to the rulers. No political position, no position of authority, was hereditary or elected, either. All those positions, from Supervisor up to Lord, had been taken, won in a contest of power.

Find the aliens . . . kill the Lord. . . .

Everyone on this world who rose at all from the muck of pawn slavery rose from the bottom through the ranks. Everyone.

How did this power operate? How did you find out if you had it?

I felt ashamed of myself for my reaction to Kronlon. I had been in bad situations before, situations in which the enemy had all the power, and I had been stalled only temporarily by those conditions. The only difference between those situations and this one was that in this one I had looked at the lay of the land and the forces of the enemy, and instead of considering the problem and working out how to beat the enemy—or at least die trying—I had instead meekly surrendered. The day I faced and accepted the fact that I had run across a tremendously powerful obstacle, not an impassable barrier, was the day I rejoined the human race.

I started talking to people, although that was a pretty limited thing. Few topics for small talk were available—the weather was always hot and humid, for example—and it was difficult to talk down to people who might be bright and alert but whose whole world was this primitive, non-mechanized existence. What could you say to people whose world view, if they had one, was that the valley was the world and the sun rose and set around it? Oh, they knew there were other Keeps, but they saw them all as being just like this one. And as for mechanization, they had seen the shuttle come and go, but that was as far as it went—after all, they were familiar with large flying insects. The concept of any machine not powered by muscle was simply beyond them.

That was the core of my problem. I didn't know enough, not by a long shot, but I knew a hell of a lot more than these natives. Also, now that I'd pulled myself together, I craved some kind of intelligent conversation. I'd always been a loner before, but there is a difference between being alone by choice and being alone by force. Conversation and diversion had always been available when I had needed it. Everything seemed stacked against me. I hadn't gotten a single break on this whole mission since waking up. But I did get one now.

Her name was Ti.

A few days after my recovery I encountered her in the village common one evening, after the last meal of the day. I had seen her a few times before, and once you saw her you couldn't forget her.

She was about 160 centimeters tall and very thin, particularly at the waist, but she had large breasts and nice buttocks and sandy brown hair—unusual in itself—down to those buttocks. A pretty, sexy young woman, you might say—except that her face was amazingly young and innocent, the kind of face not seen on a body like that in my experience. It was a pretty face, all wide-eyed and innocent. But it was the face of a child, one no more than eleven or twelve, atop that well-developed body. Though the two would eventually reconcile, the body seemed to be developing several years ahead of that face.

I could have understood the contrast more if such a thing had been common on Lilith, but it was not—at least not from this pawn sample. Here was one minor mystery that perhaps I could learn something about, and I asked a couple of my co-workers about her.

"Oh, that's Ti," one explained. "A chosen of the Bodymaster. He'll pluck her in a little while, I'd say. Only thing that's slowed it is that she's got some wild talent in her and they want to see what it'll do."

Several items of new data. I felt like I was on to something new, something that would be of value.

"What do you mean, a chosen of the Bodymaster?" I asked. "Remember, I wasn't born here."

The question got me one of those looks of incomprehension I was becoming used to, since the natives just couldn't picture any other place as being any different than Zeis Keep. But the man shrugged and answered anyway. They had reconciled themselves to me by convincing themselves that the shock to my system, which they *could* comprehend, had made me funny in the head.

"Boss Tiel, he breeds women like he breeds *snarks*," the laborer explained. *Snarks* were those hairy monsters in the pasture that were raised for their highly prized meat. "When a child, particularly a girl child, is born with looks or something else special, well, she gets marked by the Bodymaster in charge of the breeding. He brings 'em along 'til they're the way he wants 'em, then he breeds 'em with selected boys. See?"

I *did* see, sort of, although the concept repelled me more than anything yet about this foul world. Repelled, but didn't surprise.

"But her—ah—development isn't natural, is it?" I prompted.

He chuckled and held up an index finger. "See this finger? I lost it—got chopped clean away—in an accident a while back. Bled like mad. They took me to the Bodymaster, who had only to look at it to stop the blood. Then he looked at it, touched it, and I came back. It grew back out in time, good as new. Look." He wiggled it for emphasis.

"But what does that . . . ?" I began, then realized what he was saying and shook my head in wonder. He caught my look and grinned.

"Breed stock needs to make lotsa babies, needs to want to make lotsa babies," the man noted. "You see?"

I saw, all right. Slowly, to make certain her cells and nervous system were capable of standing it, this Bodymaster was somehow reaching inside her with his power, in the same way as he had ordered the finger regenerated and as Kronlon had inflicted paralysis and pain. Subtle alterations were being made, had probably been made from the point of puberty, which could only have taken place a year or so ago. Hormones stimulated, body chemistry subtly altered, so that actually he was making her unnatural, his exaggeration deforming her somewhat—but all for his purposes. Breeding stock he wanted, not show stock. For what? The beautifully colored hair, perhaps? Possibly as little as that, although another thought came to me.

"Hogi?" I prodded my laborer companion once again.

"Uh?"

"You said she had some wild talent. What kind? What can she do?"

He shrugged. "Don't know. Might not understand it, anyway. I do know that none of the Supers bother her much, not even Kronlon. A little scared, maybe, which may mean she's got really great power—but it's wild. Comes and goes. No control."

I nodded. That would explain why the powers that be had left her here a while after puberty instead of taking her into the main village or perhaps to the castle grounds. They weren't quite sure what her powers were, either, or whether she might not someday learn to control them. They wanted to see more, first, to ascertain what she could or could not do. They were afraid of her potential, which indicated great power. If it stayed wild, well, she'd become a breeder and that was that. But if she gained control, she could threaten them.

I suspected that that was the real reason for this breeding program. It must frustrate that upper class to see their own children wind up as pawns, to have to pass on their splendor and holdings to some stranger or subordinate who would take it from them. For the first time I thought I understood people like the Masters and Knights. How galling, how frustrating it must be to be like a god and know that you can't pass it on, leave it to anyone. Genetic manipulation was out, as were all the scientific tests and lab procedures of the civilized worlds. What bestowed and regulated that mysterious and terrifying Warden power had eluded technological science and would elude them as well. They would have no choice but to try and breed for it. First among themselves, of course, but that hadn't worked.

It struck me that, except for Patra, virtually all the powerful people I'd heard about were male. That might be a misleading statistic, based as it was on so small a sample, but if it held, even partly, it would mean even more problems in pure inbreeding.

Hogi at least knew enough to answer that. "Well, yes, more men than women, but lots of women have it," he assured me. "No, I hear tell that when a woman like a Master or a Duke gets with child, she loses control, becomes a wild talent while carrying the child. During that time somebody could steal her job, see?"

I *did* see. With only a few thousand positions near the top and only 471 really at the top, people in those positions were always on the spot, always being challenged by newcomers—and to put yourself in the position of being wide open to challenge for nine months would be unthinkable.

"You mean the big people don't have sex?" I asked incredulously.

"Haw. Sure. When you got the power it's easy," Hogi responded. "You get cut, you just tell your body not to bleed. You also just tell your body not to get pregnant. See?" This was all said in the boy-are-you-dumb tone he usually used when talking to me.

It all fit, though. They were breeding with the strong wild talents that occasionally cropped up among the pawns' children. Trying for power *and* control—and perhaps the key to breeding power in their own young.

But this young girl had the power, even if it *was* wild, and that was the most important thing to me. I had to know a lot more about that power, and since she was the only one around who had it that I could talk to as an equal, I determined to get to know her.

CHAPTER SIX

Ti

The next evening, I sought her out, trying to appear as casual as I could. I had been warned that she was hard to approach and difficult to talk to, but I had no problems. Sitting on a rock off by herself and out of the torchlights, she was fanning away the ever-present swarms of tiny bugs and idly chewing on a piece of *gri*, a melonlike fruit with an odd sweet-and-sour taste.

There wasn't really too much I could do without being either corny or obvious, so I just walked up close to her and said, "Hello, there."

She looked up with those huge, little girl's eyes and smiled. "Hi. Sure. Have a seat."

"My name is—" I began, but she cut me off. "Your name's Caltremon, and you come from Outside," she shot, catching me a little off-guard. Her voice, still a youthful one, more matched her face and true age than her body.

I laughed. "And how do you know all that?"

"I seen you lookin' at me," she responded playfully. "O'course, all the men look at me, but I 'specially noticed you. They say you's sick in the head. That right?"

I found myself instantly warming to her. "I was," I told her, "but I'm better now. This is not like the place I came from, and it took a lot of getting used to."

She tossed the rind back into the bushes and shifted around, pulling her knees up against her bosom and putting her arms around her legs, rocking slightly. "What's it like—Outside, I mean?" she wanted to know.

I smiled. She was so damned cute. "Nothing like here," I replied, trying to find terms she could understand. "Not at all. For one thing, it's cooler. And there aren't any pawns or supers or knights."

I could see that this was hard for her to digest. "If there ain't no pawns, who does the work?"

A fair question. "People who want to do it," I tried carefully. "And it's a different kind of work than we do here. Machines do all the really heavy stuff."

"I heard 'bout 'sheens," she said knowingly. "But somebody gotta raise 'em and breed 'em, right?"

I sighed. The usual dead end. How could you explain machines to somebody who was born and raised on a world where nothing worked and practically nothing lasted? I decided this could be used as a back way into the subject that really interested me.

"Where I come from nobody has the power," I told her. "And when a place doesn't have the power, you can change things, make things that last. Some of those are machines, and they do what the power does here."

She mulled this over, trying to sort it out, but didn't seem to understand. That was about as far as I'd gotten with anybody else, though, which indicated she had some brains.

"Why don't they have the power?" she asked.

I shrugged. "I don't know. I don't know why some people do. I don't really understand what the power is even now." Watch it, I warned myself. Be very careful. "I hear you got the power. Is that right?"

"Well, yeah, I guess so," she admitted. "Don't do me no good, though. Y'know, like you can *feel* it inside but can't talk to it. I guess that's what them others can do. They can talk to it, tell it to do things."

"But you can feel it," I prompted. "What's it feel like?"

She unclasped her arms and slid down from the rock, stretching and rubbing her behind. She slithered over and sat right next to me. "I just can feel it, that's all," she replied. "Can't you?"

I shook my head. "Nope. Either I don't have it or I don't know how to look or what to feel."

She shrugged. "Ever look?"

I considered that, and filed it for reference.

I tried to press the subject, but she'd become bored with it and didn't want to talk about it any more. I decided not to push her. I'd made an easy friend here, and I didn't want to blow my advantage all at once. There would be other nights.

I was suddenly aware that she was sitting *very* close to me, and for the first time I realized why she was attracted to me and had noticed me before. My most outstanding outsized feature would be an almost irresistible magnet to somebody being manipulated as she was. And for the first time in this body, I did start feeling the urge, but something stopped me. She was so very young, damn it all, and for her the word "pawn" took on an even greater meaning.

After a little small talk elicited no response from me she sat up and looked at me strangely. "You ain't one of them man-lovers, are you?" she asked, genuinely perplexed.

I had to laugh. "No, not that," I replied carefully. "I—well, it's just that, where I come from, somebody my age feels funny with somebody your age." *I could have a child your age,* I added to myself.

She gave me a disgusted look. "That's what I thought," she pouted. "I dunno why that's a big deal. It ain't like I never *done* it, you know. I do it lots since I come out. Master Tang said it was good to do it." She stood up, looking miffed. "Guess I'll go up to the Super, then. He don't mind."

I sighed. This combination of child-woman was hard for me to accept, let alone cope with. I was also torn by my desire not to alienate her and my mental reaction to her as a child. How can I explain it? It was as if an adolescent who was very desirable had said, "If you don't make love to me I'll hold my breath until I turn blue, so there!" The contrast between willing and sensuous woman and small child was just something I couldn't figure out how to handle, particularly when I knew that her avid sexuality was induced by cold, uncaring men who saw her as an animal, some kind of domesticated beast. It seemed, damn it, somewhat *incestuous* to take advantage of that sort of situation.

I'd like to think that the reason I gave in that night had to do with my fear of alienating her and thus jeopardizing my only avenue of gaining knowledge.

The body Security had given me was, of course, a body of opportunity. Krega had said that they went through a lot of bodies before an imprint "took," so it was pure chance that I wound up with this one—yet it proved to be my real break. Its primitive, throw-back nature gave me size and great strength, and its oversexed development had attracted Ti. In the days that followed she stayed with me and near me, at least in the evenings. On size alone I seem to have made, in her mind at least, the other men around seem inadequate. Furthermore, a playboy learns just about every variation, and variety wasn't well known on Lilith.

I kept after her, subtly and without boring her, about this power she felt and its nature. Slowly, considering her fairly short attention span, I got what I could. Late at night, with Ti lying at my side, I tried to shut out everything and everybody else and see if I, too, could "feel it."

It was an internal process, somewhat a mental process, but there was no real guide to it. Ti had been born with the power, had grown up with it, and therefore wasn't the best person to tell me exactly what to look for. The best would have been a super or higher, and they weren't going to reveal anything.

Kronlon was the key to my persistence. The man was a sadist, a petty little godlet without the brains he was born with. Yet somehow *he'd* found it, learned to use it. I will never understand the selection process for Warden worlds, I'm convinced, if a Kronlon could have been sent here instead of wiped. And sent here he'd been—or so Ti assured me. A long time ago now, of course, but that bastard had been spawned in *my* space, not here on this primitive and brutal planet.

What had he done to awaken those powers? I wondered each night. What did he feel?

Sometimes, on the border of sleep, I thought I *could* feel something stirring, something strange; but it was elusive, beyond my grasp. I was beginning to worry that it was denied me. Or perhaps the fact that this was not my body was the blocking factor. It was said to be a sense of alienness. To my mind, anyway, this body I wore, former property of the late and unlamented Cal Tremon, was alien, too—though becoming less and less so. I was not really aware of it at the time, but now, looking back, I can see more clearly.

My memories and personality were intact, but there is a biological side to us as well, one involving enzymes, hormones, and secretions. It is as if the individual, the personality, is a particularly vivid black-and-white photograph and those physiological elements add the color, the shading, the nuance. Even your sexual preferences are determined mostly by a small cluster of cells deep in the cerebrum. Such cells aren't transferred in the process with the personality; you inherit the body you get with all its physiological and chemical properties, and they change you.

Tremon's body was particularly sensitive to that sort of thing, since it was an unregulated one from the frontier. On the civilized worlds such physical and chemical properties are carefully regulated. But Tremon, the result of a random coupling of two unregulated people, was subject to all the ancient genes and the variations spawned not only by evolution but also by mutation, something spacers were particularly prone to.

Personality is built on these properties, not the other way around. Tremon was violent, aggressive, and amoral; he simply couldn't be more of the brutish male, with all that implies than he was. All these physical factors now worked on me as they had on him, and were tempered only by my own memories and personality, my old ingrained habits and cultural inhibitions. Tempered, but not damped out. Of course the longer I remained in the body, the more completely these factors would come to dominate my behavior. Already I was beginning to look back on my old life and existence with more than a little wonder, trying in vain to understand how I could have acted this way or that, or done this or that, or enjoyed this rather than that. It was becoming more and more difficult to think of that old life as my own. Terribly clear and vivid and the only past I had, but increasingly I began thinking and acting as if I, Cal Tremon, had somehow inherited from Security the memories and knowledge of a total stranger.

Within a couple of weeks of first meeting Ti, I found it difficult to understand my earlier reluctance about her. I understood on an intellectual level, of course, but on the increasingly dominant emotional level it became harder and harder to believe that those objections mattered.

Then one evening, on my way back to the village after a long, tiring day, looking forward to food and Ti, I heard the grass talking.

It was an eerie, alien sensation like nothing I'd ever experienced before; it wasn't any kind of conversation we humans could comprehend. It was as if somehow the grass was suddenly filled with colonies of living things in contact with one another, even between blades and clusters of grass. I was aware of a discomforting protest when I trod down some of the grass, and of a tiny tickle of relief when I moved on. I don't think it was intelligence I was sensing, but it was awareness, life of some sort, on a very basic, emotive level. And yet it was communication of a sort. For after a bit of walking I could sense a distant feeling of tension just ahead in the grass that I was about to step on.

It was a strange sensation, there and yet almost not there, sensed mostly because it was so pervasive, because there was just so damned much grass. The feeling excited me, even though I had to face the fact that I was tired, dirty, somewhat depressed, and just possibly was going nuts.

Ti, however, who joined me from her job at the nursery, seemed to sense something even before I told her about it. "You felt it today," she said, not asked.

I nodded. "I think so. It was—odd. Hearing the grass, sensing countless billions of tiny interconnected living things."

She didn't follow some of the big words but she knew what I meant and I saw an unexpected look of pity on her face. "You mean," she asked incredulously, "you couldn't hear it 'fore now?"

It was a revelation to her, as if suddenly discovering that the supposedly normal person she knew had been deaf all his life and had suddenly acquired hearing. It was that acute—almost like another sense, a sixth sense, one that grew and developed as the days went on.

Once I knew what to look for, I could find it everywhere.

The rocks, the trees, the animal life of this world, all sang with it over and above their existence as separate entities. It was an incredible sensation, and a beautiful one. The world sang to you, whispered to you.

People, too—although they were the most difficult partly because their own activities partially masked the effect, so quiet and subtle it was, and partly because it's almost impossible to observe a human being with the same objectivity as can be applied to a rock or tree or blade of grass. Yet each entity was also unique, and with a little concentration I could not only sense but actually mentally map a particular area with my eyes closed.

This, I realized, was the key to that mysterious power. My own Warden organisms, inside every cell, perhaps every molecule of my body, were in some way interconnected by some sort of energy to every other Warden organism. It was this interconnection I saw and felt and heard. It had to be what they all saw and felt and heard, all the ones with any vestige of the power.

A Supervisor sensed what I sensed and had the ability to send, through his own body's symbiotes, a message to yours—or to a rock's or to anything else's. A Master, then, could do it in more detail—could see the individual parts inside a human body and order changes in the way those cells operated.

When something died, or if it lost its primary form—such as when a rock was crushed—the Warden organisms died, and without them, the very structure of the thing became unstable and collapsed. A Knight, then, I realized, could somehow keep the Warden organisms alive under those conditions. But even then, the organism attacked and destabilized inorganic matter from outside its environment. Somehow I thought of antibodies, those substances in human blood that attack foreign substances such as viruses that invade our bodies. It seemed to me that the Warden organism acted much like an antibody on inorganic alien matter: it attacked, destabilized, and destroyed it.

Kreegan, then, could do the impossible—convince the Warden organism not to attack and destroy alien inorganic matter. And each rank could also keep lower ranks from communicating with the Warden organisms inside their own bodies, thus protecting them.

But what tuned you to your own symbiotes, allowed you to relay commands through them to others outside your own body? That I had yet to discover. The mere discovery that I could sense the communication while most pawns could not was the best thing that could have happened to me. I no longer felt tired or depressed. I had the talent. I needed to explore my powers, test them, learn how to use them, learn my own limits.

Perhaps I wouldn't equal the Lord; perhaps I'd need help, a valuable ally.

For now, though, it was enough to know, finally, what was what on this mad world—and to know, too, that my days of hauling mud for sixteen hours were numbered.

More than enough.

CHAPTER SEVEN

Father Bronz

Over the following days my increasing sensitivity to the silent communication absorbed me, and I tried to learn everything I could about it. None of the pawns were any help except Ti, who could feel the power but had never learned how to control or use it properly. Since one's position on Lilith was dependent on mastery of the power—and since social mobility usually led to the death of one of the contestants for a particular position—there were, needless to say, no instruction manuals.

Although I've lived with the sensation for quite some time now, it is still nearly impossible to describe. The best objective description I can give is a tremendously heightened sensitivity to an energy flow. The energy is not great and yet you can sense it, not as a static thing but as a continuous and pulsating energy flow from all things solid. Gases and water don't seem to be affected by the flow, although things living *in* the water, no matter how tiny, possess it.

The energy itself is of the same sort—that is, there's no difference between a flow from a blade of grass, a person, and the insects—and yet the patterns that it forms are unique. You can tell one blade of grass from another, a person from some other large creature; you even get different patterns from the billions of microbes we all carry inside us.

I was still experimenting when the stranger arrived in our little village. He'd apparently been there most of the day, walking around to different work parties and details, but hadn't yet reached mine. Early in the evening I finally saw him, relaxing in the common and eating some fruit.

He wore a toga of shiny white that seemed to ripple with his every move and a pair of finely crafted sandals that marked him as a man of extreme power. Yet he was sitting there at ease, eating with and socializing with us mere pawns. He was an elderly man, with a fine-lined face and carefully trimmed gray beard, but he was balding badly both in front, where only a widow's peak remained, and around the top of his head. He looked thin and trim, however, and was in good physical condition, as would be expected. His age could not be guessed, but he would have to have been at least in his seventies, perhaps years older.

For a fleeting moment the idea entered my naturally suspicious head that this might be Lord Marek Kreegan himself. Why he'd show up here at this particular time, however, was a mystery that pushed coincidence to the limit. Besides, Kreegan would be of standard height and build, as all the other people of the civilized worlds and I had been. This man seemed a bit too short and too broad to fit into that absolute category.

It was interesting to see the pawns' reaction to him. While they would not even address a supervisor and would treat such a person with abject servility, they freely approached this man and chatted with him, almost as equals. I found Ti and asked her who he was.

"He is Father Bronz," she told me.

"Well? What's that mean?" I responded, a little irritated. "Who and what is a Father Bronz?"

"He is a Master," she responded, as if that explained everything when all it did was state the obvious.

"I *know* that," I pressed bravely on, "but I've never seen pawns be so casual with anybody with the power before. They even steer a little clear of you because of your reputation. I mean, is he from the castle? Does he work for the Boss or the Duke or what?"

She laughed playfully. "Father Bronz don't work for nobody," she said scornfully. "He's a God-man."

That threw me temporarily until I realized that she wasn't referring to his power but to his job. Obviously, she meant he was a cleric of some sort, although I'd seen no sign of any real religion on Lilith. I knew clerics, of course; for some reason those cults and old superstitions still held a lot of people even on the civilized worlds. The more you tried to stamp 'em out, the more strength they seemed to gain.

I stared again at the strange old man. Odd place for a cleric, I thought. He must have some really weird religious beliefs if he's here on Lilith. Why condemn yourself here when you could be living the good life in some temple paid for by the ignorant? And, I wondered, how could a man of God, whichever one or ones it was, have risen to Master without blood on his hands?

I kept noticing the men and women going up to him, talking to him, in singles and small groups. "Why are they talking to him?" I asked her. "Are they afraid not to?" It seemed to me that if you were stumping for converts and had the power of a Master you could at least compel them to listen to your sermons—but he wasn't sermonizing. Just talking nicely.

"They tell him their troubles," Ti said, "and sometimes he can help them. He's the only one of them with the power who likes pawns."

I frowned. A confessor—or did he actually offer intercession? I considered it, but couldn't really figure out his function. More stuff to learn, I told myself. Though there was really only one way to do so, I hated even the thought of going up to someone with ten times or more Kronlon's powers.

I guess he noticed me standing there staring, for when the group thinned out, he glanced over in my direction and then gestured and called to me. "You there! You're a big, hairy fellow, aren't you? Come on over!" he called pleasantly, his voice rich and mellow. That was a charmer's voice, a con man's voice—the kind that could make a crowd do almost anything he wanted.

I had no choice but to approach him, although my nervousness must have showed.

"Don't worry," he assured me. "I don't bite, nor do I inflict pain on pawns or eat little babies for breakfast." He looked me over in the torch-light, and his eyes widened slightly. "Why, you must be Cal Tremon!"

I betrayed no outward emotion, but inwardly I tensed. I had a bad feeling about that recognition.

"I've heard much about you from, ah, other colleagues of yours who wound up here," he continued. "I was wondering what you looked like."

I didn't like the sound of *that* at all. It implied that a fair number of people around might know more about Cal Tremon's life and exploits than I did.

"Have a seat," he gestured at a small tuft of grass, "and for heaven's sake, relax! I am a man of God—you have nothing to fear from me."

I sat, thinking just how wrong he was. It wasn't his power I feared, but his knowledge that could expose me. Despite my misgivings, I loosened up a little and decided to talk to him. "I'm Tremon," I admitted. "What sort of stuff have you heard about me? And from whom?"

He smiled. "Well, all of the newer folk were to one degree or another in your former line of work. Reputations carry, you know, among people of like trades. You're a legend, Cal—I hope I may call you Cal. That Coristan raid alone guaranteed that. Single-handedly blowing the domes of the entire mining colony and making off with forty millions in jondite!" He shook his head in wonder. "With that kind of talent and those brains —not to mention money—I wonder they ever caught you."

"They put a Security assassin on my trail," I responded as glibly as I could, having never heard of Coristan and not having the slightest idea what jondite was or what it was used for. "They're the best at what they do and they rarely fail. The only reason I wasn't killed outright was that I'd had the foresight to stash the loot and have it wiped, so they needed me alive to get the key information and find it." That much was the truth; the briefing had been better on the latter-day career and psychoprofile.

The cleric nodded sagely. "Yes, the agents are almost impossible to avoid—and even if you get one, the rest are on you. You know the reigning Lord of Lilith was an agent?"

I nodded. "So I heard. Excuse me for saying so, but it's pretty odd to find a cleric out here, and particularly strange to find one who talks to thieves and murderers so matter-of-factly."

Father Bronz laughed. "No preaching, you mean? Well, I have my work and it's a little different. I *was* a preacher once, and a good one—the victim of my own success, I fear. Started with a tiny little church—perhaps twenty, thirty members—on a small frontier world, and it just grew until I was the dominant cleric of three worlds, two of them civilized!" His face turned a little vacant, his eyes slightly glassy. "Ah! The enormous sums pouring into the coffers, the cathedrals, the mass worship and blessing for a half million at a time! It was *grand!*" He sounded both nostalgic and wistful.

"What happened to bring you here, then?" I asked him.

He returned to the present and looked at me squarely. "I gained too much. Too many worshipers, too much money, which of course meant too much power. The church was uncomfortable; they passed me over for archbishop and kept sending in stupid little men to take charge. Then the congress and powers that be on a number of worlds we were just starting on got nervous, too, and started putting pressure on the church. They couldn't do anything, though—I'd broken no laws. They couldn't just demote me. I'd just pop up elsewhere, and my following and my order would have exerted their influence to return me. That would have been an unforgivable defeat, so they had the idea of posting me to missionary work in the Warden Diamond—the perfect exile, you might say. But I wouldn't go. I threatened to take my order and my following out of the church and form our own denomination. It's been done before when the church has become corrupt. Of course that's where they got me. They played a few computer games, got some trumped-up charges about misappropriation of funds and using religion for political influence, and here I am—exiled to the post I wouldn't go to voluntarily, transported like any common criminal."

I had the idea that nothing about Father Bronz was common. "And yet you still serve the church as a missionary here?" I asked incredulously.

He smiled. "My bookkeeping may have been lousy, but my motives were sincere. I believe in the religious part of my church's teachings, and I believe God uses me as His instrument in His work. The civilized church is as secular and corrupt as the governments—but not here. On Lilith it's back to basics—no ranks, no churches, just pure faith. Here I am with a large heathen population and no superior save God Almighty." He looked around at the pawns going about their evening routines and lowered his voice a bit.

"Look at them," he almost whispered. "What kind of life is this you are all leading? There's no hope here, no future, just a stagnant present. If you don't have the power you're a pawn in the literal sense of that term. But they're human beings all the same. They need hope, a promise of something better, something beyond this life. They'll not get it on Lilith, and they can't leave the place, so Eternity is their only hope of salvation. As for some—the criminal element, let's say—well, that's where people like me are needed most. Besides," he added, "they need me. Who else will hear their complaints, as pitifully small as they really are, and who else will speak for them with authority to their superiors? Just people like me. No more."

I had his number now, I thought. He was completely insane, of course, but in his tremendous guilt over his own criminality with his cult or whatever, he'd decided on reparation for that guilt. The martyr type. Save his own soul through saving others. Such men were dangerous, since they were far too fanatical to face reality, but they were useful, too. Useful in some way to these people, and perhaps a lot more useful to me.

Father Bronz looked over and saw Ti standing shyly nearby. He sighed sadly. "Oh, no," he murmured under his breath but I caught it.

My eyebrows rose in surprise. "What's the matter?"

He gestured at Ti. "It's a sin, what they're doing with her and with a lot of other fine girls. They're coming along too quick—and their fates once they're taken into the castles are even worse."

I felt a nervous tingling. I didn't like to think of that, and by common consent, the subject was never mentioned. Perhaps I didn't want to think of her leaving, at least not while I was here. She had helped pull me out of the black pit into which my mind had sunk and had provided me with a friend, a companion, a source of information and growth. We'd already been paired longer than anyone in the village could remember anyone else being. Though I didn't kid myself that it was more than my body and her body having stronger needs that only we two could fulfill, I still didn't like to think of the future. But I felt compelled to ask the questions.

"What will they do to her?" I found myself asking in spite of myself.

He sighed sadly again. "First they'll freeze her, so to speak," Father Bronz said slowly. "A growing, intelligent mind would be a liability to them, so they'll keep her in a state of perpetual childhood. Even worse than now. It's only a matter of finding the right part of the brain and carefully killing what's necessary. Most of the bodymasters are former physicians and can do it easily. Then they heighten the glandular secretions or whatever—I'm no doctor, I don't really know—and when everything's balanced, they'll stick her in a harem with similarly treated girls and experiment with baby after baby trying to find the key to the power and how to transmit it. It's almost a mania with the knights, and the bodymasters are happy to practice, to continue to experiment, in their chosen field."

I shivered slightly. "And they're doctors? I thought doctors *saved* lives and made bodies and minds whole."

He looked at me strangely. "What an odd sort you are, Tremon! Why, of course doctors are no more free from sin and corruption than you or I. There are good ones and bad ones, and most of the highly skilled bad ones wind up here, the better to test their grotesque theories. I've heard it said that the Confederacy encourages them in this, even provides offworld computer analysis of their work, in the hope they'll find out what makes the Warden organism tick."

I just shook my head, refusing to accept such a horrible thought. The Confederacy! It was crazy, insane, and perfectly logical, damn it. All other experiments had come to nothing, after all, and these were considered prison worlds. But Confederacy support or no, what Bronz was saying was bleak news indeed for poor Ti.

"How long before they—take her?" I asked, fearing the answer.

He looked carefully at her. "Well," he replied, "she's already had all the preliminary treatments. I'd say she would be overdue. You see, they can't let her go too long or she'll have to set an intellectual pattern for them to play with safely. In other words, she'd be too smart for them, too complicated. I suspect that you've accelerated their plans, if they're aware of the attachment you two have formed, since contact with an outsider like you would widen her world."

I started, not only because I might have speeded up this dread fate but also because Bronz had so easily noted that Ti and I had been having a relationship. "How'd you know about us?" I wanted to know.

He laughed. "A priest is many things, but an observer of human nature is one of the most important. I see the way she hovers there, the way she looks at you, like some eager puppy for her master. She's really smitten with you, whether you realize it or not. What are your feelings toward her?"

I thought about it. Just what *were* my feelings about Ti? I really wasn't quite sure myself. By no stretch of the imagination did I consider us mates, having any obligations for one another. I'd never found that sort of arrangement comprehensible anyway. But I *did* feel a great fondness for her, not only physically but because she had the potential of becoming a complete human being. She was bright and curious, and she picked up new concepts much more quickly than any of the other native-born of this crazy world. I wondered vaguely whether it was possible to feel paternal and lustful at the same time. That smacked of some sort of incest, even though we weren't in any way related, yet it summed up my feelings as much as anything, so I told Bronz as much.

He nodded. "I thought it might be something like that. Too bad, too, because with you she might have grown to be a hell of a woman."

I considered what he was saying. Potential, that *was* the word. Potential. That was what I'd found so attractive in her, in contrast to the milling pawns around. Yet it was her tragedy, too. I felt a sudden strong fury rising in me, which I couldn't quite understand or fully control. That potential was what they were going to take from her. So great a wave of anger swept through me that I almost trembled with raw, brutal emotion, and I had trouble controlling it.

Father Bronz just sat and watched me, a serious expression on his face. Finally, as I gained some control over myself and tried to relax, to beat down the alien emotional tide, he spoke.

"For the first time," he said softly, "I saw the real Cal Tremon there beside me; he was a frightening figure, fully as terrible as his legends. I felt it, too. Great power welling up inside, bubbling like molten rock almost to the surface. You are going to be a powerful man indeed one day, Tremon, if you learn how to channel and use that fury."

I just sat and stared strangely at him, a sudden awareness of myself and my own potential exploding in my mind. In that instant I knew Bronz, from the standpoint of a very powerful Master, had *felt* a surge in my Warden abilities. Now I understood why some would rise and some would not, and how it was done. The key was emotion—raw, terrible emotion. Up until that moment I had never suffered much from emotion, a weakness I could not afford in my old work as an agent. Here, though, the enzymes and hormones and all the rest that had made Tremon such a terror had come to the fore, almost consumed me. Bronz had felt it.

It wasn't just how much power you had, it was how much self-control went along with that power—the ability to take raw, unbridled emotion and channel it, control it, shape it with your intellect. That, possibly more than any gradations of power, was what separated the ranks on this world. That explained why Kronlon, with all his power, was such a little man and would always be. That also explained why Marek Kreegan had risen to become Lord. He had been a trained agent, at the absolute top of his profession, here, in this sort of situation.

It was growing late; most of the other pawns had already returned to their huts and were sleeping now. I was, for now, still a pawn, facing the usual long day of work. "Will you still be here tomorrow?" I asked Bronz.

He shook his head. "No, sorry. I have a long way to go and I've tarried too long here now. I'm due in Shemlon Keep, to the south of here. Still, it was good meeting you, and I've a premonition of sorts we'll meet again. A man of your power will rise quickly on this world, if properly trained and developed."

That remark was too important to pass up. "Trained," I repeated. "By whom? Who does the training?"

"Sometimes nobody, sometimes somebody who knows somebody," he replied enigmatically. "The best training, I have heard, is from the colony descended from the first scientists to visit this world, Moab Keep, but that's thousands of kilometers from here. Don't worry, you'll find somebody—the best always do."

I left him still sitting there and accompanied Ti to the hut. Even though the hour was late and it had been a long day I had difficulty getting to sleep. Thoughts of breaking free of this pawn life, with eventually finding and facing down Marek Kreegan filled my head. And I also thought of Ti, poor, naive little Ti and what they were doing to her. I had built up a whole army I wanted to get even with, many of whom I hadn't even met as yet.

CHAPTER EIGHT

Social Mobility on Lilith

I continued to practice as much as I could while continuing my menial labors. If nothing else, I told myself, these past weeks or months or however long it'd been had accomplished two things. One was to tone up and fine-tune Cal Tremon's body so that it felt not only totally natural but really mine. Furthermore, its—no, *my*—muscles developed to a degree I'd have thought impossible not so long ago. I was hefting three or more times my considerable weight without even thinking about it, the aches long gone. I had no doubt that I could easily bend solid steel bars.

But oddly, it was the second thing that I, as a trained agent, appreciated the most. I had been humbled. I had been bent, then broken, with almost ridiculous ease, and the process had been humiliating.

Now, this might be a curious thing to say, but I badly needed to be humbled. I had been cocky, eager, too sure of myself when this escapade had started. Homo superior—never beaten in an assignment. I still believed that, but the place I was superior was now forever closed to me. This was a totally alien world, a world that operated on very different rules. I was out of my element here; so if I was going to win, I had to be brought down hard in order to build up again, almost from scratch. This fact, I'm sure, was the only reason I was still alive at this point. That and the fact that, though broken in the face of seemingly unassailable power, I had lost my sense of purpose but never my will to survive.

At the end of a day shortly after Bronz's departure, I walked back to the village for the evening meal with the others. I was already well into the food when I turned and looked at the faces of the others, the dirty and tired pawns of the village, and realized that something was not quite right.

Ti wasn't there. We almost always met here and ate together, and the composition of the Keep was so regular and unvarying that the few times when she'd had to be elsewhere I had always known in advance.

I started asking around, but no one had seen her. Finally I sought out some of the people she worked with at the nursery and they only said that Kronlon had come for her around the midday meal and she had gone off with him.

I frowned. Although Kronlon wasn't above taking those he was attracted to for a little fun, this was the wrong time. Kronlon, for all his power in relation to us, was just a shade higher on the scale than we pawns, and he had his own duties to perform. I had a really bad feeling about this. I stopped eating, stood up, and walked slowly through the crowd of pawns toward the supervisor's area. This wasn't an act rational people performed, but I wasn't about to let this go.

Kronlon was in. I could see him off in his little cubbyhole drinking something—probably local beer—out of a large gourd and puffing on what could have been anything from a stinkweed cigar to happy smoke. Pawns didn't get those luxuries, so I really couldn't be certain. Since it was so unusual for anyone to approach his quarters voluntarily, he noticed the movement out of the corner of his eye and turned in surprise. When he saw who it was, his face broke into an evil grin.

"Tremon! Well, well! I kinda expected you tonight!" he called out. "Come on in, boy!"

I approached, a little cautious, since even though I could sense, feel, hear, *see* the Warden organism in just about everything, including him, I hadn't had any success in actually making use of that sense. Kronlon, it seemed to me, burned a little more brightly than others whom I'd concentrated on—or was that just nerves? You never forgot the feeling he gave you, the incredible agony he could inflict merely by willing it.

I had the fleeting impulse to back out, but it was too late and I knew it. He'd seen me, he'd invited me over—and that was a command. No matter what, I was stuck.

Kronlon sat back and eyed me with an amused smirk. "Lookin' for your little bitch, huh? Missin' your bed partner?" His eyes flashed with cruel amusement. I knew he was baiting me, the son of a bitch.

I felt a warm, uncharacteristic rush of anger rising within me, but it was partially canceled out by my fear of him. I just nodded and stayed silent.

Kronlon laughed, enjoying his power and position. Here I was a giant of a man who could physically break him in two and he was my master as surely as if I were tiny and weak, like Ti. He roared with laughter and took another gulp of his beer. "She's gone, boy!" he told me. "Gone forever. You better get used to an empty bed for a while, son, 'cause she ain't never comin' back and you may as well get somebody new. Poor big ol' Cal's just got screwed." He laughed again.

My fury and frustration was growing almost beyond my control. All this time I'd been bossed and terrorized by this moronic sadist and I was becoming fed up with it.

"Where has she gone—sir?" I managed, still held back by the threat of that terrible power within him.

My hesitant tone and manner caused him even more amusement. "You really feel somethin' for her, don't you?" he responded, as if this made his news all the more a cruel joke. "Well, boy, I got a message midmornin' to fetch her and bring her up to the Castle. She didn't wanta come, I'll tell you, but hell, she ain't got no choice." His stare suddenly became slightly vacant, his tone more serious. "Ain't nobody got any choice in anything," he added. I realized that Kronlon never liked to think along those lines. He covered his own fear and debasement by his cruelty and sadism, the only things his tiny ego really had.

I should have felt some pity for him, but all I could see was a petty little man who had neither the right nor the qualification to wash the feet of the people whom he terrorized from his position of power. I was starting to boil.

"You know what they're gonna do to her?" he taunted. "Turn her into a human cow, Tremon. You know what a cow is, don't you? Big tits, no brains!" He roared at his joke.

"You slimy son of a bitch," I said evenly.

He continued laughing for a moment, and I wasn't sure he had heard me, nor, at that point, did I even *care* if he had. I was mad, howling, seething mad, perhaps crazy mad, too. I no longer cared what this worm, this lowest of the low, could do, what pain he could inflict. Agony was a price I was suddenly willing to pay if I could just snap his slimy neck.

He had heard. "What's that you said, boy? Somethin' on your mind? Why, hell, I'll give you somethin' else to think about, by damn!" He was almost shouting now, and he stood up. There was no mistaking it now—that sense of the Warden organism within him was stronger, more intense, *brighter* somehow, now. It was rising within him.

"Hell, boy!" he roared. "Maybe I'll fix you so's you won't get so worked up no more about no women! How'd you like t'be a gelding, boy? I can fix it, I can! I can fix you!"

Then hit the force of that agony, that searing pain in every cell of my body. I reeled back, staggering, but this time that terrible pain only fueled my anger and resentment. I exploded, no longer a thinking being, but a mass of raw emotions, a hatred such as I had never known all concentrated on this one terrible little man.

I stumbled and fell to my knees; yet as that animal fury took complete control, I no longer felt the pain the way I had. It lessened, still agonizing but somehow no longer relevant.

Slowly, deliberately, I pulled myself to my feet and took a step toward him.

Kronlon's bushy eyebrows rose in surprise; his expression showed confusion, then concentration as he threw everything he had at me.

I bellowed, a ferocious primal roar of rage that echoed throughout the whole village, then charged the startled and suddenly very frightened supervisor.

He retreated a couple of steps, then came up against the table he was using and almost fell back onto it. I was on him in an instant, my huge hands around his beefy throat. Kronlon had taught me more than the true meaning of fear; he'd taught me absolute, single-minded hatred.

He struggled to pry my hands loose from his throat. Somewhere in the dim recesses of my mind I was aware that the pain, the agony, was fading now, fading fast. It didn't matter. It wasn't relevant.

I felt a surge of energy grow within me, a strange, tangible power like some terrible fist. But before I could even comprehend what was happening, the tension broke and flowed outward from me, outward to the man whom I had pinned against the table. There was a searing burst of light and heat so intense I let him go and reeled backward. I recovered quickly but was still stunned as my head came up to see the supervisor lit in a strange glow, like some eerie supernatural flame.

And then he started decomposing before my eyes.

It was a gruesome sight, but one that, given my mental state, I could view without thought and, suddenly, without feeling of any kind. His skin fell from him, then his tissues, and finally the skeleton itself, which first glowed with a terrible brightness, then faded.

As my senses started to return, I just stood there, gaping at the impossible scene I had just witnessed. Finally I approached the place where Kronlon had stood and stared at it in the near darkness.

Everything, literally everything that was solid or liquid on Lilith burned with the tiny glow of Warden organisms. Everything—the table, the grass, the dirt, the rocks, the trees, even the lamp post. Everything. Everything but the grayish powder that now coated part of the table and a little of the ground beneath it.

All that was left of Kronlon.

Intellectually I was aware that I had caused it, but deep down, I could not believe it. The truth was incredible, impossible. Somehow, in my animal fury, my own Warden organisms had picked up that emotional power and transmitted it to those in Kronlon's own cells. Burned them up. Killed them.

I turned, stunned, suddenly aware that I was not alone. A crowd of villagers stood just outside, gaping in shocked silence at the scene, scared but unmoving—almost, it seemed, afraid to breathe. As I walked toward them, they quickly drew back, their fear a real and tangible thing. Fear not of Kronlon or of retribution.

Fear of me.

"Wait!" I called out. "Please! Don't be afraid! I'm not—like him. I won't hurt you! I'm your friend. I'm one of you. I live among you, work among you."

My protestations were in vain. Clearly I was *not* one of them any more. I was a man with the power. I had separated myself from them forever, drawn an unbridgeable gap between my own existence and their eternal toil.

"It doesn't have to be like this," I almost pleaded with them. "It doesn't *have* to be a tyranny. Kronlon's gone, and I am not Kronlon."

Torlok, an elderly man in a village where most never survived that long, was something of an authority figure; he ambled forward. The others were shrinking from me as if I had some terrible disease. Even Torlok would only come so far, but he was old and experienced and past a lot of caring about men and women with the power.

"Sir, you must go now," he croaked. "You are no longer one of us."

"Torlok—" I began, but he put up a hand.

"If you please, sir. When Kronlon does not check in tomorrow morning they will send someone to see why. They will find out why and they will send us another Kronlon. Things have changed only for you, not for us."

"You could leave," I pointed out. "You have until at least midday."

Torlok sighed. "Sir, you think you understand, but you do not. You are still new on this world of ours. You say flee—but where to? To another Keep run the same? To the wild to live in near starvation with the savages, unprotected from the nobles and the wild's own beasts? Or perhaps to be hunted down like some sporting beast?" He shook his head. "No, there will be no change for us. You must go now. You must go to the Castle, tell them what you have done. You belong to their life now, not ours.

You cannot go back. We cannot go forward. Go—before you unknowingly bring the wrath of the Masters upon us. If you feel anything at all for us, go—go now."

I stared at them for a moment, not quite believing what I was hearing. They were fools, I thought, who deserved their miserable lot. They actually preferred it to any sort of challenge!

Well, let them go back to their miserable lives, I told myself. This mention of the Castle reminded me that I had more than one good reason for going there. As Kronlon had said, we didn't have a choice, any of us, least of all me in this situation.

The adrenaline was ebbing, though, and I no longer felt as cocksure and all-powerful as I had only moments before. I turned and looked off into the distance, up at that fairy-tale place built into the side of the hill. Somewhere in there was Ti.

Without another word, I turned my back on the crowd that had disowned me and walked silently out of the village, out across the grassy fields toward the Castle.

Before I was halfway there I'd come down completely from the high that the power and emotional fury had given me. Now my intellectual self, my old self, was able to assume control once more—not necessarily for the better, I realized.

Up to that point I had never been anywhere near the Castle. The only people I knew who had were those like Kronlon who weren't exactly the chatty sort. I had no idea how many people were there, and of what potential power. The Knight and his family were there, of course, most of the time, and I already knew that I was no match for a Master, let alone a Knight. I wondered if I was even a match for a trained person of Supervisor rank. Kronlon was where he was because of the kind of person he had been—petty, mean, cruel, and stupid. I suspected that the first three might not matter so much, but the last was unforgivable.

I began to think that individuals like Kronlon, with a little power and small mind, were actually the sacrificial lambs. Somebody had to do that kind of work. But the risk always existed that one of the pawns who had been abused was potentially as strong or stronger than the Supervisor. When that happened, you'd probably scratch one Supervisor.

That observation led to a different line of thought. If I had been merely as strong as Kronlon, we'd have fought to a draw. If I had been *slightly* stronger, well, he'd be in terrible pain but probably alive. Master strength, at the very least.

Master strength . . . yes, but untrained. I was unable to muster that power on command, automatically, as even Kronlon could. More like Ti, I supposed, at least at this point. I wondered if that had been the reason for the caution about her. Had she at some point gotten mad and fried somebody to atoms? Somehow done so, and yet been unable to repeat the act.

I stopped in the darkened field. Was I in fact one of the elect, or, like

Ti, merely a Wild Talent? That was the most sobering question I had asked myself on the journey and the most disquieting.

All those nights I had sat there, sensing the Warden organism even as I felt it now in everything around me, trying to make it do something, anything—just bend a blade of grass. I'd failed miserably, despite intense concentration and force of will. And yet I had willed a man to decompose into dust and he had done so. How? Why?

It wasn't the absence of thought, although that was certainly true in this case, since the rulers, even those like Kronlon, could accomplish such things effortlessly and at their command. Yet there was no communication with the Warden organism itself, not really. The little buggers didn't think, they reacted to stimulus. External stimulus. If the power didn't depend on thought, but could be consciously mustered, then what was it?

The answer was so obvious I had only to ask the question of myself in order to be able to answer it. It was emotion, of course. My hatred, my sheer contempt and loathing for Kronlon had triggered the Warden organisms in my own body to transmit that devastating energy signal to the organisms in his.

Hatred, fear, love . . . all these emotions triggered chemical actions in various parts of the body, including most particularly the brain. These chemicals, then, were the catalyst that the Warden organism, living symbiotically in each and every cell of my body, needed to trigger its own powers. Emotion, reduced to its chemical products and by-products, was what was needed—and that explained a lot. Training, then, in the use of these powers was really concerned with controlling areas of the brain and body normally beyond control, much as yoga and other disciplines.

The criminals who were sent here were a bundle of messed-up psyches and unbalanced, often uncontrolled emotions. In the main, those born here were more naturally balanced as a result of their static society. Furthermore they were born with the Warden organism already growing and multiplying with their cells, in a better balance with their host's bodies; thus they were more like the creatures of Lilith, in perfect balance with the organism rather than alien to it. Outsiders, then, would naturally have the edge in triggering these odd powers. Ironically, while my cold, trained, logical mind had been unable to do a thing with this power, Cal Tremon's emotional imbalances—that new part of me that made me alien from myself—had done the job so well.

I resumed walking, but slowly, reflecting on what I knew and still didn't know. It was perhaps two hours before I reached the carved stone stairs leading, in a series of switchbacks, up to the Castle itself. For the first time in a very long time I was aware of and a little ashamed of my nakedness, my dirt and grime, my wild and savage appearance that was unfit for civilized company. Those up there in the Castle were civilized, no doubt about that. Perhaps not sane by any known definition, but certainly civilized—perhaps even cultured.

I wondered what I was supposed to do now and cursed myself for not asking someone back in the village. Did you just go up and knock and say, "Hello, I'm Cal Tremon. I just killed Supervisor Kronlon and I want to join your club?" What were the procedures here?

There seemed nothing to do but climb the stairs and wing it.

CHAPTER NINE

The Castle

It was an imposing structure, I had to admit that. Nothing like it had existed in the civilized worlds for a thousand years or so, if then, except in children's fantasies.

And they lived happily ever after . . .

Towers rose on either side of the main gateway, a huge double door of some bronze-colored wood that filled a massive stone arch. Windows in various parts of the place, which looked big enough to house several hundred, were all of stained glass and alit with the varying colors of the artist's hand. Judging from the lights, I deduced that at least the inhabitants were still up and I wouldn't be waking anybody.

I looked around for some simpler entrance, but it seemed as if the huge wooden door was it. I wondered whether every knight on Lilith had such a building, or whether this was the aberration of Boss Tiel. Certainly on Lilith there was nothing that walls and gates would keep out to be feared by one of such power.

There being no bell, apparently, nor any other system for summoning those inside, I pounded on the great wooden doors as hard as I could without hurting myself.

I hardly expected an immediate response, and I didn't get one. Vaguely, through the thick stone walls and gate, I could hear the sound of a crowd and some music, which meant I had to compete with some interior function. Still, I kept banging away, resting a bit between tries, although I was beginning to think I might have to camp out on the Knight's doorstep until the Castle opened for business in the morning.

With all my muscles I could pound pretty good, and somebody did eventually hear the pounding. I heard a voice from above me call out, "Hey! You, there! What the hell do you want?"

I jumped slightly, then turned to locate the speaker. He was standing at one of the small tower windows. He was too far away for me to see his features and how he might be dressed, or to get any idea of his rank.

I shrugged to myself. What the hell. "I'm Cal Tremon, sir!" I responded in my loudest, boomiest voice. "I just disintegrated one of your supervisors and I was told in no uncertain terms to get my ass up here."

The man hesitated a moment, as if considering what to do. Finally he called, "Just a moment! I'll have somebody come down and take care of you!"

I shrugged again. I sure wasn't going anyplace until they came, having no place to go. I wondered what was going on inside. For all I knew I was speaking to the lowest servant in the place—or to the big boss himself.

After a few minutes the huge wooden doors creaked open a bit and a woman emerged. She was tall and thin and had an almost aristocratic bearing about her. Years ago she'd probably been a really pretty woman, but she was now well into middle age and that usually didn't wear well on this kind of primitive world. Her hair was white and her face more wrinkled than even her age should have permitted.

What was important was that she was fully dressed in a long dress or robe of deep-purple silk embroidered with gold—an impressive uniform. At least a Master, I told myself, feeling even more helpless and not a little embarrassed by my appearance.

She approached me and walked around me, examining me as if I were some prize animal stock. Her nose twitched a bit, indicating that mingling with the common stock was not altogether to her taste. She smelled of perfumes too sweet to remember the time long ago when she must have been out in the muck herself.

Finally she straightened up, stood back, and took the overall view. I decided it was better to say nothing until she did. No use in blowing protocol.

Finally she said, "So you killed Kronlon, eh?"

I nodded. "Yes, ma'am."

"Gior said you claimed to have, ah, disintegrated him or some such term?"

I could only nod again. "That's true. He decomposed into dust at my touch."

She nodded back thoughtfully, more to herself than to me. "You use those cultured words freely," she noted, a trace of surprise in her voice. "Disintegrate. Decompose. And your speech is cultured. You are from Outside?"

I grimaced, knowing her thoughts on my filthy appearance. "Yes, ma'am. I've been here some time—how long I'm not sure."

She put her hand to her chin in a gesture of deep thought. "What were you when you were Outside, Tremon?"

I tried to look as innocent as possible. "I was a, ah, gentleman privateer, ma'am."

She snickered. "A pirate, you mean."

"For political motives," I replied. "The Confederacy had a basic concept that I disagreed with and I took action against it."

"Indeed? And what concept was that?"

"Why, this notion of equality," I responded, still sounding as innocently insincere as I could. This was far more my game. After all this time I was back in my own element. "The Confederacy attempts to make everyone equal in all things, and to have everyone share equally in all its wealth. I believe that some people are simply more equal than others and acted accordingly."

She was silent for a moment; then suddenly she broke into deep, throaty laughter. "Tremon, you *are* amusing," she said at last. "I do believe you will be a welcome addition to the Keep. Please come in—we'll see about making you look and feel a bit more in keeping with your background."

She turned and walked inside; I followed, feeling quite a bit better. After all this time of slavery and subjugation I was beginning to feel more like myself again.

The entry hall was alit with oil lamps of some sort, giving it a bright but flickering appearance. The place was damp and seemingly a lot chillier than anything I'd felt since arriving on Lilith. But the cold dissipated as we entered the main hall, actually something of an enclosed courtyard. It was large—perhaps forty meters square—and covered with an ornate floor made up of tens of thousands of tiny square tiles in different colors that formed a number of pleasing designs. In the center of the place was a waterfall, incredibly—not a big one, but a waterfall nonetheless. The water spurted from some fissure in the rock far above us and cascaded into a pool that frothed with the action of falling water but did not overflow, indicating an outlet or many of them. I gaped in wonder at such a thing, which was in many ways quite beautiful and impressive and, more interesting, highly creative. Whoever had designed this place really knew his stuff.

My hostess noticed my admiring gaze. "It *is* nice, isn't it?" she noted in a friendly tone. "Most impressive, really. I never quite tire of it. Under us the water is channeled into a number of different conduits, where it's stored for fresh water, boiled for steam power and hot water, sent through the Castle for use everywhere. The excess runs off into an underground stream." She laughed again. "All the comforts of civilization, my dear boy." She gestured as she walked, and I continued to follow her.

Occasionally we passed people in the stone tunnel-like corridors that fanned out from the central hall. I was conscious of a lot of side glances and outright stares from the men and women whom we passed, but nobody stopped or questioned us. Many of the people were simply dressed, often in nothing more than a simple kilt and sandals or grass skirt, occasionally topped by flowing robes of varying colors and designs. Others wore odd-looking shirts, pants, and heavy boots, indicating a variety of ranks. None, however, was naked. Simple innocence ended with the pawn world most of these people probably seldom, if ever, encountered.

But, simple or complex in dress and rank, they all looked clean, neat, well-groomed, and, well, *soft* compared to the people I'd known up to now. This was civilization indeed, and I felt like a barbarian crashing a formal party.

I was led finally to a modest room off one of the corridors; it came complete with wooden door and inside bolt. The room was certainly nothing fancy by any Outside standards, but was heaven to somebody who'd spent the past few months crammed into a communal tree hut. It was perhaps five by seven meters and contained a small table on which sat an oil lamp plus a closetlike recess with three deep drawers that rose from the floor before opening up into a reasonable hanging space. In the center stood a bed. A real bed, complete with silken sheets and fluffy-looking pillows. It had been an awfully long time since I'd seen a real bed.

The floor was carpeted with some sort of fur, possibly from the *nur*, the large spiderlike giants raised by one Zeis village. It felt really nice and cozy.

"This will be your room until you complete your tests and begin training," my hostess told me. "After testing and training we'll know just where you should be put." She looked at me, and her nose twitched a bit again. "However, before you make use of it we'll have to get that accumulated filth off you. Goodness! Don't pawns *ever* bathe any more?"

"They do," I assured her. "But under more primitive conditions—and their work load doesn't allow bathing on a regular basis."

She shrugged. "Well, *you* will bathe, Tremon, and tonight. Come along, I'll set you up for it. Then I've got to return to the Banquet Hall. It's not often we have a party here with so many guests, and I'm afraid you're not as important as that to me."

I took her comment without insult, since I could see her point. Comparative luxury or not, life in the Castle was probably as dull as everything else about this world, so social events would be like drugs to the addict for those born Outside who knew a better, more interesting life.

She took me to the Baths, a series of small recessed pools with steaming hot water in them. Like the entry hall, the Baths were well tiled and styled by someone more artist than architect; the combination of tiny tiles and the smallest bricks I'd ever seen made the place classically elegant.

Some young women of Supervisor rank, judging from their leafy skirts with little else adorning them, waited for us. My hostess quickly turned me over to them. It was one of the most unusual, though pleasant, baths I'd ever had. I'd have been somewhat embarrassed back in the civilized worlds or even on the frontier, but after months as a pawn being in a hot pool with a bevy of attractive young women was something I didn't mind one bit.

I was scrubbed all over by gentle, experienced hands using a frothy soap of some kind that was lightly scented; then I was given an expert rubdown and my nails clipped and trimmed, my beard and hair expertly cut and styled. If there was a more wrenching experience I'd never heard of it —from squalor to luxury in a matter of hours. I was enjoying the sensation thoroughly, feeling better and more relaxed than I'd felt since awakening aboard that prison ship. Even now, only an hour or two into this new life, those months of slave labor as a pawn seemed a distant nightmare, as if it had happened to someone else.

The women would answer no questions and seemed as expert in turning attempts at friendly conversation into inconsequential nothings as they were in bathing and giving manicures.

Finally I was led back to my room and left alone, the door closed behind me. I didn't lock it; there seemed no reason. I just flopped on that great bed—the most wonderful bed ever made, I quickly decided—and let myself relax completely. As I was drifting off to sleep, somewhere in a corner of my mind Ti's face and form seemed to peer out and look accusingly at me. I remembered no more.

CHAPTER TEN

Dr. Pohn and Master Artur

They let me sleep late and I did. I rarely if ever remembered my dreams, but that night was beyond all experience. I am convinced that to this day it was the deepest sleep I'd ever experienced. When I finally did awaken, it was as if a signal had been given by some means. More than likely somebody had been posted in some hidden recess to watch me throughout the night. That must have been boring as hell.

At any rate, I'd barely opened my eyes when a bell sounded somewhere far off and there was a knock on my door, which I answered with a dreamy "Enter if you will." I had overslept to extremes and felt that I'd never really wake up.

The door opened and a young boy, certainly no more than ten or eleven, stuck his head in. "Please remain here for a while," he said in a pleasant, boyish tenor. "Breakfast is being brought to you."

I just nodded, and the door closed again. I wondered whether it was a good idea to tell them that I couldn't go anyplace right now if my life depended on it. Every muscle ached, every part of my mind was filled with sponge and cobwebs. I had more than slept off my months of toil, I'd slept for the first time free of the constant and intangible tension and uncertainty that life had produced.

I lay there, occupying myself as I could by trying to locate the peephole, which wasn't difficult. In order to take in the entire room, it had to be above and probably opposite me as well. A cursory figuring of the proper angles led me to the small discolored brick niche that almost certainly had a human eye behind it.

Breakfast arrived shortly, and I struggled up to meet it. It was a relatively simple affair, true—just some wheat toast, jellies, a few small sweet-rolls, and a glass of juice—but after the gruel I'd been fed the past few months, it looked like heaven. My greatest need was the mug of hot—well, I wasn't sure what it was, but it tasted something like mocha and was obviously a strong stimulant. Everything tasted simply wonderful and did the trick.

By the time young attendants of Supervisor rank had cleared my little portable breakfast table and taken it away, I felt ready for anything and anybody. The sight of people with the power acting as the most menial of servants fit my idea of what the Castle *had* to be like. From past experience in the service, I knew a general or admiral was boss, the authority figure to be feared and respected. But at Military Systems Command, for example, junior generals and admirals were only glorified messengers. Power wasn't just what you had, it was always what you had compared to those around you.

Still, the Supervisor class had it easy compared to the masses on Lilith. Their toil was dignified, civilized, and most of all, comfortable. Still, the youth of many of them marked them as native-born, and also reminded me that Ti, too, was somewhere here in the Castle. It would be delicate, but I had to see how she was faring and to help if I could. In a sense I owed all this to her.

All set for my introduction into society, I hadn't long to wait before my guide and evaluator appeared. He hadn't knocked, a sign of extreme rank, and he was something to see. Cal Tremon was a huge man, but this chap was equally large and as well proportioned, although a lot of his body was hidden by gold-braided clothing of the deepest black—a rather fancy shirt and tailored pants, the latter held up by a shiny, thick belt and tucked into equally shiny and impressive black boots.

The man himself was clean-shaven except for a thick and droopy mustache. He had a rough, experienced face, burned and etched by sun and wind. His imposing gray eyebrows set off the coldest pair of jet-black eyes I'd *ever* seen. His hair, carefully cut and manicured, was full and somewhat curly, the gray of it marking the type of man he was rather than his age—he might have been thirty or sixty for all anyone could tell.

I knew in an instant this was a dangerous man, one whose fierceness and aristocratic bearing made the late, unlamented Kronlon look as threatening as Ti. I stood up and bowed slightly, feeling we might as well get off to a good start.

"I am Master Artur," he said, in a voice so low and thunderous that it alone would be intimidating enough to make most people jump when it sounded. Worse, I was convinced that this was Artur's nice, *pleasant* voice. I really didn't want to see this old boy mad, at least not at me.

"I am Keep Sergeant-at-Arms," he continued, looking me over. I could not fathom what might be going through his brain.

"I am Cal Tremon," I responded, hoping that was sufficient.

He nodded. "So you fried old Kronlon, did you? Well, good riddance to the little rat anyway. I never did like him much, although he did his job well enough. Well, enough of that. I'm to take you over to Medical and then we'll put you through your paces. Feel up to it?"

I nodded, although still a little hung over from my long sleep. "Now is as good a time as any," I responded, and bowed again slightly.

"Come along." He gestured with his hand, and with that he turned and walked briskly out the door. I followed as best I could, noting the big man's proud, military-style gait. He was no native of Lilith, I decided, and I wondered just who and what he had been.

The Castle was far more alive during the day, with hordes of people all over, many on cleanup and maintenance errands, but a lot seemingly just milling around. They all seemed so neat and clean and civilized, though, that they produced an odd set of comparisons in my mind. What these people were to the civilized worlds, ancient Greece of our ancestral world must have been to those of the early industrial revolution. Technologically primitive did not mean truly primitive at all.

Still, the technology that was in evidence was shock enough. Since coming to Lilith I'd been conditioned to believe that such clothing and buildings and things of this nature just weren't possible here. That's why people slept inside *bunti* trees and wore nothing. Now I was beginning to appreciate the other side of the power the Warden organism could bestow —the power that was fundamental to civilized thought and society.

The power to alter one's environment for one's own ends—that was the key denied to the pawns, the element that kept them in abject misery and slavery. The capricious rules of the Warden organism said that such a power was reserved to a select few.

I *did* notice, though, the slight traces of fear in these people's faces as Artur passed, the sideward glances and forced attempts not to appear to be looking at us. No doubt about it—they were terrified of him, as were the few Masters we encountered.

Artur dropped me at Medical and told them where to find him when they were through. They just nodded respectfully and said as little as possible, but you could feel the relief when the big man left the room. They measured, poked, and probed as best they could, having no Outside instrumentation. They *did* have some clever substitutions, though, fashioned, apparently, out of things in the environment itself. A clinging sort of vine from which they appeared to be able to read my blood pressure; a small yellow leaf whose color change to red showed to experienced eyes my body temperature. All these and more were dutifully recorded with reed pens on some thin, leafy substance that served for paper.

All of these men and women were Supervisor class, though. Only after they were through with the preliminaries and satisfied did they call in their own chief. He was a small, pudgy, middle-aged man who had the look of the civilized worlds about him without the physical standards exactingly carried through. He wore a soft white satiny robe and sandals, apparently because that was what was comfortable.

"I am Dr. Pohn," he began in the usual medical manner. He picked up the sheets and glanced idly at them. "I see you're disgustingly normal. Believe it or not, just about everybody is, you know. That's the Warden organism's trade-off to us for living off our bodies. Damage almost anywhere except the brain itself is corrected, new limbs grown, and so forth. And the viruses here are too alien for any of us to have to worry about. Still, we go through the forms. You never know when you're going to find someone unusual. Besides, we're interested in comparative readings from people such as you who have demonstrated abilities with the power."

I nodded, remembering now that Tiel was obsessed with breeding a class with the power. This, then, would be the man in charge of the Knight's pet project.

"Were you a doctor—before?" I asked, both curious and trying to be friendly.

He smiled. "Outside? Yes, yes, of course. But it was a far different thing there, you know. All those computer diagnosticians, automatic surgery, and yes, despite all, some diseases to cure if we could. Here I give physicals and administer native-distilled medication when needed for minor aches and pains and nervous strain. Otherwise, I'm engaged mostly in research on the Warden organism itself."

That was interesting, even if I did think I knew what he meant. "Have you found out anything new?" I asked carefully.

He shrugged. "A little, but it's slow work. There *are* certain physiological and chemical factors common to those with it, but isolating them, let alone duplicating them—particularly in people not born with them—is beyond me. Perhaps with all my old laboratories and analytical computers I could do something, maybe even on Lord Kreegan's satellite base, but here I am forced to be slow and primitive, I fear."

I perked up. "Satellite base?"

"Oh, yes. Didn't you know? The Medusans built it for him years ago. Since it's Medusan, our own little pet Wardens won't touch it, since it already has their cousins, who are much nicer about machines and such. He lives there most of the time."

I doubted that very much. Although Kreegan might go there when he needed things, he'd be far too exposed to the Confederacy on such a satellite, liable to get blown out of the sky at any time. If I were Kreegan, I decided, I'd almost never go there. Rather I'd let underlings take the risk and just use it as my chief communications and command center with the other Warden worlds and Outside.

There was nothing more to be gained from that tack, but I wondered if I could draw him out a little in his project. "Interesting what you say about common chemical factors," I said casually. "I had come to the conclusion that emotion triggered my surge of power and that the chemicals released into my body when I was really mad were the catalyst."

"Very astute," he responded, beaming a little. Clearly he enjoyed his subject. "Yes, emotion is the key, as you will find out. But each individual's threshold level for release of those chemicals is very different, nor are the amounts the same—yet the Warden organism is very demanding of its precise catalyst. Chemical triggering *and* will is the key. Your anger gave you the *power* to kill; your will to kill him directed and released it. I have often suspected that the initial trigger is what we've always called the 'killer instinct,' for want of a better psychological term. Everybody on Lilith really has the latent power, but not everyone the force of will to use it. That's why pawns remain pawns, I suspect."

"You said you were trying to duplicate the catalysts in those who didn't have it, or didn't have it in sufficient quantities," I prompted. "How?"

He shrugged and got up, obviously pleased with my interest. "Come on, I'll show you."

We walked out and down the hall a short way, then entered a larger chamber. I stopped, a little stunned at the sight. There were a dozen slabs, equally spaced, with bedding on top of each. On each slab there appeared to be a sleeping or comatose young girl. I looked hard and spotted Ti's distinctive form far off on the slab opposite us, but while my heart felt a twinge I clamped down hard on myself so as not to betray anything I didn't have to. Not yet, not yet, I told myself.

"Are they—still alive?" I asked, hesitant, a little fearful of his answers.

He nodded. "Oh, yes, very much so. These are pawn girls who've shown flashes of strong power, usually right around puberty, but have proved incapable of repeating it, or at least of doing anything by force of will. Between their first and twelfth menstrual periods girls undergo physiochemical changes far more radical than do boys at the same stage in their lives. Since a lot of these chemical changes trigger Warden phenomena, we tend to monitor all the young girls in the Keep at that stage. In these girls it was exceptionally strong, as you might guess from their highly overdeveloped bodies."

"I thought *you* did that," I blurted, then tried to cover. "I knew one of these girls. That's why I'm so interested." At least that much was the truth.

He appeared to be a little surprised, but accepted the statement without further thought. "Oh, no. The condition's a by-product. I believe that during this critical change in the body, the Warden organism gets confused, misfires, or receives the wrong instructions—or misinterprets the chemical stimuli it does receive. Not all girls experience this, by any means. One in a hundred, at best, and out of these, one in another hundred show strong power and bodily misdevelopment. Those are the ones we test and measure and keep a close watch on, although the very unpredictability of the power during that stage limits me. I could be killed or maimed during such an involuntary exercise of the power, and though I'm willing to risk it, Sir Tiel is not. Therefore we leave them in pawn villages until the danger is past. Which one did you know, by the way?"

I pointed to Ti. "That one, over there."

"Oh, of course. She's the newest, so it's most likely. I'm still doing a preliminary analysis on her, so I can't say much as yet, but she had the most potential of any I've seen. All sorts of phenomena around her, including the most severe. Among other things, she crippled half a dozen people around her, including her mother."

I shook my head in wonder. Little Ti a crippler? It didn't seem possible, I told myself. Still, it made me slightly uneasy, too. I'd slept with her a great deal in the past few months, and if she'd still had any of that wild power I could have been harmed, too.

"What are you doing with them now?" I wanted to know.

"Testing and measurement, as I said," Pohn replied. "All Masters and above have the power to see within others. Rank is mostly a matter of fine-tuning your reception, you might say, in our little society. A Supervisor senses, and therefore controls, only the total organism. You killed Kronlon, it's true, but you couldn't discriminate enough to affect just, say, his arm. I can isolate even more than that, much more. What I used to do with microscopes and microsurgery techniques I can now do without any mechanical aid. By concentration and study I can actually follow a single white blood cell completely through the circulatory system—and divert it, slow it, alter it, even destroy it. You can sense the Warden organism in everything, can't you?"

I nodded.

"Well, imagine being able to isolate individual cells in any organism. That's what a Master can do. Naturally, without my medical training they'd have no idea what they were doing, so my knowledge gives me the edge here. Masters have different skills based on knowing what they are looking for and what they want to accomplish. All the power of a Marek Kreegan will do you no good at all if you don't have the knowledge and the fine touch, the skill or art, to make full use of it. That's why you see the power used so often for purely destructive ends. To destroy something is easy and requires far less knowledge or skill."

I could see his point, and thought that many doctors back on the civilized worlds would envy his power as much as he envied their technology. To be able to look into the human body, to focus on any part of it one wanted, to study it at will in the most exacting and intimate ways possible—none but sophisticated medical computers Outside could accomplish anything like it, and the doctors and technicians controlling them had to trust them, never knowing exactly what it was the computers saw as they probed and analyzed.

Pohn, however, knew.

"They're so still," I noted. "Drugged?"

He shook his head. "Oh my, no! That would simply complicate things. No, I simply applied a block to certain areas of the brain, one I can remove at will. They go into deep coma and I can then study them, probe, do whatever I want or need to do. Of the batch, I'm looking for ones with key enzymes in sufficient quantities perhaps to trigger the power. Those I'll work with until I feel I can trigger them at will; then I'll start trying to educate and train them as best we can. Kria there, for example, can now dissolve solid rock at my command." He pointed at one girl near the door.

I frowned. I had a bad, uneasy feeling about all this and about Pohn in general. Why was a doctor like this on Lilith at all? I asked myself. Did he perhaps have an unhealthy fondness for little girls? Or did he perhaps experiment capriciously on such people back Outside? I knew him now, although I'd never met him or heard of him before. There have always been people like Dr. Pohn in human history, the monsters whose thirst for experimentation caused a total disregard for any concept of morality. Shades of the old story about the man who'd created a bloodthirsty monster, leaving the question of who truly was the monster—the thing, or the man who created it?

These young girls—reduced to zombies, biological specimens, perhaps playthings for this man's sport. I thought of Ti in his hands and didn't like what I was thinking at all. Still, I said nothing of my feelings. Instead I asked, "I assume you're trying breeding experiments, too?"

He nodded. "Oh, yes. Based on the idea that the proper chemical in the proper amount is an inherited and inheritable characteristic. Frankly, I doubt it is more than one in many factors, but Sir Tiel is obsessed with the idea. I'm afraid that his level of biological sophistication is about on a par with the belief of spontaneous generation, but what can I do? I work for the man, and he's a skillful and able administrator. I humor him; he indulges me. What's the harm?"

What's the harm? I thought sourly. What, indeed? As long as you didn't regard any of these girls as more than lumps of flesh, no higher or lower than the great insects raised and bred in the Keep. *That* was the barbarity at the core of this civilization, I told myself. Only a select few were people.

Precisely the underlying philosophy you'd expect on a world run by the most brilliant criminal masterminds humanity had spawned. Men like Dr. Pohn, sociopathic and probably psychopathic—and men like Cal Tremon, pirate and mass murderer, I reminded myself.

"We really have to ring for Artur now," Pohn said, turning and leaving the chamber. I followed him. "I'm afraid I've taken much too long with you, and it doesn't pay to get him too angry."

"This Artur—what did he do? Outside, I mean?"

"To get here?" the doctor chuckled. "Oh, I don't know the details. He was somebody very big in the Confederacy military hierarchy, I think. A general, maybe, or an admiral. Ignited the atmosphere of some planet years ago, as I remember. Killed a few billion people. Something like that. Always said he was scapegoated for doing somebody else's dirty work. That's all I know. A nasty man, though."

I had to agree. *Killed a few billion people . . .*

Given enough time I'd remember who he was, I was sure of that. I'd also remember that the comment on the death toll meant as little to Dr. Pohn as if the death toll had been in cockroaches.

CHAPTER ELEVEN

Choosing a Different Road

Master Artur was prompt and didn't seem the least put-out. He was just as cold and mean as always, with no trace of anything more or less. I began to wonder if the man were human.

For the next hour or so we went on a tour of the Castle, armed with a nicely drawn map that Artur handed to me. The place was very logically laid out more or less in a D shape, with corridors fanning out in all directions to main function halls and rooms, each of which were also connected in the rear semi-circle by service passages. Along each corridor were living quarters, storage, and other necessities, including group bathrooms. The corridors were arranged somewhat on a caste basis, with the bulk of them devoted to the Supervisor class that did the real work of the place, then the two on either side of the central passage for Master rank, and the center of course leading to Sir Tiel's luxurious quarters and those of his immediate family.

Not shown on the map, I noticed, were the inevitable secret passages between rooms and those perhaps above and below as well, such as the one from which they spied on me. Their absence didn't surprise me, but I decided that I really wanted to know more about them.

Outside the Castle Artur's pride and joy was quartered in a large compound against the side of the hills. It was almost a stockade, made of great logs with catwalks and guard towers that reminded me of some primitive fortress. Artur had been totally cold, dry, and formal during our tour and seemed distant from everything and everybody, but now he seemed to warm and those chilly eyes lit up.

"Not a part of the regular tour," he told me, "but I have to go down and check them out anyway, so you might as well come along."

"Them" turned out to be enclosed herds of great insects the likes of which I had not really seen before on Lilith or anywhere else. Trained Supervisor-grade personnel scurried about when Artur approached, so by the time we entered the huge compound they were all set and waiting for him. Lines of them, rows and rows of them, in tight quarters but nonetheless mighty impressive.

They sat there in formation, huge *wuks,* as they were called, their bodies a bright green with a whitish underbelly; they were fully three or four meters long on six thick, powerful bent legs, their heads dominated by great luminous ovoid eyes flanking a curled, whiplike proboscis that concealed a nasty, beaklike mouth. Their skins were perfectly smooth, but I got the impression of a strong skeleton just beneath that made them far less fragile than they looked.

Each had a saddle tied to it between the first and second pair of legs; it was an elaborate seat with a hard back and an X-shaped restraint to cover their riders and hold them in. The riders, in black pants and boots, were both male and female, but all looked tough, hard, and well-disciplined. There was an array of what I could only guess were weapons, from pikes and staffs to what might very well have been blowguns. They were situated so that the restrained rider could get at them easily and quickly.

"I am impressed," I told Artur (and I wasn't kidding). "But this looks like an army to me—mounted cavalry. I wouldn't think you'd need an army here."

Artur chuckled. "Oh, yes, indeed we do," he responded. "You see, basically in order to move up in this society you have to kill somebody—be stronger than they were. Now, *you* tell *me*—if you were Sir Tiel, would you keep going day after day in challenges against everybody who thinks he can knock you off? Of course not. And neither do any of the other knights. And what do you get for it? A lot of bowing and scraping, of course, but mostly a shitload of administrative headaches. There are probably hundreds of masters stronger than most of the knights, maybe even stronger than the Duke himself, but they just don't want the job. A lot do, though. So I'm charged with seeing that it's a bit more difficult to challenge the Knight of the Keep—a policeman, you might say. And if one knight wants something another knight has, well, they can challenge knight to knight—but they'd probably end up either dead or in a draw, so there's no profit in it. So we fight a little. Anybody who wants anything from *this* Keep has to either bargain for it in a nice way or fight for it—and that's where these troops come in."

I nodded, my view of Lilith changing a bit once more. At first I couldn't see why they'd have fighting on a local scale, but then I realized that it was the safety valve, you might say. These squabbles tended to keep the most dangerous of people on Lilith—the psychopaths, war-lovers, violence-prone troublemakers, that sort—occupied. If they liked to beat one another's brains in, give them a forum for doing so, an outlet for their violence that didn't mess up the nice, neat system. I could see an astute administrator, particularly one with a lot of troublesome, violence-prone people, actually starting a war with a neighbor now and again just to relieve the tension—and perhaps the boredom.

"The *wuks*," Artur was saying, "use those big hind legs of theirs to leap high into the air if they want to, with the soldier aboard. That's why the people are strapped in, but have their arms free. They can jump behind static ground lines with ease, making fixed fortifications useless. Up on the hill, there—you can see all those holes, almost like a honeycomb—are my *besils*, swift flyers that are, so to speak, my air force. Combine them with ground troops and you have a force that, properly employed, is almost invincible." He said that last not in a bragging tone but with the ring of truth and conviction about it. The key phrase was "properly employed." I had no doubt that Artur was one hell of a good field general.

A neat system, I had to admit. The knights, fat and comfortable, didn't want to challenge each other. The lack of any kind of instant communication meant that the acquisition of large areas, the consolidation of Keeps under one rule, would be difficult and profitless to maintain. And any challenger to the knight would first have to get past the Castle and its defenses—no mean feat. No matter what power anybody had, an arrow or spear would still kill him if it landed properly—would kill even Marek Kreegan himself.

I could just see knights sitting around at parties given by one or another of them making bets on whose army was best, whose commander was most skillful. I was willing to bet that Artur had won a lot of those wagers.

We walked back to the Castle after Artur's formal inspection. Off in the distance I could see the pawns, countless numbers of them, working in the fields and tending the herds. Only then did I think of them on an emotional level. I had been out there only a day before, yet already the social gulf separating us was an almost solid, impenetrable barrier. There seemed something wrong about that and something profound, as well, that said a lot about the ruling classes and the ruled; but I couldn't put my finger on it. Still, I was closer to them than to people like Artur and Pohn. But I was no match for the lowest, stupidest supervisor stablehand in the place.

We went to the supervisors' dining hall, and I suddenly realized how hungry I was. It had been many hours since that light breakfast, and even though I'd done little to work anything off, I was used to a lot more bulk.

"I will leave you here," Artur told me. "For the next few days, you have the run of the Castle. Relax, talk to people, learn the system. When we're ready, you'll start classes to see how your power can be developed." His furry brows narrowed a little and he looked at me hard. "Don't get too cocksure in those classes, boy. Remember, it's not just a test of power and will but an intelligence test, too. Remember where Kronlon wound up." And with that he was gone.

I was dimly aware that I had been given a kindness by this strange, aristocratic man. I pondered his words as I ate heartily the best meal I'd had in months, and I think I understood what he was saying.

They wanted you to develop what powers you had, of course, the better to fit into the system and serve the bosses. But suppose you did *too* well. If you proved out stronger than a Master, say, would your host and boss suffer you to live? Not likely. But it wouldn't do to slack, either—or you would wind up out in the muck with the pawns. Tricky indeed, this social system.

I spent the next couple of days making friends with some of the Castle staff, exploring the Castle and its many byways and learning what I could about the passages, somewhat euphemistically referred to as "service corri-

dors," not shown on the maps. From casual friendships I learned several
things I had to know, not the least of which was that the party held the
night I'd arrived on the scene was in honor of Marek Kreegan himself, in
on one of his surprise tours. Nobody had seen him—not even those who
served at the fete could say what the Lord of Lilith looked like. I had the
strong impression that not even the man who owned the place knew
which of his guests was Kreegan, whose powers to cloud minds was legendary and whose passion for anonymity was absolute. Duke Kosaru was
the nominal guest of honor, but they all knew that Kreegan had been
there.

Was he still here? I couldn't help but wonder and looked suspiciously at
all those of Master class I came in contact with who were not obviously of
Zeis Keep.

I also dropped in on Medical from time to time, mostly to see what, if
anything, was to happen to those girls on the slabs, particularly Ti. I could
hardly understand my fixation with her; in the past I'd always been coldly
detached toward sexual partners and even friends. Most were shallow individuals anyway, and those who weren't were a danger to me of one sort or
another, as I might have been set after one or another of the exceptional
ones at some point. That worried me, really, since I always had such a
clear idea of who I was, what I wanted, and what my place in the universe was.

Cal Tremon, what was your body making me into? Was I in fact no
longer immune from the emotional factors I always believed had set me
apart from the rest of humanity?

Most of my attempts to see Pohn failed. He was a busy man, it seemed,
and hard to catch in any one spot. A doctor on a world where nobody got
sick and where almost all injuries healed themselves perfectly or regenerated what was missing had a lot of time for research, and I knew some of
the directions that research was taking. I *did* learn from his assistants that
he was responsible for the supercreatures of Artur's force, selective breeding and genetic manipulation by sheer force of will alone accomplishing
wonders. Anybody that godlike could hardly resist doing the same to
people.

I *did* catch him in one afternoon, though, and he was happy to see me.
Apparently I was one of the few who seemed truly interested in his work,
but I realized I was treading on eggshells around him. In his own way he
was at least as dangerous as Artur, if only because his powers were more
far-reaching and far more subtle.

Finally, though, we were again in that eerie, funereal room with the
twelve comatose girls. I saw that Ti was still among them.

"How do they eat?" I asked him. "How do you keep them from developing circulatory problems, all the troubles inherent in not moving? For
that matter, how do they go to the bathroom?"

He chuckled. "It's a matter of routine," he explained. "I and my assistants handle each of them at four-hour intervals. It's quite simple. Watch."

With that he went over to the nearest unconscious girl, made a cursory examination of her, then stepped back a little.

"Kira, sit up," he coaxed more than ordered. The girl, still dead to the world, eyes closed and breathing regularly, sat up. It was a ghoulish sight, as if a corpse had suddenly reanimated itself without ever really coming to life.

"Open your eyes, Kira," he instructed, still using a gentle tone, and she did; but it was clear there was no thought behind the large, pretty brown eyes revealed there.

"Get out of bed and stand next to it, Kira," Pohn instructed, and again, with a smooth, fluid motion and no wasted moves, she did as she was told. I, who had killed without thinking about it more than once and had seen a lot of horrors in my life, shivered slightly.

"She's like a machine, an android," I said.

Pohn nodded. "Yes, yes, that's pretty much it," he agreed. "But an android is as complex as the human body. Here, with techniques like these, I will one day learn the secret of the Warden organism. With subjects like these I have already gone further than I dared hope when I started."

"Are they—aware—of what is happening?" I asked him.

"Oh, no, no, no," he assured me. "That would be far too cruel. With a lot of experimentation I have determined the location of what I might call the key neural connectors, although that's a layman's simplification. Their thinking part remains as if in the deepest sleep, while the rest, their physical part, can be awakened and stimulated—I call it external motivation—to do things their conscious minds could not. Here, I'll show you. Kira, follow me one step behind me, stopping when I stop and walking when I walk."

The girl followed him out the door like a shadow, and I followed them. We wound up in a small lab whose walls were the solid natural bedrock of the mountain itself, rough and unfinished. He positioned her at least three meters from one of these blank, rocky walls.

"During that key puberty period, Kira was able to influence the growth of plants—they grew almost as you watched—and she actually made small earthquakes in her local vicinity. Then the power passed, as it does in all but a few, and I wound up with her here. Working with her, I've been able to discover a large number of chemical stimuli to certain areas of the brain. She supplies the power and the stimuli, I supply the willpower." He looked around the barren room. "Do you sense the Warden organism here?"

It had become almost second nature to sense that odd feeling of life all around, even in the most passive and inanimate of things. I felt it, of course, in every molecule of the rock that framed the room, and nodded to him.

"Good. Now watch. Kira, about two meters up on the far wall I want you to hollow out a fifty-centimeter cube from the rock with your mind." He stood back, and for some reason I shrank back as far as I could.

I was aware that Pohn was concentrating on her, more than likely triggering those stimuli, those enzymes or whatever that built up the power.

"*Now,* Kira," he breathed.

What happened was almost anticlimactic. No crackle of lightning, no rumblings or anything like that. It was just that . . . well . . .

I heard a click and then a sound like falling plaster or dirt dislodged over the side of a precipice. Just a little sound—but there was now a cube of roughly fifty centimeters cut into the wall, with a heap of fine powder inside.

Dr. Pohn went over and brushed the powder out and gestured for me to approach. I was a little nervous about getting in the way of that kind of power, but I did examine the hollow the girl had created at Pohn's direction. It was perfectly smooth, very regular, with no sign of how it had been formed.

"Just proof that the potential is in all of us," he told me. "More, I think, in women than in men for some reason. At least the women seem stronger in their powers, although more erratic. I have girls in there who could possibly reduce this castle to dust if properly stimulated and motivated."

"It would seem to me that the Boss and his superiors might find you something of a threat, Doctor," I noted.

He laughed and shook his head from side to side. "Oh, no. I'm quite strong, quite powerful, but I have no taste for knighthood. It would end my work, really. I'm no risk because they all know of my lack of ambition with regard to their jobs. In fact, they encourage my work because it might help them. Master Artur, for example, is quite interested in one of the girls, who, we think, might well be able to freeze an attacking army, perhaps even dissolve it."

We walked back to the "morgue" as we talked, the zombielike Kira following obediently.

"Which one?" I asked, feeling a little queasy.

"That one," he replied, pointing, as I suspected, directly at Ti.

I was becoming pretty good at locating the secret passages. Oh, I'll admit I didn't try the ones they'd guard and booby-trap, the ones leading to Sir Tiel's quarters, but the rest were more than handy. You could almost live inside the small passages and corridors in the walls, although you'd have trouble avoiding the others who used them regularly—some on business (such as spying) and some just for fun, such as voyeurism. Everybody knew about them, of course, but few really thought much about them.

My lessons started about a week after I arrived at the Castle, and they were what I was most interested in. My tutor was Vola Tighe, sister of the elderly matron who'd admitted me in the first place. Unlike her sister, though, Vola was far more serious and businesslike and seemed to have a better idea of herself and her duties. Still, outwardly they might have been twins and may well have been.

"The key is chemical stimuli, as you know," she told me. "The *trick* is to be enough in control of yourself that you can reach inside your own head and trigger exactly what you need when you want it, then direct the result by force of will. Everyone on Lilith has this potential, but it is psychology that makes the difference. Not everyone on Lilith—not most, thank heavens—possesses the concentration, willpower, sheer intelligence to learn and execute the techniques properly."

"Dr. Pohn thinks otherwise," I pointed out. "He thinks we're born with different levels of stimuli and most of us can only do so much."

"That pervert," she responded in disgust. "He was a quack even back on the frontier. He's just a sadist with a fondness for poor little girls, and don't you forget it. The Boss indulges him—partly because he fears him, I think, but mostly because Pohn feeds him the scientific nonsense to back up what Sir Tiel wants to hear. I think it's simply *disgusting* what he does up there to those poor little girls; it's very much like what he got caught doing that caused him to be sent here in the first place. But as long as he restricts himself to pawns, he's safe."

As long as he restricts himself to pawns . . . I thought back to my own condemnation of the villagers, my almost identical feelings, and really couldn't see what was wrong with the logic. And yet somewhere there *had* to be a flaw, for the wrongness of this casual attitude toward the majority of Lilith's population nagged at me. On the civilized worlds it was different, I told myself. There the majority was *Homo superior*, perfect in mind and body, sharing equally in the work and in the good life, the utopian dream realized. There the inferiors were cast out to the frontier, or ferreted out and eliminated by ones like me and killed or . . .

Or sent to the Warden Diamond.

If Vola was right and Pohn wrong, though, I told myself, it meant that the potential to turn this class-infested tyranny into a true paradise was possible, and perhaps the result most to be wished. The parallels with human history generally seemed to apply here. Those with the power had always enslaved the masses and gathered the wealth for their own ends until finally the masses rose up against the unfairness and the revolution came, casting the tyrants out. With human civilization, the enormous explosion of technology had put most manual labor into the history books and a master computer in everyone's pocket. Control of technology had been the key to human advances; control of the Warden power here would be the equivalent. If everyone on Lilith could be taught the power, then the Dr. Pohns of this world would quickly be eradicated. I realized then that Vola didn't understand this extension of her own logic, didn't follow the implications to their ultimate conclusions, but I knew now what sort of cause I might devote my life to after . . . what?

After I became Lord of Lilith.

I turned back to my lessons.

* * *

Most of the preliminaries were basic stuff, a lot of esoteric biology, a lot of Warden history, that sort of thing. Most of it I knew, and some of the mental conditioning exercises were pretty similar to those I underwent in training as an agent. It was absurdly easy—and obviously only preparatory to the real thing. What I lacked for the first few days was the key, the catalyst. I could already regulate a lot of my autonomic functions—heartbeat, respiration—and could deaden pain centers, that sort of thing. It took a little adjustment with a new body, but once you knew how, it was easy to reassume control. But these people weren't mental marvels or miracle workers; there was an edge they had and I needed it.

I had made such progress, though, that by the fourth day Vola decided I was ready. She entered my study cell with a small gourd brazier and ignited a fire under it. From a small skin pouch on her hip, she poured a transparent golden liquid into the gourd and allowed it to boil. The vapors alone were pretty odd and made me feel somewhat light-headed.

Satisfied that it was right, she turned to me. "This is a drug," she explained needlessly. "It is distilled from a somewhat poisonous plant, the *huda'i*, found in the wild. The early science team that was stranded here started experimenting with all the wildlife, for they realized they had to understand their environment in order to live in it. This particular mixture provides the best catalyst they found for the Warden organism, causing a permanent change in you over a period of time—several dozen administrations, at least. The carefully measured dosage, given at exacting intervals, changes a key element within your cellular structure, giving a message, as it were, to the Warden organisms inside to direct a slightly different enzyme balance. Drink it down, completely if you can; if it is too hot for you, let it cool slightly. The heat simply aids absorption into your bloodstream."

I nodded and told her I understood. Inwardly I was elated. *This* was the edge, the key to real power. I drank the steaming liquid eagerly, burning my tongue slightly as I did so, but I didn't mind. It tasted bitter and nasty, but I'd expected it to be even worse. The potion made sense, in a way. It was a natural product of Lilith, it contained Warden organisms in its own molecules, and it was the natural complement to what I'd been told about how this all worked.

The only question I had, one not likely to find an easy answer, was how the hell anybody had ever come up with it. You could ask that about most great discoveries, though, I admit. Accident, probably.

The stuff burned inside me, but I felt no immediate effects. I looked at Vola. "If this is truly a chemical key, then why won't it work for everybody? Why wouldn't it work for the pawns?"

She smiled a little patronizingly. "It has only slight, random, and usually destructive effects on pawns. We have found that you have to have reached a state of power without its aid before it will work. Your action with the unfortunate supervisor prepared the way, made your brain willing to accept what is now being done. You see, this is the next test. Anyone not of the power will die from the poison."

I coughed a little and looked at her in surprise. "Now is a fine time to tell me that!"

"Sit back and relax," she instructed, an undertone of amusement in her voice. "Let it take control."

I *could* feel the potion start to work now, causing an odd, slightly hallucinogenic effect. The dimensions of the room seemed to be wrong, for one thing, and Vola herself, even the little brazier she was now putting away, seemed slightly fuzzy, distorted. I felt slightly flushed, as if I had a mild fever, and I realized I was sweating heavily.

Vola came over, put her hand on my face, turning it slightly, then examined my eyes. She nodded to herself, then stepped back. "Now," she said, her voice sounding hollow and like an echo in my ears, "let's see how strong you really are."

The distorting effect seemed to pass rather quickly, to be replaced with a different sense that might be equally false. Suddenly everything seemed sharper, more detailed and focused, than I could ever remember in my life. I had been slightly sighted, it appeared, and now I could fully see.

I saw more than room and its human and inanimate contents; I also saw the Warden organism. Saw it and heard it, sort of, but in a way I'd never known before. For the first time I realized how Dr. Pohn could literally see into cells, or the physicist into the very molecules. The whole universe seemed open to me, big and small, depending on the focus of my will, and I could see any part of it no matter how tiny. It was a heady, godlike feeling like nothing any human off Lilith could possibly imagine. And I kept thinking, *this is no drug-induced hallucination, no distortion of the senses —this is for real!*

More important than sensing the Warden organism in other things, I was equally if not more aware of it within myself. The incredibly minute living things were within me, were one with me, part of me. I reached out and touched them and felt them return that mental touch, felt a sense of pleasure and excitement within those tiny creatures at the recognition of their existence. And yet the Wardens within me were also part of a larger organism, the organism that was everything on this crazy planet, all linked, all one, in communication as the cells of the body are in communication with their parts and with the cells around them.

"Now you see how it feels," I heard Vola's voice as if from some distant place. "Now you know the truth of the power. Now you can use it, shape it, bend it to your will and your direction."

I turned and looked at her as if seeing her for the first time. Kronlon had acquired a shine, an intangible brightness you more felt than saw, when he'd mustered his limited powers against me. Vola, too, shone, but her light was so much more intense than Kronlon's that it made him seem less than a pawn, less than a tree or blade of grass. It was not a physical shining; another observer would have seen nothing. It was instead an inner burning sensed by the tiny microorganisms within my very cells and related to me.

She pointed, a radiant, supernatural being, at a small wicker-type chair in a corner of the cell, and I followed her arm to focus upon it.

"Look not at the chair," she instructed, "but *within* it. Make contact with the host within."

Doing so was absurdly easy, requiring no thought at all. I just looked and lo! I *knew* that chair, was one with that chair, saw how it was made and how its very molecules were bound together.

"Order the chair to decompose, but do not kill that which is within," Vola ordered. "Release it to become again what it was."

I frowned for a moment, trying to understand exactly what she was saying. Then suddenly, I saw the whole pattern in her meaning. The chair was alive, bound together as an organism by someone's commands, the Warden organism there going against its nature to hold itself in that pattern and remain a chair. The geometry of the pattern was clear to me, and it was hardly a gesture to release it, to snap the pattern and allow the organism within to redirect the cells of the chair—somehow still living, although long separated from its parent plants—to their normal state.

The chair decomposed rapidly, but did not come apart. As old patterns were dissolved, new patterns were woven, patterns that were instinctive to the tiny things within it. The visible effect was as if the chair had dissolved into dust, then swirled around, the tiny dust particles coming together in a new series of shapes that were somehow *right*.

Where the chair had stood were now the stalks of seven plants, the parent plants from which the reeds that had made up the chair had been cut. They were living plants, and they were drawing from the stone floor beneath them to gain what was necessary to sustain themselves.

"Now," Vola breathed, sounding slightly impressed, "put the chair back together again."

That stopped me cold. Hell, that pattern was so complex it was almost unbelievable. I could undo it, of course, but to put it back—that was something else again.

Damned killjoy, I thought sourly. Until now it was so much fun to be a god.

"The next lesson," she told me. "Power without knowledge or skill is always destructive. You can unmake with ease, but it takes a lot of study to build instead of destroy."

"But how?" I cried in frustration. "How can I know how to build, to create?"

She laughed. "Could you have physically made that chair?" she asked me. "Could you have taken an axe, cut the right stalks to the right lengths, then bound them together physically to make such a thing?"

I thought about it. Could I? "No," I had to respond. "I'm not a carpenter."

"And that is the way of Lilith, as elsewhere," she told me. "To use the power well in a specialized area is important but requires memorizing the proper patterns and then some practice. But we have an advantage here that those who do not have the power lack," she went on, and I was aware she went to the door, stepped out, then came back in with an identical chair, placing it near the plant stalks in the corner. She stepped back.

"Look at the chair," she ordered. "Be one with it. Know its pattern."

I did, and it was far easier than last time now that I knew just what to look for.

"Now, using the chair as a model, put the other chair back together," she instructed.

I frowned. Having just been pulled down to earth from godhood, I was now being ordered to elevate myself again.

"Is that possible?" I managed.

"It is if you are powerful enough," she responded. "Supervisors can destroy and, to a limited extent, stabilize things they make. You have already shown yourself a Supervisor. But the supervisor, like the pawn, must build or physically make everything himself. A Master may do more. A Master may take the very elements that make something up and rearrange them to suit himself. Are you a Master, Cal Tremon? Can you be a Master?"

She was pushing, I realized, and I hesitated within myself before going further. We were beyond this lesson, I suspected, beyond whatever we were supposed to prove. Had I in fact done what Artur cautioned against —done what I was supposed to do too effortlessly, too well? Should I make this attempt she demanded of me?

The hell with it, I told myself. Let's see just what I'm made of, whether the computer that selected me as the best person for the job knew its stuff. If I had the potential to be a Master, and I'd better, I wanted to know it. I'd spent too long marking time in the mud and the muck and I was impatient.

I stared at the chair again, saw its pattern, how it was bound up and tied together. Now I looked at the strange tubular plants growing where the other chair had been, and I again linked with the Warden organism within them while trying not to lose the contact and, well, *communion,* with the chair. It was a tricky juggling act, since the molecular structure was the same for both and it was hard not to confuse them.

I ordered the Wardens in the plants to disunite once again, to break down as they had before, untying their current plant pattern. Keeping a mostly mental eye on them, I concentrated hard on the existing chair, the pattern, the way it was bound up and tied together.

There were a lot of false starts, a lot of confusion; at one point I almost had the chair dissolving instead of the plants recombining. I don't know how long it took, but finally I succeeded. Two chairs stood there side by side, looking like twins from the same mass-produced, computer-controlled factory. I was sweating like mad and my head throbbed, but I had done it. Totally exhausted, I sank to the floor and gasped for breath. Vola, however, was more than pleased.

"I didn't think I could do it," I admitted, breathing as hard as if I had been lifting heavy stones.

"You are strong indeed, Cal Tremon," she responded. "Very strong. Many of my past students have risen to be Masters, but only four have ever accomplished that exercise on one dosage. Most never are able to do it, and they remain supervisors. Many, like your Kronlon, could not even decompose the chair without killing the organisms within. Others, the bulk of them, manage that much—and no more. A *very* few can do the reassembly, but only four before—now five—have done it on the first try. It will become easier now each time you do it, although the pattern for such a chair is simple compared to most other things."

"The other four," I pressed, feeling completely washed out. "Anybody I know?"

She shrugged. "My nephew, Boss Tiel, for one," she replied. "Also Dr. Pohn and Master Artur. And Marek Kreegan."

My head came up. "What? You taught *him?*"

She nodded. "Long ago, of course. I was very young then, no more than sixteen or seventeen, but I was here, as I have always been. I am one of the rare ones, Tremon—a native of considerable power."

That was interesting, but the information about Kreegan was more so. This explained why he returned here off and on and why he might permit a party in his honor here, of all places. Decades ago Kreegan, too, had been landed right here in Zeis Keep, had worked in those same fields, had been brought to the Castle—if there was a Castle in those days—and had been trained by a very young Vola. There was too much going on here for it to be chance. The Confederacy had arranged this, of course. Picked the man who most matched Kreegan's old agent profile and sent him to the same places under the same conditions. I could see their thinking clearly now, and I had to admit there was nothing wrong with it.

"I'll bet you made the chair the first time," I said.

She grinned and winked at me.

"Tell me about Kreegan," I pressed. "What's he like?"

She stood up and stood back a moment, studying me. "A lot like you, Cal Tremon. An awful lot like you." But she would say no more, leaving me to recover from my increasingly nasty headache as the effects of the drug wore off. Power was not without its price.

CHAPTER TWELVE

Too Dangerous to Have Around

I slept fitfully, wrestling with my headache, and awoke several times to the stillness around me. Several times I thought someone had come into the room, and once I had a strong feeling that at least one individual was actually in the room standing next to the bed, looking down at me in deep thought. A mysterious figure, a wraith, yet huge, looming, dark, indistinct, powerful—the stuff of which children's nightmares are made, yet so compelling you hesitate to open your eyes and see if anybody's really there.

I cursed myself for this reaction, for giving in to primal fears I never even knew I had, but that terrible feeling remained. Finally I shamed myself into a peek, but the room was dark and apparently empty.

I was just about to turn over and try and get back to sleep when my ears picked up a slight sound near the door. I froze, half in caution and half in—I was ashamed to admit to myself—fear of that nameless childish boogeyman.

"Tremon!" I heard a soft, female whisper.

Suddenly wide awake, I sat up cautiously. Fear had given way to puzzled curiosity now that another presence was tangible.

"Here!" I whispered.

A figure approached easily, not at all bothered by the darkness, and crouched down beside me. Although I could see only a slight form in the near-total darkness, I knew it was Vola.

"What's the matter?" I whispered.

"Tremon, you have to get out of here," she told me. "They're going to kill you before morning. There has just been a meeting about you with all the big shots present."

I remembered Artur's warning. So I *had* gone too far for prudence despite all the logic at my command.

"Now, listen carefully," she continued. "I'm not going to let them do it. Not even if what they say is true. I've seen your kind of potential too rarely here, and I won't see it nipped in the bud."

I frowned and sat on the side of the bed. "What did they say?"

"That you aren't Cal Tremon," she whispered. "That you're some sort of assassin sent here by the Confederacy to kill Lord Kreegan."

"*What!*" I exclaimed, perhaps a bit too loudly. All traces of fatigue and headache vanished as the adrenaline started flowing.

"Shhh . . . I don't know how much time we have—maybe none," she cautioned. "Still, I like you enough to give you a fighting chance." She hesitated a moment. "Is it true?"

I owed her an answer, but this wasn't the time for honor. "I don't know what they're talking about," I replied as sincerely as I could. "Hell, my prints, genetic coding—everything is on file. You ought to know I couldn't be anybody *but* me, and believe me, the *last* thing Cal Tremon could be is a Confederacy stooge."

"Maybe," she responded uncertainly. "But even in-system the Cerbrians swap bodies all the time, so I wouldn't depend too much on that defense. Look, it doesn't matter to me, I—what was that?"

We both remained perfectly still, not even breathing. Whatever she'd heard, though, I couldn't make out, and we both relaxed, although only slightly.

"Look, you have to go now," she said urgently.

"Go? Where?"

"I don't know," she responded truthfully. "Away. Away from Zeis Keep entirely. Into the wild, I suppose. If you survive the wild and bide your time, make your way south to Moab Keep, find the Masters there, who are a sort of religious order descended from the original scientists who were stuck here. There and the wild are the only places you'll be safe, and only at Moab can you complete your training. It won't be easy. You'll probably die anyway, or be caught by Artur and his agents, but at least you've got a chance. Stay here and you're dead by sunup, I promise you."

"I'll go now," I told her.

"Do you know how to get out at night?" she asked.

"I know," I told her. "I make it a point to locate all the exits as soon as I'm in a place."

"You'll have to avoid the other organized Keeps," she cautioned me. "The knights will all have the word in a few days, all over the planet. Now go. Fast and far!"

I grabbed her and hugged her. "Vola, fine lady, I won't forget this."

She laughed softly. "I really think you might make it," she said with a mixture of sincerity and wonder. "I really think you might. I have to admit I sort of hope you do."

I left her and eased out into the hallway, which was dimly lit by two lanterns far down on either side. I knew the way out, but I wasn't about to take it right away. Instead, I waited in a darkened recess until I saw Vola leave and go the other way. Maybe she *was* doing me the biggest favor of my Lilith existence, but I never trusted anyone completely.

Once she'd gone, I sneaked back into the room and used the bedding and pillows to make a rough form in the bed. Then I went out and down to one of the small holes that accessed the service corridors and crept back toward the room on the level above it. I located the peephole with some difficulty in the pitch darkness only by knowing where it had to be and by counting the number of such holes from my entry back to the room. I wanted to see what would happen next. Zeis Keep was a large area; I could hardly clear it before the alarm went out anyway, so I didn't intend to try, not right away. First I would see if anyone *did* come in the night to do me in—and if so, who. If not, I was fully prepared to return to the room in midmorning and face down Vola.

The fact that they'd somehow gotten word I was an agent was important enough.

There probably weren't three or four people in the whole Confederacy who would have known, and everyone but my counterpart hovering up there somewhere would have been mindwiped of the knowledge. Then I remembered the penetration of Military System Command's core computers and realized that somewhere in there the information could be pieced together. What they had done once they could very well have done again. For all I knew, the Confederacy was currently at war with those mysterious aliens.

But the fact that they'd pieced together some facts and come to the correct conclusion about my status didn't mean they were totally convinced of it. This could merely be a test to see if I really would jump. At this point I was determined to play by my own rules.

Suddenly I heard noises in the corridor. Two, maybe more, people walking with firm, confident steps toward me. I heard them now below, just outside the door to my room, then saw the door open cautiously. There were three of them, I decided, two of whom stepped into the room while the third remained outside. One was Artur—he was hard to miss. The other was a rather ordinary man of middle years who was obviously from the civilized worlds. He, too, was dressed as a Master and held a small lantern which lit the room with an eerie glow.

"He's gone!" the stranger whispered unbelievingly.

"*What?*" Artur thundered; then he stalked over to the bed and violently ripped the fluffed-up bedding away. He spun around angrily, and I had never seen as nasty a look as he radiated then. "Someone tipped him off. I'll know who and I'll make him pay, by God!"

"You will do nothing of the kind," said the third man, out of sight outside the door. His voice had an odd quality, somewhat diffuse and unfocused, almost mechanical; it hardly sounded human at all. "He is a fully trained and capable agent. One of their best, we must assume, perhaps *the* best of the current crop. I think he realized he overplayed his hand this afternoon. We will have to find him, Artur. I charge you with that task. You find him while he's still weak and vulnerable and untrained, or he'll fry you with a glance and eat you for breakfast. Right now he is a minor nuisance, but potentially he is the most dangerous man on this planet, possibly as dangerous or more so than I. You find him and kill him, Artur—or one day he will seek out and kill us all."

Artur bowed subserviently, his face impassive to that threat, which did a lot for my ego and hopes. And then the dark Master uttered words that chilled me beyond belief.

"Yes, My Lord Kreegan."

I cursed inwardly that I had no way of getting a look at the Lord of Lilith himself without his also getting a look at me.

Artur gestured to the other man. "Come on, let's roll out the troops. We have work to do. He's got to cross a lot of open area within the Keep to get to the wild, and he'll be moving fast to beat the sun. We may catch him yet."

With that, both men left and I heard their boots against the stone and tile floor clicking swiftly away. Still I did not move, nor did I intend to do so for quite some time. Artur was right, of course—there was almost no way at all I could cover the distance from the Castle to the wild in the remaining darkness, and to be caught in daylight with all the pawns out would be to be absolutely trapped. No, I intended to stay right where I was for the next hour or two, then to exist by day inside the corridors of the Castle itself. I would flee, yes, but as prepared as I could and on my own terms and schedule, not theirs.

I spent most of the day hidden from everyone I could, and this proved easier than most people would think. The Castle would be the last place in which they would look for me, the last place they expected me to be. Trained cops and agents might have thought of it, but these were mostly petty crooks, naive natives, and a couple of tough old ex-military birds like Artur. Several times I ran into people, but I just looked like I belonged and nobody really noticed. All I was really concerned about was minimizing my visibility and not running into anybody who knew me. I even managed to liberate a meal or two from the ones packaged for on-duty personnel, so I was hardly uncomfortable.

Still, I didn't want to make the mistake of vastly underestimating my opponents, either. If Kreegan was still around, and I had no reason to believe he was not, he would at least block the exits as an afterthought. That wouldn't entail much—just posting a couple of supervisors at every exit, particularly those from the service corridors. Getting out would be no picnic, and I really couldn't afford a week within the walls. Each hour increased the risk of discovery and pushed my luck.

I checked all the possibilities, made my decisions, and was all set for the onset of darkness. Farewell, Zeis Keep, may you rot in the muck. I'd never see this place again, that was for sure.

That thought suddenly brought me up short. Ti. She was still here, up there with that butchering sadist and his experiments.

I didn't know exactly why, but late in the afternoon, I made my way back to Medical. From experience I knew that just about everybody in Dr. Pohn's little shop of horrors knocked off work early. There really wasn't much reason not to go there, and the only real danger I faced was running into Pohn himself. Now that I knew the potential of a Master I had no desire to meet up with Pohn in an adversary role. I'd timed my arrival pretty much for supper, in the hopes that my route would be clear, and I was lucky. There appeared to be nobody in the Medical area.

I stole quickly into the area that I would always think of as the morgue and saw the twelve silent sleepers there. Hurrying over to Ti's tiny, still form, I looked down at her, trying to think clearly. Up until this point I'd thought of this as more of a goodbye visit than anything else. But now, looking down at her, I knew that I couldn't leave her here to Pohn's tender mercies.

I looked around at the others in the gathering gloom. No lights needed here, but the darkness made the place look even more like a repository for the dead. And they were dead, I thought sadly. The walking dead. What ancient superstition could conjure up only as a nightmare, the twisted sciences of Lilith had made a reality. I wanted to take them all with me, and would have if I could. Surely what one madman had done others not so mad could undo—but there was no way.

Without even thinking about it, I picked Ti up from the slab and carried her back to my service corridor hideaway. She seemed to weigh almost nothing; except for her shallow and almost imperceptible breathing, she was like a doll, a mannequin rather than a person. Picking her up again, I made my way toward my planned escape route, figuring I'd reach it at just about the point of total darkness. I had almost reached the point below the Castle's left wall when it occurred to me that I had done something monumentally stupid in carrying Ti off. If anyone came back to that lab and saw her missing, they'd realize I was still on the grounds.

Still, leaving her here now would be cold-blooded murder. Moreover, it wouldn't gain me anything, since she'd still be missed upstairs. No, stupid or not, the deed was done and I was committed now.

Although leaving Ti would have weighed on my conscience, what I was about to do didn't bother me in the slightest. Somewhere there are classifications of crimes against others such as murder, and this came under the heading of "necessary."

Just outside the small tunnel I was in was the Keep itself, the outside world—and two young paramilitary supervisors from Artur's force. If either of them so much as knew where I was, they could inflict pain and stop me dead, at least long enough to raise an alarm. I had now to get by without any of that happening, and that meant killing the guards. I wished for the power that had allowed me to fry Kronlon, to reconstruct a chair from basic cells, but that was denied me now. I was faced with the problem of eliminating two threats who didn't even have to touch me to get me—yet I had to get both of them.

I had the benefit of surprise, of course. They weren't telepaths, nor did they have any special powers that would betray me any more than if they were two normal humans. And the knowledge of their power and my lack of it made them supremely confident.

I had several different plans for drawing them near enough to get, but it suddenly occurred to me that I had the almost perfect diversion in Ti— if in fact I could control her actions as simply as Pohn had. I certainly intended to find out. I put her down on the cold stone, confident that I was far enough away from the exit not to be overheard.

"Ti, open your eyes," I commanded in a hushed tone.

Her eyelids flickered slightly, then opened. I breathed a sigh of relief in the discovery that this wasn't going to be as difficult as I thought, although tricky.

"Ti, stand up and face me."

She did as instructed, and I began to feel a little better. Still, I didn't know how many instructions in sequence she could carry out.

"Ti, softly say hello."

"Hello," she responded dully, without a trace of life in her tone. Its very woodenness made me shiver slightly.

Well, now was the time to see how complex the instructions could be.
"Ti, I want you to walk two steps forward, stop, turn around, raise your
right hand, and say 'come here,'" I instructed. Those were enough separate instructions to tell me what I wanted to know.

She paused a moment after I gave the orders, then walked two steps forward, turned around, and did everything perfectly. I got a sort of erotic
thrill from seeing her do it. The ultimate adolescent male fantasy, I
reflected—except that it bordered on necrophilia.

The only other thing left to check was whether this was similar to a
case of hypnotism and if the effect could be delayed.

I gave her a couple of minor instructions, then told her not to carry
them out unless I said the word "escape." Then I said the word and she
did them, after which I tried a couple of other random instructions, then
said "escape" once again. She immediately carried out my original commands, so I was satisfied.

I had deliberately picked this exit because a fairly large rock stood right
near the entrance. Now, I felt, I had the best way of using all the elements, and I began to think that perhaps bringing Ti along hadn't been
such a bad idea after all.

"Listen carefully, Ti," I said. "Forget all previous instructions. When
you hear me say the word 'trap' you will do the following. . . ."

It was dark outside the mouth of the cave into which the service corridor dumped. The two guards, a young man and an older woman, each
wearing the black cape, pants, and boots of soldiers in Artur's force, sat
around looking very bored. They had been there quite a while and had
exhausted most of what small talk they could muster, yet they couldn't do
much else but stand guard for fear that someone would get by them or,
worse, that Master Artur would make a surprise inspection and find them
doing something other than their military duty.

Still, each sat with the relaxed air of someone who is certain that the
quarry is long gone and nothing whatever is going to happen. It was,
then, with considerable surprise that they heard someone emerge from the
small tunnel mouth. They both jumped to their feet, whirled, and advanced with tense curiosity.

"It's—it's a girl," the female guard said in wonder. Her companion nodded and called out, "Who are you? What are you doing here?" His voice
possessed the confidence of authority; he was secure that he had the power
to meet challenges.

The tiny figure, several meters away, seemed to start, then silently
slipped behind the large rock near the cave opening, vanishing from view.

"What kind of children's trick is this?" the man muttered, irritated.

The other was not so easily lulled. "Take it easy. It could be a trap of
some kind. Remember, somebody tipped him off to run. Let's just give her
a jolt."

"Aw, you're too nervous," the man griped, but he was still unsure enough not to advance.

"There. That should have fixed her," the woman said confidently.

"I don't hear any groaning," the man responded, becoming a little nervous himself now. "Did you get her?"

"I'm sure I did," she assured him. "Come on. Somebody that little probably passed out."

They advanced cautiously, turned behind the rock, and saw the girl, apparently unconscious, stiff and flat against the rock.

"Jeez, Marl, what'd you *do* to her?" the man asked, concerned. "She looks like she's dead."

They both approached the still form against the rock, no longer cautious. When their heads were but inches apart I leaped with a yell from the other side of the rock, and before either could recover from the freeze surprise brings, I brought their two heads together as hard as I could, knocking them down with my spring as I did so.

I hadn't done that sort of thing that way since practicing with androids in training, but by God, it worked. Timing was the key, I told myself, feeling satisfied. Timing and a little knowledge of the weaknesses in human psyches.

The man was dead, I saw. The woman seemed to be still alive, but was bleeding from the scalp. Quickly and quietly I snapped her neck and then dragged both of them into the cave and hid them as securely as I could. I wanted no alarms now, and the uncertainty over their disappearance, when it was discovered, would still raise alarms in the wrong places.

Artur, after all, was charged with Castle security and would not be sure whether the two had been surprised by someone coming out or by someone going *in*. I counted on that, and on the general feeling these people would have that someone with the voluntary powers of a mere pawn could have neutralized and physically killed two trained supervisors.

I wondered idly why the hell I hadn't done *that* to Kronlon long ago. This damned world had sapped my self-confidence; I was only now feeling like myself again.

Picking up Ti for speed's sake, I made my way out of the Castle and down into the valley below.

Now for the first time the map Intelligence had arranged to be imprinted in my head came in handy. Wild areas, not under any knight or other administrative control—jungle and forest and mountains and swamp—lay as buffers between the keeps.

The Keep itself was easy to navigate in the darkness. The villagers were mostly bedding down for the night or relaxing after eating, so no one would be in the fields except for herdsmen, who could easily be bypassed.

Zeis was a bowllike valley on three sides and ran up against a swampy and somewhat unhealthy lake on the fourth. The lake was definitely out— I had no desire to navigate through unknown water in daylight, let alone in darkness. Who knew what quagmires and hostile creatures were about? That meant going over or through the mountains, which was almost as bad. Naked, without tools, and carrying Ti along, I would be restricted to well-worn trails that were probably staked out by Artur's boys.

The map in my head told me I had at least a six-hundred-meter climb ahead of me, at which point I'd have to descend almost that far to make a forest on the other side. Unfortunately, though the map included both physical and political information, it was no road map. I would have to ferret out the trails myself, and I couldn't be too choosy about the ones I found, either.

It was easy to find the trails, although none looked particularly well-worn. The network of pathways in the Keep all led to them in the end, of course A number of times I'd had to flatten when great flying *besils* with mounted riders flew past. Their buzzing sounded like a great series of motors in operation, but they were too large and cumbersome to be more than a deterrent patrol. To spot anybody while atop those creatures would take a lot of luck indeed. But if someone on the ground sounded an alarm, they'd be on me in a moment, and then I'd be totally defenseless.

If the trail I finally made was typical, at least I knew I wouldn't have problems mountain climbing. Obviously designed for cart traffic, it was wide, with a great many broad switchbacks. Those switchbacks, though, would make anyone on the path plainly obvious to guards further up, and I worried a little about this. After all, this wasn't like escaping from some armed force; these adversaries merely had to see you to knock you off the path with a strong glance.

All I could do was start up the trail as rapidly and cautiously as possible and then trust to a little luck and the fact that the hunt would still be a day stale at this point. By this point I had Ti clinging to me piggyback and was certain that her grip would never falter.

I was about a quarter of the way up and feeling pretty confident when I heard voices below. I froze, listening, but they were still far below me and, from what I could determine, on foot. The sounds of voices carried along here but with little definition, so I really couldn't tell who they were—as if I needed to know who'd be walking a trail like this in the dark so late in the evening.

After deciding that my best course was simply to keep ahead of them, I resumed my climb. A few minutes later I realized I was also hearing other voices from the trail. These sounded like the voices of two women, whereas those below me had both definitely been male—of that I was certain. I now realized that Artur had done the most obvious thing under the conditions Lilith and the geography of the Keep imposed on him. At intervals, probably somewhat at random, one team would start down the trail. A little later, another would start up, and they would cross somewhere in between. On a trail like this anybody else would be caught in between.

I tried to judge how far away from me the pair coming down were. It was almost impossible. So I had to take the chance that perhaps they were far enough up to allow me to make the edge of the accumulating fog that always shrouded the sky of Zeis Keep because of the inversion caused by the mountain ring. The fog had been thickening and lowering as the night wore on. I hurried to reach the almost tangible blanket of gray I could see perhaps two turns of the trail ahead of me, the blanket that currently masked me from the descenders' view as they were masked from mine.

Without Ti I would have been more agile, but she had become something of a crusade, an obligation to me now. I was determined that she would at least awaken and be whole once again. She no longer weighed nothing. I was becoming tired, and forty-two kilos was beginning to have a real effect on my back and neck muscles.

I had only one more switchback to go until I reached the edge of the cloud cover, but I was to be denied it, I now realized. The sound of the women's voices was coming in quite clear and I could see an eerie, disembodied glow from a yellow lantern one of them was obviously carrying. I looked around for a place to hide, but the trail had been cut into sheer bedrock, the only thing at its outer edge except air and a long, long hard fall was a small sculpted rim that obviously served to keep wheeled carts from slipping over.

I had no time and no choice: the rim would have to do. I was about to see just how strong and able this Cal Tremon body was, I thought sourly.

I worried about the men below me, but they were the least of my problems, I realized. It was pretty damned dark up here, and their light would not carry far.

As carefully as I could, I eased myself and my burden over the side and held on to the trail rim with both hands, otherwise dangling free. The drag from Ti on my back became so great I almost cried out, but I hadn't gone through all that training for nothing, nor had a week or so of soft living undone months of hard toil. I managed to keep myself hanging there; how long until I lost my grip and dropped off, I couldn't tell.

Again I counted on normal human behavior to help me—and I needed all the help I could get. These people had been walking the trail, up and down, down and up, for all their shift, and they were likely to be more bored than totally vigilant, like the two guards at the Castle had been.

They came out of the clouds, walking slowly down the trail. One of them idly picked up a pebble and tossed it over the side, barely missing me only one level and one switchback below them.

"Well, we finally got outta that stinkin' mist," one of the women noted with relief.

"Yeah, let the guys get soaked," the other one cracked. "Maybe if we take it slow enough it'll be dawn and we'll be relieved before we havta go up again."

"You said it," the first one agreed. "I've had it with this mountain business. Me for a hot meal, bath, and bed, and I don't care in what order."

They were very close now, around the turn and coming back toward my precarious and increasingly agonizing perch. All I could think of was *Don't stop! Just don't stop!* But there is a law governing such things and stop they did, not more than three or four meters from where my aching, raw hands were visible if they cared to look.

"Hey! Look! I see 'em coming!" one noted, pointing—I could see the arm and finger outstretched, far too close for comfort.

"Wanna wait here for 'em?"

No, no, you don't want to do that! I thought and prayed so loud that if there had been any such thing as ESP receptivity here they would certainly have heard me.

"You mean stall?" the other responded, thinking it over. "Naah. Why bother? Let's get this over with."

As they both turned and left the ledge, I chanced a glance downward to see where the approaching men were. Too close, I decided. Their lantern was already lighting the way only a couple of levels below me, and the women's own light would expose me when they made the turn. I would have to time my move pretty well and do it silently. I judged the light from their lantern that was thrown forward against the curve of the switchback to be about twenty or so meters further on and watched it grow brighter and brighter.

I almost blew it, for they actually came in view just as I hoisted myself and my heavy burden up and over onto the roadway, flattening there and freezing as still as Ti.

"You hear something?" one of them asked the other.

"Yeah," the other replied suspiciously. "Sounded just ahead. Let's take it slow and easy."

Not too slow, I wished, nor too cautious. I had to get up and start moving before the men got too close—and never had I felt less like moving. My neck and back ached, and my arms felt as if they were disjointed and incapable of anything. I summoned what reserve strength I had and tried some mental exercises to sponge away as much of the discomfort and ache as possible. Controlling my pain centers was no trick, but it was a false control, of course. My muscles and joints were in such pain because they had been pushed to the edge of endurance, and no longer feeling the warnings of the body didn't lessen that fact. I wondered how much further it was to the top, and whether I was up to it. I didn't even want to think about meeting yet another patrol on its way down or at the top. Judging by the light and sound, I made my way up toward the still-inviting fog, and made it.

The going was a lot slower now, since I couldn't see three meters in front of me, and the air became suddenly very wet and sticky. Still, I welcomed the gray cloak as a friend and ally, the first and only one I had ever had on this insane world.

I wasn't worried about the men approaching from below. Being human and bored, they would stop and exchange small talk with the women coming down; that would buy me a few precious minutes to add to the distance. Their lantern would be little help once they made the dew line, so they'd be going as slowly as I. If I ran into no one else and if I could just make it over the top before the sun came up, I felt I might just get away.

The sky was certainly getting light by the time I reached the summit, but by then I really didn't care any more. From this point on I'd be descending toward the wild—too early for any commercial traffic, I hoped—and into whatever brush there might be. I was out on my feet, every step a horrible experience, but I drove myself, knowing that I had to make it down, had to make it to cover, before the day really began. I hoped there would be only light patrols on this side of the range—if any at all. Not that they wouldn't be looking for me here, but with limited manpower Artur would concentrate mainly on keeping me bottled up. Only when they discovered the dead guards would their search become frantic, and only after that would they begin to widen it into places they did not control.

At least I hoped so.

I was soaked through by the time I made it to the lower edge of the dew line, had been for a couple of hours. For the first time since being on Lilith, the combination of wetness, a light wind, and the slight elevation threw a genuine chill into me. It was getting really light now; the sun, I was sure, was going to peek through any minute now and perhaps burn off some of this cloud cover.

Now, out of the thick mountain-bred fog, I could see ahead of me my first real view on Lilith of a place other than Zeis Keep. There were rolling, thickly forested hills, it appeared, the trees and hilltops peeking out a dark blue-green from trapped pockets of thick ground fog. The place had an eerie stillness about it, and I felt certain that I would at least make it to the shelter of those trees.

I could no longer carry Ti, and ordered her to let go of my back and walk beside me. Though she could keep up by running if she had to, I took it slowly and carefully nonetheless. The stone path was slick and wet, and I wanted no accidents for either of us, not now—not when I had accomplished my immediate goal.

The sun was well up and warming the place into a steam bath before I finally decided I couldn't take any more and picked a spot not far from the road that seemed well concealed from prying eyes and barren of any obvious threat from natural causes. I sensitized Ti with a series of commands so that she would remain listening and would wake me if she heard anyone or anything approaching, then settled down under tree and bush cover on the grass and rock-strewn forest floor and let myself relax for the first time. No matter how rotten I felt, I *did* feel a strong sense of accomplishment.

I'd escaped! I'd made it! I was, for the first time in this body, once more a free man, a free agent! It felt really good.

Deep down, though, that nagging little voice I always carried with me sang a different tune. *All right, superhuman,* it mocked. *So now you're naked and unarmed in a strange and hostile world whose inhabitants are all raised against you, saddled with a robot-like girl, and you've got no place to go and no help to do anything else. All right, Homo superior— now what do you do?*

There was only one response to that. I fell into the deepest of sleeps.

CHAPTER THIRTEEN

Some Interested Parties

How long I slept there I have no idea, but it was late in the day when I awoke, feeling none too good. My body still ached, at least those parts that weren't already numb, and the uneven, rocky ground hadn't helped matters much. Still, I felt now as if I could do all right as long as I didn't have to climb any more mountains or carry Ti.

I realized that at least we wouldn't starve. Warden had described Lilith as something like Paradise, and in that he hadn't been far wrong. All the cultivated food of the Keeps came originally from plants that grew in the wild, and though the naturally grown stuff wouldn't taste as good or be as perfect there should be enough to sustain us.

But sustain us for what? The trouble with breaking out of a prison is that all of your energies are directed toward the breakout. What you're going to do once outside is vague and nebulous and never very practical. Such was the case here. Moab was roughly 4,800 kilometers south-southeast of where I was—a nice hike under any circumstances, and when the powers that be were hunting for you, it might as well be on another planet.

And they *were* hunting. Just sitting there in the few minutes after waking up I could see, far off, huge black leathery shapes, two great wings supporting a giant, wormlike body whose head was a mass of tendrils, combing along the sides of the road. Besils from Artur's force, without a doubt. I sat there and admired the way the riders could control the beasts, so that they didn't seem to fly in any normal fashion at all but rather to swim and flow, snakelike, through the air.

I had to make plans, both immediate and long-range, whether I wanted to or not. I certainly couldn't stay where I was; for one thing, we needed to find food, and for another, it was too close to the road directly to Zeis for me to remain long. The more distance I could put between Artur and me the better.

Nor would the trip be as comfortable as it would by necessity be leisurely. I was already becoming aware that chairs and castles weren't the only things held in Warden patterns—the entire Keep was under such a pattern. Lilith was a world where plants and insects thrived, but there'd been no mammalian or reptilian development. The microbes were unimportant; aside from the Warden organism itself, all the microscopic beasties were far too alien to affect human beings. But the insects swarmed and bred and swarmed some more in millions of shapes and sizes. In Zeis Keep, the minor insects and pests were in some way locked out, absent. Now I found myself in a world where millions of things, many quite small, flew and crawled and creeped and hopped. I already had several small itchy bites from something or other, and a close examination of Ti showed more of the same.

True, though I had only a few hundred meters' walk into the brush to find familiar, edible melons and berries, only a few were usable. The natural food chain here was oriented toward the insects, not people; and insects infested whatever was ripe for the picking. Nonetheless, I found enough to feel reasonable again and scooped and broke up enough to hand-feed to Ti. Water was less of a problem, since there were small pools and rivulets everywhere. Some of it looked pretty scummy, but I didn't hesitate simply because I knew that my little Wardens—and Ti's—would protect us from the worst.

Only after these necessities were taken care of did I allow myself to think beyond to what I was actually going to do next. I simply couldn't manage to reach Moab Keep, help Ti, and stay out of Artur's clutches all on my own. I needed help—friends, people who could do more than I. But whom did I know on Lilith that wasn't either out to get me or locked inside Zeis Keep? The answer was obvious but unnerving.

I was somehow going to have to find Father Bronz and talk him into helping me. If the old priest wouldn't do it for me, I reasoned, he might do it for Ti, whom, I recalled, he had said he knew and for whom he had expressed some affection. Bronz it was—but where? I tried to remember. It had been a couple of weeks since I'd seen him, but he *had* mentioned where he was going next. South, he'd said—and that was good, because that meant along this road. Shemlon Keep, I thought he'd said, making his rounds.

The map in my head clicked into play once more, and I easily located Shemlon, about twenty kilometers down this road, or off it.

Near dusk we started walking, not on the road but parallel to it, choosing whatever cover we could find from random patrols and routine courier and other service. The road was lightly traveled, but during the late afternoon a few carts passed and even a few individuals, almost all masters, heading one way or the other. I had no illusions that word of me would not have reached Shemlon long before now; the aerial *besils* would have been active.

A long and dangerous trip, yes, but it didn't bother me very much. At least now I had some place to go and some reason for going there.

* * *

It took several days of lying low and several nights of slow walking to reach the border of Shemlon Keep. During that time we had occasional problems finding edible food, but in the main Lilith proved bountiful. I wouldn't like to have had to feed a mob, but for just two of us it proved fairly easy going.

Shemlon was definitely quite different than Zeis. For one thing, the hills seemed to vanish into a nearly flat plain, much of which appeared to be thinly covered with water. A more careful examination showed that they were growing *rasti*, a reddish, ricelike grain that was something of a Zeis staple. Now I knew where it came from.

There was but one village, it appeared, a large complex of hollow *bunti* huts arranged in a huge circle around the main building—a large mansion that appeared to be painted adobe. The mansion was about as primitive as Tiel's castle had been—eighty or a hundred rooms at least, in an odd geometrical assemblage of yellow-brown cubicles that looked as if it shouldn't stay up. Shemlon was obviously much smaller in terms of personnel than Zeis, although it might have been as large in area. It could have been the economics of the operation or it could mean that the knight here was simply lower in rank, perhaps slightly less powerful, than Tiel.

The layout worried me, though, since I'd spent a lot of time getting here and it had been some time since Bronz had been at Zeis. He had probably already been here and left. With but a single large village, I could hardly pass myself off as a pawn among them. I had to resort to extreme measures. My survival was at stake. So I bided my time for a day, checking out the layout and seeing who worked where, then selected a spot and finally a single individual working off by himself. He seemed to be repairing a gate on some sort of channel that fed river water to the paddies.

Leaving Ti well hidden at the edge of the bush, I stepped out near dusk, a time when most of the field hands had already returned to their village and the repairman was getting ready to depart himself. I stepped out plain as could be and walked boldly toward him. His nakedness showed him to be a pawn, albeit a skilled worker of some sort, and my casual manner and rough appearance did nothing to arouse alarm.

I walked up to him with a wave and a nod. "Hi," I said, really friendly. "I'm new here, and I think some people played me for a sucker, sending me over into the mud. When I got back there was nobody left in the field."

The man looked up, a rough old face with a beard flecked with gray, and chuckled. "Yeah, I know how it is. You wait up a moment and I'll take you in."

I nodded appreciatively. It had all gone so easily that I really hated myself for what I would have to do. This was an ugly business and an ugly world.

We exchanged a little small talk, and then I got to the point. "You know, I was a Catholic back Outside. Somebody told me there was a traveling priest around. Was that just more kidding?"

"Aw, no, he's for real," the old man replied. "Was through here not far back. Too bad you missed him. He probably won't be back until after the harvest, several months from now."

I looked surprised. "Where would he go?"

"Other Keeps," the old man replied matter-of-factly. "He's probably just getting to Mola Keep, way off to the west there, right 'bout now. He's a good man, though I don't take much stock in his beliefs."

"How long ago was he here?" I pressed. "I mean, when did he leave?"

"Day before yesterday—say, what's that to you?"

I sighed. "Because I'm Cal Tremon," I told him, and while he was still looking surprised, I killed him—as quickly and painlessly as I could. Killed him and carried his limp and lifeless body back to the bush so that, perhaps, he wouldn't be missed for a while.

The map in my head clicked again and I saw where Mola was—another thirty kilometers, by a side road. Not a long ride, no more than two days by *ak*-cart, the method Bronz likely used, but another long, wet, itchy, hungry walk all the same.

I felt bad about killing the old man. Certain people wouldn't bother me in the least—the upper classes here in particular, ones like Artur and Pohn and Tiel and Marek Kreegan. I felt no remorse for Kronlon, yet I mourned the old man, so casual and friendly, so totally innocent in all this. Mourned him, yet accepted the necessity of doing what I had done. I could hardly have walked back to the village with him, and any other behavior would have had him telling stories about me, stories that would be all too plain if he were pressed by a supervisor.

Still, I couldn't forget the look in his eyes when I'd said my name, a look that would haunt me for a long time. A look that said he hadn't the slightest idea who or what a Cal Tremon was.

Another two days of cautious walking. Another two days of insect bites, rotten fruit, stale water, thunderstorms I couldn't hide from, mud I couldn't avoid, bruises, and sore feet. The only good point about leaving Zeis Keep was that now I could really see the sky, which was a deep blue streaked with hints of red and violet, filled with but not totally blotted out by brownish clouds. By night you could sometimes see stars, a sight both reassuring and sad as well. Stars I could never again reach. Stars forever closed to me.

I was still three or four kilometers from Mola Keep when I spotted a small camp just off the road. This was highly unusual. I was curious to see what this was all about, curious and suspicious as well. Were they perhaps throwing up roadblocks now?

There was a small campfire, out now and glowing slightly, and a fairly fancy-looking bedroll. I looked at the *ak*, the huge rounded creature with the tiny head you could barely see almost dwarfing the cart it normally pulled. Though it was still, it looked alive and in good shape, as did the cart. Not a breakdown, then, I told myself—but one person alone, asleep out here in the wild. One person of some rank—a Master, probably.

Leaving Ti again in the protection of the bush, I crept as close as I dared, wanting to check out who or what this person might be. Definitely a man, snoring fit to wake the dead. I felt hope rise within me. It couldn't be, I told myself. He'd be too far ahead, and in any event wouldn't have any reason not to make Mola—but sure enough, there he was.

I had found Father Bronz.

In my excitement I made a rustling noise that, considering the level of snoring, shouldn't even have been heard. Suddenly his eyes opened. Lying still, he cocked his head, a slightly puzzled expression on his face.

"Father Bronz," I called to him in a loud whisper. "It's me—Cal Tremon!"

The priest chuckled, sat up, yawned and stretched, then rubbed his eyes and looked around. I stepped cautiously out into the open. I had no real reason to trust the man, but all things considered, I had no choice *but* to place myself in his hands.

"Tremon!" he croaked, still sounding half asleep. "About time you got here. I'd about given you up."

CHAPTER FOURTEEN

Savages and Amazons

I just stood there dumbstruck, staring at him. Finally I managed, "You were *expecting* me?"

He looked around. "Why else would I stay in such a wondrous natural hotel?" he grumbled sarcastically. "Come on over and sit. I'll put on some tea."

I walked toward him, then stopped. "I've forgotten Ti!" I exclaimed, mostly to myself.

"I have tea here," he responded, sounding confused.

"No, no. Ti. The girl."

He laughed. "Well, well! So you *did* take her! There was some question as to what happened."

I decided to fetch her before getting the details. At least I was no longer alone and I hadn't been incinerated or otherwise molested, so whatever game Bronz was playing was in my favor.

I carried her back to Bronz's camp and he rose and walked over to her immediately, doing a fairly good imitation of Dr. Pohn but with far more compassion and concern. "That bastard," he muttered. "May he rot in hell forever." He closed his eyes and placed his hand on her forehead.

"Can you do anything for her?" I asked, genuinely concerned. "She's nothing more than a living robot right now."

He sighed and thought for a moment. "If I were a doctor, yes, I *could*. If I knew my biology a little better, maybe. I can see where he's meddled, all right, but I don't dare risk doing anything myself. I might cause permanent brain damage or even kill her. No, we'll have to find help for her, that's all."

"Not at a Keep," I responded hesitatingly. "All they'd do is give her back to Dr. Pohn."

"No, not at a Keep," he agreed, thinking. "Not you, either. We have to get you someplace safe where you can get some help and Ti can get some expert care, though. I did anticipate the problems we'd have finding friends and allies and a hideout, although I didn't realize I'd have this kind of difficulty." He sighed again and went back over to the rekindled small fire, taking the gourd of water from the flame and adding some ground leaves from a pouch on his belt—one of several, I noted.

"Come on over and sit down," he invited. "It'll be ready in a few minutes and we have some time to kill anyway."

I did as instructed, already feeling a little better. I wanted to know a little more about Father Bronz, though.

"You said that you anticipated our needing a hideout, that you were waiting for me," I noted. "Maybe you better explain a little."

He chuckled. "Son, I was late getting out of Zeis. They had all the bigwigs coming for a party and it was decided that I should attend. Besides, the Duke and I are old friends—I occasionally do him some favors."

"I remember the night," I told him. "It was the night I killed Kronlon and graduated, you might say. I thought you were long gone, though."

"I'd intended to be," he responded, pouring tea into two smaller, nicely carved gourd cups. "Politics is everything around here, though. Well, that got me a couple of days late into Shemlon, and I was still there when couriers from Zeis arrived with the news that you had been condemned to death but had escaped and were now a wanted fugitive. You are really hot, as they say, my son. Any pawn that even *helps* them get you won't ever have to work or feel a supervisor's wrath again."

I nodded. Just what I expected, but it eased my conscience a little about killing the old man.

"Anyway," Bronz continued, "it didn't take much in the way of brains to figure that you'd need a friend and I was the only friend outside the Keep you had. So I was very noisy in spreading word around where I was going next. I didn't want you to try finding me in Shemlon, considering how much of a single entity the whole village setup is, so I traveled down the road about halfway to Mola, then camped here some time yesterday. I was willing to wait until somebody asked questions or until you showed up, whichever came first. But I *do* have to put in at Mola, if only for appearance sake, you know."

"You figured out my movements so easily," I pointed out, "I wonder why Artur hasn't?"

"Oh, I'm sure the thought crossed his mind," Bronz replied cheerily. "I've been getting a careful inspection from some of those flyers, and a fellow by here earlier gave me your description and told me how to report you I wouldn't worry, though. I'm one of *them*, son! To them I'm an old friend of the Duke's, a familiar old face. It might occur to them that you'd seek me out, but it would *never* occur to them that I wouldn't immediately fry your gizzard or turn you in."

I sipped the tea. "But you're not?"

"Of course not," he replied, sounding a bit miffed. "Would I have gone to all this trouble if I were? No, my son, in this bastion of the most primitive age of man on old Earth I'm reviving a two-thousand-year-old church custom for you! It's called sanctuary. Back in ancient times, on our ancestral planet, the church was a power unto itself, a political power with a lot of force and clout, yet separate from the temporal powers because we owed our allegiance not to kings but to God. Political criminals in particular, but really anybody who was being chased, could run into a church or cathedral and claim sanctuary, and the church would protect that person from temporal retribution. Well, you're asking for sanctuary, and how can I, as a Christian, turn you down? I've had it up to here with this godless tyranny anyway. And besides," he added with a wink and a smile, "I've been bored to tears for ten years."

I laughed and finished my tea, whereupon he poured me more.

"Now, then," he said, settling back once more, "just what do you want to do?"

"I want to restore Ti, of course," I responded, "but beyond that, I want to complete my treatments and training. They said I was at least Master class, and I want to reach that level badly. I want the opportunity to go as far as I can with the Warden power."

He nodded. "That's reasonable. And the fact that you put Ti first—that in fact you vastly complicated your escape to get her out—is a real mark in your favor. But suppose I can get you to Moab Keep, to that crazy group down there, and you get all the power you can. Suppose you become a Master plus—Knight level, maybe. Then what?"

"Well . . ." I thought about his question, which was a fair one. Just what *did* I want to do? "I think, one day, if I have the power, I'd like to go back to Zeis Keep and take it for my own. Then—well, we'll see."

He chuckled. "So you have designs on a knighthood, huh? Well, maybe you'll make it, Cal. Maybe you will . . . Still, first things first. We have to get you to help, we have to get Ti to help, and then somehow we have to get you down to Moab."

I nodded, looking serious and feeling worse. It was all well and good to spout dreams, but the reality was a naked and mud-caked man sipping tea beside a small fire.

"I'll have to put in my appearance ahead, as I mentioned," Father

Bronz said. "I've got a little extra here and you should be fairly comfortable for a couple of days. I figure if you can avoid all the traps and patrols to get this far, you certainly can just lie low."

"And then what?" I pressed, not liking to be so out of control of things and feeling a little helpless.

He grinned. "Once I reach the Keep I can pull a favor or two, send a little message to certain parties. I'll work out a rendezvous and we can take it from there."

"Certain parties? I thought this bound-up world wouldn't stand a resistance."

"Oh, they're not anything of the kind," he replied. "No, indeed. They're savages."

CHAPTER FIFTEEN

A Dialogue

Two days, longer and worse on the nerves than any since I'd started this trip, I spent doing absolutely nothing near where I'd originally discovered Father Bronz. I certainly trusted the odd priest far more than I had at the beginning. Not only did I have little choice in the matter, but if I hadn't seen Artur's grim face by this point, then Bronz wouldn't be the one to turn me in. Now the anxiety was mostly that something would happen to him before he could aid me.

I needn't have worried, though. Bronz held a position on Lilith that, though perhaps not unique, was enviable in the extreme. He went where he wanted and did what he wanted without being answerable to anyone, not even to his church superiors. As a well-known face among the keeps, he was always welcomed and never threatened. As a friend of the Duke and most of the more powerful knights in the east-central region of Lilith's single enormous continent, he was unlikely to be touched even by the most powerful psychopaths, since they, too, respected those more powerful than themselves. The price of all this, though, was that, though a Master himself, Bronz was simply not a threat to anybody else's position. As a priest, he seemed sincerely to care for the down-trodden, seeing his role in life as one of the very rare bridges between the elites in their castles and manor houses and the pawns condemned to eternal serfdom. His message of an all-powerful being who promised a heavenly life in the Hereafter to those who were good in this life appealed to the ruling classes, as a major official religion always appealed to such groups. And yet his faith, no matter how wrong or misplaced it might be, was the only rock of sanity for the pawns, their only hope. They suffered under the ultimate tyranny on Lilith: the ruling class was revolution-proof because the masses were born without the ability to use the Warden power.

Bronz returned late in the evening of the second day, looking very tired but satisfied. "All set," he told me. "We'll have to do some traveling, though. Our rendezvous is about two days' ride from here, and that's exactly how long we have in which to make it. It's pretty hairy with the patrols right now, and they won't wait. Let's get going."

"Now?" I responded, feeling a little rushed after two days of marking time. "It's almost dark, and you look all in. I don't want to lose you—not now."

He grinned feebly. "Yes, now. I have some straw and my bedding, so we'll be able to hide Ti and, with some difficulty, your giant frame. But you're right—I am dead tired after doing five days' ministry in two as well as the usual politicking. That's why we go now. You can do the driving while I get a little sleep."

I was startled. "Me? But you drive these damned things by talking to them, Warden-style! I can't do that!"

"Oh, Sheeba's a nice big bugger, she is," Bronz responded casually. "She doesn't need any kick in the pants, and once we get to the split down here a ways there aren't any turnoffs we need concern ourselves with for thirty kilometers or more, so she'll just plod right along."

"Why do you even need me, then?" I asked, still apprehensive.

"To stand guard, to wake me if there's any trouble, and if we are stopped by a patrol, to run like hell—but loudly."

And it was as simple as that. The huge beetlelike creature Father Bronz called Sheeba was as docile and plodding as he said and kept right to the road. The worst problem I had, other than contending with the priest's snores, was seeing every kind of terrible threat in the shadows. Twice I woke Bronz, convinced I'd seen something large shadowing us, once from the side of the road, once from the air. But after the second, his patience wore thin. "Grow up and be a big boy, Tremon. You're much too old to be scared of the dark. Listen for the bugs, boy. As long as you can hear the bugs there's nobody around."

The truth was I felt more than physically naked standing in the ak-cart looking at nothing except an occasional star that peeked through the ever-present clouds. But the ever-present crescendo of insect noises, a background I'd gotten so used to by this time I'd just about tuned it out of my conscious, never ceased.

Bronz awoke before dawn on his own, and we stopped for tea.

"Damned nuisance, this place," the priest muttered. "You can't take food with you, it rots in a day unless you have a couple of agriculture masters around to see it shipped safely and some others to store it properly. Me, I get along by roadside pickings and save my Warden energies for my gourds and teas."

I took the hint, and shortly before dawn was on a foraging expedition into the bush. I didn't come back with much, since I dared not risk going too far from the road, but it was enough—a few melons, a handful or two of berries. Bronz worked some of his Warden magic on them so that we were able to keep a tiny supply, but clearly his area of expertise, if he had one, lay elsewhere.

Daylight was the time of greatest risk. Although Bronz had chosen a route that took us away from the more congested Keeps and where the wild was dominant, we came upon the occasional traveler nonetheless.

Scrunching down in the cart, covering myself with straw and bedding as best I could, I had to stay there, still as possible, praying I could keep from coughing or sneezing or moving no matter how long the conversation (and some were *very* long). Most were supervisors, some with *ak*-carts of their own, who were delivering something from one Keep to another, but there was an occasional master as well. All were worrisome, since I doubted if Father Bronz would kill even to protect me. But the masters were the most irritating, since they possibly could outdo Bronz himself.

One time we even ran into an actual roadblock, the one thing we never expected, which indicated just how far afield Artur was willing to go. Fortunately, Father Bronz knew the two guards and talked us through it. Since I didn't really have a low opinion of Artur, I suspect that if those two mentioned in their report they passed Bronz without conducting an inspection there would be two fewer guards from Zeis Keep, no matter how reliable the priest was deemed to be.

It was like that all over, though, I knew. Act as if you own the place, betray no anxiety, and you can get away with the damnedest things, even in a crowd.

Most of the time, though, the road was empty, so Bronz and I could talk—and did we ever. There was little else to do, and I was anxious to learn.

"You don't much like the system on Lilith, I note," he commented once.

I gave a dry laugh. "Stratified oppression, a tiny ruling class in permanent power—mostly the best criminal minds humanity has produced. I think it stinks."

"What would you do, then?" he came back, sounding amused. "What sort of system would, say, Lord Cal Tremon impose that would supplant this one?"

"The Warden organism makes that tough," I replied carefully. "Obviously power corrupts"—Bronz gave me a hurt look—"most people," I rescued myself. "The people with the power are generally the most corrupt to begin with, since outsiders tend to have a higher degree of this power, and only the corrupt are sent here."

He smiled. "So corruption cometh to Paradise, and the snakes rule Eden, is that it? Get rid of the snakes and Eden returns?"

"You're mocking me. No, I don't believe that and you know it. But a more enlightened leadership could produce a better standard of living for the pawns without all this torture and degradation."

"Could it?" he mused. "I wonder. This is a complex planet, but I think

118 THE FOUR LORDS OF THE DIAMOND

you are being too one-dimensional on its limitations. You think of the Warden organism only in terms of the power it gives some people. You must recognize it as a *total* fact of life for *everything* on Lilith, not merely for who's got the power. The Warden organism is a peculiarity of the evolution of this world; it was not designed for human beings. It is just a freak of nature that we're able to tap into it."

"What do you mean?"

"Think of the Warden beast as a regulator, a balancer that evolved of necessity here. Exactly why it evolved is not for me to say, but my best guess would be that this world, for much of its past, went through some pretty violent changes. I don't know the nature of them, but there are reptiles, mammals, crystalline creatures of some sort—all sorts of creatures on the other Warden worlds that are not found here. Here only the insect was able to survive, it being the most adaptable and, ironically, the least likely to change. But I suspect that even the insects and the plants were threatened by whatever changes the planet underwent, so much so that there evolved a mechanism in nature to keep things stable—at equilibrium, you might say. *Why* the planet needs to be kept in that state is another question for which I don't have any answers, but it does. In some funny way the planet *needs* this ecosystem, at least to survive. That's the reason for the Warden organism."

"You talk as if the planet itself were alive."

He nodded slowly. "I have often found it more convenient to think that way. Look, when man originally set out from Earth centuries ago he expected to find very alien worlds. What did he find? Mostly worlds that were crater-strewn and dead, gas giants, frozen rock piles, and occasionally a planet that perhaps was a mess but could be terraformed. Most of the livable planets not needing a lot of work were already inhabited, some by mere plants and animals but some by other species. And yet—no matter how crazy the biology was or the ecosystem balance or the patterns of thought and behavior of nonhumans—they were all *comprehensible*. We could say, 'Oh, yes, the Alphans are tentacled protoplasmic blobs, but look at the environment they evolved in, look how we trace it thus and so, and look how the environmental conditions shaped their cultures, their ways of thinking, and so forth.' Their own cultures and ways of life might have been so crazy that we couldn't find anything in common with them, couldn't follow their reasoning at all, but taken as a whole they were all *comprehensible*. We never met a world so alien we couldn't at least understand, under the laws of physical and social science, how it got that way. Not until Lilith and her sisters."

I looked around at the foliage, at the deep blue sky, and at the remains of melon and berries. "Frankly, I can't see where you're heading," I told him. "In terms of familiarity, this world is more familiar than many I've been on."

He nodded. "Superficial familiarity, yes. These insects are all unique to Lilith, but they are recognizably insects. The plants are recognizably plants, since an atmosphere that will support us requires photosynthesis for complex plant life. But consider. The Warden Diamond is a statistical absurdity. Four worlds, *all* within the life-supporting range of a sun just right for them. Four worlds very close together—the distance between Charon and Medusa is only about 150 million kilometers, practically next door, with two goodies in between—almost as if they'd been placed there just for us. The idea is simply absurd. You know the slim ratio of solar systems to even terraformable worlds. And yet here they are, right in our way, and each with a tiny, inexplicable little additive that damned well keeps us here."

"You're giving the old argument—that the Wardens are all artificial," I pointed out. "You know there's never been any evidence of that."

"That's true," Father Bronz admitted, "but remember what I said about comprehensibility? It seems to be that, in this enormous universe of which we know so little, we are handcuffed by our rigid concepts. What we have here is something that's not comprehensible—truly alien—and so we ignore it, dismiss it, forget it. These planets do not fit our cosmology, so we dismiss them as aberrations of chance and forget about it. My feeling is that anything you find that can't be explained by your cosmology means that your cosmology's got some holes in it."

"The hand of God, perhaps?" I retorted, not meaning to make fun of his religion but unable to refute him, either.

He didn't laugh or take offense. "Since I believe that the universe was created by God and that He is everywhere and in everything and everyone, yes. I have often reflected that the Wardens might be here simply to slap down our smugness. But God is supremely logical, remember. The Wardens fit the rest of the universe somehow, of that I am convinced, even if they don't fit our perception of it. But we're off the track. I was discussing why your fine dream of returning Lilith to Paradise is impossible to realize."

I chuckled. "I didn't mind the digression. What else do we have to do, anyway?"

He shrugged. "Who knows? Discussion may be vital or it may be inconsequential. I have a feeling that you are somehow driven to command this world. You'll probably get killed in the attempt, of course, but if you survive—well, at least it's interesting to fence with you and see what you have in mind."

"Lord Tremon," I laughed. "Boy! Wouldn't *that* give the Confederacy heartburn!"

"You're no more Cal Tremon than I'm Marek Kreegan," Bronz came back casually. "We might as well stop the pretense, since nobody believes in it any more—and I never did."

I froze. "What do you mean?"

"You're on the wanted list here because Kreegan got information from his Confederacy agents that you were a plant, a spy, an assassin sent here to get him. You and I both know it's true. You're far too idealistic and ethical and all that to be somebody like Tremon, who was the sort of fellow who enjoyed making chopped hamburger out of his still-living enemies with carving knives. I knew that the first time we met, back in Zeis, just talking to you. You're too well-educated, too well-bred for Tremon—not to mention, of course, that you're too much a product of your culture. Who are you, anyway, by the way?"

I considered what he said, then thought about what it meant to me. I really didn't need to keep up the pretense any more. Kreegan knew it, Artur knew it—hell, *everybody* knew it.

"My name doesn't matter, does it?" I replied carefully. "I no longer exist as him. I'm Cal Tremon now and forever; I'm just not the Cal Tremon in the court dockets. And since this is his body, I'm more of him than I'd have believed."

He nodded. "All right, Cal it is. But you are an agent?"

"Assassin grade," I answered truthfully. "But it's not quite what you think. You and I know that, once down here and locked here forever, the only reason I'd have for killing Kreegan would be to challenge him for Lord of the Diamond. No, I'm here for something quite different."

"I find it interesting that they finally got that personality transfer process down mechanically. On Cerberus it's a product of the Warden organism, as physical shape-change adaptation is to Medusa and reality perception to Charon."

"You knew they were working on something like that?" I prodded suspiciously.

He nodded. "Sure. I told you I used to be a really influential power, didn't I? A few of the people involved in the research were Catholics who were very worried about the theological implications—the soul and all that. Frankly, though, not only I but the church as a whole dismissed the entire question as impossible. See what I mean about cosmologies not fitting facts?"

His story didn't ring altogether true, as I knew how absolute the security had been on the process, but I had to let it stand. Maybe my only ally on Lilith was holding out on me—but I was holding out on him, too.

"So you say it isn't Kreegan you're after," he went on, changing the direction of the conversation. "Then what? What is so vital that the Confederacy is willing to sacrifice one of their best just to find out about it, and what would force you to remain true to that end once you got here?"

Then I told him about the aliens, the penetration of the top levels of Military Systems Command, the whole story. It seemed the best course—and he might know something.

When I finished, he just sighed, then said, "Well, now . . . alien enemies, huh? Using the Four Lords . . . Damned clever beasts, you must admit that, to understand us so well."

I was disappointed. If anyone other than those at the very top of the hierarchy would know about the aliens, I felt certain Bronz would. "You've heard nothing about this?"

"Oh, yes, rumors," he responded. "I didn't put much stock in them, partly because of Kreegan. He's not like the others. He came here voluntarily, of his own free will, after serving the Confederacy well and loyally for his whole life. The revenge that would motivate the others would be lacking in him."

My heart sank. Wasted. All of it, me, wasted here. Bronz was right—it had to be one of the other Lords.

But . . . did it?

"That might be true," I admitted, "but do *you* know why an otherwise sane and even superior man like Kreegan would volunteer to come to a place like this? And could such a man be kept ignorant of things as momentous as the aliens even if he *weren't* directly involved at the start?"

Bronz thought it over. "Hmm . . . You're suggesting that maybe Kreegan is the kingpin? It's possible, of course. Suppose, for example, such a man as he became thoroughly disillusioned with his job, with his employers, with the system he helped perpetuate? Suppose that somewhere in his work he stumbled over the aliens. It would explain much. It would explain, for example, how the aliens instantly knew so much about us, how they were able to use the Warden worlds to their advantage. Kreegan would be ideal for establishing, even masterminding an operation such as you describe—and it would take time. He'd have to work his way up, like the rest of us. Maybe with a little alien help, of course, but it would still take time. Then, once in power, they'd start to implement their plans."

"I'd originally been thinking along similar lines," I told him. "But it *would* mean that our aliens were supremely confident we could be counted on to overlook them for the years it would take. And they would have to have much patience."

Bronz shrugged. "Perhaps they do. And *did* you find them? How much *did* they learn before one of their fancy machines finally got caught? It seems to me that, if your guess is right and these aliens are too nonhuman to do much of anything themselves, and if they knew they were well hidden or well disguised, this was the best route."

"The only thing wrong with such a neat picture," I said, "is in Kreegan's character itself. He's a good deal older than I am, but he came from the same place. Our lives parallel to a remarkable degree, even to the type of work we did. I just can't see what would so disillusion him about the Confederacy that he'd want to destroy it, devote his whole life to doing so."

"Well, now, you've got a point there," Bronz came back, "but it's not the point you think you made. I can see an awful lot to be disillusioned about in the Confederacy. I think perhaps you have Kreegan a little backward. I could just as easily picture him as a totally committed idealist willing to do anything for his cause. Out of that background I can envision a man who just might commit his very soul to such a project, not for gain but in an idealistic crusade."

"I think you're crazy," I told him. "An idealist would have certainly changed the system on Lilith. At the very least pawns would be far better off, the ruling class taken down several pegs."

Father Bronz laughed and shook his head in wonder. "You poor soul. Let's look at Lilith first, in light of all I've said. The social system is *not* merely determined by individual power. It is determined by the need to have Lilith support a nonindigenous human population, something she was simply not designed to do. The Warden organism defends the planetary ecosystem—the plant and animal balance, the rocks, the swamps, the air and water—against change. It struggles to retain an equilibrium. Total balance. *We're* the aliens here, the incomprehensible ones, son. We have power, yes, but it's of a very limited nature. We cannot reshape this planet, but can only adapt to its existing conditions. The Warden beasties won't let us. Now, dump thirteen million totally wrong aliens here and see what happens."

I couldn't see where he was going and said so.

"It's so *simple*," he responded. "You're so used to technology as the answer to all ills that you don't see what we're faced with here. All of human history is the history of technology, of using that technology so that man can change his environment to suit himself. And we have. On Earth we changed the course of rivers, we bent sun and wind and whatever it took to our ends. We leveled mountains when they were inconvenient, and built them where we wanted. We created lakes, cut down whole forests, tamed the entire planet. Then we went out to the stars and did the same thing. Terraforming. Genetic engineering. Using our technology, we changed whole planets; we even changed ourselves. Man's history is warring with his environment and winning that war. But, son, on Lilith—and only on Lilith—man cannot declare war. He *must* live within the environment that was already here. On Lilith the environment won. One lonely skirmish, true, but we were whipped. Beaten. We can't fight it. We can build a castle, yes, and get insects to carry us to and fro, but we can make only minor dents, dents that would be instantly erased if they weren't being constantly maintained.

"You see, son, Lilith's the boss here, thanks to Warden's bug. We all dance to her tune or compromise with her, but she's the boss. And yet we must feed and house thirteen million people. We must support thirteen million alien interlopers on a land not meant for them and on which we can't really perform more than cosmetic changes. Somebody has to grow the food and ship it. Somebody has to raise the great insect beasts and keep them domesticated. The economy must be kept going, for if those thirteen million were suddenly left entirely to their own devices they'd go out and eat and drink their fill and denude the melon groves. They'd fight each other as savage hunters and gatherers, the most primitive of tribal structures, and all but the toughest would die.

"Don't you see, son? Nobody enjoys the kind of hard labor it takes to keep the system going—but *name me another that would work*. Without technology at our disposal, we are condemned to mass muscle power."

I was appalled. "Are you claiming that there's no other way to do it?" "Nope. There are lots of other ways, all more cruel and worse than this one. There may well be a better way, but I don't know it. I suspect that's the way Kreegan sees it, too. I'm sure he doesn't *like* the system, since it's so much like the Confederacy—if we're right about him, that is—but unlike the Confederacy, he, like me, can't see any better way."

I couldn't believe what I was hearing. To have all one's basic beliefs challenged in an offhanded manner like this was a bit much. "What do you mean, this system is so much like the Confederacy?" I challenged. "I certainly can't see any similarities."

Father Bronz snorted contemptuously. "Then you do not see what you see. Consider the so-called civilized worlds. Most of humanity have been equalized into a stagnant sameness beyond belief. On a given planet everybody looks pretty much the same, talks pretty much the same, eats, sleeps, works, plays pretty much the same. They're pawns, all of them. They think the same. And they are taught that they are happy, content, at the pinnacle of human achievement, the good life for all, and they believe it. It's true they are coddled more, their cages are gilded, but they are pawns all the same. The only real difference between their pawns and ours is that ours know that they are pawns and understand the truth of the whole system. Your civilized worlds are so perfectly programmed to think the same that they are never even allowed to face the truth."

"It's a pretty comfortable pawnship," I pointed out, not really conceding his point but allowing his terms for argument's sake.

"Comfortable? I suppose so. Like pet canaries, maybe. Those are small birds that live in cages in people's homes, in case you don't know—not on the civilized worlds, of course, where pets are not thought of. But at any rate these birds are born in cages; they are fed there, and their cages are regularly cleaned by their owners. They know no other life. They know that somebody provides them with all they need to exist, and having no other expectations, they want for no more. In exchange, they chirp comfortably and provide companionship to lonely frontiersmen. Not only is no canary ever going to engineer a breakout of that cage, but he's not even going to imagine, let alone design and build, a better life. He can't even conceive of such a thing."

"Those are animals," I pointed out. "Like Sheeba here."

"Animals, yes," he acknowledged, "but so are the humans of the civilized worlds. Pets. Everybody has an apartment that is just so in size, just so in furnishings, just so in every way the same. They look the same and wear the same clothes, as if it mattered, and they perform jobs designed to keep the system going. Then they return to their identical cubicles, get immersed in entertainment that involves them totally in some formula story that's all about their own world, offering nothing new in thought, idea, concept. Most of their free time they spend on drugs in some happy, unproductive never-never land. Their arts, their literature, their very traditions are all inherited from history. They have none of their own. We've equalized them too much for that—equalized out love and ambition and creativity, too. Whenever equality is imposed as an absolute, it is always equalized at the least common denominator, and historically, the least common denominator of mankind has been quite low indeed."

"We still advance," I pointed out. "We still come up with new ideas, new innovations."

"Yes, that's true," Bronz admitted. "But you see, my son, that's not from the civilized worlds. The masters of those worlds, the Outside supervisors and knights and dukes and lords, know that they can't let progress die completely or they die and their power with it. So we have the frontier, and we have selective breeding of exceptional individuals. The elite, working in the castles of Outside."

"We don't have those ranks and positions and you know it," I retorted.

He gave a loud guffaw. "The *hell* you say! And what then, pray tell, are *you*? What is Marek Kreegan? What, for that matter, am I? Do you know what my *real* crime was, Tremon? I reintroduced not merely religion but the concepts of love, of spirituality, to those pawns. I gave them something new, a rediscovery of their humanity. And it threatened the system! I was—removed. As long as I was on the frontier giving aid and comfort to the miserable and the uncomfortable, why, I was fine. Let the churches be. But when I started making headway on the civilized worlds— oh, no, then I was dangerous. I had to be removed or I might accomplish the unthinkable. I might awaken those pawns from their total environmental entertainment mods and drug stupors and show them they didn't have to be trained canaries any more, they could be individual human beings—like me. Like you. Like the ruling class. And I got slapped down."

"For a man with that idea of the civilized worlds, you are mighty complacent about this one," I noted.

He shrugged. "Here it is necessary—at least until somebody comes up with something better and has the power and will to enforce it and make it work. But back home—oh, no. Man is master of his environment, but he is also the slave of the technocratic class that rules so cleverly that the slaves don't even know they're slaves. What of complacency? Aren't you guilty of the reverse, Cal? Aren't you raring to change Lilith, but totally complacent about the civilized worlds? Son, the time for carrying out the orders of your superior are over. You're calling your own tune now. You can think what you like. It provides a fascinating contrast, does it not? Here on Lilith man is enslaved in body yet free to think, to love, to dance, to tell stories, whatever. The *mind* is free, although the body's in chains— just like much of human history. Back where we come from it's not the body they own—hell, they *made* it—it's the mind. Nobody's enslaving your mind any more, boy. Use it to solve your own, not their, problems."

I recoiled from the dialogue. I didn't like to think about what Bronz was saying, for if I lost my belief in my own culture and the rightness of it, I had nothing else, nothing left. Worse, if what he said was true, then what had my whole life been? Tracking down those who didn't fit, ferreting out those who would challenge, subvert, or topple the system on which the civilized worlds were based.

If what he said was true, then in the context of the civilized worlds, I was . . .

Kronlon.

Could it be true? I asked myself unbelievingly. If so, did Marek Kreegan go out one day to find the enemy and come face to face with himself?

What had Marek Kreegan been like, Vola?

A lot like you, Cal Tremon. An awful lot like you . . .

CHAPTER SIXTEEN

Sumiko O'Higgins and the Seven Covens

A few hours after darkness on the second night we made the rendezvous point. Until now I'd left myself entirely in Father Bronz's hands, but now I wanted information.

"Who are these—savages?" I asked. "And what can they do for us?"

"Cal, the savages in these parts—in fact, in most parts I've seen—aren't savage, except to members of a Keep," he told me. "They are the misfits. People with the power but untrained, people with no power but determined never to work the fields their whole lives, renegades, political outcasts like yourself, and of course their children. I picked this group because of its relative power. They are strong and highly skilled, if somewhat anarchistic."

"I thought you said that wouldn't work here," I taunted, feeling good that I'd scored at least once.

"Oh, it doesn't," he responded airily. "Not on a large scale, anyway. Not even on a small one, really, but people can be made to *think* they're in an anarchy if that's what they want. On a *very* small scale they can be truly savages, of course—but they meet the fate of all true savages. They die young and usually violently. No, these folks have an organization and powerful people, but they are, ah, a bit unorthodox."

Father Bronz crossed himself when he said that last, and it was such an interesting reaction I had to press it. I'd seen him do that only a very few times, such as just before and just after the roadblock.

"These people are dangerous, then?"

He nodded. "Very. You might say that we—that is, they and I—are in the same business. Competitors."

"Another church?"

He chuckled. "In a sense, yes. They are the opposition, my lad, and you don't know how it galls me to have to use them, let alone trust them. They are witches, you see, and worship Satan."

I had to laugh. "*Witches?* Oh, come on, now."

"Witches," he acknowledged gravely. "I don't know why that should surprise you. Let's just say you were of a magical or romantic bent. Take a look at Lilith then. A spoiled Eden. Now, instead of Warden organisms and mathematical constructs, chemical catalysts and the other stuff of science we take so much for granted, replace it with the word *magic*. The upper classes, those with the power, then become magicians, wizards, sorcerers. Utilizing the Warden organism as you tell me you did, on that chair for example. A thing of nature? How about a 'magic spell' instead? *You* know what runs this world, and how, and I know, but do most people? Without that knowledge, isn't it a world of wizards and magic spells?"

I saw his point, although it didn't cheer me. "So we're being placed in the hands of people who believe all this?"

He nodded. "So watch your step. They're doing this mostly because it gives 'em a kick to have a priest ask a favor of Satanists. But *they* believe it, and they don't have much of a sense of humor about it, either. Some of 'em can fry you, too, so watch that sharp tongue."

I shut up. Whatever craziness these people believed, no matter how absurd it might be, they were the only hope I had.

We waited for the Satanist party.

They appeared without our having ever detected their presence. At one moment we were just lounging by the cart, relaxing and hoping that one of Lilith's frequent and violent thunderstorms, which was looming close on the horizon, would not hit where we were when I was suddenly aware of a number of people standing around us. I jumped up and turned in fighting posture, but quickly relaxed when Bronz seemed less concerned.

They were all women, about a dozen of them, some with the look of the civilized worlds about them—but certainly different-looking in this context. Their hair was cut very, very short, and their faces and skins had that rough, weathered look pawns get, although these women were not pawns. All wore some sort of breechclout that as nearly as I could tell was made of some tough and weathered leaf, held on by carefully braided and tied ropelike vines. On a loop of that vine, each bore some sort of weapon—a stone axe, some kind of mineral-carved knife, or in at least two cases, bows and flint-tipped arrows.

One of them, a large woman who was tall and imposing, was the exception to the hair rule, her long, silky-black hair reaching down past her buttocks. She was obviously the leader and radiated a charismatic confidence you could almost feel. Not that she could fail to dominate any scene she was in; at more than two meters in height, she was almost as big as I was.

"Well, well, Father Bronz," she said, her voice deep and rich. "So this is the fugitive in trouble." She looked at me and I felt as if I were being examined by some scientist unpleased with the odor and look of her specimen. She turned back to the priest. "You said something about a girl. Was that just a papist lie?"

"Oh, stow it, Sumiko," Bronz growled. "You know me better than that. She's in the cart."

A flick of the leader's head and three of the other women rushed to the cart, pulled the straw off Ti, and gently removed her.

"Sons of bitches," the leader snorted in genuine anger and stalked over to the comatose girl. She repeated what Bronz had done when he'd first seen her, placing her hands on Ti's forehead and concentrating hard. After a moment she drew back, opened her eyes, and turned again to face us. "What bastard did this?" she almost snarled.

"Pohn, over at Zeis," Bronz responded wearily. "You've heard the stories, and now you know they're true."

She nodded gravely. "Someday, I promise you, I will get that worm in my hands and I will slowly, very slowly, dissect him as he watches."

"Can you do anything for her?" I put in, both concerned and piqued at being ignored.

She nodded thoughtfully. "I think so. A little. At least I can bring her out of it, but there's the danger of clotting or brain damage if she's not gotten to a doctor—a real one who knows just what repairs to make. From what I can see of the spell, Pohn is less powerful than I am, but he's damned tricky and clever." She gestured to us and started walking. The other women put Ti back in the cart, and one jumped up behind Sheeba, saying nothing. The cart started, and so did the witch queen—that was the only way I could think of her. We followed off into the bush of the wild.

As we walked, Bronz turned to me and said, softly, "Well, now you've met her. Sumiko O'Higgins, chief witch and a regular loving charmer."

"She is—ah—formidable," I returned.

"That she is," he agreed. "Still, she's strong. If anybody can help Ti and you, she can."

"I don't think I made a good first impression or something," I noted. "She certainly seemed less than pleased with me."

He chuckled. "Sumiko doesn't like men very much. But don't worry. This is strictly business."

I didn't feel reassured. "Will she really help me?" I pressed. "I mean, all things considered, she's got us where she wants us."

"Don't worry," he responded, "you're perfectly safe. Satanists pride themselves, oddly, on their honor. They simply don't break agreements and commitments once made. Besides, she hates the Keeps more than anyone I know, and you're a refugee wanted by the higher-ups. That gives you status here."

"I hope so," I said dubiously. "Who *is* she, anyway? She's at least a Master herself."

He nodded. "Probably more. And with no formal training whatsoever. If she'd gotten some, she might have been ripe for Lord, but that wouldn't fit her personality."

We walked along for some time, losing sight of the cart and of any trace of the road or anything remotely familiar. We were in fact prisoners of the witch-queen's whims. I hoped fervently that Bronz was right about her, but I still remembered his cross and prayer. This was definitely the first human being I'd seen that Father Bronz feared.

We walked on for some time—how long I couldn't tell, since the life on Lilith and the abnormally long days and nights had played hell with what little time sense I retained. Finally, though, we arrived at our host's encampment, a jungle enclave that was quite different from any of the Keeps that I'd seen. The houses were made not from *bunti* but from strong wood and bamboolike reeds, the pointed thatched roofs from some woven straw. The arrangement was a bit odd: thirteen such "houses" were arranged in a large circle around a clearing in the center of which was a pit, a fireplace for central cooking, and some sort of stone cairn. The inhabitants of the village seemed most active in the dark; they were going about their tasks as we entered the village, and I noticed that the population was larger than I'd expected—sixty, perhaps more—and that all were women. The lack of men anywhere only served to increase my nervousness.

The cart had already arrived by some other route. The women doing whatever they were doing by the flickering light of the low central fire and a number of gourd lanterns filled with the flammable juices of several plants paid us no real mind as we entered. A few glances up of obvious idle curiosity, but no more. Clearly we were not only expected but weren't even big news. I noticed that most of the women were naked and unadorned, marking them as pawns. Apparently the ranking members of the tribe, Supervisor level and above, had *all* come out to meet us. That told me that they felt their village secure but hadn't been any too trusting of us.

The leader called out to a couple of women, and instructions started flying all over the place. Father Bronz and I decided that we were somehow redundant at the moment and just stood back out of the way, watching.

A covering was removed from the central area near the fire, revealing a large stone slab with what might have been a carved recess in it. It looked like a cross between a birdbath and one of those damned tables in Pohn's chamber of horrors. The fire was being stoked, and now Ti's inert form was brought from the cart and placed in the recess in the stone. Twelve women, ten of them apparently pawns, formed a circle around the comatose girl, almost blocking her from view.

I turned to Bronz and asked, "What the hell is going on here?"

"That's what it is, all right—hell," he sighed. "They're going to try and bring Ti out of the state she is in, but being Satanists, they will do it as a religious ceremony. This is hard on me, understand, but these women are deluded rather than evil and I'm a pragmatist. Sumiko was the only one I knew with this much power and some medical knowledge who wasn't on the other side or too far away to do us any good."

I shrugged. Satanism and Catholicism were one and the same to me, both remnants of ancient superstitions and power structures no longer relevant to modern times. Still, I conceded to myself, if this mumbo jumbo allowed them to concentrate and focus their powers to help Ti, well, so be it.

The twelve started chanting. I couldn't really catch the words, but if they *were* words, I think it was a language I didn't know.

They chanted for some time, until it started to get boring, but just when I'd settled down to relax, Sumiko O'Higgins entered from one of the huts. She was something to see, draped in black robes and a cape, wearing what appeared to be a carved upside-down cross on some sort of vine necklace.

As she approached the circle of chanting women, the fire, which had almost died out, burst back into explosive life with a force all its own, an action that startled me. It was an eerie effect, all the more so since I knew that the Warden organism died in fire just as all others I'd ever known did, and thus that fire business couldn't be a Warden power trick.

O'Higgins closed the circle by her presence and joined the chant, then dominated it, eyes seemingly closed, arms stretched out to the sky, appearing almost in a trancelike state. Suddenly the chant was stilled, leaving only the sounds of the massive insects of Lilith. I didn't even hear anybody breathe or cough.

"Oh, Satan, Lord of Darkness, hear our prayer!" she chanted.

"Gather, darkness!" the others responded.

"Oh, great one who combats the totalitarianism of church and government, work within us and hear our plea!"

"Hear our plea," echoed the others.

She opened her eyes and lowered her arms slowly, then placed both hands on Ti's unmoving head. "Give us strength to heal this girl," she prayed, then closed her eyes again, still touching Ti's head, apparently reentering the trancelike state. It was difficult to tell if she was faking it or was really in a trance. I began to have some doubts about this procedure, but there really was no alternative. I glanced over at Father Bonz and saw him just looking on and sadly shaking his head.

The tableau in the center court seemed frozen for some time, and I understood that, no matter what their odd beliefs, O'Higgins and maybe some of the others were probing, analyzing, perhaps even making repairs.

Suddenly the witch queen let go and stepped back, raising her arms once again. "Oh, Satan, Prince of Darkness, rightful King of the Universe, we give thanks!" she almost shouted, and the litany was repeated by the others. The fire flared again into near-blinding brilliance, then almost died, causing the strong impression of a tangible darkness closing in, embracing all of us there in the village. I felt a little chill despite the heat and humidity, I have to admit. I could well understand how this sort of thing could attract followers.

"From light into darkness, from dark knowledge the final victory," she intoned, and then it was broken, as if by some signal. All thirteen of the women stood a little unsteadily, appearing to have gone through some strenuous physical labor.

O'Higgins recovered quickly, though, and walked back to the still unmoving form of Ti, placing hands again on her head. She nodded to herself, then called for others to bear Ti to one of the huts. As they were carrying out her orders, she turned and walked over to us.

'Well, Bronz, your side couldn't do a damned thing," she noted.

Bronz shrugged. "You did what was necessary?"

'I undid what I could," she admitted, "but I told you that that butchering bastard was really good and really clever. She'll be all right for a while, though—in fact better than all right, since I had to bypass a lot of Pohn's knots and create alternate routes that might not hold up. There'll be a rush, though—she'll probably feel like she can topple mountains, even though in reality she'll be quite weak until she gets a lot more exercise and regular food, and I fear the repair job won't hold forever."

'You mean," I put in, "that she'll eventually lapse back into that state?"

She nodded. "Remember the way the system works," she said. "The Warden organisms have a single idea of what is natural. Those with the power can convince Wardens that something else is what they want to do —and that's what Pohn did. Her Wardens want to put her back into that state because he's fooled them into thinking that it's normal. I bypassed the nerve blocks by using parts of the brain not normally used at all, but the Wardens will perceive my meddling as an injury, like a broken arm. They will rush to fix it, put it right. They'll be battling my own work with some localized Wardens, but the barriers will eventually break down. It'll take somebody as expert in cranial medicine *and*/or more powerful than Dr. Pohn to put her completely right, although that could be accomplished in a matter of minutes by such a person."

I frowned. "How long, then, will she—wake up?"

She shrugged. "A few days, maybe a week. No more. It'll go slowly, so there's no sure way to tell."

I groaned in frustration. "Then what the hell was the use of all this? Who could really heal her in that length of time?"

She looked at me, slightly surprised at my tone. "You really care? About a small female?"

"He cares," Bronz put in, saving me from making nasty comments to my host. "He escaped from Zeis and he could have done it a lot easier without bringing her. Instead he's lugged her with him everywhere, fed her, cleaned her—you name it."

She looked at me again, this time nodding slightly, and for the first time I felt like I'd attained the status of human being in her eyes. "If she means that much to you," she said to me, "then perhaps something *can* be done. There's only one place I know of for sure, though, that could do the job, and it's pretty far away."

"Moab Keep," Father Bronz added, nodding. "I suspected as much. But four thousand kilometers, Sumiko! How in God's name can we possibly get her there in under a year? Let alone Tremon here, who needs to take the full treatment."

She grinned evilly. "Not in *God's* name, Augie. But the answer's obvious—we fly. A *besil* can do three, maybe four hundred kilometers a night, resting days, so we're talking ten days at the outside. That sound a lot more possible?"

"*Besils!*" Bronz scoffed. "Since when do you have access to any domesticated *besils* capable of carrying passengers?"

"I don't—now," she admitted. "I expect that if we need *besils*, though, we can get them pretty easily courtesy of Zeis Keep."

I jumped. "What!"

She shrugged. "Either you slipped up somewhere, Augie, or *he* did. It doesn't matter. We're partially surrounded by Zeis troopers right now, and I expect them to come in at sunup, when they can see what they're doing."

I whirled around, staring at the darkness in nervous anticipation. When I realized that neither of the other two seemed in any way concerned by that news, I just grew a little more paranoid about them.

I turned to Father Bronz, who was cocking his head slightly, as if listening for something. Finally he said, "How many do you make them?"

"No more than twenty or thirty, all on *besils*," she responded casually. "I'd suppose somebody's gone back for more, but he's not about to commit more than a fraction of his force. Some of the other knights might get the idea to exploit the weakness and attack Zeis."

Bronz nodded agreement. "Then we'll face no more than forty, a fifth or so of his force. I agree. Okay, forty people at arms, with Artur almost a certainty and, say, two other masters?"

She nodded. "That's about it."

"*Wait* a minute!" I exploded. "It may not be important to *you*, but they're after the girl and me! You can't fight a force like that!"

Sumiko O'Higgins shook her head slowly in disgust. "Now, isn't that just like a man! Look, you just go cower someplace and maybe get some sleep and leave the worrying to me."

"But—but—they're all highly trained soldiers, all of 'em at least supervisors and with more masters than you've got here!" I sputtered. "How do you expect to defeat them?"

"Just don't you worry about it," she replied condescendingly. "We—Father Bronz and I—have a lot of work to do between now and dawn. A good thing the God-lovers and we Satanists can get together and agree on one sort of cooperative venture," she added. "*Atheists! Pgh!*"

Father Bronz added, "She knows what she's doing, Cal," in his most reassuring tone. If it hadn't been for the under-the-breath addition of "I hope" to his statement I just might have believed him.

As it was, I just stayed there, not feeling at all sleepy, seeing Master Artur's fierce mustachioed gaze behind every darkness-shielded bush and tree in the jungle.

CHAPTER SEVENTEEN

I Do Believe in Witches—I Do, I Do!

Needless to say, I got very little sleep that night. Of course nobody in the witch village seemed to sleep at night, although they were all rather expert at ignoring anybody they didn't want to see and I was a nonperson in their eyes.

The best I could do was occasionally check on Ti, who when I peeked in for the third or fourth time was not only breathing deeply and regularly, as if in normal sleep, but actually gave out a moan and turned over by herself. That sight alone made this whole business all worthwhile— provided, of course, I lived through the next day.

Although I knew little about witchcraft and remembered less, from the village itself I made a few deductions. Thirteen, the unlucky number because it was the number at the Christians' Last Supper, was naturally a positive number for devil-worshipers. Thirteen women in the coven, then, which explained the number at the ceremony. Thirteen large huts, too, although there were far more than that number living here communally. I never could get an exact count, but I was willing to wager that whatever it was, the number was a multiple of thirteen.

Witch, of course, was a female term. If my old children's stories meant anything, a male witch would be called a warlock, but for some reason you just about never heard about them. They were more mischievous, less powerful, somehow. I remembered that Father Bronz's faith limited the priesthood to males in most cases, which might explain female dominance in Satanism, but it also occurred to me that Dr. Pohn had said that women tended to have more of the power than men, particularly wild talents. I wondered about the hierarchy itself on Lilith now. How many of the knights were female? I wondered. Half? Or a majority? Despite the fact that Tiel was the knight at Zeis, it was Vola who taught me, as she had taught Artur and Marek Kreegan. Artur, Dr. Pohn, and Father Bronz notwithstanding, it suddenly seemed to me that an extraordinary number of the staff of the Castle had been female, and the first master I'd met after arriving on Lilith had been a woman, as had at least half of Artur's soldiers.

Even in my statistically small sample, then, the women were numerically superior to the men. Perhaps Pohn had more reason to confine his experiments to young women than just perversion.

I looked around again at these—witches. Dismiss the religious cultism, the "savage" label, all the rest, and reduce it to what was known. Their chief was one who had the power in spades—Bronz had said she might be in Kreegan's class had she had training, but as I knew only too well, such power even untrained can be enormous if emotionally aroused, and hate was one of the best emotions for that sort of thing. Sumiko O'Higgins hated Zeis, if only for the principle of the thing—Zeis had Pohn, and Pohn had done a number on Ti, a woman.

These others . . . Even though most *looked* like pawns, were they? There was something here I was missing, unless Satan, Prince of Darkness, really had something here. Something had kept this tempting target for Keeps all around safe and secure—so secure O'Higgins dared bring her most powerful personnel to collect us.

It was getting close to dawn, and I was becoming more and more nervous. O'Higgins and Father Bronz had been at it all night, making plans of some kind or another—an odd couple if there ever was one, I decided—and finally the priest emerged from a hut and came over to me. "You look lousy," he said.

"You don't look so bright and eager either," I responded glumly. "But how'd you expect me to sleep through something like *this*?"

He sat down wearily. "I need some strong tea to wake me up," he muttered, more to himself than to me. "She's really got something here. I have to hand it to her. I don't know if it'll work or not, but if it does, it's almost revolutionary. No, it *is* revolutionary."

I stared at him. "Give. What are you talking about?"

"You remember our talks on the balance on Lilith? Well, she seems to have something that upsets that balance, at least a little."

I frowned. "What do you mean?"

"You see these women? All virgins, believe it or not, at least with men. All exhibited strong wild talents at puberty, although most subsided to pawn status, as per normal, after a few months to a year."

"You can't tell me O'Higgins is a virgin," I commented.

He chuckled. "Hard to say. I doubt if she's ever been to bed with a man, if that's what you mean, and that's all that seems to count in this business. There may be something to the old legend of virgins having more power in magical things—in a purely biological sense, Lilith style, I mean. Perhaps some very tiny chemical changes were not introduced. I don't know. But Sumiko got this idea, after combing the savages of the wild, that it was so. She may be crazy but she's not stupid. She was once a pretty good biochemist Outside, so don't sell her short no matter what her crazy beliefs now. At any rate, when she got sent to Lilith she didn't stay a pawn very long. Hot-blooded. Got so damned mad she not only fried her supervisor but stalked angrily out of a Keep to the west of here, glowing, it's said, like a firecracker from the Warden power, injuring or killing anybody who even tried to get in her way."

"None of that catalyst?" I responded unbelievingly.

He shook his head. "None. Now you see what I mean. She was in the wild for a while before she even found out about the stuff. She wasn't just a biochemist, Cal—she was a botanist. It took her months, but she found out what the catalyst was and worked out her own methods for distilling it. How she did it without tools, without a lab, and without even the facilities of a Keep we'll never know—sheer guts and willpower, I'd say. Cal, I don't know what she's come up with, but it isn't quite the nice, pure stuff you and I got, so it isn't as effective, but it works. She recruited all these women when they were very young, just for their wild-talent potential—and, I suspect, their sexual orientation. For short periods of time—I don't know duration—she can dose every woman here with the stuff. Awaken all their old wild talents. Use the cult beliefs and discipline to shape and direct them." He sighed. "You know, in an hour or two I think old Artur may be in for a big surprise."

I thought about what he said and it gave me some immediate hope, but the more I thought about it the more I realized its long-term implications.

Pawns were hardly celibate—Ti, for example, would never make a witch for *this* group—but if O'Higgins really *did* have this stuff it was the equivalent of a fusion bomb to Lilith.

"Bronz, how many women does she have here?"

He was resting, and for a moment I thought he was asleep. But one eye opened. "Thirteen times thirteen. What did you expect?"

One hundred and sixty-nine women, I thought. All handpicked by somebody who knew exactly what she was doing and what she was looking for. All with demonstrated wild talents of major proportions, and with a little chemical aid to awaken those locked-away powers; all fiercely loyal to their leader and mother figure.

"She hasn't got a Satanist nut cult here," I said aloud, "she's got the kernel of a revolutionary army."

"So it took you that long to figure all that out?" Father Bronz muttered sleepily.

The facts weren't all that reassuring. I really wasn't quite sure if I'd like a world fashioned by Sumiko O'Higgins as well as I liked the one run by Marek Kreegan. I wondered idly what the witch-queen's offense had been to have her sent here. Nothing pleasant, that was for sure.

As the sun rose the entire company of witches went through what appeared to be a solemn ceremony that involved, as far as I could see, cursing the sun for rising and spoiling the lovely night and asking for Satan's aid in the coming fight. In the center area, over the restoked fire, a giant gourd caldron bubbled and hissed.

After morning "prayers," each and every one of the women approached the caldron and, with an incantation, drank the hot, foul-smelling liquid from a crudely fashioned dipper. I felt helpless in the coming fight and wished for some of that brew, but Bronz would have none of it.

"Sumiko says the stuff would play hell with your nervous system," he told me. "I'm not sure I believe it, but we're the guests here. You just stay back and watch what happens—and keep out of the way. They'll have spears, poison darts, blowguns, bows and arrows, and even crossbows. Your duty is to stay down and out of the way. If you get killed, then all this will have been for nothing."

I started to argue, but his logic was unassailable. I went to Ti's hut, now emptied of its other occupants, and looked down at her.

She moaned, turned over, and opened her eyes, seeing me. "Hi," she muttered weakly.

"Hi, yourself," I responded, not bothering to hide my big grin. "You know where you are?"

She groaned and tried to sit up, failed the first time, then managed it. "Sort of," she told me. "It was—kinda like a crazy dream. I was sound asleep, and I knew I was sound asleep, but I could hear stuff when there was stuff to hear and see stuff when my eyes were open. It was all dreamy like, though, not real." She hesitated a second, looking puzzled and serious. "But it *was* real, wasn't it, Cal? All of it? That creepy doctor, that horrible room, you rescuing me, Father Bronz, witches—they really *are* witches, aren't they, Cal?"

I nodded. "Sort of. At least *they* think they are."

She stared at me with the kind of expression I had never seen anyone give me before. "You could've got out real easy, but you took me," she whispered, low and almost to herself. Her voice broke slightly and she said, "Oh, Cal, hold me! Hug me! Please!"

I went to her and gently squeezed, but she grabbed on to me and hugged and kissed me as hard and strong as she could. Finally she gasped and I saw tears in her eyes. "I love you, Cal," she almost sobbed, and hugged me again.

I looked at her strangely for a moment, not quite comprehending her actions nor my reactions. "I—I love you too, my little Ti," I replied, then held her close and hugged her, a sense of wonder and amazement coming over me at the realization that, incredibly, what I'd just said was true.

The village seemed deserted. I could see only the smoking remains of the fire and an empty gourd-pot. Not a sign of life, although all around I could hear the ever-present insect chorus.

And then the sound stopped.

It was eerie, incredible. For a moment I thought I had gone deaf, so absolute was the silence in contrast with what I was used to. Not a sound, not a whisper. Even the wind had stopped.

Suddenly, from all around came the sound of incredibly loud, piercing screeches, and a sudden wind whipped the trees from all over. I remained in the hut, conscious that I could do no more, but I was damned well going to see what I could see. Ti, although still very weak, was equally determined once the situation was explained to her, and when I objected to her nearness to the doorway she objected to *my* being too exposed. I surrendered and we both watched, cautiously.

The *besils* rose effortlessly from cover a hundred meters or so from the witch village. Although I couldn't see anything in back of me, I was aware from how they were deployed that they must have the place encircled.

I marveled at how the creatures seemed to rise incredibly smoothly as if on some invisible hoist, then hover there, nearly motionless, about twenty meters up, just beyond the treetops.

One *besil* glided slowly out of the formation and approached the center of the village, almost over the caldron, then descended to a point only four or five meters above the ground. I was marveling at how effortlessly the creature moved, but then the rider drew my attention.

"Artur," I heard Ti gasp. And in fact it *was* the Sergeant at Arms of Zeis Keep, his icy power radiating like a living thing.

"Witches!" he shouted gruffly. "I wish to speak with your leader! We have no need to do battle here today!"

Suddenly, as if popping up from nowhere, Sumiko O'Higgins stood there in full robes and regalia, facing him. I had no idea how she got there without being seen.

"Speak, armsman!" she called back. "Speak and begone! You have no right or business here!"

Artur laughed evilly, although I could tell he was slightly disconcerted by her sudden appearance and defiant tone. "Right? *Might* makes right, madam, as well you know. You and your colony exist here at the sufferance of the Grand Duke because you do us occasional service, but it is for that reason alone that I might spare you. You err, too, madam, in saying I have no business here. No less than my Lord Marek Kreegan has charged me to return with Cal Tremon, the fugitive who is now in your charge. Surrender him to me and we will depart in peace. All will be as it has been."

"*Just* Tremon? You don't wish the girl as well?" the witch queen responded, and I had a sudden queasy feeling that she was striking a deal to her liking but definitely not to mine.

Artur laughed again. "Keep the girl if you wish," he responded airily. "We will even make certain she is fully restored. It is Tremon we must have, and it is Tremon we *will* have."

"I don't like your tone, armsman," O'Higgins responded. "You are so used to wielding absolute power that your arrogance will be your undoing. We do *not* exist here at the sufferance of Grand Duke Kobé or anyone else. Marek Kreegan is *your* Lord, but mine is Satan Mafkrieg, Prince of Darkness, King of the Underworld, and no other."

He ignored the commentary, but I heard Ti mutter under her breath, "Atta girl, witchie! Give him a taste of his own big mouth!"

Artur shrugged, looking very formidable and splendid on his great black beast. "I take it, then, that you will not voluntarily surrender the fugitive?"

"I have no love for him," the witch responded, "but I have far less for you and your masters. If you attack, you will be utterly and completely destroyed. The choice is yours."

Artur just glared at her a moment. Then with an almost imperceptible nudge of the big man's foot, the *besil* floated back to its place in the waiting formation. Sumiko O'Higgins just stood there, and while I marveled at her courage I thought she had acted in a pretty stupid fashion, all things considered.

Suddenly, as mysteriously as Sumiko had appeared, the rest of the witches were all there, spread out in an almost unbroken circle around the perimeter of the village, facing outward toward the attackers. None appeared to have any weapons.

Artur gave a hand gesture, and the two *besils* on either side of him glided forward, their riders aiming pretty nasty-looking fixed crossbows, like artillery pieces, mounted in front of them on their saddles. All four, by their positioning, fixed on Sumiko O'Higgins as they closed in, then fired almost in unison, the arrows flying with enormous force toward the black-garbed figure below.

I started to cry out, but instantly the witch queen waved her hand idly and all four arrows landed in the grass, neatly framing her. Then suddenly every third or fourth woman in the long human circle turned inward, and O'Higgins gestured again with her right arm at the four soldiers.

What followed was incredible. Although the men were bound in by thick, secure straps, they were hurled from their saddles as if plucked by a giant hand, then dashed to the ground below with a force far in excess of gravity. None of them moved.

Artur roared in anger, and the other soldiers closed in and started letting loose their terrible arsenal—spears, arrows, and all sorts of other stuff rapidly flew back and forth across the field—taking point-blank aim at the circle of women. An incredible hail of lethal stuff rained down upon the witches.

It all missed.

Now Sumiko was gesturing again, making some sort of symbol with her hands. *Besils* screamed, and several dropped out of the sky like stones, crashing to earth and taking their riders with them.

I was beginning to admit that the woman had something here.

Artur was fit to be tied, of course, but he gestured for his troops to regroup. It had occurred to him, as it had to me, that nothing nasty happened to you unless you broke that circle of human bodies, and he was re-organizing to meet that fact.

"Fire at the circle from the outside!" I heard him yell. "Knock 'em down!"

Now all the witches were turned outward once again, and Sumiko O'Higgins moved to the center of the open space, practically atop the altar or whatever it was. She shouted a single command and all the women turned inward, facing her, fixing their gazes upon her. I was puzzled but a lot less worried. Artur, I thought, was learning even more than I was today.

"Oh, Satan, King of All!" she shouted, and seemed to assume that trancelike state once more. "Mass thy power in thy servant's hands, that these unbelievers be brought to heel!"

Artur's troops formed a circle outside the witches' circle and prepared to let loose again. I braced for whatever would happen and watched as the witch-queen's head suddenly shot skyward, eyes open but still in some sort of hypnotic state; her arms were outstretched, as if they were weapons aimed at the *besils*. She started to turn now, opposite the circling beasts and soldiers, and while I could see nothing, heat began crackling around that flying circle, the kind of odd internal fire I'd seen once before, when Kronlon had fried. I looked briefly at the circle of women and saw their equally hypnotic gaze resting entirely on their leader.

"They're transmitting through her!" I gasped. "They're channeling their fear and hatred into O'Higgins!"

A number of missiles from the enemy were loosed and some reached their targets. A few women were struck and fell, bleeding, unconscious, or perhaps dead, but the rest never wavered, never even looked at their fallen sisters. The concentration was absolute.

One by one, as her invisible touch reached them, the soldiers of Zeis Keep were fried to dust in their saddles, or in some cases knocked completely out of the air. I saw that Artur himself had fallen back and was now shouting for the others to break rank and join him. It was all of three or four minutes since the attack had started, and less than half of his company remained.

"All right, witch!" he shouted. "As I said, might is all, and right now it is on your side! But when word of this reaches the Keeps, the force raised against you will be more powerful than this world has ever known! Enjoy your victory—for what it is worth!" And with that he was gone.

The witch-queen's arms came down and made another sign; then the spell or whatever was broken. Women staggered, some fell, and others now bent down to attend to their fallen comrades.

O'Higgins snapped out of her trance in an instant and was all command. "See to the wounded!" she shouted. "I want a fatality count as quick as possible!" She turned and stalked over toward the hut in which Ti and I were hidden.

"Wow!" Ti breathed. "I never saw or heard anything like *that* before."

She giggled. "That look on Artur's face was worth all of it, too! Many's the pawn at Zeis would've given his life to see this whippin'!"

"Don't sell him short," I told her. "He's lost a battle, not a war. He came up against a weapon he didn't know existed and he paid the price, but he's not licked by any means. He wasn't kidding when he threatened to come back with a super-army. They have to stamp out power like this or they'll never sleep easy again in their castles."

I saw Father Bronz emerge from a nearby hut looking suitably impressed. He and Sumiko O'Higgins quickly joined us in the hut.

"How many did you get?" she asked the priest.

"Six, maybe," he responded. "The rest had to be destroyed. Is it enough?"

"Hardly," she snapped. "But it'll have to do."

"Don't blame *me*," he retorted. "*You* shot 'em down. All I did was pick 'em back up."

I looked at the two in confusion. "What the *hell* are you two talking about?" I wanted to know. "Where *were* you during the battle, Father?"

He laughed. "Picking up the pieces. We needed *besils*. So while Sumiko and her witchy friends got the riders, I was able to grab control of six of them."

O'Higgins nodded. "That's what this was all about. That's why I permitted Artur to find the village in the first place. I'd hoped for more, though—at least a dozen."

"You'd've *had* a dozen if you hadn't fried or smacked down some," Bronz responded. "That was an amazing sight. Sumiko, I really underestimated you. Even when you told me last night I still couldn't believe that what you said was true, not in *that* way. Accumulated broadcasted Warden power! Incredible!"

She shrugged. "There's nothing in the rules against it. The Wardens don't really know the difference between a human cell, a plant cell, and a copper molecule, except that their genetic code or whatever they use for one acts on what they're in to keep it that way. If we can 'talk,' so to speak, to the Warden organism inside anything and tell it to do something it doesn't like to do—reprogram it, as it were—we can tell it to do other things, too. It's just like a computer, Augie. You can program it to do *anything* if you can figure out how."

"You're too modest," he replied sincerely, obviously not just flattering her. "It's a monumental discovery. Something entirely new, entirely different. It'll do for Lilith what the Industrial Revolution did for primitive man!"

She gave what I can only describe as a derisive snigger. "Perhaps," she responded, "*if* I decide to give it to people, and *if* it can be handled and managed on a planetary scale."

I was awestruck by the implications, which made Bronz's arguments against social revolution on Lilith obsolete. "But you have the means here to destroy the hierarchy! The pawns can have the power to run their own affairs!"

She sniffed. "And what makes you think they'll do the job any better than the ones doing it now? Maybe worse."

I shrugged off her cynicism as darker thoughts intruded. "He'll be back, you know. Artur, I mean. With a *hell* of a force. What are you going to do?"

"Nothing, dear boy," she responded. "Absolutely nothing. That surprises you? Well, would you believe that this place can't even be *detected* unless I wish it? Oh, they'll come back, of course. Maybe even with a couple of knights or even the old Duke himself. They'll fly around and around and they'll comb the ground with troops and they'll simply not see us. It will drive them mad, but they can land right in the middle of the heath out there and they won't see the village. How do you think we survived *this* long?"

Bronz himself shook his head in amazement. "Sumiko, the consolidation of Warden power I'm willing to accept, since my mind can at least explain it, but that's impossible!"

She laughed wickedly and tweaked his cheek. "Augie, you're a fine little fellow even if you are everything I can't stand, but keep believing that, won't you? It'll make life a lot simpler."

"But *how*, Sumiko?" he demanded to know. "*How?*"

She just smiled and said, "Well, the only thing I can tell you that'll get you thinking is that the Warden organism is in every single molecule of every cell in your body, the brain included. I haven't discovered any miracle formula here, Augie! All I did was sit down with the little beastie and learn how to talk to it properly."

"Father Bronz!" Ti shouted; he turned, then lit up as he saw her. She ran to him and gave him a big hug, which he returned, smiling. "Well, well, well!" he responded. "So we have our little Ti back with us once again!"

"And that points up the urgency of our getting a move on," Sumiko put in. "I'm going to go check the casualties and see what can be done. You all better get some rest—the defenses are already all reset. We have a long night's ride ahead of us, the first of many, and everybody should be well-rested."

Bronz stared at her. "We?"

She nodded. "I've been meaning for some time to find out what those old fools at Moab know that maybe I don't," she told us. "I think that now the cat's out of the bag about us here I had better find out all I can. Besides, I better be along to see that there are no relapses."

I glanced over at Father Bronz. "You're coming too, I hope. I'm not sure I want to face ten days with just the witches for protection."

He chuckled. "Sure. I intended to, in any event. It's been a great many years since I was at Moab, and my curiosity is aroused. But don't expect miracles down there. They know more about the Warden organisms than anybody except maybe Sumiko—now that I've seen her in action—but they are not selfless scientists. There have been some, uh, unfortunate changes over the years down there."

CHAPTER EIGHTEEN

Moab Keep

The worst part of the journey was riding the *besils* themselves. The creatures were ugly, they stank, and they oozed a really nasty gluelike ichor when under stress—not to mention occasionally giving out with one of those earsplitting shrieks that seemed to come from somewhere deep within them. We were all inexperienced riders, too, and the sensation was much like getting whipped in all directions at once, that apparently seamless, fluid motion of theirs feeling quite different if you were actually on a *besil* back.

Still, the creatures were selectively bred types, born and raised for this sort of work, and they seemed never to tire. They were also easy to care for, since they foraged for themselves in the jungle below, eating almost anything that wouldn't eat them first, plant or animal. Being large animals, though, they ate often, and that slowed us down. They needed three times their considerable weight per day to keep going at any reasonable pace.

Still, the kilometers passed swiftly beneath us, although I saw less of the countryside than I would have liked. In order to maintain security, and to avoid meeting a lot of possibly bad company, we headed almost due east to the coast and skirted it, somewhat out from land, heading in for an encampment only when and where the wild reached the sea and gave us cover. The ocean was dotted with numerous uninhabited islands, but none provided the large amount of food our *besils* required, so some risk was necessary.

Our witches afforded us some protection, of course. I suspect that was the only reason we encountered so little in the way of other traffic on the way south. But though we could take care of individuals who might chance upon us we had nothing like the massed force to withstand an assault of the type Artur had mounted on the witch village. Sumiko couldn't even take her full "core" coven, since the most we could safely fit on and strap into a *besil* saddle was two, and Ti and I had one, O'Higgins and Bronz each had one of their own, and the other three held two of the aproned witches apiece. We had no control over the *besils* ourselves, either; Bronz and O'Higgins did the driving for all of us.

Days were spent in foraging, resting, and checking bearings. It was not

a totally friendly group, with the witches paying little mind or heed to Ti
or me and Father Bronz devoting most of his time, apparently without success. to trying to discover the nature of Sumiko O'Higgins's remarkable
discoveries about the Warden organism.

I confess I was never really sure about the witch queen. A genius, certainly, with the single-mindedness to set herself impossible problems and
then work them out. A pragmatist, too, who was putting her discoveries to
use building up some sort of superior army—for what it was hard to say.
Discussing the plants and animals of Lilith, the Warden organism, and
some rather odd ideas about the relationships between plant and animal
biochemistry, she was as expert and as dry as a university professor. But
whenever you started feeling that her Satanism was a sham, a device to accomplish some kind of psychological goal with her followers, or simply a
means to an end, she would drop into a discussion of it with an unmistakable fervor and sincerity. Ti and I talked about her at length, and both
of us were convinced that either she was one of the truly great actresses of
all times or she really believed that junk.

I was able to pump Father Bronz a bit more on her, although he admitted his own knowledge was sketchy. She was the daughter of scientists,
experts in the biological aspects of terraforming, and from what little we
could gather, was something of an experiment herself, having been genetically manipulated in some way in an attempt to produce a superior
being, an alternative to the civilized worlds for a rougher, frontier life.
They had certainly produced *someone* unique, but I wondered what the
psychological effects of growing up knowing you were just experiment
77-A in Mommy and Daddy's lab might be. Exactly what the crime was
that got her sent to Lilith was unknown, but it was of truly major proportions and left inside her a legacy of hatred and revenge directed toward
the civilized worlds. In point of fact, she was the quintessential Lord of
the Diamond personality I'd come to expect, yet she disdained even that.
To her, Marek Kreegan and the Confederacy were two sides of the same
coin.

The relationship between Ti and me continued to develop, and I felt
things within me that I had never known were there. In some ways it disturbed me—that a man of pure intellect could form such strong emotional
attachments seemed somehow an admission of my weakness, an internal
accusation that I was human when I had always clung to the notion that I
was a superior human being above all those animalistic drives affecting the
common herd. She was certainly not the type of woman I had ever
thought myself attracted to. Bright, yes, but totally uneducated, highly
emotional, and in some sense very vulnerable.

Still, I felt better with her here, awake, laughing and oohing and
aahing and having fun like a kid with a new toy. It was as if I'd had a
painful hole inside me, one that had been there so long that I wasn't even
aware of it, had considered the ache and emptiness normal and not at all
unusual, but now the hole was filled. The relief, the feeling of health and

wholeness, was indescribably good. We were complementary in some ways, too—she was my hold, my perspective, on Lilith, where I would live out my life, and I was her window to a wider and far different universe than she could now comprehend.

It took eleven days to reach Moab, with a little dodging of congested areas, neither pushing ourselves or taking chances. Moab Keep itself was below us now, a huge island in a great, broad tropical bay. Almost on the equator, it was insufferably hot and humid; but, looking down upon it, I could see why it had been selected.

The first manned expedition to Lilith had no idea what it would be getting itself into. It needed a base, one that would provide a good sample of the flora and fauna of Lilith without exposing the group to unknown dangers. The huge island of Moab was their choice, a place large and lush enough to provide a small lab and base for travel to other parts of the world but isolated enough with its high cliff walls and broad expanse of bay all around to be defensible against attack.

Time and knowledge had reshaped it only slightly. You could see cleared areas for agriculture, and lines of fruit trees too straight and regular to be haphazard. On a bluff almost in the center of the island was the headquarters for those who still lived and worked on the island. The hard rock of the bluff itself had been hewn out by the most primitive labor methods to build what was needed, a great rock temple that looked neither crude nor uncomfortable. In fact, it made Zeis's Castle seem like a small and fragile structure, although Moab had none of the fanciful design of Sir Tiel's edifice. It was straight, modern, utilitarian, functional—and huge.

Still, Father Bronz had warned us that this was not exactly all it seemed. The science of the founders was still here, for sure, and there was no authoritarian hierarchy such as the other Keeps maintained, but the purpose for the enclave had drastically changed as it became more isolated from the outside world. Today the thousands of men and women below carried on their work in the name of some odd mystical religion that seemed anachronistically out of the dawn of man. In their years of studying Lilith they had come not merely to anthropomorphize it, as Father Bronz tended to do, but actually to regard it as a living, thinking creature, a god now sleeping that would someday awaken.

In other words, here was another nut cult, although one not formed from the history of humanity but rather by the conditions of Lilith itself.

We landed atop the great bluff and immediately attendants came from stairwells to attend to the *besils*. For a moment I thought we were being attacked, so rapidly did they come forth, but it quickly became obvious that we were on the Moab equivalent of a helipad.

I took note of the appearance of the attendants. Many were of civilized worlds standards, and all had some of the look within them. Many were naked, others lightly dressed, and all seemed young, yet none of them had the look or bearing of pawns. All were neatly groomed and had that scrubbed look.

Father Bronz, the only one of us who had been here before, took the lead, and we followed him to one of the nearby stairwells.

"I have to say that they don't seem at all worried or even curious about us," I noted to him. "It's almost as if we were expected."

"We probably are," he replied. "Remember, these people know all we've been able to find out about this crazy world. Their grandparents were the original colonists, and they and their children discovered the Warden organism, the Warden powers, the various drugs and potions we all use. They designed and perfected the methods by which anything can be done here." He glanced over at Sumiko O'Higgins. "They're unassailable and they know it. Even from you, my dear, I think."

She just looked at him expressionlessly and didn't reply. Even though I owed my life and my existence here to her I would never feel comfortable around her and would certainly never completely trust her.

We were met at the bottom of the long, winding stone stairs by a woman in flowing pure-white robes. She didn't look very old, but her billowing hair was snow white and her eyes a deep blue, while her complexion showed that she just about never ventured out into the sunlight. It was an odd appearance, sort of like one of Father Bronz's angels.

"I bid you greetings, Father Bronz, you and your friends," she said, her voice soft and musical.

Bronz gave a slight bow. "My lady, I am happy to see that I am remembered," he responded somewhat formally. "May I present my companions to you?"

She turned and looked at us, not critically, but not curiously, either. "I already know them all. I am Director Komu. I will see you all to quarters that have already been prepared for you where you may rest and refresh yourselves. Later on today I will arrange for a tour of the Institute, and tomorrow is soon enough to get down to business."

I looked at her, then at Ti. "Lady Komu, I thank you for your hospitality," I said, trying to be as politely formal as seemed required here, "but my own young lady here has need of medical assistance. She's already been feeling particularly sleepy and numb."

The director went over to Ti and looked at her thoughtfully for a moment, not touching or doing anything we could see. Finally she said, "Yes, I see. Please don't worry about it—we will fix you up in no time at all." She turned. "Now, if you will follow me."

The place inside was, if anything, more impressive than outside. The walls and floors were all tiled in light, micalike panels that seemed slightly translucent and behind which some light source glowed. It wasn't electrical, of course, but neither was it the kind of localized and flickering light that oil lanterns would give off. In fact the place looked as if it were back in the Outside. I was about to ask about it when Sumiko O'Higgins beat me to it.

"This is most impressive, particularly the lighting," she noted. "How do you do it?"

"Oh, a simple matter, really," the director responded airily. "The light source is a lumen distilled from various self-illuminating insects common to Lilith. The power source is somewhat complex, but based very much on the same principle the insects themselves use to brighten the material. The basis of the power is friction, fed by water power. Whoever told you such things were impossible on Lilith, dear?"

There was no reply to that, and I was beginning to see that I would have to revise my world picture once again. There certainly *wasn't* anything in the rules governing Lilith to prohibit a lot of classical power sources; the limitation was that there were very few people who could talk the Warden organism into holding in new shapes of waterwheels and the like.

Our rooms were luxurious, furnished with fine hand-carved wood and a large bed that was as close to a stuffed mattress as I had seen on Lilith. The common baths were similar to those at the Castle, large tile-lined troughs filled with very hot, bubbly water that soothed as well as cleaned. I felt both more human and totally relaxed at the finish, and Ti had quite a time with the first bath she'd ever experienced other than those in pools of rainwater or rivers. She was tired, though, and I just about had to carry her back to the room. She was awake enough to find the bed too soft and strange for her liking and for a while considered sleeping on the floor, which she finally did. As soon as she was asleep, though, I placed her on the satiny sheets and stretched out beside her. I hadn't realized what sort of tension I'd been under the past almost two weeks, though, and I was soon out cold.

CHAPTER NINETEEN

The Wizards of Moab Keep

We toured the huge Institute, as they called it, as evening fell. Not Ti— she was still tired and her body was continuing to fight Dr. Pohn's handiwork, so I decided to let her sleep.

Everyone at the Institute seemed to live well, in Lilith terms. They seemed bright, alive, highly civilized, and happy. We saw the laboratories used by plant and animal experts to study all they could, revealing cleverly fashioned if primitive tools of the trade, including wooden microscopes whose lenses were actually quite good, and to my surprise, even a limited number of metal tools that looked like they'd been manufactured in major factories. I remarked on them, and was reminded that Lords such as Kreegan could actually stabilize a limited amount of alien matter, making it resistant to the Warden organism's attack. The intrasystem shuttle-craft, for example, that had landed me on Lilith and carried me to Zeis Keep was one such example, and a pretty hairy and delicate one at that.

The food prepared for us was also excellent, although I recognized almost nothing except the melons. I was told that the meat was from certain kinds of domesticated large insects; specially bred types of plants and plant products provided many of the other dishes and a variety of beverages that, if not really beer and wine, served as excellent substitutes.

It seemed to me that the full potential of Lilith was exercised only here, at the Institute. Comfort, civilization, worthwhile work—all were possible here. This world didn't need to be the horror house it primarily was, not if those with the power were to use it more wisely and well.

Why, I began to wonder, wasn't it, then?

The next morning Ti was taken down to their Medical Section, which was a much more complex setup than Dr. Pohn's, although the doctors there used some of the same techniques for a lot of the routine measurements. The doctor, a woman named Telar who frankly didn't look much older than Ti, let alone old enough to be a doctor, placed Ti on a comfortable but rigid table, felt key points all over her body, then touched her patient's forehead in that classic manner and closed her eyes briefly. Less than thirty seconds later she nodded, opened her eyes again, and smiled.

Ti, who was neither drugged nor instructed to do anything more than lie still, looked puzzled. "When will you start?" she asked nervously.

Telar laughed. "I've finished. That's it."

We both stared. "That's *it*?" I echoed.

She nodded. "Oh, I'd like to take a quick look at you as well. You never know."

"That's all right," I told her. "I'm fine." I started making all sorts of excuses at that point, since I was just reminded that there was something extra up there somewhere in my brain, an organic transmitter I might not have worried about if it had been anywhere else—but this doctor would spot it for sure.

Frankly, I hadn't really thought of it much since the early days. I don't even know why I didn't take advantage at that point of the opportunity to have it removed, to make myself a totally free and private agent. Perhaps, after thinking of you up there for a while as an enemy, I was now reluctant to cut this last umbilical to my former life and self. To cast it out, and you with it, would be the final and absolute rejection of everything I'd lived for all my life, and I wasn't quite willing to do that as yet. Not yet. If the information went directly to Intelligence, that would be one thing, but it went to me—that other me sitting up there somewhere, looking in. My Siamese twin.

Not yet, I decided. Not yet.

Classes started shortly after. They decided that both Ti and I would undergo as much training as we could take, although separately, of course. Only the basic stuff could be group-administered, and I'd already had that. I was curious to see what Ti might come up with, and hopeful, too.

I had been somewhat nervous when told that they were a religious cult, but aside from a few offhand references and the fact that there were occasional prayers, like before meals, and temple hours, when the staff went off somewhere and did whatever they did, there was no pushing of the faith, no mumbo-jumbo, and no attempt either to convert us or to indoctrinate us with their beliefs. Their religion interested me no more than the faiths of Bronz or O'Higgins did, and I was thankful for its lack of intrusiveness.

Of the others who had come with us I saw nothing. About two weeks into the training I was informed that the witches had gone, returning to their strange village, but Father Bronz was said to be involved in some project of his own at the Institute, something that required the use of their massive handwritten library scrolls and some of their lab facilities. I wondered idly whether he, now seeing that it was possible, was trying to crack the O'Higgins secret.

I made easy progress in the use of the power itself, but I began to realize that things would still be very slow, since, as Ti's example had so graphically pointed out, just having the power to do something wasn't enough. You needed the knowledge to apply it properly, and that could take years.

Still, a lot could be done in general terms, and it became absurdly easy for me to do so. Weaving patterns, duplicating patterns as I had with the chair, were simple as long as we were talking inanimate objects. O'Higgins had likened the Warden organism to some sort of alien organic computer, and that was a pretty good analogy. But not a lot of little computers, all components in a single, massively preprogrammed organism.

"Think of them," one of my instructors said, "as cells of Mother Lilith. Your own cells all contain DNA spirals encoded with your entire genetic makeup. Also, one part of that complex code tells that particular cell how to behave, how to form and grow and act and react as part of the whole. The Warden cells, as we call them, are like those in your own body. They are preprogrammed with an impossibly complex picture of how this planet should be, and each one knows its own place or part in that whole. What we do is slightly mutate the Warden cell. Essentially, we feed it false data and fool it into doing what we want instead of what it wants. Because our action is extremely localized when compared to the whole of Lilith, and because we can concentrate our willpower on such a tiny spot, we are able to do so. Not on a large scale, of course, but on a relatively localized scale."

I looked around at the sumptuous surroundings of the Institute. "Localized?"

My instructor just nodded. "Consider the mass of the planet. Consider the number of molecules that go into its composition. A colony of Wardens for every molecule. Now, do you think this is more than a tiny aberration, a benign cancer, as it were?"

I saw the point.

The more I practiced, the easier everything became. Although I was a little put off when I discovered that most of the silky cloth I'd seen was made from worm spit, I soon dismissed that as another cultural prejudice and had my own clothing with the option and ability to make more. Burning holes in rock and shaping those holes to suit my design also proved very easy: you just told the Wardens governing the molecules to disengage. Unfortunately, the skill aspect again came into play here, and I decided that I was cut out to be neither an engineer nor an architect. What I had done to Kronlon, the Institute considered an abuse of power, since what it seemed to amount to was an overloading of the Warden input circuits. They burned themselves out in some manner.

Classes in combat emphasized defense, but took a lot of the mystery out of what I'd seen. Knowing the proper points in an opponent's nervous system was as important in the mental combat of Warden cells as in physical stuff like judo. The trick was to keep total control over your own Wardens while knocking out those of your opponent, a really nasty task requiring not only that you have more willpower and self-control than your opponent but also that you have an enormous ability to concentrate on several things at once.

I learned as much as I could learn, and although I felt elated when they no longer gave me the potion and I grew stronger still, I realized that only experience could fine-tune my skills. The key test of my power was when they brought two small steel rods from Medusa, which, though containing Warden organisms as well, was a thing alien to our Lilith parent strain and beyond my ability to communicate with.

I was aware, though, that Warden cells were already attacking the alien matter, much as antibodies attacked a virus in the bloodstream, trying to break it down, even eat it, in some mysterious way.

Here there was no pattern to solve or imitate. I somehow had to work out a form of protection, some sort of message that would keep this metal from corroding to dust under the Warden cell onslaught. I failed miserably time after time. There seemed nothing to grab on to, nothing I could even reprogram to protect the alien matter, which even to me had a somewhat dark, dead appearance in contrast to all of the Warden-alive matter around me.

After two days the stuff crumbled into dust.

I was discouraged, feeling somehow inadequate. To have come so far and not to go the last little bit to rank me near the top in potential on this world was tremendously depressing. If I could not solve this last problem, I knew I would be no match for the Dukes, let alone for Marek Kreegan.

Ti tried to console me. But, living here at the Institute at a higher level than she'd ever dreamed of, or known was possible, she had a more limited ambition than I. Her own lessons had helped somewhat; as both Sumiko O'Higgins and Dr. Pohn had intimated, the power was at least latent in everyone. But even with all the training, her power was limited more to the Supervisor level, although she certainly could use it more discriminatingly and effectively than the Supervisors I'd known. The only thing they could offer beyond that was something of the witch methods: if she were truly consumed with emotion toward something, her power could be multiplied; but to make it controlled and effective she'd need temporary augmentation from the potion. Even then it would be only a destructive power and very limited.

This aspect worried me a bit at first, since she *was* highly emotional and I was more than a little concerned that lovemaking would cause problems. Occasionally it did, but not anything serious, since she would never aim anything destructive, even subconsciously, at me. If ever we had a falling out, I was strong enough on reflex alone to protect myself. Still, occasionally when we *did* make love and her power ran a bit wild, the earth really *did* move.

Her powers, particularly with my help, allowed her to create her own clothes, which was particularly important to one brought up in the pawn world of the Keeps, where clothing was status. Still, she had enough of an understanding of the Warden power to understand my problem and my frustration, and did think of it. In fact she came up with part of the solution.

"Look," she said to me one day, "the problem is that Warden cells ridin' dust and everything else in the air just rush in to eat this metal stuff, right?"

I nodded glumly. "And I can't stop it because that metal stuff, as you call it, doesn't have anything I can talk to, let alone control."

"Why not talk to the attacking stuff, then?" she wanted to know. "Why not talk them out of it?"

I was about to respond that that was a ridiculous idea when I suddenly realized it wasn't crazy at all. Not in the way she meant, of course, but suddenly I saw the key; it was so ridiculously simple I didn't know why I hadn't thought of it before.

Talk to the attacking cells . . . Sure. But since the attack was continuous and from all quarters, just protecting something the size of a nail would be a full-time job. But if the metal was coated in some Lilith substance and the Warden cells in that coating were told not to attack . . . Accomplishing that would not be all that easy. In fact, the process was hideously complex, but it was the right answer. When you extended the concept to a really complex piece of machinery, it became a nightmare, clearly, a lot of practice and hard thought was needed.

The Institute people were pleased, and so was I, though. Few were ever able to master the stabilization of metals on *any* scale, and I felt as if the Confederacy had certainly made its point about me. I knew now that what they'd done was feed Marek Kreegan's entire file into their computers, and that alone was why I had been selected. My life, profession, outlook, you name it, had most paralleled his—therefore I was most likely to attain the potential of Lord.

I *had* learned, though, that I was not the only one with that power and potential besides Kreegan. A number of people, as many as forty or fifty, would qualify. Kreegan simply embodied not only the greatest single power on the planet but also the greatest single power who had the will and capacity to rule and the skills to pull it off. And that, of course, was what it all boiled down to—not power, but skill. The question was brought home to me by one of my most advanced instructors when she asked, "Well, now that you have joined the circle of the elect, what will you do with your powers?"

It was a good question. I now had the power, all right, all of it. I didn't have to fear this planet and its petty leadership any longer, and I had a good deal to live for, embodied in Ti and my hopes for a comfortable future.

But just what *were* our skills? Ti was trained mostly to run a nursery, to look after small children, and I certainly intended her to exercise that skill with our own children. But what *could* I do? What was I trained to do? Kill people efficiently. Solve sophisticated technological crimes—here on a planet where the technology was not at issue. In point of fact, the only jobs on a world like this I was in any way qualified for were ones like Artur's, but the challenge of fighting for the sport of my employers didn't appeal to me. In defense of employers or for a cause, yes, but not just to let out aggressions and give the violent folks something to do.

It was the same problem that had faced Marek Kreegan at this stage in his own life, I reflected, and his own conclusion was the only one that I, too, could reach. We were more alike than even I had realized, and our faces somehow seemed bound up together. What in fact did he have that I did not? Experience, of course. He'd worked his way up. I was already a Master, although a Master of nothing in particular. The next step, administratively speaking, was Knight. From Knight to Duke. And finally, with all that experience behind me, from Duke to Lord.

For the first time I understood a bit of Marek Kreegan. He hadn't necessarily come to Lilith to take over and run it. He had become the Lord of Lilith, one of the Four Lords of the Diamond, simply because he wasn't qualified to do anything else. It was absurd, but there it was. Kronlon's own words came echoing back once more. None of us has any choice.

It had been twelve weeks since we'd come to Moab Keep, and I was beginning to realize there was nothing more they could teach me here. The next step was up to me, and my own destiny lay elsewhere. So far I'd learned a great deal about myself but almost nothing that I'd been sent here for. I knew nothing at all about the aliens, nor did I even know what Marek Kreegan looked like these days. To go further I would have to take a knighthood, and to do that I'd need an army and some advisors closer to the scene of things.

Once again I sought out Father Bronz.

The priest looked fit and well-rested and seemed happy to see me. We shook hands and then embraced warmly. I realized that, although he'd kept his distance from me, he nonetheless had kept careful track of my progress.

"So—a Master now, with the potential of a Lord!" he laughed. "I told you I wanted to be remembered when you took over!"

I returned the laughter. "But that's a long way off," I responded. "Marek Kreegan must be getting old now, so he might not even be around by the time I feel confident enough to take him on. Still, I have to take the first step, and for that I'll need help."

"You're going to try for a knighthood, then," he said matter-of-factly. "I could have guessed as much. But your normal channel is denied you. You can't apprentice yourself to some Knight as a Master and bide your time. Nobody's going to take you on."

"I thought of that," I told him. "No, I'll have to go for it in one stroke. I'll have to take on a force, defeat it, and then face down the Knight."

"A good trick," Bronz admitted. "And where are you going to get the fighting force to get in the front door?"

"I've thought about that. It seems to me that I've only got one avenue to take there, and I'll need your help. You and I watched, many long weeks ago, a relatively small and unarmed force take on and defeat an elite corps. I think the whole bunch of them could take an army."

"Perhaps," he replied thoughtfully, "but she'd never go for it. Her whole force to take a Keep so a *man* could rule? You saw Sumiko."

"I saw her. Saw her and studied her. I think she's itching for a fight. I think that's why she came here, to perfect her methods. I think she'd welcome such a test."

"At random, yes," he said. "Just for the hell of it, or to prove her theories. But not for you, Cal me boy. Not for you."

"If her test is Zeis Keep?"

He stood there, dumbstruck at the idea. Finally he said, "You don't want to take the easy way out, do you? Zeis isn't a small, weak nothing of a Keep—it's one of the big ones. Important enough to be designated a shuttle landing point, which is why all the bigwigs pass through there. And you've got Artur fighting defense on his home ground. Remember the *geography* of that place?"

"I remember," I told him. "Still, it *has* to be Zeis. I think Dr. Pohn is the one individual object of her hatred that would tempt her, don't you? And from the point of view of location, it's close enough for her without a lot of logistical problems."

He considered the proposal. "She might buy it," he admitted, "but are you sure you can take *her?* Once she fights for Zeis and wins, if she *can* take it, do you think she's going to hand the place over to you?"

"I don't know," I responded honestly. "I don't even know if I can take Boss Tiel. I've never even met him. But I think I have to try."

"I think you do," Bronz concluded, more to himself than to me. "I don't know. I'll send out some feelers to Sumiko and see if she'll buy it, or at least agree to talk about it. And I think I can reach Duke Kisorn, at least. Talk him into letting you try."

"But what about Marek Kreegan? Will *he* stay out of it? After all, he's the man who put the price on my head to begin with."

"Oh, I'm sure Kreegan will keep hands off," Father Bronz told me confidently. "He'll want to see just what you can do at this stage, in order to evaluate the true threat to himself and his own power. But *if* we talk Sumiko into this, and *if* you or she beats Tiel, and *if* you can beat her, *then* you will have to worry about Kreegan. You sure you want to start this? That's a lot of ifs, and once you start, you aren't going to be able to stop. You'll be the initiator, and responsible."

"You think I'm nuts, don't you?" I asked him. "You think I should just settle down here and read all the books and raise a family and say to hell with it, don't you?"

"I didn't say that," Bronz replied in a tone that implied exactly that.

"I can't," I told him. "I'm just not made that way."

"We'll see." Father Bronz sighed deeply. "I'll start the wheels in motion. May God have mercy on your soul."

CHAPTER TWENTY

Council of War

It all came together so easily and quickly that I was almost suspicious about it.

The witch's village seemed to have changed not at all from the last time I'd been there, although now I was far more sensitized to the entire Warden environment and everything looked a little new and different. I felt a mild, discomforting dizziness that I couldn't really put my finger on. Father Bronz explained to me that he'd felt it from the first visit, an aftereffect of the process by which Sumiko O'Higgins stayed hidden from the outside world.

"They take turns," he told me. "One of them at Master grade and a coven of twelve others, all satiated with Sumiko's juice, standing ever vigilant. Nothing short of a planetary satellite photo would be able to see what's down here, and even that doesn't seem to work—the place is well camouflaged from the air, and a couple of distorting inversion layers add to the effect. That's why she chose the place."

She'd been confident that Artur would not be able to return and find it after his defeat, and she'd been right. Basically, it was a message sent by that particular guardian pack of thirteen to all around simply not to notice the place. It was neither invisibility nor any form of telepathy, but it was a formidable mental barrier all the same.

From what Father Bronz was able to tell me, O'Higgins seemed more than delighted with the idea. She said something about needing a "test piece" anyway. Furthermore, she held particular grudges against Zeis Keep not only because Dr. Pohn was there but also because Artur had killed two of her witches in the attack.

But even though she had replaced the two dead ones, there was still a strong numerical problem in going against Zeis. Many of her procedures were far more effective defensively than offensively, since techniques such as the circle, which I'd seen in operation, and the "mind clouding" were not really much use to a mobile, advancing force. They would be able to take out *some* of Artur's forces, but not all; in close quarters her pawns, even amplified slightly, would be no match for Artur's trained and experienced Supervisors and Masters. Their strength was a group strength. Artur now knew this, having been bloodied, and would take measures to counter it. With perhaps a thousand witches Sumiko was invulnerable, but with a hundred and sixty-nine she needed support.

Again it was Father Bronz, showing a most interesting bent for Machiavellian political maneuvering, to the rescue. At our final meeting were not only the priest, the witches, and myself but also three strange women wearing colorful, flowing garb. Except for their manners and dress they looked rather ordinary, with common backgrounds of the civilized worlds in their features. Nonetheless, the immediate impression was that these were no ordinary inhabitants of Lilith, not even Masters. They were . . . something else.

As we sat around eating small, tasty pastries and drinking mild local wine, Father Bronz made the introductions. First Sumiko, then me; then he turned to the three strange women.

"May I introduce Boss Rognival of Lakk Keep," he said, pointing to the most overdressed of the women, "and her administrative assistant, the Lady Tona, and her sergeant-at-arms, the Lady Kysil."

Although they were all fighting for their own interests rather than for mine, I never really felt so left out of an operation that would decide my future as I did at this one. I stared at the three women in curiosity not only as to what they were doing here but also because I'd never seen a knight before. Except for the slight fur trim and a small jewel on a headband of some kind, she didn't look so superhuman. I had to admit, though, that the Warden power burned and shone a little brighter inside her. The map in my head clicked in again, and I saw that Lakk Keep was a very small one several kilometers due west of Zeis—across that formidable-looking swamp.

"Let's get down to business," Rognival said sharply, her tone tough and crisp. "We are going to attack and take Zeis Keep. The witch here has her own reasons and some old grudges to settle; the young man over there has ambition, and I—well, let's just say that Lakk is a very small Keep almost surrounded by a pretty lousy swamp. It wasn't always that way. I used to have four kilometers square of choice *vai* cropland on what is now the Zeis side of the swamp. Tiel and Artur took it as well as the pawns that worked it from me over nine years ago, reducing me to the island of Lakk, which though it has several melon orchards and some *snark* pastureland, is hardly self-sufficient. I became, in effect, Tiel's vassal, and I've hated him for it. Until now, though, I've had insufficient forces to attack across the swamp, and I no longer have the clout necessary to get allies. You're my chance to get back my land, my self-sufficiency, and my self-respect."

O'Higgins warmed a little to her. I could see Father Bronz's thinking in all this—a female knight who hated Zeis. Perfect.

Too perfect, I decided instantly. Something smelled wrong about this. *Very* wrong. It seemed all too convenient, all too pat. I felt uneasily that somebody was setting me up, and that somebody had to be Father Bronz.

Ever since I'd escaped from Zeis and found him, he had been in total charge of my life, a charge he seemed willing and eager to accept. As much as anything the Cal Tremon who sat in the council here was by now a product of Bronz's own machinations, as was this whole carefully orchestrated exercise. What the hell *was* his game, anyway?

I'd done what checking I could given my limited contacts with others on this world, and they'd all borne out the image of a roving Master, a priest not merely deposed but defrocked by his church, who had been around as long as everybody could remember. And yet it was that last that bothered me. Nobody ever remembered the priest saying a service or a mass or whatever it was they did, nor carrying out any real priest-type functions at all. I certainly had never seen him do so, nor did we have anything but his word as to his life Outside, his background and reason for being here.

Still, if he were with Boss Tiel and Kreegan and that bunch, why had he gone to so much trouble over me? Why not just turn me in and get on with it? If he was someone high up on the social scale masquerading as a lowly priest, why make certain I reached the Institute and received the best training and experience possible on Lilith? If he had his own ambitions I would be a threat to him, if not at this point then some time in the future.

But if indeed he was what he said he was, what were his motives? A staunch defender of the system on Lilith, he nonetheless was using its greatest threat, the witches, to put into power a man who hated that system mainly me.

I looked around at their faces as they earnestly discussed the coming campaign. I paid only slight attention to what they were saying, as, ironically, I was the least important person at this council of war in terms of the outcome, although of course I would fight. O'Higgins, the possibly Lord-class psychopath with the power to amplify, combine, and direct

Warden power at will. Rognival, who wanted revenge for her earlier loss and her territory back. Bronz . . .

In thinking of him I'd once used the term Machiavellian. If I remembered my studies at all, that ancient mind was never the leader himself but merely an advisor—an advisor who was the *real* ruler while his prince took all the heat and did all the dirty work. Was I perhaps his prince-designate? Or were all three of us somehow in that category? With patience and almost diabolical cleverness, could he perhaps dream of controlling the whole sector indirectly through its rulers, then, perhaps with O'Higgins' discoveries, going on to take the whole planet? What could even a Marek Kreegan do about it? He would only strike at princes, never at the wandering priest and advisor.

It was a good plan, perhaps a brilliant one. I told myself that if I survived all this and attained the knighthood, I wouldn't be quite the pawn in his game that he counted on.

The council broke up in seemingly good spirits, having arrived at a plan that looked pretty good—at least in theory. We would see how well it worked out when human beings faced down each other.

Returning to the hut where Ti and I were spending our time until the dawn of battle, I was surprised not to find her there. She had little interest in or understanding of the battle strategy, and the witches were only mildly communicative, but she'd certainly gone somewhere and all I could do was wait.

It was close to dark when she returned, looking a little haggard and worried. "What's wrong?" I asked, concerned. "Where have you been?"

"Spying," she sighed and sank down.

"Huh? How's that?"

She nodded. "I don't like these women," she told me. "There's something creepy about 'em." She looked up at me, concerned. "When is the battle?"

"Three days from now," I told her. "At dawn."

She shook her head. "This O'Higgins may've been nice an' all, but she's real crazy, Cal. I went over an' got real close to one group havin' a meeting of some kind. They never saw me, don't worry. Anyways, I had to listen real hard, but I heard most of it." She shivered.

I frowned. "What did you hear that upset you so much?"

She leaned forward, whispering as low as she could. "They ain't gonna keep to their side, Cal. Once they win, they're gonna kill you *and* Father Bronz. They'll give that lady knight whatever she wants to keep her off their backs for a while, but they mean to take Zeis for themselves. They were talkin' about the beginnin' of the purge. What's a purge, Cal?"

I told her.

She nodded. "That's kinda what I thought. The purge of Lilith, they said. Near as I can make out, it means they're gonna kill all the men in Zeis and turn it into a witch's keep."

I had the sinking feeling I'd known most of this all along. I just hadn't

wanted to admit it. "Don't worry." I tried to console her with a confidence
I didn't feel. "Father Bronz and I aren't going to allow ourselves to get
cornered like that. And that old witch couldn't do it, anyway. Marek
Kreegan and the other top bosses would close in before she could get
started."

Ti shook her head violently from side to side. "You think so, but they
know that, too. They're nuts, not stupid. They say O'Higgins is already
more powerful than Lord Kreegan, and with the power juice—potion of
Satan, they called it—stronger than any army that could come against
them. They say she's so strong she's already stabilized two laster guns or
something like that from Outside."

Laster guns . . . "Laser pistols?" I prompted, sounding a little weak despite my false front.

She nodded. "Yeah. That's it. Oh, Cal, what're we gonna *do?*"

All I knew to do at that moment was hold her tight and hug her and try
and make her worry fade just a little. But sometime in the next two days I
would have to have a long talk with Father Bronz.

The priest frowned. "She can stabilize laser pistols, huh? Then she *is* as
strong as Kreegan. That poses a problem." We were far outside the witch's
camp, officially in the danger zone but out of it as far as our current needs
went.

"That's not the half of it," I told him. "On a world like Lilith, a simple
small stungun would make you a king. A pawn could knock off a Lord if
there was the element of surprise. I know *I* could, and this world's full of
expert killers."

Bronz nodded thoughtfully. "It's a little late to change our game plan,
and I'm not sure she would allow it to be changed now. Still, we're not
without resources." His eyes brightened a bit and a ghost of a smile came
to his lips. "I have to say that I am not totally shocked or surprised by any
of this. I anticipated something like it, and I planned for it."

Instead of cheering me, his comment worried me a little more. "Just
who *are* you, Bronz? What's your game in all this?"

He sighed. "Cal, you have no reason to believe me, but several to trust
me. I could have killed you at any time, particularly in the early days
when you were ignorant and helpless. I didn't. I helped you and Ti, too,
as much as it was in my power to do so. Will you concede that?"

I nodded, not quite conceding the point.

"Then I must ask you to trust me until the battle's done," he went on.
"You must stay as far away from O'Higgins as possible. She's the only person that one of your power has to fear. Wait. When it's all over, all
worked out, you'll know everything, I promise. Know and understand everything, and profit by it."

"Whose side are you on, Father Bronz?" I asked suspiciously. "Can't
you at least tell me that?"

He smiled. "I'm on my side, Cal. You must understand that. But it is fortunate that your side and my side do not conflict but rather converge here. You have my solemn word on that. Trust me now, this one time more, and all will be clear."

"I'll try," I sighed, "because there's not much else I can do."

He laughed easily and slapped me on the back. "Come, let's go back. Why don't you go in and try to make a baby with that pretty mate of yours? It may be your last chance for a while. In two days' time that mind of yours will tell *you* the answer. I won't even have to explain it, I suspect. Just remember that I really *do* like you, son. You're going to be Lord of Lilith one day if you watch your back."

I just stared back at him and did not reply, but I couldn't help wondering if by that time the Lordship would be worth taking.

CHAPTER TWENTY-ONE

The Battle of Zeis Keep

A prince does not fight commoners. His own battle is reserved for those of equal or superior rank. As a result, my initial job in all this was to stand and watch. Only after the armies had done their worst and the battle decided would I myself face the challenge of entering the Castle through the front door and walking down that forbidden central hallway. Oddly, I would have preferred to have participated in the battle, since this was the sort of thing I'd devoted my life to. As much as it might shock some of the soft elements of the civilized worlds, I enjoyed it. But I'd graduated now, beyond being the lone assassin, beyond the foot soldier and cavalry. Now those others, the soldiers and fighters, sallied forth in my name.

We walked, Ti and I, down the cloud-covered path where, a short time ago that somehow seemed a lifetime, I had borne her still body past the guards and out of Zeis Keep. We were returning, under our own power and of our own free will, dressed as Master and Supervisor in the same color and design material, indicating we were a wedded pair.

Just after emerging from the clouds on the downslope, the whole of Zeis Keep was illuminated in the dawn-lit sky. It was the same impressive, fairy-talelike place I remembered.

I heard Ti give a sharp intake of breath. "It's *beautiful!*" she gasped, then looked over at me, apparently concerned that she was sounding too childlike. Finally she decided that she didn't *care*. "I was born down there," she said, pointing to the area of our old village. "There was a lot of bad there, but I'm part of *it* and it's part of *me*. Can you understand?"

I nodded, although there was no place that could claim my own soul as Zeis claimed hers. I was the product of an alien society of strange forms and structures made by computer design and formed and shaped by plastic. Still, I had a reaction as close to hers as I could come, and one that was totally alien to my old nature and lifelong philosophy. I pulled her against my side and hugged her. "This can all be ours," I breathed, wondering as I said it whether in that moment I had ceased to be what I had been and joined the race of Lilith.

We sat on a high ledge and relaxed. Ti was holding a woven basket made of some strawlike material, and she now pulled out its contents—a gourd pot, two smaller gourds, a flint, some of Father Bronz's *quar* leaves, which would burn hot but slow, and some of his tea. Runoff from the mountains caused small waterfalls all along, so water was no problem. Also in the basket were some of the small pastries and a cheeselike substance made from some insects in a manner I didn't ever want to know.

I had to chuckle. It seemed absurd to have a picnic while watching a battle.

An advance guard of witches had "swept" the trails prior to sunrise, so we weren't due for any unpleasant surprises—not, at least, until the battle started. We could see the whole area, from the swamps to the Castle, a perfect vantage point. Still, everything seemed very tiny and far away. I wished we were closer.

Ti rummaged in her basket and came up with two collapsing wooden tubes. I stared at them in wonder, then turned them over in my hands. They were small telescopes, actually monoculars.

"Where did these come from?" I asked her wonderingly.

She gave me a satisfied smirk. "I made friends with a supervisor from Lakk, the Lady Tona's *besil* pilot. When I spotted one on his belt, I asked about 'em, and got two. Thought we might need 'em."

I was impressed. I had the bad habit of continually underestimating Ti and mentally kicking myself for it later. I'd actually tried to get her to stay behind, but that proved impossible. I was beginning to think she deliberately cultivated that childlike vulnerability so that she'd have an edge on everybody else, Warden power or not.

I put one to my right eye and studied the field. "Things should be popping any moment now," I said tensely.

"Things are popping already," she responded. "Look down there, near Artur's fort. See?"

I trained my monocular on the spot, wishing I had something with better focusing and a stronger glass. "I don't see—wait! Yes, I do too!"

They were there, already lined up in a neat formation, the great hopping *vuks*, their huge bulks almost invisible at this distance against the green of the valley. Behind them a formidable array of foot soldiers stood in perfect military formation.

I shifted my glass to the *besil* pens cut in the mountain above the stockade and saw signs of frantic movement. They would come shooting out of there, I knew, at some signal from the ground. Idly I wondered where Artur would be.

Next I looked at the Castle. The great door was shut, I could see, and red flags were flying from the pointed towers. I thought I could see figures on those towers, but it was pretty far to be sure. What was certain was that no pawns were in the fields or anywhere to be seen. They had been withdrawn to the base of the mountains, as far from battle as possible, to await the outcome.

I studied the trail heads next, down on the valley floor below. During the night the witches had infiltrated and now they stood, linked in a line rather than a circle, facing inward, at each point.

There was no way to carry out any movements of this sort without your enemy knowing about it, so nobody had made much of a secret of their movements. The witches had dispatched the guard and stood in such a way that they might reinforce each other if necessary, but though Artur could probably wipe out any coven of thirteen with his forces, this would be an open invitation for the coming Lakk forces to overrun his rear. Artur, I decided, would take his chances with the divided witches until he met and defeated the Lakks. The way his forces were now moving, I was sure he intended to meet the invader as close to the swamps as possible, fighting in the air over the dank and treacherous terrain and forcing the Lakks to land on solid ground piecemeal. There they could be mopped up in small batches before they could regroup into a major fighting force.

What we'd seen in front of the stockade had merely been the reserves, a bit more than half his force that could be thrown in where needed or committed against individual groups of witches if need be. It was really good military thinking, and I could see at a glance why Artur was held in such respect and why Zeis was considered unassailable by Lakk.

But there were only seven roads into the Keep, and each was blocked by thirteen witches. That left seventy-eight witches, and those seventy-eight were a tremendous amplified and coalesced Warden force. Zeis was the model of what you'd want to defend in a military sense, but its strength lay in the impossibility of establishing a beachhead against it. If a large enough force could be landed on solid ground, it would be the defenders who would be rolled back into a trap, totally surrounded by mountains.

"There go the *besils!*" Ti shouted excitedly. I didn't need the monocular to see the great dark shapes flow out of their mountain stable lair. The riders were braced in special combat saddles that also supported long, pointed wooden lances. I looked out over the fog-shrouded swamp, seeing nothing for a moment. Then, out of the murky grayness, a long, slow line of *besils* appeared. Unlike Artur's *besils,* whose underbellies were dyed a reddish color, these were yellow underneath, the color of Lakk.

They came in slow and low, cautious until they had a full field of vision. Inside the valley, despite some wisps of ground fog, the eternal clouds had retreated past the thousand-meter mark, plenty of room for an aerial duel.

The Zeis *besils* neared the swamp, then stopped, their great wings beating so fast to keep them in place they were totally invisible. I never understood how anything that big flew, anyway.

The attacking formation split now, one-third going left, another third right, while the center column pushed ahead, accelerating suddenly and with great speed. Hundreds of black, swift shapes weaved in and out, parrying and thrusting, lances attempting to score a hit either at the underbelly of the enemy *besils* or at the riders atop them. It was a battle in three dimensions at crazy angles and speeds and with sudden whiplike motions.

While the vanguard of Zeis *besils* were occupied, the swamp itself seemed to come alive, eerie shapes moving to and fro in the fog. Emerging now were the great twelve-legged, hairy *snarks,* raised for fur and used in stews by the people of Lilith. These creatures of that swamplike terrain were somehow able to avoid sinking into the muck and mire by shifting their centers of gravity at will. Herbivores, they were totally harmless to people but they made effective troop carriers when a swamp was to be the battleground, and Lakk Keep had bred them for just that purpose.

The great, hopping, green *wuks* leaped into action from the Zeis side, aiming at going so high and landing so exactly that they would come down right on top of the fragile *snarks,* spilling them and their contents into the swamp. It should have worked, had the *snarks* contained combat soldiers, but this time was different.

The *snarks* stopped suddenly, as if waiting for certain death, but the proud and lordly *wuks* were the ones that seemed to reel in mid-hop as if struck by gunfire and topple over, out of control, to the ground below.

The *snarks* contained not soldiers but chemically enhanced witches, all concentrated on the center *snark,* where the leader was knocking *wuks* out of the air with a gesture. Seeing what was happening, Artur quickly shifted. Realizing from the pattern in which his *wuks* were falling that a central and single power was picking them off, he committed a section of his reserves to fan out across the entire basin, to keep a great distance from one another and to fan out over a wide enough front to divide the witches' fire. Their concentrated power had only one metaphorical barrel, and it couldn't point everywhere at once.

Besils, too, were screeching and falling all over the place, unable to help either side in the battle below but keeping the other from also doing so. It was bloody carnage all around, and Artur's plan was working to an extent. A *wuk* struck one of the witch-laden *snarks,* pulling up incredibly at the last minute so that it hit with its powerful hind legs out. The great spiderlike creature collapsed as if made of thin sticks, dragging its complement of passengers into the muddy quagmire—and diminishing Sumiko O'Higgins' power by a small amount. From where we were, it was impossible to see how many were on any given *snark,* but considering the number of the beasts it had to be four or five at least. The whole scene was stunning, an eerie ballet of death and destruction as it might have been centuries ago on mother Earth.

The *wuk* maneuver had weakened the witch force, but most of them had made solid land and were quickly descending and assembling into their groups. Some would not have their full complement, but since all worked with, through, and at the direction of Sumiko O'Higgins, however many managed to land would have impressive force indeed.

Suddenly the grass blazed in front of the landing witches, a huge wall of fire across the entire field, blinding everyone for a moment.

Warden power was being used against Warden power now, I knew.

After a moment's panic, the witches regrouped. Then, incredibly, a whirlwind of dirt like a great, gigantic plow shot up along the fire line, damping the fire, although small patches continued to burn. The witches advanced now, in a broad semicircle. I didn't know exactly how many there were, but it was fifty or more, I was sure. Sumiko had bragged that she could level the Castle with less.

Now fire was turned against the defenders. A terribly thin, bright wall of flame shot out from beyond the firebreak they'd just created, then started moving, widening out in an ever-increasing semicircle, pushing ground forces back and revealing large, dark holes that were obviously pits to trap invaders who advanced that far.

I frowned and turned my tiny telescope on the reserves, still sitting in front of the stockade. "He's going to lose," I muttered, more to myself than to Ti, "unless he sends those reserves in fast. They've got their beachhead. Why don't they move?"

Ti didn't answer, and I couldn't keep my eyes off the unfolding spectacle.

I turned again to the swamp, where hordes of *snarks* were now appearing, landing troops of Lakk behind the witches' screen. I looked again to the reserves, still poised but unmoving, and shook my head. "They can't be this incompetent," I told myself. "Why the hell doesn't he move before the beachhead is totally established?"

I heard Ti gasp. "The *besils* have stopped fighting!" she cried. "Look!"

I turned my gaze in that direction and saw that it was true. The survivors of the initial encounter, perhaps forty or so out of an initial hundred or more, had disengaged, but neither side was retreating.

"They—they're regrouping together!" I rasped, amazed. "What the hell . . . ?"

I heard the sound of a tremendous explosion below, its roar echoing back and forth across the mountains, its very existence so jarring that I was forced to look for it. An explosion? Here?

I looked at a great puff of smoke near the front of the witch line, then saw soldiers *behind* the witches wading into them and attacking them! Suddenly the reserves moved, the explosion an apparent cue. The reserve *besils* flew out of their mountainside nests and the *wuks* and ground troops started deploying—but not toward the invaders.

"Look, they're going after the witch groups guarding the trails!" I yelled, mouth agape. Still, I forced my attention back to the beachhead, only to see the unmistakable signs of slaughter. A wall of fire now trapped

the witches between their own defensive wall and the attackers, formed
and started to close in on them.

Disorganized and confused, the witches dropped their own firebreak
and started forward into Zeis proper, on the run. Now the *besils*, both yellow and red-colored, started moving in on them, dividing them. Bright
flashes told me that Warden power was being used on them, killing them
as they ran, as they tried to comprehend what was happening.

Below, the reserves were taking something of a beating from the power
of the covens, but it wasn't a hundred and sixty-nine witches to forty
besils now, as it had been back in the witch village. It was more like
twenty *besils* plus a dozen *wuks* and running, well-armed ground troops
against thirteen witches in each case. It was costly to take them out, but
even though they took half the attackers with them, the witches went
down—went down and were mercilessly hacked to death.

I put down the monocular and looked at Ti for a moment. She seemed
to sense it and turned to look at me, the stricken and confused look on her
face mirroring, I'm sure, my own.

"The Lakks attacked the witches," she said wonderingly. "The two
sides joined up. Cal, what's going *on* here? Have we been taken for
suckers?"

I shook my head dully. "No, honey. Well, yes, I guess we *have*. It's
kind of crushing, though, finally to understand all this. *Damn!*" I smacked
my fist in my other hand. "I don't know why I didn't figure it out from
the start—at least from a few days ago, when I had all the pieces."

"But they were fightin' for us, weren't they? They were gonna get us
Zeis Keep!"

I shook my head slowly and sadly and squeezed her hand. "Baby, I
doubt if *anybody* down there gives a damn about us one way or the other.
I doubt if they have since the decision was made to fight." I let her go and
smacked my fist in my left hand again. "Pawns!" I muttered. "God damn
it! All this way, all this far—and still pawns!"

She looked at me uncomprehendingly. "Wha . . . ?"

I sighed and got up. "Come on. Let's take a nice long walk down to the
Castle. Don't worry. Nobody's going to stop us or probably even notice
our existence."

With Ti still confused, we started on down.

CHAPTER TWENTY-TWO

First Lord of the Diamond

The extent of the carnage was enormous. The massacre of the witches had
been most thorough, more gruesome than any autopsy.

It took over two hours to reach the Castle, and by that time even the mop-up had been completed. Yellow and red forces were methodically surveying the field, helping those who could be helped, cleaning up the debris. It would be a long, tough job.

As I expected, Father Bronz and a number of others were sitting in wicker chairs outside the Castle's gates, relaxing, eating, and drinking. I recognized Vola and her sister, Dola, Boss Rognival and the Ladies Tona and Kysil, and Master Artur. The others were not familiar to me but wore designs indicating they were of Zeis. One of them—a small, frail-looking man, bald and wizened—was dressed as elaborately in ornate silken tunic, heavy boots; he wore atop his head a tiara with a single large blue gem similar to, but not identical to, the one Rognival wore. Another man, dressed in a manner similar to the older, thin one but wearing mostly gold colors, as well as a wide-brimmed hat, relaxed nearby. He was an older man, with neatly trimmed gray beard, certainly once of the civilized worlds. Although he was many years my senior he looked to be in nearly perfect physical condition.

Father Bronz spotted us. "Cal! Ti! Please come over!" he called pleasantly, and we did. Up close Bronz looked dead tired, and very, very old. He's put on at least ten years this morning, I thought. Still, he rose wearily from his chair, took my hand warmly, then kissed Ti on the forehead. Only then did he turn and nod toward the others.

"Some of these fine people you know," he began, "but I don't think you ever met Sir Honlon Tiel." The thin old man nodded in my direction, and I could only stare at him. So *that* was the knight I was to take on, I thought glumly. The Boss of Zeis Keep. The Warden cells glowed more in Artur than in him.

"The gentleman in gold there is Grand Duke Kobé," Bronz continued, and the other also nodded. He also introduced the others, but they were all of Zeis's ruling group. Then he turned back to me. "I assume you understand everything now?"

"Pretty much," I told him. "I can't say it makes me happy to be used in such a way, though. I feel like the child promised the new toy he's always wanted for his birthday, only to have nobody even come to his party, let alone getting the gift."

Bronz laughed. "Oh, come now! It's not all that bad."

"Will somebody," Ti interrupted in an even but slightly angry voice, "*please* tell me what the hell is going on here?"

I looked at her and sighed. "Ti, may I present Marek Kreegan, Lord of Lilith, First Lord of the Diamond?"

The fact that she gasped when Father Bronz bowed indicated she still had a lot to learn.

The full explanation came later, after we'd bathed, changed, and sat down to a sumptuous feast in the great hall of the Castle. Ti still hadn't recovered from the shock of Father Bronz's true identity, but given that, she had managed to figure out the basics, I'll give her that. And she was mad as hell.

Still, I wanted to hear the tale from the man who had planned it all.

"From the top, then," agreed Marek Kreegan. "Of course, we had a problem. Lilith, as I told you long ago, is a rigid ecosystem in which we humans play no part. Its economy is fragile, its ability to support a large population in the wild very much in doubt without Warden protection of the masses. The pawns don't enjoy a wonderful life—but who does? The ruling class, always, that's who. Because while everybody would love to be king, if everybody *was* a king there'd be no labor to support this monarch. The civilized worlds are no different, only thanks to technology on a massive scale the standard of living for their pawns is higher than is currently possible on Lilith."

"I still can't see the masses on the civilized worlds as pawns with a privileged class," I responded.

His eyebrows rose. "Oh? Were you born in that body?"

"You know I wasn't," I growled.

"Exactly. The Merton Process, right? Potential immortality for anybody and everybody, right? But will the masses get it? Of course not! For the same reason that cures for the big three diseases that kill people have been withheld. We are at maximum and the frontier can expand only so fast. New planets take decades to develop, particularly to the point of self-sufficiency. Cal, no system can survive if its population doesn't die. Nor is the Merton Process any cure-all, since you need a body for it. That means massive cloning—a couple of *trillion* clones. Ridiculous. They have to be raised and supported by some biomechanical means until needed. But the *leaders* of the Confederacy, now—that's a different matter. They're already immunized against diseases people don't even know are killing them. They get age-retardant processes like mad. And when they finally *do* wear out, they now have the Merton Process to keep 'em going for an infinite number of cycles. The masses count, in Confederacy society, only in the plural. Masses. Averages. Everything's an average. Only the elite get the plums. Exactly the same as here."

"I'll agree with you to a point," I admitted, "but leadership is available to those who wish it."

Again he laughed. "Really? You think so? You think you got where you were because of willpower and dedication? Hell, man, you were *bred* for it. They designed and manufactured you as they would any tool they needed, because they needed it. The same as they did me."

"But you crossed them up," I noted. "That's why *you're* here."

He shrugged good-naturedly. "The trouble with their system is that their human tools have to be smart guys and they have to be thrown out into the cold, cruel world to do their jobs. Eventually we wise up and have to be eliminated ourselves before we become a threat. That's done by promotion to the inner circle—if they can fit you someplace—or sometimes by just having a junior knock you off. Hell, they can do it just by having you show up at the Security Clinic for normal processing, then instead of feeding you your past and what you need, reducing you to the common pawn vegetable with a nice little job as a widget monitor or something. I discovered this fact almost too late and mostly by accident, and I ran like hell."

"To Lilith," I noted. "Why in heaven's name *Lilith?*" Everybody at the table laughed at that, except of course the native-born.

"I'm not going to tell you," he responded. "At least not until we've gotten that damned organic transmitter removed from your skull and until you've been around enough to know whose side you're really on."

"The aliens," I muttered, feeling like my last secrets were being stripped from me. He even knew about the transmitter.

He grinned and shrugged. "Let's just say, ah, powerful friends of mine —of all Warden citizens, but mostly of the Four Lords of the Diamond. Anyway, it must surely have occurred to you that any civilization able to penetrate the security chamber of Military Systems Command would have no trouble at all finding out about the Merton Process. And report same to me, who knows better than anybody how the great minds of the Confederacy run. I know they'd zero in on Lilith because I was running the place, and that the only logical person to send would be someone whose own past and career matched mine as closely as possible."

I said nothing to this because I'd been a lot slower than he was giving me credit for, a fact I didn't like at all.

"Well, anyway, we knew you were coming," continued the Lord of Lilith, "and, Confederacy Intelligence being what it is, I had to figure that any agent sent down here would most logically duplicate my own initial situation as closely as possible, since they were setting one assassin to catch another. That meant Zeis Keep, since I had started here. That meant I just had to wait until Zeis got a new prisoner. Then you turned up. After your seasoning, I stepped in to size you up a bit and tantalize you as well. It was pretty clear to me that you were somewhat in the doldrums and needed a swift kick in the pants you couldn't wear then to get moving. Ti was the all-too-obvious leverage."

I glanced over at Ti, and she bristled. The full implications of what a "pawn" really was were dawning on her, and she didn't like it one bit.

"So, anyway," he went on, "I had already established myself in your mind as the only independent spirit on Lilith and told you pretty much where I was heading. Then I came back here and ordered Dr. Pohn to take Ti. I figured that, if you were anything like me, you'd get so damned mad you'd come after her, and that meant you'd have to have a Warden explosion. You were already ripe—I could see it in you."

"And if it hadn't happened?"

He smiled. "Then you weren't any good to me *or* to the Confederacy and you would have been abandoned to plant beans for the rest of your life. But of course it *did* happen, the night of the banquet. When Dola came and told us here, we immediately made plans on what we'd do next.

We had to expose you to Dr. Pohn at his worst, for example, and Ti in that totally helpless condition at his villainous mercy. We had to show you not only Master Artur but his troops and beasts as well—Artur usually doesn't show newcomers around personally, you know—so you'd realize it'd take an armed force to come after Zeis Keep. And of course we had to test you for Warden potential and give you a taste of what that power is like without actually giving you that power right off. Vola took care of that, then also got you on the run with that wonderful piece of midnight theatrics. I of course was nowhere near at the time, since I already had to be far to the south to lay my trail for you to follow."

"But I heard a voice . . ."

"Duke Kobé, I'm afraid, using a reed tube," he responded. Kobé shrugged apologetically. "It was important that natural early suspicions about me be allayed. I *couldn't* be Kreegan in the hallways and also have gone to several Keeps in the time allowed, not without you finding out about it. I counted on you to file that away in your mind. On the other hand, I had to be the only person to whom you could turn for help."

"You took a chance there," I noted, nettled by his manner. "I could just have gone to the wild."

"I *never* took a chance with you," he replied. "If at any time you hadn't been up to the job for one reason or another I could simply quit and find somebody else. But I had some insurance in Ti, here."

She shot him a glance that, had she had my Warden power, would have demolished the hall.

"Remember," Kreegan said, "I'm forty years your senior, but we came out of the same background, went through the same training, did the same job for the same bosses. Oh, the faces and names change occasionally, but it's always the same bosses. It's a stratified and static society with a system it believes works. As a result, *I knew how you thought*. I could simply put myself in your place, decide what I'd have done, and act accordingly."

"How were you so sure I'd take Ti, though?"

Again he grinned. "Well, first of all, your reaction to Ti had been strong enough to trigger the Warden effect and get you to the Castle. So you *had* to be emotionally attached to her. Additionally, Dr. Pohn was an inducement if you cared anything about her. However, just in case you suddenly turned into the total pragmatist of your self-image, Vola mixed a mild hypnotic herb in with the first batch of juice; this—reinforced your tendencies, shall we say. I needed Ti. She was essential. You *had* to take her, since she was the only possible inducement for Sumiko O'Higgins to get involved."

"Did you get her?" I asked.

He nodded. "But that's getting ahead of things. You must understand the threat she represented. She was a psychopath such as comes along only once in a century or more, thank heavens. There are some monsters who, when caught, deserve to be exterminated and had better be. Sumiko was one such. Had she not been caught in a fluke accident, she'd have accomplished the actual genetic code of the Institute for Biological Stability that determines the future look of the civilized worlds. Not just the look—well, you know how much genetics can really determine."

"You just got through telling me that the civilized worlds needed changing," I pointed out.

"Change, perhaps," he replied, "but—monsters, Cal. Monsters in standard civilized world guise. They should have gotten rid of her, wiped her, vaporized her—but instead they sent her to Lilith, on the theory that anybody that smart might come up with something unusual. And she sure did!"

I nodded. "I got a whiff of her plans, thanks to Ti."

"Not the half of it," Kreegan told me. "You have no idea what a brilliance that twisted mind had. To tailor-made mutations in existing organisms. Mental genetic engineering! We had word of her activities, of course. She was hardly quiet about her recruiting of young women, that sort of thing. They performed human sacrifices, too, there in that village common. The same stone on which Ti rested was designed to hold a living human being; the grooves there were to drain off the blood, which they would all then drink. She was sick, Cal. Sick and enough of a genius to pull it all off. We had to stop her—but thanks to her brilliance, we couldn't even find her."

I nodded again, seeing it all. "And, as Artur proved, she was unassailable even if you had been able to find her."

The sergeant-at-arms grumbled to himself.

"That's about it," Kreegan agreed. "Understand, she had discovered nothing that the Institute didn't already know about, but the Institute goes to a lot of trouble to keep things stable here. Using you and particularly Ti, I was able to get us all to her village. There I could tantalize her enough that I felt sure she'd come with us to the Institute—and come she did. A lot of evaluation went on there, without her knowledge, although she also learned from the library things she needed to know. Shortcuts, so to speak. We had to give her crumbs just to keep her as long as we could. Afterward, we had long discussions on what to do, the extent of her power, that sort of thing. We felt we'd given her enough new material for her to grow overconfident, and so it only remained to play the trump card —offer her a chance to find out how strong she really was. We made the bait as irresistible as possible."

"The object, in other words, was to create a situation by which Sumiko would leave her protective haven, split her forces, and not suspect that the enemy was not merely Zeis but everyone else."

"That is true," Boss Rognival put in. "And the cost was great. We truly had to fight one another until they all landed on the beachhead. That was difficult but unavoidable. Regardless, we deployed sufficiently to allow *some* Zeis forces to get through and knock out as many witches as possible. Weaken her. But we could not close in on her forces and destroy them until the bitch herself was dead."

"Just out of curiosity, Kreegan, how *did* you kill her?" I asked.

"Oh, I had several options," he replied. "As a last resort we had, thanks to the Institute, enough of the amplifier potion to mass me, the Duke, here, two knights, and about forty Masters against her—but we didn't have to, for which I'm thankful. I had no idea how powerful she really was—still don't—and I didn't want to find out. It was you, Cal, who gave me the idea."

I started. "Me?"

He nodded. "When you told me about her laser pistol. I figured she'd have it with her for insurance, and particularly for afterward. Look, only a Lord can stabilize offworld metal. You know that. That gives you some idea of her power."

I frowned. "But what does that . . . ?"

"Come on, Cal! If *you* were in my shoes, and had my power, and if *you* knew she had a laser pistol on her, what would *you* do? Particularly knowing that her entire mind, her whole concentration, was elsewhere?"

My mouth fell open in surprise as I realized what he had done. "You concentrated on nothing but that pistol," I told him. "You undid the Warden pattern on the insulating coating. The Warden cells in the area would start immediately attacking the pistol."

He smiled and nodded. "Yep. It exposed the power supply, which overloaded and exploded. She had it tucked in her belt at the time. I'll tell you, I sweated blood waiting for that to happen. I was only going to give it another few minutes before we switched to a mass attack and damn the consequences. But it blew, praise God, and the bang was the signal for everybody to stop fighting, join hands, and take those witches from all quarters."

"You still took a terrible chance," I noted. "It could have gone off any time—maybe hours later. And you yourself said your mass attack might not have been strong enough."

"I'll admit I had a third backup," he said tiredly. "The Wardens act fast, but not *that* fast. If all else had failed, my orbital satellite would have released a null-missile right into Zeis. Everyone and everything would have been atomized, but of course so would all the witches. That's how seriously I took the threat."

That answered all the questions.

"What about this Father Bronz act?" I asked him. "You couldn't just invent the character."

"Oh, I've been Father Bronz for ten years," he told us. "It's the easiest way to get around inconspicuously." He paused. "Of course I'll have to undergo some physical changes now and find a new persona." He sighed. "Too bad, too. Old Father Bronz really did some good. I've been considering asking for some real clergy here."

I let the topic go and finally asked him the most important question. "What about me?" I asked. "What happens now?"

"You'll do fine," he assured me. "Stay here as a Master for a while and get some experience, then either outlive the Boss, here, or go find yourself a weak Knight and start it all. You're going to be at least a Duke someday, maybe even Lord. I told you. It took me seventeen years."

"I'll beat your record," I told him, not at all jokingly.

He stared at me hard. "I think you might at that."

Dinner broke up soon after that, with Kreegan saying that he was catching the shuttle when it put down the next day. "Business," he told us. "Four Lords business."

And Boss Tiel, to my surprise, had a few words for me as well. "I'd like you to stay here," he told me sincerely. "I'm an old man now, Tremon. You could take me out right now, as you originally planned. But a number of the Masters, Artur in particular, are strong, and you might take *me* out only to find yourself losing, on experience alone, to somebody else. Maybe even Rognival, who'd love to swap that island for Zeis. A couple of years here, though, learning technique and the full use of your power, making contacts, doing the proper politics, and you'll have the knighthood by acclamation. You're the best qualified. Artur's a great soldier but a lousy administrator. The others are pretty much the same. No talent or no ambition. It's up to you, of course, but you've impressed me."

I told him I'd think about it, but I knew the answer. I would stay, of course, because that was the path to my own ambition most open to me and because of Ti. She'd never like or forgive many of these people, but as she said, she was a part of Zeis.

Finally, I sought out Dr. Pohn. I still didn't like the little son of a bitch, and I knew that he'd be one of the first to go in the Tremon regime that was coming. Still, now I needed him.

The next afternoon he would undertake a little Warden-style operation. Okay, my twin and counterpart up there somewhere—I failed miserably. I got played for a sucker. I learned nothing about your precious aliens, and Lord Marek Kreegan, curse his black soul, remains Lord of Lilith and First Lord of the Diamond. But that's it. I've done all I can do for now and I find myself less and less anxious to do you any more favors. Up yours, Confederacy! Maybe when I become Lord of Lilith I won't like those aliens; but then again, maybe I will. But whether or not I feed you any information will be based on my own assessment at the time, from the viewpoint of my own interests.

Cal Tremon, none too respectfully, resigns.

CHAPTER TWENTY-THREE

A Little Unfinished Business

The air was warm and moist. We'd just had another of Lilith's nasty little thunderstorms, and the cloud ceiling was extremely low. Nonetheless, the shuttle arrived right on schedule—as if it would stand up Lord Marek Kreegan.

I had spent most of the night calming Ti down. "I hate that man," she kept saying over and over. In a sense, she'd lost as much as I had, and her world picture now included bitterness. As much as Sumiko O'Higgins had upset her, she could not forgive the man who had caused her to fall into the hands of Dr. Pohn, to degrade her so much for somebody else's cause. She felt as if she'd been raped by Marek Kreegan, more so than if he'd assaulted her sexually. It was a total violation, and she'd be a long time getting the stain off her soul.

Still, she was learning. She was there with me when the shuttlecraft landed to the west of the Castle as it always did, appearing out of the clouds and settling to the ground. The elaborate set of airlocks and safeguards came into play, although they were less necessary with Kreegan on board.

Kreegan still wore his old priest's robe, but I knew it would soon be exchanged for something else. I might not even know him the next time I saw him, although I felt sure I'd recognize that man anywhere. And one day, Kreegan, I told myself, we'd have more than a little chat.

Duke Kobé remained behind, although usually he was the one who used the shuttle. I wondered idly if Kreegan hadn't made one mistake this time after all, since he knew that the broadcaster had been in place until this afternoon. It was entirely possible that the orbiting Confederacy troops would blast his little shuttle. But no, I told myself. They wouldn't do it because that would involve a choice of record. That's why they hired —created—people like me. Nobody up there would want to take the open responsibility without clearing it back to the Confederacy itself, and by that time Kreegan would have vanished to who knew where?

Besides, he had powerful friends. Would they permit him to be blown to bits? I doubted it. He was their most valuable ally, the man who knew how the Confederacy establishment thought. The aliens wouldn't want to lose him.

He waved, smiled, and entered the shuttle, and the stairway retracted. I heard the soft whir of the engines starting up again, and, slowly at first, it started to lift.

"Cal," I heard Ti say beside me.

"Yes, hon?" I responded and looked at her.

In that moment something in my head seemed to explode. My Warden cells seemed to flare, and the energy flowed from me, maximum energy, beyond my control, flowing straight at Ti! But she didn't burn, nor even do more than shake slightly. Instead she turned and looked directly at that lifting body, heading slowly up into the clouds, cautiously trying to clear the mountains before full thrust.

I stood transfixed, unable to move, think, breathe.

The sound of the shuttle engines varied slightly, coughed, then sounded very, very wrong.

There was a sudden explosion, and a brightness in the clouds, and then, tumbling down, crashing again and again against the rocky mountainside, the shuttle plunged. It struck bottom with a thunderous roar and suddenly was bathed in a terrible glow, too bright to look at. Ti turned away, and I felt myself abruptly freed from that mysterious, terrible hold.

I turned, stunned, first in the direction of the shuttle, but it was now just a smoldering, bubbling and hissing mass of molten metal. Soon it, too, would be gone. When it cooled enough, I knew, the Warden cells would begin their relentless attack on the alien matter, reducing it to dust in a matter of days.

I turned back to Ti in shock. "Wha— What the hell did you *do?*"

She smiled, as evil and self-satisfied a smile as I had ever seen on another human being.

"Back at the witch village a few days ago—you remember?"

I could only nod dully.

"I swiped some of that potion. I drank it *all* this morning, just before coming down here. I was lucky. I was hopin' to surprise you and be able to use your power before you could stop me. And I did."

"But—but *how?*"

"Last night after dinner I talked a lot with Duke Kobé and Boss Tiel," she told me. "I asked 'em a few simple questions. One of 'em was how they kept the shuttle level. Kobé was particularly nice about showin' me. Drew me a picture of somethin' called a geoscope or some such. I asked him if the shuttle had a thing like that and he told me it did, but not like that. He told me what it looked like. And using your power, I just did the same thing to the shuttle that Kreegan did to Sumiko's gun. I just took the spell off."

"But—but it would be in a vacuum chamber!" I protested. "It shouldn't have made any difference."

"She did more than that, young man," said a voice behind me. I whirled and saw Duke Kobé standing there, looking more thoughtful than angry. "You sure as *hell* have some power, son, and she hated old Marek worse than anybody should be hated by anybody, that's for sure. I could see it, feel it, but I couldn't do a damned thing about it."

"What do you mean?" I asked, feeling suddenly totally drained.

He shook his head in wonder. "The gyros didn't get him, no matter what she thinks. She punched a hole with Warden cell material clear through the outer hull and right through the power supply!"

I sat down on the grass. "Oh, my God!"

"If nothing else, you can see now that even Sumiko didn't have an idea of just what the power of a Lord could do," the Duke noted.

I thought he was taking the death of Marek Kreegan pretty lightly and told him so.

He just smiled. "It's the way of Lilith," he said philosophically. "I did all the administrative work for the whole damned planet plus, yet I was still his toady. No, son, I had no love for Marek Kreegan."

"Cal is Lord now!" Ti exclaimed forcefully. I could still feel her tug on me, but knowing what was going on, I found I could block it.

Kobé shook his head slowly from side to side. "No, little clever and ambitious one. He's not. *He* didn't kill Marek Kreegan—you did. I doubt if he could muster that much hate on his own. No, the position is open, pending someone claiming it and being able to hold on to it. That'll take weeks, at least. In the meantime, I'll act in his stead." He sighed. "Damn. Guess I'll have to attend that damned conference now myself."

Ti flared at him, but I was now able to dampen her rage. In a few hours, I knew, the effect would wear off. In the meantime, I had to keep a really close watch on her.

I looked up at her, still a little stunned. "You don't have any more of that juice, do you?"

She looked a little hurt at the question and stared down at me. "Would *I* lie to you?"

EPILOGUE

The man came out of it slowly, only vaguely aware of who and where he was. He removed the headset almost idly and rubbed his temples. He had a headache that was killing him.

He looked around the control cubicle for some time, as if not believing that he was really here, on the picket ship, in his own lab, and not down there somewhere, on Lilith.

Finally he managed something of a recovery. "Computer?"

"Responding," a calm, male voice responded.

"You now have the raw data and the data filtered through me," he noted. "Any conclusions?"

"For the first time the connection between the aliens and the Lords of the Diamond is confirmed," the computer responded. "I also have an awful lot of data that asks more questions than it answers. Not enough now—but we do have another report in. I might also point out, sir, that Marek Kreegan knew only about Cal Tremon, so this might well mean that they do not suspect the other three."

"That's something," he admitted grumpily. "Did you say we had another?"

"Yes, sir. Cerberus. Because of the peculiar nature of the Warden cell there it was not possible to do the organic mind-link, but we imposed a command on that subject agent to report when able and then forget he reported. It is a technological culture, sir, so that was possible. I believe we have a full accounting. Would you like me to play it for you?"

"Yes—*no!*" he shot back, a little angry. "Give me a little bit, will you?"

"If you have a headache and natural fatigue, sir, I can provide the needed counters in window slot number two."

He nodded. "All right, do it. But give me a little."

He couldn't tell the computer that the headache didn't matter, that the fatigue didn't matter, that none of that mattered. What troubled him was far deeper and far more upsetting.

Cal Tremon, he wondered, are you really *me?* Would I have acted that way, would I have done things that way? Why are you a stranger to me, Cal Tremon? Are you not my twin?

Marek Kreegan's account and version of the Confederacy bothered him, too, if not as much. It was unthinkable to believe that way. It would make all this a lie, a joke. It was unacceptable.

Still, he told himself, perhaps this was an aberration. Cal Tremon's body, his hormones, whatever, affected the mind. It *had* to.

Suddenly, instead of fearing the Cerberus report, he needed it, and badly. He *had* to know. Was Cal Tremon the aberration—or was he truly seeing himself?

If so, could he face the stranger in these four mirrors?

He settled back in the chair and sipped a drink. Finally, he sighed. "All right. Run Cerberus."

"Acknowledged," the computer responded. "Recorders on. But if I may say so, sir, it would be of great help if you would put on your headset."

He sighed, picked up the fragile crown, put it on and adjusted it for maximum comfort, then settled back, wondering why his hands seemed to be shaking so.

Mirror, mirror, in the mind . . .
Would I lie to you?

CERBERUS:
A Wolf in the Fold

*For Richard Witter,
another unsung living legend
to whom the SF community
owes a great deal*

CONTENTS

Beginning Again

I

There was not supposed to be fear in the structured and ordered society of the civilized worlds; there was some sort of law against it. Clearly, there was nothing *to* fear any more. And in a society like that, somebody who knew the true folly of complacency could get away with almost anything.

Tonowah Resort was the standard for a standardized society. Golden beaches washed by warm, sparkling water and, set back from the ocean, a line of high-rise luxury hotels surrounded by exotic tropical plants and containing any sort of diversion that anybody might desire—from the traditional swimming, fishing, gambling, dancing, and whatever to the most exotic pleasure machines of a mechanized society. Leisure was big business in the Confederacy, where the basic manual-labor jobs were all totally computerized and human beings held jobs only because their leaders limited their absolute technology so people would have something to do.

Genetic and social engineering, of course, had reached the state of the art. People did not look alike. Experiments had demonstrated that such a direction tended to kill self-esteem in identical-looking people and cause them to strive, somehow, for the most bizarre ways to prove their uniqueness. Nonetheless, variety was kept within bounds. Still, people were all physically beautiful, the men uniformly trim, lean, muscular, and handsome, the women exquisitely formed and stunning. Both sexes were generally of uniform height, about 180 centimeters give or take a few, and had a uniform bronzed skin tone. Previous racial and ethnic features merged into an average without extremes. Their family was the State, the all-powerful Confederacy that controlled some seven thousand six hundred and forty-two worlds over a third of the Milky Way Galaxy; the worlds themselves had been terraformed to conform as much as possible one to another. Medical science had progressed to the point that much of what ailed people could be easily repaired, replaced, or cured. An individ-

ual could remain young and beautiful until he died, quickly, quietly, at
an age approaching a hundred.

Children were unknown on the civilized worlds. Engineers did all the
work and maintained the population stability at all times. Children were
born in Confederacy labs and raised in Confederacy group families in
which they were carefully monitored, carefully raised and controlled, so
that they thought as the Confederacy wished them to think and behaved,
as the Confederacy wished them to behave. Needed proclivities could be
genetically programmed, and the child then raised with all he or she
needed to become the scientist, the engineer, the artist, the entertainer, or,
perhaps, the soldier the Confederacy required. All were not equal, of
course, but living in the civilized worlds required only average intelligence, and only the specialized jobs required geniuses. Besides, overly
bright people might become bored or question the values and way of life
of the civilized worlds.

There were, of course, aberrations, but these were very few and far between; in fact, the society of the civilized worlds was the most egalitarian
society ever known to Man. Places were found outside the structure for
obvious aberrations. For those few who weren't detected until too late, a
small, specialized group known as Assassins ferreted out the rotten apples
and eliminated the threat.

There were worlds beyond the civilized worlds—the frontier, where
nothing had yet been standardized. The best Confederacy analyses had
predicted early on that a society such as the civilized worlds bred stagnancy and loss of creativity and drive, thus ending innovation and racial
growth and eventually leading to the destruction of the human race from
internal rot. To prevent all that, a small percentage of humanity was permitted to keep pushing outward, discovering and conquering new worlds
and living in a more primitive style. Still subject to random gene mixing in
the old tried and true ways, people out on the frontier were still very
different-looking. Tight control was not exercised, for the Confederacy was
not looking to make things easy out there. Hardship, deprivation, fierce
competition, and aggression—all forced innovation, which was the safety
valve for humanity, the system had worked for nine centuries because
none were left to oppose the Confederacy—no alien races that could not be
subjugated or eliminated easily, no competing empires that could threaten
Man and his own empire.

Until now.

Until the nightmare theoreticians had warned about came to pass.
Until there had come an enemy that so exploited the complacent egotism
of the Confederacy that it could penetrate almost at will.

Juna Rhae 137 Decorator knew nothing of this. She was merely one of
the products of the civilized worlds, a person whose job it was to meet
with citizens wishing to alter their dwelling's appearance. She would sit
down and discuss new layouts with them, run them and their psych
profiles through her computers, and come up with new and different inte

rior designs that would please her clients. As her name implied, she had been raised for this job, and since the Confederacy made few mistakes, she loved it and could think of no other citizen she would rather be. She was at Tonowah Resort just relaxing for a week, since she knew she would be busy for some time thereafter. She was about to face the greatest challenge of her career, a redesign of a Children's Family Center on Kuro that was switching its function from raising engineers to raising botanists, who, Confederacy computers projected, would be in short supply in about twenty years. Interior decorating was extremely important to career-based Family Centers, so she was looking forward to the challenge and was gratified by the confidence placed in her. Still, it would be a long time between vacations.

She had been swimming in the golden surf of Tonowah and just lying relaxed on the sand. Finally feeling relaxed and refreshed, she headed back to her luxury suite to shower and order a meal before deciding on the evening's activity. Once back in her room, she washed quickly and phoned for a meal—a real gourmet-type treat, she decided, at least for tonight. While waiting for her order, she was punching up clothing designs on the aptly named Fashion Plate, a device that contained over three million complete clothing elements with which to create personally designed outfits. Juna, like most people at resorts, dispensed with clothing during the day but wanted something stunning, complimentary, but casual for evening wear. In social situations she liked to be an object of attention, and it took clothes to accomplish that when everybody was gorgeous.

She completed the outfit, based upon a clinging evening dress of sparkling emerald green, and punched in the code knowing that it would be manufactured and would appear in her clothing delivery slot within half an hour.

The door buzzed, and she called for them to enter. A man dressed entirely in white stepped in, carrying a covered golden tray. Resorts anachronistically retained human serving staffs, an extra touch of luxury; the men and women in the service industry loved what they were doing and would never do anything else.

He entered, not even glancing at her nakedness, put the tray down for a moment on a table, then picked it up again with both hands and triggered little switches on both sides. She heard a short buzz, and from under the tray dropped thin, strong supports. The man deftly triggered what he alone knew was there, and the tray became the centerpiece on an elegant, modern dining table. He then lifted the cover, and she gasped and smiled at the delights thus revealed.

Though much meal preparation was roboticized, the chefs were top creative artists, designing new food delicacies all the time, and certain parts of such meals were even supervised and partly created by hand. Top hotels and resorts provided real food, not the synthetics and simulations of day-to-day life. She tasted the first dish, smiled as if enraptured, and nodded to the waiter that all was excellent. He returned her smile, bowed, then turned and left.

When he returned more than half an hour later, she was out cold on the sofa. He went over to her, checked her physical condition, nodded absently to himself, then went back out and wheeled in a large laundry cart. He picked up her limp, naked body and placed it in the cart, covering her with some linen. Looking around, he spotted the lighted Fashion Plate and walked over to it and punched *Cancel*, then went to the master control panel and punched the *Clean-and-make-up room* button, which lit up. Satisfied, he pushed the cart easily out the sliding door and down the broad corridor toward the service entrance.

She awoke slowly, groggily, not comprehending what had happened to her. The last she remembered she had been eating that wonderful meal when suddenly she'd felt incredibly tired and dizzy. She had wondered if she'd been overdoing things and had leaned back on the couch to get hold of herself for a moment—and now, suddenly, she was . . .

Where?

It was a featureless plastic room of some kind—very small, walls and ceiling glowing for illumination, and furnished only with the tiny, primitive cot on which she lay. A section of the wall shimmered slightly, and she stared, curious but naively unfearful, as a man stepped into the room. Her eyes widened in surprise at his chunky build and primitive dress, and particularly at his long, curly hair and bushy beard, both flecked with gray. He was certainly not from the civilized worlds, she knew, and wondered what on earth was going on.

She started to get up but he motioned against it. "Just relax," he urged in a voice low and rough and yet somehow clinically detached, like a doctor's. "You are Juna Rhae 137 Decorator?"

She nodded, growing more and more curious.

He nodded, more to himself than to her. "Okay, then, you're the right one."

"The right one for what?" she wanted to know, feeling much better now. "Who are you? And where is this?"

"I'm Hurl Bogen, although that means nothing to you. As to where you are, you're in a space station in the Warden Diamond."

She sat up and frowned. "The Warden Diamond? Isn't that some sort of . . . penal colony or something for frontier folk?"

He grinned. "Sort of, you might say. In which case you know what that makes me."

She stared at him. "How did I get here?"

"We kidnapped you," he responded matter-of-factly. "You'd be surprised how handy it is to have an agent in the resort service union. Everybody goes to a resort sooner or later. We drugged your food and our agent smuggled you out and offworld to a waiting ship, which brought you here. You've been here almost a day."

She had to chuckle. "This is some sort of resort game, right? A live-in thriller show? Things like this don't happen in real life."

The grin widened. "Oh, they happen, all right. We just make sure nobody much knows about it, and even if the Confederacy does find out, *they* make sure you never hear about it, either. No use panicking everybody."

"But *why?*"

"A fair question," he admitted. "Think of it this way. The Warden planets are a good prison because when you go there you catch a kind of disease that won't live outside the system. If you leave, you die. This—disease—it changes you, too. Makes you not quite human any more. Now, figure only the best of the worst get sent here. The rest get zapped or mindwiped or something. So what you have are four worlds full of folks with no love for humanity, being not quite human themselves. Now, figure some nonhuman race stumbles on humans and knows the two—them and the humans—will never get along. But the humans don't know yet that these aliens are around. You following me?"

She nodded, still not taking all this very seriously. She tried to remember if she'd ordered an experience program like this, but gave up. If she had, she wouldn't recognize what was going on as part of the program anyway.

"All right, so these aliens gotta know as much about humans as possible before they're discovered. They're much too nonhuman to go at it direct, and the Confederacy's much too regimented for raising human agents. So what do they do? They find out about the Warden Diamond; they contact us and kinda hire us to do their dirty work for 'em. We're the best at that sort of thing—and down the road the payoff can be pretty good. Maybe getting rid of this Warden curse. You get it now?"

"Assuming for a moment I believe all this, which I most definitely do not," she responded, "where does that leave me? You just said yourself that none of your people can leave your worlds. And why a decorator, anyway? Why not a general or a security tech?"

"Oh, we got those too, of course. But you're right—we can't leave, not yet. But our friends, they got some real nice technology, they do. You'll see one of their robots in a minute. So human it's scary. That waiter who got you was a robot, too. A perfect replacement for the real person who once held that job."

"Robots," she scoffed. "They wouldn't fool anybody very long. Too many people know them."

The grin returned. "Sure—if they were just programmed and dropped in cold. But they're not. Duplicated in their nasty little minds will be every memory, every personality trait, every like and dislike, every good and bad thought you ever had. They'll be *you*, but they'll also take orders from us, and they'll be able to think and compute at many thousands of times the speed of you or me. They scare me sometimes because they could become us and replace us entirely. Lucky their makers aren't interested in that sort of thing."

She was beginning to feel uneasy now for the first time. Not only was this show very real—she would expect that—but it was passive, talky, not the kind of thriller show anybody would make up. But the alternative, that it *was* real, was too horrible to consider.

"So you can replace people with perfect robots," she managed. "So why a decorator?"

"One of our clerical agents spotted your entry in the routine contracts a few weeks ago. Consider, Juna Rhae, that your next job is to redo a child factory. A place where they're reprogramming to raise little botanists instead of little engineers, I think. Now, suppose *we* could do a little extra reprogramming there while you were going around replanning the place?"

She shuddered. This was too horrible for a horror script.

"Now," he continued, "we're set up. The moment you entered the Warden Diamond you were infected. Given a massive overdose of the pure stuff. Saturated with the Cerberan brand of the Warden bug. It'll take a while before you'll notice anything, several days or more, but it's already there, settling into every cell in your body."

The door shimmered again and through it stepped a woman, a woman of the civilized worlds, a woman more than vaguely familiar to her although she appeared blank, stiff, almost zombielike.

Bogen turned and nodded to the newcomer, then turned back to her. "Recognize this woman?"

She stared, feeling fear for the first time now. "It—it's *me,*" she breathed.

Her other self reached out and pulled her to her feet with an iron grip. The strength in that one hand was beyond any human. The robot Juna Rhae took the human's hands and held them in a viselike grip with one hand while the other arm held her firmly around her waist. This hurt too much to be a show. She would never have ordered something like this!

"We Cerberans," Bogen said softly, "swap minds, you see."

2

The man reclined on a soft bedlike couch before an instrument-laden cluster in a small inner chamber of the space vehicle; he was wired, through some sort of helmet device, to the instruments around him. He looked tired, disturbed, and anxious.

'Hold it!" he called out.

The massive computer all around him seemed to pause for a brief moment. "Something wrong?" the computer asked, sounding genuinely concerned.

He sat up on the recliner. "Let me take a break before starting this next one. I don't think I can take two right on top of one another right now.

Let me walk around, talk to a few people, generally relax, maybe even get some sleep. Then I'll be ready. The Confederacy is not going to fall if I wait ten or twelve hours."

"As you wish," the computer responded. "However, I do think that time is of the essence. This might be the one that tells us what we need to know."

"Maybe," the man sighed, taking off the helmet. "But we've been rotting here the better part of a year with nothing much to do. Another few hours won't mean anything. We'll probably need all four anyway, and nobody knows when the next two will come in."

"All that you say is logical and true," the computer admitted. "Still, I cannot help but wonder if your hesitancy is less governed by such practical matters."

"Huh? What do you mean?"

"The Lilith account has disturbed you a great deal. I can tell it by your body-function monitors."

He sighed. "You're right. Hell, that was *me*, remember. Me when I went down, and somebody I hardly knew at all when he reported. It's kind of a shock to discover that you don't know yourself at all."

"Still, the work must continue," the computer noted. "You are putting off the Cerberus report because you fear it. That is not a healthy situation."

"I'll *take* it!" he snapped. "Just give me a little breathing room!"

"As you wish. Shutting down module."

The man rose and walked back to his living quarters. He needed some depressant, he told himself. The pills were there, but he rejected them as not what he wanted. Human company. Civilized company from the civilized worlds, from the culture in which he'd been raised. A drink in the picket-ship bar, perhaps. Or two. Or more. And human beings . . .

On Lilith things had gone both right and wrong. Right because the job had been done, but wrong in that the man had changed, or been changed, by his experiences, by his isolation, by his hatred of his other self up in space.

Two reports had come in almost at the same time. Lilith was taken first, and it shook the watcher's self-confidence and self-image. Nothing had happened the way it should have. The mission was on track, but in the process his own ego had somehow gotten derailed.

Cerberus would be the second report, and he was very nervous about facing it. He didn't fear for the mission—that was a different matter. He feared what he might find out about himself. But after a night in the ship's lounge and a fitful sleep that didn't help at all, he knew he would go back, knew he would undergo the process. He feared neither death nor any enemy, and in fact had only now found the one thing he *did* fear.

Himself.

And so he finally approached the reclining chair once again. Slowly, hesitantly, he relaxed, and the computer lowered the small probes which he placed around his head; the computer then administered the measured injections and began the master readout.

For a while he floated in a semihypnotic fog, but slowly the images began forming in his brain as they had before. Only now they seemed more definite, clearer, more like his own thoughts.

The drugs and small neural probes did their job. His own mind and personality receded, replaced by a similar, yet oddly different pattern.

"The agent is aware that no transmitter was possible with Cerberus," the computer reminded him. "It was necessary to land the needed equipment at predetermined points by remote and, at the time of cerebral imprinting, to place an absolute command to report at intervals. Subjectively, however, the process to you will be the same."

The agent didn't react, didn't think, just accepted the information. He was no longer himself, but someone else, someone like him and yet in many ways quite different.

"The agent is commanded to report," the computer ordered, sending the command deep into his own mind, a mind no longer his own. What would follow would be a sort of total recall from the mind of his counterpart down below, which his own mind would sort, classify, and edit into a coherent narrative, a narrative in the form of a report.

Recorders clicked on.

The man in the chair cleared his throat several times. It still took more than three hours to get him to do more than mumble some odd words or sounds, but computers are nothing if not patient, knowing that the man's mind was receiving a massive amount of data and struggling to cope with it.

Finally, though, as if in a dream, the man began to speak.

CHAPTER ONE

Rebirth

After being briefed by Commander Krega and a little preparation to put my own affairs in order—this would be a long assignment—I checked into the Confederacy Security Clinic. I'd been here many times before, of course, but not knowingly for this purpose. Mostly, this was where they programmed you with whatever information you'd need for a mission and where, too, you were "reintegrated." Naturally, the kind of work I did was often extralegal—a term I prefer to illegal, which implies criminal intent. All agents had their own experience of a mission wiped from their minds whenever it involved sensitive matters.

It may seem like a strange life, going about not knowing where you have been or what you've done, but it has its compensations. Because any potential enemy, military or political, knows you've been wiped, you can live a fairly normal, relaxed life outside of a mission structure. There's no purpose in coming after you—you have no knowledge of what you've done or why or for whom. In exchange for those blanks, an agent of the Confederacy lives a life of luxury and ease, with an almost unlimited supply of money and with all the comforts supplied. They have sensors in you that they constantly monitor and decide when you need a good refresher. I often wondered just how sophisticated those sensors were. The idea of having a whole security staff see all my debauchery and indiscretions used to worry me, but after a while I learned to ignore it. The life offered in exchange is just too nice. Besides, what could I do about it, anyway?

But when a mission came up it wasn't practical to forgo all the past experience you'd had. A wipe without storage simply wouldn't have been very practical, since a good agent gets better by not repeating his mistakes. So in the Security Clinic they kept everything you ever experienced on tap, and the first thing you did was go and get the rest of you put back so you would be whole for whatever they'd dreamed up this time.

It always amazed me when I got up from that chair with my past fully restored. Even the clear memories of the things I'd done always amazed me—I of all people had done this or that. The only difference this time, I knew, was that the process would be taken one step further. Not only would the complete me get up from that table, but the same memory pattern would be impressed on other minds, other bodies—as many as needed until a take was achieved.

I wondered what they'd be like, those four other versions of myself. Physically different, probably—the kind of offenders they got here weren't usually from the civilized worlds, where people had basically been standardized in the name of equality. No, these people would come from the frontier, from the traders and miners and freebooters that existed at the edge of expansion. They were certainly necessary in an expanding culture, since a high degree of individuality, self-reliance, originality, and creativity was required in the dangerous situations in which they lived.

The damned probe hurt like hell. Usually there was just some tingling, then a sensation much like sleep, and I woke up a few minutes later in the chair, myself once again. This time the tingling became a painful physical force that seemed to enter my skull, bounce around, then seize control of my head. It was as if a giant fist had grabbed my brain and squeezed, then released, then squeezed again in excruciating pulses. Instead of drifting off to sleep, I passed out.

I woke up and groaned slightly. The throbbing was gone, but the memory was still all too current and all too real. It was several minutes, I think, before I found enough strength to sit up.

The old memories flooded back as usual, and again I amazed myself by recalling my past exploits. I wondered if my surrogate selves would get similar treatment, considering they couldn't be wiped after this mission. That realization caused me to make a mental note that those surrogates would almost certainly have to be killed if they did receive my entire memory pattern. Otherwise, a lot of secrets would be loose on the Warden Diamond, many in the hands of people who'd know just what sort of use to make of them. No sooner had I had that thought than I had the odd feeling of *wrongness*. I looked around the small room in which I'd awakened and realized immediately the source of that feeling.

This wasn't the Security Clinic, wasn't any place I'd ever seen before. A tiny cubicle, about twelve cubic meters total, including the slightly higher than normal ceiling. In it was a small cot on which I'd awakened, a small basin and next to it a standard food port, and in the wall, a pull-down toilet. That was it. Nothing else—or was there?

I looked around and spotted the most obvious easily. Yes, I couldn't make a move without being visually and probably aurally monitored. The door was almost invisible and there was certainly no way to open it from inside. I knew immediately what sort of room I was in.

It was a prison cell.

Far worse than that, I could feel a faint vibration that had no single source. It wasn't irritating; in fact it was so dim as to be hardly noticeable, but I knew what it was. I was aboard a ship, moving somewhere through space. I stood up, reeling a bit from a slight bout of dizziness that soon passed, and looked down at my body. Looked down—and got what I think is the greatest shock of my life.

A woman's body. A Confederacy-standard woman at that. At that moment a tremendous shock and revulsion ran through me. First and foremost I was most solidly and assuredly male and liked things that way, but, worse, that body told me the most horrible of facts. I was not the original but a surrogate. *I'm one of them!* I thought in sheer panic. I sat back down on the cot, telling myself that it just wasn't possible. I knew who I was, remembered every bit, every detail of my life and work.

The shock gave way to anger and frustration. Not only was this female body foreign to me and my personality, but that very mind and personality wasn't real but a copy, an imitation of somebody else entirely, somebody still around, alive, possibly monitoring my every move, perhaps my every thought. I hated him then, hated him with a pathological force beyond reason. He would sit there comfortable and safe, in his man's body, watching me work, watching me do it all—and, when the mission was over, he'd go home for debriefing, return to that easy life, while I—

They were going to dump me on a world of the Warden Diamond, trap me like some kind of master criminal, imprison me there, hold me there for the rest of my life—of this body's life, anyway. And then? When my job was done? I'd said it myself upon awakening—passed my own sentence. The things I knew! I would be monitored at all times, of course.

Monitored and killed if I blew any of those secrets. Killed in any event at the completion of the assignment just for insurance's sake.

Well, I told myself, the system worked both ways. I knew how *he* thought, how *they* thought. This monitoring worked both ways. I was going to be a tough son of a bitch to kill. No, I thought, suddenly morose once more, not son. Did I in fact *want* to live the rest of my life in this body? I really didn't know. Not now, certainly—and not ever, deep down. And yet the tiniest of suspicions rested in the back of my mind that my attitude might be just what they had in mind. The perfect double trap for me. If that was the case, they were mistaken. If I began believing for one minute that they did this to me just so I wouldn't want to outlive my mission, I'd live a thousand years just to spite them. There was probably no such plot, though, I knew. Either they had an ulterior motive having to do with the mission that caused this, or they just didn't consider it one way or the other. I wished I knew.

But what about now, in any event? For now I'd bide my time, hold my peace, and adjust as best I could. Odd, in a way, how very *ordinary* and *normal* I felt. Arms, legs, head, all in the same places. A lot lighter in weight, yes, but that was relative; and being a little weaker in the arms wasn't anything you really noticed, particularly not in a barren prison cell. Only occasionally did I feel protrusions where none had been before, or the lack of something that had always been there. I knew here in an isolated cell I wouldn't be aware of the differences. Only later, down there, on whatever hellhole they dumped me, around lots of other people—*then* things would get rough.

I was very dry after waking and located a small water tap and cup in the wall just above the basin. I drank a good deal. Naturally, it went right through me, whereupon I discovered that having to piss was the same feeling only I now had to do it sitting down. I pulled down the toilet and sat and relieved myself—and got yet another shock.

The thing worked by skin contact—don't ask me how. I'm not one of the tech brains. It was not as good as a neural program, but it allowed them to talk to me in total privacy, even send me pictures only I could see and hear.

"I hope by now you are over the initial shock of who and what you are," Krega's voice came to me, so loud and clear it seemed impossible that none of the monitors could hear. "As you recall, the Merton Process of personality transfer is rather wasteful of bodies—roughly thirty die for one take, as it were—and of the first four that did take, one was this woman. We decided to use her for several reasons. She will put any Warden authorities off their guard if there's been any sort of leak about you, and Cerberus, the planet to which you are being sent, has unique properties that make your sex and age totally irrelevant. To calm you down, I suspect, I should tell you right off that Cerberans enjoy a natural form of the Merton Process—in fact we got the process partially by studies on Cerberus. In other words, you can expect to change bodies once or often down there, as well as sex, age, and all the rest."

I gave a half-startled cry at this thought and stood up, causing the toilet to flap back into the wall and flush. It worried me for a moment that I might have wiped the briefing; but because my old professional self was re-emerging, I knew that I would have to wait before finding out just to ward off any suspicion by my unseen jailers.

I walked back to the cot and sat down once again, but my mood had abruptly changed. Body switchers. That changed everything! I was suddenly *alive* again, alive and excited.

I'd had some nasty shocks, but the worst one was merely temporary. The other—the discovery that I wasn't who I thought I was but some artificial creation—was still there. The old life, the life I remembered even though I really hadn't personally experienced it, was gone forever. No more civilized worlds, no more casinos and beautiful women and all the money I could spend. And yet, as I sat there, I adjusted. That was why they'd picked me from the start. My ability to adjust and adapt to almost anything.

Memory, thought, personality—those were the individual, not the body that intelligence wore. *I was still me!* This was no different than a biological disguise of a particularly sophisticated sort. As to whom was really me— it seemed to me that this personality, these memories, were no more that other fellow's than my own. Until I got up from that chair back at the Security Clinic I'd really been somebody else anyway. A lot of me, my memories and training, had been missing. That old between-missions me was the artificial one, the created me. He, that nonentity playboy that presently did not exist, was the artificial personality. The real me was bottled up in storage in their psychosurgical computers and allowed to come out only when they needed it—and for good reason. Unlocked, I was as much a danger to the power structure as I was to whoever they set me against.

And I was good. The best, Krega had called me. That's why I was here, now, in this body, in this cell, on this ship. And I wouldn't be wiped this time—and now I was sure I would not permit them to kill me, either. Suddenly I no longer felt hatred toward that other me out there someplace. In fact I found I could no longer feel much of anything for him at all. When this was all over he'd be wiped once more—perhaps killed himself if my brother agents on the Diamond and I found out too much. At best he'd return to being that stagnant milquetoast. Not me. I'd still be here, still live on, the *real* one. A whole person. I would be more complete than he would.

I was under no illusions, though. Kill me they would, if they could, if I didn't do their bidding. They'd do it automatically, by robot satellite and without qualms. But my vulnerability would only last a short time—even less on Cerberus than elsewhere, since they would have to find out *who* I was as well and without the aid of biotracers or any other physiological gadget. I wondered how they were going to get me to report. I remembered Krega saying something about a thing implanted in the brain, but the moment I switched bodies that was useless. Probably there was some deep psychocommand to report, perhaps with the aid of agents or paid accomplices on Cerberus. I would get to that matter when I could. Until then, I'd do their dirty work for them. I had no choice, as they undoubtedly knew. During that vulnerable stage—who knew how long?—I was their property. After—well, we'd see.

The thrill of the challenge took over, as it always did. The puzzle to be solved, the objectives to be accomplished. I liked to win, and it was even easier when you felt nothing about the cause, just the challenge of the problem and the opponent and the physical and intellectual effort needed to meet that challenge. Find out about the alien menace. The outcome no longer concerned me directly, since I would be trapped on a Warden world from now on. If the aliens won the coming confrontation, the Wardens would survive as allies. If they lost—well, it would only maintain the status quo. This reduced the alien question to an abstract problem for me and made my situation perfect.

The other assignment created a similar situation. Seek out the Lord of Cerberus and kill him if I could. In a sense doing so would be more difficult, since I'd be operating on unfamiliar ground and would therefore require time and possibly allies. Another challenge. If I get him, I'd only increase my power and position on Cerberus. If he got me instead, then I wouldn't give a damn because I'd be dead. But the thought of losing is abhorrent to me. That set the contest in the best terms, from my point of view. Trackdown assassination was the ultimate game, since you won or you died and never had to live with the thought that you'd lost.

It suddenly occurred to me that the only real difference that probably existed between me and this Lord of the Diamond was that I was working *for* the law and he—or she—against it. But no, that wasn't right, either. On his world *he* was the law and I would be working against it. Perfect again. Dead heat on moral grounds.

The only thing that really bothered me was the disadvantage of not having a psychoprogram with everything I needed to know all neatly laid out for me in my mind. Probably, I thought, they hadn't done it this time because they'd had me on the table in four new bodies with four separate missions, and the transfer process to a new body was hard enough without trying to add anything afterward. Still, the omission put me in a deep pit. I sure hoped that the rest of that contact briefing recording hadn't wiped when I'd gotten up. It would be all I had.

Food came—a hot tray of tasteless muck with a thin plastic fork and knife that would dissolve into a sticky puddle in an hour or so, then dry up into a talclike powder. Standard for prisoners.

This being my first meal in some time, it wasn't long before I had to go once again, and so I faced convincingly my moment of truth with the toilet that talked.

"Now, as to this process"—Krega's voice, picking up right where we left off, gave me a tremendous feeling of relief—"we had to brief you this way because the transfer process is delicate enough as it is. Don't worry about it, though—it's permanent. We just prefer to allow as much time as possible for your brain patterns to fit in and adapt without subjecting the brain to further shock. Besides, we haven't the time to allow you to completely 'set in,' as it were. This will have to do, and I profoundly regret it, for I feel you have the trickiest task of the four."

I felt the old thrill creep in. The challenge . . . the challenge!

"As I said, your objective world is Cerberus. Like all the Diamond colonies, Cerberus is a madhouse. Third out from the Warden sun of the four Warden worlds, it is subject to seasons and ranges from a tropical equatorial zone to frozen polar caps. The most peculiar thing from a physical standpoint about the world is that it is a water world with no above-surface land masses. It is, however, a world abundant in life. The geological history is unknown, but apparently the sea covering was quite slow and the massive numbers of plants in its distant geological past kept their heads above water, so to speak. Thus almost half of the surface is covered with giant plants interwoven into complex networks, some with trunks tens of kilometers around—necessary support, since they are rooted in the seabed from a hundred meters to an impossible two to three kilometers below. The cities and towns of Cerberus are built atop these plants.

"No additional physical descriptions will be adequate, and you will be well briefed below by the governing officials upon landing. However, we feel a complete physical-political map would be useful and are thus going to imprint that map on your mind now."

I felt a sharp back pain, then a wave of dizziness and nausea that quickly cleared. Whereupon I found that I did in fact have a detailed map of the entirety of Cerberus in my head. It would be very handy. There followed a fast stream of facts on the place. It was roughly 40,000 kilometers around the equator, and its gravity was 1.02 norm, so close I'd hardly notice it. Equatorial and summer temperatures were a pleasant 26 to 27 degrees centigrade, mid-latitude spring and fall were between 12 and 13 degrees centigrade, chilly but not uncomfortable, and polar regions and mid-latitude winters could drop as low as 25 below, although the sea cover and the location of settlements along warm currents that the great plants also followed usually kept it well above that and relatively ice-free even in the worst of times.

A day was 23.65 standard hours, close enough to cause no major disruptions in my biological schedule, a pretty normal environment—if you liked water, anyway.

Cerberus was industrialized—I could hardly wait to see factories in the treetops—but lacked heavy metals or easily obtainable hard resources of any sort. Most of its ore and other needed industrial materials came from Medusa in exchange for finished goods, and from mines on the many moons of a gas giant much farther out. While technological, the Confederacy kept close tabs on what was built on Cerberus, and the industry, though good, was forcibly kept in obsolete channels. In effect this was the best of news, since there wouldn't be a machine on Cerberus I didn't know intimately or couldn't get complete details on from above. To ensure some technological retardation, there was the Warden organism, whose fancy name nobody used or remembered. It got into literally *every-thing*, right down to the molecules in a grain of sand, and it resisted "imported" materials—that is, materials that did not also have Warden organisms inside. Thanks to early exploration spreading the contagion from Lilith, this meant not only the four Warden worlds but, to my surprise, the seven barren but mineral-rich moons of the ringed giant Momrath, outside the zone of life. For some reason the Warden bug could still live where no others could, even way out there, but no further. Beyond Momrath the things died as they did going out-system.

"The Lord of Cerberus is Wagant Laroo," Krega's voice went on. "He was an important Confederacy politician until about thirty years ago, when he grew too ambitious and forgot his sacred oaths, taking his sector from the paths of civilization into his own private kingdom. As befitted his position and former contributions to the Confederacy, he was given the option of death or Warden exile; he chose the latter. He is a megalomaniac with delusions of godhood, but do not underestimate him. He has one of the most brilliant organizational minds the Confederacy ever produced, and it is coupled with total amorality and absolute ruthlessness. His power and rule extend far beyond Cerberus, for many antisocials within the Confederacy use Cerberus as a storehouse for hidden records, location of loot, and even the storage of blackmail. I fear I must warn you that, if the impossible happened and there was some sort of leak about you, he will know of it. No security is perfect, and this possibility must be considered."

I nodded to myself. Despite Krega's patriotic phrasing, few if any top Confederacy politicians were immune to scandal or blackmail on some level, and this guy was a master.

"Finding Laroo might well be impossible," Krega warned. "Cerberus has the Warden organism, but it is a mutated strain. More of this will be explained on orientation, but you must trust to the fact that bodies are as interchangeable as clothes on Cerberus. So even if you saw Laroo, had him pointed out to you and shook his hand, you could not be absolutely certain it was really he, and even less certain that it would still be he days, hours, even minutes later."

That didn't really bother me much. For one thing, if Laroo had this kind of dictatorial control somebody always had to know who he was or he couldn't give the orders and expect to be obeyed. Furthermore, a man like that would love the actual trappings and exercise of power. Then too, Laroo couldn't be at all certain who *I* might be a few minutes, days, or weeks later, either.

"At last count there were approximately 18,700,000 people on Cerberus," Krega went on. "This is not a large population, but it has a very high growth rate. There are more jobs and space than people even now.

Since the advent of Laroo's rule the population has been expanding at a rate that almost doubles it every twenty years or so. We believe that only part of this population push is economic, though. Much of it, we think, is because, on a world of body switchers, the potential for immortality exists if there is a constant and available supply of young bodies. Laroo seems to have some control over this process, which is the ultimate political leverage. Naturally, this also means that, short of being killed, Laroo could literally rule forever."

Immortality, I thought, and the idea sounded very pleasant. How long will *you* live, my other original self? I, sir, had an infinite answer to that one. Perhaps this was not such a terrible assignment after all.

Krega had a lot more routine stuff for me, but finally the lecture was over and I simply got off the john and heard it flush. The next time I used it, I discovered that this time the message had been flushed as well. Because it had been a direct neural transmission, even with the interruption, it had taken only a minute or two for the whole thing.

Efficient, the Security boys, I told myself. Even my ever-vigilant jailers on the other end of those lenses and mikes would have no idea I was anybody other than who I was supposed to be.

As to who I was, that had come in a rush as well. I was Qwin Zhang, forty-one, former freighter loadmaster and expert smuggler, a virtuoso of the computerized loading and inspection system. A technological crook— that fit many of my own skills perfectly.

I lay back on the cot and put myself in a slight trance to better sort out the information I'd received. Qwin *did* bother me a bit. I could follow her life and career without ever really getting a handle on her. Born and bred to her job, normal Confederacy upbringing, no signs of any deviation from the normal path millions of others followed, the path set out for them from birth that they were not only *expected* to follow but *designed* to follow. I mentally followed the steps in her routine life and found nothing unusual, nothing to show what I was looking for.

And yet she stole. Stole expertly, methodically, and efficiently, even using the computer routing systems not only to shave cargo loads but actually to misdeliver them to waiting fencing operations out on the frontier. Stole almost from the start of her career, and so well she was caught only when a freak accident on a freighter with a bit more cargo than it was supposed to have caused a total inventory and alerted Security. She'd been probed and poked and studied, but there seemed little there. She'd stolen because she could, because the opportunity was there. She felt no guilt, no remorse for this "crime against civilization," and didn't seem to have any clear idea of what she would one day do with all that money had she gotten away with it.

Where was the corruption point? I couldn't find it, nor could the psych boys. What dreams had you had, Qwin Zhang? I mused. What event disillusioned you or turned you from the paths of righteousness? Some exotic love affair? If so, it wasn't anywhere to be found in what they gave me.

Not much interest or history in sex of *any* sort. Perhaps the answer was there, somewhere in somebody's sexual theories of abnormal psychology, but it didn't really show.

Still, she'd been a nonentity. Her crimes depended on that, and such crimes were hidden, never publicized, lest others get ideas. Because she had had a norm body and looks and an average personality, it was unlikely anyone on Cerberus would ever have heard of her. That suited me just fine. The last thing I wanted was to bump into one of her old buddies down there. I wouldn't have the memories to match.

CHAPTER TWO

Transportation and Exposure

Except for regular meals there was no way to keep track of time, but it was a fairly long trip. They weren't wasting any money transporting prisoners by the fastest available routes, that was for sure.

Finally, though, we docked with the base ship a third of a light-year out from the Warden system. I knew it not so much by any sensation inside my cloister but by the lack of it—the vibration that had been my constant companion disappeared. Still, the routine wasn't varied. I suppose they were waiting for a large enough contingent from around the galaxy to make the final trip worthwhile.

All I could do was sit and go over the data again and again until I was comfortable with all of it. I reflected more than once that I probably wasn't very far from my old body (that's how I'd come to think of it). I wondered if he didn't occasionally come down to take a peek at me, at least from idle curiosity—me and the three others who were probably here also.

I had time to reflect on my knowledge of the Warden system, the reasons for its perfection as a prison. I had not, of course, swallowed that line whole—there was no such thing as a perfect prison, but this had to be close. Shortly after I was dropped on Cerberus I'd be infected with an oddball submicroscopic organism that would set up housekeeping in every cell of my body. There it would live, feeding off me, even earning its keep by keeping disease organisms, infections, and the like in check. The one thing that stuff had was a will to live, and it survived only if you did.

But it needed something, some trace element or some such that was only present in the Warden system. Nobody knew what and nobody had been able to do any real work to find out, but whatever it needed was found only in the Warden system. The element wasn't in the air, because in shuttles run between the worlds of the Diamond you could breathe the purified, mechanically produced stuff with no ill effects. Not in the food, either. They'd checked that. It was possible for one of the Warden people to live comfortably on synthetics in a totally isolated lab like a planetary space station. But get too far away, even with Warden food and Warden air, and the organism died. Since it had modified your cells to make itself at home, and those cells depended on the organism to keep working properly, you died, too—painfully and slowly, in horrible agony. That distance was roughly a quarter of a light-year out-system, which explained the location of the base ship.

All four worlds were more than climatologically different, too. The organism was consistent in what it did to you on each planet, but—possibly due to distance from the sun, since that seemed to be the determining factor in its life—it did different things to you depending on which world you were first exposed to it. Whatever it did stuck in just that fashion even if you later went to a different Warden world.

The organism seemed somehow to be vaguely telepathic in some way, although nobody could explain how. It certainly wasn't intelligent; at least it always behaved predictably. Still, most of the changes seemed to involve the colony in one person affecting the colony in another—or others. You provided the conscious control, if you could, and that determined your relative power over others and theirs over you. A pretty simple system, even if inexplicable.

I regretted not knowing more about Cerberus. This was far less briefing information than I was used to, although I understood their caution. It would cost me time, possibly a lot of it, to learn the ropes there and find out everything I needed to know to do my job.

About a day after I arrived—four meals' worth—there was a lurching and a lot of banging around that forced me to the cot and made me slightly seasick. Still, I wasn't disappointed; the activity meant they were making up consignments and readying for the in-system drop of these cells. I faced this idea with mixed emotions. On the one hand, I wanted desperately to be out of this little box, which provided nothing but endless, terrible boredom. On the other, when I next got out of the box it would be into a much larger and more attractive cell—the planet Cerberus itself, no less a jail for being an entire planet.

Shortly after all the banging started, it stopped. After a short, expectant pause, I felt again a more pronounced vibration than before, indicating movement. Either I was on a much smaller vessel or located nearer the drives.

Still, it took another four interminable days, twelve meals, to reach our destination. Long, certainly—but also fast for a sublight carrier, probably a modified and totally automated freighter.

The vibration stopped, and I knew we were in orbit. Again I had that dual feeling of trapped doom and exhilaration.

A crackling sound and a speaker I'd never known was there came to life. "Attention, all prisoners," it commanded, its voice a metallic parody of a man's baritone. "We have achieved orbit around the planet Cerberus in the Warden system." For the first time it occurred to me that others were also being sent down—logical, of course, but I'd never really considered it before. I knew what they all must be going through, considering my own feelings. Probably a hundred times mine, since at least I was going in with my eyes open, even if I was no more a volunteer than they had been. I wondered for a fleeting instant about Lord Laroo. Once he too sat here, naked in a common cell, feeling these same feelings and facing the same unknown future as we. He had started as low as I—lower, in fact, as a prisoner—and now he ran the place. Nobody had given the position to him on a platter, nobody had elected him. He'd gone in, naked and isolated as I was, and he'd conquered. And I certainly considered myself superior to such as Wagant Laroo.

That very line of thinking started me slightly. Was that *me*, aiming at becoming a criminal chief?

"In a moment," the voice continued, "the doors to your cells will slide open and you will be able to leave. We strongly recommend you do so, since thirty seconds after the doors open they will close again and a vacuum pump will begin sterilization operations within the cells, operations fatal to anyone who remains."

Nice touch, I reflected. Not only did it ensure against breakouts en route, but you moved or you died on their schedule. I couldn't help wondering if anyone had chosen death.

"Immediately after you enter the main corridor," the voice continued, "you will stand in place until the cell doors close once again. Do not attempt to move from in front of your cell door until it closes or automatic guard equipment will vaporize you. There will be no talking in the corridor. Anyone breaking silence or failing to obey orders precisely will be instantly dealt with. You will receive further instructions once the doors close. Ready to depart—*now!*"

The door slid open and I wasted no time in stepping out. A small white box, complete with marks for feet, showed you where to stand; I did as instructed, galling as all this was. There was something to being totally naked and isolated on a ship controlled only by computer that humbled you more than was right. It created a sense of total futility.

I could still look around and saw that I'd been right. The thing was basically a long sealed hall along the sides of which had been attached the little cells. I looked up and down and counted maybe a dozen, certainly no more than fifteen. The cream of the crop, I thought sourly. A dozen naked and bedraggled men and women—an equal number of each—beaten prisoners about to be dropped and left. I wondered why these had been chosen rather than wiped, considering the transportation expense alone. What had the computers and psych boys found in these dejected specimens that dictated they should live? *They* didn't know, that was for sure. I wondered who did.

The doors snapped shut. I waited expectantly, perhaps to hear the scream of somebody who didn't move fast enough as the air was pumped out, but there was no hint of melodrama. If anybody had taken that way out, the fact was not evident.

"At my command," the voice barked from speakers along the ceiling, "you will turn right and walk slowly, in single file, as far forward as you can. There you will find a special shuttle that will take you to the surface. You will take seats from the front first, leaving no empty seats between you. Strap yourselves in immediately."

I could hear some grumbling from the others, and suddenly small laser beams shot out, hitting the deck with an audibly nasty hiss down the line of people but hitting no one. The grumbling stopped.

The voice, pausing for this show of force, now took up its instructions with no reference to the demonstration. None was needed.

"Right turn now!" it commanded, and we did as instructed. "Walk slowly forward to the shuttle as instructed."

We walked silently, definitely in no hurry. The metal floor of the corridor was damned cold, though, and this made the shuttle at least preferable to this damned refrigerator.

The shuttle itself was surprisingly comfortable and modern, although the seats weren't made for naked bodies. I sat about six rows back and attached the safety straps, then waited until everyone had been seated and done the same. The shuttle itself could seat about twenty-four, but there were just thirteen of us, eight—no, *seven* males and six females. I kept forgetting who I was and what I was, and I scolded myself mentally for it. This was not the time for any lapses. The next day or two would be the most dangerous of all for me, since our new class would get a great deal of attention and they'd be particularly interested in any of those who didn't seem to be what they appeared.

The hatch closed automatically, followed by the hiss of pressurization. Then without further fanfare came a violent lurch and we were free of the transport and on our way down. The shuttle was much too modern and comfortable for mere prisoner transport, I told myself. This, then, was one of the interplanetary ships regularly used for transportation between worlds of the Warden Diamond.

The overhead speakers crackled, and a pleasant, human-sounding male voice came on. It was a great improvement. "Welcome to Cerberus," he said, sounding for all the world as if he meant it. "As has no doubt been explained to you, Cerberus is your final destination and new home. Although you will be unable to leave this solar system, once you get off below you will no longer be prisoners but citizens of the Warden Diamond. Confederacy rule ended when you entered this shuttle, one of many owned by the Warden worlds in common. The System Council is a corporate entity fully recognized as internally sovereign by the Confederacy and has its own seat in Congress. Each of the four worlds of our system is under its own sovereign and independent government."

The voice paused for a moment, and I reflected that it was odd not to hear anyone commenting, cheering, grumbling, or anything else. You could cut the tension with a knife, and I admit I felt it as much as the others.

"No matter who or what you've been in the past," the voice continued, "no matter what you've done or what your previous status was, you are now and forever citizens of Cerberus, nothing more—or less. You are no longer in any way prisoners and nothing you have done in the past will follow you here. You start with a clean slate and a clean record, and only what you do from this point on, as Cerberans, will matter."

Fair enough, I thought. The contrast in tone between this and the mechanical horror we'd first been exposed to was startling.

"We will be landing shortly," the voice continued, and I could feel the braking being applied and hear the whine as stabilizers deployed for in-atmosphere flight. "We would appreciate your getting off quickly after the hatch opens, as we must service this craft and return it to normal service. A government representative will meet you and take you to a place where you can get clothing, a good meal, and orientation. Please cooperate with this person and give no trouble. It wouldn't be a bright idea to start off on the wrong foot your first day on your new world."

Even a psycho could go along with them when the instructions were put that way, I told myself. They had such a *nice* way of making threats. Well, this was a world made up of and run by people just like those on the shuttle.

We made a long, slow approach, the pilot taking no chances, then finally settled into a berth of some sort. The caution warnings blinked out and the airlock hissed; when the hatches slid open, we undid our safety harnesses and got up, moving slowly and quietly toward the open area. This was it!

We filed slowly out into a long and modern passenger ramp, which was totally covered but not heated. It was chilly, and that sped us along. None of us could really think of the chill, though; all had been pushed out by a single, overriding fact.

The moment that chill had hit us, the moment that air reached our skin and nostrils and entered our bodies, we were systematically being invaded by a submicroscopic organism that was our new, and final, jailer. We were here, and free, but we were, from this moment on, also stuck.

CHAPTER THREE

Orientation and Placement

We entered a small lounge, and were greeted by two men and a woman, all dressed like soldiers in tight-fitting khaki uniforms and boots, although we quickly learned they were not military. We were given robes and sandals as a temporary measure; then our names were checked against a clipboard list and we were quickly ushered out of the terminal to a waiting air-bus. Robe or not, it was damned cold and the bus's heating system, though good, was hardly comfortable.

We lifted quickly and swung out away from the terminal, and with this maneuver we had our first look at our new world. It was a strange vista—the ocean gleaming in the sunlight to our right and the "shoreline" to our left, but shore it definitely was not. Rather, it was a dense-looking forest of reddish-brown and orange trees topped with huge, broad leaves of varying shapes and sizes. At many points the trees had been partially or completely cut into. Clearly, people lived inside the trunks themselves—you could see sunlight reflected off windows. Here was a surrealist's vision, this great forest with trunks half resembling ancient, gnarled trees of tremendous size and half resembling a complex of modern office buildings. Often we could see where some of the great trunks branched, one had been cut off horizontally and then refinished or surfaced with some glossy material, providing landing platforms and entryways.

The woman in charge saw us gaping and smiled. Picking up a small PA mike, she became an impromptu tour guide. "Welcome to Cerberus. My name is Kerar, and my two associates are Monash and Silka. You are in the Borough of MaDell. We use boroughs here because the nature of the living space makes anything as dense as a big city nearly impossible. Fortunately, with efficient transit we are able to link up areas sufficient to make cities in economic terms, and that's what we call boroughs. As you can see, there is no land whatsoever on Cerberus. Biologists tell us that people were once tree-dwelling creatures. Here, of necessity, we have returned to our origins."

I kept looking out the window at the eerie tree-land. Somehow the whole place looked like a piece of furniture I once owned, with a support pole and several flat, clover-like surfaces surrounding the stem as small shelves. Of course, this was much larger and rougher-looking, and not all the "shelves" were flat or barren, but it still had that look about it.

"You are seeing many different types of trees," Kerar continued. "There are over five thousand varieties of big trees on Cerberus, with about eighty different types in MaDell alone. As you can see, many types can be used extensively as dwellings, since much of the circulatory system goes around the outside of the trunk, allowing the trees to be hollowed out without killing them. A few are naturally hollow, although the outer bark in most parts is up to eight meters thick. They can support an enormous amount of weight because they get much thicker below the water's surface, and, over the millions of years they evolved, they also support each other. Master botanists have a special place here because they are responsible for telling us how many branches can be cut off for building and landing zones, and which ones, and also which architect's ideas for tree dwellings are practical and which are not. Mistakes can be costly. The death of one key tree might well undermine the support for a dozen, even hundreds more, in a mushroom effect that might kill our whole community."

I could see the point she was making—don't mess around with the trees. I wondered how many of the earliest pioneers had, and what sort of damage they'd wrought.

I looked out toward the ocean and caught sight of many boats, some quite large, others obviously pleasure craft—even some sailboats. Looking back into that fantastic jungle, I caught sight of a huge, imposing structure up ahead, a gleaming, modern building many stories tall sitting atop one of the cut-off sections, which, I was to learn, were called mesas on Cerberus.

"Up ahead is the government center for the borough," our guide informed us. "That is where we are heading."

We were ushered into the place and guided past curious onlookers to a tenth-floor room. There waiting for us was a hot buffet lunch. I frankly didn't recognize much of what was there, but after all that time on prison food it tasted just great. After we had eaten, while we were all just sitting around enjoying that stuffed feeling, an efficient little man came in and took our measurements. Within an hour he was back with some bundles, which turned out to be underwear, a pullover thick shirt, work pants, heavy socks, and low boots. Also included were belts and a full range of cosmetics and toiletries. In twos we were taken down the hall to a full lavatory complete with showers, which we all happily used; then we put on our clean, new clothes. I had little trouble with so simple an outfit despite the gender problem, but was thankful that my hair had been cut very short, prison-style. Come to think of it, though, Kerar's was short, too, although professionally cut and styled.

Finally, now that we were feeling human again, they decided we were ready for the full briefing. We sat in folding chairs while our guide gave us the basic stuff.

"The first world to be explored in the Warden system was Lilith," she began. "Lilith is a beautiful world, like a tropical garden. From their base camp, the first Exploiter Teams reached and set up bases on the other three Warden worlds, as well as examining the moons of Momrath, a huge gas giant further out. What they didn't know was that they were carrying an organism from Lilith, an alien thing like no other."

Briefly she recounted how the organism at last had struck Lilith, wiping out all manufactured things and reducing the population to primitive savages. Machines wouldn't work there, and the entire society was nontechnological. I couldn't help but think of my poor counterpart on Lilith. I was good, yes—the best. But I was born and raised and existed my entire life in a highly technological society. How would I be able to function in a nontechnological one? Would I be able to? I wondered, and felt more relieved that it wasn't my problem.

"The organism," Kerar went on, "was carried to the other places, where it thrived and mutated. There are many theories on this, the most logical being that it reacts to the sun's relative energy and perhaps the amount of solar wind itself, but nobody really knows. Here, as you can see, it did not destroy machines. On Lilith, its native world, it adapted men to the planet, made them a part of Lilith's ecosystem. Here *it* had to be the one to adapt, and it did. It's inside you now, moving in, making itself comfortable, settling down in every molecule of your body."

We all stirred at this unpleasant thought, which we'd managed to push to the back of our minds until now. It was funny—I didn't *feel* any different. No dizziness, no signs of anything out of the ordinary.

"Early scientists had the idea that the organism had some sort of collective intelligence," Kerar told us. "It became obvious that every single tiny subviral form was somehow in contact with every other one. We now know that they were only partly right. It *is* one organism, each one like a part of a cell to a huge body, but it doesn't *think*. Its behavior patterns are well known and quite consistent. Once you know how it acts, it will never surprise you.

"On Lilith, this intercommunication led to some people getting tremendous power, since the organism there exists in literally every molecule of solid matter. Some there can simply will a hole to be cut in rock, for example, or cause trees, fruit, even people to mutate. This works because some minds are so strong that they can transmit their will through the Warden organisms in their own body to others in people and things nearby. Here we have a different effect."

Again there were murmurs, and again I thought of my poor counterpart. Such a world would seem to be one of magic, and there magic alone worked.

"On Cerberus," our guide continued, "the organism is also in every molecule of solid matter. We've found it in tree samples taken by divers a full kilometer below the surface of the sea, and in the sea and air creatures themselves. As on Lilith, it doesn't like things that don't have Warden organisms inside them, and it will invade them as it has you. It seems to have a much easier time with organic molecules, though, particularly ones in living creatures, because it adapts to you with little trouble. Put a manufactured item from, say, the Confederacy here, though, and it will try and invade that, too—not very successfully. The stuff just doesn't work and usually falls apart. Fortunately, it doesn't care which kind of Warden creature is there, at least on Cerberus, so we can import raw materials, finished products, and food from our fraternal worlds, and with the exception of Lilith, export our goods to them. The Lilith original just won't take anything that upsets the primitive nature of the planet.

"Now, there are some good things about this invasion of your body. For one thing, since it depends on you to give it what it needs to live, it keeps you in tip-top shape. It purges your body of disease, so nobody gets sick. It cleans out the blood vessels and directs cellular repairs, so you don't get cancer, heart attacks, strokes, or whatever. Even things like drugs and alcohol, for the most part, will be purged before they can have any effect—with the exception of solids from the Warden system, and those are very rare and restricted. The worst you can do to yourself is get a little fat or out of condition. And of course the organism cannot retard the aging process, although even there it keeps you in far better shape far longer than normal."

That was an interesting benefit, I told myself. Still, no more getting drunk or high or using any kind of recreational drugs. This was a *clean* world.

Kerar looked at us and smiled a bit, pausing before dropping the other shoe, the one only she truly knew about. "However, you are fortunate to have been sent to Cerberus. Only the best are sent here. No murderers, no persons with violent histories. This is not a violent world, and for very good reason. You see, only we here on Cerberus have the potential of living forever."

There it was—along with an interesting additional bit of information. No violent criminals. I wondered why.

When the rest of the group had caught hold of itself, she continued her orientation. "I told you that on Lilith people could contact and command Warden organisms, and control and change them. That does not happen here. However, all the Warden organisms here are in constant contact with others, with proximity being the guide. The closer you are to somebody or something else, the more contact the Warden organism has with the other. When you are awake, your consciousness controls those within your body and there is no problem and no effect. But if you are tired, sleepy, or asleep, or in semiconscious or unconscious state, the Warden organisms reach out to others near them." She paused a moment, choosing her words carefully. "I'll give you an example, with the understanding that we know *what* happens but we have never discovered exactly *how* it happens.

"Let's say I go to sleep here next to you, and you fall asleep too. Unlike those on Lilith, Warden organisms here tend to communicate mostly with those in complementary positions, so those inside you don't communicate with, or link with, or whatever it is they do, those in rocks, trees, and the like the same way they do to those in other people. Freed from conscious restraint, the Wardens in *your* body would link with the Wardens in *my* body. This linkage would become strongest during the short periods of sleep when we aren't dreaming. If two of those periods match—mine and yours—the Warden organisms in your brain and mine would link, and, for reasons we don't understand, start to exchange information. Now, remember, I told you that the creatures are in every molecule and actually can cleanse, change, repair, or replace parts of your body to keep you healthy. In the same way, as a by-product of their very nature, they change the molecules in *your* cerebral cortex to *my* code and mine to yours, even adjusting the brain-wave pattern to match. It's done in a matter of minutes. Since memory is chemically stored and electrically retrieved, this means a total change of information within the brain. So you wake up with *my* memories and personality, and *I* wake up with yours. In effect, we have switched bodies."

"Then why don't they switch *all* the information?" a bearded young man to my left asked skeptically. "You should have hormonal imbalances, differentials in respiration and blood pressure—enough wrong commands tailored for the wrong body to cause it to be very wrong and very sick."

"Agreed," she responded. "Good question. The answer is simply that in the early days some of that happened, but it no longer does. The Warden organism is incredibly adaptable, and it exchanges information with other parts of itself, even with other organisms outside its physical form. It learned. As to *why* it wants to do so—well, we don't know. We're not even sure it does. The person may be a by-product of its unique life form. It may be some necessary adjustment to keep itself going in the Cerberan atmosphere. We don't know. I'm not sure we ever will. But it does happen, it has, and it almost certainly will continue."

"Have *you* ever switched bodies?" another skeptic asked.

She smiled. "Many times. I am a native, unlike you. The switching phenomenon comes with puberty—a rite of passage here, you might say. Adolescents here undergo many switches, particularly since that age is more highly emotional and so control is more difficult. Besides, what adolescent could resist the experimentation? Boys curious about what it's like to be a girl, vice versa—that sort of thing. I often wonder what it would be like to be trapped at birth in a particular gender and body. I, for example, was born male, but by the age of sixteen, having been in three male and two female bodies, I found myself more comfortable, somehow, as a female. I found a female who felt more comfortable as a male and we slept together and settled it. However, don't think we run around swapping bodies as often as we change clothes. We don't. Oh, some of us change often, and there are occasional marriages where the partners switch around constantly, but those cases are rare."

A thought had occurred to me early in her talk and I wanted to get the question out before it slipped away. "You said it takes several minutes to exchange minds during this sleep," I noted. "What happens if you're awakened in the middle of it?"

"Normally, once the exchange begins it can't be stopped—you remain comatose, as it were, even if the building's burning down," she replied. "However, there are cases—very rare—when this happens. You're right to bring it up, since it occurs only among people from Outside like yourselves. The odds, I should emphasize, are one in a million, even to you. The transfer is all at once, so to speak, so all of the molecules in your brain start their rearrangement together. If you are jolted awake early in the process, you'll have a dim remembrance of that other life which will usually fade. If this happens late in the transfer, you'll have a period of psychological problems, a sort of schizophrenia, but that too will pass and the dominant information will control. But if the process is just about exactly half over, then both of you will be in both bodies. There is a lot of extra space in the cerebrum and the new information will slowly shift to the unused parts, creating either a total split personality—two minds in one body, alternating—or a merger into a new personality that is a combination of both. And, understand, this will be the case for *both* bodies. But I wouldn't worry; there have been less than twenty such cases in the history of Cerberus. You almost have to do it deliberately, and nobody wants that."

I nodded. Those seemed like favorable odds. She returned to her basic briefing once more, with a new question from a woman on the end.

"What happens," she was asked, "when a switch occurs to someone in a critically skilled field? I mean, suppose your doctor now has the mind of your janitor? How can you tell?"

"That was an early problem," we were told. "In a nontechnological age or setting, like Lilith's, it probably wouldn't have been solvable. Fortunately, tiny electrical patterns in the brain set up to handle our specific memories are unique to each individual. The new brain adjusts to the new pattern. We have sensitive devices able to read and record that distinctive electrical 'signature,' and you'll find them all over the place. Before you leave here today we'll take your imprint and this will open your account in the master planetary computer. Early imprint reading devices were quite bulky, but now it's a simple device quickly and easily used, and it is used for everything. There is no money here, for example. You are paid according to job and status directly into your computer account. Any time you wish to make a purchase, your imprint is read and compared to your identity card. As you can see, it is virtually impossible for anyone to masquerade as someone else, since it is a crime not to report a body change within eight hours of its occurrence." She paused for a moment, then added, "For a society founded by what the Confederacy calls criminals, Cerberus has probably the most crime-free civilization in man's history."

I could see that this thought disturbed some of the others, and it disturbed me to an extent, too. In the most literal sense of the word, this was probably the most totalitarian society ever built. Not that crime here was impossible—the society was computer-dependent, and anything computer-dependent could be manipulated. But the system had few weak spots, and the ultimate penalty of death for crimes was even more terrifying here, in a society where it might be possible to move from body to body and stay young—if there was a supply of bodies, and if the government let you.

Were there old people here? I wondered. And if not, where did all the new, fresh bodies come from?

After another meal, they interviewed each of us in turn and had us take some basic placement tests, a few of which were familiar. The interview went smoothly enough, since their file on Qwin Zhang was no better than the one fed me and I could be creative where necessary with little fear of tripping up. But the personality tests, both written and by machine, were much, much more difficult. I had spent many months in classes and exercises learning how to get around such things, how to give the examiners the picture I wanted them to have—it involved knowing everything from the theory of testing to the exact nature of the psych probe machines used, as well as self-hypnotism and total body control—and I felt reasonably certain that nothing thrown at me was not properly and correctly countered.

Later still we were holographically photographed and fingerprinted, had our retinal patterns taken, that sort of thing, and were also hooked up to a large machine the operative part of which looked like a test pilot's crash helmet. This, then, was the imprint-taker. A bit later we were taken in and a small headset with three fingerlike probes was lowered on our foreheads and a check made on a computer screen. Apparently the big apparatus was used only for the recording of the imprint; the little device would be the familiar control mechanism for checking it. There was no sensation with either device, and therefore no way to figure out how they operated, something I very much wanted to know. Unless you could fool or defeat that system any authority could trace your life exactly—where you were, whom you were with, what you bought, literally everything.

In the evening they brought in cots for us. Apparently we were to remain there several days—until the Warden organism had "acclimated" itself to us—while they decided what to do with us. A book on the basic organization of the planet was provided, too. Dry but fascinating reading, including a great deal of detail about the social and economic structure.

Politically there were several hundred boroughs, each with a central administration. Some were quite small, others huge, and seemed to be based on economic specialties as much as anything. The Chief Administrator of each borough was elected by the Chairmen of the Syndicate Councils in each borough. The syndicates were also economic units, composed of corporations of similar types, all apparently privately owned stock companies. The economic system was, then, basic corporate syndicalism. It works rather simply, really: all the like companies—steel, say—get together to form a syndicate headed by a government specialist on steel. The needs of the government and the private sectors are spelled out, and each steel company is given a share of all that business based on its size and productivity, guaranteeing it business and a profit, that margin also set by the syndicate and government expert—the Steel Minister, let's call him. The only competitive factor is that a corporation within the syndicate which markedly increases productivity—does a better job, in other words, perhaps for less and thereby increasing its profits—will get a bigger share of the next quarter's business.

Extend this to every single raw materials and basic manufacturing business and you have a command economy, thoroughly under government control and management, that nonetheless rewards innovation and is profit-motivated. Only on the retail level would there be independent businesspeople, but even they would be under government control, since with profit margins fixed all wholesale prices would also be fixed. Then, using something as simple as borough zoning and business licenses, the government could apportion retail outlets where the people and need was. Because no money changed hands and the government handled even the simplest purchases electronically, there could be no hidden bank accounts, no stash of cash, nor even much barter—since all commodities would be allocated by and kept track of by the syndicates.

Nice and neat. No wonder there were so few crimes, even without the ultimate punishment angle.

From the individual's viewpoint, he or she was a free employee. But since the ultimate control was the governments, you'd better not make the syndicate mad or you might find yourself unemployed—and being unemployed for more than three months for reasons other than medical in this society was a crime punishable by forced labor. It seemed that those basic raw materials came mostly from mines and works on several moons of Momrath, and the mining syndicate was always eager for new workers.

To do anything you needed your identity card, which contained all your physical data, including your photo, but no name or personal details. That was on a programmable little microchip in the card itself which could be changed automatically should someone else find himself or herself in your body. Not to report a change was a crime punishable by being locked in an undesirable body and packed off to a lifetime of meaningful labor under the shine of beautiful Momrath.

The next day I asked our hosts how it would be possible to lock someone into a body, and was told that some people, through sheer concentration and force of will, could essentially "cut off" your Warden beasties from sufficient contact to make a switch. These people, called judges, were on call to the government; they didn't judge but merely carried out sentences. Top judges working together could actually force a transfer, too.

And of course there it was. Older, undesirable bodies were always around, and you could reward the faithful with a young, new body while shipping the malefactor off to Momrath until he or she dropped dead.

Chief industries were light manufacturing in general, computers and computer design, weapons, tools, all manner of wood products, seafood protein, and fertilizer. They even exported some of this stuff beyond the Warden system, something I hadn't realized was possible. It was even possible to "sterilize" some types of things, mostly inorganic compounds, and keep them together and working. That led to an obvious connection. That very human robot that had broken into the defense computers, for example. Was it possible that somewhere here among the more primitive machines, at least one place was turning out these sophisticated robots to some alien-supplied design? And if so, was there here some sort of programming genius capable of turning out robots so real they would fool even close friends and family, as had the alien robot? It sounded and felt right. No violent criminals here, they said. Only technological ones. The best.

By our fourth day all of us were becoming bored and restless. As much as could be learned in any brief period had already been taught us, so obviously we were being kept here at this point only for reasons not yet revealed by our hosts. For me, the wait was getting dangerous, since several of the prisoners had formed casual liaisons and I'd been propositioned repeatedly. Pressure mounted as I became a "challenge" to a couple of the men. I had no desire for any such experience, not in *this* body, but the situation was causing a social gap to open between me and the others. I wanted this waiting over with and for us to be out in the world as soon as possible.

I also wanted classification, something they certainly should have been able to do long before now, considering all the tests. I'd tried to angle the aptitude parts heavily toward computers and math, since not only was that consistent with the individual I was supposed to be but also that was where the greatest potential for moving up and finding out things might be. Besides, I'd listed a high level of expertise on many of the older-type computers in use here.

Near the end of the fourth day it hit me just what we *were* waiting for. Obviously, if some measure of control was needed, they didn't want to throw us Cerberan virgins out before we knew just what the Warden facts of life would be. Close proximity, they'd said.

All those cots all close together.

Acclimation, they'd told us, took three or four days, so it was about right. They were waiting, then, until the morning when all or most of us woke up in different bodies.

That thought brought up a mental dilemma for me. If we had to switch to leave, I'd rather leave as a man—but because of the personal problem I noted, I'd been sleeping off in a corner nearest the other women but more or less to myself. How many days would it take? I wondered. And did I have the skill and the guts to get on with this? I finally decided I had to give it a try or be trapped on the wrong side. So I picked my man carefully with an eye to age, looks, physical condition, and the like. Fortunately, my candidate, Hull Bruska, was a shy, somewhat gentle-seeming man who had caused me the least problems. His crime was even more remote from people than Qwin's had been. Apparently he'd managed electronically to tap and shift small parts of planetary budgets into frontier accounts, all from a small repair service on one of the civilized worlds. He was somewhat proud of his accomplishment, and not at all hesitant to talk about it. The cause of his downfall, ironically, was that he was too successful. Too much money showed up in the accounts of several frontier banks, the kind that attracts security police just because of the size of the assets. Obviously he needed to use more than the four banks he did to spread it out. When a bank's assets quadruple in less than two years without apparent cause, you *know* somebody's going to ask how, but Bruska's forte was machines, not the fine points of getting away with the spoils.

Curiously, he had no real plans for the money. He'd done it, he told me, mostly out of boredom. After nine years of repair and redesign of financial computers he'd simply worked it out as a mental exercise, "more or less for fun." Then when he'd put his plan into action just to see if it would work, and it had, doing it again became sort of irresistible, almost to see how much he could get away with. "I wasn't really hurting anybody," he explained, "and there was a tiny bit of satisfaction in fooling the whole Confederacy, of putting one over on them. Kinda made them human."

I liked Bruska, who also enjoyed talking about himself enough that we never got through the hand-holding stage that night. He was shy enough as a man that maybe, I hoped, becoming a woman would open up a whole new social life for him.

We slept very close, my cot against a wall and his next to mine to minimize any risks on my part. I fell asleep that night hoping against hope I'd get lucky, and quickly.

DATA REPORT INTERRUPTION. END TRANSMISSION DIRECT TRANSCEIVER. AS SUBJECT LEFT ORIGINAL BODY, ORGANIC TRANSMITTER LINK BROKEN. SUBSEQUENT REPORTS VIA READOUT BY SUBCONSCIOUS DEEP-PROBE HYPNOTIC COMMAND INTO DEVICES SUPPLIED, CUED, NATIVE AGENTS IN OUR EMPLOY. RUN NEXT SEQUENCE READOUT. SUBJECT UNAWARE OF COMPULSION OR READOUT.

CHAPTER FOUR

Settling In

All but four of us changed bodies during that fourth night. Luck being with me, I was once again young, male, and Confederacy standard, although Bruska didn't really accept the swap with good grace. They separated all of us quickly to minimize the trauma, and I was assured that good psychs would help those who needed it to adjust.

They did a complete set of tests once again, mostly on the psych side, to determine if any of us not showing severe distress were actually hiding it. Naturally I passed with flying colors. I was overjoyed at my carefully planned result.

I also found that the two most objectionable men had changed with their female partners during that night, which I considered poetic justice. Let them find out how unpleasant men like them could be from the other side; then perhaps if they got to be men again they'd be better and more considerate.

The small ID card was simply placed in a slot. I was told it would work from *any* slot for it, in stores or even to unlock doors, if you first called the number of the Identity Placement Bureau and told them which slot you were using. Basically, Bruska's name and computer code were erased from the little chip and mine were placed there. They did a check with the brain-reading machine to make sure all worked okay, and it had, so at last I was given an assignment.

"Tooker Compucorp in Medlam needs programmers," I was told, "and your experience fits that bill. Two hundred units have been credited to your account compliments of the government, which will be enough to get you there and get you settled. It's a good company and a good location if you like the tropics. Warm there most of the year."

And with little more than this and some instructions on how to buy things like clothes and tickets and who to see, I was off.

I found that the little three-pronged gadgets were literally everywhere. To get on the shuttle to Medlam you walked up, put your card in the slot, and put on the little device. If everything checked, the fare was deducted from your account and your card returned to you, and in this case a physical ticket was printed. Very efficient and very simple.

I also found that a number of small purchases worked just with the card —newspapers, confections, that sort of thing.

It was a long ride with a lot of stops and several times I had to keep myself from dozing off—the situation could get serious if somebody else was dozing, too. Fortunately the shuttle had a small food service dispensing system where you could get stimulant drinks, including a Cerberan version of coffee and another of tea, and snacks. I drank a lot of stimulant drinks along the way and needed all of them.

I arrived late in the afternoon, but got a robocab to the Tooker offices anyway on the off-chance that I wouldn't be too late for that day.

The place was imposing, that was for sure. Glassy windows lined towering tree trunks all around, and in between, cradled like some play treehouse for the impossibly rich, an imposing all-glass-fronted office building that connected to all the vast trunks. This, then, was Tooker.

The main offices had already closed for the day, but the night staff was very cordial and recommended a nearby hotel for the night. The hotel, entirely in a massive trunk, was modern and luxurious inside. Nervously, I called the Central Banking number to see how much I still had left after all this, and was surprised and relieved to find that I still had 168.72 units in my account.

The only unusual thing about the room was that there was a switch in the headboard of the bed with a sign that read: TURN BEFORE SLEEPING. I discovered that turning it raised plating around the bed from floor to ceiling, plates of some thin but firm plasticlike substance through which ran metal threads of some sort.

Claustrophobia, then, was a real problem on Cerberus. The shield was obviously there to ensure a good night's sleep with no unexpected exchanges. I wondered what sort of distance would be the maximum range for a sleep exchange and decided I'd have to know that. I asked one of the desk employees about it, and he, upon finding I was new, told me that the shields weren't necessary in the hotel and that almost nobody used them, but they were there because some big shots became paranoid. Although in some cases, an exchange could take place at up to twenty meters, the walls, floor, and ceiling of all rooms were treated to shield. That made me feel a little better, and I didn't use the shield again that evening.

The room vision monitors were no help, since they seemed composed of years-old bad programming from the civilized worlds and some really horrible and amateurish local programming, but I got a print-out of the local paper and looked it over. Not much there, either—not big-city scope at all; more like the vacuous weeklies produced in some rural areas. The only unique item was a small column back with the classifieds for personals and announcements called "switched," followed by a double column of names—maybe a dozen pairs. One way to know who your friends really were here, I reflected.

In fact, the ads were the only things of real interest. There was evidently a small but thriving competitive sector on consumer goods allowed between the corporations, assuring a variety of goods at less than totally uniform prices. On the civilized worlds, of course, there were few brands of anything. For example, the best tested and most recommended toothpaste was everybody's toothpaste, perhaps in three or four flavors, and there were no brands or competition. Here there was, for the first time since I'd been on the frontier, and I found I kind of liked it.

There were also banks, although they were not such full-service institutions as those with which I was familiar. Apparently you could take some of your units out of the master account and place it with a bank at interest, and also borrow money from such banks. There was therefore a semi-independent subeconomy here, and that too was worth noting.

Judging from the want ads, Tooker was the big employer, but many other places also advertised, so some movement was possible on one's own. The independent merchants advertised a lot for part-time help, too, suggesting some economic disparity and also indicating that, even if the executive offices closed in the late afternoon, Tooker operated around the clock in many divisions.

To my surprise, some churches were listed—in fact, a fair number of them for just about every belief under the sun, including some new to me that sounded pretty bizarre. Also part-time schools to better yourself or your position, lots of the usual stuff like that.

That brought up a point, and I checked the local phone directory. No schools for the young were listed anywhere, nor were there any headings for day care or other services for children or parents. Obviously I still had gaps to fill in for this new culture.

Medlam, being subtropical, seemed to have a number of resorts and tourist-oriented stuff, including several for "Thrilling Charter Bork Hunts!" whatever a bork was.

Interestingly, nowhere, not in the briefing, not in the guide book, nor anywhere else was there reference to Wagant Laroo. The Lord of Cerberus certainly kept a low profile.

The next day I checked out bright and early and showed up at the Tooker personnel office. They were expecting me and quickly processed me into the corporation. The job was thirty-eight hours a week at 2.75 units per hour, although that could increase up to 9.00 units with seniority in my assistant's position and even more should I move up. I definitely intended on moving up. I was told, too, that I was a Class I Individual, which was reserved for those with special skills. Class I's kept the same job regardless of body. Class II's kept the same *job* regardless of who was inside the body. There was also a Class III for unskilled workers who could switch jobs if they and their employers agreed—a sort of safety valve, I guessed. Idly I asked what happened if a I and II switched, and was told matter-of-factly that in that case the decision on who did what was made by the government, usually getting judges to switch them back forcibly.

"Take my advice if you're the kind that likes switching around," the personnel manager told me. "Switch only with the other I's. It's simpler and causes no trouble."

"I doubt if I'll do much switching in the near future," I assured him. "Not voluntarily, anyway."

He nodded. "Just remember the possibilities and guard against them, and you never will switch unless you want to, and then only with *whom* you want. And when you're gettin' older and want a new start—well, that's up to you. Stay clean, work hard, and make yourself indispensable or at least important—that is the best insurance. Make 'em *want* to give you a new body every thirty years or so. That's the best way."

I nodded soberly. "Thanks. I'll remember that." Of course I had no intention of settling into a regular routine for that long a time. But I *did* need some time like that, time to get to know people and get to know the world and the society. Patience is the greatest of virtues if you're going to subvert a society, and there's no substitute for preparation.

I would like to say that during the next four months I did all sorts of daring and exciting things, but the truth is that there are only brief moments like that in a job like mine—all the rest is boring, plodding stuff. The corporation provided me with subsidized housing—a comfortable tree-lined flat with full kitchen, air conditioning, and the rest that was quite pleasant. The job they started me at was anything but demanding, and the speed with which I "assisted" designers in improving new circuit designs marked me quickly for bigger and better things, particularly since I was careful to let my superiors take the credit while keeping evidence of who really did the work—evidence they knew about. This put them in my debt without my seeming threatening. I could have hogged full credit and had not. In a word, I was becoming indispensable, at least to the next level above me, like the man said. It was child's play, actually, since the designs used on Cerberus were a good ten or even twenty years out of date and quite limited in one area. No self-aware computers of any kind were allowed here. That was really the key to retardation in the Warden Diamond, and a clever one on the part of the Confederacy, which was very real, even here. You didn't have to land or even enter the atmosphere to wipe an entire borough off the face of the planet, and they'd do that as an object lesson if they got wind of any bending of the rules.

In point of fact, that very primitiveness imposed on the planet aided me over many other technological masterminds, since most or all of them were trained and developed on machines too advanced for here. There were very few of us, really, who could do the utmost with the older designs.

I made a number of friends and quickly became a social gadfly. The corporation had a lot of teams competing against other corporate employee teams in just about every sport I knew. After working out regularly and fine-tuning this body I now wore, I excelled at them, as usual, though I was never able to get myself up to the physical peak of my original body.

Bork hunting, however, I passed on, at least for the time. It seemed that bork were monstrous, nasty creatures that inhabited the oceans, seemed to be composed entirely of teeth, and occasionally grew large enough to swallow boats whole. They had a natural dislike of everything and everybody and were even known to attack boats just for being there and sometimes even to snare a low-flying shuttle. Hunting them just required too many specialized skills, and that sport had no initial appeal for me. Though bork were nasty, the oceans contained an enormous number of creatures that had some commercial uses, from unicellular protein creatures that linked together into floating beds kilometers long to smaller sea creatures that provided edible meat, skins, and other such things. Bork hunting might be a thrill for some, but to the ocean harvesting corporations it was a commercial necessity.

The flying creatures with such names as geeks and gops, made me wonder just what sort of person first named all these things. The flying things, mostly small, served the function of insects on other worlds, cross-pollinating this jungle from the top. In addition, there were a few predatory fliers that were monsters, too. One giant flier with a thick barrel-like body about a meter around had a neck more than three meters long and a wingspread of more than ten meters. Its head looked like a nightmare of blazing reptilian eyes and sharp teeth, but nobody much paid attention to them as long as they didn't come too close. These were carrion eaters mostly, and they remained aloft over the oceans much of the time.

Body switching was rare, although I was approached once or twice in a casual way. Every once in a while somebody new would show up who would turn out to be somebody old after all. Although few people switched—except for the occasional couple that switched almost nightly, always with each other—the subject was nonetheless a regular topic of conversation in lounges and at parties. The possibility was always there, around you, even if you didn't see it. You were reminded of it constantly when you went home or stayed at a hotel on a company trip, and you always slept shielded and alone, no matter how friendly or intimate you became with others.

There were some topics nobody really referred to, though. One was children—you just didn't discuss it—and second was advancing age. Few people you met looked any older than forty, and those who looked the oldest seemed much more jittery and under a lot more pressure than most.

Body switching ended any sort of sexual stereotypes, to a greater extent even than on the civilized worlds. When gender could so easily be exchanged, it seemed silly to think of separate sexual roles, particularly since it seemed that all the women I met had been sterilized. That, too, interested me—this was true of both sexes on the civilized worlds, where all breeding was done in bio breeding centers, but the actuality seemed particularly peculiar here. So when I saw the pregnant girl, I was drawn irresistibly to her.

I had taken to frequenting a small store near the docks which specialized in entertainment electronics and which seemed to have some sort of a remarkable underground connection stretching off-world at some point that got a lot of the latest performances from the civilized worlds. Here was a piece of home, a place where you might run into other former prisoners, now exiles like myself, there also to get a little taste and memory of what was lost.

She was there one day, looking over the latest selections. A tiny young woman—it was impossible to think of her other than as a girl. From her looks, she could hardly have been out of her mid-teens. She had extremely long reddish-brown hair, perhaps a meter or more in length, that was held loosely with a brightly sparkling headband.

Actually, I wouldn't have known she was pregnant except for Otah, the owner of the place. I happened to be talking gadgets with him, as usual, when I spotted her. "Hmmm. Cute. Never saw *her* around here before."

"You stay away from that one," Otah warned gravely. "She's with child."

I frowned. "First time I've heard *that* here. I was beginning to wonder how any of the natives came about. But what's the taboo?"

"Pregnant. Don't you know? It's not a condition, it's a Class II occupation."

Well, there it was at last. "It's a *job*? She makes a living having babies?"

He nodded. "Hell of a thing, ain't it? There's a whole colony of them down off Akeba. There's some that love it, but most of 'em would kill to switch bodies outta there. Once you're that, you're *that*. Best to keep 'em on a business basis only."

I had to chuckle. "What do they do? Steal your soul?"

He looked stricken. "Don't say that. Some of 'em's desperate enough to do most anything."

I couldn't help but chuckle at his caution and wonder just what could be so horrible. I *did* sort of wonder about the whole idea, though. Cloning was certainly within the allowable technology, if they wanted to spend the massive setup costs. Instead they seemed to have opted to take a percentage of young women, probably selected for genetic characteristics, and paid them to have kids. It seemed to me that, except for the birth itself, the major problem would be boredom—or perhaps being harried to death with a nursery full.

Certainly I'd never heard of motherhood being something horrible. On some of the more primitive frontier worlds it was something of an occupation and had been since the dawn of time. This was a piece of the social puzzle I had wanted to fill in, and here was the opportunity.

In order not to alarm Otah, I didn't approach her in the shop, but surreptitiously followed her when she left. After some window-shopping, she went to a sidewalk café and sat down at one of the outside tables, apparently enjoying the sun and salt spray. I allowed her to order, then casually walked up and into the café patio, and stopped as if seeing her for the first time.

"Well, hello!" I said. "I just saw you in Otah's."

She smiled and nodded. "Yes, I saw you in there, too." She gestured. "Care to join me?"

"Glad to," I responded, and sat down. "Qwin Zhang," I introduced myself.

"I'm Sanda Tyne," she told me. "You're from the civilized worlds, aren't you? Outside?"

I nodded. "How did you know? My looks?"

"Oh, no. Your accent. We have a couple of Outside girls at Akeba House. You can always tell."

"I hadn't been aware I had an accent," I told her honestly, filing *that* one away for future work. Analyze speech patterns and do comparative analysis to eliminate accent when needed. "Still, you say you have a couple of people from offworld at—Akeba House, was it?" I paused for a carefully measured moment. "You know, Otah told me to stay in the back of the shop while you were there. He acted like you had some kind of terrible disease or something."

She laughed, a nice, musical laugh that complemented her low, sexy voice. "I know," she told me, then made her face up into a caricature of Otah's and lowered her voice still more. "Stay away from her. She makes *babies!*"

I had to laugh at the perfect imitation. "That's about it. Maybe I'm naive, but what's so horrible? If somebody didn't do it at the dawn of time we wouldn't be here."

She sighed, then seemed to turn a little more serious. "Oh, it's not that it's bad. It's not great, either. True, you get an almost unlimited expense

account, and you live pretty good—Akeba House is like a really great
high-class hotel—but after a while it gets to be a pain. Some of us get
picked as little girls, but most of us chose it when we had to. At fourteen
they come and tell you sterilization or motherhood, and some, like me, got
dumb and chose the latter. For a while it's a lot of fun—particularly the
early stuff. But after several years and several babies the whole thing gets
very boring. You're sick for months every morning, and you're restricted in
what you can eat, drink, or even do. And you become limited. You learn
how to make, have, and raise babies, and that's it. You can't get out once
you're in, as you can with any other job. You're stuck. And when you see
other women, like the ones you grew up with, with good jobs really doing
something with their lives, you think you wasted it all, blew it."

I nodded, more or less understanding her point. "You're pretty frank
with a stranger," I noted.

She shrugged. "Why not?"

There wasn't a good response to that one. "Why this taboo on talking
about kids, though?"

She looked at me strangely. "Right off the boat, aren't you? Hell, think
about it. Ever seen any old people?"

"No. I assume the bodies wind up on mines someplace."

She nodded. "You got it. And where do the new bodies come from? A
certain percentage come from us, that's where. A baby a year, every year,
and only a small population growth. It's tough. They take most of 'em
away from us after only a year—a real heartbreaker, too. Most of us send
'em all away to government child-care centers so we don't have to go
through any more pain than we have to. Have 'em, nurse 'em, then forget
'em. Some get hardened to it, but some just get sick of it or fed up. You're
trapped, though, and you just keep at it until the docs say you gotta stop.
Then you get a fresh young body if you have done well and made your
life quota."

I had to admit it was sounding less and less pleasant. I was beginning to
see why Laroo's assumption of power had been accompanied by a population increase all out of proportion to the numbers. Although the system
probably predated him, he would order stepped-up life quotas strictly out
of paranoia. The top leadership's one nightmare would be a declining
birthrate.

"Surely you can quit. A simple operation—"

She laughed derisively. "Sure. And forget all about being reborn into a
new body. Because you lack any useful skills, there's only the dirtiest
labor jobs to make any sort of a living, and that would be only if they let
you. Most likely you'd just not find a job, be declared a vagrant, and then
it's a one-way trip to the mines, or maybe they'd just knock you off. Those
mines are mostly automated—most folks don't think too many people are
really sent anywhere."

More information to file, but the subject was becoming increasingly unpleasant. "I don't know about that lack of useful skills, though," I told her. "You have a pretty good vocabulary."

She shrugged. "Mostly self-taught. You get bored and have to do something. A lot of girls are artists or try and write stuff or things like that. Me, I just read and watch Otah's bootlegs. Hell, I'm just twenty, bore four kids with another comin' in six months, and I'm already climbing the walls. I got fifteen, maybe twenty more years of this before they let me out. And you know what they'll do? Give me another fifteen-year-old girl's body and put me back at it again! After twenty years I'd be an expert at nothin' but motherhood."

The bitterness and frustration in her voice was very real, and for the first time I understood Otah's attitude and the attitude of most Cerberans toward both the mothers and the subject of children. Nobody liked to think of children, since they realized that was where their new bodies would come from. Having once been young themselves, they really didn't like to think they were robbing some kid of a lifetime, advancing him or her from fifteen to forty-five in one step, perhaps condemning him or her to death or forced labor on some airless moon. They knew—but they wanted to live, wanted *their* new bodies, and so they just didn't talk about it, tried not to think about it, on the grounds that facts ignored were not facts at all. Seeing those who bore those children brought up all the guilt, so they were treated in the same way as people with some horrible disease. And they *did* carry such a plague—it was called conscience.

What this told me was that they had already sold their souls. Sold them to Wagant Laroo. The population of Cerberus took on a whole new light for me that day, there in the bright sunshine and salt air. I remembered old horror stories of vampires—the living dead who drank the blood of the living to survive, to be immortal. And that's what Cerberus really was—a planet of vampires.

You're lucky to be sent to Cerberus. Here you might live forever!

Yeah, in absolute slavery to a government that could grant you eternal life—at the cost of an innocent child's life—or take it away.

"I don't understand why they don't just invest in cloning," I told her. "They would still control the bodies and thus the people."

"They can't," she told me. "The Warden organism can't cope with a clone in the early stages. The natural way's the only way on any of the Diamond worlds."

Well, so much for the easy way out, I told myself. Still, there had to be better ways than this. Better managed with less heartbreak. I took a fresh look at Sanda Tyne. Tragic figure, perhaps, but the ultimate vampire herself.

"I would think the lure of eternal life wouldn't be enough for some people," I noted. "Some might prefer death."

"Not outside the motherhood," she responded. "And inside, yes, you're right. But they monitor us *very* carefully for signs of depression and suicidal tendencies. Almost nobody really goes through with it—maybe two or three a year. The rest—well, I guess the will to live is too strong. And if you try it and don't make it, they can put you through the ringer. You don't have to have much of a brain to do what we do. They take you into a little room, point a little laser probe here"—she pointed to her forehead—"and *zap!* You walk around with this nice little smile on your face and you don't do or think of nothin', but you can still have babies." She shivered. "I think I'd rather die than that—but you see? The penalty for *not* dyin' is so much worse."

What a cheery afternoon I'm having, I thought sourly. Still, I truly understood and sympathized with Sanda and the others like her. There *were* better ways, I felt sure. Not less cruel, perhaps, to some of the children, for there would be a revolution here if the new bodies for old potential was destroyed, but at least for the people like Sanda. A technological world should allow mothers to be anything they wanted as well, and it should be able to meet its need not only to grow but also to replace. There was a simple system that would at least put the responsibility where it belonged.

Everyone could be forced to bear his own replacement. *Then* he alone would have the option of killing his offspring or himself in the normal way. And, with body switching, assuming sterility was ended, everyone *could* bear his own replacement. That was the only fair way. It wouldn't end cruelty to the kids who got stuck as replacements, but far fewer would take that option—and nobody could sweep the responsibility under a mental rug.

This body-switching business sounded great at the beginning, but I was beginning now to see it for what it was—a disease. A disease that was population-wide and *required* a totalitarian system to maintain.

This realization made my assignment easier—and more urgent. I no longer had any thought whatsoever about *not* doing away with Wagant Laroo. And, at least for the period of time needed to create a real social revolution on Cerberus, I intended to be Lord myself.

CHAPTER FIVE

A Glimmer of a Plan

Over the next few weeks I continued to meet with Sanda, whom I not only felt sorry for but genuinely liked. She seemed to enjoy the company of someone from a place she would never see and a background she could hardly imagine—one who treated her as a person, not a pariah. I was, however, becoming restless and a little impatient. By this point I felt I had enough contacts and enough elements put together to get into action. But

I lacked the proper starting point, the opening I needed to have any chance of success.

My long-range objective was clear: locate and kill Wagant Laroo, then somehow assume political control of the syndicalist machinery that would allow me to retailor this world for the better. The fact that my plan dovetailed with the wishes of the Confederacy was all to the good, since I didn't want any problems from that quarter and I knew that somehow they were keeping tabs on me, probably with the aid of blackmailable agents down there—exiles with family or something else to lose back home.

My experience at Tooker convinced me that computer and robotic science on Cerberus was too far behind the Confederacy to be directly linked to the alien robots, but I still had suspicions. At least a few really good minds in the organic computer field had wound up here. Though their names occasionally cropped up in shoptalk at parties and the like, they were nowhere in evidence. Of course Tooker wasn't the only or even the largest computer firm on Cerberus, but it was definitely a middle-weight in the economic mainstream, unlikely to be left out of any major deals. Part of the trouble was I was still too low down in the hierarchical ranks to even hear the rumors of anything so secret.

Therefore, several steps had to be taken before I could even consider Laroo, one being I first had to make friends in high places who could be of help with such information as well as with favors. I also needed considerably more money than I had or could easily make—and some way to conceal it if I *could* figure out a way. Not that I couldn't steal money from banks—that was relatively easy with this computer system. The trouble was, money had to be put somewhere. In an all-electronic currency system it would show a conspicuous bulge. To disguise a stash properly would take a major operation with major resources. In other words, it would take a fortune to steal and hide a fortune.

Finally, after money and influence, I'd need somebody on the inside of Laroo's top operation. No mean trick. But that was the last of my problems and was contingent on the other two.

I traveled to Akeba one weekend mostly thinking these dark thoughts and hoping something would break my way. I had to go down there now to see Sanda, who was starting to show and so was generally restricted to her area, more by social custom than by any firm law.

Akeba House was a huge complex located on its own network. It resembled the hotel I'd stayed in my first night in town. I could see a swimming pool, various game courts, and other resortlike additions, and was told there were more such inside. But it was restricted territory, so I could get only to the gate.

Sanda had left a message for me at the gatehouse that she was down on the docks. I took the public elevator down. Just outside the compound was a small complex of commercial trawlers and bork-hunting boats, mostly the commercial type that protected the watermen rather than the sports charter type.

Sanda, out on a dock next to a formidable-looking hunter-killer boat, spotted me, called, and waved. I ambled over, wondering what she was doing down here.

"Qwin! Come on! I want you to meet Dylan Kohl!" she told me, and together we boarded the boat. It was sleek and functional with twenty-five centimeters or more of armor plate, a retractable hydrofoil, and a nasty-looking cannon. The vessel looked more like a warship than a commercial boat. I'd never been on one before, but found it fascinating.

Dylan Kohl turned out to be a tall, tanned, muscular-looking young woman wearing a sunshade, dark glasses, some very brief shorts and tennis shoes. Smoking a huge, fat Charon-import cigar, she was working on some sort of electronics console near the forward turret. At our approach, she dropped a small tool and turned to meet us.

"So you're Qwin," she said, her voice low and hard, putting out a hand. "I've heard a lot about you."

I shook the hand. A hell of a grip, I noted. "And you're Dylan Kohl, about whom I've never heard a word up to this moment," I responded.

She laughed. "Well, until you came along I was the only conversation Sanda had on a more than business basis outside the House."

"Dylan's a rare hope," Sanda added. "She's the only person I know who ever got out of the motherhood."

That raised my eyebrows. "Oh? And how'd you manage that? I've been hearing how impossible it was."

"Is," Dylan told me. "I cheated. I did it crooked, I admit, but I never regretted doing so. I drugged my way out."

"Drugged? Even caffeine and other stimulants usually get pushed out in an hour or less."

She nodded. "Some drugs work. Stuff distilled from Warden plants, particularly ones from Lilith. Strictly controlled, government use only— but I managed to get a little of a hypnotic. Let's not go into how. Swapped with a Class II dockworker."

We walked back to the aft section behind the pilot house, which had been set up as a sun deck while in port. I settled into a chair and so did Sanda. Dylan went below and returned with some refreshing-looking drinks laced with fruit. She then stretched out on a collapsible chaise longue. I tried the drink—a little too sweet for my taste, but not at all bad.

Dylan's hard, determined manner contrasted sharply with Sanda's. No matter what body she'd originally had, it was hard to imagine her as a professional mother.

"This dock down here did it," she began. "Watching the boats go in and out, hearing the stories, seeing the expressions on the faces of those who went out and came back every day. I don't know. Something in my head, I guess. I've had a lot of lovers, but I've been married to the sea ever since I can remember. It showed, I think—the water people would always talk to me. We had the same feelings. One of 'em finally took a risk and smuggled me out on a run. I was hooked. I knew that no matter what happened somehow I had to work the boats. Just shows that if you have enough smarts and you want something bad enough you can get it. I keep telling Sanda that when she's down."

I smiled and nodded. I was beginning to like Dylan Kohl quite a bit. Although I didn't share her love for the sea, in general attitudes her mind paralleled my own.

"This is your boat, I take it?"

She nodded. "Every rivet and plate. Once I was out of the House I was determined to make myself a Class I secure, and to do it with boat work. I'd go out with 'em on my own from time to time, filling in where they needed help while doing my dock cleanup job. When openings came along, I got signed on as crew. There are usually openings in this business, but you gotta be crazy to be in it to begin with. On a world where everybody's trying to live forever I love a job where you get to be captain by surviving long enough. Eventually you either have your own boat or get swallowed whole or in little pieces. I wouldn't have it any other way."

"You're the captain, then?"

She nodded. "Shorter time than most, I'm told. Four years. I'm the sole survivor of her original crew of six. They were a pretty sloppy bunch, though—it's why I picked 'em."

Here was one tough woman, I told myself. And, I guess, you had to be in this kind of business. As she said, most Cerberans tried as hard as they could to stay away from any sort of danger, with death feared far more than any place where people died naturally and normally. But in her business you constantly courted danger. It was often fatal business.

"Ever been on a bork hunt?" she asked.

I shook my head slowly from side to side. "No, never really had the inclination after seeing the pictures."

"Aw, there's nothing like it," she enthused. "Going in and cut against the thing at thirty to forty knots, your skill, knowledge, and reflexes against the monster's. You don't feel bad about killing them, either—they're so nasty and good-for-nothing. And you're saving the lives and livelihood of the salts who work the deeps. You feel good about it—and I am good at it. In seven months now as cap I haven't lost a crew member. Why, just the other day we were down off Laroo's Island and we—"

"What!" I exclaimed, almost rising to my feet. "Where?"

She stopped and appeared slightly annoyed at being interrupted. "Why, Laroo's Island. It's a little out of my territory, about a hundred and forty kilometers southeast of here, but we got to chasing a big one. A real challenge. You get like that."

"You mean Wagant Laroo?"

"There's two?"

Suddenly I was *very* interested in bork hunting.

Carefully, though, I steered the conversation away from Laroo and back into her tales of the hunt, which she obviously enjoyed repeating to a new audience. I could see Sanda with stars in her eyes at hearing all this. Even if she didn't feel like hunting borks, Dylan Kohl was the embodiment of her ideal. The hero-worship went really deep.

Inwardly, though, I felt some excitement and mentally checked my programmed map of Cerberus—nothing marked "Laroo's Island" on it. Taking a look to the southeast of Akeba, I detected only a couple of possibilities, isolated groves of great trees separated from the main body by perhaps thirty or more kilometers.

I began to see an unseen overhand in my current position and location. The Warden worlds weren't as free of some Confederacy machinations as they liked to think.

I saw more of Dylan after that, generally but not always accompanied by Sanda, and eventually eked out more information on Laroo's Island. The Lord of Cerberus was a secretive man, one who enjoyed power but not the celebrity that usually went with it. The island was neither the headquarters of the government nor his official residence, but he was there as often as possible. The place was reputed to be truly grand, the ultimate in resorts. It was also constantly patrolled by air and ship, approaches monitored by just about every known surveillance system. If somehow you beat it, you then had to pass a brain scan to keep from getting creamed automatically. It was in fact as nearly impregnable a fortress as the Lord of the Diamond, Boss of all Bosses, Chairman of the Council of Syndicates, could design.

Like all absolute dictators, Wagant Laroo feared assassination the most —and more than any others, since that was the only way of getting rid of him or allowing his syndicate chiefs to move up to the top themselves. He himself had gotten the job by judicious and legally untraceable eliminations.

Well, I didn't want to wait twenty or thirty years to move up the ladder. Not only did I not have *that* much patience, but there was more of a chance that something would go wrong in such a slow rise than by the more direct route. But the challenge was becoming irresistible on its own merits. The little-seen political boss in his impregnable fortress! Just perfect.

All the elements were now in place for a break when it presented itself, and it did so a bit sooner than expected, judging by the worried expression on Turgan Sugal's face. Sugal was the Tooker plant manager, a pretty good one who took an extraordinary interest in every facet of the business. Even those of us on the lowest end of the seniority scale knew him, for he was always about, checking on us, making suggestions, socializing, playing on all the company teams. He was, in fact, a very popular boss, and highly accessible. He'd been around a while, too. Although his current body was barely thirty, he was said to be almost a hundred years old.

He looked the hundred, though, when he dropped down to my department to tell me he wouldn't be able to play in the company cordball game that evening. I was captain of the team.

"What's the matter?" I asked him, genuinely concerned. "You look like a man about to have his head chopped off."

"Not quite that bad," he responded glumly, "but bad enough. We just got the next quarter's production quota and allocations from the syndicate. They're sky-high. At the same time they're yanking several key people from me for some big project upstairs. Khamgirt's been out to get me for years, and he's dropped the whole load on my shoulders. I don't see how we can meet the quotas with a reduced force, and it's my neck if we don't."

"Can't you lay off some of the stuff to the other plants?" I asked. "Or get some help from them on personnel, anyway?"

He shook his head. "Normally, yeah, but Khamgirt really means business this time and he's refused. He's never liked my way of doing business, anyway, and canning me has always been a big goal." He paused and chuckled. "And you thought when you were the boss you didn't have to worry about this kind of shit any more, didn't you?"

I returned the chuckle. "No, I know the score very well. Remember, I had a long life and job before I ever got to this planet."

He nodded. "Yeah. That's right—you're from Outside. I keep forgetting. Maybe that's why you're easier to talk to, huh?"

"A damn sight cheaper than a psych, anyway," I joked, but my mind was already working. Here it was, I could *feel* it. Here was the break, the start in the chain that would eventually lead me to Wagant Laroo.

"Tell me, Mr. Sugal," I said slowly, choosing my pace with care, "how would things go next quarter if President Khamgirt wasn't president any more?"

He paused and looked at me quizzically. "What are you suggesting? That I kill him? That's damned hard and you know it."

That statement gave me an inward chuckle, since Khamgirt was a little enough fish that I could probably have taken him out effortlessly. But I hardly wanted to betray myself as a pro in that area. Not yet. Too many other nervous bosses would see me as a threat.

"Uh-uh," I answered him. "I'm talking about getting *him* canned."

Sugal snorted derisively. "Hell, Zhang, you'd have to prove gross incompetence, direct and prolonged mismanagement, or criminal intent against the state—and as much as I hate the son of a bitch, I don't think he's guilty of any of those things."

"Whether he is or isn't is beside the point," I told him. "Suppose I could hang one of those on him anyway?"

"Are you crazy? What you're saying is impossible!" he responded, but he sat down.

"Not only not impossible, but not even that hard if a little luck is riding with me—and it usually is. I'm pretty sure such a thing has been done before, many times. I studied the histories of a lot of our syndicate bosses

and corporation presidents. This is a technological world founded by technological criminals, Mr. Sugal. Founded by them and run by them."

He shook his head in disbelief. "That's absurd. I would have heard
about it."

"Would they tell you? So you could do it to them? Look, even Laroo
has been on Cerberus less time than you've been around by far, and look
what happened to him."

Sugal considered that. "How would you do it?"

"Given, say, a week and a little inside information, I'll know exactly. I
have a rough plan in mind, but it'll need fine-tuning, the kind that can
only come when it has a specific objective and target."

He looked at me somewhat uneasily. "And why would you do this? For
me? Don't give me that bull."

"No, for me. What would happen to your position if I could do it?
Where would that leave you?"

"Probably as a senior vice-president," he told me. "Higher up, certainly,
particularly since I'd know it was coming when nobody else did and
would be able to pave the way. I know how to do it, but the only opening
to the top I had a chance at Khamgirt took. Still, as I said before, what's
in it for you? I can hardly promote you to plant manager so suddenly."

"No, I don't want much of an advancement," I told him. "In fact, I'm
thinking of a differect direction for myself. One safe for you. Do you
know Hroyasail?"

Again he was caught a little off-guard, which was fine. "Yeah, it's one
of our subsidiaries. Harvests *skrit* offshore. We use some of the chemicals
from it in making insulators. Why?"

"I want it," I told him. "Right now the place doesn't even have a president. A company accountant comes down three or four times a year from
the home office and that's about it."

"Sure. Something that small usually doesn't need one."

"I think it does. Me. And the position's already provided for, at least on
the organizational chart. All it needs is certification by a senior official.
You could do that as plant manager—but I'd prefer it coming from a senior
vice-president, say."

"Now what in hell would you want that for?"

"My own reasons. But it's a nonthreatening position. The kind of job
they'll give *you* if Khamgirt gets his way and you fail to meet quota. A
pasture job. It pays well, has few responsibilities, has no experience pre-
requisites, and is still within the company. And of course as a company
president I'd love to drop around occasionally and gossip with a senior
vice-president of my parent corporation."

He thought it over. "Supposing—just supposing—you could pull it off.
And, again just supposing, I could finagle that post for you. Would I have
to watch my own back, then?"

"No," I responded as sincerely as I could. "I'm not interested in your
job, present or future. That kind of stuff would drive me nuts. This is a

company world and I'm just not the company type. Believe me, Mr. Sugal, nothing in any of my plans would in any way harm you now or in the future. I like and admire you—but we're two different sorts with two different directions to follow."

"I think I believe you," he told me, still sounding uneasy, "but I'm still not sure if I shouldn't be afraid of you."

"What can you lose? They have you at their mercy now. *I'm* going to do something, not you. You alone will know that I did it—but neither of us will be able to ever use the information against the other because that's the only way both of us can ever be incriminated. If I fail, you're no worse off than you are now. If I succeed, we both get what we want. How about it?"

"I'll believe you can do it when I see it done," he said skeptically, "but I can't see anything against it, either."

I grinned. "You provide me with a few important bits of information, and I'll almost guarantee it. A deal's a deal." I looked at my watch. "And now, if you'll excuse me, I'm going down to change for the game. Sure you won't play?"

He shook his head. "Big meeting tonight with the area managers. But— good luck."

"I try and keep luck out of it, sir," I told him.

CHAPTER SIX

Preparations

Sanda Tyne, Dylan Kohl, Turgan Sugal, and, yes, even fat Otah. Especially him. The elements were all there.

The first thing I did was drop down to a store and buy an armload of electric slates. I needed a lot of plotting and planning with hard copy, but I wanted no trace whatsoever to remain after. No innocent slips of paper, no idle tracing to betray me. When the deed was accomplished, I'd have to stay well protected. The scam would be absolute and it would work, but those higher up, far beyond Khamgirt, would smell a rat somewhere, if only because they were variations of people like me and would have a nose for it. They'd know what had occurred was a frame, but even as they allowed Khamgirt to be led away to oblivion of some kind they'd be searching for the culprit. Khamgirt wouldn't be sacked because they believed him guilty, but for being so sloppy as to allow such a dirty trick to be played on him.

Dylan had exploited much the same weakness in the system when she had broken free of the motherhood by using a drug most people had never heard about or believed existed. I had no access to such substances, and even if I might get some that wasn't what I wanted. Any controlled substances, particularly those from offworld, could be traced by a determined group of investigators. The key to this plan as it developed was that, even if they figured it out, they would reject the explanation because of its very absurdity. I liked that touch.

Even as Sugal got me what I wanted to know—information on night shifts in certain parts of Tooker, various routine business transfer codes, and facts about certain basic computers supplied by Tooker to borough agencies—I started out to complete my subtle recruitment. This was not something that could be done alone, although I would have preferred to do it that way. But what had to be accomplished in very little time was too spread out and complex for any one person to manage. Furthermore, I wanted no chance of interruptions by third parties who might have to be dealt with, so I had to control everybody in the area for a stated period of time. That would be tough. However, I had some things to offer, and some interested parties to offer them to.

By now I had Dylan's measure pretty well and was certain of her ability to keep things quiet, including herself, and of her guts to pull off her assignment. Sanda was the problem. Now over seven months pregnant, she had little freedom of movement, and her life in that cloister was beyond my checking. She'd go along with my plan, of course, but I had to trust Dylan's judgment that she'd keep her mouth shut about it.

I decided on Dylan first, just because I needed her final evaluation on my pregnant potential weak link.

I had to wait for the weekend to get down there, though, because I needed the time with the information Sugal supplied to work things out. Also after a day chasing borks or at least patrolling for them and then cleaning and checking the boat, Dylan was not very lively company in the evenings. In one way we were incompatible: anybody who liked getting up at dawn to go to work was a bit strange and incomprehensible in my book.

I arranged to meet her at a small club in town to make sure that Sanda wouldn't be around. We'd met like this a couple of times before, just to be social—and we had gotten *very* social the last time—but this meeting would be slightly different. She was a very attractive woman, though, and even more so when she dressed for a night on the town rather than a day on the sea.

We ordered dinner and mostly exchanged small talk, then ate and went out to a small cabaret and did a little drinking and dancing. At the end of the evening, we went over to her apartment as we had before, but this time I had something additional in mind.

And at the right moment as I judged it, while we lay there, relaxed, I finally got to the point. In fact, she provided the opening. "You seemed distracted, far away tonight," she noted. "Something wrong with you? Or is it me?"

"No, nothing's wrong," I assured her, "but, yes, you're right. Dylan, it's time I came out in the open, I think, and I hope I know you well enough to trust you."

She sat up and looked at me, half puzzled, half expectant.

"Dylan, we've gotten to know each other quite well. I think we somehow complement each other. And we've talked freely about ourselves, I think. Still, what do you know about me?"

"You're Qwin Zhang, you're a computer programmer for Tooker, and you came from Outside," she replied. "And you've been an awful lot of places across the galaxy. You were loadmaster on a spaceship. And, according to some friends I know, your name is female on the civilized worlds. So? You trying to say you were once a woman? So what?"

"I came here as a woman, yes," I told her, taking the big gamble, "but I wasn't born in that body. It was Qwin Zhang's body—but I'm not Qwin Zhang. Not the original one, anyway."

"I thought only Cerberans could do that."

"It's a different process. A mechanical one, basically. But I wasn't a criminal and I wasn't a loadmaster."

She was staring at me, fascinated but not apprehensive. "So? Who *are* you, then, and what *did* you do?"

"I killed people the Confederacy wanted killed," I told her. "I tracked them down, found them out, and killed them."

There was a sharp intake of breath, but no other reaction. Finally she asked, "And they sent you here to kill someone?"

I nodded. "Yes. But it's someone who needs it, and since I'm stuck here the same as everybody else, that's important. They might try and kill me if I didn't, but that's beside the point. I'm confident enough they wouldn't succeed, and what they want is what I want, too."

"Who?" she asked.

"Wagant Laroo," I told her.

She whistled. "They don't think small, do they? And neither do you. Well, at least that explains why you were so interested in Laroo's Island."

I nodded. "I'm going to do it, Dylan. Nothing is more certain than that —although there are still a lot of steps in the way, and so a lot of time will pass before I can do it. Still it *will* happen. *Nobody* is invulnerable, not even me."

"Any particular reason why?"

"Problems. It seems Laroo and the other Lords of the Diamond made a deal with some aliens to help conquer the Confederacy. I don't have real affection one way or the other for the Confederacy, but I have a lot for the human race."

"These—aliens. What are they like?"

"We don't know," I told her. "All we do know is they're so nonhuman that there's no way they can do their own dirty work. That's why the Four Lords were hired. I'm sure they figure they'll get revenge and be on the winning side, but we don't know about these aliens. After they crack the

Confederacy they might just decide they don't need *us* any more, either. They're trying to find out all they can about these creatures, whoever and whatever they are, but the only common link is the Warden Diamond. And one way of at least throwing a curve is to eliminate the Four Lords as currently constituted. A power struggle would disrupt things, buy time—and the new Lords might not be so thrilled about cooperating with and trusting these allies. I drew Laroo. But after seeing how he runs things here, I'd like a shot at him anyway. There are better, freer ways to run things than this, ones that don't cost people so much of their self-respect. You only have to think of the motherhood to know what I mean."

"I'm not too sure I follow that last bit, but the rest I understand," she said. "I don't think anybody, not even the Four Lords, can commit people like me to help these aliens. All I keep thinking about is a race of sly, clever borks."

"Perhaps," I told her. "Or they might be a lot more appealing—it makes no difference. We don't know anything except that they're *very* nonhuman. Until I get a lot more assurances, that's all I need to know. We here in the Warden Diamond are sitting ducks when they don't need us any more. A civilization capable of crossing space and subtle enough to hire the Four Lords isn't one I could trust with my future."

She was silent for a moment, finally lighting one of those big cigars that took a fair share of her pay. Finally, in a haze of smoke, she asked softly, "Qwin? Why are you telling *me* this?"

"The first step is influence. I need influential friends in high places who can give me information. Dylan, who owns your boat?"

"Hroyasail, of course. Why?"

"Who's president of Hroyasail?"

"Nobody. I told you that."

I nodded. "Suppose *I* was president of Hroyasail? Set the salaries, got better parts, newer equipment—the best."

"What the hell are you talking about?"

"Suppose we *ran* Hroyasail, you and I. Not just a captain whose job can be cut by some bureaucrat, but really running the place. Boss. Sound interesting?"

"Go on."

"I need you to make that possible. You and one other. I'm talking about something criminal, but nobody gets killed or, I hope, even hurt. What I have in mind will take some guts, but I know you have that. Are you willing?"

"I don't know what the hell you're talking about."

"I'm going to get the president of Tooker fired. I'm going to totally discredit him. As a result, certain high-placed officials will move up and be grateful to me. They'll give me Hroyasail and a big bank account and information when I need it. See?"

"You can *do* that?"

I smiled. "Easily. If they haven't changed the fire alarm system in the borough in the past three years."

"*What!*"

I spent the night with Dylan, and over breakfast we discussed the other problem. "Unless you can think of somebody quickly who I would trust, and you *could* trust, for an operation like this, we'll need Sanda as well," I told her. "She's got brains and spunk, and she can do the job, I think. But can we rely on her not to talk? I can't get into Akeba House to see what she's like away from the rest of us. You were there once. What do you think?"

"She'd be a good choice," she agreed. "She's got the biggest crush on you I've ever seen. But to do what you're proposing—I don't think the temptation is possible for her to resist. She'll blow it there."

"If I promise her a way out of the Motherhood free and clear at a later date? Right now I *need* her where she is. I need that expense account she has, and that anonymity as well. But when we're done, I can get her out."

"I don't know. The promise of something later versus something now isn't easy to handle when you're faced with it."

"I think *I* can handle that part," I assured her. "The question is, if I trick her back into her own body, will she blow the thing just for spite?"

"Nobody can say," she said honestly. "But my gut instinct is that she wouldn't. She's got it bad for you. For that matter, so do I, damn it. Qwin, is that all I am to you? Somebody to accomplish your mission, then be paid off?"

I took her hand and squeezed it. "No," I responded gently. "No, you're a lot more than that. And so is Sanda."

She smiled. "I wish I knew for sure. I really do. Somebody like you is a little out of my league, you know, and way out of Sanda's. You were born, bred, and trained for your job. People trust you and don't know why. People confide in you and don't know why. Women fall for you and don't know why. I wonder whether even you know what about you is real."

"In the past, in the old days, you'd be right," I responded honestly. "But not here now, and for the future on Cerberus. This is my home now. My permanent home, and my life. It's different now, Dylan, and so am I. Look, I've just put my life in your hands by what I've told you. You can see that, surely?"

"Well, there *is* that," she admitted, and finished her breakfast.

On Dylan's advice, I decided to talk to Sanda alone first, then let her go talk to Dylan afterward. I decided not to be as honest with her as I had been with Dylan, mostly because I was less sure of her abilities to keep things quiet.

"Dylan and I are going to try to do something very risky," I told her.

"Basically, I've got a setup that could put me in control of Hroyasail if the law can be successfully bent, shall we say."

She was interested and fascinated. I could see the romance of it all catching on inside her. This was the kind of thing "real world" people did, not the mothers of Akeba House.

"Now," I continued carefully, "before I go any further, I have to warn you of something. This is no game. If I tell you more, you'll hold both my life and Dylan's in your hands because they'll kill us if there's any leak, if there's even the slightest *suspicion*. That means no talking to anyone except for the two of us—and no excitement, no betrayal of even the fact that you have secrets to keep, or you'll do us in. We need help, but not if you don't think you can handle it. Understand?"

She nodded. "You're afraid I can't keep it to myself?"

"There's nothing personal, but both you and Dylan have told me about life inside that harem, and it sounds like harems throughout past history. You sit around, you talk, you gossip, you know each other so well you note when something's not right with somebody else and the word gets spread all over. Be very honest—do you think you could keep something like this to yourself?"

"I think I can," she responded.

"Not think. *Know!* Be absolutely sure of yourself or it stops here and we find somebody else."

"I'm sure. I wouldn't—couldn't—do anything that might hurt you or Dylan."

"All right, then. We really *do* need you on this for what you can tell me even now. You had some nurse's training?"

She nodded. "We all do. Some more than others, but I got interested. Dylan knows more than me, though. She was at it longer."

I nodded. "All I need is some basic information right now. The first question is, have you ever been hypnotized?"

She nodded. "Sure. We do it all the time for deliveries, since we can't use much in the way of anesthetics. Not too many folks on Cerberus will come anywhere near hypnotism, though."

That was certainly true. You put total control of what body you wore and what body you would wear into someone else's hands, and *that* was something you didn't do lightly. Not here.

"All right," I told her, "now—Dylan told me that on special occasions some of the mothers would switch so those in the late stages of pregnancy could go out. Just a temporary courtesy."

"That's right. It's not usual, but we've all done it."

"Good. Can you think of anybody you might be able to switch with for a full day and night?"

She thought a moment. "Yeah. I guess so. Marga, maybe, although I'd owe her one. When would this be?"

"Two weeks from now. Friday evening through Saturday evening or maybe Sunday morning."

"I'll work it out."

"Good. Talk it over with Dylan, too, all you want. I'm going to be doing dry runs and setups all week. Next weekend I'll work out a little test or two to see if there are any kinks in company security. Now, two more things." I fished a couple of papers from my pocket and handed them to her. She looked at them quizzically.

"What are these?"

"Remember Otah?"

"Yeah?"

"Well, he does a lot of interesting bootlegs other than just entertainment," I told her. "If *I* came in with those, though, he might get suspicious, and the money would still be missing from my account. I want you —or somebody else who won't ask questions and can act for you—to go into Otah's place with those and ask for those specific parts. Tell him they are required spares for a surprise fire inspection at Akeba House. Tell him that they have to be exactly like those on the sheet because of special equipment in the House. If he presses further, act ignorant of any more, but insist he make those specific parts, without variations and without substitutions."

She looked at the diagrams, then turned them first one way, then upside down. "It won't be hard to pretend ignorance. What are they?"

"Computer memory chips," I told her. "I need 'em as soon as possible, but definitely within a week. Understand?"

She nodded. "He makes these things?"

"He can have them made."

"How much should I pay for them?"

"You have almost unlimited credit, you said. It's why I've let you buy me so many dinners. The price'll be high, since the transaction is under the counter. Probably two or three hundred units each."

She whistled. "Wow."

"Too steep for you?"

"No, but it's more than I'm ever used to paying."

"Will it show up in your personal account?"

"Oh, no. We don't have them. It's another way they keep us barefoot and pregnant. It's the House account."

I nodded to myself, then pulled her close and kissed her. "You know," I said, "I never realized before how sexy a pregnant woman can be to a man."

By God, I told myself, this crazy, insane, totally absurd plot was going to work!

"Tell me about nuraform," I asked them on the boat Friday night.

"It's an anesthetic, one of the few that works here," Dylan replied. "A couple of whiffs and you'll go out like a light for twenty minutes or so— but you won't be able to change bodies with it. That's why it's approved at all. Major operations and stuff like that, or on-the-job accidents where somebody's in great pain. But it's a controlled substance. Doctors and medical personnel only."

"That's no trouble," I replied. "The company dispensary keeps some around. I can steal it pretty easy."

"Why bother?" she asked me, and pulled a small magnakey from her pocket. "We always carry a small supply on the boats."

I not only could have kissed her, I did.

"But what good's nuraform?" Sanda asked. "I mean, you can't switch with it, and if somebody's knocked out with it they'll know."

"Not if they're asleep," I told her. "Look, let's go on to other phases of this operation. What about the chips?"

"He took the job," Sanda told me, "although it required some real haggling, and I had to do a lot of squirming. I also had to borrow Marga's body to get in there, so I'm really going to have to find something to get her."

"You figure that out and I'll get it," I assured her. "Now—when will you have them?"

"Tuesday. He was pretty firm about that, no matter what. I can send a messenger then, because it's prepaid."

"Okay. I'll need 'em Tuesday evening, and I'll drop down to pick them up. We're looking good—fewer hitches than I'd ever dreamed. You can do wonders when you're doing a dirty deed for the boss. The amount of information I've gotten would have taken a year of hard and risky work."

"I still say you're crazy and this plan's insane," Dylan said, shaking her head. "It's so crazy and so complicated it can't possibly work."

"You think they make this kind of operation easy? Look, every corporation president, every syndicate boss, got where he was by doing the insane and crooked thing at just the right time. Even with that, their investigators will know they've been had. Within two weeks they'll have figured out how it was done—although, hopefully, not who did it, since I'm not even the one getting rewarded at the end but pastured instead. No, they'll come up with the right solution, all right, but the scheme is so crazy they won't believe it themselves, and that'll stop that. As for its being complicated—yes, I don't like that. The more complicated something is, the more likely it is to go wrong. But at least there are provisions almost to the end to back out at any point, so if we do our jobs properly there's minimal risk of getting caught. Don't worry about that part—just worry about your own."

"I am," Dylan responded glumly.

"Look, let's go through the key rehearsal now. Just think about this, both of you. If it works, you, Dylan, will have your own boat under nobody's supervision and no real worries—independent and secure. And you, Sanda, I promise—if all goes as planned, we're going to liberate you from the motherhood and do it so slickly that nobody will bat an eyelash. If you can be patient and not jump the gun, the three of us might wind up running this damned world in a couple of years."

Neither of them believed that, but they believed in me and that was enough. It usually was. Only this time, for a change, I wasn't just pulling a con to set up a mission. I really meant business.

"Now, let's see what sort of hypnotic subjects you are," I said.

Sanda went under quickly and easily. Dylan resisted somewhat, and I could understand why and sympathize with her. After a long struggle she was who and what she wanted to be. Hypnosis was a threat to that. It took a good deal of smooth and soothing talk finally to get her to the point where she was willing.

Sanda had romance to gain and absolutely nothing to lose in this whole business—if we weren't caught on the spot. Dylan, on the other hand, had relatively little to gain but was risking all that she held dear in this business. She wasn't really doing this for herself, but for me, and I knew it.

I knew the routine well from past operations and had had a lot of practice. I'd also used Tooker's computers to do a lot of medical research on exactly how to handle this particular ticklish business, but actually doing so would not be easy.

Being there alone in a boat lounge with two attractive women in deep hypnosis was something of a kinky turn-on, but that feeling passed in a minute. This was business. In the Confederacy there were drugs and devices that could do this much better. But I was prevented from using the first by the Warden organism and didn't have access to the second. That's why we learned hypnosis from the start. You never had the right stuff around when you really needed it.

They both seemed to be asleep in their chairs, and I went over to Dylan first. "Dylan, you will listen to my voice and nothing else, listen and trust me and do exactly as I say. Do you understand?"

"Yes." Sleepily, faraway.

"Answer my questions truthfully, Dylan."

"I will."

"Would you ever betray me or my mission?"

"I don't think so."

"Dylan, why are you willing to do this?"

"Because you want it."

"But why is that so important? Why should you take risks for me?"

"Because I—"

"Yes?"

"I think I love you."

Love. A fascinating word and feeling. One I had used many times but still didn't quite understand myself. Certainly love was usually an abstract concept on Cerberus.

"You *do* love me, don't you?"

"Yes."

"Very much. Very deeply. More than you've ever loved anyone, more than you love yourself."

"Yes."

"You would trust me with your body, even your life."

"Yes."

"And I could trust you with my body, my life."

"You could."

I moved over to Sanda and repeated some of the process.

"Would you betray us or our mission?"

"No," she assured me. "Never."

"Have you told anyone in the House about this?"

"No."

"Has anyone there suspected you were up to something? Asked questions?"

"One or two."

"And what did you tell them?"

"I said I was in love with you and that you were in love with me."

"Did they believe you and press no more?"

"They were envious," she told me. "They ask me about you."

"And what do you tell them?"

"I tell them you came from Outside and you work for Tooker."

"And what else?"

The next segment was more than a little embarrassing to me personally. The romantic fantasies this lonely and bored young woman had concocted were graphic and hard to believe, and the image of me as someone approaching godhood was beyond any technique I'd ever studied. Still, it was satisfactory. They would understand those fantasies for what they were and put down a lot of her nervous excitement to meeting me.

Her emotional patterns were at once simpler and more complex than Dylan's or the average person's. She loved, truly loved, Dylan, but she worshiped me.

Confederacy agents are born and bred to their jobs and are as perfect as the biological and social sciences can make them for doing whatever needs to be done.

As a youngster in the game I'd been amazed at how easily people could be turned, how malleable they were in emotions and will if only the right words were said at the right times, the right buttons pushed. It was something I'd never really thought about, something that came almost instinctively. Even now it still amazed me. Two women were in love with me and were willing to risk their necks and who knew what else for me.

Even when they *knew*, as Dylan knew, they still went along. And yet standing there looking at the two women, I felt something that I had never really felt before, the stirrings of care, of concern, of real affection and appreciation for these two. Perhaps, I reflected, not quite understanding myself, I too could love.

But business came first.

I almost held my breath before this next one, since without it the whole thing would fall and have to be postponed. And time was running out on Turgan Sugal, and therefore on me.

I had them both open their eyes and rise, facing me. I instructed them to turn and face each other.

"Feel inside yourselves," I instructed. "Feel your mind. Feel the Wardens in your mind, calling out, connecting you one to the other, talking to each other mind to mind. Think of nothing else, concentrate on nothing else, but feel, hear, as they reach out, your mind to the other. Can you feel it?"

"Yes," they both answered in unison.

"Dylan, you wish to be in Sanda's body. You wish it more than anything else in the world. It is a beautiful body, not a mother's body, and it is the ideal body you have always dreamed of. You want to be in that body. Flow into it, Dylan. Become Sanda's body. Sanda, you will not resist. You *want* to exchange bodies with Dylan. You will flow into hers as she into yours. And when your bodies have changed, you will both go back and sit in your chairs, still in a deep hypnotic sleep."

Apparently when both were hypnotized and so instructed the exchange went more quickly and smoothly than in the "natural" way. Or so the computers had told me, although they also warned that, once complete, it would take another ten minutes or so to set in. Actually, although consciously the exchange was complete at that point, it took up to seventy-two hours for a true set, but that wasn't what I was after. All I wanted was a mental exchange, no more.

In less than ten minutes both women moved—and sat in each other's chairs. Dylan was now Sanda, and Sanda was now Dylan.

I went over to the new Dylan. "Dylan? Can you hear me?"

"Yes."

"Now, listen carefully. Soon I will awaken you, but you will still remain in a deep hypnotic sleep, even though awakened. And when you awaken, you will do the following exactly . . ."

Although I was a master of autohypnosis and had even gotten to the point of sensing the Wardens inside my own body, this was a bit too tricky to trust just to myself. So when she awakened, I allowed her to put *me* under, and the process was repeated, with me going into Dylan's old body and Sanda into mine. We were then all awakened, still under, and were able to compare notes, reactions, and the like. It looked like complete conscious control even in the short time allowed, and that satisfied me. We switched back again and Dylan brought me out, then I brought the two of them out, along with some handy posthypnotic suggestions. The suggestions wouldn't last more than a day or two, but tended to be of the self-reinforcing type, in which each of them would put herself under and repeat quite a lot over and over. It was an advanced form of hypnosis with limited use, but it was more than handy for memorizing things to do and to calm nerves.

All that afternoon we went over the plan again and again, until I was satisfied that all three of us had what we were to do down pat. Sanda had received permission to spend the night on the boat as long as she was in safe and enclosed quarters—their organization was run by a few incurable romantics, too—and we had a fancy dinner sent down from town which we ate on the aft deck.

"One thing puzzles me," Dylan remarked. "It seems to me you had all the elements to make this plan first. Which came first—the elements or the plan?"

I laughed. "The elements, of course. The plan was tailored for what I *could* do and what my friends, associates, and close partners—you two— could do. It was a matter of stating the problem when it came up—Sugal's subtle forced ouster—and then putting together all I had, all that I could have, and matching it up to the chinks I'd already found in this society's armor. So far it's all worked out—but if my research was wrong and something doesn't go right, well, I'll try a different plan. Plans are easy—this one took only a few minutes—but execution's the hard part, since you never really know what's possible until you try it. Like tonight."

Tonight would be yet another test, really, and it would depend on me more than anything. All those two had to do was go to sleep, shielded from each other. I'd have a more difficult task, and all my plans and theories depended on it. It was logical, my computers told me, but there wasn't much medical evidence to back it up—for obvious reasons, I knew.

Which is why I sat, in a deep but aware hypnotic trance, in the same room as Dylan but unshielded—yet a good five meters from her bed. Sat and reached out and felt the creatures in my mind. It was an eerie sensation, really. There was no sight, sound, or smell to betray the Warden organism, but when you were deeply under—and occasionally while you were in a really deep sleep—you could hear them, sense them, talking.

Not talking in any sense that we understand, but there was some sort of communication, some sort of linkage, as if one could sense the individual cells comparing information elsewhere. An energy network, intangible, invisible, yet very much there, creating a sense of linkage not only between minds but between literally *everything* solid around you.

Under hypnotic control I was able to tune out much of it, all but Dylan's sleeping form, which seemed almost to *burn* with the tiny tendrils of immeasurably small energy linking one Warden organism to another. I could feel myself being almost physically drawn to her, interconnecting with every part of her body, linking mind to mind, arms to arms, legs to legs, heart to heart. At this point, more deep than I'd ever been, I understood a bit more how those on Lilith must feel who could command, send messages through that network. One could also wonder, too, how such a creature as the Warden could have evolved, how it could possibly exist at all, on worlds otherwise not so different from many man had conquered, and far less alien than most. What are you? Who are you? Why do you exist?

And there seemed to be a faint answer somewhere, from all around.

We exist! We live! We are! That is enough!

Dylan had gone from lighter, dream-filled sleep to that period people went through several times a night. Rigid, deep, dreamless. Her Wardens burned bright, talking, singing along fields of invisible force—hers to mine and mine to hers. And for the first time conscious as it happened, we changed. It was a strange experience, but not a terrifying one. There was something eerily satisfying about it, my body building up a tension and then the core of my being flowing along those fields of force toward that sleeping body and the core of hers to mine, providing a wondrous feeling I could not then and can not now describe.

I arose in the body of Dylan Kohl, feeling somehow exhilarated, high, powerful. I went over to the dressing table, took the small bottle there and crept over to my old body, sleeping uneasily in the lounge chair. Carefully I placed it under his nose and pressed the stud, releasing a tiny whiff of vapor, which was quickly inhaled.

The body sagged slightly and the breathing became deeper, a bit labored but no real problem.

I shook him. "Dylan? Wake up." I shook harder. "Wake up, Dylan!" I almost shouted in his ear, and there was no reaction.

Satisfied, I clicked on the stopwatch, then tried moving the body. Though Dylan was a strong woman, she was still weaker than I was used to being as a man; I tried all sorts of ways to rouse the sleeper but got nowhere.

Finally I sat down on the bed to wait it out, going over every few minutes and trying again to rouse the unconscious form. About the fourth or fifth time I tried, the figure groaned a little and turned slightly. I reached over and clicked off the watch. Twenty-four minutes and a few odd seconds. Time enough.

Another minute or so, and I was able to shake Dylan awake. He shook his head and rubbed his eyes for a moment, seemingly unable to get his bearings, then sighed and looked at me. "So it *does* work."

I nodded. "Twenty-four minutes, with my additional body weight. I'll bet it's longer for your body. Any ill effects?"

"I feel dead tired but otherwise nothing much," Dylan replied.

"Now it's your turn," I said. "Hippogryph."

The posthypnotic command took effect, sending her under quickly. With only a minimal briefing—we'd been over this again and again earlier in the day—I went back over to the bed and stretched out. It was several minutes before I could relax enough to drift into sleep. The old excitement, the old fun of this sort of thing was rising fully in me once again.

We were able to get a reversal on me in under three hours, which was very good indeed, and then I tiptoed quietly into Sanda's partitioned and shielded side to do much the same thing. I was tired, yes, but the hypnotic state was somewhat restful in and of itself and this was far more important. I could call on mental reserves when necessary.

I didn't use the nuraform on Sanda, since I didn't need to—my body had already proven out—and I didn't want any risks in her condition to *her* body.

Sensorily, her body was also far different from Dylan's or my own. The fetus inside her was far enough along that even now it had its own unique Warden pattern, one that I could sense, although it's own Wardens were out of reach to me, much as the Wardens in the molecules of the ship itself or the dock or the bed. It was a curious feeling.

Arising in her body was also something of a shock, as I was very much aware of the pregnancy and the vast differences in my new body, a body in a condition far stranger than merely the gender change from male to female and back again. My awakening on the prison ship that first time had almost been disappointing in that it felt so *little* different. Sanda was a far more startling experience.

But I had proved my theory and the heart of the scam. Proved it absolutely. I didn't know why someone else hadn't thought of it, too—but then again, maybe someone had. If so, it would take a rare sneaky mind like my own, since it required a knowledge of hypnotism and the body as well, and had involved an *awful* lot of homework that I would have found nearly impossible had I not worked at Tooker and had its vast computer system to play with.

Sanda's body was a marvel to me; I don't know how anybody can cope with it. It was awkward, and I felt bloated, and there were other sensations a bit too odd to describe. I began to get some appreciation of why she wanted out of this routine, although I couldn't believe it was like this most of the time. Still, I had to hang on for a bit, bring Sanda, now in my body, around and awake, and check out the one nagging doubt I had about my chosen personnel.

It was the first time she'd been in a man's body and awake and under control, unlike the hypnotic experiment earlier on the deck. She took some delight in the body, and in exploring it. I suspected the additional contrast between the body I was now in, in the condition it was—roughly eight months pregnant—and my own top physical form only added to her pleasure.

"Can't I stay like this a while?" he pleaded. "It feels so—*free!*"

I shook my head sadly. "No, not now. You have to learn how to exchange for next week, and it's already close to dawn."

"Oh, please! Just for one day? You don't know what it *means!*"

"I think I do," I sympathized, "but, no. Control, Sanda. We'll do this again tomorrow night if the House is willing to let you stay another night, as I suspect they will. We don't have much time, and we have a lot of practice to do."

He pouted. It was amusing to see the characteristics of Sanda in my body, as it had tickled me to see some legit switchers in similar circumstances. We learn our sexual and personality moves early on, and even on a body-switch world these come through—on people with a clear sexual identity, such as the three of us.

"I think we ought to get to this," I told him. "It's getting late, and you might get your wish by just keeping me up a little longer." I was somewhat concerned. The unfamiliar-feeling body would cause enough problems, but I was becoming more and more awake. Sanda, in this body, had had a lot more sleep than Dylan or I had had.

Sanda seemed to sense that, too, and seemed determined to keep the argument going until it would go his way by default. Realizing this, I snapped, "Will I have this problem again next week, when our lives depend on it?"

That brought him up short, and sounding a little apologetic, he replied, "Look. I'm sorry. I won't cross you up."

"I know you won't," I said softly, then said, "Hippogryph."

Thank heavens for posthypnotic suggestion, I thought with relief. That was my ace in the hole for the next weekend too, of course. I crossed my fingers on that one, lay down, and tried to get some sleep, which was a long time coming. The longer it took the more afraid I became of being trapped in this body, and the harder it was to get to sleep because of that fear. I finally managed, though, cheating a bit with some autohypnosis.

The sun was bright and it was late in the morning when Sanda, again herself, somewhat ruefully awakened me.

One more day of rehearsal, going over everything again and again, testing things out again and again, and one more night of testing, this time with Dylan doing the double switching, and we were as ready as we'd ever be. If Otah was as good as his word, I had one extra setup to accomplish on my own, and then a little sadistic fun, and we'd be ready for Friday afternoon.

CHAPTER SEVEN

Final Set-up and Much Prayer

Tuesday afternoon, while I was still at work, I got a call from Sanda telling me that a package had just been delivered to her at Akeba House. After I knocked off for the day, I went down there to get it.

I met her at the gatehouse, and we walked along the wood walk to the sea. We looked down on the Hroyasail fleet, already tied up below, but I wasn't about to disturb Dylan at this point. She had her work to do and I had mine.

"I still can't believe there's a whole business in supplying special parts for computers and stuff like that," Sanda told me.

I grinned. "There's always some service like that, and people like Otah to provide it."

"But what would anyone use it for, except maybe to commit a crime?"

"Some of it's undoubtedly for that, but not much, or the authorities would shut 'em down," I told her. "A lot of it is for people making their own modifications in their own home or business equipment—modifications not approved by the manufacturer, who wants to control everything about his machines. Some of it is to modify stock security systems so somebody can't get the master keys and defeat them. And some of it, like our cover story, is due to people forgetting to fix stuff that's required by borough code, like fire and police alarms, because they were lazy or because they were too cheap to get a maintenance contract, only to be caught with their pants down when inspectors pull a surprise."

She shrugged and looked suspiciously at the unopened parcel. "How can you be sure it'll work? Or that Otah hasn't cheated you by supplying some standard part?"

"He wouldn't stay in business long if he did that, but if he has, then the plan won't work and we'll have to figure out something else, that's all."

"Why so many, then?"

I grinned wider. "Because the breakdown has to look natural. These are the same standard chips used in the old and venerable system this borough's had for years, only with slight changes. They're designed to react to different loads on the system. We can't just have something break once—they'll just come and fix it. We have to have a repeated series of breakdowns, and that means we have one go bad, get fixed, then another go, and so forth."

"But won't that attract suspicion, too?"

"You don't know machines. When one part goes, others often follow. No, the more failures they find, the more the blame will be laid to the antiquated system finally giving up under the strain of years. Trust me—it's my business."

She put her arm around me. "I do trust you, Qwin. It's just all so—so incredible. I could never have come up with an idea as crazy as this."

"Yeah," I said. "That's why people like me—the good guys and the crooks—get away with so much. The average person, even the average law enforcer, just doesn't have the kind of mind to figure out things like this."

"You'd think they'd learn."

"They did," I told her. "They created a corps of specialists in the Confederacy for people who thought like this, to catch them."

"Sounds fascinating. But surely somebody by now would have designed a foolproof system."

I had to laugh. "The ultimate foolproof system is invented every year or two and has been since the dawn of time. It usually lasts only until the next genius figures out how to beat it."

Even you, Wagant Laroo, I thought, looking out across the ocean to the southeast. *No fortress has ever proven impregnable, nor is the best security without flaw. I'm coming for you, Wagant Laroo. One day, step by step, I'm coming. And not even your alien friends will be able to save you from me.*

Despite my glib assurances to Sanda, I didn't trust any bootlegger for anything. Wednesday I checked out the circuits in the lab. It was a fascinating business, a computer so small you could hardly see it with the naked eye, but it was naturally centuries out of date. What could be done with computers now was nothing short of awesome—but it hadn't been done, out of fear by power-loving, weak-kneed leaders who feared just who or what would be in control of humanity if they went too far. Here on Cerberus, where the system was even more retarded, I suspect that scientists from centuries earlier could probably have understood what I was doing.

Human history had always been like that—centuries, even millennia, of incredibly slow, creeping advance, followed by a few centuries of exponential multiplication of knowledge, followed by a collapse, a setback, and more lengthy periods of backwardness. We are hardly as backward as some, but the analogy still held. This was not an age of great advancement, if only for political reasons, nor the century for it. We were Neanderthals, primitives who could set the air conditioner on in our caves and drive comfortably down to the dinosaur pits.

The chips checked out perfectly. Otah's people had done a good job, and now it was up to me to be worthy.

Wednesday evening I checked out a company flier, which wasn't unusual, since I was due the next day in Comora, about a hundred and ten kilometers north, for a reorganizational meeting—standard stuff. What wasn't standard was where I went that evening after changing into a Tooker Service Systems uniform and, with a little easy sleight of hand, picking up an official repairman's tool kit.

My first stop was an apartment complex eight kilometers west of the main plant. My authentic Tooker ID badge got me easy entry—they didn't even take note of the name, just that its face and mine matched—and soon I was in the manager's office.

"The entire city master alarm system is undergoing an overhaul," I told her. "We've been having breakdowns all up and down the line. You can't really tell if the damn stuff goes bad until it does, but they want me to check the line anyway."

"Go ahead," she told me, not really concerned. "It's on level four, just above waterline."

I nodded, told her thanks, then added, "This system's so much of an antique maybe they'll get sick of these things and put in a new one."

"Ha!" she exclaimed. "Not until the Municipal Building itself burns down, or the fancy homes fill with water!"

I took the service elevator down and quickly found the master line that routed the fire alarm system to each floor and each room. One weakness of the system I'd spotted right away was the fact that people had to build in the trees—they couldn't kill the trees or replace them for lack of a foundation. And since the bulk of the plants were underwater, the tops were generally hollow and the circulatory systems were not extensive, as well as being exposed to the sun.

In other words, no matter how inert the materials used inside the tree buildings themselves, the outer bark was highly flammable, and was covered by a municipal alarm system. Although it was almost impossible to set fire to anything inside the man-made structures, you were always completely surrounded by the tree and had a fair way to go to exit. Fire would be a severe problem, with smoke potentially blocking all the exits.

The computer fire alarm system, then, was designed to detect any temperature rise anywhere in the exposed tree by the use of a selective monitoring system at all levels above the waterline. Other than this early warning system, the only real escape was by the chutes, which could shoot you from any hall to the waterline. These areas had special systems to keep them free of smoke and were for the most part in the center, where everything was man-made and insulated.

There were few fires, and even fewer than ever amounted to anything. Hence the alarm system as such had been mostly ignored for years, considering borough budgets.

I was not out to start any fires. I ran a systems check, stopping at predetermined points, and then replaced the tiny, almost microscopic chips with specific ones I'd brought with me, being careful even to spray a bit of dust and gunk on them so that there would be no evidence of replacement. Anyone removing one would probably complain about how dirty the area was and remark that it was no wonder the chips had gone bad.

I'd never done this with a fire alarm system before, but I'd done similar things countless times to security systems far more complex and technologically advanced than this. I'd never been found out once—even when they suspected what had been done.

It took less than half an hour to place all my key chips, but I had more stops to make, hitting the usual maintenance route mapped on the shop board. In the other places I did absolutely nothing, but anyone checking on the mysterious serviceman would find that he'd done nothing not routine and that in fact the servicing had been ordered and logged. I knew it had: I'd slipped the order in myself, then made sure it wouldn't come up on the assignment board so I could take it.

Modern man, I'm convinced, is vulnerable to any competent engineer. We depend on the computer to total our purchases, rarely checking each item for accuracy, and we rely on it for inventory, for security, for remembering to turn out the lights and remembering to keep the temperature in our homes at the same level no matter what. We trust them so much and take them so much for granted that most people can be had by simply nudging a computer to suggest what you want.

By the time I'd reached the fire department I was well satisfied and had made about thirty stops on this particular system. According to service records at Tooker, false alarms were relatively common at almost every station, averaging two a week, so systems checks were routine—and pointless. At the fire station I removed and replaced the rest of my bootleg load in several places, and then left for the plant once again. Changing back to my normal clothes, I used my company pass to get back into inventory, where I replaced the tool kit and threw the uniform into the company laundry chute.

Then I went home.

The next morning I flew up to my conference, returned in the afternoon, and checked out early, going back down to maintenance and punching up their service record.

Two chips had gone bad at an apartment complex eight kilometers west of the plant, one around noon and the other not too long before I checked. The repair personnel were still on the job for that one. I smiled to myself, nodded, and went home for an early dinner.

By Friday there had been seven failures within the system, some at the apartment house, some through the system and apparently in the master control at the fire station, ringing every alarm on that particular string. There had also been one false alarm at another apartment—one I wasn't responsible for but had hoped for, considering the average two a week. It would keep my tampering from being obvious, although I couldn't imagine why any investigator or Tooker tech would even consider that somebody had gone to a lot of trouble and expense to ring false alarms.

I worked late on Thursday night, partly to catch up from the time lost at the meetings earlier in the week and partly because everybody was putting in at least one long day these days—we were *really* understaffed. Sugal had no idea where they went or what they were working on, but a rundown of the people pulled told me a little. All were junior staff like me, and every one of them had been involved in the field of organic computers, which were banned on Cerberus, before being sent here. It was only six, but they were all exiles, all experts in the same field, and all good minds. And, all of their forwarding addresses were care of the corporation headquarters building—a forwarding box service. Interesting. Obviously something was going on. Something I wanted to know about.

Late that evening, stretching my legs, I just happened to meet the night janitorial supervisory staff coming on. Most of the cleaning was automated, but the rules required a few human beings to make sure all was working right, since self-aware computers were banned on the planet. I looked at the men and women coming on, skilled technicians themselves, and noted that some of them looked tired.

During the day on Friday all hell broke loose in the fire control computer, with false alarms all over the place and the whole system going crazy. It took half of Tooker Service to track down the problem and replace the bad parts, but by early evening they had completed the job, fortunately—since most people worked regular days like me, and thus weren't there when all this happened.

Only the few night workers, most of whom lived in an apartment about eight kilometers west of the plant, went through hell. Few of them got any sleep at all, poor things.

According to the readouts, the system really *was* in awful shape. I hadn't caused nearly all that happened to that system on Friday afternoon. Apparently my defects triggered breakdowns in *real* defects within the system. I had hoped for that but hadn't planned on it. The system really *was* in dire need of replacement.

While all those people were having problems, I managed to finish early, thanks to my extra-long day the day before. At a little before four I walked down to the main entrance for a previously scheduled VIP tour. Like most, this VIP tour had no VIPs; many of us took friends on little demo tours to show off, and the company encouraged such things as good public relations.

Dylan had put in sick for the day, so she had plenty of sleep and was in fine shape for the evening. With her was a tiny, thin olive-skinned beauty with long jet-black hair and eyes I'd never seen before. I had to stop and shake my head in wonder. I'd *never* get used to this switching stuff.

"Sanda?" I ventured.

She smiled and nodded. "You wouldn't believe what this is going to cost you. I think you're going to have to wine, dine, and romance half of Akeba House."

I thought about it. "Doesn't sound too terrifying." I looked at both of them, sensing an inward nervousness in each that they were only partly successful in masking. I hugged both of them and whispered, "Don't worry so much. It's going great."

Beyond the public rooms, a scan was necessary to make certain that only authorized employees passed beyond certain points. Since I had prearranged the tour, which wasn't that unusual, entry caused no problems at all. Basically, you faced a door, put the headpiece on, then inserted your identicard in the slot. If all was okay, the door opened and you walked into a small antechamber, whereupon the door closed behind you. You then slotted the card again and the second door would open, admitting you—in the same way as an airlock did.

If the more than four thousand Tooker employees had to do this, they would be all day just getting to work, so the internal computers simply recognized your body features and all you did was put your card in the slot. Scanning took a couple of minutes, and since the system was tied to the master computer—which, I discovered, was in orbit and linked to the entire surface by a series of satellites—it was also advisable to discourage an expensive overload of any local system. Scans within Tooker were required only in high security areas.

That, of course, was a second flaw. Not only because they didn't use full scan everywhere, but also because you could walk right past all those security areas, outside, separated only by a floor-to-ceiling sheet of thick, unbreakable, and alarmed plastiglass. For extra security, you could see the whole of the security areas from this walk—although of course you couldn't get to anything going on inside or even get close enough to figure out what was going on. Computers monitored the inside of those areas to make certain that nobody except those properly scanned could enter, and the list of those so authorized was quite short.

We stood outside one such area while I acted the guide. Some of the staff were still huddled over consoles and transceivers, although they were thinning out as the end of the workday approached.

"This area controls the local banking system," I told them. "Eleven borough small banks keep all their transaction records here, and shift money and assets between them. Of course it's just a bank link to the master computer, where all our electronic money is stored, but that master computer holds only the total assets of every person and corporation. These machines hold where that money came from and where it's to go, and can effect a transfer of funds within the master accounts with a simple set of coded orders. The codes are pretty simple—so much so that anybody who could get to one of the register machines there could steal millions in moments."

"Then why aren't they made more complicated?" Sanda asked.

"Because, since everybody's money is in the master computer, any unusual bulge in it, or any pattern of smaller bulges, would flag the central banking authorities that something was funny and promote an investigation." We'd actually been over this material before, but with people still around we needed to complete the grand tour.

Her question, besides being a normal one, pointed up the second flaw in the system. It would be *damned* hard, beyond all but the best computer minds in the galaxy armed with unlimited resources, to get away with any sort of money theft on Cerberus. It *better* be—I was counting on everybody in the system being competent.

Down a long hall from the banking center was a small group of conference rooms. I selected one I knew wasn't scheduled for anything and opened the door. It was the usual small meeting room—rostrum, round table of nice, polished wood, and five comfortable executive chairs. You could lock the room from the inside for privacy, but not from the outside. There was no need.

We entered and locked the door, and in a matter of minutes I had put both of them under. Oddly, Sanda was the hardest to hypnotize—she was just too excited.

Dylan had brought two small bottles of nuraform from the ship medi-kit, and I gave one to Sanda. Under as she was, I had her repeat the procedure and everything she was to do exactly, then gave her all the added cautions. I also added a suggestion that she felt neither nervous nor excited and would calmly and coolly perform her duties.

We left her in the conference room and I took Dylan up two levels to the company accounting section, also a security area. Almost everybody was gone now which made it even easier.

The bosses were long gone for the weekend, so I used Sugal's office as Dylan's waiting area. Again I made her go through her own procedure exactly, then left her.

I returned to the main level and took out not one but three identicards and one at a time, put them in the slot, allowing the equipment to act as if a person were going through each time. I used a rear exit to avoid any undue attention, although I had a cover story ready if I needed one. The third card was mine, of course, and I walked out with that one.

The computer not only didn't scan for exiting but didn't even look at you. Fire regulations required a fast exit, and the only reason for using the two women's cards was that there now would be a record of both of them leaving the building with me.

The nervous excitement was rising in me, too, and I considered a little autohypnosis to calm myself down. After all, I had a tough thing to do, too.

I had to go someplace and eat dinner.

CHAPTER EIGHT

Execution

Not only did I have a nice dinner, but I had it with two lovely women. Both were people I'd met socially off and on, and neither really looked like Dylan or the body Sanda was now using. That wasn't really important. If anybody wanted to check, they'd run my record for Friday night and see that I'd taken my two known close friends on a stock VIP tour, exited with them, then dined with them, on me. The restaurant used was a dark and unfamiliar one, and if anybody was to ask, the most anybody would remember was that I'd dined there in the company of two lovely ladies.

I had a tough time keeping my mind on their conversation, though. I knew what must be happening back at Tooker, and what would occur not too long from now. I realized that, despite my glib assertions, what was going to be happening was damned risky and by no means a sure thing. Now, sitting there at dinner, I could think of hundreds of things that could go wrong, and the more I considered them, the more certain I became that one or another of them *would* go wrong. Both Dylan and Sanda had been saying to me over and over how it was impossible, how absurd the whole idea was, how fraught with peril, but I'd talked, charmed, and hypnotized my way out of worrying about their warnings.

Unfortunately, they were right.

Still, that plan was in motion now. There was no way to stop it, nor would I if I could have at this point.

The best, Krega had called me. And how had I become the best? By taking insane risks, doing the absurd and the impossible, and getting away with it.

The trouble was, one of these days my luck was going to catch up with me. Tonight, perhaps?

What they had to do was damned tricky.

One of the women with me said something and I snapped out of my reverie. "Huh? Sorry. Just tired, I'm afraid."

"Poor darling! All I was saying was that Mural over in Accounting joined one of those body-swapping clubs. I mean, Jora and I swap a lot with each other because we contrast so well, but I'm not sure I could be somebody else every day without much control over what. I wonder what drives people to that?"

"Bored people, mostly," I told her, "and ones with real weird needs. I've heard some of those clubs are regular orgies."

"Hmmm! Who'd think *that* of somebody like Mural! I guess you can never tell . . ."

The janitorial staff for the executive floors of Tooker checked in for work. All were grumbling, yawning, and damned sleepy, but none had called in sick. Had it been midweek they might have, but as it was Friday, they would have the weekend to sleep off those damned false alarms. Besides, a supervisor for cleaning robots was rarely needed for anything anyway, and once their crew got to the security areas, not even a supervisor could catch them taking a little catnap.

"You've been working too hard lately," she said.

I nodded. "They've got us on double shifts some nights," I told the two of them. "Some big deal has taken some of our key people just when the quota's been upped. I've even got to go in tomorrow."

"Oh, you poor man! Well, we'll have to take you home and tuck you in early."

At a little after eleven, the janitorial supervisor finally reached the banking section. He was more than happy at the prospect; he'd been nodding off almost constantly. He went up to the entry doors, switched on the scanner, waited a couple of minutes, then put his card in the slot. Then he placed his special card, taken from the safety vault far below, in the slot as well, so the doors would admit the cleaning robots. Instructing the machines as to what to do—and what not to do, particularly in the area he was going to be—he drifted over to a large chair, positioned it so that it was hidden from direct view of the windows by some consoles, and settled in for a little sleep.

Sanda, alerted by the noise, waited until he was clearly inside, then pulled a wheeled chair out and down the hall to the area near the door. From this point she could see much of the room, although she could barely see the form of the already sleeping supervisor. Relaxing, concentrating as only her hypnotized state would allow, she felt the Wardens in her mind reach out. The distance between her and the sleeping man was more than eleven meters, and she could feel some interference from the Wardens in the machinery and even the plastiglass that caused a bit of a focusing problem, but finally she had it. It helped that there were no shields here, and no other human beings on the floor. Slowly at first, then more positively, she felt the fields of force from her own Wardens reach out, touch, and link with those of the sleeping man.

My mind is your mind, my arms are your arms, my legs are your legs, my heart is your heart . . .

Twenty minutes later and several floors above Sanda, another tired janitor entered another security area, first by having herself scanned, then using the special card that allowed seventy seconds for the cleaning robots to enter. Since the floors were all sealed except to those in the scanning computers, such as the janitor, the gap was never considered a threat by security analysts.

"Home at last, Qwin! Thanks for a beautiful evening. I'm only sorry you're so tired and have to work tomorrow. We could have an even more perfect evening."

I looked at both of them, then at my watch. "Well, I'm not *that* tired."

Sanda was in the janitor's body. The cleaning equipment softly hummed, doing its business all around the banking room, but that was it. Getting up, and knowing exactly where to look, Sanda saw the form of her former self still asleep in the chair outside the door. Now came the most sensitive and riskiest part of the operation, and the most discretionary. She could simply proceed with her job and risk the sleeper awakening, but the door had been relatively silent and its noise would probably be masked by the sounds of the cleaning equipment. She decided on a mild risk for more insurance, found the passkey for the robot equipment, went over to the door, and inserted the card. The door slid open, and she walked out. Taking the ten anxious paces to the sleeping form, she then picked up the nuraform in the small bottle next to the chair and, holding it under the sleeper's nose, saw its vapors inhaled and the figure slump.

She immediately put the bottle down and ran back into the banking room. Seven seconds later, the doors snapped shut once more. With an additional check of the sleeper and a check of the wall clock, she went over to a console and began performing instructions on it she did not understand but carried out just as she had been taught.

Above, in accounting, Dylan fretted nervously as the young woman inside the security area made no move to take a nap but went on checking the operation of all the machines. Five minutes passed, then ten. Finally, though, the woman picked a spot of floor behind the consoles and stretched out, using her jacket for a pillow. She did not go to sleep as easily or quickly as her counterpart below, but eventually she lapsed into it. Only then could Dylan set up as Sanda had below and begin the laborious process.

Sanda's part had been completed in only nine minutes, and she was satisfied. Now came the hard part—waiting. She placed herself in a deeper trance by a combination of autohypnosis reinforced by posthypnotic suggestion, and in full view of the sleeping form outside the plastiglass, waited in the chair for the nuraform to wear off and the sleeper to go into the characteristic deeper sleep of those who have just come out of nuraform.

Inside the sleeping, small form it took thirty-seven minutes for the nuraform to cycle out of the system, aided by Warden rejection, whereupon she began the process of switching bodies again.

Almost an hour had elapsed before Dylan could make her exchange. Once inside, she checked and saw that she'd positioned her body correctly and there had been no problems. The janitor still slept.

She decided, though, to take a chance on not using the nuraform. This was a light, troubled sleeper who might easily be awakened by the necessity of opening the doors. She went quickly to the consoles and, as Sanda had, followed instructions to the letter. It took less than five minutes to complete the job, and reconcile Sanda's alterations with those going on on a floor below.

Checking often her sleeping charge outside the room, she had several nervous moments when the figure shifted, but so far so good. She stretched back out on the floor, relaxed, and let her mind flow toward the other outside the plastiglass. Her own body was so tired and achy she feared she might accidentally go to sleep herself.

Sanda awoke back in the chair outside the plastiglass with a splitting headache and some double vision. It had been *her* body, after all, that had been nuraformed.

She looked into the glass—and froze, as the janitor's body shifted slightly and he awoke and looked around, a puzzled expression on his face. He stood up, looking not in her direction but rather at the cleaning equipment on the far side of the room.

He barked an order to it and it started to move toward him. Taking the noise as her only cue, Sanda slid out of the chair and pushed it away, down the hall, literally on her knees, one eye always on the janitor. It was a nervous time, but she was saved partly by his lack of suspicion and partly by the fact that the interior lights of the banking section reflected off the plastiglass, masking much of what went on in the darkened hallway. Once or twice he seemed to look in her direction and she froze, but then he'd just look away at something else or shake his head and yawn, and that was that.

Not until she was back in the conference room, though, and with the door closed and latched behind her, did she allow herself to relax and nurse her still aching head. She was just about to congratulate herself when she realized that she'd left the nuraform bottle right there, next to the door. Her nerves overcame her conditioning, but she had enough common sense to know there was nothing she could do about it now.

Back in the banking section, the janitor gathered up his machines, yawned, stretched once more, and wondered a bit about some strange feelings and after-impressions in his head. Putting them down to his exhaustion, he gathered his cleaning crew and brought them out the door once again.

The sweeping machine turned and started down the hall, sweeping up the tiny bottle and sucking it inside with the rest of the garbage.

It was more than two hours later before Dylan could make the switch, two anxious hours when it appeared that at any moment the sleeper would awake or, worse, Dylan would fall asleep herself. Still, she managed the switch, and back in the accounting room, thanks partly to the tiredness of the janitor's body and partly to the reclining form, there was no awakening. Dylan was able to return to her office hideaway and relax.

I in turn knew nothing of this at the time, but I finally kissed my two alibis off and settled down to a nervous wait. My greatest fear was that one or both couldn't make the original switch or the switch back without awakening the sleepers. I had never doubted that both janitors would take the snooze; they usually did anyway, and my false alarms just ensured that this night wouldn't be the exception.

I had also exempted, on the janitor's schedule, both the meeting room and Sugal's office. This wasn't unusual—those areas weren't to be used until Monday, anyway, and with a half crew on for the weekend they would be cleaned at that time.

I got a little sleep, but not much, and showed up at Tooker about 6:00 A.M. Very early, but not totally unusual in these hard-pressed days. You either worked really late or you worked early. I'd established an irregular enough pattern so that the records wouldn't show anything particularly odd.

Once in the still mostly deserted building, I headed for my office and picked up the phone. No outside calls would be possible until eight, when the master building control computer came back on to normal, but the inter-office system worked regardless. I rang Sugal's office, letting it ring twice, then hanging up and dialing again.

"Qwin?" I heard Dylan's anxious voice and felt some relief.

"Yeah. Who else? How'd it go?"

"Hairy, you bastard. I'd much rather hunt borks."

I laughed. "But you did it?"

"Yeah, it's done, although I still don't believe it. Sanda?"

"I haven't called yet. I'll do that in a minute."

"Look, isn't somebody going to be coming in here shortly? When can I leave this mausoleum? I'm starving to death!"

"You know the routine. At seven-thirty the public function elevators will revert to normal, and you're on the office level. Just take the first car at seven-thirty down to the main level and use the emergency exit I told you about. No card needed."

That was true, for the fire code—but it *would* snap her picture along with day and time. That was no problem at all, though. As soon as they were both through, I'd use the handy little code Sugal supplied to erase the recording.

I gave her some encouraging words and rang the conference room with the same signal. The second time I called, Sanda answered, even more breathless than Dylan had been.

"How'd it go?"

She told me the whole story, of how the man had awakened and she had left the bottle there and, later, when the janitor had cleared the floor, it wasn't there any more. I calmed her, noting that he cleaned and polished the halls with that equipment, too.

Calmed of that particular fear, she was otherwise gushing. "It was," she told me, "the most exciting time of my whole life. More, even, than my first baby!"

I had to laugh at that, then reminded her of the exit procedures, and made certain that she, too, would be out of the building by seven forty-five. That was when I was going to take care of that little security record.

I sat back, feeling satisfied. They'd both been right: the plan had been absurd and certain to fail, so many variables beyond our control, all that. But it *had* worked. Worked perfectly. And the two women and I all had wonderful alibis.

I'd had all sorts of fallback positions in case something had gone wrong, including convincing cover stories for both of them to use about being locked in the building and all that. But that would have caused a lot of suspicion and might have blown the whole thing even if they were believed by the night janitors and security people. Nothing had to be used. Free and clear.

At seven forty-five I cleared the security recording.

At eight the Chief of Security checked, found a blank recording, and was satisfied that nobody had passed. By that time I was actually doing a little work, although I planned to knock off by ten. I was tired, damn it.

The whole plan looked crazy on paper, and it was; yet it was also tailor-made for the weaknesses inherent in the system. The conviction that nothing save orders from legal judges could change you against your will had made it possible to do just that with the janitors, under the circumstances of the deserted, familiar halls of the building.

But the final item that made it all possible was the certainty in every Cerberan mind that even if you could electronically steal money you couldn't get away with it, and that therefore nobody would bother to try. A few early and prominent examples sufficed.

The beauty of the plot was that nobody who did anything had any easily visible motive, and the man who did wouldn't have the slightest idea how the caper had been accomplished.

CHAPTER NINE

Aftermath and Reset

Sunday afternoon on the boat the three of us, with Sanda back in her own body, held something of a party to celebrate. I was particularly proud of Sanda, whose major reaction was that she wanted to do that kind of thing again. Dylan was more serious about it all; she knew the risks and the improbabilities of the thing as much as I did. We were a lot alike, Dylan and I, despite our very different backgrounds, except she was far more practical than I. Like those who would investigate this caper, she was fully capable of working out the details and dreaming it up, but she would never have gone through with it on her own. Had she not been in on it, she wouldn't have believed anybody would have. That, of course, was the ace in the hole for those investigative types.

"Look," I told her. "The people who run this world—the corporation presidents, syndicate bosses, central administration—are the survivors. They are the ones who were audacious enough and smart enough to pull off their own operations and eliminate their competition—and lucky enough to get away with it. There's a share of luck in all success stories, and only the unlucky ones make the headlines."

"Well, we were lucky this time," she responded, "and we did it. Your luck's bound to run out sometime, though. If it had last night, *your* mind wouldn't be going to the moons of Momrath—Sanda's and mine would. She can do what she wants, but that is *it* for me. I'm not risking my neck on your harebrained schemes any more."

"You won't have to," I assured her as sincerely as possible. "Help, yes. We're all partners in this, we three. But this sort of thing you do once. From here on in it'll be something different—and only I can accomplish the final objective."

"You're still going after Wagant Laroo?"

I nodded. "I've got to, for many reasons."

"And if you get yourself blown away?"

I smiled. "Then I'll try again. They'll just send in another me, and another, until the job gets done."

That afternoon I also filled Sanda in on the rest of the truth about me. After what she'd gone through, I thought she had a right to know. I admit I was soothing Dylan with my promise of no more risk to her. I really didn't know what was going to happen next, and who or what I'd need, but it certainly would involve at least her boat. Concerning the promise that we three were partners as long as we were together, though, I was dead serious. I really did like and admire these two very different women, such a contrast to, say, those two I'd spent the evening with Friday night, with their shallow dreams and shallow fantasies about body-swapping clubs and office gossip.

The next few weeks were nerve-racking. I had depended on the system being efficiently and competently run by people who understood the criminal mind because they too each had one. But after the success of our mission I was beginning to fear that I had been too subtle.

However, late one afternoon Turgan Sugal came down to see me, looking like a man who had suddenly found eternal life and fortune. "They suspended Khamgirt today," he told me.

"Oh?" I tried to sound playfully ignorant, but inside I felt a rising sense of satisfaction.

"Seems he had a hidden gambling vice. He was in hock up to his ass and still owed, so he had been siphoning off corporation money and spreading it thin in a lot of small bank accounts. A banking securities check a few days ago turned up the account pattern in the banking records, and they traced it to him."

"Well, what do you know about that!" I replied sarcastically.

He stopped for a moment. "It *was* you, wasn't it?" he managed, as if struck by a sudden revelation. "You—*framed* him? How?"

"Me? I didn't do any such thing," I replied with mock seriousness. "Hell, do you realize what it would take to fake something like that? Impossible!" And then I broke into loud laughter.

He laughed along with me for a moment, then stopped and stared at me strangely. "Just what the hell did you *do* to get sent here, anyway?"

"The usual. Computer fraud."

"How the hell did they ever catch you?"

"The same way they caught Khamgirt," I told him. "That's what gave me the idea."

He whistled. "Well, I'll be damned. All right, I won't ask any more. Things are pretty turbulent right now, and there's an investigation of the whole thing, since Khamgirt has not only denied everything but has passed a truth scan."

"Sure. They *know* it's a frame. But that won't help him. Oh, don't worry—they won't kill him or send him to the mines or anything like that. They'll pasture him, with a slap on the wrist. Not for embezzlement. They'll know he was had. For getting framed. That means he is not only unable to protect himself and his secrets but vulnerable. The syndicates don't allow you to make mistakes. Just remember that when you get on the high and mighty side."

He nodded. "Makes sense. But what if they figure it out and trace the whole thing back to us?"

"What do you mean, *us?*" I shot back. "You weren't involved except in supplying some information they can't specifically trace to anybody in upper management. And I really wouldn't worry about it in any event. They'll have some grudging respect for whoever pulled this off. It was a risky operation that took a lot of luck, but it worked. They might figure out *how* it was done, but never who did it. Just relax and take advantage. I assume you'll be moving up?"

"That's what I came to see you about. They've asked me to fill in as corporate comptroller while the comptroller assumes the acting presidency. I'm finally leaving this place—and none too soon, either. We can't possibly make Khamgirt's artificially high quotas this quarter. Fortunately, as comptroller, I'll be able to adjust those to a more realistic figure on a temporary basis, maybe even show the board of directors that Khamgirt was conducting a vendetta against us. They'll be happy to believe anything of him now."

"And how soon am I paid?" I asked him slowly.

He paused a moment. "Give me a month to get a handle on the operation there. Then I can act—they won't find it surprising for me to reward several old associates. It's done all the time, to put our men into the underpositions. That's the earliest I dare move."

I nodded. "Fine with me. I have a lot of work to do here before I leave, anyway—*company* work, don't get that stricken look. But there are two other things."

He started looking uneasy again. "What do you mean? We had a deal."

I nodded. "And I'll stick to it. The other two are in the form of favors. One is simply that I be able to get an appointment, maybe a business lunch, with the acting corporate comptroller once in a while. Just to keep my hand in and find out the latest company gossip."

He relaxed a bit. "That's easy enough."

"The second's a very different favor, and it's not a requirement or condition. If necessary I can handle it in an underhanded manner, but it would be easier if you could do it normally."

"Go ahead."

"There's a young woman who did us both a real service, and she's stuck in the motherhood and doesn't want to be. That's bad enough, but she's extremely bright and talented and has a lot of guts. I'd like to get her out —I kind of owe it to her."

He thought for a moment. "I can see your reasons, but it's pretty tough, you know. I don't know of anybody with the power to do it unless you could force a judgment—catching somebody committing a crime against her. And that'd be pretty rough on her."

I nodded. "Just thought I'd ask in case there was some way out."

"Look, tell you what. Give me some time on this, a couple of months at least, and I'll see if anything can be done. Fair enough?"

I agreed. "It'll wait. She'll have sixty days' leave coming soon, so it's not *that* pressing. Only if you can't, tell me, won't you? And don't you want her name and address?"

He grinned. "Don't need it. I keep very good track of my employees."

That brought a little feeling of admiration from me. Still, I felt compelled to nail him down a bit.

"As you can see, I'm a good friend—and a loyal one, Mr. Sugal. I won't cross you now or in the future as long as you don't cross me either. Just remember we have a mutual stake in each other's protection. If you get in trouble, a psych probe could smoke *me* out. If *I* do, the reverse is true. So we have a stake in each other's welfare."

"Funny," he replied. "I was about to give the same speech to you."

Events proceeded in a slow, relaxed fashion after that, but right on schedule. Sugal was promoted, and within the month Tooker quotas were slashed and an industrial investigation team from the government evaluated maximum production potential with the staff we had against the quotas imposed and declared the quotas unrealistic and false. That gave us a great deal of breathing space.

Also during this period a particular fire district had a completely new alarm system installed, and our night janitorial supervisory staff was changed and its cleaning methods modified. Several staff members, including me, were discreetly questioned, known associates, that sort of thing. The investigators found nothing, of course, and the heat was off as quickly as it had appeared.

At the end of the month Sanda had her baby, a little girl, and within a week after was looking and sounding more like her old self again. I'd told her I was working on her problem, but that it might take time, and she seemed to accept that. After our little caper, she had the utmost trust and confidence in my ability to deliver—and of course that meant I felt honor-bound to do so.

Shortly afterward Tooker was reorganized, with a new manager appointed and many of my colleagues and co-workers promoted, moved around, and in a few cases, canned—particularly if they had been known Khamgirt people. As for me, I was made president of Hroyasail Limited, a wholly owned Tooker subsidiary. The job paid extremely well, but as I knew, wasn't all that necessary, being one of those ornamental posts mostly used to pasture people like Khamgirt. My promotion raised no eyebrows, since it was explained as a personal decision based on my relationship with Dylan.

And so it was I had the upper offices of the Akeba marina cleaned and redecorated. There I was, a company president in less than a year—never mind that it was a dead-end job. Technically I was in charge of a fleet of four hunter-killer boats and sixty-two trawlers, plus assorted warehouses and processing centers for the catch.

The offices were a three-story affair overlooking the harbor and perched in the branches of a couple of huge trees. One branch had been cut and a deck put on it that extended, bridgelike, back to the offices, so there was a clear walk down to the boats themselves.

The lower floors contained basic administration and records processing and the initial holding tanks for the skrit, a reddish little creature somewhere between a plant and an animal whose internal body chemistry provided, among other things, chemicals that made superb electrical conductors. Once a week or so, more often if business was good, a big industrial flier would arrive, take the tank off to Tooker for processing, and then drop off a new, empty one.

The upper floor, however, had been closed off since the last president, at least eight years before. I spent Tooker's expense money lavishly, fixing up not only a comfortable office suite but also a huge luxury apartment with all the amenities. I moved in quickly. Shortly after, Dylan moved in as well, and we drew up and filed a marriage contract. Marriages were not usual nor necessary on Cerberus and existed mostly among people belonging to religious communities, but there were reasons for this one. On a practical level, it clearly defined joint and separate property and allowed us to establish a joint credit line. In that sense, it fulfilled my original promise of full partnership, and her position in Hroyasail suddenly became, as the boss's spouse, one of greatest among equals.

And of course our relationship made my request for the Hroyasail position all the more credible to any suspicious onlookers. But there was more to it than that. I felt comfortable around Dylan, and not as comfortable away from her. She was a close friend and absolute confidante, and I'd never had that close a relationship. It was more than that. Being with her felt *good,* somehow—having her there, to know she was there even when we were in different parts of the place doing different things. However, this dependency bothered me, because up until now I'd considered myself immune to such human emotional weaknesses.

We slept together as a couple, too, causing frequent body switches that bothered neither of us. As Class I's we did our regular job no matter who looked like who, and the experience brought us closer than any couple I could remember.

As for Dylan—well, all I can say is that I seemed to fit into a hollow space in her life, possibly left over from her previous career in the motherhood. She needed someone very close, and sleeping together without shields was more important to her than to me.

The only two things that bothered me were her cigars, which were pretty smelly even with the blower system on full, and the fact that most mornings she'd go out on that damned boat and risk her life. I wasn't on my post more than a couple of weeks when they brought the first bodies back, mangled and bleeding if the sailors had been lucky, or in parts in body bags if they hadn't been. I didn't want to see Dylan come home like that, but I couldn't talk her out of it. It was her life, in her blood, and no matter how she felt about me I knew I'd always come second to the sea.

Sanda, of course, was the extra element in all this, but it wasn't really so bad. Both Dylan and I were nearby now, constantly within a quick elevator ride of Akeba House. So Sanda couldn't have been happier, although there was a wistful envy inside her that she could witness this but was prohibited by virtue of the motherhood from its paradoxical freedom and stability.

I had heard a few times from Sugal, who was digging into the comptroller's post so solidly that it looked like the "acting" titles for all of the board would soon be removed and the positions made permanent. Khamgirt, as I predicted, had been convicted of the charge, placed on probation, and pastured to president of a regional shipping line that was also a Tooker subsidiary.

Things were going well for me, but I resisted the temptation just to let things slide. There was still Wagant Laroo to catch, and all I could do was keep my eyes and ears open and wait for a new break.

CHAPTER TEN

A Bork Hunt

My worries over Dylan increased with each injury, and yet I understood her well enough to know that protesting was useless. Sanda, on the other hand, had gotten the bug bad from her exploit with me and was just dying for some more action.

We were sitting around the place one evening, just talking and relaxing, when Sanda brought the subject up after hearing a few new accounts from Dylan, who never tired of the subject.

"It sounds so thrilling," she told us. "I'd give almost anything to go out just once."

"You'd probably be bored stiff," Dylan told her. "After all, we don't have hunts and attacks every day—thank heaven."

"Still—just to be out there speeding across the waves, with the feeling that danger could come from anywhere—I've heard all your stories so often I can see it in my dreams. Instead, well, my leave's almost up. Next week it's back to the House and the hormones." The thought of that really depressed her.

"You know you can't go, though," I noted sympathetically. "You're certified valuable to the state. No risks allowed."

"I know, I know," she sighed and sank into depression.

Though this wasn't the first time the subject had come up, this had been the worst and most persistent round. I could see Sanda was getting to Dylan, partly out of friendship but also because she too had once been in the girl's position.

Later that evening, after Sanda was asleep in the guest room, we lay there, not saying much. Finally I said, "You're thinking about Sanda."

She nodded. "I can't help it. I look at her, listen to her, and all I can see and hear is me a few years ago. Anything on getting her out?"

"No, and you know it. Sugal's pulled every string he can find and it just isn't done. The only cases on record are ones in which a syndicate boss wants a private breeder, so to speak, to control his own kids—or for Laroo's own purposes. It's a dead end. Maybe I can come up with something of my own, but I've gone through all the possibilities and the system's just against me. Unless I can crack that master computer I can't do much, and to crack the computer I'd have to replace Laroo."

"What about the drug angle? It's the way I got out."

"And they closed that loophole after you," I noted. "After your switch they had a big debate and decided that there was nothing in the rules to use against you, so they let you go, but then they made some new rules. Any switch from the 'valuable to the state' category has to be voluntary on both sides now or either one can seek a judgment to reverse it."

"We could let her use one of our bodies now and then. That's something."

"Yeah, that's true, but not for the boats and you know it. If anything happened to either one of our bodies under those conditions we'd automatically wind up in the motherhood ourselves—permanently, regardless of our Class I status." I sighed in frustration. "That's the hell of this system. In some places, in human history and even out on the frontier, motherhood's not only voluntary but a normal and *respected* thing. Even on other Warden worlds, I hear. But the bosses are afraid that the birthrate would decline low enough that it wouldn't sustain their need for new bodies as well as maintaining normal population growth. As long as *they* control and raise the babies they also control who lives forever and who dies—the ultimate control on this society."

"Hey! Don't forget, I was raised that way," she reminded me. "So was Sanda. They don't do a bad job."

"No, they don't," I had to admit. "And don't forget that my state raised me, too. It's going through and picking the kids who'll live and the kid who'll die that gets to me. Sure, sixty percent get a good upbringing, but it's that other forty percent that gets me. And as long as the system's a depersonalized to the average Cerberan as the birthing centers are in th civilized worlds, they'll never fully face up to what they're doing—killin kids for their bodies."

"Are *you* going to turn down a new body when your turn comes?"

I chuckled sourly. "Hell, no. That's the heart of this system. Even i opponents can't resist taking advantage of its benefits. Still, it probably won't matter to either of us, anyway. I'll probably get my fool head blown off in the next scam and you'll wind up lunch for a bork. What you said about me is also true for you—our luck can't last forever."

"I've been thinking along similar lines," she said. "I mean it—we're two of a kind. My luck's been astounding for the past few years, but it can't hold out forever. And I know that one of these days you're going to go off to do battle against Wagant Laroo, and one of these times it isn't going to work out. That's why I wanted this. Why I am, right now, having the time of my life. We're doomed, the both of us, doing the jobs we love, and every day might be the last. You feel that, too."

I nodded slowly. "I know."

"So you see, if we're professional risk-takers, why can't we take a risk with Sanda on the boat?"

"My instincts just go against it," I told her honestly. "I can't explain why."

"Look, I'm going to tell you a story. It's about a girl genetically tested and selected while still very young. One that the genetic experts said had all the right and none of the wrong genes. So when she was very young, she was taken out of the normal group and put in a special school composed entirely of other little girls and isolated from the mainstream of society. She received no more formal education, but instead was subjected to ceaseless propaganda on the wonderfulness of having babies, the duty to society and civilization to do so, and how to have them and give them prenatal and postnatal care. By thirteen she was capable of having them, but didn't yet, although she had been introduced to sex, sexual pleasures, and all the rest, while the mental conditioning reached such a fever pitch that she wanted desperately nothing but the life of the motherhood. She was also mentally and physically conditioned to a life of leisure and to the idea that she was in the most important class on all Cerberus."

She paused for a moment, a distant, wistful look on her face, and I said nothing. Finally she continued.

"So the girl finally passed her preliminary nursing and midwife exams and reached her fifteenth birthday, and they sent her to Akeba House. The next few months were an absolute heaven—anything and everything she wanted, plus the excitement of new people, trips into the cities, the resort and all that. And of course they arranged for her to become pregnant. That wasn't bad, either, although it's pretty dispassionate in the doctor's office. She felt herself change and marveled at the miracle within her. And finally the baby came—pretty rough the first time, but that didn't matter. And there was this beautiful baby boy, clinging, nursing, crying.

"And then one day, in about the second month, they came and took the baby away. They didn't"—she paused, her voice getting choked with emotion at the remembered pain—"they didn't even tell her. Just came and took him and that was that. And then they said go, take two months' leave and do anything you want—then come back. You have to have roughly a baby a year."

She sighed and I thought I saw the glimmer of a tear, the first time I'd ever seen Dylan cry.

"And so," she went on in that wavering, distant tone, "she ran to the others, her friends, for consolation, and got none. Either they were hardened to the system or they'd given up and were reconciled to it. The House staff also was very little consolation, finally offering to send me to a psych center so I'd adjust and be happy doing nothing but having babies. I couldn't accept that, either, so I sort of gave up. Gave up and gave in, like they all do. But Akeba House was located on an outcrop, and there was a small harbor on one side. I used to watch the hunters go out, and my mind went with them every time, as Sanda's does now. I became their friend, except for the times when I was obviously pregnant and they shunned me like a disease. Finally, during my leave time—after my fifth child—one of them, a very compassionate man I'll never forget, said much what you did just now—hell, you and he were a lot alike, really. He could be killed tomorrow and probably would be someday, so if risks were his business, well, he'd smuggle me aboard—and he did.

"And you know—nothing much happened. We sighted a bork, yes, but another boat took it and chased it out of view. The whole thing was pretty dull, really—but to me it was everything. It made me *alive* again, Qwin. I determined to get out of the motherhood, and I worked and schemed and plotted and took my opportunities just like you—and it worked. If it hadn't been for that joyride, though, I'd still be up there at the House, still having babies and gazing out at the sea, as Sanda is now. Wasting—just like she is. Do you understand now?"

I turned over and hugged her and held her close. "Yes, Dylan, I understand." I sighed. "So when are you going to take her?"

"Day after tomorrow. I wouldn't want it on my conscience that I killed a baby, too."

"All right. If your mind's made up. But please consider the matter again before you do. You're risking that sea, you know."

"Yeah, I know. Call me dumb or a softie or whatever. But I risked it for you, too. Maybe the luck'll hold one more time. The chances of getting caught are a lot slimmer this time. I've got a good crew. They won't talk, because it'd mark them as disloyals and they'd never get another berth."

"Your mind's made up, then?"

She nodded. "Absolutely."

"Then I'm coming along, too."

She sat up. "You? After I've been trying to get you out for weeks now?"

"Well, maybe if the president's along the responsibility will be spread a bit."

"No," she said firmly. "Come on if you want—hell, I'd love to see you. But there's only one person in charge of a boat, and that's the captain. One person in charge absolutely, and one person who's responsible for all aboard and their actions. That's the law and that's the way it has to be. Understand?"

"Okay, Captain," I responded, and kissed her.

It was a foul morning with intermittent rain and mist, so that you were hardly aware it was past dawn. The sea looked choppy and the boats all rode up and down uneasily on the water. That worried me, but Dylan was actually in better spirits because of it.

"We'll all be in rain gear, so if anybody happens to be spying from Akeba House they'll get no clues, not with these slickers and with her hair tucked up under the rain hat."

She had briefed her crew the day before in the privacy of the open sea. Nobody had objected. They knew her almost as well as I did, if not better, and she had their absolute respect.

The boat had a name—*Thunder Dancer*—but it was usually used only officially. Informally, it was always "Dylan's boat" or just "the boat."

We stayed inside the aft cabin where we had schemed and plotted not that long before, and a crewman fitted us with life jackets and briefed us. Dylan, at the wheel, was busy and we respected that.

"You can both swim, can't you?" the crewman asked, half joking.

"Yeah, although I'm not sure how far and how fast," I responded. "It's a shame we have to go out on such a rotten day."

He laughed. "Oh, this is a *good* day. You ought to be here when we get in really rough weather. Waves over the bow, and even we crewmen puking as we hold it together. Don't worry about this, though. The front's only three or four kilometers out, and we're going a lot farther than that today. We should have warm and sunny weather by midmorning."

And, somewhat to my surprise, we did.

It was an education to watch the fleet move out, the trawlers chugging along slowly with two hunter-killers as escorts while we, as one of the two point boats, cleared the harbor and its buoys and flashing lights. We suddenly rose on two skilike rails, thus tilting the whole boat back as it poured on the speed, suddenly freed of having the bulk of its mass push against the water.

"I have to be at station," the crewman told us. "You can go up to the bridge now if you want, but hold on to the handrails at all times."

I looked aft at the rapidly receding shoreline, half hidden in fog and mist, and at the wide wake we were leaving. The shoreline itself appeared ghostly, the great mass of trees rising from the water in and out of fog, punctured only by some distant lights.

"Oh, God! Isn't this *great!*" Sanda enthused, rushing from one window to another. She was like a little kid again, squealing, oohing, aahing, and just having a grand old time.

And there I was, the grand old veteran space pilot, feeling funny in my stomach. But that old me had been in a different body. Still, Dylan had come out on occasion in this body and seemingly had had no trouble, so that wasn't the whole explanation.

"Let's go up to the bridge," I suggested as we broke through the squall line and were suddenly hit by sunlight.

"Great! Lead on!"

We walked through the interior, past the electronic detection gear and biomonitors that would locate the masses of *skrit* on or near the surface and would also warn of borks, through the small galley and up a small set of steps to the bridge itself. There Dylan was sitting, relaxed, in the broad, comfortable captain's chair with an idle hand on the wheel, looking out. She turned as we entered and smiled. "Well! How do you like it so far?"

"Tremendous!" Sanda enthused. "Oh, Dylan, I can never repay you for this."

Dylan took her hand from the wheel, got up, and hugged Sanda. The look on our captain's face said that the attitude alone was more than payment enough.

"Hey!" I yelled. "Who's driving?"

Dylan laughed. "The autopilot, of course. I've programmed in the course and set it for automatic after we lifted. No more attention required until we get to our zone for the day."

I felt a bit foolish and even a little ashamed. The same guy who bearded lions in their dens and was confident of taking on Wagant Laroo, who'd piloted starships through trackless voids, was damned scared out here in an alien ocean with no land closer than two kilometers straight down.

"You look a little green," she joked, looking in my direction. "If I were the mean sort I'd find some really rough water and give you a workout—but don't worry, I love you and I won't."

The rest of the morning we sat around talking, occasionally bringing Dylan a cup of coffee or light snack from the mini-galley or doing the same for the crew.

And she'd been right. After a while it got to be damned boring. Not for Sanda, who climbed all over the boat, getting explanations from the gun crews, and lessons from the electronics experts, and asking a million questions. For me, though, and basically for the crew as well, there was nothing exciting about skimming along the ocean at thirty-six knots with nothing anywhere in sight.

Still, they all had within them some extra sense, some deep love for the sea, the boat, and their lives here. They were happy, content, at peace out here in a way I could not understand, perhaps could *never* really figure out.

The ocean itself, though, had a certain academic fascination. It was different colors in different places, and there were obvious currents you could literally feel, as if the temperature rose and fell in a moment depending on what invisible part of the water you were in. In the distance you could actually see the storm front now moving "inland," and out a little farther to the northeast you could fully see a thunderstorm, dense rain, high, bomblike clouds, and lightning all included, while you yourself were basking in the sunlight of a cloudless sky.

The pattern was generally the same for the boats. We had gone to a sector southeast of Medlam allocated by the Cerberan Coast Guard so that each company had its own area for the day, then had started a wide, circular sweep of the zone, going round and round in ever-smaller circles as the instruments looked for skrit.

"Still no skrit in commercial quantity," a speaker told us, "but we've got a bork on scope."

Dylan was suddenly all business. "Does he look interested in us?"

"Nope. Not particularly. Big one, though. Four, maybe five tons. About twelve hundred meters south-southwest and at about twenty meters depth. Not going much of anywhere, maybe going to come up for some sun is all."

"Well, keep an eye on him," she ordered, "and warn me of any changes in behavior." She walked out onto the outer deck around the bridge and I followed. The wind from our speed was pretty fierce, although there was a windshield just forward of the real bridge and actually an auxiliary wheel. She stared out at the open sea, as did I, but I could see nothing.

"Yup. There he is," she said unemotionally as she pointed. I squinted in the indicated direction but could see little. I began to wonder if she was putting me on or if my eyes weren't as good as hers.

"I don't see a thing."

"See—way off there? Look real hard in the sky. Squint a little against the reflection, or put on your dark glasses."

I put on the glasses, which I didn't particularly find comfortable, and tried to see. "Look in the sky?"

She nodded. "See those little black specks?"

I tried very hard, and *thought* I could see what she meant. "Uh-huh."

"They're geeks," she told me.

I tried to remember what a geek was. Some kind of flying horror, I seemed to recall. A carrion-eater. "Do they always follow borks?"

She nodded. "They're too lazy to make kills for themselves, and borks are greedy killers who are not too efficient about disposing of their kill. Oddly enough, the bork feeds mostly on skrit, which is why we have the problems we do, but it attacks and takes bites out of almost everything, including other borks. Some sort of natural balance, really. The borks feed the flying creatures and several other sea creatures by the kills they make and don't or can't consume. That's why we even have limits on the number of borks we can kill."

"He's turning," came the voice on the speaker. "We've got the bed pretty well located now and he's heading right toward it. I've sent a slow-down order to the fleet. Shall we engage?"

She looked thoughtful. "Call Karel. Ask if she's in any position to assist a runaway."

There was a short pause, and I gathered by their manner that it was better just to stand out of the way, and let them do what they knew how to do so well. I had an uneasy feeling about all this, though. I kept hearing that "four, maybe five tons" over and over again.

"Karel says she's about twenty minutes away, and escort's about forty." She looked at me. "Where's Sanda?"

"In the lounge, last I checked."

She turned back to the speaker. "Make sure the passenger is secure inside, then tell Karel to pour it on. Gun crews to full alert status. Stand by to close." She went to the outside wheel and reached to one side, flipping a switch. The boat slowed noticeably. Then, one hand on the wheel and the other on the throttle, a stick with a big black ball on top, she took full control of the boat from the autopilot.

"You better go inside and get strapped in," she told me. "We're at least going to have to turn the bastard and I don't want to lose you."

I nodded absently, feeling a little tightness in my stomach. Lots of nasty things and nastier situations I could handle, but out here on the open sea facing a creature I'd only seen pictures of, I was totally at the mercy of Dylan and her crew. We were closing on the thing. I could clearly see the nasty-looking geeks, about half a dozen of them, circling a dark patch in the water.

"Qwin! Please!"

"All right, all right. I don't want to distract you. I was just wondering why they called them borks."

At that moment the sea ahead of us exploded with an elephantine mass at least three times the size of the boat. An enormous slit opened, revealing a tremendous cavity lined with sharp teeth and wriggling, wormlike tendrils. "BOOOOAAAAARK!" it roared, so loud that it echoed like thunder across the open sea and almost burst my eardrums.

"Ask a stupid question," I muttered, turned, and dashed for the lounge. Sanda was already there, strapped into a chair and watching out the window. I joined her, almost getting thrown against the side by the sudden change in the boat's direction.

Sanda's expression was stupefied and vacant, her mouth open, and when I got myself into a seat and stared out the window I probably looked about the same myself. "Oh, man!" she breathed.

The entire side of the ship seemed dominated by the monstrous reddish-brown thing that continued to show more and more of itself. I couldn't translate what I was seeing to the pictures and diagrams I'd seen of the things.

Out of the water on either side rose four huge tentacles with bony spikes all over. The tentacles alone looked as if they could pick up and crush the boat, and those bony protrusions looked as if they could easily penetrate not only the plastiglass but the armor plating itself. Worse, I knew that the entire surface of the bork's skin was tremendously sticky and abrasive at the same time, so that the merest touch could rip flesh from bone.

And we were slowly cruising by now, as if on a sightseeing tour!

Suddenly I heard the engine rev up, whining as if it were strained to the limit. We had been moving so slowly that we were actually hardly up on our hydrofoil skis at all. Then the guns let loose, shaking the ship from stem to stem and sending cups and such flying. The guns were explosive projectiles; you couldn't use a disrupter system on something mostly underwater because you might not be able to stop the effect. Besides, a weaker laser wouldn't put a dent in something this size, whose vital organs were always well underwater and away from direct attack by boats.

I had to admit that for the first time in my life I felt not only helpless but terrified.

The shells struck the thing and exploded with enormous force, releasing not only a powerful explosive charge but also some kind of electrical one as well. The creature roared and moved faster than I would have believed anything that big could possibly move. But still we remained, just crawling past.

With a splash I thought might sink us by itself, the thing had appeared to retreat and dive at the same time, but I was suspicious of this respite. We waited tensely.

Suddenly we were jerked almost out of our restraining straps as the full power of the engines was released at once and the ship almost jumped out of the water.

In a matter of no more than a couple of seconds, the bork rose with a roar and enfolded an area of ocean astern of us. I realized with a sinking feeling that that area of sea was where we had just been.

The aft gun opened up with a full series of shots, pouring it into the great beast. With its computer laser-guidance system it must have poured twenty or more exploding charges into the thing, and they barely made a dent in it.

Again the bork seemed to shrivel and sink beneath the waves. Outside somewhere over the roar of all the action I kept hearing fierce, loud cries of "Geek! Geek!" like some sort of bizarre cheerleading squad—which in a way it was.

So much for how creatures on Cerberus got their names.

For more than half an hour we played cat and mouse with the beast, luring, feinting, and shooting at it with enough ordnance to totally obliterate a medium-sized city. After a while you could see the areas of the creature that had been shot away, and occasional wounds still bubbling and hissing from the electrochemicals shot into it that water would not extinguish. But no matter how many times it was hit, there seemed to be another section just as nasty and virtually untouched.

I did finally realize what Dylan was doing, though. She was doing her job—pulling the bork further and further away from the skrit that had to be commercially harvested. All I could do was admire her skill, timing, and guts. I recall thinking, *And they have charter boats for people to do this for fun?*

How far away had she pulled it? I began to wonder. Possibly several kilometers. But while it was clear to me that we were faster in the long run than the bork, we didn't have the ordnance to kill the monstrosity alone. For all that we were doing, we were hitting nonvital parts.

Suddenly, after all this cat-and-mouse stuff, Dylan gunned the engine and we sped up and away from the monster, this time not firing. I wondered if she was going to break off. Then suddenly she made a steep turn, and in that turn I could see another boat like ours—Karel certainly—making a similar turn toward the great beast, which, because it hadn't been shot at the last time had not done its fantastic quick vanishing act.

It had in fact seen the other boat and ours turn and was standing its ground, confident of itself despite all the harm we'd done to it.

We started closing fast—so fast I was afraid we were going to crash right into the thing. Mentally I could see only one of those great bony tentacles crashing down into us, bringing oblivion in the deeps. But as the thing made ready for its swipes I heard four sharp pops from each side of the boat, and we suddenly made a turn so sharp it seemed certain to capsize us. The turn put the aft lounge in full view of the thing, and it seemed that the world was full of nothing but the most disgusting gullet imaginable.

Suddenly the sea behind us erupted in a tremendous series of blasts, tearing into the monster, which roared its terrible defiance. We could see the second boat launch its own torpedoes, the nice kind that went by air or water and did what you told them to do.

I saw two literally jump out of the water and go right down the monster's throat!

Already we had some distance on the thing, which still looked like a floating city. Suddenly, though, it was ripped by two tremendous explosions and seemed almost to fly apart, bits and pieces several meters long of bloody skin, bone, and tentacle flying every which way, some almost far enough to reach our boat. At that moment I saw Karel's boat appear off to our side, though quite a bit astern, and heard above the death throes of the monster a foghornlike signal which we answered.

Confirmed kill.

You could hear the yells and cheers from the men and women on our boat, too—and maybe even a little from Sanda and me.

Sanda seemed to collapse, then shook her head in wonder. "Wow! I read all the books, heard all the stories, saw all the roomvision specials, but nothing was ever like this! Compared to this, what we did for you was a piece of cake!" She paused and looked at me oddly. "You all right?"

"I think I wet my pants," I croaked.

A bit later I managed to get hold of myself, clean up, and go forward to see Dylan. This trip had been an education for me, all right, and one I would remember until my death. I had discovered that I *could* be that scared, and I also finally realized that Dylan not only did this every day but did it routinely, as a matter of course. I had a new, almost awed respect for her courage now. If there was anybody I ever dreamed of wanting at my back, it was definitely Dylan Kohl.

The rest of the day, such as it was, was uneventful. No more borks—although we had one sighting—and no more chases. Just playing shepherd to the fleet of trawlers hauling in the rich, reddish skrit. It was a boring afternoon, and I loved every boring minute of it. The efficient trawlers were quick about their work, reaching capacity in less than two hours. Together, we and the fleet headed for home.

My emotions were more mixed now than they had been earlier. As much admiration as I had for Dylan and the others who did this day in and day out, this sort of tension had to take its toll on all of them. If anything, I had underestimated the danger of the job. I was going to be worried more and more about her as I replayed this experience in my mind again and again.

We reached the harbor uneventfully and settled down into the water, pulling smoothly to the dock. Dylan supervised the securing of the mooring lines to the boat and then came back to see us. "Better wait until dark before getting off," she cautioned Sanda. "That way nobody's going to be sure if you went with us or came on after."

She nodded, and I stood up. "I hope you'll excuse me for not staying as well, but I have to put my foot on dry, solid wood or something or I'll go nuts." My whole body felt as if it were permanently vibrating.

Sanda rose and gave Dylan a big hug and kiss. "Oh, I love you for this! By God, I'm gonna beat the motherhood if it kills me!"

Dylan looked at me. "See?"

I nodded understandingly and took off, heading for the gangplank and dock. I had no sooner walked out than I stopped dead in my tracks. Two unfamiliar people were standing there at the end of the gangplank, and they had the look that seems universal for their kind anywhere in the galaxy. I felt a sinking sensation in my stomach and tensed up as bad as I had during the bork hunt.

The two, a man and a woman, walked on board and stopped, looking at me. One flashed a badge and said softly, "CID. I caution you to remain where you are and not make a sound." He nodded to the woman, who walked aft to the lounge, then in the door.

"After you," said the male cop. I turned, and walked back into the lounge with him.

The two women were both there, having mistaken the woman's approach for my return.

"Which of you is Captain Kohl?" the female cop asked.

"I am!" Sanda spoke up bravely.

"No, I am," responded Dylan, looking then at Sanda with a sadness in her eyes and voice. "It's no good. They'll have to scan us both anyway."

"Look," I said, trying to sound indignant, "I'm the president of this company. What seems to be the trouble, officers?"

"Captain Kohl is charged with willfully violating Section 623½, Universal Penal Code," the man responded. "Knowingly subjecting an individual classified as an asset to the state to extreme danger."

"This is ridiculous!" I sputtered. "Both of these women work for me."

"Stow it," the woman snapped at me. "We know who the girl is."

"I'm afraid I'll have to ask you both to come down to the station with us," the male cop added. Then, turning to me, he cautioned, "Please don't interfere. The penalties are quite severe for that."

"Can I go with them, then? I'm married to the captain."

"I don't see why not. But no funny business."

"There won't be," I assured them, feeling that all was suddenly very wrong; that for once luck had run out—not on me, but on the one I cared for most. I would have loved to have pulled some funny business and wouldn't have hesitated in the slightest to do so, but there seemed absolutely nothing I could do, funny or otherwise, except tag along.

CHAPTER ELEVEN

A Judgment

On the way in, I cautioned both of them to say nothing. Dylan squeezed my hand and Sanda's. "It's all right," she said simply. "I knew what I was doing, and I'm not sorry for it even now. Maybe it's a fair exchange, although not one I'd have made willingly. I've had five years of living. Now maybe it's somebody else's turn."

"Don't talk like that!" I scolded her. "It's not the end of the world."

"It's the end of *my* world," she almost whispered.

Once in the stationhouse, in a corner of the Municipal Building, both women were taken into a small room where their card imprints and scans were taken. I was not able to follow, but simply had to pace back and forth in a small waiting area. Even the bork hunt paled before my feelings now, which were at an all-time low. After about half an hour, they let me see Dylan for a few minutes while they processed their records and did whatever cops did. Sanda was being held in a separate room, and I didn't see her.

"Well, it's over," she sighed.

"Huh? What do you mean?"

"They've been laying for me, Qwin. Laying for me for, I guess, five years. They didn't like the fact that I wormed my way out of the mother-

hood, so they've been waiting for a chance to get me. A clerk in the office
—one I know, one who's worked there almost as long as I have—was a
plant. They had something on her. An old criminal conviction or something, and she was too low in skill level to be considered vital. She had to
catch me or when she reached the mandatory age it was the mines for
her."

I shook my head in disbelief. "Five *years?*"

She nodded. "They needed an example. There's been a lot of rumblings
in the motherhood since I sneaked out. I was their symbol of hope—and I
knew it. The authorities *had* to get me, no matter how long it took. They
said their psychological profiles indicated I'd do exactly what I did sooner
or later, and they were sure right."

"What happens now?" I asked her, both concerned and mad as hell at a
system that would wait this long to hang somebody.

"Judgment," she told me. "The witness, the cops, and the scans proved
their case automatically."

My mind was racing. "Who sentences you? What kind of rank?"

"A professional judgment panel. Thirteen of them. I'm scheduled to
meet them in a little less than an hour. They don't usually hold proceedings this late, but they're making a special case for me."

I thought of all the men in high places I knew. "Is there someone I can
call? Someone who can intercede?"

She shook her head. "I don't think so. Maybe after, but not now. We
don't even know what the sentence is yet—could be almost anything. All I
know is that it was planned and directed years ago." She looked up at me.
"Don't blame yourself! I did it, all of my own free will. I'm totally responsible."

"I let you do it."

She smiled, a ghost of that old smile. "You couldn't have stopped me
and you know it."

"Will they let me in? Will they hear any mitigating statements?"

She shrugged. "I don't know."

We waited together nervously until they called her name.

The judgment chamber was much like any other courtroom except for
the thirteen black-robed men and women up there behind a curved table.
Since only one had a mike, it was clear that there was a presiding officer.
They let me in and I took a seat, noting Sanda in a chair forward of the
rest of the seats, which were empty. Sanda looked as if she'd been crying a
little, or maybe a lot, but she seemed composed now.

"The State versus Dylan Zhang Kohl," intoned the chief judge, as if
there were other cases. "Will the prisoner please rise and approach the
bench?"

Dylan stood up and confidently did as she was told, looking the chief
judge right in the eye. *Good for you, gal!* I thought.

"Dylan Zhang Kohl, you have been found guilty on the evidence

which we have judged to be true and incontrovertible that you did willfully and knowingly violate Section 623½, Cerberan Universal Penal
Code. Can you find any reason for sentence to be deferred or mitigated?"
    "No, your honor," she said firmly.
    I cursed and fidgeted like mad in my seat. Twice in one day I felt real
fear, and twice in one day a total sense of helplessness.
    "Will Sanda Tyne approach the bench?"
    Sanda, looking tiny and nervous, did so, standing next to Dylan. I saw
that Dylan took Sanda's hand and squeezed it affectionately, as if to reassure her.
    "Sanda Tyne, we find that you did knowingly and willfully violate
the Articles of Syndication applicable to Akeba House. This we have
judged true and incontrovertible on the evidence. Can you find any reason
for sentence to be deferred or mitigated?"
    "I talked her into it," she pleaded bravely. "I kept after her and after
her. It's all my fault!"
    "We have considered all the factors involved, including having both
your psychological profiles analyzed completely. One of the principal articles of the code, particularly considering the past history of this planet and
many of its founding parents, is that the criminal act is not something to
be judged in and of itself, but in the context of society. One can, for example, go into one of the private banks and plead for a thousand units,
without credit, collateral, or any obvious means of payback. If the bank
then gives you the loan anyway, and you default, it is not your responsibility but the bank's. Now, say you desperately needed the money, for a
matter of life and death, and you conveyed this to a bank officer. The
officer is sympathetic but should deny your loan because it would injure
his employer, and therefore his depositors, and therefore the state. Everyone who had deposits in good faith at that bank would pay for his error.
    "But let us suppose that his heart was touched by your plea, and he
then arranged for you to get to a console so that you could steal the
money. You are desperate, and you do so, thereby committing a criminal
act. But who is truly committing the more serious crime? The one who
steals, or the one who allows and arranges for the person to steal? This
court recognizes this principle, so enshrined in our laws and principles,
and in that context applies it to judgment in this case. Examining your
psychological profile, we find you, Sanda Tyne, to be a secondary party to
this violation, as you did not stow away on the boat or enter it without the
permission of its captain.
    "This court has studied both your records and has arrived at what we
believe is a fair and just verdict. It is the sentence of this court that the
two of you exchange bodies by means of judgment, and so be locked into
those bodies. We further hold that you, Dylan Kohl, will assume the responsibilities of the Tyne body and are therefore not to assume your former position or take any other employ. In view of your psychological
profile we further direct that you be taken after judgment to the Borough

of Medlam's Public Psychology Section and undergo a series of specific treatments to be set by this court for yours and the public's good."

I jumped up. "You're not going to turn my wife into a vegetable!" I screamed.

The judge paused, and all thirteen gave me the dirtiest locks I ever got from anybody. *Well, you've blown it now,* I told myself, but I didn't care any more.

"You are the spouse of the prisoner Dylan Kohl?"

"Yes, I am, and—"

"Silence! Or I will have you removed and charged!" He paused for a moment to see if I would take the challenge, but I got back a little of my self-control and managed to hold on for a moment.

"Now, then," the judge continued, sounding deliberative but satisfied, "let me state to you, sir, that the days of such things, except in extreme cases, are past. For your benefit, I will outline and explain what we mean."

"Please," I almost begged, shaking a little.

"We believe that the profile of Dylan Kohl indicates a possibility of suicide. We will prevent that, as well as other acts possibly harmful to herself or to others. Everything we do will be in the nature of protections such as that or compulsion to ensure that the sentence is carried out. Her memory, personality, and general freedom of movement will not be impaired, since to do anything else would not be a punishment at all. Does this satisfy you?"

It didn't, but what could I say? Well, there was always one thing, while I had the judge's ear. "Your honor, we are married and we truly love each other. Could she not continue to live with me? Even with her other occupation, she knows my business better than I do and could make a contribution to its management without costing the company or the state anything. It would be a shame to waste this expertise."

I saw the judges whispering among themselves until finally the whisper, like a ripple, reached the chief judge. He looked slightly surprised and a bit uncomfortable, but he considered whatever it was, then turned back to me.

"My colleagues seem to go along with you—to a point. In such a relationship, which is quite rare on this planet, it has been maintained by some of my learned colleagues that an absolute sentence would punish *you,* who have been charged with nothing. Furthermore, it appears that no matter how removed our society seems, there are still some romantics among us. Let me ask you—have you ever had a full physical examination?"

I thought a bit. "Yes, your honor. When I was first on the planet, and again the first week of my employment."

"I see. I note that your form is close to the standard for the civilized worlds, and such are generally sterile. Do you know if you have the capacity to father children?"

"I am told I do, your honor," I answered. "Although the product of some genetic engineering, this body is of the frontier."

Again came conversation, again the whispers and the ripples, the nods and gestures. Finally the chief judge announced, "Well, we find an equitable solution here, we believe, one that is in accord with our past history and is in the interest of fairness. It is quite out of the ordinary, but we feel that if it sets a precedent it will be a rare one, considering the circumstances of the case and the example. We therefore place the prisoner in the Childbearers and Rearers Syndicate, subject to all its codes, rules, articles and provisions, but assign her to you rather than to a specific Guild House, for so long as you choose, with the following provisions.

"One, that you yourself in no way cause the prisoner to violate any of those codes, rules, articles, and provisions. Two, that you perform the duties normally done by insemination at the Guild Houses, or arrange for insemination in case she cannot fulfill her quota. Three, that you assume absolutely all financial burdens, and that the prisoner shall have no credit, no money, and no possessions under law except those which you provide. All joint assets currently in both names or in her name shall be transferred to you alone, and her card shall be invalid for any purchases or other transactions, making her a total dependent. Four, she shall be totally subject to your authority, carrying out any such duties large or small that you permit so long as she follows the guild code, rules, articles, and provisions. Five, should you ever no longer wish her company or services, she must immediately report to and enroll in the nearest Guild House, transferring all authority to the Guild House. Do you understand the terms?"

"Yes, your honor." I sure did. It was the most degrading and demeaning sentence I'd ever heard in my whole life, one that could only have been pronounced on this dirty planet. It was in fact the worst punishment they could mete out to her, considering her independent spirit. Suddenly she was reduced not merely to the chattel of Akeba House but to outright slavery. Still, I *had* to agree, it being as good a deal as I thought could be made at this time. But someday, Cerberus, I was going to correct it all. Correct it, and pay them back for this. They might temporarily break her. But that only spurred me on to break their whole goddamned rotten system.

"Sentence on Dylan Zhang Kohl is therefore pronounced and ratified," the judge was saying. "Prisoner will remain in custody and undergo full sentencing as soon as practicable, preferably within the next few hours. Release is set at ten hundred tomorrow morning, at which time she will be released to your custody, Qwin Zhang."

I nodded and sat back down.

"Sanda Tyne," the judge continued, "you shall be judged and locked into the body now possessed by Dylan Kohl. It is further directed that you undergo a process of psychological conditioning at the Borough of Medlam's Public Psychology Section as prescribed by this court, and that you be reduced to the status of mendicant. Any employment you might find is restricted to the most menial of Class II occupations, and permanently fixed in the lowest position at the minimum wage prescribed by law. This sentence is to be carried out expeditiously, and not later than ten hundred tomorrow morning. This court is now adjourned. Prisoners will report to chambers for initial judgment."

The thirteen filed out, and a cop came up and escorted the two women through a door to one side of the judge's dais. Neither of them looked back in my direction.

I was frankly more concerned with Dylan than with Sanda. As head of Hroyasail, I could hire her even if I was limited in what I could pay her or do for her, so she wouldn't face the fate of others in the mendicant class —a free one-way trip to Momrath. I worried, though, if having her around in that body would bother Dylan.

I waited anxiously in the anteroom of the Municipal Building at ten hundred. I didn't have long to wait. I soon saw both of my women, looking very much the same, walk out and head toward me. Both were stopped, asked to sign something, and then given their cards.

Dylan, now in Sanda's slim sandy-haired form, was through first and came up to me. "Hi," she managed weakly.

"Hi, yourself," I responded, and kissed her. "Was it bad?"

"Not really. I don't even remember most of it. No, the bad stuff's to come. I can't believe the sons of bitches actually *gave* me to you!"

"It's not a precedent," I told her, "and not restricted to women, either. It's also done for Syndicate bosses, it seems, and Laroo. Some of 'em have private harems, male or female. It's based on their first principle—you own your mind but the state owns all our bodies."

"Maybe mostly, but they own a little of my mind, too. I don't think they missed a trick to humiliate me. I can't cause myself or anyone else physical harm. The way the psychs adjusted my mind, I'll almost go into heat, like some animal, to get pregnant right on their schedule. I can't even leave your side without permission, and if I'm left in the apartment I must stay there. I can't set foot on a boat, even if it's docked, permission or no. All that sort of shit."

"I'm so very sorry. I'll make it as easy on you as I can," I soothed.

She managed a wan smile. "I know you will. Look, I told you I took the risk freely. We crapped out this time, that's all. Look on the bright side: you won't have to worry any more about my getting killed, and those bastards turned me into an adolescent sex fantasy all for you."

"I didn't ask for that."

"I know." She turned. "Here's Sanda."

Our other woman looked *really* stricken, filled with guilt, a guilt I knew would surface not only every time she looked at Dylan but also every time she looked in a mirror. She had done her idol in, and that was her true punishment.

Dylan grabbed her and hugged her. "Don't feel so bad! Don't feel so guilty! No more babies for you, no more prisoner! And we're still to- gether!" She turned back to me. "You *can* find a job for her, can't you?"

I nodded, feeling relieved that *that* was out of the way. "Sure." I looked around. "Let's get out of this place."

We walked out into the sunshine and sea breeze, and I hailed a cab to take us back to the dock. When we got out, Dylan looked up at Akeba House, out on the promontory. "There *is* one requirement they made that I have to observe, permission or no," she told me. "I have to go up to the House in the next few days and, before an assembly of the women there, tell what happened to me and recant my crimes in front of them. That'll be the hardest thing."

We entered the old, familiar apartment. "You can set that up now and get it over with," I noted, gesturing toward the phone.

She went over, took out her card, put it in the slot, and waited. Noth- ing happened. She sighed and turned to me. "You'll have to dial for me," she said wearily. "With no credit of any kind I can't even make a simple phone call."

I tried to console her. "I'm going after Laroo and this whole rotten sys- tem. You're gonna be free and on the seas once more someday. I swear it."

I was going to try as hard as hell to make her believe that, too.

CHAPTER TWELVE

Project Phoenix

Dylan's luck had gone down the drain, but mine was still holding up. She went up to the House for her obligatory purging, then stayed around a bit, with my blessings, looking up some old friends, getting some consola- tion and advice, and doing some general talking. Misery loves company, as Sanda pointed out, and deep down, nobody was more miserable than Dylan. Still, when she finally returned, it was with some interesting news. Sanda, after all, had been spending her leave with us and had hardly checked in up there at all.

"There's a couple of women there under Cloister," she told me. "New people I never heard of before. Really gorgeous, too."

"What's Cloister?"

"It means they're restricted to the grounds of the House, and they've had their cards completely lifted. They can't leave the place. It's usually only done by the Syndicate as punishment for offenses, but they don't seem to be like that at all. In fact you'll never guess where they come from."

I shrugged. "What's the mystery?"

"They're from Laroo's Island," she told me. "They were some of his—what? Courtesans? Harem? Whatever."

The news piqued my interest for several reasons. "What did they do? Have a falling out with the old bastard? Or did he just get tired of them?"

"They're not sure. One day—zap! The whole bunch were picked up and shipped to Houses up and down the coast under Cloister. They say they think it's because of some big deal that Laroo's using the island for. According to them lots of new faces and equipment were coming in—and have been for the past few months."

She shook her head negatively. "But one of them saw a name on a stack of boxes—Tooker boxes."

Better and better. "What was the name?"

"Project Phoenix."

I punched up the encyclopedia on the roomvision monitor and checked the word. A legendary bird from ancient Earth cultures that was totally reborn by being completely consumed in flames.

"Can you go back up to the House whenever you want?"

"As a Syndicate member, sure."

"I want you to do just that. Get to know these women. Find out as discreetly as possible everything you can about Laroo and his island and this mysterious project."

"As you wish," she responded. "But I should warn you if you have any new schemes in your head. One of the things they psyched into me might foul you up. I cannot tell a lie. Not only not to you, not to *anybody*."

I considered that. "Can you not tell the truth? I mean, if somebody asks you a question and you don't want to give the answer, can you withhold it?"

She thought about it. "Yeah, sure. Otherwise anybody could pump me about you, and that would be illegal."

"Well, use your common sense, but if anybody asks you a question the answer to which would cause any problems, tell them you aren't permitted to answer that."

"As you wish," she repeated again in that rote tone.

I looked at her. "What's that 'as you wish' stuff?"

"Conditioning. Any order or direction you give me that doesn't violate Syndicate rules or my other conditioning I *must* obey. Don't look so upset —you can't change the rules. You can't even order me to disregard them, because they thought of that, damn them! I have—a—a *compulsion to serve*. They have made me a totally passive individual and I will, well, suffer mentally if I'm not ordered about, set to tasks—in a word, dominated. Every time you give me an order and I respond I get—well, a feeling of pleasure, of well-being, of importance. I'm a human robot—I exist to serve you, and you must let me. You must—for me."

I looked at her strangely. Was this the same Dylan Kohl who only a day before had coolly faced down one of the most horrible monsters of the sea? Was this the independent, gutsy schemer who got out of the motherhood, worked her way to captain, and helped rig a computer? It didn't seem so. They had certainly done something to her. Something in its own way more horrible than the lobotomies the judge said were no longer civilized. In more than one sense, this was a far crueler thing to do. I didn't know how to handle it.

"What sort of tasks?" I wanted to know.

"Prepare your meals, clean, run errands. Anything and everything. Qwin, I know this is hard on you, and you must know it's hard on me, but it's done. I accept it, and you must, too. Otherwise send me away to the House and forget me."

"Never—unless you want it."

"Qwin, I no longer have wants. Wants have been forbidden me. They stripped the wants away and left only a series of needs. I need to serve. I need to do my work as a mother. I want nothing. If you choose to keep me naked constantly scrubbing the apartment, that is what I will do, and what I *must* do."

"Damn! There must be some crooked psychs I can pressure into getting this lifted!"

"No. These compulsions are so deep-planted that to remove them other than in the precise manner that they were applied would destroy my mind and make me a permanent vegetable—and that precise manner is stored in the master computer alone. They didn't even have just one tech do it, but many, one at a time, so it couldn't be reconstructed; that is the added hold they have. They alone can restore me. As long as I am a good example to the motherhood of what happens if you try and change your lot, I will remain this way. I would be this way even at the House, only subject to the orders of all the women of the motherhood."

That master computer again! I *had* to crack Wagant Laroo! I just *had* to!

I pulled all my strings at Tooker, starting with Sugal, with whom I had a cordial lunch.

"You want something. You always do when you come up," he told me, sounding not in the least put out.

"What's Project Phoenix?"

He started. "Where did you hear *that* name?"

"I heard it. I want to know what it is."

His voice lowered to a whisper and he grew increasingly nervous. "Man! You're dealing with high explosives here!"

"Still, Turgan, by hook or by crook I *will* know about it."

He sighed. "If you heard of it at all, I suppose you will. But not here. In a public place. I'll get you the information."

He was as good as his word, although even he really didn't know what was going on. Nor in fact did I depend entirely on him. I pulled every string and called in any IOUs I had, as well as using the ever-fascinating Tooker computer network, to which I still had access, to build my own

CERBERUS: A Wolf in the Fold

picture. The elements, spread out in front of me in my office, gave a story that would emerge only through deduction and analysis.

Item: As I had already known, every single computer expert pulled from Tooker at the start of the last quarter had been expert in some form of organic computering. Most major organic computers and work on them had been banned long ago by the Confederacy, after some of the early creations, centuries ago, became more than human and almost took over humanity. That bitter, bloody, and costly war had made such work feared to this day. Those who dabbled in it were wiped or—sent to Cerberus? From Sugal and other sources I determined that we weren't the only one tapped for such minds.

Item: A couple of months earlier than this, major construction began on Laroo's Island, partly to create a place for shuttle landings to be made in safety there. But a whole hell of a lot more than that was in progress, to judge from the crews and raw materials ordered.

Item: Interfaces between Tooker's master computer—and other corporations' master computers—were established on a high and unbreakable scramble, relayed by satellite. The relay system's other end pointed to Laroo's Island, although officially it was interconnected to the Lord of the Diamond's command space station in orbit around Cerberus. That raised an interesting question: if the work was so super-secret, why *not* the space station? It was almost as large as the island, and if one allowed for the shuttle dock, power plant, and fixed structures on the island, it was a damn sight bigger in usable space.

Item: Interestingly, Hroyasail's own area for trawling had been increased by almost 50 percent shortly before I took over, something I never would have noticed if it hadn't been reflected in the quota plan for the quarter, a document I was only now getting to know intimately. Seaprince of Coborn, about the same distance south of Laroo's Island as we were north, had an equal increase. A look at corporation affiliates and a check with the previous quarter's quota plan showed that an entire Tooker trawling operation, Emyasail, was in the previous quarter's plan but was totally missing now. Its area had been given to Hroyasail, which was natural, and Seaprince, which was most unnatural, since Seaprince was a Compworld Corporation subsidiary, not one of Tooker's. You didn't hand valuable territory to a competitor that close voluntarily, so Compworld had to have given something really major in return and nothing like that showed in the books. In fact records showed that Tooker's *skrit* harvest since the quarter began was down sharply, indicating a dip into the reserves by next year. So it wasn't voluntary, and only the government could force such a move.

These facts alone, put together with what only I really knew of anyone likely to compile them, painted a stark picture.

Item: The only folks anybody knew about now using uncannily human organic computers were our aliens and their spy robots, robots known to have a connection with the Warden Diamond. That was why I was here.

But the alien robots were so good that no research project would be really necessary on them—and even if it was, it wouldn't be carried out here, not on Cerberus or any other Warden world, and certainly not by any of our people, who were definitely behind the aliens in this area.

And yet the conclusion was inescapable: Wagant Laroo had converted his former retreat and resort into an organic computer laboratory, staffed with the best of his own that he could find and supplied by Emyasail's trawlers. Why trawlers and gunboats and not by air? Well, for one thing it would attract less attention and give the appearance to onlookers of business as usual in Emyasail's area. Also, there appeared to be some paranoia about many aircraft in the vicinity of Laroo's Island.

I paced back and forth for several days and also talked the matter over with Dylan, who, having less background in this sort of thing than I did, came up even more of a blank. However, her more parochial outlook gave me the key I was looking for. "Why are you assuming the aliens have anything to do with it?" she asked me. "Why isn't this just a new scheme by Wagant Laroo?"

That stopped me cold. Suddenly all the pieces fell into place, and I had at least part of the picture. "No," I told her, "the aliens have everything to do with this—only they don't know it!"

"Huh?"

I sat down. "Okay, we know that these aliens are able to make facsimiles of people, people with jobs in sensitive places they have to gain access to. We know that these organic robots are so good they fool literally everybody. Not just the machines that check to see who's who, but everybody. Close friends. Lovers. People they've known for years. And they even pass brain scans!" I was getting excited now. "Of course! Of course! How could I be so blind?"

She looked concerned. "What do you mean?"

"Okay, so first your agents pick out the person they want to duplicate. They find their records, take holographic pictures, you name it. And from that, our alien friends create an organic robot—grow is a more apt term, if I remember correctly—that is absolutely physically identical to the target. Absolutely. Except, of course, being artificial it has whatever additional characteristics its designers want—eyes that see into infrared and ultraviolet, enormous strength if need be. Since it's made up of incredibly tough material instead of cells, with a skin more or less grafted on top, and powered perhaps by drawing energy from the fields that surround us—microwaves, magnetic fields, I don't know what—it can survive even a vacuum. The one that penetrated Military Systems Command seemed to have the power to change its components into other designs—it actually launched itself into space. And yet it fooled everybody! Bled the right blood when it had to, knew all the right answers, duplicated the personality, right down to the littlest habit, of the person it was pretending to be. And there's only one way it could have done that."

"All right, how?"

"It *was* the person it was pretending to be."

She shook her head in wonder. "You're not making any sense. Was it a robot or a person?"

"A robot. An absolutely perfect robot whose components could provide it with whatever it needed, either as a mimic or as a device for fulfilling its mission or getting away. An incredible machine made from tiny unicellular computers that can control independently what they are and do—trillions of them, perhaps. But the aliens solved the problem we never did, and never allowed ourselves the research time to do—they discovered how to preprogram the things indelibly, so they'd be free and complete individuals yet never deviate from their programming, which was to spy on us. So now they build them in our images, and—what? They bring them to Cerberus. No, not Cerberus, probably to the space station."

Dylan frowned, puzzled. "You mean they're around here?"

I shook my head. "No, what happens next has to be something like this. The target is snatched—kidnapped. Probably on vacation. At least at a time when he or she won't be missed for up to a couple of weeks. The victim is brought to the station and infected with the Cerberan version of the Warden organism and allowed to season there. Then—Dylan, you remember that drug you stole to get out of the motherhood?'

She nodded. "I—I got it off a shuttle pilot."

"Great! It's coming together nicely. So, after seasoning, their target is given some of this drug and introduced to the similarly infected robot facsimile. The target's mind and personality goes into the robot's, but the robot is already preprogrammed as an agent."

"As they programmed me," Dylan said emotionlessly.

I nodded. "Only a far more sophisticated method. A psych machine wouldn't do the job, since they need the complete person—and only that person's attitude is changed. No, it's in the original programming of the robot when it's made by the aliens, of that I'm sure."

"But how can this robot return and replace the original?" she asked. "Wouldn't the Warden organism destroy it when it left?"

"No, not necessarily. Remember, there are several items, several products that even now can be sterilized. Apparently these robots can too. Basically, all they do is get out of the system. The Wardens die, but so adaptable are the quasi-cellular components of the robot that they can make immediate repairs. The target returns to work from 'vacation,' the absolutely perfect agent-spy. It's beautiful."

"It sounds too much like what happened to me," she noted.

"I'm sorry," I said gently. "I was admiring a finely crafted gem. I don't want to make light of the human tragedy involved. Still, considering the size and complexity of the Confederacy, it'd be almost impossible to block them all out, and the major damage has probably already been done."

"And Laroo's Project Phoenix?"

I considered it a moment. "There's only one possibility I can come up with, and it's a terrifying one in some respects. The aliens have no reason to use the island, and less reason to use people who know less about their robots than they do. To put any of their operation directly on a Warden world would eventually tip off the Confederacy anyway, and they know the Wardens are 'hot' for them right now. No, for the answer you have to think as Wagant Laroo thinks, from the perspective of the Warden Diamond, and the answer becomes obvious."

"Not to me it doesn't," she said.

"All right—all along we've wondered just what the aliens could offer the Four Lords other than revenge. Well, here's the payoff. When they win, the Four Lords, and those others whom they choose—maybe even the whole population of all four worlds—will be given new bodies. Perfect bodies, those of organic robots. You see what the Four Lords were offered? A way out. Escape. The freedom to leave. If these agent robots can do it, anybody can. But there's a hitch, one that necessarily paranoid Lords like Laroo would immediately think of."

"I can follow this part. What's to stop these aliens from preprogramming the payoff robots as well, so they have a population of superhuman slaves?"

"Very good. High marks. So here you're given a way of escape and you dare not use it. What would *you* do?"

She thought a moment. "Study theirs and build my own."

"All right. But it's unlikely that you could do it without such a massive plant that the Confederacy watchers wouldn't take notice. Besides, it might well involve construction materials or support materials not found anywhere in the Warden Diamond, maybe unknown to anybody on our side at this point. What if you couldn't build one?"

"Well, I guess you'd order a few you didn't need as agents from the aliens, who have to trust your judgment in these matters, and use them."

"Right again! But these will come preprogrammed by a method unknown to our science. To make them work you have to find out how they are programmed and eliminate the programming. No mean trick, since it's probably integrated with instructions on how the robots function and those you have to keep. The best you can do is hope. Gather everything you can, and everybody who might know something about it, lock 'em up on the island with the robots, lab, computer links, and whatever, and try and find an answer. And that's what Project Phoenix is all about."

"Laroo's not only getting back at the Confederacy," Dylan said in an almost awed tone, "but double-crossing the aliens, too!"

I nodded. "I have to admire the old boy for that, anyway. And it's probably not just Laroo but all the Four Lords. And I think I know, at least, how the robots are getting in and out, too. It has to be in the shuttle system. But aside from the Diamond they go only one other place—the moons of Momrath. Out there someplace, possibly inside those moons' orbits, alien and Warden human meet."

I sat back, feeling satisfied. In one moment I'd solved at least half the Warden puzzle. I didn't know anything about the aliens, true, and I had no idea as to the nature and scope of their plot, but I now understood, I felt certain, much of the Warden connection.

"And what good does it do you to know these things?" Dylan asked. "You can't do anything about them."

Good old practical Dylan! Her comment was on the mark. What *could* I do?

Or more accurately, what did I *want* to do?

Kill Laroo and topple the system, yes—but even if I figured out how, did I really want Project Phoenix to fail?

At the moment I knew only one thing. The biggest deal in Warden history was happening out there on Laroo's Island—and I wanted in on it.

CHAPTER THIRTEEN

The Easy Way Into an Impregnable Fort

A few days later I had Karel take me out in her boat and go through all the routine motions, but this time we went almost as far south as we dared go. I remembered Dylan's comment about chasing a bork to within sight of Laroo's Island, and I had questioned her on the incident. I felt certain we could get as far chasing an imaginary one as she had chasing a real one.

The "island" was really pretty far out in the ocean, far from any sight of land and exactly the kind of place a dictator would love as a refuge. It was a small stand of major trees, giving an area of perhaps a hundred or so square kilometers. Not a really big place. At some point this grove had obviously been connected to the main body, but something had happened, probably ages ago, leaving only isolated islands of trees out here now. There were several dozen in the area, none really close enough to be within sight of the others; still, they pointed like a wavering arrow toward our familiar "mainland" bunch.

We skirted the island just outside the main computer defense perimeter, an area clearly visible on electronic scans of the place. It was a mass of orange, purple, and gold foliage atop the thick, blackish trunks, and even from our vantage point of almost fifteen kilometers out, my spotting scopes revealed an extraordinary building in the center of the mass. Gleaming silvery in the sun, sort of like a fantasy castle or some kind of modernistic sculpture, it was both anachronistic and futuristic. The exiled concubines and even Dylan herself had given rough descriptions of it, but these paled before the actual sight.

Still, thanks to Dylan and contacts throughout the Motherhood, at other Houses where Laroo's women had been sent, I knew it pretty well.

Knew, at least, the basic room layouts and the locations of the elevators, the key power plant, the basic defense systems, and things like that. From it all, I concluded that it was as close to an impregnable fortress as was possible to build on Cerberus.

The electronic screens were not only domelike over the place but also went down to a depth of more than two kilometers—right down to the ocean floor itself. With a few million units of the right equipment and a force that would be more than obvious, it might be possible to tunnel under the screens, but even then it would be risky once you were through the initial barrier. There were not only inner defense screens but physical ones as well. Both robotic and manned gunboats constantly were patrolling.

Karel, a big, muscular woman with a deep, rich voice, was all too happy to help, and she at least suspected what I might be up to. She and Dylan were very different to look at, but they shared a lot deep down and had been close to partners for more than three years.

"Suppose we drove borks in there? Lots of them?" I suggested, thinking of various plans.

She laughed at the idea. "Sure would be fun, but it wouldn't get you in. There *are* ways to attract borks, for sure, but those screens are pretty powerful. You'd need a regular stampede even to make a dent, and if two of *our* boats in skilled hands can usually finish one, you wouldn't believe what the defenses there can do, even to a dozen."

I nodded. "Yeah, I know. But—say! Did you say there were ways of *attracting* borks?"

She nodded. "Certain high-pitched sounds, and certain odors in the water that simulate a *skrit* colony. You might draw three or four, if you were lucky, but no more. They aren't as common as all *that* around here. If they were, there'd be no way for the *skrit* to survive and reproduce."

I nodded idly, but I was already thinking. When we got back to shore I'd do a bit more, and see what could be done. I was sure that given enough time—and I had no idea how much time I had—I could have gotten through those screens, but that would have gotten me only to the island—where just about every step required a brain scan.

No, there *had* to be some easier way.

"Dylan?"

"Yes, Qwin?"

"How do those torpedoes on the boats work? I mean, how do they explode?"

"A detonation device screwed in the side, with a minicomputer aboard. You tell it when to arm and when to explode by remote control."

"Uh-huh. And how do you know one from the other? I mean, how can you use a single remote to trigger the whole bunch?"

"Why, you don't. Each uses the same frequency and all the torpedo are universal. Each also comes with a code stamped on it. You just read the code for each into your transmitter, then fire them by the code numbers, which is all they'll answer to. Once you have the numbers in your weapons control computer you don't really need to know anything else."

I nodded. "And who feeds the new numbers in? Do you take 'em off the invoices or bills of lading when new ones arrive, or what?"

"Are you kidding? Would *you* trust your life to a bill of lading? No, each captain loads each torpedo into his or her own boat, then physically reads the numbers off and puts them personally into the weapons control computer."

"Uh-huh. And where's this number stamped?"

"On the detonator hatch. A small door that's welded shut after the minicomputer for each is placed inside. Go down and see for yourself in the warehouse here."

I did—and liked what I found. They didn't bother to stamp each number on the door, just stenciled it on. Talking with others, I found that, indeed, sometimes the numbers were wrong, but there was a test code to check it that would send back an acknowledging signal to the weapons control computer verifying the number. It was a rather simple test: you just took a number like, say, FG7654-321AA and changed the last A to a T.

I found the information most interesting, and asked Dylan a few more key questions. "The minicomputers come preprogrammed and the doors welded shut. I assume, then, that they're shipped live, so to speak?"

She nodded. "There's no danger. A test must be run to arm them, no code is ever duplicated or used again, the frequency used is used only for that purpose, and the transmitters are controlled devices built into the gunboats. Why this interest in torpedoes all of a sudden? Are you planning something?"

"What you don't know can't violate your psych commands," I told her. "Of *course* I'm planning something."

"Just changing the codes won't work," she noted. "They wouldn't pass the test."

I grinned. "What's the transmitting range on these things?"

"As an additional safety measure, only three kilometers. That's more than enough for a good captain."

"And more than enough for me, my darling," I responded, and kissed her.

The next day I dropped by Tooker and checked the shipping section and bills of lading. Even if Emyasail was now working only for Laroo, it was still *our* company and supplied via our transit routes. And of course they needed torpedoes in case they ran into a bork or two on their way to Laroo's Island anyway.

Nobody kept a large stock of the things on hand—no matter how safe they were claimed to be; they terrified the fire department, and even local governments didn't like to think of all those explosives in one place. A little warehouse fire and you could wipe a whole section off the map.

I *did* have to wait, though, a bit impatiently, for over ten days until Emyasail put in another order, and then it was for only twenty. Still, that was enough, considering that they would at best be replacing used ones in the tubes, not completely refitting the boats.

A bit of creative routing on the forms made sure that these torpedoes would come first to Hroyasail and little ol' me.

Dylan could have nothing more to do with this one. She would be prohibited from assisting in anything that would almost certainly cause someone to come to harm. Sanda, however, was only too glad to help out.

I had been worried about Dylan's reaction to having Sanda around, but the true problem had turned out to be the reverse. Sanda felt tremendous guilt and remorse and blamed herself completely for what had happened, and she really didn't want to face me or, particularly, Dylan any more than necessary. I had put her to work as a maintenance worker around the docks, refinishing the wharf, painting the boats, stuff like that, and she seemed content with her lot. Now, however, I had a different sort of painting to do, and it had to be done quickly and quietly.

The flaw in their torpedo system was that, since there was little to be perverted concerning them, they'd standardized it. Thus Sanda and I, working through the night with Emyasail's new torpedoes, were able to remove the numbers and, with some expert stenciling, replace them. I had some admiration for the manufacturing process: those numbers were *baked* on and hard as hell to get off, but my trusty computers at Tooker had come up with a solvent, and I had no trouble with a replacement stencil and paint, although the numbers would not be on as solidly as before. Oh, they'd *look* right, but they weren't as permanent. I hoped nothing rubbed off during the transshipment.

Sanda was puzzled, but there was a slight glow of excitement in her as she realized another operation was underway. "I don't see what good switching the numbers will do," she commented, sounding more curious than anything else. "I mean, they just won't test out and they'll be rejected, like those three over there of ours."

I grinned. "But they *will* test out," I told her. "We aren't just changing numbers. We are exchanging the numbers. All the numbers are still good, just for the wrong torpedoes. When they load these and test them, they'll get a response from their computers—from the torpedoes in the warehouse —but the computer won't know that, or at least won't tell. So they'll sail off with a batch of torpedoes that will test out perfectly, but when they have to use them, they won't work."

"Sounds like you're gonna blow up the dock instead," she noted.

"No. It's highly unlikely that any borks will come within three kilometers of land. The danger zone's out past five kilometers. And that's too far.

Still, if there's a really thorough investigation, I can always blow the docks —from one of our boats."

She stared at me, looking slightly shocked. "Oh," she said.

Rigging the torpedoes was only part of the problem. The other was making certain that there would be an occasion to use them. For that, I began a thorough search for everything that turned borks on.

It turned out that the most reliable and effective means were pretty simple—some soluble sulfides would draw them if they were anywhere close and would drive them into something of a frenzy (as if that weren't their normal state anyway). But for long-range attraction, I needed something more. Again the solution was rather simple. Like marine creatures on many worlds, the borks were supersensitive to ultra-high-frequency sounds and apparently used them for territorial claims, fights, lovemaking (hard to imagine with something like that, but, then again, there were a lot of borks), and such. The vocabulary was not extensive, but it was clearly known, so much so that various boat engines and the like were made to specific noise standards to avoid any such sounds within their operating ranges.

On such a simple idea I didn't go the circuitous route, but simply got some modified UHF broadcasters from Otah myself, then worked with them, a circuit diagram, and some easy modifications of tiny programmable chips to create a remote transceiver that I could tune to any selective frequency from anywhere within an area of fifty to a hundred kilometers. Various shops specializing in special underwater gear provided easy cases that could be adapted to the transmitters without much problem. A couple of chemical supply houses sold various standard compounds that together would in my makeshift kitchen lab create one hell of a glue to reinforce the magnets on the inside of the case. I didn't want the things falling off under battle stress, as magnets might risk—and a magnet powerful enough to stay regardless would be a magnet powerful enough to be detected by ship's instruments. More electronic modification and I had a small charge I could also set off by remote control—enough to melt the little transmitters into a nondescript goo, but not enough to cause harm to the hull.

Although they were curious, I dared not tell Dylan or the boat captains and crews what I was doing, since in Dylan's case she might try and stop me because of her prohibition against any violence, while the boat people would hardly be enthusiastic about my possibly doing in several of their own. I didn't like that prospect much myself, but more was at stake here than a few lives. This was Laroo I was going against, not some minor executive or fire department employee. At least my way they had a chance and so did I. Simply to have sabotaged the boats might not accomplish what I wanted, but would certainly alert Laroo and his security forces that somebody nasty was up to something.

But I would need somebody to help me plant the things and that meant Sanda—and I wasn't 100 percent certain of her. Up to now she had gone along, it was true, but before I actually put anything into practice I had to be certain she wouldn't cross me up at the wrong time—not by choice, I knew, but I had no real idea what *her* psych inhibitors and commands were. So I had to see somebody who could tell me.

Most doctors were pretty bored on Cerberus; the Warden organism was extremely efficient at keeping the natives ultra-healthy. Still, some were around for emergency services and for research, and one group, considering the culture, was absolutely necessary and always busy—the group I was most concerned with, the psychiatrists.

Almost all were exiles, of course, sent here for a variety of infractions. Most were not averse to a little under-the-table money for private work of a less-than-official nature. A large number of people, some otherwise quite ordinary, recommended Dr. Svarc Dumonia as the ultimate psych expert who would do anything for an extra unit, so it was he I went to see, taking Dylan along—not because I felt he could help her, but because it would make seeing him more natural, and the big fee look legitimate. Dylan, however, would undergo an extensive series of mostly useless tests while Dumonia and I had our real little chat.

He was a thin, wiry, nervous little man who wore horn-rimmed glasses, something I took particular note of, since everyone on Cerberus had eyesight in the same condition as the rest of their bodies—near perfect. He caught my glance and shrugged.

"The glasses. Oh, call them an affectation. I'd like to think I wear 'em—the panes are perfectly clear, of course—to be more of an individual, to stand out in the crowd. Truth was, I'd been getting a tad nearsighted back home and never seemed to have the time to have the matter attended to. I just got some glasses, liked the look, and kept wearing them. After I got here I felt unnatural without 'em."

I smiled slightly and took a seat in his office. My record of never meeting a psych who didn't need a psych was holding firm.

"Doctor," I began carefully, "I'm here so I can understand more about the process of psychological conditioning. As you're aware, I live with its results almost constantly."

He nodded and flipped through a folder. "Hmmm . . . interesting treatment, I must say. Highly creative. The design team that worked out your wife's pattern had to be one of the best. It's a highly skilled profession, you know, and getting the results you want from what's ordered is often nearly impossible. Every time you implant *anything* beyond, say, a simple command, as in say, posthypnotic suggestion but making it permanent, you're taking risks with the entire mind, the entire personality. Information is filed scattershot throughout the brain in tiny electrochemical bytes, you know. It's put together up front by the cerebral cortex, which reaches at the speed of light for whatever it needs to create holographic memory, personality, whatever. To do something this complex takes—well, not technicians but *artisans*."

"Some artisans," I muttered. "They destroyed her."

"Oh, sorry. Didn't mean to offend, but when you're in the business and you see it as a mathematical abstract rather than in human terms it's, well, like admiring a skillful heart restoration back home. If you don't know the person, you admire the work in isolation, even if afterward you find that the person died."

I accepted that notion, or at least understood it. "Still, she was changed into someone, well, very different. The result seems somehow more awful than death or imprisonment."

"Oh, no! Actually, it's not that way at all. Back home, where both of us come from, the procedure is so common you probably met hundreds, even thousands of people with some psych work and never knew it. In psychiatry, for example, we can actually go in and get at the deep psychoses, do things our forefathers never dreamed of. There are no more hopeless cases in my profession. And in the case of your wife, think of the alternatives. *You* might not agree that she did anything wrong or that the law or judges were just, but who does in any society? Isn't that why we're both here?"

I had to smile and nod at that.

"Well, in your wife's case, from the point of view of society, they took someone who violated the law and made her into a productive member of that society who won't violate any laws. Not the important ones, anyway."

"Important to whom?"

"To the state, of course. To understand my job, you have to remember that our task is to restore abnormal people to normal. Normality isn't an objective standard, but rather a subjective term imposed by each society on its people by laws and culture. Ancient cultures used to sacrifice people to appease the gods. In those societies, anybody who objected to that sacrifice or doubted the existence of the gods wasn't normal. The social fabric of the civilized worlds would be horribly abnormal to many of our own ancestors, but it's ours. We were born into it and accept most of its values, even if we question or violate one or two. Cerberan culture is nothing but a modification of the civilized worlds' own culture adapted to local conditions and limitations. Deep down you can understand that."

This line of conversation was making me slightly uncomfortable, and I couldn't really figure out why.

"Now, in your wife's case," he continued, "we have somebody with a couple of problems from the state's point of view that made her abnormal. First, she escaped from the motherhood, something which is culturally forbidden and which held the threat of undermining a basic underpinning of Cerberan society. But since everybody here in any position got there by getting away with breaking the rules—and she had only bent them slightly —they couldn't do much to her at that point without questioning their basic values and themselves. Besides, she overcompensated for her previous cloistered life by taking on a profession most Cerberans consider suicidal."

"Overcompensated?"

He nodded. "Sure. The unhappy ones in the motherhood are basically of two kinds—those really unfit for the role, who are usually given psych treatments, and the romantics. Extremely bright and very limited by her assigned role, Dylan had only one view of outside, in this case outside her House—that dock and those adventurous seamen. She fantasized about what she knew and could see, and that really was Hroyasail. But when she *did* get out and *did* attain her dreams, they weren't all they were cracked up to be. The fantasy was far more romantic than the reality. It was either as dull as the motherhood or horribly life-threatening, and when you take risks like that day after day, knowing the odds, even *that* becomes unsatisfying. Like most people who work on the boats, she was really past caring. The motherhood was dull and repressive, and her fantasy was dull and in its own way equally repressive. So she continued going through the motions without much hope for the future, knowing that sooner or later her luck would run out and she'd be killed. Being killed in her work became her new romantic fantasy."

I was a bit shocked at this. "You mean she was suicidal?"

He looked back down at his charts. "In a sense, yes. Oh, she wouldn't try to kill herself, but she herself must have told you that you get to be captain mostly by attrition. Everybody likes thrills, but with the kind of odds in *her* business you have to have a death wish. It shows up clearly in her profile."

I shook my head in wonder. "I can't believe that of her."

"Oh, it's true. What in fact her profile suggests she really wanted was to be what she is—a mother. But a *complete* mother, one who not only bears but raises her children, frontier-style. In fact, for all her rationalization, the addition of a new factor in her life, when her odds were surely running low, was the final trigger for her to take the action she did."

"New factor?"

He nodded. "You. She fell in love with you. And suddenly she found it more and more difficult to go out on her daily hunts. For the first time she started getting scared because she no longer was content to die at the helm, so to speak. When you restored her will to live, you shortened her odds of surviving to a tiny fraction. She couldn't *consciously* face this, but her subconscious knew, and that's why she decided to give in—to violate the law—and take the girl Sanda along that day. She was at her peak, of course, because she had both you and Sanda to protect, but you have no idea the risk you took that day. Half of her, I'm sure, considered the idea of going down with those she loved, a tidy and romantic ending. She didn't, because she loved you too much."

"You're saying she knew she'd get caught?"

"I'm saying she wanted to get caught. If she hadn't been caught this time she'd have done something else. She wanted out so she would no longer be faced with inevitable death and separation from you."

I felt at once touched, uncomfortable, and incredulous. "But she could have quit. We'd have created a place for her with the company."

"No, no. She couldn't consciously face that either. I suspect that the idea never entered her head, since she also feared losing you. You admired her courage, even as you feared for her life. She was afraid that any such move would be interpreted as cowardice on your part and might leave her without you—and that was the only thing that mattered to her. You."

"But that's ridiculous! I wouldn't have—"

"You probably wouldn't," he agreed, "but the human mind is more than a computer, which is why we have psychiatrists at all. We're individualists, with emotions and a streak of irrational thinking that both makes us humans great and is our biggest weakness."

"I still can't really accept this," I told him.

"Ah! Love!" he sighed. "Our craziest failing. It has almost been eliminated on the civilized worlds, and it's pretty damned rare here on Cerberus, too. But give it half a chance, give it a little crack to slip into and it raises its head nonetheless. Look, Zhang, I can tell you really don't like Cerberan culture very much, but next to the frontier the Warden worlds— all of them—allow one thing that makes them, I think, better places. Here we still dream, we still fantasize and romanticize. On the civilized worlds they've eradicated that, and they know it. That's why the frontier's a continuing operation. It's the only place where people can still dream. All of humankind's advances—since the precursor of Man came down from the trees on ancient primordial Earth—have resulted from dreams, fantasies, imagination. Dylan broke free of the motherhood for a dream—she found a way. But as with the civilized worlds, which were begun with the most glorious of dreams in mind, the reality proved less than that. Hollow. If you search inside yourself *you* know it, too."

I gave a dry, humorless chuckle. "I can see how you wound up here."

He gave a genuine chuckle in return. "They made a mistake on me. Sent me off to the frontier because they had a shortage of medical officers for a short tour. When I returned to the civilized worlds I couldn't believe how hollow and empty they were—the same places I loved and yearned for only a year before. I became convinced that civilization as I knew it would continue of its own momentum much as other ancient empires had continued, but being hollow, it was also fragile. I knew that we'd crack against any good assault from outside, and I started a campaign to restore some vigor, some mental health." He spread his arms. "And here I am. And know what? I really haven't been that sorry about it."

"Suit yourself," I told him. "I certainly see your point, even if I don't accept your conclusions on the civilized worlds or on Dylan."

"An interesting metaphor, one that appeals to me. Your wife and our old civilization. History will eventually prove me right on the civilized worlds, but I can prove my point on Dylan easily."

"How could you do that? From reading psych profiles taken in only one night?"

He grinned like a man about to lower the noose. "No, because I know from your cover application on her what she told you was done to her. I knew in a minute it couldn't have been like that—that sort of complete turnaround takes weeks, maybe months, if it can be done at all. So I just got the test results on her, and they confirmed my suspicions."

"Which are?"

"Considering the time, it was a masterful job, as I said, but it was hardly *that* extensive. Dylan believes they did all of it—she is convinced of that. But what the psychs did was far slighter and more subtle. They simply gave her a nudge here, a tap there, a *very* subtle working of her subconscious desires, ones she herself was not fully willing to admit to herself. She did the rest to convince herself and you that those things she wanted to do and be were involuntarily imposed from above. Look, Zhang, if we could do such a complete job on somebody like her overnight, the syndicates would put us all through the ringer and you know it."

"Are you telling me that there's no psych command that says she has to obey my every wish? No psych plant against going out on the boats?"

"I'm saying there is not. The first, the obedience thing, comes partly from her early training and psyche, partly from inner needs, and partly out of her very real total dependence on you financially. She is convinced there *is* such a command, but it comes from her own subconscious—and is no less real because it does. Furthermore, there is absolutely nothing preventing her from going near the boats except the laws governing the motherhood, but it's a damn good way of not having to face up to the fact that she doesn't *want* to go any more. You see, she's taken the things she doesn't want to face and transferred them to a third party—the psych. That way *she* can accept it, and that way *you* have to accept her."

I had half risen from the chair, but now I sat back down again. "What you're saying is that she's living in a fantasy world completely now. One of her own making."

"Somewhat," he agreed. "Now, we can schedule a series of sessions that will allow her to accept the truth, but it may take time. With your help we can bring her face to face with herself again, so she'll be a whole person. Nonetheless, she'll be more the *present* Dylan than the past one—you understand that?"

I nodded, feeling slightly dazed. "All right. We'll schedule it. But I'm stunned. What psych commands *did* they put in?"

"Well, the prohibition against taking any human life is real and pretty standard for sentencing," he told me. "It protects her and you. She's also got a command that prohibits her from ever leaving the motherhood of her own accord again, although that's mostly reinforcing—under judgment she can't switch bodies anyway. The rest, as I said, is all subtle. The brain triggers hormones and the like. Reinforcing her natural drives, so to speak, as defined by that body. This has the nice by-product of reinforcing her feelings for you, which is damned clever, since that in turn feeds her psychoses and gives them the force of commands, too."

"From what you're saying, maybe we shouldn't snap her out of it," I noted. "You claim she's happy."

"No. She'll never be happy until she *realizes* that this is what she wants and until she is convinced that what she wants is also all right with you. Not doing something about these convictions, particularly the second, could in the long run turn her into the very robot she thinks she is. Which is fine for the state and the state's psychs, but not for her or for you."

"Okay, you convinced me. But what about my original purpose for coming?"

"Sanda Tyne. An interesting case, quite unlike Dylan, you know. She's one of those never really cut out for the motherhood, but she hasn't nearly the intelligence potential nor the vision to really be somebody in the outside world, although she has great dreams. She enjoys thrills and adventure, but only as a child might, with no real understanding of the dangers to herself or to others. As with Dylan and with all the best psych work, they simply took what was there and used it, although in her case they more or less froze it. Hard as it is to believe, Sanda is more psyched than Dylan."

"What!"

He nodded. "She feels no real guilt about what happened to Dylan. Not really. In fact she's somewhat disappointed that she didn't replace Dylan in your life; she still hopes to one day. That's the limit of her ambition and vision—and now you understand why she doesn't call on you both more often."

"Jealousy?"

"Envy, mostly. Her whole life has been nothing but envy. The grass is *always* greener to her. Physically and intellectually she might have lived for twenty years, but emotionally she's somewhere around eight or nine. The psychs merely damped down whatever ambition was left and much of that active imagination. They reinforced the envy, but also lay down prohibitions about doing anything about it. The way they have her damped and oriented, she'll be perfectly happy chipping paint and collecting garbage, secure in the knowledge that someday her prince—you—will come to her."

"What about that business concerning harm to self or others? You said it was standard?"

"True, but there's only so much you can do in a few hours, and they did a lot. Much the same thing was accomplished by the other conditioning, as I mentioned. She isn't going to hurt Dylan because that might alienate you. Besides, she's sure you'll dump Dylan sooner or later and come down and see the errors of your ways. She isn't going to hurt you because she's patient, as long as she's near you. And secure in the knowledge that she'll win in the end, she's hardly going to do anything to herself. That being the case, no prohibition was necessary. In fact I can foresee only one way in which she could harm *anybody* for the rest of her judgment, and only one, so you're safe."

'Oh? What's that?"

'If you asked her to. She'll do anything to demonstrate to you the mistake she thinks you made."

I grinned, feeling a bit more comfortable. "No chance of that, of course."

"Of course," Dumonia agreed.

The torpedoes had been rerouted to Emyasail, where they were supposed to be all along, and my devices were ready. Confident now of Sanda's complete cooperation, we went down one evening to scout out the place and found it similar in layout to Hroyasail. It would be, I told myself, considering it was built by the same parent corporation at the same time for the same purposes.

Of course there were guards all over the place, and all sorts of electronic security as well, but it was oriented toward the warehouses.

Sanda, like all Cerberans, knew how to swim. When you lived in giant trees with an eternal ocean always underneath, that was one thing you absolutely learned from the start.

We were using just basic wet suits and snorkels. I wanted no giveaways should there be underwater devices for picking up sounds like mechanical rebreathers or an underwater cycle. As a check, we donned the suits and, starting from more than two hundred meters beyond the docks, actually swam up to and under the boats, checking out the lay of the land. We found some small sensors along the docks themselves, but not only was there nothing to keep us from the bottom of the boats but the area was floodlit so they were nicely silhouetted.

But then why should Laroo suspect sabotage? What would be gained? It was sure to be discovered. But even if it wasn't, it would just slow him down slightly—he could get boats from other places, if need be. The only irreplaceable stuff, the organic robots, would come in from space to his new landing pad. Anybody else would be more interested in the warehouses, which were heavily guarded, than in the boats—since, any good security officer would reason, why would anybody attack them? Not only expendable, but you'd lose the cargo to the depths. Nothing to gain.

They were wrong.

The next night Sanda and I returned, this time with the bag of little goodies I had made up from Otah's materials and other sources. We easily and silently affixed the devices not only to the gunboats but to several of the biggest trawlers as well.

The work went so easily, in fact, that Sanda was more than a little disappointed. It was exhausting, yes, but not thrilling. It was in fact as easy as writing a letter.

The devices triggered at different points, and I arranged for them to be triggered from our boats when we came within range during routine operations. Nobody on our boats knew, of course, that they were doing anything like that, but that didn't matter. The one thing I couldn't control was when those defective torpedoes would be loaded and used. I could only give them an intermittently bad bork problem that would cause torpedoes to be used up at a fearful rate. Otherwise, all I could do was go about my normal routine and wait it out. I wouldn't even hear the horror stories. I just hoped that the aftermath of their troubles would, otherwise unbidden, wash right over me. It was the easiest, if least certain, way.

The best way of doing what you want to do, of course, is to create a situation wherein your enemy invites you, even commands you, to do precisely what you wanted to do in the first place—which was the plot here. If *that* worked out, then the solution of how to get into Laroo's fortress would work out, too. The easiest way into an impregnable fortress is to be invited in by the owner.

CHAPTER FOURTEEN

Facts About Myself, Some Psych Work, and Fruition

During the waiting period, Dylan began her sessions with Dumonia—and so did I, since convincing her that I loved her no matter what incarnation was at the heart of the whole thing. It was true. I *did* love her, and if frontier wife was her new goal, then that was fine with me. I wanted her to be happy, and as Dr. Dumonia had noted, under the present circumstances she was not. What was intended was to give her a sense of *security* —which in its own way was somewhat ironic. I was arranging to kill Wagant Laroo and at the same time trying to make Dylan *secure.*

What was really interesting about the process was that during a few sessions some of her visions of me and my earlier caper slipped out, as inevitably they would. Although I was paying Dumonia enough to ensure he kept his medical ethics about him, I was more than slightly amused when I discovered that he totally misread this one as another of Dylan's romantic fantasies in which I had somehow become involved. That computer fraud scheme had been so nutty and unbelievable that even her psych refused to believe it. That, of course, had been precisely why I had done it the way I had.

Naturally, during the process, I had to undergo a bit myself, but I wasn't really worried. My early training and conditioning automatically switched in under such probes, giving the psychs whatever information I wanted them to have. My probing also wasn't deep, but was only directed toward my feelings about Dylan and so I was on relatively safe ground. At the end of the second session with the psych and his machines, however, I got one shock.

"Did you know you have two surface-planted command impulses?" he asked me. "Been to a psych before?"

"No," I answered, slightly worried. "I know of *one* that should be there. Basic data about Cerberus. It was a new process they were trying with me to help people get acclimated."

He nodded. "We got that. Some of it, anyway. Quite thorough. But there's another."

I frowned and leaned forward. "Another?"

He nodded. "Actually, as I said, two. Two commands, in addition to the briefing."

I was beginning to get worried, not only because I didn't know what these were—all my agent conditioning would be beyond these machines—but also because they might betray me and who I really was. "Do you know what they are?"

"One is treasonous," he replied, sounding as objective as he did when discussing mundane matters. "It appears to be a command to kill Wagant Laroo if you can. Actually more of a reinforcement—designed to make you detest him enough to kill him. Very nice job, really. I wonder if every new exile is being sent in with this sort of conditioning? Still, I wouldn't worry about it. The readouts state that you're really not violent or self-destructive. Though this impulse is enough to ensure that you're never going to love the state and its glorious leader, it's no stronger than your common impulses, which would be to damp down the actuality. We'd *all* like to kill *somebody* at one time or another, but few of us do. The impulse is no stronger than that. Unless you have a specific pre-Cerberan reason for wanting to do him in? Revenge?"

"No," I responded smoothly. "Nothing like that. I never met the man, never even *heard* of him until I was told I was being sent here."

"All right. But that makes the second one all the more puzzling."

"Huh?"

"Basically it boils down to an instruction to call your office every so often when the opportunity's offered you, then forget all about doing so. Do *you* understand that?"

Instantly I *did* understand, but the trouble was finding a way to explain it away, all the while mentally kicking myself for not thinking of this before. The sons of bitches! Of course! How could they track me, know what I was doing on Cerberus? The organic transmitter would cease functioning the moment I switched bodies. The answer was simple and staring me in the face, but I'd been too cocky to think of it before.

There were other agents here somewhere. Probably local people, perhaps with something they wanted from outside, or perhaps exiles with close friends, family, something to lose back home. Blackmailable, to a degree. How many times had one of these come to me, perhaps when I was walking alone or on the road, and told me to call the office? Lead me, then, to a transceiver of some sort so I could send my doings up to my other self, sitting there off the Warden system.

Done it, then promptly forgot it.

"I think I understand," I told him. "My—ah, previous activities, well, they involved some complex dealings and some people in high places. These people need certain—codes, basically, to continue to enjoy what I no longer can. This, I think, is a form of blackmail."

He smiled blandly at me. "You're a plant, aren't you? A Confederacy agent. Oh, don't look startled. You're not the first, nor the last. Don't worry, I won't rat on you. In fact it wouldn't matter much if I did, all things considered. Your profile indicates you are highly independent, and that Cerberus, and particularly Dylan, has changed you, as something always does. They keep trying though."

I sat back and sighed. "How did you know?"

"From the start—Qwin Zhang. Woman's name. Woman's body, when you came down. But you're no woman. You've never been one, except for that brief and quite brilliant cover entrance. There are differences in the brain scans between males and females. Not ones you'd really notice, but not only am I an expert, I'm also on a world where such swapping goes on all the time, so I see all sort of switches. Remember the physiological differences between the sexes. The brain governs them, and while new patterns might emerge, there are always traces of the old. Not in your case, though. So from your appearance here, I infer that the Confederacy's finally figured out how to do what we can do naturally."

"Not exactly," I told him. "The attrition rate's high. But they're working on it."

"Fascinating. They'll have to suppress the knowledge, you know, except perhaps for the leadership and essential people. They'll have to—such switching would disrupt their society enormously, perhaps beyond repair." He smiled at the thought. "Well, it's no big thing, since the Confederacy still has the unsolvable problem. Anybody capable enough to really cause damage as an agent that they send to a Warden world changes into one of the Warden Diamond's best and most dangerous citizens. Tell me, do you really intend to kill Laroo?"

"I *should* kill you," I noted icily. "You're the most dangerous man on this planet to me. More than Laroo."

"But you won't," he responded confidently. "For one thing, that would add lots of complications to whatever you're doing now. For another, it would draw attention to you, even if you got away with it, since you'd be linked to me by your scheduled visits. I doubt if a man like you could stand being under a microscope right now. And finally, I think you realize that I couldn't care *less* if you bump off Laroo, or settle down and enjoy life, or take over the whole damned place. If you did, it'd be a change, anyway. You must believe me, Zhang, when I tell you that you're the seventh agent I've met and I haven't turned one in yet. You surely must realize by now that my own fatal psychological flaw is that I'm a romantic revolutionary anarchist with no guts, but with a taste for the good life. If you weren't sure I would stay bought, you wouldn't have come to me in the first place."

I relaxed, in spite of my old instincts. He was right, of course—and it was unlikely that I could do anything *but* trust him. This was a smart man who'd protect himself.

"Can you remove that 'call the office' command? At least the part about forgetting I did it?"

"Sadly, no. Not with what I have. However, both commands are simple enough that they could be canceled out."

"Huh? What do you mean?"

"Well, using the level and intensity of the patterns I have here, I could lay on a new set of commands of absolutely equal strength. For example, I could lay on one that said you *liked* Wagant Laroo and had good feelings whenever his name was mentioned. This would negate the other. If I phrased the command exactly right, you'd wind up in a love-hate relationship that would cancel. As for the other—well, I could give an equal command that you will *not* use a transceiver for off-planet communication. Same effect. You'd still go when called, but you wouldn't tell 'em anything."

"I'm not too concerned about those," I told him. "At least not now. Later I might want to have that call command negated; right now it might be useful, although I'm not sure how. But I want to remember doing it, and what I did. Any tricks there?"

"After the fact, perhaps. After all, it's all there, in your memory. You're just barred from consciously recollecting it. I suspect that with a very strong neutral field under a psych converter, together with a hypnotic series, for example, we might be able to get the information out of you and recorded. When you awoke you still wouldn't be able to remember it, but you could then examine the recording and get the data no matter what."

"All right," I told him. "Let's do it."

The trick worked, after a fashion. I really don't know what is being transmitted even now, you bastards, but I now know how it's done and by whom. And how damnably obvious the whole thing was once the truth was out.

Who better to have such a spatial link with you than old fat, friendly Otah? An electronics shop with blackmarket connections. No wonder Otah could get whatever he needed in the way of bootleg gear! That's how you pay him, right? Very clever. I should have thought of it as soon as I figured out that you had something to do with my being sent to Medlam, so close to Laroo's Island, in the first place. Medlam, and associated with Tooker, a corporation well suited to my talents. And waiting there, where you knew I'd eventually go, was Otah.

Well, it didn't matter now. In fact it helped. Now at least I knew who —and when.

* * *

Three weeks had passed since my dirty deeds at Emyasail, and I was beginning to feel nervous. Something, I felt sure, should have happened by now. I began to turn my mind to more direct, less devious, but more risky alternatives.

The one bright spot was Dylan, whose treatment was really helping. I'll say this for Dumonia: although he is crazy as a loon and more amoral and cynical than I am, he really knows his stuff. I began to believe that in his own field he was one of the most brilliant men I had ever known. This is not to say that Dylan was anything like back to normal, but she was more comfortable with herself and with me, more like a real human being, and she seemed happier. Dumonia explained that he could do a lot, but the key breakthrough eluded him, the point of her own insecurity regarding me. It was a wall he couldn't get past, a wall erected of her deep-rooted conviction that without the pity angle I would not like her as she wanted to be and would tire of her and leave. She was very wrong, of course, but her fear was deeply rooted in her understanding of the culture from which I came and the culture of Cerberus in which she had been raised—cultures minimizing close personal attachments and emotional factors. In the Cerberan culture you held your power and position by the favors owed you or by blackmail or by some other hook. So the idea of such things not being necessary was a cultural gap that seemed impossible to bridge. In reversed circumstances, I could see myself having the same hang-ups.

"If she weren't under judgment, there *are* things that might be used," Dumonia told me. "Unorthodox, maybe dangerous things, but quite effective. But as long as she's trapped in that body we're stuck."

That thought depressed me a bit, since I most wanted the old Dylan back, a partner I could deal with as an equal, almost the part of me I'd gotten used to having. It was peculiar that I, the consummate loner, born and bred to be above such things and never before touched by them, should suddenly have this need, almost a craving, for someone else. I instinctively knew that it was my Achilles' heel. Still, the fact that I had these weaknesses, didn't matter to me as much as it had, and there was also the corner of my mind that said that everyone, even me at my old top form, had flaws and weaknesses anyway. Nobody was immune. The important thing was to recognize your own and get to know them so that perhaps they could also work *for* you.

A few days later, when I'd just about given up, my scam paid off. I was visited in midmorning at my Hroyasail office by a big, burly man whose dark eyes indicated an intelligence his general appearance belied.

"I'm Hurl Bogen," he introduced himself, offering his hand, which I shook, then gestured for him to have a seat.

"What can I do for you, Mr. Bogen?"

"I'm the security coordinator for Chairman Laroo," he told me, and my heart almost stopped. This was either very good or bad news. "You know he has an island resort south of here?"

I nodded. "I'm afraid I've even taken a vicarious look at it from one of our boats," I told him honestly. If he didn't already know that he should have. "Just out of curiosity."

He grinned. "Yeah, lots of folks do. I don't blame 'em and I don't worry about it. Basically, though, we've run into a big problem with a project we're working on over there and we need your help. We've contracted with Emyasail to keep steady supplies coming and going to and from the island, and it's worked out fine until a couple of weeks ago. We got just creamed by borks—never saw so many of 'em in my life. We got most of 'em, but they did a pretty good job on Emyasail's fleet. We're down to a dozen trawlers, all smaller types, and just one gunboat."

I feigned shock. "But hell, how many borks could you *have*? Those were good crews, and we haven't had any problems of that sort. Matter of fact, we've been pretty damned peaceful around here the last few weeks, with only one or two reported and only one actual engagement."

He nodded ruefully. "No wonder. They were all down our way. The bio boys say that something attracted them down there, possibly a run of some chemical in subsurface currents. Rotten luck."

I held my breath. "How many people were lost?"

"We were pretty lucky there, although we did lose a dozen or so. Luck of the job, really. You should know that. But the main thing is, we no longer have enough boats to meet our supply needs. We've limped along with what we had for a while, using some air supply for the emergency stuff, but we really need some boats. Not trawlers—we're commandeering some big freighters now—but gunboats. We need a full four to make it out to the island okay."

"I can understand that," I replied, "but I've only got the four here myself."

"We need one of 'em," he told me matter-of-factly. "We're also pulling one each from two other companies along the coast here. You'll have to make do with three." It wasn't a request but a command.

I sighed. "All right. But I'm responsible for those boats and crews and I don't like the idea of a high-risk bork area being worked by four crews unused to each other." I pretended to think for a moment. "Look, for your safety as well as ours, why not do this instead? Pull all four of my boats and crews off—that is, let Hroyasail take over entirely from Emyasail. We'll use your surviving Emyasail boat and the other two to fill in here. The Emyasail skipper knows the territory around here, and putting three crews from three spots into a routine trawling and protection operation is a lot safer than cargo."

He considered my suggestion. "Makes sense," he admitted. "In fact I'll recommend it if you and your crews check out okay."

My eyebrows went up. "Check out? Come on, Mr. Bogen. You're a security man. You've already checked us out."

He smiled and gave a slight shrug. "Well, yes. Your boats and crews check out nicely, I admit. You, however, are a question mark to me, Mr. Zhang. You don't fit. You don't quite add up to me. Your psychological profile feels funny. I have the funny feeling I should take the rest of Hroyasail and not you."

"What! I don't understand."

"Don't ask me why. It's just a gut feeling. Still, my gut feelings are often correct. Besides, we don't really *need* you, you know."

This guy was good. I hadn't quite counted on this and I had to make some split-second decisions on him based on risky and incomplete data.

"Look," I said. "What do you think I am? A Confederacy spy or something? You have my old records."

"Yes, we do. And more completely than you can believe. We find your whole personality and profile too much at variance from Qwin Zhang's to dismiss." Then he thought for a moment, as if wrestling with himself, while I suppressed my rising tension. *Damn* Security for that sex switch! First Dumonia, now the infinitely more dangerous Bogen, smelled a rat because of it.

"Tell you what," he said at last. "I don't know your game, Zhang, nor whether you're who or what you say you are. But I'll admit I'm curious— and more than curious, I'm interested. So I'm going to take a mild risk and let you come along. What throws me is that your current profiles indicate a strong, almost overriding attachment to your wife, and she to you. That's enough of a lever for now."

I relaxed, pleased that I hadn't had to play any trump cards at this point and take some real risks. "When do you want us to move down?"

"Day after tomorrow," he told me. "Brief your crews, then switch over your computer nets." He stood up and again shook my hand. "I don't know why, but I have the feeling this is going to be very, very interesting."

I nodded. "Somehow I think so, too, Mr. Bogen. Now, if you'll excuse me, I have a lot of work to do. I want to brief my crews this afternoon and make the adjustments with Tooker."

"The day after tomorrow, then, at Emyasail." And he was gone.

I sighed, and didn't like the vibrations I got from Bogen at all. I think I knew the final step he'd taken in deciding to invite me along, and it was another one of those gut feelings. We had stared into each other's eyes— and seen each other there. One good pro always deserves another. That would mean that he'd be out to get me, perhaps out to give me enough rope.

One against one, Bogen, I thought, feeling better than I should. With the best man winning.

Moving down was no real problem since we were taking only the gunboats and the administrative staff. The layout was similar to the one we had, except the upstairs offices weren't in very good shape and hadn't been used for more than storage for some time. Dylan threw herself into getting the place into at least reasonable shape, although for the first week we felt more as if we were camping out than being in familiar surroundings, cooking over a small portable stove and sleeping on a mattress on the floor. I offered to get her some help, but she was determined to do everything herself and seemed to really enjoy it.

One major change was the large number of scanning machines you had to pass through to go just about anywhere. We all had to have new imprints taken for the benefit of the security system. I had no intention of trying that security system. I was in the big leagues here, and the schemes that had brought me to this point were no longer valid. Bogen would have me under a microscope, and I had no intention of giving him an opening unless it was on my terms. A dozen lives had already been spent getting me here; I felt a strong sense of responsibility to those innocents to do what I had been sent here to do. I owed them at least that.

Dylan suspected I had somehow engineered my way here. Hell, she more than suspected—she had worked with me before and had given me the initial information about it. Only her feeling that I would not deliberately cause the deaths of any innocents kept the peace. I had no intention of ever telling her differently.

One of the first things I had to do, though, was check the torpedoes still in the weapons warehouse against my little list of serial numbers. None of my old numbers were still there, but since we'd come down with a full load of our own in our boats I felt safe.

The stuff we ferried out to the island varied from the usual stuff—food, general electronic and maintenance supplies, that sort of thing—to major communications and computer links and lots of biolab stuff. The fact that so much was still going out, along with an occasional new face from one of the corporations, told me that Laroo wasn't having a lot of success with Project Phoenix. Still, though I was allowed to ride the boats out to the island and back, I had not been permitted off the island dock and was closely watched at all times when I went over. The strange, futuristic structure in the center appeared even more imposing close up, but that was as near as I could get.

I kept going through everything I knew or had surmised or deduced and what I was seeing, though, and I understood the dead end I was at. Merely having access to the island dock wasn't enough, but even if I managed to sneak in I'd be caught in short order, as would anybody else I might send.

"I'm frustrated," I admitted to Dylan one day. "I'm at a dead end, and I can't figure out any way to proceed. I've been here a year now and I've accomplished a great deal—but now I'm stuck. The most frustrating thing is to be this close to all of it and not be able to move."

"You're still bent on killing Laroo, aren't you?" she responded. "I wish I could help you, but I couldn't and wouldn't. You know I can't be a party to taking a human life."

I nodded and squeezed her hand. "I know. Still, killing isn't my major objective. I want to find out about those robots. I don't like the idea of a legion of those things, all under Laroo and Bogen and perhaps the others of the Four Lords, unleashed on the Confederacy. Those things are so perfect they scare the hell out of me. If they could negate the obedience programming, that would in and of itself create a new form of life, human-looking but not at all human. Imagine such people able to think with the speed of a super-computer, literally able to control every 'cell' of their bodies, to give them whatever they want—the ability to fly, to survive in a vacuum, and all the rest. People like that mentally reduced to great super-computers in human form with only one drive, their own ultimate drive—power. They'd be nearly immortal, too—and if they ever *did* have problems or wanted a new shape or mass, they would just return here and take on a new one."

"Surely the Confederacy could track them down and destroy them!"

"Maybe. I keep remembering that one of them got into the most absolutely secure area of the Confederacy, survived all the traps and both human and robot security personnel, and was caught and destroyed in the end only because its programming demanded that it report back to the Warden Diamond. It was basically a senior clerk! Put the best, the crookedest, the nastiest minds of the Warden Diamond in those forms and—well, Dr. Dumonia suggested that the Confederacy was fragile, continuing to be a success mostly because it had never met a real challenge to it. These people alone would be a challenge. Put them together with a sophisticated alien culture and it could very well be the end of all we know. I've got to stop him, Dylan."

"You're sure he can do it, then? Did you ever think that maybe these aliens are advanced enough so that the tools simply aren't available here to get around their creations?"

I thought it over. "The Four Lords' reach goes far beyond the Warden Diamond. Although trapped here themselves, they have powerful people all over the Confederacy in their pockets."

"But would they dare it? I mean, they know the Confederacy knows about their robots, right? And Laroo can't risk tipping the aliens off, either, to what he's doing. Doesn't the fact that he's doing the research here rather than having it carried on outside show that he doesn't want to risk getting anybody outside involved?"

"I think you may be right," I told her. "Okay, let's make a few assumptions based on what we know. First, the work's being done here. Second, despite unlimited Cerberan—and maybe Diamond—resources, and the best scientific minds around, he hasn't been able to crack it yet. The Four Lords are also in a bind: they risk the intervention of the Confederacy, and they also are risking relations with their allies." I leaned over and kissed her. "Maybe you're right. Maybe they *can't* solve their problem without outside help, and they can't get that help."

We sat there silent for a while as I considered all my options and all my possibilities. What *did* I know, and what didn't I know?

I wanted to get on the island and into the project. If in fact it was a project of the Four Lords rather than just Laroo's, as seemed likely, knocking off Laroo wouldn't matter a bit in the long run. Bogen or somebody else in this highly organized society would simply slip in and keep things going.

So what, then, did I really want to accomplish? I wanted the project abandoned, at least for now. I wanted to be in a position to change this rotten world a little, make it more human, while at the same time protecting what was important to me. Most important, I wanted to wind up a good guy to the Cerberans, to the Four Lords, and to the Confederacy all at the same time.

The idea floated in and I grabbed it, turned it first this way, then that, then decided it was so crazy it couldn't possibly work—just like the first one. I would have to be *right* on a lot of close, perhaps uncallable calls, 100 percent of the way. If I was wrong just once in this whole thing I was a dead duck.

"Dylan?"

"Yes, Qwin?"

"Suppose—now just suppose—that there was a way to put a stop to this, at least for now. Put a stop to it, cause a minor revolution that would change Cerberus to a more open and humane society, and put us on top of it?"

"You're getting crazy again. I can see it."

I nodded. "But suppose all that was possible—and if everything worked, we would kill no one, not even Wagant Laroo?"

She laughed. "Are the odds as bad as the Tooker operation?"

"Worse. I would estimate that right up to the end, to the very last second, the odds would be five to one for discovery, double-cross, or even death. The odds of the whole thing coming off might be a hundred to one, or a thousand to one, or even worse. Depending on where and when things go wrong, it could mean anything from packing up and forgetting all about it through a really nasty judgment to death or Momrath, which is much the same thing. The risks start the moment I put the plan into operation, and after that it might not be stoppable."

She looked at me with that puzzled fascination she'd shown in the past, a flash of the old Dylan indeed. "I know you want to do it anyway. What's stopping you?"

I drew her to me. "You don't know?"

She sighed. "The alternatives, I guess, should be considered. If you don't do it, you'll wonder about it for all time, and if anything really terrible like what you were saying comes to pass, you'll never forgive yourself. I'm not sure I could, either. I don't know much about your Confederacy or what it's like outside or even on other Warden worlds, but sometimes I think we're the last two really true human beings around."

"But what about you?" I responded gently. "It might be the end of all this."

"Then it's the end. If we continue the way we are, our relationship will be hollow anyway. I'll have kids and they'll be taken away, as always. And they aren't very likely to lift my judgment, so in twenty years or so I'll be ready for Momrath or whatever it is they do to the expendables. What kind of life is that?" She stared seriously into my eyes. "You go ahead—and if my psych blocks won't interfere, include me in. You understand? If anything goes wrong, and it probably will, I don't want to keep going. One big gamble for the two of us. Everything we want—or we go out together."

I grabbed her and pulled her to me and kissed her long and hard, and we made love as if it might be the last time we would ever have the chance.

The final, the ultimate scam was about to begin.

CHAPTER FIFTEEN

Laroo's Island

I walked into the dockside security office with a sense of doom, yet also with a feeling of intense excitement, as if my whole life had prepared me for this moment. Enough of the idea was necessarily left to improvisation, and knowing I was going up against the best the planet had to offer added to the challenge of it all.

The security officer was surprised to see me, since we had no shipments today, but he just nodded and looked curiously at me.

"I want you to get in touch with Security Coordinator Bogen," I told him. "I want to see him as soon as possible."

"Bogen's on the island," the man responded. "Besides, anything about security concerning you is more my problem than his."

"No offense, but you're too small. Besides, it's not a breach. You're a good cop, Hanak, but this is out of your league."

That nettled him. "What the hell are you spouting off about, Zhang?"

"Radio Bogen and tell him I want to talk to him right away. Just *do* it, Hanak, will you? It won't cost you anything."

"He won't see you," he sneered back at me. "He has more important things to do."

"If you send this message just the way I dictate it, I guarantee you I'll not only see him, but he'll break the galactic record to get to me."

"So what's this big, important message?"

"Tell him . . ." Here goes. "Tell him that he'll never solve the deprogramming problem no matter how much time, money, and effort he puts in Project Phoenix. Tell him I can do it."

Hanak stared at me. "You ain't supposed to know about that."

"Just send it. And let me know when he wants the meeting. I have work to do back in my office." And with that I turned and walked out the door and back to the administrative complex. I had no doubt that Bogen would take the bait. None at all. I figured I'd hear the explosion from the office, and I wasn't far wrong.

Just a few minutes after I'd settled back down to try and get some work done, Hanak rushed in to see me.

"Well, big shot," he said, "I sent it out to the island and they threw a half-dozen shit fits. Bogen's up on the satellite but he's coming back down, personal, just like you wanted. You're to meet him in ninety minutes."

I nodded and grinned at him. "Where?"

"In his office in the Castle."

"On the island?"

"What other castle is there?" He paused a moment, looking at me strangely. "You know, Zhang, you're either the dumbest guy I ever met or the nerviest. Which are you?"

I gave him a wide, toothy grin. "Guess!"

It was harder to get a crew on this day off than I'd figured, but with backup and emergency services I was able to muster a gunboat crew in about half an hour, leave a note for Dylan reading simply, "It's started," and head for the island.

Bogen, although coming from the space station, would probably arrive before or at least at the same time as I did, assuming he left right after sending his reply. In point of fact, his "ninety minutes" was unrealistic for me to make, short of flying over, which security really wasn't prepared for. Even at top speed of something around seventy kilometers an hour, the boat would take almost ninety minutes just to reach the island, and we'd had a half-hour delay in starting. That was just fine with me. I liked to keep people waiting and fuming a bit—knocks them off balance and makes them somewhat emotional in a situation where I'm perfectly rational and as calm as I can be given my training.

Still, it seemed like an eternity crossing that stretch of ocean. I kept having nightmares about being attacked by a bork on the way over and having the whole thing end right there.

The crossing, though, was uneventful, and soon the shining tower of the Castle hove into view, rising eerily up out of the trees. The sky was darkening, and I could feel a slight chill that told me that rain was due. It hardly bothered me. The executioner might care what sort of day it was, but not his victim.

We pulled up to the island dock and secured quickly. I walked off and up to the security building in back.

"Zhang," I told the duty officer. "Here to see Bogen."

She checked a screen and nodded. "You're cleared to his office and no other areas. Pick up your escort at the security gate."

"Escort, huh? Well, well!" I turned and walked out, then over to the gate I'd never gone through before. I had to put on a scanner to enter. Finally it confirmed that I was me and slid open, allowing me to step into a second chamber, where the procedure was repeated. Finally a far gate opened, and I walked through, meeting two khaki-clad and very serious members of the National Police, both very large men and both heavily armed.

"Walk between us and don't deviate from our path," one of them ordered. I gestured for him to lead the way. As we walked along the tree-lined paths I couldn't help but notice the special security systems all over the place and the fact that just about every step we took was being closely watched by somebody. Still, we were almost to the Castle when we had to get through yet another double gate with scan, and from there we walked on into the inner courtyard.

I was impressed. Although artificially surfaced like the docks and landing areas, and made from careful cutting of the trees, the area around the Castle was something I hadn't seen since leaving the Confederacy. They had imported sod from somewhere—probably Lilith, since that was supposedly the garden planet—and there was a huge, brilliant green lawn complete with exotic plants and flowers. I was impressed a little more with Laroo; this was the sort of thing *I* would have done in his position, but few others would have.

After another scan at the Castle entrance as we approached, we were inside double sliding doors. I had to admit, despite the tales from the concubines, I wasn't prepared for what I saw. We walked through huge open areas with incredibly opulent furnishings. Beautiful rugs and carpeting blended into furlike couches, chairs, and recliners. On the walls were beautiful works of original—I supposed—artwork that matched the mood of the rooms. The only jarring note was the policemen standing guard just about everywhere, that plus the knowledge that cameras were following us everywhere and seeing everything.

I never saw any stairways, although they might well be somewhere if only for safety reasons. We went up in a large elevator that was basically a glass tube wrapped completely around its supporting pole. Very neat, I thought. *They* control access to and egress from the elevators, can see you at all times, and make sure you go only where you're supposed to.

We got off on what I thought was either the fourth or fifth floor, walked across to the main building on a small ramp—which had emerged when we stopped there and pulled back into the wall once we were clear, another nice touch—and down another corridor. This floor was filled with rooms resembling national museums, complete with display cases and lighting. Weapons, coins, and gems from many worlds were all there in their respective places. I was more than impressed. I knew, too, that this stuff wasn't Wagant Laroo's—it was just put in his charge. Everything here was a type of object that could survive Warden sterilization from the Cerberan organism, and all of it belonged to somebody else, put here for safekeeping until its owner needed it or was in a position to enjoy it. I began to appreciate just what Bogen secured most of the time.

Finally we reached the end of the hall and a door slid back to reveal a modern office waiting room, complete with receptionist but lacking, I noticed, anything to read or look at.

My two guards flanked me while I presented myself. The receptionist nodded at my name. "Go right in. Director Bogen is waiting for you."

"I'll bet," I muttered and walked to the inner office door, then turned and looked back at my guards. "Not coming?"

They said nothing, so I opened the door and stepped inside.

It was a small, cramped office, one that looked really lived in—all sorts of books, magazines, print-outs, you name it were scattered over the place, practically obscuring an L-style office desk with computer access terminals on one side and a pile of papers and other stuff, even a dictawriter, on the other. Bogen, dressed in casual work clothes, needed a shower and shave. Clearly he wasn't prepared for this, and his eyes had an angry look.

"Clear that junk away and sit down," he snapped, gesturing to a chair. I did so and just looked at him.

"Well?" he shot. "Just what kind of shit are you trying to pull on me, Zhang, or whatever your name really is?"

"I wanted to prove a point about your operation, and I think I proved it to your satisfaction," I told him, controlling heart rate, blood pressure, and everything else, to keep as calm and relaxed as was humanly possible.

"That my security stinks? Is that it? Look, it's easy for you to have picked up that Project Phoenix name just from some of the stuff around the docks, and maybe to guess a little that we're doing some kind of biological experiments out here. But you put your finger on the heart of the research, and that just isn't possible. Aside from the Chairman, me, and six or seven other people on Cerberus—and the other three Lords—there's nobody, and I mean nobody, who knows what we're doing who ever gets off this island. I want to know how you know, and I want to know why you told me you knew, before I have you killed."

"Charming," I responded dryly. "I'll bet that line is a big hit with all the girls."

"Cut the clown act, Zhang! I'm in no mood for it."

"Would you believe I deduced it?"

"Ha! From what? You'd have to know more than almost anybody on this planet to do that."

"I do," I replied coolly. "I'm not *from* this planet. And to judge from your accent, neither are you originally. I know about the aliens, Bogen. The aliens and their fancy robots."

"How *could* you know? Or are you admitting you're a Confederacy agent, like I thought?"

"I'm an agent," I admitted. "My old employer was the Assassination Bureau of Security. They took me and using a process that seems to have been developed based on what happens here on Cerberus, they put me in Qwin Zhang's body and sent me here."

"For what specific purpose?"

"Basically because they already suspected how the robots were so perfectly programmed," I told him, lying profusely and knowing that I was being monitored by lie-detection gear of the first water. That was all right. I had been trained to fool the best of them.

"That's bullshit and you know it!" he shot back. "If they knew that they'd be on us like a ton of bricks, connections or no connections."

"They know," I assured him. "And I'm almost certainly not the only one here, although I don't personally know of any others. Sure, they could knock down your fancy space station, maybe fry this island with a deep beam—but what would that get 'em? They want the aliens, Bogen, and Cerberus is the only place so far where they have a direct link to them. They'll fry us, maybe the whole damned planet, one of these days, that's for sure—but not as long as they can gain as much or more than they lose."

Bogen chuckled. "Well, they'll have a long wait for that. I don't think even Laroo's ever met one. If any of the Four Lords have, it's probably Kreegan of Lilith. This whole thing was his idea, anyway."

"It's to our advantage not to let anybody know that—to *our* advantage, really. I don't want to be fried, Bogen."

"It won't make any difference to you, anyway," he noted. "You're a dead man right now."

"I doubt it," I responded, sounding less than upset by his threats. "Now, I'm going to make a point, and I think you're intelligent enough to realize that it's the truth. I *could* have just reported my findings on Project Phoenix to the Confederacy and let them take drastic action. I didn't. Instead I reported them to you."

"Go on."

"You know the old problem with agents sent to the Wardens. We're trapped here, same as you."

"They must have been pretty sure of you, since they could hardly keep any kind of trace on you from body to body," he noted.

"They were—and with good reason. I was born and bred for a job like this. It is the sole reason for my existence, what I live, eat, sleep, and breathe for. Once the objective's accomplished, there's no further reason for living. You've heard of the assassins before."

He nodded. "Met a couple, and I agree. Fanatics. I think old man Kreegan used to be one, in fact. So I know what you are and what you're like. I know out of your own mouth you're the most dangerous man on Cerberus to me and my boss."

"But they screwed up," I told him. "Believe me, it surprised me as much or more than it's gonna surprise them, but they slipped up. This place—well, it changed me, too. I have something to live for beyond the mission—or rather, some*one*."

Bogen seemed to relax a bit. I saw, though, that one eye kept glancing down at something beyond my field of vision. The lie-detector screen, probably. "So now you want in and you're trying to bargain with us, right? But you've got no cards."

"I think I do," I responded carefully. "The fact is, they were so sneaky they put in a deep psych command for me to report and forget I reported. I didn't even know that until I put my wife and myself under Dumonia up in Medlam."

Bogen tensed. "Then you might already have reported."

I shook my head from side to side. "No, not this much, anyway. My last report was more than two months ago, and I haven't been near the agent who can trigger the command. But I know who he is now, so they don't own me any more."

"Who?"

"Does it matter? If you nab him, they'll just establish a dozen more, ones we don't know. No, from the point at which I learned of all this stuff, I started getting ideas of my own. First, I definitely wanted in. I don't like being a prisoner any more than you or any of the rest of us, and I don't like living under the Confederacy's gun. Whether I succeeded or failed, I was a dead man—and I don't want to be dead, Bogen, and I don't want the kind of stasis my life's now in, which was the other alternative. So that got me to thinking about you and Laroo and Project Phoenix. It occurred to me that you're dealing with a product of alien technology using people who have no experience even in our end of things. Organic computing's on the proscribed list, as you know, so there are few experts in it, and those who are, are basically industrially oriented, toward the parts the Confederacy *does* use. You don't have the people or the years of research and development to solve the problem, and I think you know it."

"All right. I'm not about to grant that, but I'll admit progress has been almost nil. We know *what*, but there's just no way to take the programming out selectively—and if you take it all out, you destroy it, since life support and all the other normal functions are part of the programming molecules within each tiny cell. Basically you need a full-blown organic computer to do the job, and we haven't been allowed to get near those things in hundreds of years, not since the war."

I nodded. "There's only one place other than the aliens where the kind of expertise you need exists at all. You know it and I know it. I'm sure you've sicced some of your robots on it, but the data are too diffuse to get at. It might take years to put it all together, even assuming you can break the codes. I don't think you feel like you have years to spare."

"Go on."

"Security. Confederacy Security. They could easily tap the data, put it together, and send it to as complex a computing network as necessary to solve the problem. *They* use organic computers, you know. Not like these

—not at all like these. But they *do* use them in their ships and modules. *They* could solve your problem for you."

He laughed. "And just like that—you ask 'em and they comply, right? Don't be ridiculous!"

I relaxed a little. "Not at all. I told you I knew who the communications agent was. If I walk in there and force him to put me through, there'll be no force, no coercion, and no forgetting. Now, just suppose I call upstairs and tell them I've got a crack at stealing one of the alien robots?"

"What!"

"Uh-huh. And I tell them how I'm going to do it. I'm going to clear it of all prior programming, then take control myself. Let my mind go into it and bring it—and me—out of Cerberus."

"They won't swallow it."

"I think they will. Remember, they don't have any way to check on the truth of what I'm saying, and the mere fact that I'll be coming to them with this will prove an unbroken line. I'm a pretty good hypnotic subject when I want to be. Let's say I tell 'em some of the robot programming is being done on this island—they already know almost as much anyway— and that I've wormed my way into the project through my Tooker associations. Some of the experts working on the project don't like the idea of working for unknown aliens, and I've got some underground help—if I can get a robot out. And the only way to ensure that is to walk out as one. They'll buy it. It sounds just like me."

He thought it over. "Too risky."

"There's no risk, if you think about it. They already know that the Cerberans are involved in the programming, and it doesn't take a master detective to figure that it has to be the space station and the island. I'm giving them a convincing scenario that meshes with my previous reports and also with what they already know. They themselves then have the choice. Either they okay the plan and give the solution to me—if *they* can solve it— or they turn me down as too much of a risk for that kind of information. I think I know them. As long as they know they have the power to destroy this whole planet, they'll okay it. The temptation, the bait, will be too great."

"Supposing they do? What happens to Cerberus when you don't deliver?"

"We have the key, and that solves the problem. Beyond that—well, I would assume protection for my wife and myself, perhaps eventually cleared robot bodies of our own. And if the Confederacy makes a move to atomize Cerberus, we'll have a lot of advance warning. You just can't make that kind of decision easily, so we'll have the opportunity to call on those aliens for help."

"And if they won't?"

"Then at least *we* get away."

He thought it over some more. "Well, what you say is true—up to a point. My only concern is that, unbeknownst even to you, this is a subtle Confederacy plot."

"Huh? What could I do to you?"

"Oh, not you. But suppose they use all this to get an authorization for planetary destruction? Suppose that's what they really want—direct cause they can get through the Councils? Their primary, maybe only, objective is to bring these aliens out of the woodwork. Maybe the authorized destruction of Cerberus is the way they're planning to do that—and we have no guarantees the aliens will protect us, or be able to. It seems to me that if they could defeat the Confederacy militarily they wouldn't have needed us in the first place."

It was a glum thought, one I hadn't really considered. As sneaky as my bosses had been, *was* this, then, their goal? Certainly it would be the ultimate goal, to smoke them out. I didn't like to think of the idea that they expected it all along, though, from me.

"It's a possibility. A risk. A big risk, I admit. But which is the bigger risk? *Not* to try it, not to crack this programming code, and still be sitting here when they eventually *do* get around to excising us? It's going to happen. You know it and I know it. If they go along, at least we have a chance—all of us."

Bogen sighed and shook his head, but all his belligerence was gone. "This is too big a decision for me to make, you know. I'm going to have to buck this to Laroo. You, too, probably."

"Suits me fine."

I sent back word with the boat crew that I would be remaining at least overnight, and gave Dylan some encouraging news, in the simplest form of code. I didn't really care if Bogen's people figured it out or not; if he didn't have some foreknowledge of me and my nature he didn't deserve to be in the business.

Then I waited for Bogen to call his boss, and finally he returned. "Okay," he said, "he's coming in tomorrow afternoon. Earliest he can get away. You're to stay here as his guest until he hears you out and makes a final decision."

"What about my wife?" I asked, somewhat concerned. "She has no credit, remember."

"She'll be all right through tomorrow. My people will be there if she needs anything. After that, well, we'll see. Remember, your future and hers are hanging by a thread right now."

Didn't I know it! Still, I was committed now. "Well, since I'm either in or dead, mind letting me see one of these wonders of the universe?"

He thought it over. "Sure. Why not. Come on."

We rode down in one of the transparent elevators, far beyond the ground floor and into the vast trunk of the main support tree itself.

The lab facilities down there were quite modern and impressive. Along the way I ran into several old Tooker employees who saw and greeted me, but Bogen wasn't in the mood to let me renew old friendships.

The center of all this activity was an eerie lab in two parts, with a monitoring and control panel of unfamiliar design on one side and a series of small booths along an entire wall. A young and very attractive woman with long black hair trailing down over her traditional lab coat was checking a series of readings on one of the machines as we entered. She glanced up, saw Bogen, and rose to meet us.

"Here's the best mind on Cerberus, and one of the best in the whole galaxy," Bogen beamed.

She smiled and put out a hand. "Zyra Merton," she introduced herself.

I was startled even as I shook the thin, delicate hand. "Qwin Zhang. Did you say Merton?"

She laughed pleasantly. "Yes. You've heard the name?"

"I sure have. Somehow, though, my vision was always of some little old man with wild hair and a beard."

"Well, I *am* pretty old," she replied good-humoredly. "In fact, I'm close to a hundred and eighty. The reason why I came here, almost ninety years ago, was not only to study the Warden processes on Cerberus but also because it was at the time the only way to save my life. However, I assure you that I am and have always been a woman, and I've never once had a beard."

I laughed back. She was charming, and a surprising answer to the question of just who Merton really was.

"But tell me, where did you hear my name?" she asked.

"I'm a product of what the Confederacy calls the Merton Process," I told her.

She seemed very interested. "You mean they solved the problems? It cost too many lives and too many people's sanity ever to be very practical, I thought. I abandoned that research when I turned entirely to researching Cerberan processes. That was—let me see—fifty years or so ago."

"Well, they solved some of it," I told her. "Not the attrition rate, though."

She looked disappointed and a bit angry. "Damn them! Damn me! My biggest regret has always been that I developed the thing to begin with and sent out the data in so incomplete a form. Still, in those days there were few people here, and not much technology or governmental structure, and I was dependent on outside support to get anywhere. Still, I'd like to give you a complete psych scan sometime, just to find out how far they *did* go with it. It's a dead end beyond what you say, I fear."

I decided not to tell her how much of a success the Confederacy thought it was. Out of respect for my counterparts on Lilith, Medusa, and Charon, I didn't want to blow too much right now.

"I'll be glad to—sometime," I told her sincerely. If I could trust anybody on this crazy ball it was probably her, if only for her scientific detachment.

"Zhang's interested in our friends," Bogen told her. "Can you give us a bit of a demonstration?"

She nodded. "Glad to. Got one that's just about ripe."

"Ripe?"

"Finished. Complete. Ready to go." She went back to her instruments and punched in a series of instructions. A slight buzzer sounded over one of the booths, and a red light came on. After a moment the red light went out and was replaced by an amber standby, then a green.

She left her panel, went over, and opened the door to one of the booths. The sight revealed startled me. It was the body of a tall, muscular man to civilized worlds' norm. He looked recently dead.

"Two one two six seven—awake and step out," she instructed.

The cadaver stirred, opened its eyes, and looked around, and into its whole body came an eerie sense of life, of full animation. It walked out of the box, suddenly appearing very natural.

I went over and looked at him. Doing so made me a little uncomfortable, because suddenly it was a person and not a thing I was eyeing as I would a piece of sculpture.

"The most amazing marriage of organic chemistry, computer, and molecular biology I have ever seen or known," Merton told me.

"This is a robot?"

She nodded. "They don't come packaged exactly like this, I should tell you. They arrive in a roughly humanoid shape and with the same mass, but that's about all. From cell samples supplied us, we're able to graft an entire skin onto it so perfectly that it is an exact duplicate of whoever's cell we use. The material we use for it is similar to the stuff used on the entire device, but it's capable of following and using the genetic code of the original. When we have the original subject handy, it can add in moments any scars, blemishes, or oddities to make itself a complete duplicate."

"How the hell can you make something like this?" I gasped.

"We don't, and can't. The Confederacy could if it wanted to. Even then, the design would be different. It takes very little time in close examination to see these devices are the product of a society and culture that is extremely alien to our own. Not that scientific laws are violated—they aren't. But the whole evolution of science up to this point came from a far different series of steps."

"Where do they come from, then?"

She shrugged. "We have only a few here, partly for seasoning and partly for experimental purposes. They don't let us have too many, and only when we have a specific individual in mind. They're pretty careful."

"But the whole thing is done here? All the mind-changing?"

"Oh, no. It can be done anywhere in the Warden system out to a point roughly one hundred and sixty million kilometers beyond the orbit of Momrath. Just as long as it's done in an atmosphere containing only Cerberan Wardens. I don't know the details."

"And this doesn't disturb you? That we're using these to spy on the Confederacy?"

"Not really. Why should it? Everything that government does turns to dust or ashes, including the people. We have an entirely new, fresh technology here from an entirely nonhuman evolution, and that's far more interesting. I can hardly blame them for not announcing themselves to the Confederacy. Every alien race we've ever touched we've murdered, literally or culturally."

"You sound like you would have gotten sentenced here if you hadn't come voluntarily," I noted.

"Probably," she laughed. "We'll never know. But it worked out, anyway."

I stared at her, thinking hard. "And *you* haven't been able to solve the programming riddle? If *you* can't, can anybody?"

She looked questioningly at Bogen, who nodded, and then she turned back to me. "It's not all that simple. Here, let's go over to the scope."

We walked over to the instrument cluster. "I don't recognize any of this," I told her. "Whose is it? Your own design?"

"No. It's supplied by the makers, too. That's part of the problem. Here. Look in the screen."

I looked, and saw a close-up of a cell. No, not a cell. Some sort of unicellular animal, it seemed, like the amoeba.

"That's a cellular unit from one of the robots," she told me. "It really isn't a cell, although it acts like one. It's a complete self-contained microcomputer using organic molecules and an organic structure." She fiddled with a dial and the tiny thing was gone, replaced by a horde of tiny things swimming in a clear river.

"The molecular chemistry itself's a nightmare," she told me. "It's not that we're seeing anything unusual. No special elements we've never seen before, nothing like that. But they're put together in a way I couldn't even imagine. There is in fact no way I know to build or grow something like that, composed of all those elements and compounds, and make it work. For example, I can take carbon chains and sulfur and zinc, potassium, magnesium, and a hundred other compounds and elements and put them together—but never would I get something like *that*." She shifted the focus to the cellular wall and blew it up almost impossibly large. "See those tiny little hairlike things? They're the electrical connectors to the surrounding cells. Like nerves, yet not like them. Connected up, they form a *conscious communications system* from cell to cell. The brain can tell any cell, or any cell group, what it wants the little bugger to do, look like—you name it, and it can do it. Mimic almost anything. Even functional things. Impossible. Inconceivable. Even in our best bad old days of the robot war we had nothing that could do that. We might have had, though, had they not banned further research and development."

"I get the point. What you're telling me is that even the Confederacy couldn't reprogram or deprogram the things."

"Nothing of the sort! Given one of these, they probably could. But we—we're at a dead end. We are able to see how it's done, but we can't do it—or undo it—ourselves. And most important, we can't tell the necessary programming from the unnecessary stuff. See?"

I *did* see. "But you think the Confederacy could?"

"Only because they have bigger, faster, quasi-organic devices themselves. I doubt if they could *duplicate* this, but they could probably tell it what to do. That's why each cell has a self-destruct switch. If it's incapacitated or in danger of capture, it simply melts down. All of it."

"Seen enough?" Bogen asked impatiently.

I nodded. "For now, anyway. I'm impressed, I have to say that." I was more than impressed. The damned things scared me to death.

CHAPTER SIXTEEN

Wagant Laroo

I spent an extremely comfortable night in one of the guest rooms, surrounded by old masters and sleeping in the kind of computer-controlled luxury I'd almost forgotten existed. I slept late, knowing I might need all my wits about me, and had a sumptuous brunch; then, with the permission of the National Police, and under their extremely watchful eyes, I toured the collections upstairs. All in all it was a fascinating day as well as providing solutions to enough unsolved spectacular thefts to earn any cop a seat in the hall of fame, if they have one.

In the late afternoon a flier approached and landed on the front lawn I still found so nice. Out stepped five men, each carrying a briefcase. There was nothing particularly unusual about any of them, so I could only stare out the window and wonder which was Laroo.

That, it seemed, was the real trick.

"You never know which one of the party is him," Bogen warned me. "He has about two dozen people that are so good at acting that they actually represent him at various functions, and he usually travels with a group. He can be any one of them—and you're never sure if you're talking to the real one or not."

That made me a little nervous. "So the real one might not be here at all."

"Oh, one of 'em's him, I guarantee. This is that kind of decision. The best way is just to treat *any* of 'em as if he were Laroo. The real one'll get everything."

I nodded uneasily, and we went down to the Lord of the Diamond's elaborate office. The idea that Laroo played such tricks made me a bit uneasy. Another thing that could go wrong, I thought nervously.

I was ushered in and introduced to a tall, handsome man with prematurely white hair that gave him the look of a distinguished politician. I looked over at the others. One of them was short and fat and looked a little like Otah, but hardly anything like I imagined the Lord of Cerberus should look. *I'd* pick that one, I noted to myself. Nobody could ever take somebody who looked like that seriously as a dictator. I looked around at the others sitting there, relaxed, eyes on me. I wondered if *they* knew who was who right now.

I went up to the Laroo indicated, stopped, and bowed slightly.

He put out his hand and flashed a politician's smile. "You don't have to go through that shit," he told me pleasantly. "We're all businessmen here. Here, have a seat and make yourself comfortable."

I did as instructed. He just sat there a moment, looking me over. "So you're a First-Class Assassin," he finally said.

"Was," I responded, relaxing a bit. "I'm no longer interested in that part of the work."

"I've viewed the tape of your conversation with Bogen yesterday and checked the instrument readings. It seems we have a truly valuable and interesting man in you, Zhang. I'm curious, though. If you volunteered for all this, why did you turn yourself around?"

"I didn't volunteer," I told him truthfully. "I was nominated, elected, put to sleep, briefed, and woke up on the prison ship."

He laughed at that. "Sounds like 'em, all right. And now you're in business for yourself. Well, I have a few more questions of a more practical nature."

"Fire away."

"First, assuming we let you go ahead with this, what guarantees do we have that you won't double-cross us?"

It was my turn to laugh. "Double-cross *you?* All by myself? Look, turn it around. Once I've done it, what guarantee do *I* have that you won't then decide just to terminate me?"

"Fair enough. So we're starting on the basis of mutual trust. A good foundation. You know what *we* expect to gain. What about you? What do *you* want out of this?"

"Well, before we go anywhere with this, I'd like my wife's judgment set aside. She's got some mental problems and the judgment stands in the way of solving them. That comes before anything—as a gesture of trust. Also, I'm going to need her, since she's the only check I have that the Confederacy's agents won't pull a fast one on me."

Wagant Laroo seemed more than a little amused, as did the others. I noted with some discomfort that their reactions to my statements were virtually simultaneous—and identical.

"You know, I like you, Zhant, or whatever your name really is. Here you are, a prisoner on my island, and with a flick of a finger I could sweep you away as if you'd never been. Considering this, you start demanding terms and advance payment! I really do like that."

"If you accept my idea, then it's perfectly reasonable," I told him. "If you don't, then I'm gone anyway."

He nodded, liking the answer. "That's true. You already know I'm interested, or I wouldn't have interrupted my very busy schedule to get here. More, there's an extra feeling of urgency on my part to accomplish something, purely for my own protection. Marek Kreegan, Lord of Lilith, was assassinated yesterday."

"What!" I felt a rise of excitement within me that I could not suppress.

He nodded gravely. "Actually, it was something of a fluke, I'm told, but it was a direct result of the Confederacy putting somebody there to do it. I, and the other planetary leaders, must assume that there are Confederacy assassins out to get all of us, a clever and backhanded way to strike at us. Tell me, wasn't that really *your* assignment?"

Honesty was the best policy. Besides, they probably had already burglarized Dumonia's office and records anyway. "Yes, it was. Deep down there's still a psych command to that effect in my brain, but if you'll check with Dr. Dumonia he'll tell you it isn't an imperative in any way—and I have already changed my game plan. I would have anyway after discovering that. I don't like people, even those people, messing with my mind."

"I think I believe you," he told me. "But that doesn't alter the fact that you're probably not the only one."

"Almost certainly not," I agreed, feeding his paranoia with the truth. "They told me at the time that there might be others."

"Exactly. That means Project Phoenix is even more urgent in my case. You know, I was giving your proposal much thought, and I got to wondering why I shouldn't just have a robot made of you. That would most certainly assure your loyalty, honesty, and cooperation."

I felt a tinge of panic. That was a line I'd thought of as one of the major risks—and one I had no real counter for.

"It won't work," I lied as smoothly and convincingly as I could. "The kind of mental training I had for my entire life would be placed into direct conflict with the robotic programming. An internal war would ensue, and at best, insanity."

He thought it over. "Maybe. Maybe not. I don't know. We've never had someone of your unique training and upbringing before. Still, I can see the logic in it, and I'll check it out with a psych. Go get some dinner now—Bogen will show you where—while we discuss this and while I check out that particular point."

The interview was over, but I didn't feel too good about it nor did I feel much like eating. Bogen, who stuck with me, seemed quite satisfied with himself, so I knew immediately where the idea had come from. After killing some after-dinner time, we were summoned back into the five presences, this time with even less ceremony.

"All right," Laroo began, "you win this round. We contacted five of the top psychs in the area, including your own, and two out of five agreed with you while the other three weren't sure. All things considered, I can take the chance on you right now. I also toyed with the idea of replacing your wife—a very simple procedure, really."

I tensed, but said nothing.

"However," he continued, "Dumonia said that doing so would eventually turn you into a suicidal assassin of the first rank, which would mean killing you immediately. It's still an attractive idea—and you might consider that you won't know if and when I decide to do it—but I won't for now. The fact is, your kind of mind comes along all too seldom around here, and your type is one I find fascinating and useful."

"Aside from the fact that if you replaced Dylan I'd know the first time we swapped minds, assuming I survived the swap."

He sighed. "Yes, that *is* the compelling reason. See what I mean? You think right. And because you think right, I'm inclined to give you a chance. I'm inclined to let you try."

I relaxed. Second big hurdle crossed. "When?"

"As soon as possible," he told me. "Ordinarily I'd take this up at the semiannual meeting of the Lords of the Diamond, which is the day after tomorrow, but with Kreegan gone I can no longer afford the luxury of committee decisions. *He* usually made them, anyway. I will, however, bring the matter up at the time." He rose, as if to dismiss me.

"My wife," I reminded him. "The down payment."

He hesitated, then sighed. "Very well. Call Dumonia when you get back to shore. I'll arrange things through him. Get it done quickly. But the psych commands and network remain. You understand that? And the credit dependency. If she tries to get out of the motherhood again, I'll fix it so she'll beg for mercy—and you, too. Also, her life as well as yours is in your hands as of now. *One* cross, *one* little slip by either of you, *one* thing going even slightly off—even if it's something beyond your doing or control—and both of you won't be dead, but you'll wish you were. You understand?"

I nodded seriously, noting the vicious undertone in his voice. It was an edge, a *very* slight chilling undertone, that had been absent before. I realized suddenly that I was facing the real Wagant Laroo, although I hadn't the first time, and I felt the odds tilt very slightly back to me. I could recognize him if I was careful. Could pick him out in his room full of doubles. Those others, that first one, were damned good actors, but the kind of emotional undertone here had to be, I felt, unique to the real one.

Bogen suddenly paled as a worthy opponent in my eyes. I could see him shrink into insignificance in my mind, a minor-league security chief. Wagant Laroo was the most chillingly dangerous human being I had ever met. I never doubted for a second his threat, or his ability to make good on it.

CHAPTER SEVENTEEN

Creative Psych and Proposition Time

"I still can't believe you managed it," Dylan told me on the way over to Dumonia's. "My God, Qwin! In one year you've come here, framed a big shot, become a company president, wormed your way into a high-level security project, and now you've even managed to get a judgment reversed—a judgment not too many months old!"

I nodded and smiled, but that dark edge that came in when things were underway and out of control was irrepressible. "Still, we're only halfway home. The trickiest parts are yet to come, and this guy Laroo really bothers me. Dylan, I looked at him and I knew real fear, real danger. These Four Lords are the best of their kind, an ultimate evolutionary type. The whole Warden Diamond concept was the dumbest thing the Confederacy ever accomplished. I see that now. They put the absolute best, most brilliant criminal psychopaths together on one spot. The survivor of such struggles has to be the perfection of their kind—thoroughly brilliant, totally amoral, totally ruthless. He thought of every way to screw me up just while I was sitting there, and I think he knows, or at least suspects, what I'm up to."

"But you talked yourself out of his traps," she pointed out, "and he went along with you. If he's *that* good, why did he?"

"I think I know. Consider his position. His biggest weakness is his fear that at any moment his enormous and growing power may be snuffed out. It was already a fear before, but now that one of the Four Lords is gone, it has become an obsession. He has the best minds on Cerberus working on his ultimate solution—including Merton, who may be one of the best minds in that area, period. And they can't crack it. He *needs* Project Phoenix. So even figuring on a double-cross of some kind, he's willing to let me go ahead anyway. He has no choice. The only thing he can do is let me go all the way, using Merton and the others to uncover my tricks, in the hopes that I'll still solve the problem for him. It's the ultimate challenge, Dylan. He's betting his ego against mine that he can outfox me before I can outfox him."

"You're sure he knows you're planning something?"

I nodded. "He knows. Like Bogen said, you get a gut feeling, pro to pro. Like the gut feelings you relied on most heavily in the bork hunts. He knows simply because of the bottom line. Once I deliver, he has everything to fear from me and nothing to gain by keeping me around. We both understand that. He knows I'll have to pull something, and he is betting he can figure it out. That's why the free leash right now, the giving in to my conditions. It doesn't matter—as long as I deliver the goods."

She looked at me. "*Can* you deliver?"

I shrugged. "I haven't the slightest idea. That'll be up to Otah and my brother and Krega and those above *him.* In the end, I have to bet on their being able to come up with the solution to the problem."

She just nodded and turned and looked back out the window of the helicab.

Soon we arrived at Dumonia's offices and were quickly ushered in. Laroo had wasted no time in setting all this up, since he saw assassins in every corner. He was probably right.

Dumonia, too, seemed impressed. While Dylan was off with the thirteen judges assembled on Laroo's orders just for this purpose, we sat, relaxed, and talked. I liked Dumonia, although I didn't trust him.

"Well, so you blew the lid off your cover," he noted casually.

I nodded. "Why not? It was always shaky anyway. And frankly, if *you* knew, it'd eventually get out in any event."

He winced. "Am I *that* disreputable?"

"For all I know, you're exactly what you seem to be. Or you *could* be Wagant Laroo himself. On this world, who can tell?"

He found the idea amusing. "That's the most common problem we face, you know, here on Cerberus. Paranoia. Fear of who's who. It's the thing that keeps the people in line. We have a really nasty element in our population, courtesy of the Confederacy, but it takes something like that to keep us as peaceful and relatively crime-free as we are. That and the threat of a judgment, or death, if caught. I suspect that that's why I love this place so much. Think of the *business!*"

I had thought a lot about Svarc Dumonia over the past several weeks, and had been extra careful even in choosing him. The man was a total contradiction—a totally amoral, cynical person with criminal tendencies in the mass and abstract sense, yet totally devoted to helping and curing his individual patients.

"Just your idea that I might be Laroo is a good example," he said. "Total paranoia reigns. But I'm *not* Laroo. I couldn't ever *be* Laroo, for the very simple reason that I hate governments. I hate *all* institutions, from the Confederacy to the Cerberan government to the local medical society. Organized anthills, all of 'em. Designed to stifle and straitjacket the individual human spirit, and doing a damned good job as well. Religions are just as bad, maybe worse. Dogma. You have to believe this; you have to behave like that. Run around wasting time in silly rituals instead of being productive. You know we have a hundred and seventy different faiths in Medlam alone? Everything from the Catholic Church and Orthodox Judaism—consider the problems with sex changing, circumcision, and the rest *they* face in our changeable world—to local nut cults that believe the gods are sleeping inside Cerberus and will awaken to take us to the Millennium someday."

"You're an anarchist, then."

"Oh, I suppose. A comfortable, upper-class anarchist of a sort, wearing tailored suits and having a seaside resort home I can get to in my private flier. That's where the old philosophers went wrong, you know. Anarchism isn't the way for the masses. Hell, they *want* to be led, or they wouldn't keep tolerating and creating all these new bureaucratic institutions to tell them what to think. It's an individual philosophy. You compromise, becoming as much of an anarchist as you can without worrying about man in the collective. The only thing you can do in the collective sense is to shake them up periodically, give 'em a revolutionary kick in the pants. It never lasts—it creates its own dogmas and bureaucracies. But the shake-up is healthy. When the Confederacy got so institutionalized that even a little revolt here and there was impossible, that's when dry rot set in."

I began to see where he was heading. "And you think I'm a local revolutionary?"

"Oh, you'll probably get your fool head blown off, but maybe you'll give 'em a kick. Eventually you'll become what you destroy even if you succeed, but then some new smart ass will come along and do the same to you. It'll keep the juices flowing for the long run."

I accepted that. I *liked* Dumonia, although not necessarily all that he said or believed. I certainly couldn't see myself as another Laroo and said so.

"But you *are*," he responded. "You told me you felt real apprehension and fear when you met him. Know why? Because you looked at Laroo and knew, deep down, that you were looking at yourself. Knew that you were looking straight into the eyes of somebody whose mind worked just like yours."

"I don't worship power."

"Because you've never had that degree of power, so you can't really imagine what it might do to you. But you *do* love it. Every time you took on an opponent, a system, something, and won, you exercised power and demonstrated your mastery over those people, that system."

"I hope not. I sincerely hope you're wrong. But tell you what. In the incredibly unlikely event that I ever get to be Lord of Cerberus, I'll continue to see you often just to have you kick me in the rear. How's that?"

He didn't laugh. "No, you won't. You won't like, or will choose not to believe, what I tell you, and you'll eventually grow sick of it. I *know*. You see, twenty years ago I had almost this identical conversation with Wagant Laroo."

"What!"

He nodded. "I've seen 'em come and go. I helped put him in, and I'll help put *you* in if I can, but nothing will change."

"How do you stay alive, Doc?"

He grinned. "My little secret. But remember, everybody now running this place has at one time or another been a patient of mine."

"Including me," I muttered, more to myself than him. I suddenly realized that here in this office was truly the smartest, most devious man on Cerberus—and oddly, not one to be feared, at least yet. Dumonia could have been Lord any time he wanted, but he didn't want it. Running a place was against his religion.

"Well, let's get on to more direct matters," I suggested, feeling more and more uncomfortable. "You said that if Dylan were out of judgment you might effect a complete cure. Well, that's going to be the case. Now, what needs to be done?"

He assumed a more professional tone. "Frankly, the easiest thing to do is to stop here and let it ride. The safest, too. She's quite a bit better now. She knows who she is and what she is and understands herself pretty well. Most of her old personality is back, and some of the confidence, too. The remaining block is that she's scared deep down of losing you. If not now, then years down the pike. Not by violence, which seems likely—she could accept that, I think. She lived with friends and co-workers dying for five years. But, well, losing your *heart*, so to speak. There's really only one way to show her it's a groundless fear, and it involves tremendous risk to both of you."

"I'm rolling for all the marbles now, Doc," I told him. "What's a little more risk at this stage?"

He sat back, thinking. "All right. You've heard of Cerberan-induced schizophrenia? A misnomer, by the way, since it not only has nothing to do with schizophrenia, it doesn't even have any related symptoms."

"I'm not really sure," I told him honestly.

"Well, in very rare, freak instances during the personality transfer process, we wind up with one of two very strange conditions. If we can control the transference between two minds and interrupt it at a precise spot, the data from both minds will be present equally in both brains, so to speak. We have more than enough room in there, you know. The two primary results are either eventual merging of the two into one new personality after a period of acute identity crisis, or winding up with two complete, distinct personalities in each body, alternating. Timing, mental and physical setup, and the like, is crucial and not guaranteed."

"I think I remember hearing something about it. Early on, in the briefings after I came."

He nodded. "Very rare—but we can do it in the lab. The problem is that every individual is physically different, and the time tolerances are incredibly fine to get any result, let alone the desired one. And there's very little margin for error. We've occasionally been able to get the splits to merge, but that's about it. The process is irreversible and permanent."

"And just what does this have to do with Dylan?"

"Well, barring the discovery of mental telepathy in practical form, the only way to reassure her totally—if you really are sincere and her fears are groundless—is to try something akin to this process. Control it, and stop the transference *just short* of the induced split. This will put a strong imprint from the other person in each mind. It'll be as if you could read each other's innermost thoughts and secrets—which is why almost nobody has the guts to try it. No more secrets, period. None. But if timed correctly, it'll fade over a period of weeks, leaving only the original personality and the intimate memory of knowing the other. If we could do this with the two of you, she would *know,* would have been inside your head so to speak, and there would be no more doubting you—if you really don't, deep down give cause for the doubt. For a brief time, a few days at least, she would have total access to your mind, memories, and personalities inside her own head—and you, hers."

I whistled. "That's a pretty nasty load. Do I even know *myself* what I really want or feel?"

"Yes. You see the risk. And there's the additional one. To be really effective, the timing is crucial, and as I said, individual factors not all quantifiable come into play, making it an educated guess. Split or merger is a very real possibility."

"I see. And what are the odds of something going wrong like that?"

"Fifty-fifty, frankly."

I sighed. "I see. And, just on the off-chance I still wanted this, and Dylan was willing too, how much prep time would you need? How much notice?"

"At least a day. Several weeks would be better, since I'd have to cancel a lot of my appointments, but it'll be worth it. I haven't done anything like this in a long, long time."

"How many times *have* you done it in your twenty or thirty years of practice?"

He thought a moment. "Four, I think."

"And how many times did it succeed?"

"Well, that's relative. Two worked, and two caused the induced state I mentioned. Of the two that worked, one couple became the closest duo I'd ever known, and seemed to almost reach nirvana."

"And the other?"

"Wound up hating each other's guts. That was partly my fault. I really didn't dig deep enough into one of 'em."

"We'll have to think about this," I told him. "It's a big step. And right now I can't afford to have anything less than a clear head. It's a pretty drastic step."

He nodded. "That's understandable. But I might mention something that might come in handy, maybe not. The brain-scan devices have a preset pattern they look for, allowing for variances if bodies have been switched in the electrical and chemical requirements of the new body. It's a points-of-similarity thing, like partial fingerprints. If it gets twenty points of similarity with what's recorded, it says it's you. Under *any* of the induced states, at least for a period of days, the scan machines would recognize those points in either mind. I've been playing with that idea for years, but never had a use for it. Maybe you will."

I looked at him strangely, then had to laugh. "You old anarchist bastard!"

"Things are so bright and clear again," Dylan told me as we sped away from the office. "You don't realize how much you see and hear the Warden organisms between people and things until you're deprived of that contact for the first time in your life. It's like being blind and then suddenly being able to see again."

I could only partly understand that. True, I was aware of the things, and you *could* feel 'em and hear 'em if you concentrated, but they'd become just something that was, something you damped out and never gave a thought to. And that of course may have been what she really meant. You don't notice the noises of the sea, but if they stopped, you sure would.

"You've got to watch yourself now, though," she warned. "You can wake up automatically inducted into the motherhood some morning."

I laughed and kissed her. "Don't worry about it. I can always get my body back if I want to."

We went on to talk about a lot of things, including Dumonia's radical ideas.

"You'd be willing to do that?" she asked. "For me?"

"If that was what you wanted and needed," I assured her. "That is, if we survive the next few days."

She hugged me. "Then we don't have to. Just knowing that you would is more than enough for me. Partner."

"Lover," I retorted, and hugged her back.

Otah's shop hadn't changed at all, nor had Otah himself. He hadn't seen me in some time, though, and looked surprised and pleased to see me, although less so at the sight of Dylan. Still, he pulled himself up as straight as he could and came over to us.

"Qwin! How delightful! I'd given you up for dead!"

"I'll bet," I responded dryly, then gestured with my head to Dylan. "This is my wife, Dylan Kohl."

"Your wi— Well, I'll be damned! And to think you two first met here!"

"We didn't," Dylan told him. "That was somebody else, same body."

That news befuddled him a bit, which I took as a good sign. That meant that Otah had no idea what I had transmitted, or he'd have known of Dylan, Sanda, and the rest. He didn't listen—or couldn't.

"Well, what can I do for you two this lovely day?" he asked pleasantly, and I could see that behind that fat face his mind was trying to figure out how to separate the two of us so he could force a report.

"You can can the act, Otah," I responded, a slight edge in my voice. "I know about the transmissions. I know you get your black-market electronics from the Confederacy somehow in exchange for triggering folks like me."

He laughed nervously. "Why, Qwin! That's insane!"

"No, it's true—and you know it, I know it, even Dylan knows it. Otah, this has grown bigger than you, bigger than the bootleg stuff. I need to call in. I need to call in *now*, consciously, and with full knowledge and memory of the call. You understand?"

"I don't have the slightest idea what you're talking about!"

"No more games!" I snapped. "If you want to keep this sham up, fine. There are other sources. But you'll be long gone to Momrath for inconveniencing me, I promise you. Otah, I'm in the middle of Wagant Laroo's own circle, including the man himself. One word about your off-planet bootlegging activities and you know what will happen."

He sputtered and swallowed hard. "You wouldn't."

"In a minute. Now, let's stop this old school uniform stuff, huh? We got to be friends because that was how you got your payoffs. You used me, and that means I can now use you—or discard you. Which will it be?"

He swallowed hard, shook his head, and sighed. "Come on, it was nothing personal, Qwin. You gotta believe that. I always liked you. It was just —well, *business.*"

"The transceiver, Otah. Let's get this over with. I can only promise you that if you go along, with no funny business, no one will ever know. But we're stuck for time. We're being followed, and I had to get a doctor to remove a couple of small tracking devices placed under our skins without our knowledge. We're going on a real shopping spree and celebration today, hitting all our old haunts, and you're one. But if we take too long here, they'll know."

He looked around nervously. "Come on in the back," he turned and we followed.

The workshop was the usual mess, out of which he dug a helmetlike device and plugged it into what looked like a test bench console, then turned on the juice.

"Looks something like the brain-scan things—the big stuff," Dylan noted, and I nodded.

"It probably is something like that. Otah, without saying the magic words, how's it work?"

He shrugged. "I dunno. The transmission just goes out through the antenna on the roof I use for routine communications. I guess it's scrambled and picked up somewhere else on Cerberus, then beamed to satellite, and then to who knows where. All I know is you come in, we talk, I wait until we're alone and say—well, the key words—and you and I walk back, turn the thing on, plug it in. Then you put it on and go into a trance for a couple of minutes. Afterwards you take it off and come back out, and I spot you and make some inane comment and you pick up the conversation from there, just as if you never left."

I nodded. "Okay, good. Go on back out to the shop until I need you. Dylan can stand watch."

"Suits me," he responded nervously, and left.

I looked over the helmet. "It's a simplified version of a readout used b the Security Clinic," I told her. "It *is* something like a scan device, only it transmits the information."

"I thought that was impossible," she responded. "Nobody but you would be able to receive it."

"That's pretty much correct. Now, don't get alarmed if I go into that trance. Just let it go. Make a brief appearance out front if you want to—I want no interruptions. When I'm through, we'll see what's what."

"Qwin, who's on the other end of that thing?"

I sighed. "A computer, probably. Quasi-organic type. And eventually me."

And so that's where we stand to date. I hope you will evaluate this information and pass it on to the Operator at this point, rather than waiting for a final report which I *will* make—if I'm able.

There is a mild pause, like a break in the static. Suddenly a voice—no, not a voice, really, just an impression of one, forms in my mind.

"I will inform him that the report should be read," the computer says, "but not of its incomplete nature. He will make his own decision."

"Fair enough," I tell the computer. "How long?"

"Unknown. He is distraught over the Lilith report and has refused immediate reading of this one. Perhaps a day."

"How, then, will I get back into contact? I can't draw attention to here."

"We will contact you. Do not worry."

That's easy for you to say. You're only a machine, and you aren't down here with your neck in a noose.

END TRANSMISSION. READ OUT, HOLD FOR FURTHER INSTRUCTIONS.

The observer removed the helmet and sank back in the chair, looking and feeling exhausted. He just sat there for several minutes staring at nothing, as if unable to focus his thoughts or get hold of himself.

"You are upset again," the computer said.

He pointed at nothing. "Is that *me* down there? Is that really me? Is that me so romantically linked, so crazy and so ambitious?"

"It is you. The verifications and patterns show it so."

He chuckled dryly. "Yeah. Quantitative analysis. Boil everything down to nice, neat little numbers and symbols. It must be nice to be a computer, not to give a damn that everything you ever thought, ever believed, about yourself and your society is being ripped apart bit by bit, piece by piece."

"Both of us are the sum of our respective programming," the computer noted. "Nothing more—or less."

"Programming! Aw, what's the use? You're incapable of understanding this. I wonder if anybody is. Nobody's ever been put through this before—and shouldn't be, again."

"Nonetheless, we have learned much. If the Cerberan unit were to be terminated right now, we would be far ahead. We know now how the robots are programmed. We know that the point of contact between alien and Diamond is inside the orbit of the moons of Momrath. We also are in a position to strike a blow against those robots, even if we have not yet solved the puzzle."

"I'm not going to recommend frying Cerberus!" he snapped. "Not now, anyway."

"The station and Laroo's Island would be sufficient, don't you think, to put more of a crimp in the operation than even killing one of the Lords, or even all four?"

"Yeah, you may be right. But if I report this, they're going to recommend taking the whole planet out anyway. As Laroo, I think, pointed out, that might provoke a confrontation—and it would eliminate the robot threat. Without Cerberus, they couldn't program the things with real minds."

"Why do you hesitate? Ordinarily you would think nothing of such a step."

"Why—" He paused, sitting back down. "Yeah, why do I?" he asked himself aloud. "What's it to me?" That was his training and experience talking, but that was only his intellectual side. There was another side of him, one he had never suspected, that had now revealed itself not once but twice. With Lilith he'd finally convinced himself that it had been an aberration. He was a technological agent, and in a nontechnological society he'd had to change and compromise. But Cerberus? The excuse was gone in that situation. And yet, and yet—had only his twins down there changed?

Still, there was only one thing to do, and he knew it.

"If it makes your decision any easier," the computer put in, "the elimination of Cerberus would not stop the robot operation, only set it back. As long as any of the Cerberan variant of the Warden organism remained in alien hands, it could be used anywhere in-system. We had the indication that it already was being so used. Nor is it yet the time to provoke a confrontation. We have insufficient data yet to get such a resolution through Council for the sector's elimination. All we might accomplish at this point is a refusal to defend by the enemy, the elimination of the Warden system or its neutralization, and we would then lose all links with the enemy."

He considered that, and it made sense. "All right. Transmit the proposal and problems to Security Central and get an evaluation and recommendations."

"Being done," the computer responded.

CHAPTER EIGHTEEN

R&D—And a Split Decision

I notified Bogen that I had initiated the contact and could only wait for results. It would be a nervous time, I knew. The only bright spot was that Dylan was so much fresher, so much more alive, her old self again in spades. If it hadn't been for the noose, those next three days would have been among the happiest and most satisfying of all my time on Cerberus.

At the end of the third day, though, I received a call from someone I didn't know and from a place I couldn't guess. I knew Bogen had the phone bugged and traces all over the place, but somehow I doubted his ability to do much about this.

There was no visual, only audio. "Qwin Zhang?"

"Yes?"

"Your proposal has merit, but nothing can be done without a physical sample."

I held my breath. "How much of a sample?"

"About fifty cubic centimeters of brain tissue and another fifty of other random tissue should suffice. Is this possible?"

"I'll see," I told whoever or whatever it was. "How do I let you know?"

"We'll be in touch." The line was dead.

Dylan came in. "Who was that?"

"You know who," I responded. "Time to call Bogen from the security shack."

Bogen insisted on talking to me directly, so I got on the line.

"They contacted me. They need two tissue samples."

He nodded. "Figures. We anticipated that. Just out of curiosity, though —how did they do it? You haven't been out all day and you haven't received any phone calls or messages."

"They called. On my phone. Surely you tapped it."

He looked more than a little nervous. "We sure did. And your quarters, too. I'll check it out, but nobody called me from the monitors like they were supposed to. I don't like this at all. They shouldn't have power like that—not here."

He switched off, but I understood his concern and waited at the shack for a reply, which wasn't long in coming.

"Did you check the phone?" I asked him.

He nodded worriedly. "Sure did. No calls of any kind. And we ran the recording of our bugs in your place, too. You wouldn't be kidding us, would you, Zhang? There's nothing on that tape but normal noises. No conversation on the phone at all, although we do hear your wife come in and ask 'Who was that?' and you reply."

I whistled. I *was* impressed, and so was Bogen—although not in the same way. "So what's the answer?"

"You'll get your tissue."

"Shall I pick up or do you deliver?"

"Very funny. No, it should be picked up, if only because I want to see how they collect the sample."

"I'll get a boat started up," I told him.

"No. As a precautionary measure, Chairman Laroo has ordered that you never set foot on the island again, and security will fry you if you try."

"That wasn't part of the deal!" I protested, feeling a sinking sensation in my stomach. If Security went along, I *had* to be there.

"We changed it. You're an admitted assassin, Zhang, and we don't minimize your skills. We can't afford to take the chance."

"But I'll *have* to come in if they give me anything."

"Nope. If anything physical is required that we can't handle, you will send your wife. Between the psych implant against killing and the fact that she's native here, we feel more secure."

"I don't want to involve her! The deal's off!"

He laughed evilly. "Well, that's okay, but if it ends here, so do the both of you. You knew that when you started this. Our terms, or forget it. Now, send her over in two hours exactly."

"All right," I sighed. "We'll play it your way—for now. But wait a minute. She's of the motherhood. She's prohibited from ocean travel."

"By whom? By authority of Chairman Laroo she's been waived of that requirement. Anybody gives you trouble on it, tell 'em to call me."

"But I thought she had a psych implant against it."

"We had Dumonia remove it. It wasn't much anyway. Go ahead. We're wasting time."

I switched off, feeling less than confident now. This change in the ground rules was hairy indeed.

Dylan, however, didn't mind at all. "We're in this together, remember."

I nodded, and could do nothing but see her down to the docks and off. She was excited to be on a boat again, for she really *did* love the sea. She was gone about five hours, a time in which I became increasingly worried and nervous. When she finally returned I was still apprehensive.

"They didn't do anything to you, did they?" I asked her.

She laughed. "No. Mostly I took the wheel and had a little fun. That's a gorgeous place inside there, though. They only let me on the main floor, handed me the sealed, refrigerated case here, and marched me back."

I looked at her nervously. Would I know if they'd replaced her with a robot? Would I *know* if they'd pulled a fast one with the psych machines?

Well, I'd know the robot situation if we swapped during the night, and I felt reasonably confident that at this stage they wouldn't risk it. For the other, I'd need Dumonia—if I could trust him.

Suddenly I stopped short. "That son of a bitch!" I muttered. "That crafty old anarchist!"

She looked at me, puzzled. "What? Who?"

"Dumonia. He's ahead of both Laroo *and* me. He knew this all along, set me up for it."

Points of similarity indeed. He knew damned well what he was saying when he told me that.

We just brought the case into the apartment and then waited for more instructions, which didn't come. Finally, we got tired of waiting, caught up on some routine paperwork, and went to bed.

In the morning the case was gone. I reported the theft to Bogen, who sounded none too thrilled about it all. He'd had lenses, agents, and a full security system trained on the place, and nobody had seen a thing. Worse, at least five separate tracing devices had been placed inside the case, all of which had functioned perfectly, apparently. At least they still were— they said the case was still in the apartment. The trouble was, no amount of detection and searching could reveal it, although they finally came up with a tiny recording module, something like a tiny battery, wedged inside the floorboards.

Sure enough, it nicely broadcast exactly all five tracing signals.

Bogen was both furious and unnerved by it all. I knew damned well that a far different account would reach Laroo, one in which Bogen didn't look so bad.

I had to admire the Confederacy's other agent in this area, who seemed head and shoulders above even me, at least in audacity. In fact I was so impressed that when he called and made an appointment for us to go and see him, I could hardly wait.

The samples had been gone nine days, and during that time little of interest happened in any direction, except Bogen was becoming more impatient and threatening toward us. Both Dylan and I started becoming a little fidgety.

Finally, though, the call I'd been expecting came, and off we went, almost certainly unsuspected by Bogen and his other people.

"I always wondered how and why you thought you could talk so freely in here," I told the agent.

Dr. Dumonia smiled and nodded to the two of us. "Oh, it's a couple of modern wonders, really. The fact is, the place *is* bugged and Bogen's people are right now hearing us talk. They're just hearing something quite different. It's so pleasant to work in a technological environment that's a few decades behind what's current."

"You and your anti-Confederacy anarchism. I *knew* there was something funny about you, almost from the first, but I missed which side you were on."

"I'm on my side, of course. So are you two—on your side, that is. I'm not a fraud, and everything I told you is true. I *detest* the Confederacy.

If I could be sure these aliens of ours wouldn't eliminate our whole race I'd cheer 'em on as they attacked. There would be no better shot in the arm for humanity than a good old war, as long as the race survived to build and grow. I'm a psychiatrist and I like my creature comforts and my profession, too."

"Then why—why work for them?" Dylan asked, puzzled.

"Oh, I don't *work* for them, exactly. On Cerberus, I just about *am* the Confederacy, which I consider a delicious joke on all of them. It has to do with the way I look at history and society. Qwin here might tell you more about that. I don't really feel like philosophical chats right now, there's too much to be done. Let's just say that I use them, and they use me, and we both profit. I also use Laroo and his people and system. All to the end of living exactly the life I want, doing what I most love to do."

"I don't understand why they sent me at all," I told him honestly, and with the respect one professional offers another. "You could have done everything easier and with less risk yourself."

"Well, that's not true. If I got anywhere near Laroo, or particularly his island and his projects, I'd put myself in severe and immediate danger, and I'm just not willing to do that. As I said, my activities are designed to keep me in my own personal nirvana as long as possible. Indefinitely, I hope. So I'm not the active sort. Laroo wouldn't trust me near him or his babies simply because I know too much about him, know him too well." He grinned. "He thinks I had a partial mindwipe about that, which is the only reason I'm still here. But on a secondary level, I'm too close to the problem. I've been here too many years, know too many people. My objectivity is askew. A fresh analytical mind was needed to filter the information. Besides, this way it's *your* neck, not mine."

"But you said you didn't care if the aliens attacked," Dylan noted, still trying to figure him out. "Then why help against this thing at all?"

He became very serious. "The ultimate threat is those creatures out there. Perfect organisms, superior in every way. *Homo excelsus*. And all totally programmable. Totally. Everybody's programmed, of course, by what we call heredity and environment. But we have the ability to transcend much of that, to become what the programming never intended. That's why no totalitarian society, no matter how absolute, in the whole history of mankind has been able to eradicate the individual human spirit. These—robots—are the first true threat to that. *They can't outgrow their programming.* Speaking euphemistically, I have to say they scare the shit out of me."

We both nodded. "So where do we go from here?" I asked him.

"All right. We've analyzed and dissected and played with all those samples. I'll tell you the truth: Dr. Merton is correct. We have no idea how to duplicate that stuff, how to make it ourselves. It's beyond us. Which is all to the good, I think. I wouldn't want us in that business, either, although Lord knows they'll try. That's the bad news, sort of. The good news is that

though we can't make it or quite understand how it works, we know how
to work it, if that makes sense."

"Not a bit," I told him.

"Well, I don't know how to make a pencil, but I know how to use one.
Even if I'd never seen one before, I could still figure it out. The operation,
that is. We have an infinitely complex variation of that same idea here.
Now, if the basic obedience programming were in the very chemical
makeup of the thing, we'd be up the creek. No way to deprogram without
dissolving it. Fortunately, it's not. There *is* a programming device inside
each quasi-cell, and it's quite complex and we don't understand it at all.
However, knowing that, we can *add* programming information and be
sure that the information is transmitted and stored via the Wardens the
same way as we swap here. There's an interesting implication that the
thing is designed with Wardens in mind and might not work without
them, which may mean that these things were developed by our aliens
specifically for us here and now on Cerberus, rather than just being a variation of something common in their culture."

"So? What does this all mean?" Dylan asked impatiently.

"Well, half the samples went elsewhere and the other half stayed here,
where my lab handled the practical stuff. Wardens were essential, which
we have in abundance here. It became a fascinating exercise, really. Using
an organism we can't understand at all to influence another we can't build
or duplicate. But with the aid of computers Outside and my lab here, we
finally managed to get a readout. The chemical coding language is quite
complex and not at all human, and that's what took the time, but we
finally got it. Fortunately, the basic obedience stuff is duplicated in every
cell. In fact all the cells, whether brain or tissue, are pretty much the same
and can simply become what they need to be. The programming is rather
basic, as it would have to be, since it's serving as a single base for all the
different robot agents being sent back to all sorts of different worlds, jobs,
and conditions."

"Then you can get rid of it?" I pressed.

"Nope. But we can do the same thing I suggested as regards psych
implants. The aliens have made it impossible to separate the basics without lousing up the cell and triggering this meltdown process. But the cells
are programmable, remember. They have to be. So we can *add* programming to override these initial steps. Cancel it out completely, leaving an
unencumbered mind in a super body."

"Surely Merton would have thought of that," I pointed out.

"Undoubtedly she has," he agreed, "but she hasn't the computer capacity and resources to get a complete readout of the codes, let alone actually
break the language used. That's what stuck them. You wouldn't believe
how much time had to be devoted to *this*. Laroo was right: not every
string he could pull could commandeer that much computer time for that
long without drawing Security like a magnet."

"So we can give him what he wants," Dylan sighed. "How does that gain *us* anything?"

"Well, for starters, we'll need to give you some absolute protection. That can be accomplished simply by making it a complex psych implant using the Security system. Laroo can't break it. Nobody here could break it—or if they can, we've already lost the war. In other words, you can't give the information to 'em unless you want to, which is the only time you'll know it—and you'll just know what to do, not what you're doing. And it'll have to be done one at a time, one robot at a crack."

"But he's only allowing *me* on the island," Dylan pointed out. "Doesn't that mean he'll just make a robot out of me and have it any time he wants it, block or no block?"

"No, and there's an easy way to handle that. Very easy. We add another block, similar to the dozens Security's placed in Qwin's brain over the years, as insurance. There is no human who cannot be tortured, or chemically or mechanically made to spill his or her guts. None. So we use the same methods to make sure that such operations will be fruitless. It's what stopped Laroo from going the robot route with Qwin here right from the start. I'm sure he has some implants like this himself. It's really simple, and one they'll understand and accept right off because they all know the type. Basically, it's a psych command that erases other information if any sort of coercion is used, and can even be triggered voluntarily if need be. He won't *dare* try anything with you. He'll need you totally—and he can use his own psych staff to verify the existence of the erase commands. It protects you—and it protects us."

Dylan looked puzzled by that, but I understood him exactly. "He's telling us that not only can it be triggered voluntarily or involuntarily to erase, but it can be triggered externally, as by a Confederacy agent. Similar to what the good doctor here must have used on Laroo to ensure his own well-being."

Dumonia smiled and nodded.

"But you're *still* going to give him the answer he wants!" Dylan protested.

Dumonia kept smiling.

"Think about it, Dylan," I urged her. "You've seen the way we think long enough. Remember the cells are *programmable.*"

She considered what he said, and I was beginning to think we were going to have to spell it out. Then suddenly I saw her mouth shape into an oval. "Oooh . . . Oh, my!"

"My only regret is that Dylan's going to have to do this all alone," I grumbled. "I hate missing out on the climax of the big scam. After all, it *was* my idea."

"There's a way, you know," Dumonia reminded us softly, but I could see that eager gleam in his eyes. "I set things up in case you wanted to do so."

Dylan looked at him, then me. "I—I'm not sure I want to," she told us. "I'm a little scared of it."

"I told you there was a big risk," the psych admitted. "And I understand the cautions. First, you could split. No big deal there, as long as you wanted to stay together forever, and that's a long time. You could merge into one new personality. Or you could find out that deep down neither of you really like the other. That's particularly the case in Qwin's mind, since he was a *very* unpleasant person until he came here and found his humanity."

She nodded. "I know. That scares me the most, I guess. I love him the way he is now, but I don't think I would like the old Qwin very much at all. He sounds too much like Wagant Laroo."

I looked at her strangely. Her, too?

"There's another possibility," he suggested, sounding slightly disappointed at her reluctance. I think he really *wanted* to pull off that merger or whatever, strictly for professional curiosity or maybe just for fun. "I could manipulate the psych plants so that it would require *both* of you to complete the programming operation."

I looked up at him accusingly. "That's what they recommended right along, wasn't it? To make sure that neither of us could be held hostage to the other's cooperation."

He coughed apologetically, then shrugged and gave a wan smile. "So would I be a good doctor if I didn't point out all the interesting alternatives?"

"Then we go together, whether they like it or not," Dylan said firmly. "That's good." She hesitated. "But won't this operation point an arrow straight back to you? Won't they *know* who had to be the one to give us the information?"

"If it works, it's academic," he told us. "If it doesn't, or if anything goes wrong, well, I have contingency plans. Don't worry about me. I cover myself pretty well."

"I'll bet you do," I said dryly. "Well, let's get on with it."

As I predicted, Bogen *didn't* like the revised plan, not one bit.

"What could I do?" I asked him innocently. "Here we were going down the elevator from Dumonia's office and suddenly, bang, out go the lights for both of us. We wake up half an hour later halfway across town, with the briefing identically planted in our minds and the blocks in place. You know your men lost us."

He didn't much like *that,* either, but could only glower.

"Well, you got it, though?"

"We got it." I had already explained the terms and conditions, spelling out the protections in pretty absolute terms.

"The boss isn't gonna like this," he growled. "Too much to go wrong. Tell you what, though. Both of you come out to the island this afternoon. Bring your things—it might be a long stay."

I nodded and switched off.

"You really think Laroo will buy it?" Dylan asked worriedly. "After all, he's putting himself in the Confederacy's hands."

"He'll buy it," I assured her, "although cautiously. He doesn't have any choice, as you know who assured us."

"Imagine. The most powerful man on Cerberus, one of the four most powerful in the Diamond, and maybe one of the most powerful men around today, period—and he's scared to death."

"Or *of* it," I responded. "Let's go pack."

CHAPTER NINETEEN

The Final Scam

Dumonia and his psych computers had built a tremendously impressive psychological profile of Wagant Laroo over the years, back from when he first appeared on Cerberus. Like all the world's most powerful men throughout history, his one fear was assassination or even accidental death. This fear had actually been compounded, on Cerberus, where one had the potential of eternal life—and that was the kicker. By now Laroo felt almost omnipotent, but to feel like a god and know you were potentially mortal was unthinkable. The robot was the closest thing to total security he could ever hope to achieve. Even more, it would allow him to leave the Warden Diamond—and return—at will, thus making him certainly the most powerful man our spacefaring race had ever known. Surrounded by a small army of the more obedient sort of organic robots, he would be virtually invulnerable. Freed from all wants and needs of the flesh, and armed with a mind that could operate with the swiftness and sureness of a top computer, he would be a monster such as mankind had never known.

He knew this, and knowing this, his psych charts said, he *had* to take the risk. Add to that the knowledge that one Lord had already been done in, a Lord he obviously respected and feared—and you had the clincher.

I couldn't help but think that Dumonia had had a lot to do with my decisions. I'd been seeing him—and he'd made sure it would be him—about Sanda and Dylan before I ever made the Project Phoenix move, and then I'd done nothing until just the right psychological time—for Laroo. Then and only then had I been willing to take the ultimate risk and had done so practically without hesitation, and with Dylan's full support. I couldn't help wondering how many little pushes and suggestions I'd gotten from him even before I ever heard of him.

It really didn't matter now, though. Now everything would come together—or it would all come apart. Either way, I had no doubt he was protected. And I suspected that if we *did* fail there was a cruiser even now prepared to come in close to Cerberus and fry Laroo's Island to a crisp and us with it.

Dylan and I spent almost a full week in the Castle, mostly enjoying ourselves, although always under the watchful eyes of guards and scanners. She was fascinated by the broad, green lawn, something she frankly had never even conceived of before, and by the museums of stolen goods, many of which I could take pleasure in explaining both the history and something about the culture they came from.

When we first arrived we were taken to Dr. Merton, who ran some tests to verify our psych commands and blocks, as expected, and had done so. Unlike the first time I'd come to the Castle, I wasn't bluffing now, and they confirmed it.

We also revealed, without really knowing or understanding what it was we were describing, the type of equipment necessary for the deprogramming process. Merton checked the information over with interest, obviously understanding it, and assured us that it could be assembled quickly.

Finally, though, and without any real warning, a big transport landed on the front lawn. Out stepped five people as before, only these were far different. Dylan surveyed them curiously from the window. A teenage boy and girl. A tough-looking woman pushing forty, with short gray-brown hair. A short, wiry man of very dark complexion. And finally, a young executive type in full dress suit and black goatee.

"He has quite a collection," I said approvingly. "Nobody there I recognize, from last time or any other time."

"They walk alike," Dylan noted. "Even the women walk just like the men."

"I see what you mean. They're good actors. Damned good."

"How will we know which one is the real Laroo? Or if *any* of them are?"

"That's simple," I replied. "The real one will be the one left alive and kicking at the end."

We were summoned by National Police to the downstairs lab complex, and left immediately. All five of the newcomers, plus Merton and Bogen, awaited us in the lab, where seats had been provided—five seats.

"They even cross their legs the same," Dylan whispered, and I had to suppress a laugh.

We stopped. The goateed businessman proved the spokesman this time.

"Well, well. Qwin Zhang. I hadn't intended that we meet a second time, but you made it unavoidable."

"I'll make it worth your while," I promised him.

"You better," he growled. "I don't like people who make themselves indispensable. You should understand that."

I nodded. "You have a choice. We can call this off and all go home."

He ignored the comment and looked over at Dylan. "A pleasure. I trust all is satisfactory with you now?"

"Extremely," she responded with that old confidence. I could almost read her mind, and I loved her for it. Wagant Laroo would be a pantywaist in a bork hunt.

"You understand there'll be some, ah, tests first?"

We both nodded. "We're ready when you are," Dylan told him. "The truth is, we no more understand this than you do." She looked them all over. "Who goes first?"

"None of us. Yet." He nodded at Bogen, and the security man went out. Two technicians wheeled in a device that was pretty much what we'd described several days before to Merton. It was a hybrid, and obviously had been knocked together, but if Merton thought the thing would work, well, I was willing to trust the expert.

The machine looked essentially like three hair driers on long, thick gooseneck poles leading into a rear electronic console. They brought it in, and with Merton's help fitted it against the instrument cluster that was a permanent part of the lab. Cables—lots of them—were taken from the top rear of the console part and plugged into the instrumentation, and switches were thrown. Merton checked the whole thing out, then nodded. "It's ready."

I looked at the gadget and couldn't shake the feeling that I was about to be electrocuted. According to Merton, it was a variation of the basic psych machine itself, although without a lot of the electronics and analytical circuits. In effect, it would allow Dylan and me, if we concentrated, to send impulses from our own minds to a third. What we were going to do could have been done by computer, of course, but then they wouldn't have needed us. Chairs were brought in and placed under the gadget, and the helmets or whatever were adjusted to hover just over each one.

"Now what?" Laroo demanded.

"We need a robot," I told him. "First we feed the signal into the robot, then you slide a mind in there any good old Cerberan way."

"Merton?" he said expectantly.

The doctor walked over to one of those booths and opened it, obviously prepared for this. The robot inside didn't look like a cadaver this time, but was fully prepped and animated. Still, it had a totally vacant look that would be impossible for a human being to duplicate.

Dylan and I both gasped at the same time. "Sanda!" she breathed.

No, it wasn't Sanda, but it *was* a perfect facsimile of Sanda's current, and Dylan's old, body.

"I see I haven't underestimated the old boy," I muttered. "What a rotten trick."

Laroo—all the Laroos—looked at us with smug satisfaction. "I thought that if you were going to try any funny business, you'd be less likely with somebody you both know and like," he told us.

"You're going to kill her after this works!" Dylan accused. "You know I can't be a party to that. I *won't* be."

One of the Laroos stopped, thought a moment, and I thought I could see his eyes divert to his side. For a moment none of the others moved. Then, interestingly, I saw the teenage girl very naturally reach up and scratch her nose. Goatee paused a moment, then pretended to consider things while glancing idly at the ceiling. Finally he said, "All right. But for reasons you obviously understand, you're making a test *very* difficult— and I will not proceed without one."

I shrugged. "Don't look at me. *I'm* not the one who insisted that the psych inhibitors remain on."

"It wouldn't matter. I wouldn't do that kind of thing anyway," Dylan snapped.

Laroo sighed, and thought again. Finally he said, "Leave us for a minute, both of you. Just wait outside."

"Stuck you, didn't I?" Dylan stated smugly. I nudged her to keep her from baiting him further. Paranoia, psych profile, or not, Laroo was psychotic enough to call the whole thing off if we pushed him far enough. We left and stood outside.

"Don't bait him," I warned her. "There are some things more important to him even than this."

She just nodded and squeezed my hand. We didn't have long to wait, and were soon called back in by Dr. Merton.

"All right," Laroo said, "let's start one step at a time. First we'll just try and clear a neutral body, so to speak. Then I want Merton to check it over, see what can be done, what we can learn. Will you go that far with me?"

We looked around and found that the robot Sanda had been replaced in its booth. I looked over at Dylan and shrugged. She sighed. "What choice do we have? All right."

The robot body produced was impressive. A huge bronze giant of a man with great, bulging muscles. If any one of them looked the part of a superior human being, this male body did.

It too was as blank as you could conceive, and had to be helped to the chair by Merton and two assistants.

"I gather they don't have much basic programming when they arrive," I commented.

"Activate, deactivate, walk forward, walk back, stand, and sit—that's about it," Dr. Merton told us. "They don't need much else, although in a pinch I can feed in some basic additional commands. When you're putting a complex human mind in there, you don't need much."

I could see her point. I took the seat next to the thing and Dylan sat next to me as Merton pointed out which helmet was which.

This point was the most nerve-racking to me personally, since I knew Laroo was as close to totally evil as anyone I had ever met and I hardly trusted him a moment.

The helmets came down and I felt clamps and probes fit into place.

"All right," Dr. Merton said. "You're all set, just like you told me. Do whatever it is you do."

I relaxed, took a couple of deep breaths, heard Dylan doing much the same, then concentrated—no, *willed*—the transfer.

I felt a momentary dizziness, or disorientation, and then it was over. So quick I could hardly believe it.

"That's it," I told them. "Dylan?"

"I guess so. If that funny feeling was it."

The assistants flicked switches retracting the probe helmets and gently lifted them off our heads—all three of us. I got up, as did Dylan, and we stared again at our giant. He looked as blank as ever.

Laroo looked over at Merton. "Anything?"

"Well, we recorded *something*," she told him. "Who knows what?"

Realization came suddenly. *Countermove*, I thought. Laroo's move, really. Merton had created the Merton Process, by which I was here—and in four other places, too. A process that didn't transfer but *recorded* and *duplicated* information in the brain! If she had the key from both our minds, then Laroo no longer needed us at all. It had been a major mistake on my part. I fervently hoped that this hadn't been overlooked by Dumonia or Security.

Two assistants came up with a crazy-looking vertical hand truck, and as we watched, the giant was told to stand, then tilted forward, the platform slipped expertly under, then tilted back so it could carry the thing, which remained rigid. They wheeled him out a side door as we watched, Merton following.

"Where are they going?" I asked curiously.

"First we'll hook him up to some analytical equipment to see if the charge took—or if it did, whether or not we can see it at all," Laroo told us. "After—well, one step at a time."

Several nervous minutes passed, after which Merton reappeared. "Nothing I can measure has changed in the slightest," she told us. "As far as I can see, everything's the same."

Laroo sighed. "All right, then. We have to try a live test. Is Samash prepared?"

She nodded, went to a wall intercom, and called somewhere. I could recognize Bogen's voice, and the surprise when she said Samash. But in less than a minute an unconscious figure was wheeled into the lab, one that looked nothing like the giant. In fact he was the oldest man I'd ever seen on Cerberus, although he was probably no more than in his middle fifties.

"Samash is a technician here on the island," Laroo told us. "He's very loyal and not very bright, but he's handy. And you can see, he's more than overdue for a new body."

"Some new body," Dylan noted.

"Well, now he'll look the part."

"Is he—drugged?"

"Kabash leaves, a substance about which, if I remember, you also know something."

"Oh."

I got the picture. This was the stuff that forced a transfer if anybody else in the area had it or was receptive. Samash was wheeled into the other room, and soon Merton and the techs all emerged. "Give him, say, an hour," she said confidently. "I'll call you."

And with that, we were dismissed. As before, we were fed, and very nicely, too.

"I'm still worried about all this," Dylan commented.

"Want more?" I told her about my fears of Merton.

She sighed. "Well, we did our best, right?"

"We'll see. It isn't over yet."

An hour or so later we *were* called back and found the lab the same except that now the great giant seemed to be sleeping on the table in the center. Of the old body I saw nothing, and guessed it had died from lack of interest.

Even though the giant robot was sleeping, there was no doubt that there was a *person* inside it now. It looked natural and normal; somehow even its sleeping face was filled with an indefinable *something* that had not been there before.

"Wake him up," Laroo ordered.

Dr. Merton and the two assistants stood back, and there was a sudden, almost deafening cymbal-like sound all around. It subsided quickly, and Merton called, "Samash! Wake up!"

The body stirred, and we stepped back to the wall and held our breath. Even the Laroos seemed extremely tense.

Samash's eyes opened, and the face took on a puzzled look. He groaned, a deep bass, shook his head, and sat up on the cart and looked around. "Wha—what happened?" he managed.

"Look at yourself, Samash," Laroo told him. "See what you've become! See what I have given you!"

Samash looked and gasped, but seemed to realize instantly what had happened. He jumped off the cart, stretched, smiled, and looked around, a slight smile on his face. I didn't like the looks of that smile.

"Samash, I am Wagant Laroo. Activation Code AJ360."

The giant hesitated a moment as if puzzled, then started to laugh.

"Samash, Activation Code AJ360!" Laroo repeated uneasily.

Samash stopped laughing and started looking mean and irritated. He turned and pointed to goatee. "I don't take orders from you," he sneered. "Not any more. I don't take orders from nobody! You don't know what you did, Laroo! Sure, I know what Activation Code AJ360 means. But it don't mean nothin' to me. Not me. You fouled up this time, Laroo." He turned, ignoring us all, and said to himself, aloud, "You don't know the feeling! The power! Like a *god!*" He turned back to goatee. "Greater than you'l ever know, Laroo, whichever one of you you really are. You're *through* now!" With that he lunged for the five Laroos.

"Protect me!" screamed the teenage girl we'd rightly fingered, real panic in her voice—and to our shock the other four, plus Merton and the two assistants, all leaped upon the giant with almost blinding speed. In seconds they had pinned him to the floor.

"Oh, my God!" Dylan breathed. "They're *all* robots!"

The girl—Laroo, the real one—stepped nervously to the far wall and tripped the intercom. "This is Laroo. Security on the double!"

On the double was right: we were suddenly flooded with National Police as well as Bogen, arms drawn.

"Stand away from him!" Bogen shouted. "Let him up!"

As quickly as they were on him, they were off. Then it took only a split second for Samash himself, in one motion, to get to his feet and charge Bogen and the NPs.

He never had a chance. As lightning-fast as he was, they were even faster. Beams shot out, covering the giant's body. It was an incredible display, since any one of those beams would slice steel in two and burn, melt, or disintegrate almost anything we knew—and all they did was stop Samash. No, not even stop him, exactly—just slowed him to a crawl. He was almost at them, but they kept firing and stood their ground—and suddenly you could see the beams finally taking effect.

There was a sudden, acrid smell. Samash stopped, looked surprised and more confused than anything, and then, with a bright flash that almost blinded us, ignited and melted down into a horrid little puddle of goo. At the moment of ignition, all weapons stopped firing at the same moment, so no beam went astray—an incredible display.

"*All* of them," Dylan was saying. "Even Merton and Bogen and the cops. *All* of them."

"Except her," I noted, pointing to the still frightened face of the teenaged girl. "That's Wagant Laroo for today."

Laroo regained some of his—her—composure.

"Yes, that's right. All the important people on the island are robots," she admitted. "Normally only two of my party are, but I didn't want to take any chances this time. You can see why."

I nodded. "But you took one anyway. He almost got you, even after taking enough blast to melt the Castle."

She nodded nervously. "We'll have better precautions next time. I really didn't quite expect that."

"Well? What did you expect?" Dylan asked caustically. "You're not exactly the most popular person on Cerberus, you know, and you suddenly gave the old guy tremendous power and a real shot at you."

"Enough for now!" Laroo snapped. "Get out of here, you two! Go back upstairs until I call for you again."

If you need us again, you mean, I thought grumpily.

"Well, at least we proved the system works, I think," I noted, and both of us exited at that line, carefully stepping around the NPs, Bogen, and the still smoldering pile of goo.

"How *did* they stop him?" Dylan wondered later that evening.

"I suspect they trained a bunch of different weapons at different settings on him," I told her. "His cells kept compensating for one kind of charge and he was finally faced with too many contradictory conditions to fight at one time. One got through, damaged something vital, and triggered the self-destruct in the cell units."

She shivered. "It was horrible."

"I don't think we'd have liked Samash, either," I pointed out.

"No, not that. The fact that they're all robots. Even that nice Dr. Merton."

"I know. Even *I* didn't think of that, which shows how paranoid he really is. And damn it, they're so stinking *real!* Bogen, Merton—they were real people. Natural. Understandable. They looked, talked, acted just like normal people." I shivered a bit. "My God! No wonder they haven't found a defense against these things!"

"So now what do we do?" she asked.

I sighed. "We relax, get some sleep, and find out if we still wake up in the morning."

We *did* wake up and were served an excellent breakfast to boot. It was a good sign. After we ate, dressed, and cleaned up a bit we were summoned back down to the lab. Laroo had not changed bodies and was alone now, except for Merton, Bogen, and a figure we both recognized.

"Sanda?" Dylan called.

She saw us and smiled. "Dylan! Qwin! They told me you were here! What's this all about? I don't remember anything since I went to sleep last night back in Medlam."

Dylan and I both suddenly froze, the same idea in our heads, and Sanda, sensing something wrong, stopped too, her face falling and looking a little puzzled. "What's the matter?"

I turned to Laroo. "You did it anyway."

She shrugged. "She was here, prepped and available. We decided to see if Dr. Merton's process would work from what we took off of you."

"I gather it didn't, or we wouldn't still be here," I noted.

Sanda looked genuinely bewildered. "Qwin? Dylan? What's all this about? What are you talking about?"

"That's quite enough, Sanda," Laroo told her wearily. "Go report to housekeeping on the third level."

Suddenly Sanda's manner changed. She forgot about us and her bewilderment, turned to Laroo and bowed. "As you wish, my lord," she said, then walked out. Our eyes followed her in stunned amazement.

"How does it work, Laroo?" I asked. "I mean, what does the programming we're canceling *say?*"

"You don't know? Basically it states that you love, admire, worship, or whatever whoever gives you the activation code, and that you wish to serve only the wishes of that person or that person's designated agents. It's sort of an emotional hook, but it's unbreakable. They genuinely love me."

"Surely you don't activate all of them yourself!"

"Oh, no. But if one of my own robots is the activator, it works out to the same thing, you see. Complicated, though. Takes a computer to remember who loves whom."

"Well, I gather your process doesn't work in recording, anyway," I said, relieved, then turned to Dylan. "Don't worry about Sanda. She's still all there She's just finally in love with somebody else."

Laroo sighed. "Well, we've done what we could. Merton assures me that the language is still gibberish. There's no reason why it shouldn't record and work—but it doesn't. We tried it out not only on Sanda but on three others, varying various factors. It didn't work with any of them. I sadly have to admit that I need you."

Back to my move, I thought, and *thank you, Dr. Dumonia or whoever.*

"Ready now to take the plunge yourself?" Dylan asked Laroo.

She nodded. "But I'll need a half-hour or so in prep. However, I want to warn you—both of you. *Any* funny business, anything wrong with my programming, even accidentally—*anything*—and you won't live a moment. My robots will tear you to pieces, slowly."

"There won't be any double-cross," I assured her. "We have some stake in this ourselves, remember. We're the only two people who *can't* become those robots—and as such, we need you for new bodies at the proper time. It's an even trade."

"It better be." It was that little girl's voice, but that same threatening tone was there.

We waited anxiously for the prep.

To our surprise, the body Laroo had chosen was rather nondescript. Average in almost all respects—civilized world standard male, nothing exceptional, wouldn't stand out in a crowd.

"Still, it makes sense," I told Dylan. "The last thing he wants is to attract attention to himself."

"It's not too bad," Dylan said critically. "Looks a little like you, really."

"Thanks a lot."

In a short time the girl's body was wheeled in by Bogen and the two attendants, and off into the back room. We wasted no time at all giving the jolt to the selected body on the helmet machine, and watched that body get the same hand-truck treatment to the back.

I spent the time looking around the lab, asking Merton a few inane and useless questions and taking in what I could. Something bothered me. Laroo had given in too easily, even considering the stress. Particularly after last night. Something just felt *wrong.* It was a while, though, before I figured out what it was and whispered to Dylan. "Another trick. Don't fall for it."

She frowned and whispered back so low I could barely hear, "How do you know?"

"Those were cameras up there yesterday, I'm sure. Now they're laser cannons."

"You sure they weren't there before?"

"Sure. Otherwise they'd have used them on golden boy. They can track anything in the lab on those camera mounts."

"So he switched during the night."

"Uh-huh. Clever bastard, but hold tight. We got him." His move. No countermove.

A little over an hour later they wheeled the body back out and went through the wakeup routine again. At least this time we held our ears when the cymbals clanged. The man on the table went through much the same experience as Samash had the day before, and when he jumped to the floor, he looked around wonderingly. "Well, I'll be damned!"

Merton went up to him. "Activation Code AJ360," she said to him.

The man paused, smiled, and shook his head. "Nope. There's a little tingle when you say it, like something inside wants to be let out, but it's suppressed, all right." He sighed. "I can see now what Samash must have felt. Like a god!" He turned back to Merton. "You have no *idea* what it's like—oh, of course you do. I forget. It's—unbelievable!" He turned to us.

"Well," he said, "it works. It really works! You have no idea of the *power* I feel. It's almost a strain to slow myself down to your speed just to converse with you. Every cell in my body's *alive!* Alive and sentient! Sentient—and obedient! The power in each is phenomenal! Even I had no idea until now just how powerful and versatile these bodies were. And *no pain!* Every single body has some pain at all points after they're born. We live in it. The rush of freedom—to be totally immune to it—is almost awesome!"

"I wonder, though—if these aliens are so smart, why did they allow this loophole to slip by?" I commented. It was a genuine question that really bothered me.

He shrugged. "I don't know. That bothered me, too—but not now. Nothing," he added darkly, "will ever bother me again. Nothing and no one." He looked back at us. "Now, tell me. Give me one reason why I should allow either of you to live one moment longer."

Dylan looked up at me questioningly, as if to ask, are you *sure* this isn't Laroo?

"Trust me," I whispered beneath my breath, then turned to Laroo once more—the fake Laroo, I was convinced. "Insurance," I told him aloud, hoping his superior hearing would mistake her glance and my comment for reassurance and nothing more sinister. "Remember Samash. And that robot they caught in Military Systems Command. Hard to kill—yes. Superior? Yes. But immortal? No. Not only that, but I think I know, or can at least guess, the alien's insurance policy."

Both Merton and "Laroo" looked startled. "Go on," he urged.

"They—these robot bodies. They'll wear out. They have to, no matter how good they are. What's to prevent a little bit of that programming we dared not touch, the autonomic system's, say, from suddenly stopping at some predetermined point in time?"

He looked nervously at Merton. "Is this possible?"

She nodded. "But not insurmountable. Remember, I have recorded your and other key people's imprints. As long as you update them periodically, as they do in Confederation Intelligence, you can die over and over again—and still live again."

That explanation satisfied him, and also me. "Might I point out, though, that if somebody's not there to clear the next robotic programming, you'll have to go back into a human body again."

"Never!" he snapped. "Once you've been in one of these you can never go back. Not for an instant! Never!" He realized the implications of what he was saying. "Yes, all right. You're right. But you will remain here on the island as my permanent guests. For all time, and from body to body. You say you want to keep your children, raise them yourselves. Very well, do so here, in the midst of luxury."

"Luxury prison, you mean," Dylan responded.

He shrugged. "As you wish. But it's velvet-lined and gold-plated. You'll want for nothing here. It's the best I can do. You and I both know the Confederacy will quickly know that you played false with them. They'll want you at all costs, to erase that information which is probably easily done with a simple verbal trigger—so I can afford you no contact except with my own."

"And if they fry the island?" Dylan asked pointedly.

"They won't," he responded confidently. "Not until they're *sure*. And we'll give them corpses to look at and a really convincing story, not to mention obviously dismantling Project Phoenix. Everything back to normal. They'll believe something went wrong, all right—but it'll be convincing. Believe me."

I sighed and shrugged. "What choice have we got?"

"None," he responded smugly. At that point I noticed he was alone in the center of the room. The laser cannon opened up, and after an incredible time he too was melted. I looked over at the brownish patch left from Samesh, still there despite a strong cleanup effort. My move—success. And check.

Dylan gasped and whispered, "You were right!" Then she hesitated. "How will we know the real one?"

"We won't," I told her. "Just trust me."

We went through three more acts, each one as or more convincing than the first. Each time the robot was suddenly melted. I kept wondering if they'd all be so confident if Laroo told them what had happened to their predecessors.

The fourth one, though, another civilized worlds standard like the others and equally nondescript, was different at the end. He finally smiled when we finished the interminable wonderment conversation and sighed. "All right, that's it. Enough fun and games. I'm convinced." He turned, gestured, and we followed nervously, avoiding the puddles and eyeing those cannon suspiciously. But, this time, we all walked out of the lab.

Bogen awaited us, and bowed. "Did all go well, my lord?"

"Perfectly. Hard as it is for me to believe, it seems as if our friends here really delivered. Take good care of them, Bogen. Give them anything they want—except communication with the outside world. Understand?"

"As you wish, my lord," he responded respectfully.

We all began walking down the corridor and I started singing, softly and lightly, a ditty I neither understood nor had known before, but one I knew the function of quite well.

> "'Twas brillig, and the slithy toves
> Did gyre and gimble in the wabe;
> All mimsy were the borogoves,
> And mome raths outgrabe . . ."

Laroo stopped and turned, curious. "What's that?"

"Just a little light song from my childhood," I told him. "I've been under a hell of a lot of tension the past few weeks, remember, and it's gone now."

He shook his head in wonder. "Umph. Crazy business."

"We'll see you again, won't we?" Dylan asked him innocently.

"Oh, yes, certainly. I have no intention of leaving just yet."

"Maybe a month from now," I suggested helpfully. "At least then we could talk about our lives here."

"Why, yes, certainly. In a month." And with that we went up to the quarters level while he and Bogen went elsewhere.

Freed at last of the constant guard, we walked out onto the lawn and sat in the middle of it, basking in the sunlight and warmth, stripping down and lying next to each other. For a while we said nothing. Finally Dylan spoke. "Did we actually just take control of the Lord of Cerberus?" she asked, wonderingly.

"I'm not sure. We'll know in a month, certainly," I replied. "If he lives to get off this island, he's the real one. If not, we'll just do it again and again until we get it right. But I think he was the right one."

She giggled. "In a month. We have a whole month. Just us, here, with every wish catered to. It'll be a relief. And then . . ."

"It's all ours, honey. All Cerberus is ours. Good old Dr. Dumonia."

She looked startled. "Who?"

"Dr. Du—now why did I bring him up?"

She shrugged. "I don't know. We sure won't be needing a psych any more. Except maybe to get that implant to report out of your head."

"Yeah, but I suppose that Dr. Merton could do that as well. I hope so."

She turned to me. "You know why I love you? You did it all yourself! Without *any* outside help! You're incredible!"

"Well, the Confederacy had to go along with the plan, you know."

"Pooh. You knew it all along. Every single one of your crazy, mad, non-sensical schemes worked. In a little more than a year you went from exile to true Lord of the Diamond."

"And you're the Lady of the Diamond, remember."

She lay idly for a moment, then said, "I wonder if we'd shock anybody if we made love out here?"

"Only robots, probably," I responded, "and we know what they're worth."

She laughed. "Shocking. You know, though—remember when they suggested we put ourselves in each other's minds? Who was that, anyway?"

I shook my head. "Too long ago. I can't remember. Not important, anyway. But why do you bring *that* up?"

She laughed. "It wasn't necessary. I'm a part of you anyway now. And you, me, I believe. At least I can't get you out of my head."

END REPORT. REFER TO EVALUATION. STOP TRANSMISSION STOP STOP.

EPILOGUE

The observer leaned back, removed the helmet, and sighed. He looked weary, worn, and even a little old beyond his years, and he knew it.

"You are still disturbed," the computer noted. "I fail to see why you should be upset. It was a splendid victory, perhaps a key one for us. We will henceforth have our own spy in the ranks of the Four Lords."

He didn't reply immediately. The computer irritated him, and he couldn't quite explain that either. Computers and agents were well matched to each other, and before he had always somewhat identified with the machine. Two of a kind. Cold, emotionless, logical, a perfect analytical working team. Was he in fact irritated at the computer, he wondered, or was it that the machine was such a reflection of his own previous ego and self-image that he couldn't bear the mirror it presented? He wasn't sure, but his mind did seize for a moment on the word *previous*. Curious word. Why had he used it? Had he changed that much?

I haven't changed! he told himself, banging a clenched fist down on the armrest. *They changed. Not me!*

But they are *you,* his mind accused.

What was so different about their missions, anyway? The planets, to be sure, were far more exotic than the majority of plastic and steel worlds he was used to, but not as different as a few on the frontier. Never before had that changed him. What had—down there?

Perhaps it was the fact that they—his other selves—knew that they were down there for life. No check back in, debrief, and lay off until the next mission. No return to the good life and the best the Confederacy could offer. A last mission. No more responsibilities to the Confederacy, no more working for anyone except yourself.

All his life he'd been trained to think in the collective sense. The greatest good for the greatest number. The preservation of the civilized worlds from internal forces that threatened it. As long as humanity in the mass was bettered, they'd taught him, it hardly mattered that a few had to die, innocent or not, or even an entire planet. Bettered. Protected. Saved.

Did he really believe that any more? he asked himself.

Plastic worlds. Did they, then, breed plastic people? Was Dumonia right? Was the alien threat more of a threat because of the way we'd remade ourselves?

And yet the civilized worlds were happy places. There was no poverty, few diseases, no hunger or other forms of human misery that had plagued man through the ages. Not even the frontier, with its vast technological support, was as miserable or threatening as past frontiers had been. He was raised in that culture and, seeing the historical record, believed in it. It *was* better than anything man had ever had before. That was the trouble. The basic puzzle that haunted him. It was neither bad nor evil. It was a *good* society full of happy, healthy, well-adjusted people, on the whole.

That thought cheered him slightly. Dumonia was wrong, too, in believing that the sparks of human greatness were extinguished in such a system. They hadn't been extinguished—they merely lay dormant until needed. The Warden Diamond proved that.

Humanity's strength and hope lay in that dormancy. In the fact that under trial the reserve was there to adapt, to change, to meet new challenges. Dormant but not extinct.

That thought brightened his mood somewhat, although not completely. That was fine for the collective, but not for the individual. Not for one particular individual in five bodies.

Twice now he'd followed himself on dangerous ground. Twice he had seen himself change, in some ways radically, putting aside his self-image, his devotion to duty and ideals—even the ideals themselves. In all cases he'd violated, once and for all, his personal standards, his own sense of himself as a bedrock, the ultimate loner who uses but does not need. These, too, were dormant inside him and came out when—well, when the leash was cut. The leash that bound him to the Confederacy, its authority, principles, and ideals. He had willingly been leashed, and the cut had not been of his own making, but still it was there.

What disturbed him most of all was that he was still on that leash. That very thought was horrible, a violation of all he'd ever stood for or believed in, but it was a truth that had to be faced. Those men down there—they thought themselves trapped, and him the free man. They were wrong. And as they envied him, so he too was envying them.

But, still, there was a mission, a problem. One that even *they* had continued to serve. He could at least address that.

"Evaluation?"

"Correlations with Lilith are fascinating," the computer told him. "There are certain totally irrational common grounds."

He nodded. "I saw them."

"We'll need to get someone out to Momrath, of course, but that may have been done for us from the data sifting in. We will also have to intensify patrols throughout the Warden system, since there *are* points of contact between alien and human here somewhere."

"We should tighten up on vacation resorts back in the civilized worlds, too," he noted. "Obviously that's the key place from which they kidnap their targets. They would have to be missing for at least a week to ten days."

"That can be done only to a point," the computer pointed out. "It would be helpful to know who selects those targets. So far the grand design, the pattern, eludes me, mostly because we do not have enough identified robot agents to correlate their positions. It seems obvious, though, that the aliens are quite subtle."

"We knew that from the start. Who the hell would ever imagine an enemy alien force hiring the chief criminal elements to do all its advance work?"

"I worry that it is more than advance work. Let us postulate one or two conditions that seem reasonable from the facts, bearing in mind that we are dealing with alien minds developed in an unknown evolutionary pattern that might not follow our logic."

"Go on."

"We assume that they are either numerically inferior to our own forces or unwilling to take the casualty rates a direct attack might bring."

"That may be a wrong assumption," he pointed out. "After all, if they can make super-robots like this, they could do their fighting entirely with surrogates."

"Perhaps. But I tend to believe that the processes involved in perfecting these devices is too long, involved, laborious, and costly for such mass production. Instead, I suggest that their plot may be *entirely* on the subtle side. We have been looking too hard at the direct military option."

"Huh? What do you mean?"

"Suppose their plot is to bore from within? To weaken and disrupt key services, key facilities, the bedrock of our economic and social system? A carefully chosen and placed organic robot could do more harm for longer periods than any direct attack by planet killers. I need only look at your own psychological reactions to the Warden to see how easily and subtly we can be turned. The human race and its culture is such that it would destroy itself rather than be conquered from outside. There are parallel among the early independent planets and even earlier, in the age of na tions on a single planet. We have often come very, very close to self-de struction rather than total capitulation. A direct attacker, then, would have nothing to win."

"So you think the choice of the Four Lords was more than just a clever expediency? Hmmm . . . Laroo indicated that Kreegan was the original mastermind; and Kreegan, to be sure, had a penchant for nasty and sneaky plots and behavior." He sat back. "Now, let me get this straight. You're suggesting that the aliens never intend to attack us directly. That the war they chose is the war they are now fighting. That they aim for internal disruption and collapse by exploiting our weaknesses, rather than conquest."

"It makes the most sense."

He nodded. "And it's the least costly of the alternatives. None of *their* people are exposed or jeopardized. The Diamond, and through it the robots, do the dirty work. It's even cost-effective. Assuming you're right—analysis?"

"If the Four Lords are directing things in this manner, and choose properly and correctly, it will work. Not quickly. We might not even *know* or *realize* the extent of their success until it's too late. And with the promise of those robot bodies and the chance to escape, the end could come not by kidnapping key people and replacing them but by mobilizing the best criminal minds of the last seventy years in such bodies and loosing them on an already weakened and infiltrated Confederacy."

The prospect appalled him. "But wait a moment. Only Cerberan criminals could be used. Those on the other three worlds have other Warden variants that won't step aside to allow a Cerberan mind-switch."

"Have you forgotten the Merton Process?"

He whistled and shook his head. "Then finding the aliens, bringing them out into the open, is our only hope. And we have no guarantees that there are any of them anywhere near the Warden system. It could all be handled by robots and third parties hired by the Four Lords."

"Perhaps one of the remaining two will tell us for sure," the computer suggested hopefully. "Or if not, perhaps our in-system patrols will get lucky."

"Correlate and transmit what we've got," he ordered. "We just have to wait and see."

"Done."

The man walked back to the living quarters of the module on the great picket ship, poured himself a drink, and sat down on his bed. All that the computer had suggested disturbed him, but still he couldn't bring his mind to focus for long on the larger problem and plot.

Cal Tremon . . . Qwin Zhang . . . Ti . . . Dylan Kohl . . .

Like some song that gets stuck in your mind and you keep hearing it over and over whether you want to or not.

I can't get you out of my head.

CHARON:
A Dragon at the Gate

*For Art Saha, longtime member of First Fandom,
anthologist of exceptional taste and discernment,
and a Good Man*

CONTENTS

A Time for Reflection

I

The naril circled and positioned themselves for the kill against the backdrop of the onrushing *al*-wind. Opening their razorlike runners, which squeezed out through slits in their skins, the naril started down.

The man looked around frantically without breaking his desperate run. There was little shelter in the desolate desert landscape, and the cracked desert floor was harder than concrete.

The naril were great creatures of the air, huge, speeding black ovals with great egg-shaped eyes that made up what little face there was, tentacles behind shifting subtly to aid in flight as if a solid tail and rudder. Underneath each black horror were the two curved bony plates, almost like rockers, out of which came the deadly sharp steel-like blades with which it would slash its prey.

The man realized that there was no place left to go and decided to make what stand he could here, in the flat open land. One naril swooped down on him, impossibly fast, but he dropped to the ground and rolled an instant before the sharp blades struck, and the naril almost bit into the hard earth and spilled. No such luck, though, and the man was quickly to his feet once more, cursing that he had delayed so long. Taking a quick check of both naril, he knew that he needed both of them in front of him, not flanking as they now were, so he summoned a reserve only impending death could call up and ran at an angle to the two circling monsters.

The naril were quite intelligent, but also overconfident. They had several square kilometers of open country to play around in and never doubted the final outcome. In the meantime, this was fun.

The man stopped once more and whirled again to face his tormentors. As he had hoped, the pair had joined again and seemed to be almost hovering there in the air, their yellow, expressionless eyes watching him and concealing, he had no doubt, some great amusement.

He knew he had very little time.

From the naril point of view he seemed just to stand there, facing them, eyes closed, hands outstretched. They took this act as a gesture of surrender and submission, and, since this sort of thing was boring, moved in for the kill.

They dropped very low, only a meter or so off the desert floor, and sped toward him, relishing the kill. As they neared their intended victim there was a rumbling sound and the earth itself seemed to rupture. Around the man grew a wall of solid stone as he himself sank down into the earth behind it. The predators were so taken by surprise that each struck an opposite side of the still-growing wall. There was a shower of sparks as their sharp runners ground into the stone, but both had sufficient balance to stay aloft and veer off.

Inside the sudden pit, in the darkness surrounded by four meters of stone wall, the man heard the naril hiss in defiance and frustration. He was nearly spent; he had used up half a day's water. The fort would *have* to hold. He sank down, relishing the cool relief his tiny fortress afforded, and listened.

The naril adjusted quickly to the new conditions and tried to break down the walls, hitting them hard and at careful angles. While they managed to do some damage to the rocky fortress, they did even more damage to themselves, since their blades were of bone. They soon gave up the attempt.

Settling down on top of the structure, they blocked what little light was left to the man. He saw that he had judged the side of the pit well; both were too large to get down the chimneylike opening to him.

Ultimately, of course, one of the creatures sat on top of the opening, trailing its long tentacles down into the pit. Again the man had been exacting in his measurements, although it was terrifying to lie there in the bottom, with all light blocked, and hear those tendrils slapping and searching about just a bit above him. Finally that, too, stopped, and he relaxed a bit. He had come so far, so very far, and although momentarily safe, he felt his reserves nearly gone.

He heard the naril shift again, and then he was subjected to the ultimate indignity. Unable to reach him in any other way, they were trying to flush him out by defecating on him.

There was an angry, frustrated growl from above and then the naril moved off, allowing some light inside. He did not kid himself that they were gone. At least one still lurked outside, waiting for him to come up, while the other was most likely now up and away into whatever clouds there might be, soaking up moisture as only naril could. He would have given anything for some of that moisture in a form other than that he now wallowed in.

Clouds . . . He tried to think. What had the sky been like? His attention had been on more immediate stuff. Still, there were always *some* clouds around. High ones, of course, which contained less moisture than he would like, but *some* . . .

Concentrate . . . concentrate! If only he had the strength! With supreme effort he closed his eyes and attempted to shut out all but his sensitivity to the *wa*, an attempt made doubly difficult by the slimy naril feces being baked even more in the heat of the sun and stinking all the worse for it. He too would bake, he knew, if he did not succeed, for his crude fortress was also a crude but very effective oven.

Think . . . think! Think only of the *wa* . . .

He felt the *wa* that built his fort from the start, of course, but those he needed now to shut out. He reached out, *wa* to *wa*, his to those others, and broke free his vision onto the desert floor once more.

Of the naril there was no sign, but there were two bar-bushes nearby that hadn't been there before. Inwardly this made him smile, although he had little to smile about. The naril were intelligent animals, it was true, but barely that. It would never occur to them that bushes in a place like this were as conspicuous as the naril themselves—which is what the bushes most certainly were.

The fact that both waited, so still and patiently in the heat, confirmed his worst fears about them. Trained and under orders they most certainly were, possibly Yatek Morah's own personal hunters.

He felt the *wa* of the thick desert air around them all, but again he ignored it, reaching up, up, ever higher, hoping, praying that somewhere within his range was enough cloud to form what must be made.

It was there, of course, but terribly sparse and high up. He hoped it was enough. It *had* to be enough.

Slowly, carefully, he reached the *wa* of the cloud, of the water molecules, reached and talked to it and carefully guided and cajoled it into patterns, clumps, groups growing thicker and thicker, bringing it together centered on the tiny instant fort far below.

He wasn't sure if he had enough power, but it was all his strength and power could muster. It *had* to be enough. It just *had* to be . . .

Now fly, *wa* of the clouds, fly upward, rise toward the sun your nurturer. Rise . . . rise . . .

The two "bushes" lying in wait outside trembled, shimmered, and were naril once again. They did not quite understand what was happening, but they saw the shadow on the ground and felt its coolness. Great yellow eyes looked skyward and beheld the clouds gathering together, coalescing at hundreds of times normal speed, growing thicker and darker as they did so. The naril did not understand why it was happening, but they knew, could smell and sense, that a small but powerful thunderstorm was building just over them most unnaturally, and they felt real fear. For a moment they were poised between their fear and natural instincts and their command to pursue and kill this man, but as thunder boomed out of the strange, unnatural cloud and echoed eerily across the vast desert, fear and instinct won out. They rose into the air and sped away, toward the sunlit desert outside the boundaries of the clouds' shadow.

The rain came now, falling not heavily but steadily on the small fort and an area of approximately eighty or so meters around it. The man wasted no time in commanding the *wa* of the walls to return to form, and as the walls shrunk, he rose until he stood once more on the desert floor with no sign of structure. The naril feces still clung to him, and he shed all but his empty water flask and black skin belt, letting the rain wash him. For a minute or two he just stood there enjoying the rain and the cool relief it brought, but he knew he dared not linger. There was not much water up there, and it could give out any time.

The recovered naril, understanding that their quarry had somehow caused the storm and regaining their confidence, hovered just at the edge of the clouds, waiting for the rain to end.

The parched ground, which had seen rain perhaps two or three human generations ago and not since, could not absorb the water, and this made the hard ground slippery and treacherous going. As the man moved, the center of the storm traveled with him, keeping him in its center, while at the edges the naril moved at his pace, waiting for the rain to give out. The rain itself would foul the naril's delicate membranous wings, invisible in flight or hover, but once the rain stopped they would move once more.

The man prayed the rain would hold, and it almost did, getting him to within a hundred meters of the mountains before it started to give out. All the *wa* in the world could not conjure more rain if there was no more water to use, and he hadn't time to take the evaporation from behind him and recycle it into the diminishing cloud.

The naril, wary of more trickery and fearful that he had stopped the rain only to lure them in, held back, though, and this extra time gave him the opportunity to run for the rocky outcrops just ahead.

Seeing him sprint, one naril forgot its caution and, hissing, shot out after him, overtaking him just at the base of the rocks and striking him in the back. He flew against the rocks from the force of the blow and gave a terrible scream, but the naril had forgotten to extend its blades, and while the blow was crushing, it neither cut nor sliced.

Though dazed, he managed to crawl into a cleft in the rocks and wedge himself in as tightly as possible. Even so, he knew he was done in, out of strength at last, his bag of tricks used up, the cleft far too shallow to protect him from the naril tentacles. He was done, though; he almost didn't really care anymore. He passed out there, in the rocks, with a last thought that death at least would give him rest.

"Jatik?"

The voice seemed to come from far away. *Go away!* his mind shouted. *I am dead! Let me have my peace!*

"Jatik, you must listen to my voice," it said again, closer now, more commanding, harder to ignore. "Jatik, this is Koril. You must speak to me."

"I die," he muttered, almost angrily. "Let me go."

"Yes, you are dead," Koril's voice agreed. "You are beyond my power or anyone's to save you. Yet while your *wa* still burns and struggles against extinction within you, we may yet communicate. Please, Jatik, you were a brave man and a loyal one. Do not pass until your bravery is given meaning by your words."

He struggled, tried to remember. The words . . . The mission . . .

"Where are the others, Jatik?"

Others? "Dead. All dead."

"Then you are the last. Hurry, Jatik, for time grows short and my power to hold you weakens quickly. I must know. Did you get in? Did you see the meeting?"

Meeting . . . what meeting? He struggled. Oh, yes, the meeting. Oh, God! The meeting . . .

"I—I saw," he managed. "The Four Lords at Diamond Rock. The Four Lords and the others. Oh, God! The others!"

"Those others—think, Jatik! Hold on a bit more! The others! What were they like?"

"Horrible . . . Monstrous. They wore the cloaks of men but could not hide from us. They are terrible, Koril, terrible to behold. Spawns of some hell beyond man's imagination. Slobbering, horrible . . . Such as they were born in some hellish place far removed from man."

"The Four Lords—there is an alliance?"

"Yes, yes! Oh, God! You must destroy them, Koril! You must not let them sell man out to such as these! Horrible! You cannot know! I pray to God you never know. Their very sight was enough to drive Latir and Mohar mad."

"What do they look like, these spawns of hell? Think, Jatik! Hold on!"

"Look like! My mind holds what little it still has by putting that likeness from it. Monstrous . . . Pulp . . . Slime . . . They are evil, Koril! Evil in ways no human can comprehend. They will devour man and then they will devour the Four Lords and us. You must . . ."

"*Jatik! Jatik! Hold on!* Just a little more! *Jatik!* Come back! I need to know . . . Oh, hell, what's the use? He's gone."

Koril sighed and shook his head, then got up from beside the dead man and looked around his desert domain. The bodies of the two naril still twitched nearby where he had slain them.

He spent the better part of an hour restaging the death scene. Sooner or later he knew that some party from Diamond Rock, even now covering the trail of chase and capture, would happen here, and he wanted to make it absolutely certain that any such party would draw the obvious conclusions. Essential to him was that party's belief that the naril and Jatik had finally finished each other. They would believe it. To get even this far required one of enormous power, and even so, only seeing the dead man's rainstorm from afar and recognizing it for the signature it was had brought him here. Too late, alas, too late for poor Jatik . . .

Still, he had learned much from the dead man. Or, more properly, Jatik had confirmed his information and his worst fears. But Koril was old—old and alone now. Power he had in abundance, but there were limits to an old man's endurance even with the best of powers.

He needed a new Company, he knew, and that would not be easy to assemble, particularly under Matuze's watchful eye. While she would assume that his messengers had all failed to report, there was no question that she would recognize the dead for who they were and guess who had sent them.

Still, he knew his course was already set and his resolve was firm. No matter what the odds, it must be done. There was no getting around the shock and revulsion of Jatik's last utterances. Both he and the dead man had been born and raised on worlds far from this one, and both had seen a lot in this universe before being exiled to this hell.

Hell . . . That was Charon, true enough. Every horror in the mind of man from the beginning of time to now was here, along with a physical landscape, climate, and plant and animal life appropriate for the worst of Dante's hells.

Koril knew this for a fact, and he knew that Jatik also knew and felt it. What could a man already in hell see that so frightened him?

What sort of thing could cause a criminal imprisoned in hell with thousands of other criminals to label something unimaginably evil?

What was so monstrous that even the denizens of hell were repulsed and frightened by it?

Jatik had been a sadistic mass murderer without the slightest sense of good and evil. The very concepts had been alien to him. And yet, and yet —even he had now seen something so terrible that he *had* known evil before he died. There was a certain symmetry in that, anyway.

Still, the Four Lords had made a compact with whatever it was here on Charon. Their egos would protect them, Koril reflected sourly. For a while, anyway.

The Four Lords were evil by human standards. They were evil personified to many, including the Confederacy itself. But they had not been evil to Jatik, not in the slightest.

Just what *had* Jatik seen? Into what terrible bondage had they sold themselves and mankind on their own egomaniacal delusions of grandeur?

It was almost as hot as a human being could stand there on the hard, desolate desert, yet Koril felt a sudden chill as he turned and walked away from the body of the dead man.

2

The most frustrating thing to a great military force is to discover that it is at war only long after the first blows of the enemy have been struck. Even more frustrating is when, even after the discovery of enemy action, you simply can't find the enemy.

The Confederacy was the culmination of all human history and culture.

In the distant past, man had determined that expansion to the stars was the most interesting and preferable means of advancing civilization without racial suicide. Somehow the sporting instinct overrode all else in the human condition when the proposition was put correctly. National competition was something all people, regardless of background or ideology, could understand. They could work for, root for, and cheer on their home team against all comers.

As politics became dirtier and more and more irrational in the twentieth and twenty-first centuries, and total global annihilation grew more and more certain, man remembered that he had first set foot on the Moon because it had been sold as a sporting wager—a space race. Not that space had been ignored since—in fact, every country had been involved—but it had been a slow technocratic and military growth that sputtered here and there for lack of popular participation and support. Anybody with the spirit could try the Oregon Trail in the nineteenth century, or carve a city out of frozen Siberian tundra in the late twentieth, but the very people who were the pioneers of ancient times were excluded from this new frontier, no matter how limitless it was. The poor, the destitute, and the refugee as well as idealistic dreamers had settled and tamed the old frontiers, but they couldn't even get a ticket to the Moon in the age of space. Only the highly skilled specialist was able to get into space—or the very rich. The masses of Earth, even if they wanted to go, could not, nor did the dull and plodding development of space offer the same excitement that the space race had generated in the early explorer.

The governments of Earth came to understand this, and also saw a world of ever-increasing population and incredibly diminishing resources grow more and more apathetic toward life in general. A steady decline in living standards worldwide was something that every computer forecast as inevitable, and each group's demand that *its* country not be the one in decline put tremendous pressures on even the most totalitarian regimes and increased the pressure for total war.

Technology, however, offered a way out, a way that the various nations took reluctantly but with the realization that there was little else to do. Researchers had ultimately done the impossible and broken the universal speed limit. It was complex, and involved physics that did not contradict Einstein so much as deal in totally different areas where he was simply not relevant. The stars were open to exploration. Not that the distances were shrunk to nothing: within the first century, there were so many new places to go over such vast distances that it still took more than three years subjectively to travel from one end of man's domain to the edge of the frontier. This was still a far smaller price to pay than the generations such trips would otherwise have taken. It had, after all, taken some of the early American pioneers four to six months to reach California. But this new system had another big advantage. Building the ships and great engines needed took a lot of capital, but once built, they cost very little to operate, and size was not a factor in cost beyond air and food.

Only one world in a thousand was even terraformable, but there were *still* a lot of habitable worlds out there, and the nations of the world began to compete for them instead of for more tufts of worn-out Earth—and colonizing with incentives, so the poor and the dreamers finally got to go. It took the pressure off and provided a new spark to humanity. There was excitement and discovery in the air once more and all could be a part of it, and the resources were infinite.

But as generations were born on new worlds, generations who had never seen Earth and had only an abstract concept of what a Russia or an America or a Brazil or a Ghana was, the old concepts of nationality began to blur. Three generations later they were no longer Americans or Soviets or Brazilians but were natives of their own worlds, the only worlds they knew. Nor did the distance between worlds and the burgeoning numbers of worlds lend themselves to effective colonial government from afar. Fearful now less of destroying one another than of being left behind, cast off by the new populations on alien worlds, the old governments began to co-operate more than compete, to merge, over little more than another century, into what was in effect a single ruling instrumentality, the Confederacy, with a bureaucracy dominated by those old powers but presiding over a congress where each new world was represented.

The pooled resources and ever-expanding technology remade world after world, many into great paradises of which the people of old Earth had barely dreamed. Many diseases were wiped out; genetic manipulation made man and woman beautiful and nearly perfect. Careful genetic and cultural nudging produced a population each of whom had an equal but large slice of a very huge pie. People were bred and raised to do specific jobs, and they were the best people to do those jobs, too. It was a civilization without tension or fear—nearly a paradise. Worlds that reached such perfection were called the civilized worlds. Though wonderful places to live and work, these worlds were spiritually and culturally dead—totally stagnant.

Obviously the Confederacy could have totally controlled population and settled into this stasis, but they were the heirs to all of Earth's own history. Humanity might last in paradise for a million years, but once the spark of excitement and creativity was extinguished, it was dead, an extinct race. The answer, of course, was never to stop. Scouts would continue to be dispatched, scouts that would discover more and more worlds to settle, tame, and remake by the oddballs and misfits that even the civilized worlds occasionally created. The frontier became not merely the edge of expansion but a religion, an article of faith among the Confederacy, something that could never be allowed to stop because it alone provided the safety valve, the creativity, the spark, the purpose to human existence.

As man filled up almost a quarter of his galaxy, he ran into some alien races. Not too many—and not nearly the number many had expected—but some. There were ones that inhabited worlds that no human could ever use, and these were simply watched for signs of future threat and generally ignored. Others used the same sorts of material as man, and these were treated in an age-old way. Those that could be modified and adapted to the Confederacy's way of doing things were welcomed into it, whether or not they wanted to come. Those that could not be culturally assimilated for one reason or another were ruthlessly eliminated, as many of the Indian tribes of America and the aborigines of Tasmania had been eliminated in ancient times. Many alien worlds were primitive and some were quite advanced, but all had one thing in common: the Confederacy was bigger and stronger and more ruthless than they were.

Then one day the powers that be in the Confederacy woke up to the fact that the moment they feared had finally arrived—somebody smarter than they were had found them first.

3

He reentered his command module from the great picket ship that was always on station near the Warden Diamond, just beyond the life range of the Warden organism. Totally protected, it was a great city in space with all the amenities, offering both comfort and security. Still, none of the thousands aboard the combined research and quarantine enforcement ship knew what the man was doing there, nor could they enter or in any way discover the secrets of the module.

"You have been away more than three days," the computer chided him. "We have had an incoming data report from Charon all this time."

"I know, I know," he grumbled. "I just . . . needed some time, that was all. I needed a little contact with the Confederacy and its people." It shamed him a bit to admit that last, even to himself, such a blow was it to his self-image, but he was not the same man who had first entered this module so long ago. The experience he had shared with his counterparts on Lilith and Cerberus had changed him greatly, and he really didn't like it one bit. It wasn't as if he were getting reports from agents down there: hell, those people were *him.*

The sociopathic worlds of the Four Lords were a contradiction of every single principle and belief he'd always held so dear. It wasn't so much seeing the Confederacy and its values the way the criminals did—that was excusable, since he was dealing with psychopaths of one sort or another. But when he himself down there on those worlds began to doubt and finally fractured all those bedrock ideals—well, that was something else again.

The Confederacy did not look so good, so much like paradise, when viewed from outside, and that view was difficult to refute. He feared for his own sanity most of all, and that made him fear another report, another secondhand life, yet another insane challenge to his orderly universe. He knew it, understood it, but that didn't help much at all.

The fact was, he most of all didn't like discovering that he was as human as all the others in the human race, subject to the same fears, emotions, and failings. He had always thought himself superior, above all that. No more, no more . . .

Nor had it escaped him that he was learning too much, knew too much even at this point. He was a tool of the Confederacy, just as a saw, drill, hammer, or—well, computer—was a tool. Useful to get the job done; then, as if such a tool grew, say, radioactive, readily destroyed when the job was over. He wasn't kidding himself. They didn't even have to worry about keeping any sparks alive within him—four of him were already down there, on each of the Warden worlds.

The moment he solved the riddle of the Four Lords of the Diamond he was a dead man. His faithful computer might jettison the module into the sun or explode it, might supercharge it with electricity. The worst part was, he couldn't even opt out now, not even with a mindwipe. They'd just trot out the Merton recording, make another him, have that new him go through the same experiences—and reach the same point he was at right now.

But *he* would have to solve the puzzle first. He and he alone—not even the computer—would decide that terrible moment. It was an ironic, terrible box, and he knew it. The fate of human civilization, perhaps human life, was very much in his hands. Yet he could save them or himself—not both.

His final, agonized decisions were nonetheless a compromise. First solve the puzzle. *Then* decide what to do with that solution. What troubled him most was the nature of that decision. He suspected even now that the nature of this alien threat was not as good and evil as he had originally believed.

He sat down at the lab screen and thought a moment. "Put up a wide scan of the Lilith organism," he told the computer.

The screen in front of him lit up and showed a strange enlargement. Its closest relative was a virus, yet it was infinitely smaller, an alien abstract design of tiny lines and pits actually able to combine on an atomic level with actual molecules—*molecules!* It wasn't a real creature but a few extra chemical ingredients on the end of a molecular formula, extras that somehow didn't really change what the molecule was but nonetheless controlled it. Once organism and molecules were linked, to remove the organism from inorganic molecules was relatively simple—they were always on the end. But in carbon molecules the Warden was not at the end at all but in the middle. Remove the Warden from a carbon chain and the chain fell apart—and so did the individual it helped make up. In much the same way, the synthetics with their odd and unnatural chains attracted the Wardens as carbon molecules did, but while the Wardens wormed their way in, they couldn't stick. Synthetics disintegrated.

There was an advantage to that, from the Confederacy point of view. It kept the Four Lords and their worlds technologically far behind the Confederacy, and limited their industry to what they could take from their own worlds and from the asteroids and other space junk in the system that the Warden somehow recognized as "natural." In fact there were no important heavy metals on any of the Diamond worlds; mines on the asteroids and on the moons of the nearest gas giant, Momrath, provided the raw materials for the Warden worlds that could use *any* machines. Many down there could easily build an interstellar spacecraft, but they didn't have the materials to do so.

And yet, and yet . . .

That *thing* on the screen couldn't possibly be alive, not in any sense that any biologist understood life. More than that, it didn't *fit*, not on the Diamond. The four worlds down there were very different, yes, but every one of them—*every* one—was composed of logical, rational, carbon-based life. Most of it wasn't nearly as exotic as life on most planets in and near the Confederacy itself, yet it was consistent and logically there.

But nowhere was there any sign of anything else like the Warden organism. It didn't belong there, not on those worlds. It had no clear ancestors, no relatives, no dead ends. In fact, it had no place or reason to evolve down there.

"The remote probes—the ones that preceded the initial landings on all four worlds. Why didn't those core samples show the Warden?"

"The instruments were not really designed to look for something like it," the computer replied. "Only after they knew something was there could they find it."

"Mighty poor procedures," he noted. "The whole idea of an exploration is to find just such new threats as this."

"If a question has not been asked it will rarely be answered," the computer responded philosophically. "In other words, nobody can think of everything. Still, why the interest in the old samples? Surely you don't think the Warden organism itself can be the aliens?"

"No, of course not. It's an incredibly odd and alien thing, but even in its collective mode it's hardly capable of a consciousness. You know, there are worlds in our catalogue where this thing wouldn't really shock me or any of the scientists one bit—but not here. The thing doesn't fit here. It's as if an iceberg were suddenly found on a tropical world—it just doesn't logically belong there."

"A number of researchers and theorists have noted as much. Some have even theorized an interstellar origin—it arrived, perhaps in a meteorite, and set up housekeeping. That is the prevailing theory."

He nodded. "But why just on Lilith? Or *was* it just on Lilith? How do we *know* we were the carriers to the other three worlds? Perhaps by the time we found the thing all four had already *been* contaminated, if they were."

"It has been postulated that the Wardens existed on all four worlds, too," the computer told him. "Sampling work was taken from a base ship that was actually beyond the life range of the Warden organism. However, since plant life did not disintegrate in the Warden manner it was simply assumed that the Wardens were not yet there."

"Assumed . . . I wonder. What about the plant samples from Lilith, then?"

"I just checked on that. The fact is, *all* vegetation died in the samples from Lilith, but there were a thousand natural explanations and it was not taken as a terrible sign. It wasn't unusual enough in general surveys of alien worlds, really. Many alien plants are interdependent on organisms and conditions requiring exacting biospheres to survive—a minuscule change in pressure or temperature, for example. Although Lilith's samples died first, all of the samples died within a period of a day or two at most. This is normal and expected. You can't possibly hope to duplicate every exact condition for totally alien forms of life. Still, your proposition is now beyond proof. All four worlds have the Warden organism."

"Still, it is an interesting speculation."

"Why? If the alien-spore theory is correct, and it seems most logical, it might easily hit all four as one. That proves nothing."

"Maybe not," he murmured to himself. "Maybe . . ." He got up and walked forward to the control area. "Who's in?"

"Charon."

"Too bad. Most of all I want Medusa now, I think. I'm beginning to think the confirmation of my theories must lie there—and perhaps beyond. I suspect that Charon's not going to add any new pieces."

"You're sure you just aren't trying to avoid the experience?"

He stopped and looked around quizzically. Was he? He *did* dread this new experience, it was true, but was he kidding himself, or the computer?

He sat down in the master command chair and adjusted it for maximum comfort. The computer lowered the small probes, which he carefully placed on his head; then the thinking machine that was part of the module itself administered the measured injections and began the master readout.

For a while he floated in a semihypnotic fog, but slowly the images started forming in his brain as they had before. Only now they seemed more definite, clearer, more like his own thoughts.

The drugs and small neural probes did their job. His own mind and personality receded, replaced by a similar, yet oddly different pattern.

"The agent is commanded to report," the computer ordered, sending the command deep into his own mind, a mind no longer quite his own.

Recorders clicked on.

Slowly the man in the chair cleared his throat. He mumbled, groaned, and made odd, disjointed words and sounds as his mind received the data and coded, classified, adjusted, and sorted it all out.

Finally the man began to speak.

CHAPTER ONE

Rebirth

After Krega's talk and a little preparation to put my own affairs in order—
this would be a long one—I checked into the Confederacy Security Clinic.
I'd been here many times before, of course, but not knowingly for this
purpose. Mostly, this was where they programmed you with whatever information you'd need for a mission and where, too, you were "reintegrated." Naturally, the kind of work I did was often extralegal—a term I
prefer to "illegal," which implies criminal intent—and much of it was simply too hot ever to be known. To avoid such risks, all agents had their
own experience of a mission wiped from their minds whenever it involved
sensitive matters.

It may seem like a strange life, going about not knowing where you
have been or what you've done, but it has its compensations. Because any
potential enemy, military or political, knows you've been wiped, you can
live a fairly normal, relaxed life outside of a mission structure. There's no
purpose to coming after you—you have no knowledge of what you've done
or why or for whom. In exchange for these blanks, an agent of the Confederacy lives a life of luxury and ease, with an almost unlimited supply
of money and with all the comforts supplied. I bummed around, swam,
gambled, ate in the best restaurants, played a little semipro ball or cube—
I'm pretty good, and it keeps me in shape. I enjoyed every minute of it,
and except for my regular requalification training sessions, four-to-six-week
stints that resemble military basic training, only nastier and more sadistic,
I felt no guilt at my playboy life. The training sessions are to make sure
that your body and mind don't stagnate from all that good living. They
have sensors in you that they constantly monitor to determine when you
need a good refresher.

I often wondered just how sophisticated these sensors were. The notion
that a whole security staff could see all my debauchery and indiscretions
used to worry me, but after a while you learn to ignore it.

The life offered in trade is just too nice. Besides, what could I do about
it, anyway? People on most of the civilized worlds these days had such
sensors, although hardly to the degree and sophistication of mine. How
else could a population so vast and so spread out possibly be kept orderly,
progressive, and peaceful?

But when a mission came up it wasn't practical to forgo all that past experience. A wipe without storage simply wouldn't have been a good idea,
since a good agent gets better by not repeating his mistakes. So in the Security Clinic they had everything you ever experienced on file, and the

first thing you did was get the rest of you put back so you would be whole for whatever mission they'd dreamed up this time. I was always amazed when I rose from that chair with my past fully restored. Just the clear memories of the things I'd done always surprised me—that I, of all people, had done this or that.

The only difference this time, I knew, was that the process would be taken one step further. Not only would the complete me get up from that table, but the same memory pattern would be impressed on other minds, other bodies—as many as needed until a take was achieved.

I wondered what the others would be like, those four versions of myself. Physically different, probably—the offenders they got here didn't normally come from the civilized worlds, where people had basically been standardized in the name of equality. No, these people would be from the frontier, from the traders and miners and freebooters that always existed at the edge of expansion. They were certainly necessary in an expanding culture, since a high degree of individuality, self-reliance, originality, and creativity was required in the dangerous situations in which they lived. A stupid government would have eliminated all such, but a stupid government quickly degenerates and loses its vitality and growth potential by standardization. Utopia was for the masses, of course, but not for everyone —or it wouldn't be Utopia very long.

That was the original reason for the Warden Diamond Reserve in the first place. Some of these hard frontier people are so individualistic that they become a threat to the stability of the civilized worlds. The trouble is, anybody able to crack the fabric that holds our society together is most likely the smartest, nastiest, meanest, cleverest, most original sort of person humanity can produce—and therefore not somebody whose mind should idly be wiped clean. The Diamond, it was felt, would effectively trap people like that forever, yet allow them continued creative opportunities, which when properly monitored might still produce something of value for the Confederacy.

Of course the felons down there were anxious to please as well, since the alternative was death. Eventually such creative minds made themselves indispensable to the Confederacy and ensured their continued survival. That possibility had been foreseen, but it wasn't altogether unwelcome. Like all criminal organizations in the past, they provided services that people were convinced should be illegal or were immoral or some such, but that masses of people wanted anyway.

The damned probe hurt like hell. Usually there was just some tingling, then a sensation much like sleep, and you woke up a few minutes later in the chair yourself once again. This time the tingling became a painful physical force that seemed to enter my skull, bounce around, then seize control of my head. It was as if a giant fist had grabbed my brain and squeezed, then released, then squeezed again. Instead of drifting off to sleep, I passed out.

* * *

I woke up and groaned slightly. The throbbing was gone, but the memory was still all too current and all too real. It was several minutes, I think, before I found enough strength to sit up.

The old memories flooded back, and again I amazed myself by recalling many of my past exploits. I wondered if my surrogate selves would get similar treatment, considering that they couldn't be wiped after this mission as I could. That caused me to make a mental note that those surrogates would almost certainly have to be killed if they did have my entire memory pattern. Otherwise a lot of secrets would be loose in the Warden Diamond, many in the hands of people who'd know just what sort of use to make of them.

No sooner had I had that thought than I had an odd feeling that something was very wrong. I looked around the small room in which I'd awakened and realized immediately the source of that feeling.

This wasn't the Security Clinic, wasn't anyplace I'd ever seen before. A tiny cubicle, about twelve cubic meters total, including the slightly higher than normal ceiling. In it was a small cot on which I'd awakened, a small basin and next to it a standard food port, and in the wall, a pull-down toilet. That was it. Nothing else—or was there?

I looked around and spotted the most obvious easily. Yes, I couldn't make a move without being visually and probably aurally monitored. The door was almost invisible and there was certainly no way to open it from inside. I knew immediately where I was.

It was a prison cell.

Far worse, I could feel a faint vibration that had no single source. It wasn't irritating; in fact, it was so dim as to be hardly noticeable, but I knew what it was. I was aboard a ship, moving somewhere through space.

I stood up, reeling a little bit from a slight bout of dizziness that soon passed, and looked down at my body. It was small and lithe, almost wiry, but there was muscle there and no fat at all. I had a few rough-looking scars, but aside from the evident fact that they had been more crudely treated than by a meditech they didn't look all that unusual. The skin was naturally dark, with an almost olive complexion that was unusual but apparently quite natural. A natural-born body, then, and not one that had been genetically engineered. It would be psychologically difficult to adjust to being not merely short but small. I could only stand there, stunned, for I don't know how long.

I'm not me! my mind screamed at me. *I'm one of them—one of the surrogates!*

I sat back down on the cot, telling myself that it just wasn't possible. I knew who I was, remembered every bit, every detail, of my life and work.

My shock gave way after a while to anger—anger and frustration. I was a copy, an imitation of somebody else entirely, somebody still alive and kicking and possibly monitoring my every move, my every thought. I hated that other then, hated him with a pathological force beyond reason. He would sit there comfortable and safe, watching me work, watching me do it all—and when the mission was over, he'd go home for debriefing, return to that easy life, while I—

They were going to dump me on a world of the Warden Diamond, trap me like some kind of master criminal, imprison me there, hold me there for the rest of my life—of this body's life, anyway. And then? When my job was done? I'd said it myself upon awakening—passed my own sentence. The things I knew! I would be monitored at all times, of course. Monitored and killed if I blew any of those secrets. Killed anyway at the completion of the mission just for insurance's sake.

My training came into automatic play at that point, overriding the shock and anger. I regained control and considered everything that I knew.

Monitor? Sure, more than ever. I recalled Krega saying that there was some sort of organic linkup. Are you enjoying this, you son of a bitch? Are you getting pleasure from vicariously experiencing my reaction?

My training clicked in again. It didn't matter, I told myself. First of all, I knew just what he must be thinking—and that was an advantage. He of all people would know that I would be a damned tough son of a bitch to kill.

It was a shock to discover that you are not who you thought you were but some artificial creation. It was a shock, too, to realize that the old life, the life you remembered even if you personally didn't experience it, was gone forever. No more civilized worlds, no more casinos or beautiful women or— And yet as I sat there, I adjusted. That was what they picked men like me for from the start—our ability to adjust and adapt to almost anything.

It was not my body, but I was still me. Memory and thought and personality were the individual, not his body. This was no different than a biological disguise, I told myself, of a particularly sophisticated sort. As to who was really me—it seemed to me that this personality, these memories, were no more that other fellow's than my own. Until I got up from that chair back in the Security Clinic I'd really been somebody else anyway. A lot of me, my memories and training, had been missing. That old between-missions me was the artificial me, the created me, I thought. He, that nonentity playboy that presently did not exist, was the artificial personality. Me—the real me—was bottled up and stored in their psychosurgical computers and only allowed to come out when needed—and for good reason. Unlocked, I was as much a danger to the power structure as to whomever they set me against.

And I was good. The best, Krega had called me. That's why I was here now, in this body, in this cell, on this ship. And I wouldn't be wiped and I wouldn't be killed if I could help it. That other me, sitting there in the console—somehow I no longer hated him very much, no longer felt anything at all for him. When this was all over he'd be wiped once more—perhaps get killed himself if my brother agents on the Diamond and I found out too much. At best he'd return to being that stagnant milquetoast.

Me, on the other hand . . . I would still be here, still live on, the *real* me. I would become more complete than he would.

I was under no illusions, though. Kill me they would, if they could, if I didn't do their bidding. They'd do it automatically, by robot satellite and without qualms. *I* would. But my vulnerability would last only until I mastered my new situation and accustomed myself to my new and permanent home. I felt that with a deep sense of certainty, for I knew their methods and how they thought. I'd have to do their dirty work for them, and they knew it—but only until I could get around it. They could be beaten, even on their own turf. That was why they had people like me in the first place. To uncover those who had expertly covered over their whole lives and activities, who had managed to totally vanish from their best monitors. To uncover them and get them.

But there'd be no new expert agent sent to get me if *I* beat them. They'd just be putting somebody else in the same position.

I realized then, as they had undoubtedly figured, that I had no choice but to carry out the mission. Only so long as I was doing what they wanted would I be safe from them while still in that vulnerable position. After—well, we'd see.

The thrill of the challenge took over, as it always did. There was a puzzle to be solved, were objectives to be accomplished. I liked to win. Doing so was even easier when you felt nothing about the cause, just the challenge of the problem and the opponent and the physical and intellectual effort needed to meet that challenge. Find out about the alien menace. The outcome no longer concerned me either way, since I would be trapped on a Warden world from now on anyway. If the aliens won the coming confrontation, the Wardens would survive as allies. If they lost—well, it wouldn't make a damned bit of difference, only maintain the status quo. That meant the alien problem was purely an intellectual challenge and that made the situation perfect.

The other assignment created a similar situation. Seek out the Lord of that particular Diamond world and kill him if I could. In a sense this would be more difficult, for I'd be operating on totally unfamiliar ground and would therefore require time and possibly allies. Another challenge. And if I got him, it could only increase my own power and position over the long term. If he got me instead, of course, that would solve everybody's problem, but the thought of losing is abhorrent to me. That set the contest in the best terms, from my point of view. Trackdown and assassination was the ultimate game—either you won or you died and never had to live with the thought that you lost.

It suddenly occurred to me that the only real difference that probably existed between me and a Lord of the Diamond was that I was working *for* the law and he—or she—against it. But no, that wasn't right, either. On his world *he* was the law and I would be working against it. Fine. Dead heat on moral grounds.

The only thing wrong at this point, I reflected, was that they were starting me at a tremendous disadvantage and I disliked having more handicaps than absolutely necessary. The normal procedure was to program all pertinent information into my brain before setting me off on a mission, but they hadn't done it this time. Probably, I thought, because they had me once on the table for four separate missions, and the transfer process to a new body was hard enough without trying to add anything afterwards. Still, the outcome put me in a deep pit. I thought sourly that somebody should have thought about that.

Somebody did, but it was a while before I discovered how. About an hour after I had awakened a little bell clanged near the food port and I walked over to it. Almost instantly a hot tray appeared, along with a thin plastic fork and knife I recognized as the dissolving type. They'd melt into a sticky puddle in an hour or less, then dry up into a powder shortly after that. Standard for prisoners.

The food was lousy, but I hadn't expected better. The vitamin-enriched fruit drink with it, though, was pretty good. I made the most of the drink, keeping the thin, clear container which was *not* the dissolving type in case I wanted water later. The rest I put back in the port, and it vaporized neatly. All nice and sealed. You couldn't even draw more than a thimbleful of water at a time from the tap.

About the only thing they couldn't control was bodily functions, and a half hour or so after eating my first meal as a new man, say, I just had to go. On the far wall was a panel marked *Toilet* and a small pull ring. Simple, standard stuff, the same sort of thing you might get in a cheap cabin on a passenger liner. I pulled the ring, the thing came down—and damned if there wasn't a paper-thin probe in the recess behind it.

So I sat down on the john, leaned back against the panel, and got a brief and relief at the same time.

The thing worked by skin contact—don't ask me how. I'm not one of the tech brains. The system was not as good as a programming, but it allowed them to talk to me, even send me pictures that only I could see and hear.

"By now I hope you're over the shock of discovering who and what you are." Krega's voice came to me, seemingly forming in my brain. It was a shock to realize that not even my jailers could hear or see a thing.

"We have to brief you this way simply because the transfer process is delicate enough as it is. Oh, don't worry about it—it's permanent. But we prefer to allow as much time as possible for your brain patterns to fit in and adapt without subjecting the brain to further shock. Besides, we haven't the time to allow you to 'set in' completely, as it were. So this will have to do, and I profoundly regret it, for I feel that you have an exceptionally difficult assignment."

I felt the excitement rising within me. The challenge, the challenge . . .

"Your objective world is Charon, nearest to the sun of the Diamond colonies," the Commander's voice continued. "If there is a single place in the universe that will drive sane people mad and insane people to ecstasy, it is Charon. There is no way to adequately explain the effects of being there. You will have to find that out for yourself, and you will receive a thorough orientation briefing from Charon itself after you land.

"The imprint ability of this device is limited," he continued, "but we can send you one basic thing that may or may not be of use to you on Charon. It is a physical-political map of the entire planet, as complete and up-to-date as we could make it."

That puzzled me. Why would such a map *not* be of use? What kind of place was this, anyway? Before I could mull that over further and curse my inability to ask Krega questions, I felt a sharp pain in my back, then a short wave of dizziness and nausea. But when the discomfort cleared, I found the complete map was clearly and indelibly etched in my mind.

Following this came a stream of facts about the place not likely to be too detailed in any indoctrination lecture. The planet was roughly 42,000 kilometers at the equator—or from pole back to pole, allowing for topographic differences. Like all four Diamond worlds, Charon was basically a ball—highly unusual as planets go, even though everybody, including me, thinks of all major planets as round.

The gravity was roughly .88 norm, so I'd feel a bit lighter and be able to jump further. That would take a slight adjustment in timing, and I made a note to work on that first and foremost. Charon was a tad richer in oxygen, not really enough to matter, but it was overloaded with water vapor, which probably accounted for that extra oxygen in the first place.

The planet had a reasonable axial tilt, which normally would have meant strong seasonal changes, but 158,551,000 kilometers out from an F-type star it was basically a choice of hot, hotter, still hotter, and hotter than hell. There were no polar caps—the circulation of warm ocean water prevented it—but there *was* sometimes ice in the dead of winter in the arctic or antarctic circle regions, so even on a tremendously tropical world you *could* freeze, but as both polar regions were entirely water, it wasn't likely you'd ever get there.

Equatorial temperatures were almost at the limit of human endurance: temperatures of sixty degrees Centigrade or more had been measured there, along with near-lethal radiation levels for brief periods near the time of the sun's direct rays. There was sufficient land in the more temperate zones for the mere eleven million or so people who inhabited the place. Not that the temperate zones were all *that* temperate—in the latitudes with the largest populations temperatures still reached above fifty degrees Centigrade at midsummer and rarely fell below twenty-five degrees in the dead of winter—but they were better than that equator. The three major continental land masses, however, were spaced above, on, and just below the equator, thus keeping everybody in the hothouse. A day was about twenty-nine standard hours, not enough of a difference from that to which I was accustomed to be a real factor, and a year was a short 282 Charon days.

Three continents—one not very useful that was mountainous and had large stretches of desert blocked from rain by the landforms; the other two basically tropical rain forests where the rain damn near never stopped. Not a cheery place at all, I reflected, remembering that old Warden had named this his vision of hell. Not far off the mark.

Well, I'd better get used to loving it, I told myself. Short of suicide, I had no way to avoid calling it home.

"Charon is the only one of the Diamond worlds with a female Lord," Krega continued. "I would not, however, count on your considerable charm to tame Aeolia Matuze. She is something of a political genius, and as hard and cynical as a human can become. At one time she was actually on the Confederacy Council, and it's a sure bet that a lot of the aliens' information on our political and military structure came from her. Her crime might best be called an excess of ambition; she skillfully manipulated whole governmental forces and key individuals in the governments and military and was well on the way to pulling off something of a coup d'etat, which would have in effect substituted her for the Council. Don't laugh— she came very close. Needless to say, she was well enough connected to be sent to the Diamond, where she was fifteen years into the system before taking complete charge only four years ago. It appears that her predecessor actually retired, although we consider this so unlikely that the retirement was almost certainly forced by Matuze. Do not underestimate her! In another age and time we would probably all be worshiping her as a goddess."

Aeolia Matuze. I remembered her from the distant past and from some of my history indoctrinations. I also vaguely recall that she had died and there had actually been an official period of mourning back when I was still a kid. So now at last I knew the truth about her, and it was fascinating. A formidable opponent indeed. I had to wonder if the aristocratic beauty my mind recalled was still as stunning after nineteen years on Charon.

The rest of the briefing was pretty much routine, and after it was over I simply got off the john and pushed it back into the wall. I heard a flushing sound and, the next time I used it, discovered that my waste wasn't the only thing flushed. The direct neural transmission had taken less than a minute to transfer all the information they could pack into it. Extremely efficient, the security boys, I told myself. Even my ever-vigilant jailers on the other end of those lenses and mikes would have no idea that I was anybody other than who I was supposed to be.

As to who that was, I'd gotten my first mental picture of myself from the briefing. My impression of myself as small was very true—barely 157 centimeters tall, and a mere 46 kilos. Physically, my mind had to go back to childhood for a really good word—elfin. Small, thin, wiry, with a sharp, stern-looking face set off by ears slightly too large for it and pushed back and a healthy shock of jet-black hair trimmed almost in a pageboy style. I appeared to have little or no body hair and no facial hair beyond the dark, V-shaped eyebrows. The truth was, with some nondescript clothing I would look more like a young girl of eleven or so than the mature twenty-seven-year-old the dossier said I was. Perhaps that had been part of his problem.

For the body was that of Park Lacoch, the Butcher of Bonhomme. I remembered Park's case from recent press reports—recent to the old me, anyway. He had a real thing about women, and on the frontier he'd been an insidious terror.

The odd thing was, he'd been a colonial district administrator—that was the only reason it had taken so long to catch him. One of his duties was heading the local cops who were all-out to capture him, and he had mastery of the computer records and lab facilities of the whole place. He was by all reports a superior administrator: always in under budget, never needing excuses, well-liked by the people under him. A charmer. His big problem was that he liked to play with women in a most unapproved manner. He would abduct them, often from frontier farming areas, take them to his private labs, and systematically mutilate and torture them to death. He had done so seventeen times in one year until finally hard deductive detective work by one of his colleagues, brought in, ironically, at his own request, finally tracked him down and nailed him.

He was a textbook case for the psychs, of course. Looking like this, he had been the butt of every cruelty while growing up and had had a hard time being taken seriously by anybody. But he had a keen mind and graduated first in administration—no mean feat for a natural-born frontier human, not a genetically and culturally generated individual of the civilized worlds—and he made them pay attention by doing everything just right. Why he became the Butcher was something the press had a field day with, but the causes were certainly far more complex than pop psych. Still, so revolting had been his crimes, so against all standards of civilized behavior no matter where, that only death or exile to the Warden Diamond would have been politically acceptable. The publicity alone made his face and name notorious throughout the Confederacy, so that even a totally psyched and wiped Park Lacoch could hardly have fitted back in anywhere.

He was in fact a perfect Diamond candidate for those reasons and for his brilliance. As such, he was a near-perfect cover, but he would also be something of a liability if his notoriety followed him. Hell, I liked women in a more normal way, but it would be damned difficult to make friends with any of them if they knew Lacoch's criminal history. Well, perhaps I could devise a decent cover story to attain some degree of normalcy if it came up.

I lay back down on the cot and put myself in a light trance, going over all the briefing information, filing, sorting, thinking it all out. Particularly important were the details, large and small, of Lacoch's life and work, since I would be most vulnerable to tripping up in those areas. I also studied my host's mannerisms, nervous habits, and the like, and tried to get myself into the mind-set of a small, effeminate-looking man in a big, rough world.

By the time I reached Charon, I'd better be perfect for my own sake. Lacoch—me—would have one more lady-killing to his credit before it was all over, but I wasn't for a minute going to underestimate Aeolia Matuze.

CHAPTER TWO

Transportation and Exposure

Except for the regular meals there was no way to keep track of time, but it was a fairly long trip. They weren't wasting any money transporting prisoners by the fastest available routes, that was for sure.

Finally, though, we docked with the base ship a third of a light-year out from the Warden system. I knew it not so much by any sensation inside my cloister but from the lack of it: the vibration that had been my constant companion ceased. The routine still wasn't varied; I suppose they were waiting for a large enough contingent from around the galaxy to make the landing worthwhile. All I could do was sit and go over my data for the millionth time and occasionally reflect on the fact that I probably wasn't very far from my old body (that's how I'd come to think of it). I wondered if perhaps he didn't even come down and take a peek at me from time to time, at least from idle curiosity—me and the three others who probably were also here.

I also had time to reflect on what I knew of the Warden situation itself, the reason for its perfection as a prison. I had not, of course, swallowed that line whole—there was no such thing as the perfect prison, but this one had to come close. Shortly after I was landed on Charon and started breathing its air I would be infected with an oddball submicroscopic organism that would set up housekeeping in every cell of my body. There it would live, feeding off me, even earning its keep by keeping disease organisms, infections, and the like in check. The one thing that stuff had was a will to live, and it only lived if you did.

But it needed something, some trace element or some such that was present only in the Warden system. Nobody knew what and nobody had been able to do the real work to find out, but whatever it needed was found only in the Warden system. Whatever it was wasn't in the air, because in shuttles run between the worlds of the Diamond you breathed the purified, mechanically produced stuff to no ill effect. Not the food, either. They'd checked that. It was possible for one of the Warden people to live comfortably on synthetics in a totally isolated lab like a planetary space station. But get too far away, even with Warden food and Warden air, and the organism died. Since it had modified your cells to make itself at home, and those cells depended on the organism to keep working properly, you died, too—painfully and slowly, in horrible agony. That distance was roughly a quarter of a light-year from the system's sun, which explained the location of the base ship.

All four worlds were more than climatologically different, too. The organism was consistent in how it affected an individual on each planet, but —possibly due to distance from the sun, since that seemed to be the determining factor in its life—it did different things depending on which world an individual was first exposed. Whatever it did stuck in just that fashion even if you later went to a different world of the Diamond.

The organism seemed to be vaguely telepathic in some way, although nobody could explain how. It certainly wasn't an intelligent organism; at least it always behaved predictably. Still, most of the changes seemed to involve the colony in one person affecting the colony in another—or others. You provided the conscious control, if you could, and that determined who bossed whom. A pretty simple system, even if nobody had yet been able to explain it.

As for Charon, all I really knew about it was that it was terribly hot and rainy. I cursed again not having been fed the proper programming to fully prepare me—learning the ropes would cost time, possibly a lot of it.

Almost three days—eight meals—after I'd arrived at the base ship there was a lurching and a lot of banging around, which forced me to the cot and made me slightly seasick. Still, I wasn't disappointed. The disruption meant that they were making up the consignments and readying for the in-system drop of these cells. I faced the idea with mixed emotions. On the one hand, I wanted desperately to be out of this boring little box. On the other, when I next got out of the box it would be into a much larger and probably prettier box—Charon itself, no less a cell for being an entire planet. And while it would be more diverting, challenging, exciting, or whatever, it would also be, unlike this box, very, very final.

Shortly after the banging about started, it stopped again and, after a short, expectant pause, I again felt a vibration indicating movement— much more pronounced than before. I was now either on a much smaller vessel or nearer the drives.

Still, it took another three interminable days—nine meals—to reach our destination. Long, certainly, but also fast for a sublight carrier, probably a modified and totally automated freighter.

The vibration stopped and I knew we were in orbit. Again I had that dual feeling of trapped doom and exhilaration.

There was a crackling sound and a speaker I'd never even known was here came to life. "Attention all prisoners!" it commanded, its voice a metallic parody of a man's baritone. "We have achieved orbit around the planet Charon in the Warden system," it continued, telling me nothing I didn't already know but probably informing the others, however many there were, for the first time. I could understand what they must be going through, considering my own feelings. A hundred times mine probably, since at least I was going in with my eyes open even if no more voluntarily than they.

"In a moment," the voice continued, "the doors to your cells will slide open and you will be able to leave. We strongly recommend you do so, since thirty seconds after the doors open they will close again and a vacuum pump will begin sterilization operations within the cells which would be fatal to anyone who remains."

Nice touch, I thought. I couldn't help wondering whether anybody would choose death.

"Immediately after you enter the main corridor," the voice continued, "you will stand in place until the cell doors close once again. Do not attempt to move from in front of your cell door until it closes or automatic security equipment will vaporize you. There will be no talking in the corridor. Anyone breaking silence or failing to obey orders precisely will be dealt with instantly. You will receive further instructions once the doors close. Ready to depart—*now!*"

The door slid open and I wasted no time in stepping out. A small white box, complete with marks for feet, showed you where to stand and I did as instructed, galling as all this was. There was something about being totally naked and isolated on a ship controlled only by computer that humbled you more than was right. It produced a sense of total futility.

I could still look around and I saw that I'd been right. The ship was basically a long sealed hall along the sides of which little cells had been attached. I looked up and down and counted maybe ten or twelve prisoners no more. The cream of the crop, I thought sourly. A handful of men and women—mostly men, it seemed—naked and bedraggled, beaten now, about to be dropped off and left. I wondered why they had been chosen rather than wiped, considering the transportation costs alone. What had the computers and psych boys found in these dejected specimens that dictate they should live? *They* didn't know, that was for sure. I wondered exactly who did.

The doors snapped shut. I waited expectantly, as the air was pumped out, to hear the scream of someone who hadn't moved fast enough, but there was no hint of melodrama. If anyone had taken that way out, the fact was not evident.

"At my command," the voice barked from speakers along the ceiling, "you will turn right and walk slowly in single file, as far forward as you can. There you will find a special shuttle that will take you to the surface. You will take forward seats first, leave no empty seats between you, and immediately strap yourselves in."

I heard some muttering from a few of my fellow prisoners, and instantly a brief but very visible spurt of light shot from a side wall. It c not strike anyone but hit with an audible hiss just in front of the offenders' feet. They jumped slightly at this demonstration of power. All the grumbling and mumbling immediately ceased.

The voice, which had paused for this digression, now took up its instructions with no reference to what had taken place. None was needed.

"Right turn—*now!*" it commanded, and we did as instructed. "Walk slowly forward to the shuttle as instructed."

We walked silently, definitely in no hurry. The metal floor of the corridor was damned cold—at least the shuttle would be preferable to this damned refrigerator.

The shuttle itself was surprisingly comfortable and modern, although the seats weren't made for naked bodies. I sat about three rows back and attached the safety straps, then waited for the rest to enter. My first impression had been close, I noted. The shuttle itself could seat twenty-four, but there were only eleven of us, and only three were women.

The hatch closed automatically, followed by the hiss of pressurization. I felt a violent lurch and knew we were free of the transport and on our way down.

The shuttle was much too modern and comfortable for mere prisoner transport, I told myself. This had to be one of the interplanetary ships regularly used for transportation between the worlds of the Warden Diamond.

The overhead speakers crackled, and a much nicer female voice that actually sounded human came on. It was a great improvement.

"Welcome to Charon," the voice said, sounding for all the world like it meant it. "As has no doubt been explained to you, Charon is your final destination and new home. Although you will be unable to leave the Warden system after debarking on the planet, you will also no longer be prisoners. Rather, you will be citizens of the Warden Diamond. Confederacy rule ended the moment you entered this shuttle, one of a fleet of four shuttlecraft and sixteen freighters owned in common by the Warden Worlds. The System Council, a corporate entity fully recognized as internally sovereign by the Confederacy, has a seat in the Confederacy Congress. Each of the four worlds is under a separate administration and the government of each planet is unique and independent. No matter who you are or what you have been or done in the past, you are now citizens of Charon and nothing more—or less. Anything done prior to this moment is past history that will neither be remembered, filed, or ever again referred to. Only what you do from this point on, as citizens of Charon, Warden System, will matter."

It—or she, I wasn't really sure—paused for that much to sink in. The contrast between the attitude and tone taken now and what we'd all been subjected to previously was enormous. But if she expected me to believe that the powers-that-be on Charon didn't know anything of our past she had a very low opinion of my intelligence.

"We will arrive at the spaceport at Honuth in approximately five minutes," she told us. "You will be met there by representatives bringing clothing and then taken to an orientation center where all your questions will be answered. Please be prepared for hot, wet weather and for a level of technology below what most of you have come to expect. This is still very much a frontier world, with even more restrictions than on any frontier world you have ever known. But please don't be unduly upset by that. Charon is not without its comforts. Again, welcome to Charon."

Although the lid was off, nobody really said much for the rest of the trip. Part of the reason was that we were still conditioned by our recent imprisonment; the rest was nerves, mine included. This was it, I told myself. Here we go.

There were a few bumps on the way down, particularly once we were firmly in the atmosphere; but, overall, the ride was smooth and efficient. Then came a level-off, a slow descent, and a glide right up to and into the dock.

In less than a minute I could hear the airlock door mechanisms operating, and the indicator moved from red to orange to green. Following a pneumatic hiss, the doors rolled back.

For a moment, none of us moved, but finally those nearest the hatch stood up and walked out the open door. Sighing, I did the same.

The docking area was small but quite modern and fully air-conditioned. Walking along the glassine tubelike egress arm, I could see Charon, which did nothing to improve my spirits. It was raining like crazy, so heavily I could hardly see a thing.

The terminal was quite small but nothing like the log hut I had been expecting. The air-conditioning was positively chilling. Two very ordinary people, a man and a woman, waited for us. They were both dressed in pullover black shirts and briefs and wore thick, rubber-soled sandals. They looked more like a couple that had just gotten rained out at the beach than officials of a planetary government.

"Welcome to Charon," the woman said, and I recognized the voice as the same one in the shuttle. Remote controlled from the ground, then. "Please step over to that table, pick out clothes and sandals in your size, and put them on," she instructed in a businesslike tone.

Part of my briefing had included Park Lacoch's sizes, but I quickly discovered that all the men's clothing was too large and that I would have to go to the women's section to outfit myself. It didn't really matter—it all looked the same anyway—but I did get some idea of how Lacoch developed his nasty complex and bad identity problem.

The modified beachwear was apparently standard attire, at least here— where was it? Honuth, that was it. I wondered if the stuff was waterproof.

I dressed and was standing around waiting for the others to get similarly set when the fact really hit me. I was here, on Charon—and even as that first blast of air-conditioning had hit me, my body was being systematically invaded by an alien organism that was to be my permanent jailer.

CHAPTER THREE

Orientation

After getting dressed, we were gathered around the two greeters in the small terminal.

"All right—listen up!" the man called out, his voice almost lost in the sound of the heavy rain hitting the roof of the building. "We're going to leave here and go into town where we have set up temporary quarters for you. I strongly recommend that you follow us closely, since Charon is a world that can kill the newcomer in a minute. Mechanized transportation is not allowed in town, so we'll have to go in two coaches that are parked outside now. Don't be startled at what's pulling them, just get in the nearest one."

"Got any umbrellas?" somebody called out. The man and woman both smiled a bit but didn't reply.

I became acutely aware of my physical disadvantage in the group. Everybody, male and female, was taller than I, and so I was forced to watch our hosts from a small break in the gathering that opened and closed. The whole thing was very frustrating.

"Come on!" the woman called to us. "Don't run or rush—those sandals have fair traction, but on the slick pavement just outside they'll slip on you." With that both Charonites turned, and the man started leading us out, the woman bringing up the rear.

It wasn't just bad outside, it was worse than I had imagined—incredibly hot, almost like a steambath. The rain seemed to be pouring out of some giant faucet in the sky, so thickly was it coming down. The rigid awning to the street offered little protection thanks to a hot wind, and we were all soaked in moments. Still, the ugly climate wasn't the real shock—it was what waited for us at the curb.

Two huge wheeled coaches made entirely out of what appeared to be wood, were there: pulling each of them was a pair of monster lizards, each almost four meters tall. Well, they weren't *quite* lizards, but that was the closest you could come. They were bipedal, standing on enormous, muscular legs, balancing themselves by use of a long, thick tail. Their saurian-like heads, with unblinking eyes of burning red, were not only enormous but looked full of row after row of sharp teeth. Two small arms ended in handlike appendages now flexed in apparent anticipation—or boredom. Those hands, smaller versions of the enormous feet, were composed of three, long jointed fingers connected by webbing that made them look like giant leaves. The fingers ended in suckerlike tips. The splayed hand and foot was, as I later learned, a feature of many of the animals of Charon.

Instead of having reptilian scales, the great creatures were smooth-skinned, and colored a uniform and ridiculous-looking perfect baby blue.

Each wore an elaborate looking bridle, with a network of reins rivaling a marionette's strings in number and complexity, that stretched back into a raised driver compartment above the coach proper. The driving compartment was completely enclosed, and included a windscreen with a huge windscreen wiper.

I jumped into the nearest coach, almost slipping on the smooth paving despite the warning—that rain was so fierce it almost hurt—and found myself jammed in with five other prisoners and the male Charonite. The coach was quite comfortable, with soft, padded upholstery but it would have been a lot more comfortable with two less people.

After closing and locking the door, our coach, the lead one, started off with a strong jerk. The ride was *not* at all comfortable; extremely hard and bumpy all the way, with the coach lurching this way and that, more like a ship at sea in a storm than basic ground transportation. I saw the Charonite looking at us with some amusement, probably wondering if any of us were going to get seasick. "Don't worry, it's not a long trip. Sorry about this, but it's considered deluxe transportation here on Charon."

"This ain't Lilith—machines operate there," a big man sitting next to him grumbled. "How come all this primitive shit?"

"*Some* machines operate here, when they are permitted to," the native responded somewhat enigmatically. "Fact is, most of this misery is a sort of compromise. Machinery's so easy to foul it isn't worth a damn here anyway, so we go with what we can. For the most part though, it's this bad or worse. Better get used to losing a couple of thousand years, 'cause that's what you just did."

"Damn foolishness," the big man grumped, but the rest of us remained silent, either because we didn't know enough or out of real depression.

Within five minutes the coach rolled to a stop with a jerk even worse than the start. I thought to myself that these vehicles could use seat belts more than the space shuttles, but said nothing. My situation was still too new and I was far too green, not to mention soaked and perspiring from the heat.

It was a relief when the door was opened, since at least it let in a breeze with the rain. The Charonite emerged and stood there, almost oblivious to the rain, helping us all down and pointing to a nearby door, which we made for. Once inside that door we were all dripping wet again and a little dazed, but after a half a minute or so I got my bearings and was able to look around.

When they said the place was primitive they weren't kidding. The buildings seemed to be made mostly of various kinds of native wood, along with other plants of the area. They were well-crafted but very utilitarian, that was for sure. Along the walk of polished mosaic in front of the buildings on this side of the street, were what appeared to be wick-lamps, burning oil of some kind magnified through polished glass. The reason they didn't fall victim to the rain was ingenious: between the walk and the street a wall of some glassy substance ran the length of the street and had a roof attached to the roofs of the buildings themselves. Although there was some seepage through cracks in the walk, it was pretty well watertight —a clever idea. There was also some airflow, which felt oddly chilling, although I couldn't figure out where it came from.

Our host, as soaked as we, examined us with a sour smile, and I knew we probably looked worse than he did.

The second coach arrived shortly after, and the rest of our party joined us and went through the same drying out—not that we were dry by any means.

"It doesn't rain like this *all* the time, does it?" I asked the native.

He laughed. "No, not like this. Usually it's no more than an hour or two, but in early spring and late fall the rain sometimes lasts two, three days at a clip, dumping up to three centimeters per hour." He paused a moment for that to sink in, then added, "We do have a *good* drainage system."

They'd better, I thought, more amazed than anything else. Three days of such a downpour at that rate would come to almost *two meters* of water.

"What season is it now?" someone asked sourly.

"The middle of spring," our guide responded. "It's gonna be getting hot soon." Unfortunately he didn't say it like he was joking.

The group was led into the nearest building, which proved to be—well, rustic. It was composed of logs of some kind, including log bracing for the log ceiling, which was very high. There were wickerlike chairs around, some tables, and very little else. The building was also lit by those basic lamps, and they did a very good job I had to admit, despite the slight flickering that took some getting used to. The floor was carpeted with a rubbery-feeling tilelike substance with an elaborate grooved design—to allow water run-off, I supposed. Still, if this place didn't flood it must be well designed indeed.

Groaning, we sank into the chairs, feeling as if we'd put in a full day already despite the fact that we had actually done very little. The tension was beginning to wear off, producing a general lethargy.

"This is normally the lobby of the town's hotel," the woman told us. "We requisitioned it for a few days so that you could get acclimated. We reserved the top floor rooms for you—although I'm afraid you'll have to share two to a room for the most part. We need the lower floor for regular guests, and they're cramped as it is. The guests and townspeople will not come in here while we are using it, and for the first stages of orientation we'll take all our meals here as well. I would recommend that, pending our series of talks, you avoid any of the townspeople you might meet in the lavatory or on the stairs. Don't be mean, just don't strike up any conversations or get into any arguments. Most of them are natives here and

won't understand your lack of familiarity with Charon and it's no use getting into trouble before you know what you're getting into."

Several of us nodded in agreement on that. "What about getting out of
these wet clothes?" I asked.

"We *all* have wet clothes," she replied. "We'll try and get some dry
ones for you as soon as we have your sizes down, but for now you'll have
to make do with the ones you have."

A pretty young woman in our party shivered slightly and looked
around. "Is it my imagination or is cold air blowing in here?"

"It's not really all that cold," the man told her. "But, yes, cooler air is
circulated through a system of pipes that blows cool air from below
ground, where there are natural underground river caverns, and some
man-made ones as well. The blower system is powered by windmills located on top of the buildings, and it keeps us from frying or strangling in
stagnant air."

Pretty ingenious, I had to admit, although I couldn't help wondering
why the ban on machinery. The spaceport terminal was tiny, it was true,
but it was quite modern, electrically powered and air-conditioned, all the
rest. Technology then wasn't so much impossible on Charon as it was
banned. By whom? Matuze? No, she hadn't been in power long enough
to produce this sort of thing. This town and the culture reflected by the
male native was long-term. By the Lord of Cerberus, that was for sure—
perhaps long, long ago. That made some sense if the ruling could be enforced on a planetary scale. If only the Lord of Cerberus and those he or
she designated had access to technology and the training to use it, they
would be assured of absolute control.

"We'll let you go to your rooms first for a while," the woman was saying. "There are towels and such there, and you can get fairly dried out.
We also have robes there, so if you want to change into those you'll probably be more comfortable. Top floor, pick your own rooms and roommates,
and meet us back down here in—say, an hour for food. I know you don't
have watches, but we'll make sure you get called."

We made our way to the rear of the lobby area and discovered an alcove in the back with a spiral wooden staircase. From the other side of the
alcove, beyond two closed wooden doors, came the smells of food cooking
and people talking loudly. The bar? The restaurant? Well, it didn't matter
—yet.

I hung back. I had decided the easiest way to guarantee either that I'd
be alone in a room or at least get a random shot at it was to be last, there
being an odd number of us.

No such luck on the single, though. The big, gruff man who had made
all the sour comments along the way staked out a single and nobody
seemed inclined to argue with him. Everybody else, including two of the
women, paired off, and by the time I reached the top of the stairs only one
person remained—the pretty young woman who had asked about the air
system downstairs. I saw her down at the end of the hall looking slightly

worried and more than a little confused. She cautiously opened the last
door on the right and looked inside then turned back to see me approaching. I could tell by her expression that she wasn't thrilled by the situation.

"Looks like we're stuck together," I noted.

She thought a moment, then sighed. "What the hell—what does it matter, anyway?"

"Thanks a lot," I responded sourly and walked into the room. It was
surprisingly spacious and contained two large comfortable beds, mattresses
and all, some closet space and a sink with a cold water tap. I was surprised
at that, having expected to have to go down to a well someplace. The beds
were not made, but clean linen was folded at the foot of each along with
washcloths and towels and, as promised, a robe each.

I saw her hesitating, a little nervous, and I sympathized. "Look, if I'm
offending your morals I'll step into the closet. Somebody my size could
practically live in there."

"No, no, that's not necessary. After all, we were all naked on the shuttle coming in."

I nodded, relaxed a little, and peeled off the wet clothes and stuck them
on the towel rack to dry. I then took the towel and dried myself as best I
could, particularly my hair, which was a tangled mess, then tried the robe.
As I suspected, it was quite a bit large for me. So much for standardization. Still, I decided I could manage in it without breaking my
neck.

During this time she just stood there, watching me. I began to wonder
if she knew who her roommate was. "Something wrong?" I asked her.

For a moment she said nothing, not even acknowledging my comment
or existence. I was beginning to suspect I had somebody really ill but she
finally snapped out of it and looked at me.

"I—I'm sorry, but it's been hard for me. I feel like this is all an ugly
dream, that I'll wake up from it sometime."

I nodded sympathetically. "I know what you mean. But you can't let it
get to you. You have to figure that you're alive, and you're still you and
not some psych's dream, and that you've got a whole new start in a whole
new life. It isn't as bad as all that." But, of course, it was. She was from
the civilized worlds and probably had never even seen a frontier settlement. Her world, a world she not only had loved but had taken entirely
for granted, was now totally and irrevocably gone.

Come to think of it, so was mine.

She walked over and sat on the edge of her bed. "Oh, what's the use? It
seems to me that being dead would be better than *this*."

"No, death is never better than life. Besides, you have to consider that
you're really pretty special to the Confederacy. There's only eleven of us
out of the—what? Hundreds?—convicted at the same time. They saw
something in us that they didn't want to lose. In a sense, they're saying
we're better than almost all the people in the Confederacy."

"Different, anyway," she responded. "I don't know. I just don't. Spending the rest of my life in this rotten place." She looked me straight in the eye. "What makes you so special? What did *you* do to get here?"

Well, here it was—acid test early on. I decided to take a very mild gamble, but first a proper priming. "You know you aren't supposed to ask that."

She was beginning to relax a little now, and moved to get rid of her own wet clothes. "Something you're ashamed of?" she asked. "Funny. I never thought it mattered."

"It doesn't matter to you?"

She thought a moment as she dried her hair. "No, not really. I'm Zala Embuay, by the way."

"Park Lacoch," I responded, tensing a bit to see if it got any reaction. He—I—was pretty damned notorious.

She let it pass without a glimmer of recognition. Well, that was something, anyway.

"Well, Park Lacoch, weren't you some sort of criminal?"

"Weren't we all?"

She shook her head. "No, not me. I'm different. I may be the only person ever sent to the Warden Diamond because I was an innocent victim."

I was finding it hard to take her seriously. "How's that?"

She nodded seriously. "You've never heard of the Triana family?"

It was my turn to betray ignorance. "Nope."

"Well, the Trianas are the ranking political family on Takanna. Ever been there?"

"No, can't say I have," I admitted.

"Well, you know at least what it's like to be a ranking political family, don't you?"

You bet I did—but Lacoch would have been a little more removed. "I understand it, although I'm a frontier man myself. I've been to many of the civilized worlds but I've never actually lived on one."

"That's what I mean. You're much better equipped for someplace like this."

"The frontier's not as wild and primitive as you think," I told her. "In comparison to the civilized worlds, yes, but it's nothing at all like this. Believe me, our backgrounds may be very different but they're much more alike than either of us is to the people who were born here."

I'm not sure she accepted that truism, but she let it pass. "Well, anyway, I was raised in a government house, had a happy childhood and was being prepared for an administrative slot. Everything was going right when all of a sudden, the Security Service came in one day and arrested my designated mother and me."

I understood what she meant by that. All people of the civilized world were born *in vitro*, perfect products of genetic engineering, predesigned and predestined for their lives and careers. Each career on a civilized world was a Family, and when children were five they were given to a designated member of that Family unit to be raised and educated. "What was the charge?" I asked her, really interested now. I wondered whose territory Takanna was in.

"Well, they charged *her* with unauthorized genetic manipulation," she told me. "They claimed I was a special product—*product!*—illegally created and born."

I sat up, all ears. *This* was interesting. "You look perfectly normal to me," I assured her. "Just what were you supposed to be that you weren't supposed to be?"

"That's just it! They wouldn't tell me! They said it would be better that I didn't know, and maybe if I didn't the truth wouldn't make any difference. That's what's so frustrating about it all. How would you like to be told one day that you're a freak, but not told how or in what way?"

"And you haven't a clue? Your mother never indicated anything?"

"Nothing. I've searched and searched my whole childhood, and I haven't come up with anything that anyone found odd or unusual. I *do* admit I found the whole business of administration pretty boring, but a lot of it *is* boring. And I never saw her after the arrest, so I never got a chance to talk to anybody else who might know and would tell me."

"And for that they shipped you here?"

She nodded. "They told me it was for my own good; that I'd do all right here, that I could never fit into the civilized worlds. Just like that, I'm a convicted criminal—and here I am."

I studied her face and manner as she spoke and came to a conclusion. The tale was pretty bizarre, but it had a ring of truth to it. It was *just* the kind of thing the Confederacy would do. It would be interesting to know why she couldn't have been recultured or simply shifted elsewhere. There was no such thing as a criminal gene, of course, but there *were* hormonal and enzyme causes for a large number of physical and mental tendencies, from violence to anger to schizophrenia. If her story rang true all the way, it meant I might be sharing a room with a ticking bomb. Still, if she ever learned the complete truth about Park Lacoch she might think the same thing—and be wrong.

"Well, if it's any comfort to you, I'm something of a freak myself, as you can see," I told her. "You get cases like me out on the frontier, where there's all sorts of complications in the different planetary conditions—radiation, you name it—and most births are the old-fashioned kind, of mother and father. By 'like me' I don't really mean exactly like me, just—well, unusual."

"You do look—well, unusual," she said cautiously. "I mean, most of the frontier people seem to be so big and hairy."

I chuckled. "Well, not quite, but my small size is only part of it. Tell me, just seeing me in the clothes and now, what do I look like? How old would you say I was?"

She thought a moment. "Well, I know you're a lot older just by the way you talk, but, well, to be honest, you look like . . . well . . ."

"I look like a ten-year-old girl, right?"

She sighed. "Well, yeah. But I know you aren't. Even your voice is kinda, well, in between, though."

That was news. My voice sounded like a sharp but definite tenor to me. [I had the advantage of all that information Krega had fed into my fanny, and I was beginning to understand Park Lacoch a little more.]

"Well, I'm twenty-seven," I told her, "and I've looked this way since I was twelve. Puberty brought me pubic hair, a slightly deeper voice, and that was it. It wasn't until I was sixteen, though, that my folks were able to get me to a really good meditech. They found out that I was a mutation, a real freak. A hermaphrodite, they called it."

"A—you mean you're both sexes?"

"No, not really. I'm a man, but I'm probably the only man you'll ever meet who's a man entirely by choice. Inside I have the makings of both, but the psychs and meditechs struck a balance, and that's the way I'll stay —because I wanted it. They could have adjusted the other way and, with a minimum amount of surgery, I'd have wound up female." Poor Lacoch, I'd reflected more than once. Confused totally about his sexual identity, hung up in a limbo not of his own making, permanently small and girlish. No wonder he went nuts. The file said he even masqueraded as a young girl to lure his victims away. I wondered if he'd have been different, perhaps better off, if he'd chosen to be female instead—but he hadn't, and while seventeen victims was a terrible price, here and now, in his body, I was damned glad to be a man.

"Then, in a way you and I are alike," Zala said, fascinated. "We're both genetic freaks. The only difference is, you *know* what's wrong. I wish I did."

I nodded. "Maybe you will now. Or maybe this Warden organism will just wipe out the problem. It's supposed to do that."

The idea sobered her a bit. "I'd almost forgotten about that. Funny, I don't feel . . . well . . . *infected.*"

"Neither do I, but we are. Bet on it."

Then without warning, she returned to the original conversation. "Ah, Park?"

"Uh-huh?"

"What did you do to get here?"

I sighed. "What I did I won't do again," I told her. "It was a terrible sickness, Zala—mental illness that came from a lot of things, including my physical condition. The psychs cured me of that, though, and I've never been more sane in my life. That alone is really worth the price. I was in real hell, Zala, back home. I may be a prisoner here, but I'm free for the first time in my life. I was a district administrator, by the way, so we do have a little more in common."

She wasn't buying the stall. "Park, why won't you tell me what you did?"

I sighed. "Because if I did you wouldn't get a good night's sleep while we were together, that's why."

She thought for a moment. "You . . . killed somebody, didn't you?"
I nodded.
"A woman?"
Again I just nodded.
She hesitated. "More than one?"
Again I could only nod and wish this conversation hadn't come up.
"A lot?"
I sighed and sat back up on my bed. "Look, let's stop playing games. I really don't want to remember that part of myself. It's like I was somebody else, Zala. It was a terrible, terrible madness, a sickness. Looking back on it makes me more nauseated than people who remember it or were there. I swear to you, though, that they *have* to terminate anybody they can't cure of such madness, and the fact that I'm here proves that I'm cured. They could have sent me back on the streets with perfect confidence and in perfect safety, but my case was so notorious and I'm so physically distinctive that I would have been lynched, or worse. The Diamond was the only way out for me and, believe it or not, I'm grateful. For the first time I can be a whole human being—and that means a lot to me, even here on this pesthole."
She smiled. "Then I'm your acid test, because I don't *want* to be here. If you're lying, and you kill me, well, at least it'll be over. And if you're telling the truth, both of us will know it and maybe, together, we can survive this place."
"Sounds fair to me," I told her sincerely. A temporary alliance, anyway. I *did* have a woman left to kill, but it wasn't Zala Embuay.

They knocked on our doors shortly after that, and we trooped downstairs again like a convention of bathhouse enthusiasts. I had some trouble with the robe on the stairs, but I managed to keep from tripping.
Our hosts, in fresh black clothes of the same kind we'd been issued, but looking dry and prim, were waiting for us. In the center of the lobby area a table had been set with a lot of steaming dishes on it, and eleven place settings.
The food was all natural, which was bizarre enough, but the tastes and textures were also rather odd. I won't go into a catalogue of the meal, but I had the feeling that, with the stew anyway, we really didn't *want* to know what was in it. For the six civilized-worlds prisoners, Zala included, it was probably the first nonsynthetic, non-computer-balanced and -prepared meal they had ever had, and they showed it. The rest of us rude frontiersmen and women ate with gusto. As I said, I really didn't want to know what the stuff was, but it *was* good and highly but delicately spiced. At least the food was going to be decent here.
Our native guides obviously had either already eaten or would eat later. They busied themselves setting up a large chart stand and adjusting lights and the like until we were through.

Eating mostly in silence but feeling for the first time a lot more human, we finally finished and waited anxiously on our hosts.

The man began. "I am Garal," he introduced himself, "and this is Tiliar. We've been assigned this job by the Honuth District Supervisor, acting for and at the command of the planetary government. We are both former prisoners ourselves, so we know what you're going through. Let's start out by saying that you must have fears and odd superstitions about the Warden Diamond, and we want to assure you that those fears have no basis. You're not going to get sick—in fact, you will most likely not notice any real difference between yourselves before and yourselves here. It is true, though, that your bodies are even now altering in minute and undetectable ways. Within a few days you and the Warden organism will reach a state of what we like to call 'alliance.' Let me emphasize that you are not sick. In fact, in the five years I've been here I've *never* been sick, not once. The Wardens are far more effective than any body defense in killing off viruses and any other disease organisms you might have brought with you —the ones native here are too alien to do you any harm—as well as infection and a host of other ills. You can appreciate the fact that, in a climate like this, nobody ever gets a cold."

That brought a small chuckle from us, but it was an important aspect of this world. Back in the civilized worlds people never got sick much either, but that was due to the immediate access to the best medical facilities. Here, if Garal was to be believed, doctors and the like were simply not necessary.

"Some of you may find a little discomfort in one or two areas," Tiliar put in, "because you aren't healthy enough. Anyone who has chipped or lost a tooth, for example, may find it growing back, which can be an irritating thing. Anyone who has vision problems might experience some dizziness or slight headaches as whatever problems you had are corrected. The Warden organism doesn't just keep you from getting worse, it makes you better. And it keeps you that way. Cuts heal quickly and rarely leave a scar; even whole limbs are often regenerated if lost."

"You make it sound like we're immortal," the big prisoner with the single room commented.

"No, not immortal," she replied. "Fatal wounds Outside are fatal wounds here. The Wardens use your own body's natural abilities to keep you healthy and whole, but if your body can't fix it, well, neither can they. However, more people on Charon die from external causes than natural causes. With the Warden ability to repair and even replace brain cells, your potential lifespan in a healthy body is longer than in the civilized worlds."

Most of those at the table, Zala included, heard only the second part of that statement and seemed pleased. I was much more interested in the implication that a lot of people died here from unnatural causes. I couldn't forget the teeth on those baby blue lizards.

Our guides followed up with a general rundown of the planet, much of which I already knew. It was interesting in the context of the torrential rains to discover that there were a few deserts on the central continent, often the only places where blue sky was seen for more than brief periods. Water, it seemed, was feast or famine on Charon—mostly feast. But in those dry areas it might rain once a century. Additionally, there were violent storms, tabarwinds they were called, that were quick and deadly and could strike out of nowhere with tremendous lightning charges and winds of over 160 kilometers per hour. Much of the weather, including these storms, could not be accurately predicted since a layer in the upper atmosphere had an odd field of electrically charged particles that fouled most conventional radars, infrared cameras, and the like, while artificial electrical fields on the ground attracted the full fury of tabarwinds. I began to see a practical reason why they kept technology at a minimum level. The spaceport was immediately shut down at the first sign of such tabarwinds, and, even so, it had been hit and destroyed twice in the memory of these two people. The shuttle had special protection against many of these electrical fields, but was not totally immune.

As with all the Warden worlds, a "research" space station was maintained in orbit well outside the range of any nasty stuff, but it was closed to unauthorized personnel. It was an interesting fact that on those space stations the Warden organism would infect anyone that it came into contact with, but would leave all the inorganic material alone. Its full properties were operative only on one of the planets, and then only on people affected with the same breed of organism.

That brought us to what we really wanted to know. "In addition to the total lack of technological comforts," Garal told us, "there is a by-product of the Warden affiliation that is, well, hard to accept even after you've seen it. There's a different by-product on each of the four Diamond worlds, all relating to the fact that the tiny Wardens are, somehow, in some sort of contact or communication with one another. On Lilith, for example, some people have the power literally to move, build, or destroy mountains with a thought, by telling *their* Wardens to give orders to *other* Wardens in the rocks, trees, other people, you name it. But the degree of power an individual has is arbitrary. On Cerberus this communication is so bizarre that people can literally exchange minds with each other—and it's so universal that they often do so without meaning to. No control. On Medusa, the Warden communication is so limited that it's really only within one's own body, and causes rapid and involuntary shape-changing to meet whatever environment the person finds him or herself in. Here—well, things are a bit different but still related."

We were all silent now, raptly intent on the speaker. Here was the heart of the Charon experience—what we would become.

"As on Lilith, we have a certain power over objects and people," Tiliar jumped in, taking up the talk. "As on Cerberus, it is a mental ability rather than a physical one, and mind-to-mind contact is possible. As on Medusa, physical change is possible, but in a different sense. And, while these powers are *not* arbitrary—that is, everyone has these abilities—it takes great training and discipline to be able to use them properly, while those with the training and control *can* use them on you. That's why we cautioned you to avoid the locals for a while." She paused for a moment, carefully considering her words.

"You see," she continued after a moment, "Charon is a world out of children's stories and fairy tales. It is a world where magic works, where sorcs—sorcerers and their spells have devastating effects. And yet it is a world where none of the laws of science are violated."

This was a hard concept to digest, and several of our company muttered and shook their heads.

"I know, I know, it's hard to accept," Garal said after a while, "but the more hardheaded of you will quickly grasp the reality. Let me ask you first how you know you're here. How do you know this place looks like this place, that you look like you and we like us? How do you know it's raining?"

"We got wet," somebody mumbled, and we all laughed.

"All right, but how do you *know* you got wet? You—your personality, your memories, the thinking part of you—are really all locked up in the cerebellum and cerebral cortex. Your brain is the only real *you* that you know—and the brain is totally encased in your skull. It has no way of directly knowing what's going on at all—it doesn't even have pain centers. Every single thing you know comes to you, your brain, by remote sensors. Vision. Smell. Taste. Touch. Sound. The five senses. Each transmits information to the brain, and supports the others to tell the brain what's going on. *But what if those five senses were wrong?* There are methods of torture—and a lot of psych work, which may be the same thing—that capitalize on this. Sending you false information. There is, in fact, an ancient human religion called voodoo—that might explain it."

"A practitioner of voodoo," Tiliar explained, picking up the lecture, "took samples of your fingernails, hair, even shit, and put it on a doll. Then whatever that magician-priest did to the doll was supposed to happen to you. And why has voodoo really survived the space age? *Because it works.*"

"Aw, c'mon," the big man scoffed.

She nodded seriously. "Yes, it works. But only under two conditions. First, the intended victim must believe that the priest has this power. It doesn't even have to be strong belief, just a subconscious fear that maybe it *does* work. And second, the intended victim must be made aware that he or she is being hexed. People have been crippled, physically and mentally, and even killed by this method, as long as those two conditions are met. And it's easier than you think. Even the most rational-minded have, deep down, a streak of superstition or doubt about unknown powers. The voodoo priests are master psychs, and every visible success reinforces the belief in their powers among others."

"Of course the priest doesn't really *do* anything," Garal noted. "They just establish the psychological conditions and you do it to yourself. In a sense, you might say that voodoo is a magic force that violates no known scientific laws."

"You mean this is a voodoo world?" I asked jokingly.

They did not think me at all funny. "In a sense, yes," the man replied. "But here you can eliminate the variables completely and go a lot further. If you'll remember, I said that the Warden organisms can communicate, so to speak, with one another, even outside the body they inhabit. But it's a passive thing. They communicate, but they don't actually *say* anything. But, because they are a part of you, they can talk to you as well—and you to them. That's the trick. How well you can master communication between your own Wardens and others. In a sense, Charon is the ultimate voodoo world where belief and preparation are not really necessary."

Tiliar thought a moment. "Look, let's put it this way. Suppose some powerful person decided to turn you into a uhar—one of those big blue things that pulled the coaches. If he has the power, the training, and the self-control, he contacts the Wardens in your mind through *his* Wardens. He sends out a message—you are a uhar. Not being trained, or not possessing the mental control needed, or any combination of these things, you have no defense, no way to tell your *own* Wardens that they are receiving false data. So this idea, that you are a uhar, gets pounded into your brain, much like a forced hypnoprobe. Your senses are fooled, all the information coming into the brain now confirms that you are a four-meter-tall blue lizard—and, from *your* point of view, you *are*."

I saw Zala shiver slightly and felt some perspective was needed. "So all we are dealing with is a powerful form of hypnotism, the same kind we can achieve with machines, only we've dispensed with them to make the contact mind to mind."

"Sort of," Tiliar agreed. "But it doesn't stop there. Remember, your Wardens are in constant communication with all the other Wardens. Your own perceptions and self-image are 'broadcasting,' so to speak, to everyone else. What this means is that if *you* think you're a uhar, well then, so will everybody else. Even uhar will perceive you as uhar, since they, too, are Warden affiliated. *Every single thing will act as if the command, or spell, is real.* And since we depend on our senses for all our information, what we and everybody else perceive as real *will* be real. The more training and self-control you have in this ability, the more protected *you* will be and the more vulnerable everyone else will be. It's that simple."

"Needless to say, the better you are at it, the higher you will rise in Charon society," Garal added.

I'm not sure any of us really believed what we were being told, but we kept an open mind as it was information on how the place operated. Before I believed in any magic though, I'd have to see it demonstrated myself.

If this ability took training, it was worth going after. "Just how do we get the training needed to develop this?" I asked our hosts.

"Maybe you do, maybe you don't," Garal replied. "First of all, there's that self-control, a certain mental ability and attitude-set that you just can't teach. The fact is, most people can't handle the discipline involved, or can only handle it to a degree. Needless to say, it's also not in the best interests of the powers-that-be for everyone to develop this ability, even if they could. It is this way all over. There are few wolves and many sheep, yet the wolf rules the sheep. There are masses of people, nearly countless people, in the Confederacy, yet their entire lives, from their genetic makeup to jobs, location, even how long they will live, are in the hands of a very few. Please don't expect Charon to be any different."

That we could all understand at least. There was a government here, a government headed by the worst kind of power-mad politicians and super-crooks, and they had to preside over a society that was at least five percent as crooked and nasty as they were, or the children and grandchildren of the same sort. Such a government would not willingly share any of its power, nor dare to make it easily available. Still, I reflected, my own self-discipline and mental training and abilities were engineered to be way above the norm, and what an Aeolia Matuze and lesser lights could do, I most certainly could do as well. And there was always somebody ready to beat the system. Unofficial training would be around someplace—if it could be found, and if its price could be met.

In a way I suspected this might be something of a test. We had come to Charon with nothing but our wits; those who could secure the method and means for training and its protection and chance for upward mobility would do so. The rest would join the masses in the endless pool of eternal victims. That was, I felt sure, the challenge they were issuing us here.

Back in our room, Zala and I talked over what we'd been told the first day.

"Do you think it's for real?" she wanted to know. "Magic, hexes, voodoo—it all sounds so ridiculous!"

"Ridiculous perhaps, when put in that context, but that's the context of science. Look, they're not saying that anybody on Charon can do anything that a good psych with a battery of mechanical devices couldn't do. Believe me, I *know*." And I *did* know—but not from being on the wrong end of them as she believed.

"Yes, but that's with machines and experts . . ."

"Machines, yes," I agreed, "but don't kid yourself that the experts are any less expert here than back there. There are even psychs sent here—they're the most imaginative people you can find, but they go out of their heads more often than those in any other job. No, the only difference here is that everybody's carrying his own psych machine around inside of him—an organic machine, but still a gadget, a device."

She shivered. "What's wrong?" I asked her.

"Well, it's what you said. Psychs are the people most likely to go nuts, right? I guess it's because they not only get involved in hundreds of messed-up people's minds, but their machines give them a god complex."

"That's pretty fair," I agreed.

"Well, what you just said is that we're on a world of psychs and *everybody* is under their machines and can't get disconnected. I mean, if a psych goes nuts back home, there are other psychs and computer monitors and all the rest to catch it, pull the plug, and get him out of you, right?"

I nodded.

"But, Park—who's the monitor here? Who's around to pull the plug on these people?"

And that, of course, was the real problem. Loose in a Bedlam with the psychs crazier than the patients, and nobody to pull the plug—and no plug to be pulled. Nobody except . . . me.

It hadn't been a very trying day, but the release of tension added to the fact that none of us had gotten any real exercise for weeks, made it pretty easy to turn in fast. I had a little trouble figuring out how to extinguish the oil lamp in the room without burning myself, but I finally discovered the way the globe was latched. A tiny little cup on a long handle hanging next to the towel rack proved the easiest way to extinguish the light. It was not until days later that I found out that this was exactly what the little cuplike thing was for.

Despite my near exhaustion, I couldn't fall asleep right away. I kept thinking about Charon and the challenge it posed. Obviously I could do nothing until I was able to experience this pseudo-magic first hand and get a measure of what I was up against and what I had to learn. After that I'd have to get a job, I supposed, to develop some local contacts, to find out what I needed to know about training and rogue magicians. I would be totally ineffective until I had enough experience and expert instruction to hold my own on this crazy planet. It was entirely possible—likely, in fact—that the top politicians like Matuze weren't the top powers in magic here. I suspected the skills involved were quite different. But she would be flanked and guarded by the absolute tops, that was for sure; and the only way to her would be right through them. As a top agent, I had no doubt that I could eventually master the art enough to get by the best, but I was pragmatic enough not to think I could get through *all* of them single-handedly. No, I would need help—local help. The one thing I could be certain of was that a system like this would breed a whole raft of enemies for Matuze, and they'd all be either as criminal or as psychotic as they come—or both. The trick was to find them and organize them.

"Park?" Her voice came to me in the darkness, through the sound of the omnipresent rain on the roof.

"Yes, Zala?"

"Can I . . . would you mind if I got into your bed? Just for a while?"

I grinned in the dark. "Not afraid I'll strangle you or something."

She got up and walked over, almost stumbling, and sat on the edge of my bed. "No, I don't think so. If I really ever thought so I wouldn't have stayed in here a minute." She crawled into bed with me and snuggled close. It felt good, oddly comforting, but also a little disconcerting. I wasn't used to women that much larger than I was. Well, I'd better get used to it.

"What makes you so sure about me?" I teased, whispering. Still, it was reassuring to have the uncertainty settled so quickly.

"Oh, I don't know," she replied. "I've always been able to tell things about people."

"Things? Like what?"

"Oh, like the fact that Tiliar and Garal are a couple of hoods who don't really give a damn about us. Or that that big son of a bitch would enjoy breaking people in two just for fun."

"And what can you tell about me?"

"I—I'm not sure. There's a hardness in you somewhere, that's for sure, but you're no psycho. It's almost as if, well, if I didn't know it was impossible I'd say you weren't Park Lacoch at all but somebody very different, somebody who didn't belong in that body at all."

Her observations were dead on, and my respect for her intuitive abilities, if that's what it was, went up a hundred notches. Still, a smooth, glib cover was called for.

"In a way you're right," I told her carefully. "I'm not the same man I was all my life. Mentally, I'm the man I *should* have been all along. I owe them at least that much. The old Lacoch's dead and gone, never to return. He was executed in the psych rooms with my full and hearty cooperation." *That* was true enough, although not in the way it sounded.

"Do you still have any doubts about what you are?" she asked. "I mean, ever think of maybe having the operation?"

I laughed. "Not anymore," I told her, and proved it, both to her and to my own satisfaction.

CHAPTER FOUR

Interviews and Placement

Over the next few days we got down to learning the basics of the planet through a series of lectures that would normally be very boring—and really were—but which even the most thick-headed of us realized we needed before we took our place in this new society.

The economy of Charon was almost entirely agricultural, a combination of subsistence and plantation farming. The service industries were still very primitive. While little could be brought into the Warden Diamond from Outside—the general term for every place *except* the Warden system

—the planets themselves were not without resources, and material from one world could be shipped and used on others. There were sea creatures that could be caught and eaten that were rich in protein and minerals, and many creatures of the land could also be carefully raised for food. The skins of some of these reptilian creatures were also useful. Shipped to Cerberus, where they apparently had elaborate manufacturing facilities, they could be made into everything from the best waterproof clothing you could find to roofing and insulation materials.

I couldn't help but wonder about my Lilith counterpart. I myself was having a tough time with this nontechnological culture on Charon; I wondered if I would even survive in a world whose denizens were rabidly antitechnological. "I" was probably doing far better on Cerberus and Medusa, both of which had a technological level which, if below what I was used to, was nonetheless closer to my element.

Another export was the woodlike material that made up the rain forests and provided the foundations for Charon's buildings. Its weather-proofing properties and hardness made it desirable even on worlds that had their own trees.

So they exported a great deal of it to Medusa to pay for raw materials. Medusa controlled the asteroid and moon mining industries. The raw materials were sent to Cerberus where they were made into things they needed and could use under their peculiar conditions. All in all it was a neat and interdependent system.

The political system on Charon was also a good topic, and a most revealing one. I remembered Krega's comment that Matuze would become a goddess if she could and I was thus not as surprised as the rest.

The vast majority of the eleven million or so inhabitants of Charon were, of course, the workers who were mere citizens. In a nicely feudal arrangement, they worked for Companies—a euphemism for plantations basically—in exchange for which the Companies guaranteed their safety and all their basic needs.

There was a small town at the center of every dozen or so Companies, and the townspeople were also organized, this time into what were called Unions, based on trade, profession, or skill. The political head of each town was, interestingly but logically, the Town Accountant, whose office kept all the books not only on what the town produced or provided but what the Companies owed for those services. Although it was a barter system (until you got to the very top anyway), some money was in circulation—coins, made of some iron alloy. They were a good small currency, since without any significant metals the supply was strictly controlled by trade with Medusa.

In the Companies, the coins were used basically as rewards for exceptional work, so there was very little money there. In the towns, however, each Union had a set wage and a varying scale of who got paid what based on a number of factors; the money was used to buy some necessities —the Unions provided housing—and all luxuries, which weren't many.

The Transportation Union, of course, was planetwide and centered in Honuth; and it used the coins to buy what was needed along the way. Honuth, being the spaceport, was the largest city on Charon—although there was a freightport on the southern continent, a land just now starting to be developed—and greater Honuth consisted of maybe five thousand people. The average town was a tenth that size.

Companies and Unions were run by Managers who lived pretty well as long as they produced. The Town Accountants kept tabs on them all, and that tab was forwarded to the Board of Regents which collectively kept track of everything and got the requirements from the towns and Companies and the raw materials and finished products they needed from off-planet. The head of the Board of Regents was called the Director, and he was the top government official on Charon. A simple system, one that seemed to work.

However, there was a parallel system as well, and this one was a little bit off the beaten track. It was composed of the small number of men and women who were in command of the Warden organism and its uses. These were the people to watch. As I'd suspected, the political and "magical" ends were not necessarily the same.

At the low end of this parallel system were the apts, the students of the art, who studied under and worked for journeymen magicians, usually referred to as sorcs, which was short for sorcerers. The sorcs were represented in every Company and Union and in every Town Accountant's office, too. They protected the people who had to be protected, enforced the rules and laws, and generally gave advice and consent when asked.

Basically, the magicians and their students were the cops. They reported to a board of Bishops whose responsibilities encompassed whole planetary areas. Collectively this group was known as the Synod.

Interestingly, the Bishops were appointed by the Director, who could hire or fire them at will. I wondered how the hell Matuze could make a firing of somebody that powerful stick—and why the Bishops were in any way obedient to her in the first place—but they were. The reason was something to be found out later. Still, the system confirmed my basic idea that Matuze herself, while probably schooled in those magical arts and reasonably competent, wasn't the top witch or whatever in terms of magical power. Sooner or later I'd have to find out just what the Director's base of power was.

One thing was sure—Matuze had not only all the political power but all the respect and pomp as well. She was almost invariably referred to in ancient royal terms, such as "Her Highness" or even "Her Worship"; but she was nevertheless, the Lord, not the Lady, of the Diamond.

She liked to have her picture everywhere, that was for sure. Four different full-size portraits adorned the lobby. When the rain actually stopped for periods and we had walking tours of the town, I found her likeness almost everywhere, even on many of the coins we were shown—but not all. Older coins showed several men's faces, different men, and while I was sure she hated them I could see she was practical enough not to go to all the trouble and expense of replacing all the old currency until it was worn out—not when the mint was 160 million kilometers away.

All the portraits showed her much the way I remembered her—fairly young, attractive, somewhat aloof and aristocratic. Even though she was from the civilized worlds and conformed to the norm, there was something in that personality that even portraits caught, something that made her stand out. I couldn't help but wonder, though, if she still really looked that good.

The animal life on Charon was too diverse to keep track of, and was quite strange depending on which of the three continents you were on. Difficult as it was in rain-soaked Honuth to believe, animals existed on the parched central continent for whom rain could be disabling, even deadly.

The most important thing, from a survival viewpoint, was that the animals also possess a certain power for magic. It was on a primitive level, of course, but the carnivores, in particular, could quite often make you think they were a tree, a bush, or even a pretty flower, until you came too close. Some of the carrion-eaters in particular could project whole landscapes, disorienting and confusing travelers as well as instinct-driven herbivorous prey, causing bogs to look like rocks or land water.

"In a very real sense," Garal warned us, "walking along unprotected on Charon in broad daylight in good weather is like walking blindly in pitch-dark night, never knowing what is waiting for you, never knowing what is real and what is not."

This situation, of course, reinforced the feudal Company system. Nobody dared walk away, nor even travel from town to town, without the protection and abilities of a sorc. Charon was a deadly place indeed, well-suited for easy population control and political domination.

But Charon didn't worry me because in the long run its least common denominators were the same socio-economic factors that supported every world, even the Confederacy itself. Here, you got the training to use the power if you could—the easy way up, like being born to power or position elsewhere. Failing that, you found somebody who *did* have the power and rode up with that individual, using that person's power as your own—a slower and more delicate method than the first, but one that worked.

I realized, of course, why we were being kept in this hotel in this rain-soaked town for so long. Our hosts were waiting for the final "set in" of the Warden organism in order to demonstrate its effects—and powers. We were the cream of the criminal crop; we had to be shown explicitly who was boss first.

With one exception, that is. Zala continued to be more and more of an enigma to me. I realized very early on that she had been lying about herself, at least in part—she was never trained to be an accountant or, for that matter, in any similar profession. In just routine conversation and in discussing the briefings it became clear that her counting ability only slightly exceeded the capacity of her fingers and toes; her reading ability was similarly quite basic. That put her well outside any government, business, or scientific areas of expertise. It confined her, in fact, to the lowest job classes, not at all unusual for the frontier but very unusual for one of the civilized worlds.

But lies were the stock in trade of people sent to Charon, so the problem wasn't that she was lying but that she was a bundle of contradictions. The ego, the sense of self-worth in the job you were born to do, was central to the social fabric of the civilized worlds. Everyone had a job they did well and knew was important, even vital, and something few others could do as well. Sex was casual and recreational. There were, of course, no family units and everyone's egocentrism kept the concept of individualism a core idea. You had a circle of friends certainly, but no dependency on others in a psychological sense. The slogan "Interdependence in work, independence in self" was everywhere and was always being drummed into you.

But not Zala. Zala *needed* somebody else, and I do mean needed. She latched onto me immediately despite the distinct possibility that I was still a mass murderer of women. I had enjoyed our sexual encounters; she had required, needed them. She was simply incapable of existing, let alone surviving, on her own for very long—and that was an incredible idea for someone like me from the civilized worlds. Timid and passive, she lacked any of the egocentrism I took for granted. I didn't have any illusions that she'd chosen me because of some innate magnetic charm or superior radiance I gave off. She'd chosen me because I happened to be there, was convenient, and therefore the one.

But once I was chosen, she was totally solicitous of my welfare to the exclusion even of her own, as if she had no thoughts of her own but simply awaited my pleasure. Although her behavior was demeaning in my eyes and bothered me in the extreme, nonetheless I have to admit I got a certain charge from it, since it certainly fed my own ego beyond anything I had come to expect short of service robots.

And yet, and yet . . . How the hell did somebody like her ever get to *be* at all, particularly on the civilized worlds? And why was she sent to the Warden Diamond?

Late in the evening of the fourth day on Charon I decided to confront her. Her response, which was both embarrassed and nervous at being caught in so obvious a lie, did little to answer my basic questions about her.

"I—well, you're right," she admitted. "I'm not an administrator. But the rest is true. I am, well, what they call a bioslot Entertainer, but that isn't really quite right either. Basically, well, the planetary administrators often have guests from other planets and from the Confederacy itself. There are banquets and entertainments of course for the bigwigs—and I'm part of it. My job is—was—to provide those important people with just about anything they wanted. Keep them happy."

Now I knew what she meant. I'd seen a number of her type in just such circumstances while working on cases involving business and government bigwigs. The very sameness of the civilized worlds made them pretty dull. When you saw one you saw them all. Even the entertainments, meals and the like were standardized—in the name of equality, of course. It was a perfect and proper system, but there were still men and women in incredibly high places who had to be impressed when they dropped in on your little world, and those in the Entertainer class were the ones to do it. They planned and set up banquets that would be unique and offer exotic delicacies. They planned and performed unusual entertainments, including live dancing and even more esoteric demonstrations. And if even sex was boring they could provide really exotic demonstrations there too. So that's what Zala was—literally programmed and trained and raised to do anything and everything for other people. Cut off from that, she'd naturally latched onto the first person that would make her feel valued—me.

But these facts didn't explain what she was doing here, or why she had lied.

"As for the lie, well, it seemed better *here* to be an administrative assistant than an entertainer. They would have just thrown me in some kind of frontier-style brothel and that would have been that. I am not a whore! My profession is a valuable and honorable one—back home." Big tears started to well up in her eyes, and I found myself somehow on the defensive instead of the attack. She was really good at that.

Still, she stuck to the rest of her story. She was supposedly a genetic illegal, of what kind she hadn't been told, and she had been shipped here without a clue as to why. Shifting her to the right slot in life had cleared up one of my mysteries, but left her big one still unanswered.

On the afternoon of our fifth day, we got a taste of what was to come on Charon. Some minor tests had been performed without our knowing about them; they proved we were now fully "affiliated"—or seasoned—and ready to face the cold, cruel world. One of the tests, I discovered, involved the excellent soup we'd been served for lunch. Everybody had had some, everybody loved it; the only trouble was there hadn't been any soup.

At the end of the meal it came as a big shock when Garal stood up and announced, "We will need no service to clear this soup from the table." He waved his hand, and the soup—bowls, spoon, and tureen—suddenly and abruptly vanished. Even the spots where some had spilled a little on the tablecloth instantly vanished.

Although we'd all been warned to expect this, I'm afraid my jaw dropped as low as any other. The demonstration was incredible—unbelievable. That soup had been as real as my own right hand. And yet, we had all sat there, in reality eating absolutely nothing, and raving about it.

"Now, at last, you see what we mean," Garal said smugly. "But we need a few more examples just to give you an idea of the range." He pointed at a young, sandy-haired frontiersman. "You. Float up and over the table and hover there."

Immediately the startled man rose from his chair, still in a sitting position, floated over to about a meter above the dining table. He grew panicky and started flailing away at the air as we all gaped.

Mogar, the big brute with the single room who was sitting next to the man, reached over to the now empty chair and felt around. His IQ was obviously higher than I'd thought—it's exactly what I would have done. "Th—he's not in the chair!" the big man growled in amazement. To prove it, even to himself, he moved down one and sat in the chair.

"Stop thrashing about in the air!" Garal snapped, but the hapless floating man didn't heed him. Finally Garal, in a disgusted tone, said, "All right then—get down from there!" He snapped his fingers. The man fell into the center of the table with a loud crash, almost knocking it over. Soup wasn't the only course we'd had, and he got up a little dizzily covered in leftovers.

We were all stunned. Levitation? "I thought you said the magic wasn't real," I remarked suspiciously. "If that wasn't real—what is?"

Garal smiled. "*Now* you're getting the true measure of Charon. What *is* real here? Did that man float up, then fall? Or did he climb up under the *impression* he was floating and then fall into the food? Do *you* know?"

"*Do you?*" somebody grumbled.

He smiled. "In this case, yes, I do. But I don't always know. You have to be a real master of this always to tell what's real and what's not—and usually, even then, there's somebody around at least as good as you who can fool you. The point is, you can't trust anybody or anything on Charon. Never." He snapped his fingers once again, and we all fell smack on our behinds. The chairs we had been sitting in had all abruptly vanished.

Garal laughed. "You see? Real or illusion? Because *I* will it even *I* see what you see, perceive it as you perceive it. A perfect check on my own handiwork. Had someone come in who'd never met any of us before while you were sitting eating your soup, that person would have seen you all sitting there eating soup. They would see what you saw, smell what you smelled, the works. Why? Not because I willed the illusion, but because you believed it—and radiated it."

Zala picked herself up a little painfully and then helped me to my feet. We were all more than a little shaken.

"Enough of these children's games," our host proclaimed, "you now know exactly what you're in for. It's not really all that bad—nor is it all that easy. Spells and counterspells, mental control and discipline, those are the keys and they aren't easily learned—and even less easily tamed."

"Well how do we know what's real, then?" somebody asked.

He took the question seriously. "There is only one way to survive and prosper on Charon. Only one. You must act as if *everything* is real—even magic. You have to discard all your notions of the past and live as if you were part of a children's fairy tale. You're in a world where magic works. You're in a world where sorcery, not science, reigns, even though it knows and understands scientific principles. You're in a world where science, natural law, and even logic and common sense can be suspended at the whim of certain people. It doesn't matter if we're dealing with reality or illusion —it doesn't matter one bit. No matter what it is, *it is real to you,* and to everyone else. Look—see that pitcher of fruit juice on the table?"

We all looked at it, expecting it to vanish. It did not. Instead, Garal concentrated, half shutting his eyes, and pointed to the pitcher.

Slowly the yellow liquid inside seemed to churn, to bubble, to run through with many colors, while smoking and hissing. It was an ugly brew now, and all the more so because we had all drank from that pitcher earlier.

Garal opened his eyes and looked at us seriously. "Now, that pitcher contained one hundred percent *nui* juice and nothing else. I have just changed the contents into a deadly poison—or have I? You all *see* and *smell* the stuff, don't you?"

We all just murmured assent or nodded.

"All right, then. Stand back a bit." He walked up, carefully lifted the pitcher, and spilled a small drop on the edge of the table. It hissed and bubbled and began eating through the tablecloth and into the finish. Then he replaced the pitcher on the table.

"Now, *did* I just change that into a deadly acid, or is that still a pitcher of fruit juice?"

"It's still fruit juice," somebody said, and reached for it.

"No! Don't touch it!" Garal almost yelled; the man hesitated. "Don't you understand? It doesn't matter what it really is! It doesn't matter a bit! You all perceive it as acid—and so for you it *is* acid. If you got some on you it would burn a hole in you. Why? Because you'd subconsciously tell the Wardens in your own body that it was acid, and your cells and molecules would react accordingly. *We* believe it's acid, and so our Wardens tell those in the tablecloth and top that it's acid, and they, having no sensory apparatus of their own, believe it too, and react accordingly. Don't you see? Whether it is illusion or not, this is not simple hypnosis." He waved an arm at the room as a whole. "See all this? It's not dead. *It's alive!* The rocks and trees outside are alive. The table, walls, clothing, *everything* is alive. Alive with Wardens. And so are you and so am I.

"Wardens don't think, but they hear what you are thinking and they act accordingly. They broadcast that to all the other Wardens, and those Wardens act accordingly. That is acid because your senses tell your brain it is acid—that's hypnosis. But your brain tells the Wardens, and the others that it is acid—and that's not hypnosis. That *is* acid."

Tiliar entered from the rear accompanied by a distinguished-looking man, in his forties perhaps, wearing a long black robe adorned with golden and silver threads. He was gray-haired, an unusual sight in one so young, and had a ruddy complexion, as if he'd spent a lot of his time in a hard outdoor climate. Not *this* climate, though—he certainly was dry enough.

Garal stepped back and bowed slightly in deference to the newcomer. Both he and Tiliar treated the man with respect, the respect of subordinates to the boss.

He stopped and looked around at us, then at the acid still sputtering in the pitcher, and smiled. With no sign of concentration or effort at all, he mumbled a word and pointed to the pitcher, which immediately ceased bubbling and quickly began to transform itself back into fruit juice. Once its normal, healthy yellow color was restored, he walked over to it, picked it up, materialized a glass from somewhere, and poured juice into the glass. He then drank about half and looked satisfied, then put the glass back down on the table.

"My name is Korman," he introduced himself, his voice a mellow and pleasant baritone with an air of extreme confidence in its tone. "I'm what the locals would call the sorc—the town sorcerer. I'm also one of those who sit in the Synod, so I'm here as the official representative of the government of Charon and Her Worship, the Queen Aeolia, Lord of the Diamond. Welcome."

That was a new one. So she was queen now? Could goddess be far behind—or would that be too much even for the Synod?

"My assistants here will be setting up an interview table in the rear while we chat," he continued, "and I hope I can answer some of your questions." He paused a moment. "Oh, how inconsiderate of me!" He snapped his fingers and the chairs reappeared. In addition to ours, an almost thronelike wooden monster appeared at the head of the table. He sat in it.

We all eyed the chairs with some suspicion, which gave Korman some amusement.

"Oh, come, come," he admonished us, "please have a seat—or has nothing Garal told you sunk in as yet? Face it, *you* don't know if the chairs were always there and only seemed to vanish, or whether there never were any chairs. And does it make any difference? These chairs are solid and comfortable. They will support you. You can go completely mad here trying to decide if things like that are real. Accept what your senses tell you. Sit down, please!"

With a shrug, I sat down, and slowly, the others followed suit. Korman was right of course, it made no practical difference whatsoever whether or not the chairs were real. However, I had a pretty good idea they were—Garal just didn't look like the type to exert himself to actually carry the things out, and they had been real the previous four days.

"That's better," the wizard approved. "Now, let's begin. First of all, none of you are ordinary to us. Oh, I know, it sounds like a political snow job, but I mean it. We have a lot of ordinary people to work the farms and fields. Some of the other worlds of the Diamond waste resources like you would just throw you together with the peasants and forget about you, but not us. Each of you is here for a reason, each of you has special skills learned Outside that would take years to learn here. We don't propose to throw away any valuable talents and skills you might have just because you're new here. We don't get many Outsiders these days—you're the first small batch in more than three years—and we don't propose to have you out there picking fruit if you have something we can use."

That was something of a relief to me and probably to most of the others at the table. None of us had any desire to be peasants, and we all, for good reasons and bad, had pretty high opinions of ourselves. But Korman's statement also had an element of insecurity in it, for the challenge was clear—they would make good use of us only if we could show them a talent or skill they needed. What if everything one knew proved obsolete at Charon's quaint technological level?

"Now," he went on, "when you arrived here you were told your past was behind you, that no reference to it would be made. That is the stock speech everybody gets on all the Warden worlds, and there is a measure of truth in it. If there is anybody here who does not wish his or her past to be brought up ever again and wants a totally clean start, you are free to tell me now. We will destroy your dossier back there and you will be assigned as an unskilled laborer under any name you wish. That is your right. Anybody?"

People looked at one another, but nobody made a move or said anything. For a moment I thought Zala might, but she just took my hand and squeezed it. Nobody in this group wanted to spend the rest of his life as a melon picker in a swamp.

After a suitable pause, Korman nodded to himself. "Very well then. Your silence is consent to reopen your past—just a little. Now, one at a time I would like to interview each of you. Do not lie to me, for I will know it, I guarantee you. And if I am lied to, I will place a spell of truthfulness on you and keep it there so you will be forever incapable of lying again. You can appreciate how embarrassing that would be."

Uh-oh. I didn't like *that* at all. Still, not lying was not the same thing as telling the truth. If I could fool some of the best machines, I should have little trouble fooling a real person.

"Now, before we begin, are there any general questions you want answered?"

We looked around, mostly at one another. Finally, I decided to be the brave one. "Yeah. How do we get trained in the, ah, magical arts?"

He looked amused. "A good question. Maybe you do, and maybe you don't. Not right away, certainly—there's a certain mind-set you have to acquire over time before the training will do you much good. As long as you are in any way concerned with what is real and what is not it's hopeless. Only when you accept this world and this culture on its own terms can you begin. Your entire lives have been rooted in science, in faith in science, in belief in science and experimental evidence. Empiricism is your cultural bias. But here, where an experiment of any sort will always come out the way I decide it should, that's not valid. We'll know when—or if—you're ready, and so will you."

Somebody else had a good question. "These things we see that you and the others cause—I know everybody *here* sees 'em, but what about anybody *not* from here? Somebody from a different Warden world, maybe. Or a camera."

"Two questions," Korman replied, "and two answers. The easy one first, I think. Cameras. Cameras down here will take pictures, and no matter what is actually photographed the picture will be perceived as what was *believed* to have been photographed. Say I turn you into a uhar. This fellow here then takes your picture. He looks at the picture, and he sees a uhar. He takes the picture to a different town and shows it to somebody else. *They* see a uhar because *you* see a uhar, so the question's moot. Incidentally robotic devices don't work well down here—the electrical fields and storms of Charon will short out any known power plant I've heard of in fairly quick order. The same properties disrupt aerial or satellite surveillance. But even if a robot worked here, it would be nothing more than a guide for the blind, and one you could never fully trust because you wouldn't know all the questions to ask it."

"And somebody not from here?" the questioner prompted.

"Well, that's more complicated. Our Wardens are a mutated strain of the other Wardens. Our Wardens don't talk to the Wardens of the other three planets, just to those like themselves. So a visitor here from Lilith, say, would see things as they really are. However, on Charon our wishes have a way of partially coming true. A building must be a building, or the winds rush through and the storms will get you. It may not really be as fancy as it looks to us, but it's a building all the same. Organic matter, however, is a different story. If I turn you into a uhar, as my previous example shows, you'll believe you're a uhar. So will the Wardens in your body. Now, we don't know how they get the information, let alone the energy, but, slowly, the illusion will become the reality. Your cells will change accordingly, or be replaced. The whole complex biochemistry of the uhar is suddenly available to your Wardens. Perhaps they just contact their brethren in a real uhar, I don't know, but they draw all the information they need, and they draw energy from somewhere outside themselves and convert it to matter as needed; so, over a period of time, you will *be* a uhar. Really. And then even our visitor from Lilith will see you as such."

This was a new, exciting, and yet frightening idea. Transmutation was not something I relished. Still, something very important was involved here. The Wardens could get information, incredibly complex information —more complex and detailed than the best computers—and then act upon it, even converting energy to matter to achieve it. I mentally filed the information for future reference.

Korman looked around. "Anything else? No? Well then, let's begin. I'm sure you are anxious to get out of this place and pick up your lives. We are just as anxious to give this hotel back to its regular patrons, who are none too happy about the arrangement." He stood up and walked back to his two assistants, who had set up a folding table and placed a stack of thick file folders on it. He walked behind the table, sat down on a folding chair, and picked up the first of the dossiers. "Mojet Kaigh!" he called out.

One of the men in our group walked nervously over to the table and sat down at another folding chair placed in front. They were just slightly too far away to hear them when they talked in low tones, but normal conversation carried sufficiently so that we were all more or less in on the interview.

It was pretty routine really. Name, age, special skills and backgrounds—things like that. Then right in the middle I experienced something odd, as if, somehow, a second or two was lost—sort of *edited out*. Nobody else seemed to notice it and so I said nothing, but it was eerie nonetheless—either this was something I should know about or it was me, and the latter worried me the most.

The same thing happened during the second and third interviews—a sense of following along, hearing the routine procedure when, *blip*, there was a sudden slight difference in the scene—people slightly out of position, something like that. The more it happened, the more I became convinced that something not apparent to everyone else was happening.

Interestingly, the occurrence was repeated with each interview except one—Zala's. I followed what was going on particularly keenly, not only looking for the telltale blackout but also to see how well Korman's records jibed with Zala's own version of her life. It was pretty close, I had to admit—and there was no disorientation.

I fidgeted irritably as the boring process continued, although it was not completely without interest. Our big bully upstairs with the private room had been something of a dictator, it appeared, on an off-the-beaten-track frontier world; he had a particular fondness for grotesque maimings and the like. Although this information confirmed the man's chilling aura, it also reminded me that big, brawny, and nasty did not necessarily mean stupid. Anybody who could pull off a virtual planetary takeover and hold on for almost six years was definitely on the genius side—which is why he was here at all. Aeolia Matuze would love him—but whether he'd play ball with her was something else again.

I was kept for last, and when Korman called my name it was with a great deal of curiosity that I approached the table. Would I too suffer an "edit"?

He was pleasant and businesslike enough, as he had been with the others.

"You are Park Lacoch?"

"I am," I responded.

"You have no objections to your past being reviewed?"

I hesitated for what I judged was an appropriate length of time, then said, "No, I guess not."

He nodded. "I understand your apprehension. You are a most colorful character, Lacoch—did you know that?"

"I hardly think that's the word most people would use."

He chuckled dryly. "I daresay. Still, you're in a long line of mass murderers from respected backgrounds. They color human history and make its humdrum aspects more interesting. I gather they solved your basic problem?"

"You could say that. I was in deep psych for quite a long time, you understand. I emerged as what they call sane, but because of my notoriety I could hardly be returned to society."

"You see what I mean about colorful? Yes, that fits. Also, we could hardly ignore the fact that you've shared quarters here with a woman and have now spent a week in a town full of them and you've been nothing but civilized to all. Tell me, though, honestly—do you think that any conditions might set you off again, even the most extreme?"

I shrugged. "Who can say? I don't think so, not any more than you or anybody else. I'm pretty well at peace with myself on that score, so much so I can't even imagine myself doing such things, though I know I did."

"What about killing in general? Could you kill someone under any conditions?"

That was pretty easy. "Of course. If somebody was trying to kill me, for example. They didn't take that route out with me, sir. I wasn't programmed—I was cured."

He nodded approvingly, then looked up suddenly and straight at me, eyes wide, almost burning—a hypnotic gaze, an amazing one, but it flared for only a second and then was gone. Korman sighed and relaxed a moment. "There, we're alone now."

I jumped. "Huh?" I looked around at—well, nothing. There appeared to be a huge, smooth black wall right in back of me.

It was clearly too routine a thing for him to even be amused by my reaction. "A simple thing. When we return to the real world once more none of your compatriots will even be aware of any gap."

"So that's what happened! I noticed the jerkiness."

"I'm impressed. Almost nobody does, you know. The brain fills in the gap or explains it away. You say you noticed it with others?"

I nodded. "The first time I thought I was going a little crazy, but when it happened again and again I knew something was up."

"You noticed it with every one of them?"

I smiled, seeing his probe. "All but Zala. You didn't take her aside like this, I don't think."

He nodded approvingly. "You're quite correct. I don't think I've underestimated you, Lacoch. With training, you might even gain and control the Power yourself. You have demonstrated an abnormally early affinity."

"I'd like to give it a try," I told him sincerely—and *that* was no lie.

"We'll see. Chance has placed you in a most fortuitous position, Lacoch, and now you show even more interesting abilities. You've got a golden opportunity to go far on Charon."

"Oh? In what way?" I was both curious and a bit suspicious at all this interest. I didn't like having attention called to myself quite this early in the game.

Korman thought a moment, seeming to wrestle with some question in his mind. Whatever the dilemma, he seemed to resolve it and sighed.

"A little more than five years ago the Lord of Charon was Tulio Koril. He was a wily old rogue, and tremendously powerful. He had little stomach for the routine affairs of state—when one can be a god, how much more do bureaucracy, paperwork, and routine decisions weigh on him?"

"Why did he keep at it, then?"

"A sense of duty, of obligation, mostly. He derived no joy from it, but he saw the potential for terrible abuse in the position and felt that any of his logical successors would be a disaster—his opinion, of course, which has to be balanced against the egomania necessary to get to be Lord in the first place."

"A *Warden* man with a sense of duty and obligation?"

"There are many. I fancy myself one, in fact. You are as much an outcast as any of us, yet far more than we, you are the product of the society that cast you out. It is a society that aims overall for the common good, but to achieve that aim it requires all its citizens to take a certain viewpoint that is not necessarily the only one. Many of us are criminals by any lights, of course, but many more are criminal only because we dared take or develop a different viewpoint than the one the Confederacy favors. Throughout man's dirty history 'different' was always equated with evil, when 'different' is—well, simply 'different.' If *their* system is perfect, why do they employ detectives, assassins, and, for that matter, how the hell can they produce *us?*"

It was not a question easily answered, nor profitably responded to at this time. I said nothing.

"When first the Confederacy system was imposed, they set their assassins to execute those few who would not or could not adapt. That was centuries ago, and many millions of lives ago, and yet the unadapted are still here—and they are still out there killing. You know something, Lacoch? No matter how many they kill, no matter how many they reprogram, no matter what means they develop to control mind and body—we will still exist. Those who would shape history never learn from it, and yet if they did they would see in people like us the greatness of man, why he's out here among the stars instead of blown away by his own hand back on some dirty fly-speck of a home world. No matter how many enemies tyranny would kill, *there is always somebody else.* Always."

"I wouldn't exactly call the Confederacy a tyranny. Not when compared to the old ways."

"Well, perhaps not, but there, new ways mask the old. A society that mandates absolutely the way people must think, eat, drink, whom to love

—and whether to love—is a tyranny, even if cloaked in gold and tasting of honey."

"But if the people are happy—"

"The people of the greatest tyrannies are usually happy—or, at least, not unhappy. No tyrant in human history ever governed without the tacit support of the masses, no matter what those masses might say if the tyrant was ever overthrown. Revolutions are made by the few, the elect, those with the imagination and the intellect to penetrate the tyranny and see how things could and should be better. It is a lesson the Confederacy understands full well—that's why people like Koril and myself are here. And, no matter to what lengths they go, the Confederacy will eventually follow all other human empires and fall, either from external factors or from sheer dry rot. They are staving off the fall, but fall they will, eventually. Some of us would prefer they fall sooner than later."

"You sound like an embittered philosopher," I commented.

He shrugged. "Actually, I was a historian. Not one of those official types teaching you all the doctored-up versions of the past you were supposed to learn, but one of the real ones with access to *all* the facts, doing analyses for the Confederacy. History is a science, you know—although they don't really let you know that either. The techs are scared to death of it and put it in the same category as literature, as always. That's why hard science people are the most ignorant of it and so easily led. But, I digress from my point."

"I find this all fascinating," I told him truthfully—knowing my enemy was vital—"but you were speaking for some reason of Koril."

He nodded. "Koril is one of the old school intellectuals. He knows that the Confederacy will fall one day of its own weight and he is content to allow natural forces to do just that, even if it might be centuries in the future. There is another school, though, that believes that a quick and, if need be, violent push to oblivion will, overall, save lives and produce positive results for more people. A man can die in agonizing slowness or nearly instantly—which is more merciful to him? You see the difference in positions?"

I nodded. "Evolution or revolution—an old story. I gather this is behind Koril no longer being Lord?"   •

"It is. He was an evolution man in power at the wrong time."

I was becoming more and more interested. "The wrong time? That implies that such a revolution on such a scale is suddenly possible, something I find very hard to believe."

"About five years ago," Korman told me, "Marek Kreegan, Lord Lilith, called a special conference of the Four Lords of the Diamond. We had been contacted, it seems, by an external force that wanted our aid overthrowing the Confederacy."

"External force?" I could hardly believe it. A week on Charon and already I was finding out a lot of details I thought I would have to dig out with a sword.

"An alien force. Big. Powerful. Not really more advanced than the Confederacy but unhampered by their ideological restraints, which means they have a lot of stuff we don't. They are also—by design, we think—far fewer in number than humankind. They have a long history of getting along with other kinds of life forms, but their analysis of the culture and values of the Confederacy said that together we would just out-and-out crush them. They feel they must destroy the Confederacy, but they have no wish to destroy humankind as well."

"Do you think they could? You just said how small they were compared to us."

He shook his head sadly from side to side, more in wonder than in reaction to my question. "You see? You make an easy mistake. It's not *numbers* that are important. The Confederacy itself could destroy a planet with ten billion on it with *one* simple device, and do it with perhaps only one man and two robots. Three against ten billion—and who would win?"

"But they'd have to get to all those planets first," I pointed out.

"Any race smart enough to meet and attempt an alliance with the Four Lords—and pull it off under the noses of the picket ships and the other devices our prison system contains to keep us isolated—and who even so remains virtually unknown to the Confederacy would have few problems doing so."

I had to admit he had a point there, but I let it pass for the moment. "And the Four Lords went along with the deal?"

He nodded. "Three of them did. Kreegan came up with the master plan; the aliens will provide the technology and access; and the other worlds contribute their power, wealth, and expertise."

"I assume the one who didn't was Koril."

Again he nodded. "That's the story. He was just flat-out against the plan. He feared the aliens were only using us for a painless conquest which once undertaken, would enable them to enslave or wipe out mankind. In this he was pretty well alone. Of course, emotionally, to be a party to the overthrow of the Confederacy within your lifetime is almost irresistible, but there is an overriding practical reason as well. The Warden worlds that help will share in the rewards, even the spoils. There is very good reason to believe that these aliens are capable of curing, or at least stabilizing, the Warden organism. You understand what *that* means."

I nodded. "Escape."

"More than escape! It means we, personally, will be there to pick up the pieces. Quite an incentive! But, as I said, there is overriding practicality here. Charon is probably the least necessary of all the Warden worlds. Mostly political criminals, wrong thinkers, that type are sent here, and the plot, quite frankly, could proceed without us. Could—and would. We would be isolated, cut off as things proceeded without us. But if anything went wrong, we would be blamed along with the others, even though we took no part. That might result in the Confederacy literally destroying the Warden Diamond. But, if things succeeded, the other three would be on the winning side, with all those IOUs and means of escape, and we would be stuck here, consigned to eternal oblivion. Therefore, since we were not important to the plot, we either joined it and gained or we didn't and lost whatever the outcome. *That* was what caused the unprecedented removal of a Lord of the Diamond."

"This Koril—I gather he didn't take this lying down?"

"Hardly! It took the entire Synod's combined power to oust him, and even then he was horrible in his power. He fled, finally, to Gamush, the equatorial continent, where he had already prepared a retreat and head-quarters so well hidden none have been able to find it. Consider—a lowly apt in the magical arts could kill you with a glance. One of the village sorcs could level a castle and transform all the people into trees if he or she felt like it. The combined Synod could make a continent vanish and rearrange the oceans of the world. But that same combined Synod could only oust, not kill, Koril—and cannot locate him now. Does that give you an appreciation of the old man's power?"

I had seen little but parlor tricks on this world so far, but I could accept his examples at least as comparative allegory. "And he's still working against you."

"He is. Not effectively of late, but he is more than dangerous. He retained good friends in high places, and some of his agents even managed to penetrate meetings of the Four Lords themselves. At one point, they got past tight security of kinds you cannot imagine to witness a meeting with our alien allies themselves. The spies slipped up before they could do any harm and were all eventually tracked down and killed, but it was a *very* close call. Koril came within a hairsbreadth of killing all Four Lords and two of the aliens as well—and he wasn't even there! He was still safe down in Gamush."

It was my turn to push now. "All this is well and good—but, tell me, why are you telling me all this? I would assume it's far from common knowledge."

"You're right. Koril's fall was pictured publicly as a move to save Charon from evil ambition. We created, in the minds of the people, a portrait of him as a devil, a demon, a creature of pure powerful evil. It has been quite effective, and even useful—a force of opposition based on fear and power. It keeps the masses in line, and he can be blamed for just about anything that goes wrong."

"A bogeyman." So much for tolerating other points of view, I thought to myself.

"Yes, exactly. But a real one who remains a real threat. We would much prefer to have him be merely a myth. He's used our own propaganda against us too, to attract those unhappy with us in any way, employing the trappings of devil worship and the rest, creating an effective cult of opposition, in both senses of the word 'cult.' We cannot be truly safe and secure until Koril is destroyed."

"But I thought you said you had tried that and failed."

"Well, not exactly. There was no concerted effort to destroy him when he wasn't already forewarned and forearmed. After all, we didn't hate him or covet his job—we merely wanted him out because we could not change his mind. Had we foreseen what sort of enemy he would make—but that's hindsight. We *can* kill him—if we face him down. But to do that we have to know where he is, where that redoubt is."

I knew all this was leading somewhere, but it wasn't clear why I was the one being led there. "What's all this have to do with me?"

"I'm coming to that. First of all, he has a large minority following in his demon cult, but they are mostly useless except as information gatherers because they really believe that guff. In the aftermath of his botched assault we pretty well wiped out his effective force. He needs new people—level-headed, unclouded with superstition, and yet with some residual ties to the old values of the Confederacy. People who would be useful commanders of his demonic troops, bring fresh ideas and approaches to him, and take his side against the aliens even if they had no particular love for the Confederacy."

I began to see. "In other words, newly arrived inmates like me."

"You're the most logical. We get few newcomers these days—none of the Wardens get many, and we get the fewest of all. The nature of our atmosphere prevents most clandestine communications, and even blocks basic surveillance of us on the ground by remotes. The Confederacy has agents of one sort or another all over the Warden Diamond, but they are of almost no use here since messages are nearly impossible to get in or out except by spacecraft, which are rigidly monitored. You're the first small group we've gotten since long before Koril was deposed, so you're an absolute natural for him to approach. And of course there is a different reason as well—the real reason why we got *any* prisoners this drop. You see, due to the inevitable slip-up, the Confederacy is finally wise to the fact that we and our alien allies are plotting against it. That's *all* it knows though, and it's too little to act upon—and, I think, too late. Still, they are not stupid. They have already sent at least one top assassin to the Warden Diamond—we know that."

"*What!*" I felt a cold chill. Was I being led down the garden path to the guillotine? Had my cover been so easily blown?

He nodded. "And while we are sure only of the one, it's reasonable for us to assume that they would send more."

"But what for?" I asked, steadying my nerves as best I could. "You just said it would be nearly impossible to get information out. And anybody they'd send here would be stuck, just like us."

"It is our belief—Charon's, not the Four Lords, I might add—that they will send their best men available to each of the four worlds with the intent of killing each of the Four Lords. Doing this will, they feel, cause some disruption, and the new Lord will be a lot less sure of him or herself and perhaps less disposed toward treason. It is not much of a hope, I admit, but it's the only logical thing they *can* do while they try and find the alien enemy first."

He was uncomfortably close to the mark, and I could only feel I was being toyed with. Something inside kept shouting *"He knows! He knows!"*—but my more controlled overmind kept saying that the best way to proceed was to play along, at least for now. "And you think that one of us is a Confederacy fanatic?"

"I *know* it," he responded. "I knew it the moment I met the agent face to face."

He paused for a moment and I braced for the inevitable denouement to our little play.

"The Confederacy's agent," he said, "is Zala Embuay."

CHAPTER FIVE

A Plot, a Deal, and a Potion

"*Zala?* You've got to be joking!" I could hardly contain my emotions at this point, a mixture of incredulity, relief, and a still-lingering suspicion that I was being had. "You've got to be kidding. Without protection she wouldn't last ten minutes outside this hotel."

"That's partly the point," Korman responded, and he didn't seem to be joking. "Have you ever seen anyone so innocent, so confused, so totally *dependent?* Not the Warden Diamond sort at all. Not even the Confederacy's."

"You're saying it's all an act? A plant?" I found it hard to take this seriously from *any* viewpoint.

"Oddly enough, no. Zala is, I'm certain, exactly what we see. She's shallow, weak, more an outline of a real person than a whole human being. There is no doubt in my mind that she believes herself to be what she is utterly and has no inkling whatsoever of her true nature and purpose."

I had to laugh. "This is impossible."

"When I saw her I was immediately aware of the anomaly. The Wardens, you see, congregate in every cell, in every molecule of our being. They permeate our existence. With some training you can even see them. Sense them. *Hear* them. I'm sure you'll one day experience what I can only inadequately verbalize. But the Wardens become as highly specialized as the molecules they link up to. The brain is particularly odd. Wardens there organize in specific ways, so specialized that you can actually see a diagram of the parts of the brain. When I look at anyone—you, for instance—I see those parts distinctly, and even how they interconnect and interact. The cerebrum and the cerebral cortex are easy to define. In you, in everyone—but not in Zala."

"Huh? How's that?"

"I can't really explain it. It is outside my experience in every way. Outside anybody's, I'd guess. But organically, Zala's cerebral functions are organized very differently. It's almost as if there were *two* forebrains in there, two totally different operative centers linked to the same cerebellum, medulla, spinal cord and nervous system—but not to each other. It is definitely organic. Deliberate. And unprecedented as far as I can tell."

"You're telling me that there are two minds in one body? That's hard to swallow, although I've heard tales of multiple personalities."

"No! Not in that old sense. Multiples as we know them are psych conditions. Psychologically induced—and curable. This is not a psych condition. I'm talking about two real minds, Lacoch!"

I couldn't shake the oddest feeling that either I was dreaming this whole illogical and improbable conversation or that I had really gone suddenly insane. The thought suddenly came to me that all this was illusion, some way in which they were pulling some sort of sophisticated psyche job on me. Still, I had wits enough left to realize that no matter what the situation, my only choice was to keep playing along, at least for now. "You will understand," I said carefully, "that I find both the idea and your means of confirmation rather, ah, improbable."

He nodded. "Still, it's true and it must be acted upon. The implications of a dual mind with unknown powers are ones we can't ignore, and must know more about it. Within a matter of hours, I can get a set of master defense codes for the Confederacy, even a list of the top fifty assassins now on assignment along with the actual assignments of at least half. Our information conduits into the Confederacy are not only beyond their belief, they are almost beyond mine. Yet we have heard nothing whatsoever about a project like this, which must have been—what?—twenty years plus in the making. The perfect agent. She can be hypnoed, psyched to the gills, tortured beyond endurance and she wouldn't know or give away a thing. If we had telepathy she'd pass *that* test too. All the while the other mind, the assassin's mind, would be there, beyond reach, gathering data and picking its own time to assume control. It must be something else—it has nothing to do *but* its job. Cold, analytical genius set to one task and only one."

I thought about it. If all this were real, I could not only see his point I could almost doubt myself. Krega had never said that I'd be the only agent, and Zala might well be part of an independent effort. Telling myself I was really crazy for starting to believe all this, I still had to press on. "So you just kill her and that's that," I commented dryly.

"Oh, no! Then we would never see this other mind, never know its capabilities—and we might not catch the next one, or the next dozen, or hundred, or whatever. Not to mention that they'll be ticking bombs back in the Confederacy when all hell breaks loose and we return. We need to know a great deal more about her new type. Of course, we'd like to know just how much they really know about us at this stage."

"I thought you just told me their secrets were an open book."

He glared at me. "Some. But we—the Four Lords—are a special target of a special group. Their plans are so secret that even those who formulated them have been wiped now." He sighed. "And that brings us back to what we have dubbed 'Operation Darkquest'—which brings us back to you."

I nodded, beginning to see how all this was fitting together. Still, I couldn't resist a mild jab. "It seems to me that for a man with the powers of a god you're sounding pretty human."

Again the glare, but it softened, and his eyes lit up with just a trace of humor. "You're right, of course. It *is* something of a humbling experience, but the mind is always the best weapon no matter what sort of power one acquires."

"Now—do you mind getting down to specifics?" I pressed.

"All right, all right. We are going to assign Zala to you and you to a minor but conspicuous village post down south where Koril's cult is very strong. We feel certain Koril will contact you, indirectly of course, and sound you out. Now that you know the situation, we want you to go along with him, feed his prejudices. You and Zala will ultimately accept his deal to join him, and that will mean getting you to his redoubt."

"You feel sure he'll contact us? We'll be pretty obvious, I'd think."

"He'll contact you, all right. Maybe not right away, but he'll come. Eventually he'll contact all of you, but not all will go his way."

"I see. And you want me to somehow get the location of that fortress to you."

He nodded. "That and his future plans."

"You have some gadget for me to do all this with, I presume?"

He shook his head from side to side. "Sadly, no. Most of the usual ones won't work here, and anything I might add by my powers Koril would detect. He's that good. No, I suspect we'll have to wait until he sends you out on your first errand, or mission, or whatever. Call it a test of your resourcefulness."

I considered it. "And how am I supposed to make sure this message gets to you without getting my head blown off either by your people or Koril's?"

"Koril is your problem. As for the other, the key word is 'Darkquest.' Village sorcs and those above will know the term but not what it means. What it will do is make certain that you are not killed and that word of your capture or whatever will reach the Synod."

"It seems to me Koril's going to know at least the signal word himself— if he's as good as you say."

Korman nodded. "He will, but it will do him no good. He won't know what it means, and any of his people using it other than yourself will simply walk into capture."

That part pretty well satisfied me. "How good is this Koril in psych terms though? Am I likely to go through some sort of exercise that will betray the plot when I'm down there in *his* domain?"

"He himself is powerful enough to turn your mind to almost anything, which is the reason for the length of our session here. I have been creating blocks in your mind, selective traps and guards that will go up should he try any such thing. And if he *does* try any mind-turning, it won't take. Not for long anyway."

"But he's likely to sense the blocks," I noted.

"On most attempts, certainly," Korman agreed. "But *you*—you have been through three years of intense psych before coming here, remember. Your mind now shows many, many blocks and rechannelings to me. The extras I add won't be noticed, and that alone is what makes you so uniquely qualified—you see?"

I *did* see. Of course, the psych blocks Korman saw weren't from any Lacoch psych treatments but from my own breeding, training, and Krega's Security; but it explained a lot. If Korman could sense those blocks—but not remove them—it not only reinforced my assumed identity but quite possibly prevented him from doing some of that mind-bending on me. I remembered that earlier hypnotic gaze. "All right, I understand the plot," I told him. "What about Zala?"

"Take her along, by all means!" Korman urged. "Find out all you can from her, particularly from her alter ego which you will almost certainly see. And if you can manage it, when *you* are in position to use 'Darkquest' see if you can't manage to have her with you."

I chuckled. "This is *some* job you're giving me. I was a planetary administrator, for god's sake! Now I'm instantly supposed to be a master spy, secret agent, and the rest, pitting myself against the top power on the planet and a Confederacy assassin!"

"You don't have to accept," he said calmly. "I admit your overall qualifications aren't very good. Against the perfect psych cover and an interesting and agile mind, we must balance your lack of experience. Do you remember your old self all that well?"

I gave the required shudder. "Yes, I remember him."

"You were a master of disguise and you baffled the best police for over five years. You're not as rank an amateur as you think."

I considered that. "Still, I'm going to have to make every move right—no mistakes of any kind. One goof and I'm done, maybe for a very long time. The odds are I'm going to get killed."

"Well, that's true," he admitted casually, "but consider that you have alternatives. First, you can refuse categorically. I'll find another candidate, team Zala up with him or her, and wipe this entire conversation from your memory. You'll then be sent north, out of the way, and can spend the rest of your life toiling in the fields getting in the harvest. That's safe. Or you can accept—and get killed. Or you can accept, accomplish the mission, and find yourself very abruptly a man of immense rank and power at

the right hand of Aeolia Matuze and the Synod, a participant in the coming revolution, and sure recipient of its fruits."

I looked at him cautiously. "And I could accept, contact Koril, and really join his side."

'You could," he admitted, "and yet—why? If you win you'll be a big
shot on an isolated and primitive world forever. More likely, you will not
win, and will either grow old in frustration as we go ahead anyway—or
die in some foolish attempt on the Synod. If you can't see that Koril has
nothing to offer worth the risk, then you're not much good to me anyway."

I nodded. "All right, I'll be your boy. Overall, you don't give me much
choice, and it beats boredom. Besides, I'm kind of curious about all this
myself."

Korman smiled. "I knew you would see reason. Just remember this:
don't underestimate Koril a whit, and under no circumstances try to take
on the old boy himself or even run to us while he's anywhere in the
neighborhood. Nobody's that good. It'll take the whole Synod to nail him.
Bet on it."

"I fully intend to live through this," I assured him.

He laughed evilly. "Lacoch, if you blow this, death will be the *best* you
can expect. Now, I'm going to lower the barrier and continue asking routine questions once more. None of the others, not even my associates, will
know that this conversation has even taken place. You'll be assigned later
today and be on your way early in the morning. It's a long trip, but one
you'll find interesting. Once in Bourget, the town we're sending you to,
you'll be under the wing of Tully Kokul, the local sorc. He's a good man
and he'll orient you properly, but he won't be in on this at all. Keep it
that way—and watch out for him and his apts. We're not so sure of the
apts, and any of them have more power than you can imagine."

"I'll remember," I assured him.

There was a sudden feeling of disorientation that lasted only a fraction
of a second. I didn't turn around, but I could hear the rest of the inmates
whispering and rustling behind me.

"I think we have a number of openings for administrative types like
yourself," Korman said, now very businesslike. "You may return to the
group."

I got up and went back to the rest of them, searching for signs that any
of them were in any way aware of just how long we had been talking, but
detected nothing. Still, there were a few knowing smirks, and I remembered that Korman had had private conversations with most of the others
as well. I wondered if they had gotten the same offer that I had. I somehow doubted it—unless some of them also had unique qualifications. It
was unlikely that the sorcerer had put all his eggs in one basket.

I had to look at Zala again, with new insight, but what I had just heard
still didn't seem possible. And yet . . . It was also unlikely that the Confederacy would have put all *its* eggs in one basket either. If what Korman

suspected was true, it would place me in a very interesting position. I too wanted very much to meet this other Zala—if indeed she truly existed.

We were fed again, and then relaxed, playing some basic games, just snoozing or sitting in the lobby waiting for our hosts to return. Several times I got into conversations, but either I was too subtle or nobody wanted to discuss his experience. Finally I wound up in a corner with Zala.

"What do you think will happen to us now?" she asked me.

I shrugged. "They're going to give us jobs, I think."

"They knew I wasn't an administrator," she said nervously. "I guess they have the official records no matter what they said. He said there wasn't much call for my talents here."

"Don't worry. It'll all work out."

"I wonder if they'll split us up?" she went on, playing out her petty fears. "I wouldn't want to be split up. Not from you."

"We'll see," was all I could reply, knowing the verdict ahead of time.

It was a couple of hours before Korman returned, this time with a clipboard. He took his seat again behind the table, thumbed through some sheets, then looked up at us. We all stood, expectantly, waiting for the word. Zala seemed extremely nervous and squeezed my hand so hard she was almost cutting off circulation; some of the others looked a little anxious themselves, but others did not. I found that an interesting fact in itself.

One by one, Korman called out our names, not in the order he had used at the start, and told the various people the names of towns and jobs they were assigned to. About halfway through, he called both Zala and me, whereupon my suffering hand got squeezed even tighter as we approached.

"Park Lacoch, you were a planetary administrator, and that's quite good and useful experience, although here you won't have your fancy computers and large staffs. It'll take some getting used to, so we're going to start you off small. The town of Bourget on the southeast coast just lost its Town Accountant. It's a bit larger than we'd like to start somebody green at, but the position's open and you're here. You'll deal with four industries, twenty-one Companies. There's a civil staff there that'll break you in and get you oriented—depend on them until you learn the ropes."

"Won't there be some resentment that I got the job ahead of them?" I asked him.

"Probably a little, but not much. It's basically a local staff, all native, and they're a pretty contented lot. They do what they're told. If you're good to them and respect their experience they'll accept you."

"Sounds fair," I told him, meaning it.

"As for you, Zala Embuay," Korman continued, "you present us with a problem. Your nonaugmented literacy rate is very low, your grasp of figures basic. The best position we could find to fit your unique talents would be barmaid or chambermaid. Your entertainment and planning skills might be considerable, but they are all tailored to augmentation. Without the standard computer devices, these skills are mostly useless here. In fact, the more we considered it, the more we realized that you would be out of your element even in the bar or chamber service. You would have to learn skills taken for granted here."

I felt her tremble through the clutched hand as this was being said, all the more so because it was true. A product of a society in which robots did all the basic work and everything from the lights to the music was controlled through machines, she simply had no skills to offer here.

'Therefore, the most logical occupation for you here would be an agricultural field worker. But we feel that such a radical change to basic menial labor without some intermediate steps might not be best for you; your outworlder status could cause some disruptions among your fellow menials." Zala looked blankly at him when he said that, but I understood what he meant. Workers are happiest when they don't know what they're missing. Zala's memories and tales of the wonders of the Confederacy, while they lived with no hope of change in the wretched and primitive condition, would foster resentment—and cause all sorts of local disruptions, not to mention perhaps more converts for Koril.

'So, Zala Embuay, what shall we do with you?"

'I—don't know," she wailed, so pitifully that neither of us could be completely unmoved by her evident misery and low self-esteem.

'The best we could come up with, I'm afraid, is a rather outdated concept where you both come from," Korman continued, sounding cold and businesslike. "With Lacoch's permission, I'd like to propose you become his wifemistress."

She gave something of a gasp and I kind of started myself. "Wifemistress?" I echoed.

He nodded. "I'm rather embarrassed to bring it up. In effect it's a sort of chattel slavery. You would be pledged to Lacoch absolutely. You would live with him and be totally dependent on him for your living quarters and provisions. In exchange, you will learn and practice basic skills—cooking, cleaning, mending. Many of the villagers will take you in hand and show you these things. You will also clean and run errands in his office, whatever he requires you to do. And if need be, you may be called upon by any of the Companies or the town for supplementary labor in the harvest or maintenance."

She looked startled. "That almost sounds like a service robot."

'Something like that," Korman agreed. "But there are no robots here. Other than as a subject for experimental research, there's little we can do with you."

She started at that. "Exper . . . you mean like some kind of animal?"

He nodded gravely, then looked over at me. "Would you accept this arrangement?"

I was in something of a quandary. For anybody but Zala it sounded horrible, dehumanizing, demeaning in the extreme—but what else could she do? "If she's willing, I'll go for it," I told him.

He shifted his gaze back to her. "Well?"

"I—I'd like to go with Park, but I don't know whether I *can* . . ."

Korman grinned, made that magical wave and produced a vial of reddish-colored liquid. He handed it to her. "The oldest sorcerer's gift in magical history," he said. "If you decide to go along, both of you go up to your room and when alone, Embuay, drink this. It is pleasant-tasting and won't hurt a bit, but it'll make things a lot easier on you."

She took the vial and looked at it curiously. "What—what is it?"

"A potion," he replied. "As I said, the oldest basic formula. A love potion, the ancients would call it. Just be sure to drink it when the two of you are alone, maybe just before going to sleep."

Suddenly, again, that wall of silence and isolation came down and Korman and I were effectively alone.

"Is that *really* a love potion?" I asked him.

He chuckled. "Not to you or me if we drank it. Tastes a little like licorice. But I have prepared her mind for it, and it'll be quite effective with her because she will believe in it and that will trigger my patterns in the Wardens of her brain."

"Which one?" I couldn't resist it.

"Actually, that should be interesting," he replied, taking no note of the sarcasm. "The emotional centers and hormonal responses are in the animal, not the human part of the brain. Theoretically it should affect her no matter what—I hope. But don't count on it. If that other brain's as good as I think, it can probably control and suppress almost any emotional response." He paused for a moment. "See that she drinks it. And—well, good luck."

"I'll need it," I assured him, and I sure would. Still, all in all, things had gone better so far than my wildest dreams. If what was going on could be taken at anything close to face value, they suspected someone other than me of being, well, *me*; and they'd assigned me to keep watch on their mistaken notion. They had practically forced me into the camp of what would seem to be a natural ally—Koril—and given me the option of joining a local superpowerful resistance devoted to my own cause or betraying it, giving me entré into the presence of my quarry, Aeolia Matuze, as a trusted confidant. Hell, I couldn't lose!

Zala, though, was still and always the unknown factor. The more I analyzed her, the more I began to believe that she *couldn't* be what she seemed. Such a weak ego was unthinkable on the civilized worlds.

Later, back in our room, we sat and talked for a while. It had not been pleasant having her low self-worth so coldly and completely analyzed in the open, even if it was obvious.

"I want to go with you," she told me sincerely, "but—people as property! It's barbaric!" She took out the vial and looked at it oddly.

"You don't have to take that," I assured her. "Just come along."

She shook her head slowly, still looking at the vial. "No, I know what would happen. I'd rebel, or go crazy, and wind up worse than I am now. Maybe . . . maybe this is best for me."

"That stuff might not even work," I noted. "Not only is the idea pretty insane—a love potion—but it seems to me that it's like everything else on this crazy world—a love potion only if you think it is."

"I wonder what he meant by love potion, anyway?" she mused. "As in making love?"

"No, I don't think so. It's an ancient romantic concept. Somehow I doubt that any little bottle is going to revive that."

She removed the stopper and sniffed. "Smells like candy."

I sighed and relaxed back on the bed. "Look, stop it up for now and let's get some sleep. Bring it with you if you want. But let's get some sleep —we've got a big day ahead tomorrow."

"I—I suppose you're right. But damn it, Park, I'm scared! Scared of me, scared of that town, scared of . . . living." That last was said slowly, strangely, as if only now she was accepting the truth. I watched, curious, as she suddenly pulled the stopper back off and raised the bottle to her lips . . . and froze solid. It was odd, as if she'd made the decision, started to drink, and then become petrified in mid-motion. Still, there was movement, of a sort. Her hand, and only her hand and arm that held the vial, trembled, the little vial rising ever so slightly, then falling slightly more, as if it were at war with itself, receiving two totally different sets of commands.

I rose a bit and watched, fascinated. Two minds, Korman had said. Two minds, one central nervous system. Abruptly, the struggle stopped, and without a word, her body seemed to relax, but her face seemed vacant, expressionless. Wordlessly she stood up, walked over to the basin, and poured out the contents of the vial. Then, after putting the vial on the commode, she turned, returned to her bed, and lay down.

"Zala? Are you all right?" I asked gently, finally getting up when I had no response and going over to her. She was asleep, breathing regularly and rhythmically.

I stood there a few moments, just staring. Finally I said, aloud, "Well I'll be damned," snuffed out the light, and got into my own bed. I found it hard to sleep. It had started raining again, but the regular sound of the drops hitting the roof hardly bothered me at all.

What the hell had I just witnessed?

CHAPTER SIX

The High Road to Bourget

In the morning, Zala had no memory of the internal struggle I had witnessed, and she seemed surprised to see the goop still in the basin, practically accusing me of doing the deed.

"You did it—I watched you," I assured her. "It's for the best anyway."

She stared at me in disbelief. "*I* did? You're not just kidding me?"

"No, no kidding. Honest."

She shook her head for a moment, as if trying to remember. Finally she just sighed and shrugged. "Well, let's get on with it."

"At least packing's easy," I noted. "I hope they have more clothing at Bourget."

We went down to breakfast, a fairly ample one as usual, but Garal, our host for this, our last morning, cautioned a few of us, Zala and I among them, to eat lightly. "You're gonna have a long trip and traveling isn't very smooth around here."

Both of us took his advice. I was never much of a breakfast eater anyway, but I put away several cups of café, a very good hot caffeine drink, and a sweet roll.

When we were finished, Garal stood at the head of the table. "We will be going out individually or in small groups as transportation is available," he announced. "The rain has stopped, which means that some of you will be flying, which is a good thing. Overland to some of your villages might take days."

"Flying?" I couldn't resist voicing the surprise that everyone felt. "I thought there were few machines here."

"Well, we use the shuttle, for extremely long hauls—like intercontinental ones—but we have other means here as well," Garal responded enigmatically. "Just hold on. You'll find out soon enough."

He reached down and checked his clipboard. "All right—take nothing with you except the clothes on your back. You'll get everything you need when you get where you're going." He looked around at all of us and smiled a little evilly. "So far you've had it soft and easy. Now you're going out into the real world there, and it's gonna be a shock, I promise you. Keep your noses clean, take the advice of any locals, and take it real easy until you get the lay of the land, I warn you. That sounds like the usual advice, but it goes double here. Just remember that scrawny kid you knock down might be an apt who'll get a little irritated and wrench your guts around or at the very least cast a spell on you. And don't stare at the changelings! Just remember that anybody who happens to look funny or different got that way for a reason and the same thing could happen to you."

This last meant little to us at the time.

As the morning wore on, official-looking men and women came by and called out a name, sometimes two, and out they'd go. We were not the last to be called, but in the bottom half, which made me start to regret how lightly I'd eaten.

Our initial transport was a small enclosed buggy pulled by a single toothy uhar. It wasn't nearly as comfortable as the coach—very basic board and putty insulation—and we could feel every little bump in the very bumpy road. The uhar carts, no matter how fancy or plain, would take some getting used to; the big lizard's gait tilted you first to one side, then to the other, rather quickly, while seeming to draw you forward in tiny and continuous fits and starts.

We quickly cleared the town, then took a branch road to the north. Zala and I said very little during the journey, for there was very little to say except to voice the anxiety we both felt. With her ego it was really bad; at least I not only had a full reservoir of self-confidence, but knew in what direction the future was leading. Never had two more dissimilar people started out on an epic journey together, I reflected.

We had broken through the rain forest to a vast clearing when Zala looked out her window and gasped. Frowning, I leaned over and looked out at what she was seeing—and did a little gasping myself.

I saw a great, sleek, jet-black body topped by a head that looked like an enormous black triangle, with an enormous hornlike bony plate going back from the top of that weird head to almost halfway down the body. The head itself seemed to consist of an enormous beak and a pair of huge, round eyes that appeared to be lidless. But the real stunning part of the creature was its wings, which were barely folded and ran almost the length of the body. The wings were supported, somehow, by an apparatus and guy-wires. The thing appeared to be eating something enormous and bloody, gulping it down easily. As our buggy pulled to a stop and two people ran to get the door for us, I heard an enormous belch.

We both jumped out of the buggy and stood there, transfixed by the sight. A young woman dressed in tight, leathery black clothes and boots approached, joined us, then turned and looked back at the beast. "Magnificent, isn't she?" the newcomer enthused.

"That's one word for it," I responded. "What the hell *is* it?"

"They have a long scientific name, but we generally call 'em soarers around Charon. They're very rarely found on the ground, because it's so hard to get them aloft again. They live up above the clouds around most of the planet, just floating there above the clouds and using surprisingly little energy."

"Is the beast down here for the reason I think it's down here?" Zala managed nervously.

The woman laughed. "Oh, yes. We use the soarers for transportation.

They're very useful, although only certain areas have enough clearing, wind, and elevation to get them aloft again. They're quite friendly and intelligent, if they're raised from eggs."

"I'll bet," I replied. "And it can get back in the air from here?"

"Oh, sure. Silla's an old vet to this kind of thing. Still, they're not practical for mass transportation, and we use 'em mostly for the high-ups. You two're gonna get a real treat. Most folks never get to ride on one and the sight of one of 'em dropping through the clouds scares most folks silly."

"The thought of riding on one doesn't do wonders for me," I said uneasily, no longer regretting the light breakfast a bit.

"What do we do—climb on her back?" Zala wanted to know.

The woman laughed. "Oh, no. See? The crew's putting the passenger compartment on now. It's strapped on tight and fits between bony plates just forward of the wings—see?"

We *did* see—a fairly substantial-looking compartment, like a small cabin, was being hoisted into position with a manual winch. Two members of the ground crew, looking like tiny insects on that great body, positioned the contraption into place and then dropped straps to the ground, where others crawled under the beast and tied or buckled the straps together. A few sample pushes to make sure it was seated right and the people on top seemed satisfied and started down ladders on either side. The operation shifted forward, where a smaller compartment was being similarly mounted just in back of the thick neck.

"What do they *eat?*" Zala asked, still incredulous at the sight.

The woman shrugged. "Practically anything. They're omnivores, like us. Actually, they need very little. They're hollow-boned and amazingly light; once they catch the currents and get some altitude, they use very little energy. A ton of mixed stuff every two days or so is the usual—mostly the tops of trees, stuff like that, along with whatever's in 'em—but we give Silla extra, a couple of uhars or some other big animal, because of the energy take-off requires. They're quite effective in controlling the wild animal population, thinning forests, you name it, and they fly in heavy rain as easily as in sunshine. The wild ones just about never land, but they do come in close. Don't worry about 'em, though—they know better than to nab people, who generally don't have enough meat on 'em to be worth paying attention to, anyway."

I was very happy to hear that. "How's it flown—guided, I mean?" I asked her.

"The pilot—that's me—sits up there in that control cabin. I've got basic navigation instruments there, and the floor on both sides opens up. The early pioneers tried bridles, but they don't work and the soarers are smart anyway. A well-trained one like Silla knows what to do just from how I press my feet on which side of the neck, when to do it, and when to stop." She paused a moment, then added, "Well, it's a little more complicated than that—but I'll be in complete control."

Looking at her—she was no larger than I was and probably weighed less

—and then at the soarer over there I was not reassured, but this wasn't my party, not yet.

A crewman came running up to her. "Word is it'll start pouring again in less than twenty minutes," he told her. "Better get everybody aboard and away."

She nodded.

"I thought you said it was fine in the rain," I said.

"She is," the pilot replied, "but taking off in those winds can turn us upside down at the very least. Better get on board." She ran for the pilot's cabin.

I looked at Zala, who looked nervously back at me. "Think you can take it?" I asked her.

"I'll—try. If *she* can fly one, I can sure ride one."

We walked quickly over to the creature, following the crewman. The ladder to the passenger compartment was still in place, and he steadied it as first Zala and then I climbed up and went through an open door.

The interior was actually quite nice—heavily padded, manufactured seats much like those on the shuttle, complete with seat belts; the whole thing was lined and carpeted with what looked like fur of some kind. Aft a small compartment was clearly marked as a rest room. Although it lacked lights, some sort of self-luminous chemical tubing ran all around giving off a sufficient glow to see by and we felt pretty comfortable.

We were not the only ones in the cabin. Although I hadn't noticed earlier, an elderly woman and a tough-looking young man had climbed aboard. They were dressed in very fancy raingear, obviously of offworld design. Following them were three ground crew people, two men and a woman, including the man who had taken us "aboard," as it were. He pulled up the ladder, made a last check, then closed the door and spun a wheel locking it securely in place. The other crewman stood facing us, while the woman checked in back.

"Please fasten both lap and shoulder belts," the man told us. "While the flight's basically a smooth one, you never know what you're going to run into. Keep them fastened at all times. If you have to walk back to the lavatory, hold onto the rail and strap yourself in even in there. The cabin is not pressurized, so be prepared for a pressure differential in the ears. We have gum and mints if that troubles you. Occasionally we have to fly very high to get by some bad weather, and in that case I'll tell you to remove the oxygen masks under your seats and put them on. They are fed by manual pressurized tanks. Keep 'em on until I say it's okay."

A sudden violent lurch really shook us up; it was followed by the most chilling screech I've ever heard in my whole life. Both Zala and I jumped nervously; the crew and the two passengers took no real notice.

"Take-off positions!" the crewman yelled, and the three all strapped themselves into their seats very quickly. "Hold on, everybody! Here we go!"

At that moment I felt a sudden, violent lurch, and we were abruptly pushed against the back of our seats and simultaneously jarred up and down so hard it almost hurt. I suddenly realized that the damned thing was *running*. I glanced over at Zala, but she was all tightened up, eyes closed. Then I looked out the tiny round window to my left. It was possible to see the ground just ahead of that incredible wing, going up and down with that terrible bouncing, and then, all at once, the damned thing jumped off a cliff I hadn't known was there—and sank like a stone, throwing us forward in our seats.

As a certified pilot, both air and space, I'd experienced far worse than this, which may be why I was holding up so well. But *then* I'd been in control of a machine whose properties were known. To be perfectly honest, in that moment of forward fall all I could think was *"Well, this is it— you're dead."*

But almost as abrupt as the plunge was the sudden and violent turn and rise. At that moment I could see, with a kind of horrible fascination, just how close we'd come to the ground below.

Now we were lifting, with an eerie, rocking motion that first threw us forward, then back, as the enormous, powerful wings took us up, then paused to rest on a current of air. In another minute or two we were in the ever-present clouds, getting really bounced about. I glanced around and saw that Zala, eyes still closed, appeared very, very sick; the two other passengers were sitting quietly with no real reaction, while the crew was very relaxed. One was eating a fruit of some kind.

That terrible bouncing seemed to go on forever. Finally, we broke free, above the clouds, and into bright sunshine. Within another minute or two the creature caught a comfortable current, adjusted its course, and settled down. The experience was really strange now—after such a violent upheaval, the ride was now as smooth as glass, and nearly silent.

I looked over at Zala. "You can open your eyes now, and catch hold of your stomach," I told her. "It'll probably be like this the rest of the way." I just hoped and prayed this was an express.

One eye opened, then the other; she looked at me rather mournfully. "I'm sick," she managed.

All I could do was be sympathetic. "Just relax, calm down, and don't worry. That was a pretty rough take-off, but it's going to be like this until we get where we're going."

She didn't seem to be any more relieved. "I keep wondering what the landing is going to be like, if that was the take-off."

Good point. How the hell would something this size brake to a stop? Still, I had to have confidence since the pilot and crew did this all the time and none of the crew seemed worried.

At one point one of the crewmen took out a small carton and offered us fruit. Zala turned green at its mere mention. I almost took one, then decided for her sake that I could spare her the sight of me eating for the duration which, the crewman told us, would be a little more than five hours if we didn't run into weather problems. The thing managed an average airspeed in excess of 250 kph, a pretty respectable rate over the long haul for something this big.

The smoothness was interrupted every fifteen minutes or so by one or two sudden jolts, as those great wings compensated or switched currents, but that was about the only problem it presented.

The sky of Charon was nothing if not spectacular. Below were the dark, swirling clouds that seemed to never leave; above our clear place wasn't the sky I'd been expecting, but an odd band of reds and yellows all swirling about, almost as active as the storm clouds below. Some kind of gaseous layer that acted as a protective filter, I guessed, allowing a human-tolerable temperature below. The sun, a great, bright glob in the sky, was hot and visible through the upper layer. I guessed that the upper layer rather than the clouds below prevented much surveillance from orbit and blocked transmissions to and from the planet. I wondered what the stuff was.

Aside from my ears popping every so often, and the occasional screech from the soarer as we passed another soarer somewhere near us—I never did get more than a vague glimpse of black so I didn't get to see one in full flight—the voyage was uneventful. I took note of the other two passengers though—still fairly well-dressed even after removing their rain gear. They were obviously together, but the woman, who seemed to be going over some paperwork, rarely acknowledged or talked to the younger man. I smelled boss and bodyguard, but had no way of knowing just who they really were.

Even Zala managed to relax after a while, although she never did move during the entire trip and never really seemed to recover her color.

Finally my ears started popping a bit more regularly, and I saw that we were turning and descending very slowly. The crewmembers checked all their boxes and small hatches to make sure all was secure, then returned to their seats and strapped in.

I looked out at what I could see of the ground in front of the big wing, and was surprised to see breaks in the clouds not far off, and large patches of dark blue below. Hitting the clouds was similar to hitting them in an airship, and we experienced some rocking and a number of violent jerks as the wings worked harder to compensate for downdrafts, updrafts, and the like. The window showed moisture as we descended through a gray-white fog, then we broke suddenly into clearer air and the ground was visible below. Aside from seeing that it was green and somewhat mountainous down there, I couldn't make out much of anything.

The soarer circled, slowing a bit each time, then dropped and put its wings at an angle, abruptly braking hard. There were three or four jolts as the wings suddenly beat hard, and then one big bang—and we were down and, incredibly, motionless. For something this big, I had to admit it certainly could land much easier than it could take off.

I had to tap Zala and assure her we were down in one piece and that it was all over. She could hardly believe it, but finally opened her eyes and looked around. For the first time, she looked across me to the window and finally seemed to relax.

"Not as bad as take-off, was it?" I said cheerfully.

She shook her head. "I'll kill myself before I get on one of these again, I swear it, Park."

The wheel was spun, the hatchlike door opened, and a blast of really hot, sticky air hit us. Still, after five hours in that hotbox of the cabin, it was welcome, and it didn't seem to be raining.

The two other passengers gathered their things together and departed first. We followed, although Zala was more than a little shaky, and made it down the ladder.

I looked around the open field. A wagon was heading for the soarer with what looked like an entire butcher shop in the back—the fuel truck, I thought, amused. Off to one side, a small group of people and two coaches waited. Our fellow passengers had already reached one of them and were being greeted by very officious-looking men and women, some of whom bowed as they greeted the woman; others opened the coach door for her, while still others rushed to the soarer and retrieved what had to be baggage from a compartment under the passenger unit. Other cargo was also carried, and several buggies came right up to the soarer for it.

We just stood there, not quite knowing what to do. Finally I went over to the crewman who had been our host aboard. "Excuse me—but is this Bourget?" I asked him, praying that it was.

"Oh, yeah," he responded. "This *is* where you wanted to go, wasn't it? Our next stop's Lamasa."

"This is the place," I assured him, then thanked him and turned back to Zala. "Well, I guess we go over to that group and see if anybody's expecting us."

We walked cautiously over to the second coach, then looked expectantly at a couple of the people standing around. One young man—hardly more than a boy—grasped our situation and came over to us. "You the new Accountant?" he asked.

I felt relieved. "That's me. Park Lacoch."

He looked over expectantly at Zala. "You?"

"Zala Embuay. I'm his—assistant."

"Yeah, sure," the boy responded knowingly. "Well, if you two'll get into the coach there we'll get you into town and squared away." He looked around. "Any luggage?"

"No," I told him. "We're new to Charon. We're going to have to pick up everything we need here."

He seemed mildly interested. "Outside, huh? Funny they'd stick you here."

I shrugged and climbed into the coach. "They gave me the job and I took it. I wasn't in any position to say no."

We rode into town in silence, there not being much to say. The boy was not the driver, but stayed topside with him.

Bourget was not quite what I expected. A small village set against a very pretty bay, it was up and around low hills covered with trees. The buildings were all low and mostly painted white with reddish-brown roofs. There was nothing like the glassed-in sidewalks of Montlay or its more modern architecture. It was more like a small peasant village on one of the better frontier worlds, with the buildings made mostly of adobe and stucco of some kind, many with thatched roofs of that reddish-brown plant. Despite the clouds, it clearly didn't rain as much here as farther north, which was well and good from my point of view. There were many boats in the harbor, most with masts.

But it was *really* hot, easily over 40 degrees Centigrade, and both Zala and I were sweating profusely. I didn't know about her, but I needed a long, cold drink of something—anything.

Zala, however, was impressed. "Why, it's really *pretty,*" she commented, looking out the window at the scene.

The town was organized around a central square that had a little park in the middle and four large multipurpose buildings—each a square block around although all two stories tall—which were obviously markets, shops, and stalls. The coach pulled up across from the one of the four buildings that had a more or less solid front and stopped. The boy jumped down, opened the door, and helped us both down.

The place was lively, I'll say that. People rushing this way and that, stalls open to the outside displaying lots of fruits, vegetables, clothes, and handicrafts, and doing a fair business from the look of it.

"Come with me now," the boy instructed, and we followed. I could see that Zala had completely recovered from her flight for she was showing some anticipation at touring the market.

We entered the solid-facade building and found ourselves in a wide entry hall with a large wooden staircase situated directly in the middle. Corridors led off in all directions with what were obviously offices along them. The boy stopped and turned to us. "You wait here. I'll see if the Master is in." And with that he bounded up the stairs and was off.

Zala turned to me. "Who do you think he means?"

"Probably the local wizard," I replied. "Remember to be respectful to him. I want to get off on a good note."

"Don't worry."

We waited for the boy to return. A few people walked here and there on unknown business, but none gave us more than a passing glance. Civil servants looked the same anywhere. The one oddity was that the place was cool—at least a lot cooler than it was outside. There was certainly some kind of air circulation system at work, although what type I could not guess. Not regular air-conditioning, that was for sure—the temperature was down, but not the humidity.

Before long the boy was back. "The Master will see you," he told us, and we followed him upstairs. It was a bit warmer there, as would be expected, and as we walked to the rear of the large building I was conscious of the temperature rising.

We were ushered into an office with nothing on the door. There was an antechamber, like a waiting room, with nobody behind the desk; we went straight back to a second door which the boy opened.

We felt a surprising blast of cool, dry air as we entered. The office was large and very comfortably appointed, with a huge carved wooden desk in the center. Behind that desk sat a rather large man with an enormous white beard, as if in compensation for his mostly bald head. He was smoking a pipe.

He smiled as we entered and nodded. "Please, take seats in front of the desk here," he said pleasantly, gesturing. The chairs, large and high-backed, were modern and quite comfortable, although as the man surely knew, it's impossible for a person sitting opposite anyone behind a desk to feel on an equal footing.

The bearded man looked at the boy. "That'll be all, Gori. Shut the door on your way out."

The boy nodded and did as instructed.

"A good lad, that," the man commented. "Might make a good apt someday, if he gets over his hangup."

I couldn't imagine what the fellow was talking about, so I said, "Hangup?"

"Yes. He wants to be a fish. Oh, well—I'm Tully Kokul, chief magician and high muckety-muck of this little speck of humanity."

"Park Lacoch," I responded, "and this is Zala Embuay."

He looked at Zala, and I saw a little puzzlement come over his face, but he recovered quickly. Whatever Korman had seen, though, Kokul had just seen as well.

"I knew you were coming, Lacoch, but nobody said anything about the lady here. I—" He was about to continue when there was a knock at the door. The boy Gori entered and placed a brief-pouch on his desk, then turned and left again. "I was *wondering* about this," he muttered, as he opened it, removed two file folders, discarded one and opened and looked through the other. I could guess pretty well that those folders contained everything known on both of us, along with orders and recommendations from above.

"Humph. I'm not sure I like your status, Madame Embuay," he said almost to himself. He looked up at her. "Bourget is a pretty conservative village. Other than myself, you're the only two people here not native to Charon."

Zala looked blank, so I hazarded a guess. "Religious?"

He nodded. "Fifty, sixty years ago the Diamond had a near invasion of missionaries from all sorts of sects. The Confederacy more or less encouraged it—got the fanatics out of their hair and voluntarily exiled here for life. Bourget wasn't much of anything then—it still isn't all that much, although we now rate as a sort of local capital. This one group, the Unitites, were real fanatics and were pretty much run out of all the established towns. But their leader, a fellow named Suritani, was a real lady's man who was also pretty well practiced in the Arts. He was able to get a pretty good following, mostly female, and came here and established Bourget as a religious colony of sorts. Most everybody here's a cousin of everybody else."

"Sounds pretty liberal to me," I noted. Zala said nothing.

"Oh, it was—for the big man. But not for everybody else. The usual story. Understand, I'm the only one around who can get away with talk like this. You better respect the local beliefs so you don't step on any."

I nodded, and he went on.

"Well, anyway, you'll find most everybody stops twice a day—at eight and six—and prays together for a couple of minutes. Men and women have clearly defined, but different jobs, very strict, and men can have up to three wives. We still have more women than men by a long shot."

"Can a woman have three husbands?" Zala asked, seriously interested.

"No. I told you it was an old-style, almost throwback religion—one big god, who supposedly lives at the center of the universe, and assorted godlets who are the messengers between people and this one god. All very complex, and very strict."

"Sounds like this isn't a very good place for loyalty to the central government," I noted. "Not with a woman as Lord of Cerberus."

"You're very perceptive, Lacoch. I can see why they sent you. You're right—they simply don't accept the prevailing politics, which is always a headache to me. One of several this sect gives me, frankly. Most of them just prefer to believe Aeolia Matuze has a man who does all the thinking for her, making her a bridge, like the godlets. So far that's been okay, although there've been rumblings that our leader is going to declare her divinity and impose her own religion on the planet. If it comes to that, they may have to get a new population for Bourget, even the Company chiefs. I'm hoping that, at least, I can get a soft-pedaled exemption here."

I sympathized with his problem, and it didn't escape me that the chief sorcerer of Bourget was a ripe candidate for somebody like Koril.

"This religion is a hundred percent, then?" I asked.

He shook his head. "Nothing's ever a hundred percent. I'd say about half the people are really devout and really believe all of it, another thirty percent just do it because it's the way they were raised, and another ten go through the motions just to avoid trouble."

"That's only ninety percent," I noted.

He nodded. "The other ten are with the opposition."

"The opposition?"

"Most religions have a devil, a demon, somebody who represents evil and on which everything bad can be blamed. This one's no exception. It's called the Destroyer. Some personalities are just naturally attracted to the side of evil in such a strict society. In addition, it's a natural place for people in Bourget who chafe under the strict society—women, mostly, who have some or a lot of the Art, and know either by experience or direct knowledge that the rest of the worlds allow women not only equality, but occasionally superiority. It used to be pretty local, but lately similar cults have been cropping up all over Charon, and there's some evidence that they've been co-opted by a political opposition to the rule of Matuze."

"I'm familiar with the politics of the situation," I told him. "Still, it seems funny that the logical order's been reversed here. The establishment, which backs the existing order on Charon, is prejudiced against women in leadership positions yet has a woman at its head; the opposition, which wants women made equal like everywhere else, is falling in with a group designed to put a man back in power."

Zala followed the conversation but said nothing. I had pretty well given her the entire outline of recent history on Charon, so she at least knew the players even if she didn't seem quite able to understand the game.

"Well, it's not that simple," Kokul came back. "On most of Charon it's different, although some towns have pockets with even crazier beliefs and systems than Bourget. What we have is a three-sided system here, as in most places. Our cult with its value system; the opposition, which ties into the overall opposition; and governmental authority—which right now is you and me and just about nobody else."

I understood what he meant, and although it wasn't comforting to me, I could well understand why I'd been sent to Bourget. The stricter the local social system, the more likely that the opposition—and Koril's strength and agents—would be powerful and well-organized as well, particularly with its south-coast location and general isolation.

Although Kokul seemed casual and not a little cynical about Matuze, I was under no illusions that he could be trusted. Like me, he was from some other world and culture—and had been sent here for a reason. No matter how casual he was about the central government, there had to be the suspicion that they would hardly send a traitor or an incompetent to such a sensitive spot as Bourget.

"Enough about that," the wizard decided. "As for Bourget—well, if you can tolerate the social structure, which really isn't all that bad once you get used to it, the citizens are a pretty good, hard-working lot. We're self-sufficient in food and building materials, have a lively local handicrafts industry, and generate a fair amount of surplus income through exports. Not bad for a village of less than 5000. The climate has two seasons—hot and hotter—so outside of official circles you'll find dress ranges from little to less. We have good ground water, which is safe for all purposes, and back in the hills some really nice waterfalls, which we've harnessed as best we can for everything from cooling systems to pumps and the like—all direct mechanical, though. About the most modern machine you'll find here is a solar watch, although we do generate some minor steam power for the big jobs, mostly out in the Companies. It's surprising what good engineering will do, even without modern power sources."

I accepted his point, since it was self-evident—early man had built some stunning empires on the most basic of power sources. "So what's *my* job here?" I asked him. "And how do we get set up and get started?"

"Well, it's basically supervision, but as you're responsible for overall efficiency, the accuracy of all data and will be held accountable for any problems or errors, it's very much a hands-on job. Within a day's journey of Bourget are nine Companies, employing upwards of a thousand people and producing very valuable commodities. In town, there are thirty guilds which produce everything from clothing to handicrafts. All of them need things and I don't just mean raw materials. You are, basically, the head of the local bank. The government's syndicates meet four times a year in Montlay and decide on a fair price and profit margin for everything, and you get the official rates in a big book. The job of your office is to maintain a balance between what they get and what they provide according to the set table of values. All Company orders come to you, as do orders for their products. The trick is to make sure the Companies get only what they have paid for in products, but receive enough to get by on. If there is an imbalance in their favor, they are paid in money."

I nodded. "Sounds pretty direct. But who pays my salary, my staff, and my operating expenses?"

"Well, that's simple. The bank takes ten percent of all transactions at the time of the transaction. Half of that is your take, split along mutually agreeable lines. Naturally, in good times you make more than in bad, with each employee getting a share. The rest gets sent on to Charon's government."

I nodded. "So the more I encourage business and make it easier, by advice, suggestion, whatever, to increase production, the more we all make. A very interesting system."

"That's about it," he agreed. "If somebody's got a real problem you can send for an expert to help—paid out of your overhead, though."

That, perhaps, explained the elderly woman on the soarer. I wondered how somebody used to being the boss would like this culture, even for a short time. Still, I had a few more questions.

"Where will we live and how are we going to pick up the basics?"

"Oh, that's easy," he responded. "The share account for the T.A. kept operating in the two months since the old one died, so there's a fair amount in there now. You can draw on it downstairs—they'll be expecting you. Then just buy what you need. A house goes with the job, already furnished—Gori, that's the boy who met you, will show it to you. It's on the bay, an easy walk from here."

"Out of curiosity—who pays *you*?" I asked him.

He laughed. "Oh, nobody. The last thing I need is money." He grew more serious. "Now, the staff will break you in during the next few days—take it easy until you get the hang of it. Your first month you can use learning the ropes, since any minor mistakes can be blamed on the past two months' vacancy. We open at eight each morning, the markets and stores at nine, and we close except for a night accounting staff at four.

The businesses stay open until nine or ten, the cafés a bit later, but the nightlife's pretty poor around here. For one thing, they drink only weak beer and light wines, and the entertainment's mostly home-grown and not very good. We go for six days, then take three off, then go again."

"I would guess a small town like this is full of gossip and rumor," I noted. "I doubt if it's going to take very long to get to know these people."

"Oh, it'll be easier than that. We'll introduce the two of you at your wedding."

"*What!*" That was Zala.

"I *said* it was a conservative place. You have no job, no means of support—and you're quite attractive. I assume that you'd rather marry Park here, than be forced to marry some local with one or two others around."

"I don't want to marry anybody. I don't believe in it."

He sighed. "Look, it doesn't matter *what* you believe. You're not back on the civilized worlds now. You're not even in some freewheeling town like Montlay or Cadura. Remember, you don't have to take the ceremony very seriously since it's just for the locals' consumption."

"Then why not just say we're already married?" she wanted to know.

"Because this is the easiest way to get in with the locals. They'll get to know you, will like you respecting their local customs and beliefs, and they'll be much more likely to accept you. Just let me arrange it all, and go along. Other than that, just keep your mouth shut when you see something you don't agree with. Antagonize these people and you can find yourself in a world of trouble. I'm the strongest and most feared wizard in these parts, but I'm hardly the only one who can cast spells and work magic. There's a lot of home-grown talent around, and a lot more than can be bought. Some of them are pretty good. Unless you can develop your own powers, it's best to go along with them no matter how backward or ignorant they may seem. This is literally the key to your survival—you have to live with these people and depend on them for your necessities. It can be pretty lonely if you antagonize them from the beginning."

She seemed slightly unnerved, but a little chastened. "I'll try," was all she could promise.

CHAPTER SEVEN

Settling In

Things actually went off rather nicely, if I do say so myself. As it turned out, the accumulated back pay was more than generous, and we were both able to buy suitable toiletries, wardrobes, and the like.

The wedding took place in the town square, officiated at by one of the local priests who did a lot of prerehearsed mumbo-jumbo, and by Kokul as

State's Witness and certifier. Zala made a beautiful bride, and there was a real festival afterwards with lots of singing, dancing, presents, and goodies of all sorts, plus some nice socializing. Kokul was particularly helpful in pointing out the important people in the crowd, and I was taking careful mental notes. Even Zala, who had been expressing extreme misgivings right up to the ceremony, seemed to get into the swing of things, for later she noted that weddings were something she thought everybody should do every year or two.

As for me, I was most interested in settling down, learning the job, and doing it well. There was no percentage in acting any other way. Koril was unlikely to pop up right away, knowing certainly that Matuze would figure we were prime recruiting targets and keep a careful watch on us.

The staff was friendly and helpful, and the system, once fully laid out and demonstrated in practice, was primitive but quite effectively organized. Solar calculators and small solar computers helped, but the basic work was all done by hand and typewriter on endless sheets of accounting paper.

Zala, too, seemed to adjust, after a fashion. Local women taught her how to use the wood stove without burning herself or the house down, and the basics of domestic work. Since nothing much could be stored in this heat and under these conditions, she went to the market daily and even learned the art of bargaining. What particularly fascinated her was the very concept of handicrafts—nothing in her world or background prepared her for clothing made from scratch, designed and sewn by individuals on individual machines, or pottery hand-made on potter's wheels and hand-decorated with brush and glaze. Suddenly flung back thousands of years in cultural time, both of us were very surprised to learn that there were whole art forms devoted to such things. The products had a special sort of quality machine and mass production at its best just couldn't quite match.

My job though took more time than I'd figured, since it included trips out to the Companies to see their accountants, to plan for the future, and to examine and get to know their operations and see if there were new and better ways to do things. Money was tight because the system really wasn't designed for one person supporting two. Zala, to her credit, solved that problem by learning to use the hand loom and joining a Guild in town in which many women and some men weaved intricate patterns into blankets, bedspreads, you name it, and then sold them to the Guild for a set price per piece. The Guild, through my office, then sold them all over Charon.

The people were friendly, open, and seemed reasonably happy, and neither of us gave them any cause to get mad at us, particularly after we saw a few of the cursed and the changelings. The cursed were more prominent since they weren't bad off enough to be able to drop out of society. Mostly they just covered up as best they could, but you could always tell. A club foot, a withered arm, a scarred face, or some deformity even worse stood out rather well in a society so well protected by the interior Wardens that cuts always stopped bleeding and never left scars and even amputated limbs grew back.

The knowledge that many of our fellow townspeople could throw curses like these wasn't very comforting, and the discovery that you could actually *buy* curses in the marketplace didn't help either. One old woman who sold them in a small stall explained to me that it didn't pay as well as weaving, for example, but it was a living.

The changelings, which were beyond the power of an untrained or self-trained local (or so I was assured) were far more bizarre. Many were former apts themselves who had literally done it to themselves, either for psychological reasons or because something got away from them, or they had displeased Kokul or others of great power and training. Kokul was the best around, as he said, but each of the Companies also had a sorc of considerable power to add to the changeling population—and since, unlike Kokul, the Company sorcs were employees of the Company and not the government, they were often willing to do the cruel bidding of their employers, meting out reward and punishment with equal ease. I ached to learn something of that power, but I had neither the time nor the teacher —not at this stage of the game.

For example, there was this two-meter frog that sat on a rock just down from the town staring out to sea and smoking big, fat cigars. Well, actually, I hadn't a notion what a frog really looked like, but I read the fairy tales just like everybody else and this one sure looked like a fairy-tale frog, standing on its hind bow legs, balancing on big webbed feet.

There were others around too—halflings that were half human and half something else, almost anything else it seemed, and probably more that I never fully recognized as such because they were so completely transformed. They never came into town, though, and were generally shunned by people, although I suppose somebody had to trade with them on at least a barter basis—how else did the frog get his or her cigars? There was supposedly a small colony of them out on the point north of the town, but nobody ever went there that I could find.

I saw more of them on Company lands, since people there were more at the mercy of Company officials and the local sorc and apts. I was out at Thunderkor, a Company that was basically involved in softwood logging and milling, when I had my first direct encounter with a changeling. I was on my way back from the mill after checking production schedules, and I'd decided to walk rather than ride back to Sanroth Hall, the Company headquarters, because it was a nice day and I felt I was getting soft, when I ran into her.

She was a halfling and at one time had obviously been a very beautiful young woman. The woman's body remained, down to the lower chest, but from that point it became the bottom part of a uhar or uharlike animal, with powerful saurian legs and, coming out from the spine, the long, thick saurian tail. Her color was a leaf-green rather than the blue of the uhar clan, including her long hair which was, however, a far darker green in color. She walked with the peculiar angle that showed that the tail was needed as a counterbalance, and she was walking up the road about ten meters in front of me. At first I took her for some kind of animal—there were a great number on Charon—and she heard me despite the fact that I stopped in my tracks; she herself stopped and turned around. Her face showed more annoyance than surprise at the sight of me, and certainly no fear. Hers was a pretty face, even in its shades of green, exotic and quite sensual, though she *did* have a long, sharp horn protruding from the center of her forehead.

She stood there, and I stood there, and finally I decided that it was the better part of valor to keep on. Besides, I was more curious than fearful or repelled.

"Good morning!" I said cheerfully as I approached. After all, what else *do* you say to a half-woman, half-lizard standing in your way? "A nice day, isn't it?"

She stared at me strangely for a moment, and I wondered if she could still speak—and which half, the human or animal, was in control. That thought hadn't really occurred to me until I was too close to run.

She was large, in proportion to her saurian half, and almost towered over me. Almost everybody did, of course, even Zala, but I was used to *that* disproportion. This was more than the usual—she was certainly over two meters, even slightly bent like that.

"You're the new T.A. from Outside," she said, her voice sounding deep but otherwise quite ordinary. I was relieved.

I stopped near her, just out of range of that horn, and nodded. "Park Lacoch."

"Well? What the hell you staring at?" she snapped.

I shrugged sheepishly. "Remember, I'm new here—not just to here, but to Charon," I reminded her. "Let's just say you're a bit, ah, different, than most of the people I meet."

She laughed at that. "That's true enough. Am I the first changeling you've ever seen?"

"No, but you're the first one I've *met*," I told her.

"And?"

I wasn't sure if she was fishing for a compliment or spoiling for a fight. "And what?" I responded. "I find you—and the whole idea—fascinating."

She gave a sort of snort. "Fascinating! That's one word for it, I guess."

"You work here for Thunderkor?"

"What else? They hitch me up and I pull things they want moved. My arms aren't much use but I've got real pull in the legs."

I looked at them and wasn't in any mood to argue that point. "What did you do—before?" I asked as delicately as I could.

"Before? Hah! I was a riverwoman. Ran log floats, that kind of thing. Takes more skill than strength."

I was impressed. "I would have thought you'd have been up at Sanroth," I told her. "With your looks . . ."

She smiled grimly. "Yeah. My looks. That's what got me into trouble. I was born and bred on the river, into a family of river people. I had the talent and loved the work, ever since I was little, but everybody said I was too pretty for it, that I should get married and make babies. Hell, I loved that job. Even the men admitted I was the best—that's why they wanted me out of there. I embarrassed them."

I could see the situation in this particular culture.

"Well, anyway, one day this old guy, Jimrod Gneezer, comes down from Sanroth and sees me. Next thing I know I'm ordered up to the Hall —never been there in my life. Real Mr. Ego, too."

"I think I've met him," I told her, recalling a distinguished-looking man of middle age.

"Well, he thinks I'm supposed to swoon all over him. I tell him where to go. He gets real mad, tries to force himself, and I belted him one— knocked him cold, walked out, and went home. Next thing I know, Simber, the dirty sorc, comes down, tells me I better go back. He reminds me that he could cast a spell and I'd be Gneezer's willing slave. I tell him to go ahead, that that was the only way I'd go back to the bastard, but it turns out that the guy's got such a big head he don't like no spells for that. His pride's hurt. So Simber takes some hair and nail clippings—I couldn't stop him, he being a sorc—and the next thing I know this little brat of an apt, Isil, shows up and tells me all about how I've been given to him now and he's very creative. Yeah, very."

I whistled. "That's rough" was all I could think to say.

"Oh, I could reverse the spell, probably, by going crawling to Gneezer, but I'd rather be like this than do that. Someday I'll get even with 'em, you can count on it. But it's not so bad. They didn't mess with my head, if you know what I mean. But he sure got even. I mean, the only thing I could marry would be a bunhar, and who wants to play sexy with a lizard?"

I saw her point, and assumed a bunhar was the kind of creature she half was.

"No chance of having a different, more powerful sorc undo it?"

She shook her head. "Naw. First of all, they got a brotherhood, a code. Even the women. None of 'em will undo what another has done no matter how much they want to, because if one breaks it they all will, you see, and then where'll they be?"

It was a good point. "And none of the unofficial ones can help?"

Again the head-shake. "It's a good spell. Them amateurs can only make things worse. Besides, there seems to be something in the spell that makes it tougher. Tried it once—and that's when I got this horn. That's enough."

"Are there others like you around?" I was genuinely curious.

"Like me? Not exactly. Some others got some of the same bunhar parts, I guess, and a lot of other stuff. There's a few dozen around the Company,

I guess, of different kinds. It's a big place, so we don't see much of each other, and some of 'em are really messed up in the head by what was done to 'em. They don't do this all that much—we're the examples, see?"

I *did* see, and it made me even happier to be both a townsman with a degree of freedom and on the good side of Tully Kokul and the Charon government.

"Did you ever think of leaving?" I asked her. "I hear there are places where changelings can live together. It would probably be—easier."

"Oh, yeah, there's lots of that," she agreed, "but here's where the dungheads who did it to me are, and here's where they could remove it— or I could remove them." She flexed her very human arms and hands, and I could see that at the end of each finger was not merely a nail but a sharp, long curved talon.

"Well, I've got to be getting on," I told her, not making excuses but being honest. My transportation back to town was waiting. "It was nice, and interesting, talking to you. And if I catch your Mr. Gneezer with his hand in the till I guarantee I'll remember you when I turn him over to Master Kokul."

She chuckled evilly. "Wouldn't *that* be something, now!" She paused for breath, then said more gently, "Hey, look. If you get back over this way, stop by and see me, won't you? Most of the people here, they treat me like dirt. You're the first person in a long time who's been nice to me and treated me like—well, like a human being."

"I'll do that," I promised her. We started to go our separate ways, but I stopped and turned. "Hey—what's your name, anyway?"

"Darva," she called back. "With no family now I'm just Darva."

She took a branch path and walked away from me. I stood there for a moment, watching her lumber off—rather gracefully actually. I also made a mental note of the names Gneezer and Isil. One of these days there would be an accounting.

Months passed, and I settled in very well and really enjoyed the job. Zala taught me how to swim more expertly than I had learned as a kid, and we took full advantage of the warm bay. I also learned how to sail, although I couldn't afford a boat and had to beg or borrow one for the lessons. Zala saved up enough from her loom work to buy a pair of bicycles, obviously made off-world—on Cerberus, as it turned out—and this extended my range and gave me some much needed exercise when it didn't rain.

Large sailing ships occasionally came into the bay to pick up manufactured goods and nonperishables and drop off what we needed, and I was very impressed by them. Although strong steel ships could be built on Cerberus, which I understood was a water world, the cost of shipping that size and weight here was prohibitive. Charon's ships were made out of native hardwoods and were the more impressive for it. I noticed that the crews of these ships often contained a disproportionate number of changelings—every kind and variety I could imagine and many I couldn't. But certain forms and variations were particularly useful in rigging and setting and taking in sail, and in cargo management. The shipping guilds apparently didn't care who or what you were if you were best for the job. They mostly remained on board when in port, although once or twice I thought I saw longboats heading for Parhara Point where the changeling colony was supposed to be.

Tully Kokul I saw very infrequently—he kept mostly to himself and his "studies," and I almost never needed him. His apts occasionally got playful in the wrong places though, and I'd have to send him a note or drop in if he was there and get him to control them. They were mostly young boys—with more power than young boys should have. I wondered what he did with the talented girl apts, then reflected that somebody who could turn a young woman into a hybrid creature could easily disguise the sex of an apt if she were really promising.

I also heard very little from the central government of Charon, other than the routine correspondence and manuals necessary to my job, and that suited me just fine as well. It was with some surprise, then, that a clerk came in one day and told me that a very important visitor had arrived, and he wanted to see me in Kokul's office as soon as possible. "I'd make it possible right now," he added, shuddering slightly. "You haven't seen *him* yet."

That was enough to get me up there on the double.

Just walking into the inner office I knew what he had meant. Even before I saw the man, I could *sense* something, something decidedly wrong. It wasn't my old agent's "sixth sense" or any kind of apprehension—it was a real, tangible feeling of unease, almost of dread, like you feel just before you have to stick your hand in a damp, dark hole without knowing what's on the other side.

He was large and lean, dressed from head to foot in black leather trimmed with silver and gold designs. His face, peering out of a black hood, was lean, hard, even nasty-looking. What really struck me, though, were the eyes—there seemed to be something wrong with them, something odd and not at all human. It was as if his pupils were not solid black, but rather, transparent, like windows into some unfathomable other dimension. It was the damnedest effect I'd ever seen and it was extremely unnerving. Kokul sensed it too, and looked uneasy in his big office chair for the first time since I'd known him. This man was no ordinary man—he was Power, raw, tremendous power of an unknown sort. I noticed the man remained standing even though there were enough chairs, the better no doubt to negate the man-at-the-desk feeling. I, however, just nodded at Tully and sat down. I only came up to the strange man's chest, anyway. Never, not even with Darva, had I felt so totally small, puny, and weak.

"Park, this is Yatek Morah, from the Castle," Tully introduced us and I noticed a feeling of unease in his voice.

I stood up again and offered my hand, but Morah ignored it. I sat back down. "Any problem?" I asked as casually as I could.

"I am making a survey," the strange man replied in a voice as cold and emotionless as an assembly-line robot's. Coming from a living man it was unnerving, particularly on this planet where robots were impossible. "We are having severe security problems in most of the coastal areas. Ships have been pirated on the high seas and never been seen again. Soarers with important, even vital cargo have vanished, or suffered attack. Important people have been imperiled. As Chief of Security it is my job to put a stop to this."

I looked at Tully in genuine surprise. "First I've heard of it."

"I've had rumblings," the sorc responded. "But nothing in this area."

"That is exactly why I am here," Morah told us. "Sixty coastal settlements along the south and east have been hit, either directly or indirectly, in the last three weeks. There have also been more than two dozen incidents in the interior. Practically every community within two thousand square kilometers has been touched—except Bourget. Messages, records, you name it have been destroyed or disrupted all over—except material to or from fat, rich Bourget. Interesting coincidence, is it not?"

"I'll agree it sounds anything but a coincidence," I replied, "but I haven't a clue as to who or where. I've been here now the better part of—what?—five months and I've never seen a straighter, more basic and open culture than this."

"A culture that refuses to recognize the Queen and festers the largest cult of the Destroyer on the planet," Morah snapped back. "A culture with the resources and means to mount a widespread rebellion."

"Except that all the Unitites want is to be left alone," Kokul noted. "As far as they're concerned, they're on another planet and they'd just as soon keep it that way."

"That's about it," I agreed.

"You have made no attempts to break the Destroyer cult," the Chief of Security noted.

Kokul shrugged. "What can I do? It's a safety valve for this kind of culture, and the ones I've caught have been genuine fanatics. They have someone of great power at their heart though—they know and completely change and move as soon as I get a clue. It's as if they had somebody right in my labs."

"Perhaps they do," Morah replied. "Perhaps you have been here too long, Kokul."

The wizard's face turned red, and he stood up. I had never seen him angry before, and he was a fearsome sight. "Are you questioning my loyalty? Even you have no right to do that, Morah!"

The big, weird man was unmoved. "I have every right to do whatever necessary," he replied. However, he seemed to realize he had overstepped his diplomatic bounds if he hoped to get cooperation with a minimum of trouble, and added, "However, I am not questioning your loyalty. Were you would be brought up before the Synod, as you know. No, I merely reflect that you have been here a *very* long time. You *like* Bourget and its isolation, and as you are intimate with the people, they are also intimate with you. You may or may not have the power necessary to do what needs to be done, but you lack the will in any case. I have no such problems."

Kokul was only partially mollified, but he sat down.

"You will call a series of assemblies of all townsmen," Morah told him. "Groups of 500, in one-hour intervals—and I don't care if it *does* disrupt things for a day or two. I will make similar arrangements with the Companies. If I read these Unitites correctly, they would be more intolerant than even we of anyone discovered to be in the cult of the Destroyer. We will bring them into the open. We will let your precious villagers discover just who is who. And then we will stamp out this cult in Bourget."

"Just what are you going to do?" I asked him, still trying, and failing, to look directly into those weird eyes.

"My best troops are even now in the process of sealing off the town by both land and sea," he told us. "There will be no escape for this band of traitors. Be there for the first assembly tomorrow morning. It will probably be the only one required. I think both of you will find the exercise an educational experience."

CHAPTER EIGHT

All Hell Breaks Loose

"Who's this Yatek Morah, anyway, that he can come in and order us around like this?" Zala wanted to know.

"Chief of Security, he says, and I know little more except that Tully is scared stiff of him and he comes directly from Aeolia Matuze."

"Well, I don't think he's got any right doing this. I've got half a mind not to show up."

I stared at her, wondering a bit at her sudden show of spunk and bravado—or was it? She wasn't very good at hiding things, and in her eyes I saw a tinge of fear and uncertainty. For a brief moment I wondered if maybe there was more going on here than I realized.

"You have to go," I told her. "We all do. Anybody on the list who doesn't show up when ordered will automatically be branded an enemy of the people, and they can take whatever action they want. Besides, you saw the ships out there?"

She nodded nervously.

"I don't know how many troops he's got with him, but they're a nasty bunch and very well trained and efficient—and according to Tully they're *all* at least apts." I paused a moment to let that sink in. "Besides—aren't you just the least bit curious to see what they're going to do?"

"I—I suppose. Well, let's do it."

We left the house together and walked up the road toward the square. Everything was closed today, even the bank, and there was the general feeling of a community under sudden siege. I didn't like it—the eerie stillness, the tension so thick you could feel it, like cobwebs or dense fog oozing around, despite the fact that this was one of our few bright, rainless days.

Most of the first group had already gathered in and around the square, which nonetheless looked oddly barren without the vendors and café tables. A small stage had been erected in the center of the square, on the grassy plot where Zala and I had been ceremoniously married only five months before. The four streets leading into the square were all filled with men in the black and gold imperial uniforms of Charon. I was struck by their tough, nasty appearance and by the fact that they were all armed with very ugly-looking rifles of unfamiliar design. I looked around on top of the market buildings and the town hall and saw indications of movement, reflections in the light, everywhere. Morah was taking no chances. I had no idea what those rifles shot or their rate of fire, but I was pretty sure that, in a pinch, this force could probably mow down everyone in the square. Not a comforting thought.

Zala looked nervously at the troops and gulped, grabbing and squeezing my hand for reassurance. "Park?"

"Yeah?"

"Let's stay close to Tully in this. At least we'll have some measure of protection."

"Good idea—if we can find him in this mob." I looked around but the wizard was nowhere to be seen. "Let's try the town hall. That'll be where Morah will come from."

She nodded, and we made our way through a sea of worried faces; the people were milling around, looking at the troops, but not talking very much. We had almost reached the front door when it opened and Morah and Kokul emerged, flanked by four more troopers. Zala stopped at the sight of the security chief and gave a slight gasp as, for an instant, she saw those strange, terrible eyes. But Morah paid us no notice and, using his troopers—all four female, I noted, deliberately chosen to thumb his nose at the Unitites—to clear a path, he made his way to the stage. He really didn't need the troopers—nobody was going to stand in *that* man's way.

Tully followed him to the foot of the stage, but did not climb up on it. I started to go to him, but Zala pulled me back. "No. Let's stay against the building, near the doorway," she suggested hopefully. I looked around and could see her point. If any shooting started it was the best exit available and one I knew well.

Morah was, if anything, more imposing than ever, standing alone in the center of that platform. I could see his weird eyes survey both the crowd and the positions of his troops. There was an air of tense expectation in the crowd, as if everyone knew that something, something explosive and, perhaps, evil, was about to begin. Even Zala seemed to sense it and feel that way. As for me, hell, I was a member of the party in good standing—I could hardly wait to see how the big boys operated here. Things had been dull for too long.

Finally, Morah seemed satisfied. I suspected that he was delaying things, letting everybody become as nervous and jumpy as possible, for good, psychological reasons. This was a tenth of the town, including almost all the bigwigs, and they were going to be the example.

"Citizens of Bourget," he began, his voice tremendously amplified and echoing off the walls, lending an additional alien quality to his presence. "Thank you for coming. Charon has long valued Bourget and its industrious people who are so valuable to the whole of the planet for their products. We deeply regret these measures, and I, Yatek Morah, Chief of Security, wish to assure those of you who are loyal citizens that you have nothing to fear today. In fact, I am here precisely because there is a threat to your peace and well-being, a threat you did not know existed but one that might consume you should it go unchecked. After today enemies both of Bourget and of Charon will be unmasked, exposed, and dealt with, and we can all feel safer because of it."

He paused a moment to let that sink in. I found the softening up very impressive and quite good human psychology. Of course, very soon would come the still-hidden knife, but these were simple people and most of them probably didn't know that yet.

"I come today to tell you of treason," Morah continued. "I come today to tell you of ships falling victim to piracy, treasuries looted, important officials kidnapped and assassinated. It is a scourge that has enveloped our beloved land, although it has not as yet touched Bourget." Again the dramatic pause. "And, of course, we had to ask ourselves, why not Bourget? Is it not the richest, fattest, and most tempting target for such enemies? And yet we could not bring ourselves to believe that Bourget itself would be a party to such things. Bourget has been good to Charon, and Charon has been good to Bourget. What, then, are we to think of all this?"

Some rumblings, mumblings, and whispers could be heard in the crowd. I noticed, too, that at least a few people started looking around very uncomfortably, or were edging toward the back of the crowd. Very, very interesting.

"Obviously," the security chief continued, "our enemies are in Bourget, of Bourget, but unknown to the loyal and peace-loving people of Bourget. And if such enemies are amongst you, living amongst you, while they perpetrate such monstrous crimes, they are growing stronger, richer, more confident. Eventually, they would have taken over and dominated this community. Today we will end this threat."

More rumblings and whisperings, and I noticed the troopers coming to full alert. I was now beginning to get an idea of what Morah had in mind, remembering Garal's original statement back in orientation that a curse is only good if the victim knows about it. Well, anybody in this crowd who was involved in the underground movement sure knew—and had no way out, as a couple of women who started walking toward one of the streets found out when they were blocked and turned back by the troopers.

"What *is* he going to do?" Zala whispered to me.

"He's going to cast a spell on the evildoers," I told her. "At least, I think so."

"I am Chief of Security," Morah reminded them, "and as befits one of my titles and responsibilities, I have great power." He raised his arms up over his head and began chanting what sounded to me like nonsense syllables—but I'd witnessed such a thing before. "Concentration aids" Tully had called them, but the people called them spells.

Slowly the arms dropped, and those eerie eyes seemed to fill the stage. He stretched out his arms to the crowd, which reacted by nervously pulling back. I noticed that Tully Kokul was viewing the scene with interest but was taking no part in the proceedings.

Morah stopped his chant and froze in position, pointing both arms at the crowd. "Now and in the presence of you all," he intoned, "I do hereby curse those who would follow the Destroyer, Lord of Nothingness, and do his bidding. Let their evil traitorous presence be known to all good men and women—*now!*"

It was an amazing show. Bright yellow sparks seemed to fly from his fingers and reach out in all directions for the crowd, many of whom screamed or cried out. Many in the crowd really let out yells and raised hands to foreheads. One woman near us let out a screech and turned in fear and shock toward us, whereupon I let out an involuntary gasp. From her forehead protruded two short, stubby, demonic horns.

"Look at that!" I exclaimed, turning to Zala. "I—" then stopped dead. Zala, looking shocked and scared to death, was feeling her own pair of horns. "Oh, no! Not *you*." She looked at me in mixed fear and bewilderment. "No, I—"

But the comment was suddenly cut off, and I watched in amazement as an odd, bizarre transformation seemed to take place within her. Her body seemed to be all in motion as some power reshaped muscle and transformed her into someone else before my very eyes. I thought for a moment it was part of the spell, but a quick glance around showed that it was not. Shots rang out, and I saw several people who had rushed for one of the streets near us go down in a hail of gunfire and lie there, writhing and moaning.

"Get them, honest citizens!" Morah was ordering. "Hold them for us!"

When I looked back, the woman next to me was only barely recognizable as Zala Embuay. She seemed larger, stronger, and the face, even the eyes, while still hers, seemed to belong to someone else, someone I did not know at all. She looked at me—horns still present—and said in a crisp, low voice, "Get inside the hall—*fast!* For your own sake!"

"What the hell?" was all I could manage. Roughly she picked me up as if I were a rag doll and shoved me in the doorway. It didn't take a genius to realize that, for the first time, I was in the presence of the other, hidden Zala Embuay—but not for long. Before I could say another word she ran into the town hall and was quickly gone. For a moment I debated running after her, but I realized there was little I could do—and few places for her to run, with troops on the roof and, surely, stationed at the side exits as well. So, keeping well inside the doorway, I returned my gaze to the street.

The massacre was starting on schedule. I estimated thirty or forty people, perhaps, had suddenly sprouted horns—all female as far as I could see. The crowd, primed, acted as Morah expected, actually jumping on their erstwhile friends and relatives and helping the efficient troops to capture them.

Suddenly a series of tracerlike blasts shook the square, and there were explosions and concussions everywhere, followed immediately by the steady sounds of something I knew well. Laser pistols! But they weren't supposed to *work* on Charon!

Stun rays were playing down the square, collapsing people into little heaps by the dozens, but not far away, on the rooftops, a deadly gunfight was obviously taking place between the troops and—who? I realized I didn't know and, from my protective vantage point, I couldn't really see either.

Near the stage I saw Tully Kokul's mouth sag as he watched the scene in total amazement. The rays playing the square seemed to have no effect on him at all, nor did he seem unduly worried.

On the stage, Morah was shouting instructions to his troops and trying to rally those he could. As with Kokul, nothing happening around him seemed to touch him in the slightest, a state that attested to both men's extreme powers—and one I, also, would have found especially useful and comforting right about then.

Suddenly all the shooting stopped. The square itself looked like the scene of a grisly massacre, although I knew from the nature of the rays and from experience on the sonics that most of the people had simply been knocked cold.

Morah, suddenly aware of the silence, stopped his commands and turned to look at the rooftops.

"All right, Morah! Stay where you are until we get our people out and no additional measures will be taken," came a deep, gruff voice. "You too, Kokul. We've no desire to kill you—but we will."

The Wizard of Bourget seemed to smile a bit, then looked up at the security chief. Morah's face remained impassive as always, but his eyes and manner suggested that he was boiling inside.

"You dare face down *me?*" Morah shot back defiantly. "If that's you,

Koril I welcome the challenge. If not, I have little to fear from the likes of the rest of you!"

My heart jumped on hearing Koril's name. Koril! It was really beginning! In fact, I wondered if this wasn't all pretty well stage-managed to do just that. Maybe Matuze was becoming as bored and impatient as I was to get something moving. Well, they'd sure as hell gotten something moving now . . .

After a long pause, heavy weapons opened up from the rooftops right at Yatek Morah and the stage area. They were prevented from using real devastators since they wanted to keep the unconscious crowd alive, but the amount of ordnance that did open up would atomize anything it hit, and it hit Yatek Morah head on. Tully Kokul moved fast to the side as the entire stage area crackled, burned, turned suddenly white-hot and vanished, leaving a crater two meters deep.

Yatek Morah was still standing there where the stage had been, about four meters in mid-air. The stuff continued to pour into him, and for a moment he seemed not to notice and certainly not to be worried as he looked this way and that. I realized, however, that it was a frantic series of glances even for so impressive a power. He was holding off all that concentrated firepower by sheer force of will, aided, probably, by some very effective body-worn neutralizers, but they couldn't withstand that sort of concentrated power very long and he knew it.

Suddenly he seemed to grow and expand, becoming in an instant a huge, three-headed dragonlike monster rising up, up, out of an invisible cavity in the air just above the smoldering pit. It was a fearsome, terrifying sight as the thing grew and grew until it towered over the entire square and bathed the scene in its shadow. The firing wavered, but then picked up again and, with a defiant howl and hiss from all three heads, the terrible creature shot from sight as fast as a shuttle and quickly disappeared into the sky.

The firing stopped, leaving only a scene of incredible carnage and a vast, bubbling caldron where once the square had been. Some of the people who had been knocked out by the stun rays had been caught, inevitably, in the firing, but very few—most had drawn back during the excitement.

I had to admit I was stunned almost beyond thought, and had to call on all my training and experience to put myself back together. Things had happened very fast, and few of them were expected. First Zala—the fact that she was, perhaps had been all along, part of the opposition here and neither told me nor betrayed it in any way. And, of course, there was her transformation into someone quite different almost before my very eyes. Then the tables being turned on Morah, followed by his own incredible transformation into the terrifying three-headed dragon.

And now? I was acutely aware of how very alone I was at the moment—and how much on the *outside* of where I wanted to be *in*. I looked out into the square and listened carefully. No weapons, no sonics, no rays. It was over, whatever it was. They would come in and take their own out, now marked with the horns, and shift to new and unknown places and bases. Either I got left behind to rot or I got out there and tried to get inside.

I opened the door and walked cautiously into the street, being careful to keep close to the wall and exercising all my training and experience to make as small and difficult a target as I could for anybody who might get nervous. I admitted to myself that I would have felt much more confident with a laser pistol of my own.

Still, I had to be out here if only to make my contacts. I wondered where Zala was. If she were in this up to her neck, as it now appeared, she would be very handy—I needed some friend to bridge the gap.

For a few minutes nothing moved except a couple of the poor devils shot but not killed by the troopers near the street intersection. Obviously the ray hadn't gotten that far. The troopers themselves were mostly ugly messes, smeared over the nicely whitewashed walls.

But then, carefully, shapes began moving into the square—or what was left of it—starting with two nasty-looking things that flew down from the rooftops. Strange creatures covered with what appeared to be both fur and feathers of gold and brown. Their batlike wings did not fold into their bodies but instead semi-accordioned on their backs. Their heads were nasty, somewhat birdlike with large eyes and beaks but capable of an almost humanlike expression. They were horrors, and for a moment I feared they were some new kind of Charonese creature come to feed on carrion. But the deliberateness of their moves and their very human manner in going through and checking the unconscious and the dead showed them to be changelings. I was not really surprised at the changeling involvement, but to see two of them that looked like the same creature was more than interesting.

Huge, clawlike hands gestured beyond my line of sight, and from all four main streets they entered—a nightmarish parade of creatures that had never evolved except in the human mind. Shaggy, apelike things, things that crawled, things on four legs, walkers, hoppers, amphibians—the collection of human horrors seemed endless and terrible, all the more so because you could see in their movements and gestures, and sometimes in their features, the humanity that lay deep within them. But they were not all repulsive—some were quite beautiful and graceful, exotic creatures out of mankind's myths and imagination, as well as its nightmares.

I looked around for some sign of Zala or, perhaps, Tully Kokul, but neither were anywhere to be seen. I was suddenly acutely aware of the fact that I was very much alone in that square, the only whole and conscious human being and not marked by the spell as a friend or ally. I began to think better of the idea and edged back along the wall toward the door once more, whereupon a couple of creatures, one tentacled and snakelike, the other a gray thing like a crude stone carving noticed me and pointed. I froze, and some of the others turned in my direction. There seemed little I could do—they had the guns—so I just stood up straight, walked away from the wall, and put my hands up.

"Wait! Don't shoot!" I called to them. "I'm not a bad guy. I'm Zala's husband! You know—Zala. One of your people!"

A creature that looked something like a walking tree turned to the tentacled, snakelike thing and said something I couldn't catch. The tentacled creature said something back. I saw some shrugs and indecision from several of the more humanoid ones around as they stopped for a moment from their task of identifying those with horns and carrying them off.

The frog-man came up to them and said, clearly, "He's the T.A.—the government man here. Get rid of him!"

One of the winged creatures nodded, pulled its pistol, and aimed it at me.

"Hey! Wait a minute!" I yelled, but then something hit me real hard and I lost consciousness.

CHAPTER NINE

Changeling

I came to, slightly, but felt dizzy, weak, and my head hurt as it never had before. I know I groaned, but I was only semiconscious and still not really thinking. I was aware, though, that I was on a stretcher or litter of some kind and that I was being carried someplace very fast. I managed to open my eyes and was shocked to see that it was dark. How long had I been out?

I heard a sharp command and the stretcher bearers slowed, then stopped and put me down. There was very little light and I was in no condition to see straight, but I couldn't help thinking that the front bearer was a giant caricature of a big bird of some kind. Caricature. That was a good word for most of the changelings I had seen. The image of the white, feathered head with its huge eyes and wide, flat orange beak finally penetrated my still-foggy brain enough for me to realize the obvious—they hadn't killed me but had, for some reason, taken me with them! The game was back on track—if my head ever reassembled itself.

The bird-thing poured something into a cup from a gourd around its waist. "Drink this," it rasped in a guttural, nonhuman voice. "Go on—it'll make you feel better."

I managed to grab the cup and bring it, with the help of a humanlike white hand, to my lips. It burned a bit, but tasted much like a fruit brandy. My mouth was dry and parched and I badly needed something. I spilled a little, but only a little, then dropped back down on the stretcher.

"He'll be all right," the bird-man said to a companion I hadn't yet seen. "That'll keep him until we get to the Old Woman."

"That's all I want," replied the other, a woman's voice that sounded vaguely familiar but wasn't one I could easily place.

"Zala?" I managed weakly, voice cracking.

"Forget her," the voice responded, and then we were up and off again.

My head didn't really clear very much for the remainder of the journey, although the pain subsided into nothingness. I was semiconscious, but not really able to move or say much of anything, and the whole world seemed to have a fuzzy, dreamlike quality. I had enough wits to realize that I'd been given a drug containing a light sedative, but whether to lessen my pain or to keep me from recovering—or both—I couldn't be sure. Nor, in fact, did I much care.

Time had little meaning for me, but it was still quite dark when we slowed and approached what appeared to be a cave from which a dull fireglow shone into the blackness. Thunder sounded in the distance, and told us all that the inevitable Charonese rains would soon be upon us once more. But the cave was the destination, and they managed to carry me into it before the heavens opened.

The cave itself had a small mouth but opened into a single large chamber, although exactly how large I couldn't tell. A fire burning in the center of the chamber was the source of light. Its smoke was rising straight up, indicating some kind of air vent. If it was hot outside, it was really broiling inside, and if I had been in anything other than a drugged condition I would have gotten out of there. As it was, I could only lie there, sweating profusely, visions of being roasted on a spit dancing through my fevered brain.

There was someone else in the cave—a very old woman, it appeared, dressed all in black cloth that virtually hid her entire body, which appeared to be extremely large. She doddered up to us using a crooked stick as a cane and gestured for them to put me down where I was, which they did. Bird-man turned to the one in back of me. "All right, we're even now, Darva. I hope this is really what you want."

Darva! I'd almost forgotten about her. I hadn't really seen or talked to her after that first time, although I'd looked for her when I was out at Thunderkor. Even in my drugged state, it made me feel a little better to know that I had yet another friend among the others, one who had probably saved my life.

She moved around to where I could see her, near the old woman. Darva towered over the woman in black, who had pretty good bulk herself, although she was almost certainly human.

"I bring you my heart, Grandmother," she greeted the old woman.

The woman stood back and looked at her with ancient, dark eyes. "It is good that you are well," the old one responded in a voice cracked with age and experience. "I feared the loss of many lives."

"There were twelve of us killed," Darva told her. "That is less than we thought. And almost two hundred of them."

The old woman nodded. "That is well. But they will bring down a terror now beyond knowing or understanding. All are even now scattering to the winds and will not regroup for many weeks in special places far away. And what of you? What will you do?"

Darva sighed. "You know Isil is dead and his masters flown."

'I know," the old woman replied, a tinge of sadness in her voice. "You are a changeling forever, and no old changeling may ever return to Bourget."

'I know," Darva told her. "But what I did, I did for revenge, not out of some loyalty pledged to ones I don't even know."

'You will not join the others, then, at the appointed time?"

She shrugged. "I haven't decided as yet, Grandmother."

The old woman looked over at me. "He is the one of whom you spoke?"

Darva nodded. "He was kind to me when no one else would be. He is not like the others. I ask you now for a last favor, Grandmother."

Still fogged and semi-comatose, I could only follow the conversation, not analyze it or join in.

"Does he consent?" the old woman asked.

Darva turned and pointed to me. "See how they have hurt him? They were about to shoot him when I stopped them. Without me he would be twelve hours dead. Does that not give *me* the right?"

"Under our sacred law, it does," the old one agreed, "but he may not be the kind of person you think if your will is imposed."

"What choice will he have?" She paused. "Besides—if not he, then who? It is my reason to live."

The old woman gave a sympathetic smile. "Then that is more than reason enough." She waddled over to me and examined me clinically, like a doctor before an operation. "That's a nasty crack on the head. Skull fracture, some concussion."

Darva came over and looked down at me. She was still exotically beautiful, even the light green skin and dark green of lips and hair served to make her even more alluring. For the first time though, I noticed the nonhuman touches of the now-dead creature artist who had remade her: small pointed ears that twitched this way and that through the dark green hair, and hands that were far rougher and more beastlike than I remembered. That sharp, curved horn, perhaps fifty centimeters long, was actually a curved bone, layer upon layer presenting a sense of concentric rings leading to its sharp point. "You will be able to repair him?" she asked, worriedly.

The old woman nodded. "Oh, yes, yes. Although the blow's a serious one that would have killed many men. He has a very, very strong will to live. Good *wa*, strong *wa*, already rushing within him to repair the damage. We will help the *wa*."

"When?"

"Why not now? He is quiet. He has been given *osisi*, I perceive. That is good. He is heavily sedated, but conscious. It helps, his being awake." She turned back to Darva. "A spell of the mind will be hard. He is protected by the town sorc from such meddling. I could give you potions, though . . ."

She shook her head. "No. That will be all right. I wouldn't want it to be like that anyway."

"That is good. I will have enough problems reworking parts of his body functions, reflexes, balance centers, that sort of thing, without having to worry about the conscious mind as well." She sighed. "Well, let's get it done."

Again, I can say little about how much time passed, or exactly what was done. I know that the old woman chanted and meditated over me for a long while, and occasionally seemed to knead various parts of my head and body. I also seemed to have a bad fever, with all sorts of strange, surrealist visions passing in and out of my mind. I would come down with chills, then hot flashes, and even oddly erotic sensations ran through my whole body. They had remarked on how bad off I was, and so I didn't fight any of it. Finally, I just lapsed into an incredibly deep sleep where no odd creatures, feelings, wizards and witches penetrated.

I awoke still feeling groggy, although with no pain. It was some moments before I perceived a wrongness, somehow, about myself. I looked around the cave, but aside from a now tiny fire and a sliver of light coming in through the opening indicating it was day outside I saw nobody and nothing unusual. I fought to clear the cobwebs from my brain, and, at last, I realized a couple of things right away. First of all, I was standing up. That was really odd, since there was no way I could imagine myself rising in the dark—unless it was part of the witch's healing spells or whatever. Second, I no longer felt the least bit hot. In fact, I felt a little chilly, which was ridiculous in a cave with the fire still going.

I was suddenly very wide awake and with a very bad feeling about all this. I raised my hand to rub the last bits of sleep from my eyes and saw what I feared.

The hand was green, rough, and taloned.

"*No!*" I shouted, my voice echoing slightly around the cave walls. "Damn it!" I took a step forward, and immediately knew the whole story. I turned and looked down and back at myself. I had big, taloned lizard's feet and thickly muscled lizard's legs, not to mention a bright green tail that was almost as long as my body without the legs. Frantically I looked around the cave, then saw over in one corner something that would do for my purposes—a large piece of shiny metal. I went over to it, picked it up, and looked at myself in the fire's reflection.

Horn and all, I reflected glumly. The face and torso retained some of my former appearance, but it was an odd hybrid, a combination of the features of Park Lacoch and Darva.

I heard someone enter behind me. I put down the shiny metal and turned. It was Darva. She stopped and looked at me, a mixture of pleasure and apprehension on her face.

"Darva, why?" I asked her.

She looked a little apologetic. "I saved your life," she reminded me. "I would think you would do the same for me."

"I—I would," I told her honestly, "but how is changing me into a near double of you going to do that?"

She sighed and looked a little sad. "The only thing I lived for was revenge, and I've had that, although not the way I hoped. Now, with all this, I'm completely alone and like this forever, unless I'm changed into something even worse. The only one of my kind, Park—and never able to go home again, to see my family, to be among the few I treasure." There was a note of pleading in her voice. "Don't you see? If I had to go on alone, I'd kill myself. And there you were, and Jobrun knocked you out, then drew his pistol to shoot you. I saw it, and knew, somehow, it was destiny and that the gods had put you and me there like that for a reason."

I shook my head sadly. The truth was, I had to admit even to myself, that what she was saying was totally understandable and even reasonable. How could I even argue with her logic, no matter how I felt? Face facts, I said to myself. You'd be dead without her, so you owe her. And this way, you are still in the game, still playing. If the changelings were the heart of Koril's movement, then it was with the changelings I belonged. If there was any doubt about that I should have just stayed out of that square and helped Tully pick up the pieces as a loyal T.A. Besides, there were a lot worse things I could have been turned into—I ought to know. I had seen them in the square.

I went over to her, almost knocking over some stuff with my tail, took her hand in mine, and smiled. "I *do* understand," I told her, "and I *do* forgive you."

She looked instantly happy beyond measure.

"But you might have gotten more than you bargained for," I warned.

She didn't seem to hear the comment, but two big tears welled up in her green eyes. "I'm glad we're not going to have a fight."

I sighed. "No, no fight. I admit this is going to take some getting used to in more ways than one, but I think I can live with it."

"Let's go outside," she suggested. "We're sort of cold-blooded."

Well, that explained the slight chill, I thought. I followed her out. It was the usual hot day, with heavy humidity and great clumps of white fog covering almost everything. The heat and humidity seemed to fade slowly away, though, and I began feeling very comfortable for the first time since arriving on Charon. Suddenly I was conscious of a great hunger. "What do we eat?" I asked her.

She smiled. "Almost anything living," she replied, and I had visions of tearing small lizards limb from limb. She caught my thought and laughed.

"Oh, no. Plants, fruits, leaves, that sort of thing. Animals, too, but I prefer mine cooked the old way."

"Fair enough. Anything nearby?"

"There's a grove of fruit trees—cuaga melons—just down the hill here. Follow me."

She started off and I followed. "You say it's a grove. Any chance of our being seen? I'm pretty sure changelings aren't too popular right now."

"No, it's on the edge of Bindahar's holdings," she replied. "They won't be out this way for a couple of days, and by then we'll be long gone."

The melons were big, fat black and orange striped things, but they were very filling, although I had to get used to eating the rind as well. Either my taste sense had changed drastically—which was likely—or the humans who ate only the pulp missed something good.

We ate long and heavily. My old self—my original self—might have managed a whole melon, pulp only. The old Park Lacoch maybe a quarter of that. I ate seventeen, rinds and all, and still wasn't totally full.

"You eat a lot," Darva told me, "and whenever we can. We never get fat, though—just stronger, it seems."

"That's a fair trade," I admitted, feeling much better now. Once we'd eaten, it was time to talk of other things. Eating made me a little lazy and lethargic, and it was time to relax.

"Look—tell me a lot of things."

"Anything," she responded, obviously meaning it. "You don't know how very long it's been since I've had anybody to talk to, just friend to friend."

I nodded. "Okay. First of all, the immediate stuff. Who was the old woman who cast the spell?" Frankly, I wanted to know for more than one reason. She was the one who, at some future time, might also take it off.

"That was my great-grandmother—my real one," she told me. "She's had that power since I don't know when. Maybe since she was little. She studied with a Company sorc when she was very young, when there weren't the kinds of prejudice and tight unions they have now. But she never got the full bit. She had nine kids instead."

"I can see where that would slow you down," I admitted, "though she seemed powerful enough. But—why make me into your twin sister? Was that because her powers were limited?"

She hesitated a moment. "Well, that's not exactly true," she responded. "It's true that she had me for a model, and it's kind of tricky, making a changeling. Do it wrong and your brain's not right for the rest of you and you get crippled in the body or head. There's lots like that. So she used the same spell that bastard Isil used on me as her guide. That meant you look almost like me. But she had bunhars as models also. I was so excited I didn't even really think about it, but *she* did. You're still a male, Park—looks aside."

That was interesting. It was also ironically funny, and I had to chuckle.

"What's so funny?"

"Well, you know I wasn't born on Charon. I was sent here. Sent here by the law."

She nodded. "I know. It was the talk of Thunderkor."

"Well, I got into—trouble. I killed somebody, for no reason you—or even I, now—would think was right or sane. And the reason, when they found it, was that I was a hermaphrodite, a freak."

Her mouth formed a little circle. "Oh . . . So that's why you looked a little well, funny."

I nodded. "But they got me straightened out and happily male," I continued. "And now—look! I'm a male who looks like your sister!"

She laughed at that herself, but it brought up an interesting question. All right, I was male—but a male *what?* I asked her about it.

"I wondered about that myself," she said. "According to Grandmother, if we were to, ah, make it, right now nothing would happen. But as soon as the *wa* inside you gets the rest of you straight, it might just be that we could reproduce our own kind. It's not certain, but it's been known to happen. We might start a whole new race!" She looked thoughtful. "*Darvus Lacoehus.*"

"Sounds like a disease."

She laughed. "You know, this is wonderful, Park. I feel more alive than I have in two years!"

I could see her joy, and even feel good about it. I liked her, too. Her speech was a little rough, and occasionally became even rougher. She was uneducated and inexperienced, but she was a bright, intelligent woman whose potential had been blunted by a man's cruel ego. And she was certainly tougher and more decisive than Zala—the old Zala, anyway. I idly wondered what the new Zala was like.

"Look," I said, "you're going to have to fill me in. What the hell happened back there in Bourget? And who did it? And why?"

She sighed. "Well, for a long time there's been a devil cult. You know that?"

I nodded.

"Well, anyway, it was mostly bored and frustrated women trying to get a little of the Power. But a year or two ago, things changed. How and who did it I don't know, but they got kinda taken over by this bigger group that wants to overthrow the government. It's got a real powerful sorc behind it is all I know."

"Koril," I told her. "Used to be Lord."

"Yeah, him, I think," she agreed. "Anyway, lots of folks liked him better. You didn't have any creepy guys like that security chief, and no troopers jumping out at you. Well, this sorc also contacted all the changeling colonies. He promised them that when he got back they'd be given Tukyan, the south continent, for their own. There's few people down there now, and it's mostly still unexplored, but it's at least as nice as here, or so I'm told. Well, this was great for the changelings, who have no real life and no future here. The humans went along, too, because we'd be out of their hair. See?"

I nodded. It was very logical—and good politics on Koril's part. I was beginning to see how formidable the man was, even without his reputed super magical powers. I had to wonder how Aeolia Matuze was ever able to oust him in the first place, and how she kept her power.

In a flash, I had it—the only logical answer. She was in the job because she backed the war against the Confederacy. The other three Lords couldn't care less about Charon—Korman said as much. Who did? The only logical answer was the aliens themselves.

You didn't have any creepy guys like that security chief . . .

Whose Chief of Security *was* Yatek Morah? Matuze's? Yes, but only so long as she followed the correct line. And that meant that it was very possible that the strange man with those strange eyes, that robotlike manner, that incredible power, was not human at all. And *that* meant that, while Charon was unimportant to the war, it was, for some reason, very, very important to the aliens. Why?

Aeolia Matuze, with her great ego and dreams of godhood—the aliens would feed that, and in exchange, she would follow the alien line right where they said. It made sense. I wondered if Koril, even now, realized it? What was one Lord of the Diamond to a race prepared to disrupt and take over a thousand worlds or more?

"What'cha thinking?"

I was startled out of my reverie. "Just putting a lot of pieces together in my head. I'll explain them to you later. We're going to be together a long time, and it's a long and complicated story."

"Together," she sighed. "You don't know how good that sounds."

"First, some basics. How come I don't trip over my tail when I walk or tip over on the run? I feel pretty natural in this body."

"It was a good spell, with all the necessaries."

I nodded. That was good enough for me. "Okay then—where do we go from here?"

"Far away," she responded quickly, "and fairly fast. This place is a day's march from Bourget, but it'll soon be crawling with government troops. Probably already is. We have a number of defenses—including the ability to stand absolutely still. You'd be surprised, but big as we are, if we're all surrounded by green and stay completely still they'll run right past us."

"Handy," I told her, "but the weaponry suddenly turned a lot more modern around here than I was used to, and the good stuff has heat sensors."

She laughed. "So what? They tried them in hunting. Our body temperature's pretty much the same as our surroundings. They're nearly useless."

I hadn't thought of that angle. "Still, I'd just as soon be away from here —fast. How well do you know the land beyond this region?"

"Fair," she responded. "Worse if we get more than a hundred kilometers from here. I never traveled much. But I know where the roads are, even though we can't use them—and I have landmarks from maps in my head. They made us memorize a bunch of them."

"Good girl," I told her.

"You want to join up with the others, then?" She sounded almost disappointed.

I nodded. "I'll try and explain why as we go. There's a lot going on they don't tell you about."

"We've still got three weeks to get maybe 800 kilometers," she told me. "That's time enough to tell me everything. We were supposed to scatter and live off the land until then."

"Gives 'em plenty of time to capture some of us and force those locations out of us," I said worriedly.

"Oh, there's hundreds of rendezvous spots, and only a very small group was told of one and two alternates. Even if they pick up half the change-lings, which I doubt, we still would have an even chance that one or more of ours was still good."

"Not the odds I like, but they're the only ones we have." I looked around. The fog was coming in even more thickly. "And now's the time to make tracks for far away."

She laughed. "And even those'll be bunhar tracks."

There were, in fact, advantages to this shape.

I looked around. "I think I'm going to have to find a friendly tree," I told her. "It goes right through you on an empty stomach."

She laughed and pointed randomly. I took her advice, picked a spot, and relaxed, looking down.

"Oh, so *that's* where it is," I said aloud.

CHAPTER TEN

Decision at the Pinnacles

It was, in some ways, an idyllic three weeks, and it bothered me a bit because I thought of it as such. The fact was, I really *enjoyed* Darva, person to person, and found within myself the stirrings of feelings I never even knew I had. It was a blow to my own self-image, really, that I should feel this way. The strong, solid, emotionless agent of the Confederacy, who needed nothing and no one—ever. Who was born, bred, and trained to be above such petty human feelings as loyalty, friendship . . . love? Hadn't I been the one who couldn't even pin down the meaning of the word to Zala only a few months ago? Was it possible, I found myself wondering, that loneliness was not something only inferior people suffered? Had I, in fact, been as much an alien and an outsider to my own culture as Darva had been to hers? That thought, I knew, was dangerous. It struck at the very value system of the Confederacy which I still told myself I believed in.

But had we, in our headlong rush to perfection, somehow left holes somewhere in the human psyche? Or was it rather just a new body, a new form, new hormones and whatever that created those holes where they'd never been before? For the moment, I preferred to think the latter—although, from a practical standpoint, it made no real difference when it was happening to me.

Several times during the three weeks we roamed the jungles of Charon, I was on the brink of telling her my real identity, my real mission, but I always held back. Nothing was to be gained from doing so now, and there was always time later on. I got to know her, though, as thoroughly as I knew anybody, and I liked what I found. She was a quick study, too, entranced by my tales of the civilized worlds and the frontier she would never see. She had less trouble than I would have thought with the alien/Four Lords backdrop, although I suspect that she thought of the aliens only as a new form of changeling. When you're bright green, 215 centimeters tall, have a horn and a tail, the concepts of "alien" and "nonhuman" just don't come across quite as well. But she understood that alien did not mean form as much as mind. If, as I suspected, Morah was an alien, she was all for saving a humanity she'd never see nor ever be a part of.

Some aspects of the new form were definitely affecting my mind, though. I found myself increasingly emotional, and increasingly aware of that emotion. I still retained all my training and its gimmicks, but I felt everything with an intensity I'd never known before, both positive and negative.

Our new form, which I shortened to *darvas,* wasn't at all bad, either. We were enormously strong, and despite being large, we could indeed fade into any green underbrush, then sprint faster than any human could run. The talons were handy as weapons, although we hadn't had to use them for that, and for cutting and slicing food of no matter what sort, and they made no difference to us, since our skin was extremely thick and tough—and it shed water like a waterproof coat.

There was no question they were out looking for us, though. We saw soarers on many occasions, some coming very close to the treetops or open spaces, occasionally with troopers spray-firing into clumps of growth just to panic anything and flush it out. The roads were under constant patrol by more of those nasty-looking troopers as well as some locals. Still, as long as we didn't run into a sorc or an apt and betray ourselves, we found it little trouble to stay out of the way.

The only trouble, in fact, came near the end of our jungle exile. We had both become easily accustomed to the jungle, a fearsome place for most humans. Our hides were too tough for the insects to penetrate, and we were relatively immune to predators and strong enough to break free of vines and mud. It was, in fact, a wondrous sort of place, the kind of place where there was endless fascination, endless beauty. Although we didn't really realize it, what we were doing in psych parlance was "going wild," totally adapting to an environment for which we were, quite literally, designed.

What brought it home to us was when we ran into the bunhar. Now, we'd seen and encountered many of the large creatures of jungle and swamp, including hundreds I'd had no idea existed before, but mostly we'd managed to steer clear of them—and they seemed to accept us as well. But this one was different. I will never be sure just what we did wrong. Maybe he was just horny and smelled Darva. But, anyway, he didn't avoid us; he challenged us with a great roar and snarling teeth. In fact, he looked to me like he was *all* nice, sharp, pointed teeth.

Despite some overlarge fanglike incisors, we had the omnivore's complement in a human-type mouth and face. It was a no-win situation, but try as we might to avoid him he challenged all the more, and we realized we had a fight on our hands. Oddly, I felt a rush of adrenalin or something similar like I'd never known before. While the big saurian sat there, snarling, I found myself overcome with anger and rage—and heard similar, animalistic snarlings from Darva. Without even thinking, both of us charged the brute, who was about our size, heads down and horns straight.

The bunhar had teeth, all right, but no horn, and I don't think he was quite prepared for our sudden charge. He reared back on his tail to protect his head, and both our horns penetrated his upper chest, while our talons ripped at him. Again and again we plunged and ripped into him, and he roared in pain and anger as his blood gushed all over his chest and us. Then Darva whirled around and kicked the creature behind his right leg with her own powerful leg, rearing back on her own tail for maximum effect, and the bunhar toppled.

In a moment we were both on him, plunging our horns into his vulnerable neck and ripping out flesh and limb. The poor creature never had a chance from the start, not only because of the horn but because, even in our animal rush, we had the advantage of human fighting tactics. The creature was killed outright, and neither of us received more than a slight scratch from the foot talons as we plunged in.

But when it was dead, the anger, the rage, the sense of power without thought, continued in both of us for some time, and we drank of the dead creature's blood and ripped off and ate chunks of raw flesh until we could eat no more and it was a bloody mess. Only when the eating was done and the feeling of satisfied lethargy overtook us, did we relax. The great emotions subsided, and rational thought returned.

For a while neither of us could say anything. Finally, Darva looked at me, as blood-spattered as she, then back at the carcass that was already drawing insects and would eventually draw carrion eaters. "My god, what have we done?" she gasped.

I looked at her, then at the carcass, then back at her again. I shook my head in tired wonder. "It looks like we're more animal than even you thought."

She looked dazed, slightly horrified. "It—it wasn't the bunhar. I mean, the damned thing asked for it. It was—after." She dipped her hand in a small pool of bunhar blood, brought it up to her nose, then licked it off her fingers. "My god, Park—it felt *good!* And it tasted . . ."

"I know," I replied wearily. The whole experience was wearing off now, leaving me feeling very tired, muscles aching a bit, and aware now of my scratches. I knew she was feeling the same.

She was still in that shocked daze. "I—I've been this way for over two years, and I never felt like that before, never did anything like that before."

I nodded wearily. "Your Isil was more creative than you thought. I suspect that this was to be the next stage if you didn't cave in, as you weren't —if your Gneezer even remembered you anymore. It was probably a good idea at the time, long forgotten. If the change wouldn't do it, they would put you off in the swamps, where your animal instincts would take over. You'd go wild, either winding up with a bunhar group or crawling back to them." I paused for a moment. "Still, it's not all bad."

She looked at me strangely. "What in hell is good about it?"

"Consider. We—the two of us—killed that mass of muscle and teeth, and did it pretty easily. We *instinctively* used all our best biological weapons against him. He outweighs us by a couple of hundred kilos, probably, and he was born a predator. But we're a more fearsome predator. That maneuver that toppled him probably saved us from serious injury. It's something you did almost automatically, but it would never occur to such a pea-brain as him. We're the bosses now. The king and queen of Charon's jungles, totally adapted to our element. We have nothing whatsoever to fear while we're in that element."

"But—the blood. God! It was like a shock, an orgasm. It was like a supercharge, the ultimate drug stimulant! Even now, repelled as I am, I crave the taste of it."

She was right. So did I, and it was something that was going to be hard to ignore.

I sighed. "Well, I'd say we'll probably keep it under control, but maybe have to give into it every once in a while. We're killers now, Darva. Natural predators. It's the bill that goes with this form and we simply have to accept it."

She looked dubious. "I—I don't know. Park—what if it had been a man? One of those troopers?"

My training was coming to the fore, my mind sorting and placing the new facts and choosing inevitable courses of action. It would be far harder for Darva, I knew, far harder, but she would have to eventually accept one basic fact and live with it.

"We're no longer human, Darva," I told her flatly. "We're something else entirely. Frankly, as long as the man is an enemy, I can see no difference between spearing him and shooting him."

"Bu:—cannibalism!" She shivered.

"If I ate you, it would be cannibalism," I said realistically. "But a human is just another smart animal."

She shook her head. "I—I don't know."

"You'll have to accept it, Darv, or go nuts," I told her. "But I wouldn't worry about it. Back with our own, back in intelligent company with ready food supplies, I doubt if our condition will be any problem at all. Only out here, in the jungle."

She said nothing for a while, and we more or less slept off the experience. When we awoke it was nearly dark, but we found a stream and washed the caked blood and remains from each other, feeling a little more like rational people and less like predators after we did.

Still, she could ask, "Park—those aliens you spoke of. Aren't *we* aliens, too? Particularly now?"

I didn't really have a ready answer for that one.

Despite the moralizing, we repeated our orgy the next day—deliberately. This time we found a small female uhar with a wounded leg who had been left by her herd to die because she could no longer hunt food. Such a target of opportunity was quite literally irresistible, incredibly easy, and also easy to defend to our consciences since the creature would have died more agonizingly anyway. Still, the ease and quickness of the decision and the high emotion—"anticipation" I guess would be the word—of the kill actually bothered me more than Darva. My whole life and self-image was based on my absolute confidence in my ability to be completely in control at all times, to be able to analyze and evaluate every situation with cold, dispassionate logic. To be able to give in to such base, animal—literally animal—instincts so easily was disturbing. To enjoy the experience so much was even more disturbing.

As for the hunting and killing, humans had been doing that to animals since the dawn of time. Though the civilized worlds knew meat only as a synthetic, those on the frontier certainly knew it in the same way ancient man on ancestral Earth had. Here on Charon people made their livings hunting game and fishing and eating their catch, and those who did this work enjoyed it. The fact that the people of Montlay and Bourget, among others, had their meat ground or cut and cooked and seasoned so they no longer really thought of their meal as an animal that had to be butchered only eased their minds a bit. Darva and I were no different—we were simply eliminating the hypocrisy. Looking at it in that way we both found it much easier to move fully into our roles as predators.

The Warden organisms that governed everything inside us also seemed to take a more practical view. After only the third kill and feed I was aware of odd feelings, mostly numbness and a little discomfort in my mouth. I mentioned this to Darva, who had noted the same thing, and a quick examination showed that things *were* changing. Our teeth were becoming sharper, the front fangs growing longer and thicker. Without an additional magic spell or anything else, we were changing into true carnivores.

Such a modification could not have been in the long-range plans of an apt like Isil; the Wardens inside us, somehow, were sensing the change in our life-style and modifying us to adapt. But what exactly were they reacting to? I wondered. Was it the changed physical circumstances? That seemed unlikely—Darva had been this way for a long time, I a very short time, yet the transformation was taking place only now. It had to be the change in our *mental* attitude that triggered it, I decided. Korman said we all had the power. Maybe the process was more complex than even he thought.

But that brought up an even more mystifying question. How did the Wardens *know?* An apt like Isil, even a powerful sorc like Korman, hardly had the kind of mind that could literally reprogram every cell, order speeded growth, put every cell and every molecule together in such a pattern as to create a biologically functioning changeling. The Confederacy's computers could do the job easily, of course, although doing so was illegal. But a man or woman could just wave a magic wand here, mumble some words, and somehow, force the transmutation of a human being into something else—something that functioned.

I had here a lot of pieces of a truly great puzzle but, as yet, nothing with which to put them all together. For the first time in a long while I wondered about my counterpart, my old self, out there, somewhere, off the Warden Diamond. Was he still getting his information even though I'd been transformed? And, if he *was* getting information from all of us on the four Warden worlds, had he already been able to put those pieces together with the superior computer and Confederacy resources at his command?

I no longer hated him, certainly. Now, here, the way I was, I wasn't even sure if I envied him.

Slowly, through it all in the final week, we moved cautiously closer to the rendezvous point Darva had selected as the main target for us, the least likely to be betrayed. It was about a kilometer off a main road, in a rock cleft near a waterfall, and we approached it cautiously and in a roundabout manner. Darva was still hesitant about going at all, particularly now.

"We're happy here," she argued. "You said it yourself—we were made for the jungle and for this life. If we return, there'll only be more fighting and trouble."

"What you say is true," I admitted, "but I'm thinking of more than just you and me. For one thing, *I have to know.* I want to find out just what the hell is going on here, and I have a particular responsibility, since I know that all Charon might be destroyed, we and our precious jungle along with it. But there's more. If we win, and if this Koril's a man of his word, we can strike a blow for changelings and end this stupid discrimination. Changelings need their own land and they need the Power. Otherwise, somebody will always control and threaten us. With the Power, we could build a new race here, or many races."

I'm afraid she didn't really share my vision or my curiosity, but she understood, at least, that I could not be denied—and she wasn't going to be left out, alone, again.

We approached the rocks cautiously. I let her take the lead because she at least knew the lay of the land from the maps. She was very cautious. Fifty meters or more from the clearing, but within the sound of the roar of the falls, she froze into the immobility we both could achieve and still found hard to believe. Seeing her, I automatically froze as well.

The falls masked most sounds, so I started looking around, feeling a bit what she also felt—or sensed. It was, I knew, another one of those animal attributes we were either acquiring or discovering. There were others about. We couldn't see them or hear them but we knew with absolute certainty they were there.

Concentration on this one aspect produced an interesting sensation. I was aware that I was sensing something entirely new, outside any previous experience. For the first time, consciously, we were sensing our own Wardens—our *wa*, as the old woman had called it—and those Wardens were not isolated or alone. Somehow some threads of energy, incredibly minute, were sending and receiving signals in all directions. No, that wasn't right, either—not signals; more like an open communications link, waveforms of the most basic and microscopic sort; open channels to the trees, grass, rocks, stuff in the air—everything around us. This, then, was what the sorcs felt, what Korman could not explain to me.

The jungle was alive, both with the forms of life we could see and with the Warden organism itself. It was alive, and we were a part of it. What a glorious, heady feeling—unlike any I'd ever known.

Suddenly, I realized what exactly Darva and I were sensing. In us and most of the surroundings, the Wardens were usually passive, connected to all the other Wardens but sending and receiving nothing. But there were Wardens around through which things were now being transmitted. Not changelings—as far as Darva knew there were few with any of the Power and much of it had been blocked off by the spell. These were apts then, very minor apts, but apts nonetheless, and that meant humans.

Fine-tuning that sense of the Wardens as much as I could, I tried to locate the sources of these emanations—and did. One was about ten meters from Darva, behind a large tree. There was another about fifteen meters in the other direction and ahead of her. A third, at least, was near the waterfall—and a fourth was on top of it. It seemed absurdly simple to pick them out now, with their very different Warden patterns. But did that mean that they had also picked *us* up in the same way? Almost immediately I decided that they hadn't. Either they were totally unaware of us or they took us for bunhars. If they knew, we would have been jumped by now.

At that moment the one nearest Darva, the one behind the tree, came into view, but he wasn't looking at us or even in our direction. We were against the best natural camouflage and remained incredibly still, so he might not have seen us anyway.

He turned out to be a trooper in one of those black and gold uniforms. Looking very relaxed and very bored, he settled down under the tree, weapon still holstered. I could tell from its shape that it was a laser pistol. How I wanted one of those! Both Darva and I were efficient killing machines, it was true, but nothing could outrun a laser pistol. If I had one now, I could knock the trooper off without any personal risk at all.

I heard a short beeping sound, and the man reached to his belt and picked up a tiny transceiver. He spoke a few words into it, and I could make out that there *was* a reply, although not what the reply was. Checking in, that was all.

Unfortunately, we were not small, delicate creatures. The old Park Lacoch would have been better in this situation—tiny and catlike. We had to get away from here. I was in no danger, but Darva was too damned close. Slowly, carefully, I reached down and picked up a large rock, noting idly that even the rock radiated the Warden sense.

Darva turned her head very slowly and carefully, saw what I was doing, and gave me a careful nod; then she turned back to look at the trooper.

Quickly I heaved the rock with all my might in the opposite direction from where we stood. It was not a good throw—my hands were tough and nasty, but my arms were really very weak. Still, the rock made a clatter in back of the trooper, and he jumped to his feet and whirled around, pistol quickly drawn, then looked around suspiciously. The rock, as I said, was weakly thrown, and though it *had* landed beyond us the trooper began walking slowly toward Darva. I seemed to see the man's Wardens almost "light up," although that's not really the right word for it. I could sense those channels of communication between his own Wardens and those around him reverberating with a sense of suspicion, a message of inquiry, as it were, although I could only guess that was what it was.

Darva was crouching a bit, flattened against broad-leafed trees and bushes of the same green as she; and she would have been nearly impossible even for me to spot had I not known she was there. It was the *Warden* sense that was to be feared, not any physical ones.

For some reason he hadn't yet picked her up—possibly we were involuntarily jamming in some way through our own apprehension—but I could see that he was soon going to be close enough to her that he couldn't miss her no matter what. It also hadn't escaped my notice that he had yet to call in on his communicator.

I made up my mind in a moment, only hoping that Darva would have the presence of mind to act correctly in the split second she would have.

The man stopped no more than two or three meters from her, turned slowly, and—I realized—saw her, first with Warden sense and then, knowing she was there, by sight. He grinned. "Well, well! A changeling with the Art," he said, obviously enjoying himself.

At that moment I popped up. "Hey!" I called, then gave my huge rear legs the kick of my life.

Darva whirled as the man's head and pistol turned toward me and struck him a blow that nearly cut off his head. Then his finger pushed the firing stud, and a beam of blue-white light shot out, burning a tree far over my head.

She didn't wait, but started for me, but I ran at her and at the dead body. She looked puzzled as I reached the man and tore the pistol from his hand; then I pivoted on my tail and headed for the jungle. I could hear another man's voice yelling behind us, and heard, rather than saw, the sound of laser pistol blasts.

Darva was still ahead of me dashing back into the jungle. When I saw she was safely out of the way I stopped, assumed my camouflage stance at a good spot, and waited.

Two troopers—a man and a woman—came running into the jungle, pistols drawn. I suddenly realized how off my timing was going to be with my oversized, taloned hands, but the comfortable feel of the pistol was reassuring enough. I was the absolute best—and this was like shooting targets at ten meters. Picking my time, I squeezed off two easy, well-placed shots, putting neat little holes in both chests. Both fell backward and were quickly still. As fast as I could, I went to them, took both pistols and both utility belts with their precious chargers, then turned and followed Darva's trail.

I handed her one of the belts and a pistol, power off, and we said nothing until we were deep into the jungle and felt safe. Finally we settled back on our tails, caught our breath, and relaxed a bit. "That was close!" she wheezed.

I nodded. "But worth it, anyway."

She looked puzzled. "Worth it? Why'd you take such a chance to get those pistols?" She flexed her talons. "*We* don't need them."

"You're wrong on that," I told her. "Neither of us can outrun a communicator or a well-aimed shot." I grinned. "But neither can they."

She shook her head in wonder. "He was so—weak. Puny." She lifted up her right hand. "I caved in his skull with one quick blow."

"That you did," I agreed. "And our arms are the weakest things we have. But don't get too cocky. Humans have always been the weakest and puniest creatures on any planet they've settled, and look who's boss."

She looked over at me. "Well, I guess that's it for anyplace else. If they were at that place I'm almost positive they know the alternates."

I shook my head. "No, we've got to try them. One of them might still be good. If there's a chance, we have to take it."

"All right," she sighed, sounding disappointed; then she brightened a bit. "You know, I really did the right thing back there!"

"You sure did," I agreed. "I'm proud of you. There was no way for me to tell you what to do and you came through magnificently."

She beamed. "I guess maybe I'm cut out for this after all. You know—back there I was scared to death. And yet somehow I really enjoyed it."

"That's the way it is," I told her. "I hate to admit it, but it's fun to beat them like that. It really is."

"You know, you talk like you've done this kind of thing before," she observed. "A lot of times, just talking, you sounded like you did more than you told me about. And those two shots with that pistol! Wow!"

I sighed. "All right, I guess you should know the facts. You more than anybody." Briefly I told her about my real career, and why I had been sent to the Warden Diamond. She listened intently, nodding.

When I'd finished, she smiled. "Well, I guess that really explains a lot. And you're still on the job, even after . . ." She let the obvious trail off.

"More or less," I told her, "but not in the way you think. I wasn't kidding about reforms on Charon or the potential of the changelings. And I'm here for the rest of my life, just like you. There's very little they can do to me, although they *could*, as I said, destroy Charon. So you see why finding Koril is even more important to me. He's against the aliens—and so am I, at least from what I can see. He's my key to getting Aeolia Matuze, and also to our future here." I suddenly had a thought, checked one of the utility belts and found a communicator there. I picked it up and flipped it on.

". . . out of the bush, jumped Sormat—tore his throat out like some animal," a tinny voice said. "God! Two of 'em. Had to be. Only caught sight of one, though. Kinda looked like a bunhar. Creepy."

"What I want to know is how they managed to elude Sormie's *wa* shield," another voice came back. "Gives me the creeps. We should just get rid of these monsters."

Their signals were weakening—they were heading away from us, I could tell. The last comment made me a little mad. I looked at the communicator—a simple device, but not one I was familiar with. "Ever seen one of these before?" I asked Darva.

She came over and looked at it. "It's pretty much the same as the ones used to keep the Companies' headquarters in contact with the field workers," she replied. "A little different, but not much."

I nodded. "Military issue." I turned it over. Embossed on the back was a little logo—*Zemco, CB*. Cerberus again. The manufacturing center of the Warden Diamond. I predicted that my counterpart there would probably do quite well. "What's its range?"

"Huh?"

"About how far will it reach?"

"Oh. Well, the ones we used—maybe three, four kilometers."

I nodded. "This one's probably souped up just a little, but call it five at the top. If they're in common use on the planet, there would have to be some limits on them or nobody could talk to one another." I thought a moment. "I wonder if they're all using the same frequency?"

"You have something in mind?"

"Well, let's head for the first alternate—whichever's closest. It's possible we might be able to *hear* if it's occupied before we go in."

Some work with both belts and I managed to wrap one big combo belt around my torso, with two pistols, the communicators, and the rest all there. It wasn't very comfortable, but it was handy.

Using some vines, we managed to rig a carrier for Darva to wear the other pistol, although without practice it was more a psychological weapon than anything else. They were tricky to use.

We had a "window" of only thirty hours to allow for shifts to alternates. Every thirty hours the places would be checked to see if anybody was there or if they were staked out for the next four days, then—forget it.

We traveled, therefore, most of the night. During rest and eating breaks, we discussed what both of us had felt about the Warden organism. Our experiences were almost identical—and even the trooper she'd killed had sensed she had the power. We compared notes. She was not totally ignorant of the Warden sense from the start, although her understanding of it was cloaked in the ignorant mysticism of the natives.

"My great-grandmother, as you know, has tremendous powers," she reminded me, "and much of her knowledge was passed down. As a kid I used to do the little exercises with her and it was really a lot of fun, but I never got too far with it. It was like the Torgo"—a Charonese flute—"that my brother was given at the same age. For a while it was a toy, but it soon became boring and he never kept up his studies and practice. It's the same with the Art."

I nodded. "That doesn't explain my own sensitivity, though," I told her. "I don't think it came from the changeling spell, either. Korman said I had a natural aptitude for it and predicted I would sense the Wardens— the *wa*—as we did. That's important for a couple of reasons. It means both of us can learn it, and it means that changelings are no more limited than humans, which makes sense. We're built differently, but we're made of the same stuff and out of the same stuff." Since many of the changelings had been at least at the apt stage themselves, it was evident that what was needed was training. You could go only so far without that, after which it either wasn't usable any further or it backfired.

It was clear that the basis of the power was the ability to concentrate while sensing the Wardens in your object. Most people just wouldn't have the necessary self-control or self-confidence, but I was pretty sure I did, even now—and perhaps Darva did as well. An artistic bent and a mathematical aptitude would certainly help, of course, in doing elaborate things.

The place we were headed Darva called the Pinnacles, because of some odd rock formations. She'd never been near it, but had been shown a picture and assured me that, if she saw the real thing, she couldn't mistake it.

Initially, she had rejected the spot because it was almost astride a main road and fairly close to an inland town called Gehbrat, but it was the closest.

We approached it in the late afternoon of the next day. I checked with my little communicator and found that there *was* some intermittent traffic on it, but it was mostly road patrols. Nothing was said about the Pinnacles as a staked-out place, and there was every indication that the frequency the things were on was fixed. That didn't mean somebody clever didn't have the place staked out using different frequencies or communicators, but the information we could get was a little reassuring.

We were more than a little cautious in approaching this time. She was certainly right—you couldn't miss the place. Four jagged spires of hard rock rose a kilometer or more over the surrounding jungle, like four great arrows pointing to the sky. Near the base of the second spire from the left would be the meeting place—if it were not already "spoiled."

We approached slowly and cautiously from opposite directions, ready to take any action required, but there was no sign or sense of any stakeout. If the location had been blown, the troopers were certainly far more professional than the ones back at the waterfall had been. It took a good two hours for me to satisfy myself that there were no dangerous troopers about, although when we linked up within sight of the rendezvous, we stayed just inside the woods. Having no timepieces, we could only settle back a little and wait, hoping for a pickup.

It grew dark quickly as night overtook us. Every once in a while I'd check the radio, but all signals were either faint or very intermittent; Pinnacles was never mentioned.

A bit after dark, we saw some movement in the area and froze. I drew one of the pistols and watched nervously. My night vision was extremely good—our eyes worked best in the murky twilight of the jungle, and were most sensitive to bright light—but it was by no means nocturnal vision. Therefore, I had difficulty seeing just who or what came into view. The Warden sense vaguely tracked the newcomer, but it was impossible to really tell much about its shape.

Whoever it was crept cautiously to the center of the clearing, seemed to stop and look around, then whispered nervously, "There is thunder in the south." That was the identifying phrase Darva had been told, but while our hopes rose our caution did not let down. If Morah knew of one hideout from captives, he certainly knew many of the passwords.

I looked at Darva and gestured at the pistol. She nodded, moved away from me, then approached the dark shape. "The Destroyer builds," she whispered, giving the response.

I heard a sharp sigh. "Thank the gods!" a female voice said in low but clear tones. "Who's there?"

"Darva. Who are you?" She walked closer to the dark shape.

"I am Hemara," the other responded, "from the Valley of Cloud."

"I am from Thunderkor," Darva told her. "Come closer, so we may see each other clearly."

The other moved, and now I too could make out the shape. She was indeed a changeling, a large woman with a reddish yet very human face that differed only in that she appeared to have two large compound eyes of bright orange in place of the normal ones. She seemed to be carrying something smooth and round on her back.

Darva turned and whispered to me, "All right, you can come out. I think it's safe."

I moved from my hideaway and approached them. Up close, I could see that far more in the woman was changed than I had first noticed. Her body was black, hard, and shiny, like an insect's, and that round thing on her back was a huge black shell of some kind. She was standing on four of her eight legs—no arms—and these were also covered in a hard shell and had small pads at their tips ending in a single hard nail each. Still, she retained short-cropped humanoid black hair on her head.

The newcomer turned, looked at me, then back at Darva, then back at me again. "There are two of you?"

"Sort of," I responded. "It's a long story. Anyway, I'm Park and I'm the male."

Her very human mouth showed delighted surprise. "A pair! How wonderful!" There was a wistful note in that last, that I couldn't help but catch.

"Maybe," I told her. "For now, what's the plan to get out of here? I feel like a sitting duck."

She looked suddenly crestfallen. "I'd hoped that *you* . . ."

Darva sighed. "Just another refugee. Well, join the party and we'll wait some more."

She wasn't really constructed for the jungle, but down flat, or almost so, she could blend in pretty well with the rocks. Time passed as we talked, explaining where the pistols came from and telling her a little about ourselves—very little, really. As for Hemara, she'd been caught poaching by her Company—a very serious offense. As punishment, she was given to a Company apt as an experimental being on whom to practice. When not a plaything she was on public exhibition near the Company headquarters as a deterrent, and they had outdone themselves in providing a really nasty example. Without hands or claws she couldn't really manipulate much. Settling an interesting point, she said that the compound eye's multi-images resolved into a single image in her brain, but that she could focus on only one point. She could either see very far, but nothing close, or vice versa, and if she fixed on an object she could see only that object and its surroundings. That meant almost constantly changing focus to get a clear picture. She was a sad example of how far the cruel and insane minds that ran Charon could go, and yet she said she had seen and met worse. I probably had too, but the scene in that square after the fight had been so much of an overload that I found it hard to remember the shapes clearly.

We were joined later that evening by three more changelings. One was a man whose face was a hideous devil's mask and whose bent, winged body made him permanently bowlegged. His bat wings, however, were not functional. He was a good reminder of how volatile the Warden power could be. He'd been more or less stealing lessons, hiding himself and listening in while his local sorc instructed his apts. Then he tried experimenting on his own and had been doing very well, but one night he'd had a horrible nightmare . . .

The second creature was part long, gray limbless worm and part human torso topped by a hairless man's head. The body, perhaps five meters long, glistened and left a trail of ichor. He wouldn't tell us how he'd gotten that way, but we discovered he ate dirt.

The last one was surprisingly human, and decidedly uncomfortable with us. She was small, quite attractive, and had a distinctive pair of devil's horns. She appeared to be a nervous wreck and I'm afraid our all-changeling group didn't help her mood. Her name was Emla Quoor. She'd been in the group in the square, and she'd been terrified from that point on. There was little we could do to comfort her, except to point out that she must have some real guts and intelligence to make it this far undetected and in one piece. She looked like she'd been through hell, though, and I wasn't about to press her further. Others could do that—if we ever got picked up.

Suddenly a rumbling erupted all around us. "Oh, brother!" somebody swore. "You can't go three hours out here without getting dumped on." As the skies opened up for what promised to be the usual long deluge, everyone moved into the shelter of the trees. The way the wind whipped things up, though, there was no question but that everyone would be pretty well drenched.

Lightning swirled around the Pinnacles, lighting up the area intermittently in what, I had to admit, was an impressive scene. I looked out into the little clearing which was brightly lit by a lightning flash, then dark again. Then came a second bolt, but this time there was somebody—or something—there, standing in the middle. "There's somebody here!" I called to the others and drew my pistol.

All eyes peered nervously into the clearing—it was empty. They glared at me, but I stood firm. "Somebody *was* there," I assured them. "I do not see things." I flicked the power on the pistol to full.

Another lightning blast, and once again the figure appeared—a tall, thin human in a long black cloak and hood. Not a trooper, that was for sure. One of the others caught sight of it too, and mumbled confirmation of my sighting. All turned to look, nerves on edge.

The figure was certainly standing there now in the rain for all to see. Slowly it approached us. It came right into our midst and looked around. The impression was of a very dark human face inside the hood, but little else. Finally a woman's voice announced: "There is thunder in the south."

"The Destroyer builds," returned the stranger in a very deep female voice. She turned and nodded. "Is this all of you?"

"Us and the human girl over there," the worm-man responded.

"I am Frienta," the newcomer introduced herself. "I'm sorry to have kept you all waiting, but there are heavy patrols on the road and I decided to wait and use the storm for cover."

"You are from Koril's organization?" I asked.

"Master Koril is certainly involved, although it is not entirely his organization, or anyone's," Frienta replied curtly. "However, we have to move you and hundreds more out of the region, and that is a massive logistical effort. More than half of our people have already been caught or killed in this region, and you are not out of danger yet yourself. We must now get you quickly to an assembly point." She looked around. "Are you up to a long march in the rain?"

The human woman and the devil-man both groaned. Frienta took notice of them, then looked at our worm-man. "What about you? How fast can you travel?"

"I'll be fine," he assured her. "The wetter it is, the better."

"Well, then, our success depends on the two of you." She looked at Darva and me. "You're the biggest. Do you think you could each carry one of these?"

I looked at Darva, who shrugged. "Why not?" I replied. "But they'll have to hang on tight."

The devil-man gave a grotesque expression which I hoped was one of gratitude. The human woman seemed extremely nervous and uncertain. "Come on—climb up and get as comfortable as you can," I said, trying to sound as friendly and reassuring as possible. "I'm not poison, I don't bite—not people on my side anyway—and riding beats walking in this stuff."

The devil-man had little problem getting on Darva's back, but he apparently weighed more than he looked, given the expression on her face. Frienta went over to the human. "Come. I will help you."

She looked over at me. "I—I don't know. Maybe I can walk . . ."

"I have no time or patience for such prejudice," the strange dark women said acidly. "You too are nonhuman, as those horns attest."

The woman stepped back, obviously upset by the sudden attitude of the one whom she'd considered her only ally. Abruptly I was aware of a flaring of the Wardens within the dark woman's body, and I sensed complex message information flow from her outstretched arm to the scared woman. It was as if there were now thousands, perhaps millions of tiny weblike cords of energy linking the two.

Then, somewhat jerkily, the human walked up to me, and with Frienta's assistance, climbed on my back and clung tightly. Frienta nodded to herself, stepped back, and traced a few symbols in the air. "There!" she announced, satisfied. "You are bound there until I free you!" She turned to the rest of us. "Come! Follow me quickly! This is not the time to stay in one place!"

I was aware of the rigidity of the woman on my back, and said to Frienta, "You are an apt."

"A minor one," she responded crisply. Then we were off into the rain-soaked jungle in the midst of the darkness.

It was a long and arduous journey, taken at a good pace. Frienta, whose face I never could see clearly and whose body was masked by her black robes, proved extremely quick and agile—and apparently tireless. The extra burdens Darva and I carried soon proved to be wearing, but we had no choice but to go on. Worm-man and Hemara proved capable of some speed under adverse conditions, but none of us were cut out for this sort of thing. Frienta seemed to sense when one or more of us was spent and absolutely had to rest, and the breaks were well timed although not as frequent as we would have wished.

We walked all night through a wilderness so complete that after a while none of us had any sense of where we were, how far we'd come, or in what direction we were going. We finally reached a small clearing in the jungle where Frienta proclaimed a complete stop. We would be allowed to forage for food, each according to our own needs, then get some sleep. It was not well, she told us, to travel much in daylight and we still had a long way to go—more than two nights' march at the least.

Even relieved of our burdens, Darva and I felt exhausted, but we knew we needed strength now more than ever. We picked no fights, settling for catching and eating a number of small animals that were no real challenge and supplementing this with what wild fruits we could find. Then we slept through most of the day.

Frienta revealed no more of herself in light than in darkness—a fact that intrigued us all more and more. We felt certain she was some sort of changeling herself, but what sort we had no idea. We rotated guard positions while the others slept, but I kept the laser pistols. Most of the others didn't know how to use them and a couple simply couldn't. Besides, I didn't really fully trust anybody except Darva, who certainly didn't know how to shoot, and myself.

The next night was much like the first, although we got a break in the rain which certainly helped me a little. My human passenger said next to nothing during the entire journey, and I was glad for that. I was too tired to be conversational. During the middle of the third night we suddenly broke out onto a wide, sandy beach. We had reached the coast—the south coast again, as it turned out, but more than a hundred kilometers west of Bourget.

It was with relief that we realized that we were at the end of our journey. Our mysterious guide had taken us unerringly to the right spot through the jungle, avoiding all Companies and all but a very few roads—and also avoiding the worst of the jungle and swamps.

"We are safe now," Frienta assured us. "The encampment here is protected from interlopers by high sorcery."

I looked around. "Encampment?"

"Come," she beckoned, and we walked down the beach a little to where it curved inland, forming a small bay. It looked desolate, totally deserted, until we turned slightly inland on the bay's south side. Suddenly we found ourselves in a very large if primitive village, with tents, even fires and torchlight. It was so surprising that several of us uttered sounds of amazement; I, for one, stopped, then turned and stepped back a few meters and turned again. Desertion and silence. Walk a few steps forward, and there it was—a true camp with hundreds of beings, both changeling and human.

Frienta waved a ghostly arm. "Just find yourself a comfortable place and settle in," she told us. "Ample food to your requirements will be provided, but we are out of tents and other shelters, I fear. If you can make no arrangements, you can use the jungle in the rear. The spell covers the entire south side of the bay but only to a depth of ninety meters from the beach—so if you go beyond, into the forest, take care."

Our little group dispersed quickly as our fellow travelers found others they knew among the teeming throng of creatures on the beach. Our nervous human joined a small group of her own kind with evident relief.

Darva looked at me. "Well? What shall we do now?"

I shrugged. "Sleep, I think. Tomorrow we'll find out what comes next." I looked around at the various kinds of creatures on the beach, some of which were the stuff of real nightmares. Charon had taken criminal minds, insane minds, and given them great power. Much of that insanity could be seen reflected in its victims on the beach as well as in our former company, I reflected. Koril might prove more sympathetic, I knew; but he was still a politician, a king dethroned who wanted his position back and was willing to go to any lengths to get it. This system had been in effect when he was in charge before, and even before that, and he'd done nothing then to stop it. And that, of course, was something most of these people, the changelings in particular, would simply overlook; almost all were natives, and that alone accounted for a certain naivete to which was now added an exponential increase in trust borne of hope and desperation.

How were we different from the aliens, Darva had asked me—and I really wasn't sure of an answer. If I wasn't, then perhaps Koril saw few differences either. He would be unlikely to eliminate an external alien menace only to allow another to fester here homegrown. There was no question in my mind that these people were being used, as always. Sooner or later I knew, something would have to be done.

Darva had wandered off for a few minutes to see if anybody was around and awake whom she knew. When I saw her talking to a small group near a large tent, I decided to join her.

She looked over at me as I approached, smiled, nodded, and turned back to the trio by the fire—I saw one of them was frog-man, another the bird creature—and I strode right up to them. Before I could say anything though, the flap of the tent behind me opened and I heard a familiar voice. "Why, hello, Darva! Hi, Park! My, you look stunning in your new suit!"

I whirled about in total surprise, and looked into the face of Tully Kokul.

CHAPTER ELEVEN

Koril's Redoubt

Tully and I walked along the beach. "Tell me," I asked him, "are *you* Koril?"

He laughed. "Oh my, no! I couldn't hold a candle to him! I'm really a very simple man, Park. In ancient times I'd be the parish priest, a man looking for rest and a place to contemplate and experiment with a minimum of interference. Bourget was like a dream come true for me. Nobody around higher up to give me all sorts of orders, a peaceful village filled with good, profit-minded simple folk, and a very distant government that left us all alone. I was *extremely* happy there."

"So how come you're here, then?" I asked him. "Surely you didn't just come along for the ride."

He chuckled. "Oh no, but I'm like the pacifist who stays home, locks himself in his house while the war rages, then suddenly finds the opposing armies marching and shooting through his living room. I'm only a fair sorc, but I'm a *good* politician, Park. I knew what was going on in and around the village. I knew too that eventually the idyll would end, although I put off all decisions until the last minute. It was painful to lose— but when Matuze took over it was only a matter of time. She's a real nut case, Park. Morah keeps her protected from the Synod for his own purposes, and she's able to indulge her every crazy whim. She's sadistic, cruel, but very, very imaginative—and very ambitious. So when she took control, I more or less got my credentials from this group, although I kept a hands-off attitude almost to the last minute. It really wasn't until Morah himself showed up that I knew the game was up."

"Why not just go along with him and then settle back like before?" I asked him. "You didn't have to cut and run."

"Oh, things will never be like they were before—not after that stuff in the square. Morah's been publicly humiliated. Matuze will take it personally. If those people in Bourget have any sense—and the majority don't —they'll all cut and run. Even though they missed their targets, Bourget's going to become a big, ugly example. Permanent troops and a Synod sorc will be installed there from now on, bet on it. You won't be able to blow your nose there without permission."

I told him of my suspicions about Morah.

"Hmph. Morah an alien. Hadn't thought of that before, but it could be —providing we accept a couple of givens. One is that the aliens can catch the Warden bug themselves—Morah's just loaded and he knows how to use that power better than anybody I've ever seen. But if they *can* catch it the same as us, how'd that delegation five years back come and go without getting trapped?"

"They could have the cure," I noted. "Their whole deal with the Four Lords is predicated on that claim. What better way to prove it?"

"You may be right," he agreed, "but I'm not so sure. True, I know nothing of Morah's background, but that's not unusual. And then there's that fine show he staged at the end."

"You mean that monster he became?"

He nodded. "Get a good look at it?"

"Not really. Everything happened so fast. A multiheaded dragon, that's about all I can remember. Three heads. That's about it."

"That's fair enough. In fact, there were *four* heads, not three, and each of the four was extremely different. One was saurian, one like some great insect, one a creature of the sea, and one vaguely humanoid. See any significance?"

I shook my head. "Not really."

"Charon, Lilith, Cerberus, Medusa. The living sign of the Four Lords of the Diamond."

I gave a low whistle. "Symbolism to the very end."

"Almost the real end too," he noted. "Look, the only reason he wasn't totally fried was that he wasn't really there at all. You couldn't sense it, but I saw. The moment the first shot was fired, the one that unfortunately missed, he was off that platform and into the crowd. I lost him at that point—he cast a spell on himself so complete I couldn't tell him from the victims."

I looked around nervously. "Then he could be here with us now."

"He could, but I doubt it. He would be the only one capable of coordinating the hunt, not to mention reporting to the government. Besides, he couldn't fool Koril, so once he got here he'd just have betrayed us anyway. No, don't worry about that part. But that was quite a show all the same . . . Say, speaking of shows—how the hell did you wind up like *that*, anyway?"

Briefly I told him the sequence of events.

"Fair enough. I thought you'd have sense enough to stay in the town hall, damn it, so I didn't pay any attention to you. I was far too busy trying to keep out of the line of fire while trying to spot Morah; then I got bogged down helping with the escapes."

"How'd you know it was me here?"

He smiled. "Your *wa*—your Warden brain pattern. It's unique, distinctive, as everybody's is. Not that I remember everybody's, but you were around for months in the same building."

"What about these spells, Tully? Are they really permanent?"

He stopped and turned to look at me. "Nothing's permanent, particularly not on Charon. But it's far, far easier to add than to subtract, if you know what I mean. When you cast a changeling spell, you form a mental set of instructions in your mind and transmit them to your subject's Wardens. Those Wardens then proceed to do whatever they're instructed to do. They draw energy from somewhere—external, certainly, but where nobody's ever found out. They draw the energy in, convert it into matter often at astonishing speed, and apply the redesign."

"Yeah, but it's not just changing shape," I replied. "Hell, I need a far stronger backbone; I have a different digestive system better adapted to this; a different balance mechanism—and a million other things, big and small, that make this creature that's the new me work. You can't possibly know or think of all the little details required. It would take an extensive biomedical library complete with full biological design capabilities to do that."

He looked at me seriously. "Want the truth? I warn you, it's something we don't tell everybody."

"I sure do."

"We haven't the slightest idea how it's done, and that's the truth. Some of it, I think—the basic stuff—simply borrows from the Wardens elsewhere on the planet. Information requested and exchanged in a way we can't comprehend—it's a whole different form of life. The bunhar parts of you, the pigmentation and so on, are probably borrowed like that. In fact, we know they are—one can sense the request for and flow into the subject of that information. But when there's no equivalent, or when you have to put bunhar and human together and make the new creature work, well, that's a whole different story. The Warden organism doesn't think. It's more like a machine, waiting for instructions. It's too simple a thing to think, even if you considered all of them on the planet as a single organism. Without instructions, it's totally passive."

I could only nod and file the information away—for now. I returned to the immediate subject at hand. "But basically once you're changed you're stuck."

"Fairly much so. It took very little time to remake you, but it'd be a ticklish operation and maybe take a year or more to put you back the way you were. First of all, you'd be destroying the homes of all those billions of extra Wardens, and they have a fair survival instinct. Second, the extra mass has to go somewhere, and in general the only place it can go is back to energy. Do that wrong, or in too much of a hurry, and you get a big flash and bang and you're dead. Far easier to modify you. In fact I think some modification may be in order. I can tell by looking at both Darva and you that your spell's become somewhat unraveled, and if that isn't checked, you'll have even bigger problems."

"Huh? How's that?"

"Well, the situation's unusual, but I've seen it before. Both of you have an abnormally high sensitivity to the *wa*, and it in turn listens to you.

Without control, your subconscious, your animal parts, take over. If the trend isn't checked or modified, it'll turn both of you completely into bunhars. Tell me—have you been having any odd, ah, mental problems or urges lately?"

Sheepishly I told him of the hunting experiences in the wild.

He nodded gravely. "Well, we'll have to do something about that as soon as I can make a complete examination of you. It'll be tricky for several reasons. They're *your* Wardens, and *wa* will follow what it perceives as the will of its host first and foremost. We work by convincing it that you're some other way—by convincing *you*. In these reversions, the mind is the first to go since it's not only unnecessary to the ultimate goal but often gets in the way. The process is so slow only because it does not occur on the conscious level—and because you're around other people. If you'd missed us though, and stayed in the wild, the process would have accelerated. In a few months you'd have become a total bunhar, running with herd, and absolutely no different from a natural-born one. You were lucky."

I shivered. "Tell that to Darva, will you, Tully? That's what she wanted to do—and I almost caved in."

The changelings were being moved out in very small groups, usually by ship but occasionally even by air. Koril's network was far wider and deeper than I'd suspected.

Tully took the time we had there to work with us as much as possible. Our days were spent in a series of exacting and often extremely boring mental exercises, many of which gave us headaches. There were all sorts of effective blocking techniques as well, many based on simple self-hypnosis that I could do in a moment, that kept the growing understanding of the power within us under some sort of control.

The basics were simple. First, you couldn't make something out of nothing. There had to be Wardens there to work with. Thus, one could not materialize something out of thin air—it just wouldn't happen. But given something very small, even a rock or pile of sand, you could cause it to grow, multiply, and transform itself. You could not, however, give non-Warden life to something that had no life at the start. You could create a lot of things with simple sand, but you couldn't make it a living thing. You could, however, reshape it, then direct and motivate it, puppetlike, by your own powers of concentration.

Darva was, in many ways, a quicker study than I was, because she was taking up where she'd left off so long before. Tully warned us, though, that there was only a small chance of us growing beyond very powerful apts. since the younger you were the easier the Art was to learn. Still, *he* had learned it starting at an age not far from mine, and that spurred me on. Koril, in fact, had become perhaps the most powerful and he'd learned it after he was forty.

You would think that the more you practiced a thing the easier it would become, but in fact it became harder as we progressed, since the more ambitious you became the more complex the instructions and the more millions of Wardens had to be contacted.

Finally though, when we'd been there almost four weeks and the company had dwindled to only a handful—meaning we were soon due to depart—Tully admitted he'd taken us as far as he could under these conditions. It was not far enough, of course, but we had far more self-control and power than either of us could have hoped to have had without his help. In point of fact, we were full-fledged, if still minor, apts.

"You'll be leaving in two days," Tully told us finally. "Going south, to Gamush, on my recommendation. You should feel flattered—only apts with potential are sent there. You might even meet the big man himself."

"What about the reversion?" Darva asked nervously.

"Well, you've stabilized it. I think we caught it just in time, in fact. But down in Gamush you'll get the top professional help you need, extra training, and—who knows?"

"How will we be going?" I asked.

"Well, we've been having problems with the ships, of course. Troopers are boarding and searching every one they spot, and they have effective aerial patrols out. We've been able to fake a lot—they don't have much of a list of names, let alone changeling descriptions, but it's a slow and risky process. No, we'll get you out by air. Rather direct, I'm afraid, but the best way."

Tully's "rather direct" turned out to be an understatement. We were not built for the compartments of a soarer, but a soarer modified and controlled by a sorc could be used to transport humans up top—and changelings by having the damned thing swoop down and pick us up in its huge prehensile feet.

Though we were both sedated for the sudden "pick up," it was still one of the most frightening things I'd ever experienced. Crossing an ocean held in the grip of a great flying creature's toes is *not* guaranteed to make anybody comfortable, although, it proved more comfortable than riding in that damned cabin. Not reassuring, though, when you looked down at countless thousands of square kilometers of open ocean and knew that you could be dropped in a moment if the big flying monster had an itch—and nobody would ever know.

Our sense of security was no greater when, several hours flying time later, we crossed the barren coast of Gamush. For one thing, this was the first time I had seen a broken sky and bright sun since landing on Charon. The sky was reddish-orange, with gray clouds, and it looked really strange. The gas layer was thin enough for the real sun of the Warden system to be clearly visible—and it was a real hot one. Since our body temperatures rose or fell to adapt to the outside temperature, I began to worry about just how high that temperature could go in our kind without boiling our blood. It really was that hot, or so it felt—and incredibly dry. Below, orange and brown sand, ridged and duned, stretched as far as the eye could see.

What a world, I remembered thinking. Tropical rain forests north and south and a desert baked almost beyond imagining in the middle.

Still, there *were* creatures about. We could see them flying around; apparently wingless cylinders, but none came close enough for us to get a really good look at them. Somewhere down below, other things also must live, I realized, for those creatures to feed upon. Yet in the whole journey I never saw a single tree, shrub, or animal. Nothing but desolate sand.

We were rather rudely dropped at the end although we had trained as best we could and been prepared. There was no place for a soarer to take off from around here—not enough elevation on the dunes and no footholds —so it soared in low, stalled almost to a crawl, then dropped us a few meters into the sand. It then rapidly gained altitude until it was a small blot in the sky, and we saw those in the passenger compartment, mostly humans and human-sized creatures, parachute to the ground over a square kilometer or more. Parachuting was not a common art on Charon, but broken legs mended in a few days thanks to the Wardens.

We were met by a small group of men and women, all humans, dressed in thick yellow robes and wide-brimmed hats. They were quite efficient at moving about and gathering together the dozen or so humans and changelings that had been deposited by the soarer.

"How are you?" Darva asked, concerned.

I checked myself. "A little bruised and burned by the sand, but otherwise all right," I told her. "I feel rotten, though, and I need a drink. You?"

"Same here," she responded. "Let's see how we get out of this hole. This place is like something from the worst nightmare. It's hell itself." It was hard to disagree with that, although for her this was the first time she'd ever seen or experienced this sort of climate and desert terrain. But what she considered normal wasn't so nice, either.

One of the robed men holding a clipboard quickly checked our names, seemed satisfied, then brought us to a central spot in the sand not in any way distinguishable from any other point in the desert. They looked around, checked something or other, and suddenly we started sinking into the sand.

It was an eerie and unnerving sensation, although after the flight it was pretty tame. I held my breath as I sunk to my mouth, then continued down under.

For a brief moment my entire body was encased in sand, and I had this horrible feeling of smothering, but it soon passed as I felt cool air hit my feet and hindquarters and I realized we were entering some sort of huge passage. Spitting sand and wiping my eyes, I managed to get hold of myself and look around.

What I saw was impressive—a huge hangarlike building, well-lit with very modern industrial lights, with a lot of people running around below apparently working on or servicing a lot of stuff. What struck me most was the machinery—this place could almost be out of the civilized worlds. It was at least as modern as the shuttle—the first time I'd seen such a technological level since arriving at Montlay in what seemed like a lifetime ago.

We were standing on some kind of translucent platform on a large pistonlike device that was gradually lowering us from the opening to the huge floor. Looking up, I had to gasp as I saw a huge roof apparently composed entirely of sand with no support whatsoever. How the effect was managed I never did find out, whether by some Warden sorcery or by some sort of force field, but this clearly was why the all-powerful Charonese and their alien allies had never found the place. Hell, I wouldn't be able to find it myself again no matter what the inducement.

As we reached bottom, our greeting party quickly removed their robes and left them on the platform. A glance at them and at many of the personnel around the place showed that, down here, the mode of dress was closer to undress. I wondered how some of our moralistic Unitites were going to take that.

Another party arrived to greet us, dressed rather scantily though a couple had on medicallike garb. One of them approached Darva and me. "You are the two with the reversion problem?" she asked clinically.

We nodded. "I'm Dr. Yissim," she continued. "Follow me, please."

We followed her across part of the vast work area to a large tunnellike opening and went down it for a hundred meters or more, finally walking into a large, comfortable room that had large pads on the floor and little else.

"We're going to start your first treatment right away," she told us. "Otherwise you're going to have problems down here with fresh meat, among other things. Each of you please sit on a separate pad."

We looked at each other, shrugged, and did as instructed. The doctor stood back, looked at each of us in turn, then touched her temples and seemed to go into a light trance. I was familiar with the technique now, but it still surprised me. Hell, we'd only just arrived.

She stood still that way for several minutes, and I could sense her Warden power—her *wa*—reaching out to me. It tingled, sort of, as I suddenly felt myself under the most absolute of microscopes. Darva felt the same. Then the doctor came out of her trance, nodded to herself, and started mumbling into a small recorder I hadn't noticed before.

"Limik!" she called, and a young man came in also dressed in hospital garb. She wasted no time on amenities. "Six liters number forty," she told him, "for each of them."

He nodded, left, and in a short while returned with two large jugs full of a clear liquid. He approached us—without a flinch or without even staring oddly at us, I noticed with some satisfaction—and handed us each a jug.

"Drink all you can," Dr. Yissim instructed us. "It's basically water, which you need badly, with some additives. Drink it all if you can."

There was absolutely no problem in drinking it all. I seemed to have a bottomless reservoir.

"Master Kokul's analysis of the two of you was sent on ahead," she told us as we finished. "He's quite thorough. Now, you'll both start to feel a little sleepy, lethargic, and relaxed. Don't fight it. This is going to be a tricky series. If we don't get this exactly right from the start we could merely accelerate the process, and we don't want that. I realize you're both starved, but I want empty stomachs for now." With that, she turned and walked out of the room.

Darva looked over at me, already seeming a bit sleepy. "She's the coldest person I've ever met. We might as well be two lumps of mud."

I nodded. "I've met a lot like that. Don't let it worry you. Her type almost always know what they're doing. Let's just help it, get into the relaxation mode, and let them do their job."

Using some of the concentration and relaxation exercises Tully had taught us, we needed very little time to reach a state of quasi-sleep. We were aware of what was going on, but floating in a cloud of peace and comfort, we just didn't give a damn. In many ways it was like the state I'd been placed into before the old woman had made me a changeling.

A wall flicked, and suddenly became transparent. I saw Yissim there, along with two men and three women, all sitting at a console of some sort. They looked at us then at the console; we could see only them.

It began. It began without any of the gyrations or mumbo-jumbo everyone before had always used. You could see it, sense it, feel it, as a tremendous concentration of Warden direction flowed out from those people behind the partition to us. It was blinding, overwhelming, all-encompassing, and within seconds it was in control of my mind. I found myself involuntarily resisting, and a minor fight ensued, made worse because, thanks to Tully, we knew the blocking techniques.

Somehow I managed a slight turn so that I could see Darva, and despite my drugged state I nonetheless had a fascination for what I was seeing, a fascination that was neither shock nor horror nor anything else but just that—fascination. I found I didn't really care. Darva's body was undulating, going through rapid, fluid changes. I knew that my body was probably undergoing the same. Her torso was thickening up, her arms becoming shorter and smaller, and merging into her head, which was also changing, flowing liquidly out, taking a whole different shape.

The Wardens in our bodies, aided by the animal foundations of our brains, were fighting the treatment, fighting it effectively by accelerating the change. We were turning into true bunhars—and worse, we were gaining mass in the head and torso as we did so, mass that would be very hard to remove. This then was the loaded gun of the changeling, the reason why it was next to impossible to change back. *Reversion . . .*

I was aware my vision was changing. It was becoming impossible to focus close in, although I could still see Darva clearly and she could see me. I could see, blurrily, that I had a snout and I realized that my eyes, like hers, must be set much farther apart. It was becoming more and more difficult, though, to think at all. My mind was dying; I knew it, yet, eerily, even as it was lost I experienced less and less a sense of any loss at all.

Darva looked completely like a *bunhar* now, and she appeared very natural and normal to me. Only her eyes, set farther apart along that large, toothy snout, still retained a curious human appearance. I had only three awarenesses . . . I was hungry, yet sleepy, and there was a female over there . . .

The next few days are all but impossible to remember or describe. Basically, we were kept in a large pen with an electrified barrier, and a pool of water; once a day, a large, freshly killed creature was brought somehow into the enclosure and Darva and I devoured it greedily. Eating was followed by a period of strained sleep, in which we were both in this funny place, then we'd wake up again in the pen. Both of us were bunhars, and we operated on the most basic animal level and on no other. We had absolutely no sense of time, place, or anything. We were barely self-aware.

Slowly, though, we came out of it. Very, very slowly. Memory returned first, but it was uncoupled with conscious thought, and thus useless. Finally, we came out of one of the sleep sessions still in the strange room, and for the first time, I could think again.

Yissim's voice seemed to float in to us. "If you can understand me, stamp your right foot," she instructed.

I turned, looked at Darva, and saw that she was still very much a hundred percent bunhar. But she stamped her right foot—and so did I.

"Very good," the doctor approved. "Please do not try to talk to me or to each other. You don't have the equipment at the moment, and all you'd produce would be a loud roar. It has been a tricky, delicate operation to say the least. In order literally to save your minds we had to let the process take its course with your conscious selves decoupled. Believe me, this was necessary—but radical. You are only the third and fourth individuals we've had to use this procedure on, and we've had one success and one failure. Hopefully we will have two more successes here.

"Now," she went on, "we're going to try and bring you back, but it will be a slow, patient process. We have restored your minds, your basic humanity. Bit by bit we will restore the rest. We will be working with you, but you must do it yourselves. Our initial probe shows that we cannot impose the change on you. Were we to try a new series of spells, you would react in such a way as to literally alter your brain. Once your brain modified to the bunhar mode you would be bunhars and we could not restore memory, personality, or sentience. You must learn to control every Warden in your bodies. Every one. You must assume total control."

What proved most frustrating was that Darva and I could communicate neither with the doctors nor with each other since, I soon discovered, she was totally illiterate—a condition that simply had never occurred to me could happen.

If the situation was bizarre to us, it must have been more so to the doctors. Imagine going in every day and giving very elaborate lessons and exercises to a pair of bunhars. Still, I'll give them that much—they never once seemed to blink at the situation or treat us as anything except intelligent adults. I, for one, was more than anxious to do everything until I had it perfect—I had no wish to return to the zoo and the oblivious state of the simple saurian.

Still, it was a constant mental fight with those animal impulses. I had to stop myself continually from roaring, charging, or doing other animal things in proper bunhar fashion. I realized that part of my trouble was my concern that Darva might not make it. I wanted both of us to succeed, desperately.

The day we concentrated on our larynxes was an exciting one. Each day I was gaining more and more control over my body and my actions—becoming, very definitely, the smartest and most self-controlled bunhar in all history. The spell was a complex one, but it still boiled down to *ordering* the Wardens in our bodies to form a voice mechanism that would work in our very primitive throats. I had no idea what one would look like, or how it would work, but I was like a small child with a new toy when I felt something growing, taking shape far back in my throat, and made my first, rather basic sounds that weren't roars and growls. Still, it was not a human voice, and it came from far back in my throat, independent of my mouth—which couldn't form the words anyway. It couldn't—but this new growth could.

Darva, I heard with excitement, managed it also, although the sound was more like a deep belching sound than anything else. We were stopped there and given a chance to practice. We managed in an amazingly short time to form crude words and sentences. It was a breakthrough, and one that said we were on the way. But how long would the rest take?

I discovered in talking that Darva had had a much rougher fight with her animal self than I, and was still having trouble. Dr. Yissim now knew this too, and in a separate session one day told me, "If we are to bring her all the way back, we may have to do another radical procedure."

"Of what sort?" I rasped, my new voice sounding odd—and yet appropriate to a bunhar, if bunhars could talk—even to me.

"You are now far enough down the line to control a great deal of your body. The *wa* is powerful and controlled in you. But if we were to remove you from lab conditions, both of you would quickly revert, simply because you are so far along. She would change much before you. You might even fight it off, but I doubt if she could. You need reinforcement and the only reinforcement around comes from each other. It's called a *wa* connection, and it may be her only hope—but only you can decide on it."

"There is danger then."

She nodded. "You know how the *wa* is really one, how it is in total communication with all other *wa*."

"Yes."

"But your consciousness contains the *wa* and directs it, and this is a method by which the *wa* of one consciousness is transmitted to the other and then stabilized. A permanent link is established."

"You mean our minds would *merge?*"

"No. The *wa* is directed by thought; it is not thought itself. No, your *bodies* would merge, on the *wa*, or metaphysical, level. Anything done to one, with the aid of the other, could be easily duplicated in the other body. Her mind would give you the little extra push you would need not merely to control, but to *direct* the *wa* in your body. And conversely, your having achieved this, the process could be easily reversed. However, such a total link, similar to casting a changeling spell but far more elaborate, has a drawback. If forged effectively enough to work on this level, it cannot be broken. The *wa* of one would be the *wa* of both. If you progress to the next stage of *wa* training, it could give you enormous power. Enormous. But you would be absolutely identical. Even an injury to one would be felt by the other."

"And the danger?"

"If her *wa* instincts overwhelm you, she could drag you down with her."

"And if this is not done?"

"Then we might well, over a long period, bring you back—but she would be lost. She simply doesn't have the mental training you seem to have."

"Then let's do it," I told her.

CHAPTER TWELVE

"The *Wa* Considers You One"

I had seen very little of Koril's redoubt since our arrival, for obvious reasons, but clearly several things were going on here that I would never have anticipated or even believed from my previous experience on Charon. Gone was the mumbo-jumbo, except for some general references to spells that seemed to be here more words of convenience than words implying some mystique. Down here was a thoroughly professional and scientific base where crisp, well-trained professionals examined and stretched their knowledge of the Warden organisms' powers and peculiarities almost to the limit. The technology, though, that supported it was basically from Cerberus, the only one of the four Warden worlds where efficient and modern industrial production was possible. This place remained in operation because of its unique below-ground desert location. Koril had surveyed and picked the one point on Charon that would allow such material and facilities to work and duplicated the precise conditions here.

Obviously the place hadn't just been thrown together in the last five years since he had been deposed. This was a far longer and more ambitious project than could have been assembled by some rebel, no matter how powerful he was, and it had to be sustained by clandestine traffic even between the Warden worlds. This refuge had been set up and outfitted in the years Koril was Lord of the Diamond, and *somebody*—certainly not the Four Lords—continued to supply it with spare parts.

The computers used here were hardly the equal of anything in the Confederacy—they were, in fact, incredibly primitive—but they were certainly better than the calculators and abacuses that I had used as Town Accountant.

The level of instruction we were given indicated an enormous amount of progress on understanding the Warden organisms' mechanisms, even if the bottom line of knowing where their power and information came from remained a mystery. It was like gravity—centuries after gravity was first truly identified and quantified it was still not at all understood. Those who didn't understand *what* it was had discovered every effect and use of gravity despite their basic ignorance of just what really caused it.

The exercises were serious, complex and required an enormous amount of knowledge of a large number of disciplines in order to use them effectively. That, in fact, was why the most powerful users were either former prisoners from the Confederacy or natives trained as apts when they were very, very young. In my business, it was absolutely vital to know as much as possible—and at least a little about everything—and this gave me an enormous advantage in the training. Darva, on the other hand, had virtually no education and only limited experience with human behavior outside her own local group; that was the hang-up. My own mind control techniques and self-hypnotic abilities were crucial to the process, and my understanding of basic human behavior, particularly my own, gave me the advantage. But the spell that had made me a changeling was an imitative spell. I was locked into the spell originally used on Darva, and so the weaknesses in it, her weaknesses, were repeated in me. She could not control her *wa*, and so her *wa* was hell-bent on taking the path of least resistance. And what her *wa* did, mine duplicated, since her half-trained great grandmother had taken the short cut of linking my spell to hers. This was no matter of waving your hands and making chairs appear or disappear. I was dealing with a complex psychological and biological science involving the spin-off effects of a tiny organism that had no counterpart in human experience beyond the Warden Diamond.

Darva and I were led through as much basic training and instruction as we could take. *She* had to be "cured" before I could be, but I was the only one that could master the stuff well enough to do the job—and it was a job you really had to do for yourself. It was not simply a matter of removing the original spell either. That might have worked in the early stages, but things had gone too far. The Wardens themselves, freed from any spell, would just hurl us back into the animal world without restraint, dragging me with her.

I was certainly well enough advanced after two months to do the job, although I was also aware that mastering principles and exploring the potential to the utmost were two very different things. I could cast a spell, even produce a changeling—do just about everything Korman and his apts had demonstrated plus a lot more—but it might be years of experimentation and practice before I had it all mastered. I could read Isil's spell very easily—and the copy in myself—and even see where and how it was unraveling in the wrong direction. I even thought it was possible for me to break free myself, to sever my connection to Darva—but that would mean abandoning her. How funny! My old self wouldn't have hesitated a moment—she had been useful and good company, but she was no longer necessary to me. The old me would have discarded her at this point and concentrated on total mastery of the *wa* and the fabrication of a new, fine body. Logically that was the only course that made any sense.

And yet, I couldn't abandon her. I simply could not do it. I admit I agonized over the decision, but not because it was a hard one to make. What it would mean, though, was that I would be compromising my own mission—if, in fact, I still wanted to have one. It seemed equally logical that my best interests lay in the future course of Charon, not in the direction of the Confederacy—although, here, the two might be close. Aeolia Matuze must go, of course, and if Morah represented the aliens then he too must go. But did it have to be *me* who did it? From the looks of the place, Koril was more formidable than I could ever be.

That, of course, was the ultimate reason for my decision. My first loyalty was to myself, and I wanted Darva saved. If that somewhat compromised the rest—well, so be it. I was only part of a team here, and I had to wonder why the Confederacy even bothered to send me to a place like Charon, with so well-prepared and equipped a rebel organization.

Unless Koril too was not exactly what he seemed?

I had carried out the procedures so often in practice that when we came down to the real thing there seemed nothing to it. The staff, Yissim and the others, seemed amazed at my rapid progress. I discovered that there was a relative rating system for sorcs, I being the strongest they had seen (such as Koril and Morah), to V. Lower ratings were apts—VI to X. Tully Kokul, whom I hadn't seen nor heard from since that time on the beach, was a IV or V; Korman was a II. Normally, anyone could become a X with nominal training; apt VI was generally assumed to take one to two years for someone from Outside, like me, who had the necessary mental control, and perhaps ten years for a native raised as an apt from childhood. After VI it wasn't a matter of learning the procedure, but learning how to understand and use it, developing mental control, confidence, and accumulating knowledge to expand your range of influences. It had been barely three months since I'd begun training in Kokul's tent, and the staff easily rated me a V. Of course, the fact that I had nothing else to do, no distractions, the top instructors, and that mastering it was a matter of life or death —literally—for both Darva and myself had a lot to do with the speed, as did my own breeding, experience, and practice as an agent.

What I was going to do was, from my point of view, absurdly simple. I mentioned that the Warden sense was like open lines of energy, a communications net of infinite complexity, from me to everything around me. I was going to send complex prearranged messages—commands—to Darva's mind, to her controlling Wardens who were at the heart of our predicament. I was then going to direct her self-repair, point by point and area by area. In this I was aided by the redoubt's computer visualizations, which did a lot of the difficult preparatory work for me. It was a measure of the difference between, say, Morah and myself, that I couldn't have gone this far without the computer aids—everyone felt sure that *he* could.

I had taught Darva basic hypnotic techniques and now used them both on her and on myself. I was conscious of an audience for all this, but I couldn't see anyone. The experts would be there if needed, but otherwise would remain completely out of sight, and mind. I knew, though, that a lot of big shots were watching. Yissim had said they had learned an enormous amount of new material through our case—which, in the end, was the only reason all this was going on anyway.

The big problem had always been what to do with the extra mass. It could be reduced very slowly, over a period of perhaps years, but we hardly wanted that. I had almost 220 kilos to deal with—not an easy task. More importantly I wanted no trace of the old spell; I wanted no way that the Wardens could someday run wild again and reduce us to animals. So we had to become something with no equivalent outside my own mind.

Alone, in that now very familiar white room, I began. Hypnotized, Darva was far easier to take control of—but to be able to impose my spells so dominantly over the old that I could then wipe the old clean required tremendous concentration and mental effort. So much, in fact, that the experts believed it would be impossible ever to close those lines of communications from me to her and back again.

I cast the spell, using all the force at my command. The resistance was extremely hard and somewhat surprising. I saw immediately what the original sorcs had run into the first time they tried, and it was tremendous. But they hadn't been prepared for it, nor had they used this kind of force of will, backed by my total commitment to breaking it at all cost. What we were dealing with was, of course, at heart a psych problem—her romanticizing about the two of us in the wild—that any good psych could cure back in the civilized worlds. Here it simply had to be beaten back. I had to decouple and push back her subconscious control over her body's *wa* by making her consciously override it, then guide that force of will to my own. She was rated an apt VII, but she lacked the total commitment to break the pattern. I was supplying that.

It turned into an odd mental battle, almost a cross between a stubborn argument and rerouting points on a circuit diagram. At one and the same time I was constantly identifying and beating back her own subconsciously directed *wa* while, with her, I was trying to find any and all routes of *wa* communication between conscious mind and body and then tie them up, even dominate them, while isolating this strong, primitive influence, isolating it, and beating it back into submission. None of this had any effect on her mind or thought processes, of course; we were attacking only the *wa*, the Warden organisms giving out the wrong signal.

As the impasse became more obvious, I began talking to her, soothing her, trying to direct her, to convince her that she must not give in to this primitive, animal will. "Darva—if you have any regard, any feeling for me, you *must* help me! You must beat it back!"

"I do. You *know* I do," she responded.

"Darva—if you—love—me, let it go! You must!" The use of that word sounded odd to me, yet now I almost understood it. At least, I thought, I could *use* it. "Darva—I do this because I love you. If you know that and love me too, release! *Let it go!*" It was odd, what I had said for clinical purposes. Did I, in fact, love her? Was *that* why I was doing this?

Abruptly, the resistance broke—gave up, receded into the depths of her mind. It was so sudden and so unexpected that I wasn't prepared, and the whole force of my will flooded into her, so strong it almost knocked her out. I recovered as quickly as possible, retracing the pathways, seeing how the spell had been so neatly tied and then retied.

The rest was absurdly simple after that; I just followed the computer models I had memorized and practiced again and again. In what seemed like a matter of minutes, at best, although later I was told it was more than seven hours, we were done.

I pushed out the waste and fatty accumulations unnecessary for life rather easily, and did some internal rearranging to expel as much water and excess tissue as possible, getting the *wa* to treat it like common waste and thus assist its expulsion. The shift amounted to more than 30 kilos and looked and smelled horrible, but I was in no state at that point to appreciate it. One hundred ninety kilos were still a hell of a lot, but every bit lost made the job easier.

Diagrams, pictograms, three-dimensional views and designs both internal and external flashed through my mind from training and into hers and thus to the *wa* itself. And she was changing, flowing, redirecting to my commands. I could literally feel it, sense it, as if it were happening inside my own body.

When the job was finished I still couldn't relax because, thanks to the linkage, my body *was* in fact a mirror image of hers in every single respect, and that wasn't my intent. In fact, what took so very long was the attempt to differentiate my body from hers. There were a large number of false starts, as everything I tried to do to myself I found duplicating in her. We knew it might happen, and I hoped now she was up to the task. I could visualize only her; therefore, *she* must direct my own reconstitution while *I* concentrated on keeping her stable as she was. Doing so was difficult, because I was the stronger, but we finally worked out a system that would flow information both ways, an eerie sensation like trying to do three things at once, but one we finally mastered.

And when it was finally over, we both passed out for more than ten hours.

We both awoke, stirred, and opened our eyes. Somewhere an alarm buzzer sounded, probably to summon somebody when we awoke, I thought. Visions of computer diagrams and electrical signals pulsed in my brain, and I knew I was going to have a hell of a time getting rid of them.

"Oh, my god! It really *did* work!" Darva said, amazed. "Look at you!"

"Look at *you*," I responded. "I'm proud of you."

"We need mirrors," she decided. "Say—can you sense the *wa* between us?"

I hadn't really paid much attention, but now that she pointed it out I sensed what she meant. The links were still there, the lines of communication from nervous system to nervous system were intact.

A door opened, and Dr. Yissim and two others entered. One was a large, burly-looking man with rugged complexion and snow-white hair and moustache. I knew at a glance that he had at one time been part of the civilized worlds. He was dressed entirely in white, but not the medical whites of Yissim. His clothing was fine, tailor-fitted and almost a uniform. The other man was in every way weird.

He was small, had a goatee, wore horn-rimmed glasses—a real anomaly here, where the Wardens made certain of your eyesight and everything else—and he was dressed in a casual tweed jacket and dark blue slacks. That alone would have been enough to cause a stare, but there was something more dramatically wrong with him.

I suddenly knew how an animal that trusted its sense of smell above all else felt when confronted with its reflection in a mirror.

The man was patently there—I could see him, touch him, everything. But he had no *wa*, no Warden sense at all. On the level I had been learning to trust above all else, the Warden organism level, he simply did not exist.

"How are you feeling?" Yissim asked me.

"A little weak, otherwise fine," I told her. "We both would love a mirror, though."

"We expected that," she responded with a slight smile, then nodded to the far wall, the one that held the technician's booth. Instead of becoming clear, an indirect light made the surface a good reflector, with only a slight hint of the consoles in back. We both turned and looked at ourselves.

We were both giants, of course. That was mandated. 228.6 centimeters, the spec had called for, balancing off remaining mass. We towered over the more normal-sized people in the room, and particularly over the short little man who wasn't there.

The bone structure needed to support such a body properly, even in the slightly reduced gravity of Charon, was a bit different than the human norm, but none of it showed. Other than her size, Darva was an absolutely beautiful human-looking woman. I had taken my own visualization of what she must have looked like before Isil's changeling spell and produced what I freely admitted was an idealized version. I probably accented her female figure overmuch, but I plead guilty to doing so without shame. Hell, she'd done the same thing to me.

In fact, I hadn't the slightest idea who I looked like, but it was her idea of what the perfect man *should* be. We were both strongly over-muscled, of course—it was one fine way of compacting mass usefully—but hers only showed when she flexed, while mine showed all over. My face was broad and handsome, and overall we were very good personifications of some ancient god and goddess from man's primitive times. Both of us, of course, had tremendously long hair and I had a huge beard as well—more mass used up—but that was in an area that could be cut and trimmed.

But we were not human. She should weigh between 105 and 110 kilos, and I, perhaps 120, but we both had around 180 kilos to contend with and hair really doesn't take away that much. The balance I had placed in our tails; hers was a bit longer than mine. For pigmentation I'd selected, with her approval, a dark solid bronze, with the hair a reddish brown. She hadn't really cared—but we both agreed on anything but green.

I couldn't help but notice that her idealized man was as exaggeratedly endowed in one area as my idealized Darva was in the other. Even though the doctor was there, I had to admit I felt a little self-conscious. Well, something would have to be worked out, even with that tail in the way—but there was nothing to do about it now.

It was hard to tear our gazes away from the reflections, but finally we did and turned back to the trio, who were watching us with great interest.

"Tailed gods," the handsome older man in white commented in a pleasant, deep voice. "Fascinating. You could start a whole new religion, the two of you."

I chuckled. "I think there are enough of those as it is."

"Quite so," he agreed, then looked to Dr. Yissim expectantly.

"Oh, I'm sorry," Yissim said, sounding uncommonly flustered. "Park, Darva—this gentleman is Tulio Koril."

I felt a shock go through me. *Koril! At last!*

Yissim turned to the little man who wasn't there. "And this is Dr. Dumonia. He is a Cerberan."

We had problems with doorways made for smaller folk, and occasionally ceilings were just a tad too low. Darva bumped her head leaving the lab and I felt a shock. I hadn't bumped into anything, but I felt every ache she did. It quickly developed that there was more to our exchange than first met the eye—as we'd been warned. The lines of communication were permanent and intact, theory said, and that meant that whatever one felt, the other did too. A minor irritant, but a potential dagger at my throat nonetheless. Whatever was done to her was done likewise to me, no matter where I was. There *had* to be a range limitation—the energy channels were too tiny to carry—but as long as we were close enough to feel the *wa*, the *wa* in one body considered itself the body of the other.

"The *wa* considers you one," Yissim agreed. "You will have to be careful. Still, if you really *do* care for one another, you should be in for some unique physical sensations on the plus side, too."

I saw Darva's eyebrows rise and her lips form a slight smile. We hadn't thought of that angle—which really proved out, I might add.

We were led into a large office, the kind top executives have, complete with outer office staff, receptionists, the whole business, and we got a lot of stares. In the inner office, our tails proved useful for at least one thing. There were few chairs made for people our size but, with the tails, we didn't need them.

Koril took his seat behind a large desk in the center of the room and Dumonia took a chair next to him, facing us. Yissim had left us in the outer office, assuring us that when we returned she would have already arranged to check us out physically, and for some sort of living quarters. She offered a barber but Darva just asked for barbering tools—no use somebody getting on a ladder to do us.

Koril looked at us for a few moments without saying anything. Finally he said, "Well, you two have become some kind of celebrities around here, I must say."

"I'll bet," I responded. "Still, it's good to be back among the living again, and maybe even be able to get out and see this great place you've built here. I am amazed by it all."

"A large share of the credit goes to the good doctor here," Koril responded, nodding to the little man. "Dr. Dumonia, you see, is the man who makes sure we get our share of Cerberan manufactured goods—and training in their use. He doesn't usually come along himself, though. In fact, this is the first time I think you've *ever* been here, isn't it?"

Dumonia nodded and smiled. "Things are going down all over the system. Matters are coming to a head. It was necessary to coordinate as much as possible with our friends elsewhere, and I could only do so in person. I will admit the trip has been both fascinating and—entertaining."

We stared blankly at him. "What's all this about? And what does it have to do with us?"

Koril looked at Dumonia, who nodded and sighed. "Three days ago, in a fluke, Marek Kreegan, Lord of Lilith, was assassinated."

My heart skipped a beat, and Darva looked at me in concern. *"What!"* I exclaimed, not even realizing that Darva's heart had also fluttered for no reason she could fathom.

The Cerberan nodded. "Despite its flukish nature, such a thing could never have happened without the direct intervention of a Confederacy assassin."

I couldn't suppress my excitement. So I'd done it! Or somebody had anyway. I kind of hoped it was the other me on Lilith.

"With Kreegan's death, the brains behind the alien plot are dead as well," Dumonia went on. "But he was a good planner, so his death, in and of itself, will not affect much. His chief officer, Kobe, ran the basic system anyway and was not only in on everything but was in pretty fair agreement with Kreegan's aims, although he lacks his dead boss's imagination. Still, it is a blow. On Cerberus, I have high hopes that, within a matter of months, perhaps weeks, I will be able to gain control of the Lord of Cerberus. It is a tricky business, but I have several plots going at once and I'm confident at least one will succeed. You see, I'm the Lord of Cerberus's psych."

I burst out laughing. "You seem to be a one-man army," I told him.

"I only wish it were true," the Cerberan replied wearily. "Fortunately, you have a well-organized and equipped rebel force here on Charon—but you have additional problems. A—sorc, I think you call them—named Kokul, who knew you well, said you had a conviction that the aliens are physically here and behind the entire Charonese government. He reported this to friend Koril here, and we'd like very much to know if this is only conjecture or whether you have something to base it upon."

"A feeling, really," I answered truthfully. "But the more I'm here, the more I'm convinced of it. I've been among the humans here, high and low, and I've been among the changelings. Even the most remote and terrible changeling monstrosity retains its basic humanity somehow—some inner something I can't really put my finger on that marks them as human."

"The soul," Darva put in.

I shrugged. "I'm not sure I know what a soul is, but that's as good a word as any. Even the animals here have a certain spark. Everybody and everything—except this man Yatek Morah."

"You mean he's like me—a Warden cypher?" Dumonia asked. "As you all are to me?"

I shook my head. "No, not that. Physically he's just a man, all right, but—inside—I don't know any other way to put it—he's just not there. That soul, that essence, that intangible—it's just not there. I'm not the only one who noticed it. Tully did, too."

"It's true," Darva put in. "I saw him only briefly and from afar, but even then you could sense something—different—about him."

"Like a robot?" the Cerberan prompted.

The comment surprised me, but I had to recall that "robot" was exactly the word I'd used. "Yeah. Very much like that."

Dumonia looked at Koril, and Koril looked back; both sighed. Finally the former Lord said, "Well, that's that, then."

The Cerberan nodded. "Not from Cerberus." He turned back to us. "You see, Cerberus is the source of those cute imitative robots that are playing hell with the Confederacy. Never mind how—our powers are quite different from yours. But this Morah's no Cerberan."

"No, he certainly is not," Koril agreed, then turned to us. "You see, I *know* Yatek Morah. Or, at least, I *knew* him. He was born on Takanna, one of the civilized worlds. We were sent here at the same time, so we got to know each other pretty well. That was forty-odd years ago, of course, but he owes his present position to me. He's a cold, cruel man—but he's human."

"He *was*," Dumonia added. "Now he's far more than that."

Koril sighed. "Yes, I think our friends here confirm that. It explains a lot. It explains almost everything."

"Well it doesn't explain anything to me," Darva put in, showing her old spunk.

It didn't explain anything to me either, but I was preoccupied trying to catch hold of something I couldn't quite corner. Takanna . . . What the hell was familiar about Takanna?

"The alien robots are extremely sophisticated," Dumonia told us. "They are of a sort unknown in the Confederacy, although theoretically possible. In effect, they are quasi-immortal superhumans with the memory and personality of actual human beings."

"And this Morah—he's one of these things?" Darva responded.

"It very much appears so," the Cerberan agreed, "but it's unheard-of. As far as we know, it will only work through a Cerberan. Cerberans, you see, can swap minds—or swap bodies, if you prefer, but only with each other and with these robots. We know of no way that a Charonese could do so—or anybody else."

I put Takanna to the back of my mind for a moment to percolate, then rejoined the discussion. "There *is* a way," I told them. "Even the Confederacy knows about it. It's called the Merton Process."

Both Dumonia and Koril seemed startled, but Dumonia most of all. "Merton! How do you know that name? She is a Cerberan!"

That was news to me. "No matter. They have a process for complete mind and personality transfer from one body to another. It's terribly wasteful of bodies, but it works. I know it works."

It was Koril's turn to get into the argument. "And how do you know?"

I took a deep breath and made a decision. Why not? If not to these two —then who? "Because I went through the process. I'm not nor have I ever been Park Lacoch. He died—and I took his body."

Although Darva had known I was an agent, she hadn't known before of the mind swap and looked at me rather oddly.

Dumonia, though, beamed and turned to Koril. "See?" he said smugly.

Koril sighed and shook his head. "I'll be damned how you knew," he replied.

"Knew what?" Darva asked.

"That your friend and partner here is a Confederacy assassin, come with the expressed mission of killing Aeolia Matuze," Dumonia told her.

"Oh, that," Darva said, surprising and befuddling the two men.

"*I'd* like to know, too," I added. "I haven't exactly been very conspicuous as an agent."

"Simple," Dumonia replied. "You see, once I found out that there was an agent on Cerberus, I suspected others. When another was involved in the Kreegan matter on Lilith, I had to assume that at least one agent had been infiltrated at the same time to each of the four worlds. I looked at who was dropped, got behavioral reports, and made my decision. It was only surprising that I found you already here. I thought friend Koril was going to have to track you down all over the planet to rope you in."

I nodded, feeling a bit relieved. "And *that's* why I'm here."

"Yes—and me, too," the Cerberan responded. "You see, I believe we're running out of time. I am convinced, and so are the Confederacy security and military authorities, that the war is less than a year away. The full war. Even now it may be beyond stopping—but we must try. Removing Cerberus may be impossible, but at least we can exert some measure of control there. But the aliens seem abnormally interested in Charon. As you noted, it is not central to the plan—but it is *vital* to the aliens, for some reason—or else why introduce Morah and topple Koril for Aeolia Matuze? Well, we must remove the danger. *You* must. I can give only technical help and moral support at this point."

Koril patted him on the shoulder. "And invaluable it's been, my friend. Otherwise I should be a crazy hermit in the desert now. We'll take it from here—and soon. Still, how do we kill such a man as Morah now is? He is as powerful as I in control of the *wa*—and far less mortal."

"He can be killed," Dumonia told him. "But it will take concentrated raw power weapons. Fry him completely—melt him down. Or blow him up with the most powerful explosive you can use. Nothing else will work. Things like laser pistols, he will not only absorb but actually take in and use the energy. Melt him or blow him to bits. That's the only way. I've given you the rundown of just what these robots can do."

Koril sighed. "It is a problem. But Morah dominates the Synod, and Aeolia uses his power to rule Charon. No wonder I could not defeat them! You don't suppose . . . ? How many robots might there be?"

"Any number," Dumonia told him. "Who knows? Perhaps Matuze herself. But, remember your own power. Their minds are still the same, and their own Warden powers will be no greater than if they were human."

Koril nodded. "It's a terrible problem—here. Heavy weapons may be no good at all. Still we will work something out. We *will* act."

"Soon?"

"As soon as possible. As soon as we have even a half-decent chance to win."

"That, then, will have to do," Dumonia told him.

Suddenly I yelled, "Zala! Zala Embuay!"

Everybody turned and looked at me as if I'd gone mad. Darva's expression was even worse.

"What makes you think of *her?*" she snapped.

I didn't even recognize the tinge of jealousy. "She was from Takanna! The same world as Morah!"

Koril's eyes fixed grimly on me. "Who is this you speak of?"

"A woman who came to Charon with me," I told him. "We lived together in Bourget until the showdown there." Briefly I told him the rest—including her apparent involvement with the Destroyer's group there and her dual personality. "In fact," I added, "Korman was convinced that *she* was the Confederacy's assassin."

Koril looked at Dumonia. "Is that possible? Two of them—here?"

Dumonia shrugged. "Possibly. But nothing I know about, although, let's face it, the Confederacy and I trust each other equally—and you know what that means."

The sorcerer chuckled slightly. "This woman, then—she might be here."

"I didn't see her at Tully's encampment, nor any time since that shootout," I told him. "Still, if she's here, it might be time to get some answers to some questions."

Koril nodded. "I quite agree."

CHAPTER THIRTEEN

Kira

The huge complex beneath the desert of Gamush was indeed as impressive as it had appeared at first sight. Modern, efficient, and well-staffed, it was a mighty fortress, hidden completely from visual observation and also by more than a little subterfuge. Built as a modern lab and retreat while Koril was still in power, its location was deliberately obscured on maps and charts. Those who had been to it were saddled with spells of confusion that prevented their betraying, or even finding, the place again. By the same token, the isolated technical staff in the place was really stuck without Koril's supply missions and hardly able to betray him—or escape—even if so inclined. Tens of thousands of square kilometers of parched desert that all looked exactly the same, but in which nasty small sand predators lived—and above which the highly intelligent naril flew, ready to pounce upon and eat anything it could—were formidable barriers.

So, should Zala have been there, she was likely to be there still. Koril's clerks quickly located her. She had entered even before me and had been assigned mostly to maintenance. Poor Zala—even in the stronghold of the rebel headquarters she was deemed fit only to scrub the floors.

"Surely there can't be any connection between this woman and Morah," Darva protested as we walked down a long hall. "I mean, she can't be more than in her twenties—and Morah's been here since fifteen or more years before she was born. Their background has got to be just coincidence."

"That's pretty much what Koril figures," I told her, "but I can't buy it. There's simply too many mysteries about her even without this new connection. Add to that a link between her and somebody high up in the Charonese power structure and I can't buy coincidence. There are too many worlds out there and too few prisoners sent here for that."

"You don't still feel anything for her, do you?"

I had to laugh. "Don't worry on that score. I never really did. Oh, at first I was fascinated—Korman's two minds, all the mystery. But when Zala stayed simple, mousy, little Zala she became boring pretty quickly. Besides, we're hardly even of the same race anymore."

"Still, I'd like to go in with you."

"No! This has to be one on one. Remember, I don't look anything like I did before, so unless she's got some really good spies she'll have no link between me and the Park Lacoch she knew. That gives me a big advantage. Still, we don't know what's going to happen, and I don't want to have to worry about you."

We reached our destination. I turned and kissed Darva, then smiled. "Wish me luck."

"Depends," she responded cautiously, but let me go into the room without further protest.

The room had been set up according to my instructions, which meant one chair, a small table in front of it, and nothing else. I ducked my head, a habit I was getting used to, and entered the room.

Zala looked up. I could see a mixture of awe and fright in her face that couldn't be faked—or so I thought. I *was* pretty imposing, after all. I stood there a moment, just looking at her, as the door slid shut behind me.

She looked, I had to admit, no worse for wear. Aside from the loose-fitting blue slacks and shirt which marked her as a service worker she hadn't changed since the last time I'd seen her, there on the street so many months before. And she still had Morah's mark on her, the horns having settled in so well that they appeared almost natural.

"Zala Embuay?" I asked, sounding as officious as possible.

She nodded hesitantly, and I caught a slight gulp, but she said nothing.

"Zala, I'm going to give you some hard-fact ground rules right in the beginning," I went on. "First of all, you might notice in the far corner there two small devices. One is a camera—what is going on here is being recorded. The other is an automatic laser weapon that will follow you no matter what. The door will not open until and unless *I* say so, and it can only be operated by the person on the other end of that camera. Do you understand?"

She nodded weakly, but summoned up enough courage to ask, in a trembling voice, "Wha . . . what's this all about? What have I done?"

"I think you know. At first we thought you didn't know, but now it's been realized that you almost had to know, or at least suspect."

"I—I don't know what you're talking about."

"I think you do. Tell me, you were a member of the cult of the Destroyer in Bourget?"

She nodded hesitantly.

"Who was the leader of the cult?"

"I—I can't tell you that. It is forbidden."

"Zala, as you know well, *we* are the superiors of that organization. Hence, we already know the name."

"Then why ask me?"

I smiled. She wasn't quite as scared as she was pretending to be. "Because I want to see if *you* know."

"Of *course* I know. I *said* I was a member, didn't I?"

"Then tell me the name."

I could see thinking going on behind those frightened eyes. "I—I really can't. A spell was cast to prevent us from revealing it even if we wanted to. As protection."

Good ploy, I reflected. "You and I know that's not really true. I want the name. You won't leave here without giving it."

She shook her head in bewilderment. "I—I really can't. I *did* get a spell. I was scared . . ."

I smiled. "You can't tell me, it's true, but not because of a spell. You can't tell me because you really don't know. You don't remember any of those meetings, do you?"

"I—of course I do! That's ridiculous!"

"If you *did* remember, you'd know that the leader of the cult was disguised by a spell, as were most of the members. You couldn't know who that head was—and no spell would prevent you from telling me that. You're lying, Zala Embuay. You were never a member of that cult."

"I—of course I was! See?" She pointed to the horns. "How else could I get *these?*"

"*That* is the question we're trying to answer here. You see, in the confusion there really wasn't enough time or organization to check *everybody* against the membership rolls. They had to take anybody who suddenly sprouted a pair of horns. We've already caught a few spies." That was a complete lie, although the thought had occurred to Koril and his staff and histories had been taken. The truth was, nobody *could* really be sure, so they were simply all under observation and in no case permitted to leave or even approach the cargo areas, Zala included. "They learned that death is the least punishment a spy can expect—here."

At that moment I reached out to her and touched her *wa*, effortlessly weaving a mild demand spell. She gave a sharp cry and stood up. I had to give a slight paralyzing stroke to her legs to keep her from involuntarily bolting. I had to be dramatic while being careful not to juggle mass, since this was to be a strictly temporary spell—but that was all right. The *wa* took days, even weeks, to complete a physical change, whereas the *perception* of that change was immediate.

She watched as her hands and arms shriveled, changed, became a mottled green and brown, then larger and heavier as they turned into perfectly repulsive suckered tentacles that, to her, weighed half a ton. "No!" she screamed.

"Want a mirror to see the rest of you?" I taunted, feeling less than wonderful about all this but realizing its need. Korman said she would break only under extreme pressure, and this was certainly that.

"No! No! No!" she wailed. "Kira! Please help me! Kira! Kira!"

I suddenly felt a little better. So she *did* know! I watched and waited to see what would happen next.

Korman had told me that I would one day perceive the *wa* as he did—and I was well past that point. The two forebrains of Zala Embuay showed clearly, not just as two brains but as two distinct and particularly weird ones. From the odd, distorted *wa* sense they looked about equal, each smaller than the norm for a human. If a person had the Power, you could see the information flow from *wa* to *wa*. Zala didn't—but somebody did. Somebody, in fact, abruptly started doing the nearly impossible.

The message flares, terribly strong, flowed from the brain to the body and back again, measuring, checking the spell which showed as a spider's web of *wa* energy, then unraveling it in the same manner as I had unraveled Darva's spell and my own. Whoever was doing it—and it had to be Zala herself—was a stronger sorc than the spell, which was, of course, a simple one but still a level VI or VII. I began to wonder if this mind might be more powerful than my own, and reflected that I just might have to find out. One thing was clear—not only was the mind powerful, it was extremely well trained. When? And by whom?

I made no effort to defend the spell and it broke easily, restoring Zala quickly to her former appearance. Very briefly I saw a vision of that stronger, Amazonlike Zala of those last moments on the streets of Bourget. But the vision was fleeting and quickly gone. Kira, it appeared, was still not quite willing to meet me face to face.

Zala sat down, looking weak and shaken. I did not intend to let her get off that easily.

"Zala, who is Kira?" I asked her.

She just shook her head and wouldn't look at me directly.

"She's inside you, isn't she?" I pressed. "Kira and you share the same body, don't you? And that's why you're here, on Charon—because of Kira, *isn't that right?* Zala, what is Kira?"

She put her hands to her ears, trying to block out my voice, but it wasn't going to be that easy.

"Kira, if you can hear me, understand me, you'd better put in an appearance," I said sharply. "Your spells are good, but that was a minor one for me and I'm hardly the most powerful sorc here. Any attempt to disable that laser by spell will be instantly detected and it will fire. *Wa* takes time to weave. I don't think anybody can beat the speed of light. You'll sit here until you come out, Kira. Sit here without food, without water, in a plain and empty room in a place in the desert from which there's no escape."

Zala's head turned and looked at the laser-camera combination, but she made no attempt at it. Finally she turned to me. "Damn you! Who the hell *are* you, anyway?"

I smiled. "Why, Zala, honey, it's your old loving husband, dear old Park, in his new suit of changeling clothes. Remember me?"

That got her, more than the threats or anything. "Park?" she managed weakly. "Is that really—you?"

I bowed slightly. "It's me, all right. And if it's any consolation, you were blown from the beginning. Korman actually assigned me to keep close to you and report. He thought you were a new kind of Confederacy assassin. Your rather unique mind shines like a beacon to all who can see the *wa*, I'm afraid."

She gasped. I could tell that this was genuine news to her—and to her counterpart too, I suspected. The fact is, self-control or not, we never accurately see *ourselves* in *wa* terms. *Wa* doesn't reflect in mirrors.

"What I'm telling you is all on the level," I assured her. "Koril's had a small team trying to figure out the unique part of your brain almost from the moment you arrived. There's been some debate on the science and security staffs about you. They've let you run, so far, to see what would happen—and nothing did. So we're making it happen. Now, don't you think it's time the truth comes out? If you're working for Morah, you might as well admit it and go from there. If you're working for anybody else, we want to know. And if you're not working for anybody, we want to know just what the hell this is all about."

She shook her head, as if to clear it. "I—oh, hell. What's the use of going on any further? I'm going to tell you—unless I'm stopped."

"By Kira."

She nodded. "By Kira."

"Zala, what is Kira?"

"She—she's my sister. What I told you—you *really* are Park?—at the start was mostly true. I was an experiment. *We* were. A whole different kind of brain, they said. Two of us. Two complete people in one body. It's really funny saying that, 'cause I don't really know what it's like not to have it."

I shook my head in wonder. "But why? What was the purpose? What was the aim? Surely somebody didn't take this kind of chance just to experiment? It wouldn't be worth the risk."

She chuckled dryly. "The risk. What risk? You have too high an opinion of the Confederacy, Park. That's your trouble. You see only what's on top, out there for show, and you swallow it whole, just like most of the jerks. You think the Four Lords just sit here and run their little worlds?

Just because they're trapped here? That's a laugh. They run a lot you don't see all over the Confederacy. They're just the new examples of what's been around for thousands of years—maybe forever. A business. A business that sells things that nobody else does. Things that people say they don't want, but they really do: perversions, gambling outside the official casinos, special loans, even promotions. Fancy jewels, works of art, stuff like that is stolen or bought and a lot of it comes here, to the Diamond. They're everywhere and into everything. Drugs for bored frontier folk and space-navy people who might be out for a year or more. Anything you want they can get—anywhere—at a price."

"I'm not as naive as you think," I told her. "But go on. This syndicate, then, bred you?"

She nodded. "Bred me—and others."

That was interesting. "Others? Many others?"

She shrugged. "Who knows? We were raised independently."

"Yeah—but why? For what purpose?"

"The Confederacy has an elite force, bred to their jobs. They're called assassins, although they don't often kill. Did you know that?"

"I know something about them, yes," I admitted rather evasively.

"Well, how do you think the Four Lords got stuck here? Or most of the rest of the people, for that matter? *They*—the assassins—got them. The assassins are bred for the job, as I said, so they're almost impossible to corrupt. They love their work, and do nothing else. Their true identities aren't even known to the bureaus that employ them, and any time one is contacted, that contact is brief. After the job is done, all memory of them is wiped from even Security's minds and general records. Their anonymity is the one thing the Four Lords have never broken. Those men and women are the *only* people the high-ranking members of the Brethren, as the organization usually calls itself, are scared of. The only ones. Only one has ever been exposed and corrupted—and *he's* one of the Four Lords!"

"Marek Kreegan of Lilith," I responded. "He's dead, you know."

Her head shot up. "Dead! How?"

"A Confederacy assassin got him, it seems."

"You see, then?"

I shook my head. "No, I don't see at all. What's all this leading to?"

"The Four Lords, the entire Brethren, need people who can identify and kill these assassins before they themselves are killed. They've tried every way in the universe to crack the system, and been frustrated every time. Even Kreegan couldn't help them, for no assassin ever knows enough of the security system, which is changing anyway all the time, to break it. So, the Brethren figured, if they couldn't expose the system, they'd breed their own. Assassin killers, you might say."

I had to laugh. "*You* are an assassin killer?"

She shook her head. "No, not me. Kira. She's amazing, Park. Amazing. She learns almost anything from one lesson, and never forgets. She's got total control of her—our—body. Total. She is an analytical killing machine, and brilliant." She was saying this admiringly, but as if she were talking about someone else entirely. It was eerie. And, of course, it raised more questions than it solved.

If Zala were telling the truth, then Koril already *knew* what she was—he'd have to. And Korman probably would, too. Why didn't they? Or if they did, why all the charade? Something definitely smelled funny now, and Zala was the first suspect. She hadn't exactly proved reliable in the past.

"Zala, why two of you?" I asked. "Why *both* you and Kira?"

"Oh, that's supposed to be a safeguard if we were caught. They couldn't psych Kira, only me. They couldn't wipe her—only me."

"That only makes sense if you don't know about her yourself," I pointed out. "And of course you *had* to know."

"Oh, sure. But she's real strong. I don't really understand it, but Kira says that there's really only one of us, at least as far as memories and stuff is concerned. She can shut me off, and sometimes she does. One time I can remember a lot of things, then I can't—and sometimes I don't even know what I used to know until I know it again, if that makes any sense."

Oddly enough, it did, and it rang true. I had no idea of the biology of it —I certainly would have said two such personalities in one brain was impossible if an example wasn't sitting in front of me. But somehow, those syndicate biologists had done it. A master assassin, at least as good as the Confederacy's. Maybe better, I reflected sourly. There certainly was a mortality rate in my business, and sometimes it was impossible to explain. But if this dominant personality had all the keys to the memory core, a total understanding and command of what went on in there—which was more than anybody else did—it could literally reserve sections to itself. And add sections as needed too, I reflected. So you could get to know Zala, and hypno her, and put her under psych or mind control, and it wouldn't make a damned bit of difference.

"Kira seems to be satisfied to let you live your life, though," I pointed out. "Most of the time she just seems along for the ride."

Zala nodded. "That's right. But she's not asleep or anything like that. She's right here with me. She says that's the way we were—well, *designed,* although that makes us seem like some kind of creepy machine."

I nodded. "So when I talk to you I'm talking to her—but when *you* talk to *me* it can be just you."

"That's about it," she agreed.

"And so how'd you wind up here, on Charon?"

"Well, Kira says it looked like a fluke, but not anymore. They never really told us. They just came in one day and arrested me, that's all. *Oh!*" She suddenly started, and then I watched that strange transformation take place in her.

Unlike my earlier perception, it really was more of a mental than a physical thing, yet you could *see* it clearly. What happened was more than a complete change of personality behind those big, brown eyes—

Zala's hidden attributes were clearly displayed. In the Zala *persona* she looked weak and ordinary, but as Kira the tremendous muscles and the strength in them, matching the new strength in the eyes, seemed to stand out. Although nothing really changed, the transformation was startling.

"Hello, Kira," I said.

"Lacoch," she responded, her voice lower and very cool, almost inhuman in its lack of tone. "I think it is time we talked directly."

I relaxed back on my tail. "I'll agree to *that*. Uh—tell me. Does Zala know what's going on when you are you?"

"When I permit," she replied. "I am permitting now. There seems no reason not to."

"And when you don't—permit?"

"Then it's like she is asleep."

"Fair enough. You're willing to answer the rest of my questions?"

"We'll see. There is no penalty in asking."

I had this odd feeling that *I* was trapped in the room, not her. She had an unsettling effect on me from the start. "First of all, did Zala tell the truth?"

"She told no falsehoods," Kira responded, which was not really answering the question. I took note of that fact and went on.

"This breeding of special agents like yourself—it was entirely on Takanna?"

She nodded. "Spread the project and you spread the risk of detection. There is no need to cover up now, since the project was discovered and has probably been obliterated by now anyway."

That was interesting. "Do you know how it was finally penetrated?"

She shook her head negatively. "I suspect that it was not. I believe it was leaked—closed down by the Four Lords themselves. Zala was not penetrated. We were betrayed. A very few of us have been taken and sent here before by the Confederacy. But the Confederacy should not have known about me. The project was ended and totally destroyed years before I was caught. Ended by the Four Lords themselves. I have no direct evidence, but I believe that I am here also at the Lords' direction. Perhaps all remaining of my kind are."

I thought about that. "Then in effect you were called in to the boss in the only way they could call you in."

"It is the only possible explanation."

"All right, then, tell me—if that's true, why didn't the current or former Lord of Charon know anything about you? Korman thought you were a Confederacy assassin. Koril says he didn't even know of you until I drew attention your way. And Koril's staff says they were very curious about you—but also had no idea as to your true nature. *Why didn't they know, Za . . . Kira?*"

"At the moment, only three possibilities come to mind," she replied. "Either Koril or Matuze *didn't* know, and only one was pretending, or both do not know and this project was either not passed on to the new

Lords who took over since for some reason, or they had some purpose in keeping this information from them."

"Nobody contacted you?"

"Yes, I *was* contacted. In Bourget."

"By who?"

"Yatek Morah."

I felt the old blood flowing again. *Now* we were getting somewhere.

"When was this?"

"Less than two days after we arrived."

"Less than two days! But we were there five months before he showed himself!"

She nodded. "He instructed me in the use of the *wa*—while you were working mostly. He'd come almost every day at the start, then less often as the lessons became less instruction and more practice, as you should understand."

Yeah, I sure did. "Did you ask him what all this was for?"

"I asked him if he had a mission for me. He told me that the mission would come later, that I was now only to practice."

"And you never pressed him?"

"I do not question the orders of my superiors." It wasn't a brag, just a fact stated in that same flat, emotionless tone as the rest.

"So you were still without instructions that morning at Bourget?"

"I was. I expected to be contacted, and even made an effort to contact Morah, but he brushed me aside. I am still without orders."

"You were never in the cult?"

"No. I tried, certainly—but I was not permitted. None would even admit its existence, and it was well hidden. Of course, it was no trick to determine who was involved and where those meetings were, but since I was still learning the powers myself I had no desire to meet a superior challenge in them until I felt I was ready."

I nodded idly, mostly to myself. It all made a crazy kind of sense, but all the pieces didn't fit. Damn it, *did* Koril know, or didn't he? And, regardless, had *Korman* known, at least at the start? Morah certainly had. I needed more information—and fast.

"Tell me, Kira, who do you work for now? Whose instructions will you, must you take?"

She immediately saw the point of the question. "It is not so simple on Charon, which is why I wait and live through Zala. Here, as back home, there are factions in the Brethren, but there I was clearly on one side. Here are two coequal forces, it seems to me. Matuze ousted Koril, who was one of my Lords. Matuze has control now, but may or may not maintain it. Morah has helped me, for Matuze's faction. But realistically, I must serve Lord Koril. I am here. I have no orders, no instructions, from Morah, and I am not likely to get any. If I do not ally myself with Lord Koril against Lord Matuze, I will be killed. Logic, therefore, dictates that I serve Lord Koril. I am at his service."

The statement was so cold and emotionless I could hardly suppress a shudder. Here was someone without any sense of morality, scruples, even loyalty. It made absolutely no difference to her who she worked for.

It was time to talk to Koril.

"You've seen the recording," I said. "Any reaction?"

Koril sat back and looked thoughtful. "I vaguely remember the project," he responded after a long pause. "Very vaguely. It was started long before I was sent here, of course. But it was never considered successful. I swear to you I thought the whole operation was shut down and abandoned years ago. And this double mind thing—hell, it's unbelievable to *me*."

He sounded sincere, and I wanted to believe him. Very much.

"Still, *somebody* knew," I pointed out. "She—and others—have been working for the Brethren for years. Who knows how many and over how long? And somebody ordered it shut down. Turned her in, in fact, and arranged somehow to send her here."

Koril seemed deep in thought and only half talking to me. "The more I think about it, the more I can see a possible scenario. The project was closed down, if I remember, because its products scared the hell out of the Four Lords—particularly their top people back home. Killing machines . . . What the Zala persona said rang a bell. No loyalty. No emotions. The bottom line was, no controls. Anything that—inhuman—could be used not only against the Confederacy but also against other power centers of the Brethren. Hell, it was supposedly shut down about the time I got sent here. I only got told about it when I was on the Synod by an old planetary boss who liked to reminisce."

"But that was forty or more years ago," I noted. "She's not nearly two-thirds that old."

He nodded. "And that, my friend, means that somebody has kept the thing going *after* it was ordered closed. Somebody who kept the secret from just about everybody except his own immediate family. It would give that person a tremendous edge."

"She said something about the Triana family," I said.

He shrugged. "I don't know them, but it might be a real family and not a Brethren one. Still, you see what this means? A fifth Lord, a secret one, in the game for maybe forty years."

"Morah. It has to be Morah."

"I agree. And yet Morah closed down the thing and exposed at least one, maybe all, the remaining ones. Why?"

"Well, I can think of one reason," I told him.

"Huh?"

"With organic super-robots and an alien force behind him he didn't need them anymore. Not there, anyway."

"Perhaps. But why did he need them *here*? And why, once here, didn't he use her?"

He thought a moment. "Maybe he wasn't ready to use her yet."

It was my turn. "Huh?"

"Suppose there aren't many of these—people. Suppose there are only, maybe, four of them. You remember Morah's getaway in the square at Bourget?"

"The four-headed hydra."

"And now Kreegan's dead. Remember—Dumonia said it *wasn't* the assassin who got him. A fluke, he called it." He looked straight at me. "And Morah's seen, met with, talked with those aliens face to face."

I finally saw where he was going. "So Korman might *not* have known. Or Aeolia Matuze either."

He nodded. "The Confederacy might not be the only ones trying to knock off the Four Lords. In fact the Confederacy might just be doing Yatek Morah a favor.

"Not Four Lords of the Diamond—but one."

CHAPTER FOURTEEN

Forced Decisions

"That girl—Zala or Kira or whoever she is—worries you, doesn't she?" Darva asked.

I nodded. "Not the Zala part. There's something even likable about Zala. But ever since Korman told me about the other part of her I've wanted to meet that part—and now that I have, I'm not sure I should have forced it."

"I guess I'll never understand you," she sighed. "You force her out, then get really unhappy about it. Why? Isn't Kira more or less the same type as you?"

I whirled and felt my blood pressure go up. I paused a moment to try and get control of myself. I was going to make a nasty remark and strong denial, but Darva had really hit the nail on the head. Admitting that to myself calmed me down.

"All right. Yes, in a way. Never that cold, that unemotional, but, yes, she *is* a lot like I used to be. The way I still really think of myself. But she's me stripped down to the least common denominator. No morality, no cause, no feelings of any sort. That's what those biotechs managed with that two-mind technique. She's able to shift all her emotions, morals, feelings into Zala. It gives Kira the mind of a computer, unencumbered by any traces of—well, humanity. Zala may be dumb, shallow, and not good for much, but she's all that's human in that body and brain. And, still, when I look at Kira, talk to her, I see—me." *I see a man I used to be, sitting up there, a third of a light-year off the Warden system,* I added to myself.

And, in fact, just how different *was* Kira from that man up there? Outside of assignments, psych blocked and mostly wiped, he was really nothing more than a Zala with money. A playboy in the haunts of the rich and powerful, contributing little and totally hedonistic. The only difference between Kira and me, deep down, was that when I got all that information back before a mission, like now, I still had at my base that other man, that playboy lover of fun. Kira, on the other hand, experienced everything vicariously and never felt that her cover was anything more than that—certainly not a part of her.

The technique by which Zala/Kira had been formed remained a mystery. The medics here had poked and probed and found nothing. Her brain, aside from the Warden organisms' odd grouping, appeared normal. Nothing in medical science could pinpoint the difference in any way. And yet it was not a psych technique, or some mental aberration—the *wa* showed clearly a true biological division there somewhere.

To look into a mirror, to see such a personality—the perfect assassin—and see in all its ugliness the perfection of those qualities you always prided yourself on, this was the problem. Nor did I have the faith, the moral certitude, any more than I was on the side of right, justice, and good. Charon and its viewpoints and my own experiences here had killed that certainty, and even though I was still, for now, on the same side, I was there because the opposition repelled me, not out of any lingering loyalty to the Confederacy ideal. Had this, I wondered, happened to the others, my counterparts on Lilith, Cerberus, and Medusa? I knew this—I was more completely human now than ever before, and both the weaker for it and yet, somehow, whole as Kira was not and might never be.

Explaining all this to Darva wasn't easy. Although it helped to share it and talk it out, the fact was she could never fully understand. She hadn't been raised to *believe*.

And that, in the end, was the bottom line of difference between Kira and me. I had been a believer who lost his faith but found his humanity. She had never believed in anything, and, because of that, could never find or even fully comprehend her own humanity. I had been literally reduced to the animal on Charon and been reborn a human. Kira was reduced to the machine and locked there for all time.

In a sense, she'd forced me to take a good, hard look at myself—and in the process, I was free. The last bonds were cut. Like that little Cerberan, Dumonia, I severed my last ties to my past and stayed allied with it only because, for the moment, our interests coincided.

For the first time I reached back and examined myself, and much to my surprise, was able to locate through my own *wa* that tiny piece of organic goo in my brain. Still there. From Lacoch to changeling to bunhar to changeling again, it had somehow survived. So you're still listening, my brother out there? My . . . Kira.

*   *   *

Koril looked grim-faced. His office was littered with reports and photos, and he wasn't pleased with whatever they said.

He got straight to the point. "We have been compromised. After all these years, we've been compromised."

"Somebody got word out?"

He nodded. "Somehow. I'm not sure how. But this complex is doomed, Park. It's only a matter of time. Oh, it's safe enough against ground assault, but once its location is known they could bring in heavy stuff, off-planet stuff, and fry hell out of us."

"Then why haven't they?"

He smiled. "Funny. Basically because the Confederacy monitors the system so well. They don't have the heavy weapons on Charon to do the job, and if they tried to get them they'd be shot to hell in space. To hit us hard they'd have to bring in one of their alien friends' vessels—and that would force them into the open. But it's only a matter of time until they work out some way to fool our Wardens."

"How much time?" I asked uneasily.

"Who knows? A day? A week? A month? A minute from now? Whenever they can work it out. We can't take the chance of its being long." He sat back in his chair, and for the first time he looked very old, old and incredibly tired. "Well, perhaps it's for the best. To end it, one way or the other, once and for all. He looked up at me, the weight of his decision showing in his face. "You know, Park, for the first time I realize how I've been kidding myself all these years. I *enjoyed* this place. I loved the research, the peace, the lack of demands. I even loved being the rebel leader. It was far more of a challenge to be the opposition than to actually run the place. It's funny—always preparing but never acting. That's just what Dumonia was saying the other—son of a bitch!"

"What's the matter?"

"That old bastard! Outside of people directly under my control, Dumonia was the only one who knew precisely how to determine this base's location. He had to—his people stocked it. Why, I ought to . . ." He was turning so red I feared his rage, but he soon calmed down.

"Oh, hell," he said, "I guess he had a right. Without him I wouldn't have all this."

"You mean the *Cerberan* betrayed you?"

He nodded. "Had to be."

"But why?"

"Just to get me to move. Damn it, Park, I'm ready. I've been ready for over a year. You saw Bourget—just a little test. That's why Dumonia was here. We talked and talked and talked, and I gave him a hundred excuses, but hell, the man's a psych. He knew I would have to be pushed, and so he pushed."

I frowned. "Who *is* that man, anyway? Where does he get the resources and power he uses?"

"He's probably the most dangerous man in the Diamond, and that's saying something," Koril replied. "He could be Lord if he wanted, or just about anything else, I think. He's absolutely brilliant, particularly at making other powerful people do what he wants. Right now he has the Confederacy and who knows how much of the Diamond doing his bidding. What his motives are I can't say—but I know it's not power for its own sake. If he wanted to run things, he would. I asked him once why he was helping me and you know what he said? He said it was a relief from boredom! But, enough of him. He's kicked me hard now—and I have no choice but to act."

"You're going to try and retake control then?"

He nodded. "Now, I don't want to minimize anything. You're still new here—a little over a year total, I think. You still don't really appreciate what we're up against."

I waved my hands around. "This place is equipped to take the whole system, and your planetwide underground is effective. I can't see why you'd have a problem at this stage."

He smiled grimly. "Ah, but you see only the surface. First of all, we can't depend on the weapons here. Didn't you ever wonder why those troopers in Bourget had projectile weapons? I took a great risk with the laser stuff there. One small tabarwind and we'd have been blown to kingdom come."

"You know, ever since I've been on Charon I've heard about tabarwinds," I told him. "And yet they have to be rare. I never saw one, or met anyone who did."

"It only takes one to scare hell out of you. It's a whirling electrical storm that reaches from the ground to the ion layer surrounding the planet. Nobody knows what causes them, but they look like something out of the most fanatical of religious hells. There's even a religion based on them, if you can believe it. They just appear—no cause, no real reason we've ever found. They can be anywhere—except here, in the center of Gamush, for some reason. They follow no set path and no logic, and they vanish as quickly as they come. It can be a year between them—and then there can be dozens, even hundreds. Aside from the direct fury of the storm, almost anything electrical within a dozen or more kilometers of the storm just goes crazy. Overloads and explodes, often with a force beyond anything inherent in the exploding device. No sorcery, no force of will can stand against them. And electrical energy attracts them like a magnet."

"Sounds like an experience I can gladly skip," I told him truthfully.

"And they're more common than you think," Koril went on. "There are three right now in the north, and that's where we have to go."

I sighed. "I see. But reduced to those primitive weapons, numbers mean even more—and I think you have them. If Bourget is any indication, the masses of people here really don't give a damn who runs things."

"As usual anywhere," Koril agreed. "Oh, it's certain that we could take as much as seventy percent of the north and the few settlements on

Garrush without problems. Tukyan's hardly worth worrying about it's so primitive. I have enough powerful sorcs, trained and developed here, to carry the day, force the government to a few strongholds like Montlay and Cubera. But it makes no difference. As long as they hold the Castle they hold one of only two spaceports on the planet, and they hold the power really. The trade, the records—the whole economy. Holding that, they can disrupt the business of the planet. Things don't work right, people get hungry, or angry. And while we deteriorate sitting on our seven-tenths, they wait for reinforcements either from the other three Lords or, maybe, directly from the aliens. Basically, we take the countryside without the Castle and we take nothing we can hold. Take the Castle and the rest falls automatically into line."

"Then we must take the Castle."

Tulio Koril laughed. "Easier said than done, my rash young assassin. Far easier said than done."

We sat in a small briefing room, eight of us and Koril. I looked around at the faces there, but aside from two I didn't recognize any of them. The two I knew were Darva, of course, and Zala Embuay whose presence was unexplained. It was definitely Zala we were seeing, not Kira, but we all knew that Kira was present too.

The room was darkened, and a picture appeared on the screen of a huge, black circular stone building set atop a commanding mountain. Pagodalike, there were a series of stone porches around it at regular intervals almost all the way to the not quite flat top of the building.

"This is the Castle," Koril told us. "It is eighty meters high from ground level, but there are an additional forty meters below ground. The building is divided into fifteen levels, and has excellent drainage. Its walls are solid stone, a meter thick, reinforced with steel plating and mesh. Beneath it, inside the mountain, is a network of tunnels leading to remote, below-ground armories. You could probably blow a nice hole in it with a laser cannon, but you'd never get a second chance at it. Even so, you would have to be a genius to make that first hole, since the outer rock surface is chemically coated with a clever armorite compound developed on Cerberus. It will deflect a laser and, if you're not careful, reflect it back at you. Because of the coating, the *wa* of the Castle is inert to us. It acts like a true physical barrier to the best *wa* sense. You can't throw a spell to disperse anything or anybody behind it. Of course, they can't do it to you either—but, remember, they don't have to. They can hold on until reinforced either from other areas or from space. That topmost area is a shuttle cradle."

I had to admit the place was most impressive, although I knew of two dozen weapons that could bring it down. Of course, none were available in the Warden Diamond—and two would also destroy the planet.

"The top level is shuttle receiving," Koril continued, "and there is a series of lifts around the exterior for moving people and goods up and down, mostly by a clever counterweight system. The fourteenth floor is the living quarters of the Lord of the Diamond, her servants and whatever entourage she might permit. On the next eight floors below are special troopers and a defense force, living quarters for the rest of the top government and their staffs, and central records. The bottom five floors, all below ground level, include a supply level and warehouse with tunnel access, a special prison known as the dungeon, a reception level and general offices, and more defensive and trooper personnel. Additionally, on many of the upper levels there are governmental and experimental offices, labs, and the like. All in all, quite a complex."

Koril flipped a switch, and a schematic of the building came on.

"Get to know this. You will all have copies provided, and I want you to know every passage, service corridor, twist and turn in the place. Within the next two days I'll be putting you to the test, showing blind areas on a computer simulator. Better know your way around or you'll get quickly lost. Speed is important, but I don't want any of you in there to get lost in any way, shape, or form."

The picture flipped again, showing the bottom level and the tunnel complex.

"This is the weak spot of the Castle, if it can be said to have one," the sorcerer went on. "If you look closely, you'll realize that this is more than a complex of tunnels and caves in a mountain. This is a maze. It is certainly possible to get into the maze more than two kilometers from the Castle itself, but once in you have even more problems. There are spells and sensors everywhere. Apparent rock walls show where there is clear space, and there are literally hundreds of rock plugs that can be—and are—shifted regularly, changing the entire maze. There is, literally, no way to know the configuration of the maze at any given time. At one time, several years ago, I *did* discover the key to it and sent in some of my best people. Most of them got into the Castle, but only a handful got out again—and none lived to get back to me. You understand the meaning of that. Many of them were top sorcs. The best. Therefore, should we manage to get *in,* we're *in.* We either take the Castle or we die. No alternatives."

That outlook was pretty grim, but we all could see his point. Still, somebody had a question—I couldn't tell who.

"How will we solve the maze?" the questioner sensibly asked.

"The only advantage I have is that I know the entire area. I know what sort of things are installed and what are not, and I can orient myself even to changed circumstances. Basically, I'm betting that I can solve the maze based on my prior knowledge. If I can't, it's all over."

There was a nervous shuffling in the room at that. We were all being asked to put our necks entirely in a noose made for Koril, and were totally dependent on Koril to keep that noose from tightening.

"Now, it's inevitable we'll trip something, bringing troopers and defense forces," Koril continued, "but these don't worry me and should not worry you. None are above the level of a low-grade apt, maybe VII tops and more likely IXs. The least of you is a VII, and most of us are far higher than that. They keep the troop grade low to prevent any possible internal revolts, of course. But don't kid yourself—also in the Castle are some incredibly powerful sorcs. The tops. The best we know. With luck, there'll be no more than four or five Synod members there—they roam about much of the time. But the odds are extremely good that there will be at least that number, and we can't discount Morah. We can only hope that he's out—and then try and rig things a bit our way."

"What about Matuze?" somebody else asked.

"She'll almost certainly be in. She rarely leaves, and never for any extended visits. Without her, of course, the Castle is valueless, but I feel certain the odds are with us on that much. As for Morah, we'll stir up a big dish of trouble in the south coast region, as far from the Castle as we can. With any luck, the fracas will bring him there. Then we enter the Castle. Finally, as a distraction, there will be a general uprising and a well-coordinated but futile attack upon the Castle itself. Our own movements will be determined both by events inside and by the shuttle schedule, which we most certainly know. It puts down at four every afternoon and remains for an hour. That means we launch our south coast diversion a day before we go in. We go in at five the next day. Once we're discovered, we're committed. We must accomplish everything before that shuttle returns the next afternoon. If not, if we're held in the lower areas through then, Aeolia need only take the shuttle up to the space station and we're dead." He paused a moment, then added, "Remember, you all volunteered for this."

Well, maybe we had—but there were a lot of ifs in this proposition. If all the attacks were coordinated. If Morah could be drawn off. If there were no more Synod members in residence than we could handle ourselves. If the shuttle kept its schedule. If Aeolia Matuze was home. And if we could think, fight, and ensorcel our way through that huge building in only one full day.

I looked at Darva in the gloom and knew she was thinking the same things I was. "I really wish you wouldn't come," I told her. "You're not strong enough for the sorcs and you're a knife at my throat. They kill you, they get me."

"I have other skills," she reminded me, "not the least of which is the weapons practice I've been through here. And I'm no more a knife at your throat than you are at mine. If you're going to take me with you I don't want to get it sitting out the action someplace."

I smiled and squeezed her hand. "All right, then. It's a team we are."

Her smile in return was weak. I knew she really thought we were going to die in this, and I understood that she was willing to go, particularly if it was in the pursuit of something important.

And, I think, she understood me as well. Hell, up to the last I'd never expected to be in on the end of this thing, not directly. As it was, I was going to have more fun than I'd had in the past ten years.

CHAPTER FIFTEEN

A Walk in the Dark

We could have used four months to train for the mission; Koril gave us four days. Once he'd decided to move, he decided to *move,* and that was that. He said he'd picked each of us for a reason, but some reasons were easier than others to figure out.

I seemed to have been included because Koril, like many of the Brethren I'd hunted for most of my life, had a very high opinion of Confederacy assassins, an opinion I'd tried to reinforce in my conversations with him. I was surprised he agreed to let Darva come, but as she had pointed out, what she lacked in sorcerous powers she more than compensated for with close-quarters weaponry. She'd worked hard developing those skills, and I wouldn't want to be in the way if she wanted to go somewhere. If her opponent were equal or weaker than she in control of the *wa* force, or was prevented by one of us from using it, that opponent was dead. Zala—or, rather, Kira—was a more interesting choice, since I knew Koril trusted her no more than I did. If she was on the level, of course, she'd be invaluable—but she could also easily be our Trojan Horse, ready to betray us once we were trapped inside the Castle.

The rest were his best sorcs, as illustrated by the "K" sound that preceded their names, which they took when admitted to that fraternity of the very best. It was like a title or badge of rank—and when I finally realized that it explained a lot. Of them all, only Morah had never taken a sorc name.

Our party wasn't without interesting abilities. In addition to Darva and myself, Ku, a small, dark man with a rodentlike face, was also a changeling, although very human in appearance. He was naturally nocturnal and, additionally, had some sort of built-in sonar system which would be very useful to us—along with his unnerving ability to stick to walls and ceilings like a fly. It was obvious that, if in fact someone else had made him a changeling or not, he'd adapted for himself some most useful attributes.

Kaigh was a large, hairy bearlike man who looked naturally mean, and perhaps was. I understood he was a former Confederacy frontier officer who'd found the possibilities for graft and extortion out there irresistible. Kimil was a typical civilized worlder, younger than Koril but otherwise undistinguished. Kindel was a small, wiry woman with wickedly long nails and a shaved head. Her cold, black eyes seemed too large for her head, and were constantly in nervous motion. Krugar was a woman of the civilized worlds, in early middle age and otherwise not very distinguished from any other civilized worlder. Of us all, I realized, only Darva was native to Charon.

Darva and I were the largest and most obvious targets; I realized that from the beginning. Over the months we had managed to scale ourselves down slowly to a more moderately tall 204 centimeters, still enough to tower over the others. Of course, our appearance, although very human, was still changeling enough to mark us. We were both damned strong and surprisingly agile, and we worked at it.

We left Koril's redoubt by air, in much the same manner as we'd arrived—but this time, inside the cabin of the great flying creature and not in its claws. Zala hadn't been too excited by the idea of the trip, but apparently had been calmed or sedated in some way by Kira. I found the trip as bumpy and uncomfortable as the first time, but took it in stride. We had a schedule to keep.

We did not, of course, dare land anywhere near the Castle. Since there were no legitimate landing areas for the big creatures we could use, we made do with an area more than forty kilometers southwest of the seat of Charon's government and managed to get the big thing back off the ground ourselves.

Our equipment was surprisingly spare. Koril had risked laser pistols, with the understanding that we might have to get rid of them for any number of reasons. We also carried a small store of projectile weapons and ammunition, on which we'd practiced and been checked out at the redoubt's firing ranges long before. Darva never did quite get the art of laser pistol down well, but she was a whiz at the projectile pistols—just the reverse of me. In addition several of us, including Darva, carried that most ancient of weapons, the sword; others carried small but deadly daggers. The burly Kaigh, to my awe and fascination, carried what seemed to be a crossbow, a kind of early weapon I'd only read about but had never seen before.

We carried no papers or documents of any kind. All information had been hypnoed into our minds to save weight and problems. We all wore tough clothing of jungle green, a sort of forest version of the trooper uniforms, Darva's and mine having been specially cut and tailored for our peculiar requirements. Beyond some prepackaged food cakes and canteens, we had nothing else.

On the road we ate mostly by transmutation, a rather fascinating process. Just as Garal had changed fruit punch into acid and Korman had changed it back, so our own sorcs could take almost any vegetable matter in the jungle and make almost anything of it we desired. To this day I'm still not sure if we really were eating transmuted stuff or just leaves and the like we were fooled into believing was the good food it seemed to be. In the end, it probably made no difference. At least our bodies not only accepted the stuff but seemed to make good use of it.

We had two and a half days to reach the Castle, which was easy enough considering the distance involved. Still, the trek was through the rough of the jungle, and not even Darva and I were any longer prepared to feel completely at home there. As we approached the mountains, though, the jungle gave way first to thick forest and then to intermittent groves with bare glades and rocky outcrops. The going was steep, since we could hardly use the known roads, and tough. Much of the open spaces had to be negotiated at night. We had our first practice with Koril's little nocturnal vision spells, but still needed the more natural and nearly perfect night eyes of Ku to keep us from breaking our fool necks.

By the morning of the appointed day, we had made it to the place where we knew we'd be entering the caves. It was a good spot, really. Nearby, through a small grove of trees, was a sheer cliff and we were able to look out on the valley below. From any point we could see the top of the Castle, which looked even more fearsome in person than it did in any pictures.

We settled down to wait for the late afternoon, when the real work would begin. Standing short watches, we tried to get as much sleep as we could. With some interest I noticed that, somehow, Zala hadn't been included in the watch schedule.

I slept in short stretches, but couldn't really relax. I was simply too keyed up, although I knew that was an amateur's problem and wasn't supposed to happen to me. Early in the afternoon, before the start of one of Charon's interminable rains, I wandered down through the grove of trees to the cliffside and looked out, perhaps for the last time, on the landscape below.

And, finally, I saw a tabarwind.

The view across the valley was fifteen, maybe twenty kilometers at worst, although it was obscured by rain. The cloud cover remained above the line of hills on both sides, though, allowing fair visibility with no real resolution of fine detail on the ground. Still, there was no mistaking what I was seeing—I watched it form.

First a small area far off to the east seemed to flash on and off with upper-level lightning. But instead of the intermittent and irregular illumination within the clouds it grew quite regular and very strong, so strong that it was almost as if a bright light was shining in the center of the cloud mass. Still nothing had emerged from the cloud. Then, suddenly, the immediate area began to swirl around. I had seen something of the pattern before, although not with the central globe of increasingly steady light. Tornado, it was called, or sometimes cyclone.

From that bright center in the clouds long fingers of electricity shot down to the ground, and seconds later, reported their arrival to me with a series of loud booms that echoed back and forth across the valley. I couldn't make out much of what was under those bolts, but I felt relieved that it wasn't me.

Now, out of that bright, shining center a funnel shape seemed to emerge, not like a tornado but almost mathematically regular. A conical shape of charged—what?—moving down, surrounded by a maniacal dance of lightning all around. The yellowish cone began to change, darken, take on colors as it reached for and then touched the ground. Reds and oranges and purples swirled within but did not mix.

I could see where the ignorant might ascribe a supernatural power to such a thing. It was a swirl of color and forces, and as I watched, it flattened into an almost cylindrical shape and began to move.

Others, hearing the thunder, came and joined me at my watching place. The storm, although far off, was awesome, and everyone seemed magnetically attracted to its grim, erratic march across the valley. Everyone but Koril.

"I think it's time we went in," he said calmly.

A couple of us turned and looked in surprise at him. "But it's not nearly five yet," I noted.

He nodded. "They won't risk a shuttle landing with tabarwind conditions in the area. The automatic systems will close down completely for the duration so as not to attract the storm. That means no electricity or automatic watchdogs, no landings, nothing. And right now any laser charges are being hauled down the long tunnel away from the Castle. That means we'll be between the charges and the people who can use them, and that's fine with me. The storm's a godsend! Let's move!"

The tabarwind's almost hypnotic effect was hard to leave, but we all understood his urgency. We slipped on our packs and headed for an undistinguished grove of trees some sixty meters from our camp.

"The watch has retreated," Koril said, almost gloating. "That'll make it easy. If we can get past the interior guardpost without being seen we'll be in without a trace."

The roar of the tabarwind sounded very close, and the wind picked up to almost gale force. "Hadn't we better ditch our laser pistols?" Kimil asked nervously.

"I think not," the chief sorcerer replied. "I'm willing to take the risk. With the luck we're having, it just might mean we have 'em and nobody else will."

The spell in the grove was a good one, tightly woven and nearly impossible to detect. Few knew that the Castle had any back entrances and exits in the first place, although nobody builds a fortress without both an escape system and a hidden route of supply. This was one of four such, and the second closest to the Castle itself—but the most direct. The closest in, and most used, of these back doors actually led *away* from the Castle to the underground storerooms in natural caverns in the mountain. Though it would be the easiest to uncover and enter, an enemy force might never find the Castle from there.

Koril and two of our other sorcerers worked quickly on the spell, with a skill and ease I found fascinating and enviable. I might have their potential, but I was a long way from having their skill.

Two of the trees seemed to shrivel, wither before our eyes, then they

bent backward to reveal a solid metal door. Medusan metal, I knew—and
totally inert to us. Both door and lock were beyond our powers, but not
the rock in which the lock was imbedded. I watched as our advance team
of sorcs sent their combined energies into and around the rock, and saw
the *wa* of the rock respond as if it was some living thing, compressing
back from the locking mechanism. In a matter of minutes a hole appeared
on one side of the door large enough for an arm to go through. Koril nodded to himself, walked forward, reached in almost to his elbow, and slid
the door back. We could all see that the locking mechanism also slid back,
still in place. No alarms had been tripped because the lock had not been
tampered with.

Quickly we were inside the tunnel entrance, then waited there as the
door returned to its original position and our wizards replicated the spells
they had broken on the way in, moving the trees and the rock back into
place. A Class 1 sorc could detect the tampering if he was in any way suspicious, but I sure couldn't.

With the door shut, we were suddenly encased in total darkness, but we
were neither blind nor helpless. Ku scampered up the wall and stuck
firmly to the top of the cave. He would travel with us that way and be our
surprise insurance policy. As for us, we could see each other's distinctive
wa—Zala's twin mind was particularly visible—thus providing us with our
own outlines as well as the *wa* in the rock of the cave itself. The sight, un-
complicated by anything visual, was eerie, and useful—but not only to us.
Anyone else could see us, too.

Ku in the lead proceeded slowly about five meters ahead of us. As
silently as possible, in this configuration, we began our walk down that
long, dark tunnel, most attention focused on Ku. Koril took the lead in
our group, Darva remained the last, her attention less on Ku than on Zala,
as agreed. This was, in fact, one of Koril's little master strokes. The
weakest in power, Darva's *wa* was linked immutably to mine. If she saw
anything unusual, she could signal me with a prearranged pinch code. If
anybody tried anything on her, I'd know it immediately, too. Koril, I now
understood, had good reasons for everything he did, including bringing
both Darva and me along.

We rounded a turn in the tunnel and suddenly had some sight—a
flickering torch not in the cave itself but coming from a small room just
off it. Ku was a nervy bastard, I had to give him that much. He scampered
on the cave roof right up to that door, which didn't reach his position, and
peered cautiously in from his upside-down angle. Then, cautiously, he
made his way back to Koril.

"Two troopers," he hissed to Koril in a voice barely audible to me in the
middle of the group. "Repeaters with exploding bullets. Power's still off."

Koril nodded to him and appeared to be satisfied. Then, as Ku went on
ahead once again, the man who used to own both cave and troopers
stepped forward, almost to the open door itself, and raised his hands in
what I knew was a power gesture. He seemed immobile, frozen but majes-

tic, and yet the index finger of his outstretched right hand wriggled, telling us to proceed.

One at a time, as silently as we could, we approached Koril, then the door, then passed it, walking right under Ku. We could see the two men in the room, looking bored and occasionally glancing up at some device beyond our gaze. Neither seemed to notice us.

Once Darva was past, Koril himself finally moved, retaining his outstretched form and moving first sideways, then back to the far cave wall, past the door, under Ku, and to the rest of us waiting on the other side. Only then did he relax, move forward, and allowing Ku to go ahead once again, he led us down the tunnel and around another curve, back into the darkness once again. There was no need to explain what he had done. We all knew he had maintained the illusion of peace, quiet, and no intruders for the two men while we all passed.

We continued another forty or fifty meters when the cave opened up into a large, circular area—an obvious junction point. The trouble was, once you stepped into it the *wa* glowed brightly all around, indicating solid rock. We couldn't even tell where we'd entered. This, then, was the first of the maze traps, and a very good one it was.

The tunnel system had the intricate workings of a circuit diagram, as I knew from my earlier sessions with the diagrams and floor plans. It would be obvious to anyone getting this far that the solidness of the chamber was a blind, but you had no real clue as to which opening to take, even if you found it. Of the five tunnels that actually fed into the place, only one led towards the Castle. Another, of course, led back the way we had come. The other three were laced with very nasty traps and ultimately led to storage areas away from the Castle itself.

I slipped back to Darva. "How're you holding up?" I whispered.

"Fine, except I feel like I have to pee," she responded just as quietly. I patted her comfortingly and retook my position.

Koril looked around, then urged us back and again stretched out his arms. He began to turn, slowly, for more than a minute, making three complete circles before he stopped. Finally he said, in a very low voice, "Somebody very good's done a nice job. They're all badly booby-trapped, and they've added a new cross-tunnel about ten meters out. Okay—follow me closely and *don't* get ahead of me. Ku, no more than a couple meters at a time."

With that he made his decision, pointed his finger, and some of the *wa* to his left dissolved a bit. He walked cautiously through it, allowed Ku to go on, then waited for the rest of us. The *wa* curtain, made of some thin strands of something or other that simulated rock but were easily penetrable, slid back into place.

Slowly, cautiously, we reformed and started down the new path. After only two or three meters, though, Koril gestured for us to stop.

"Dumb shits," Koril mumbled. "They ought to know better than to use offworlder traps." He pointed to the floor, and we all could sense what he meant. All around us was *wa*—in us, in the walls, floor, and roof. Everything shone with its distinctive *wa* pattern—except an area four meters long that ran the width of the cave on the floor right in front of Koril. Inert matter meant Medusan metal, and its very lack of any sight, including *wa*, outlined it perfectly.

Ku needed no prompting; he was already on the roof of the cave and working. I saw a small laser drill snap into place, and, soon after, he was affixing a ring to the roof with an instant-bonding cement. Darva and I, being the largest, carried the miscellaneous packs, and she was already ahead of me. The rope, made from some really nasty jungle vines in Koril's shops, tested out at over 500 kilos. For our sake I hoped it still did.

Kindel was nearest me, and I whispered to her, "What would we do without Ku?"

"Why, we'd turn another of us into something like him," she replied matter-of-factly.

"Oh," was all I could manage, and turned back to watch the work. The system was simple enough—grab the rope and swing across the pressure-sensitive floor plate to the other side. It wasn't quite as easy as all that though—the roof of the cave was less than three meters high, while the plate was four across. Since the rope couldn't touch the plate, that meant you needed good speed and a slight jump at the end. It would be tricky indeed.

It was a nervous eternity as each of us made our crossing, but we were all trained professionals. We had only one close call, and no other problems. I made it very easily, almost to my surprise, and the thought struck me that, if Kira were a double agent, primed to betray us, she could do so very convincingly now. She didn't, though, demonstrating that nice timing and power she tried so hard to hide.

In fact, only the tiny Kindel needed several swings until she felt confident enough to let go, and, even then, only fast action by Ku overhead pushed her the last few precious centimeters.

We all waited while Ku used his little laser tool to cut the knot and retrieve the rope, then return, cut off and bring back the ring also. Again, anyone who passed by would have to be looking for something to find any sign that we had been here.

Much of the rest of the tunnel was arranged with other traps, some easier to spot than others. A few were actually powered and thus not active, but most were basic, mechanical types that were bad enough. Each caused a little heart trouble but each had its answer in our packs, and none deterred us.

We found countless blind junctions too, and in each we had to rely on Koril's old experience and the probing sense of the top sorcs. Approaching one, though, we were held up by Koril from entering. We had reached areas close to the Castle—and now we were going to face the real problems.

For one thing, *this* junction had traffic; a fair amount by the sound of it.

Troopers and maintenance personnel pushing dollies of various things to
and fro, or so it seemed. There was never a lag of more than a minute or
so between such sounds, hardly enough time to enter, determine the right
path, and move on through.

Koril was still deeply in thought when the power returned. A band of
light came alive all up and down the corridors, illuminating us dimly but
completely—and illuminating the junction as well. We moved quickly
back into the tunnel, just in time to miss four red-clad people emerging
from another tunnel mouth on the run, pushing a large yellow cart filled
with cases of something or other across the open space, and into another
opening. They never glanced in our direction.

"Well, we made it a lot farther than I thought, thanks to the tabarwind," Koril sighed. "Now the real fun begins. We're less than fifty meters from the bottom floor of the Castle right now. These tunnels lead to
the art storage rooms, the precious metals rooms, and the like. That one to
the right, there, at two o'clock, leads to the Castle." He stopped, and we
all froze as yet another team came through, this time with what sounded
like a powered vehicle of some kind. As the last sounds were receding, he
continued.

"The booby traps have got to be down by now. I'm not sure anybody
ever expected anyone to get this far undetected. I'm not sure I ever did.
I've had an education in security myself these past hours. Now, I know
you're all tired but we have to push on. I'm sure all this fuss is over the attack that has surely been launched by now, and all hell is breaking loose.
That means they'll be coming up or down here any moment now. We
can't stay here and we can't go on. I think—"

Just as he said that last a small powered tractor towing a trailer entered
the junction point, paused a moment, then turned our way and started
right toward us.

Pistols were out in a moment, and Koril hardly had time to hiss "Don't
miss!" as the thing chugged into view. There were only two people in the
cab, both dressed in maintenance red. We shot them so fast I can't even
describe what they looked like. In another moment Ku dropped from the
roof into the open cab, kicked the corpses out of the way, and brought the
tractor to a stop.

"Quickly!" Koril said. "Park. Darva. Kaigh. You're the biggest and
strongest. Get those crates off this thing!"

We hustled to do as instructed. The damned things were heavy, but not
beyond any two of us, and we had them off the trailer and to the side of
the little chugging train in a couple of minutes. During that time we nervously ignored other traffic sounds behind us. We were just far enough
around the bend, we hoped, not to be noticed—unless somebody else
wanted to come up our way.

Koril wasted no time on sorcery. He opened his laser pistol to wide scan
and disintegrated the crates to white powder, taking the risk that the electronic springlike sound would be unheard or obscured by traffic noise.

Quickly we climbed into the back trailer. Ku then stuck the small service cab into reverse, backed out carefully into the junction point, made the turn, then moved into the tunnel that headed for the Castle. We never knew what was in those crates.

Ku drove like a madman and hardly hesitated when we approached some troopers and maintenance personnel on foot. To my surprise they just stepped against the wall and let us by without a glance. A little further on, we passed a similar tractor going the other way. Ku waved, so did the red-clad driver of the other vehicle, and we passed with a few centimeters to spare.

Koril laughed out loud. "The fools! They figure we're troopers. Well, we are! Weapons at the ready! This is gonna get hairy in a minute!"

With that, we entered the bottom floor of the Castle, a huge open area supported by rock pillars. Hundreds of men and women clad in red or black were there, and a number of vehicles and trailers were about.

We pulled in between some painted lines on the floor and Ku brought us to a stop. Koril, brimming with confidence, winked. "Now I'll show you why bureaucracy is so evil." He jumped down, holstered his pistol, and walked briskly towards a gold-braided black-clad trooper, an officer of some kind and by his *wa* a powerful man.

The former Lord of the Diamond walked right up to him, started talking to him, and the trooper nodded, then pointed and said something back. Koril saluted and returned to us, hardly suppressing a grin. "Okay—out! We don't have to walk up. We're going to take Lift 4."

A little numbly we complied, and followed him across the busy floor to the doors of a huge open lift. I wasn't used to such a primitive device, but remembered that Koril had said these were moved by counterweight, not by any electrical power. They had to be—otherwise in a power outage they would be useless.

We stood there, looking about nervously, not quite believing what we were doing and feeling we stuck out like a sore thumb in our green uniforms. I couldn't stand it any more than the rest, and eased up to Koril. "All right—how the hell did you manage this?"

He smiled and winked. "I just walked up to the chief operations officer there, told him we were a special security patrol ordered to defensive positions, and asked him for the quickest way to our station."

"And he told you?"

"Sure. Why not?"

I wasn't the only one shaking my head in wonder as the big lift descended, stopped, and form-fitted itself neatly into the indentation for it in the floor. There were a number of hand carts on it, mostly empty, with security troopers and maintenance personnel on them, all of whom paid us no mind whatsoever. I admit, though, that at least I, and almost certainly most of us, were close to being nervous wrecks at this point. Still, this was just the sort of stunt I might improvise if this were *my* old stamping grounds. I knew that our greatest danger until we got off wasn't from these faceless men and women but from somebody's nerve springing in our group and giving us away.

When the lift was cleared we stepped uneasily on, only to find that several troopers also came up, pushing carts with cases of what looked like ammunition for the projectile weapons and, possibly, laser pistol power packs. No sooner were they on than a loud gong sounded overhead, and we started up, one floor at a time. The system was obviously designed for slow ascent and descent. It would stop on every floor no matter what.

The next floor, and most of the others, were not open spaces like the warehouse level but instead opened on access corridors that went down a few meters, then branched off to the right and left. Security guards were visible on each level, wearing special color-coded passes which, I was acutely and suddenly aware, we did *not* have.

The troopers with us didn't seem to notice, but when one cart got off at the fifth level the security men *did* check badges. At the seventh level when the rest exited, badges were given an even greater scrutiny. Alone and rising, I shouted to Koril, "Badges!"

He nodded and patted his pistol in its holster. It was pretty clear that we'd have to take his lead and use brute force—and, once we did, all hell would break loose. As we cleared Level 9 he whispered, "Draw weapons and shoot as soon as you're able!"

At Level 10, the topmost point you could go on these lifts without full security clearance, eight armed security guards waited for us with very ugly-looking projectile weapons. Even if they didn't suspect us, and they probably did, they would be ready to shoot anyone on the lift at the slightest provocation.

As our heads came up over the floor and into the clear, I shouted, "Wait! Don't shoot!" The guards naturally hesitated at that, and that was all we needed. As our shoulders cleared we opened wide rapid fire with the laser pistols. None of them had a chance against such concentrated fire.

"Everybody off—fast!" Koril shouted. "When they don't give the go-ahead signal this thing'll drop like a stone!" We needed no other urging; the last of us was off before the lift leveled with the floor—and just in time, too. Apparently the guards above had the locking mechanism, and with no guard to throw it the big platform rumbled and dropped immediately from view.

Kaigh looked back at the gaping hole and shook his head. "Close." We all turned our attention back to Koril, who was looking around critically.

Finally he said, "This is the primary guard floor for the upper levels. There'll be some fifty, sixty people here even if the rest were drawn off by the outside attack. I doubt, though, if we could walk through to the main stair without getting slaughtered. Park, Darva, Kira—stay in the middle of our circle. No firing even if fired upon. Bluff, bravado, and conventional weapons will no longer get us anywhere."

We knew what he meant and quickly formed up, allowing the sorcs to surround us. But neither Darva nor I put down our weapons. In the last analysis, something was better than nothing. Still, we'd gone through this procedure, and for now, I was certainly willing to let the pros do what they did best. What bothered me most was that what they were going to do was form an actual circle as we moved. Should anyone in the circle fall, breaking contact, one of us would have to complete the connection and quickly. Otherwise, instead of the pooled power of the highly trained Class 1 sorcs assembled by Koril, there would be only individuals—possibly capable of protecting themselves, but hardly me.

The circle was formed quickly, but we didn't start right away. The concentration required to link the *wa* of so many powerful minds was enormous. Darva, Kira, and I looked around nervously, and I know they were wondering why our unseen enemy hadn't charged. I could see why with no difficulty. The entry corridor dead-ended about twenty meters in, and you had to turn either right or left. From the diagrams I knew we had to go left to get to where we had to go—and so would any defenders. With the lift behind us, troopers on all lower floors, and safety seals in place above, we couldn't retreat, not even climb up or down, nor could we remain for long or that lift would return with really nasty goodies just for us. Any defender would naturally prefer to stake out a route of inevitable march by an invader than attack in this confined space, where we had good shots ourselves.

"The *wa* is one," Koril chanted. "The *wa* is one." The others repeated the chant, again and again, until they were all in sync. It was eerie. Still, we'd all seen Tully Kokul, a mere 4 or 5, shrug off laser pistol shots aimed directly at him. This was an infinitely more powerful group—the combined wills and power of the best Charon had to offer outside of the Synod. In fact, I realized, this was exactly what the Synod itself was, and why these sorcs were here. They would be the new Synod—if we survived a wall of bullets and who knew what else and then reached the Synod itself, one floor above and almost certainly waiting.

Even I could sense the enormous power of the circle Koril and the others had created. All around us was a wall of *wa*, acting magnetically. We would see how well it repelled—for we started to move.

Troopers were waiting for us down both halls, of course. As soon as we turned left, then right again to walk together in very tight quarters, the troops from the wing on the right moved in behind us. They were cool and quite professional, I had to give them that. They let us get ten meters or more down that long, seventy-meter straight path, before they opened up. Both Darva and I froze for a moment when they did, and almost killed us all—for the circle kept moving, steadily, as it had to.

Enough of those primitive but deadly missiles were fired from remote positions and from gun stations along the hallway that paint flew, hundreds of holes seemed to appear all around in the walls, and the air seemed to grow almost solid. Yet, as we continued to move, not a single one seemed able to strike us, either directly or by ricochet.

The circle, acting as one, stopped about halfway; the others were in a trancelike state, seemingly oblivious to the horror that was being unleashed on us. No matter what, none of the three of us in the middle could keep from flinching and ducking, and it took a mighty amount of will power to just stand there, and try and match the motions or lack of them that the sorcerers' circle made.

The reason they stopped was soon clear. A massive wall of *wa*-force emerged from the circle and reached out in all directions from us. It was an almost blinding, overwhelming sense of force and power, more power than I had ever felt before in anything or anybody. It was almost a living thing, like that tabarwind, but totally invisible to any who could not sense the *wa*. It struck out at those with the weapons in an ever-widening circle, touched those weapons and controlled them.

Sometime I will work out the physics of what they did, but basically they did to the weapons what would have happened to Darva and me had we immediately tried to significantly reduce our mass after my final transformation. The reaction was similar, with much heat being generated— and in projectile weapons the ammunition always has an explosive charge.

One by one, as the force met them and took hold, those weapons started blowing up. Troopers screamed in pain, and several came charging right at us in blind fury, hoping to break the circle by sheer physical force. Our own weapons had not been affected. Picking our shots carefully and going between the shoulders of the sorc circle, we calmly shot the hell out of those attackers. There weren't very many after the first batch from front and rear. To make sure we wouldn't have any spell problems, we all used laser weapons. At this range, even Darva couldn't miss, and she seemed particularly proud of herself as she gave me a wink and a big grin. I glanced over at Kira, who was all grim and businesslike. Well, to hell with her. What good was it to be good at something if you couldn't enjoy your work?

We started moving once again, but we were all ready for it now. We inside the circle kept a clear line of fire, though, not only because of the threat of more hall attacks but also because we'd have to pass some of the gun stations and offices. From that close, a man could physically hurl himself into the circle.

Nobody did, though. We reached an abandoned gun platform at the base of a wide set of stairs. Wide—but not wide enough to accommodate a circle our size, and steep enough so that we couldn't really see much of anything on the next floor. Whoever designed this place had put a lot of thought into it.

I reached into my pack and brought out four small silvery globes, each with a thin metal band around its middle. Almost as if on an unspoken command, the circle broke and the sorcs took up the defensive positions at the end of the hall which, until a few moments ago, had been occupied by troopers—in some cases they had to push still smoldering bodies out of the way. At almost the same moment a trooper came down the stairs, opening fire. I heard some yells, but Kira acted with blinding speed and sliced the man almost in two. He collapsed in a bloody heap and fell to the base of the stairs.

Without looking back at casualties, I rushed to the bottom of the stairs, twisted the ring on the first globe, and threw it underhanded to the top. Without waiting, I did the same for the second. The first went off before I could manage the third. It produced such a bang and shock wave I was almost knocked over. I took no chances, throwing number three before the second went off, and number four immediately after I'd regained my balance. Only then did I look around.

Class 1 sorcs or not, they were human beings and they had been startled and surprised by the gunman. Kaigh was certainly dead, and Krugar was clutching her bloody side near her right hip. Now we were seven—down to four good sorcs, but what the hell else could we do?

We had already delayed too long for the concussion grenades to be one hundred percent effective, and we had to press on. It was Kira, who started the run up the stairs, and we had no choice but to abandon Krugar and charge up behind her, all weapons drawn. The only optimistic thing I could think about at this point was, well, at least the place wasn't sealed enough to permit a gas trap.

I half expected Kira to be gone by the time I made the next floor, but there she was, two more dead troopers at her feet. We were still theoretically three floors from Aeolia Matuze—if she was there at all—but we were now beyond the security cordon and into the offices, living quarters, and labs of the Synod and top bureaucrats.

The eleventh floor resembled a hotel complex with all the doors shut tight. Nice, modern, comfortable—and because these were offices and quarters, it wasn't really possible to tell what was what. They changed a lot, as would be expected.

Koril paused to take a breather. "Krugar is in good enough shape to try some self-repair and maybe hold off anybody coming at us from below," he said between puffs. "Whew! I'm not as young as I used to be, that's for sure." He sighed. "Well, I'm not worried about troopers anymore. I think we can probably walk straight down this hall with no problems—but shoot anything that moves anyway."

"You don't think they'll make any more attempts?" I asked him worriedly.

He shook his head. "They know that anybody who can get this far is no slouch. No. Any members of the Synod here will have retreated to the thirteenth floor reception area. They'll be waiting for us there."

I looked at the others. "Are you and the other three enough?"

He shrugged. "Depends on how many are there and who they are. We've been damned lucky so far. Let's hope our luck holds out."

It was preparedness, the training of the sorcs, and a lot of inside information as well as skill and brass that had brought us this far, but in the end Koril was right. We *had* been lucky, too. He was certainly right, also, about the rest of the way. None of those doors opened, and we were unobstructed in our walk to the eleventh and twelfth floors. We could all hear, though, the floors below being occupied as soon as we left. *They* had the lift system, after all. They just didn't want to shoot up the official quarters. The troopers had already failed—now it was up to their bosses. In one sense, I suspected that the troopers, particularly the officers, were now very much on our side. If we failed, their own failures would have to be accounted for to those very same bosses. No, I decided, for that reason more than any other, they'd stay out of the rest of this fight.

Koril paused at the bottom of the stairway to the thirteenth level. "All right—Ku, Kimil, Kindel, stick close to me. You know what you must do. The rest of you follow us up, but stay out of it. None of your weapons will mean much now."

We understood what he meant. Our part was at least theoretically finished. All we could do was needlessly guard the back door.

Koril took in a deep breath, let it out slowly, then turned and started slowly up the stairs. One by one the sorcs followed him, then Kira, Darva, and myself. I don't know what I was expecting to see at the top, but it wasn't a sumptuously furnished empty room.

The large chamber was entirely crimson. The ancient-looking chairs upholstered in some silken material were ornamented with metal studs of a bright golden color that were inlaid in the dark native woods; the tables were equally antique and polished to a mirrorlike sheen. The carpet, too, was crimson, although of some thick, plush hair that the *wa* said was not native to Charon. In the center was a golden path, marked by two golden stripes of colored cloth woven into the rest and leading up to a raised platform. The platform itself was almost like a stage, with a huge wooden throne in the center of the same polished material and upholstered in the same deep red, but this time encrusted with what looked like—and turned out to be—enormous precious stones from all over the known galaxy. Two slightly smaller and more recessed but similar chairs flanked the big one. Behind the whole thing, eleven similar chairs were arranged in a permanent semi-circle. The entire stage area was decorated with gold-embroidered crimson drapes, hanging loosely around the back and tied back at the front.

We all stood there gazing about the room. I couldn't suppress a low whistle. "Like something out of an ancient fairy tale," I remarked.

Koril looked around, his eyes ablaze. "More power than those ancient kings had is represented here," he responded seriously. "This is the seat of Charon's government. I used to sit on that throne, remember. I *know*." That wistful, almost dreamlike quality left his voice. "She's redecorated since I left, though. In a way it's too bad. I had some great works of art looted from the Confederacy's top museums on those draped walls. Still, all in all, it's a nice touch."

"Skip the interior decoration comments," Kira broke in. "Where the hell's the enemy?"

At that moment I detected slight movement behind the thrones, and I saw Kira's laser pistol come up. Koril quickly forced her hand down. "No use in burning the place down—unless you have to," he told her. "You can't harm these with that toy."

From behind the chairs five shapes emerged. All wore gold-embroidered robes of that same crimson as the room, and all wore scarlet hoods as well. They looked eerie and impressive, as they were supposed to.

Koril smiled a bit and with a flick of the wrist beckoned his three associate sorcs together in line, hands linked.

The figures walked out to the front of the stage and stood there, also in a line but not touching one another. Three of the five were women. One was Korman I saw—the only familiar face. None looked particularly worried.

"Just the five of you?" Koril said pleasantly. "I'm shocked."

"More than enough for the lot of *you*," Korman responded for the group. "We don't spend quite as much time here as we did in your day, Tulio. We don't have to." With that, all five levitated a meter or so above the stage and moved out just beyond it. All of us gasped at this, for we all realized it was no Warden trick. They were really doing it.

"Parlor tricks, Dieter?" Koril scoffed. "I thought we were beyond *that*."

"No parlor trick," one of the women answered him. "We are not as you knew us, Tulio. We are immortal, as powerful in body as in *wa*, with minds clearer than your merely human minds could ever be."

"So *that's* how she kept your allegiance," Koril responded. "With the new model alien robot bodies. You serve her now because you are *programmed* to serve! No longer humans—but mere machines."

"We are not 'mere machines,' Tulio," Korman replied. "I'll admit I have never heard 'programmed' used as a curseword before, but you are wrong. We were among those who freely chose to throw you out, Tulio. Freely. And none of us has ever regretted it. Should we choose, we could leave this place. Really leave, Tulio. The *wa* within us dies as it would in you, but leaves us alive and whole—and more than human."

"May we—examine those fancy new clothes of yours?" Koril asked, and all of us understood that he didn't mean literally.

"Go ahead. We can fool any scanner, rig any test—but look at us as we really are. Be our guest, Tulio—and the rest of you. You are powerful ones indeed to have come this far. But no tricks."

Koril had a pained expression. "Would I insult your intelligence?" With that, all four of them reached out their Warden senses to the five who still floated, impossibly, in the air.

"You see our superiority," Korman continued, not so much bragging as being rather matter of fact about it all. "You are a good man, Tulio. You served Charon well and the Brethren before that. Don't you see that the revolution is *now?* Are you so old and blind and prejudiced that you can't realize that your ideals can become reality now—out there? With you?"

They were very, very confident, I thought. Almost unsettlingly so, yet I also understood that this sort of overconfidence can kill you. I had no idea what Koril had up his sleeve at this point, but I motioned to Darva and we edged away toward a far wall, well away from the area between the two groups of sorcs. Suddenly I had a thought, and leaned over and whispered to her, "See that alcove to the left of the stage? I bet that goes up to You-Know-Who."

She nodded. "Seems likely. When do you want to try for it?"

"Good girl. But not until they've started doing whatever they're doing. They'll probably ignore us—I hope. We're certainly no threat to them."

"I'll follow your lead," she whispered, and we turned back to watch whatever was going to happen.

"Well, Tulio?" Korman was saying. "It's yours. It's for all four of you, in fact. Immortal, superior bodies—free to escape this prison. Free to run an empire."

Koril smiled. "So it's an empire now, is it? And who would I be in this? Lord—or preprogrammed servant?"

Korman shrugged. "Your old position is, of course, already taken. But you would lead the Synod, as a matter of course. You never really liked being Lord anyway."

Koril sighed. "That's true enough. And yet I feel I cannot take your offer for two reasons. I do not trust those alien friends of yours as much as you do—though I'm sure I would once I got my new, improved body. Without a guarantee you cannot give, that of an unmolested mind, I can hardly accept. And, as for the second reason—do you remember Jatik?"

Korman looked puzzled, then brightened for a moment. "Of course. Little weasel of a man. Sorc for Diamond Rock. As bizarre a psychopath as we've ever had here on Charon. Killed in the desert, if I remember."

Koril nodded. "Killed coming to me. But he made his report, Dieter, before he died. He saw those friends of yours, those aliens. Tell me, Dieter—what would a man like that find so terrifying that he would brand it pure evil? It is a question that has troubled me, and driven me on, these past several years. More than anything, it's why I'm here."

Korman laughed. "Evil? The Lord of Satan, Agent of the Destroyer asks *me* about evil? What would that little psycho know about evil, anyway? Different, yes—incredibly so. Alien in many senses of that word. But *evil?* The former Lord of the Diamond, Lord of the Most Sacred Order of Brethren talks of *evil?*" And again he laughed.

"Now!" Koril yelled. At that moment all laughing stopped as a wall of Warden force at least the equal of what I had seen below lashed out with blinding speed right at Korman. Taken aback, he had only a simple shield himself and so he burst into flame before our very eyes, flame so intense I could not bear to look at it.

The others, less intent on Koril's speech and less confident than their leader of their own powers—after all, all of them hadn't been able to kill Koril alone the last time, or even keep him prisoner—struck back. Ignoring the flaming Korman, who toppled to the floor and continued melting into an acrid puddle, each of *our* sorcs took on the four remaining head to head.

I wasn't sure how they had managed to melt a robot of the type that had penetrated Military Systems Command and outsmarted all the Confederacy's best security devices, but I wasn't about to stay around and ask questions. I moved slowly and cautiously towards that alcove, and Darva followed. We were, as we had hoped, totally ignored.

Still, I stopped when we reached the alcove and looked back. It was no longer just *wa* being traded, willpower against willpower. The Synod sorcs were coming straight on, but the four, under Koril's direction, began twisting, turning, forming a careful mathematical pattern. Such was its nature and intricacy that it actually began disturbing the air between the two sets of antagonists. Incredibly I saw ripples there, then crackles of real, visible energy—electrical bolts forming and shooting, at first randomly and then *laterally.*

"Oh, by the gods! They're creating their own tabarwind!" Darva exclaimed.

"Let's get the hell out of here!" I responded, and we ducked into the alcove.

Frankly, the place didn't match the exterior. It was dark and dank and smelly. There were all sorts of pieces of furniture and stuff as well as controls for the curtains and whatever else was in the room. Still, far in back was indeed a service corridor which ran in one direction to a lift, clearly visible. Obviously the service entrance. We picked the other direction, as roars and howls of thunder and the crackle of raw energy sounded behind us. What was happening in that room back there would have been the sight of a lifetime—but it would almost certainly have ended ours.

Sure enough, at the end of the corridor a wooden stair led upward. We both hesitated at the bottom, then Darva looked at me. "Where's Kira or Zala or whatever the hell she is?"

I shook my head. "I don't know. I didn't really notice. Back there, I suppose. Hell, forget her—now." I took the lead and walked slowly and carefully up the stairs, laser pistol drawn.

I reached the top, stopped, and waited for Darva. I don't know quite who or what I expected up there, but it sure as hell wasn't Yatek Morah.

CHAPTER SIXTEEN

Twists and Turns

Darva fired before I could stop her, but Morah merely shrugged off the shots and dissipated the energy harmlessly. He was still dressed as I remembered him—in his black trooper uniform, although he had added a red-lined cape of the same material. His eyes were still bizarre and almost impossible to look at.

"Put away those things," he told us, gesturing at the pistols. "They are of no use here—and there is no need for them."

I sighed and holstered mine. Darva, uncertain, did the same. I looked at him, then at Darva, and sized up the situation. "Does 'Darkquest' mean anything to you?"

Darva looked blank, but Morah actually chuckled. "Now where'd you learn *that* little phrase?"

"I'm it. Park Lacoch. The same boy Korman threw to the wolves a year ago."

Morah sounded genuinely amused. "And of what use is that information to me now? I already know the true nature of Embuay, and I also know the location of Koril's base."

"That may be true, but it's not my problem," I responded casually. "I was given a job to do, and the first chance I got I did it."

That comment, and my calm manner, seemed to give him pause. "You may be right at that."

"Look—I could've taken the safe way out at Bourget, but I didn't. I deliberately got myself caught and wound up a changeling. Whether or not you no longer need the information, it says something about me, I think. I've paid a pretty high price to be just a redundancy."

Darva looked at me strangely. "What the hell are you talking about?"

"Sorry, honey. I'm a bottom-line pragmatist. I'll explain it all to you later. Let's just say Morah and I aren't necessarily the opponents we might seem to be."

She looked at Morah with obvious distaste. "Your girl Zala sure wasn't any help to you, you know."

Morah nodded, and I felt a little relieved that she was at least going along with me for now.

"It *is* true that the girl's been something of a disappointment so far," the Chief of Security admitted. "Is she with you?"

"Back there—someplace," I told him. "We didn't exactly want to stick around for the fireworks."

"Yes, well, I can understand that," he responded, sounding a little nervous and preoccupied. "How many are down there?"

"Koril and three others, all damned good," I told him truthfully. "Plus your girl, of course, if she survived all that."

"Hmmm . . . Yes. I see . . ."

He looked and sounded worried, and it gave me no end of satisfaction to see such emotions in him. His appearance, manner, and those damnable eyes all carried such an air of overwhelming power that I would have sworn he was above such things.

"How come you aren't down helping out your fellow—whatevers?" Darva asked, sensing the same thing.

"I am not required to," he said simply. "I am not on the Synod."

"*What!* But Koril said—" I began, but he cut me short.

"I told you before I was Chief of Security. I just did not tell you *whose* security."

"Oh, gods!" Darva breathed. "He's working directly for *them!*"

Morah cocked his head. "The battle is over downstairs," he told us matter-of-factly. "We are about to have visitors. I suggest we three all go into that room over there and remain *very* silent."

I hesitated a moment. "Who won?"

"If the Synod had won, we wouldn't have to get into this room, now would we?"

That was good enough for me. I followed him. Darva, shrugging, did the same. I knew she was still trying to figure out which side we were on now. As for me, I was trying to figure out Morah's motives in all this. Clearly, as chief representative of the aliens on Charon, it was in his best interest to keep Matuze on her throne. Yet, here we were, about to let Koril have her.

There wasn't time for questions, though; we barely got the door closed when we heard somebody slowly mounting that final stairway. The newcomer sounded tired, perhaps weak and wounded, but he came steadily on. One man. One only. I knew who it had to be.

We heard him pause at the top of the stairs, and I could visualize him looking around cautiously. Finally, he walked past our door and away from us, his footsteps receding.

I turned to Morah. "You're letting him have her."

"Perhaps. Perhaps not. But—wait!"

A second, quieter tread could be heard on the stairs. Whoever it was was far lighter and more cautious than the first. We held our breaths a moment, then Morah let out a small sigh and beckoned us back in the room. On the far side was a rather pretty landscape of some world I'd never seen. He pressed a neatly hidden stud on it and the painting moved down silently revealing a one-way mirror.

It was a huge, comfortable living room, beautifully furnished and with good use of open space. Sculpture and paintings were around as well, and

I clearly recognized some as lost art treasures of man's past. Originals, too, I knew instinctively.

Sitting on a divan, dressed casually in slacks, sandals, and a purple sleeveless shirt, was Aeolia Matuze. Unmistakably Matuze, looking every bit as good as her pictures. Very casually relaxed, legs crossed, she was smoking a cigarette in a long holder. She looked neither worried nor apprehensive.

"I assume this is soundproof?" I said in a low tone to Morah.

He nodded. "Absolutely. But I have a one way mike connection in."

"She looks awfully good for her age," I noted. "Robot?"

"Oh, no. Spell. I don't think we're quite ready for a robot Lord of the Diamond as yet."

"Why not just make everybody robots?" Darva said acidly. "That would make your job obsolete."

"You misunderstand our motives," Morah replied, shaking off the sarcastic tone. "The robots are weapons, and, in a sense, bribes; but they have their limitations as well. As weapons and bribes, they are valuable for the superior abilities they give. But they are sure death for a people and a civilization because of what they take away. Someday, perhaps, you will understand that. But—watch."

"Do you know what's gonna happen?" Darva asked him.

He shook his head from side to side. "Not the slightest idea. But it should be—interesting. You see, those entire quarters are wa-inert. Not only is there no wa in anything, the chemical treatment dampens out any wa sense you might have. It is quite a complex treatment and has to be—imported, if you understand."

I nodded. "That's why you don't have it all over this place."

"That, and the fact that it's very hard to manufacture and doesn't work with many surfaces. Still—here we go."

Aeolia Matuze leaned forward and flicked some ashes into an ornate standing ash tray, then turned toward the door to our right. A figure entered, a figure only recognizable with effort.

His clothing was scorched, and his face—all his exposed skin—was blackened as if by prolonged desert exposure. He was a terrible, and terrifying sight. He stood there in the doorway unsteadily, and stared at the woman.

Aeolia Matuze looked up in surprise. "Toolie! Oh, you *poor* dear! Whatever did they *do* to you?"

"It's been a long time, Aeolia," said Tulio Koril wearily.

"Oh, my! Come! Sit down in a chair and relax! Can I get you a drink or anything?"

We were dumbfounded by the scene, but Koril just chuckled dryly. "Got some of that wine? The good white?"

She stood up, went over to a small bar, reached behind, took out a bottle, opened it, and poured him a large glass; then she took it over to him.

He accepted it, drank some in big gulps, then slowly sipped it. It *did* seem to relax him.

Aeolia Matuze sat back on the couch so she was pretty well facing him, then just watched him. She showed no fear, no shock, or horror at her predecessor's visit, which of course implied that either there was something we didn't know going on or, at the very least, something Koril sure as hell didn't. I remembered Morah's comment that, in there, both of them were equals in *wa*, having none at all.

Aeolia Matuze looked genuinely concerned. "Tell me—the burns. Do they hurt much?"

He shrugged. "Not so bad. More stiff than anything else. I think I'm still in a little bit of shock, but it's nothing I can't handle."

She nodded and appeared satisfied. "You know, I loved you for years, but never more than today. What you did was impossible, Toolie. No other man alive could have made it up here."

"You knew I'd come back."

She nodded. "I knew that if anybody could, you would. Tell me, how did you get by the Synod? They could rip iron bars, shoot into space—why, you wouldn't believe it. And they still had all their powers!"

"That was your problem," Koril told her, taking another sip of wine. "If they didn't keep their *wa* power, they were valueless as Synod members. If they did, then they had to have the *wa* in their molecules as sure as you and me. And *wa* is *wa*."

"But they are virtually impervious!"

He chuckled. "Know what we're made of, Aeolia? Chemicals. Know what rock is made of? More chemicals. The rule is that if you're matter you have to be made of *something*. Chemicals. A specific mix of chemicals. And once you know how something's put together, and you know there's *wa* in each molecule; that stuff, whatever it was, was no different than natural flesh. No different. And I happened to have a sample of the stuff ahead of time. I had it analyzed. It actually surprised me. The movement of just one little atom in its basic material caused it to change into another equally bizarre substance—but one that burned and melted quite nicely. Isn't it nice, Aeolia, to know that even sorcery is nothing more than basic chemistry?"

She laughed, seemingly delighted with his explanation. "How clever of you! I'll bet the reception room's a mess."

"It'll need a little more than mere redecorating," he agreed. "At least I'm happy now you got those paintings out of there."

Darva shook her head wonderingly. "They're talking like they're old buddies! Wasn't he here to *kill* her?"

"Perhaps," Morah replied. "But they were married for twenty-seven years."

Both Darva's and my own mouth flew open but no sound came out.

". . . two left alive down there," Koril was saying. "They're in worse shape than I am. They're backstage, but I told them not to come up just yet."

Matuze looked satisfied. "Tell me, Toolie—why now? I thought you'd be stuck forever down there in your desert hideaway, particularly with all those *delicious* toys we allowed to get through."

That startled the sorcerer. "Allowed?"

She smiled sweetly. "Toolie! Who knows you better than I do? Do you *really* think you could have gotten all that stuff from offworld all this time without our help? It was far cheaper and easier to keep you occupied at what you love best than to try any all-out fight. In a few more months' time, your return would have been academic anyway. Our delicious little war is well underway."

Koril looked absolutely devastated by the obvious truth of what she was telling him. He had as much as admitted his failings to me. I now more than suspected that Dumonia had caught onto the plot and that had been why he'd finally decided to push. But Koril wasn't about to mention the Cerberan, I'll give him that.

"It has to do with evil, Aeolia. Evil."

She laughed. "*Evil?* What in the *world* are you talking about?"

And, once more, he repeated the words that seemed to have haunted him since they were first uttered by the hapless Jatik.

She listened intently, but without any obvious reaction. Finally, when he'd completed his story, she said, "That's the most utter and complete nonsense I've ever heard! They're—odd—I admit, but they're not *evil*. What *is* evil, anyway, except somebody's arbitrary idea of what's wrong? Isn't that what you fought the Confederacy about? Aren't *our* ideas evil by everyone else's standards? Do *you* feel evil, Toolie? I don't."

But Koril did not reply. Slowly he seemed to stiffen, then relax. The wineglass dropped from his fingers and bounced on the rug, spilling a little of the remainder.

"Toolie?" she inquired sweetly. "Toolie?" Getting no response, she stood up and went over to him, then bent down and examined him carefully. Satisfied, she nodded and looked around the empty room.

"Morah!" she snapped, her tone suddenly cold and imperious. "I know you're spying around here someplace! Clean up this mess and get this *garbage* out of my living room!"

"She *poisoned* him!" Darva gasped. "All this way and he lets her poison him!"

"No," I told her. "He surrendered. When he got all the way up here he just couldn't do it—and she knew it. She sure knew him, all right!"

Darva just shook her head sadly. "So simple. So powerful, so smart a man."

"Oddly enough, those are exactly the qualities in humans that are worth preserving," Morah added enigmatically. "You'll see. But—wait. The play isn't over yet."

Aeolia Matuze was up and striding around the room like a mad woman. "Morah! Somebody! Attend me! It will be necessary to arrange the executions of those below and those troops who failed me! Where the hell *is* everybody?"

"Here." A cold, female voice came from behind her. She whirled and looked very surprised and not the least bit annoyed.

"Who the hell are *you?*" Aeolia Matuze snapped.

"We're the new Queen of Charon," Zala/Kira replied as she shot Aeolia Matuze three times. The Lord of Charon toppled and fell, a look of total surprise and bewilderment frozen forever on her face.

I looked at Morah. "She expected you to guard her."

He nodded. "She never could get it through her head who I worked for," he replied, as we watched the woman we both knew walk over, check Koril first, then Aeolia Matuze.

Yatek Morah sighed and turned away from the window. We did the same. "What now?" I asked him.

He smiled. "That depends on you. The remainder of Koril's surviving Class I's will pretty well fill out the Synod."

Darva turned and pointed back at the glass. "But *she's* not qualified to run Charon! Zala's a helpless wimp and Kira's a mechanized assassin!"

"I'm aware of that," Morah replied. "Think of this, Lacoch. You're the Confederacy's assassin. Don't bother to deny it. Nobody else in your batch showed any real promise. I arranged that whole sideshow at Bourget on that assumption." He made a backhanded gesture at the glass. "Her type is now obsolete. It has served its purpose. I've called the few surviving ones to the Diamond. The robots are better, more reliable, and harder to kill."

"Koril thought you wanted to be Supreme Lord of all the Diamond," I told him.

"That ambition had crossed my mind when I had my agents on Takanna keep a small version of this bioagent project going many years ago," he admitted. "However, that prospect no longer interests me. It has become rather—small. Petty, even. No longer worth going after. It has been so for quite some time."

"And Zala?"

He chuckled. "That's up to you. Kira is *extremely* good at what she does, but that's all she does. Zala—well, she trusts you. And she'll need the help of a lot of people she trusts to put things back together and get the government straightened out once more. You're an assassin. She's an assassin. It will be interesting to see who, in the end, is the better."

"You're offering me a shot at being Lord of Charon," I said, a little in awe of the possibilities. I turned to Darva. "Remember those dreams we had? Of changing things for the better, of a virgin continent for the changelings?"

She looked at me strangely. "You mean you'd *do* it? But it'd be on *his* terms and at *his* pleasure."

I turned to Morah. "From what I've seen I could have a very brief tenure myself."

"She was power-mad, you know. She was about to proclaim herself Supreme Goddess of a new, true, and only religion. She was no longer rational enough to do what she was supposed to do—run Charon. As for me and my employers, we frankly don't *care* how the humans run each other on Charon. Our motives—but no, that must wait. I know from reports from Lilith that you carry within you, perhaps still, a sort of organic transmitter. You will eliminate it, or I will. Then, I think, you can be told the whole story. Then you can make your own decisions. For now I must go and tend to our new queen."

For a while we just stood there, not saying anything to one another. Finally Darva asked, "Well? After all this, you're gonna do it? Or what?"

I smiled and kissed her, then looked back at the glass. Zala was there now, not Kira, and she was doing a happy little dance between the bodies. I stared at her, not quite knowing what to do next.

Finally I sighed and said, "Well, I'm of two minds about this . . ."

EPILOGUE

The man in the chair came out of it slowly. He lifted the probes from his head and pushed the apparatus away, but just sat there for a while, as if in a daze.

"Are you all right?" the computer asked him, sounding genuinely concerned.

"Yeah, as good as I'll ever be again, I guess. It gets worse and worse. Now I'm considering joining the enemy!"

"Differing circumstances, an additional year in an alien environment under trapped conditions—it is not totally unexpected. They are not you. They are different people."

The man chuckled mirthlessly. "Maybe. Maybe. At any rate—you saw and heard?"

"It is obvious. Do you wish to file a report and make a recommendation now?"

The man seemed startled. "Huh? No. Of course not! Some pieces are still missing, and while I'm pretty sure I know what is going on I'm still not at all sure how to stop it."

"Time is of the essence now," the computer reminded him. "You heard Matuze. A matter of months. That means they are probably all in place even now."

"And we've yet to find the aliens. We've yet to see what one looks like. We've yet to determine their defensive force and how near it is. Pretty near, I'd guess."

"I believe you do not wish to act," the computer responded. "You know why the aliens are here, their interest in the Warden Diamond specifically, the method by which the Confederacy is to be attacked and just about when—there is more than enough evidence to act."

"Evidence! Deduction! Not a shred of real evidence!"

"Considering the extreme circumstances and the consistency cf the deductions on three worlds now, I'd say you were more than justified."

"*No!*" the man protested. "I want to be absolutely certain! There are millions of lives at stake here!"

"In the Warden Diamond. But there are thousands of times that at stake elsewhere."

"It's not as easy as you make it seem. That's why they just don't let *you* make the decisions. We still have *some* time. And maybe we can figure out some way so nobody has to die."

"You *have* changed," the computer chided. "I feel obligated to make an emergency summary report. You will add your conclusions."

"Not yet. All right—look. Let me get to the ship's library and labs for a day or so. I also want to check out communications. I have a strong feeling I can track the alien fleet."

"I don't believe you. You're just stalling. You have become assimilated with your counterparts."

"Three days. Even you will have to admit that three days won't hurt anything. Besides, the solution is so outrageous they wouldn't believe it now anyway. Even *you* must admit that much."

The computer actually hesitated a moment. Finally it said, "All right. Three days. What can you possibly expect to turn up in three days?"

"Just watch. And I'll want to run Medusa before we finish up."

"But Medusa is not complete."

"Makes no difference. Medusa's the key to it all. Be ready when I return."

He walked back, showered, dressed, then approached the security door that both interlocked him to and isolated him from the giant picket ship. He pressed the identplate; the door refused to open. Angrily, he turned and yelled at the empty air, "All right! Let me out, you bastard. We had an agreement!"

"Do you really know what you're going to do, or are you just grasping at straws?" the computer's disembodied voice asked him.

"Look—am I a prisoner or the agent in charge?" he shot back angrily.

"You *will* come back?"

"Of course I will! Where the hell am I going to run?"

"What are you planning?"

"I'm—oh, let's just say I'm of two minds about it right now."

"Well . . ."

"Would I lie to you?"

There was a second pause, and then the door opened.

MEDUSA:
A Tiger by the Tail

For Walt Liebscher, the elfish Puck of science fiction for over forty years. Those who haven't met him or read him have been missing something unique and wonderful.

CONTENTS

Beginning of the End Game

I

There is nothing quite like the sensation of calling your worst enemy up for a friendly little chat. The face appeared on the little screen, although such communication often dispensed with visuals. In this case, both sides were curious to see what the other looked like.

He looked at the face on that screen and understood immediately why everyone who had seen it feared it. It was the handsome face of a man in middle age, trim, lean, and somewhat military, but the eyes got you right away. They seemed hollowed, like a skull's eyes, yet not empty—they burned with an undefinable *something* that seemed both eerie and impossible.

"Yatek Morah here," said the man with the strange eyes. "Who are you and why do you demand to speak to me?"

The man on the other end gave a slight smile. He was on a huge floating city in space, a picket ship and base camp for those who guarded the four prison worlds of the Warden Diamond, a third of a light-year out and beyond the range of the Warden's own peculiar weapons. "I think you know who I am," he told Morah.

The strange man's brow furrowed a bit in puzzlement, but, suddenly, he nodded and gave a slight smile of his own. "So the puppet master is finally out in the open."

"Look who's talking!"

Morah gave a slight shrug. "So what is it you wish of me?"

"I'm trying to save a minimum of fifty or sixty million lives—including your own," he told the man with the burning eyes. "Perhaps a great many more than that."

Morah's smile widened. "Are you certain that it is we who are in danger? Or, in fact, that *anyone* is."

"Let's not beat around the bush. I know who you are—at least who and what you *claim* to be. I have been observing your behavior of late, particularly that in the Castle on Charon. You claim to be Chief of Security for our hidden friends here in the Diamond, and I'm willing to accept you at your word—for now. I certainly hope you're telling the truth."

Morah sat back and thought a moment. Finally he said, "It appears you know a great deal indeed. How much *do* you know?"

"I know why your alien friends are there. I know pretty well where they *have* to be. I know the nature and purpose of the Warden Diamond and its interesting little beasties. And I know for a fact that your bosses will fight like hell against any move against the Warden Diamond. Furthermore, I know that *my* bosses will make just such a move when my report is analyzed. What I *don't* know is how strong a resistance your bosses can put up; but they are defending a relatively small position against the resources of an enormous interstellar entity, one which, if you are truly Morah, you know well. In the end, things could become horribly bloody for both sides. Perhaps your bosses could get a number of our worlds and your robots will mess up a hundred more—but we'd get the Diamond. And I mean totally. That means that, no matter what we lose, you and your bosses lose more."

Yatek Morah remained impassive to the logic, but still appeared interested in the overall conversation. "So what do you propose?"

"I think we should talk. By 'we' I mean your bosses and mine. I think we'd better reach some accommodation short of total war."

"Indeed? But if you know so much, my friend, you must also realize that the very existence of this little exercise came about because my bosses, as you call them, in consultation with our people, determined that the Confederacy can *never* reach an accommodation with another spacefaring race. So we'll have our little conference, and both sides will say all the right things, and then we'll sign some sort of treaty or somesuch guaranteeing this or that; but the Confederacy will not honor that any longer than it feels it has to. They will send in their little missionaries, and they will find that they have come across a civilization so alien that they won't be able to understand it or its motives."

"Do you?"

Morah shrugged. "I know and accept them, even if I do not completely understand them. I doubt if any human ever will—nor they us. We are the products of two so totally alien histories that I doubt if even an academic acceptance of one another's motives and attitudes is possible. On an individual basis, perhaps—on a collective basis, never. The Confederacy simply cannot tolerate something that powerful that is also inscrutably different, particularly with a pronounced technological edge. They would attack, and you know it."

He made no reply to that, because he could find no flaw in the argument. Morah was simply presenting human history from its beginnings. Such was the nature of the beast—as he should know, being human himself. So instead he changed the subject slightly. "Is there another way? I am in something of a trap myself, you know. My bosses are demanding a report. My own computer analyzer had to be talked into letting me out the door of my lab to come up here and make a call—and it never would have done so if it thought I was going to call you. When I return, I will have a matter of hours, perhaps a couple of days, to make a report. I will be forced to make it. And then the whole thing will be out of my hands. I am running out of time, and that's why I'm coming to you."

"What do you want of me?"

"Options," he told the strange, powerful man. "Solving your little puzzle was simple. Solving the bigger problem is something beyond me."

Morah seemed deeply impressed. Still, he said, "You realize that I could prevent you from making that report."

"Possibly," he agreed. "But it would do no good. The raw data has already been shifted, and they have a Merton impression of me. They could, with some trouble, go through this entire thing again in a very safe area, and come up with the same report. Besides, I doubt if they would believe I died accidentally—so killing me would tip more of your hand."

"The problems of killing you safely and convincingly are hardly insurmountable, but what you say is true. Doing so would buy very little time. But I'm not certain you *do* have the total picture. It would be a pity to sacrifice the Warden Diamond, but only a local tragedy. You have failed to consider all the implications of what you have learned. And, it is true, things are iffy should that happen. But there is at least a forty-percent chance that such an outcome would not adversely affect my bosses' plans and hopes at all. There is more than a ninety-percent chance that it will not *completely* be a washout from their point of view."

That disturbed him a bit. "How long would they need for a hundred-percent success rate? In other words, how much time are we talking about?"

"To do things right—decades. A century, perhaps. I know what you're thinking. Too long. But the alternative will not be the disaster to my people you counted on, only a major inconvenience."

He nodded glumly. "And if they are—inconvenienced? What sort of price will they exact on the Confederacy?"

"A terrible one. We had hoped from the beginning to avoid any sort of major bloodshed, although, I admit, the prospect of fouling up the Confederacy has great appeal for us. Foul them up, perhaps try and overthrow them from within, yes—but not all-out war. That prospect appeals not at all to the thinking ones among us, and is exciting only to the naive and the totally psychotic." The frown came back a bit. "I wonder, though, just how much of the truth you really *do* know."

He sat back in his chair, unable to keep a little bit of smugness from his expression and tone, and told Morah the basics. The Chief of Security was impressed.

"Your theory has some holes," he told the man on the picket ship, "but I am extremely impressed. You certainly know . . . enough. More than enough. I'm afraid we all vastly underestimated you. Not merely your agents down here in the Diamond, but their boss as well. Particularly their boss."

"Then you, too, have some holes in what *you* know," he came back. "One particularly major one. But I'll give you that one as a gift—you'll find out sooner or later anyway, and it might help you in plotting a course. All of them—all four—are not my agents. All four are quite literally me. The Merton Process, remember."

It had been a complex and elaborate plot by the Confederacy, to counter, in part, an even more complex and enormous plot by their enemy. The Confederacy had been fat and complacent all those centuries, and then, suddenly, it had been confronted with evidence that an alien power of superior technology had discovered them, had fashioned such perfect robots to replace key personnel that absolutely no known method would detect them, and that the Confederacy was, in fact, under some sort of systemized attack. The focus of the attack was the Warden Diamond, four human-habitable worlds used as prison planets for the most brilliant criminal and perverted political minds. The perfect prison, since all four worlds were contaminated by an organism that fed, somehow, off energy available only within the Warden system. The organism invaded the bodies of all who landed there, mutating them and giving them strange powers; but it also imprisoned them, as the organism could not survive far from the Warden system's sun—and neither could anyone it inhabited.

But placing the top criminal minds and political deviants together on four worlds in contact with one another had created the most powerful criminal center ever known, one whose tentacles spread far from the Warden system and continued to run the criminal underworld of a thousand planets remotely, and more efficiently, than ever before. But all these masterminds were trapped, and they hated the Confederacy for that trap.

Into that situation had come the aliens. Technologically superior to the Confederacy, they were numerically inferior and so alien that they could neither take on the Confederacy openly and win nor do so secretly. Then they encountered the Warden Diamond and realized what the four worlds held. A deal was struck. The heads of the four worlds—the most powerful and ruthless criminal minds alive—the Four Lords of the Diamond were approached with a proposition. Use their own power and the technology of the aliens, together with their knowledge of mankind and the Confederacy, and subvert it. Cause so much trouble, so much disruption, that the Confederacy would be too concerned with its own problems to even think of the Warden Diamond.

Marek Kreegan, Lord of Lilith, himself a former agent for the Confederacy, came up with a detailed plan for replacing key personnel all over the Confederacy with the impossible robots. Through Wagant Laroo's operation on Cerberus, the robots themselves were first primed with the minds of the very people they would replace. The Cerberans could swap minds as a byproduct of the Warden organism and also had Dr. Merton, creator of the mechanical-mind-exchange process being used experimentally by the Confederacy, to make it work right. Aeolia Matuze of Charon ran a world where almost anything could be easily hidden, so it served as the meeting place between aliens and agents—and as Morah's base of operations. Finally, Talant Ypsir, Lord of Medusa, provided the hardware, raw materials, and in-system transportation of alien technology —and, perhaps, even the aliens themselves. Each of the Lords also controlled vast underworld organizations within the Confederacy itself.

Kreegan hoped to avoid a terrible war, but he intended to disrupt and perhaps break up the Confederacy itself, leaving a fragmented bunch of worlds he and his fellow Lords could take over. The aliens had promised that, in return for removing the Confederacy's threat, they would provide a means to escape from the Warden Diamond and its insidious organism.

But when a robot's cover had been blown, and it had demonstrated its superior capabilities, the Confederacy quickly caught on to the plot and came up with one of its own. To send an agent down on the Warden worlds was not enough. The Lords controlled their worlds; besides, any agent down there was trapped, too, and soon would figure out which side best represented his future.

But, using the Merton Process, the mind of their top agent was simultaneously placed in the bodies of four convicted criminals with long histories; each was sent to one of the four Warden worlds. Also implanted within each was the means by which whatever they saw and did would be transmitted to their original agent, in orbit on the picket ship. With the aid of a sophisticated analytical computer, it was hoped he would be able to piece together the puzzle of the Warden Diamond. In the meantime, his own personality should add psychological reinforcement to the command given the agents down below—kill the Four Lords, disrupt their timetable, buy time for the Confederacy.

But as the agent watched, even experienced, each of his counterparts' lives on Lilith, Cerberus, and Charon, he had also watched as his counterparts—himself—threw aside their basic values, their loyalties, the precepts of the Confederacy which he/they had accepted and to which he/they had devoted a lifetime. Now, convinced he'd figured out the plot and being pressured by his computer and his superiors, he was telling Morah this. It was not self-confidence that made him tell the mysterious, still unseen aliens' Security Chief the secret; rather, it was to inspire confidence. Morah knew and had close at hand at least one of "him"—Park Lacoch of Charon. Now Morah would know just who he was really dealing with.

The Security Chief was suitably impressed. "All of them you? Fascinating. In a sense, it's taking Kreegan's robots one step farther. All right—I agree *we* could probably strike a deal. But I suspect if you've lived those lives along with them, you're not quite the man they sent any more—and they know it. I know the first for a fact, for we are having this conversation. I infer the second from your own statements. You do not expect to survive the next encounter in your lab. So that leaves me nowhere, you see. Any deal we might strike is certain to have no validity to your bosses. Still, I am touched by your attempt—and by your devotion. You do not have to go back into that lab, you know."

The agent looked squarely at the screen, into those weird eyes that none could look into in person. "If you know me at all, you know that I do. My title is Assassin, but I am no hired killer. I have a job to do—if I can."

"Just hypothetically—if you *can* survive this last entry and the report, what would you do? Where would you go? Not back to the Confederacy, surely."

He grinned. "Are you making a hypothetical job offer?"

"Perhaps. I hope you *do* survive. It would be most interesting to talk to you at length."

He laughed. "You have only to talk to Park. Or Cal Tremon. Or Qwin Zhang. Or—hmm . . . I'll be damned. I don't know what name I've got on Medusa. I haven't gotten to that one yet."

Morah was impressed. "You figured out all you have without Medusa? You have an amazing mind."

"I was bred for it." He sighed. "If I survive, we will meet, and soon. If I do not, then the others, different as they now are, will carry on."

"It would be fascinating to have the five of you together. That is something to think about."

"Fascinating, yes," he admitted, "but I'm not sure I'd be the one in the group who'd be the most popular."

"Perhaps. Perhaps. I suspect we would have four equally clever, equally ambitious, but different individuals. Still, I thank you for your warning and your offer. I will convey the details to the proper authorities. I, too, hope that massive war can be avoided—but wiser heads than mine will be needed." He paused. "Good luck, my enemy," he added sincerely, then broke the connection.

He sat there, just staring at the blank console, for several minutes. *You have not considered all the implications . . .*

He was missing something. Morah had been too casual, too sure of himself. One piece, one vital piece, remained. Perhaps it would be found on Medusa. It had to be.

Mirror, mirror . . .

He didn't want to go back into that room. Death waited there, death not only for himself but for millions more at the least.

I'm of two minds about this . . .

Morah's attitude, now—was it bluff and bravado? Would he pull something? Or was he serious in his hard confidence?

Would I lie to you?

Sighing, he rose from his chair and walked back to the lab cubicle attached to the rear of the picket ship.

The door to the cubicle he generally called his lab opened for him and then hissed closed with a strange finality. The entire module was attached to the picket ship, but was internally controlled by its own computer. Everything was independent of the ship if need be—power, air, and air-filtration systems, it even had its own food synthesizer. The door was, of necessity, also an airlock; the place was essentially a container with a universal interlock, carried in a space freighter and then eased into its niche in the picket ship by a small tug. Since the module did not have its own propulsion system, it was definitely stuck there until its securing seals were released and it could be backed out by a tug.

The controlling computer recognized only him, and would be resistant to any entry attempt by another—and lethal should the intruder succeed. The trouble was, he knew, the computer had been specially programmed for this mission by the Security Police, and not all that programming was directed toward his safety, survival, and comfort.

"You were not gone very long this time," the computer remarked through speakers in the wall. It sounded surprised.

"There wasn't much to do," he told it, sounding tired. "And even less I *could* do."

"You made a call to one of the space stations in the Warden Diamond," it noted, "on a scrambler circuit. Why? And who did you call?"

"I'm not answerable to you—you're a machine!" he snapped, then got hold of himself a bit. "That is why the two of us, and not you alone, are on this mission."

"Why didn't you use me for the call? It would have been simple."

"And on the record," he noted. "Let us face it, my cold companion, you do not work for me but for Security."

"But so do you," the computer noted. "We both have the same job to do."

He nodded absently. "I agree. And you probably have never comprehended why I'm needed at all. But I'll tell you why, my synthetic friend. They don't trust *you* any more than they trust *me*, for one thing. They fear thinking machines, which is why we never developed the type of organic robot the aliens use. Or, rather, we did once—and lived to regret it."

"They *would* be superior," the computer responded thoughtfully. "But be that as it may, as long as they control my programming and restrict my self-programming, I'm not a threat to them."

"No, but that's not really why I'm here. Left to your own devices—pardon the pun—you would simply carry out the mission literally, with no regard for consequences or politics or psychology. You would deliver information even if doing so meant the loss of billions of lives. I, on the other hand, can subjectively filter those findings and weigh more factors than the bare mission outline. And that's why they trust me more than you—even though they hardly trust me, which is why you are here. We guard and check one another. We're not partners, you know—we are actually antagonists."

"Not so," the computer responded. "You and I both have the same mission from the same source. It is *not* our job to evaluate the information subjectively, only to report the truth. The evaluation will be made by others—many others, better equipped to do so. You are assuming a godlike egocentric personality that is neither warranted nor justified. Now—who did you call?"

"Yatek Morah," he responded.

"Why?"

"I wanted him to know that I knew. I wanted his masters to know that as well. I find war inevitable. However, I also find that his side loses everything, while we lose a great deal but hardly all. It was my decision to face him with that fact and to give the ball to him, as it were. Either he and his masters come up with a solution, or war *is* inevitable."

"This is a questionable tactic, but it is done. How did he take it?"

"That's just the trouble. He took it. It didn't seem to worry him or bother him. That's what I had to know. He *is*, I believe, sincerely interested in avoiding war for his own purposes, but he is not worried about it from the viewpoint of those who employ him. It was the one thing I could not get from the field reports—a direct sense of how the aliens view the war threat."

"It was only a viewing scanner on a single individual," the computer noted. "He could be bluffing. All things considered, how else *could* he react?"

He shook his head slowly from side to side. "No. Call it gut instinct, call it hunch or intuition, or whatever you wish—but also call it, too, experience. Reading the length of pauses, the slight tone of voice, the subtle shifts in the body to bad news and flawless reasoning. There is still something missing in our information. He as much as said it himself."

"That is interesting, however. He confirmed the basics?"

He nodded. "We're right—dead on. That was the other reason for the call. Still, I feel no joy in it—for if we're completely right, then what factor has been overlooked? To have all one's deductions and inferences confirmed is gratifying. But to discover that, being right on the wildest stretches of logic, you have missed a factor that they consider decisive—that is frustrating."

"I believe I understand. This is what made you return, was it not? You fear the Confederacy and me as much as the aliens—perhaps more. Yet you came back. Such conviction, when faced with your brilliant deductions, carries weight. All right. We are missing a factor. What is it?"

"There's no way to know. Morah came out and told me that I'd not carried my deductions to their logical conclusions." He sighed and drummed his fingers against a desk top. "It must have to do with the nature of the aliens. He called them incomprehensible, basically, yet he said he understood what they were doing. That means it is a question not of deed but *motivation*." The fist slammed down hard on the desk. "But we *know* their motivation, dammit! It *has* to be!" Again he struggled to get hold of himself.

"We are still handicapped in one way," the computer noted. "We have not yet met the aliens, not yet seen them. We still know nothing about them other than the inference that they breathe an atmosphere similar to human norm, and are comfortable within normal temperature ranges."

He nodded. "That's the problem. And *that* I'm not likely to get from Medusa, either, unless there's some miracle. A psychotic killer who sees them thinks of them as evil. A psychotic Lord thinks of them as funny-looking but hardly evil, just self-interested. And intellects like Kreegan and Morah see them as a positive force. And that's all we really know, isn't it? After all this . . ."

"No race lasts long enough to reach the stars and do all that this one has done unless it first acts in its own self-interest," the computer noted. "We can probably dismiss the evil concept of the criminal on one of dozens of bases, the most probable being that these aliens are subjectively terrifying to look at, or smell putrid, or something of that sort. It is hardly likely that their evolution, even given some of the same basics as human-kind, is anything like that of humans."

He nodded. "I keep thinking of Morah's inhuman eyes. He claims he is not a robot and that he is the same Yatek Morah sentenced to the Dia-mond more than forty years ago. We need not believe him, and should not, but let's for a moment take his statements at face value. If he *is* who and what he claims to be—then why those eyes?"

"A Warden modification, possibly self-induced for effect. He could do it easily on Charon."

"Perhaps. But, perhaps, too, those eyes mean something more. What does he see with them? And how? A broader spectrum, perhaps? I don't think they are totally for effect. For protection, maybe? I wonder . . ."

"Still, the bottom line remains your report," the computer noted. "I will admit that I, too, am somewhat curious, even though I have the basics."

"Medusa first. Let's complete the set. Maybe my missing piece will be found there. Or, maybe, what I experience will jog my mind to see those missing implications. It can't hurt."

"But Talant Ypsir lives. The mission is incomplete there."

"We are beyond caring about the Lords of the Diamond now, I think, except, perhaps, in some sort of solution if one is possible. I need informa-tion. Medusa will have the most direct contacts with the aliens. Let me get the information I need."

"But whether or not it is there, you will still make your report after that?"

He nodded. "I'll make my report." He got up and walked forward to the central console, then sat down in the large padded chair and adjusted it for maximum comfort. "Are you ready?"

"Yes." The computer lowered the probes, which the agent carefully attached to his forehead. Now he simply lay back and relaxed, hardly feeling the computer-induced injection that cleared his mind and established the proper state for receipt and filtration of this kind of information.

Thanks to an organic module inside the brain of his other self down there on Medusa, every single thing that had happened to that other self was transmitted to the computer as raw data. Now it would be fed into the mind of the original in the chair, filtered—the basics and unimportant matter discarded by his own mind—and that other self would give a basic report both to the agent in the chair and to the computer as if the man were there in that room—which, in a very broad and very odd sense, he was.

The drugs and small neural probes did their job. His own mind and personality receded, replaced by a similar, yet oddly different pattern.

"The agent is commanded to report," the computer ordered, sending the command deep into the agent's mind, a mind no longer quite his own.

Recorders clicked on.

Slowly, the man in the chair cleared his throat. He mumbled, groaned, and made odd, disjointed words and sounds, as his mind received, coded, and classified the incoming data, adjusted it all, and sorted it out.

Finally, the man began to speak.

CHAPTER ONE

Rebirth

After Krega's talk and a little preparation to put my own affairs in order—this would be a long one—I checked into the Confederacy Security Clinic. I'd been here many times before, of course—but not knowingly for this purpose. Mostly, this was where they programmed you with whatever information you'd need for a mission and where, too, you were "reintegrated." Naturally, the kind of work I did was often extralegal, a term I prefer to illegal, which implies criminal intent—and much of it was simply too hot to ever be known. To avoid such risks, all agents, of course, had their own experience of sensitive missions wiped from their minds when they were over.

It may seem like a strange life, going about not knowing where you have been or what you've done, but it has its compensations. Because any potential enemy, military or political, knows you've been wiped, you can live a fairly normal, relaxed life outside of a mission structure. There's no purpose in coming after you—you have no knowledge of what you've done, or why, or for whom. In exchange for these blanks, an agent of the Confederacy lives a life of luxury and ease, with an almost unlimited supply of money, and with all the comforts supplied I bummed around, swam, gambled, ate in the best restaurants, played a little semi-pro ball or cube—I'm pretty good, and the exercise keeps me in shape. I enjoyed every minute of it, and except for my regular requalification training sessions— four- to six-week stints that resemble military basic training only nastier and more sadistic—I felt no guilt over my playboy life. The training sessions, of course, make sure that your body and mind don't stagnate from all that good living. They implant sensors in you that they constantly monitor and decide when you need a good refresher.

I often wondered just how sophisticated those sensors were. Having a whole security staff witness all my debauchery and indiscretions once worried me, but after a while I learned to ignore it.

The life offered in trade is just too nice. Besides, what could I do about it? People on most of the civilized worlds these days had such sensors, although hardly to the degree and sophistication of mine. How else could a population so vast and so spread out possibly be kept orderly, progressive, and peaceful?

But, of course, when a mission came up you couldn't afford to forego all that past experience you'd had. A wipe without storage simply wouldn't have been very practical, since a good agent gets better by not repeating his mistakes. In the Security Clinic they had everything you ever experienced, and the first thing you did was go and get the rest of you put back so you would be whole for whatever mission they'd dreamed up this time.

I was always amazed when I got up from that chair with my past fully restored. Clear as my memory was once again, it was hard to believe that *I*, of all people, had done this or that.

The only difference this time, I knew, was that the process would be taken one step further. Not only would the complete "me" get up from that table, but the same memory pattern would be impressed on other minds, other bodies—as many as needed until a "take" was achieved.

I wondered what they'd be like, those four other versions of myself. Physically different, probably—the offenders on the Warden Diamond weren't usually from the civilized worlds, where people had basically been standardized in the name of equality. No, these people would come from the frontier, from among the traders and miners and freebooters who operated there, and who were, of course, necessary in an expanding culture since a high degree of individuality, self-reliance, originality, and creativity was required in the dangerous environment in which they lived. A stupid government would have eliminated all such, but a stupid government degenerates into stagnancy or loses its vitality and growth potential by standardization. Utopia was for the masses, of course, but not for everyone or it wouldn't *be* Utopia very long.

That, of course, was the original reason for the Warden Diamond Reserve. Some of these hardy frontier people are so individualistic that they become a threat to the stability of the civilized worlds. The trouble is, anybody able to crack the fabric that holds our society together has, most likely, the smartest, nastiest, most original sort of mind humanity can produce—and, therefore, he is not somebody who should be idly wiped clean. The Diamond, it was felt, would effectively trap those individuals forever, yet allow them continued creative opportunities. Properly monitored, they might still produce something of value for the Confederacy—if only an idea, a thought, a way of looking at something that nobody else could evolve.

Of course, these felons were anxious to please, since the alternative was death. Eventually such creative minds made themselves indispensable to the Confederacy and insured their continued survival. The possibility had been foreseen—but it wasn't altogether unwelcome, either. Like all criminal organizations in the past, this one provided services that people were convinced should be illegal or were immoral or somesuch, but which masses of people wanted anyway.

The damned probe hurt like hell. Usually there was just some tingling, then a sensation much like sleep. You woke up a few minutes later in the chair, once again yourself. This time the tingling became a painful physical force that seemed to enter my skull, bounce around, then seize control of my head. It was as if a huge, giant fist had grabbed my brain and squeezed, then released, then squeezed again, in excruciating pulses. Instead of drifting off to sleep, I passed out.

I woke up and groaned slightly. The throbbing was gone, but the memory was still all too current and all too real. It was several minutes, I think, before I found enough strength to sit up.

The old memories flooded back, and again I was amazed at many of my past exploits. Considering my surrogate selves couldn't be wiped after this mission as could I, I made a mental note that those surrogates would almost certainly have to be killed if they did have my entire memory pattern. Otherwise, a lot of secrets would be loose on the Warden Diamond, many in the hands of people who'd know just what sort of use to make of them.

No sooner had I had that thought than I had the odd feeling of wrongness. I looked around the small room in which I'd awakened and realized immediately the source of that feeling.

This wasn't the Security Clinic, wasn't anyplace I'd ever seen before. A tiny cubicle, about twelve cubic meters total, including the slightly higher than normal ceiling. In it was a small cot on which I'd awakened, a small basin, next to which was a standard food port, and, in the wall, a pulldown toilet. That was it. Nothing else—or was there?

I looked around and easily spotted the obvious. Yes, I couldn't make a move without being visually and probably aurally monitored. The door was almost invisible and there was certainly no way to open it from inside. I knew immediately where I was.

I was in a prison cell.

Far worse than that, I could feel a faint vibration that had no single source. It wasn't irritating; in fact, it was so dim as to be hardly noticeable, but I knew what it was. I was aboard a ship, moving somewhere through space.

I stood up, reeling a bit from a slight bout of dizziness that soon passed, and examined my body. It was smaller, lighter, thinner than I was used to, but it was clearly the body of a male of the civilized worlds. What made it different, or unusual compared to my own, didn't hit me right away, but I finally put my finger on it. It was its unspoiled, unmarked newness, a body not yet in full development—not even much pubic hair. It was the body of someone extremely young. It wasn't *my* body, and I could only stand there, stunned, for I don't know how long.

I'm not me! my mind screamed at me. *I'm one of* them—*one of the surrogates!* I sat back down on the cot, telling myself that it just wasn't possible. I knew who I was, remembered every bit, every detail, of my life and work.

The shock gave way after a while to anger—anger and frustration. I was a copy, an imitation of somebody else entirely, somebody still alive and kicking and perhaps monitoring my every move, my every thought. I hated that other then, hated him with a pathological force that was beyond reason. He would sit there comfortable and safe, watching me work, watching me do it all—and, when it was over, he'd go home for debriefing, return to that easy life, while I . . .

They were going to dump me on a world of the Warden Diamond, trap me like some kind of master criminal, imprison me there for the rest of my life—of this body's life, anyway. And then? When my job was done? I'd said it myself upon awakening, passed my own sentence. The things I knew! I would be monitored at all times, of course. Monitored and killed if I blew any of those secrets—killed anyway at the completion of it, for insurance sake.

My training came into automatic play at that point, overriding the shock and anger. I regained control and considered all that I knew.

Monitor? Sure—more than ever. I recalled Krega saying that there was some sort of organic linkup. Are you enjoying this, you son of a bitch? Are you getting pleasure from vicariously experiencing my reaction?

My training clicked in again, dampening me down. It didn't matter, I told myself. First of all, I knew what he must be thinking—and that was an advantage. *He,* of all people, would know that I would be a damned tough son of a bitch to kill.

It was a shock to discover that you were not who you thought you were but some artificial creation. It was a shock, too, to realize that the old life, the life you remembered even if you, personally, didn't experience it, was gone forever. No more civilized worlds, no more casinos and beautiful women and all the money you could spend. And yet—and yet, as I sat there, I adjusted. That was what they picked men like me for from the start—our ability to adjust and adapt to almost anything.

It was not my body, but I was still me. Memory and thought and personality were an individual, not his body. This was no different from a biological disguise, I told myself, of a particularly sophisticated sort. As to who was really me—it seemed to me that this personality, these memories, were no more that other fellow's than my own. Until I got up from that chair back in the Security Clinic I'd really been somebody else anyway. A lot of me, my memories and training, had been missing. That old between-missions me was the artificial me, the created me, I thought. He, that nonentity playboy that presently did not exist, was the artificial personality. Me—the real me—was bottled up and stored in their psychosurgical computers and only allowed to come out when they needed it—and for good reason. Unlocked, I was as much a danger to the power structure as to whomever they set me against.

And I was good. The best, Krega had called me. That's why I was here, now, in this body, in this cell, on this ship. And I wouldn't be wiped and I wouldn't be killed if I could help it. That other me, sitting there in the console—somehow I no longer hated him very much, no longer felt anything at all for him. When this was all over he'd be wiped once more—perhaps even killed himself if my brother agents and I on the Diamond found out too much. At best he'd return to being that stagnant milquetoast.

Me, on the other hand . . . Me. I would still be here, still live on, the *real* me. I would become more complete than he would.

I was under no illusions, though. Kill me they would, if they could, if I didn't do their bidding. They'd do it automatically, from robot satellite, and without a qualm. I would. But my vulnerability would last only until I mastered my new situation and my new and permanent home. I felt that with a deep sense of certainty—for I knew their methods and how they thought. I'd have to do their dirty work for them, and they knew it—but only until I could get around it. They could be beaten, even on their own turf. That was why they had people like me in the first place—to uncover those who expertly covered over their whole lives and activities, who managed to totally vanish from their best monitors. To uncover them and get them. But there'd be no new expert agent sent to get me if I beat them. They'd just be putting somebody else in the same position.

I realized then, as they had undoubtedly figured, that I had no choice but to carry out the mission. As long as I was doing what they wanted I would be safe from them while still in that vulnerable stage. After—well, we'd see.

The thrill of the challenge took over, as it always did: the puzzle to be solved; the objectives to be accomplished. I liked to win, and it was even easier if you felt nothing about the cause—then it was just the challenge of the problem and the opponent and the physical and intellectual effort needed to meet that challenge. Find out about the alien menace. The outcome no longer concerned me either way—I was trapped on a Warden world from now on anyway. If the aliens won the coming confrontation, the Wardens would survive as allies. If they lost—well, it wouldn't make a damned bit of difference, only continue the current situation. Thus, the alien problem was purely an intellectual challenge and that made it perfect.

The other problem created a similar situation. Seek out the Lord of the particular Diamond world and kill him if I could. In a sense doing so would be more difficult, for I'd be operating on totally unfamiliar ground and would, therefore, require time and, perhaps, allies. Another challenge. And, if I got him, it could only increase my own power and position in the long run. If he got me instead, of course, that would solve everybody's problem—but the thought of losing is abhorrent to me. That set the contest in the best terms, from my point of view. Trackdown assassination was the ultimate game, since you won or you died and did not have to live with the thought that you lost.

It suddenly occurred to me that the only real difference that probably existed between me and a Lord of the Diamond was that I was working *for* the law and he—or she—against it. But, no, that wasn't right, either. On his world *he* was the law and I would be working against that. Fine. Dead heat on moral grounds.

The only thing wrong at this point, I reflected, was that they were starting me at a tremendous disadvantage and I disliked having more than necessary. The normal procedure was to program all pertinent information into my brain before they sent me off on a mission—but they hadn't done it this time. Probably, I thought, because they had me on the table once for four separate missions—and the transfer process, to a new body, was hard enough without trying to add anything afterward. Still, knowing this put me in a deep pit. I thought sourly that somebody should have thought of that.

Somebody did, but it was a while before I discovered how. About an hour after I had awakened a little bell clanged near the food port and I walked over to it. Almost instantly a hot tray appeared, along with a thin plastic fork and knife that I recognized as the dissolving type. They'd melt into a sticky puddle in an hour or less, then dry up and become a dry powder shortly after that. Standard for prisoners.

The food was lousy but I hadn't expected better. The vitamin-enriched fruit drink with it, though, was pretty good, and I made the most of it. I kept the thin, clear container, which was *not* the dissolving type, in case I wanted water later. The rest I put back in the port, and it vaporized neatly. All nice and sealed. You couldn't even draw more than a thimble full of water at a time from the tap.

About the only thing they couldn't control was my bodily functions, and a half-hour or so after eating my first meal as what you might call a new man, I just had to go. I tugged on the toilet pull ring on the far wall, the unit came down—and damned if there wasn't a small, paper-thin probe in the recess behind it. And so, I sat down on the john, leaned back against the panel, and got a brief and relief at the same time.

The thing worked by skin contact—don't ask me how. I'm not one of the tech brains. It was not as good as a programming, but it allowed them to talk to me, even send me pictures that only I could see and hear.

"By now I hope you're over the shock of discovering who and what you are," Krega's voice came to me, seemingly forming in my brain. It was a shock to realize that not even my jailers could hear or see a thing.

"We have to brief you this way simply because the transfer process is delicate enough as it is. Oh, don't worry about it—it's permanent. But we prefer to allow as much time as possible for your brain patterns to fit in and adapt without subjecting the brain to further shock and we haven't the time to allow you to 'set in' completely, as it were. This method will have to do, and I profoundly regret it, for I feel that you have a difficult enough assignment as is, perhaps impossible."

I felt the excitement rising within me. The challenge, the challenge . . .

"Your objective world is Medusa, farthest out from the sun of the Diamond colonies," the Commander's voice continued. "If there is a single place in the universe where man can live but wouldn't want to, it's Medusa. Old Warden, who discovered the system, said he named the place after the mythological creature that turned men to stone because anybody who'd want to live there had to have rocks in his head. That's pretty close to the truth.

"The imprint ability of this device is limited," he continued, "but we can send you one basic thing that may—or may not—be of use to you on Medusa. It is a physical-political map of the entire planet as complete and up-to-date as we could make it."

That puzzled me. Why would such a map *not* be of use? Before I could consider the matter further, and curse my inability to ask Krega questions, I felt a sharp back pain, then a short wave of dizziness and nausea. When the haze cleared, I found that I had the complete map clearly and indelibly etched in my mind.

There followed a stream of facts about the place. The planet was roughly 46,000 kilometers both around the equator—and in polar circumference, allowing for topographic differences. Like all four Diamond worlds, it was basically a ball—highly unusual as planets go, even though everybody, including me, thinks of all major planets as spherical.

The gravity was roughly 1.2 norm, so I would have to adjust to being a bit slower and heavier than usual. That would take a slight adjustment in timing, and I made a note to work on that first thing. Its atmosphere was within a few hundredths of a percentage point of human standard—far too little difference to be noticeable, since nobody I know ever actually experienced that human standard in real life.

Medusa's axial tilt of roughly 22° gave the world strong seasonal changes under normal circumstances, but at over three hundred million kilometers from its F-type sun it was, at best, a tad chilly. In point of fact, something like seventy percent of Medusa was so glaciated that it consisted of just two large polar caps with a sandwich of real planet in between on both sides of the equator. Its day was a bit long, but not more than an hour off the standard and hardly a matter of concern. What *was* a concern was that those wonderful tropic temperatures were something around 10° C at the equator or at midsummer, and that could drop to −20 at the tropic extremes in midwinter. But the life zone *did* extend for some distance beyond that—up and down to a jagged glacial line at roughly 35° latitude, give or take a few degrees, and in that subtropical zone at midwinter a brisk −80° C. Some climate! I sincerely hoped that they provided free insulated gear from the moment of arrival, particularly since that map in my head said that a number of cities were located in the coldest areas.

Continents were pretty much irrelevant, since the seas were frozen down to the habitable zones all the time and down to almost the tropic lines half the year. There were three distinct habitable land masses that I could see from the map, though, so you might as well say three very wide and very thin continents. Throughout the habitable latitudes there was a lot of mountain that didn't help the climate much, and a huge amount of forest, all of which seemed to be various evergreen types. Nothing familiar, of course, but familiar types in any cold climate.

A rocky, terribly cold, hostile world. Calling it human-habitable was stretching things a bit, no matter the air you breathed. About the only thing of interest was that Medusa, of all places, showed the only evidence of vulcanism on any of the Warden worlds. No volcanoes—but that would be too much, anyway, for any person to stand. But there were large thermal pools, hot springs, and even geysers in the midst of the barren wastes, some in the coldest regions. Obviously there was something hot beneath many parts of the surface.

There *was* animal life, though—mostly mammals, it seemed, of a great many varieties. That figured, really—only mammals could survive that kind of climate. Some were nasty, some harmless, some a little of both, but nothing alive could be taken for granted on such a fierce, harsh place where just staying alive took tremendous effort.

Well, I'd better start loving it, I told myself. Short of suicide, there was no way to avoid calling it home. At least it was a supposedly modern and industrialized world, so there *would* be creature comforts.

"Medusa is ruled with an iron hand by Talant Ypsir, a former member of the Confederacy Council. Ypsir attempted to engineer a coup of sorts more than thirty-five years ago. It was hushed up, and he dropped from sight and disappeared from the news, but the object of his coup was to make fundamental changes in the way the civilized worlds, and even the frontier, were organized and administered. His system was so brutal and so naked a grab for absolute personal power that he eventually shocked even his most ardent adherents who betrayed him. Unlike Charon's Aeolia Matuze, also once a Council member, Ypsir was never popular or trusted, but he had an absolute genius for bureaucratic organization and was at one time head of the civil service. Be warned that he and his minions run Medusa with the same brutal, methodical system he once hoped to impose on all mankind, and that the cities are models of efficiency, as is the economy, but in every way absolutely under his control. His government controls *only* the organized settlements, however—although that is the bulk of the more than twelve million people estimated to be Medusa's current population. As his industries are fueled from the mines on the moons of Momrath, the gas giant that is the next planet out from Medusa, and there is little in that wilderness except water and wood, he makes no effort to extend his authority to that wild area."

I remembered Matuze well, but I had to admit I'd never heard of this Ypsir. Well, it was long ago and the Council was pretty large. Besides, who the hell ever knows the head of the civil service anyway?

As to who I was, I got my first mental picture of myself from the briefing, and it was a bit of a shock. I'd had a sense of being younger, true —but the body I now wore was little more than fourteen, barely into puberty. It was, however, a civilized-world-norm body, and that was good enough although it was from Halstansir, a world I didn't know. I could infer a lot, though, simply from the skin, basic build, and facial features. I was now relatively tall and thin, with a burnt-orange complexion, and the boyish face had jet-black hair but no trace of sideburns or beard, almond-shaped black eyes, and fairly thick, flat nose over broad lips. It was a strong, handsome face and body—but very, very young-looking.

So what was a fourteen-year-old boy doing on his way to the Diamond? Well, Tarin Bul of Halstansir was a rather exceptional young lad. The son of a local administrator, he'd been raised in pampered splendor. But Halstansir's Council member, a man named Daca Kra, had apparently used the boy's father as a scapegoat in a minor scandal, exposing him to ridicule and personal ruin. The older Bul just couldn't stand it, and, refusing psych treatment, killed himself instead. Such things happened occasionally particularly on the upper political levels. What *didn't* happen, even occasionally, was what the boy, who just about worshiped his father, had done then. Taking advantage of the natural sympathy of the first families of Halstansir, Tarin Bul had plotted, planned, and trained to get to a reception for Daca Kra—where he'd assassinated the Councillor, in mid-handshake, by the rather quaint and ugly method of disemboweling the man with a sword used in physical training. The boy was a prepubescent twelve at the time, which caused more problems than the nearly unprecedented assassination.

Of course we picked him up and got him off-planet, where we had him evaluated by psychs, but he'd withdrawn from the world into a better one of his own imagination after carrying out the kill. The psychs could hardly reach him at all, though they spent a lot of time trying. Normally they would have simply done a complete wipe of his mind and built a new personality, but Kra's family used some influence of its own. So now

Tarin Bul was out of his shell and on his way to Medusa—but not really. Bul had died as soon as my mind displaced his. *I* was now Tarin Bul, and I wondered how an ex-Councillor would take to a boy who'd killed one of his colleagues.

Still, that would be a ways off as yet. I could see certain real advantages in the body—not the least of which was the fact that I had an extra thirty years or so on my life—but there would also be disadvantages as well. There would be the tendency to treat me as a child—and, because it was my cover, I had to go along to a certain extent. But though children get a bit more license than adults in simple behavioral areas, they are also subject to more rigid social controls. That realization led me onto the path of determining my best and most effective persona. The fact that Bul was a male of the civilized worlds born to a political family meant his IQ and general formative education would be expected to be well above average. The fact that he'd engineered a successful assassination and survived, even being sent to the Warden Diamond, was another plus. I would have no trouble convincing anyone that I was quite a bit older than my years, which eased the problem quite a bit. Being a tough, smart kid would be an easy and useful role to play.

I lay back down on the cot and put myself in a light trance, going over all the briefing information, filing, sorting, thinking everything out. Particularly important were the details, large and small, of Bul's short life and family, since it was in that area I'd be most vulnerable to a trip-up. I also studied his mannerisms, nervous habits, and the like, and tried to get myself into the mind-set of a small but deadly assassin.

By the time I reached Medusa I knew I'd *better* be perfect for my own sake. I had another assassination to add to Tarin Bul's total still to come, and though I hoped they would underestimate me, I did not for one moment underestimate Talant Ypsir.

CHAPTER TWO

Transportation and Exposure

Except for the regular meals I had no way to keep track of time, but it was a fairly long trip. Nobody was wasting any money transporting prisoners by the fastest available routes, that was for sure.

Finally, though, we docked with the base ship a third of a light-year out from the Warden system. I understood the situation not so much by any sensation inside my cloister but from the lack of it—the vibration that had been my constant companion stopped. Still the routine wasn't varied—I assumed they were waiting for a large enough contingent from around the galaxy to make the landing worthwhile. For now, I could only sit and go over my data for the millionth time and, occasionally, reflect on the fact that I probably wasn't very far from my old body—as I'd come to think of it. I wondered if, perhaps, he didn't even come down and take a peek at me from time to time, at least from idle curiosity—me and the three others who probably were here as well.

I also had time to reflect on what I knew of the Warden situation itself, the reason for its perfection as a prison. I had not, of course, swallowed that whole. Though there was no such thing as the perfect prison, this one had to be close. Shortly after I was landed on Medusa and started wading in and breathing its air I would be infected with an oddball submicroscopic organism that would set up housekeeping in every cell of my body. There it would live, feeding off me, even earning its keep by keeping disease organisms, infections, and the like in check. The one thing that stuff had was a will to live and it only lived if you did.

But the organism needed something, some trace element or somesuch that was only present in the Warden system. Nobody knew what and nobody had been able to do the real work necessary to find out, but whatever it needed—other than you—was found only in the Warden system. Whatever it was wasn't in the air, because they ran shuttles between the worlds of the Diamond and in them you breathed the purified, mechanically produced stuff with no ill effect. Not in the food, either. They'd tried that. It was possible for one of the Warden people to live comfortably on synthetics in a totally isolated lab such as a planetary space station. But get too far away, even with Warden food and Warden air, and the organism died. Since it had modified your cells to make itself at home, and those cells depended on the organism to keep working properly, you died, too—painfully and slowly, in horrible agony. That distance was roughly a quarter of a light-year from the sun, which explained the location of the base ship.

All four worlds were more than climatologically different. The organism acted consistently in what it did to you on each planet. But—possibly because of distance from the sun, which seemed to be the determining factor in its life, the organism did different things to you depending on which world you were first exposed to it. Whatever it did stuck in just that fashion even if you went to a different world of the Diamond.

The organism seemed to be vaguely telepathic, although nobody could explain quite how. It certainly wasn't an intelligent organism, though it behaved predictably. Still, most of the changes seemed to involve the colony in one person affecting the colony in another—or others. The individual provided the conscious control, if he could, and that determined who bossed whom. A pretty simple system, even if nobody had yet been able to explain it. I vaguely understood, though, that Medusans were unique in the Diamond in that the Warden organism colony inside you affected you alone in some way, not others. Well, we would have to see.

As for Medusa itself, all I really knew about it was that it was terribly cold and hostile. I cursed again at not having been fed the proper programming to prepare me fully—it would cost time, possibly a lot, just to learn the ropes.

Almost six days—seventeen meals—after I'd arrived at the base ship there was a lurching and a lot of banging around that forced me to the cot and made me slightly seasick. Still, I wasn't disappointed—it meant that they were making up the consignments and readying for the in-system drop of these cells. I faced what was to come with mixed emotions. On one hand, I desperately wanted to be out of this little box that had provided nothing but endless, terrible boredom for such a long time. The problem was, though, that when I next got out of the box I would just be in a much larger and probably more comfortable box—Medusa itself, no less a cell for being an entire planet. And if my new situation would provide diversion, challenge, excitement, or whatever, lacking in this box, it might also prove, unlike this box, very, very final.

Shortly after the banging started, it stopped again. After a short, expectant pause, I felt a vibration indicating movement. It was much more pronounced than before, telling me that I was either on a much smaller vessel or located nearer the drives.

Still, another five interminable days—fifteen meals—passed before we reached our destination. Long, certainly, but also fast for a sublight carrier, probably a modified and totally automated freighter. Then the vibrations stopped and I knew we were in orbit. Again I had those mixed feelings of trapped doom and exhilaration.

There was a crackling sound and a speaker I'd never even known was there came to life.

"Attention all prisoners!" it commanded; the voice was a metallic parody of a man's baritone. "We have achieved orbit around the planet Medusa in the Warden system." Nothing I didn't know, but the announcement was, I reflected, probably telling the others, however many there were, for the first time. I could understand what they must be going through, although, I was lucky to be going in with my eyes open even if no more voluntarily.

"In a moment," the voice continued, "the doors to your cells will slide open and you will be able to leave. We strongly recommend you do so, since thirty seconds after the doors open they will close again and a vacuum pump will begin sterilization operations within the cells which would be fatal to anyone who remains."

Nice touch, I thought. Not only did that insure against breakouts en route, you moved or you died on their schedule. I couldn't help wonder whether anybody chose death.

"Immediately after you enter the main corridor," the voice continued, "you will stand in place until the cell doors close. Do not attempt to move from in front of your cell door until it closes or automatic guard equipment will vaporize you. There will be no talking in the corridor. Anyone breaking silence or failing to obey orders precisely will be dealt with instantly. You will receive further instructions once the doors close. Ready to depart—*now!*"

The door slid open, and I wasted no time in stepping out. A small white box, complete with marks for feet, indicated where you were to stand. I did as instructed, galling as all this was. There was something to being totally naked and isolated on a ship controlled only by computer that humbled you more than was right. I experienced a sense of total futility.

I could still look around and realized that I'd been right. The place where we stood was basically a long sealed hall along whose sides the little cells had been attached. I looked up and down and counted maybe ten or twelve, no more. The cream of the crop, I thought sourly. A handful of men and women, naked and bedraggled, beaten prisoners now, about to be dropped off and left. I wondered why my companions had been chosen rather than wiped, considering the transportation costs alone. What had the computers and psych boys found in these dejected specimens that dictated that they should live? *They* didn't know, that was for sure. I wondered exactly who did.

The doors snapped shut. I waited expectantly, perhaps to hear the scream of somebody who didn't move fast enough as the air was pumped out, but there was no hint of melodrama. If anybody had taken that way out, it was not evident.

"At my command," the voice barked from speakers along the ceiling, "you will turn right and walk, slowly, in single file, as far forward as you can. There you will find a special shuttle that will bring you to the surface. You will take seats from front to back, leaving no empty seats between you, and immediately strap yourselves in."

I heard some muttering from a couple of my fellow prisoners. Instantly a brief but very visible spurt of light from a side wall hit with an audible hiss just in front of the offenders' feet. They jumped slightly at this demonstration of power, but all the grumbling and mumbling ceased.

The voice had paused for this interruption, but now took up its instructions with no reference to it. None was needed.

"Right turn—*now!*" it commanded, and we did as instructed. "Walk slowly forward to the shuttle as instructed."

We walked silently, definitely in no hurry. The metal floor of the corridor was damned cold, which made the shuttle preferable to this damned refrigerator. The shuttle itself was surprisingly comfortable and modern, although the seats weren't made for naked bodies. I sat about three rows back and attached the safety straps, then waited for the others to enter. My first impression had been close, I noted. The shuttle itself could seat twenty-four, but there were only nine of us—six men and three women.

The hatch closed automatically and I heard the hiss of pressurization. Then, without further fanfare, came a violent lurch and we were free of the transport and on our way down.

The shuttle was much too modern and comfortable for mere prisoner transport, I told myself. This, then, had to be one of the interplanetary ships regularly used for transportation between the worlds of the Warden Diamond.

The overhead speakers crackled, and a much nicer female voice that actually sounded human came on. It was a great improvement.

"Welcome to Medusa." The voice sounded like a cool, urbane tour guide. "As has no doubt been explained to you, Medusa is your final destination and new home. Although you will be unable to leave the Warden system after debarking on the planet, you will also no longer be prisoners, but, rather, citizens of the Warden Diamond. Confederacy rule ended the moment you entered this shuttle, which is owned in common by the Warden worlds, and is one of a fleet of four shuttlecraft and sixteen freighters. The System Council is a corporate entity recognized by the Confederacy as fully and internally self-governing, and it even has a seat in the Confederacy Congress. Each of the four worlds is under a separate administration, and the government of each planet is unique and independent. No matter who you are or what you have been or done in the past, you are now citizens of Medusa and nothing more—or less. Anything done prior to right now is past history that will neither be remembered, filed, or ever again referred to. Only what you do from this point, as citizens of Medusa, Warden system, will matter."

Yeah, sure buddy. And I also still believe in fairies. If they expected me to believe that the powers-that-be on Medusa didn't know anything about our past and didn't keep good records, they had a very low opinion of my intelligence.

"We will arrive at the spaceport at Gray Basin, Medusa, in approximately five minutes," the shuttle voice told us. "There you will be met by representatives of the government, given protective clothing, and then taken to a sheltered center where all your questions will be answered. Please be prepared for extreme cold; Gray Basin is in the northern hemisphere, which is now in winter season, and conditions are extremely harsh. Do not lose your guides or go out on your own. The climate at this time of year can prove lethal in a very short time to new arrivals. Although technologically quite comfortable, Medusa is somewhat primitive by the standards of the so-called civilized worlds, and the physical requirements of Medusans differ from those of other humans. Therefore, expect to find the interiors of buildings quite cold. A special place just for you has been prepared, and you will be taken there. Our government is a model of efficiency, necessary for this harsh world; please do not disregard its authority. Again, welcome to Medusa."

Although the lid was off, nobody really said much for the rest of the trip—partly because we were still conditioned by our so recent imprisonment; the rest was nerves. Me included. This was it, I told myself. Here we go.

The descent was extremely bumpy once we hit the atmosphere, but whoever was at the controls knew his or her business. Despite the turbulent air, the pilot managed a nice descent, then glided right up to and into the dock.

In less than a minute I could hear the airlock door mechanisms operating, and the indicator went from red to orange to green. There was a pneumatic hiss, then the doors rolled back. For a moment, none of us moved. Finally, those nearest the hatch stood up and walked out the open door. Sighing, I got up and did the same.

The walkway was bitter cold. We were all stark naked, so there was no time to think as we ran for the terminal. A man and a woman waited for us just as we came inside, by which time I was already turning blue. They shouted at us to get over to a table and take protective clothing as quickly as possible and put it on. None of us needed any urging. Although it was pretty tough finding anything in my size, I did the best I could. I saw that the stuff was standard thermal underclothing, then parka, pants, and soft boots all lined with some sort of fur, with matching fur-lined gloves. Getting them on helped, but I was so damned cold I knew it would take some time to thaw out.

"As soon as you're dressed, line up here!" the woman shouted in a commanding, drill-instructor-type voice.

I did as instructed, feeling a bit as if I was back in training. Only when I was standing there did the reality hit me. Here I was, on Medusa—and even as that first blast of frigid air had hit me, my body was being systematically invaded by an alien organism that was to be my permanent jailer.

CHAPTER THREE

Orientation

The couple who had met us looked lean, tough, and mean. They radiated an arrogant sort of cold, businesslike power. Both were dressed in fatigue-green uniforms and wore rubber-soled black shoes, but the uniforms were rather light and did not seem to offer much protection against the cold. In fact, these two were dressed in such a way that you'd swear the ambient temperature in the terminal was not below freezing but rather somewhere in the temperate range. Their uniforms bore sewn insignia of rank—if they followed the usual standard here, the man was a sergeant, the woman a corporal—and an odd-looking, snakelike insignia on their right pockets, but that was it.

We all lined up, turned, and looked at the couple, who stared back at us as if we were some kind of disgusting specimens for a lab dissection. I took an instant dislike to them both.

"I'm Sergeant Gorn," the man said. With his clipped, officious voice he sounded like every sergeant I'd ever heard. "This is Corporal Sugra. We are orientation leaders and medical technicians for your group. I think you are as dressed as we can manage. Don't worry if you have size problems—everyone does. When you become more acclimated to Medusa, you will be issued a full set of tailored clothing. First we must transfer you to the orientation center, so follow me and we will board a bus just outside." With that he started walking and, after a moment's hesitation, we all followed. The corporal brought up the rear.

The bus was of an odd magnetic-drive design, with hard, molded seats, two strings of internal lights, and not much else. There was no operator and, as we quickly discovered, no heat. It was built like a fort, though, so we would be sheltered from the noisy wind and thickly blowing snow if not from the biting cold. As soon as the last of us boarded, the corporal took a card out of one of her pockets and stuck it in a slot in the front panel of the bus. The doors closed with a *whoosh* and we were off rather smoothly and quickly, emerging from the tunnel into Medusa proper.

The spaceport was located some distance from the town. We managed to run out of the blizzard after some ten or fifteen minutes and gained a little visibility of a world that was still totally snow-covered. I could see high mountains off in the distance, grim and foreboding. There was no sign of life out there, though—I had no idea how much snow was there, but it was more than I'd ever seen outside of a polar ice cap.

The bus, however, was an impressive vehicle, smooth and sturdy, that apparently was guided along some sort of under-snow tracking system. The system made sense, for no matter how high the snow piled up the bus would glide just above it.

We slowed, suddenly, but without any jerking, and approached a large building that loomed up out of the sea of white. We stopped, waited, then started up again, stopped again, waited, then glided on, the tracking system now clearly visible ahead.

Sgt. Gorn picked up the microphone. "We are entering the west gate of the city of Gray Basin," he informed us. "Because of the unpleasant weather around here, much of the city is built underground—in fact, under the permafrost. The two stops we made were to clear force fields, without which the gates would be open to wild animals and other unpleasant creatures that do, in fact, roam that landscape you have seen."

We took another turn, then came to a complicated track-switching area. The bus stopped, then cautiously proceeded once again as a series of lights changed on all the tracks; the bus eased onto one of them. We moved along another two or three minutes at a slow but steady speed, then emerged from the tunnel and into the city of Gray Basin proper, which was as modern-looking as the bus. It seemed to go on forever.

"The city is not in a cavern," Gorn informed us, "but is built in the same manner as are the domed cities on some of the most hostile frontier worlds. In fact, it's something of a domed city upside down, in that we built the city and then roofed it over. Most Medusan cities not on or near the equator are built like this. Gray Basin has a population of seventeen thousand and is the commercial center of the north."

The map in my head showed me pretty much where I was. The eastern continental land mass, it seemed, and at about 38° north latitude. On most worlds this would be a fairly pleasant climate; here, it was tundra.

Despite my warm clothing, the cold was beginning to get to me. I had spent the last several weeks in perfect climate control, and my body was not used to this kind of extreme. Even in the bus, where things should be fairly stable in temperature, it was still damned *cold*.

We wound through streets past neat-looking modular apartment buildings and what must have been office buildings and shops, finally pulling up at a blocky, monolithic four-story building made out of some blackish stone. The doors hissed open.

"Please follow us into the building," Gorn said. Despite the "please," it still sounded like the command it was. "Do not hold back. You will have to climb two flights of stairs. Do not get lost."

We followed the same route-step as before, entering the building and walking down a wide corridor with offices and other corridors branching off to the right and left of us. We then reached a stairway and climbed it, keeping up with Gorn as best we could. I think most of us were a bit surprised to be winded by a mere two-story climb, our sedentary imprisonment notwithstanding. Not only were we all out of condition, but the slightly heavier gravity was telling.

The blast of warm air when we entered the first room on the third floor was as unexpected as it was tremendously welcome. Despite my clothing, I frankly hadn't realized how terribly cold I was until the pain that the heat generated hit me. It took a few minutes before I could really think of anything else and look around.

The first room, the heated one, was fairly large and furnished in a utilitarian manner, with long, hard folding tables and collapsible chairs and not much else. There were no windows, a fact our hosts were quick to explain.

"Just take seats anywhere and get accustomed to the temperature change," Gorn told us. "This room and the three adjoining rooms have been raised to 21° for your initial comfort. These are the only directly heated rooms, so stay within them at all times. We chose this area to heat because, with no windows or other outside vents, it is the most efficient system." He walked over to a nearby door. "If you'll come in here, I'll show you the rest of the place."

We followed—slowly, still not recovered completely from exposure—and found that the second room was a large barrackslike area with eight double bunks, four on each side of the hall. The mattresses appeared to be paper-thin and none too comfortable, but I'd seen worse. The place was well-maintained, although obviously seldom used. Beyond was a third large room, with a large common shower and three open standard toilets, plus four small sinks with mirrors. Again it looked seldom-used, but serviceable.

We followed Sgt. Gorn back to the "lounge" area and took seats. As yet nobody had removed his thermal clothing and I had no inclination to do so myself. I felt as if I would never be warm again.

It was Cpl. Sugra's turn at us. She looked like a lot of women cops I've met in my work—not unattractive, but hard, cold, and worldly; her voice matched. For the first time I could look at her and Gorn and see a bit beyond the manner and the uniforms. Their complexions, which at the spaceport and on the bus were a granitelike gray, now seemed lighter, almost orange. There was a certain toughness to their skin, which, on close inspection, resembled the hides of great animals. Soft they were not.

"I'm Corporal Sugra," she began, reintroducing herself. "Sergeant Gorn and I will be with you over the next week. We will be staying right down the hall from this complex and will be available to answer your questions and give you basic preparation. At various times others from the government will come in to talk about specific areas. Now, we understand you have just come from a bitter experience, and you are now most concerned about what this new world is like and what it both has for you and will do for you."

And *to* me, I thought.

"First of all, is there anyone here who does not know why Medusa and the other worlds of the Warden Diamond are used by the Confederacy for exile?" She paused a moment, then seemed satisfied that we all knew at least the basics.

"The micro-organism that is now within all of your bodies will be making itself at home. Please don't be alarmed. You will find there is no sensation, no feeling at all that anything is different. In fact, you will probably feel increasingly *better* as this process goes on because, despite the best medical care, the human system is riddled with disease and physical problems of one sort or another. Since the Warden organism depends on you for its place to live, it wants that place to be in as good a condition as possible. So it will repair what is wrong, make more efficient that which is inefficient, and will not only cure you of any diseases or infections you might have but prevent any new ones. That's how it pays you back; it's a good deal."

A big, gruff-looking man near me gave a low cough. "Yeah—but what's *our* price?" he grumbled.

"There is no . . . price, as you call it," she responded. "As you may know, it is theorized that the Warden organism was native only to the planet Lilith and was spread by early explorers to the other three worlds, where it mutated to survive. Some people on Lilith have the power to order the Wardens around, inflicting pain and pleasure and in some cases even creating and destroying through willpower alone. On Charon this ability is even more pronounced, with physical and mental power giving those trained in controlling their Wardens almost magical abilities over themselves and others. On Cerberus minds are actually exchanged between the people as a by-product of the Warden organism. In all cases there are more positives than minuses in the by-products. But here on Medusa survival dominates all other things. The organism here is more colonial in nature, sticking to whatever it's in and not bothering with others."

"You can't be saying that there's no effect," a skeptical woman put in.

"No, there is an effect, but it is limited to each individual. It is also universal and automatic, so that no willpower or training is required. Everyone can use it equally, making Medusa a far better place. What it did to us, what it is doing to you, is totally altering your basic biochemistry. We look human, we act human; but under the microscope we are not human. Here, on Medusa, the Warden colonies survive in us only as long as we ourselves survive. So the colonies mutated humanity here to survive the climate, no matter what. The changes are far more extensive and comprehensive than on the other three planets. Our entire cellular structure is modified, with each Warden colony in each cell in total and complete control, ready to act at a moment's notice, either independently or collectively as required."

"To what end?" I asked, genuinely curious. "What does it do?"

"Instant adaptation to whatever the needs of the organism are," she told us. "We can survive almost any temperature extreme. Our bodies can consume and use almost any substance to provide whatever energy is needed under any conditions. We could go stark naked into that snowy wilderness you saw coming in and we would neither freeze nor starve. Water is our only requirement. We can adapt to extremes of radiation, drink boiling water, even walk barefoot on hot coals. Medusans are in every way superior to humanity, or even to those of the other three worlds. Instant evolution, it's been called. What we need, we have or become. As I say, the system is automatic—no thought or direction is required."

"That's why the bus and buildings were unheated," I thought aloud. "You don't need heat."

She nodded. "Natural insulation is enough to keep everything fairly uniform and comfortable for us. These uniforms mark our station and rank, and provide such handy things as pockets. They in no way provide protection, because we don't need any—and neither will you."

She paused to let that sink in a bit, then looked over at Sgt. Gorn and nodded to him. He took up the briefing.

"For now you will remain in these specially heated and insulated quarters," he told us. "Over the course of a week, the Warden organism will make Medusans out of you physically. Our purpose is to make you Medusans socially and politically as well. We have here a society that is one of man's old dreams. Every single man, woman, and child here is superior in every physical way. To that our current First Minister, Talant Ypsir, has added his considerable skills at political organization and social engineering to create a highly advanced society. On Lilith or Charon you might wind up as primitive migrant workers. Here we are technologically advanced, with all that implies. Your place in our society will be determined by your mind and skills, not by any physical or technological limitations. This world looks harsh, I know, but once it no longer threatens you it becomes a world of wonder and beauty and comfort. You are lucky to be Medusans, considering the alternatives."

I wondered about that.

The barracks-style setup meant we nine would get to know one another pretty well, at least in a superficial sense. Although one couple preferred not to talk at all about their pasts, from the six who would it was clear that this was a very unusual crop. Every single one of the six—seven, including my cover—had killed at least one other human being in a cold and premeditated way. I suspected that all nine of us represented the most violent kinds of criminal minds. No smugglers or embezzlers here—we were the cream of the crop.

As the "kid" in the group, I found the others curiously kind and protective toward me, almost to a one. Those who have never encountered real criminals before might find that a bit hard to believe; but, in fact, most criminals are pretty nice, ordinary people except for one little area. All these people were extraordinary, because in contrast to my—Tarin Bul's—rather direct and sloppy job, they had all killed in extremely clever technological ways.

Just how Talant Ypsir planned to turn such people into model citizens of his new superior society we all discovered the next day. A tall man came in, looking granite-gray in the same way Gorn and Sugra had when we'd first met them. He introduced himself as Solon Kabaye, Gray Basin's Political Commissioner. His uniform was all black but still styled in the military manner. He had gold braid on his sleeves and a golden-colored belt. On his pocket was the obvious government symbol—a stylized woman's head with a hair full of what had to be snakes. His manner was easygoing and conversational, like that of most politicians; I may have been the only one to notice his skin color change from that light gray to the oranger shade of Gorn and Sugra. Here was a graphic indication that something inside him worked very differently from anything we were accustomed to.

"I'm going to be basic and blunt," he told us, "because that's the best way to start. Let's go over a couple of facts right away, shall we? First—you're stuck. There is no escape from Medusa, no place to run. Therefore, you'd best get used to the world as quickly as possible and settle in as best you can. Your future—the rest of your lives—is here, tied to Medusa. The system works, and it works well. It takes into account our planetary assets, our inherent problems and limitations as Warden citizens, and it gives a strong measure of prosperity to the people. The system evolved over the past century, as various ideas were tried and discarded. This one works. You didn't ask to be here—but you put yourselves here by your own actions. We didn't ask for you, either. Frankly, unless you possess some new technological knowledge that could be of use to us, you're not really needed here. So we have to find out just where you fit—then you fit. You either fit, or you take that last step into the deferred oblivion from which coming here saved you. That's the bottom line."

This was tough talk, and very discomforting as well. Still, it was also very professionally timed. We were stuck here, on an alien world, waiting for a something we couldn't see, hear, or feel to take over our bodies. Quite simply, we had no real options. After the first night they had even taken away the thermal wear while we slept, leaving us with nothing but flimsy white hospital-type gowns. Try to run now, boy, out into a frigid wilderness.

"Sounds like the Confederacy," Turnel, the ruddy, gruff resident grouch of our group noted half under his breath. Of course Kabaye heard him and smiled slightly.

"Perhaps it does. The Confederacy is a society that exists because it works. That doesn't make it the *best* society, or the most efficient, or anything else, but it's there because it works for the majority of people."

"Well, we're the minority," noted Edala, a tough, worldly woman prisoner.

"True," Kabaye agreed. "We all are. I was born and raised in the Confederacy, same as you. So was Talant Ypsir, our First Minister. And now we're here, and you're here, and, ironically, folks like the First Minister and myself find ourselves the government rather than opposed to the government. We're faced with the same problems as the Confederacy, and we have additional problems because of Medusa's limitations. Our advantage, though, is that Medusa is the wealthiest of the Warden worlds since we control the raw-materials sources, and, with a Warden organism not trying to get in the way of building stuff, we can best exploit these resources. So, let me tell you the score here and then I'll tell you how you fit in."

The "score," as it were, was that we came from a somewhat totalitarian society that believed in the basic goodness of man to a *very* totalitarian society run by men and women who were convinced that humans would always, given a choice, do the wrong thing. Therefore, a society tightly and rigidly controlled, in which all the rules were known and posted and no violations were tolerated, was Ypsir's new vision. It turned out to be not nearly as new as he thought, but a very old idea indeed.

There were less than thirteen million Medusans, scattered around the so-called temperate zones in small, enclosed cities and towns linked by magne-bus and a freight service using the same tracks. Electric power was generated basically by geothermal wells, and the location and size of the cities were determined by just how much power was available. Medusa controlled the Diamond's freighter fleet, digging raw materials out of the mineral-rich moons of the next nearest neighbor out-system, the great ringed gas giant Momrath. These were unloaded at specific freight terminals strategically located around the planet so that the cities could be most economically served. The reason for cities like Gray Basin was not only their large geothermal sources of power, but also because, being so far north, magne-tracks could be laid over the permanently frozen ocean to the north and thus connect continents. Air travel was available, but it was expensive, subject to frequent nasty weather conditions, and not practical for heavy freight.

Some of the cities were quite large, but most had between fifty and a hundred thousand people. All were self-contained, and all nonequatorial ones were, like Gray Basin, dug in rather than built on the surface; and each one specialized in just a few industries. Gray Basin, for example, specialized in transportation and related industries on the surface. All of the magne-buses, some of the freight containers, and much of the buried guidance track were made here. One town built computers—a surprise to me, since I'd assumed that such things would be strictly prohibited by the Confederacy guardians. A few specialized in food production and distribution, mostly synthetics and food imported from Lilith and Charon. It *was* true, as Sugra had told us, that we could eat almost anything—yet, as Kabaye was quick to point out, the fact that we could eat human flesh did not mean that we preferred it to steak. Being able to eat something was not the same as either liking it or enjoying it.

Clearly Medusa's economy worked closely with that of Cerberus, next in-system. The Cerberans helped design the products Medusa made, and handled just about all the computer software, as well as taking raw materials like basic steel, plastics, and the like we turned out and making things that were of use on their and other worlds but not here. For example, the very concept of a speedboat was ridiculous on Medusa, but on the Cerberan water world speedboats were in great demand.

The factories and industries of Medusa were basically automated, but there was a job for every human. Natives went to state schools from ages four to twelve, then were examined in a number of areas including aptitudes and intelligence potential and placed in the particular training track for which they were most suited. This was a bit more ponderous than the Confederacy's method of breeding you to your job, but it served the same purpose.

Also contrary to Confederacy custom, families were maintained for those early years, although they were often nontraditional and always state-determined. Group marriages and group families were the rule, partly because of the need to bear and raise children and partly in the name of "efficiency," a word of which I was already tiring.

There were forty-four wage steps, or grades possible, although the top four grades were strictly top government personnel and there was only one Grade 44, naturally.

The easiest way to think of the society, I reflected, was as if everybody—every man, woman, and child—were in the military, attached to a mission section. Within that section were most of the grades, with grade reflecting rank and, therefore, power. The state, or your section of it, provided com-

mon meal facilities, food, clothing, and shelter, and also made available
the amenities that could be bought with the money you made. The pay
seemed relatively low until you remembered that all the basics were taken
care of and anything you earned could be spent on luxuries.

There were three shifts a day, each running eight hours, with the hours
adjusted for the differences from Confederacy norm. The work week was
six days, with the seventh off, but different industries took different days
off so there was no universal off day. To make sure all worked well and
smoothly, there was the Monitor Service.

I suspected it was this Monitor Service idea that got Talant Ypsir his
one-way ticket from the Confederacy to the Diamond. Though I doubt if
it would work on a thousand worlds spread over a quarter of a galaxy, the
system worked fine, it seemed, on Medusa, though none of us liked it,
least of all me.

Every single room in every single city and town was monitored. Not
just the rooms, but the streets, alleyways, buses, you name it. Just about
every single thing anyone said or did was monitored and recorded by a
master computer or, really, the huge computer bank that was actually in
orbit around the planet. Whoever wrote the computer program should be
tortured to death.

Now, obviously, not even the galaxy's greatest computer could really analyze all that data, and this was where Ypsir was diabolically clever. The
Monitor Service, a sort of police force that ran this system and was generally just called TMS, programmed the computers to look for certain things
—phrases, actions, who except for them knew what?—that would cause a
computer to "flag" you. Then a human TMS agent would sit down and
with the computer's aid review anything about you he or she wanted, then
haul you in to see why you were acting so funny or being so subversive.
Nobody knew what the flag codes were, and a certain amount of totally
random harassment was maintained by TMS just so the bright guys
couldn't figure them out.

The system, as Kabaye pointed out proudly, did, in fact, work. Productivity was extremely high, absenteeism and shirking extremely low. Crime
was almost nonexistent, except for the rare crime of passion which the
computer couldn't flag in time to stop. But even if you managed to commit
it, as soon as the crime was discovered the TMS could call up the whole
scene and see exactly what was what.

Violators were tried in secret by TMS courts, extremely quickly it
seemed, and given punishment ranging from demotion to being handed
over to the psychs—many of whom were Confederacy crooks and sadists
sentenced here themselves—for whatever they felt like doing to your mind.
The ultimate punishment, for treason, was what was known as Ultimate
Demotion—you were shipped off on a very unpleasant one-way trip to the
mines of Momrath's moons.

It was an ugly system, and extremely difficult to fight or circumvent unless you knew exactly where the monitor devices were and what would

and would not constitute a flag. That made it a near-impossible challenge, particularly for a kid whose background would suggest that he not be allowed too near any world leaders. In a sense, though, I liked it. Not only was this a real challenge, perhaps my supreme challenge; but Medusa was, after all, my type of world—technologically oriented and dependent on that technology. If I *could* find a way, too, the system would actually help. TMS, and, therefore, Talant Ypsir, must be pretty damn confident and secure.

But the more complex the challenge, the more I would have to know, and learn. This would not be easy by any means, and no mistakes would be tolerated by the system. It would take some time, perhaps a very long time, before I could confidently know enough to act.

After Kabaye's visit conversation was muted and sullen, to say the least. There were a number of attempts to figure out where the monitors were in the various rooms, but none of us found one that night.

Still, the third day's lessons proved to be pretty instructive as, one by one, even our most private whispers of the day before were repeated back to us by our hosts. Here was an effective demonstration of how efficient the fixed system really was—it selectively picked up one whisper even when masked by other whispers as well as fairly loud sounds. I was most interested in seeing pictures to check the angle and, therefore, locate the monitors; but we were shown none. We reached a general consensus that we were in one hell of a planetary jail cell, but there was nothing, at least for now, that any of us could do about it.

On the fourth day, we were tested and interviewed. Various officious-looking clerks wearing the same kind of military garb as Gorn and Sugra subjected us individually to a battery of tests that took much of the day. They then conducted general interviews.

At the end of the whole thing, each of us was taken into a small room we hadn't known about for a final interview.

She said her name was Dr. Crouda, and I knew immediately by her whites and her medical insignia that she had to be a psych. That really didn't bother me—not only was I trained and fortified against the general run of psych tricks, but I was in some ways the creation of the best psychs in the Confederacy. What I needed, though, was a good performance that would cement my cover and do me the most good overall.

She motioned me to a chair, sat back behind a small desk, and looked over my files for a moment. "You are Tarin Bul?"

I shuffled with kid fidgets in my seat. "Yes, ma'am."

"And you are fourteen?"

I nodded. "A few months ago. I'm not too sure of the time. It's been a real long time since I could remember anything but prisons and psychs—beg pardon, ma'am."

She nodded and couldn't suppress a slight smile. "I understand perfectly. Did you know that as far as we can tell you are the youngest person ever sent to the Warden Diamond?"

"I sorta guessed that," I answered truthfully.

"Your education and training and your genetic inclinations are toward administrative work, but you're hardly ready at your age. You realize that, don't you?"

Again I could only nod. "I understand." Right now, in the normal course of things, Tarin Bul would still be in school.

She sighed and looked over her reports. Real written files, I noted. How novel. "Now, your tests show a true inclination for math and a strong grasp of computer principles and operations. Have you given any thought to what you'd like to be?"

I thought a moment, choosing the best tack. Finally I settled on the one I thought most in character. "Lord of the Diamond," I told her.

Again the smile. "Well, I understand that. But, realistically, considering your abbreviated education and your likes and dislikes—is there anything you really find yourself drawn to?"

I thought a moment. "Yes, ma'am. Freighter pilot." That wasn't much of a risk, since it was right in character—but, oh how I wished I really *were* a freighter pilot! Money, mobility, status, and a lot more.

"That's not unreasonable," she said, thinking it over, "but you are a long way from the age at which you could even enter pilot training." She paused and threw me the typical psych curve. "Have you ever had any sexual experiences either with girls or with boys?"

I acted shocked. "No, ma'am!"

"What do you think of girls?"

I shrugged. "Oh, they're okay."

She nodded to herself and scribbled something, then asked, "How do you feel about being here? Being sent here, I mean?"

Again I shrugged. "Beats bein' dead, I guess. I haven't seen enough of this world to tell otherwise."

Again the nod and the scribble. "I think we have enough for now—Tarin, isn't it? You may go. Tomorrow someone will be in to talk to you, and then we'll know where you're going."

For now that sounded fair enough. I left.

I hadn't really had any problems with that battery they threw at me earlier I had seen such tests before and understood exactly how they were weighted and scored. I had skewed my aptitudes upward in certain specific areas, like electronics and mechanics, as well as computers, while keeping the Tarin Bul background as consistent with what would be expected of my breeding and training. I could see and understand their problem with me, though. The fact was, I was too old to fit directly into their fixed planetary training system and too young to go to work properly. The best I could do was present myself as some sort of smart-ass genius and hope for the best.

On the fourth day my skin turned an orange-brown, as did that of four of the others. In a sense the change excited me, since I knew now for the first time that something major really *was* happening inside me; but it gave me a chilling feeling as well.

Gorn and Sugra were obviously pleased by the development, and the morning was spent with the five of us undergoing a few physical tests. The first one was simple and basic. I was dressed only in the flimsy hospital gown, when they took me out into that cold corridor and down to the first level of the building. For a while I thought they were pulling some kind of fast one—I felt a chill when the door opened and we stepped out, but the chill was rapidly replaced with a feeling of growing warmth and comfort, until I felt perfectly normal once again.

I was not normal, though, which I realized just by looking at the backs of my hands. The burnt orange quickly faded out, replaced by a more neutral grayish coloration. And yet, I *felt* normal—felt just fine, thank you, and as human as ever.

The first level was now staffed with a receptionist and a few people moved in and out; but the place was by no means crowded. We were the object of a few stares, but little else.

Satisfied that we felt all right, Gorn led the five of us outside into the street. Again there was that slightly chilling feeling, followed by a comforting warmth, and that was that. I felt warm as toast and perfectly comfortable despite the fact I was barefoot and wearing nothing more than a glorified bedsheet. In a sense, the test was reassuring, since some of the fear of the unknown and uncontrollable vanished with the realization that I really didn't feel unusual or extraordinary or different.

Satisfied with our progress, they led us back to our quarters. When I entered, I felt a really strong blast of heat, which faded as quickly as had the chill, leaving me feeling pretty much as I had in the street outside. Now at least I felt like a Medusan. I still wished they would tell us everything about this Warden transformation—I was quite sure they were withholding a lot of information on the theory that what you didn't know you couldn't use—but there was no way to approach the problem directly. I'd have to wait and learn in the streets, or by accident, dammit.

That afternoon those of us who had "acclimated"—as they called it— were summoned, one by one, into the small office. When my turn came I walked in, expecting another psych, but found instead a man I'd never seen before.

"Tarin Bul? I am Staff Supervisor Trin of the Transport Workers Guild. I'm told you have ambitions to be a pilot."

My emotions soared. "Yes, sir!"

"Well, that's possible. Your literacy level is off the scale, your mathematical level nearly that, and you have a command of computer theory far beyond any expectations. But your education is still not really advanced, and you'll need some more height and a couple of years of age before we can enroll you in pilot's school, if we do. However, you have been assigned to the Guild. Now, don't get your hopes up. You're coming in rather awkwardly—considering your age and experience, or lack of it. You don't quite fit. Nor do your tests really indicate a direction or focus. That means you're in the right Guild for your ambitions, but at the lowest level. We can't put you in school—you're too old for the integrated program and too young for advanced training. Therefore, it has been decided that you will be given a position—we call them slots—at the lowest level of the Guild, as well as administered self-study computer courses in a number of areas to allow you some preparation for the future."

I nodded seriously. The rating wasn't as good as it could have been, but it was more than enough to start.

'The lowest levels require hard, unpleasant, boring work," he warned. "But you will be observed and, if you do well both at work and in your courses, you will be advanced accordingly. Whether you are advanced to pilot or driver training, or to some other area, will depend on your work habits, diligence, your supervisor's ratings, and how well you integrate yourself into our system. Understand?"

'Ah, yes, sir. Um . . . how old do you have to be to enter pilot's school?"

He smiled. "The minimum age is sixteen, the average age eighteen. The program is one year, then there's an additional year of in-service apprentice work before you can be considered for full licensing."

I nodded. Still, while trying to convince the man that I was more than eager to work my way up and please everybody for the next two years, the back of my mind said "two years" in a far different tone. Two years was a long, long time. . . .

CHAPTER FOUR

Workin' on the Railroad

The next day I was given a small card that bore a number and a symbol on the front and had a series of dots of some magnetic material on the back. The symbol was a bolt of lightning flanked by two solid black lines —rails, it seemed. The symbol of the Transportation Guild. True to their word at the initial briefing, I also received a set of tailored uniforms in my size. They were in the satiny red color of the Guild and bore the same symbol on the pocket. A small suitcase contained some basic toiletries, including, I found, a razor, something I wouldn't need for a while. Also included was a pair of red rubber-soled shoes, just to improve footing on the smooth floors and sidewalks of the city.

The card contained my name, new address, Guild, work assignment, and various control numbers. It was even my bankbook. The Central Bank of Gray Basin held an account in my name. Every time I wanted to pay for something I had to stick my card in the appropriate slot and the amount would automatically be deducted from my account. I was impressed. Pretty much like home, although my bank stake was only a hundred units.

The basic currency was the unit—work unit, I assumed—which was broken into a hundred smaller divisions called bits. A pretty standard decimal system. Things must be fairly cheap.

Beyond that I received some insincere "good lucks" from Gorn and Sugra and some far more sincere ones from my eight comrades, now all tuned, or acclimated, to the Warden organism. I picked up a bus-route map of the city that told me how to get to where I had to be, and that was it. Clutching my small overnight case, I was out the door and on the streets of the big city.

Once temperature was no longer a problem, the city seemed much like those domed cities I'd been in on several other worlds. Factories and such were easy to spot by their design, but mostly because their exhaust vents went straight up to the illuminated ceiling and on through it. With temperatures fairly well equalized inside and out, there was no problem with frost, although occasional ice crystals floated in the air. Curiously, my breath did not show in the cold. I wondered just what the hell that bug had made us into, since I was pretty sure I was still a warm-blooded mammal.

The buses were pretty easy to find, and in their automated style worked very well. The locals seemed to be guided by single magnetic strips buried within the street paving itself and ran on rubberized tires—synthetic, of course. They had sensors at the clearly marked and color-coded bus stops and would stop if anyone was within the painted stop zones. The door was something of a turnstile, unlocking when you stuck your card in the side slot and passing you through without giving any opportunity for a second person to sneak by—an interesting indication to me that this place wasn't as crime-free and rock honest as had been made out. I suspected a lot of petty crimes were attempted even by ordinarily honest folk. It was just about the only way you had to feel like you were getting back at the system.

The bus was not only comfortable, it had a handy map above the windshield that illuminated where it was on its route and where the transfer points were. With that and my own set of directions I had no trouble crossing town, changing twice and winding up exactly where I was supposed to be. There was something, certainly, to be said for Medusan efficiency.

During the ride I just sat back and studied the city and the people. They looked a rather ordinary lot, all dressed in these identical uniforms, color- and badge-coded as to guild and grade. It took no real detective work to figure out that the militarylike rank and uniforms of Gorn and Sugra were those of the dreaded TMS, who certainly had to socialize only among their own. Whenever a green fatigue uniform was visible, you could see everybody else pretending to ignore it but shying away fast. And

TMS people, of course, radiated arrogant disdain for the masses and joy in knowing they were powerful and feared. The cops were certainly the enemy here, and for good reason. I had never seen a system with police force more in control of things. Idly I wondered how you entered TMS—and who were *they* afraid of?

Around the city's core, with its office buildings and cooperative shops and markets and central terminal, the residential and manufacturing areas were arranged in something of a pie-wedge design. The wedges seemed to alternate between heavy industry and residential units, all of which were four-story affairs composed of what looked like identical apartments. I later learned this was not the case, however. Family units had one room per family member over twelve, so some were fairly large suites; and the top grades had pretty swanky suites just for themselves.

My own destination was T-26, a unit that looked much like all the others. I punched the stop button and jumped off as the building number went past the window, which meant I had to backtrack a block. I hesitated only a moment, then walked up and entered the main entrance.

The place was like a dormitory. The ground floor had a lobby with computer screens giving general information, including schedule changes and even sports scores. A pair of double doors led to a common dining hall. Apparently the residents of the building ate here, cafeteria-style, although the food was certainly prepared elsewhere. There wasn't much room for a kitchen.

Doors on either side led to communal stores. There was a small pharmacy, a tailor, a shoe shop, and the like. Apparently they were only open one hour on each side of each shift change. They also couldn't be very large, I told myself, as it wouldn't be efficient to have actual stores in each building unit. Each was staffed by one clerk, who simply took in what you had—shoes to be fixed, for example, or an order for toiletries and such—then sent them to a central store which had the shoes fixed or filled the order. What you wanted was ready when you came back from a shift. Not a bad system. If it wasn't for TMS I might actually be impressed by this place, I told myself.

There was a small elevator cage at each end of the hall, too, I noticed, so I would not have to climb the stairs.

My instructions said I was to report first to T-26, Room 404—which, I assumed, was on the fourth floor—and get settled. I would be contacted there and told where to go and what to do next.

Room 404 was where it should logically have been. Since there was no key, only a card slot, I inserted my card and the door slid open.

It was a small room, about five meters by four, but it had been sensibly laid out by somebody who'd obviously done hotel work. The two beds looked comfortable and standard—after the cell and then those barracks cots they looked wonderful—and there were two reasonably spacious closets, plenty of drawers along the wall opposite the beds, and a CRT terminal that was unfamiliar in design but pretty easy to figure out.

A side door led to a toilet, shower, and basin, which, I saw, we shared with the room next to us. I say "we" simply because when I looked in the closets, then in the drawers, somebody's stuff was already in them. The owner didn't appear to be much bigger than I from the size of the clothes, but I'd have to wait and see.

Although the room monitors were cleverly concealed to blend in with the surroundings, they weren't hard to locate. The one in the bathroom was in the center of the overhead light, and the one in the main room was almost certainly integrated into the centrally located smoke and fire detector. I wondered idly if they had the closets covered. Though the idea seemed pretty ridiculous they probably did. Ypsir and his TMS apparently had that kind of mind.

I checked the computer terminal for messages but there were none apparent. I didn't yet have the codes needed to call up the less routine stuff. Since I had received no instructions beyond coming here and waiting, I put my stuff away in an empty drawer and stowed the overnight bag in one of the closets, then went back to the terminal and gave it a good going-over. It was extremely primitive by my standards, but *did* have the basics, both keyboard and voxcoder for two-way communication. The thing was a combination terminal and telephone, possibly even a picturephone. Considering the obvious technical limitations the Confederacy imposed on the Warden Diamond, this really was a slick piece of homegrown work. After deciding I didn't have the proper tools to disassemble the frame and see what really made the machine tick, I abandoned it for the time being, walked over to the bed, leaned back, and relaxed in the nice, downy softness. I promptly fell asleep.

I was awakened perhaps two hours later by the sound of the door *whooshing* back to admit someone. Deciding that discretion was the better part of valor and all that, I remained motionless, curious to see who it might be. My eyes opened wide and I sat straight up when I saw the newcomer. I really hadn't been prepared for this.

"Oh, hello!" she said, spotting me. "You must be Tarin Bul."

The girl was very young—I couldn't really tell how young—quite small and slightly built, hair cropped as short as my own. I was still sitting up in bed, staring, mouth agape, trying to adjust to the fact that she was a she, when she started removing her uniform.

"Hey!" I cried out, feeling very awkward indeed. I was no prude, but societies have rules and the one I came from wasn't quite *this* casual.

She stopped, a little puzzled. "What's the matter?" And she meant it.

"Um—you're taking off your clothes in front of a perfect stranger."

The idea struck her as funny. "Oh, you're supposed to take yours off, too. The Monitor should have told you. I guess somebody's asleep at the switch today." She finished removing the last of her clothing, which she folded into a small ball, then opened a drawer, from which she removed a plastic bag, stuffing in the clothes. "Below Supervisor grade it's not permitted to wear uniforms in your home dorm. Don't you know *that?*"

I shook my head slowly, trying to decide if I was being put on. My wits returning, I realized that what she was telling me made perfect sense from the TMS viewpoint. You couldn't carry in anything without taking it out of your clothing first, and being totally nude was the ultimate invasion of privacy, somehow. Now, I'd gone nude in mixed company many times, usually on plush resort worlds with seaside villas, and never thought anything of it. But this was a whole different kind of experience, and it took some getting used to.

She held out the bag. "Come on—before the Monitor sees you. Off and in the bag."

I sighed and decided that it wouldn't be in character if I caved in too easily. "But—you're a *girl!*" I was suddenly very cautious, mentally. The mere fact that I *hadn't* been called on such a rule indicated to me that they were observing my behavior and how I acclimated socially. The fact that I was fourteen was some protection, but it wasn't total. I had to assume that any government capable of putting a superhuman robot in the most secret rooms of Military Systems Command could easily know about the Merton Process and deduce the truth given half a chance.

She stood up straight and shook her head at me in wonder. "Are all people Outside so shy and upset by so simple a thing?"

Her question told me two facts straight off, if she was indeed what she seemed. First, she was a native of this world, and, second, I was the first person from "Outside"—that is, outside the Warden Diamond, and maybe even outside of Medusa—she'd ever met. Ordinarily such knowledge would give me some advantage and leeway in slips, but I couldn't assume that whoever was monitoring me was as inexperienced or naive.

I sighed, gave in, and removed my clothes, tossing them into the common bag. She tied the bag off and left it on the floor. "I'm Ching Lu Kor,' she introduced herself. "Ah—you *are* Tarin Bul?"

I nodded nervously. "Uh huh."

She looked me over mock-critically. "You're not so bad. I always heard people Outside were all soft and flabby, but you look pretty good."

I shuffled nervously, creating my proper *persona* as I went. "Uh—I haven't had a lot of exercise in a while, but I made do."

She sat down on the corner of the bed opposite mine. "What'd you do to get sent here? Or shouldn't I ask that?"

I shrugged and sat back on my bed. "I executed the murderer of my father." I told her. "Nobody else would."

She frowned and appeared to be a little taken aback by that. Clearly a crime of that magnitude was hard for someone brought up in a totalitarian world like Medusa to fathom. But clearly she understood the implications of the act, even if it seemed impossible to her. She even seemed impressed. A romantic, I decided.

"Are you hungry?" she asked suddenly, getting away from the subject.

"I'm starved—I've just come off shift. You're lucky—no work until 1600 to-morrow." She jumped up from the bed. "Come on. We have to drop off the laundry anyway. Then you can tell me all about Outside, and I can tell you all about here."

That seemed a fair trade, but I decided some hesitation was in order. "We go eat—like this?"

She laughed. "You really *are* hung up, aren't you? They'll have a psych on you if you don't relax a little." She turned and waved at the room. "Besides, somebody's *always* looking at you anyway. What's the difference?"

She had a point there. I let her pick up the clothes bag and followed her out the door, then stopped. "Hey—what about the cards?"

Obviously I had said something funny again. "You don't need cards in your own *home*," she responded as she headed for the stairs.

She was certainly right about nudity. Old, young, male, female—everyone walked about and sat and talked with no inhibitions at all. Here and there would be people in uniform, either somebody with rank who wanted everybody else to remember it or those still coming in from work or leaving for it. Apparently there were staggered start times for the shifts within the two-hour active period, probably to ease the mass-transit load.

The cafeteria was about half full, with the usual eating-place bustle and unintelligible mass-conversation buzz. There were no menu choices, I found—you went up, punched a button, got a covered tray, then went to a table and sat down. Water and a selection of three beverages at a self-service area in the center of the cafeteria provided the only option.

The food was unfamiliar but tasted pretty good. I was never very fussy about food and was certainly no gourmet, so I adjusted to this as easily as if I'd eaten the stuff all my life. After the jail mush and blocky slop of the reception center it was a real pleasure to have a recognizable plate with entrée, vegetables, and dessert. The meat seemed a standard synthetic, but the fruit and vegetable appeared fresh. I remembered that Medusa imported a fair amount of food from the warmer worlds. Keep the masses happy, I thought, even if they *can* eat tree bark.

I was struck by a number of things as I sat there eating, including at least one fact that amazed me. Here were these people in the most totalitarian society I'd ever known or experienced, and they were sitting back, relaxed, talking, looking, and sounding for all the world like any cafeteria crowd anyplace—except, of course, for their bare hides. Far from making me relax more about Medusa, the observation that here was a totalitarian society that *worked*—worked so well that the generations born and raised into it felt completely at ease—made me nervous. I had to admit that Talant Ypsir might be an unpleasant individual, but he was damned smart.

My other observations were on the more practical side. Medusans *looked* about as human as anybody else, particularly a frontier world population. Yet subtle differences that might otherwise go unnoticed were immediately apparent to an Outsider such as myself. The skin textures seemed far more leathery, somehow; the hair was also far stiffer, wiry. Even the eyes seemed somehow different, almost as if shaped by a master sculptor out of marble, without the shine and liquidity of human eyes.

I knew that I, too, now shared these characteristics, yet I felt perfectly normal, not in the least bit changed. My skin had the same look as the skin of those around me, yet it felt normal, soft, and natural to me.

A third observation was that I was the youngest-looking person in the cafeteria, although several very young people were there. Well, nothing to do but get to know my roommate a bit more. She certainly seemed anxious to get to know me.

"How old are you?" she asked. "They told me you were young, but I figured you'd be my age."

My eyebrows rose. "How old *are* you?"

"Sixteen two weeks ago," she told me proudly. "That's when I started work here."

"Well, I'm close to fifteen." I answered her initial question, stretching the truth a bit. There's far less of a gap between fifteen and sixteen than between fourteen and sixteen. I wanted to press a bit further on her comment, though. "Who told you about me? And how come you and me are together here?"

She sighed. "They really didn't tell you *anything*, did they? Okay, three weeks ago I was just graduated and still in Huang Bay—that's way south of here—with my family. I knew I was going to get assigned soon, though, and, sure enough, my orders came through. I was inducted into the Transport Guild and sent here to start work. About a week ago I was called down to the Supervisor's office and told that I was being paired with one Tarin Bul, a young man sent here from Outside, and that the two of us would work as a pair thereafter. They also told me you'd have some ideas and ways I might find strange—and that's certainly true. In fact, all this is still a little strange to me, although it's the same kind of setup I grew up in. My assignment's inside, though, and away from the water."

"Huang Bay's on the equator, then?" I knew where it was exactly thanks to the handy map in my head, but it was a logical question.

She nodded. "Nearly, anyway. It's a lot prettier than here, with all sorts of flowers and trees. Not that this is really bad, though. No animal or insect problems, and the fruit's fresher." She paused a moment. "Still, I kind of miss home and family and all that."

I understood perfectly. Although I'd never been raised in any sort of family atmosphere, or had any close personal attachments, I could well see how someone who had been would be very lonely and homesick in this situation. That she accepted the wrench in her life so unquestioningly, said something important about the society. That wrench also explained why she was glad to see me.

We put our trays in the disposal, dropped the laundry by the small window that now had a uniformed attendant, then went back upstairs. We would see the rest of the place later; now it was time to get to know each other better, and for me to start learning the rules.

Apparently once the door was activated by a card the first time it opened when it recognized you, because the room door slid back and we walked in. First Ching checked the room terminal, then, finding it still blank, sank back down on the bed and looked at me. It was far too soon for me to do anything but sit on the other. I didn't wait for an opening, though.

"You said downstairs that we were paired—does that mean what I think it does?" I asked her.

"Depends on what you think it means. Everybody's paired who hasn't started or joined a family group. From here on in, we do everything together. Eat, sleep, go out, work—even our cards have identical account codes, so we can spend each other's money."

I gave a wan smile. "What if we don't get along?"

"Oh, we will. The State ran us through a lot of checks with their big computers and came up with us. The State doesn't make mistakes."

I certainly hoped that wasn't true; frankly, I knew it wasn't. But what the hell. "That might be true for native-born Medusans, but they can't know as much about me as they do about somebody born and raised here." And how! At least—I hoped not.

She seemed upset. "You mean you don't like me?"

"Now, I didn't say that. I think I could learn to like you a lot, but I don't really know you yet, and you don't know me. And I don't know Medusa at all—which should be obvious."

My seeming honesty calmed her a little. "I guess you're right. But there's so little *to* know about Medusa."

"That's only because you were born and raised here. What you take for granted I don't recognize at all. This pairing, for example—is it always a girl and a boy?"

My question got her giggling a bit again. "That's silly. You put *any* two in a pair and one of 'em's gonna be a girl."

"How's that?" Now I was genuinely confused. There was something here I was missing, and it was tough to find.

She sighed and tried to summon patience without sounding patronizing, but she didn't quite make it. "I still don't see what your problem is. I mean, I was a boy once myself and it was no big thing."

"What!" But with my surprise came the dawn, and with a lot more gingerly asked half-questions I managed to find the key. The key was the basic Warden precept on Medusa: survival.

Unlike the rest of the Warden Diamond, on Medusa the Warden organism was not all-pervasive. It depended upon the living creatures, plant and animal, of Medusa for its survival. On places like Lilith and Charon the little buggers were in the rocks and trees and everything, but here they concentrated only on animal life forms—and they changed those life forms to insure their own survival. That meant Wardens couldn't reproduce beyond their host's capacity without deforming that host and making the host less likely to survive in general. Thus, there was a premium on making certain that the bisexual humans—and animals, too, it seemed—reproduced as well.

Children were born basically neuter, although physiologically they would be classed as female, I suppose. When puberty hit, between ten and thirteen years of age, they acquired sexual characteristics based on the group with which they lived and with whom they most frequently associated. The vast majority, perhaps seventy-five percent, of the people of Medusa were female since you needed more females than males to assure regular reproduction.

Frankly, I hadn't been out in Medusan society enough for this concept to have sunk in, but, thinking back to the groupings on the buses and even in the cafeteria, it *had* seemed that there were an awful lot of women. . . .

"Let me get this straight," I said at last, trying to sort things out. "If we were to, say, join one of these group families, and it already had its share of men, I might change sex?"

She nodded. "Sure. Happens all the time. Nobody thinks much of it, really."

"Well, I do," I told her. "Everywhere else, even in the Diamond, I'm told, if you're born male you stay male and if you're born female you stay female. This system is going to take some getting used to."

The sociological implications were staggering, but beyond that it raised a broader question: if the Warden organism could undertake as major a change as *that* in, apparently, a very short time, what else could it do? The potential was there for making Medusans totally self-determining malleables—if they could control the Wardens, rather than being controlled by them. If that were somehow possible, you could literally change your appearance by willpower, become anybody—or the semblance of any thing—you wanted. I raised the possibility with her.

"There're always stories about that sort of stuff, like out with the Wild Ones but nobody I know has ever seen it. Not because you *order* it, anyway. Sometimes that kind of thing just *happens*, but it's nothing anybody can control."

The whole idea excited me. Anything that can just happen can somehow be controlled, particularly on a world with computers, psychs, and other modern mind- and body-control techniques. I would bet my life that Ypsir either had top researchers working on it or else had already figured out the means to do it. Of course, if that were true then you couldn't trust anybody's appearance. But I could understand why the ability would be very sparingly used and the very idea of it tightly suppressed, even ridiculed. A total society of malleables would bring this totalitarian state crashing down easily. I was beginning to see some possibilities here after all. But I couldn't dwell on the subject. Not now, particularly.

"The Wild Ones? Who are they?"

"Crazy people," she told me. "Savages. They live out there in the wild, outside the State. They're a pretty primitive, pitiful bunch, very super- stitious and spending all their time just staying alive. I know—I've seen some of 'em."

I frowned, more interested than puzzled, but appearances were every- thing in this business. "But where did they come from? I mean, are they exiles from the State? Castoffs? Runaways? What?"

She shrugged. "Nobody's sure, but they've been there since before the State was even founded. Most likely they're the descendants of early set- tlers, explorers, or whatever, who got cut off from civilization."

I didn't really believe that, but I *could* believe they were people—and the children and grandchildren of people—who just couldn't abide the State and its increasing control and had opted out. I had no doubt they were as primitive as Ching described them—this was a hard, nasty world— but some would consider that life preferable to this fishbowl existence. It was handy to know they were there, and helpful, too, to know that the Medusan State extended only to the cities, towns, and transport networks and left most of the rest of the planet wild and free. I didn't particularly like the idea of grubbing in snow for branches and roots, but knowing this gave me an option—and on Medusa, right then, I badly needed options of any kind, even unappealing ones.

I turned the conversation back to Ching. Best not to dwell on anything of real interest, lest unseen watchers grow suspicious. There would be plenty of time to extract additional information in bits and pieces.

"How come you're here in a basic job?" I asked her. "I *know* why I'm here—I don't quite fit anyplace right now, and won't until I'm older. But you were born here. What kind of job is it you have, anyway?"

She was more comfortable on this subject. "I—we—clean and restock trains and occasionally buses. It's pretty easy work, really."

I was surprised again. "Don't they have robots to do that sort of thing?"

She giggled yet again. "No, silly! Oh sure, they use industrial robots a lot, but in complicated passenger places like trains and buses it takes a human to clean up after another human. Besides, the State doesn't believe that just because a machine *can* do a job it is good or healthy for machines to do it."

That sounded like a recitation of holy writ, but it was okay with me. We were both janitors—so what? But she hadn't answered my first ques- tion.

"You're a smart girl," I told her, only partly flattering her, "and you speak very well. You have an educated vocabulary. So how come you're down here with us low-graders?"

She sighed and looked a little uncomfortable.

"If you'd rather not tell me, I will understand," I said soothingly.

"No, it's all right. I'm adjusted to it now. And yes, you're right, they say my IQ's way up there—but it's not much good to me. You see, back a long time ago, maybe when I was born or even before, something funny happened in my head. They say it's like a short circuit in an electrical line, only the affected area is so tiny they can't find it and fix it. In most things I'm just as normal as anybody else. But when I look at words, or bunches of letters, they get all mixed up, somehow." She pointed to the computer terminal. "I can do fine on that thing with voxcoder. But I look at the keys and they all just sorta run around in my head. I can understand the voice line, but I get all mixed up when anything's printed on the screen." She shook her head sadly and sighed once more. "So you're looking at the smartest illiterate on Medusa, I guess."

I could understand her problem—and the State's. In a technological society, it was necessary to know how to read. No matter how you cut it, it was necessary to read the repair manuals, or trace an engineering diagram, or follow procedures for getting out of a burning building. On any of the civilized worlds she might have been treated, although this sort of thing— "dyslexia," it was called—had never been wiped out. Still, it didn't quite make sense to me, considering the holy Wardens.

"How come the Wardens don't fix it?" I asked her. "I thought nobody gets sick or has problems."

She shrugged. "The experts they sent me to say it's because I was born with it. Maybe it was the way I was made up, and the Wardens think that's the way I should be. They finally said that even if they found it and fixed it my Wardens would probably un-fix it, 'cause they think the way it is, is the way it should be. I learned to accept my handicap, but it drove me crazy, mainly 'cause I was smarter than most of them who got good test grades and are now in school working toward good jobs."

I could sympathize with her on several counts. Anybody could sympathize with the frustration of being smart and also restricted, but I realized that this Warden business was kind of tricky on birth defects. It proved to me that only genetically engineered humans were truly moral or practical —not that I needed any proof, since I was the product of genetic engineering myself and so was Tarin Bul.

"So does that mean you're stuck being a waitress or janitor or something else like that?" I asked her. "Doing those jobs machines can't or don't do but which require no reading?"

"Oh, I can do a little better than that, if I prove it," she answered confidently. "After all, if I can *talk* to a computer and the computer can *talk* back I can still use it okay. But, yeah, you're right. Beyond a certain point there are lots of jobs I *could* do but literate persons could do a little faster or more efficiently, so they get the jobs. But that's not what I'm supposed to do anyway, after a while. Why do you think they paired us, anyway?"

I thought a moment. "Because neither of us fit?"

She laughed at that. "No—well, maybe. I hadn't thought of that. But eventually we're supposed to found a family group. I'll be the Base Mother—I'll maintain the house and take care of the kids. And I'll be able to teach 'em when they're young, and nobody's gonna mind if I need a vox to do the budget. It's not so bad. Better than being in a dead-end job, or any of the alternatives, like being a Goodtime Girl or working the mines of the moons of Momrath."

Aha! Another set of pieces fall into place. "Then, in a way, we're married. At our age!"

She gave me a big smile. "I guess you can say that. Sort of. Why? When do people marry Outside?"

"Well, mostly they don't," I told her honestly. "Most people are genetically engineered to do a particular thing and to do it better than anything else. You were raised by specialists and trained for what you're going to do, then you do it. But, yeah, there are *some* marriages." All types, too, but there was no use complicating things for her. "Most people don't bother, though."

She nodded. "They teach us something about Outside, but it's really hard to imagine anyplace else than here. I know a couple of people who've been to Cerberus, and that's strange enough. They switch minds and bodies all the time and live on trees in the water. Crazy."

Body-switching, I thought. My counterpart there must be having a field day. "That sounds pretty weird to me, too," I assured her. "But maybe one day I'll see it. They think when I'm old enough I can become a pilot."

That romanticism lurking inside her peered out of her face again. "A pilot. Wow. Have you ever flown anything before?"

I shook my head from side to side. "No," I lied, "not really. Oh, my father occasionally let me take the controls once we were underway, and I know everything there is to know about flying. But, I mean, I was just twelve when I got arrested."

That brought my past back into focus, and, as I suspected, she was trying not to think in that direction. Still, she asked, "If you were born in a lab or something and raised in a group, how could you have a father?"

That was an intelligent question. I was becoming more and more impressed with her. "Those of us in certain positions, like politics and administration, have to have some kind of family so we can learn how things work and make the personal contacts we need," I explained. "So, when we're five, we're adopted by someone in the position we're intended to be in someday. Sometimes it's just business, but sometimes we grow real close, like me and my father." Acting time, boy—give a good performance. Face turns angry, maybe a hint of bitterness in my voice. "Yeah —like me and my father," I repeated slowly.

She looked suddenly nervous. "I'm sorry. I won't bring it up again unless *you* want to."

I snapped out of my mood. At least the performance was good enough for her. "No, that's all right. He was a great man and I don't want to forget him—ever. But that was long ago and it's over. Here and now is what's important." I paused for dramatic effect, then cleared my throat, sniffled a little, and changed the subject. "What about these Goodtime Girls? What are they?"

She seemed relieved at the opportunity to get out of a sticky situation. I hoped I'd just laid to rest a lot of otherwise inevitable prying about a past I really didn't have, the area most likely to trip me up. "Goodtime Girls is a general title for the entertainer class. It's a dead end, but they're put under psych so they don't think much." She shivered. "I don't want to talk about them. They're necessary, of course, and serve a need of the State, but it's not anything I'd like." She suddenly yawned, tried to repress it, couldn't, then shook her head. "Sorry. It's getting near my bedtime, I guess. I usually like to sleep in the middle of the off-time, so I have time before work to do things. If you want to do it differently we'll have to work something out."

"That's all right," I assured her. "I'll adjust to your schedule for now. You get some sleep—I'll manage. If I can't drift off, maybe I'll just explore the dorm for a while and see whatall is here. I'll need a couple of days to make the shift to this sleep time."

She nodded sleepily and yawned again. "If you do go out, don't go beyond the inside of the dorm, though. It's a rule that pairs should do everything together." Again a yawn.

"That's all right. I'll be good," I assured her good-naturedly. "I have a good teacher."

I let her crawl into bed and she was soon fast asleep. I did not go out, at least not then. Instead I just lay there, thinking about all the new material I had to sort through, what I had learned, what I had to work with, and what potentialities might be here for mischief.

Ching was going to be an invaluable asset at the start, that was for sure. She was smart, romantic, and a knowledgeable native guide. But in the long run she would be a problem. You can't overthrow a system or set up the assassination of a Lord of the Diamond when you have for a constant companion someone raised always to believe in and trust in the system. As a romantic, she might easily wind up falling in love with me—which would be okay—but that would also mean that she might just turn me in to TMS for my own good.

There were ways, although they'd take some time and ingenuity. But talk about long-range planning! The only way to separate Ching and myself, obviously, was to get her pregnant and stick her home with the kid. And I was only fourteen and a half years old and still technically a virgin. . . .

CHAPTER FIVE

A Friendly Chat with TMS

My job was, in fact, as easy as Ching had made it out to be. Machines still did the real work—we just guided and directed them and made complete inspections of the passenger cars, buses, and train-crew quarters simply because humans will stick things and drop things and wedge things in places no machine would ever think of looking, let alone cleaning. How many times was I guilty of sticking stuff under a seat or between cushions just because it was convenient? It might be healthy if everyone had to spend a couple of months cleaning trains and buses before being allowed to ride them.

Ching was so happy to have a friend at last and something solid to hang on to that she was far more pleasure than inconvenience. Hoping to get us involved in Guild hobbies and recreational activities, she took full advantage of our off time to show me the city and its services and frills, which were quite a bit more elaborate than I had expected.

Gray Basin was nicely laid out once you understood the initial logic of it, and this, she assured me, was pretty much how all cities on Medusa were laid out, even the ones above ground. Just about everything was prefabricated, which allowed for expansion, change, and growth with a minimum of displacement and trauma. Everything, everywhere, just sort of fit together.

There was theater, well-mounted if heavy on the musical fluff mixed with propaganda and duty to the State, and you could punch up an extensive library of books on your dorm terminal, even order a hard copy for delivery for a small sum. The books were heavy on technical and practical subjects and not much on literature and politics, for obvious reasons—no use contaminating fresh minds.

Far less fettered were art galleries, which contained some of the finest human art and sculpture anywhere—no surprise, because most of them had been stolen from the best museums of the Confederacy and were here more or less on protective loan. A substantial native art group was allowed to do just about anything without State interference as long as the themes weren't political, at least, not political in a way that contradicted the official line. There was music, too, even an entire Medusan symphony orchestra—one of many, I was assured—that fascinated me by performing great compositions from man's far past that I had never heard or heard of, as well as newer and more experimental stuff. I had to admit that, somehow, living people creating music was somehow better, more alive and pleasing, than the expert and flawless computer musicons I had grown used to in the Confederacy. The musicians had their own guild, headed by a woman who, it was said, had come to Medusa voluntarily. An expert musicologist and musician herself, she was an anachronism back in the Confederacy, but she had known Talant Ypsir and had joined him in exile when he offered the carrot of a real, primitive, wide-open musical program that would be planetwide.

As for our own dorm, it had its own basic activities, and we had use of Guild common facilities like gyms and playing fields. A number of sports teams were organized around both intra-guild and inter-guild rivalries, and they certainly were a help both in meeting other people regardless of grade and for keeping in shape. In fact, the only Guild that didn't seem to have teams or outside activities was TMS. I was told that they *had* tried it, once, in a campaign to give them a friendlier, more human face, but it had been a disastrous failure. You just can't relax and have fun with a group whose members could do nasty things to you if you so much as protested a call.

Besides, even TMS didn't find it much of a challenge to win every game they played, no matter how lousy they'd played. So, they kept to themselves, being their normal prying, lousy selves, and everyone tried to ignore them as much as possible.

In truth, working and playing with Ching, I almost *did* feel fourteen years old once again, and I really enjoyed it—but not to the point of not concentrating on my main task, which was to put together a plan that would eventually dispose of Talant Ypsir. I pretty much gave up my ideas of doing anything beyond that—although that was surely enough!—because of the restrictive nature of the society. They could be entertaining aliens and churning out humanoid superrobots in every third office building in Gray Basin, and I would neither know it or have any real way of finding out.

Still, any move against the government of Medusa would have to be based upon what was, as of now, only a theoretical possibility. The society was locked in too tight, and was too well run, to do any real damage unless the monitor system could be negated. To do that, I would somehow have to learn if this malleability principle was really possible, and, if so, how to take advantage of it myself.

Just how closely we were monitored was brought home at our every-other-week private sessions with a liaison between the Guild and TMS. We were generally asked to explain this or that action or comment we had made, often out in the open. I quickly understood that this was not really an inquisition, nor were we accused of sedition or any sort of wrongdoing —it was merely a reminder that we were always observed, and, as such, better just start totally accepting the system and thinking and acting right at all times.

Close to the end of my third month on Medusa I had become increasingly aware of changes in both Ching and myself—physiological changes that were hard to ignore. When I'd first met her, she'd been thin and spindly and, while cute, not really what you'd call well endowed. She was filling out now, and it didn't take long to realize that this was no late pubescent growth but a direct Warden action in reaction to my stimulus. She was fast becoming an extremely sexy woman with all the right equipment. Clearly the hormonal triggers the Wardens employed to bring about the physical changes were also having the expected psychological effects.

As for me, I was undergoing the same sort of transformation. I was filling out, becoming hard, lean, and muscular, sprouting body hair, and experiencing substantial sexual sensations. This helped my overall plan in the sense that I was beginning to look less like a fourteen-year-old kid. It also helped in that playing the role of the sexually repressed kid was driving me nuts anyway. Still, I was kind of nervous. It was within my acting abilities to simulate almost anything, but the role of a fourteen-year-old inexperienced virgin might well be beyond me. Fortunately, it was Ching who finally brought up the subject, and also allayed my real fears on that score.

"Tarin?"

"Uh huh?"

"Do you feel—anything—when you look at me?"

I thought a moment. "You're a pretty girl and a good friend."

"No, I mean—well, *beyond* that. I do when I look at you most times. Real funny feelings, if you know what I mean."

"Maybe," I answered cautiously.

"Uh . . . Tarin? Have you ever . . . made love to a girl before?"

I acted startled at the question. "I was twelve when they arrested me. When did I ever have a chance?" I hesitated a moment. "Have *you?*"

She looked suitably shocked. "Oh, *no!* What do you think I am? A Goodtime Girl?"

I laughed, walked over to her, and patted her soothingly. "Take it easy. So we're both new at it." Or very good liars, I thought. Still, she sounded sincere, which made the job much simpler. In a society where sex is generally available to all, one of the more boring things is watching two people make it through some kind of closed-circuit hookup. Even if TMS got their jollies that way, we'd be such a small and uninteresting lot considering the whole population it would hardly be worth noticing. But if she were experienced, *she* could tell.

And so, finally, tentatively, we made love, and that was a real mental release for me. As for Ching, she was in fact awkward and inexperienced and the whole thing was new to her, but she wound up with a happy and radiant high the likes of which I'd never seen before. In the days that followed the psychological changes in her were incredible. She was happier, far more self-confident, and given to spontaneous and automatic displays of affection, even on the job. This was a bit embarrassing at times; I wasn't used to such displays, let's face it, nor to any kind of attachment. I'd always been a loner and proud of it—you had to be in my kind of business.

But we had sex a lot, which only reinforced everything.

On a different note, I found an electronics hobby club sponsored by the Guild, and actively joined it. It occurred to me that this was the best way I had to see the engineering philosophy behind Medusa's society, and it would give me access to the tools to counter that technological threat when the time finally came.

That time was bothering me, though. Here it was three months along and I was really not ready to begin. I was still outside the establishment, still denied the tools and positions I needed, and even more cemented into the fairly pleasant daily regimen of low-grade Guild work. I had as much information and as much access to tools and technology as I needed to perform my duties, and I would get no more without some really dramatic or radical changes, changes I simply could not initiate.

Interestingly enough, TMS provided me with the kick in the rear I needed. We were returning from work one day, holding hands and talking about nothing much, coming across the street from the bus stop to the dorm, when a small vehicle pulled up across the street and its driver looked over at us. Now, individual vehicles were rare enough to cause attention and apprehension, and there was no mistaking the military green of the woman at the controls or that look of inner power on her face.

We tried to ignore her as best we could, but the TMS agent got out of the car and walked briskly and confidently toward us. When it became obvious that we were the object of her attention, we stopped. Ching gripped my hand so tightly I thought it was going to be pulled off.

"Tarin Bul?" the Monitor asked, although she knew who I was from the time she'd left her headquarters.

I nodded. "Yes?"

"This is a routine check. Ching Lu Kor, you will proceed to the dorm and go through your normal routine. He should be back in a few hours."

"Shouldn't I go with him?" Ching protested. "I mean, we're paired. . . ."

Brave girl, I thought, but I said, "No, it's all right, I'm sure this is just routine, Ching. You go on. I'll tell you all about it when I get back."

She let go of my hand, hesitantly, and seemed to appeal to the Monitor with her eyes—but met only a steely blank response. The Monitor turned and walked back to the car and I followed, after kissing Ching lightly and giving her a reassuring pat and squeeze. But she was still standing there, looking frightened and upset, as the Monitor and I climbed into the car and sped smoothly out and away from the Guild sector.

It was the first time I'd been in an independent vehicle since coming to Medusa, and I paid a good deal of attention to how the officer drove the car. It seemed a simple affair, basically electric-powered and limited to city duty, with a small steering wheel and one-knob accelerator and brake. There was also an on-off switch, I noted, but no key or code pad. These TMS folks were pretty confident.

I knew I was supposed to be terrified and all that, but I couldn't bring

myself to look or act that way. The fact was, this was the first odd or unusual thing that had happened to me since I'd started work at the Guild
and it sure broke the monotony. Besides, maybe the experience would
yield some new information. One thing was sure—it was no routine check
as the agent had said; I'd seen a lot of folks picked up for those routine
checks, and they always took the pair or family as a group and never,
never sent a personal car for them.

We went through and beyond downtown, to a small, low, black building on our right. We turned into a back alley on the side of the building,
then made a sharp left and actually drove inside, gliding smoothly into a
prepared stall in a garage with automatic hookups for recharging, energiz-
ing, and cold protection that came out and started work the moment we
stopped and the "off" switch was flipped. The cold-weather protection was
something I was well aware of; machinery wasn't as tolerant of temperature as we Medusans, and special care had to be taken to make sure they
worked correctly in our lovely climate.

"Follow me," the Monitor instructed, and I did, walking with her to a
nearby elevator, then into it, and up two floors. The doors slid back to reveal a somewhat familiar scene to me—squad rooms looked like squad
rooms the galaxy over.

My Monitor, who still hadn't so much as given me a name and who
wore only one stripe, checked in with the desk sergeant, then turned to
me. "Your card." She held out her hand, and I gave it to her, and she, in
turn, gave it to the desk sergeant. Now I was stuck here until they wanted
to let me leave.

We walked behind the desk and down a hall that led to a complex of
offices, mostly with arcane names on the door. I became a little nervous
when we stopped in front of a door marked SUBVERSIVE COUNTERIN-
TELLIGENCE and walked in. That was too close to home. I felt a twinge
as I considered that an enemy who could penetrate your deepest military
headquarters might just get a leak as to an agent being dropped in their
midst.

I followed my Monitor in, closing the door behind me—an old-fashioned
one, I noted, with coded lock. The office was large and impressive, a big
room with a desk in the center that was larger than could possibly be useful, a comfortable chair behind it, and just about nothing else. People
stood before whoever belonged to this office, and probably at attention.

The chair turned and I saw that it held a tall, strong-looking woman,
military-type, wearing not stripes but a major's leaf. A big shot indeed. I
was both more worried and suitably impressed.

The private approached the desk in good military fashion, came to attention, and saluted. "The citizen Tarin Bul, as ordered!" she snapped.

The major nodded casually and did not bother to return the salute.
"That'll be all, private. You may leave us."

"As you wish!" the Monitor returned smartly, then did an about-face
and walked past me to the door and was out. I was now alone with a big

cheese in TMS circles here in Gray Basin, where, I understood, there was only one general and two colonels. That made this one a Department Chief—Grade 30 or better for sure.

I just stood there, well back from the desk, looking uncomfortable and curious. For a while the major just looked back at me. Finally she said, "Come here."

I approached the desk, which still put some distance between us. Not much on the desk, either, I noted. This was a show office to impress not only folks like me but the lower-downs. The real work of this department was done elsewhere.

Again the stare. Finally she asked, "How do you like Medusa, Bul?"

I shrugged. "Better than a lot of places, I guess. I don't have any complaints, except maybe that the job I've got's a little boring."

She nodded, not at all taken aback by my less than cringing attitude. Here was a pro, I realized from the start—but, well, so was I. Still, my demeanor was not easily overlooked. "You're not nervous at being brought in here like this?"

"Should I be?" I countered. "Your people should know better than anybody that I haven't been a bad boy."

That brought a very slight smile to the corners of her mouth. "That is probably true, but it doesn't necessarily mean anything. Maybe we think your thoughts are impure."

"They are," I assured her, "but they're no threat to Medusa."

She seemed a little taken aback by my statement, but didn't let it get to her. Clearly she was used to dealing with a different sort of personality than mine. Well, who knew? But either I acted in character or correctly from her point of view—and I'd been on the other side of a desk like that too many times not to know exactly what that point of view was—or I triggered a greater suspicion. I was a new boy on the planet, no matter what, and I could not be expected to react like the natives.

She sat there a moment, looking me over thoughtfully. "You're a bright boy. I almost think that you are not what you seem."

That was uncomfortably close. She knew her business. "I haven't been around long enough to fake much," I retorted. "But I've gone through more cop interrogations and psych sessions than most old people have."

She sighed. "Fourteen going on forty . . . Your situation is—unique, I admit. I know that politics played a part in your coming to us, but I suspect it was also the uniqueness of your situation. They didn't know what to do with you." She paused, then asked, "What *are* we going to do with you?"

"Is there any reason for not letting me continue to live my life?" I returned, a little surprised at this attitude. "Or isn't it permitted to ask why I was brought here?"

"Ordinarily, no. And you weren't brought here for anything you've done, Tarin Bul. In fact, you've been something of a model citizen. But sitting here, talking to you personally, I get this *feeling* about you. There is just something about you that smells . . . dangerous. Why do you smell dangerous, Tarin Bul?"

I shrugged and looked as innocent as can be. "I don't know what you are talking about, Major. I *did* execute a man, but that was simple justice. Others that came in with me would willingly kill for no real reason."

She shook her head negatively. "No, that's not it. Something about you is . . . odd. I suspect that this is what was smelled by the Confederacy and their psychs as well. That is the reason they sent you to the Diamond, although, somehow, I feel we would all be better off if you weren't Medusan." She sighed again. "That is in the simple way of a warning, Bul. I'm going to be watching you extra carefully."

"I assumed I was being watched extra carefully anyway, considering I'm a newcomer."

She did not respond to that for a moment, but finally got to the point. "Have you been . . . contacted by anyone we should know about?"

The question was surprising. "Don't *you* know?"

"Can the bullshit, Bul!" she snapped. "Answer the question!"

"I wasn't being funny," I assured her. "You've got to admit that's a pretty weird question for Medusa, though."

Her anger subsided as she realized that, of course, I was right. She had already admitted by her very question that this system wasn't nearly as infallible as they claimed, nor as all-inclusive. It was a potentially damaging admission, and one I valued highly. "Just answer yes or no," she said at last.

"No," I responded honestly. "At least, not by anybody outside my normal life and job. What *is* this about, Major?"

"Some of the others who came here with you have been contacted by subversives," she said in another, even more startling admission. "None of them are now in Gray Basin except you, but it's my job to find out if these enemies of the people have spread to us. Logically, they would contact you if they were."

"I've heard nothing about them or this," I answered truthfully. I didn't add that I could see the all-powerful TMS's terrible embarrassment at anything like this. Subversives meant those opposed to Ypsir, TMS, and the system—natural enough, but in a society this regimented and monitored, allegedly perfect in its enforcement procedures, even a minor flaw would be a matter of great concern. Clearly somebody had found that flaw. On at least a verbal level somebody was operating against the Medusan government and had somehow circumvented their fancy computers, monitors, flags, and recorders. That meant more than a real genius at electronics—that meant an inside job. It meant that the leader of this thing had to be either a highly placed government official or somebody fairly high up in TMS.

"They call themselves simply the Opposition," she told me. "We don't think there are many of them, but the smaller and more cell-like their organization the more difficult it is to destroy. Since you have not been contacted, we must assume that they are not yet in Gray Basin." She paused a moment for effect. As I said, a real pro. "How would you and your pairmate like a promotion, Bul?"

Surprise followed surprise, and I could hardly repress my excitement. At last some room to move. I could almost guess what was coming next. "You know we would," I told her. "And what's the price?"

Again that faint smile. "The price could be very high indeed, Bul. Two of those who came in with you are dead now. One joined them but was not very clever. The other refused them—and was executed by them, we believe. A third joined, slipped, and tried to bluff things out with us. She was given to our psychs. She had a very strong mind and will and fought to the bitter end. Still, we got some information from her, but at the cost of her own mind. She's now a Goodtime Girl for her city government. She smiles a lot and does whatever she's told—she would jump off a building or behead herself if asked—but she doesn't exactly *think* any more."

I'm afraid the sudden hoarseness in my voice wasn't at all feigned. Frankly, I could stand death. It was a part of the risk my profession always ran, and one that all of us accepted. I also had no real fear of routine psych probes or even physical torture. I was trained and prepped by the best for that. But I have to admit that a total assault on my mind, enough to break it, *was* possible. So although they would still get no information from such an effort, they could, in fact, destroy me mentally. It was always a possibility, one that revolted me.

"Do you want to become a Goodtime Girl, Bul?" she asked, sensing my discomfort.

"No. Of course not," I told her, my voice weak.

"Well, here is what we are going to do. Two of those people were in the city of Rochande, more than sixteen hundred kilometers southwest of here. It so happens we run three trains between Gray Basin and Rochande, two of which are freights. It is the passenger-freight combination train that interests us, since we have some information that at least one contact was made on that train. We intend to assign you to that train, on a regular basis, as a normal promotion. Since the trip, with preparation and cleanup, takes a full shift, you will have two residences, one here and one there, and work different directions on alternate days. We believe that, sooner or later, either on the train or at Rochande, you will be contacted."

It figured. Bait. But the actual routine sounded like fun, and it would give me the first opening in my own little campaign. "And when—if—I'm contacted?"

"You will join. You will go along with what they ask. We don't want you to just report a contact. We want you to join the organization, perhaps for some time. We want to know who these people—this cell—are. We want their leader, because she will be the only one with enough information to take us further."

I nodded as several questions immediately leaped to mind. "Ah, Major,

I may not be very old but I was trained for organization and administration. I know how these political things work. First of all, I will *never* know their real names, most likely, and only one of them will know mine, unless we run across each other by accident in the street or on the job."

"But you'll know what they look like and you're a bright boy. You'll be able to figure out a lot of information about many of them. Somebody will make a slip about her family, or somebody else will betray knowledge that will indicate her Guild, at least. Eventually we'll have pictures from your description to match with our computers, and we'll come up with a fair number of them. Don't worry—we understand the limits of this work better than you do."

"All right, I'll accept that. But the one that *they* killed worries me. That means they have some way to check sincerity. One of 'em's probably either a psych or a technician for a psych lab. That's going to be hard to fake."

She gave that smile again. "You *are* a bright boy. Your objection can be very easily disposed of. The equipment has to be basic and portable. They can't possibly do a full job on you. The solution is very simple, then—you tell them all about this meeting and you tell them about me."

"*Huh?*"

"You tell them you're playing along with us, but you really sympathize with them. That will be the truth—don't bother to deny it. The ambivalence will be enough to confuse their devices, our psychs assure me. You're still new enough and fresh enough to cause no problem on that score."

I frowned and looked nervous at the suggestion, although she was perfectly correct and it was exactly what I was planning to do anyway. "How sure are you about that?"

"Very," she assured me. "Believe me, we have the best here. And it worked before. The third one, the one whose mind is gone, was one of ours. Unfortunately for her, she went too far over to their side and tried to double-cross us. In that case, what happened to her will happen to you, Bul. Remember that."

I shivered. "I'll remember," I assured her. "But—sooner or later they'll rig some way to make a final test, and that'll be with the full gear. I'll have to go through that before I'll really know who they are."

She nodded. "We anticipate that, although we have no direct knowledge. There is some evidence that this operation is Confederacy-backed, by person or persons unknown elsewhere in the Diamond who are, if not in the Confederacy's employ, at least working against us. When that kind of test comes, you will be ready. The one who went before you passed it, we think—with the help of our own people. If you get into trouble on that, we will give you a basic psych overlay that will fool them. We're certain it will, since it will simply build on those anti-State parts of your own nature and background. We will make a rebel out of you, and then we will unmake it."

I could hardly tell her that I could make any psych probe read exactly what I wanted, probably including their best. "All right—I understand so far. But if this works so well, why did they kill one of us?"

"She wasn't working for us, directly. We mishandled the situation and have learned from our mistake. We made no mistakes the second time—except that she got to the point where she decided to play *us* for suckers. You're our third, Bul. We have all the prep techniques down pat now, and we've covered our trail on the last two very well. Nobody, and I mean nobody, except you and me knows about this arrangement right now. At the proper time, two others in TMS, one a top psych, will be informed—and that will be all. There is no recording in this office, no record at all of what happened here. A very convincing and totally fictional dressing-down for a minor infraction is being substituted."

"Okay. I admit I'm very bored cleaning buses and I would sure like some more credit. Besides I can play a pretty good part. It wasn't easy getting into that reception back on Halstansir, you know, particularly carrying a sword."

She liked that. I wondered if she were native, as her accent suggested, or a convict. Probably I would never know.

"I am glad you approve, Bul—but you realize you have no choice in this matter?"

I nodded. "I've had very few choices in my life."

"Now, we'll get on to the procedures for reporting. You will not report to or trust your terminal or other TMS officers. I will give you a code which can be keyed from any terminal. It is simply a variation on getting your credit and debit statement from the Central Bank—and it *will* give you that. But it will also be a signal to me. Key it, and I will know, and you will be picked up for a routine interrogation as you were today. Understand?"

I nodded. "One thing, though—what about Ching?"

"While we have been having this talk, Ching was picked up and taken to the psych used only by my special branch. Oh, don't look so worried—there will be no change. All we've done is to reinforce a weakness already obvious in her. She practically worships you now. From this point, that will simply dominate. You'll notice no change, nor will she even be aware that she's been to a psych—as far as she's concerned, she'll have been waiting for you in your room all this time. But she will be very uncritical of your attitudes and inclinations on the social and political front. She was born and raised here. As a loyal native, she would have turned you in for your own good, or reported anything odd to us. She won't now. If you say to betray the government, she will go along with you. If you join the Opposition, she will go along and accept it. And if you later betray the Opposition, she will think all the more highly of you for it. They will have no trouble passing her on that basis. That is one reason we thought of her as a logical pair-mate for you. As with most totally frustrated people, she is an incurable fantasizing romantic."

I didn't like the idea of messing with Ching's mind—she had enough problems as it was—but it didn't seem too bad, and it would keep her out of trouble as long as I was all right. However, she would now be exposed to exactly the same dangers—and fate—from either side that I faced, and she was not well prepared for it. I liked her too much not to worry about what might happen, but I *was* a professional. If it had to be, it had to be—and, if it came down to her or me, I knew I would have no such romantic notions.

CHAPTER SIX

The Disloyal Opposition

Ching was, as promised, no different on my return than when I'd left her and, also as advertised, she told me that she'd been waiting in the room for me worriedly for the previous few hours. If I hadn't been told differently, I would have sworn she was narrating the correct version of events, rather than just what she was told to remember.

Two days later we were both summoned to the Guild Hall for an audience with a top-grade supervisor. I played the surprised worker that Ching genuinely was. There we were informed that we had shown ourselves more than capable of higher positions. Effective immediately, we were being promoted to In-Service Passenger Attendants, Grade 6, and would shortly be assigned for a week of training and evaluation. Since we'd been Grade 3s (I never did learn what 1s and 2s were—I could hardly imagine anything lower than bus cleaners) this was a substantial jump, although it was, of course, contingent on our successful training and initial job performance evaluations. The job actually only warranted a Grade 5, but the extra bump was given because we would now have two homes many kilometers apart, and would have double toiletries and the like. At our previous level you owned virtually nothing at all—you couldn't afford it—but, while we wouldn't be very well off compared to many others, we would now have a bit left over from basic expenses for luxuries.

We presented our cards, which were run through a computer and popped back to us apparently unchanged, but we knew that the information now reflected increased grade and status. We also had two days until our new shift, an afternoon one, would properly cycle so we could join our crew. We actually had some time to kill and made the most of it. Ching was particularly excited and pleased by the turn of events, and I tried as hard as I could to share in her joy and excitement. Doing so was tough when you knew what was really going on.

Two days later we went down to the main passenger terminal and found Shift Supervisor Morphy, a distinguished-looking woman in early middle age who looked a little like civilized worlders. A native most defi-nicely, I decided, but a child or grandchild of a civilized worlder and a frontier type. These were very common on Medusa.

The job wasn't very glamorous or exciting, despite the fancy titles. Basically we patrolled the cars, wiping passenger's noses, answering their stupid questions, explaining how to get food or drink or how to operate the seat terminals as well as making sure that all the amenities were working properly. In some ways this was worse than cleaning buses. In that job, I mostly stood around and goofed off while seeing that the cleaning machines did their jobs properly, while here I was constantly exposed to the public and observed by shift supervisors as I walked from one end of the train to the other and back. And I had to be *very* neat, and *very* clean, and always smile, smile. . . .

In one way the job was similar to tracking down and confronting criminals. Both were filled with repetition and long, boring stretches, yet both were at the same time interesting and disgusting.

Our train usually had two or three passenger cars and the rest freight. The freight level remained constant but the passenger car number increased or decreased according to demand. In the first week we had one six-car passenger train and another that had only one, but never did we have a run with none.

The training period was really grating at times, with every little thing criticized. I almost belted Morphy more than once. The week seemed to last forever. Finally, though, we were on our own and less closely supervised, and things eased up a bit.

Train crews had distinctive uniforms, nicely tailored and with overly large insignia on them. Since a lot of our own Guild's members used the trains to get to and from where they were needed, there had to be some way to tell the specific train's crew from others in transportation. We looked, in fact, pretty elegant by Medusan standards, but that was par for the course. I remember a fancy resort once, long ago, that used a lot of human attendants just to give the place a more elegant and personal feel, and the best-dressed people in the joint were the doorman and the waiters.

Our new room in Rochande was virtually identical to the one back in Gray Basin, the only difference being that it was on the third, not the fourth, floor and the beds were against the left rather than the right wall. A mirror image, basically, to remind us where we were.

Rochande, however, was quite different from Gray Basin if only because of its geography. It was a food-distribution center for the region, and, therefore, a space-freight port. It was also pretty far south, comparatively speaking, and while the winter still hit it was neither long nor hard, and the city was on the surface rather than dug in and roofed over. There were also huge forests around, and quite a number of exotic plants, which gave the place a whole different feel, even if the city's pie-shaped design and dull, blocky architecture was depressingly familiar.

The trip south, once through the electronic barricades of Gray Basin, was interesting, too. You could see the climate gradually change as you

moved south, with occasional breaks in the thinning snow patches, showing hardy grasses at first, then some bushes, and eventually increasingly
larger trees. Finally we were more or less out of the hard winter and into a
more temperate zone. The world was not nearly as bad as Gray Basin
made it seem, though there was not a sign of cultivation or even roads in
sight for the entire distance. More than the climate and vegetation
changes, that was the true contrast on Medusa, one brought home with
every trip. In the cities and towns, and on the sleek, smooth, modern
trains, you were in a highly technological, modern society though a regimented one. Outside the cities was a primitive world.

It was a world that was said to have genuine threats although I'd been
able to learn very little about it. Basically, the people were very secure in
their modern pockets on this wilderness world and most of them had
never been beyond their society's protection. What exactly was cut there,
other than wild and vicious animals, some of whom could change their
shape, was really unknown. I found the stories about shape-changing most
interesting and made it a point to research those animals as much as I
could with the library access on the terminal. Apparently the Medusans
didn't even like to study these creatures, at least not publicly. If, in fact,
some of those creatures could shape-change—something not even alluded
to in the descriptions—I could see why Medusan authorities wouldn't
want the opportunity to plant ideas like mine into crooked heads.

The dominant life forms were mammals, however, something I found
interesting but logical—reptiles couldn't really have much of a future on a
world as cold as this, and insects would have too short a developmental
season each year to do more than fill an ecological niche. Even the ocean
creatures, as far as was known, were air-breathing mammals, since, apparently, the algae and plankton that would support a real fishy evolution
was low, and the seas were relatively shallow.

The familiar pattern of animal development was here, though, with one
vegetarian species called vettas eating mostly grasses and another called
tubros eating mostly leaves and other parts of trees, apparently instinctively trimming but not killing. The big, nasty brutes were the harrar,
who mostly ate vettas and tubros. There were several hundred subspecies
of the two vegetarian types, and several varieties of harrar. The rest of the
animal kingdom was varied, vast, and mostly invisible, but fitted into the
normal balance of nature in totally expected ways. I concentrated on the
dominant life forms, except for the smaller creatures that were poisonous
or nasty, because I hoped to find some clues in the big ones to what I was
looking for.

As for looks, the vettas had large, flat, toothy bills, big, round eyes, short
necks, and legs that were very wide, clawed, and padded, and yet they
could move when they had to, at speeds up to forty kilometers per hour
for short distances. The tubros had long, thin snouts, necks that bent in
all directions and were longer than their bodies, and enormous, clawed
limbs that were almost handlike. Their tails somewhat resembled their

necks, and they occasionally used these tails as decoys when checking to see if the coast was clear. Apparently the tails came out if bitten. Tubros weren't very fast, but they could climb trees in a flash and could sleep either right side up or upside down, clinging to strong branches or trunks. Vettas had no real defense except their speed; tubros, however, could be nasty when cornered, and could use that tail of theirs like a whip.

The harrar was the hardest to pin down. Mostly it looked like a huge, undulating mass of fur, skin, and taloned feet that were almost birdlike. It generally walked, looking ridiculous, on those legs; but when it caught prey, two small, nasty hands in that fur were strong enough to tear heads off. Somewhere in that lump was the biggest mouth relative to body size that I'd ever seen, with row upon row of teeth. The harrar interested me the most, since it was, according to the legends, a shape-changer. This critter would need to eat a lot to feed that big body, and it could hardly climb trees or outrun anything going forty kilometers per hour.

The sea creatures seemed to mirror those on land, except that there were more levels with far greater interdependence, starting with the little slugs that ate bacterialike organisms near the surface and also scavenged the bottom, up to water-born counterparts of the vettas and tubros. Despite smooth sides and flippers and fins, these looked very much like their land counterparts—but were omnivores, eating smaller animals as well as surface and bottom water plants. There was also an amphibious version of the harrar, which appeared to be a one-ton or more lump of gray or black with dorsal and tail fins, little beady eyes, a big, big mouth—and little else. This sea carnivore, called makhara, seemed totally unable to cope with swift prey—yet it had to do pretty well to keep that mass of fat happy. How did it do it? How, in fact, could it even grab its prey? These questions, too, were not only unanswered in the texts, they were unasked.

There were no tubros north of the twenty-eighth parallel, where the trees became too small or intermittent to support such life. But there were snow vettas able to burrow under meters of snow and ice to get at whatever was down there, and harrar to hunt them. That, too, was interesting. Lots of stuff on the unique life cycle of the snow vetta, nothing but a mention that the harrar were there. That implied that there were no snow harrar, and again brought up an interesting question: how did the dark, bulky, ungainly *harrar* ever catch its quota of snow *vetta*, many of whom spent most of their time burrowing deep beneath the snows?

Ching, to my surprise, became interested in some of my studies. It was amazing to me that someone born and raised on Medusa knew so little about the bulk of the planet. But she was aware of her ignorance—after first confessing that, until I looked into these things, she'd never even thought about them—and eager to fill the gap.

One thing was for sure—they were really scared of those harrar, even in the highest councils of Medusa. You had only to think of the double energy guard around Gray Basin's entrances, and even Rochande had a double perimeter fence of the same lethal energy barrier around it. Of course, such a system, for the protection of the public—sold and accepted as such —also kept the people tightly inside their monitored cities and protected trains. Even those trains were sealed compartments, totally insulated from the outside world, almost as if they were spacecraft sealing off their occupants from some lethal, alien environment.

Man had always triumphed over the most vicious and lethal carnivores on world after world. Yet here it seemed almost as if the legendary harrar were allowed to breed and roam and multiply; and they probably were, not so much from technological as from political motives. Raised in insulated cradle-to-grave technological pockets, most Medusans probably couldn't survive a day without those conveniences they took for granted. This suited the Medusan authorities very well indeed.

Whether the doing of Ypsir or of his predecessor, this was a unique society and something of a work of genius, based on the fact that Lilith and Charon supplied so much food there was no necessity to raise any on Medusa, and technology had maintained the closed culture of Medusa and fed it.

We worked some six weeks with nothing happening, and I was beginning to grow bored and worried and fidgety once more. Neither TMS nor this mysterious Opposition I only half believed in had surfaced, and I was beginning to wrack my brain once more for a different opening.

Ching dismissed my irritation as moodiness, something she was used to by now, but I was determined to do something to get me off dead center and beat the system. Of course, just when I'd given up all hope or belief in the Opposition, I heard from them. And heard is the right word, although they took a leaf from Krega's notebook.

We had a separate crew's toilet on the train, just forward of the first passenger car, and, as usual, I went there to take a piss. Such occasions were one of the very few times I was separated not only from Ching, who had to keep working while I went and vice versa, but also from the supervisors and general passengers. There was, of course, a monitoring device in the john.

"Tarin Bul?" I heard the voice, electronically distorted, and looked up and around, puzzled. I'd been called by vox on the terminal many times, but the voices had never sounded as inhuman as this.

"Yes?"

"We've been watching you, Tarin Bul."

"Aren't you always?" I cracked, zipping up my pants and going to the washbasin.

"We are not TMS," the voice told me. "We do not like TMS very much. We suspect that, by now, you don't like them much, either."

I shrugged and washed my hands. "I'm damned if I do and damned if I don't on that one," I told the voice sincerely. "If this is a test by TMS and I say I don't like them, I'll get picked up and asked why. If, on the other hand, I say I just love TMS, they'll pick me up for sure and rush me to the nearest psych. So I'll pass on the answer, and unless there's something else I've got to go back to work."

"We are not TMS," the voice told me. "We are in opposition to the TMS and the current government of Medusa. We are powerful enough to feed a false signal, recorded earlier, of you sitting on the toilet to TMS monitors while we use this channel to talk to you."

"Says you," I retorted.

"You're no native, programmed to this life. Why do you not accept what we say?"

"For one thing, if you're that powerful you don't need me. And if you *do* need me, and are that powerful, then you're either phony or pretty incompetent rebels."

"We *don't* need you," the voice responded. "We *want* you. That is a different thing. The more people in more guilds we have, the stronger we become, the better able to manage this world after it is ours. You in particular have two attributes of value to us. You have mobility due to your job, which is invaluable in our society. And, you are not a native of this world, and sooner or later it will drive you crazy."

"Maybe it already has," I said, retaining my skeptical tone. "But let's say, just for the sake of argument, that I believe you're who and what you say. What good does it do me?"

"Listen carefully, for we will say this only once, and time is short. Someone will soon miss you and come in demanding to know why you are not back at work. You have one chance and one chance only to join us. At your next layover at Rochande you have a day off. Go to the matinee show at the Grand Theater that day. Sit in the balcony. Leave to go to the bathroom halfway through the first act. We will contact you."

"And my pair-mate?"

"Not at the first meeting. Later we will arrange for her as well. This communication is ended. Guard your comments."

And, with that, things were, allegedly, back to normal. I left quickly and returned to work. Ching noticed that I seemed cheerier than I had for weeks, but couldn't figure out why.

We always went out for a special meal and a show on our day off and when I suggested the Grand, Ching wasn't the least surprised. As instructed long ago, I keyed in the code on my terminal that told me how much credit we had for our day on the town—and simultaneously let my TMS contact know that things had, finally, started to roll. I had no intention of double-crossing either side until I'd gotten what I wanted from this assignment, and certainly not until I could get away with it.

When you're sitting in the middle of a dark and crowded theater you can instantly make yourself a villain in a number of ways, but the worst is to go to the bathroom in the middle of the show. I finally made it to the aisle through the curses and dirty looks—made worse by the sure and certain knowledge that I'd be back—and proceeded to the upper lobby, where the large rest room was located. As I passed the last row of seats—far more sparsely populated since they were so far from the screen you might as well have dialed the show on your terminal—a hand shot out from a darkened seat, grabbed my arm, and pulled me over with such force I almost lost my balance.

All I could really tell about her was that she was tall, lean, and looked to be a pure civilized worlder. "Listen, Bul," she whispered, "just sit down and make like you're watching the show. Let me do the talking."

"Fair enough," I whispered back, and sat.

"Are you still interested in our organization?"

"I still don't believe in it," I told her, "but I'm here, at least out of curiosity."

"That's enough—for now. Just two blocks north of this theater is a small café, the Gringol. Go there after the show. Order what you like from the menu. Wait for us. We will take care of things from that point on, both with you and with TMS. If you are not there, you will never hear from us again. Now get up and go to the toilet."

I started to open my mouth and respond, then thought better of it, and did as instructed.

Ching and I watched the rest of the show, then wandered outside, where it was still light but would not be for much longer. I suggested a walk to get the kinks out of my leg. In the middle of the second block north of the theater, I spotted the small sign for the Gringol and turned to Ching. "I'm getting hungry. Want to get something?"

"Sure. Why not? Got anyplace in mind? How flush are we?"

"Not very," I told her, and that was the truth, despite the extra cash. "Let's see what this café has." The maneuver was nice and smooth and natural, and she didn't suspect a thing.

The place was small and dimly lit, although, of course, that would not matter to TMS and its ever-present monitors. Still, in a world with cafeteria sameness, the occasional trip to a restaurant or café, with an actual menu from which to select meals, was a real treat. Sometimes, the food in small places like this was even prepared by humans with their own special recipes, mostly Warden exiles or those with recipes passed down from exiles and pioneers.

"Looks expensive," Ching said dubiously. "Are you sure we can afford this?"

"Probably not, but what the hell," I responded, picking a small two-person table in the back and sitting down. The place was almost empty, although a few more people drifted in as we sat. A human waitress arrived from the back and handed us small menus. There weren't *that* many choices, but the few available promised to be "special recipes found nowhere else on Medusa": a Cerberan algae steak, an unusual Charon fruit plate, and other Warden specialties, including some meat dishes, I noted. The menu bragged that nothing used was synthetic. I doubted that, but at least such a declaration meant they'd try hard to make you believe it. The prices were fairly reasonable, so when the waitress suggested a special Lilith wine I looked at Ching, then sprang for it.

Frankly, I was surprised at the suggestion, considering our obvious youth. The wine arrived and was poured from a small wooden flask. I picked mine up, looked at Ching, and smiled. "Ever had alcohol before?" "No," she admitted, "but I've always been curious about it."

"Well, you'll know why you haven't. Try it." I sipped mine, and she drank hers as if it were a glass of water, then made a curious face. "It tastes—funny."

It was actually a very good wine, considering I had no idea what it was fermented from, that tasted like a high-class white from the civilized worlds. "You don't like it?"

"No—I mean, yes. It's just—different."

The waitress was soon back to take our order, and we gave it and relaxed. It occurred to me that either the wine or something in the food might contain a drug, but that didn't worry me. I expected it.

I looked over at Ching, who was already looking a little glassy-eyed and just smiling and staring at me. She was small and alcohol was new to her and would hit her. She sighed, "I feel real good. Relaxed." She reached for the flask, poured more wine, and drank it fairly quickly. I was still sipping my first glass, of course, feeling fairly human and normal for the first time since I woke up on that prison ship.

Whoever this Opposition was, they were a most civilized underground. While whatever it was, was somewhere in the meal, they let us finish it before our consciousness just sort of faded out without either of us even noticing. Half expecting it, I could have established mental defenses to block the effects—but that would have defeated the whole plan anyway.

I awoke in a smelly tunnel, with several dark forms hovering near me. The place smelled really cruddy, like raw sewage, and it took no brains at all to figure out that I was somewhere down in the drainage system under the city.

Whatever they used was no more than a light hypnotic; I could break it fairly easily, but that wasn't something Tarin Bul was supposed to be able to do, and so I simply rearranged my mind-set while keeping myself under at about the same level as the drug or whatever—but with autohypnosis replacing the substance. If agents could be subdued by such simple chemical means there'd be no use breeding them and training them so extensively.

I could not quite make out the dark shapes, even though they were very close. Either they wore some all-encompassing black hooded garments or they were using some sort of disrupter field.

"He wakes to level one," a woman's voice said.

"It is time, then," another—a gruff man's voice—responded. "Here—let me check." He kneeled down very close to me, and a black, ghostly arm and hand opened one of my eyes, checked my pulse, and did other routine checks. He got back up, seeming satisfied. "It's okay, Sister 657, you want to take him?"

"Tarin Bul—do you hear us?" the woman's voice asked softly.

"Yes," I responded dully.

"You understand that this is your point of no return? That you may tell us now to restore you and nothing more will ever be said nor will you hear from us again? But, if you continue, you are committed to us, and should you compromise or betray the Opposition you will forfeit your life."

"I understand," I told them. "I did not come here to turn away."

They seemed to like that. "Very well," Sister 657 said, "then rise and follow us."

I did as instructed, thankfully noting that I had been on a dry wooden platform and not in that gunk below. We were, in fact, walking on catwalks over the river of sludge, somewhere beneath Rochande in a maze even those who worked in it would need a map to negotiate. Not these folks, though; they knew just where they were going. Despite the twists and turns, I was pretty sure I could get back to where we started, but that knowledge did me no good. I had no assurance that that starting spot was anywhere near the café, since I had no idea how long I'd been out.

Finally we made a turn and walked over a temporary catwalk maybe three meters long. It led to an opening in the tunnel wall beyond which was a dimly lit room full of maintenance equipment. Several more dark shapes were in evidence, perhaps a dozen in all including my captors, which was a good thing. With all the ropes and probes and cables and patch can about, there wouldn't be room in the place for many more.

They sat me down on a crate in front of them, whereupon I relaxed. The stuff they gave me would be out of my system by now anyway, and they'd be the first to realize that.

Sister 657 seemed to be the leader. Nice touch, that, just the camaraderie title and a simple number. The odds were that her number made her very high up indeed—I assumed, correctly as it turned out, that the numbers referred to cell and city and only one to the individual's within the cell.

"Behold a possible brother," Sister 657 intoned. I hoped I wasn't in for a night of silly mumbo-jumbo and secret lodge stuff. "We give him the number 6137. He is awake, alert, and open to questions."

"Brother—why do you want to oppose the government?" a woman in the back asked me.

"It's pretty dull," I responded, which got a few chuckles.

"Brother—why do you wish to join us?" another woman asked.

"*You* recruited *me*," I pointed out. "Right now you're the only game in town, so, okay, I'll join up. But I really don't know what you stand for, and maybe your ideas on running Medusa are worse than the government's."

Some whispers around, as if I'd said something I shouldn't, but I intended to be blunt. What little I could pick out seemed to concern how cocksure and self-confident I was for one so young.

"He makes a good point," Sister 657 broke in, defusing the whispers. "We have told him nothing of ourselves. Perhaps we should before going any further." She turned to me. "Brother 6137, we don't bother with oaths, handshakes, or ceremonies. That's for the superstitious masses. However, I should tell you that, like most groups of this sort, we are more united in our opposition to the current government than we are in what to replace it with. Still, a lot more can be done with this world than this society permits, and it can be done effectively without having the government watch you go to the bathroom. We are strong, powerful, and well-positioned; but the means of overthrow has, as yet, eluded us. Right now we concentrate on getting recruits, gaining as much technical information on the local level as possible in each place, and establishing ourselves in each major population center on Medusa. It is a start."

I nodded. "But you can just as easily become a powerful debating society," I pointed out. "Look, I was born and bred to politics. Had things gone differently for me, in a few years I'd have been in planetary administration instead of sitting here waiting on passengers. Don't patronize me or think of me as a kid. I leave that to the people I want to underestimate me. For example, I think you should know that TMS knows you're in Rochande and put me out as bait."

There was a lot of shuffling and gasping at that one. Finally the leader asked, "Are you sure you know what you just said?"

I nodded. "Why hide it? You snuffed one of theirs and they got some information from another, and I was the logical bait. So they bumped me to a job that would bring me here. Frankly, I was getting sick and tired waiting for you people."

"He admits to working for TMS!" a woman almost shouted. "Remove him—now!"

"If I were a really effective TMS agent or plant the last thing I would have done would have been to tell you what I just did," I pointed out—falsely, as a matter of fact. The outburst worried me. Amateurs. Damned play-at-revolution amateurs! I had hoped for better.

"And will you tell TMS that you have contacted us, and joined us?" Sister 657 asked.

I nodded. "Sure. And you'll have to cook up something occasionally for me to feed that stonelike major or they'll pick me up and put me under a psych machine. They did that to one of your own—I don't know any names—a few months back, another newcomer like me, breaking her mind. I don't want anything like that happening to me, so if you're as powerful as you say you are I expect protection."

The man—possibly the only male other than myself—rose for the first time. "You make good sense, young man. You are very clever. Perhaps too clever. I almost wonder about you. The Cerberans, it is said, can make robots in any shape or form that cannot be told from humans. Ones that can assume the characteristics of any of the four Warden worlds."

"I'm no robot," I assured him, "but that information interests me." I paused, as if thinking over some weighty matters, then showed by my face and manner that I had made a decision. "In point of fact, I'm going to tell you something that isn't even on my records. Something Medusa, and, I suspect, Halstansir doesn't really know. I was a ringer back home. I didn't come out of the administrative breeding pool nor out of their schools. Do you think a high-class administrator could have managed to get into a reception and chop off a top politician's head with a sword? No, for reasons that are old history and have no business with you or anybody else any more, I came out of the assassin's pool."

There. A nice white lie that allowed me to be a little more of myself while at the same time protected my real identity and purpose. Who knows? My logic was so good maybe the kid *had* been from my old school at that. I'd like to think so. It disturbs me that an amateur could have pulled off that job so neatly.

And they bought it, hook, line, and sinker, just because it *did* make good sense. My first meeting, and already I'd engineered at least a social promotion for myself. As I said, amateurs.

"This explains a lot about you and your manner," Sister 657 said. "If this is so, then you are a far more valued recruit than I—we—had originally hoped for." Interesting slip, that. It implied that I knew her and she knew me, and I didn't know that many older folks on Medusa. She seemed unaware of her slip, though, and continued.

"Our time is run for this matter," she told us. "I propose we administer a small hypnotic and replace him at the café. Later, this week or early next, 6137, you will be called to the company psych for a routine check. There one of our people will add her own little bit to your testing, and we will check out your facts. If you prove out, then you will join our group, leaving for meetings in the same manner, but without the drug, from various small cafés. Objections?"

I shook my head. "Not on the psych stuff, no. But I suggest we continue to use the Gringol, at least for me. It wouldn't make any sense at all to compromise other cafés and similar places, since I am both being watched and obliged to report to TMS. Everybody else can use different spots—but keep me on the café. Eventually they'll put a transmitter on me somewhere, probably one I know about and one I won't, but I assume you have some kind of scanning for that sort of thing. If not, the next time or two, I'll show you how to build one. They'll assume any failure in the gadgets is your doing, anyway."

"Why do I feel *we* just joined *him?*" a woman in the front said grumpily.

I smiled.

* * *

They were smooth, I'll say that. Ching had passed out, but with the careful administering of additional doses of the hypnotic—a native plant, since anything else would be quickly negated by the Wardens—she was hardly aware that time passed at all. Nicely susceptible to the hypnotics, as most people are, she accepted a reasonable romantic scenario set in and near the café that, the Opposition assured me, would be supported in TMS records.

I dutifully keyed in the major on the terminal later that night, and, sure enough, the next day, after returning to Gray Basin and getting something to eat, TMS had another "random pickup," this time of both of us, although we were separated, once at headquarters.

The major, whose name, I learned, was Hocrow, was more than interested in my account, which, no doubt, was being checked and verified by countless scanners and sensors. No doubt, indeed—because she not only had a chair for me this time, she insisted I sit in it. Still, I had no worries about them, either—not only could I control just about all my important bodily indicators to make those machines read any way I wanted, I insured things by telling nothing but the truth, leaving out, of course, some of the inconvenient details.

"We have monitors along that whole area under the café, and in every maintenance room," the major grumbled, "and we did a total check when it was obvious you could have gone nowhere else. They showed nothing. How is it possible?"

"One sewer looks exactly like another," I pointed out, "and most of it is totally uninhabited most of the time. It's pretty easy to patch in and substitute an old recording of a sewer doing what sewers do."

She nodded. "And all the monitors are on one cable down there, to save money. I could make them all independent, which would compound their troubles no end, but that would be a rather obvious ploy."

"Not to mention the fact that, unless you did it to the whole city, something that would not only be obvious but would cost a fortune and disrupt the place for months, they could just move to a different sewer. But surely you already knew they were in the sewers."

"We did. It is the most logical place, anyway. But any attempt to breach that cable should set up all sorts of flags in Control."

"Well, there are two possibilities there. One is that they have somebody in Control who can be at just the right spot to cover up this sort of thing when needed. The second possibility is that you've simply been outclassed technically. This system of yours is pretty sophisticated, but it would be easy for a Confederacy tech team to beat and you know that better than I do."

"Are you suggesting that the Confederacy is behind this group?"

"It seems likely—but indirectly. Maybe they supply the smarts from someplace like the picket ship or their own satellites, but the people are home-grown. I don't know—for all their technical wizardry, they seemed to me like kids playing a game, sort of a more dangerous version of trying to beat the automatic doors on the buses and trains. They're *playing* at revolution, at least the ones I saw were."

Hocrow looked at me strangely for a moment. "Is what you told them about actually being a bred assassin true?"

"Yeah, it's true. Big money was paid, too. I was a long-range hidden gun in a power play my father planned. They got the jump on him before he was ready or I was old enough to be a factor, and I admit I was too young—too emotional—then."

"Then you wouldn't avenge your father's death if it happened now?"

"Oh, sure I would—but I wouldn't have been caught."

She mulled that over, just sitting there, looking up at the ceiling for quite some time. Finally she nodded to herself. "That's what was bothering me so much about you before. It fits. It explains a lot." She gave that icy smile again. "It seems you are misplaced. You should be in TMS."

I raised my eyebrows. "I thought I *was*. Otherwise, what are we doing here?"

She sighed. "One thing does bother me. If you have your preliminary training and all that special design, how will we ever know which side you are really on?"

I chuckled. "No matter what, I have limited experience. If you and your entire staff of monitors, psychs, and the like can't be sure of me, then your system's too shaky to have any hope of long-term survival anyway. Either you can do the job or you should give it up."

That was blunt, almost daring talk, but it was also guaranteed to play directly to a solid cop's ego because, frankly, it was true. The fact that I was trained to beat any system didn't mean I couldn't be beat. It only meant they had to be up to the job.

"Now, what about this psych exam?" I asked her. "Can you get me by it?"

"It should be relatively easy for someone with your supposed abilities," she mocked. "Still, we can do a little reinforcing before you leave here, with your help. I have a tech on call."

"That'll do," I told her. "But you're not going to do anything crazy like pick up any of the café staff, are you? They all have to be in on it, at least in another cell that supports mine. I'd just trail and track 'em, if possible. My own intention is to make myself invaluable enough to the organization that I'll be passed ever upward. If everybody's as amateurish as these people, you have no real problem, only an irritant. So what if they can play games with the system as long as they're still trapped in it? But if, at the top levels, there's somebody or some group really able to use what they've got, then I want to meet them."

She looked at me with those steely eyes. "Why?"

I grinned. "Because I want your job. Because, maybe, I'd like to be First Minister before I'm forty. Or, maybe, the guy who tells the First Minister what to do."

"Ambitious, aren't you?"

I shrugged. "I'm young."

CHAPTER SEVEN

Working Both Sides of the Street

The psych job was no big problem. In fact, the hardest thing about it was not betraying how much more I knew about the tech's machines than she did. Still, as someone allegedly under psych probes for over a year after the murder, I could be expected to have a certain amount of familiarity and expertise.

The routine psych exam was designed to catch problems before they developed into something that might cause real trouble for the Guild and the system. I did learn, by casual conversation while taking the exam, a bit of interesting additional information to file.

There was no psych school on Medusa; all psychs native to the Warden system were trained on Cerberus. It stood to reason, therefore, that this Opposition might also have Cerberan origins. I had no evidence, of course, but such a level of technological expertise combined with such an amateurish and naive set of people led to the inescapable conclusion that we— the Opposition, that is—were the arm of a widespread, Confederacy-backed underground whose main objective, at least on Medusa, was to get organized and remain in waiting until needed.

I got along well with the cell members, particularly once I disdained that silly robe, hood, and veil the rest of them used. Hell, they all knew who I was anyway, so why fool with that sort of stuff? To my disappointment, most of them were also in the Transport Guild—I wanted to broaden my base—although at least two were fairly high up. But they were such eager amateurs, that I felt I had to more or less lead them along and also maybe dangle some bait for the higher-ups. Therefore, at one meeting I dropped a real bombshell. They were doing their usual debating-society stuff about the problems in breaking the system as opposed to crawling around in the cracks when I interrupted. "I think I'm pretty clear on how to destroy totally TMS's hold on Medusa." All of a sudden you could have heard a pin drop.

"So? What master plot has the superkid come up with now?" one of them finally asked.

"Let me tell you about the harrar," I began. "They're too big not to eat all the time, and too big and fat ever to catch anything. Yet there are plenty of harrar in the wild. You remember some of the old wives' tales about them?"

They nodded and shook their heads and mumbled and finally somebody said, "But nobody believes that crap."

"On a world that's been settled for this short a time, there's almost always a good reason for those tales," I pointed out. "And the harrar itself fits in perfectly. They can change shape. They can make themselves look like other, more familiar things and then just sit there until prey comes near. Maybe they even attract it. But they change shape all the same. On a more primitive basis, I think the tubros have a little of this ability as well. They have a tail that looks like their necks with a ball of fat on the end of it. Why? A neck with no head, or a ball of fat, isn't going to fool any predator worth its salt. I think they make that ball of fat look just like their pointy heads, when they have to. All of them change color to fit their background, as do almost all the animals on Medusa. Hell, even *we* do that, sort of."

"But that's animals," somebody noted. "What's that to do with us, even if it *is* true?"

"I think humans can do it, too. The fact is, the Warden cells that make up our bodies are basic living cells for plants and animals. They're not like normal human, plant, or animal cells, but they're more like each other than like normal cells. They protect us from cold and heat and even from starvation, within limits. Given air and water we can live anywhere and on most anything if we had to. Nature is really pretty consistent. Shape-changing is simply a practical survival characteristic the Wardens could develop."

"Then why can't we do it?" somebody wanted to know.

"Because we don't know how. I suspect that if we were out in the wild the ability would come more or less naturally. But it *does* exist, even here. I've seen scars heal almost while I was watching them. I've seen three people I knew change sex so absolutely you'd swear they were born with that new sex. If we can accomplish something that total, we can surely make changes with any face and form."

"That may be," Sister 657 put in, "but nobody can control these things so it does no one any good."

"I think they *can* be controlled. I think the harrar and the tubros' tail tell us it's possible. With them it's probably instinctive, but the ability is there. It's only a matter of our finding out how to do it. I'm convinced the government knows. They went to a lot of trouble to suppress any idea that it's possible because they know it is. Their system is one based on visual and audio surveillance. Anybody who looked and sounded just like somebody else could use the card of whoever they appeared to be. Replace somebody—almost anybody roughly your size—and you can walk where he or she would walk and the monitors would never pick up the substitution. A lot of TMS's offices, for example, have no monitors themselves. The watchers don't like to be watched, and they need a few places off the record sometimes. A relatively small group of malleable people could walk into TMS as prisoners and wind up replacing everybody in top authority. A coordinated effort could collapse the system beyond easy repair."

"He makes it sound so easy," our other male member grumbled.

"No, it's not easy, and the plan is not without risk. Some people would die. A lot of homework would be necessary to keep detection away as long as possible. But our group has enough people placed in top levels to phony those records now—they're using the same principle I'm referring to, only in a more limited way. They understand that a totalitarian government is dependent on its technology for its controls and is secure only as long as that technology works and remains in their hands. They're going slightly nuts just because we beat the system, even though we haven't done anything threatening to them. Take away their system's confidence in knowing that the person on their recordings is really that person and you have rabid, absolute paranoia and fear on the part of the leadership. Shake it and it topples. It's more fragile than you've been brought up to think."

This set off a furious debate that was ended by Sister 657 with the comment, "All this might be true—if such body control is really possible. And that's a big if."

"I'm not so sure it is," I replied. "Look, we're pretty low down on the Opposition chart right now, but somebody up top is very bright and very well placed. If we can get this idea kicked far enough upstairs we might find out for sure. Can you arrange it?"

"I'll try," she assured me, "but I still think it's nothing but a fairy tale."

I had been on Medusa for more than six months when I finally got an answer. I'll say this for them—whoever was at the top was cautious in the extreme. The information, when it came, was both good and bad at the same time, and not something that could be used immediately.

Yes, all humans on Medusa were potentially malleable, but in order to accomplish a change, you first almost literally had to develop a sense of the Wardens and their connections, one to another. Once you had this sense—this ability to "talk" to your Wardens—you could, through hypnosis or psych machine, perform what was needed to be performed. The trouble was, nobody had ever found out how you accomplished it. Oh, it was possible, and had been done, but those who could do it could not explain how they did it, or even accurately describe the sensation. Nor had they been able to teach others. And unless you had that "sense of communication," as they called it, all the hypnos and psych machines in the world couldn't do a damned thing.

There was a general feeling that people who had the ability were born with it, at least as a latent ability that could not be learned. The government spent some time looking for those people, spiriting them away to a special compound far from anything and anybody else. They had hoped to breed the ability, but that plan had fallen flat. There were reports that many of the Wild Ones could do it, and often did, but whether this was voluntary or a response to the harsh conditions under which they lived was unknown.

Stimulus-response, that was the answer; but what stimulated this "sense" into action? Find the stimulus and you had the key—but Opposition sources had failed to find it and hardly believed in it, at least for the record. Still, if either certain social conditions or psychs could induce sex changes, then there *had* to be a way to induce the rest of it.

Certainly this same "sense" was responsible for the fabled powers of the leaders of Lilith, although there, too, the power was not for the masses and could not be acquired. You either had it or you didn't. That thought was depressing, since the same sort of thing might be the case here. Neither I nor anybody I knew might have that ability.

On Charon and Cerberus, though, everybody had it, at least to a degree. On Charon a person required training; on Cerberus the ability was involuntary, automatic, and universal. The lack of consistency between the three other worlds didn't help in finding a Medusan key.

Although I'd been warned about it, I can remember the shock at my first experience with the sex-change business. It wasn't some gradual thing —one person slowly changing—it was dramatic, taking place entirely in a matter of days. Medusan society was certainly the least sexist in any sense I could remember. Oh, certainly, there was complete sexual equality on the civilized worlds, but the two sexes still were physically different, hormonally different, and it was never really possible for one sex to understand the other totally. Neither sex had ever been the other. On Medusa you could be one or the other, either according to some odd formula the Wardens had or because you wanted to through psych sessions—and that was the key to my theory, the clincher. If something so drastic as sexual change could be induced, *any* change could be induced, if only you had the key.

This brought me to the Wild Ones. Nobody really seemed to know much about them except that they had a primitive hunter-gatherer tribal society. There were no romantic legends about them on Medusa; the very thought of living away from power and transportation and automated meals terrified even the bravest Medusan. That was irritating, but understandable. What was less understandable was why the Medusan government allowed Wild Ones at all. They served no apparent purpose, contributed nothing to the society—although, it's true, they also took nothing from it—and remained a totally uncontrolled, independent element who owned the wilderness portion of the world, and that meant the bulk of it. I knew from bitter experience that totalitarian minds like those of Ypsir and his associates would find the very existence of such bands intolerable. Their psychology simply wouldn't allow people to remain so free and unfettered for long. Of that I was absolutely certain, unless one of three conditions existed: (1) they performed a useful, valuable, or essential service to the government—highly unlikely; (2) they did not exist—even more unlikely; or (3) no matter what Medusa could do, they couldn't catch them.

And now I had reliable reports from above somewhere that the Wild Ones were reputed shape-changers, that they were at least on equal terms with the harrar. So, logically, the third choice seemed the most probable. Medusa wanted them, but had been singularly unsuccessful in catching those primitive folk. That conclusion led, too, to the question of just how primitive they might be, but this was something I could only learn by going and seeing for myself. If they were indeed a bunch of tribal types munching roots and grunting, I'd be stuck with them and out of luck.

Right now working both sides of the street had its advantages for me, but that, too, couldn't last forever. Major Hocrow would keep me going on the leash only as long as I was feeding her information that was either useful or might lead to useful information. If too long a dry spell came along, or if she decided that was all I could get, I knew my future wasn't too bright no matter what her assertions were as to my ultimate destiny. She was a good agent, with just the right nose for trouble, and she smelled a rat in me.

On the other hand, no matter how disappointing a debating forum these so-called rebels were, they were scared enough of the Medusan government and TMS to kill at the first sign of a double cross. Since they were such nervous amateurs, it wouldn't take much to push at least a couple of them over the edge against me. The man in the middle is always living on borrowed time.

About the only bright spot was that both sides realized I was not sentimental enough for them to use Ching against me. I was really fond of her. As hard as that was to admit, I also had to admit that I was really far more comfortable with her around, even if she was just *there*, doing something else quietly in the same room, than on the few occasions when I was alone. I liked to think that my feelings were more paternal than anything else. It was deadly for anyone in my line of work to ever form real attachments—and never more so than here and now. I was convinced I was above really needing other people except as tools or means to ends, but I did sort of realize that Ching needed me.

It would have been ridiculous and unfair to drag her to the café at irregular intervals while in Rochande, then knock her out for a period and try and cover. Not only was doing so impractical, the routine would soon become something she would do anything to avoid. Actually, it was Hocrow's tech who came up with the answer, with my help. Ching already knew I was up to something with TMS, and she trusted me. Therefore I was able to put her under the second time at Hocrow's and use the tech to reinforce the hypno. With a simple posthypnotic command I could make her either a totally loyal member of Medusan society or a totally committed Opposition member, pretty much going along with whatever I was playing at the time—only believing in it. Since we already knew their screening procedures, it was pretty easy to fake her past the Opposition's security checks.

In the meantime, the routine continued. Ching was bright enough to understand that my position, and thus, hers as well, was precarious at all times. I had to admit that I was not fond of that situation. I felt a little guilty at having thrust her into it, but, dammit, I hadn't *asked* for her.

Winter snows gave way, at last, to spring, and yet the situation dragged on, with me stuck at a stone wall. I *knew* my proposal for revolution was valid, and I was even more certain that those in the top levels of the Opposition not only agreed but had the means, somehow, to crack that needed stimulus. The only real question was why they didn't act. Certainly it wasn't out of fear of failure—what they had now was dead-ended and stagnating—but something else. If, in fact, I was correct about the off-planet origins of that leadership, it might mean that we were waiting for a concerted, multiplanet effort—but that wouldn't do any good here, I knew. These people simply didn't have adequate training, nor did we really know what sort of "soldiers" they would be if push came to shove.

And yet, I was curiously reluctant to move on my own. I was still trapped by the system as well, and I didn't like it at all. Sooner or later, I began to understand, I would have to break free, and take the chances beyond the simple ones I had taken to date. But somehow I was reluctant to do it. I had so little data. If only I knew more about the Wild Ones! I couldn't help but wonder if my counterparts on the other three worlds were feeling this frustrated. In a perverse sort of way I kind of hoped they were—I wouldn't like to be the only flop.

Not that I really gave a damn about the mission any more, though I was very slow to realize that. When I had awakened on that ship, even before planetfall, I had pretty much closed my mind to the dear old Confederacy and its causes and ways. It was odd how easy it was to slam the door on a lifetime—but then, *I* wasn't the one who slammed the door. They threw me out, then slammed it shut behind me.

Still, the primary objective of the mission and my own personal objective remained the same. I wanted the Medusan system overthrown, and I wouldn't have minded knocking off Talant Ypsir one bit. And yet, here I was, months in, stalled and half-beaten. Damn it all, I didn't even know where Ypsir was, and I had no means to get to him if I did.

What was happening to me down here? What was I changing into? In my quest for the key to physical metamorphosis, had I, somehow, had a mental metamorphosis that slipped right by unnoticed?

As had happened before, my next play was forced on me by factors beyond my control. It began with the summons to a particularly urgent meeting of the Opposition, one which all cell members were expected to attend. I was actually a little excited by the summons—maybe, just maybe, somebody had finally decided to move.

What I found in the maintenance room was not just my cell, but five separate cells, perhaps sixty people, all crowded into a place that could hardly hold one-third that number. Up front somebody had set up a screen and small recorder. A sense of extreme tension pervaded the air, yet few speculated or even said much to one another. The cells were uncomfortable being this packed together, and not just in the physical sense.

A tall woman from one of the other cells, all masked and robed as usual—even Ching was so disguised, although I still refused—looked around, took a count, then, satisfied, began by asking for quiet. The request was quickly granted by the uncomfortable crowd. Ching and I climbed up in the back on top of some crates so we could get out of the crush and still see at least the top part of the screen.

"We have been directed by our leadership board to gather you here and play this recording for you," the woman told us. "None of us have any more idea of what it contains than you do. Therefore, we will proceed to find out as quickly as possible. I am told that the recording card will destroy itself as it plays, so there can be no repeats." She punched the card into the recorder, and the screen flickered to life.

They could have saved themselves the trouble of a screen for all it was worth. It simply showed a man, masked and robed himself, sitting at a desk. It was impossible to tell anything about the scene, even the planet of origin, and it was obvious from the start that even the voice was distorted.

"Fellow comrades in opposition to the Lords of the Diamond," he began, "I bring you greetings. As some of you may have guessed, you are a part not only of a planetwide organization but a systemwide group devoted to the overthrow of all Four Lords of the Diamond."

There were gasps and some rumbling in the crowd.

"All of you have your personal reasons for wishing to overthrow the Medusan system, reasons we well understand. Simply because you are a part of a larger plan, please do not for one moment think that your own hopes and objectives are not part of that plan," the man went on. "Events have a way of overtaking plans, however, and that has happened in this case. The Confederacy itself is taking an active hand against the Four Lords, and has some chance of success. It is time, therefore, to explain to you all a little of what this is about.

"An alien race, totally alien to anything we know, discovered humanity before humanity discovered it. That race is somehow bound up with our homeland, the Warden system itself, and they are very clever and have a very good understanding of the way people work. Instead of warring with the Confederacy, they contacted the Four Lords, who jointly accepted a contract to destroy human civilization outside of the Diamond."

A lot more whispering and rustling now, and I could hear some snatches that included the words "mad" and "insult" and the like. Clearly this cloistered group, few or none of whom had ever known anyplace except the Warden Diamond, either didn't believe the man or they couldn't care less about the aliens. This reaction was understandable, and, I found, exactly what the speaker had anticipated. Either he was a psych or he had some good ones prepare the talk.

"Now, I know this doesn't seem to apply to you, but the fact is, it does. The Four Lords have made this contract and they are in the process of carrying it out. Their means are irrelevant to you, since they are worked against non-Diamond people, but those means depended on secrecy to the very last minute. Now that secrecy is blown. The Confederacy knows. Knows, but not enough. They are left with two options. We are one. The Four Lords must go, and be replaced by more honest, Warden-oriented people who will work for the Diamond and not on some sort of mass revenge. But we are no tools of the Confederacy, I assure you. We do this for our own good."

Nice dramatic pause here, I thought.

"The second and only remaining option as to the overthrow of the Four Lords and the consequent flushing out of these aliens is simple. The Confederacy, if it can not achieve or see the first, will not hesitate to do on a mass scale what they fail to do on a simple scale. They propose to incinerate the four Warden Diamond worlds totally and kill every living person and thing upon them."

Another pause and much agitation and some really loud comments rose from the crowd. It sounded angry and upset.

"They have the power to do this. They have the means. And those aliens won't save us. If they could, they wouldn't have needed the Four Lords in the first place. Therefore, this organization of good, serious men and women of the Diamond, very different on each world but nonetheless there, was formed not to save the Confederacy, which means nothing to us, but to save our homes, our worlds, our very lives. The Four Lords will not back down. They are in this to the death, since anything less than the aliens' total victory will destroy them. And since we know very little about them ourselves, we have no reason to think that, even in the case of a now improbable alien and Four Lords victory, those aliens would then be friendly to us. We have no choice.

"However, each planet is different, and must be dealt with by different methods—and is best dealt with by the natives of those worlds. Therefore, the members of Medusa's Opposition must now sit back, reflect, and discuss the situation among themselves. Cells will be asked within no more than two weeks to propose plans for action. Those plans will be examined and coordinated by us, and then a single master plan will be developed. We will win. We must win. I leave you now to discuss the situation in your individual cells. With your help, Medusa, TMS, and the very idea of monitors that strangles the world will be vanquished within a year."

With that the recording stopped, and there was instant pandemonium that took the group leader some time to quiet down to a dull roar. Finally she got enough of a lull to yell, "Discussion will be in individual cell groups. Those with numbers beginning in four will file out first, then those with six, following your cell leaders. Those in my cell will remain here! Do it now!"

Everyone stood around for a few moments, then a small group of four started toward the exit, followed by the rest, still grumbling and talking. As for me, I was reasonably excited by this development, since it meant action in the foreseeable future. I could just imagine the furious debates that would ensue when we met in private from now on. But something still bothered me a little. Was it *really* true that they had no plan, or was this simply a test? And would the truth sell to these folks?

I saw Sister 657, and turned to Ching. "What do you think?"

She shrugged. "It's hard to believe."

"It's true," I told her. "I knew it before I ever got to Medusa."

She thought about that one for a moment. Finally she said, "But *is* it any of our business, really? I'm not sure I even know what he means by aliens. and as for the Confederacy, all Outside is just a fairy tale to us, anyway."

I expected more of this logic when we assembled in our cell meeting. A lot more. What could you expect from people who weren't even sure what wild animals lived on their own native world? What did the concept of "alien' mean to them, anyway? Cerberan or Charonese was as alien as they could probably think. The idea that somebody, somewhere, could or would give an order and be willing and able to blow up a world was incomprehensibly abstract. I suspected that the Opposition leader had his hands full. I could tell just from his accent that he was a transportee himself, probably from the civilized worlds. His fancy, wood-paneled office wasn't in the Medusan style, at least none I'd ever seen, leading to the inescapable conclusion that our leaders were Cerberan or Charonese, not Medusan. That would also be the ultimate conclusion of the group, I knew—and would cause even more intense antileadership feelings. For the first time these play rebels were being asked to do something, possibly to put their lives on the line, and they would do anything to avoid that.

Our group was going out, and I jumped down and helped Ching down as well. We turned and followed the others, bringing up the rear of the group. I moved only a few paces outside the door when I stopped and ducked back inside. Ching, startled, looked at me. "What's the matter?"

"TMS!" I shouted so that everybody could hear. "It's a trap!"

The monitors also heard my echoed warning, because there was the sudden sound of an amplified official voice. "This is TMS! Everyone inside that room will come out, one by one, hands on heads, starting exactly one minute from now! We will gas anyone left after the rest have emerged, so there is no reason to hold back. You are trapped, and there is no way out. You have fifty seconds!"

Ching looked at me, scared and confused. "What will we do?"

I peered back out the door and saw perhaps a dozen agents, lined up on both sides of the catwalk about ten meters on either side of the temporary bridge. I had never seen TMS monitors armed with anything more lethal than a night stick, but these held very familiar-looking laser weapons.

I turned back to Ching and lowered my voice. "Now, listen carefully. I'm going to try and bluff us out of here with Hocrow's name. At the very least that should get us taken to her." I turned and looked at the remaining Opposition members in the room. Most had their hoods off and defeat registered all over their faces and in their mannerisms. They were sheep who'd do what they were told, like good little children, now that they'd been caught.

"Thirty seconds!"

"Damn!" I swore. "No, that Hocrow thing won't work except as a diversion. She's got to be behind this, at least partly. That means I'm no longer useful to her. We'll get psyched with the sheep. We've got to escape."

"Twenty seconds!"

"Escape? *How?*" Ching's whole expression showed that the very concept was alien to her. On Medusa, you were raised from birth to believe that there was no escape.

"I'm going to get one of those guns, then go over the rail into the sewer. Follow me if you want, but it's gonna be rough."

"Ten seconds!"

"But—where can we go?"

"Only one place. It's that or the Goodtime Girls, love. Ready?"

She nodded.

"Come out *now!*"

I walked out, hands above my head, and Ching followed. The rest of the cell walked behind us, looking very dejected. I could now see the others who'd gone before us lined up on both sides, and I couldn't help but be disgusted at the sight. Not a single weapon was aimed at them; in fact, nobody was even looking at them. Yet there they stood, hands meekly over heads, waiting for the rest of the sheep. Well, by God, they had one rabid dog in this bunch. Still, I couldn't believe that these were the shock troops of a real rebellion. If they had any guts or weren't so completely conditioned by their society, they could have easily taken all those TMS agents and their weapons. *Escape? Where?* Rule one: first escape, then go where they aren't.

Thanks to the illuminated stripes on its top, you could see a pretty long ways up and down the pipe, and the dozen TMS agents were all I saw. Only two on each side held laser weapons, short rifles from the looks of them.

"Get over against the wall with your traitorous friends!" snapped the laser-armed woman closest to me.

"Hey! I'm with Major Hocrow—I'm her inside man!" I protested.

"Major Hocrow is under arrest, just like you," the monitor snapped back. "You'll meet her in traitor's hell!"

Oho! Well, that was interesting. At least it meant that Hocrow was either being done in by a subordinate who was walking into her job or she really was with the Opposition and was one of those who ran cover for us. I would never know which, but the comment removed any last doubts I had about what I was going to do. There was no reprieve, and, once out of here, no chance at all.

I walked on past the monitor with the nasty tone, who, I saw, was no longer even looking at us but idly holding the rifle while gazing at the people coming behind us. I was about the same size as the monitor, but I had several advantages, not the least of which was that I wasn't conditioned by Medusa and I knew how to use that fancy rifle.

I whirled, pushed, and knocked her head into the rail, then reached out and grabbed the rifle from her loose grip as she struck.

In one motion I ducked, came up with the rifle, using it to push Ching on past, then opened fire on the line of monitors across from me. The beam, set to kill, sliced through them all pretty neatly, leaving just one weapon and four unarmed monitors at my back.

Men and women screamed at the violence that was not and had never been a part of their lives. I grabbed the groggy monitor I'd pushed into the rail in a hammer grip and, using her as a shield, started firing at the others.

I still would have failed, though, if three of the sheep still pressed against the wall hadn't made a split-second decision and rushed out. The officer holding the laser rifle on the far end was pushed into the muck, toppling nicely over the rail. The other three monitors, looking not just stunned but actually stricken, had eyes only for my rifle—and they stood still as stone.

"Thanks!" I called out to the three who'd come to my aid. "I couldn't have done it without you!" One of them waved, and I looked over at Ching. "You all right?"

"You—you *killed* them!"

"It's my job. I'll tell you about it sometime. Right now we have to get out of here—fast." I looked up and down at the Opposition members, some of whom still had their hands over their heads. I could sympathize, sort of. What they'd just seen was impossible, and that's why it'd worked. The monitors were simply too self-assured and too relaxed, too confident that the sheep would all be meek. They reacted very slowly, and, amateurishly, they had their rifles on narrow-beam kill, which allowed me to get that whole neat row with a single shot. Even the monitors were products of Medusa, conditioned to certain kinds of behavior and confident in their total mastery over the common herd.

I pushed my prisoner into the others and freed myself of any physical restrictions. The monitor rubbed her head and looked at me with a mixture of fear and confusion. "You better let us have that! There is no escape. Your entire organization is broken."

I smiled at her, which confused her all the more. "Okay, you Opposition members, listen up!" I yelled. "They're picking up our people all over the city, maybe all over the planet. You have only three choices. You can kill yourselves, go with the monitors, or come with me!"

"Come with you? Where?" somebody yelled back nervously.

"Outside! In the bush and the wild! It's the only place to run!"

That suggestion stopped them for a moment. I let them mull over the implications, but only for a short period. We had to move fast, before we were missed. This group of monitors was the usual bunch of egomaniacal incompetents, but TMS had much better than these, and it wouldn't take very long for their best to set out after us. I wanted to be long gone by then. "Anybody here know where the sewers dump outside the city and how to get there from here?"

"I know 'em pretty well," one of the three who'd pushed at the right moment called back. "I think I can get us out of here."

"Who's coming? I have to know *now!*"

It didn't surprise me that only the three who'd showed any guts wanted to come. Counting Ching, who was still looking pretty scared and confused herself, and me, that was five out of almost sixty. Some rebels!

"You three come up with me!" I called, then turned to Ching. "Coming?"

She was frightened and shocked, but she nodded affirmatively. "I go with you."

"Good girl!" I looked at the three. All were women, and one was familiar. "Well! Morphy! I *thought* you'd have the guts!"

Our demanding shift supervisor looked sheepish. "You knew?"

"Almost from the start. Introductions later, though." I flicked the rifle field to wide scan. "This won't hurt anybody," I said loud enough for all to hear, "just knock you out for a couple of minutes. I gotta say, though, that you deserve what you're going to get from TMS." I looked around. "Last chance." Nobody moved.

I fired first at the side with the monitors, then turned as the others on the other side screamed once more and started to panic. They all dropped in their tracks, although they were going to be a pain to crawl over on the catwalk.

I looked at them, feeling oddly confident and solid with the rifle in my hand. Four women and me. That could make the wild easier to take, that was for sure.

"C'mon, tribe!" I said, and we started picking our way through the unconscious bodies toward the clear area of the tunnel.

CHAPTER EIGHT

The Wild Ones

When we'd gotten pretty far from the fallen crowd, I stopped and turned to them. I had had the foresight to pick up the other rifle as we'd moved by the dead monitor on the end, as well as a power pack from the monitor's belt, but the charges were still limited and I was pretty sure I was the only one who knew how to fire the things.

"Okay—now things get messy," I told them. "They'll have squads all through this tunnel, and we're going to have to crawl in the muck below the catwalks and keep very still when they pass near so they go right on past. Understand?"

They nodded. I looked at the one who had said she knew the sewage system, a very attractive woman perhaps in her early twenties. "You said you knew these sewers. Can we get near a train at the exit point?"

She looked startled. "I thought you said we were going out with the garbage."

"Argue later. But for the record, now that we've said that it's exactly where they'll look for us. Remember, they've got all sorts of scanners in these tunnels, too, and they'll all be looking for us. I've looked at their regular locations, though, which depend on the power cables, and they're all located above the catwalks. If we're quiet enough, and careful enough, they won't see us down in the muck below. They have fixed focal lengths, so anything below the catwalks is a blur. Let's move—you lead. Morphy, you know what I'm thinking?"

She nodded. "Let's try it."

"Okay. Follow the leader, no talking unless I tell you. Let's go, gang—over and into the muck." One by one they complied, although not without some real hesitation. The stuff was really awful, thicker than I would have thought and close to waist-deep.

I couldn't resist thinking we were in deep shit, but it was the only odd-ball thought I allowed myself and it was too literally true to be funny. I had deliberately returned along the route we'd taken from the café, on the theory that those monitoring devices might still be out of commission, but I couldn't depend on it. This mission would be played by ear, and first we had to get to an exit point—a long, long way in the sewage.

The next several hours were nervous ones, although my hopes that the initial escape route was still blocked were borne out. Several times we stood right under squads of TMS herding Opposition members to exit points, and several more times we huddled in the stinking muck as small, very efficient armed patrols double-timed above us. We were all pretty well covered with the stuff and slipping and sliding as we moved, and it was clear we couldn't keep this up indefinitely.

So far we'd been extremely lucky. My escape was still something of a miracle, but it simply proved that when you have even one potential wolf you don't send sheep out to capture other sheep, even if the sheep you send are arrogant bastards. After the initial escape, we were protected by the flaw in their visual monitoring system and the very complexity of master sewage drains under a city of close to 350,000. There were probably a couple of thousand kilometers of drainage tunnels under the city, and TMS simply couldn't cover more than a fraction of that with its personnel. They had to wait for us to make a mistake, to betray our position, so they could concentrate their forces in that area.

I was proud of all four of my companions, who held together under some of the worst conditions I could think of, not only physically but mentally, knowing that just one little mistake would betray us to these overhead monitors. The monitors, I was sure, were all staffed by real live people as well as by the computers.

Finally, I had to ask the one who was supposed to know the tunnels if she really did. Frankly, none of us could take much more of this, and, sooner or later, we would certainly be found. "How much farther to the trains?"

"At the rate we're going, maybe an hour more," she whispered.

I didn't like the sound of that. "How long to any kind of exit near the city border?"

She thought a moment. "From the sector numbers at the last junction, maybe ten minutes to a drainage outlet. But there'll be an energy barrier there."

"I'll chance it. We can't take much more of this. Lead on."

She shrugged.

What seemed like an hour later we came close to the outlet. I could hear the thing rushing like a falls, and we were now waist high in sewage, which was developing a fairly strong current. There were no catwalks in the direction of the outlet, so there would be maybe thirty meters when we'd be fully exposed. There would certainly be a visual monitor up there, if only as a final check on animal entry should the energy barriers fail.

I tried to angle myself as best I could to see what the outlet looked like, but all I could see was the sewage dropping into some sort of sludge pool below and the unmistakable light purple of an energy barrier. "I wonder if that barrier is beyond the drop," I said aloud. "If it is, we might be able to go over the falls and then, beneath the surface, under the barrier. Do you know how much of a drop it is?"

She shook her head from side to side. "It varies. This plant is located in an old stone quarry. It might not be much of a drop but the holding pool could be fifty meters deep."

I gave a low whistle. "Well, that washes that idea, I guess. Let's go for the transport terminal after all."

At that moment, from just ahead of us there came the sound of many feet running in step, which then ceased abruptly. I heard a lot of shuffling around not too far down from us and saw the glare of spotlights on the sludge below. Obviously I'd blown it—the monitors here had to be a lot better than most.

"All right! We know you're down there!" a sharp woman's voice called. "Come out now, one at a time, or we'll come down and get you. And if we have to get into that slop we will not take you alive!"

I looked at my four companions. "What'll we *do*?" Ching asked, looking to me as if I had all the answers.

I sighed. "Nothing to do, really. Can you all swim?"

They nodded, which helped.

"Then take a deep breath, launch yourselves into this muck, and stay below it, letting the current take you over."

Morphy looked down uncomfortably at the muck. *"Under it?"*

"The whole way. It shouldn't be for long. Either that or they'll be here in a couple of minutes. We're already so stinking this won't make much of a difference." I took a deep breath, let it out, took another, let a little out, and ducked under, hugging onto my two rifles for dear life.

It was a miserable experience to top all other miserable experiences, particularly since I had to keep my eyes closed. All I could tell was that I was moving, with agonizing slowness; but aside from trying to stay below the surface without knowing if in fact I was doing that, I also couldn't be sure I was being carried with the current. I finally decided I'd hold out until I either fell, got knocked cold by the energy barrier, or had to come up for air, in which case I'd come up shooting.

It seemed as if I had been down for an eternity, when, oddly, the sludge seemed to thin and I felt less pressure to breathe. Then, suddenly, I broke the surface not from the top but in front of me, and I had to duck very quickly to pass just under the energy barrier. Then I was falling, and falling fast, still in the midst of a sludge river. I lost both rifles in the fall, which was at least twenty meters, then struck the main pool below, arms out to try and cushion what I sincerely believed would be a crippling or fatal impact.

I went into the pool effortlessly, and continued down for a bit with the momentum. I instinctively angled myself, treating the pool as common water, and arched back up again, breaking the surface.

There was no current in the pool, which was surrounded on three sides by sheer rock walls. Down at the far end was the structure of what had to be the automated treatment plant. It wasn't much—Medusa didn't really care what happened to the environment outside—but it operated in sunlight only, mixing the raw sewage with natural water and forcing it out into a river that led directly to the ocean. Just enough to keep the stuff from backing up and contaminating the natural water supply of the city.

The damlike structure wasn't very high, and I headed for its sloping white concrete wall. I reached it quickly, and crawled out onto it. Gasping for breath, I decided to make for the top of the thing, which was only about seven or eight meters above on the slanted surface. I would wait there as long as I could to see if anybody else made it through, but I knew that TMS would be out here as soon as that squad leader figured out what we'd done and radioed back to headquarters.

I was halfway up before I realized that I hadn't exactly swum that distance conventionally and even now was climbing the wall in a most unconventional manner. My arms, now a dark sludge-brown, were almost flipperlike! I realized that, somehow, I'd changed—and fast. There would be time for more self-examination later, I decided—but first I had to make the top or it was all for nothing.

I waited there nervously, but not for very long. My eyes quickly adjusted to the near darkness, and I soon saw two other shapes pop up and make for the wall, then a third.

When the first one got to the edge of the retaining pool and climbed out, I got something of a shock. It was a weird, inhuman sort of monster, all black and shiny, with an angular head, flippers, and a pair of strong, webbed hind legs. The creature began to crawl up toward me, wiggling up on its belly, and I almost recoiled in alarm until I suddenly realized that my own arms resembled those others. A second one made it and started the climb as the first one almost reached me, caught sight of me, and cried out in fear.

"Don't worry!" I called back. "It's just me! The Wardens changed us to live in that muck! Get up here—all of you! We'll change back soon enough if we get away from this!"

The others had similar reactions, but got talked up nonetheless.

I looked at them, and could see their skin begin to lose some of its shimmer and start to—well, ooze, as if our bodies were made of a puttylike substance that had a mind of its own. Strangely, I felt a little better about that—here was a stimulus with proof! If you placed yourself in an untenable environment, you changed. You changed into whatever would allow you to survive. This certainly explained the Wild Ones' ability to escape from TMS, and probably accounted for the shape-change legends as well. The Wild Ones used the ability to hide and to survive.

If I could just get my hands on a psych machine and convince somebody he was in a different sort of environment, it would work—but still not under real control. You would become an improvised monster, whatever your Wardens required for your survival.

But how did the Wardens understand just what you needed in that instant you needed it? And from where did they get the incredibly sophisticated knowledge of biology to accomplish the change so quickly?

We waited another five minutes, and I checked the roll. Ching had made it, although she was terribly confused and terrified by the shape change. Morphy had come through and one other, whose name I still didn't know. Our guide through the sewers, though, was not here.

We were becoming "human" again, and quickly, as the Wardens inside us sensed our changing environment. In fact, we were becoming our old selves, indicating that either the original pattern was always reverted to when the Wardens were "at rest" or that a strong sense of self-identity would reimpose it. The one thing that was not coming back was hair, I noted; and our skin remained that dark brown of the "monsters" we had briefly become.

It was fascinating to watch my own arms slowly flow, change, rearrange back into the more familiar patterns. When we were humanoid enough to have full upright muscle control, I took one last look for a fourth head in the pool. Nothing. "We have to get moving. I think I see a patrol over there on the far side."

Morphy looked at me, then back at the pool. "But we're still one short!"

"Can't be helped. Either she couldn't change or she got plugged or caught. Either way, we can't help her by getting caught or shot ourselves. Let's move!"

The one whose name I still didn't know looked puzzled and confused. "Where? Where do we go now?"

I sighed. "Somewhere else, of course. Follow me!" Then I was off along the top of the plant. Coming on some steps on the other side, I started down as laser tracers started illuminating the night. Once we hit the rather shallow river below, I just ran into it and waded across to the other side, not even checking to see if the others were following. I didn't have the time, and if they weren't there, I couldn't do anything about it anyway. I was heading for the forest located just on the other side of the river, and I wasn't going to stop for anything until I made the cover of those trees.

Suddenly I heard Morphy's voice yell, "Drop!" and I didn't wait to find out why. I dropped right into the water, which, by this time, was not deep enough to cover my body. After I was down, I raised my head a little and looked up, seeing what Morphy had seen. A small illuminated bubble with two TMS monitors in it was flying almost noiselessly down the river, shining a spotlight on the whole river course. I made a quick check to see that everybody was, indeed, down, then froze as the thing approached, passed right over us, and continued on. In this light, and with this shallow, rocky bed, we had to look like rocks to a copter going any speed at all. But I was pretty sure this wasn't something TMS did every day; we were being pursued.

When the lights disappeared, I stood up again and we all made it to the far bank and the cover of the trees. I finally allowed myself to let up a bit and collapsed on the ground. The others did the same, and it was a little while before any of us could talk.

Finally I said, "Well, the age of miracles has returned. We got away with it sure enough."

Morphy looked back at me with a grim expression, then at the other two. Except for our coloration and the total absence of any body hair, we all looked pretty much as we had, although the transformation or whatever it was had split our flimsy clothes as well. "Stark naked, in an unknown wilderness, hunted like wild animals, and without a hair to our name, and he thinks he's winning!"

"Not to mention starving to death," the strange woman put in.

I grinned. "I am. We are—will—win. We didn't go through all this to lose now. And if that tumble in the sludge didn't teach you that we are survival machines, I don't know what will. But I think we'll have to get as far from here as we can tonight. I don't think they'll hunt us very far or long—it just isn't worth it, even though we're all going to be pretty wanted by this group."

"After those others tell about what you did back there when we were first captured, I'd say they'll want *you* more than anybody," Morphy replied. "What you did to those monitors wasn't—*human*. I wonder if even you realize that you knocked over the armed monitor, grabbed her rifle, turned, killed four monitors, then whirled back to cover the others in something under five seconds?"

"Five sec—" I was struck speechless for a moment. No wonder the job had seemed so easy! Five seconds for the entire thing! In my original fine-tuned body, *maybe*, just maybe, I could have done it, but here and now . . . knowing what to do and making your body do it are two different things. Ask any fifty-year-old space pilot. And yet, the answer to it was obvious.

"I knew what to do," I told her, "and the Wardens supplied the rest. I was under such tremendous tension, picking my position and mentally preparing for the moves, that the Wardens must have made the necessary survival adjustment—the same principle that turned us into whatever it was we had turned into briefly back there. If you had the knowledge and the will it would've worked for you, too. So you see, we're not exactly helpless out here. We carry our protection with us. We were made for this planet—I almost said *designed* for it, and maybe that's right—and *this* is Medusa, not those comfortable, sealed prisons we call cities here."

"That was some . . . strange thing that happened to us, you can't say it wasn't," our mystery woman put in. "I never heard of anybody changing into anything else before, except maybe sex."

"That's true," I admitted, "but the system's designed against it. We're all kept in artificial, stable environments where that sort of thing just won't happen. Even so, I'm sure it has, maybe when somebody's gotten into an accident or was in danger of drowning or something. Transformations may occur every day. But if so, those people are rescued, hustled off to psychs, and put right. Even memories are sponged from the minds of people involved directly or of the people who observed it. And, by the way, I think we ought to know who you are. I'm Tarin Bul."

"Angi Patma, Construction Guild," she responded.

We made introductions all around. I was particularly concerned with the usually outgoing Ching, who now seemed quiet and sullen, still in shock. I walked over to her. "Come on—we're gonna be fine," I soothed.

She looked up at me. "I know."

I frowned. "What's wrong, hon? I was proud of you!"

She was silent for a moment. Finally she said, "You killed four people, Tarin. Killed. And you're not even a little sorry about it."

I sighed. "Listen, Ching—I had to do it. It was the only way. When someone is marching you off to your death, and happy to do it, he forfeits his own right to life. Those survivors—they're still going to get those fifty-five or so who remained. None of them are going to be left alive, at least not without destroyed minds. That is a worse crime in my book. Remember, these people were picked for TMS for the same reason everybody else on Medusa is picked for his job. They *like* bullying, scaring, and even killing people."

"Don't you?"

That stopped me for a moment. The fact was, I really do love my job, of course. But there *was* a difference. At least, I hoped there was. "I'm not interested in bullying or scaring anybody, except for that kind of person. People who like to hurt other people is who I hunt and get. That's not so bad, is it?"

She didn't seem sure, and the more I thought about it, neither was I. From birth I had been raised to believe in the Confederacy, in its perfection and its ideals. But, in that context, what *was* my job, anyway? The same as TMS here? To track down those who posed a threat to the Confederacy's system—or who abused or perverted it—and send them to psychs, or to the Warden Diamond, or, on rare occasions, to their deaths. True, most of the Confederacy was a far better system than Ypsir's Medusa, but the people here did in fact believe in that system, including those in TMS. In *their* minds they were no different from me. Did that make us different—or the same? Medusa was nothing if not a perversion—a distorted mirror image—of the Confederacy's system and dreams. That must have been why I felt so uncomfortable with it.

I rose to my feet. "Let's get walking. They'll have foot patrols through here anytime now, and we've already stayed too long. Let's make all the time at night we can. We can talk on the way."

They *did* send a few patrols and copters after us, and we saw or heard them from time to time, but they made no more than a minimum effort, which simply wasn't good enough. To their minds, being out in the wild was tantamount to being dead anyway, and nobody was really worth the kind of effort that would have been needed to track us down. Again it was Medusa's own system that allowed us our freedom, although what sort of freedom remained to be seen.

The biology texts hadn't revealed the half of Medusa's natural history, though. Not only were there hundreds, perhaps thousands, of different plants large and small, but the forests literally teemed with animal life. All of it was strange-looking on the surface, but at the same time very much like many other planets. Perhaps the theory that ecosystems developed under nearly identical conditions came out much the same way was true. Here, as elsewhere, trees were clearly trees and insects clearly bugs—and they served the same functions.

The first real concern wasn't eluding a ho-hum pursuit, but finding food. Coming into spring in the "tropical" regions meant that there were a number of berries and fruits around, but little looked ripe and all was unknown to me.

"How do we know what's safe and what's not?" Angi complained, hungry like the rest of us.

"I think it's simple," I told them all. "At least, it should be. If there's anything *really* lethal around it should produce some kind of warning that our Wardens will trigger. That berry, there, for example, smells really foul, and I wouldn't touch it. Even my initial indoctrination, though, said that we *could* eat almost anything, with the Wardens converting the substance into what we and they really need. I'd say, for now, we just pick something that at least seems practical to eat and eat it."

It took some time, though, and a lot of guts, before we decided to go through with a test. The leaves and unripe fruits tasted from bitter to lousy, but once we started eating we found it difficult to stop until we felt full. All of us suffered a bit from stomach aches and the runs that night but after a somewhat fitful sleep on the open ground we all awoke feeling much better. After that our Wardens adjusted even more to our new situation and provided the guidance we needed—much as I'd hoped. Some stuff that tasted lousy the first time tended to taste quite good after that, while other stuff just tasted worse and worse. With that neat sorting and classification system to go on, we had no more trouble, although I confess that Ching wasn't the only one who dreamed of good meat and fresh fruit.

Well, we wouldn't starve, so the next thing was to adapt our lifestyle to this new environment. Clothing proved unnecessary, as always, and after what we'd been through modesty was no longer a factor. Shelter from the cold rains and occasional ice-pellet storms was provided by the forests and, if necessary, we could rig portable lean-tos from branches and the broad leaves of a prevalent bush. In point of fact I had the survival training and the means to make permanent dwellings, if necessary, but I had no intention of founding a village at this point. We had three months before the first snows, with the best weather yet to come, to find the Wild Ones. That had to be our first priority.

Over several days I made a broad circle around Rochande and then headed toward the coast which that handy map in my head said was there. From that point, and using the sun for direction, I could determine our approximate location and chart where we were going.

The first few weeks were education weeks. We learned what we could eat, where it was most likely to grow, and what caused problems. I gave a small seminar in survival skills—building lean-tos, that sort of thing—and we also learned the habits of many of the animals. The tree-dwelling tubros were all around, but if you didn't bother them they wouldn't bother you. The vettas stayed mostly in the clearings and on the plains, so we tended to avoid such places. We had not met a harrar as yet, and I, for one, had no intention of doing so if I could help it.

Then there were the occasional thermal areas. The place wasn't full of them, but they were far more numerous than I originally would have guessed. Geyser holes, bubbling mudpots, and fumeroles turned up in the damnedest places and, occasionally, we even came across a hot thermal pool. Once you got used to the sulfurous stink, these pools were very handy for bathing. We even tried some experiments in wrapping all sorts of food in leaf bags and boiling them.

We also got to know one another better than I think any of us had ever known anyone before. I will say this for all three of them—they were inwardly tough. Though complaints were numerous they had by and large accepted their lot fatalistically and began to look upon this new life as some sort of great adventure. I wondered, though, if they would have fared so confidently or so well had I not been there to teach them a few tricks of the trade.

There was no more purpose in concealment, and I explained to them just who and what I was. In a sense the explanation seemed to reassure them, and the fact that I was a professional agent somehow seemed to soften Ching's initial revulsion at my killings. It became less of a radical change in me than a reversion to form, and she seemed better able to accept that.

We lapsed into a total familiarity so easily I often wondered if the Wardens had anything to do with it. Morphy became "just Bura," Ching was still Ching, and Angi's last name I just about forgot. As for me, I accepted everybody calling me by Ching's pet name for me—Tari—and we became just one big family.

The fifty-five who remained behind continued to weigh heavily on me, though, and I decided to find out why they stayed and these didn't.

Bura, it seemed, was a native but had once been much higher in the Guild. Years earlier she had married into a family group that included another exile to the Diamond, a rough-and-tumble man built like an ox who had a horrible temper with those outside his own family group but was kind and gentle at home. Still, she admired his independent spirit, his disdain for TMS and the system, and, I suspect, she damn near worshiped him. One day he had one too many run-ins with TMS, of course, and he'd blown up and literally snapped a monitor in two. Most of the family, to save their own skins, were willing to testify against him as to his murderous instincts and to his inability to "assimilate" into Medusan society. Bura refused, for which she was transferred halfway around the world and demoted to a passenger-service shift supervisor with no hope of advancing any further. At that she'd gotten off lucky, but when the psych she was sent to by TMS for adjustment instead introduced her to the Opposition, she was more than ready and willing and quickly rose to cell leader—Sister 657, of course.

Angi had a less understandable background. Born and raised on Medusa, and never to her knowledge having had any contact with Diamond transportees, she nonetheless was always somebody who didn't quite fit. As a kid she'd beaten the bus fares and done some minor shoplifting—for which she was never caught—and she'd qualified for training as a civil engineer. The subject fascinated her, but the restrictions, the lack of creativity, the sheer sameness imposed from above, had always gotten to her, so she'd never progressed very far. When you built just one way, and all of the tough problems had already been solved, it was a pretty dull profession. She'd been doing quality-control supervision for a massive repair of the bus system in a sector of Rochande—"real thrilling work," she called it without enthusiasm. Again it was a routine psych exam that introduced her to the Opposition, and she joined simply because it was another something different to do. She had been the one who had pushed the armed monitor over the rail—"strictly on impulse," she told us.

None knew the other courageous woman, the one who had led us out of the city only to be denied freedom and life herself, but all of us agreed that, no matter where—or whether—she was at the moment, she was and would always be a member of our family.

Family is exactly what we became in those early days of Medusa's spring. On a world whose culture was based upon the group marriage, there was no real jealousy or bad feelings between any of the women, and certainly not from me. In fact, this period of isolation, just the four of us living much as man's ancestors must have lived back on the ancient home world of man a million years ago, was in many respects the best time of my entire life. It was during this period that, I think, I turned my back once and for all on the Confederacy.

We made our way in zigzag fashion from coast to interior thermal areas and back again, developing a sense of where the thermal regions were. We headed north because Bura's long tenure on the trains had shown her that some Wild Ones definitely lived between Rochande and Gray Basin. She had caught glimpses of manlike shapes in the distance several times—in the direction of the coast. Occasionally we would find traces of habitation, signs of a temporary encampment, but there seemed no way at all to tell how warm or cold the trail.

Ultimately we never found them—they found us. Exactly how long we were alone in our wandering tribal existence I don't know, but summer was definitely upon us when, one day, stepping into a clearing, we suddenly found ourselves surrounded by several new people.

The group consisted of one man and six women, at least one of whom appeared quite pregnant. Like us, they were dark-skinned and hairless, a condition that looked quite natural and normal to us now. All wore skirts of some reddish or black hair and all bore homemade bows and spears. Obviously from their manner they'd been observing us for some time, but they said nothing and made no move toward us when they showed themselves. They just stood there, looking hard at our little group. We, of course, looked back.

Finally I shrugged, put up my hands palms out. "We're friends. We mean you no harm."

For a while they made no response, and gave no indication that they understood my words, and I grew nervous that there might be some sort of language gap. No telling what sort of culture people raised in this wild would develop. But, finally, one of the women asked, "What tribe do you come from? Where are your tribal marks?"

"No tribe," I responded, feeling relieved. "Or, say, rather, that we are our own tribe."

"Outcasts," one of the others hissed, in a tone that did not indicate approval.

"Not from a tribe," I said quickly. "We escaped from the cities."

They showed some surprise at that, the first real emotion I'd seen any of them display. I had never really dealt with a primitive group before, and I was winging it, hoping I wouldn't put my foot in my mouth. Those weapons looked pretty grim. One of the women whispered to the one who appeared to be their leader, "The demons live in those places. It is a demon trick."

The leader shrugged off the comment. "What do you wish here?"

"A tribe," I responded, trying to get as much into the mind-set as I could. "A place to belong, to learn the ways of the world and the ways of a great tribe of people."

That seemed to be the right response, because the leader nodded sagely to herself. She seemed to think it over, then made her decision—which, I noted, was final no matter what the others thought. "You will come with us. We are the People of the Rock. We will take you to our camp, where the Elders will decide."

"That sounds good to us," I told her, and, with that, they all turned and started back into the forest. I looked at the others, shrugged, and followed.

CHAPTER NINE

The Demons of the Mount

They had not mentioned that they were several days from this camp of theirs, and that didn't become apparent for some time. They allowed us to follow them, all right, but kept themselves apart, not talking to us any more than they had to and occasionally taking suspicious glances at us when they thought we weren't looking. It was clear that, while a leader's decision was absolute and to be obeyed, it didn't mean you had to agree with it.

They carried sacks of some kind of skin, in which were various supplies, bows, extra spear points, that sort of thing, but no food. That they foraged for, much as we had, although they had a dietary element that we'd lacked to this point. They hunted vettas and tubros, and did it expertly, considering the primitiveness of their equipment. They could stake out a place silently for an hour or more, seemingly not moving at all. But when a vetta, for example, came close they would rise around it in a circle, tossing spears and shooting arrows with precision and lightning speed, bringing the panicked animal down. Then they would disembowel it with a different, even nastier sort of spear. The vettas, too, were Warden creatures, and you had to kill them quickly or repairs would begin.

Once they were sure the animal was dead they would skewer it on a couple of spears and carry it between two of them, the poles expertly balanced on their shoulders, until they came to a thermal pool. There, experts wielded stone axes in butchering the animal into various small parts which were then wrapped in leaves and cooked in the thermal pools. As one who had, at one time or another, eaten natural meat on frontier worlds, it wasn't more than a curiosity to me, but to my three wives it was a sickening experience. Butchering an animal is not pretty, and none of the three had ever seen it done before or even thought about it. I had to work pretty hard to prevent them from showing their disgust.

"You have to have real guts," I told them, "like you did back in the escape. If they offer any to us, take it and eat it. You don't have to like it, and you can be disgusted by it, but we need them."

"I don't know why we need anybody," Ching protested. "We were doing pretty good, I think, and we were *happy*."

"Vettas are happy until they're caught and killed," I retorted. "We're more than animals, Ching. We're human beings—and human beings have to grow and learn. That's why we need them."

We *were* offered some of the kill, after the rest had taken their pick of the best cuts, and I complimented them on their great skill as hunters—which also seemed to please them. I think they knew that my three city-dwelling companions were upset by the hunt and kill, and were vastly amused by their reactions as they tried to bite into the chunks of meat. Angi, whose motto seemed to be "I'll try anything once" was the most successful; Bura ate as little as she thought she could get away with and looked extremely uncomfortable; Ching finally forced a mouthful down, but she just couldn't conceal her disgust and refused to eat any more. I didn't press her; I thought throwing up would be in the worst of taste.

I was relieved to see that our tribal hosts were taking things so well, and I began to suspect that some of them, at least, were neither as naive nor as ignorant as they pretended to be.

They had a ceremony at the end of the meal that seemed to have solemn religious overtones. Dead vetta would not keep; only the skin was savable, and you had to strip off the meat and bone from it completely and "cure" the skin in the thermal pool. When the host died, the Wardens began to die as well, and decomposition was swift. I had found this the case with fruit and berries, although not with cut wood and leaves. It was almost as if the Wardens were determined to keep a very clean, almost antiseptic, wilderness, yet knew enough to leave behind those parts that were useful to man.

The ceremony itself was interesting and, as usual with such rites, incomprehensible to me. It involved praying and chanting over the remains, with the leader eventually casting what couldn't be saved into the thermal pool in the manner of an offering, or sacrifice. I wanted very much to know more about such ceremonies and beliefs, if only to keep from stepping on toes, but didn't dare ask right now. There was time enough for that later.

Two more days of travel to the northwest, which included some more hunting, lay the camp. On the way, we approached and actually crossed the tracks of our old train; it brought a twinge of nostalgia to Bura, at least, and certainly to Ching.

The camp was far more than that. Nestled up against the mountains, invisible from anywhere on the ground beyond, it was in every sense a small city. A large circle of stones, some placed by humans, some natural, forming an area more than a kilometer in diameter inside the "walls," guarded the camp from the ground and from the wind, although the roofless area inside was open to the elements. A small stone amphitheater was carved out of the rock floor in the center of the interior—with what my old training told me might be an altar at the bottom. This and a fire pit dominated the place, but there were many conical small dwellings made of skin and supported by strong but temporary wooden beams all over. The bulk of the population was not below in the common yard, but above, actually within the sheer rock wall behind, in what appeared to be dozens of caves. They were all over the wall, high and low, and there were no ladders—only small, well-worn hand- and footholds carved into the sides of the wall. Tribal members, however, scurried up and down that wall and in and out of the caves as if they were born to it.

At the base of the cliff, at ground level was a single cave, a bit larger than the others. Through obviously manmade channels, streams from the snow melt above flowed down in small matched waterfalls to holding pools on both sides of the camp. From there the water was either diverted for use within the compound or allowed to overflow and run off through outlets in the protective wall.

Angi, in particular, was impressed. "This is one hell of a job of civil engineering, mostly done by hand."

"Remember, we're not dealing with a long time period here," I reminded her and the others as well. "The two Medusas were only really completely closed off to each other forty or fifty years ago. It's entirely possible that some of the original pioneers are still alive here."

It was, in fact, this dichotomy between the inevitable pioneer resourcefulness and the primitive, religion-based lifestyle of these people that bothered me the most.

We were told to wait near the amphitheater, and we could only stand there and look around.

"How many people would you say live here?" I asked our engineer.

She thought for a moment. "Hard to say. Depends on how deep those caves are and what kind of chambers are inside, although I doubt if they're too big. This is metamorphic rock, not sedimentary."

"Make a guess."

"A hundred. Maybe a hundred and fifty."

I nodded. "That's about my guess at the top end."

"It's so *small* for a town," Ching put in.

"Uh uh," I responded. "It's too *large*. How do you feed a hundred and fifty people when you can't store food? If those tents there were out on the plain, near the vettas, or in the forest, maybe I could see it. A population this small might be supported there. But we're half a day from any grazing or edible forest land. There's something pretty fishy going on here."

Various people, almost all women and all with those tribal skirts, went here and there and up and down, always giving us curious looks, but we were left pretty much alone for quite a while. Finally somebody seemed to remember us, and a pregnant woman—not the one with the hunting party —emerged from one of the skin tents, and walked over to us. "Come with me," she said. "The Elders will see you now."

I gave a let-me-do-the-talking glance at the other three, hoping that was a good idea, and, not surprisingly, the woman led us over to the ground-level cave.

The first surprise were the torches, nicely aligned and lit along the walls of the cave. This was the first exposed fire we'd seen the Wild Ones use, and really the first real flame we'd seen in a long time.

The cave went back pretty far in the cliff, causing some mental revision of how extensive the interiors could be. More interesting, perhaps ten meters in there appeared an abrupt boundary in the cave wall. The first part of the cave was natural, but the rest of it beyond the boundary had been carved with modern tools, probably a laser cannon.

About a hundred and twenty meters in, the cave opened into a large rectangular chamber, perhaps fifteen by ten and with a five-meter ceiling. Only half of the room, however, was usable; about five meters into the room the floor suddenly stopped and we were looking at a fast-flowing river. Beyond the river, again another five meters, was a recess in the rock, carved by laser—you could tell by the neat squared-off corners. Inside the recess stood three large wooden chairs, with no sign of how anyone would get into or out of that recess. But get in they did—two very old women and an equally aged man sat there, looking at us. I think they were the oldest people I'd ever seen, but they were very much alert and looking at us.

So Elders was not a title of respect but a literal one.

All three were as hairless as everybody else, but their skin was a stretched and wrinkled light gray, like the surrounding rock. In the torch-light they looked eerily impressive.

I glanced around, but could see no sign of our guide—or anybody else. We were alone with the wizened Elders of the People of the Rock.

"What is your name, boy?" one of the women asked in a cracked, high-pitched voice.

"I am called Tari, and also Tarin Bul," I responded.

"But those are not your true names."

I was a little surprised, particularly since this was not a question but a statement of fact. "It is not," I admitted. "However, it is my name now and the only one by which I go."

"You are not a native." The words, again fact and not question, were uttered by the man, whose voice was scarcely different from the old woman's.

"No. I was sent here from the Confederacy."

"As a convict?"

At last! A real question! I had begun to worry. "Against my will, yes." That was true enough. No use telling them any more than I had to for now.

"These women are your family?" That was the third one.

"They are."

There was a pause, then the man said, "You told the pilgrims you fled Rockande. Why?"

As concisely as I could, I told them about the Opposition, its betrayal, and our narrow escape. I went into no detail as to motives, just presented the bare facts, concluding with our long search in the wild for others. They sat impassively, but I could tell that their eyes were bright and alive with both intelligence and interest. When I finished I expected more questions on our lives, but that was apparently not of further interest.

"What did the pilgrims tell you this place was?" the first woman asked.

"They just said they were taking us to their tribal camp."

That response brought a chuckle from all three. "Camp. Very good," the second woman commented. "Well—what do you think of this camp?"

"I think it is not a camp or a tribal village," I answered.

"Indeed? Why not?"

"You can't possibly feed all who are here. And you called the hunting party pilgrims."

"Very good, very good," the old man approved. "You are correct. This is not a camp. It is more in the nature of a religious retreat. Does that disturb you?"

"No. As long as we're not to be sacrifices."

They seemed to like that reply; it started them chuckling again. Finally the first woman asked, "What do you expect of your life here in the wild? Why did you seek out those whom the city dwellers call Wild Ones?"

Well, they sure didn't try to pretend they were ignorant or naive. "Knowledge," I told them. "Much of this world is in bondage, and the people don't even all realize it. The city dwellers are becoming about as human as vettas, and not nearly as free. Or, like the tubros, they cling to their safe, secure havens where they don't have to think and only have to do what they are told to be provided with their basic needs."

"And this is wrong?"

"We think it is. This Lord of Medusa is evil. He has killed the spirit inside people that makes them human—and he enjoys it. Worse, he has gotten Medusa involved in a clandestine war against the Confederacy itself that might possibly destroy the entire planet."

"And you think you four can stop him?"

"I think we can try," I told them honestly. "I think I would rather try than do nothing."

They thought that one over. Finally the second woman asked me, "In this world picture of human, vettas, and tubros you paint—how do you paint yourselves?"

I smiled. "We escaped. Fifty-five went meekly to their mind-deaths. We are harrars, of course."

They all nodded and did not return the smile. The man said, "In our past we, too, dreamed of destroying that evil system and freeing Medusa for the people. We three were adults fifty-one years ago when the cities were enclosed and the early monitor systems installed. Only one of us—myself—was born here, and I was born before this place became a prison and a madhouse. Less than a thousand, including us, escaped planetwide in the pogrom that resulted in what you have today. But we were clever. Like you, we escaped with nothing at all."

I nodded, having figured as much. "But this place—it was built before the crackdown?"

"It was. Not all of it, of course—just this cave and the network in back of it. Call it an escape place, if you like. Records of its very existence were expunged from Medusa's files after the pogrom was inevitable but before it took place. From here, with our hands and those of others, we carved the rest."

"It's very impressive," I told them, and meant it. "Running water, something of a sewage system, shelter—very impressive. But badly located to support any size population."

"Oh, we don't wish a large population," the first woman told us. "That would attract attention. It is neither our purpose nor intent to support anything more here than you see, particularly now. You see, at one time we had such dreams as you have. But did you think that Talant Ypsir created the system and initiated the pogrom? He did not. He was still high and mighty back in the Outside at the time it was initiated. He only refined it, made it even more complete. He is the third Lord since it began and each one has been worse than the one who came before. The first two died by assassination—and the second one was a true reformer who intended to reverse the changes and reconcile Medusans with their land. He was, instead, seduced by the same handy drug as his predecessor and successor—absolute power. It is not enough to kill the Lord. It is not enough to kill the Lord's Council. To accomplish what you wish would require the failure of all technological support of the cities, transport, and space. The population would have to be forced *en masse* into the wild, whether they wanted to go or not. And that is something that cannot be. *They* have the arms and the means to see that it does not."

"And so, with this realization," the man picked up, "we decided that we could only ignore them as they now ignore us. Build a new and different culture suited to the land outside their system."

"But their system will come for you one day," I pointed out. "In the end, it will engulf you because it must."

"Perhaps. We think not. We hope not. But our way is the only possible way."

"But it isn't!" I protested. "Your goal *can* be achieved. The potential is here. How many—ah, Wild Ones are there now?"

"We prefer Free Tribes," the first woman told me. "There are between thirty and forty thousand worldwide. That is an estimate, of course—our communication lines are primitive."

Thirty to forty thousand! What an army that would make! If only . . . "Such a force could infiltrate and take the major cities, cripple the industry and transportation network, and destroy the balance of Medusan control."

"How? Ten thousand near-naked savages, most of whom think even a flashlight is magic and who have never seen a light switch or things made of steel and plastic?"

"I believe it can be done, with training. I believe it can be done because I believe in the possibility of self-controlled body malleability. That is what I am looking for here."

They remained silent—as if thinking about what I just said. They didn't seem very surprised one way or the other about my assertion of controlled malleability. Finally the first woman said, "Foolish one! Do you not think your idea has not been thought of before? From the start it was the only reasonable course. But at the beginning we were disorganized, scattered refugees, without the numbers or abilities. An entire generation was mercilessly hunted all over the planet, and it learned how to survive—but in the wild. The next generation was born here and had nothing but what seemed like fanciful tales of magic. The generation after that, the current one, feels no kinship whatever to the city dwellers—they are demons. Now we have the numbers, but not the will. We built the culture that keeps them alive and holds them together, but it is a primitive one. If we had ten thousand, perhaps even five thousand, people like you four, perhaps we could do it. But the gap between your cultures and your minds and theirs is too great."

I was not prepared to concede the point, but I was very interested in the implications of what she said. "Then controlled malleability is possible."

They didn't answer me; instead, the second woman asked, "Well, what are we to do with you, then? You will never fit into this culture. You will never accept it, and your efforts will bring the others down upon it. You cannot return to the cities. So for now, you will have to stay with us as our guests—but you will not disrupt the people or their customs or beliefs, understand? Until we decide what to do with you you are welcome to our hospitality. But we are perfectly willing, and capable, of terminating you as well. Do you understand?"

I nodded. "I think we do."

"Then, for now, this audience is finished." With that intonation a small boat appeared from the left inside the cave, showing just how you *did* get to the other side and in and out. The underground river, diverted through here, was apparently deep and navigable. The craft was basically a wooden rowboat, with a separate and overlarge tiller. Inside sat a tall, stately-looking woman. "Get in—all of you," she commanded.

I looked at the other three, then complied. There was no use in pressing anything with the Elders right now, and time was needed to find the information I sought.

Fortunately the current was with us in this direction, so the oars were secured and the pilot let the river take us with it. We left the cavern, then went around a fairly sharp bend, and came to another landing, but didn't stop there. We passed several more such landings, with tunnels leading off in both directions, before we reached the one the pilot wanted. She tied off the boat with a rope, then jumped out and helped us up onto the rocky floor. We were led back along a narrow cave that seemed mostly natural, but which opened into a fairly large chamber. By torchlight we could see it contained a thick floor of some strawlike material, a few crude handmade wooden chairs, a small writing desk but nothing to write with, and very little else. It did, however, have a crude water system; a streamlet issuing from a small rock fissure was channeled into and along a trough. The stream was pretty swift, and it exited through another small fissure at the other end of the room. Just before that exit point was a crude, handrubbed toilet top.

"The water is fresh and pure," our guide explained. "The current is swift enough so that waste products will be swiftly carried away. Food will be brought to you shortly, and regularly. Please stay here until the Elders decide what to do with you. Swimming in the river is not recommended, however. The river's eventual outlet is the larger waterfall in the courtyard, and the drop is more than forty meters into stone." With that, she turned and was gone.

Bura looked after her for a moment, then turned to me. "I gather we're prisoners, then?"

"Looks like it," I had to admit. "But these people know what I want to know. However, maybe they're right. Maybe we can't make our revolution. But I *still* want to know how to change my form to suit me at will. Whether we can build an army or not, that knowledge would sure increase *our* options."

Ching looked around and shook her head. "I knew we should have just stayed in the forest. They're gonna let us rot here until we're as old as they are."

I went over to her, hugged her, and gave her a small kiss. "No they won't. For one thing, they just don't know what to do with us right now. Give them some time. I don't think they want to be like TMS and the city people, and that's just what they'd be like if they killed us. Besides," I added with a wink, "if we got out of the Rochande sewers, what's this place?"

It quickly developed that Ching's fears were grossly misplaced. While we were, in fact, being held prisoner, our time was not to be wasted in some dank cell inside a mountain but in what proved to be quite an education for all of us. And the food was good—an odd sort of fishy-tasting mammal as a main course, but supplemented with good fresh fruit and the tastiest edible leaves. A very small portable power plant from the old days still worked; it was used for a small hydroponics setup entirely within the mountain that fed the staff. What else it might power I didn't know.

We were regularly visited by various people who knew an awful lot about Medusa and its history and ways; they brought with them bound hard copies of much computer data now denied the citizens of Medusa's cities, not to mention large, laboriously handwritten chronicles of the Wild Ones—sorry, the Free Tribes—and their customs.

The first Lord of Medusa to close off the society was a former naval admiral named Kasikian, who had led an abortive and hushed-up coup attempt at Military Systems Command. A lifelong career military man, and a strong disciplinarian, this civilized worlder, born and bred to command, had taken charge on Medusa. He had started out organizing the small freighter fleet, having been given the job by virtue of his vast experience. But he eventually drew to him a number of other military types, plus a lot of disaffected, and this time his *coup d'état* worked flawlessly. After a period of consolidation, Kasikian began reorganizing Medusan society along military lines, with strict ranks, grades, and chains of command. He was an efficient organizer no matter what his political ideas may have been; it was he who modernized and expanded the industries of Medusa, and he who built the space stations that now circled all four Warden worlds. Ironically, his effect was most dramatic on Cerberus, which was transformed from a primitive water world to an industrial giant that took what Medusa produced and made it into whatever the Diamond needed.

But after two coup attempts against him, Kasikian became increasingly paranoid, and so was born of his fears and Cerberan computer skills the original monitor system. The society was even more rigidly structured and controlled in military fashion. As a final gesture, realizing he could never extend total control over the people unless they were consolidated in the key cities and kept there, he ordered the pogrom: those who would not commit themselves fully to his system and his government and come into the cities were to be ruthlessly exterminated.

The Elders had explained that less than a thousand survived the bloodbath that followed, most fleeing to a few key pre-prepared places such as the one we were now in, places that had been erased from the records and were, to all outward appearances, just new, small primitive enclaves. Still, Kasikian ordered those few escapees ruthlessly hunted down, no matter what the cost, and he became so obsessed with that mission that he was careless at home. A young officer who was an aide to one of the admiral's top associates managed to get him as he relaxed in his luxurious command quarters and kill him.

But this young officer, motivated by idealism and revulsion for bloodshed, became pretty bloody himself as he and his followers hunted down and executed all those in the top five grades of the admiral's government. By the time Tolakah, new Lord of the Diamond, felt secure, his hands were as bloody as the admiral's—and he not only grew as paranoid, but was soon seduced by his power. The other Lords, particularly Cerberus', used his paranoia and love of power for their own ends. They needed what Medusa put out, and the system there suited them just fine.

But the monitor system worried Tolakah. He and his own people had managed to get around it, so he knew how vulnerable it was. As a result, he was delighted to get Talant Ypsir, an expert in administration whose ideas on how societies should be organized closely paralleled the late Kasikian's. Using the computer talent on Cerberus, Ypsir plugged the holes and created a nearly ironclad society—but not for Tolakah's benefit. Tolakah, in fact, was personally beheaded by Ypsir while the administrative specialist was showing him the master computers in the orbiting space station that totally sealed the society. Complicity with the other Lords was probable; they distrusted the erratic Tolakah, and preferred someone who *knew* he was as corrupt as the others, and enjoyed it.

In the meantime, the last of the survivors of the pogrom managed to gather in the various secret places, and decided on an organization for their society in the wild. Dominant among them was Dr. Kura Hsiu, a cultural anthropologist by trade, who'd come to Medusa as a life study of the Warden organism's effect on society. She was particularly drawn by the idea of a society where people changed sex as routinely as they changed their clothes, and she considered the work worth the sacrifice. But not now—as a fugitive and exile in the wild. She realized that the remnants were no match for Medusa's power, but Ypsir seemed to be lapsing into a tolerance as long as they didn't bother or interfere with him. Medusa was too big a planet for it to be worth tracking down that small a group, which the last two Lords had both considered dispersed and neutralized.

Dr. Hsiu realized that the new generation would be born in the bush, and that they would be culturally far removed from their own children, and so she set about creating a society that would allow the Wild Ones to grow and develop as a native culture, free of all past cultural pollutants. In many ways, it was the greatest task, experiment, and opportunity for an anthropologist in history.

The greater family, or tribal system, seemed the only logical way to go. Groups would have to be large enough to support one another, yet small enough to move with the weather and the food and still not attract Ypsir's attention. A simple system, based primarily on age, was developed and taught—the younger would respect and follow the Elder's lead, and eventually, if they lived long enough, they, too, would run things. Originally intended just to keep the first generation in guiding control as long as possible, the tradition became quickly institutionalized in the harsh land.

Since political unity beyond the tribal system was impossible, the only basic overlay that would unite the tribes in any way would be a religious one. So the few centers of refuge became holy shrines, and a system of simple belief based on many religions was established.

Early on, though, the religion had taken an odd turn. Instead of worshiping some anthropomorphic god, the religion turned inward, to planet worship, of all things. God lived not in the heavens but inside the earth itself, one god for each world. This seemed logical to the young ones, for did not the Elders say that the heavens were filled with stars and planets and that humans went between them? If God was not in space, then, where was she?

The original Elders went along with the theory because it worked; Dr. Hsiu herself noted that similar faiths in one form or another existed on all three of the other Warden worlds. Later Elders came to believe in it, and most, but not all, now did.

By the second generation in the wild, things had become pretty institutionalized. The Free Tribes everywhere prayed in the direction of the Mount of God, a particularly high peak in the frozen north said to be the backbone of God the Mother Medusa Herself. This explained both the ritualized prayers and the sacrifice of the animal remains back into the pool —a return to Mother Medusa.

The religious centers became retreats for study and meditation, as well as old-age homes for the most elderly, and also places where those who were pregnant came to give birth, if they could. This explained the pregnant woman with the hunting party, and as well why so many in the courtyard had been pregnant.

As to why the Mount of God was chosen, that particularly piqued my interest. It was said that a hunting party had stumbled upon it shortly after the pogrom was in full swing and the hunt was on, and had battled "fierce demons who seemed to besiege the mount but could not climb upon it; demons more horrible to behold than the human mind can comprehend." These "demons" got a number of the party, but the rest took refuge on the mountain where they had what can only be described as a classic religious experience. They claimed that somehow they had actually touched the mind of God, and as a result of that experience *they had found themselves able to change their shape, form, or gender at will*. This was apparently the beginning of the change toward planet-worship, and their experience was borne out by others who made the journey in their footsteps.

Here was God, then, in a tangible but not easily accessible form, under constant attack by terrible demons who wanted to destroy Her but could not climb the mountain to do so. The demons were terrible enough in taking a fearsome toll of the curious, the pilgrims, and all others; but the experience of anyone able to make it to the mountain and then back off again was the same—a sense that they had talked with God, and had acquired the power to control every damned cell in their bodies by sheer force of will.

I could certainly see why the revolution of malleables would be a real pain today for other than cultural reasons. Whatever those animals or creatures were that the accounts called demons, they were terrible and deadly—and very real. I felt sure of that. It would be tough getting enough people to that mountain, and back. Still, that mountain had *something*, some strange power that not only conferred this ability for life but also convinced a lot of hard-headed scientific materialists of the claptrap of this silly religion.

I knew then where I had to go next. Surprisingly, the Elders agreed.

"Yes, you must go," said the first woman, who I thought might well have been Dr. Hsiu. "You alone are the key to your family's salvation. Without your drive and relentless will the other three would settle down and accept this culture. They dream your dreams because they love you. If, then, you make the Great Pilgrimage, and survive the demon trial, you will come mind to mind with God and you will *know*. Then will your life picture and world picture be irrevocably changed, as ours was. And, if you must still dream your ambitions after that, you will at least find the power that you seek."

I smiled and nodded. "I think, though, that we should have more training in the use of the primitive weapons here first. I don't want anybody killed out of ignorance."

"We?"

"Why, yes. All four of us. We are together in this, one."

"No."

I looked puzzled and felt angry. "Why not? Give me one good reason for it!"

"I will give you two. Your wife Angi is four months with child. Your wife Bura is three months with child. They must remain here for the term."

"Well I'll be damned!" I said, genuinely surprised and shocked. "It never occurred to me. It really didn't." Even after all this time on Medusa, the idea of natural birth as opposed to scientifically controlled laboratory birth was simply not connected in my mind. "But why didn't they tell me?"

"They did not want you to know as long as you were bent on your killing mission. Pregnancy does not show as much on us as on normal humans at this stage, nor does it produce any of the negative symptoms that normal human first-trimester gestation does." She paused for a moment. "They were going to tell you and I stopped them. But now you know, and now you must make your decision. Go to the Mount of God, or remain to raise your children with those who love you."

My mind was racing at all this, and I felt a little angry and betrayed that they hadn't told me straight off—but, then, they had been behaving a little odd lately and I'd simply passed it off.

"What about Ching?" I asked. "If the other two are pregnant, then she sure should be. We've been together a lot longer."

"As far as we can tell, no, but on Medusa a pregnancy usually has to be fairly well along before we know for certain. We believe she is determined to go where you go, do what you do, no matter what; being with child would prevent that. On Medusa, a solid mind-set *not* to get pregnant is sufficient to leave it that way."

I thought it all out, trying to decide if the new situation really made a difference. It did, dammit, but I also had my own responsibilities to consider beyond the family. What good would it do to remain and have lots of kids and then look up one day to see a Confederacy world destroyer bearing down on Medusa, wiping out all of us and our futures? If anything I thought, this made it even *more* urgent that I find the means to get to Talant Ypsir.

Or was I just kidding myself?

"How long will it take to get to the mountain?" I asked her.

"Seven weeks—and it is in the north and east."

Fourteen weeks round trip. It was possible, anyway, to get there and back in the period before Angi was due. "Weapons?"

"Do you know how to use the sword?"

I almost laughed out loud. Considering Tarin Bul's background, the question was a joke. But I wasn't really Tarin Bul. "I've fenced for sport," I told her, "but not with swords."

"That's the best I can do. We have no pistols or rifles. The swords are hand-made, melted down and remolded from some useless metal artifacts we found here."

"I can handle it," I assured her. I was pretty sure I could handle any weapon, and I'd have weeks to get used to it. "And Ching?"

"Are you sure she will go with you?"

"*You* are," I pointed out.

She chuckled. "Yes, I am. She may choose what she wishes or feels comfortable with. You will go with a small group of sincere pilgrims, including a doubter or two going to see for themselves, and these will include experienced spear and bow masters."

"These . . . demons. What are they like?"

"They are almost impossible to describe. But to reach the Mount you must cross an ever-frozen inlet of the ocean. There is no other way that is practical. They live there, in the waters under the ice, and can break through and grab you and drag you down as you cross. Their tentacles are tenacious, and their great mouths are on top of their heads. They are terrifying, and deadly, but remember this—hurt them and they will retreat. They do not like being hurt. But it is difficult to hurt them through their armor."

I frowned. "They have shells?"

"No. Armor. They wear some sort of hard protective suit that is impervious to our weapons. Aim for the tentacles, eyes, and mouth. It is the only way."

Armor? On a creature living in the frozen sea? Or a tough suit that would act like armor, perhaps . . .

Now I knew for certain that my choice was made. I would have to go. Unless I was completely and utterly wrong, the challenge was irresistible.

I was going to meet our damned, elusive aliens—and find out just what the hell they were doing up there that started a religion.

CHAPTER TEN

The Goddess Medusa

"What're *you* mad about?" Bura wanted to know. "You're the one who's leaving."

"Well, at least I expected you to try and talk me out of it," I retorted.

Angi looked me right in the eyes. "Would it matter? Would you not go if we cried and pleaded?"

I sighed. "Probably not. I *have* to go."

"And we understand that," Bura said. "We don't like it, but we know you well enough by now. There's something inside you, something eating away, that just isn't going to go away. It's just . . ." Her voice trailed off and she turned away.

I reached out and put my hand on her shoulder. "I know. The children to come. You can't believe how rotten I feel leaving you now—but, with luck, I'll be back in fourteen weeks. If it was much longer I'd wait until after, you know that."

"You probably would," Angi agreed, "and you'd slowly go nuts. You know it and we know it. So—go. But . . . come back to us, Tari."

I admit I was starting to feel a little teary myself, and I hugged and kissed them both, and they hugged and kissed Ching. I turned to my original pair-mate. "I still wish you wouldn't come. They need you here. Particularly if—"

"I go where you go," she said once again. "I'm not going to sit here and not know."

"All right, then," I sighed, "let's get going."

We walked out to the courtyard, where the rest of the party was gathering. With Ching and myself it was a group of fourteen, led by an experienced northerner named Hono. Like the others, she'd been born in the wild; the Free Tribes tended to keep to one name if doing so didn't lead to confusion. We had been practicing with the group for several days, and I had to admit that Ching seemed to have a better handle on spear and bow than I did. Yet using my increased muscle power and some of my fencing steps and moves, I could wield the sword very effectively in close quarters. It was a close quarters weapon only, though, and I sorely missed those two laser rifles at the bottom of the slag pit.

There was one more round of emotional good-byes, and attempts on all parts to pretend that things were really just fine and normal, but both Ching and I were glad when we left the compound and our people behind. It wasn't a question of out of sight out of mind, but, rather, a strong feeling inside me that if I didn't get out of there soon I would be unable to leave. Having found a closeness and an emotional bond I had never before even conceived of, I was now turning my back on it and going back to work for a system in which I no longer had any faith. I liked to tell myself, and Ching, that we were doing this for ourselves and for the planet's protection and not for any outside force or government. But there was still both the love of challenge which was part of my personality and the uneasy sense that three more of me—one each on Charon, Lilith, and Cerberus—were leading different lives with similar objectives. It would be intolerable for me to fail if any one of them were to succeed. I wished I knew more about them and their fates.

At least we didn't have to walk all the way. Four sleds pulled by tame vettas awaited, large enough to carry us and our weapons, tools, and portable shelters. The vettas raised their odd-looking heads and snapped their wide, flat bills at us as we approached, but that was just their form of recognition.

The sleds proved efficient, though neither comfortable nor fast, since we were traveling long ways over grass and rocks and the vettas, restrained in their harness, could use their power but not their speed and grace. The trip was bumpy as hell, but it beat walking and carrying the stuff.

Ching remained pretty tense and quiet—clearly she disapproved of the trip, of leaving the others, and of most everything concerning my objectives. She wanted to sit back, meld into one or another of the Free Tribes, and just live out her life. The war, the aliens, the Four Lords themselves seemed at best distant, at worst unreal or incomprehensible to her. But she did understand that she had a family and, away from TMS and the guilds and modern Medusan society in general, was enjoying a sense of personal freedom she had never known before. The primitiveness of her new life style really didn't bother her. The sense of oppression—a sense she'd been born and raised with—had lifted from her, giving her what she wanted; Bura, Angi, and I gave her what she needed.

And yet, here she was.

The Elders had spoken of a cultural gap between the Free Tribes and me that might never be bridged; here, too, I felt, was another gap that remained despite all our closeness and intimacy. Ching could never understand why I had to go; I could never understand why she had to follow— but I could no more stand in the way of what she had to do than I could allow her and the others to stand in my way. In that sense, as the days passed out in the bush and the air grew colder with the northern journey, we did more or less affect a practical sort of thaw. We did not understand each other, and we knew it; but we respected each other, and, for that time and place, that would have to be enough.

We fell in with a small hunting group backed by the trip leader, Hono, and also including Quarl, Sitzter, and Tyne. Neither Ching nor I were very good or effective hunters, needless to say, and I doubt if Ching could bring herself to kill for food—although she had grown used to the idea enough to be able to eat an animal when it was no longer recognizable as what it was—so we were dependent on our little group for our nourishment. The four hunters were easy, likable, and outgoing people with a feel for life, but, as the Elders had warned, they were of and from a different world, space, and time from me. Medusa had made the stone age not only possible but somewhat antiseptic—and how very easily humans had reverted to that primitive state.

Ching was aware of the gap between us and them as I was. They plied us both with honest questions about our former lives and worlds, but they accepted only little bits of it. The trains they saw from time to time, and because they understood natural magnetism in its basic form they could stretch their minds at least to accept the idea that great magnets could pull trains from point to point. Of course that wasn't the way the trains worked or used magnetism, but it didn't really matter. Of monitors, psychs, computers, and long-range communications, though, they had no real understanding or grasp, and they accepted stories of such things with a grain of salt. As to how and why large numbers of people would willingly seal themselves in cities and never hunt or explore or live in the bush—that was really beyond them.

I began to understand the problem the Elders had posed for me, as much as I hated to admit it. Although intelligent and resourceful, these people were in many ways like small children on the frontier. You could make one *look* like a city dweller, but he would find it impossible to cope with the simple, everyday things of modern technological living. By the time he learned, assuming he wasn't run over by a bus first, he'd have long since exposed himself to the authorities.

By the end of our journey, I was more than willing to give up my dream of an army of malleables infiltrating and destroying the Medusan cities. It just wasn't going to work. I wasn't going to overthrow the system by that means, and perhaps not at all—that task would have to be left to others. Certainly there were others, I had to remind myself. Krega had never said I'd be the only agent, and it would be foolish for them to have put all their eggs in my lone basket. Somebody had trained and equipped the Opposition; so even if its members were now ineffectual, the leadership was more than competent. They would try again, and again, until they came up with the right combination. At least, I had to hope so. This planet was too well organized and the system too tight for it to be so easily overthrown by just one man.

But that did not diminish the other objectives. Whatever we were going toward was very much connected to all that had happened before, to all the reasons I was here to begin with, and, most certainly, it was connected to the ultimate fate of me and my family—and of Medusa itself. This knowledge simply had to be acquired, no matter what the cost.

We were in sight of the mountains when we had to abandon the sleds and really get to work ourselves. That mountain view was deceptive.

Three days of hard, dangerous walking remained, the last day over pack ice. The last hunt had been tough, and still we had left little to toss back to Mother Medusa. From here on in, any food we might find would be sheer luck.

The barren wasteland before us was frightening enough. Up here, in the far north, glaciation was omnipresent—the whole thing was a massive ice sheet—with jagged ice ridges piled up making anything except foot travel impossible, and foot travel itself difficult. The air was crisp and clear, but there was a steady wind blowing small, localized ice-crystal storms all over.

Our period of danger from the "demons" would start now, since under all this stuff was a jagged and irregular coastline that you simply couldn't tell from the frozen ocean. The last day we would be almost literally walking on water, which posed real dangers, since underneath all this ice the ocean was being whipped into a frenzy by thermal currents. The ice right above them might be thin enough to cause a human to fall through. The wonder was that anybody had ever found and crossed this desolate, frozen horror in the first place.

We used hand-made snowshoes provided back at the citadel and strapped our feet into boots made from the skin and hair of tubros and quite literally woven into the snowshoes themselves. Yet, amazing as it might seem, the windy cold that probably approached minus 60° C. was only slightly annoying. What sort of internal changes had been wrought inside us by the Wardens to keep us and them alive I couldn't guess, although I noticed our appetites had greatly increased as it grew colder and we had all built up noticeable amounts of fat all over our bodies. It seemed amazing that we could survive such cold, but I realized that on many worlds other animals, including a large number of mammals, survived conditions at least this extreme and even thrived in them. I doubted if any of us would ever thrive in such a place as this, but we endured.

The Mount of God was not difficult to find in this expanse. Its glacier-covered slopes rose up as a white monolith before us, dwarfing surrounding mountains that were pretty high themselves. Just looking at it was to experience a strong sense of awe and wonder. It was easy to see how the mountain came to be known as Medusa's backbone. Weathering and glaciation had worn and shaped the top so that it did sort of resemble the backbone of some great four-legged beast.

Our Wardens had to work overtime to keep us warm and comfortable, and to protect our eyes and other exposed areas. Two weeks earlier, all of us, male and female, had begun sprouting hair all over our bodies including on our faces—and now that hair and our skin was turning to milky white against the white landscape. The most interesting and occasionally irritating change was that our eyelids grew quickly transparent. So soon we walked across the ice with our eyes shut against the wind and ice crystals and still saw perfectly well.

It was hell, however, to try and sleep that way no matter how dark it became. Not that any sleep was really comfortable on that icy landscape, or very long. It was just something else in the way of hardships to get used to, and I was doubly impressed with the dedication of those who made this pilgrimage out of faith or to confront and allay their doubts, instead of out of foolish curiosity, as I was doing.

On that last, cold trek, it took only a few hours for our first casualty. One of the group simply walked over an area that looked for all the world like the rest of the frozen landscape, and it gave way beneath her, swallowing her instantly. By the time we reached the spot and were arguing over whether or not we could do anything the water had already started to refreeze.

We lost two more just getting to the final inlet before the mountain itself, a second to another hidden soft spot in the ice, a third to a crevasse that suddenly opened up as two ice packs shifted subtly, then closed in again, crushing the woman to death.

Now we were nine for the final stretch, and I could only shake my head and look back at the horrible landscape we had already traversed. "And, just think, we have to cross that stretch again to get back."

Almost as I said those words the ice gave way beneath my feet and I felt myself falling, as if through a trapdoor. I screamed out and raised my hands, but I was in over my head before I felt strong hands grip mine and hold me, attempt to pull me up, and not quite make it. I knew in that instant that I'd had it—I was going to drown—but almost as I reconciled myself to that fate I felt myself being lifted back up out of the hole and onto the ice.

I wasn't very lucid for a while there, but I remember seeing a stricken and anxious-looking Ching—and also Quarl and Sitzter—fussing over me. I drifted in a fog as my body fought the one enemy the Wardens could not overcome so easily—shock. It was some time before I came out of it. It was dark, and I was in a *wapti*—one of the portable skin tents—covered by fur and skin. A serious-looking Hono entered and glanced at me, then smiled when she saw I was awake. "Welcome back."

I coughed. "Thanks. How long was I out?"

"A couple of hours. You've been rambling something fierce, but I think you are self-repairing nicely now. You should be all right by morning, I think, if you made it this far."

"I'll make it," I assured her. "I'm not going to spend one more day on this stuff than I have to."

She nodded and seemed satisfied, then pointed near me. I turned my head and saw Ching, out cold and snoring slightly, alongside me. "She was the one who saved you," Hono told me. "I never saw anybody move so fast whose own life wasn't at stake. She was on you, grabbed hold of your arms, and held you while yelling at us until we could reach you. She used up a lot of strength, but she actually got your head above water herself."

I looked over at her, sleeping so soundly, and felt an emotional tide rising within me. "And I tried so hard to talk her out of coming."

"She loves you very much. I think she would give her life to save yours. In fact, I know she would. You have something very rare and valuable and important, Tari. Cherish it."

I should have been happy, proud, overjoyed at something like that. Why then did I feel so much like a heel?

This is it, I told myself, and meant it this time. Having come this far we'll go the rest of the way, and back again, but this is it. Sorry, you bastards, my job stops with this one. No more. When we leave here we will return to the citadel, bear and raise those babies and make more, and carve out a new life for *all* of us. They had let me go because they loved me. Ching had come along because she loved me. And me, good old selfish me, had I given them anything other than mere sperm in return? For the first time, really, I took a good, hard, objective look at myself and I didn't like what I saw. It took something like this to make me realize my egomania, my selfish drives, my all-consuming love affair with myself. But I wasn't above love—I needed it. I needed them. And love, I now understood, wasn't just something you received as a matter of right, but something you gave in equal measure.

I was no longer the most important person in my life. Three others were now paramount, and I swore that I would never forget that again. And, with that sincere vow, I managed, finally, to drift back into a fitful and uncomfortable sleep.

The next day dawned ugly. Gray clouds had moved in with relatively warmer air and there was the possibility of snow. Hono didn't like it any more than the rest of us, but she was pragmatic about things.

"We have two choices," she told us in a small group meeting that dawn. "Either we stay here another day or we press on to the Mountain. What do you say?"

Tyne, who usually said little, really decided for us. "That's hard weather coming, perhaps a front of some kind. It's been known to storm for days, even weeks, up here, once conditions are right. If that's so, our chances are better on the solid mountain than staying here—no matter how lousy things may seem."

"Then we go," Hono declared. "Anyone want to do otherwise?" She looked around, but nobody else responded. Frankly, by this time we just wanted to get this thing over with. Even some of the most faithful could be heard muttering that morning that sacred places should be easier to get to.

As for me, Ching sensed the change inside me. I think I was successful in convincing her it wasn't any back-from-the-dead conversion but a genuine reassessment. My thoughts on the sacred mountain, however, were still all business. Hard to reach, yes, and terribly dangerous—a fluke that anybody on this planet ever found it. A perfect place for an alien base, perhaps an entire hidden alien outpost or city.

We started out under thickening clouds and were soon encrusted with ice particles, although the snow remained aloft for the moment. The last crossing was relatively smooth compared to the previous two days' worth, but considering the landforms, its smoothness said that the ice was relatively thin, the water beneath warmer, and thus, far more dangerous.

Still, it was midday and the first snowflakes had begun to fall before anything happened.

It looked for all the world like another one of those damned holes, and we might have just put it down to that, except this time it happened right in front of me and I had a clear view.

What pulled Yorder down through the ice was not any natural soft spot, but something below. One moment she was walking there, then she *stopped* and turned to look back at me—and something, I couldn't tell what, broke through right beneath her and just sucked her down with tremendous force.

The others came running, but there was nothing any of us could do. Nonetheless, I brought out my primitive bronze sword and crouched, looking around. "They're under the ice!" I called. "Let's keep moving! Don't stop for anything or they'll break through and grab us! Those suckers are *fast!*"

They sure were—I had no sooner pulled myself up and started on when the ice exploded around us in the building wind and snowstorm. The eight of us fixed our weapons and assumed a protective formation while continuing to move.

"They're striking at random!" Hono shouted. "Tari's right—move! And don't stop for anything unless you can kill it!"

We made our way across the ice as the enemy started playing a psychological game with us. Using the now swirling snow as a cover, they would pop up and break the ice at random points all around us, again and again, ahead and behind and on all sides, occasionally even showing large, dark shapes looming in the whiteness for brief periods.

They don't like to be hurt. . . .

They *were* really playing games with us, and I think we all knew it. A patrol, most likely, just a small roving guard detachment; they were bored, and now they had something to play with.

Several times the dark masses would hold on the surface long enough for one of our three remaining archers to get off a shot or two, but hitting anything under these conditions was nearly impossible.

Of course, game or not, these wretched conditions certainly didn't help the "demon" patrol, either. I doubted whether they could see any better in this crap than we could, and if they had any kind of tracking devices below us they either didn't work on us or were too scrambled by the weather conditions to allow any accurate mark. They were also, obviously, forbidden to use modern arms—almost certainly because such a report would eventually get back to others in the Free Tribes and blow their demonic cover.

Still I wanted to see one. No wonder all our surveillance and all our monitoring hadn't detected them—and no wonder they required a life zone very close to human requirements yet were physically unable to move among us without bulky suits. Air-breathing, water-dwelling mammals! How I'd like to see one!

I got my wish as the ice erupted just ahead of me and one overconfident creature pushed up halfway through the surface with a roar. It was so close I made a slash at it with the sword, and struck the tip of a waving tentacle. The air was suddenly filled with a terrible high-pitched scream of agony that echoed across the ice as it dropped back into the water with blinding speed. And I almost regretted getting my wish.

The pear-shaped head was ringed with extremely long tentacles, perhaps three meters or more, covered with thousands of tiny little suckers. Below the tentacles were two huge heart-shaped pads of some wet, glistening material that must have been eyes. Where the head met the body, there were at least two visible pairs of stalklike arms or legs or whatever that terminated in scissorlike claws from elbow to end. The skin itself looked almost like a thing separately alive, a mottled, sickly yellow and purple that seemed to me to be constantly in motion, although, I told myself, that could just be water draining from it. The creature certainly earned its demon reputation—it was the most grotesque living horror I'd ever seen. Whatever evolution had produced such creatures had been brutal indeed, and if they weren't killing machines nothing in nature ever was.

Although I saw only a bit of the upper torso, there was no question that the old Elder had been right—the torso, at least, was covered by a metallic-looking suit of some kind, which resembled a chitinous exoskeleton. But I'd never seen an exoskeleton with a metal ring at the top and obvious vacuum connectors around it.

I didn't stop to question the thing, or shout my impressions to anybody else, but all of a sudden I knew I was glad of the side I was on. I had seen no sign of a mouth or nose, but the roaring when they broke through indicated to me that they had a lot of their equipment elsewhere.

Their mouths are on top. . . .

After I'd struck a glancing blow to the one, though, they stopped playing their game. Obviously they were not going to take any more risks now that their self-confidence was shaken a bit. That scream may have been just a normal yelp of pain to them, but if it translated at all into human terms, the emotion in it was unmistakable. They sure didn't like to be hurt.

The attacks became more cautious and intermittent now, and, therefore, easier to fend off. At the same time the snow seemed to slack off for a moment, and we saw how close we were to the first outcrop of the mountain itself. With a shout we broke and ran for it, taking our chances, but running a cautious, zigzag pattern that gave the creatures less opportunity to preplan an opening. More than that, the ice was becoming thicker now as it packed up against the rock wall of the mountainside, and that made following us even more difficult. I wondered if the things could move on land at all, but finally decided that they must be able to do so.

When the last of us reached the solidity of the mountain itself, even though its ice-encrusted side was not distinguishable from the pack ice, we all dropped in sheer exhaustion from the tension of the run. "Safe!" Ching sighed.

A sudden buzzing sound, impossibly loud and ugly, came from the direction of the ice. Wearily, Hono and I crawled up to see what was making it.

"Archers!" Hono screamed. "They're coming for us!"

All the tension flooded back as the archers jumped up and moved forward. There was still snow falling, but it was light, and we had about a kilometer's visibility. Out there, on the ice, we could see four of the creatures rise from the ice and into the air, where they grouped, suspended as neatly as a neg-grav car or copter.

Ching joined us, saw them, and gasped. "Are they using some kind of flying belt or what?"

I shook my head in wonder. "I don't think so, honey. The bastards have wings!"

She frowned. "Where are the tentacles? Those huge things . . . ?"

Hono pointed. "They're still there—see? But they retract, somehow, into the head, making a short ring of horns. Demon's horns!"

"They're well out of range of my bow," Quarl said in frustration. "Are they coming on, or not?"

"I'm not sure," Hono responded, "but this is getting on my nerves. I wish they'd do *something*."

"They are," I said softly. "They're showing us what they can do, more or less. I don't think they *are* coming—I think they're just giving us a demonstration that they'll still be there when we come back."

Hono shook her head in wonder. "What creatures can these be that are so insane? Part creature of the sea, part insect that flies and crawls, and is that thing hanging down a tentacle or some sort of tail?"

"They're all of it, and probably more," I responded. "They're living, breathing, thinking creatures that look as if they were put together by a committee, but put together for every environment, every weather or climatic condition, every land form or sea type. Given the kinds of air and temperatures within our broad range. I think they could live on any world I've ever seen. They sure scare the hell right out of me."

"Those are no demons," Hono said flatly, surprising me. "I don't know what they are, but they are no demons."

I nodded. "You're right on that. They're a smart, tricky, clever race from out there in the stars somewhere."

Ching looked at me in mixed shock and surprise. "Then *those* are the aliens we were told of?"

"Some of them, anyway. I suspect these are bred for just this kind of job. Manufactured to survive up here and kill anybody who comes along. If *we* can genetically breed what we need, there's no reason they can't go one step further."

"But then they should have the city weapons, or worse," Sitzter noted. "If they have such things, why do they not just sit back where they are and blast us off of here?"

I was wondering that myself. It didn't make sense for them to expose themselves like this and yet have no backup of their own equivalent of laser pistols and whatever, which would make short work of us. "Maybe— I know this sounds crazy, but just maybe it isn't *allowed* around here," I suggested. "It looks like they don't like to come on the mountain for some reason, either, so I think we're safe for now—until we start back, anyway." I turned and looked at the imposing Mount of God, most of it hidden in cloud. "Shall we see what's so special about this mountain, then?"

Hono grinned. "As long as we are in the area, why not?"

We climbed up and away from the aliens, and soon the buzzing faded, then stopped altogether. What they were going to do I had no idea, but I had new respect for those Free Tribesmen who'd made it here and back. No wonder most of them became highly respected priests and shamans of their tribes.

Once anybody reached the sacred mountain the instructions became pretty vague—just climb away from the flats a bit, everybody had said, then spend one night there, and that would be it.

We had lost just about everything except those weapons we retained and the hair skirts and snowshoe boots we wore, and which we now had to discard to climb. It took less than two hours before we came on an area that was small, reasonably flat, and had, surprisingly, some exposed rock, rock that looked far darker and mineral-rich than the usual stuff found on Medusa. But it provided a sheltered area, with something of a rock overhang—if we trusted the ice on top to stay put—and seemed as good a place as any to camp out. The wind and snow were whipping themselves up anyway, and there didn't seem much point in further exploration during the few remaining hours of daylight. We did, however, look around the small redoubt and found some signs that we were far from the first to ever reach it or spend the night there. In some of the exposed rock, for example, were carved designs, petroglyphs of some sort, although most of them were pretty obscure and it was impossible to take any meaning from them.

Ching examined the drawings with fascination. "What do you think they used to carve them? The lines are so deep and smooth it almost looks as if they were carved by some weapon or machine."

I nodded, but hadn't a clue.

The petroglyphs were useful for an hour's diversion, but that was about it. The wind was up, the snow blowing all around us, and it was growing dark. We eight survivors gathered around mostly for comfort rather than conversation.

"You know, I've been thinking about these aliens," Ching commented, snuggling up to me.

"Who hasn't?"

"No, I mean those retractable tentacles on their heads. Remind you of anything?"

For a moment I didn't know what she was talking about, then, suddenly, it hit me. Medusa. The symbol of the planet and its government, taken from some ancient human religion. The woman with live snakes for hair. "Yeah, I see what you mean," I told her. "But if I remember right, you were supposed to turn to stone if you looked at Medusa. They finally killed her by making her look at her own face in a mirror or something."

And that, oddly, was very appropriate to me, in a perverse sort of way. Medusa, the planet, had been my mirror; it had reflected all that was wrong or corrupt in me and all that was wrong or corrupt in my society. How odd that such an effect would happen here, on a world filled with those kicked out of my old society and their offspring. I couldn't help but wonder if the whole Warden system didn't have that effect. This was a bad world indeed, an evil world, far worse than the banal sameness of the civilized worlds, yet it served, it served. . . .

Sitting there, holding Ching close to me and reflecting on all of life as one was supposed to on a holy mountain, I drifted off into sleep. It was a deep, almost hypnotic sleep, partially a result of the release of tension from the day's horrors, but it was not dreamless. In fact, it was filled with images, stray thoughts, and odd sensations that made no sense.

I dreamed that I was in the presence of something great, something that was very, very young yet eons old—an alien force that was neither friendly nor unfriendly, neither monstrous nor beautiful, but strangely detached and indifferent to all around it.

There was a great energy and vitality to it, and a tremendous sense of self-importance. It was a believer in gods, for it was a god and a true one, as its very existence proved—for did not all else in the universe, both matter and energy, exist to serve, feed, and nurture it? It was worshiped, yes, by lessers with some small grain of intelligence, yet had no sense of obligation or caring for those who worshiped it. It was worshiped because it was a god, and gods were so far above mortal beings that worship was simply the natural way of things. All who did not recognize this and worship and serve would die, of course, as it never died; but the inevitability of their death was not so much a threat as a matter-of-fact statement of belief. Ultimatums were for lessers and were, in fact, not really understood by it, nor were threats or any other petty human emotions. These things would be because that was the natural order, the way things *were*.

I had no sense of the thing's shape or form, and calling what I perceived thoughts was not really correct. Rather, these attitudes were simply radiated from its mind into mine, and translated there—inadequately—into terms I could grasp.

Beyond that initial perception, the impressions were beyond any hope of translation by my mind; here were concepts too alien, too complex, too fast for me to grab hold of, let alone understand. Only the vastness of its intellect, and that curious feeling of ancient newness pervaded my consciousness. I had the feeling of falling, falling into the mind of the thing itself and there was a danger of being engulfed, swallowed by that which was totally incomprehensible. My mind shut it out, refused to allow the tremendous onrush of sensory input so alien to humanity that it could not even be correlated. In a sense, I had the feeling that the thing was aware of me, yet mostly indifferent to my existence. Or—maybe not. I felt a gentle nudge, a mental shift from it that swept me away from its tremendous, unfathomable presence, and I found myself shrinking, shrinking into nothingness, into a microbial world. No, I was not merely swept there—I was *relegated* to it by imperious decree.

And, slowly, I became aware once more of my body, but not in the normal way. It was as if, suddenly, a new sense was opened to me, allowing me somehow to see, hear, feel every single part of my body.

I heard the Warden colonies within me sing to one another, and while the sound was incomprehensible the sensation was pleasing and powerful. The Wardens, I realized, were in constant communication, cell to cell, throughout my entire body, yet they were not, in any normal sense, alive. Information was flowing in their song, though, information flowing into my body and into the Wardens from some source I could not trace.

I knew I was still dreaming, yet, strangely, I felt wide awake, my mind never clearer or more sensitive. Somehow, I knew, I could interrupt and tap that flow, even if I could not understand it. And, in this new way of seeing, I realized, for the first time, just how unhuman I had become. Each cell an individual, each cell infinitely programmable, operating as a whole but not limited to it. The information for almost any order was there the information for any transformation of any cell, group of cells, or the entire organism in fact, and while I could not understand the source of that information or the language the Wardens used to govern the cells and cellular interaction, I could speak to them, mentally, and they would respond.

When I awoke it was dawn. Things looked the same. Everything and everybody looked the same, and yet . . . Awake, fully conscious, I could still see, still sense the Wardens inside of me. Something very strange had in fact happened in the night I'd spent on the mountain—I had become my dream. Not the dream of the god-thing, but the dream of a new and formless creature, whose collective *consciousness* totally owned and controlled his body and every cell in it. The last link not only with the Confederacy but with any sort of humanity as I knew or understood it had been cut.

In a real sense, I was as alien as those terrors on the ice.

CHAPTER ELEVEN

Saints Are Not Gods

The reaction to all this varied a bit with the other seven on the mountain-top, but it was clear that we had all been profoundly changed by the experience. The few who were willing to come out of the clouds and compare notes, such as Hono, Ching, and myself, found that our primary encounters with the *presence*, whatever it was, were quite different and highly subjective, though the discovery of our own bodies and the Wardens within was almost exactly the same.

"But what was it?" Ching wanted to know. "I mean—is it really a god?"

"Most of the others have no doubts whatsoever," I noted, also gesturing a little for some caution. I didn't want to start any fights over theology at this point, and lowered my voice to a whisper. "I think, somehow, we were in contact with the alien mind. Or *an* alien mind, or something. I think their power plant and base is under here somewhere, and somehow, maybe through the Warden organism, we connected."

"But the thoughts and pictures were so *strange*. . . ."

I nodded. "That's why we call 'em aliens. We were somehow inside a mind so different from ours, with so little in common, that we could hear each other, maybe be aware of each other, but make no real common connection. If you were born unable to see and then, for a short period, saw a picture of a forest from the air with no explanation of what it was, that would be akin to what we experienced."

"And how we—feel—now?"

"Somehow that connection sensitized us to the Wardens. When we contacted that other mind, it was through the Wardens, somehow. And when we broke contact with it, our brains had been taught how to keep in contact with those in our own bodies. Honey, we haven't changed a bit. *Everybody* on Medusa is like this. But we're some of the very few aware of the fact."

"Hey! Tari! Look at me!" Hono's voice called, and we all turned and gasped at what we saw. It wasn't Hono at all, but a beautiful, stately goddess, the epitome of grace and beauty and strength—an angel. "I just pictured this in my mind and told my body what that picture was—and I had it!"

Just like that, I thought wonderingly. As simple as that.

We spent the rest of the morning experimenting and found that there was little we couldn't do if we willed it. Hair came and went, sex changed and changed again in a matter of minutes, in a curious process that seemed much like stop-motion photography. What you willed you could become, and the others could watch it happen. It was, in a sense, a new art form. Even mass seemed unimportant; the Wardens not only obeyed commands, but seemed able to reduce size if needed or create more cells out of energy. To be sure, it was easier to create the new mass than to get rid of it, since getting rid of it turned out to be extremely painful, but to some it was worth the price.

Since making such changes demanded a tremendous knowledge of biology, biophysics, biochemistry, you name it—knowledge all of us lacked—it became obvious that the Wardens translated the mental visions into reality by drawing on a vast body of knowledge beyond us. Where? I wondered. Some vast, high-speed computer someplace was feeding the things. It had to be.

Was the computer in fact what we had somehow connected with the night before? An alien computer, whose programming would also be so alien and so complex it would appear to us as a godlike superbeing? It was a good theory, anyway, and a computer had to be located someplace. That, in turn, would mean that the Warden organism was not a natural thing at all, but something artificial, something introduced into the environment of the four worlds. And who but those ugly bastards out there on the ice could have done that?

So they were here, below the waters, perhaps by choice, when the first exploiter teams arrived. They hadn't discovered the place—they had been here all along. Did that mean, then, that *they* could do this as well as we— or better? The combined powers of all four worlds, perhaps—shape-changing, body-switching, the power to create and destroy by sheer force of will . . .

But if that were true, then why the robots? Why deal with the Four Lords at all, for that matter—let alone allow them to run their clandestine war against the Confederacy? And why that dangerous game of cat-and-mouse on the ice?

The clearer things became, the muddier they became. I was fascinated by the problem and hoped to spend a lot of time on it, but only in an intellectual capacity. I was still sincere about my vow, and this was my retirement mission—although it had a wonderful payoff.

"We have talked with God, and She has made us Her angels!" Quarl whooped with pride and glee, and that seemed to be the general consensus. Only the more pragmatic Hono, a doubter to begin with and with a somewhat wider intellectual horizon than the rest, was anywhere near restrained. Yet even she was exultant with the new power, which was as good or greater than promised.

"It has occurred to me that the Elders have been here and have received this gift," she remarked to me. "Ugly old crones, aren't they?"

I grasped her meaning at once, for the same thought had also occurred to me. Although this ability might fade with age or lack of regular workouts, the fact was that it was almost impossible to accept those Elders' appearances as more than theatrical façades at this point. The others, too, understood the implications, and I was glad to pounce on them.

"Think about what that means," I warned them. "This power is to be used when necessary, and only for good, not to frighten or amuse yourself or others. You have great power, but you also have a sacred trust now. This isn't something that can be passed on or taught. We all earned it. Now we must return to use it wisely."

That statement sobered them a bit, as I hoped. I was anxious to leave before too much of the day was gone. New power or no, I didn't want to cross that stretch at night with our horror-show friends out there waiting for us, and I really didn't care to spend another night on this mountain. Once the connection had been established it would be easier the next time, and a few of us were far enough into madness now that no added exposure was needed.

Hono picked up her spear. "We walk down, then."

I thought a moment. "No. Maybe we don't. Let me try a little experiment here. Be brave, and don't be *too* surprised if it doesn't work." I looked at Ching, winked, then concentrated, drawing on my long practice of mind control and autohypnosis.

At once I began to change. I knew it, could see it, feel it, even as I willed it, and I knew that the message was adequate even as the process started.

The others, Ching included, watched in amazement at the transformation as my hunch paid off. Somewhere in that Warden computer there were the blueprints for a very large creature that flew.

"What is it?" several cried in alarm.

"How the hell do I know?" I croaked back. "But it has talons to pick up and rend prey, and it *flies*. Draw upon yourselves, become this thing as I did, and have a little faith. Then we'll *fly* back over that cold waste!"

That very thought—of flying strongly for a day or less rather than three days of dangerous walking—was enough. Now, for the first time, I could see in the others the creature I had willed up from some unknown source. Great, black man-sized birds, with oddly human eyes and curious, twisted beaks and taloned, powerful feet that could grab and rend if need be.

"Now what?" somebody called out.

"Let the Wardens do the work!" I called back. "We want to fly, so we will fly!" Awkwardly I walked out of the protected rock shelter and into a pretty strong wind. The drop was not sheer, but the ice-covered ground did fall away fairly fast. If this didn't work, I was going to be a bug spot down there someplace, that was for sure. And yet, I had to be first. Mind control and autohypnosis would provide the relaxation and confidence I knew I'd need, control the others sorely lacked. But if I took off, if I flew, faith would no longer be necessary, and would be replaced in them by will.

I concentrated for a moment, then looked out again and could *see* the air as clearly divided layers and swirls. Not as something solid—I could still see *through* it—but rather as differences in *textures,* a softness here, a bright clarity rushing through there. "Take off with a strong leap into the wind." I told them, then summoned up my courage and leaped, spreading my great wings as I did so.

I plunged down at an angle, barely skimming the tops of the slope, and only my mental control kept me from panicking and crashing. Down, down, and then I let loose the last of the tenseness and—as I'd told them—allowed the Wardens, replacing the bird's instinct, to take over. I bottomed out the drop and glided upward at an equal angle, up into empty, cloud-filled skies! *I flew!*

Ching, to her credit, got over her amazement quickly and followed my lead as I watched from above with nervous eyes. Oddly, she had an easier time of it than I had. Perhaps, I thought, there's more to faith than I'd thought. Then, one by one, the rest launched themselves, and I circled nervously and waited for them.

Once in the air, most were exultant, like little children, doing loops and swirls and having a grand time. I finally had to move to herd them in, reminding them, "We have a long way to go—don't waste your energy. You're not immortal, just powerful!"

"And strong," Hono shouted back. "We are truly blessed!" But she accepted my lead as we formed up close together and headed back out toward the ice.

I hadn't taken the low ceiling into consideration. We were still certainly within easy sight of the ground, as I didn't want to risk bodies as large and relatively cumbersome as ours controlled by novices in any real storm.

Since those creatures on the ice could see us if they were looking for us, or had some simple radar scan, I wanted to get up some speed to put as much distance as possible between them and us. The air currents helped a great deal; though we had a little trouble with firm control, there were levels where we could just rest on the currents and let them carry us, with a minimum expenditure of effort.

"There're our demons!" Hono snarled, looking down and to the west. "Looks to be the same four. I don't think they see us."

"Let's keep it that way," I responded. "We don't have the time or the experience to tangle with them."

"They killed four of us!" Sitzter protested angrily. "And who knows how many others? We are powerful, strong, and blessed by Mother Medusa! We should avenge our sisters!"

"No!" I shouted. "Dammit, if *we* can do this the odds are *they* can, too!" But my warning was too late. The madness that power brings and the religious fervor that had been kindled on the mountain was just too much for them, and, after all, they were hunters. First Sitzter, then Hono, and finally the others peeled off and made for the four large, dark forms below.

I picked up my speed and made a dangerous turn, trying to cut them off and steer them away. "This is madness!" I cried, but they were beyond talking now—and the aliens below had now spotted us.

Hono had taken the lead, as befitted her role as master hunter and group leader, and dove on the four dark forms. The aliens suddenly shot up into the air and dispersed, then hovered in an obviously preplanned diamond formation that allowed each to come to the aid of the others. I had a pretty strong feeling that these were pros who had been through situations like this many times before. I didn't like it at all. A strange idea popped into my head that these four, out here like this, were bait in a subtle trap as well as a discouragement to any mass movement to the sacred mountain.

Hono approached the lead alien, whose pressure suit, complete with some sort of backpack, was now clearly visible. The alien didn't let her get very close. The creatures looked really strange now, with just fifty centimeters of each of their ten tentacles showing. Those tentacles were three meters long and apparently independent of one another. Hono was coming at the hovering alien at great speed, but the alien never wavered, never even moved, until the great bird was almost upon it. Then, suddenly, the creature zipped a few carefully measured meters to one side, enough for Hono to miss and also to render her unable to break her forward momentum. Tentacles shot out not only from the target creature but from the next closest, and they hit home. Hono whirled in midair and great feathers flew off in all directions. Clearly she was totally off balance and she plunged like a stone to the ground.

Quarl and Sitzter flew right behind her, and the other three behind them. Suddenly the sky was a mass of feathers, screams, and flying tentacles extended to full length, skillfully and independently wielded with expert skill.

I pulled up, seeing Ching following behind me, and tried to create a diversion for the others. It worked to an extent, pulling one alien's attention off the furiously attacking great birds and allowing a gap in their tight tentacle-tip-to-tentacle-tip formation. But instead of using the opportunity to escape, Tyne and Sitzter went after the exposed alien. Tyne grabbed hold of a snaking tentacle with her talons and, while it wasn't really clear who had whom, she managed to yank the alien off balance and whip it to one side. The alien let out one of those piercing screams, and fun time was over.

A dozen more suddenly shot up through the ice, and these bore small handlebar-shaped devices held between two forward tentacles. Energy shot from the nub of the "bars," the newcomers being totally uncaring whether they hit their own or us.

That was enough. Tyne was down with her alien, and Sitzter and two others soon after. I decided there was nothing I could do and swooped up and away, toward the cloud bank overhead. Suddenly I heard Ching scream, "Tari! Watch out!" I immediately dropped, rolled, and sped off in another direction, but not before I saw Ching take the beam that had been meant for me and drop like the others to the sea floor. Then I suddenly made a complete upturn as a handy current came by and shot like a rocket up into the clouds.

I remained there for some time, trying to decide what to do next. Certainly the game had been over ever since Tyne had grabbed that one alien soldier, and they suddenly brought up their reinforcements with their equivalent of hand weapons. The indiscriminate way the gunners had used their weapons could indicate a callous disregard for individual lives, but somehow I didn't think so. The beam seemed very wide field, and if it were a death weapon it would be better suited to large battles or simply to clean away all comers across the ice from fixed positions. No, it was almost certainly a stun weapon, which meant they were even now cleaning up on the ice below, checking unconscious bodies, both theirs and ours, for signs of life.

That they were killers was clear from their earlier actions, but I didn't believe they were indiscriminate killers. Otherwise why give the prey what could only be seen as a sporting chance, provided that prey didn't threaten the lives of one or more of them?

I knew I had to have one more look, perhaps several more, and I came out of the clouds cautiously, ever on the alert to duck back into them. A dozen or so aliens were on the ice below, as I expected, setting bodies out in a row and examining them. Three alien bodies were visible, along with our own people, who were, I noted, rapidly reverting to their human forms. They didn't see me, and I didn't drop down too close, getting back up into the cloud cover again and circling around.

I counted six half-bird, half-human bodies down there, which meant at least one other besides me had gotten away—but I had no real way of telling who. I was pretty certain, though, that Ching had been hit, and that was my main concern. I liked Hono and most of the others, but they had brought this upon themselves despite my best efforts and were in any event impossible to save. The only hope I had was that, after a while, perhaps near darkness, the aliens would relax enough so that I might try a dive-snatch-and-grab operation on Ching. I had no idea if she or any of the others were dead or alive, but I had to assume that they survived until evidence proved otherwise. My only practical question was how long I could maintain this form and this energy level.

Quick dips in and out of the clouds revealed to me that some, at least, were alive. They moved occasionally, and were quickly slapped down by fast tentacles or pushed back by one of the four scissorlike appendages growing from the trunk.

If one were alive that raised my hopes that all might be. With the great self-repair abilities we all had, almost any survival was as good as not being injured at all.

The aliens were very professional and very methodical about the whole thing, but they were, I thought, pretty casual with people who could change into something else, perhaps even into aliens. That would be what

I would do if it were me down there. But over the next hour or two, the most any of the captives, now totally restored to human form, did was sit up. These weren't like my fifty-five sheep back in the sewers, so it stood to reason that if they didn't change and try and fight their way out they couldn't. If the Warden organism was, as I suspected, an extension of some alien computer, then obviously the connection between the computer and the captives had either been switched off or turned way down. The real question was what the aliens were waiting for. If they were just going to kill the captives, they could have done that long before and been gone to wherever they were most comfortable. But if they meant to take the crew prisoners, for some sort of questioning, they showed no inclination either to bring up transport or move them to safer and more secure quarters. They seemed, in fact, to be waiting for something. As sentinels they were also pros, their weapons and stations positioned so I could make out Ching in the group below. But I had no prayer of reaching her and getting back out without being shot myself.

Still, I waited, just out of their sight, I hoped just out of their reach, unwilling to abandon Ching unless I was certain there was no chance I could help her. If she was the price of all this discovery, I told myself sincerely, then the price was too high.

Finally, what they were waiting for arrived, and it was not at all what I expected. A large transport copter, specially outfitted for extreme-cold-weather use, came rushing out of the south, green and red running lights blinking and two large headlights slanting down on the ice itself. With growing apprehension, I watched the vehicle approach. Then I saw TMS markings on its side. It set down near the group, hovering just a few centimeters above the surface that could not have supported its dead weight. Carefully, one at a time, four TMS monitors climbed out onto the ice, laser pistols in hand. They gave hardly a glance or nod at the alien sentries, but went straight to the prisoners who, one by one, were taken to the copter and rudely pushed inside.

Although the copter was large enough to hold all that weight, it would certainly have a far slower return than it did coming out from wherever it was. I hoped that I could either follow it or get a good idea of its destination before my energy gave out. The copter rose slowly from the alien camp, hovered at about forty meters, and, staying below the thick clouds, started off. I followed as cautiously as I could, but it quickly became clear that I could never really keep up or even catch them. At one point just before they applied full power, I managed to get close enough to read the base city's name around the TMS shield on both doors.

Centrum.

I had never been to Centrum, nor met anyone who had, but I had heard the stories about it. The map in my head showed that it was far to the south, almost on the equator itself, and on the west coast—a distance of more than ten thousand kilometers. It was ridiculous even to *think* that the copter had come from there—it would have taken days at its average speed—but Gray Basin was close indeed, by air, perhaps three hundred and fifty or four hundred kilometers south, or about two hours' copter time with a full load.

Wearily, I turned and headed for Gray Basin, heading first due south so I could pick up some map landmarks. It would take me considerably longer than two hours to make the city, even with cooperative air currents and good weather, neither of which was a certainty. I still had no idea how much longer I could last.

A shape joined me in the darkness. I was already bone-tired and totally depressed, just going on sheer automatics, or I would have noticed it before it came close. When it did level out next to me, I was too weary even to take evasive measures, but, fortunately, it wasn't necessary.

"Tari?"

"That you, Quarl?"

"Yeah. Uh—dammit, I'm sorry, Tari."

"We're all sorry. I'm sorry, you're sorry, the rest of 'em are *really* sorry, it doesn't make any difference. What is, is, Quarl. We go on from there."

"We'll never catch them, you know."

I sighed. "I know. But I think I know where they're going, and that'll have to do. At least it's a city I know backward and forward, so I may be able to slip in and out of it without much trouble."

"You mean *we*. I'm going, too. They're my friends, too, Tari."

"No, Quarl. It wouldn't work. They'd pick you up in a second no matter what your powers. It's a whole different world in there, a world that's built to keep everybody in, to see what everybody's doing all the time. I know that world, and I know how it works. You don't. They'd have you in ten minutes."

"Then I will make them pay dearly for those ten minutes!" she spat, "but I am going in."

"I'd kill you first, Quarl, if I could, for the sake of the others."

"Huh?"

"They wouldn't kill you. They'd knock you out, knock you down like they did the others back there on the ice. Then they'd take you to a place that is truly hell, where men can steal your mind and soul and learn everything you know."

"I can not be tortured so easily!"

I sighed. How do you explain a psych complex to a stone-age woman? "There's no torture. No pain at all. You just can't know what they can do. And when they get you, they'll find out that I'm there and then they'll get me. It's no good, Quarl. I have to do this alone."

"You sound strange, Tari. Not like a brave one going after his own, but more like one who has lost all hope."

"No, I haven't gone that far, Quarl, but you're right. First of all, I'm tired. I'm on my last energy reserves, and the dawn and the landmarks tell me that I've got at least two more hours to go. And, yes, I would rather go home."

"But you go anyway. You do not seem surprised."

"I'm not. Somehow, I knew that it would eventually end, that it would come down to this, a final chase, a final hunt. Just when I found what I really wanted and was ready to give it all up." I chuckled dryly to myself. "It just wasn't meant to be, Quarl. I could *see* happiness, hold it in my hands, but I could not realize that I had what I wanted most in the world until it was no longer there."

"Among my people, the Kuzmas, there is a strong belief in fate and destiny for all people," Quarl told me. "Each of us is born to that destiny, but knows not what it is. So I can understand your feelings, my friend from the stars. But perhaps you will win, hey? Anything worth your life's devotion is worth risking death for."

Perhaps she was right, I thought. Those fifty-five back in the sewers—play revolutionaries, children daring the fire and kidding themselves—came down to their moment of truth. But the cause was proven not worth their miserable lives, even though they would suffer horribly. No risk, no gain.

But I *had* apparently impressed Quarl enough that she endangered the whole mission. "What do you wish me to do, Tari?" she asked.

"Go back to the citadel. Tell them what happened. Tell them that the demons are not demons but beings from the stars who work with the city people and have great weapons. Warn them of that. And tell them exactly what happened to all of us as far as you know it. Leave nothing out, make nothing look better or worse than it is. See Angi and Bura. Tell them—tell them that I love them both very much, and that if there is any way to do so I will return to them. See that they and my children are cared for."

"Until you return."

"Yes," I responded in a litanous monotone, "until I return."

Quarl saw me almost to Gray Basin, then flew off to the south and west. I saw the city in the distance, looking ugly in the late summer when no snow or ice covered it, leaving only that brutal gray roof and the stacks peering from it. It stretched out as far as the eye could see, and I hated every square meter of it.

Still, I settled down directly on that roof and found a place that didn't look *too* uncomfortable. I let myself relax for the first time, allowing my skin, bones, every cell of my body, to revert to my old form. I was too damned tired to do anything, but I forced myself to sit and think for a moment.

The copter was from Centrum, yet it was undeniably headed here. Why? Why a Centrum copter, anyway—and what was it doing this far north? Medusan government business, most likely—unless they had a Centrum copter near all major cities to differentiate national from local authorities.

And if that was the case, then all of the prisoners would be in the hands of the central government, not the local TMS office. They would probably be shifted to Centrum for disposition. That made sense. They knew a lot about a lot of things, including the sacred mountain, the malleability trick and its possibilities. They also had experience with the aliens at close hand. These wouldn't be things that Ypsir's people would like a regional psych office or the usual TMS monitors to come across. Too many might get ideas of their own, and there'd be somebody around who would be from Outside as well, somebody who would equate those demons with alien creatures and draw some interesting conclusions. No, the prisoners would be taken directly to party headquarters at Centrum, a bastion of protection, and handled by people who already knew the terrible secrets these prisoners could spill.

How would they get them there? The train was out—too long and too public. And air traffic seemed limited to local practical vehicles like the copters, which would be too slow. That brought Gray Basin back into focus, for it had one thing several other cities and towns of relatively equal importance and distance did not have.

It had a spaceport.

I stood up wearily. I was just barely atop the city, and when I entered it, I would have to do so from below. The access points from the roof were among the most heavily monitored places of all, and I knew it. Still, I wasn't so far gone that I couldn't use the vantage point to some advantage. I climbed up a ladder atop a large and dormant stack and looked out in the direction of the spaceport. I could just barely see it, off in the distance: a small cluster of warehouses and a tiny terminal in an ovoid pattern around the landing pad that was otherwise in the middle of nothingness.

There definitely was no ship in.

How long I had I didn't know, but I realized it would be better to lose them through sleeping than to lose them by rushing in as tired as I was. Ironically, I was going from the stone age back to my most nasty and sophisticated technological self for this mission, and, even then, I'd be taking risk after unacceptable risk. I had to rest and renew myself, so I went back and lay down as the sun rose high over the sealed city beneath and was soon asleep.

I hated going in yet again. I hated risking all, with the odds so totally stacked against me, knowing that even if I got away with anything myself the odds of saving Ching were very slim indeed.

But damn my filthy hide, I just couldn't resist the challenge.

CHAPTER TWELVE

Into the Lion's Den

I didn't sleep nearly as long as I needed, but it was a good, solid sleep and just what I needed to restore my confidence and get my brain working again.

Entering the city wasn't much of a problem, but once in, I wasn't at all sure what I could do. The only thing certain was that my theory of breaking the system by transformation was about to get a real test. The trouble was, I would have to be slow and careful to have any reasonable chance, and I just didn't have the time for that.

Having served in the city in Transportation proved invaluable. Of course, to enter I simply waited for a train to come up and stop, then I walked in with the train when they turned off the energy barriers to admit it. Once inside the entry tunnel, though, I was in the yards for the trains and had to make my way carefully to the passenger section. Having worked the station, I knew where the monitor cameras were located and where the inevitable "dead" zones were, although they were hardly conveniently located for my purposes. At this point, naked and hairless, I was an easy mark for a monitor and a sure flag, so getting into position without being observed was time-consuming.

I was counting on the Rochande passenger train, my old workhorse, to come in late. There were inevitably a number of TMS personnel on board, not for patrol but either coming back from some training mission or arriving after assignment to Gray Basin. It would still be a ticklish operation, requiring a lot of luck, but overall I'd had more than my share of that lately and had to trust that I'd get a bit more.

There was a spot between the passenger platform and the automatic baggage-handling section that was part of the freight operation which did not overlap two cameras. By a zigzag route I managed to make it across the yards and take a position behind a moving stair that was at the far end of the passenger section. For the first time it hit me that I would have to kill a few people if I went ahead with this; although I wouldn't feel too badly about TMS or government personnel, an innocent or two would also be necessary. I didn't really like doing that, but could only remember again the fifty-five who wouldn't try to escape and who were, in many ways, typical not only of the people here but of the whole system I was fighting.

I had a pretty clear plan, based on my observations and experiences during my life here. It is in the nature of my business, and of my mind, to file just about everything away, even when it serves no apparent purpose. You never know when you'll have to use one trivial or not-so-trivial item or another.

The initial move would be ticklish. There was a clock overhanging the passenger-discharge section that said I had to remain there, undiscovered, for at least two hours. To make my move too early might blow the whole scheme. Several station personnel passed very near me at various times, but thanks to my new Warden sense and my own self-control I was able to remain hidden in the shadows. At least, no alarms went off.

Finally, it was only ten minutes before the train was due, and I was starting to get nervous. None of the station people had passed in almost half an hour, and I needed one, my first innocent victim, any time now. The train was actually within earshot, stopped for the barriers, before I got my chance. A grade-four passenger-service agent walked from the baggage office up toward the platform. As she passed, I moved fast and silent from my shadowy place.

The deed was done in a couple of seconds. I had created a sharp, serrated ridge of cartilage on my arm and reinforced the muscle. I decapitated her rather cleanly, then had a nervous moment as the head started rolling out almost into camera range. I grabbed it, but it was messy and unpleasant.

I had timed the maneuver perfectly and applied just the right amount of force. Decapitation sounds terrible, and it is; but considering the Warden's amazing powers you had to strike an immediate, certain death blow or you'd have it. The other advantage was that the shock caused the body's Wardens to snap into futile action to seal the wound, so surprisingly little bleeding occurred.

I made no attempt to duplicate her features more than roughly; I hadn't seen them long enough in presentable condition to do so. Still, I managed it, displacing some of my extra mass into height to manage to fit, however uncomfortably, into the clothes which were, mercifully, close enough to the color of Medusan blood to mask the stains somewhat. The girl's sandals, however, would never fit without a lot of work, and I didn't even try. None of this disguise really had to last for very long.

I had an uneasy moment when it looked as if two others were going to walk back by my hiding place with its grisly contents, but, fortunately, at that moment the train rounded the bend and slid into its slip. Everybody snapped to professional attention.

My luck had held up to this point, but now I'd need more. I waited until the train was completely in and docked, then watched the doors slide open and the passengers begin to emerge. When I spotted two TMS uniforms with duffels I went into my act, fully aware that the others would also see, but counting on the usual mob inclination on Medusa to let TMS handle things whenever there was a question of responsibility. I pulled the trunk of the woman's body out a bit, so an arm and leg were showing, then stepped out myself and cried, hysterically, *"Monitors! Come here! Please hurry!"*

Nobody calls a cop on Medusa unless there's terrible trouble. I saw the two young faces, a man and a woman, glance over at me, look puzzled for a minute, then follow my arm that pointed to the exposed limbs. They dropped their duffels and trotted over to me.

"What's the matter?" the woman asked, sounding more concerned than nasty.

"T-there's a body there!" I stuttered, sounding scared to death. Both of them looked shocked, then turned and knelt down as I angled myself so that the moving stair shielded me from the platform. By then most of the people had gone up and we had no curious gawkers, but there was certain to be a couple of curious train people pretty quickly.

The two monitors were pushovers. I managed to chop them both cold before they realized what had happened, then killed them a bit more cleanly but no less efficiently. I had to move damned fast—their bags were still on the platform, and the camera would at least have seen that.

I quickly got rid of the transport clothing and pulled off the man's monitor uniform. I was working against time and just barely got it right. Fortunately, the man was not too far off my size, so I was able to adjust myself for a reasonable, if slightly uncomfortable, fit. It only had to *look* presentable.

I took the risk of rolling the bodies out and under the train when a quick peek showed, incredibly, nobody looking in my direction or even, it seemed, aware that anything was going on. Then I walked back out onto the platform, picked up a bag, turned, and called back loudly, "Okay, I'll meet you in the main terminal!" Hoisting the bag on my shoulder, I then took the moving stairs myself.

The main terminal was, of course, still pretty busy, and that helped a lot. I needed another switch, one not so easily traced, and quickly, but no opportunity presented itself. I walked into the lavatory, looked through the bag, found some evidence that this private was a new transfer to Gray Basin, and decided to take a chance, at least for the moment. The train wouldn't be turning around until it was cleaned and serviced, about two or three hours. If they didn't look for that passenger agent too hard, I might have some time before the bodies were discovered. Such callous murder was so totally alien to this society they would search everywhere for the missing agent before looking for a body. The other recruit was almost certainly new herself and unlikely to be missed immediately, either. If, and it was a big if, the computer hadn't flagged the two of them dropping their bags and running out of view. But who could know?

Using the private's card, I took the bus to TMS headquarters. I needed another TMS body because, again, I bore only a vague resemblance to the dead monitor. Luckily, I knew Gray Basin's TMS building pretty well, including, thanks to the probably late Major Hocrow, many of its own dead areas.

I got off a couple of blocks before reaching headquarters and managed to toss the bag into a trash receptacle before walking boldly down to the building. If only the people knew how many dead zones there were in any major city there'd be hell to pay, I thought with some amusement. The alley with the trash bin had a camera, but it was mounted high on a wall and easily seen. So by just keeping the trash bin between me and it I couldn't be seen. They still might send somebody to check the trash, of course, but by then I'd be somebody else—I hoped.

I entered by the garage rather than the front door, my uniform being sufficient to get no more than nods from a few monitors.

There was a single camera mounted on a slowly rotating and wide-open mount in the center of the car-maintenance garage. A piece of cake. I just walked along until I found a monitor checking a car for something, struck up a mild conversation, then, when the camera and mark were easily in the right positions, chopped him. This time I had had a few minutes to study the intended victim's features and the luxury of a less messy kill, so I had no trouble in duplicating her features. She was a fairly large woman and things fit pretty well, and, under the car, I was able to change quickly and efficiently into her uniform.

I found the replication trick a cinch, at least as far as I knew. Just concentrate on the victim, match his or her Warden configuration to yours, and let your Wardens emulate the pattern. It was kind of weird to feel hair grow out rapidly on my head, and to watch flesh act as if it were something independently alive and fluid; but the actual change was so damned easy, now that I had a few minutes.

When I climbed out from under the car I was the private, to all onlookers, anyway, and again I timed the camera just right to stash the body in the car's trunk. With any luck, it might be a couple of days before the body was found, and I didn't need that long.

Satisfied, I took out "my" card, called the elevator, and rode up to the desk and central processing area I knew so well. This was always a busy area, and the risk I ran here had mostly to do with meeting some friend of the person I was supposed to be. I couldn't hold that kind of pose for a moment against somebody who knew the original well.

The important thing, though, was to look and act as if you belong and you're working on somebody's instructions. Usually that's enough to get by in public areas, where people just don't expect this sort of thing. I went in back to the small compartments, each with its own terminal, that TMS monitors used when filing reports. I picked an empty one, flicked on the terminal, and started.

While I expected no trouble in breaking the simple computer codes generally used, I was surprised to find that these terminals needed no codes at all. You just stuck in your card, which certified that you were a legitimate TMS monitor, and that was enough when the computer monitor checked appearance against file. No fingerprints, no retinal check, just a simple method for a society that took far too much for granted.

I punched up KOR—CHING—LU and then sat back and waited for the data to come up on the screen. I scrolled quickly through the basics to the last entry, which was what I wanted:

ARRESTED 1416 OFFICERS CENTRUM 17–9–51. PROCESSED GB TMS 0355 18–9–51, JUDG UD, SUBJ. REF. CENTRUM DISTRICT, REL. CENTRUM CUST. 0922 18–9, DEPT. 41 IV GB 1705. CASE CLOSED. REF. #37–6589234.

It wasn't hard to figure out what had happened. Ching had been brought here in the early morning, processed, judged guilty and sentenced to UD—Ultimate Demotion—then turned over to Centrum officially. She was to leave at 1705—in less than an hour. The computer didn't say how, but it had to be via the shuttle. I punched the reference number given and got a similar readout:

HONO, W–O UNCLASS., ARRESTED 1416 OFFICERS CENTRUM 17–9–51. The rest of the listing was identical to Ching's, except, of course, that the end reference referenced Ching's case. So they were both going out on the shuttle. Well, maybe I should, too.

Bluff and bravado will only get you so far, but it does wonders in a tightly regimented society. I walked out the front door without any problem and headed for the bus to the central terminal. I wasn't about to risk trying for a TMS car—the motor pool authorizations would be pretty tightly watched. Then I stopped, cursed myself, walked around to the garage, and found the car with the body still hidden inside. This, of course, *had* to be *her* car, and that would make things easy—if the damned thing worked.

It did, and I was soon out of the garage and heading toward a city gate, a dead body under the back seat and a really irritating squeal coming from somewhere in front that had obviously been the reason for the service.

I reached the road gate to the space terminal with no problem, but had to get out, present my card to the monitoring machine, and tell it that I was going out to the terminal with some special paperwork that some other monitor had forgotten. It was a routine enough thing, and I had no trouble getting the barriers lowered quickly.

The shuttle was already in, and I made it with almost twenty minutes to spare. I hadn't been back here since arriving on Medusa, but the place hadn't changed much. It was small and cramped and not very impressive, since passengers were infrequent. I saw only a couple, both official-looking, sitting around now. No sign of Ching or Hono, though, let alone of the arresting officers. For the first time I began to fear that I'd blown it.

My confusion must have been all too apparent, for one of the government employees waiting to board, a white-haired man of middle age, stood up and came over to me. "Something the matter, young woman?"

I was a little startled for a moment, since I'd forgotten I was playing a woman at this point. Actually, this was the first conversation I had had with anyone since assuming this identity, and the change had almost slipped my mind.

"Yes, sir. I have some papers that never got cleared for a couple of prisoners supposed to go out to Centrum, and now I don't see 'em." The voice sounded funny, but more or less female, which was all that mattered on a world like this.

He frowned. "Let me see them."

I was ready. I had made hard copies of several forms with the dispositions of Ching's and Hono's cases for just such an eventuality. They wouldn't fool a monitor, but they'd get by a bureaucrat, I hoped.

He looked them over, smiled, then handed them back. "Well, it's easy to see why. They departed on the eighteenth—that was yesterday."

I was thunderstruck, and for a moment my self-control failed. I hadn't slept a few hours, I'd slept almost a day and a half on that city roof!

I must have looked really crushed—as I was—because the government man said, "You're going to have some problems, huh?"

I nodded, thinking as fast as I could. "Yes, sir. I'm pretty new here, and while I just was told by my boss to get these things down here, when I come back with them and they see the wrong date it won't be my sergeant who gets the blame. Discipline's pretty rough up here, too."

He seemed genuinely touched. "Give me your card."

"Sir?"

"I said, give me your card. Let me see what I can do."

I was afraid he was going to call me in and try and square a nonexistent mission with an unknown superior, but I had no choice. I did, however, eye the exit. I was outside the city here, and all I really needed was some running room. Unfortunately, I was also in the most heavily monitored type of buildings on Medusa—since it was exposed to the outside—and one connected to live evaluators with automatic rifles all over the place. If I made a run for the door now they'd hit the alarm; if I stood here, I was probably trapped. The only thing I could think of was to let this scene run its course and take a last-gasp chance at a panic escape when the right time came.

The man was back from a small office in a couple of minutes and he was smiling as he handed back my card. "I think we can arrange for you to complete your mission, Monitor. I'll square things with your superior, since you're not due back on duty until 0800 tomorrow anyway." He winked. "Nobody will ever know, huh?"

I was thunderstruck. "Then you'll take the papers with you to Centrum and see that they're delivered?"

"Oh, my, no. I'm not going to Centrum, unfortunately. But there's plenty of room on the shuttle, and I've logged you as my guest as far as Centrum, with a return on the morning flight. The trip is still going to cost you some money you probably don't have—Centrum's not cheap—but you'll get there and back and be able to deposit your papers with no one the wiser at your end, since I've cleared it on my personal assurance."

I could hardly believe this. "You mean you want me to come with you?"

He nodded. "And better hurry. We're about to board. Well? How about it?"

I considered his offer. Out there was freedom. The shuttle meant new dangers, and I was probably too late to do much anyway, even if I could find them. Still, I'd come this far, and this seemed the only sensible thing to do under the circumstances, so I nodded. "All right, sir—and thanks."

Of course, the question I had weighed was not that hard to answer. Nobody, and I mean *nobody*, has this kind of luck. When too many things keep going right, you just have to know you're being had. I don't know whose bodies they'd found, or where my slip had come, but somebody had gotten a lot of laughs at seeing me do my routine, knowing all the while that I was a day late and didn't realize it.

Obviously escape was out. They'd never let me make the door, and it would be a very uncomfortable ride. It seemed to me that going along with things would at least bring me close to Ching and Hono, even if very dangerously, and I was still not without resources.

The shuttle was the same comfortable craft I remembered, only now there were only the two government bureaucrats and myself aboard. The takeoff was smooth and effortless, although not without the press of many gravities into the soft foam seats and the unsettling but thrilling feeling when the boost was cut off.

"Dunecal, next stop, five minutes," the speaker said crisply. "Remain in your seats and strapped in at all times." That surprised me, since I'd assumed we were going directly to Centrum, where my welcoming committee would be waiting. But, sure enough, we descended smoothly and were soon in Dunecal, main city of the central continent, and my benefactor's destination. He wished me well, and departed, acting for all the world as if he had no idea who or what I really was—and he may not have known, I reflected.

"Loading passengers now," the speaker announced. "Centrum next stop."

I thought about jumping ship at this point, but there seemed no purpose to it. I was hooked and was being reeled in slowly for the amusement of whatever sportsman was on the other end.

Three passengers boarded at Dunecal, a man and woman in government black and another young woman whose looks were so startlingly different I almost had to stare.

Women on Medusa were no beauties. Oh, once you got used to them they were fine, but all were chunky, and had a masculine muscularity about them. There was, after all, a chance that anybody could flip from one sex to the other and so the average person was a bit of both, really. I had frankly almost forgotten the difference between normal human and Medusan females until this young woman came on.

She was certainly Medusan—her casual clothes would not have been sufficient protection for anybody else—but, then again, she wasn't. Her olive skin looked far softer than the tough hide we all took for granted. She was built as few women I'd met were built and had mastered all the right sexy moves. She also had a sweet, sexy smile on her very pretty face and her hair was longer than normal and light brown—the first of such a color I'd ever seen on Medusa, and one I'd rarely seen anywhere else, for that matter.

"Take that seat and strap in, Tix," the man instructed.

She smiled. "Oh, yes, my lord," she said in a childish-sounding yet sexy voice, and did as instructed. I noticed she never stopped smiling and just about never took her eyes off him. The other two strapped themselves in and the man noticed me staring at the young woman.

"Never seen a Goodtime Girl before, huh?" he called out conversationally.

I shook my head. "No, sir. I'm from Gray Basin, and we don't see any there."

"I daresay," he answered with pride. "You just arrest 'em and send 'em to us and we make 'em." He chuckled at that.

I responded with a smile I didn't feel. There was something creepy about Tix, something *unnatural*.

I'd heard mentions of Goodtime Girls, of course. Everybody had. Entertainers, consorts, concubines, and a little of everything else, it was said—mostly for the entertainment and gratification of the bigwigs. But nobody I had ever talked to had actually seen one, or really knew anything about them except that theirs was a different kind of job. I always wondered why, on a planet ninety-percent female, there weren't Goodtime Boys.

The man proved chatty. Either he, too, was ignorant of who I was or he was putting on a mighty fine act. I gave him my cover story, with the truth when explaining what I was doing on the shuttle. He seemed to accept it.

Goodtime Girls, it seemed, weren't employees, they were slaves. Oh, he didn't call Tix that, but it was clear that all the euphemisms were standins for the word "slave." They had been convicted of crimes against the state and sentenced to Ultimate Demotion. Most UDs, as he called them, were sent off to the mines of Momrath's moons, but a few were selected and turned into Goodtime Girls by expert psychs in the government's Criminal Division. "Some of 'em are real artists," he told me proudly. "You wouldn't believe what Tix looked like before they worked on her."

"There are no Goodtime Boys?" I couldn't resist asking.

He shook his head from side to side. "Nope. Something in the process having to do with our little buggers the Wardens. When they remove the psyche or whatever it is they take out, the subject's invariably locked in as female." He gave a leer in Tix's direction, and she nearly shivered with delight. "Not that I mind that a bit."

I had to repress the urge to shiver. In all the barbaric acts of mankind, the worst was certainly abject slavery, and probably the worst of the worst was to create willing, natural slaves with a psych guide and a psych machine. The system seemed terribly perverted, somehow, as well as downright crazy. Why have slaves on a world where robots were happily employed? The only possible answer was instant ego-gratification for the kind of mentality that worshiped only power. This guy had been "given" Tix by the government for doing such wonderful work and reaching a government grade level that warranted a Goodtime Girl. He took her with him as a highly visible status symbol, and because he got his jollies having a personal slave to order about. It was the ultimate reflection of the sickness of this society, I thought sadly. What kind of a place was it that was run by people who had psych-created fawning slaves the way influential people in other societies owned great gems or great works of art?

I repressed a sudden urge to kill the fellow and his companion right then and there, and maybe the Goodtime Girl, too, although, in more than one sense, she was already dead.

About twenty minutes after takeoff the speaker came on. "Please remain strapped in your seats. We are about to dock."

The man and woman both frowned, and she turned to him. "That's odd. I didn't feel any deceleration."

He nodded. "I wonder if something's wrong?"

There were no windows, so there was no way of knowing, but I tensed up. Here we go, I thought, and got myself mentally ready for any move that could be made.

I felt a shudder and vibration, then three quick deceleration bursts, and we slid neatly into the dock. There was a hissing, and then the rear door slid open. The man unbuckled himself and walked over to the door, looking out, still puzzled. "This isn't Centrum," he said, confused. "I think this is the space station."

I unbuckled myself, sighed, stood up and walked back to the door. "Just go back to your seat," I told him, "and relax. I think this is my stop."

CHAPTER THIRTEEN

A Victim of Philosophy

The lock was of the modern, standardized type, with the shuttle docked in space against a long tubular entryway into the space station itself. I knew that all four planets had such stations, and that the Four Lords made good use of them. The master computer for Medusa was here, for example, but I was unprepared for the enormity of the place. It had good artificial gravity, perhaps a bit lighter than I'd become used to. From the entry tube you could look out through a transparent strip and see the gigantic structure stretching away from you on all sides. It was more than a mere space station; it was more like a small floating city several kilometers across, large enough to be self-sufficient in those things that would support a sizable population.

At the end of the long walk up the entry tube I came upon a second airlock chamber, which I entered without hesitation. If they'd meant to kill me they could have done so far more easily and less messily elsewhere. This second lock was pretty much an insurance measure against premature leak and emergencies, but it also served as a neat security cell. Up top was the ever-present monitor, almost certainly with a real person on the other end, and a series of small and unfamiliar-looking projections that could have been either decontamination or weapons.

The first door closed behind me, but the second did not open right away. Suddenly those projections flooded the chamber with a pale blue force field that had a rather odd effect on me. The sensation must have been similar to that of being suddenly struck deaf or blind or both, yet I could see and hear perfectly well. What I no longer could do was sense or contact the Wardens within my own body. They had cut off communications, somehow, and, in so doing, had reverted me to my original form. I could see and feel it happening, with no powers except my own brain.

The ray cut off quickly, and the outer door opened. I found it very difficult to move, though, as if heavy weights had suddenly been placed all over me. I wasn't quite sure what they were doing, but I guessed that they, not I, were now sending to the Wardens in my body somehow, and they were telling them to produce this sensation. It was quite effective. I could still move and act normally, but any quick or sustained actions would be beyond me. I had walked into the trap, and now they had me good. I had a vague thought that I should have made a run for it back at Gray Basin, no matter what the risks, but it was a little late for that now.

A strong-faced Medusan woman in government black waited for me in the reception lounge, along with a monitor sergeant armed with some sort of small, light sidearm. It was certainly no laser weapon, and I guessed it to be some sort of stun gun, which made perfect sense in this situation. You could shoot hostages as well as the hostage-takers with no fear of permanent injury to either, and you were unlikely to burn accidental holes in the space-station wall.

"I am Sugah Fallon," the woman announced, "director of this installation. You are, I would guess, the one called Tarin Bul, although I expect that that's not your real name, either."

"It will do," I told her wearily. "I see you know a lot more about the Warden organism than even I expected."

She smiled. "Research into the possibilities is never-ending, Bul. You would be amazed at the things we can do these days. Come. It must be days since you ate, so we'll attend to that first." With my every move physically restricted, I had little choice but to follow her. Besides I *was* starved, I had to admit.

The food was good, and it was fresh. "We grow it all ourselves," Fallon told me with some pride. "In fact, we support a staff here of over two thousand permanent party personnel plus half again as many on transient business. It is from here that the entire monitoring system is guided. All the records are here, and all are centrally coordinated and beamed by satellite to every city on the planet. Our laboratories and technical specialists are drawn from all four Diamond worlds, and are the best in their fields."

I really *was* impressed. "I'd like to see the whole thing sometime," I said dryly.

"Oh, perhaps you might, but we will show you only a few departments today, I think. You'll be fascinated by what we're doing in those areas, I think."

"Alien psychology?"

She laughed. "No, sorry, that's off limits. You understand we have to be somewhat circumspect with you since we know that you carry some sort of broadcaster inside your head. Until that goes I'm afraid your movements will be rather limited here."

"How do you know about that?" I asked, not bothering to deny it. This wasn't a fishing expedition—they knew a whole hell of a lot.

"We know a bit from some of your compatriots. You may be interested to know that the agent sent to Lilith *did* manage to kill Marek Kreegan, although in a rather oblique way, and that Aeolia Matuze of Charon is also dead, partly thanks to your man there. On Cerberus, though, your man failed, and did a most interesting thing—he joined our side without even making a real attempt at Laroo."

That *was* news, most of it welcome. Two out of four wasn't bad at all, everything considered. Her comment further indicated that none of the other three had revealed that they were, in fact, the same person as myself. I wondered about the turncoat on Cerberus, though—was his conversion sincere, or some sort of ongoing ruse? The fact that he was alive and apparently influential indicated to me that he couldn't be counted out.

"I suppose it's too late for me to defect," I said half-seriously.

"I'm afraid so. Defections under duress are *so* undependable. It really was nothing personal, either, that you failed. You accomplished a tremendous amount that we would have thought impossible, and you've caused a major reassessment of our entire monitoring system. In fact, if you hadn't attacked the Altavar on your way out, you would still be free and a tremendous threat to us. Even so, you could have escaped. You have a weak spot, a sentimental streak, that your compatriots seem to lack. It's what's done you in."

I shrugged. "I owed it to them to see what I could do. Besides, if I couldn't pull it off, I was neutralized anyway, with no hope of ever really doing anything beyond living with the Wild Ones. Call it the testing of a theory—and the theory proved wrong. I simply underestimated the system. Just out of curiosity, though, I'd like to know when you got on to me."

"We knew you were in Gray Basin when we sent somebody to check on the missing monitor at the station," she told me. "However, we really didn't have any idea of who you were until you punched Ching Lu Kor into the computer. Since the monitor you were pretending to be didn't have knowledge of, interest in, or anything to do with that case, it raised a flag here. From that point on, of course, we had you. We were pretty certain it *was* you, since few others would have the combination of nerve and timing to pull off such a thing even that far." She paused, then added, "You should have kept switching identities every hour or so."

I nodded, then added, "I could still have gotten away if I hadn't misjudged how long I'd slept. That was my key mistake and I admit it. One little mistake in a long string of successes, but that's all you get in this business."

"That's why the system always wins. We can make a hundred mistakes, but you can make only one."

"Tell that to those two you said are dead."

The comment didn't faze her. "Their systems were quite different from ours. Technology doesn't even work on Lilith, and it's easily negated by a strong mind on Charon. They will have to develop systems better suited to their own homes as we have evolved this one."

"I'm not very impressed with this one," I told her. "It's a dull, stupefying world of sheep you've created down there, people without drive, ambition, or guts. And for the elite on top, human slaves kept as status pets— like something out of the Dark Ages of man."

She didn't take offense. Her reply, in fact, was indirect and at first I didn't see where she was going. "Tell me one thing that's puzzled me, Tarin Bul or whatever your name is. Just one thing. I know you've been conditioned so that we can't get any information from you by force, but I *would* like to know the answer to one question."

"Perhaps. What is it?"

"Why?"

"Why what?" I was very confused.

"Are you really as blindly naive as you say you are, or is there a real reason why you continued doggedly on your mission once you were here?"

"I told you I found your system repugnant."

"Do you really? And what are the civilized worlds if not an enormous collection of sheep, bred to be happy, bred to do their specific jobs without complaint, and also without ambition or imagination. They look prettier, that's all—but they don't have to survive the hard climate of Medusa. What you see down there is simply a local adaptation, a reflection of the civilized worlds themselves. And do you know why? Because most people *are* sheep and are perfectly content to be led if they are guaranteed security, a home, job, protection, and a full belly. In the whole history of humankind, whenever people demanded democracy and total independence and got it, they were willing and eager to trade their precious freedom for security—every time. Every time. To the strong-willed, the people who knew what to do and had the guts to do it. The people who prize personal power above all else."

"We don't have cameras in people's bathrooms," I responded lamely.

"Because you don't *need* cameras in the bathroom. You've had centuries of the best biotechnology around to breed out all thoughts of deviant activity, and a barrier not of energy but of tens of thousands of light-years of space to keep out social contamination. The few who slip by, people like you, are sent here. That's why so many of them wind up in charge, and why the system here is a reflection of the civilized worlds. We grew up there, too, Bul, so it's the system we know and understand best. We're the people most fit to rule, not by our own say-so, but the Confederacy's. That's why we got sent here."

I opened my mouth to reply, but nothing came out. There had to be a flaw in the logic somewhere, but I could find none. However, accepting her thesis didn't make things any more pleasant. "If I admit the point, then all I can say is that the system itself is corrupt, bankrupt, and wrong, whether it's here or in the Confederacy."

"Then you *are* naive. Both Medusa and the Confederacy have given the masses exactly what all the social reformers have clamored for all these years—peace, plenty, economic and social equality, *security*. All other alternatives that are not variations of the plan have resulted in mass privation. You saw nothing wrong with the Confederacy while you were there because you were a part of the power structure, not one of the sheep. You chafed here because we tried to make you a sheep. But if you'd come in as a government official, perhaps a monitor officer, you'd have felt right at home."

"I doubt that now," I told her. "I have lost my faith."

"Then, perhaps, that's why you really did what you did. Think about it. You could have been home free, yet you persisted. You could have turned back at several points, yet you came on against hopeless odds. That isn't the act of a trained Confederacy assassin, even a disillusioned one. You came willingly because you know what I say is true. You cannot accept the system in any form, yet you accept the fact that it is the best one. For one like you, living as a savage in a dead-end existence would eventually drive you crazy, yet you could not embrace the system. You didn't really come after us to rescue anyone, Bul. You came here to surrender, and you did. There is no place in this world for one like you, and you know it."

I didn't want to believe that what she said was true, and I would not admit her conclusions no matter what. I had no desire for suicide, no need to purge myself. She had it only partly right, I realized, and I would not give her the satisfaction of admitting even that to her. I could *not* exist on Medusa; there *was* no place on it for one like me. I came either to destroy the system or die trying.

Or was I just kidding myself?

"What happens to me now?" I asked her.

"Well, first I think we should give you something of an education. I think, perhaps, we should first take you to your friends. It should be interesting to see your reactions to our rather unique art form."

* * *

We stood on a walk overlooking a vast expanse of plant growth. In many ways it was reminiscent of a resort complex back in the civilized worlds, with white sandy beaches, small pools of clear water fed by artfully constructed artificial waterfalls, and a safe but beautiful flower-filled planned jungle.

"The First Minister's personal pleasure garden," Fallon told me. "A place to totally relax and get away from it all."

I squinted and looked down. "There are people down there."

She nodded. "The garden is staffed by several dozen Goodtime Girls," she told me. "They are there to fulfill his every wish, indulge his every whim, as well as keep the place in perfect condition."

"At least in the Confederacy we don't turn people into robotized slaves," I noted acidly. That was one clear difference.

"Oh, no, you don't," Fallon admitted. "However, you killed four people in cold blood just to get this far, and who knows how many others over your career? The Confederacy takes the so-called criminals people like you catch and either totally wipes their minds and rebuilds childlike, menial personalities, or they totally remake your psyche into their own image if they can. In extremely violent cases, they simply kill the people. They send only the best to the Warden Diamond, but only because they have done something unusual or creative—or are highly connected politically, which is the most important factor in being sent here, since someday those determining the criminals' fates may be caught doing something naughty and sent down themselves. The difference between the Council and the Congress and the so-called criminals like Talant Ypsir and Aeolia Matuze, two former government members, is only that Ypsir and Matuze made some enemies and so were prosecuted. They're no different from any other Confederacy rulers. The personality goes with the job."

"But—slaves out of some thirteen-year-old boy's wet dreams?"

"They serve a purpose. All are criminals by *our* standards. Their guilt is not in doubt in the least. The strongest and cleverest we send to the moors of Momrath—*our* Warden Diamond, you might say. The rest, the ones who cannot be trusted to continue at all, we either kill or change. We change them. We make them useful. In many ways we're more humane than the Confederacy. Come."

We walked back into the main station complex and past a door that read PSYCH SECTION, AUTHORIZED PERSONNEL ONLY. I knew what the next stop was. My faithful armed guard, who had not so much uttered a word or changed her dour expression, followed.

"Originally the idea was just to change the mind-set into something useful," Fallon continued, seemingly enjoying the grand tour she was giving me. "We have, after all, a lot more menial jobs than the civilized worlds. But we discovered that when we did a wipe on a Medusan, a funny thing happened. The body, whether male or female, reverted to a primal female form as well." We stopped in front of a door, which opened for us. We entered an observation room for a psych machine. "Recognize the subject in the chair?" she asked me.

I looked hard. Connected as she was to all sorts of tubes, sensors, and the like, it was at first difficult to get a good look at the woman "on the couch," as psychs liked to call it. Still, I recognized the general facial features and form quite well. "Ching," I sighed.

She nodded. "We're almost to the state we call 'at rest' in our process here. You can see that the skin is abnormally soft and pliant, there is no hair or any blemish or unusual feature. The basic form is female but not unusually so."

I nodded, feeling sick again. So this was what this business was all about. They were going to take great pleasure in making me watch, and I knew they could force me whether I wanted to or not.

"It's actually rather unfortunate that all Medusans reach this base female pliancy. It would be useful to have some Goodtime Boys. But don't think that all Goodtime Girls are mere sex objects. I'm afraid many of our top male administrators prefer to use them that way, as does the First Minister, but there can be a number of different types. My two, for example, are like very muscular young boys, very cute. Female, of course, but you'd hardly know. It's the new art form I was talking about. The artists are our top psychs, who can actually feed information through the psych machines to the Wardens within a body, once all mental resistance is eliminated. Goodtime Girls to order, according to preference. All still smart, able to learn all sorts of things as instructed, and all totally and completely devoted to their owners."

"Who is . . . she being made up for?" I asked, my previous meal turning sour in my stomach as I watched.

"Haval Kunser. He is my counterpart on the planet itself, you might say. He runs the administrative side of the government. Both of us are equals, just below the First Minister, who sets the policies we carry out. Of course, Hav probably won't keep her. He'll give her to somebody as a reward or something. We even export a few to the other Diamond worlds. Ah! I see the psych is ready. Now watch."

"I don't want to see any more," I snapped.

"What you want is of no concern," she responded coolly. "I can freeze you in place and make you, so shut up. Whining doesn't become a Confederacy assassin."

And, of course, she was right. How different, really, was this from the young woman I'd killed on the train platform? The only real difference was that I hadn't *known* that woman. Maybe Fallon *was* right, after a fashion, I told myself. The more I looked at myself coldly and dispassionately, the less I liked what I saw.

The process was fascinating to watch, in a macabre sort of way. The same fluidity I had used to become a bird and a bunch of people was now being used on Ching's body, but not by her. She was effectively dead, I knew, although I couldn't accept that fact emotionally yet. How many deaths *had* I caused in just this operation? Krega had said twenty or thirty minds were destroyed for nothing just getting one "take" in the Merton Process that had put a recording of my mind into Tarin Bul's body.

Ching had always been short, slightly built, like many Medusan women, but now she was—well, changing before my eyes. She did not grow in height but weight was redistributed to the hips and bust, and her whole body was becoming sleekly redesigned. The head was modified far less, although her slightly too large ears were trimmed back and her face was softened and slightly rounded at the mouth and chin. When they were done, I could still recognize Ching on the table, but probably nobody else could have.

Hair was added, but only on the head, and it grew with astonishing, almost comical speed—a light reddish brown in color, which surprised me. I had to admit I was fascinated even though revolted. "Hair color can be changed?"

"And eyes. Actually, anything can be almost anything. That is the beauty of it."

In a few more minutes Ching was physically complete. I could see the shadowy form of the psych punching in and controlling and mixing small recording modules. The last step—the mental buildup. Finally she was detached from the machine and all its connectors and left there in what looked like normal sleep. The lights came up, and I saw her stir.

"Now, you remember her," Fallon said, "and you saw it all. Now observe her as she awakens there."

It didn't take long. The woman I'd known as Ching stirred, smiled, then opened her eyes, smiled wider, sat up, stretched, and looked wonderingly around the psych lab as if she'd never seen it before and had no idea what it was, which was probably the case.

Fallon flipped an intercom switch. "Girl?"

She looked up in happy anticipation. "Yes, mistress?"

"What are you called, girl?"

"I am called Cheer, mistress. Please let me serve you."

"Go through the rear door. There you will find a wardrobe. Pick out whatever clothing you feel is proper for you, use whatever cosmetics and jewelry you like, and brush your hair. Then go through the *next* door and stand and wait there until I come."

"As you command, mistress. I live to serve." And, with that, smile still on her face, she jumped down and walked out of the psych chamber and into the other room.

Fallon turned to me. "Well? What do you think?"

"Very impressive, but if this is to soften me up to spill all or something, it won't work. I'm not *that* impressed."

"You should be. She was, I understand, quite a fighter under the psych probes. We got very little information out of her on her life with or without you. However, she couldn't avoid giving us information and impressions on you, since you were the reason for her resistance. Come. Let's go into the other room."

We walked down the corridor to a rather bare office that didn't seem as if it were being used for much of anything, and waited. All I wanted now was to get this over with and get down to my ultimate fate. All this was leading somewhere, I knew. I wanted to know where.

In short order Ching appeared and then smiled and bowed low. "How do I please you, mistress?"

Fallon looked her over. She was a truly tiny and curvaceous beauty now, that was for sure; her moves were sexy and provocative. Her voice had a throaty tone that seemed at once sensuous and childish. Hell, I'd once been a thirteen-year-old boy myself.

She had chosen some small golden earrings, a matching necklace, and a silvery clinging slit dress, and she had expertly and discreetly applied some lip rouge and eye makeup, and painted her newly created long fingernails to match the lips.

Fallon turned to me with a slight grin. "Well? How does she please you?"

"She looks . . . stunning," I managed.

"Want to see her do tricks?"

"No, I—"

"Cheer—get down on all fours and lick the man's feet."

I started to protest, but "Cheer" joyfully and immediately complied. The exercise was disgusting, somehow unclean, and I stood there only because I had to.

"That's enough, girl. Get back up."

"Yes, mistress." In a moment she was back up and looking expectantly at Fallon.

"Now, go out this door. There you will meet a man dressed like me. He will be your master and will tell you what else to do. Now—go."

"At once, mistress." She was gone.

"Definitely a giveaway," Fallon commented, mostly to herself. "The kind who provides company for visiting dignitaries and the like and does dances on tables." She looked over at me. "Useful to others, though. She's frozen, just like that, for just about her whole life. No external aging, no physical changes that aren't internal adjustments to climate or weather conditions, no attitudinal changes. If she got lost or separated down there, she'd plead with people to return her to her master. She'll give pleasure, and only in serving her master will she find pleasure. Now, isn't that better than the mines or death or a permanent job as a janitor someplace?"

"I'm not convinced," I told her. "I don't think I'll ever be convinced."

"Probably not," Fallon agreed cheerfully, "but it's the way of the world. Come—we have one more interim stop."

Again we walked out into the corridor and went down to yet another office, this one obviously used and cluttered with all sorts of stuff. Fallon rooted through a desk drawer and finally came up with what looked like, and was, an artist's sketch pad. She flipped over a few sheets, and I could see that there were, indeed, drawings in pencil and ink on them. Finally she found the one she wanted, held it up, and handed the pad to me. I looked at the image.

"What do you think?" she asked.

The drawing, a very good drawing by a very skilled artist, was of a stunningly beautiful woman, perhaps the most stunning vision of womanhood I'd ever seen. Rendered in colored pencils, the drawing showed a dark-skinned beauty with long mixed blond and light brown hair, two very large and sexy dark green eyes, set in perhaps the most sensual face I could imagine. The body was large, lean, sexy, and sleek, but the sexual organs were very exaggerated. The artist had drawn multiple views, including one of the figure crouching, animal-like, like some perfect primal savage, wearing some sort of spotted animal skin. It was an incredible vision, a bestial sex machine. Even though it was only a cartoon in colored pencils, I felt the intent in the artist's skilled strokes and could only whistle.

Fallon nodded. "I'm glad you approve. This has been the First Minister's special project for some time, although he's been waiting for just the right time to translate it into reality."

"Ypsir drew these? He's quite talented, no pun intended."

"Yes, he is—in quite a number of ways. And, yes, he drew that, in addition to working with our best artist psych for better than half a year to create the mental and emotional sets. The hormonal is obvious. The primal savage, the perfect and uncorrupted natural woman, he calls her. I wish sometimes I'd been built like that."

"You'd have a terrible backache," I noted.

She shrugged. "She's far more than a mere Goodtime Girl. He calls her Ass, by the way. His strong male libido is as firm as your own, I might note. She'll be his constant companion, his mark of perfection, you might say. He owns many great works of art stolen from the finest museums in the Confederacy, but he intends her as his prize possession. Everyone will drool with envy, but she will be totally and absolutely committed to and devoted to him. A tamed wild animal, you might say, totally passive, yet with the wild streak that will make her all the more exotic, and with a bit of a twist. Like a good devoted tamed thing of the wild, she will do whatever is necessary to protect him. Here is a multipurpose, totally sensuous creature that is also a work of art."

I nodded. I understood Ypsir pretty well after this; he was certainly the most slimy soul I could ever remember coming across. "I see," I said.

"I don't think you do," Fallon responded. "I think you don't fully appreciate the First Minister's sense of justice. Not just anyone would do for Ass, of course. He likes to be reminded constantly that he is in total control, so she is to be a symbol of his superior position, his superior system, and his basic invulnerability to the Confederacy and its schemes. Ass, you see, is not for her ample posterior, but rather, short for assassin."

"No!" I screamed, and tried to lunge at her. The monitor behind just put me out with a single brief and localized shot.

I was strapped to the psych machine, feeling pure fear for the first time in my life. Not anxiety, not concern, but real fear. I did not fear death—never had—but this was something else. I always feared going under a psych for a total wipe; there was always the chance that something of me might yet remain, might *know*, and that was the ultimate horror to me.

Fallon and two techs completed the attachments of my numb body to the "couch," and she stepped back. "This will be most interesting," she said, enjoying my discomfort. "You have not only a unique destiny and vision but Jorgash, the psych back there and our top psych on all Medusa, will be renowned as a brilliant artist and technician for the results."

"Bastards," I tried to snarl, but very little came out.

"You can see the First Minister's point of view," she went on. "Not only will he have his dream, but he will know that his dream was once one of the Confederacy's top assassins, one devoted to killing him at all costs. You will be a constant reminder and reassurance to him of the impotence of the Confederacy here, and, in a real mark of irony, you will be his most devoted slave and bodyguard. He has ordered the entire changing process visually recorded, by the way, so he can if he wishes prove to anyone—including your precious Security—that you were, indeed, their big-shot assassin. Talant Ypsir will be here tomorrow, by the way, on his way to a Four Lords conference called on the satellite of Lilith. I spoke to him just now, and he wants me to set up video recording in a studio room, so he can put you through *all* your paces before he leaves. And you'll get your wish, really. Not only will you reach the Lord of Medusa, you will meet the others as well. He surely won't be able to resist showing you off to them, perhaps even bringing you into the meeting on a gold leash like the pet you'll be."

Damn her! She was enjoying every minute of this!

"Good-bye, Tarin Bul or whatever your name *really* is. I'm sure you realize that all this is going to your control as well, and so do we. Therefore, the first thing to be done is locate that little organic transmitter in you and excise it. But maybe we'll send your control a copy of Talant's recording session. Wouldn't that be true justice?" And, with that, she walked out and the door hissed behind her.

I could not move, literally. All I could do was die a little each second as I heard the master psych turning on various devices.

Suddenly I felt another presence in my head. It was the start of the psych process, of course, but merely the preliminary test of my blocks and defenses, set up by the best psychs in the Confederacy. I could not be broken, nor could they—my mind, however, could be destroyed just like anyone else's, perhaps with a lot more effort. In fact, my immunity to psychs in general was now the root of my greatest fear. What if they didn't get it

690 THE FOUR LORDS OF THE DIAMOND

all? What if there was one tiny corner that was still me, unable to act or do anything, yet *there* . . . ?

I heard a recording cube slip into place in the dark. It begins, I thought, and steeled myself.

But it wasn't the beginning. Instead a thin, reedy man's voice began feeding directly into my brain. "Listen, agent," he said, "I am Jorgash, the psych in this project. Like all other Medusan psychs, I was trained at an institute on Cerberus, the only such institute for psychs in the Diamond. It is run by a master. Neither he nor we have any taste for the Four Lords, for Talant Ypsir, for this incredible alien alliance that might well destroy us all, or for the rest of it. We did not train to be torturers, but healers. Long ago we established our control over many of the top-level bureaucrats of Medusa, since Ypsir insists they all undergo psych loyalty reinforcement to him. We gained control of Laroo on Cerberus in that way, with the help of your comrade there. But that is out for Ypsir himself he won't come near a psych machine. Since he was once in an accident with Fallon and Kunser and at their mercy—and they saved him—those are the only two others he trusts implicitly. They won't undergo psych, either, for any reason.

"It would be relatively simple to kill Ypsir, but that would do no good. Unless Ypsir, Fallon, and Kunser are all killed—and in a relatively short time—the elimination of one will simply elevate another. Fallon, in particular, is adept enough at the couch to create others outside our influence, as could Kunser. They make it their business to know. They do not trust *any* psych, but neither do they suspect that almost all of us are involved. But before any can move toward an effective takeover of the entire system, we will need all three dead close together. Accomplishing this will be difficult —may be impossible. The three are rarely together, with Fallon and Kunser meeting only twice over the past three years and only once with Ypsir present. I say this so as not to encourage you unduly."

I felt some hope rise in spite of myself. Was this just a trick of a master psych or was this for real? I had no way of knowing.

"I cannot save you," Jorgash continued. "I could not save your friends. But their minds didn't have your strength or your core identity, built up and reinforced by master psychs. If I did not execute this program almost exactly as Ypsir tailored it, if any of the original you remained even on the subconscious level, it would show. It would show physically; you couldn't help it, and that is exactly what a cautious Ypsir will be looking for. What I propose to do I frankly admit I have never done before, and understand only in theory. If my master teacher were here he could do it easily; he created the process long ago, for other purposes and for other times.

"What I propose to do is to push whatever of your core identity I can into a specific recess so remote from consciousness that it might as well not be there. It won't be measurable in any way, and, in addition, all communication between the matrixed area and the rest of your brain will be cut. It is a delicate operation—the difference between obliterating this core and storing it thus is a measurement best expressed as a forty-place decimal point. Even I won't know if I hit it right or not, nor exactly what was saved—if anything. But what I am trying to save is your total hatred and contempt for the Medusan system and particularly for those people who would do this sort of thing to human beings. If your hatred is strong enough, if your thirst for revenge is strong enough, it *might* just survive, although so buried, and cut off that even you will not know it is there. In theory, if this part of you remains, a single stimulus could be used to trigger it, reconnect it to your psyche. The stimulus I will give you and reinforce is a situation in which *all three* principals are in your presence simultaneously. If I succeed, your blind hatred will rush out and you will then kill all three or die in the attempt.

"Now, this is a long shot. One of the three may die, in which case you may find yourself in the presence of the other two and not have your rage triggered. Or all three might never be together in your presence, in which case, again, it will not trigger. But all three *have* been together and may well be again, particularly under war conditions. It may be a week, a month, a year, ten years. We can't know. But we can hope, and that is the chance I must take."

A chance *he* must take!

"What you will be after you kill them, assuming you do and survive, I cannot say. Most likely the action will bring about a total release, after which you will again and always be what Ypsir has made you. You might become a wild beast. But you might have rational potential, depending on how much of you survives. Regardless, so thorough will the physical transformation and freeze be that you will physically, hormonally, and emotionally become what I intend to make of you. That I promise, although it is no comfort. Under a really good psych you might be restored intellectually, although, of course, as a new and different person with no past memories. I can do no less and still convince Ypsir and his test battery. Again, this may all fail—even my teacher succeeded only with fewer than ten percent of his subjects—but I *can* offer you, and your control, the hope that that beautiful creature by Ypsir's side is in fact a ticking bomb that if triggered, could create such a power vacuum on Medusa that those under our control would assume power. I must proceed now, and I am sorry, but I hope this is some comfort. I have already spotted the absolutely ingenious organic transmitter in your brain, so I know your control has this information, too. Now only he and I will know. Time is short and the process long and arduous. Forgive me, Bul, or whatever your name is. Good-bye."

Searing pain inside my head . . . Feel like I'm going to implode . . . Oh, God! I—

TRANSMISSION TERMINATED. TRANSMITTER DESTROYED.

He came out of it slowly, and shivered a bit as he lifted the probes from his head.

"That was most unpleasant," the computer said.

He chuckled. "Well, God bless Dumonia, bless his devious hide. We might get something yet."

"You seem remarkably fit for one who just underwent a wrenching defeat, faced his worst fear, and stared at mental savagery. Better, in fact, than you came out of the last three. I fear for your sanity."

"You needn't," he assured the computer. "It doesn't matter, anyway. I have to argue with you, though, on the failure. We've finally met our aliens, gotten their names, and confirmed some of my wildest and least certain deductions."

"Then you have solved the enigma?"

"I *think* so. Morah's comments still worry me. I still have that gaping feeling, not that I'm wrong, but that I've missed something. That was confirmed by Ypsir's own attitudes just now."

"But we never saw Ypsir."

"We didn't have to. But he's a slick old greasy bastard, an old Confederacy politician, remember, and here he was about to make a recording that he intended to flaunt to the Confederacy. That's confidence. You don't flaunt something like that if you expect to get into a losing war soon. Yet he knows the relative strength and power of the Confederacy military. He is depraved, vicious, and almost inhuman, but he's not stupid. Even with two of the Four Lords gone and the scheme blown wide open—they knew about us, note—he still expects to win. Why? Unless our fundamental assumption about these aliens, these Altavar, are wrong."

"You think there will be a war, then?"

"I'm almost positive. Actually, it's pretty odd, but the best chance of avoiding war was the man who doesn't fit, Marek Kreegan. I wish now he had lived instead of this slime ball Ypsir."

"I do not understand. He was a traitor."

"He remains the one who doesn't fit. Look at the Four Lords. One is a classic gangster, a master hoodlum, and the other two were former politicians so corrupt they crawled. And then there's Kreegan. What the hell was he really doing there? And how did he come to be accepted as an equal Lord by the other three? Remember, we just learned that the other Lords actually deposed Ypsir's predecessor because they found him too much the reformer and not really corrupt enough to share in the running of their criminal empire. Everybody keeps going back to Kreegan, too—the only man who wasn't shown corrupt, and who they all seemed to depend upon even though they had no reason to. Not only did he not come from the criminal class—he was self-exiled, remember—but Lilith has the least to offer the hidden war. Yet there he is, at the forefront, the leader."

"He did not seem admirable to me."

He chuckled. "Maybe not, but he sure reminded me of me, and vice versa. I look at Kreegan and I see a man on a mission, a very long and complex mission, not a corrupt criminal."

"There is no record he was on a mission."

"Not for us. Well, maybe for us—but not officially. I think Kreegan, somewhere, on some other mission, stumbled on the aliens. I don't know how, and I doubt if we ever will, but he found out what was going on years before we knew. Decades, perhaps, since there's some evidence those aliens have been here all along."

"Would it not have been more effective to report this information?" the computer asked.

"Report it? With what? He probably had no physical evidence. The Confederacy only believed it when they couldn't avoid the truth, and even now they tread softly and slowly through the Warden Diamond rather than hitting hard and fast when the evidence that this is the heart of the conspiracy is right at hand. They would have declared Kreegan insane and destroyed him or sent him to the Diamond anyway. And so he played his role to the hilt, worked hard for twenty years—*twenty years!*—and finally became Lord of Lilith so he could take control of events. I think we killed the greatest Confederacy agent in human history before his plans came out."

"You think he was setting the aliens up for the kill, then?"

"Oh, no. If anything, I think he was totally committed to his covert war against the Confederacy, using those damned robots. He preferred a weakened, shaky, off-balance Confederacy to an actual war. That's just what he was trying to do, in fact. I'd bet on it. And that fits in with Ypsir and Morah. I think these Altavar are stronger than we dreamed. I think Kreegan assessed them as the probable victors in an all-out war, with huge masses of humanity killed. Sure! It fits! He had to choose between a covert war that would dismember the Confederacy or an all-out interstellar conflict he felt we could not win."

"Are you going to include that in your report?"

"No. They wouldn't believe it, anyway, and if they did they wouldn't understand. It makes no difference in any event, except that explanation lays to rest a few of my remaining questions. He's gone, and only Morah, who is good but really hasn't the skills of a Kreegan, is holding things off right now. Somewhere along the line, Morah and Kreegan met, and Morah, the brilliant master criminal, developed a Kreegan-style sense of what had to be done. He came around to Kreegan's point of view. He is doing what he can, but he knows he isn't up to the job. Damn!" He sat deep in thought for a moment. Finally he said, "Call Morah. Tell him to keep that meeting in session, that I'll get back to him as soon as I have consulted with my superiors."

"That is easily done. Has it occurred to you that they all are together in a highly vulnerable and exposed space station around Lilith at this time? Just one well-placed shot . . ."

"And then we would have to deal blind with the Altavar, and I'm not even sure we *can*. Besides, with what will you shoot them down?"

"This picket ship has more than enough armament for such a simple task."

He chuckled. "So man can triumph over computer after all. How the hell do you suppose Altavar have gotten in and out of system, not to mention those robots? Where would be the first place you'd try out and test those robots to see if they really could fool everybody?"

"Oh. You mean that this ship is under their control and in their hands. That is a most unpleasant thought."

"Bet on it. If you need any further confirmation, just remember that I sat down in a comm chair up there, punched in Morah's name and planet, and got a connection in seconds. No hunting around, no guesswork. The comm people knew who he was and exactly where he was at that point."

"I could detonate this module, at least protecting our information."

"I certainly hope not. Right now I'm the only one from the Confederacy that Morah or any of the others will trust at all. They know me, in one form or another. I'm right there with them. I'm Cal Tremon, Park Lacoch, and Qwin Zhang, but uncontaminated by Wardens. I'm the only man they're going to believe, because I'm the only one they have expert evaluation of." He laughed. "I don't think you're going to get to kill me anyway, old friend."

"It is not my intention to do so unless the mission is compromised."

"Maybe, maybe you just don't know it. But it's irrelevant." He got up from the chair and moved back to the desk area, pulling down a pen and a pad of paper. He always used pen and paper for his notes rather than a terminal. You never knew who or what was listening in on a terminal, but if you ate your notes you knew exactly where they were and in what form. Old habits were hard to break now.

He was at it for some time, until, finally, slips of paper, cards, and scribbled notations were scattered all over the place. Finally he picked them up, looking them over, put them in an odd pile, smiled, then nodded. He reached up and pulled down the special comcode set.

"Open Security Channel R," he instructed the computer. "Tightbeam, scramble, top security code. Let's let them in on the fun."

It took several minutes to establish communications through the various secret links over such vast distances, but because these signals traveled in the same oblique interdimensional way as the spaceships, communication was virtually instantaneous at this high-priority level. Once the phone was answered at the other end, that is, and all the information was matched to decode what was going in.

"Go ahead, Warden Control," came a very slightly distorted voice from the speaker. "This is Papa speaking."

"Hello, Krega! You sound tired."

"I was sound asleep when your call came in, and I'm taking a couple of pills now to wake up. I assume this is some other special request you want —like the Cerberan thing?"

"No. This is my report. I have the strong feeling that something important is still missing, but I have no way of finding out what it is. Instead, I have assembled everything that I do know and all that my deductions lead to. I think I have enough information to allow us to act and I think time might be of the essence now. There is a war council going on in the Diamond right now, and I think our time's about run out."

"All hell's breaking loose throughout the civilized worlds," Commander Krega told him. "That sleep you got me out of was the first I'd tried in four days. It's chaos! Supply ships routed wrongly, causing factories on a dozen worlds to shut down for lack of raw material, causing dozens more to have to ration food and other vital materials because the ships didn't arrive. Even some naval units have opened fire on one another! The number of those damned robots—and the scale of the operation—is massive, Control! Massive! There must be thousands of them, all at different, usually routine posts along the lines of communications, shipping, you name it. Our Confederacy holds together by total interdependence. You know that."

He nodded and couldn't suppress a slight smile. So Morah had put Kreegan's war into operation unilaterally, as well as mobilizing the vast political and criminal organizations the Four Lords controlled. "How are you holding out?" he asked, almost hoping for a really bad answer.

"We're coping—but barely!" Krega told him. "We were prepared for this kind of thing, considering what we already knew, but the scale is beyond anything we imagined—and it's devilishly clever. The people they took over are very minor, routine links in complex chains, but they're at just the right point to make a minor mistake on a shipping order, or routing order, or even battle order. And so damn minor the mistakes are hell to track down. They didn't go for the admiral, instead they went for a minor clerk who types up or sends out the admiral's orders. We can hold now, but there are already food riots in many places and I doubt if we can stopgap this for long. You're right about the time business. If you can't give us an out, we've got no choice but to take out the whole Warden Diamond—now."

"I'm not sure you can, Papa," he said bluntly. "We missed it on these aliens. Evidence shows they're every bit as strong or even stronger than we are. Hold on to your hat. You aren't gonna believe all this."

"Well, get going, then. But I'm not sure I go along with that military-strength idea. Logic argues against it."

He smiled wanly. Why are aliens evil to a psychotic murderer? That question bothered the Charonese, who didn't answer it. He could.

Evil is when a race casually contemplates genocide against another not because another race is a threat but because it is inconvenient.

He was about to begin his report when something occurred to him. "Papa? Tell me one thing I don't know. Our other prime operative down there, this Dr. Dumonia. Who the hell *is* he, really?"

"Him? Former Chief, Psychiatric Section, Confederacy Criminal Division. Not under that name, of course. He devised a lot of the techniques we still use on agents like you."

"And he retired to *Cerberus?*"

"Why not? He's in a volatile profession, Control. All a psych ever sees are really sick minds. They finally just get fed up and can't do it any more, or they crack themselves. He was a little of both. Well, we couldn't kill him, after his invaluable services, and we couldn't use a psych machine on *him*—he's so good with one of those things he's invulnerable to them. So we gave him a complete cover identity and he picked Cerberus, where he could establish a mild private practice and work when he felt like it on either criminal or normal people with problems. He's pretty sour and disillusioned about the Confederacy, but he's not fond of the Four Lords, either. This alien thing really got to him, so he came out of retirement and set up an organization for us."

"I'm glad he stayed on *our* side."

Krega laughed now. "He'd better. He's got a few little organic devices similar to that transmitter we used with your people inside him, including a couple of a new design that he doesn't know about. If he ever became a threat a remote signal from a flyby would splatter him from Cerberus halfway to the Confederacy."

There was no real answer to that. After a moment of dead air, Control reshuffled his notes. "Ready to report."

"Standing by to record. On my mark . . . Go!"

2

A great deal of the information in this report is deduction, not direct observation. However, I must point out firmly that every deduction made here is not only logical in the context of the Diamond and our known situation, each and every deduction holds true for all four worlds. I feel that the information presented as fact herein is true and correct and borne out by remote personal observation. Let's begin by addressing the broad points of the extraordinarily complex and subtle puzzle that is the Warden Diamond itself.

Point 1: No matter what, it is obvious that the four Diamond worlds are not natural. Each of the four worlds was certainly within the known "life zone" before being transformed into its present state, but mere location in the life zone is not sufficient to guarantee any conditions remotely survivable. This obvious terraforming process of all four would have been easily confirmed had normal scientific thoroughness been applied to the Diamond worlds, but since the appearance of the Warden organism, with its bizarre effects and by-products, such an examination was not possible in the early years and would be subverted by the locals at the present stage of development. Still, from sheer deduction it is obvious that the worlds were extensively terraformed, and I will offer but a few of the abounding examples to prove my point. For example, there is no evidence that any of the planets are the products of natural evolution. While there are different examples of the dominant life form on each world, there are no clear primal orders—each class of plant and animal is unique and in place.

Despite the fact that any naturally evolving life on the four worlds would have to have a common origin—the plants, for example, are too close to one another and to ones familiar to us—the dominant type of animal life on each is without serious competition and without any sign that the other three forms existed except in minor phyla. Thus, the cold-blooded reptile dominates on the warmest planet, the insect is virtually alone on the lushest, as is the water-breather on the world that is mostly sea, and the large mammal on the coldest planet is the dominant form on both land and sea. In other words, despite a certain common origin, four different kinds of life dominate four different worlds with the other forms either eliminated or reduced to minor and static roles. Frankly, the whole thing smells more like some sort of experiment than any chance occurrence—which form is best for what, perhaps. To accept current biology on all four worlds is beyond my credulity range.

Point 2: All of the flora and fauna on all four worlds logically match with our carbon-based life system, and all are integrated in biologically expected and balanced ways, except for the omnipresent Warden organism, which is unique unto itself. Here is a totally different kind of life that has no microbial relatives yet is static enough that its properties and behavior on each world is uniform and predictable. Such an organism might be expected to mutate with lightning speed—after all, this is the common theory applied to the three worlds other than Lilith, that *we* spread the organism and it instantly mutated to meet the differing conditions. So I am asked to accept an organism that mutates instantly and perfectly to other planets, yet shows not the slightest sign of mutation or deviation on any of the four themselves. I find this biologically inconceivable. Therefore, I am forced to the conclusion that the Warden organism is an artificially created form of life superimposed on all four worlds by a common intelligence.

The Warden organism is far too simple a creature to do more than cause an illness or two, yet it is integral to all four worlds and symbiotically matched to them. On Lilith the Warden organism obviously serves as a sort of planetary manager, keeping the ecosystem stable and static; this is what led to the prevailing view of a single source. I submit that evidence exists in ample amounts that the organism is equally the planetary manager of the other three worlds, and that a little hard research will show this to be so. We drew our original conclusions about the Warden organism because of its widely variable effects on humans and human perception and ability. But the Warden organism was not created and does not exist with humans in mind at all—it is there to keep the ecosystems of the four worlds within certain stable tolerances—in effect, to eliminate as many variables as possible.

Charon and Medusa further demonstrate that the Warden organism, while chemically rather simple, has the ability to act collectively and to draw upon a vast amount of complex knowledge. This is less obvious on Cerberus and Lilith, but I can cite examples there as well, and I need only note how fast it is able to regenerate damaged and lost tissue in humans on all four worlds. But how is it able to draw upon and use such knowledge?

At first I was drawn to the hypothesis of a collective intelligence for the organism—that is, each colony represented a cell or collection of cells in communication with other colonies, or cells, making up a single and physically discorporeal entity. I find no evidence to support this supposition, though, and much to support the conclusion that this is not true. People of Charon travel to Medusa, and vice versa, with no ill effects, although, surely, the distance between planets would be more than enough to sever their Wardens from any such planetary consciousness. On Lilith, for example, people can directly perceive the lines of communication between Warden colonies, yet they can perceive nothing of this while on other Warden worlds. Nor, in fact, could I conceive of such organisms even collectively storing and analyzing so many quadrillion-plus data bits just to do some fairly complex regenerations.

But when I thought of the Wardens not in terms of cells but rather in terms of neural transmitters and receivers, the system made far more sense. Consider the nerve endings in your index finger. They serve only one function really—they transmit information to the brain. Burn them and the irritation reaches the brain, and the brain then transmits back through the same network corrective measures to repair the burn. Warden colonies, then, are the neural transmitters and receivers of information, remote sensors to a central brain source. Such a brain must in fact be a tremendously versatile computer of near infinite capacity. This theory then fits in with everything else.

Everything all four worlds say about the Warden organisms on each also belies an external power source, as has been hypothesized as the reason for the so-called "Warden Limit" after which the Wardens run amok and destroy their hosts. The Wardens have been shown to be able to draw whatever they needed from the host for normal operation. On those rare occasions when more was demanded of them than the host could provide, they have shown a limited ability to make energy-to-matter and matter-to-energy conversions, although they are clearly not specifically designed to do so and, when demanded, this causes pain, discomfort, or danger to the host. Such an organism, unless far too much was demanded of it, would hardly self-destruct for the reasons supposed.

However, when you realize that the Warden organism is, in fact, too simple an organism to do *anything* for itself, being merely a transmitter and receiver, what the limit implies is the limit of its ability to transmit and receive information from its computer.

It is equally obvious that four different frequencies, perhaps four entirely separate transmitters, are in operation. This is why a Cerberan, for example, appears "Warden-dead" to a Charonese, who sees the Warden network in everything and everyone on his own world. But where are the brain's transmitters and receivers—the Wardens' base station, as it were? I suspect that there is a central computer outside the Diamond zone itself, perhaps on or beyond Momrath, although that gas giant with its rings and thousands of moons would be the most logical and logically placed location. This would transmit, in turn, to central areas, or subcomputers, on each of the four worlds, which would in turn directly govern those worlds. The two-tiered system would be extravagant, but it is one way of explaining why there is a fixed quarter of a light-year distance for travel from all four Diamond worlds, yet Cerberans can travel to Charon, for example, cut from their own planetary net but not from the central computer.

On Medusa there is a "sacred mountain," and, remaining there overnight, one is subjected to nightmarish alien dreams and sensations only to awaken the next day with a far greater control of the Wardens in his own body. This mountain, I am convinced, is over the central processor for Medusa's Wardens. Medusans are already plugged into their Warden network, but here, so close to maximum signal, their Wardens are far more excited than elsewhere. The experience is somewhat akin to, I believe, what communications scientists call "front-end overload," in which a signal too powerful for the electronics of a transceiver will produce a blasting but unintelligible signal. However, the human brain, which has some control over its Wardens, reacts to this overload much as protective circuits would in electronics—it recoils and damps the overload down. The tremendously high level of excitation the overload produced in the Wardens, however, makes the host far more aware of them and their energy flow.

I am convinced that such points exist on the other three planets. I note, for example, that on all four worlds there are curiously similar religions based on planet worship, of a god who resides inside the world and is the source of all power for that world. If we were able to transport the entirety of Lilith's population to its central processing facility, I am convinced that everyone would share the powers now limited to a few. The few who do, in fact, are mostly transportees to the planet who are likely to be more conscious of the energy flow than those born with it in place. I shudder to think, however, of what such an overload would do to a Cerberan— madness, perhaps, or constant, uncontrollable body-changing, or perhaps the merging of minds into a single mass entity.

Point 3: We are faced, then, with an incredibly advanced civilization technologically, far beyond anything we can imagine, a civilization that can terraform four worlds, and stabilize and maintain them with a single clever device (the Wardens), yet does not apparently use them for anything. Although these aliens, who are apparently called the Altavar, maintain a token force near the Medusan processing center, and probably near the others as well, I do not believe they inhabit any of the four worlds in any numbers. One of my counterparts theorized them as air-breathing water mammals, but I find it difficult to see how such a civilization could have developed such a high degree of technological advancement if limited to water. Indeed, the few Altavar that I saw, via my remote, appeared equally at home in air and sea, and probably would also be on land. These, of course, were bred to the conditions in which they had to live and work, and are most certainly not representative of the Altavar masses in form of capabilities. Perhaps they are a token force, not guards or soldiers but on-site mechanics or engineers for the processor who simply relieve their boredom with random attacks on any who venture close.

Now, since they went to all this trouble but do not at this time inhabit the four worlds in the broad understanding of that term, it remains to be determined why the project was undertaken at all. Certainly it has all the earmarks of a carefully established scientific experiment, but if this is so, they made no attempt to remove an inconstant variable when introduced—humans—even though they could have easily done so, and in a manner convincing enough that we wouldn't have bothered with further settlement.

Since they do not use the worlds now, they either had use of them in the past, in which case they couldn't care less about humans being there now, or they have a use for them in the *future*, in which case they would care a great deal about our being there. Since they obviously do not care about present use, but are still very much around and involved in an action against the Confederacy, their use of the Diamond is obviously in the future.

It bothered me from the start that the aliens, who allegedly could not take our form or infiltrate directly, could still immediately know all about our civilization and go just to the Four Lords, the only people likely to be on their side against us. Obviously, therefore, they came specifically to the Diamond, or were called there by the small permanent party when we landed on the places, and *then* discovered us. So we have a small cadre of aliens in place when we suddenly show up, which greatly surprised them. One can imagine the problem the small base parties faced. It would take some time to report our arrival and have experts from wherever good little Altavar come from get here. Meanwhile, of course, the Warden organism was invading and trying to cope with this new element and threatening to destroy or transform the first exploiter teams. If I were in charge of such a base, I would play for time, and the best way to play for time would be to do what I could—and fast—to hold a representative segment of this new race for study while discouraging further approach and settlement. They did this by simply adding human beings to the program of their central computer, making the Warden, in effect, an alien disease that had terrible effects not only on "alien" life forms but also on "alien" machinery. It was a clever and resourceful ploy, and we fell for it hook, line, and sinker.

The Altavar, obviously, were pleased with the arrangement and pleased that it had so obviously worked, and felt no need to go further at this time. I suspect, though, that they were as surprised as we were at the odd and peculiar by-products the Wardens produced in human beings. I don't think that those by-products, those bizarre powers, were programmed in, for their best interest would be in leaving us trapped but still ourselves, both for study and for control. It's simply possible that the bicelectrical system that powers the human body operates within the same sort of range as the Warden transmitters, or fairly close. This would explain why some people have more powers than others, and some have little or none, on three of the worlds, anyway. You might say both our brains and nervous systems and their quasi-organic machines work on the same wavelengths.

A side thought is somewhat illuminating and a little disturbing. In effect, the Warden invasion of human bodies made the humans on the Diamond creatures of the master computer just as the plants and animals and probably anything and everything else are. Everything from simple biology and biophysics all the way to the content of those human minds was sent to that computer. This information would give them all they needed in the way of human nature, human politics, human beliefs, and human history as well. This is how they learned so much about us without having to pay us a visit.

This means, too, that they knew about our agents as soon as they were "assimilated" into the Warden computer system. Knew about our entire plot, in fact. So either they never made use of this information, which is possible, or they really find the Four Lords and their operation irrelevant to them. They certainly did nothing to tell the Four Lords of our plans, nor to inform them of any of our operations. They did nothing to warn or save Kreegan or Matuze, and they did nothing to warn Laroo or to keep him from coming under our control and influence. In point of fact, they must have known about Laroo's treachery to them, but made no effort even to block the information on their damned robots from coming to us for analysis. They supply the robot masters to Cerberus, yet don't really care if we know about it or even find a way to subvert the process. I find all this enlightening, and disturbing. It implies that they feel they have sufficient defenses to be invulnerable to attack on *their* interests—as opposed to those of the Four Lords and the people of the Diamond—and also that this entire sabotage war and its robot campaign are not something initiated by them but entirely conceived of and run by the Four Lords.

But if they can defend easily, why allow this odd and diabolically clever campaign against us in the first place, one that would almost certainly attract attention to themselves when it was put into operation or prematurely revealed, as happened?

The only possible answer is that several years ago the Altavar decided that they had at this time to make use of the Warden Diamond, and that we would get in the way. They decided, I believe, to attack the Confederacy in an all-out and brutal campaign of genocide but were talked out of it, or at least convinced to defer it, by Marek Kreegan. The evidence for this is all over my alter-ego experiences and can be examined at leisure, but that evidence is inescapable. Kreegan, then, is a rather odd sort of hero. Fearing racial extermination and wholesale destruction of planetary populations in a defensive war against a foe technologically superior to us and unknown to us in the ways that count—including the location of their worlds and fleet—he sold them on a different sort of campaign, one that would strike at the very heart of the political and economic union of the worlds of the Confederacy, causing us to turn inward, to be unable to retain our unity, which is our only strength. It would cost countless lives, of course, and push much of humanity back into harsh barbarism, but we would survive. The other Lords bought the plan for revenge, and because it held out the promise of escape, to leave the Warden Diamond and be the ones to pick up the shattered pieces of the Confederacy. The Altavar bought it simply because it accomplished the same purpose as all-out war but much more cheaply. It is also clear that they didn't have much faith in the plan's success, but were willing to give the Four Lords just enough time and material support to try it just in case.

Point 4: The aliens have decided we must be taken out, yet they have perfect confidence that they can lick us in any such war. Why, then, are we a threat to them at all? We don't know where to hit them back, nor do we know enough about them to pose anything like the threat to their civilization that they are to ours. Therefore, we *can* interfere in some way that will cause them real trouble. As of now, the only point at which our two civilizations intersect is the Diamond. Obviously, they fear we can destroy it, or badly louse it up, and this must be of central importance to them. Saving the Diamond is their one priority here, the reason they were willing to buy Kreegan's plot at all. So what *is* the Warden Diamond to them that they want it so badly? To go to these lengths it must be something of great racial importance to them, a matter of life and death.

The Altavar can breathe the same air we do. They are almost certainly made up of carbon chains in a way that will be unusual, but still very understandable to our biologists. Therefore, it's fairly easy to find their same racial least common denominators—they must be the same as ours. These three LCDs are food, shelter, and reproduction.

I think we can dismiss food out of hand. The amount of protein and other food products that these four worlds could produce is insignificant in the light of an interstellar civilization's needs. Besides, if they can work energy-to-matter conversions, they'll never starve.

Shelter is an obvious possibility. These four worlds were deliberately terraformed and stabilized, so they obviously were intended to be settled. But a population that could be settled on four normal-sized planets is pretty small and hardly worth interstellar war to protect. Considering the number of terraformable planets humanity has found just in its galactic quadrant, total war over the colonization rights to four worlds we couldn't use anyway because of the Warden organism just doesn't make any sort of logical sense.

That leaves reproduction. Defense of their young would make the behavior and attitudes they've exhibited so far totally comprehensible. Assuming their total alienness—evidence indicates that their thinking would be very strange to us, as you might expect—we might extend that to their biology as well. There is no reason to believe that their reproductive method is anything like our own. If we accept the Diamond as a breeding center, though, we must assume they reproduce very seldom or very, very slowly. If so, they are almost certainly extremely long-lived, and, by inference, this would indicate that the number of their eggs, or whatever, is enormous to require four worlds. The Warden organism, then, might be a protective device, keeping conditions for the eggs optimal while also defending them against basic threats. Its defensive capabilities may be very great, and the eggs must be deep inside the planets themselves. I suspect that the fact that there is geothermal activity only on the frigid world of Medusa is evidence that only there is some sort of temperature regulation necessary. They need it warm.

Point 5: Assuming this reproductive function, a number of very interesting possibilities arise. While protecting their young is the *only* solution that logic admits, then the Diamond worlds are there not only as needed protection for the eggs but also to serve as carefully controlled biomes for the young to settle. It's a fascinating concept—colonizing worlds by first terraforming them, then planting the eggs which, when they hatch, will become the perfectly adapted indigenous population of those worlds, complete with the Warden computer links to teach them all they need to know. I admit, however, to be missing a key element here, since all this implies that space travel and terraforming and computers are essential to their reproduction. It is patently absurd to think of such a race, since how did it get born or evolve in the first place?

Of course, if we just accept the idea that their civilization is far older than ours, this problem partly resolves itself. After all, human beings now reproduce in technologically perfect genetic engineering laboratories throughout the civilized worlds. A race just coming upon the civilized worlds and ignorant of our history and of observing the "natural" way on a frontier world or the Diamond might well have the same puzzle the Altavar present to me here. They would wonder how we ever reproduced before we had the technology the bioengineering labs implies. Much the same must be at work here. This is not how they evolved or how nature intended them to breed, but it is the way they choose to do it now—

because, for them, it's better, easier, more efficient, or whatever. Take your choice.

Summary: The aliens created the Diamond worlds as incubators and new homes for their young. They are slow-breeding and long-lived, and thus this must represent a whole new generation for a large mass of Altavar. They can not retreat or back down without abandoning their young, and while I doubt that the Diamond is the *only* breeding ground for them, it is of sufficiently large size and scope that anything interfering with the hatching and development of the young would be tantamount to genocide in their minds.

When humans showed up, the aliens used their mechanism—the Warden organism—and their planetary computers to understand, evaluate, and assess our entire civilization. As long as the hatching, or whatever it is, was sufficiently far off, they had plenty of time in which to do so. But we obliged them by sending our greatest criminal minds and political and social deviants to the Diamond, and their attitudes shaped the human societies that grew on all four worlds. As a result, their picture of us is rather negatively slanted, to say the least. The hatch time approached—although it may still be a decade or even longer away—and they had to decide what to do. Whether for science, or study, or just out of scientific mercy, they contacted the Four Lords with a view to saving the Diamond population. But it was then also communicated to the Lords that the rest of humanity was simply too great a threat and would have to be wiped out.

Kreegan, upon becoming Lord of Lilith, came up with and proposed his own scheme to the Altavar, who were willing to let him try it but neither expected it to work nor concerned themselves with the fates of the Four Lords. But because the Four Lords made a mistake, the Altavar now feel backed against a wall. To their minds, delaying much longer will risk genocide of *their* young, and if it's them or us, they'll naturally choose us. They know our military strengths and weaknesses, our weaponry, our military mind, and everything else an enemy dreams of knowing. Apparently none of that worries them. They are confident that they can crush us, and I believe they will attempt to do so by preemptive strike, after the Four Lords campaign has wreaked as much damage and disruption as it can. I think we are no more than weeks, and perhaps only days, away from a total war that may result in the near elimination of human—or perhaps both—civilizations.

Conclusions and Recommendations: I think they not only can beat us, but I suspect they have fought at least one such war before. They are too supremely confident. However, we as a race would survive. We are too numerous and located on too many worlds over too much space to be wiped out totally. Pushed back into barbarism, the collapse of interstellar civilization and the death of at least a third of humanity would be the least I would expect in such a conflict, but we would survive. Our only recourse would be that we could, obviously, destroy the Diamond with a concerted, possibly suicidal all-out revenge attack—the thing they fear most, and so do I. Such an attack would enrage them and rob them of their next generation; it would be our last blow, but much of their force would remain intact.

I may be totally wrong, and they may think in so alien a manner that they will not react in a way I can predict, but I feel I must point out how *we* would react under such circumstances and urge that we act as if they're more like us emotionally than unlike us. If the situation were reversed: if humans beat the hell out of the Altavar but, in the process, the Altavar managed to destroy every human being's ability to create children by any means, thereby ending the race in slow agony, *we* would then seek out Altavar wherever they were, in their ships, on their worlds, and once they were beaten and defenseless, we would then systematically wipe them out to the last one. In other words, destroying the Diamond might well result in total human genocide.

Obviously I'm telling you that we can not win in this situation. If you refuse to face that fact, refuse to accept my report and its conclusions, then I believe both races could die. The impossible, the unthinkable, *will* happen. When man first went into space and colonized other worlds, a great pressure was lifted from the collective psyche. The human race would not be totally destroyed by itself in war, at least not easily. And when, finally, we grew so large and so expansive and merged into the single system that the Confederacy represents, we thought we had put any possibility of racial destruction behind us. People could die, even whole suns could explode and take their worlds and populations with them, but humanity would survive.

If this chain is now started, it will be impossible to stop. We have finally come face to face with the horror once again, and we have only ugly choices.

The Four Lords are now meeting in Council and are waiting for my call. The only hope we have is to do everything right, and, therefore, it is essential that you follow all of my recommendations immediately and without fail.

(1) No matter how this sabotage campaign is going, it is essential that only reports of complete disarray and disaster reach this picket ship, which is totally infiltrated with the robots. At all times from this point the Four Lords and the Altavar must be convinced that Kreegan's war is *winning*, that his plan is working perfectly. If the Altavar receive the slightest hint that it is not, they will probably launch a massive preemptive strike on us.

(2) Negotiations must be opened immediately. I will be the go-between, because, having three surviving alter egos down there, I will be one they will trust. However, we must be linked directly to the Confederacy Inner Council, who must all be on call to appear on visual transmission. It must be clear that they are dealing with someone—me—who speaks for the Council and that I have the force sufficient to make my agreements binding on the Confederacy.

(3) As much of the fleet as can be depended upon not to be needed

for emergency actions against the current war campaign must be rushed to the Diamond on full alert. Only with the threat of immediate destruction of the Diamond will we have any leverage at all. Put your best military minds in that fleet and get it here—fast, and on full war alert. You can expect ship-to-ship attack if negotiations fail or if they decide to test us.

(4) No matter what you think of the Four Lords and their organizations, they are not stupid and they will not be lulled into any false agreements. They know that their own worlds are on the line, which will keep them honest, but as agents of the Altavar they also know our real position, which isn't great. They have also, obviously, been promised safe evacuation in the event of an attack by us, so they are only concerned about their populations, not their own hides. I must warn the Council that the demands the Altavar will make will be stiff and severe. We must negotiate and be prepared to give up a great deal, perhaps much that we hold dear. But we must find a solution that will result in the Altavar feeling safe and secure—and we must mean it and guarantee it with our actions, not just words. They know us too well to accept our promises or a treaty.

This is Warden Control, awaiting your decision and instructions.

3

"Well? What do you think?"

"It is the only logical solution given the data," the computer replied.

"You should have been a computer."

"High praise. Well, they got it now. How do you think they'll take it?"

"They will refuse to accept your conclusions, of course, but they will play along with you and the Four Lords for now. Did you expect anything else?"

He shrugged. "I don't know. I doubt it. Given what you know, can you compute the current probabilities of all-out war?"

"Too many variables. But I would say you have a ten-percent chance of pulling something out of this."

He sighed. "Ten percent. I guess that'll have to do. Wake me when they call back." He paused a moment. "Well, it doesn't look like *you* will be ordered to kill me, anyway."

The computer did not reply.

It took them almost five hours to reach some kind of consensus, which, considering the complexity of the Confederacy and its bureaucracy, was almost miraculous time.

"We can arrange for a complete visual hookup," Krega told him, "but we'll have to do an open broadcast. I suppose that doesn't matter, since they *should* be able to see and hear your communication with Base."

He nodded. "They will insist on a remote location. I will try and stall to give the fleet as much time to position itself as I can, but I must have one secure line and this is the only one I'm reasonably sure about. The computer tells me that I can transmit back to this module from anywhere within the Warden system and that it will do the rest. The Council stays on the public and visual band; you stay on this one, and if I have to get word to the Council I will tell you and you will personally tell the Council."

"Agreed. Uh—if you go down there you're going to be stuck along with the rest, you know."

"I'm not worried by the prospect. However, I don't believe that it's necessarily true, either. I think they now have their Warden organism under pretty complete control. No matter, though. This is a time of ugly choices, and given the choice of being blown to hell in a war or having to live on a Diamond world, my choice is pretty well made. Commander, no matter what, I'm convinced that, after this, all that we know will never be the same again."

He switched off, then turned to the other side. "Get me Morah on the Lilith satellite."

It took only a couple of minutes to fetch the dark, eerie Chief of Security. "We had about given you up," Morah told him.

"These things take time. Your moves against the Confederacy are having major disastrous effects and they're worried, but they want to talk." Briefly he outlined his proposal for himself as negotiator with the Council following by direct link, site to be selected.

Morah thought the proposition over. "This is not simply a trick to bring up the fleet?"

"We don't have to. A major task force has been lying only a couple of days off the Diamond for weeks, waiting for any hard evidence from me so they could act. They're going to come in reasonably close no matter what, but I think the Council will keep its word as long as we keep talking. It seems to me that delay now is in the best interests of the Altavar as well, since we are already in position while they can use the extra time to position their own forces."

Morah seemed to consider the idea, then nodded absently. "All right, then. But any move by the task force to attack positions on the Diamond will terminate everything right then and there. You understand?"

"I understand. You name the place and time."

"Boojum is the seventh moon of Momrath. We have an all-purpose communications center there, with sufficient room and comfortable facilities. Can you reach it by 1600 standard time tomorrow?"

He nodded. "I'll be there, along with the comm codes needed to plug us all in. However, I want certain people present from the Diamond as well."

"Oh? Who?"

"First, I want a senior Altavar empowered to deal for its people. The Council insists on it. Second, I'm not clear on the political situation on the Diamond itself right now. Who will represent Charon?"

'I will, as temporary, or acting Lord," Morah replied. "Kobé will represent Lilith, and the two surviving Lords the other two."

'I'll have to have a psych named Dumonia from Cerberus there."

'Indeed? Why? Who is he?"

'One of my wild cards. Dumonia is Lord of Cerberus but neither you nor Laroo realize it. Laroo is nothing more than an unnecessary puppet at this point." He enjoyed the total sense of shock and surprise Morah conveyed. *Score one,* he thought with satisfaction. Now Morah could not be so absolutely certain of anything. "I also would like, if possible, Park Lacoch from Charon, Cal Tremon from Lilith, and Qwin Zhang from Cerberus present."

Morah found that amusing. "Indeed? And which side do they represent?"

"Good faith," he responded. "You were going to bring Lacoch anyway, so why not have them all? Who better to evaluate my own sincerity and behavior?"

"Done, then."

"I notice you aren't surprised that I want nobody from Medusa except Ypsir."

Morah cleared his throat and seemed a bit embarrassed. "We are all well aware of what happened on Medusa. I'm afraid Ypsir hasn't stopped crowing about it yet. A most brilliant and ruthless but totally unpleasant man, the sort of man that turned us against the Confederacy in the old days." He frowned thoughtfully. "Um—it will be unavoidable that you and Ypsir and his—pet—will meet. I can assume no personal vendetta as long as we are negotiating?"

"Until we are finished with this business, yes. The stakes here are much too high to allow myself the luxury of personal revenge right now."

Morah looked back into the screen with those piercing, inhuman eyes. "I have the strange feeling that you are not telling me all."

He grinned. "Tell me, if you don't mind—where did you pick up those interesting eyes."

Morah paused for a moment, then said softly, "I went to the Mount once too often."

It was arranged that he would go by picket boat to Momrath. The boat would be completely automated except for him, and would return automatically without him and be totally sterilized. Later, he was assured, if he could leave the Diamond at all, he would be picked up.

Curiously, he found himself reluctant to leave what, only the day before, he had regarded as his tomb.

"We will be in continuous touch," the computer assured him.

He nodded absently, checking again his small travel kit.

"Um, if you don't mind, would you answer one question for me?" the computer asked. "I have been wondering about it."

"Go ahead. I thought you knew everything."

"How did you know that a battle fleet lay only two days off the Diamond? I knew, of course, but that information was deliberately kept from you. Did you deduce it?"

"Oh, no," he responded breezily, "I hadn't a clue. I was bluffing."

"Oh."

And with that, he left the cabin with no trouble and traveled down many decks in the picket ship to the patrol-boat bay. The boat was no luxury yacht, but it was extremely fast and had the ability to "skip" in and out of real space in short bursts of only a fraction of a second. Unlike the lazy freighters that took many days to traverse the distance, he would make his assigned rendezvous in just twenty-five hours.

He felt a curious sense of detachment from the proceedings after this point. The final phase, and, in a sense, the final scam, was on its way, working itself out to conclusion. One misstep and not only he but everything and everyone might go up, and he knew it. The fact that he'd failed on Medusa and had succeeded only by flukes on Lilith and Charon bothered him a bit. This whole mission had shaken his self-confidence a bit, although, he had to admit, he had never tackled so ambitious a project before. Indeed, no human being in living memory had ever shouldered such responsibility.

Something still bothered him about his deductions and conclusions, and he knew what it was. His solution of the maze in the Diamond was too pat, his aliens assumed to be too predictably like humans in their thinking. It was all too damned pat. Life was never pat.

He slept on the problem, and awoke nine hours later with a vague idea of what was wrong. It was the animals and plants, he realized. Familiar forms, bisexual and asexual. Since they obviously weren't created for human viewing, they must reflect the general lines of thinking of the Altavar, who would draw on their own background and experience. No matter how bizarre the Altavar looked, how different their evolutionary roots from those of man, they must have evolved in roughly similar environments. They were highly consistent in their makeups of the worlds, yet here was a basic inconsistency. His view of them did not conform to the kinds of worlds they built.

The screens picked up the vistas he passed, and recorded them for later viewing. He amused himself by punching up all four Diamond worlds, now in anything but a diamond configuration, and blowing up the images as best he could. None of them really showed much in the way of surface features at this distance, but he found himself oddly transported to each as he looked at its disk. So odd, so unusual, so exotic . . . So deadly.

If they're really homes for Altavar young, why the hell did they tolerate human populations in the millions on them?

Questions with no easy or clear answers like that one disturbed him. For most of his life, the Confederacy had been his rock, and he had believed in it. He, himself, had caught some of the very people down there on those four worlds, sending them to what he believed to be a hellish prison. He still wasn't very impressed with the Four Lords and their minions or with the systems they had developed; but, he knew, he felt no real difference when looking at the Diamond or at the Confederacy. He felt like a confirmed atheist in the midst of a vast and grandiose cathedral, able to appreciate the skill and art that went into its construction but feeling pretty sure it wasn't worth the effort.

In many ways he identified almost completely with Marek Kreegan, who must have had similar thoughts upon coming to the Diamond, and, most likely, even before. That priestly role was more than mere disguise, it was a subtle and humorous tweaking of the man's nose at Man's odd and distorted attempt at building institutions that served him. How many thousands, or tens of thousands, of years had Mankind been trying to build the right institutions? How many had slaved in faith at that building, and how many, even now, deluded themselves as they always had that, *this time*, they'd gotten it right?

Once upon a time sixty percent of the people didn't believe in their system. Only twelve percent thought there might be something better than the system they hated, something worth bothering to fight about. Loss of faith equaled loss of hope, then, in that large a segment of the population, and it didn't, in historical retrospect, seem out of line. People tended to extremes, and hope was a very mild extreme when faith became impossible, while despair was easy and all the way down the other end of the scale.

He pounded his fist on the console hard enough to hurt his hand. "Tarin Bul" had given in to despair, yet had died with slight hope. Qwin Zhang had risked everything on hope, and won. Park Lacoch had refused to be seduced by a good and happy life when he knew that others he did not even know depended on his actions. Cal Tremon had been used and abused by practically everyone for their own purposes, yet he had never surrendered.

Four people, four distinct individuals, who were, in every sense of the word, sides of himself. He hoped, he *thought,* he had learned something valuable, something the Confederacy had never meant to teach him. Now it was his turn.

The great orb that was Momrath filled the screens early on in the trip, and he watched it grow closer with eerie fascination. Ringed gas giants were always the most beautiful of places, and, in more than one sense, the most forbidding as well. At least two moons of the great planet were large or larger than any of the Diamond worlds, yet he went not to them but to small and frozen Boojum. Well, Momrath had been the one place he hadn't visited, in a sense, as yet, and it seemed appropriate that it be *his* world.

He settled back to await the landing, still deep in reflection.

Task Force Delta was composed of four "war stations," each surrounded and protected by a formidable battle group. Clustered around the barbell-shaped station that was the nerve center and computer control for its awesome firepower were hundreds of "modules," each complete in and of itself. Most were unmanned; war these days was very much a remote-controlled affair, with battle group leaders merely choosing from a list of tactics, giving their battle group computers the objectives, and letting everything else run itself. Not a single one of the modules was intended for defense; the battle group provided that. Yet among all the clusters, there were weapons that could take out selected cities on remote worlds, could level a mountain range or even disintegrate all carbon-based life forms within a proscribed radius while doing no other damage. Other modules could ignite atmospheres with sufficient combustible gasses in them, while still others could literally split planets in two.

One such station could wipe out an entire solar system, leaving nothing but debris, gasses, and assorted space junk to orbit the sun, or could, in fact, even explode that sun. There were only six such stations in operation throughout the vast Confederacy, and four of them were concentrated here in the task force, the largest ever assembled.

The protective battle group was composed of fifty defensive ships, called cruisers after ancient seagoing vessels none could remember at this stage, built along the same lines as the war stations. But their modules consisted of hundreds of scouts, probes, and fighters, again almost all needing no human hand or brain, capable of taking continuous streams of orders from their base cruisers or, in the event the cruiser was destroyed, from any cruiser or the war station itself. Nothing else was needed; the combined firepower and mobility of a cruiser was equal to an entire planetary attack force, complete with human and robot troops that could land on and occupy a cleared stretch of land and hold it until relieved provided the cruiser's modules continued their air and space cover. As well, the human marines inside their battle machines could be so effective that a squad might be able to take and destroy a medium-sized city, even if the city were defended with laser weapons, immune to the lethal energy rain their supporting fighters could unleash.

In theory the task force was as close to invulnerable as could be imagined, combined with the punch of an irresistible force. The only trouble was, its powers, weapons, programming, and tactics had never been tested under real battle conditions. For several centuries the Confederacy military had been almost exclusively devoted to policing itself.

A forward cruiser, still more than a light-year off the Diamond, launched four probe modules, one to each of the four Warden worlds. They sped off, skipping in and out of subspacial modes, in a near-random approach to the system, their next direction determined only after they came out for that brief moment and saw where they were. With no humans or other living organisms aboard to worry about, they made the trip in less than an hour.

Stern-faced men and women born and bred to the art of war sat in the center of the battle group, watching the four probes track on a great battle screen showing the entire probable sector of engagement, while subsidiary screens scrolled data slow enough for the human observers to see, although the data was far behind the reality being fed back to the master battle computer.

In precision drill, the four small steely blue-black modules arrived off each of their four target worlds simultaneously and quickly closed on their targets. Their armament consisted entirely of defensive screens and scramblers for potential adversaries; they were the forerunners, the testers of defenses and the data-bearers to the command and control center far off but closing.

"Measuring abnormal large energy flow between the four worlds," a comtech reported to the battle room. "Our probes also report scanning on an unusual band, origin each of the four targets."

"Very well," the admiral responded. "Close to minimum safety zone on each world. All photo recorders on. Commence evasive action on scans."

As soon as the order was given it was done. The admiral wanted to know how well his hardware could be tracked after it was first discovered.

It could track very well indeed, it seemed, and the odd sensors kept pace effortlessly with the variations in course and speed; even shields and jamming techniques had no effect.

They approached within twelve hundred kilometers of the respective planetary surfaces, not too far above the orbits of the space stations of the Four Lords.

All data ceased on all boards simultaneously. Startled comtechs and observers leaped to their consoles and ran every kind of data check they could, to no avail. There seemed no question that, on all four worlds simultaneously, something had fired and totally destroyed the probes.

They ran back the last few seconds frame by frame, looking for what happened, but could see nothing and had to call upon the computers for help. Ultimately the computers could simulate what could not be seen. It had been an electrical beam, a jagged pencil line of force looking more like natural lightning than something fired from any kind of known weapon, reaching up and out from an unknown point below the upper atmospheric layers of each world and striking each probe, destroying it instantly. Only a single burst had been used in each case, the burst lasting mere milliseconds yet packing enough punch to destroy the heavily armored probes completely.

Commander, Special Task Force, sighed and shook his head. "Well, we know that we'll have a fight when we go in," he said with professional objectivity.

Five seconds after the probes were destroyed, all Confederacy satellites around the Warden Diamond were taken out, leaving only one channel of outside communication unjammed.

He had to admit that while the rock wasn't much it offered a really fine view. The great multicolored orb of Momrath filled the sky of Boojum, and the small probe boat settled into a cradle dock on the bumpy and drab surface. The setting made it seem as if the moon and ship were about to be swallowed by a sea of yellows, blues, and magentas.

He donned a spacesuit and depressurized the cabin, waiting for the lights to tell him he could open the hatch. The cradle dock was built for the blocky, rectangular freighters rather than for the small passenger craft he had used, so there was really no way to mate boat to airlock. He noted two of the Warden shuttlecraft parked in the rear of the bay, but was surprised not to see any ship of unfamiliar design. Either the Altavar hadn't arrived as yet, or it utilized a different and less obvious mode of transportation.

As soon as he was at the hangar-level airlock, a small tug emerged from a recess in the far wall and eased up to his ship, grabbing hold with a dual tractor beam and then easing it into an out-of-the-way parking space. He hoped he'd remembered to tell them that the thing would automatically take back off on command of the picket ship in an hour or two, then shrugged off the thought. What good was taking over an enemy ship like the picket ship if your spies were incompetents? He shouldn't be expected to do *everything*.

The light turned green and he opened the hatch, stepped inside the chamber, closed and hit reseal behind him, and waited for the light on the inner door to open. He was reminded a bit of that dual airlock in Ypsir's space palace. Sure enough, there was even a camera here, and some of those odd projections.

He barely had time to reflect on the implications when he was bathed in an energy field from those same projections, just as his counterpart had been back on Medusa. It was over quickly and caused him no unpleasantness; in fact, he felt no sensation out of the ordinary at all. He couldn't help wondering what all that was about, then. An automatic precaution? If it were some kind of decontamination, it would have been better served if they'd waited until he took off the spacesuit.

The inner lock's guide light turned green, and he opened it and walked into a fairly large locker room. He quickly removed his suit, then opened his small travel bag and donned rubber-soled boots, work pants, and a casual shirt. He checked the small transceiver's power, then left it in the case along with a change of clothes and his toiletries, then picked up the bag and walked out of the locker room and down a small utilitarian hall to an elevator. He felt a bit light but not uncomfortably so; they were using a gravity field inside the place.

The elevator was of the sealed type, so he had only the indicator lights to show how far he was being taken. Not too far, as it turned out. While there appeared to be at least eight levels to the place, he went down only to the third one before a door rolled back.

Yaʒek Morah, wearing a shining black outfit complete with a rather effective crimson-lined cape, stood there to greet him.

He had been used to thinking of Morah as a large man, but, he found, they were both about the same size. The eyes hadn't changed much, though, and were still hard to look at.

He stepped out of the elevator and did not offer his hand. Instead he stood there, looking at Morah. "So."

"Welcome to Boojum, sir," Morah responded, sounding fairly friendly. "Odd name, isn't it? The outer planets and moons were named for some follow-up scout's favorite fairy stories, I think. Rather obscure." He paused a moment. "Speaking of obscure—just what do we call you?"

He shrugged. "Call me Mr. Carroll. That'll do, and it's certainly appropriate both to history and to our current situation."

"Good enough," the Security Chief responded, apparently not aware of the irony in name or tone. "Follow me and I'll give you the grand tour. It's not much, I'm afraid—this is a mining colony, after all, not a luxury spa. Oh, you might be relieved to know that that shower bath we gave you has an interesting effect. The Warden organisms, which are thicker than dirt on this rockpile, will totally ignore you. That should relieve your mind."

He couldn't help smiling at that. "As easy as that. Well, I'll be damned." He followed the man in black down the corridor.

Morah first showed him his room, a small cubicle less than a third the size of his module on the picket ship, but it would do. He thought about retaining his bag, then decided not to and tossed it on the bed. "Better let your people know not to touch that bag without me around," he warned Morah. "A few things in there can be very unpleasant if you don't know exactly how to talk to them."

"Although this is nominally Ypsir's territory, I am in complete command here," the security chief assured him. "You are currently under what might best be expressed as diplomatic immunity. None of your things, or your person, will be touched; whoever touches them will answer to me."

He accepted that, and they proceeded. "The Lords are staying along here, in rooms similar to yours," Morah told him. "The others are sharing a dorm normally used by mine security personnel. I'm afraid there's been a lot of grumbling as to the accommodations, but only Ypsir has a livable place here."

"It'll do," he assured the other man. "I've been in worse."

A small central area between the single rooms and the dorm had been set up with a large conference table and comfortable chairs. "This is our meeting hall," Morah told him, "and, I'm afraid, also our dining hall, although the food comes from Ypsir's personal kitchen and is quite good."

The three people assembled in the room when they entered all turned to look at the newcomers. One of them looked so shocked he appeared to be having a heart attack. "You!" he gasped.

He smiled. "Hello, Zhang. I see nobody warned you." He turned to the other two. "Doctor, I am most happy to see you here, and I'd like to thank you for all your help." Dumonia bowed and shrugged. The third man he didn't recognize at all. He was a tall, thin, white-haired man of indeterminate age. About the only thing that could be told about him was that he was certainly a Medusan. "And you are?"

"Haval Kunser, Chief Administrator of Medusa," the man responded smoothly, putting out his hand.

He took it and shook it warmly, replying, "It's *very* good to meet you. I know you only by reputation."

He turned back to Zhang, who looked only slightly less stricken. "Are you going to drop dead or shoot me or relax and have a drink?" he asked his Cerberan counterpart.

"Well, what do you expect?" Qwin Zhang responded tartly. "I'm still not over the other two yet."

His eyebrows went up. "They're here, then?"

"Everyone is here," Morah told him. "We can proceed after dinner if you like."

"The Altavar?"

"Two levels down. Not only do they prefer it down there, but I'm afraid they stink like a three-day-old corpse. Our body odor is similarly offensive to them, so you can understand the separation considering the cramped quarters. I'll certainly take you down and introduce you if you want to verify that they're here, but I think otherwise we should let them sit in by remote, for, ah, mutual comfort. Don't answer until you've smelled them."

He chuckled. "All right, I have no objection to the remote, although I *am* going to have to verify their physical presence. I'm afraid that some in the Council simply don't believe in them."

"Understandable. Through that door there, and we'll meet the others." They walked into a large room that looked more like a barracks than anything else, in which several people were sitting and talking or reading or writing. All heads turned as they entered, followed by Zhang and Dumonia, and he saw immediately that Zhang's reaction was not going to be unique. Tremon, for one, was so startled he stood up and banged his head on an upper bunk.

"Tremon and Lacoch you know," Morah said pleasantly, "and the others are either associates of theirs or aides of the Four Lords like Kunser. Communications, coordination, and a subsidiary meeting room with visual facilities have been set up on the level below us. It's all ready, Mr. Carroll."

Tremon and Lacoch both shook their heads at that. "Mr. *Who?*" Lacoch muttered, but did not press the matter. He looked over at two others

near them and smiled and bowed slightly. "Darva and Dylan. Charmed."
The two women stared back at him in puzzlement. He looked over at
Tremon. "No Ti?"

Tremon looked a little stunned. "So it *did* work!"

"Better than you could ever know," he responded softly, then turned to
Morah. "I'll give your techs the codes to open everything to the Council so
they can make the proper checks and set up a time. I'm not sure how
many on the Council we managed to get together but it'll be a working
majority. Then I'd like to meet privately with my three former operatives,
if that's possible, and separately with you, Doctor. Then I'll go down with
you to meet the Altavar, Morah, and we can get started."

Morah looked a little uncomfortable. "Um, I believe all that can be arranged, but I would recommend eating before going down to meet the Altavar Lord Ypsir has invited you to dine with him in his private suite
above us." He paused a moment. "Nothing says you have to accept, you
know."

He thought about it. "Does he know the full extent of who and what I
am?"

"No. I thought it would be . . . judicious not to tell him. And although
he has this whole place wired up, my own people are controlling everything there."

"I thank you for that. In that case, I'll accept his invitation. Oh, don't
worry. I'll be a good boy."

Morah thought a moment, then nodded. "Very well. I will so inform
him. It is now—let's see, 1720. Give me the comcode and I will see to the
checks with my people, and also arrange for you not to be disturbed in the
meeting room until . . . shall we say, 1900? We'll set your dinner date for
then. After, or in the early morning, you can meet the Altavar. Shall we
set negotiations to begin at, oh, 1000 tomorrow morning? That will
also give the Council plenty of time, and my men can hook up the Altavar
and Council visuals. How does that sound?"

He nodded. "Excellent." He turned to his counterparts. "You three want
to come outside with me? I think we have some talking to do. Of course
the ladies can come, too, if you wish."

He stood there looking at them as they studied him. Tremon was still a
big, muscular brute of a man, just as he remembered him, and Lacoch still
had a somewhat reptilian cast to him, including a tail. Zhang was in the
body of a young civilized worlder, and looked much like he did himself,
although he was certainly physically older and felt ancient. He found it
interesting that neither of the two with their ladies there had included
them in on this reunion, although it saved making explanations.

"I assume we're being totally bugged, so I won't say anything I don't
want Morah to know," he began. "I want to start by stating flatly that I
was with you all the way on your worlds. I know you very well, and you
know me."

They were fascinated that, after all the different events that had happened to them, they found it difficult not to begin speaking at the same time, and one quite often could complete another's statements.

Still, he let them get their resentment out, and, perhaps, their pride as well. Zhang pretty much said why he didn't want Dylan in the room when he stated, "Hell, you were there, sort of, all the time. Every time we made love, you did it, too. That's not an easy thing to face, or to explain to her."

"Then don't," he suggested. "Let's get this straight. We are *all* individuals. I am Mr. Carroll, for reasons only you three probably understand. You're Tremon, and you're Lacoch, and you're Zhang. I think the easiest way to explain it to others is to explain it in more natural terms."

They all nodded and said, as one, "Quadruplets."

"Why not? It's closer to the truth now, anyway. Have you all been briefed on the situation?"

They nodded, but he found they were still a bit sketchy and he filled in the details. It was surprising, once they got down to business, how quickly the anger and hurt and resentment vanished and they worked almost as a team. Finally, though, Lacoch asked the loaded question. "Where's our man on Medusa?"

He sighed. "Three hits, one miss. Not a bad record."

"Dead, then?"

He nodded. "Yes, dead. But his information was the clincher. Damn it, though, I'll always feel guilty about that. After I got the report from you, Lacoch, on Charon, I had it pretty well down. If I had gone directly to Medusa at that time, instead of delaying as I did, he'd still be alive. It was that close."

Tremon whistled. "You know, I think all of us hated your guts up until today. I know I did." The others nodded understandingly. "But, with you here, in the middle of this shit, I think we got off lucky. Not the Medusan, of course, but three of us, anyway. We're the individuals, and we're the free ones living our own lives. You got nothing, nobody, not even the Confederacy in a pinch, and you got all the crosses."

"And yet you've really changed," Lacoch put in, again getting nods. "We all sense it. Sure, *we* changed, but you were with all three of us and you still got the load. The big load. That's what this is all about, isn't it?"

He grinned. "In a way, yes. If we never had this meeting, never had this talk, none of us would be really free of the others and you know it. Now you—all of you—are free and only I am not. If this all works out, I think the four of us will do very well indeed as . . . brothers. If not—well, who knows what will happen to any of us?"

They accepted that in silence for a moment. Finally Tremon said, "The Council will never bargain in good faith. You know that."

He sighed. "Not yet they won't. Not without the shedding of blood on both sides. I'm going to do my best, though, tomorrow, to put it together. We'll see. At least you of all people understand my motives and loyalties."

"I think we do," they all said softly. The meeting broke up a little after that, and Dumonia was summoned to the conference room. The little man with the needless glasses and nervous ticks didn't try to conceal his position of strength from him, but he *was* curious.

"You are really the original of all of them?"

He nodded. "If original is the right word. And I experienced all that they experienced, Doctor, but without any little memory tricks. You might tell me, though, how the hell you managed to erase yourself from Zhang's mind. I thought any tinkering like that was damned near impossible with my—his—mind."

Dumonia smiled. "And who do you think created many of those techniques in the first place?"

He sighed. "I wish you'd been on Ypsir's satellite a couple of days ago. I assume that you're behind the Opposition projects there?"

He nodded. "But what happened that you wished for me?"

Briefly, he told Dumonia and asked, "What's your long-term prognosis?"

"Well, Jorgash is among the best I ever taught, if that's any consolation, and your kind of mind is best for that procedure, but—and it is a big but— he would have to guess on your mental blocks and patterns where I would know. In any event, I would counsel you to think of Bul as dead, for dead he certainly is. I realize your guilt but I also know this Ypsir. He knows that you were Control for Bul, and that's why you've been invited to dinner tonight. You should understand him, too, to an extent, and realize that if you *had* been in time to intercede, he would have accidentally on purpose done it anyway. The only real human being in Ypsir's mental universe is himself. Everyone else is either a tool or an enemy authority. To the enemy authority—and to himself—he must continually prove that he is better, stronger, superior. You are the tool of that authority, the Confederacy, and, therefore, you represent it. If I were you I would not go to dinner tonight."

"Why? You think he means me harm?"

"He is not so foolish. But if you cannot accept the fact that this Tarin Bul is dead, as dead as if he had been shot through the heart, and that this new person is exactly that, a new and different person you do not know and have never met, he will torture you horribly. You must put aside your guilt, for it is misplaced. There is nothing you could have done to stop this. *Nothing.* You would only have hastened it. In the case of Bul, you must abandon hope with that guilt. Otherwise, cancel and eat here with us."

He nodded. "I'll handle it. But what should my reaction be?"

"You are not yourself here!" the psych snapped. "You are not even the Confederacy! You are all of mankind, and all of the Diamond as well! You've been elected, without your consent, to a post that makes you more nonhuman than these Altavar things! You must be above all human concerns, all personal concerns, for the duration of this conference! If not, you are lost."

He nodded and smiled wanly. "Then you know at least as much as I do about this."

"I know what Laroo knows, and that is quite a lot. I assume that you are here because you know, too. If you don't, then God help us all."

He sighed. "Well, I don't pretend to have all the answers, or, maybe, any answers at all, Doctor, but you've convinced me I have to go to dinner tonight."

"Eh?"

"If I can't handle Talant Ypsir's mad egomania, how the hell can I handle tomorrow?"

5

After the cramped quarters below, he was surprised at the size of Ypsir's apartment. Surely the man hardly ever visited Boojum, and so this place spoke volumes about the man's mind. Ypsir must have a place like this on every damned one of these moons, he assumed.

He entered a main hall and turned into a room at the sound of conversation. They were there, all of them, the old and the new, and he recognized the ones on sight that he had not yet met. The tall, distinguished man with the snow white hair was Duke Kobé, new Lord of Lilith. The tall, muscular, handsome man was Laroo, in his robot body totally indistinguishable at this point from a normal human one. Morah was there, too, temporarily representing Charon. He made a mental note to ask him sometime what happened to his pretty little killer. And over there, laughing and joking, a distinguished-looking civilized worlder with incongruous flaming red hair and mustache, his eyes mischievous-looking and flanked by "laugh lines," dressed in deep black and gold. He just had to be Talant Ypsir.

Scampering around were four scantily clad young women of inordinate beauty and sexual endowments, supplying *hors d'oeuvres*, replenishing glasses, lighting Kobé's Lilithian cigars, all with a smile and an adoring expression. Goodtime Girls, happily plying their trade. Idly he wondered if they were always here, waiting for that incredibly rare occasion when their master might show up, or whether they were part of his traveling party.

Ypsir spotted him, grinned a politician's grin, and made his way over to him, hand out. "Well, well! So you're the man who's going to save the universe!" His manner was joking, not sarcastic-sounding, and he recognized the man's public *persona* in an instant. The eternal baby-kissing hypocritical politician, the crook who knows full well he's got everything in the bag. He snapped his finger and a Goodtime Girl was immediately at hand, eagerly awaiting a command. "Get Mr.—Carroll, I believe?—a *homau* and a tray of those little sausage things with the cheese inside."

The girl was quick to obey and was soon back with both. He sipped the sweet drink and took a small sausage on a toothpick and tasted it. The drink was a bit sweet for him—he recognized it as some blend of Charonese fruits and alcohol—but the appetizer was quite good.

Ypsir engaged him in a small talk for some time, and he found it remarkably easy to do. His indignation and outright hatred were still there, of course, but under complete control. He doubted if he'd ever met someone so internally corrupt and evil, but he'd tracked down and caught a bunch of very unpleasant types in the past, and quite often he'd had a meal with them and been forced to endure their bizarre lifestyles and values.

All the men in the room except himself were in that class, he realized. Laroo had been the criminal boss of a dozen worlds; Morah had run the criminal brotherhood's scientific branch, which included projects that would probably make the Goodtime Girls seem tame. Kobé had in his youth been a master of the robot and computerized alarm systems, personally looting more works of art by great masters from impregnable fortresses —or so they were thought to be—than any other single human being. And yet, oddly, he felt almost a kinship with those three, whose careers were based upon disdain for the very values he now disdained, and who, beyond that, were at least sane enough to live in the real universe.

Of them all, only Talant Ypsir hoped he would fail to stop the impending war. Dumonia had been most specific about that point. Ypsir saw the destruction of the Confederacy, and perhaps the whole non-Warden branch of humanity, as something very much to be desired. He was assured of survival with his harem, and that was all that mattered to him. He did not consider the Altavar any threat, because they did not interfere with him or threaten what he considered important. In fact, to Talant Ypsir the entire alien race was just another tool against his enemies.

Ypsir held up a finger and grinned broadly, ever the jovial, friendly politician, only his incredibly cold eyes betraying anything of his inner self. "Wait here! I want to show you my most precious possession!" And, with that, he ducked from the room.

He heard the others whispering admiringly of what they knew was coming. But when Talant Ypsir re-entered, in spectacular fashion, he was aware that the eyes of the other Lords—Morah's inhuman, burning orbs in particular—were all upon him and not on the newcomer to the room. To Ypsir, this was fun torture; to the others, it was very much a test of his own self-control and resolve. If he blew it now, there would *be* no tomorrow morning.

She was almost inhuman in her wild, exotic, sensuous beauty, far beyond the sketches he'd seen in Fallon's office. Despite all his knowledge and feelings, he was almost overcome by wanton desire, by pure lust, and that, he realized later, was the key.

You must think of her as someone you do not know and have never met.

It was easier to do than he'd believed.

She entered on all fours, playfully tugging at a golden leash held by Ypsir, whose face showed absolute ecstasy and triumph. Ypsir was having a doubly fine time, not only tweaking this outsider's nose and, by so doing, the Confederacy's, but also showing off to the other Lords, his political equals, with an air of *I have her and you never can or will.*

Ypsir and the girl halted just inside the entrance door, and she rolled over and then partly propped herself up on one arm, legs crossed, and looked up at them with those enormous green eyes, at once sexy and, somehow, wild as well.

She was, he thought lustfully in spite of himself, the ten best pornographic performances ever given all rolled up into one. She was quite literally *designed* to create instant envy and lust, and he could only stare at her. She looked straight into his face and there was no glimmer of any recognition at all, but there was a vibrancy, a fire in those eyes that was not in any of the Goodtime Girls.

Ypsir looked down at her with pride. "Tell the nice men your name," he urged softly, as if talking to a trained animal or a child.

"I'm Ass," she purred. "I'm a *baaad* Ass."

"And why are you named Ass?"

"'Cause Ass was 'sassin. Ass try to kill Master."

He was under control now, perfectly so, and glanced out of the corner of his eye at the others. They were still looking only at him.

"And what happened when you tried?"

"Master too smart. Master too wise for Ass. Master *so* generous. Master no kill Ass. Master no hurt Ass. Master make Ass *love* him. Master take ugly, evil 'sassin, make into Ass, to love Master."

Despite the depravity of the scene, this was becoming interesting, he thought. If they retold her that much, how much *did* she know of her former self? Not enough to recognize him, certainly. This was different from what he expected, yet it was consistent. *Ypsir wanted her to know.*

"Do you remember who you were?"

She looked slightly confused by that one. "Ass not 'member old self. Ass no want to 'member."

"Are you happy now, Ass?"

"Oh, yes!"

"Would you want to be anybody else—anybody or anything in the whole wide universe?"

"No, no, no, no, no. Ass loves being Ass. Feels *so* good."

Ypsir looked up straight at him. "Your former agent."

"Very creative," he responded dryly, sipping at his drink. "And very lovely. Maybe we missed a bet, Lord Ypsir. Maybe we should have made *you* into a gorgeous beauty like that instead of sending you to Medusa. That's what *you* would have done with you."

Ypsir's face clouded, and he literally shook with emotion, his inner self coming out in the twisting of his face, in his expression, in his every mannerism. It was a frightening, totally evil visage, a demonic creature that could no longer hide behind the mask of the cheery politician for very long.

He was about to add more, but felt Morah's arm touch his and thought better of it. He'd done his job, and that was all that mattered, but he took a strong pleasure in twisting Talant Ypsir's vision of beauty back upon him by applying the Medusan's standards to himself.

Ypsir took a minute or so to regain control, and slowly that terrible demon faded and the cheery politician was back with only a nasty leer remaining. He knew now, though, that he was in complete control, and his self-confidence, which had been badly wavering, flowed back into him in a grand surge. He also now knew that, while he still couldn't believe in a god, he would always afterward believe in the existence of pure evil.

The rest of the evening was strained, but he found the right balance that not only Morah but the other Lords could approve. Not that Ypsir didn't try, parading Ass, making her do pretty disgusting and degrading things, and pushing him as far as the Medusan could push using her, but to no avail. Ypsir fought his war with grand and ugly gestures; he fought back with sarcasm and flip comments, and totally frustrated the great Lord of Medusa. It was a very rare evening, really, he told himself, equally unpleasant and rewarding.

Morah got him out of there as soon as dessert was finished, though. Ypsir would be boiling, horribly mad for hours after. Still, the Charonese was more than impressed by his behavior, and seemed to regard him even more as an equal now than before.

"He will kill you if and when he can," Morah warned him. "Ypsir is not used to losing face so badly. Only the presence of the other Lords restrained him tonight, for his object is not ours."

He nodded. "Shall we meet the Altavar now? I don't care how foul they smell—they almost have to be a breath of fresh air compared to the company we've been keeping this night."

"Come with me," Yatek Morah said.

The smell *was* pervasive and pretty much as Morah had warned. On a full stomach it almost made him gag, and he restrained the impulse to do so only with the greatest difficulty and discomfort.

The Altavar were not quite what he expected. They bore a general kinship to the demons of the ice, but only a kinship, in the same sense that Ass was generically related to Commander Krega.

The first thing that struck him was the sheer alienness of the special quarters for the three Altavar. The lighting was subdued, the furniture odd and blocky and totally unfamiliar in form or function, and there was an odd, figure-eight shaped pool of water to one side. He knew the creatures were watching him with interest, but he couldn't really tell how. The retractable tentacles and odd, heart-shaped pads on their "heads" were familiar, but their bodies trailed into a large, nearly formless mass that seemed constantly in motion. They did not walk, but oozed as they moved, leaving a slender trail of slime behind them. Obviously none of these creatures could fly, or move very fast at all.

The one nearest to him and Morah moved to a small device and extended a flowing stalklike appendage until it reached the box and actually seemed to enter it through a small compartment on the side. A speaker crackled.

"So this is the one who caused so much trouble, Morah." The voice, totally electronically synthesized, sounded eerie as the dank enclosure added reverb to its already inhuman tones.

Morah bowed slightly, although whether or not the gesture had any meaning to the creatures couldn't be known. "He wished to meet you prior to the talks."

"Why?"

The question seemed addressed to either one of them, and so he answered. "Partly curiosity. Partly to add to my knowledge. And partly because protocol demanded it."

"Ah, yes, protocol," the alien replied. "It seems important to your people." It paused a moment. "You hold yourself well. In many ways you remind us of the one called Kreegan."

"We were from the same place and in the same profession originally," he told the Altavar. "I suspect we thought more alike than either of us would have admitted. You respected Kreegan, I know. I hope that I may earn a measure of that respect tomorrow."

"You and he wished to save your people. This is a normal and natural thing to us, and we weakened out of our compassion. We hope sincerely that we did not err on that basis, for the cost will be far greater to you and infinitely greater to us if we did. It was our original intent, you know, to eliminate a number of your worlds in a carefully measured pattern so that your technological capabilities would be broken for at least three centuries. This would have allowed us the necessary time to complete this phase of our task."

He was appalled at this revelation, and the casual way in which it was delivered, appalled as Marek Kreegan must have been many years ago when, assuming his rank as Lord of Lilith, he had first met this or some similar Altavar. Say there were nine hundred human worlds, seven hundred of them the civilized worlds. Three billion per civilized world, and an average of a half-billion for the others, would be— The Altavar was talking about eliminating over one *trillion*, three hundred and twenty *billion* people! And now, the creature had said, the risk was far greater than that!

He drew in his breath and swallowed hard. "Let me get this straight.

You wished to eliminate over a trillion of us so that we could not interfere with your activities for three centuries?"

"It has worked in the past," the Altavar said calmly. "The last time we did not do it with a civilization it cost us dearly in time, lives, and materiel, and your own civilization is easily ten times the largest we have encountered before."

So calm, so natural and normal, so clearly confirming much of his thesis about the Altavar and their motives.

"We hope that this time we may reason with your leaders, and avoid all war but this may not be possible," the creature continued. "We have studied your people well, and we understand you."

"Do you, really? I wonder." All he could see was not a terrible, gruesome alien form and stench, only an entire race of Talant Ypsirs, shorn of any need to be cheery, political, or human in any sense. The Medusans called them demons with no real understanding of how right they were.

"We know your concern," the Altavar told him. "Once, you see, our race was much like yours. We grew from a single world not unlike your own, although, obviously, evolution took a different path. We breathe the same sort of air, we drink and are made up of the same water. Our cells would be understandable to your biologists. Only the most warlike, competitive races survive to expand, so do not think us any different from you there, either. We, too, had our empire of several hundred worlds. And when faced with threat, we, too, fought. Because our history is so much like your own, we know full well what your Confederacy will do, how it will behave. But we are far older than your kind. Our objectives have changed, our purpose is firm and sure, our entire race committed to a single set of goals and objectives, while yours exists only to exist and to no real purpose. We desire none of your worlds. We desire none of your territory, nor your people.

"But your people will never believe that, for they know no higher purpose. They will not accept, or countenance, our great task, nor understand it. This is sad, for if there was any way to avoid the spilling of blood we would do so. That, we think, is why we were willing to allow Kreegan his chance. That and the fact that we had the luxury of time. We still have some time, but we fear his plan has achieved instead this current situation. Tomorrow we will begin to resolve it."

He nodded. "Yes. Tomorrow. Thank you for speaking to me." He looked at Morah, who nodded, turned, and walked out without another word. He followed, remembering that the Altavar didn't stand on protocol.

It took a little while of breathing good air before his stomach would settle down enough to have any sort of conversation. Morah waited patiently for him to recover.

"Well, did you find any surprises in your pet theories?"

He thought a moment. "Yes and no. It depends on just how well that thing translates. I heard the right words, but words can mean different things to different people."

"Tell me," the security chief said, "just out of curiosity—and if you can without giving away your own position. Just why do you think that the Altavar are so obsessed with the Diamond?"

"Huh? I assumed it had something to do with reproduction, but if I heard that thing correctly it may not. What did I miss?"

Morah thought his answer over carefully. "Then my guess was correct. You are a good agent, Carroll, and you have the most brilliant deductive mind I have ever encountered, Kreegan included. Do not feel badly. You labor under a handicap impossible to overcome."

"I knew I missed something—but you still haven't told me what yet."

"I think not. Not at this time. If anything, the true answer would make even the slender hope of settlement impossible. Reproduction is a good theory, and you should stick with it. The Council will understand it, perhaps accept it, and it will do as a basis for negotiations. The true answer, however, they will never accept, for they share your fatal flaw—and mine, too, for I had to be shown to believe."

He looked at Morah, frowning. "Then at least tell me the flaw."

"These are aliens, Mr. Carroll. They are, as the old one said, far closer to us than their hideous appearance and smelly hides admit, but they are alien all the same. They were shaped by a history that went vastly different from ours, and they reacted in a way, I suspect, that we could not. It should be obvious that their values, their institutions, their way of looking at things is very different from our own and would require a mind-wrenching adjustment to understand."

"Do *you* understand it?"

"Sometimes I think I do, but I cannot really say so truthfully. I know what they are doing, and why they are doing it, but that is not the same thing as understanding it. I think it is time we both turn in, Mr. Carroll. Tomorrow, we settle it, and, in a sense, I fear that the hopes of Kreegan and, in fact, myself, will be dashed. I know those people too well, those high and mighty Confederacy leaders. You see Talant Ypsir and see a monster. I look at the Council and the Congress and the planetary leaders and I see a great gathering of Talant Ypsirs, and would-be Talant Ypsirs if they thought they could get away with it. That is the true reason they established the Warden Diamond; you have only to recognize it yourself. They wanted a place of security, refuge, and escape in case *they* were caught. The Four Lords of the Diamond are not truly any different from the Nine Hundred Lords of the Confederacy, who are merely greater hypocrites." He turned to go, and the agent reached out and softly took hold of his arm for a moment.

"Morah—I have to know. Just whose side are you on? What is your ultimate game? You hate the Confederacy, but you have the same contempt for the Four Lords and the Diamond systems. You hoped that Kreegan could save humanity, yet you work for the aliens. What is your game?"

The chief of security sighed. "Once I had a game, Mr. Carroll. I don't any longer. I am trapped in a near-endless madhouse of a universe I did not make and cannot control or truly influence. From our viewpoint the Altavar are incredibly wise and totally insane, but insanity itself is a matter of degree. I am certainly insane by the standards of the Confederacy. Think of me as you would yourself. Neither of us asked to be here, nor did we fight for the responsibility that has been dropped upon us. Both of us do what we must because we are here, not because we are even the best people to be here. And, being totally insane ourselves, while we do not wish the ruin, carnage, and senseless violence that impends, we will both, wearily and without joy, work like hell to pick up the pieces."

"That's a pretty shitty universe you live in."

Morah grinned. "I wouldn't bring this up tomorrow, but, for the record, the Altavar have three sexes. One contributes sperm, one egg, into a third who bears the young. And given a near-perfect medical knowledge, they live about three times as long as we do." And with that, Yatek Morah went off to bed.

6

The conference was an awkward affair, but it was the best that could be done on short notice. He wondered from the start why such a minor moon, ill-suited for this sort of thing, should have been chosen, but suspected it might have been to accommodate the Altavar.

The technicians had rigged a screen at each end of the "conference room" and a similar setup, but not two-way, for the aides and assistants and others in the dorm next door. Inside the room sat the four current Lords of the Diamond dressed in their best, or most dramatic, as well as Dumonia and "Mr. Carroll," the last two facing the rest despite the fact that Laroo was really Dumonia's surrogate. Morah, it seemed, didn't fully believe his statements on Dumonia's power and neither recognized it nor told the others. Dumonia, for his part, was happy to be there as a representative of the Confederacy, although he found that concept highly amusing.

To the Lords' right, on the screen, was an Altavar, possibly the same one he'd spoken to the night before. To their left the screen showed two men and a woman, all civilized worlders, dressed in formal robes of office. These were the senior ranking members of the Council, the rest of whom watched on a larger screen in an adjoining room back in the Confederacy.

He surveyed the Four Lords and shuffled his note cards nervously. Several times he tried to catch Ypsir's eye, but while the Medusan kept taking sidelong glances at him he otherwise would not acknowledge the agent's existence.

When both sides' comtechs certified all was ready, Morah began the meeting, as he represented not only Charon but also, to some extent, the Altavar themselves.

"These proceedings are open at ten hundred Base Mean Time. I am

Yatek Morah, acting Lord of Charon. To my right is Talant Ypsir, Lord of Medusa, then Wagant Laroo, Lord of Cerberus, and, finally, Duke Hamano Kobé, Lord of Lilith. We speak with full authority for the populations of the Warden Diamond. Across from me sit Mr. Lewis Carroll, authorized agent of the Confederacy, and Antonini Dumonia, the Confederacy's resident agent on the Warden Diamond." Morah kept a straight face but Dumonia almost broke up. "Representing the Party Council are Senators Klon Luge, Morakar O'Higgins, and Surenda Quapiere. Representing the Altavar Managerial Project staff and with full authority to represent all Altavar involved in this spacial sector is Hadakim Soog. The name is an attempt to represent the actual name in our speech, and is used simply because the Altavar translating devices will recognize those syllables and transliterate them into Altavar and vice versa. There being no neutral parties present, I will assume the chairmanship for the time being, if there is no objection."

Nobody spoke or moved.

"Very well, then," Morah continued, "we will proceed. Mr. Carroll, will you please state your position?"

He smiled and nodded. "There is no use going into all the circumstances that brought us to this point. If we didn't all know them, and if it wasn't now a matter of record at all governments concerned, we wouldn't be here. It is the Confederacy's position that there is nothing here to fight about, put as simply and bluntly as possible. As far as we can determine, the interest of the Altavar is entirely in the Warden system, as are the interests of the Four Lords of the Diamond. The Confederacy is a very large group not in conflict with the Altavar or any other territory, and, therefore, believes that this matter may be settled simply. We are prepared to cede and concede to the Altavar sovereignty of the Warden solar system for a distance of twenty light-years from its sun, and we are further prepared to guarantee that no people or vessels not now belonging to those in residence in the system will encroach upon this zone, nor will Altavar access or egress from the system be in any way impeded even if it cuts through regions under Confederacy sovereignty. The four worlds known as the Warden Diamond, and their possessions and colonies, will be given free, unconditional, unilateral independence and may work out whatever arrangement they like with the Altavar. If the Altavar are sincere in stating that they have no interest in Confederacy space beyond the Warden system, this should be sufficient. Any violations, of course, would constitute an immediate act of war, but the vastness of the surrounding zone would provide ample warning."

He looked around to see how this was being taken—he had hashed it out on the security band well into the night with the Council and Krega— but saw no emotion whatever on the intent listeners. Well, not quite all— Ypsir was cleaning his nails with a small pen knife.

"In exchange for this," he continued, "the Confederacy expects an immediate and total cessation of hostilities now underway against it by the

Four Lords of the Diamond with the acquiescence of the Altavar, with-drawal of all such agents to the Warden Diamond, and a formal agree-ment that any future territorial or interest conflicts between the Confed-eration and the Altavar be settled by arbitration with both sides renouncing the use of force against the other. We feel this is more than fair."

Morah waited a moment to see if he was finished, then saw his nod that he was. "Very well, then," the Charonese said, "do you have anything to add, Doctor?"

Dumonia shook his head negatively.

"All right. I sense some objections among the Four Lords, but I will defer them at this time, and ask the Council to confirm this offer."

"We do," Luge's voice came to them after a momentary delay caused not by interstellar communications but by the lag from the subspace relay they were using on the picket ship. "In fact, the offer was approved twenty-one to four by the full Council and thus is binding upon us if ac-cepted."

Morah nodded and turned to the impassive Altavar. "Manager Soog, are you prepared at this time to answer the offer?"

"We are," the eerie synthesized voice responded. "We would very much like to accept the offer, which answers our basic needs and our ob-jections to the current arrangement. However, we feel we cannot do so. The history of the human race argues against you, Confederacy. It is a most consistent record, no matter the technological or social levels. From the very beginnings of your history you have shown yourselves to be to-tally intolerant of those who are different. The record is a clear record of repression. Treaties are signed and sworn to and systematically violated at the first opportunity. You persecuted your own for a mild difference in skin color or bone structure, or because some worshiped a different god, or even the same god by different names. Treaties between nations held only so long as both nations felt so strong that they could destroy the other. Not once do we see social or political agreements made and held by mu-tual respect, only by mutual fear—and then with all the efforts of both sides devoted to destroying even that balance.

"You took these attitudes with you into space," the creature went on, "and continued them for a while, until the years and the practicalities of distance and the advance of technology merged you racially and cul-turally. Still, the fact of this merger only caused redirection of this trait. Fully a dozen nonhuman races were discovered in your outward expan-sion. None equaled your power or emulated your culture. Five you utterly destroyed simply because you could not understand them. The other seven you conquered ruthlessly, and imposed your culture and your system upon them by force. With two of those you first concluded treaties of peace and friendship and the exchange of ambassadors and technical skills, because they were spacefaring races. But as soon as you decided that they could be no threat to you, you ruthlessly rushed in upon them and crushed them, ignoring your treaties. Understand that we do not necessarily condemn this trait, nor condone it, for it is natural to an expanding spacefaring culture and we have seen it before. We were even guilty of it ourselves, once. But you see where this leaves us in the current situation.

"Your treaties are worthless, until you know our strength and power, knowledge those treaties buy you because they buy you whatever time is needed. Sovereignty so easily given away may be more easily taken back. Nor can your military and government leaders rest easy as long as we are hidden behind a shield of their ignorance. Unless we show you all, you will try all the more by any means to learn and thus interfere. If we *did* show you, either you would determine us too weak and thus rush in to crush us, or we would be too strong, in which case you would spare no effort to catch up, then surpass us technologically and militarily. Your proposal, then, simply buys you the time you need to gain advantage, or it puts off the war, allowing you to build up and improve your forces. It offers us nothing of substance, and we must reject it."

The three Councillors looked extremely distressed and uncomfortable at this assessment, and Dumonia leaned over and whispered to the agent, "Take 'em off the hook, son. They're outclassed."

He nodded. "Then do the Altavar have a counterproposal to avoid war?"

The creature did not hesitate. "We see only one possible guarantee of our own security and safety. The Confederacy will turn over to us control of all spacecraft of whatever size or type capable of interstellar travel, and will build no more. All interstellar travel and communications between human worlds and all forces capable of harming us will be entirely under our control and supervision for a period of three hundred and fifty years from the date of commencement of the agreement. We will guarantee to maintain all existing passenger and freight routes and establish whatever added schedules are needed for the maintenance of the economy and the well-being of the people. We will not interfere in the internal political affairs of the Confederacy in any way. Expansion or the possession or control of any spacial weapons for the interdicted period will not be permitted."

The Councillors gasped, and all Four Lords smiled knowingly. "But— that would leave the entire human race totally and completely at the mercy of a race and culture of which we know nothing, having to trust all your promises at face value!" Senator Luge exclaimed. "Surely you can't be serious!"

"You proposed to cut loose unilaterally fifty million plus people who are Confederacy citizens under law and put them under these people, you know," Talant Ypsir snapped. "If it's good enough for us, it should be good enough for you!"

Morah let the outburst pass, and the Councillors ignored it. "These are negotiations in progress," he reminded them all. "Let us keep our decorum. Manager Soog?"

"Can the Senator or his advisors suggest any other way we can guarantee our security?" the alien asked.

"Our word is—" the Senator started, but the alien cut him off.

"Your word is valueless. Even you know this. Even as these proceedings begin, a vast and powerful war fleet is within range of the Warden system. On the very eve of negotiations it launched four military probes of advanced design against us. We know what your word is worth, Senator."

There was consternation and frantic whispering on the Council's side. Finally Luge seemed to calm everyone down and turned back to the camera. "May we have a recess to discuss a counteroffer?"

Morah looked around. "Is there any objection? No? For how long, then, Senator?"

"One—uh, sorry, two hours."

"Agents? Manager? Lords? No objection?"

"Let them have their meeting," Laroo snarled. "It'll probably be hilarious."

"Very well, then. This meeting is in recess for two hours and will reconvene at twelve thirty standard."

Both screens winked out, and everybody seemed to relax. Both Ypsir and Laroo seemed extremely pleased by the way things had gone; Kobé was as impassive as Morah, who looked over at the two opposite him and asked, "Well? Do you think it's still possible to reach any sort of agreement?"

"I doubt it. Not until we've gone through the bloody motions. How about it, Morah? Will they understand a show of force and resistance, or will they simply go all-out?"

"They understand the game, if that's what you mean. How they will play is anybody's guess and is certainly beyond my ability to predict. However, they have gone along with it this far, and that is an achievement."

The agent rose from the table. "I have to call my people."

He gave it to them straight, but they didn't really believe him. Not all of it. He was surprised at the start that they had accepted most of his report as gospel—certainly the computer had backed him up, and their own analysis of the same data seemed to have reinforced it. What they could not accept was the concept that the Altavar were in any sense militarily superior to the Confederacy. In weaponry, yes, but not in total weapons systems or firepower.

"But what kind of a solution can you have?" he asked, frustrated. "Nothing less than their offer will give them the security they want, and we can't possibly accept it."

"We think we were more than fair in our initial offer," Luge replied, "and it is still the only offer we can live with. Ypsir certainly has a nerve suggesting we can't turn over the Diamond to the Altavar—by their own admission now they are in a state of open rebellion. But these squishy, tentacled things give me the creeps. We all wish we had something other than the Diamond to hold over them, but we don't. We don't know their power or their forces. In one respect, old squirmy had us pegged. Power and fear of power is the only thing that really counts in situations like this. I know you think they can beat us, but we can't see any way that's possible. The only way to get us the information we need, and to learn the true situation once and for all, the Council feels, is a demonstration attack."

He sighed. "I thought as much, but I'm against it. I don't know what it is, but I have this crazy feeling that the Altavar, and Morah, are laughing at us."

"Bluff. They have no place to even hide a fleet, and even if the Diamond is extremely well defended, as we think, they are entirely on the defensive there. Any fleet of theirs capable of menacing the Diamond would be weeks, perhaps months away. Since the Diamond is all-important to them, we must put it in jeopardy. This will force their fleet, if in fact they have one, out into the open to counter us, or it will reveal their bluff. Either way, we'll know what we're facing."

"But if you attack the Diamond you lose the only card we have," he pointed out.

"Not the Diamond. Not entirely. Just one. One of the four worlds. A demonstration of power—for both sides. If they can keep us from doing it, then we'll know something. If they cannot, they risk losing the other three, one at a time, unless they agree to our original terms. This way we destroy a quarter of their eggs or whatever, but leave them three quarters. Unless they choose not to call us, in which case the bluff is revealed and we are in complete control. We still feel that if they could have destroyed us, they would have done so at the outset. The fact that they are talking at all indicates our original hypothesis is correct."

He shook his head sadly. "I was afraid it would come to this, but I hoped not. You will have to give the ultimatum yourself—I simply cannot bring myself to do it." He hesitated a moment. "You intend to target Medusa, is that correct?"

Luge looked slightly surprised, then nodded. "Yes. It has the smallest population, is the system's industrial base, and is also, in fact, the only world where hard evidence of an Altavar colony exists. Eliminate Medusa and you eliminate the technological base of the Diamond. None of the others could support the needed factories."

"I'll need details," he said softly.

"What you suggest will cost you far more than it will cost us," the Altavar told the Council. "Perhaps it was destined to be this way. But there will be no limited, demonstration wars. If a Diamond world is destroyed, then we will take appropriate action to bring this matter to a conclusion."

"You ask us to take your word for your honesty and trustworthiness with nothing whatever to support it," the agent interjected, trying to avoid what he was beginning to believe could not be avoided. "You say that our racial histories are not as different as they are similar. You surely must appreciate, then, that a civilization with over nine hundred worlds cannot totally capitulate on the word, the promise, the threat of one opponent whose entire race and history are a blank to us."

"We know," Soog responded, and there seemed genuine sadness and regret in that electronic voice. "We have known that all along. That is why generally we simply make an all-out comprehensive attack. It is far less costly to our side, yet comes down to the same thing."

"But if you felt this way all along, why didn't you do it here?" Luge responded sharply, thinking he had scored a point.

"If you were faced with this prospect, and there was but a five-percent chance this could all be avoided, would you not try?" the Altavar asked him. "We saw that one chance, and allowed ourselves to be convinced of it. It was a mistake, and many more will die because of that mistake, yet we are not sorry we made it. To have *not* taken the opportunity would have always left the question begging—did we wipe out so many countless intelligent beings for nothing?"

"I'm sorry," Senator Luge said, not sounding very sorry at all, "but we simply cannot accept your unsupported threats. If you can stop us from destroying one of the worlds, then do so. If you cannot, then you better call all this off and accept our terms before we do."

Morah, sounding very nervous, broke into the proceedings. "How long before you strike? The Altavar must have time to deliberate this matter and take it up in full."

The Council could understand that. They would have had the same problems, and the Altavar probably had greater distances to figure in, and, perhaps, a slower communications system. "Beginning at 2400 this night, we will allow exactly seven standard days for deliberation," Luge told them. "Then we will either have a settlement, or we will commence offensive operations—unless the Altavar can come up with a counteroffer we can accept in the meantime. This channel will be kept open, and our agent will remain on the scene, in case anything must get through to us."

"Seven days!" Morah thundered, rising to his feet. "But we cannot possibly evacuate a world in seven days! Using the entire Warden fleet, with pressurized freight containers, we couldn't hope to evacuate a tenth of the population of the smallest world!"

Luge nodded. "This is a demonstration, not an intentional bloodbath. We have many grievances against the Four Lords, but have no wish to destroy the innocent. We are operating on contingency plans made up when the task force was dispatched, and thus, we have provided for some of this. Sixteen transports, capable of moving twenty thousand people each, with drives capable of making interplanetary trips in one to two hours, are available. If you move only the people, at the most rapid rate, you ought to be able to make four trips a day even with loading and unloading. All ships are automated and computer-driven, but will be commanded by anyone you designate to obey voice orders. The ships will be on station in orbit off Medusa within hours—if the Altavar defenses don't shoot them down. If you start as soon as they arrive, and mobilize the rest of the Diamond fleet, and cram them in as best you can, you *can* evacuate the planet. Or you can settle this now."

Talant Ypsir was up and screaming as he heard the target. "You can't! You bastards! You swine! You hellish spawn of animals! That is *my* world you are talking about! *Mine!* Not the Altavar! It is *mine* and *I will not let you rob me of it!*" The combined effect of his inner nature and the Medusan peculiarities of the Warden organism started to change his appearance. He became, in that instant, something terrible, horrible, loathsome to behold, a monstrous, ever-changing vision of evil itself. The creature turned to the agent who sat, impassive, across the table, while next to him Dumonia watched the change with horrid fascination. *"You!"* Ypsir screamed, pointing a rotting, crawling finger at the agent. *"You put them up to this!* I will *kill* you, *kill* you, *kill*—" He made to launch himself across the table.

Yatek Morah turned in the same instant, a laser pistol in his hand, and pointed it at Ypsir. "Oh, shut up, Talant," he sighed wearily, and pulled the trigger. Ypsir collapsed instantly into unconsciousness and slid beneath the table. They all looked down at the crumpled heap and saw it slowly changing back to the familiar face they knew, the expression alone soon becoming the only measure of the hate that was inside him.

Kunser entered the room from the back dorm in an instant, but they all saw immediately that he was not threatening. "Let me get a couple of people in here and get him back upstairs," he pleaded. "We have a lot of work to do."

Morah nodded and holstered the weapon. "We will move everyone we can to the southern continent of Charon at the start," he told the Medusan assistant. "If time becomes short, we'll start putting them down wherever we can on Lilith. Cerberus simply can't handle any such loads. Tell Ypsir when he wakes up that he can settle scores in eight days. If he does anything else than exactly what this meeting decides, or in any way makes trouble before that point, he will meet the fate of his predecessor instantly. Remind him that we do not need to know where he is or what he is doing, that the Altavar can and will simply order his Wardens to consume him if *any* of the rest of us say so. Is that clear?"

Everyone else in the room was just getting over their stunned and shocked feelings at the proceedings when Ypsir was finally carried out and away. Even Luge remained frozen on the screen, horrified and shocked by his first direct look at what the Warden organism could do.

Only Morah remained completely in control. "These proceedings are now in indefinite recess. All parties agree that commencing seven days from 2400 this night a state of war will exist between the Altavar on the one hand and the Confederacy on the other."

Luge seemed to snap out of it. "Any move against us prior to that point will result in even more dire consequences," he warned. "We are allowing this period not only in hopes of a diplomatic solution but also out of common decency and mercy. If any attempt is made during this period, or is perceived by us to be made, we will abandon our plans and instead all modules will be directed by the task force with the intent of inducing the sun to nova."

The others on both sides looked particularly shocked by the threat, but the Altavar seemed to take it in stride. "That would be most interesting," it noted coldly. "However, it would cause quite a lot more problems than we are currently prepared to handle. We will, therefore, uphold the waiting period. But make no mistake on this, Senators. Neither you nor the Confederacy will survive many hours after you know just what you have done."

The agent who called himself Mr. Carroll frowned and looked nervously at the Altavar on the screen. What an odd way to put it, he couldn't help thinking. What a *very* odd way to put it. . . .

7

Talant Ypsir spent most of his time brooding on his palatial orbiting satellite, but he did not interfere with the evacuation nor prevent his aides and infrastructure from doing what had to be done. For himself, though, he spent almost all of his time in his pleasure garden accompanied only by Ass, emerging only briefly to make certain that the station itself would be moved from orbit by tug.

The transports, too, were built on the modular concept, so it was relatively easy for the great ships to break into small compartments and move down to various collection points on the surface. These were troop transports, designed to hold half of what they were being asked to hold; but in a war without troops they could be spared by the Confederacy, which was, according to Commander Krega, still confident that the Altavar bluff would break at the last minute.

The Medusan population proved unusually easy to move. Virtually all of them had been born and raised to obey the orders of the monitors and their superiors, so while they grumbled and complained a lot they did pretty much as they were told. There was some panic in the big cities, among groups who simply would not believe that there was a threat. Others suddenly lost faith when their well-ordered society was proven incapable of protecting them, but these were quickly quelled by monitors with efficient brutality. It was also simply stated that those who did not want to go could remain—but their lives would probably be abnormally short.

Mr. Carroll was particularly concerned about the colonies of Wild Ones. They were too spread out for all of them to be contacted easily, and most disbelieved the news if they heard it and fled into the wild. Finally, he commandeered a shuttle craft and went down to a particular settlement he knew well.

The shuttle landed not in a cradle but on a flat, something it really wasn't designed to do but could because the possibility of an emergency landing always existed. The door opened and he emerged, the only one aboard, dressed in a protective orange spacesuit with the helmet removed. Still, he wore goggles and a small respirator as he walked up to the rock cliff with the twin waterfalls, aware for the first time of just how hard this land really was on one not redesigned as a Medusan.

The courtyard was deserted, as he'd expected, but he didn't hesitate a moment, walking up to the one ground-level cave and inside as far back as he could. The torches were still lit, which told him that people were in fact still here somewhere. He cursed himself for not bringing some additional light source. The last time he'd been here he'd been riding along in a Medusan body and hadn't realized just how damned dark and dangerous the path was.

As he'd hoped, the three elders waited for him across the underground river, eying him without suspicion or fear. He stopped and faced them.

The old woman on the right spoke. "So you have come back after all."

The comment startled him. "You know who I am?"

"Your body is Warden-dead, yet your spirit shines through," the other woman told him. "Your walk, your manner, your turn of speech is the same."

"Then you know why I have come."

"We know," the first woman responded. "We will not stop anyone from leaving anywhere on this world, but we will not go."

"They're going to do it," he warned. "They're really going to do it. The kind of heat and thermal radiation they will use will melt the very crust of this planet. I know you understand what that means. No Warden power is going to save you, and the way the Altavar are acting, they can't save you, either."

"We know, and yet to go would be to call our lives and beliefs that we have held for so many years a lie," the man put in. "When they do as you say, we trust in the God of Medusa to save us, or take us, as is Her will. But no matter what happens there, they will unleash upon themselves a power greater than the pitiful Confederacy can conceive, and She will be angry. We place our faith in Her."

He sighed. "If you want to be martyrs, I can't stop you. But you have fifty thousand people across this world, and they are your responsibility, too. They can survive, if we know where they are, and if we can get to them some word that we can be trusted."

"It is impossible to notify them all in the time remaining," the first woman pointed out, "but surely more than half have knowledge of what is to come. Some will go, and none will be stopped from going. It is the same here."

"You have explained to the pilgrims here that they are likely to die in two days?"

"We put it to them just that way," the man assured him. "We told them that physical death was almost a certainty. Only a very few said that they would like to go, and most of them have not changed their minds."

"There are two here, though, who should go. I think even you must realize *that*."

A few moments later one of the small boats came, bearing two occupants he knew well. They stared at him in frightened bewilderment. He helped them out of the boat, and was immediately aware that both were obviously pregnant, Bura Morphy exceedingly so. Both Bura and Angi just gaped at him. Finally Bura said, "They told us Tari had returned. Who are you?"

"Tari is dead. You know that," he responded sadly. "I am his—father, in a sense—and his brother."

Angi gasped, realizing before Bura the implications of that. During the weeks in the wilderness, Tarin Bul had told them of his origin. "You are the man who . . ." It was all she could manage.

He nodded. "I am. You can't possibly understand this now, but you must believe me. I was with you in the sewers under Rochande, and with you in the wilderness. I was with you when you came to the citadel, and with Tarin Bul until the moment of his death. I am not Tarin Bul, but he is with me. I have come to get you."

"They say they're going to blow up the planet. Is that true?" Bura asked him.

"That's true."

"And nothing can stop it?"

"I tried—Lord, how I tried! But we have an enormous group of men and women who are in the strange position of being totally confident of their power and scared to death at one and the same time. We are trying to save those we can. You carry what future there is for Tarin Bul inside you. Don't kill him completely. Come with me."

They looked nervous and uncertain. Bura's hand took Angi's and squeezed it tightly. "A pack of mad harrar couldn't keep us here one more minute if we have a way to get off."

He grinned. "Fine," he said, and turned back to the elders. "You may not want to leave, but may I address the others here? Give them one last immediate chance?"

"You have our permission," the first woman said. "Go to the courtyard, and we will send them to you."

His speech was impassioned, eloquent, convincing, and mostly futile. Out of perhaps two hundred, only seventeen—all, it turned out, refugees and escapees from the cities—took his offer of escape. He could tell that others, perhaps many others, wanted to go, but were being held back not so much by physical means as by an odd sort of peer pressure. The phenomenon was new to him, and frightened him a little, but he could do no more.

Not a single one of them had ever been on a spacecraft before, and he had some trouble making the adjustments in restraints and in calming nerves before he could take off. Fifteen of the seventeen were female, all of whom were at least seven months pregnant. The citadel, he knew, was a place where tribes within a week's journey came when it was time for women to bear their young.

Once over their initial fears, they seemed to enjoy the ride. As time grew shorter and shorter, though, and the evacuation fell more and more behind schedule, he knew that the shuttle would be needed desperately elsewhere. He headed for the Cerberan space station, calling ahead to Dumonia's people to take on his passengers for now. Ypsir's Medusan station was already beyond the plane of the Cerberan orbit on its way instream by tug, but even if it had been available he wouldn't have used it. He knew full well what would happen if it were known to Talant Ypsir, as it would be, that two wives of Tarin Bul, pregnant with his children, were within the Lord of Medusa's station—all that really remained of Ypsir's formerly absolute power.

He was surprised to find Dumonia personally waiting for him when he arrived, and after he got the refugees as settled as possible they had a short time to talk. Dumonia had an easy and relaxed style and the perfect manner, and their talk was pretty wide-ranging, considering the time limit the agent had for turnaround. Dumonia saw the human angle.

"You know," he said, "that this thing can only end in one of two ways now. Either there will be no more Diamond, or no more Confederacy."

"Mr. Carroll" nodded. "I'm well aware of that. If there's no more Confederacy we're still alive, but in a hell of a fix with no more imports and the Altavar no longer in hiding. On the other hand, if there's no more Diamond we've just done a lot of work for nothing."

Dumonia grinned. "I think not. You must understand that the Confederacy is ripe for collapse. It won't take an awful lot to bring that about. Making so many worlds so interdependent has left them far too vulnerable. I'm sure that's what Kreegan had in mind when he dreamed up this human-replacement business. Unfortunately for all of us, such action was not enough, and if it hadn't been a desperation scheme it would have been obvious from the start. As fragile and corrupt as the system is, it is still firm enough to keep together a massive population spread out over impossible distances. In its own way the Confederacy was quite amazing, eclipsing any empire in humanity's past. But it *needs* collapsing—all empires do, after they have peaked, or humanity grows stale and dies."

The agent nodded. "I've come to pretty much the same conclusion myself. It seems horrible, though, that so many will have to die."

"It's always been the case. Back in the very old days when we were only on one planet with simple weapons, occasional wars—even with bows, arrows, and spears—spurred progress. But it is no different, really, if your population dies by the sword or by a fusion bomb, or laser blast, or any other of our modern ways. Still, we finally reached the point on that old world where we couldn't afford big wars any more without wiping ourselves out. So we replaced them with small, limited wars, until even these became too sophisticated for any sort of control. Space took much of the pressure off—colonization did that. But political needs and technology unified us, made a human empire of more than nine hundred worlds possible—and kept us in place for a few centuries. Now it falls under the new barbarians."

"The Altavar strike me as inhuman, and really frightening, but not as barbarians. I wish I understood them better. I'm not even sure I understand their actions now. Why not strike—if they can? Or if they can defend Medusa, why allow all this?"

"I don't know," the psych told him. "The Four Lords really don't know, either—except Morah, I think. I doubt if Kreegan knew, although perhaps he did. They, too, bought a bill of goods. The Altavar convinced them that they were no threat to the Diamond, perhaps simply by demonstrating that they'd been here all the time. The Four Lords were attracted to a war by remote control, one with no seeming risk and a lot of rewards, including escape, since the Altavar demonstrated to them early on that they could control the Warden organism. Even those robots are totally operated by a variation of the same little creature, each responsive to its own self-contained programming so it can come and go as it pleases. You know, the Confederacy managed to bypass and even reprogram Laroo and others since, yet they really don't know how the damned things work. Thanks to Merton and her colleagues we knew where the computer-control center was and figured a different but effective input-output system for it, but we still did it by counterprogramming, feeding self-canceling instructions. We couldn't build one if we tried, nor create our own total-control mechanism."

He nodded. "You joined our side—for which I'm eternally grateful, by the way—because you feared the aliens. Now what do you think?"

Dumonia shrugged. "Who knows? In science, one takes what *is*, not what one would like things to be. In the end, perhaps because of the actions of both of us, we've come down to war anyway. If the aliens lose, so do we—end of problem. If the aliens win, then we must deal with them and with our own future. Obviously, I am cheering for the aliens even though I don't trust them one little tentacle-tip. You must understand, for a man who has devoted his entire life to learning what he can—and that's precious little, I assure you—of the workings of the human mind and personality, to be suddenly faced at my age with the necessity of learning the workings of a wholly different complex creature, was and is a bit intimidating."

"But if we survive—and have to go it alone—we must look forward. Suppose the Altavar really do let us alone on the three remaining worlds. What then?"

"I began my little operation out of a sense of personal survival," the psych replied, "but it later expanded, as you know. Ultimately, I hoped for a better, more free and open society on all the Diamond worlds. Turn them loose, with these strange powers, and see what could be built. It's more than enough challenge for an old man, don't you think?"

He nodded and grinned. "And for a younger one, too, I think. But what about the Medusans? I wonder if the destruction of Medusa might not also destroy their own potential and actual power. And, if not, whether or not they'll breed true to Medusa or to Charon or wherever else their children are born."

"We'll have to wait and see on that. However, I suspect that the computer for them is the same as the one for us. Probably one of those huge moons of Momrath, broadcasting and receiving on all four frequencies no matter what. In that case, they will retain their potential and breed true. Charon will become a biracial society, which will bear close watching. Eventually we must learn the Warden secrets and go out again from here, of course, but each of the three worlds can handle many times their present population. You could put half a billion or more on Cerberus yet, and perhaps three billion or more on each of the other two. The survivors will have several generations to solve the problems, and with far less ignorance than we've all had up to now. Show some bright minds that a thing is possible and sooner or later they'll drive themselves mad until they learn how to do it. That's what makes us humans something pretty special."

It was almost time to leave, but he had one more question. "What about Ypsir's girl? What if we could get her away from him—or if she freed herself?"

He sighed. "Jorgash is an expert on the Medusan variants. He tells me flatly that the process absolutely locks in the physiological design so that it cannot be changed at all. I suspect the computer treats them as trees or animals or such—things that must be kept stable. Remember, that's what the Wardens are actually for. Now, assuming your computer would let us, we could take that Tarin Bul recording you used for your report and feed it back into her, but consider the consequences. That body, those revised genetics, that hormonal makeup would, I think, drive you nuts. Still, she was made out of Tarin Bul's body, and the intellectual capacity is still very much there. The challenge is, at the moment, quite academic, but I'm fascinated by what *could* be done. Someone with her looks, moves, and drives and your superior intellect might potentially be running all our lives in a couple of years. It's something to think about."

"I think about it a lot," he told the psych master, "but I'll think about it more if I'm still alive and kicking three days from now. I have to go."

As he stood up to leave, Dumonia put a hand on his shoulder and added, in a concerned tone, "Watch out for Ypsir, boy. He was always *for* the war, remember—so bad is his hatred of the Confederacy—and now that war's come, but at a price he never expected to pay. He'll never forgive the Altavar for that, but he's very smart and knows it might be a long time before he can get revenge there. Thus, all of his hatred, all of his frustration, almost certainly will be taken out on you and your brothers here. Right now he's probably spending all his time thinking of how to get his revenge on you. Not by killing you—that's not his style and would give him only brief satisfaction. It will be something horrible, and far worse than we can imagine."

He nodded and shook the little psych's hand warmly. "I know that and I'll remember. If we're still around."

"Yes," Dumonia repeated grimly, "if we're still around. Empires never go quietly."

He was back on Boojum on the night before the deadline expired, as instructed by both the Confederacy and Morah. He opened his secure channel to Krega, a channel so secure that the field enveloping him would not allow any recording device, or even someone standing right next to him, to understand a word either way.

"There has been no reconsideration?" he asked, hoping against hope. "They're still behind in evacuation, and there are between fifty and a hundred thousand people we just can't get off under any circumstances."

"There has been no reconsideration on this end," Krega told him. "In fact, it's been difficult just to restrain some of our people, particularly the military, to this limited engagement. However, it's going to be awfully bloody. We have monitored some traffic not on our control system at various random points around the civilized worlds. They duck in and out of light before we can get to them, but some of them are pretty big. They haven't budged on your side?"

"Not a bit. I talked to Morah and to the Altavar and they're both firm—you might say even *eager*, on Morah's part. However, that unauthorized traffic gives me bad feelings. There's been no sign of any fleet massing here—I still haven't seen an Altavar ship, not even one to take off the party on Medusa. I don't think they're going to take on the task force head-to-head."

"We have a computer projection on their potential, even assuming a tenth of our firepower, and it's scary," Krega admitted. "Security and Military Systems Command have used the week to shift to remote backup positions. Unless this is more bluff, we think they have dispersed rather than massed their forces for hit-and-run. If we had ten war stations we could destroy hundreds of planets. We have to hit them in one spot—yours, I'm sorry to say, but it's the only one we have. They can hit us wherever we're not. Come in, destroy a weakly defended planet someplace, then get out fast. Choose another equally vulnerable. We can't guard them all. We'd need eighteen hundred cruisers to do a strong defense of all the worlds and we have less than three hundred. Sounded like a lot when we built them."

And that was that. "They're willing to accept the possibility of a protracted bloodbath of those proportions?"

Krega chuckled dryly. "Son, maybe you're still naive. The Council, the Congress, all the top people are in the best, most well-protected rear areas. They'll die of old age before *they're* in jeopardy. Face facts—they've got to win no matter *what* the cost."

No matter what the cost . . . Yes, he reflected sourly, that was the bottom line. Fallon had been right. Korman had been right. They'd *all* been right. The Warden Diamond wasn't the opposite of the Confederacy, nor were the Four Lords of the Diamond the opposites of the Council. No, they were merely reflections of the Confederacy, allowing for local conditions. That was it—the break was now complete, total, and irrevocable.

"Good-bye, Papa," he said, meaning it.

"Good-bye, Control," Krega responded and broke the contact.

He threw the security transceiver as hard as he could at the nearest wall. It bounced off and clattered and rolled back to his feet.

The task force was already alerted. There was only an hour to go.

8

Morah turned and nodded to him as he entered the cramped meeting room. "Welcome, Mr. Carroll," he said calmly, sounding in a good mood. "Have a seat. Some of my staff are here and we thought we would make use of the transmission facilities and these screens to watch what happens now. Unfortunately, Altavar ships are simply not built for such as us, and the command center itself bears little resemblance to anything we could make use of. I have arranged to couple in our own devices to theirs so that we can, shall we say, watch the show."

Morah's manner irritated him. He could not really figure out the man, who moved so rapidly from tired philosopher to master agent to an almost Ypsir-like disregard for suffering and destruction. Still, until this was resolved, he was more or less along for the ride and would have to make the best of it.

A half-dozen others were seated around the table, some with small terminals, others with primitive pads and paper, but all looked more interested than worried by what might well take place. Most, but not all, were Charonese. Medusans were conspicuously absent, though.

One screen displayed the familiar computer plot showing the tactical disposition of the task force, the Diamond worlds, and representations of moving traffic and satellites. The plot extended to Momrath, but not beyond.

The task force had split into three sections. Two battle groups with their attendant cruiser protection had moved well away from the main force and were station keeping at right angles to the task force and the sun. The main battle group, with two war stations, was rapidly beginning to close on the target, its obvious move designed to draw out an enemy fleet and to draw and test interplanetary defenses, since all operations could have been carried out from any distance within a light-year of the target.

He frowned. "From the looks of it the Altavar are putting up no resistance at all," he noted aloud.

Morah sat back in his chair and watched the screen. "There will be no resistance to the objective except from fixed planetary defenses, which will become increasingly costly to the task force the more they close," he told the agent. "However, the subsidiary battle groups will be engaged at the proper time."

"Then there *are* forces in the area! Where?"

"You'll see them when the time comes, Mr. Carroll. Be patient. We are about to bear witness to a sight no humans and few living Altavar have ever seen. We have remote cameras stationed in-system and will be able to see things firsthand on the other screen. All of this, of course, is contingent on the Confederacy task force doing exactly what it said it would. If they try to double-cross us with a mass attack on all four worlds or any one other than Medusa, or if they come at us here, the script may change drastically. I *do* expect some attempt at the moons here, but as long as the main attack is centered on Medusa I believe we are in no danger."

As the standard clock hit 2400, there was a sharp, anticipatory taking in of breath by all concerned, but nothing happened immediately. The task force continued to close, now well within the orbit of Orpheus, the farthest out planet in the Warden system.

At 2403 the task force slowed, then came to a complete stop between Orpheus and Oedipus, next in of the planets, as shown in the total system insert, and the cruisers deployed in protective formations around the two main war stations. Suddenly buzzers sounded, and they could see a great number of tiny pinpricks of white light emerge from the war stations in a steady stream that lasted several seconds, then halted. The field, resembling an onrushing meteor storm, was on the big in-system board in a matter of seconds.

Streamers of blue light appeared in great numbers, lashing out from the moons of Momrath at the onrushing storm of modules. About a third of the modules broke from the main stream and headed toward the source of the fire, but the defenders were taking a tremendous toll. "The fools clustered them too closely together," Morah sneered.

And it was true. Bright flashes occurred all through the field and its breakaway segment, followed by tiny white lights winking out all over the place. The blue streams were moving so fast the eye could hardly follow them, but they were well directed and found their targets.

"Second wave away and dispersing!" an aide at a terminal called, and eyes went back to the insert. The new modular attack appeared to be about the same in number as the first, but it spread into an extremely wide field that was almost impossible for the boards to track properly. They were now coming in from all directions.

"That's more like it," Yatek Morah mumbled to himself.

He could only look at Morah and the others in wonder. Quite rightly, some of those modules were aimed directly at them, yet they didn't seem the least bit concerned. He sighed and gave himself a fatalistic shrug. Either they were safe, or they were not—but, in either case, as much as he'd like to be out there in a ship under his control, he was stuck.

"Open camera screens," Morah ordered, and on the rear screen a series of views appeared. One was a long shot from a position far enough from Medusa to show it only as a greenish-white disk, the view polarized enough so that the night side of the planet showed dully but completely as well. Then there were six smaller views, some from orbit around Medusa, others apparently on the planet's surface. One showed a city that might have been Rochande but also might have been any one of a dozen others, while another showed a long shot of the sacred mountain in the far north, a location he recognized well.

"The defensive shields are holding just fine," Morah commented to nobody in particular. "However, we can't possibly get all the probes if we're to save Momrath's bases as well as give cover to the other three planets." He turned toward the camera viewscreens and pointed. "There! See the sky near that plains view?"

They all looked, and could see clear streaks in the otherwise blemishless dark blue sky, streaks leaving a reddish-white trail. Now there were more and more of them, almost filling the skies as the attack modules separated after entering the atmosphere and split into a hundred equally deadly weapons each.

Massive explosions showed on each view, with huge domes of crackling energy ballooned up and out. One of the cameras was knocked out, but was quickly replaced by another. Obviously there were enough located all over the planet for them to get at least one good surface view.

The full disk view showed thousands of tiny bursts of light all over the globe, as if it were covered with windows and now suddenly had internal light, each window representing a lethal energy weapon of enormous destructive potential.

He glanced over at the situations board and saw, to his surprise, new formations in a new color, yellow, approaching the system from all directions in a coordinated circle. There was no way to tell their size or design from the board codes, but there were a *hell* of a lot of them, at least a number equal to the total task force. "The Altavar are closing for attack," he said to the others, all of whom were watching the merciless bombardment of Medusa.

Morah took a glance back at the board. "Yes. They made it very easy on us, giving us the week. It allowed us to plot their probable attack pattern and to position our own forces so that they could emerge from hyperspace at precisely predetermined points. They will engage only the two smaller reserve task forces, however; the main body's job is to restrict the main enemy force to its original target."

"But with a force like that they could have defended the whole damned system!" he almost yelled in fury. "They're *deliberately* throwing Medusa *away!" Why? Why? What have I missed?*

The Altavar fleet split into three sections, two of which moved to create a ball-shaped attack formation around each of the reserve task forces, the main body moving steadily on toward a position near Momrath.

From their movements, it appeared that the Altavar had ships that were smaller than the Confederacy's cruisers, perhaps much smaller, but with far greater speed and maneuverability at sublight speeds. They moved so quickly and precisely into their ball-shaped attack pattern and began closing in what seemed like one motion that the bigger Confederacy ships had no chance to get out of the way or disperse. Instead the cruisers positioned themselves in a classical defense and began counterattacking the Altavar formation immediately. The fury and totality of the engagement was such that the board became a riot of colors, both white and yellow, and it quit making any attempt at showing the actual action.

In a sense it seemed an almost romantic vision of war, the ship-to-ship battle of long ago, but he knew it was not. The board itself showed a vast distance, and those ships probably never would see one another, except on boards like this one that were far more detailed and localized. Nor, probably, were very many lives at stake. This was not really man-to-man or even ship-to-ship, it was computer versus computer, technology versus technology, and it was some time before it was clear who was going to win. The Altavar's smaller, speedier, easier-to-turn and harder-to-hit ships, supported by computers whose programs were based not on problem theories but actual combat, had the edge, assuming the forces were basically equal in strength.

The main task force between Orpheus and Oedipus regrouped, studying the side conflicts and learning from them, but made no move to press inward or engage the main Altavar force, which was clearly now not headed for a direct engagement but rather was establishing a large and formidable defensive perimeter inside the Diamond itself. The task force threw a number of lethal modules at the defenders, but they were easily neutralized. The main concentration continued to be upon Medusa for the moment.

But with both reserve battle groups now showing bright yellow circles blinking on and off, meaning that the Altavar had broken the back of that force, the main task-force commander was not about to continue a methodical demonstration of increasing power against a largely deserted planet. He opted to put an end to Medusa and then, if need be, engage the main task force before the victorious remnants of the two main Altavar groups that were mopping up their battles could regroup and join the defenders.

The agent felt a great deal of admiration for the task-force commander, whoever he or she was, for having the good sense and guts not to split up that force and aid the reserves, thereby weakening their own double group to Altavar attack. That admiral understood full well that the alien main group was there to defend the other three planets and, possibly, Momrath, and could not afford to leave those targets open to close and join battle with the Confederacy task force. As soon as Medusa was taken care of, then the task force would have to close on the now defending Altavar.

Only two cameras on the surface of Medusa were still working, and one was up in the north, where energy weapons were melting the glacial ice with ease. For the first time in a long while, perhaps since shortly after the surface was created, there was open ocean on most of the planet, and much of it was boiling.

"Salvo seven. This should be it!" somebody called, and at that moment the last surface cameras went.

He could see them at the citadel, those proud and foolish Wild Ones, praying to their god as the searing heat and energy hit them. At least it had been quick. At least that . . .

And now simultaneously deployed special warheads went off simultaneously around the entire globe of Medusa, their heat so intense the very atmosphere was inflamed, and the crust began to melt. Great sheets of steam rose from the oceans and the ice, and the world turned slowly from bright white to a dull crimson as the magma underlying the Medusan surface was freed and fed by the material at the top.

It was a gruesome sight that yet so fascinated him that he couldn't take his eyes off it.

"Any moment now . . ." Morah said expectantly, then: "There! It's begun!"

He stared hard at the image, now blood red, and for a moment saw nothing he hadn't expected to see. Abruptly, he frowned and rubbed his eyes, as the image seemed to lose its consistency and become fuzzy and distorted. Medusa seemed no longer to be a disk at all, but some sort of stretchy blob of reddish-brown goo going off in all directions. And it seemed to be growing abnormally larger, until it was twice the size it had been, and he could only scratch his chin and mutter, "Now, what the hell?"

The glob seemed to flow in a single direction, then separate into two distinct masses, one of which clearly again was a planetary body of Medusa's size. The other mass, however, of almost equal size, congealed and writhed and twisted—and *moved.* Moved outward, gaining speed as it did so, *moving toward the Confederation task force* that immediately began throwing everything it had at the onrushing mass.

The Altavar fleet, in a wide, inverted V, moved in behind it, matching speed and direction.

"Close-up!" Morah snapped. "I want a close-up on the Coldah!"

His staff did what they could, and found at least one view from somewhere out-system that showed the mass of the writhing, terrible planet-sized thing that had emerged from the bombarded planet.

It was a monstrous, ever-changing shape, mostly energy but with some matter, taking no clearly defined substance for more than a second before changing into something else, like a mad ball of lightning gone completely berserk. And yet it was not berserk—its course and speed were deliberate, and it continued to close on the fleet, ignoring all that was being thrown at it, absorbing module after module that could destroy a planet.

It was on the fleet before any counteraction could be taken, just wading in, shooting off tens of thousands of tendrils of fire and flame into the hearts of the ships, exploding whatever ordnance they still carried. Both war stations went up in blazes that matched Medusa itself, but much of the outer task force, beyond immediate reach of the Coldah's tentacles, began to fan out and those were now engaged by Altavar ships from the edges of the great fleet's wedge.

The agent angrily pounded his fist on the table. "Of course! Of course!" he muttered to himself. "Why the hell didn't *I* think of that? Not one species—two! That wasn't the damned Altavar computer I sensed on Medusa, it was the mind of this other thing!"

Morah couldn't take his eyes off the pictures, but nodded. "Yes, two. The Altavar serve and protect the Coldah."

"This—this Coldah. What the hell *is* it? What's it made of? How can the damned thing even exist?"

"We don't know. The Altavar, who have been studying it for thousands of years, don't know, either. They're not many in number, these Coldah, so we have no idea how numerous they might be or even if they are native to this galaxy or even this universe. They roam solitarily throughout the vastness of space until they come upon a world of the size and type and position they need for whatever it is they do. Long ago, thousands of years ago, when the Altavar were an expanding empire like the Confederacy, one came into an Altavar system and made one of their worlds its home. They are energy, they are matter, they are whatever they choose to be whenever they choose to be. In settling into that Altavar world, they killed three billion inhabitants. Naturally, that started a long and dirty war."

He nodded, seeing the possibilities.

"Of course," the security chief went on, "they attacked that first Coldah much as we just did, and with similar results. They made the thing irritable. It went right through their forces to another inhabited world and did the same thing. They continued to fight it, to chase it, to harass it as much as possible while trying to learn as much about it as they could. It became an obsession with the Altavar, as, of course, it would with us. But while the Coldah don't like company they *can* communicate with one another over great distances, and after a few centuries more of them showed up in the Altavar systems. Eventually the Coldah learned to anticipate the Altavar attacks and take measures ahead of time. The Altavar losses were gigantic, and they finally had to stop their continual, useless war and take stock, learn a bit more, then try again. Every time they failed. For thousands of years they failed. They learned a lot, though. When the Coldah inhabited a planet, it added little or no mass, apparently remaining in an energy state, and it sent out colonies of organisms to create within it a disguise of sorts—a perfect, natural disguise."

"The Warden organism," he breathed.

"The concept is not unknown in nature. As to why they always prefer our kinds of planets, and remake them into our kinds of planets, nobody really knows. They are the classic alien—so different from anything we know, any form of life we know, any life origins we can understand, that they are totally incomprehensible to us. Your man on Medusa once made a fringe contact with this one. Do you remember it?"

He nodded. "I thought it was the computer."

"What was your impression?"

He thought a moment. "It was aware of me, but didn't have much of an opinion about it. I got the impression of a sense of utter superiority out of the thing, and I had the feeling it noted me, then flicked me aside as we would a fly."

"I have been—far deeper—in contact over the years," Morah told him, "and I find it an impossible, frustrating task. I'm not even certain that what we get into our minds really correlates with the real Coldah. There is an undeniable sense of power—and why not? They have it, that's for sure. Beyond that—who knows? They are certainly aware we exist, and they are even aware of who their friends are, but that's about it. Perhaps, one day, we *will* know, but I somehow doubt it. All we can do is study them and learn what we can. They're impossible creatures, but whatever they do they seem to obey the laws just as we do. They just might know a few more laws than we do."

The viewscreens were blank now, except for the long-shot view of Medusa, still molten hot yet cooling even now, swaddling itself in an incredibly thick and violent layer of clouds. He turned to the plot board, which showed no white dots or forms whatsoever and yellow forms only in the mop-up battle operations. It was over. The greatest task force ever assembled by man had been met, and bested, partly by a better assembled force that had an easier time on the defense, and partly by a creature they could neither understand nor believe in even as it was killing them.

"Where's this thing going now?" he asked Morah.

The security chief shrugged. "Wherever it wants. Probably to another of our planets, to burrow in once again. They go from system to system until they find a planet within our life zone around a stable sun, then they burrow in and remake the surface out of matter and energy. It's never the same twice, but always something familiar to us, even the atmosphere. It'll stay there a thousand years unless disturbed, as this one was, then rise again, move on, find the next planet, and start it all again. You know, when they leave on their own they do virtually no damage to the planetary systems their little symbiotic riders create? They just leave 'em. I think a number of mysteries about how so many worlds have formed within our life tolerances may be answered by the Coldah. As random as they are, most of the planets they use are not initially inhabitable, but they leave them that way. Once they leave their little symbiotes don't destruct, as they do when in residence and taken away, but just sort of fade out. Normal evolution follows." He chuckled. "You know, it's even just possible that our own race, and the Altavar, grew up over the millions of years because of Coldah lifestyles. It's a fascinating concept."

"But the Altavar—they fought these things. And now they seem almost to protect them."

"That's true," Morah agreed, telling one of his aides in an aside to get them all strong drinks, "but in the thousands of years they fought and studied the Coldah, a funny thing happened. Somewhere along the line they got tired of it, just got sick of futile head-knocking, and sort of mentally surrendered to the big bastards. To the Altavar, the Coldah became their whole life, and in a probably gradual switch they came not only to accept the existence of these creatures but to actually work *with* them. Don't ask me to explain it—it's certainly religious, or mystic, in a way, and those are unexplainable even when we're talking about *our* faiths, yet they are coldly and scientifically devoted to the great project, as they call it. They protect the Coldah from outside interference whenever possible, and they try with their fleets to nudge the Coldah into worlds that need some work. Don't ask me how that's possible, but the Coldah, once the Altavar started helping rather than fighting, seemed to go along with it."

He nodded. "But not here."

"Well, it was impossible, for one thing. When the Coldah originally came to the Warden system we were still stuck knee-deep on old Mother Earth. These four worlds were pretty piss-poor rock piles with nasty atmospheres and surface pressures, just perfect. And when a particularly big, fat, Coldah arrived, it did something the Altavar, with all their experience, had never seen before. It reproduced by fission. It made triplets, in fact, and the one old and three new ones entered into the four Diamond worlds. Shortly after, they released, or made and released, or whatever, their little beasties, and they went to work on the world, making it over. Lilith, with the original mama Coldah, had the most rigid system imposed on it. Then the Altavar moved in. In the years they have studied, fought, then served the Coldah, they learned a lot. They can make their own Wardens, and they can give orders to these synthesized versions, too. Within limits, they can even play games with the Coldah versions, and they did here. Looking at the climates, they elevated one species on each to dominance."

"I figured that much out. Reptiles on the warmest world, insects on the lushest, water breathers on the wettest, and mammals on the coldest."

"Right. Part of their own grand project, really. Since the Coldah *can* leave, although not arrive, with a minimum of fuss—it's sort of like a big mist rising, they tell me—leaving the worlds to natural laws, they've been trying to influence their direction. It's a very long-term concept, naturally, but they are really trying to learn what factors and conditions produce intelligence one place and not another. It's pretty complex. Of course, our arrival screwed up the project here."

"And because, somehow, the electrochemical wavelengths on which the human brain operates were just slightly off the wavelengths used by the Coldah to command the Warden organisms, we developed these wild talents." He paused for a moment, then added, "I assume the Altavar are nowhere near those wavelengths?"

Morah chuckled. "No. Oh, they can tune in, as it were, mechanically, but not biologically."

He whistled low and grabbed a drink as it arrived, drinking a bit more in one gulp than he should. He needed it. Finally he said, "Then *we* became the project."

"Yes. *We* became the project. But in order to control it, and to minimize interference between ourselves and the Coldah, the Confederacy was in the way. The Coldah are headed, generally, in our direction—or back to it, I don't know which. The idea of *our* race, who can, as it were, tune in on at least one Coldah band, threatened the Altavar, their lifestyle, their system of beliefs. I think they were actually afraid that, if we followed the same pattern as they did, we could eventually establish contact, even *rapport* with the Coldah. Maybe we can, although I think they may simply be too alien ever to understand or communicate with on more than a basic level."

He smiled wanly and shook his head in wonder. "Then, to the Altavar, *we* were the demons. *They* were scared of us stealing their gods. If the results weren't so tragic they'd be almost funny, you know that?" He thought a moment. "But if we were that much of a threat to them, the snake that could steal their Eden, why not just wipe out everybody but the project people—the Diamond?"

"They intended to do just that, as the old Altavar told us. But they are an enormous, mostly mobile population, spread out over half a galaxy, wherever there are Coldah. They faced an empire of vast proportions and unknown capabilities. They had to know how we thought, what our tactics were like, how we'd fight, all the rest. They had time. It's still three hundred years until the scheduled hatching, or breakout, or whatever it is the Coldah do. It was over four hundred when we first arrived here. They spent fifty years or more just getting to know us through the Wardens, watching us work, and realizing just how different our relationship to the Wardens was from theirs, and only then did they really send for their fleet, which must be assembled from incredible distances and then can only be spared in small pieces. It was easier for them to establish factories on worlds beyond the Confederacy, even Warden worlds themselves, and build the force they needed, along with using the Wardens to breed the Altavar necessary for the fight. By the time they had their fleet and their military ready, Kreegan was Lord of Lilith."

"And he stumbled on the whole truth?"

"Much as I did. On each world there was one point, one weakness, that was the Coldah's window to the outside. Don't ask me how it works or why, I don't know. But there was one point, usually in an inaccessible and nasty place on the globe, where this happened. On Lilith it's very near the north pole. On Charon it's a small island off the southern continent. I don't know how Kreegan happened on the north pole, but considering that the descendants of the original exploiter team had set up a planet-worship religion on Lilith they must have put him on to it. The signal strength, as it were, at each of those points is so strong it bleeds over directly onto ours, exciting our own Wardens and our brain's awareness and control."

"No wonder, then, Kreegan became Lord."

Morah nodded. "Local Altavar, bred for the conditions and for unobtrusiveness, try to discourage anyone from getting too close without blowing their cover, often masquerading as wild animals themselves. They mostly staff monitoring and control devices to keep tabs on the Coldah, whose signals increase consistently until they leave. By that monitor they can predict the Coldah's eventual behavior and be ready for it."

He thought a moment. "Then the ice demons weren't the only ones. There were those nasty beasties in the Charonese desert with tentacles, too, if I remember."

"Oh, the narils. Actually, they're not Altavar, but Altavar pets, in a way. An attempt to breed an animal with their own biochemical structure that was sensitive to the Warden frequencies. It worked only slightly, though. Some got into the wild and adapted themselves to the desert, that's all. The Cerberan bork is another botched attempt, only that time their result scared them so much they haven't tried it again."

"I still don't understand why they'd go for Kreegan's plan, though."

"Oh, that's simple. They still weren't quite ready to tackle us yet. They were pretty sure he couldn't succeed, but he hit it off with them for some reason, and they agreed to go along simply because, no matter what, it would give them the strategic and military information they craved. If it worked, so much the better. But they couldn't stand for us in any event, a race with a powerful empire that also could reach, and even make use of, the Coldah and their symbiotes without a lot of mechanical aids."

"So what will they do to the Confederacy now—and to us?"

Morah sighed. "They will use small but deadly forces to hit weakly defended planets throughout the Confederacy. Eventually the remnants of this fleet not concerned with the Medusan Coldah's new habitat and settlement will join in scattered action. They will collapse the empire back into planetbound barbarism, but on hundreds of worlds. The Confederacy itself will continue to hold fanatically, all the while contracting to a defensible size and base, but they will be effectively neutralized for a long time. What they will eventually do, or become, you and I will never know, my friend. We'll be long dead."

"And the Diamond?"

"The Altavar computers can stabilize the Medusan variety for a while, perhaps rebuilding Medusa or, more likely, just letting it go. We will settle the Medusans on Lilith and Charon, and progressively we'll switch the programming on them over from Medusa to whatever new world they settle upon, if not with the current generation, then with their children. The Altavar will be around, but remain as unobtrusive as possible, for the next three centuries. Then, one after another, the Coldah will emerge in natural fashion, and, theoretically, our Warden powers will die out and we'll be just plain folks again. Or maybe we won't. Whether or not the Medusan young become Charonese or Lilithians or remain their own kind even with the Coldah gone and with subtle suggestion from the Altavar master computers will tell us a lot. If they *do* continue to breed true, then the Coldah's leaving will have no effect. If we, in those three centuries, can learn how to keep those Wardens alive, or replace them with synthetic equivalents as the Altavar now could do if they wanted, we Warden Diamond races could emerge as true, spacefaring, *Homo excelsius*. The Altavar can make their Wardens do whatever they want by mechanical processes. *We* can do it with sheer willpower, and remake ourselves if we like."

He nodded slowly. "And you were a biologist."

"I *am* a biologist. Sooner or later, working with the Altavar, I will know enough, or my staff will, aided by the computers of Cerberus, now free to expand their potential. We must build up our industry again quickly, and that is the first and vital task. We have the work force with the necessary skills in the Medusans, but we must rebuild the factories, out here first, then in space. The technological brains are all over the Diamond, and now the lid on technological development the Confederacy imposed is gone."

"You're certain the Altavar won't interfere?"

"So long as they perceive no threat from us, they will not. This is long-term planning, Mr. Carroll. It will take years to rebuild the industry and expand reasonable production. We have three centuries to do it all and learn what we have to learn. At the end of that time, if we have fathomed the full secrets of the Warden organism, we will sit here on our three remaining worlds in relative savagery and wave good-bye to the Coldah and the Altavar. Then we will go out ourselves, and see what of humanity survives and rebuild our civilization in strength, not ignorance. It is a challenge not only for us who will start this work but for our children and grandchildren who will complete it. And if we do our job right, they'll do it without the mistakes of the past rising again to stupefy human civilization. A race that can, by force of will, become any creature it needs to, destroy mountains with a finger and a push of will, and change bodies, sex, or whatever it is at any time will be a new type of creature, or creatures."

Yatek Morah leaned back, drained his drink, then pulled out and lit a Charonese cigar. Then he added, "Next time, we *will* be the demons—or the gods. And what about you, Mr. Carroll? Where do you fit in to this unique new future?"

He leaned back comfortably and put his feet up on the table. "I think I have some unique qualifications in your grand scheme, Morah. I think I'm going to fit in fine around here, all four of me. But first a little unfinished business, if you'll do me a little favor."

"We'll see. Now that *you* know it all, I still have a nagging feeling that there's something you haven't been telling me."

"Oh, it's nothing important," he assured the security chief, "except to me."

9

He had spent a little time on Cerberus with Qwin and Dylan, who had been more than willing to take in Bura and Angi and delighted to add two children of a "close relative" to the family. Both Medusan children were finally delivered and looked like normal, healthy Cerberan children, although Dylan complained somewhat enviously over the easy and relatively painless way in which Medusans gave birth. At least children conceived on Medusa bred true to form despite the loss of the Coldah, although the Altavar were, of course, still feeding supplementary data the Medusan Wardens needed to everyone through the Snark computer network.

The Altavar, without asking, did in fact randomly cut a number of Medusans off from the computer, and were somewhat distressed to find that, while the subjects' Wardens became inert, they did not die off at all. Clearly there was something different about the human-Warden relationship, or something brand new was developing in the system, some new and unique variation of human life. For now he depended on Morah and his staff to keep the Altavar from getting *too* distressed at that.

The huge picket ship had been brought in-system, to an orbit between Medusa and Momrath, and was now being converted into a massive space factory as quickly as could be accomplished, while new industries, with some grudging Altavar support, were rising on the natural moons of Momrath itself.

Dumonia had also been grudging as he assumed the public title and office of Lord of Cerberus, but it was now necessary. Working with much of Morah's team, however, he tended to delegate much of the actual running to Qwin Zhang.

Park and Darva had taken a little, short vacation to a small island off the southwest coast of the southern Charonese continent on the suggestion of Mr. Carroll. With a little training and work with Dumonia-trained psychs, they would certainly soon be fully in position to assume control of Charon, something that Morah very much desired for them. As he'd told Park before, the security chief had higher goals than being Lord himself, and, in fact, running the place only got in his way.

Cal Tremon, too, got a sudden yen to get away for a while and do some exploring, first. He might, he was saying, go all the way to Lilith's north pole. Then, perhaps, with an extended vacation back in the tropics talking with the scientific enclave there, he'd be ready for what he wanted to do next.

After keeping himself busy in this way, Mr. Carroll set course once again for Charon, against all advice. Talant Ypsir was still there, still very much alive, and still pretty vicious, all the more so because his people were learning a new life, one without omnipresent cameras and microphones and computer controls. Such things were needed elsewhere in the industrial rebuilding, and nothing new in that line would be produced for years.

It was with a sense of *déjà vu*, then, that Carroll eased his shuttle into the dock of Ypsir's still vast and impressive space station, now in orbit around Charon. He had not really left it since the war, allowing his less bitter alter ego, Haval Kunser, to organize things below.

The airlock signaled clear, and he walked into the tube and up to the second lock, getting into the small chamber and standing ready. There was the usual energy spray, but it didn't bother him this time. He'd already checked with the Altavar and found that, in fact, his body was as infested with Wardens—Altavar-created and artificial and with a neutral program—as anybody else. Ypsir's ray could do nothing to deaden or neutralize the already inert.

Two security monitors met him on the other side, more out of curiosity than anything else.

"Name?" one snapped.

"Lewis Carroll."

"What is your purpose here?"

"I wish to pay a call on First Minister Ypsir," he told them. "I represent the Four Lords in Council and we have need of your fancy computer here."

They looked uncertain, and he knew how much the mighty had fallen by their reaction. He decided to go easy on them. "Call Fallon. She'll know what to do," he suggested.

They nodded and seemed appreciative of the buck-passing suggestion. He sat and waited calmly for fifteen minutes or so until she came. She had never met him before, but he knew her, and she had heard more than enough about him from Ypsir. "Well! You're either a very big fool or you really have nerve, coming here," she told him.

He grinned, and it unsettled her a bit. At that moment an alarm rang, and a speaker broke in to state, "Administrator Kunser docking at Gate Three."

Fallon frowned. "Damn! What does *he* want up here now, of all times?"

"Why don't we go see?" he suggested. "In fact, I called him to come up. I'm representing the Four Lords in Council, with three votes already taken, and I'm here to arrange things with the fourth. Why don't we go collect him and we can all save time and see the First Minister at once."

She frowned. "Okay, but I still think you're nuts."

Kunser was as puzzled as Fallon, but right now, dependent on the good-will of the other Lords, he was in no position to disobey an official request. He was surprised to see Carroll, though, although somewhat pleased. The agent could almost read his mind. *Morah's getting rid of his only threat this way.* But both he and Fallon were civil to the agent, and that was for the best. Both seemed interested in what would happen when Carroll met Ypsir, though.

To everyone's surprise, Ypsir, in a spacious office, was all smiles and cor-diality, the politician supreme. In a corner, on satin pillows, reclined the stunning Ass.

"Well, now, what's all this about a vote and my computer?" the First Minister wanted to know.

"They need it. Its capacity is probably the largest in the Diamond, and it's doing nothing but running this station right now," he told them. "The fact is, this station can be maintained on a much smaller and more basic model Cerberus can and will supply. There are few manufactured goods right now, and we need them desperately. The picket ship is being quickly outfitted, but it's going to need your computer to control the in-dustry we're putting into her. Nothing else will do the job, and we can't make any more major computers until we have the picket running."

"They had their nerve, voting without me," Ypsir complained.

He shrugged. "We tried. You didn't answer the call. That's why Morah sent me here."

Ypsir smiled. *One of the reasons,* he thought, in accord with his two as-sistants, but he said, "Well, I don't like it but I'm hardly in a position to object at this point. One hopes that the Cerberan techs can do it without having to shut down this station."

"I'm sure they can."

"Have you met Ass?" Ypsir asked suddenly.

He smiled and nodded. "Yes, I have. In more ways than one, First Minister. You see, using the Merton Process, *I* was Tarin Bul."

Talant Ypsir's face broke into a wide grin that became a real belly laugh. "Oh, my, but that's perfect! That's wonderful!" he chortled.

"The matter of the computer is not the only reason I'm here," Carroll added. "I've decided that I need a better position than errand boy for the Four Lords."

Ypsir, savoring the irony, hardly heard him. Instead he turned to Ass and said, "Did you hear that, my pretty? *You* were once *him!*"

Showing puzzlement and confusion, she looked up at the agent, but said nothing.

"Ass?" the agent called to her. "Do you know who these people are? This is Haval Kunser, and *this* is Sugah Fallon, and *that* is Talant Ypsir."

Her eyes grew even larger, and her mouth dropped a bit, and then she frowned, shook her head, and looked up again.

"I decided I'd either be dead or the Lord of Medusans," Carroll told her, but she wasn't really listening to him.

Talant Ypsir's head was torn from his body before the bodies of Fallon and Kunser had hit the floor.

About the Author

JACK L. CHALKER was born in Norfolk, Virginia, on December 17, 1944, but was raised and has spent most of his life in Baltimore, Maryland. He learned to read almost from the moment of entering school, and by working odd jobs amassed a large book collection by the time he was in junior high school, a collection now too large for containment in his quarters. Science fiction, history, and geography all fascinated him early on, interests that continue.

Chalker joined the Washington Science Fiction Association in 1958 and began publishing an amateur SF journal, *Mirage*, in 1960. After high school he decided to be a trial lawyer, but money problems and the lack of a firm caused him to switch to teaching. He holds bachelor degrees in history and English, and an M.L.A. from the Johns Hopkins University. He taught history and geography in the Baltimore public schools between 1966 and 1978, and now makes his living as a freelance writer. Additionally, out of the amateur journals he founded a publishing house, The Mirage Press, Ltd., devoted to nonfiction and bibliographic works on science fiction and fantasy. This company has produced more than twenty books in the last nine years. His hobbies include esoteric audio, travel, working on science-fiction convention committees, and guest lecturing on SF to institutions such as the Smithsonian. He is an active conservationist and National Parks supporter, and he has an intensive love of ferryboats, with the avowed goal of riding every ferry in the world. In fact, in 1978 he was married to Eva Whitley on an ancient ferryboat in mid-river. They live in the Catoctin Mountain region of western Maryland with their son David.